Wilbur Smith was born in Central Africa in 1933. He was educated at Michaelhouse and Rhodes University.

He became a full-time writer in 1964 after the successful publication of *When the Lion Feeds*, and has since written thirty novels, all meticulously researched on his numerous expeditions worldwide. His books are now translated into twenty-six different languages.

He owns a farm and game reserve and has an abiding concern for the peoples and wildlife of his native continent, an interest strongly reflected in his novels.

Also by Wilbur Smith

THE COURTNEYS

When the Lion Feeds
The Sound of Thunder
A Sparrow Falls
Birds of Prey
Monsoon
Blue Horizon

THE COURTNEYS OF AFRICA

The Burning Shore
Power of the Sword
Rage
A Time to Die
Golden Fox

THE BALLANTYNE NOVELS

A Falcon Flies
Men of Men
The Angels Weep
The Leopard Hunts in Darkness

Also

The Dark of the Sun
Shout at the Devil
Gold Mine
The Diamond Hunters
The Sunbird
Eagle in the Sky
The Eye of the Tiger
Cry Wolf
Hungry as the Sea
Wild Justice
Elephant Song
River God
The Seventh Scroll
Warlock

WILBUR SMITH

RAGE
&
SHOUT AT
THE DEVIL

PAN BOOKS

Rage first published 1987 by William Heinemann.
First published in paperback 1988 by Pan Books.
Shout at the Devil first published 1968 by William Heinemann.
First published in paperback 1970 by Pan Books.

This omnibus first published 2006 by Pan Books
an imprint of Pan Macmillan Ltd
Pan Macmillan, 20 New Wharf Road, London N1 9RR
Basingstoke and Oxford
Associated companies throughout the world
www.panmacmillan.com

ISBN-13: 978-0-330-44681-5
ISBN-10: 0-330-44681-9

1 3 5 7 9 8 6 4 2

A CIP catalogue record for this book is available from
the British Library.

Typeset by SetSystems Ltd, Saffron Walden, Essex
Printed and bound in Great Britain by
Mackays of Chatham plc, Chatham, Kent

RAGE

I dedicate this book to my wife, Danielle

Hand in hand we have crossed the continents of this earth,
But none of them was as broad as my love for you.

Together we have voyaged on all the oceans,
But none was as deep as my love for you.

Tara Courtney had not worn white since her wedding day. Green was her favourite colour, for it best set off her thick chestnut hair.

However, the white dress she wore today made her feel like a bride again, tremulous and a little afraid but with a sense of joy and deep commitment. She had a touch of ivory lace at the cuffs and the high neckline, and had brushed her hair until it crackled with ruby lights in the bright Cape sunshine. Excitement had rouged her cheeks and although she had carried four children, her waist was slim as a virgin's. So the wide sash of funereal black that she wore over one shoulder was all the more incongruous: youth and beauty decked in the trappings of mourning. Despite her emotional turmoil, she stood with her hands clasped in front of her and her head bowed, silent and still.

She was only one of almost fifty women, all dressed in white, all draped with the black sashes, all in the same attitude of mourning, who stood at carefully spaced intervals along the pavement opposite the main entrance of the parliament buildings of the Union of South Africa.

Nearly all of the women were young matrons from Tara's own set, wealthy, privileged and bored by the undemanding tenor of their lives. Many of them had joined the protest for the excitement of defying established authority and outraging their peers. Some were seeking to regain the attentions of their husbands which after the first decade or so of marriage were jaded by familiarity and fixed more on business or golf and other extra-marital activity. There was, however, a hard nucleus to the movement consisting mostly of the older women, but including a few of the younger ones like Tara and Molly Broadhurst. These were moved only by revulsion at injustice. Tara had tried to express her feelings at the press conference that morning when a woman reporter from the *Cape Argus* had demanded of her, 'Why are you doing this, Mrs Courtney?' and she had replied, 'Because I don't like bullies, and I don't like cheats.' For her that attitude was partially vindicated now.

'Here comes the big bad wolf,' the woman who stood five paces on Tara's right said softly. 'Brace up, girls!' Molly Broadhurst was one of the founders of the Black Sash, a small determined woman in her early thirties whom Tara greatly admired and strove to emulate.

A black Chevrolet with government licence plates had drawn up at the corner of Parliament Square and four men climbed out onto the pavement. One was a police photographer and he went to work immediately, moving quickly down the line of white-clad, black-draped women with his Hasselblad camera, photographing each of them. He was followed by two of the others brandishing notebooks. Though they were dressed in dark, ill-cut business suits, their clumpy black shoes were regulation police issue and their actions were brusque and businesslike as they passed down the ranks demanding and noting the names and addresses of each of the protesters. Tara, who was fast becoming something of an expert, guessed that they probably ranked as sergeants in the Special Branch, but the fourth man she knew by name and by sight, as did most of the others.

He was dressed in a light grey summer suit with brown brogues, a plain maroon tie and a grey fedora hat. Though of average height and unremarkable features, his mouth was wide and friendly, his smile easy as he lifted his hat to Molly.

'Good morning, Mrs Broadhurst. You are early. The procession won't arrive for another hour yet.'

'Are you going to arrest us all again today, Inspector?' Molly demanded tartly.

'Perish the thought.' The inspector raised an eyebrow. 'It's a free country, you know.'

'You could have fooled me.'

'Naughty Mrs Broadhurst!' He shook his head. 'You are trying to provoke me.' His English was excellent, with only a faint trace of an Afrikaans accent.

'No, Inspector. We are protesting the blatant gerrymandering of this perverse government, the erosion of the rule of law, and the abrogation of the basic human rights of the majority of our fellow South Africans merely on the grounds of the colour of their skins.'

'I think, Mrs Broadhurst, you are repeating yourself. You told me all this last time we met.' The inspector chuckled. 'Next you'll actually be demanding that I arrest you again. Let's not spoil this grand occasion—'

'The opening of this parliament, dedicated as it is to injustice and oppression, is a cause for lament not celebration.'

The inspector tipped the brim of his hat, but beneath his flippant attitude was a real respect and perhaps even a little admiration.

'Carry on, Mrs Broadhurst,' he murmured. 'I'm sure we'll meet again soon,' and he sauntered on until he came opposite Tara.

'Good morning to you, Mrs Courtney.' He paused, and this time his admiration was unconcealed. 'What does your illustrious husband think of your treasonable behaviour?'

'Is it treason to oppose the excesses of the National Party and its legislation based on race and colour, Inspector?'

His gaze dropped for a moment to her bosom, large and yet finely shaped beneath the white lace, and then returned to her face.

3

'You are much too pretty for this nonsense,' he said. 'Leave it to the grey-headed old prunes. Go home where you belong and look after your babies.'

'Your masculine arrogance is insufferable, Inspector.' She flushed with anger, unaware that it heightened the looks he had just complimented.

'I wish all traitoresses looked the way you do. It would make my job a great deal more congenial. Thank you, Mrs Courtney.' He smiled infuriatingly and moved on.

'Don't let him rattle you, my dear,' Molly called softly. 'He's an expert at it. We are protesting passively. Remember Mahatma Gandhi.'

With an effort Tara controlled her anger, and reassumed the attitude of the penitent. On the pavement behind her the crowds of spectators began to gather. The rank of white-clad women became the object of curiosity and amusement, of some approbation and a great deal of hostility.

'Goddamn Commies,' a middle-aged man growled at Tara. 'You want to hand the country over to a bunch of savages. You should be locked up, the whole lot of you.' He was well dressed, and his speech cultivated. He even wore the small brass tin-hat insignia in his lapel to signify that he had served with the volunteer forces during the war against Fascism. His attitude was a reminder of just how much tacit support the ruling National Party enjoyed even amongst the English-speaking white community.

Tara bit her lip and forced herself to remain silent, head bowed, even when the outburst earned a ragged ironical cheer from some of the coloured people in the growing crowd.

It was getting hot now, the sunshine had a flat Mediterranean brilliance, and though the mattress of cloud was building up above the great flat-topped bastion of Table Mountain, heralding the rise of the south-easter, the wind had not yet reached the city that crouched below it. By now the crowd was dense and noisy, and Tara was jostled, she suspected deliberately. She kept her composure and concentrated on the building across the road from where she stood.

Designed by Sir Herbert Baker, that paragon of Imperial architects, it was massive and imposing, red brick colonnaded in shimmering white – far from Tara's own modern taste, which inclined to uncluttered space and lines, to glass and light Scandinavian pine furnishing. The building seemed to epitomize all that was inflexible and out-dated from the past, all that Tara wanted to see torn down and discarded.

Her thoughts were broken by the rising hum of expectation from the crowd around her.

'Here they come,' Molly called, and the crowd surged and swayed and broke into cheers. There was the clatter of hoofs on the hard-metalled roadway and the mounted police escort trotted up the avenue, pennants fluttering gaily at the tips of their lances, expert horsemen on matched chargers whose hides gleamed like burnished metal in the sunlight.

The open coaches rumbled along behind them. In the first of these rode the Governor-General and the Prime Minister. There he was, Daniel Malan, champion of the Afrikaners, with his forbidding almost froglike features, a man whose only consideration and declared intent was to keep his *Volk* supreme in Africa for a thousand years, and no price was for him too high.

Tara stared at him with palpable hatred, for he embodied all that she found repellent in the government which now held sway over the land and the peoples that she loved so dearly. As the coach swept past where she stood, their eyes met for a fleeting moment and she tried to convey the strength of her feelings, but he glanced at her without a flicker of acknowledgement, not even a shadow of annoyance, in his brooding gaze. He had looked at her and had not seen her, and now her anger was tinged with despair.

'What must be done to make these people even listen?' she wondered, but now the dignitaries had dismounted from the carriages and were standing to attention during the playing of the national anthems. And though Tara did not know it then, it was the last time 'The King' would be played at the opening of a South African Parliament.

The band ended with a fanfare of trumpets and the cabinet ministers followed the Governor-General and the Prime Minister through the massive front entrance doors. They were followed in turn by the Opposition frontbenchers. This was the moment Tara had been dreading, for her own close family now formed part of the procession. Next behind the Leader of the Opposition came Tara's own father with her stepmother on his arm. They made the most striking couple in the long procession, her father tall and dignified as a patriarchal lion, while on his arm Centaine de Thiry Courtney-Malcomess was slim and graceful in a yellow silk dress that was perfect for the occasion, a jaunty brimless hat on her small neat head with a veil over one eye; she seemed not a year older than Tara herself, though everybody knew she had been named Centaine because she had been born on the first day of the twentieth century.

Tara thought she had escaped unnoticed, for none of them had known she intended joining the protest, but at the top of the broad staircase the procession was held up for a moment and before she entered the doorway Centaine turned deliberately and looked back. From her vantage point she could see over the heads of the escort and the other dignitaries in the procession, and from across the road she caught Tara's eye and held it for a moment. Although her expression did not alter, the strength of her disapproval was even at that range like a slap in Tara's face.

For Centaine the honour, dignity and good name of the family were of paramount importance. She had warned Tara repeatedly about making a public spectacle of herself and flouting Centaine was a perilous business, for she was not only Tara's stepmother but her mother-in-law as well, and the doyenne of the Courtney family and fortune.

Halfway up the staircase behind her Shasa Courtney saw the direction and force of his mother's gaze, and turning quickly to follow it saw Tara, his wife, in the rank of black-sashed protesters. When she had told him that morning at breakfast that she would not be joining him at the opening ceremony, Shasa had barely looked up from the financial pages of the morning newspaper.

'Suit yourself, my dear. It will be a bit of a bore,' he had murmured. 'But I would like another cup of coffee, when you have a moment.'

Now when he recognized her, he smiled slightly and shook his head in mock despair, as though she were a child discovered in some naughty prank, and then he turned away as the procession moved forward once again.

He was almost impossibly handsome, and the black eyepatch gave him a debonair piratical look that most women found intriguing and challenging. Together they were renowned as the handsomest young couple in Cape Town society. Yet it was strange how the passage of a few short years had caused the flames of their love to sink into a puddle of grey ash.

'Suit yourself, my dear,' he had said, as he did so often these days.

The last back-benchers in the procession disappeared into the House, the mounted escort and empty carriages trotted away and the crowds began to break up. The demonstration was over.

'Are you coming, Tara?' Molly called, but Tara shook her head.

'Have to meet Shasa,' she said. 'See you on Friday

7

afternoon.' Tara slipped the wide black sash off over her head, folded it and placed it in her handbag as she threaded her way through the dispersing crowd. She crossed the road.

She saw no irony in now presenting her parliamentary pass to the doorman at the visitors' entrance and entering the institution against whose actions she had been so vigorously protesting. She climbed the side staircase and looked into the visitors' gallery. It was packed with wives and important guests, and she looked over their heads down into the panelled chamber below to the rows of sombre-suited members on their green leather-covered benches, all involved in the impressive ritual of parliament. However, she knew that the speeches would be trivial, platitudinous and boring to the point of pain, and she had been standing in the street since early morning. She needed to visit the ladies' room as a matter of extreme urgency.

She smiled at the usher and withdrew surreptitiously, then turned and hurried away down the wide-panelled corridor. When she had finished in the ladies' room, she headed for her father's office, which she used as her own.

As she turned the corner she almost collided with a man coming in the opposite direction. She checked only just in time, and saw that he was a tall black man dressed in the uniform of a parliamentary servant. She would have passed on with a nod and a smile, when it occurred to her that a servant should not have been in this section of the building during the time when the House was in session, for the offices of the Prime Minister and the Leader of the Opposition were at the end of the corridor. Then again, although the servant carried a mop and pail, there was something about him that was neither menial nor servile and she looked sharply at his face.

She felt an electric tingle of recognition. It had been many years, but she could never forget that face – the features of an Egyptian pharaoh, noble and fierce, the dark

8

eyes alive with intelligence. He was still one of the finest-looking men she had ever seen, and she remembered his voice, deep and thrilling so that the memory of it made her shiver slightly. She even remembered his words: 'There is a generation, whose teeth are as swords ... to devour the poor from the earth.'

It was this man who had given her the first glimmer of understanding as to what it was like to be born black in South Africa. Her true commitment dated from that distant meeting. This man had changed her life with a few words.

She stopped, blocking his path, and tried to find some way to convey her feelings to him, but her throat had closed and she found she was trembling from the shock. The instant he knew he had been recognized, he changed, like a leopard coming on guard as it becomes aware of the hunters. Tara sensed she was in danger, for a sense of African cruelty invested him, but she was unafraid.

'I am a friend,' she said softly, and stood aside to let him pass. 'Our cause is the same.'

He did not move for a moment, but stared at her. She knew that he would never forget her again, his scrutiny seemed to set her skin on fire, and then he nodded.

'I know you,' he acknowledged, and once again his voice made her shiver, deep and melodious, filled with the rhythm and cadence of Africa. 'We will meet again.'

Then he passed on and without a backward glance disappeared around the corner of the panelled corridor. She stood staring after him, and her heart was pounding, her breath burned the back of her throat.

'Moses Gama,' she whispered his name aloud. 'Messiah and warrior of Africa—' then she paused and shook her head. 'What are you doing here, in this of all places?'

The possibilities intrigued and stirred her, for now she knew with a deep instinct that the crusade was afoot, and she longed to be part of it. She wanted to do more than merely stand on a street corner with a black sash draped over her shoulder. She knew Moses Gama had only to crook his finger and she would follow him, she and ten million others.

'We will meet again,' he had promised, and she believed him.

Light with joy she went on down the passageway. She had her own key to her father's office and as she fitted it to the lock, her eyes were on a level with the brass plate:

COLONEL BLAINE MALCOMESS
DEPUTY LEADER OF THE OPPOSITION

With surprise she found that the lock was already opened, and she pushed the door wide and went in.

Centaine Courtney-Malcomess turned from the window beyond the desk to confront her. 'I have been waiting for you, young lady.' Centaine's French accent was an affectation that annoyed Tara. She has been back to France just once in thirty-five years, she thought, and lifted her chin defiantly.

'Don't toss your head at me, Tara *chérie*,' Centaine went on. 'When you act like a child, you must expect to be treated as a child.'

'No, Mater, you are wrong. I do not expect you to treat me as a child, not now or ever. I am a married woman of thirty-three years of age, the mother of four children and the mistress of my own establishment.'

Centaine sighed. 'All right,' she nodded. 'My concern made me ill-mannered, and I apologize. Let's not make this discussion any more difficult for each other than it already is.'

'I was not aware that we needed to discuss anything.'

'Sit down, Tara,' Centaine ordered, and Tara obeyed instinctively and then was annoyed with herself for doing so. Centaine took her father's chair behind the desk, and

Tara resented that also – it was Daddy's chair and this woman had no right to it.

'You have just told me that you are a wife with four children,' Centaine spoke quietly. 'Would you not agree that you have a duty—'

'My children are well cared for,' Tara flared at her. 'You cannot accuse me of that.'

'And what about your husband and your marriage?'

'What about Shasa?' Tara was immediately defensive.

'You tell me,' Centaine invited.

'It's none of your business.'

'Oh, but it is,' Centaine contradicted her. 'I have devoted my entire life to Shasa. I plan for him to be one of the leaders of this nation.' She paused and a dreamy glaze covered her eyes for a moment, and she seemed to squint slightly. Tara had noticed that expression before, whenever Centaine was in deep thought, and now she wanted to break in upon it as brutally as she could.

'That's impossible and you know it.'

Centaine's eyes snapped back into focus and she glared at Tara. 'Nothing is impossible – not for me, not for us.'

'Oh yes it is,' Tara gloated. 'You know as well as I do that the Nationalists have gerrymandered the electorate, that they have even loaded the Senate with their own appointees. They are in power for ever. Never again will anyone who is not one of them, an Afrikaner Nationalist, ever be this country's leader, not until the revolution – and when that is over, the leader will be a black man.' Tara broke off and thought for an instant of Moses Gama.

'You are naïve,' Centaine snapped. 'You do not understand these things. Your talk of revolution is childish and irresponsible.'

'Have it your own way, Mater. But deep down you know it's so. Your darling Shasa will never fulfil your dream. Even he is beginning to sense the futility of being in Opposition for ever. He is losing interest in the impossible. I wouldn't be surprised if he decides not to contest the next election, gives up the political aspirations that you have foisted on him and simply goes off to make himself another trillion pounds.'

'No.' Centaine shook her head. 'He won't give up. He is a fighter like I am.'

'He'll never be even a cabinet minister, let alone Prime Minister,' Tara stated flatly.

'If you believe that, then you are no wife for my son,' Centaine said.

'You said it,' Tara said softly. 'You said it, not me.'

'Oh, Tara, my dear, I am sorry.' Centaine reached across the desk but it was too broad for her to touch Tara's hand. 'Forgive me. I lost my temper. All this is so desperately important to me. I feel it so deeply, but I did not mean to antagonize you. I want only to help you – I am so worried about you and Shasa. I want to help, Tara. Won't you let me help you?'

'I don't see that we need help,' Tara lied sweetly. 'Shasa and I are perfectly happy. We have four lovely children—'

Centaine made an impatient gesture. 'Tara, you and I haven't always seen eye to eye. But I am your friend, I truly am. I want the best for you and Shasa and the little ones. Won't you let me help you?'

'How, Mater? By giving us money? You have already given us ten or twenty million – or is it thirty million pounds? I lose track sometimes.'

'Won't you let me share my experience with you? Won't you listen to my advice?'

'Yes, Mater, I'll listen. I don't promise to take it, but I'll listen to it.'

'Firstly, Tara dear, you must give up these crazy left-wing activities. You bring the whole family into disrepute. You make a spectacle of yourself, and therefore of us, by dressing up and standing on street corners. Apart from that, it is positively dangerous. The Suppression of Communism Act is now law. You could be declared a Communist, and placed under a banning order. Just consider that, you would become a non-person, deprived of all human rights and dignity. Then there is Shasa's political career. What you do reflects on him.'

'Mater, I promised to listen,' Tara said stonily. 'But now I withdraw that promise. I know what I am doing.' She stood up and moved to the door where she paused and looked back. 'Did you ever think, Centaine Courtney-Malcomess, that my mother died of a broken heart, and it was your blatant adultery with my father that broke it for her? Yet you can sit there smugly and advise me how to conduct my life, so as not to disgrace you and your precious son.' She went out and closed the heavy teak door softly behind her.

Shasa Courtney lolled on the Opposition front bench with his hands pushed deeply into his pockets, his legs thrust out and crossed at the ankles, and listened intently to the Minister of Police outlining the legislation which he intended bringing before the House during the current session.

The Minister of Police was the youngest member of the cabinet, a man of approximately the same age as Shasa, which was extraordinary. The Afrikaner revered age and mistrusted the inexperience and impetuosity of youth. The average age of the other members of the Nationalist cabinet could not be less than sixty-five years, Shasa reflected, and yet here was Manfred De La Rey standing before them, a mere stripling of less than forty years, setting out the general contents of the Criminal Law Amendment Bill which he would be proposing and shepherding through its various stages.

'He is asking for the right to declare a state of emergency which will put the police above the law, without appeal to the courts,' Blaine Malcomess grunted beside him, and Shasa nodded without looking at his father-in-law. Instead he was watching the man across the floor.

Manfred De La Rey was speaking in Afrikaans, as he usually did. His English was heavily accented and laboured, and he spoke it unwillingly, making only the barest gesture towards the bilingualism of the House. On the other hand, when speaking in his mother tongue, he was eloquent and persuasive, his oratorical attitudes and devices were so skilled as to seem entirely natural and more than once he raised a chuckle of exasperated admiration from the opposition benches and a chorus of '*Hoor, hoor!*' from his own party.

'The fellow has a damned cheek.' Blaine Malcomess shook his head. 'He is asking for the right to suspend the rule of law and impose a police state at the whim of the ruling party. We'll have to fight that tooth and nail.'

'My word!' Shasa agreed mildly, but he found himself envying the other man, and yet mysteriously drawn to him. It was strange how their two destinies seemed to be inexorably linked.

He had first met Manfred De La Rey twenty years ago, and for no apparent reason the two of them had flown at each other on the spot like young game cocks and fought a bloody bout of fisticuffs. Shasa grimaced at the way it had ended, the drubbing he had received still rankled even after all that time. Since then their paths had crossed and recrossed.

In 1936 they had both been on the national team that went to Adolf Hitler's Olympic Games in Berlin, but it had been Manfred De La Rey in the boxing ring who collected the only gold medal the team had won, while Shasa returned empty-handed. They had hotly and acrimoniously contested the same seat in the 1948 elections that had seen the National Party come sweeping to power, and again it was Manfred De La Rey who had won the seat and taken his place in parliament, while Shasa had to wait for a by-election in a safe United Party constituency to secure his own place on the Opposition benches from which to confront his rival once again. Now Manfred was a minister, a position that Shasa coveted with all his heart, and with his undoubted brilliance and oratorical skills together with growing political acumen and a solid power base within the party, Manfred De La Rey's future must be unbounded.

Envy, admiration and furious antagonism – that was what Shasa Courtney felt as he listened to the man across the floor from him, and he studied him intently.

Manfred De La Rey still had a boxer's physique, wide shoulders and powerful neck, but he was thickening around the waist and his jawline was beginning to blur with flesh. He wasn't keeping himself in shape and hard muscle was turning flabby. Shasa glanced down at his own lean hips and greyhound belly with self-satisfaction and then concentrated again on his adversary.

Manfred De La Rey's nose was twisted and there was a gleaming white scar through one of his dark eyebrows, injuries he had received in the boxing ring. However, his eyes were a strange pale colour, like yellow topaz, implacable as the eyes of a cat and yet with the fire of his fine intellect in their depths. Like all the Nationalist cabinet ministers, with the exception of the Prime Minister himself, he was a highly educated and brilliant man, devout and dedicated, totally convinced of the divine right of his party and his *Volk*.

'They truly believe they are God's instruments on earth. That's what makes them so damned dangerous.' Shasa smiled grimly as Manfred finished speaking and sat down to the roar of approval from his own side of the House. They were waving order papers, and the Prime Minister leaned across to pat Manfred's shoulder, while a dozen congratulatory notes were passed to him from the back benches.

Shasa used this distraction to murmur an excuse to his father-in-law. 'You won't need me for the rest of the day, but if you do, you'll know where to find me.' Then he stood up, bowed to the Speaker and, as unobtrusively as possible, headed for the exit. However, Shasa was six foot one inch tall, and with the black patch over one eye and his dark waving hair and good looks he drew more than a few speculative glances from the younger women in the visitors' gallery, and a hostile appraisal from the Government benches.

Manfred De La Rey glanced up from the note he was reading as Shasa passed, and the look they exchanged was intent but enigmatic. Then Shasa was out of the chamber and he shrugged off his jacket and slung it over his shoulder as he acknowledged the salute of the doorman and went out into the sunshine.

Shasa did not keep an office in the parliament building, for the seven-storey Centaine House, the headquarters of the Courtney Mining and Finance Co. Ltd., was just two minutes' walk across the gardens. As he strode along under the oaks he mentally changed hats, doffing his political topper for the businessman's homburg. Shasa kept his life in separate compartments, and he had trained himself to concentrate on each in its turn, without ever allowing his energy to dissipate by spreading it too thinly.

By the time he crossed the road in front of St George's Cathedral and went into the revolving glass front door of Centaine House, he was thinking of finance and mining, juggling figures and choices, weighing factual reports against his own instincts, and enjoying the game of money as hugely as he had the rituals and confrontations on the floor of the Houses of Parliament.

The two pretty girls at the reception desk in the entrance lobby with its marbled floors and columns burst into radiant smiles.

'Good afternoon, Mr Courtney,' they chorused, and he

16

devastated them with his smile as he crossed to the lifts. His reaction to them was instinctive; he liked pretty females around him, although he would never touch one of his own people. Somehow that would have been incestuous, and unsporting for they would not have been able to refuse him, too much like shooting a sitting bird. Still the two young females at the desk sighed and rolled their eyes as the lift doors closed on him.

Janet, his secretary, had heard the lift and was waiting as the doors opened. She was more Shasa's type – mature and poised, groomed and efficient, and though she made little attempt to conceal her adoration, Shasa's self-imposed rules prevailed here also.

'What have we got, Janet?' he demanded, and as she followed him across the ante-chamber to his own office, she read off his appointments for the rest of the afternoon.

He went first to the ticker-tape in the corner and ran the closing prices through his fingers. Anglos had dropped two shillings, it was almost time to buy again.

'Ring Allen and put him off. I'm not ready for him yet,' he told Janet and went to his desk. 'Give me fifteen minutes and then get David Abrahams on the phone.'

As she left the room Shasa settled to the pile of telex sheets and urgent messages that she had left on his blotter. He worked swiftly through them, undistracted by the magnificent view of Table Mountain through the window on the opposite wall, and when one of the phones rang he was ready for David.

'Hello, Davie, what's happening in Jo'burg?' It was a rhetorical question, he knew what was happening and what he was going to do about it. The daily reports and estimates were amongst the pile on his desk, but he listened carefully to David's résumé.

David was group managing director. He had been with Shasa since varsity days and he was as close to Shasa as no other person, with the exception of Centaine, had come.

Although the H'ani Diamond Mine near Windhoek in the north was still the fountainhead of the company's prosperity, and had been for the thirty-two years since Centaine Courtney had discovered it, under Shasa's direction the company had expanded and diversified until he had been forced to move the executive headquarters from Windhoek to Johannesburg. Johannesburg was the commercial centre of the country and the move was inevitable, but Johannesburg was also a bleak, heartless and unattractive city. Centaine Courtney-Malcomess refused to leave the beautiful Cape of Good Hope to live there, so the company's financial and administrative headquarters remained in Cape Town. It was a clumsy and costly duplication, but Centaine always got her way. Moreover, it was convenient for Shasa to be so close to parliament and as he loved the Cape as much as she did he did not try to change her mind.

Shasa and David spoke for ten minutes before Shasa said, 'Right, we can't decide on this on the phone. I'll come up to you.'

'When?'

'Tomorrow afternoon. Sean has a rugby match at ten in the morning. I can't miss it. I promised him.'

David was silent a moment as he considered the relative importance of a schoolboy's sporting achievement against the possible investment of something over ten million pounds in the development of the company's options on the new Orange Free State goldfields.

'Give me a ring before you take off,' David agreed with resignation. 'I'll meet you at the airfield myself.'

Shasa hung up and checked his wristwatch. He wanted to get back to Weltevreden in time to spend an hour with the children before their bath and dinner. He could finish his work after his own dinner. He began to pack the remaining papers on his desk into his black crocodile-skin

Hermès briefcase, when Janet tapped on the inter-leading door and came into his office.

'I'm sorry, sir. This has just been delivered by hand. A parliamentary messenger, and he said it was very urgent.'

Shasa took the heavy-quality envelope from her. It was the type of expensive stationery reserved for use by members of the cabinet and the flap was embossed with the coat of arms of the Union, the quartered shield and rampant antelopes supporting it with the motto in the ribbon beneath *Ex Unitate Vires* – Strength through Unity.

'Thank you, Janet.' He broke the flap with his thumb and took out a single sheet of notepaper. It was headed: 'Office of the Minister of Police', and the message was handwritten in Afrikaans.

Dear Mr Courtney,

Knowing of your interest in hunting, an important personage has asked me to invite you to a springbok hunt on his ranch over the coming weekend. There is an airstrip on the property and the coordinates are as follows: 28°32'S 26°16'E.

I can assure you of good sport and interesting company. Please let me know if you are able to attend.

Sincerely,

Manfred De La Rey.

Shasa grinned and whistled softly through his teeth as he went to the large-scale map on the wall and checked the coordinates. The note amounted to a summons, and he could guess at the identity of the important personage. He saw that the ranch was in the Orange Free State just south of the goldfields at Welkom, and it would mean only a minor detour off his return course from Johannesburg to reach it.

'I wonder what they are up to now,' he mused, and he

felt a prickle of anticipation. It was the kind of mystery he thoroughly enjoyed, and he scribbled a reply on a sheet of his personal note-paper.

> Thank you for your kind invitation to hunt with you this weekend. Please convey my acceptance to our host and I look forward to the hunting.

As he sealed the envelope he muttered, 'In fact, you'd have to nail both my feet to the ground to keep me away.'

I n his green Jaguar SS sports car, Shasa drove through the massive white-painted gateway of Weltevreden. The pediment had been designed and executed in 1790 by Anton Anreith, the Dutch East India Company's architect and sculptor, and such an exquisite work of art was a fitting entrance to the estate.

Since Centaine had handed the estate over to him and gone to live with Blaine Malcomess on the far side of the Constantia Berg mountains, Shasa had lavished the same love and care upon Weltevreden as she had before. The name translated from the Dutch as 'Well Satisfied' and that was how Shasa felt as he slowed the Jaguar to a walking pace, so as not to blow dust over the vineyards that flanked the road.

The harvest was in full swing, and the headscarves of the women working down the rows of shoulder-high vines were bright spots of colour that vied with the leaves of red and gold. They straightened up to smile and wave as Shasa passed, and the men, doubled under the overflowing baskets of red grapes, grinned at him also.

Young Sean was on one of the wagons in the centre of the field, walking the draught horses slowly, keeping pace with the harvest. The wagon was piled high with ripe grapes that glowed like rubies where the powdery bloom had been rubbed from their skin.

When he saw his father, Sean tossed the reins to the driver who had been tactfully supervising him, and leapt over the side of the wagon and raced down the rows of vines to intercept the green Jaguar. He was only eleven years old, but big for his age. He had inherited his mother's clear shining skin and Shasa's looks, and although his limbs were sturdy, he ran like an antelope, springy and quick on his feet. Watching him Shasa felt that his heart might burst with pride.

Sean flung open the passenger door of the Jag and tumbled into the seat, where he abruptly recovered his dignity.

'Good evening, Papa,' he said, and Shasa put an arm around his shoulders and hugged him.

'Hello, sport. How did it go today?'

They drove down past the winery and the stables and Shasa parked in the converted barn where he kept his collection of a dozen vintage cars. The Jaguar had been a gift from Centaine and he favoured it even over the 1928 Phantom I Rolls-Royce with Hooper coachwork beside which he parked it.

The other children had witnessed his arrival from the nursery windows and came pelting down across the lawns to meet him. Michael, the youngest boy, was leading, with Garrick, his middle son, a good five lengths back. Less than a year separated each of the boys. Michael was the dreamer of the family, a fey child who at nine years of age could lose himself for hours in *Treasure Island* or spend an afternoon with his box of water-colours, lost to all else in the world. Shasa embraced him as affectionately as he had his eldest, and then Garrick came up, wheezing with asthma, pale-faced and skinny, with wispy hair that stuck up in spikes.

'Good afternoon, Papa,' he stuttered. He really was an

ugly little brat, Shasa thought, and where the hell did he get them from, the asthma and the stutter?

'Hello, Garrick.' Shasa never called him 'son' or 'my boy' or 'sport' as he did the other two. It was always simply 'Garrick' and he patted the top of his head lightly. It never occurred to him to embrace the child, the little beggar still peed his bed and he was ten years old.

Shasa turned with relief to meet his daughter.

'Come on, my angel, come to your daddy!' And she flew into his arms and shrieked with rapture as he swung her high, then wrapped both arms around his neck and showered warm wet kisses on his face.

'What does my angel want to do now?' Shasa asked, without lowering her to earth.

'I wanna wide,' Isabella declared, and she was already wearing her new jodhpurs.

'Then wide we shall,' Shasa agreed. Whenever Tara accused him of encouraging her lisp, he protested, 'She's only a baby.'

'She's a calculating little vixen who knows exactly how to twist you around her little finger – and you let her do it.'

Now he swung her up on to his shoulders, and she sat astride his neck and took a handful of his hair to steady herself while she bounced up and down chanting, 'I love my daddy.'

'Come on, everybody,' Shasa ordered. 'We are going for a wide before dinner.'

Sean was too big and grown up to hold hands, but he kept jealously close to Shasa's right side; Michael was on his left clinging unashamedly to Shasa's hand, while Garrick trailed five paces behind looking up adoringly at his father.

'I came first in arithmetic today, Daddy,' Garrick said softly, but in all the shouting and laughter Shasa didn't hear him.

The grooms had the horses saddled up already, for the

evening ride was a family ritual. In the saddle room Shasa slipped off his city shoes and changed them for old well-polished riding boots before he lifted Isabella onto the back of her plump little piebald Shetland. Then he went up into the saddle of his own stallion and took Isabella's lead rein from the groom.

'Company, forward – walk, march, trot!' He gave the cavalry command and pumped his hand over his head, a gesture which always reduced Isabella to squeals of delight, and they clattered out of the stableyard.

They made the familiar circuit of the estate, stopping to talk with any of the coloured boss-boys they met, and exchanging shouted greetings with the gangs of labourers trudging home from the vineyards. Sean discussed the harvest with his father in adult terms, sitting straight and important in the saddle, until Isabella, feeling left out, intervened and immediately Shasa leaned over to listen deferentially to what she had to tell him.

The boys ended the ride as always with a mad gallop across the polo fields and up the hill to the stables. Sean, riding like a centaur, was far ahead of the rest of them, Michael was too gentle to use the whip and Garrick bounced awkwardly in the saddle. Despite Shasa's drilling, his seat was atrocious with toes and elbows sticking out at odd angles.

'He rides like a sack of potatoes,' Shasa thought with irritation, following them at the sedate pace set by Isabella's portly Shetland on the lead rein. Shasa was an international polo player, and he took his middle son's maladroit seat as a personal affront.

Tara was in the kitchen overseeing the last-minute details for dinner when they came trooping in. She looked up and greeted Shasa casually.

'Good day?' She was wearing those appalling trousers in faded blue denim which Shasa detested. He liked feminine women.

'Not bad,' he answered, trying to divest himself of Isabella who was still wrapped around his neck. He dislodged her and handed her over to Nanny.

'We are twelve for dinner.' Tara turned her attention back to the Malay chef who was standing by dutifully.

'Twelve?' Shasa asked sharply.

'I invited the Broadhursts at the last moment.'

'Oh, God,' Shasa groaned.

'I wanted some stimulating conversation at the table for a change, not just horses and shooting and business.'

'Last time she came to dinner your and Molly's stimulating conversation broke the party up before nine o'clock.' Shasa glanced at his wristwatch. 'I'd better think about dressing.'

'Daddy, will you feed me?' Isabella called from the children's dining-room beyond the kitchen.

'You are a big girl, angel,' he answered. 'You must learn to feed yourself.'

'I can feed myself – I just like it better when you do it. Please, Daddy, pretty please a trillion times.'

'A trillion?' Shasa asked. 'I am bid one trillion – any advance on a trillion?' but he went to her summons.

'You spoil her,' Tara said. 'She's becoming impossible.'

'I know,' said Shasa. 'You keep telling me.'

Shasa shaved quickly while his coloured valet laid out his dinner-jacket in the dressing-room and put the platinum and sapphire studs into his dress shirt. Despite Tara's vehement protests he always insisted on black tie for dinner.

'It's so stuffy and old-fashioned and snobby.'

'It's civilized,' he contradicted her.

When he was dressed, he crossed the wide corridor strewn with oriental carpets, the walls hung with a gallery of Thomas Baines water-colours, tapped on Tara's door and went in to her invitation.

Tara had moved into this suite while she was carrying

24

Isabella, and had stayed here. Last year she had redecorated it, removing the velvet drapes and George II and Louis XIV furniture, the Qum silk carpets and the magnificent oils by De Jong and Naudé, stripping the flocked wallpaper and sanding the golden patina off the yellow-wood floor until it looked like plain deal.

Now the walls were stark white with only a single enormous painting facing the bed; it was a monstrosity of geometrical shapes in primary colours in the style of Miró, but executed by an unknown art student at the Cape Town University Art School and of no value. To Shasa's mind paintings should be pleasing decorations but at the same time good long-term investments. This thing was neither.

The furniture Tara had chosen for her boudoir was made of angular stainless steel and glass, and there was very little of it. The bed was almost flat on the bare boards of the floor.

'It's Swedish decor,' she had explained.

'Send it back to Sweden,' he had advised her.

Now he perched on one of the steel chairs and lit a cigarette. She frowned at him in the mirror.

'Forgive me.' He stood up and went to flick the cigarette out of the window. 'I'll be working late after dinner,' he turned back to her, 'and I wanted to warn you before I forget that I'm flying up to Jo'burg tomorrow afternoon and I'll be away for a few days, maybe five or six.'

'Fine.' She pursed her lips as she applied her lipstick, a pale mauve shade that he disliked intensely.

'One other thing, Tara. Lord Littleton's bank is preparing to underwrite the share issue for our possible new development on the Orange Free State goldfields. I would take it as a personal favour if you and Molly could refrain from waving your black sashes in his face and from regaling him with merry tales of white injustice and bloody black revolution.'

25

'I can't speak for Molly, but I promise to be good.'

'Why don't you wear your diamonds tonight?' he changed the subject. 'They look so good on you.'

She hadn't worn the suite of yellow diamonds from the H'ani Mine since she had joined the Sash movement. They made her feel like Marie Antoinette.

'Not tonight,' she said. 'They are a little garish, it's really just a family dinner party.' She dusted her nose with the puff and looked at him in the mirror.

'Why don't you go down, dear. Your precious Lord Littleton will be arriving at any moment.'

'I just want to tuck Bella up first.' He came to stand behind her.

They stared at each other in the mirror, seriously.

'What happened to us, Tara?' he asked softly.

'I don't know what you mean, dear,' she replied, but she looked down and adjusted the front of her dress carefully.

'I'll see you downstairs,' he said. 'Don't be too long, and do make a fuss of Littleton. He's important, and he likes the girlies.'

After he had closed the door Tara stared at it for a moment, then she repeated his question aloud. 'What happened to us, Shasa? It's quite simple really. I just grew up and lost patience with the trivialities with which you fill your life.'

On the way down she looked in on the children. Isabella was asleep with teddy on top of her face. Tara saved her daughter from suffocation and went to the boys' rooms. Only Michael was still awake. He was reading.

'Lights out!' she ordered.

'Oh, Mater, just to the end of the chapter.'

'Out!'

'Just this page.'

'Out, I said!' And she kissed him lovingly.

At the head of the staircase she drew a deep breath like a diver on the high board, smiled brightly and went down into the blue drawing-room where the first guests were already sipping sherry.

Lord Littleton was much better value than she had expected – tall, silver-haired and benign.

'Do you shoot?' she asked at the first opportunity.

'Can't stand the sight of blood, me dear.'

'Do you ride?'

'Horses?' he snorted. 'Stupid bloody animals.'

'I think you and I are going to be good friends,' she said.

There were many rooms in Weltevreden that Tara disliked; the dining-room she actively hated with all those heads of long-dead animals that Shasa had massacred staring down from the walls with glass eyes. Tonight she took a chance and seated Molly on the other side of Littleton and within minutes Molly had him hooting with delighted laughter.

When they left the men with the port and Hauptmanns and went through to the ladies' room, Molly pulled Tara aside, bubbling over with excitement.

'I've been dying to get you alone all evening,' she whispered. 'You'll never guess who is in the Cape at this very moment.'

'Tell me.'

'The Secretary of the African National Congress – that's who. Moses Gama, that's who.'

Tara went very still and pale and stared at her.

'He's coming to our home to talk to a small group of us, Tara. I invited him, and he especially asked for you to be present. I didn't know you knew him.'

'I met him only once—' she corrected herself, 'twice.'

'Can you come?' Molly insisted. 'It'll be best if Shasa does not know about it, you understand.'

'When?'

'Saturday evening, eight o'clock.'

'Shasa will be away and I'll be there,' Tara said. 'I wouldn't miss it for the world.'

Sean Courtney was the stalwart of the Western Province Preparatory School First XIV, or Wet Pups, as the school was known. Quick and strong, he ran in four tries against the Rondebosch juniors and converted them himself, while his father and two younger brothers stood on the touchline and yelled encouragement.

After the final whistle blew Shasa lingered just long enough to congratulate his son, with an effort restraining himself from hugging the sweaty grinning youngster with grass stains on his white shorts and a graze on one knee. A display like that in front of Sean's peers would have mortified him horribly. Instead they shook hands.

'Well played, sport. I'm proud of you,' he said. 'Sorry about this weekend, but I'll make it up to you.' And although the expression of regret was sincere, Shasa felt a buoyancy of his spirits as he drove out to the airfield at Youngsfield. Dicky, his erk, had the aircraft out of the hangar and ready for him on the hardstand.

Shasa climbed out of the Jaguar and stood with his hands in his pockets and the cigarette in the corner of his mouth, staring at the sleek machine with rapture.

It was a DH98 Mosquito fighter-bomber. Shasa had bought it at one of the RAF disposal sales at Biggin Hill and had it completely stripped and overhauled by De Havilland trained riggers. He had even had them re-glue the sandwich construction of the wooden bodywork with the new Araldite wonder glue. The original Rodux adhesives had proved unreliable under tropical conditions. Stripped of all armaments and military fittings, the Mosquito's already formidable performance had been considerably enhanced. Not even Courtney Mining could afford one of the new civilian jet-engined aircraft, but this was the next best thing.

The beautiful machine crouched on the hardstand like a falcon at bate, the twin Rolls-Royce Merlin engines ready to roar into life and hurtle her into the blue. Blue was her colour, sky blue and silver; she shone in the bright Cape sunlight and on her fuselage where once the RAF roundel had been was now emblazoned the Courtney Company logo, a stylized silver diamond, its facets entwined with the Company's initials.

'How is the port number two magneto?' Shasa demanded of Dicky as he sauntered across in his oily overalls. The little man bridled.

'Ticking over like a sewing machine,' he answered. He loved the machine even more than Shasa did, and any imperfection, no matter how minor, wounded him deeply. When Shasa reported one, he took it very badly. He helped Shasa load his briefcase, overnight bag and guncase into the bomb bay, which had been converted into a luggage compartment.

'All tanks are full,' he said, and stood aside looking superior as Shasa insisted on checking them visually, and then made a fuss of his walk-around inspection.

'She'll do,' Shasa agreed at last and could not resist stroking the wing, as though it were the limb of a lovely woman.

Shasa switched to oxygen at eleven thousand feet and levelled out at Angels twenty, grinning into his oxygen mask at the old Air Force slang. He tuned her for cruise, carefully watching the exhaust gas temperatures and engine revs, and then settled back to enjoy it.

Enjoy was too mild a term for it. Flying was an exultation of spirit and a fever in his blood. The immense lion-tawny continent drifted by beneath him, washed by a million suns and burned by the hot herb-scented Karoo winds, its ancient hide riven and wrinkled and scarred with donga and canyon and dried riverbed. Only up here, high above it, did Shasa truly realize how much he was a part of it, how deep was his love for it. Yet it was a hard land and cruel, and it bred hard men, black and white, and he knew that he was one of them. There is no place for weaklings here, he thought, only the strong can flourish.

Perhaps it was the pure oxygen he breathed, enhanced by the ecstasy of flight, but his mind seemed clearer up here. Issues that had been obscure became lucid, uncertainties resolved, and the hours sped away as swiftly as the lovely machine streaked across the blue so that when he landed at Johannesburg's civilian airport, he knew with certainty what had to be done. David Abrahams was waiting for him, lanky and skinny as ever, but he was balding a little and he had taken to wearing gold-rimmed spectacles which gave him a perpetually startled expression. Shasa jumped down off the wing of the Mosquito and they embraced happily. They were closer than brothers. Then David patted the aircraft's wing.

'When do I get to fly her again?' he asked wistfully. David had got a DFC in the Western Desert and a bar to it in Italy. He had been credited with nine kills and ended the war as a wing commander, while Shasa had been a mere squadron leader when he had lost his eye in Abyssinia and been invalided home.

'She's too good for you,' Shasa told him and slung his luggage into the back seat of David's Cadillac.

As David drove out through the airfield gates they exchanged family news. David was married to Mathilda Janine, Tara Courtney's younger sister, so David and Shasa were brothers-in-law. Shasa boasted about Sean and Isabella without mentioning his other two sons and then they went on to the real objects of their meeting.

These, in order of importance, were, first, the decision whether or not to exercise the option on the new Silver River mining prospect in the Orange Free State. Then there was the trouble with the company's chemical factory on the Natal coast. A local pressure group was kicking up a rumpus about poisoning the sea bed and reefs in the area where the factory was discharging effluent into the sea. And, finally, there was David's crazy fixation, from which Shasa was finding it difficult to dislodge him, that they should spend something over a quarter of a million pounds on one of those new elephantine electric calculators.

'The Yanks did all the calculations for the atomic bomb with one of them,' David argued. 'And they call them computers, not calculators,' he corrected Shasa.

'Come on, Davie, what are we going to blow up?' Shasa protested. 'I'm not designing an A-bomb.'

'Anglo-American have one. It's the wave of the future, Shasa. We'd better be on it.'

'It's a quarter-million-pound wave, old son,' Shasa pointed out. 'Just when we need every penny for Silver River.'

'If we'd had one of these computers to analyse the geological drilling reports from Silver River, we'd have already saved ourselves almost the entire cost of the thing, and we'd be a lot more certain of our final decision than we are now.'

'How can a machine be better than a human brain?'

'Just come and have a look at it,' David pleaded. 'The university has just installed an IBM 701. I have arranged a demonstration for you this afternoon.'

'OK, Davie,' Shasa capitulated. 'I'll look, but that doesn't mean I'm buying.'

The IBM supervisor in the basement of the engineering faculty building was no more than twenty-six years of age.

'They're all kids,' David explained. 'It's a young people's science.'

The supervisor shook hands with Shasa, and then removed her horn-rimmed spectacles. Suddenly Shasa's interest in electronic computers burgeoned. Her eyes were clear bright green and her hair was the colour of wild honey made from mimosa blossom. She wore a green sweater of tight-fitting angora wool, and a tartan skirt which left her smooth tanned calves bare. It was immediately obvious that she was an expert, and she answered all Shasa's questions without hesitation in a tantalizing Southern drawl.

'Marylee has a Masters in electrical engineering from MIT,' David murmured, and Shasa's initial attraction was spiced with respect.

'It's so damned big,' he protested. 'It fills the entire basement. The ruddy thing is the size of a four-bedroomed house.'

'Cooling,' Marylee explained. 'The heat build-up is enormous. Most of the bulk is oil cooling baffles.'

'What are you processing at the moment?'

'Professor Dart's archaeological material from the Sterk-fontein Caves. We are correlating about two hundred thousand observations of his against over a million from the sites in East Africa.'

'How long will that take you?'

'We started the run twenty minutes ago, we'll finish it before we shut down at five o'clock.'

'That's in fifteen minutes,' Shasa chuckled. 'You're having me on!'

'I wouldn't mind,' she murmured speculatively, and when she smiled her mouth was wide and moist and kissable.

'You say you shut down at five?' he asked. 'When do you start up again?'

'Eight tomorrow morning.'

'And the machine stands idle overnight?'

Marylee glanced down the length of the basement. David was at the other end watching the print-out and the hum of the computer covered their voices.

'That's right. It will stand idle all tonight. Just like me.' Clearly she was a lady who knew exactly what she wanted, and how to get it. She looked at him directly, challengingly.

'We can't have that.' Shasa shook his head seriously.

32

'One thing my mummy taught me was "Waste not, want not". I know a place called the Stardust. The band is far beyond belief. I will wager a pound to a weekend in Paris that I can dance you until you plead for mercy.'

'It's a bet,' she agreed as seriously. 'But do you cheat?'

'Of course,' he answered. David was coming back and Shasa went on smoothly and professionally. 'What about running costs?'

'All in, including insurance and depreciation, a little under four thousand pounds a month,' she told him with a matching businesslike expression.

As they said goodbye and shook hands, she slipped a card into Shasa's palm. 'My address,' she murmured.

'Eight o'clock?' he asked.

'I'll be there,' she agreed.

In the Cadillac, Shasa lit a cigarette and blew a perfect smoke ring that exploded silently against the windscreen.

'OK, Davie, contact the Dean of Engineering first thing tomorrow. Offer to hire that monster all its down time from five o'clock in the evening until eight the next morning, and weekends also. Offer him four thousand a month and point out that he'll get the use of it for free. We'll be paying all his costs.'

David turned to him with a startled expression and almost drove up onto the pavement, then corrected with a wild swing of the wheel.

'Why didn't I think of that?' he wondered when he had the Cadillac under control.

'You have to get up earlier.' Shasa grinned and then went on, 'Once we know how much time we will need on the thing, we'll sublet the surplus time to a couple of other non-competitor companies who must be thinking about buying a computer themselves. That way we'll get our own usage free, and when IBM have improved the design and made the damned thing smaller, then we will buy our own.'

'Son of a gun.' David shook his head in awe. 'Son of a gun.' Then with sudden inspiration, 'I'll get young Marylee on our payroll—'

'No,' said Shasa sharply. 'Get someone else.'

David glanced at him again and his excitement faded. He knew his brother-in-law too well.

'You won't be taking up Matty's invitation to dinner this evening, will you?' he asked morosely.

'Not this evening,' Shasa agreed. 'Give her my love and apologies.'

'Just be careful. It's a small town and you are a marked man,' David warned as he dropped Shasa off at the Carlton Hotel, where the company kept a permanent suite. 'Do you think you will be fit for work tomorrow?'

'Eight o'clock,' Shasa told him. 'Sharp!'

By mutual agreement the dance competition at the Stardust was declared a draw, and Shasa and Marylee got back to his Carlton suite a little after midnight.

Her body was young and smooth and hard and just before she drifted off to sleep with her thick honey-coloured hair spread on his bare chest, she whispered drowsily, 'Well, I guess that's about the only thing my IBM 701 can't do for me.'

Shasa was in the Courtney mining offices fifteen minutes before David the next morning. He liked to keep everybody on their toes. Their offices occupied the entire third floor of the Standard Bank building in Commissioner Street. Although Shasa owned a prime piece of real estate on the corner of Diagonal Street opposite the stock exchange and within yelling distance of Anglo-American Corporation's head office, he hadn't yet got around to building on it; any spare money in the company always seemed to be ear-marked for mining options or extensions or other income-producing enterprises.

The young blood on the Courtney executive board was

judicially leavened with a few grey heads. Dr Twentyman-Jones was still there, in an old-fashioned black alpaca jacket and string tie, hiding his affection for Shasa behind a mournful expression. He had run the very first prospect on the H'ani diamond mine for Centaine back in the early twenties and was one of the three most·experienced and gifted mining consultants in southern Africa, which meant the world.

David's father Abraham Abrahams was still head of the legal section, perched up beside his son, bright and chirpy as a little silver sparrow. His files were piled high on the table in front of him, but he seldom had to refer to them. With half a dozen other newcomers whom Centaine and Shasa between them had hand picked, it was a balanced and functional team.

'Let's talk about the Courtney chemical plant at Chaka's Bay first.' Shasa brought the meeting to order. 'How much meat is there in the beef against us, Abe?'

'We are running hot sulphuric acid into the sea at a rate of between eleven and sixteen tons per day at a concentration of one in ten thousand,' Abe Abrahams told him matter-of-factly. 'I've had an independent marine biologist do a report on it for us.' He tapped the document. 'It isn't good. We have altered the pH for five miles along the coastline.'

'You haven't circulated this report?' Shasa asked sharply.

'What do you think?' Abe shook his head.

'All right, David. What will it cost us to modify the manufacturing procedure on the fertilizer division to dispose of the acid waste some other way?'

'There are two possible modifications,' David told him. 'The simplest and cheapest is trucking the effluent in tankers, but then we have to find another dumping ground. The ideal solution is recycling the acid.'

'Costs?'

'One hundred thousand pounds per annum for the tankers – one shot of almost three times that for the other way.'

'A year's profits down the drain,' Shasa said. 'That's not acceptable. Who is this Pearson woman that is heading up the protest? Can we reason with her?'

Abe shook his head. 'We have tried. She is holding the whole committee together. Without her they would crumble.'

'What is her position?'

'Her husband owns the local bakery.'

'Buy it,' said Shasa. 'If he won't sell, let him know discreetly that we will open another bakery in competition and subsidize its product. I want this Pearson woman far away and long ago. Any questions?' He looked down the table. Everybody was busy making notes, nobody looked at him and he wanted to ask them reasonably, 'All right, gentlemen, are you prepared to spend three hundred thousand pounds to give a good home to the oysters and the sea urchins of Chaka's Bay?'

'No questions!' he nodded instead. 'All right, let's take on the big one now. Silver River.'

They all shifted in their seats, and there was simultaneous and nervous exhalation of breath.

'Gentlemen, we have all read and studied Dr Twentyman-Jones's geological report based on his drilling on the property. It is a superb piece of work, and I don't have to tell you that it's the best opinion you'll get on Harley Street. Now I want to hear from each of you your own opinions as departmental heads. Can we start with you, Rupert?'

Rupert Horn was the junior member of the executive team. As Treasurer and Chief Accountant he filled in the financial background.

'If we let the option lapse, we shall be writing off the two point three million that we have spent on exploration

36

over the last eighteen months. If we take up the option it will mean an initial payment of four million on signature.'

'We can cover that from the rainy-day account,' Shasa intervened.

'We are holding four point three million in the provisional fund,' Rupert Horn agreed. 'We have it invested in Escom seven per cent Stock at present, but once we utilize that fund we will be in an extremely exposed position.'

One after the other, in ascending order of seniority, Shasa's managers gave their views as seen from their own departments, and David put it all together at the end.

'So it seems that we have twenty-six days remaining on the option, and four million to pay if we take it up. That is going to leave us bare-bummed, and facing development costs of three million pounds for the main shaft alone, plus another five million for plant, interest and running costs to see us into the production phase, four years from now in 1956.' He stopped and they all watched intently while Shasa selected a cigarette and tapped it lightly on the lid of his gold case.

Shasa's expression was deadly serious. He knew better than any of them that the decision could destroy the company or take it up onto a new high plateau, and nobody could make that decision for him. He was up on the lonely pinnacle of command.

'We know there is gold down there,' he spoke at last. 'A thick rich reef of it. If we reach it, it will go on producing for the next fifty years. However, gold is standing at thirty-five dollars an ounce. The Americans have pegged it, they have threatened to keep the price there for all time. Thirty-five dollars an ounce – and it will cost us between twenty and twenty-five an ounce to go down that deep and bring it to the surface. A slim margin, gentlemen, much too slim.'

He lit the cigarette, and they all sighed and relaxed, at the same time disappointed and relieved. It would have been glorious to make the charge, but disastrous to have failed. Now they would never know. But Shasa hadn't finished. He blew a spinning smoke-ring down the length of the table, and went on.

'However, I don't think the Americans are going to be able to keep the lid on the gold price much longer. Their hatred of gold is emotional, not based on economic reality. I know, deep down in my guts, that the day is not far off when we will see gold at sixty dollars and one day, sooner than any of us think, it will be a hundred and fifty dollars – perhaps even two hundred!' They stirred with disbelief, and Twentyman-Jones looked as though he might break down and weep in the face of such wild optimism, but Shasa ignored him and turned to Abe Abrahams.

'Abe, at noon on the eighteenth of next month, twelve hours before the option expires, you will hand over a cheque for four million to the owners of Silver River farms, and take possession of the property in the name of a company to be formed.' Shasa turned to David. 'At the same time we will simultaneously open subscription lists on the Johannesburg and London Stock Exchanges for ten million one-pound shares in the Silver River gold-mining property. You and Dr Twentyman-Jones will start today drawing up the prospectus. Courtney Mining will register the property in the name of the new company in return for the balance of five million shares transferred into our name. We will also be responsible for the management and development.' Quickly, succinctly, Shasa laid out the structure, financing and management of the new company, and more than once these wily seasoned campaigners glanced up from their notepads in blatant admiration of some deft and unusual touch he added to the scheme.

'Is there anything I have left out?' Shasa asked at the end, and when they shook their heads, he grinned. David was reminded strongly of the movie he and Matty had taken the children to see the previous Saturday afternoon,

The Sea Hawk, though the eye-patch made Shasa look even more piratical than Errol Flynn had done in the title role.

'The founder of our company, Mme Centaine de Thiry Courtney-Malcomess, has never approved of the consumption of alcohol in the boardroom. However—' Still grinning, Shasa nodded at David, who went to open the main doors of the boardroom and a secretary wheeled in a trolley on which the rows of glasses clinked and the green bottles of Dom Perignon swished in their silver ice-buckets. 'Old customs give way to new,' Shasa said, and drew the first cork with a discreet pop.

Shasa throttled back the Rolls-Royce engines and the Mosquito sank down through the ribbons of scattered cirrus cloud, and the endless golden plains of the high African shield came up to meet her. Off to the west Shasa could just make out the clustered buildings of the mining town of Welkom, centre of the Orange Free State goldfields. Founded only a few years previously, when the vast Anglo-American Corporation began opening up these fields, it was already a model town of over a hundred thousand persons.

Shasa unclipped his oxygen mask and let it dangle on his chest as he leaned forward on his straps and peered ahead through the windshield ahead of the Mosquito's blue nose.

He picked out the tiny steel tower of the drilling rig almost lost in the immensity of the dusty plain, and using it as a landmark traced the gossamer thread of fences that enclosed the Silver River farms – eleven thousand acres, most of it bare and undeveloped. It was amazing that the geologists of the big mining houses had overlooked this little pocket, but then nobody could have reasonably expected the gold reef to spur off like that – that is, nobody but Twentyman-Jones and Shasa Courtney.

Yet the reef was as far beneath the earth as the Mosquito now circled above it. It seemed impossible that any human endeavour would be able to burrow down that deep, but already Shasa could see in his imagination the tall headgear of the Silver River main towering two hundred feet above the bleak plain, with its shaft stabbing down a mile and more into the underground river of precious metal.

'And the Yanks can't hold out for ever – they will have to let gold go free,' he told himself.

He stood the Mosquito on one wing and on the instrument panel the gyrocompass revolved smoothly. Shasa lifted the wing and she was precisely on her new heading of 125°.

'Fifteen minutes, with these winds,' he grunted, as he marked the large-scale map on his knee, and the fine exaltation of spirit stayed with him for the remainder of the flight until he saw the dark pencil-line of smoke rising into the still air dead ahead. They had put up a smoke beacon to guide him in.

There was a Dakota parked in front of the lonely galvanized iron-clad hangar at the end of the strip. The big aircraft had Air Force markings. The runway was of rolled yellow clay, hard and smooth and the Mosquito settled to it with barely a jolt. It had taken endless practice to develop that sort of distance judgement after he had lost the eye.

Shasa slid back the canopy and taxied towards the hangar. There was a green Ford pick-up near the mast of the windsock, and a lone figure dressed in khaki shorts and shirt stood beside the smoke pot, fists clenched on his hips, watching Shasa taxi up and cut the engines. Then as Shasa jumped down, he stepped forward and offered his right hand, but his expression, solemn and reserved, was at odds with the welcoming gesture.

'Good afternoon, Minister.' Shasa was as unsmiling and their grip was hard but brief. Then as Shasa looked deeply into Manfred De La Rey's pale eyes, he had a strange feeling of déjà vu, of having stared into those same eyes in desperate circumstances before. He had to shake his head slightly to be rid of it.

'I am glad for both our sakes that you were able to come. Can I help you with your bags?' Manfred De La Rey asked.

'Don't worry. I can manage.' Shasa went back to tie down and secure the Mosquito and fetch his luggage from the bomb bay, while Manfred doused the smoke pot.

'You brought your own rifle,' Manfred remarked. 'What is it?'

'Seven millimetre Remington magnum.' Shasa swung the luggage into the back of the truck and stepped up into the passenger door of the Ford.

'Perfect for this type of shooting,' Manfred approved as he started the truck. 'Long shots over flat ground.' He swung on to the track and they drove for a few minutes in silence.

'The Prime Minister could not come,' he said. 'He intended to be here, but he sent a letter for you. It confirms that I speak with his authority.'

'I'll accept that.' Shasa kept a straight face.

'The Minister of Finance is here, and the Minister of Agriculture is our host – this is his farm. One of the biggest in the Free State.'

'I am impressed.'

'Yes,' Manfred nodded. 'I think you will be.' He stared hard at Shasa. 'Is it not strange how you and I seem doomed always to confront each other?'

'It had crossed my mind,' Shasa admitted.

'Do you think there is some reason for it – something of which we are unaware?' Manfred insisted, and Shasa shrugged.

'I shouldn't think so – coincidence only.' The reply seemed to disappoint Manfred.

'Has your mother never spoken about me?'

Shasa looked startled. 'My mother! Good Lord, I don't think so. She may have mentioned you casually – why do you ask?'

Manfred seemed not to have heard, he looked ahead. 'There is the homestead,' he said, with a finality that closed the subject.

The track breasted the rim of a shallow valley and the homestead nestled below them. Here the water must be near the surface for the pasturage was lush and green and the skeletal steel towers of a dozen windmills were scattered down the valley. A plantation of eucalyptus trees surrounded the homestead, and beyond it stood substantial outbuildings, all freshly painted and in good repair. Twenty or more brand-new tractors were lined up before one of the long garages, and there were flocks of fat sheep on the pastures. The plain beyond the homestead reaching almost to the horizon was already ploughed, thousands of acres of chocolate loam ready for sowing with maize seed. This was the heart land of Afrikanerdom, this was where the support of the National Party was solid and unwavering, and it was the reason why under the Nationalists the electoral areas had been re-demarcated to swing the centres of power away from the urban concentrations of population to favour these rural constituencies. That was why the Nationalists would stay in power for ever, and Shasa grimaced sourly. Immediately Manfred glanced at him, but Shasa offered no explanation and they drove down to the homestead and parked in the farm yard.

There were a dozen men sitting at the long yellow-wood kitchen table, smoking and drinking coffee and chatting while the women hovered in attendance. The men rose to welcome Shasa and he went down the table shaking hands with each of them and exchanging polite, if not effusive greetings.

Shasa knew every one of them. He had faced all of them across the floor of the House and had lashed most of them with his tongue, and in return had been attacked and vilified by each of them, but now they made room for him at the table and the hostess poured strong black coffee for him and placed a dish of sweet cakes and hard-baked rusks in front of him. They all treated him with that innate courtesy and hospitality that is the hallmark of the Afrikaner. Though they were dressed in rough hunting clothing and pretended to be bluff and simple farmers, they were in reality a group of shrewd and adroit politicians, amongst the richest and most powerful men in the land.

Shasa spoke their language perfectly, understood the most heavily veiled references and laughed at their private jokes, but he was not one of them. He was the *rooinek*, the traditional enemy, and subtly they had closed their ranks against him.

When he had drunk his coffee his host, the Minister of Agriculture, told him, 'I will show you to your room. You will want to change and unpack your rifle. We will hunt as soon as it is cooler.'

A little after four o'clock, they set out in a procession of pick-up trucks, the elder, more important men riding in the cabs while the others stood in the open backs of the trucks. The cavalcade climbed out of the valley, skirted the ploughed lands and then sped out across the plains towards a line of low hills on the horizon.

They saw game now, small herds of springbok far out on the plain like a fine dusting of cinnamon powder on the pale earth, but the trucks raced on, slowing only as they reached the foot of the rocky hills. The lead truck stopped for a moment and two of the hunters jumped down and scrambled into a shallow donga.

43

'Good luck! Shoot straight,' they called to them as they passed and a few hundred yards further the convoy stopped again to let another pair take up their positions.

Within half an hour all of the huntsmen had been hidden in an irregular extended line below the ragged range of hills. Manfred De La Rey and Shasa had been placed together in a cluster of broken grey rock, and they squatted down to wait with their rifles across their laps, staring out across the flats that were speckled with darker scrub.

The trucks, driven by the teenage sons of their host, headed out in a wide circle until they were merely specks against the pale glare of the horizon, each marked by the ostrich feather of dust it drew behind it. Then they turned back towards the hills, travelling more slowly, not much above walking pace, as they began to move the scattered herds of antelope ahead of them.

Shasa and Manfred had almost an hour to wait for the driven game to come within rifle shot, and they chatted in a desultory, seemingly aimless manner, at first touching only lightly on politics, but rather discussing their host, the Minister of Agriculture, and the other guests. Then quite subtly Manfred changed the direction of their talk and remarked on how little real difference existed between the policies and aspirations of the governing National Party and Shasa's own Opposition United Party.

'If you examine it carefully, our differences are only those of style and degree. We both want to keep South Africa safe for the white man and for European civilization. We both know that for all of us *apartheid* is a matter of life and death. Without it we will all drown in the black sea. Since the death of Smuts, your party has moved sharply towards our own thinking, and the leftists and liberals have begun to split away from you.'

Shasa was noncommittal, but the point was apt and painful. There were deep cracks appearing in his own party, and every day it became more apparent that they would never again form the government of this land. However, he was intrigued to know where Manfred De La Rey was leading. He had learned never to underestimate his adversary, and he sensed that he was being artfully prepared for the true purpose of this invitation. It was quite obvious that their host had manoeuvred to place them together, and that every other member of the party was privy to the business afoot. Shasa spoke little, conceding nothing, and waited with rising anticipation for the lurking beast to reveal its shape.

'You know that we have entrenched the language and culture of the English-speaking South Africans. There will never be any attempt to erode those rights – we look upon all English speakers of good will who consider themselves South Africans first as our brothers. Our destinies are linked with chains of steel—' Manfred broke off, and lifted his binoculars to his eyes. 'They are moving in closer now,' he murmured. 'We had better get ready.' He lowered the binoculars and smiled carefully at Shasa. 'I have heard that you shoot well. I look forward to a demonstration.'

Shasa was disappointed. He had wanted to know where the carefully rehearsed recital had been heading, but now he hid his impatience behind that easy smile of his and opened the breech of the rifle across his lap.

'You are right in one thing, Minister,' he said. 'We are linked together with chains of steel. Let us hope the weight of them doesn't draw us all under.' He saw a strange flash in those topaz yellow eyes, of anger or triumph, he was not certain, and it lasted only an instant.

'I will fire only on a line from dead ahead towards the right,' Manfred said. 'You only in an arc to the left. Agreed?'

'Agreed,' Shasa nodded, although he felt a prickle of irritation at being out-manoeuvred so soon and so easily. Manfred had carefully placed himself to cover the right flank, the natural side for a right-handed marksman to swing.

'You will need the advantage,' Shasa thought grimly and asked aloud, 'I hear you also are a fine shot. What about a small wager on the bag?'

'I do not gamble,' Manfred replied easily. 'That is a device of the devil, but I will count the bag with interest,' and Shasa was reminded of just how puritanical was the extreme Calvinism that Manfred De La Rey practised.

Carefully Shasa loaded his rifle. He had hand-loaded his own cartridges for he never trusted mass-produced factory ammunition. The shiny brass cases were filled with a charge of Norma powder that would drive the Nosler Partition bullet at well over three thousand feet a second. The special construction of the bullet would ensure that it mushroomed perfectly on impact.

He worked the bolt and then raised the weapon to his shoulder and used the telescopic sight to scan the plain. The pick-up trucks were less than a mile away, gently weaving back and forth, to prevent the herds breaking back, keeping them moving slowly down towards the line of hills and the hunters hidden below them. Shasa blinked his eye rapidly to clear his vision, and he could make out each individual animal in the herds of antelope trotting ahead of the vehicles.

They were light as smoke, and they rippled like cloud shadow across the plain. Trotting daintily with heads held high and with their horns shaped like perfect miniature lyres, they were graceful and indescribably lovely.

Without stereoscopic vision Shasa had difficulty in judging distance, but he had developed the knack of defining relative size and added to this a kind of sixth sense that enabled him to pilot an aircraft, strike a polo ball, or shoot as well as any fully sighted person.

The nearest of the approaching antelope were almost at extreme range when there was a crackle of rifle fire from further down the line and immediately the herds exploded into silent airy flight. Each tiny creature danced and bounced on long legs no thicker than a man's thumb. Seeming no longer bounded by the dictates of gravity, every fluid leap blurring against the matching background of parched earth, they tumbled and shot into the mirage-quivering air in the spectacular display of aerobatics that gave them their name, and down each of their backs a frosty mane came erect and shone with their alarm.

It was more difficult than trying to bring down a rocketing grouse with a spreading pattern of shot, imposs-ible to hold the darting ethereal shapes in the cross-hairs of the lens, fruitless to aim directly at the swift creatures – necessary rather to aim at the empty space where they would be a microsecond later when the supersonic bullet reached them.

With some men shooting well is skill learned with much practice and concentration. With Shasa it was a talent that he had been born with. As he turned his upper body, the long barrel pointed exactly where he was looking and the cross-hairs of the telescopic sight moved smoothly in the centre of his vision and settled on the nimble body of a racing antelope as it went bounding high in the air. Shasa was not conscious of squeezing the trigger, the rifle seemed to fire of its own accord and the recoil drove into his shoulder at precisely the correct instant.

The ram died in the air, turned over by the bullet so his snowy belly flashed in the sunlight, somersaulting to the impetus of the tiny metal capsule as it lanced his heart, and he fell and rolled horned head over dainty hoofs as he hit the earth and lay still.

Shasa worked the bolt and picked up another running creature and the rifle fired again and the sharp stink of burned powder prickled his nostrils. He kept shooting until the barrel was hot enough to raise blisters and his eardrums ached to the crackle of shot.

Then the last of the herds were gone past them and over the hills behind them, and the gunfire died away. Shasa unloaded the cartridges that remained in his rifle and looked at Manfred De La Rey.

'Eight,' Manfred said, 'and two wounded.' It was amazing how those tiny creatures could carry away a misplaced bullet. They would have to follow them up. It was unthinkable to allow a wounded animal to suffer unnecessarily.

'Eight is a good score,' Shasa told him. 'You can be pleased with your shooting.'

'And you?' Manfred asked. 'How many?'

'Twelve,' Shasa answered expressionlessly.

'How many wounded?' Manfred hid his chagrin well enough.

'Oh.' Shasa smiled at last. 'I don't wound animals — I shoot where I aim.' That was enough. He did not have to rub in salt.

Shasa left him and walked out to the nearest carcass. The springbok lay on its side and in death the deep fold of skin along its back had opened and from it the snowy plume started erect. Shasa went down on one knee and stroked the lovely plume. From the glands in the fold of skin had exuded reddish-brown musk, and Shasa parted the long plume and rubbed the secretion with his forefinger, then raised it to his face and inhaled the honey-scented aroma. It smelled more like a flower than an animal. Then the hunter's melancholy came upon him, and he mourned the beautiful little creature he had killed.

'Thank you for dying for me.' He whispered the ancient Bushman prayer that Centaine had taught him so long ago, and yet the sadness was pleasure, and deep inside him the atavistic urge of the hunter was for the moment replete.

In the cool of the evening the men gathered around the
pits of glowing embers in front of the homestead. The
braaivleis, or meat bake, was a ritual that followed
the hunt; the men did the cooking while the women were
relegated to the preparation of salads and pudding at the
long trestle tables on the stoep. The game had been
marinated or larded or made into spiced sausage and the
livers, kidneys and tripes were treated to jealously guarded
recipes before they were laid upon the coals in the grilling
pit, while the self-appointed chefs kept the heat of the fires
from becoming oppressive with liberal draughts of *mampoer*,
the pungent peach brandy.

A scratch band of coloured farm labourers belted out
traditional country airs on banjo and concertina and some
of the guests danced on the wide front stoep. A few of the
younger women were very interesting, and Shasa eyed them
thoughtfully. They were tanned and glowing with health
and an unsophisticated sensuality that was made all the
more appealing by the fact of their Calvinist upbringing.
Their untouchability and probable virginity made them
even more attractive to Shasa, who enjoyed the chase as
much as the kill.

However, there was too much at stake here to risk giving
the slightest offence. He avoided the shy but calculating
glances that some of them cast in his direction, and avoided
just as scrupulously the savage peach brandy and filled his
glass with ginger ale. He knew he would need all his wits
before the night was ended.

When their appetites, sharpened on the hunting veld,
had been blunted by the steaming platters piled with grilled
venison, and the leftovers had been carried away delightedly to the servants' quarters, Shasa found himself sitting
at the end of the long stoep furthest from the band. Manfred
De La Rey was sitting opposite him, and the two other
ministers of the government sprawled contentedly in their
deep lounging chairs flanking him. Despite their relaxed

attitudes, they watched him warily from the corners of their eyes.

'The main business is about to begin,' Shasa decided, and almost immediately Manfred stirred.

'I was telling Meneer Courtney that in many ways we are very close,' Manfred started quietly, and his colleagues nodded sagely. 'We all want to protect this land and preserve all that is fine and worthwhile in it.

'God has chosen us as guardians – it is our duty to protect all its peoples, and make certain that the identity of each group and each separate culture is kept intact, and apart from the others.'

It was the party line, this notion of divine selection, and Shasa had heard it all a hundred times before; so although he nodded and made small noncommittal sounds, he was becoming restless.

'There is still much to be done,' Manfred told him. 'After the next election we will have great labours ahead of us, we are the masons building a social edifice that will stand for a thousand years. A model society in which each group will have its place, and will not intrude upon the space of others, a broad and stable pyramid forming a unique society.' They were all silent then for a while, contemplating the beauty of the vision, and though Shasa kept his expression neutral, still he smiled inwardly at the apt metaphor of a pyramid. There was no doubt in any of their minds as to which group was divinely ordained to occupy the pinnacle.

'And yet there are enemies?' The Minister of Agriculture cued Manfred.

'There are enemies, within and without. They will become more vociferous and dangerous as the work goes ahead. The closer we come to success, the more avid they become to prevent us achieving it.'

'Already they are gathering.'

'Yes,' Manfred agreed. 'And even old and traditional friends are warning and threatening us. America, who should know better, racked by her own racial problems, the unnatural aspirations of the negroes they brought as slaves from Africa. Even Britain with her Mau Mau troubles in Kenya and the disintegration of her Indian Empire wishes to dictate to us and divert us from the course we know is right.'

'They believe us to be weak and vulnerable.'

'They already hint at an arms embargo, denying us the weapons to defend ourselves against the dark enemy that is gathering in the shadows.'

'They are right,' Manfred cut in brusquely. 'We are weak and militarily disorganized. We are at the mercy of their threats—'

'We have to change this.' The Finance Minister spoke harshly. 'We must make ourselves strong.'

'At the next budget the defence allocation will be fifty million pounds, while by the end of the decade it will be a billion.'

'We must put ourselves above their threats of sanction and boycott and embargo.'

'Strength through Unity, *Ex Unitate Vires*,' said Manfred De La Rey. 'And yet by tradition and preference, the Afrikaner people have been farmers and country folk. Because of the discrimination which was practised against us for a hundred years and more, we have been excluded from the marketplace of commerce and industry and we have not learned the skills which come so readily to our English-speaking countrymen.' Manfred paused, glanced at the other two, as if for approval, and then went on. 'What this country needs desperately is the wealth to make our vision come true. It is a massive undertaking for which we lack the skills. We need a special type of man.' They were all looking keenly at Shasa now. 'We need a man with the vigour of youth but the experience of age, a man with proven genius for finance and organization. We can find no member of our own party with those attributes.'

Shasa stared at them. What they were suggesting was outrageous. He had grown up in the shadow of Jan Christiaan Smuts and had a natural and unshakeable allegiance to the party that Smuts, that great and good man, had founded. He opened his mouth to answer angrily, but Manfred De La Rey raised his hand to stop him.

'Hear me out,' he said. 'The person chosen for this patriotic work would be immediately given a senior cabinet appointment which the Prime Minister would create specifically for him. He would become Minister of Mines and Industry.'

Shasa closed his mouth slowly. How carefully they must have studied him, and how accurately they had analysed him and arrived at his price. The very foundations of his political beliefs and principles were shaken, and the walls cracked through. They had led him up into a high place and shown him the prize that was his for the taking.

At twenty thousand feet Shasa levelled the Mosquito and trimmed for cruise. He increased the flow of oxygen into his mask to sharpen his brain. He had four hours' flying time to Youngsfield, four hours to think it all out carefully, and he tried to divorce himself from the passions and emotions which still swept him along and attempt instead to reach his decision logically – but the excitement intruded upon his meditations. The prospect of wielding vast powers, building up an arsenal that would make his country supreme in Africa and a force in the world was awe-inspiring. That was power. The thought of it all made him slightly light-headed, for it was all there at last, everything he had ever dreamed of. He had only to reach out his hand and seize the moment. Yet what would be the cost in honour and pride – how would he explain to men who trusted him?

Then abruptly he thought of Blaine Malcomess, his mentor and adviser, the man who had stood in the place of his own father all these years. What would he think of this dreadful betrayal that Shasa was contemplating?

'I can do more good by joining them, Blaine,' he whispered into his mask. 'I can help change and moderate them from within more effectively than in opposition, for now I will have the power—' but he knew he was prevaricating, and all else was dross.

It all came down to that one thing in the end, the power – and he knew that although Blaine Malcomess would never condone what he would see as treachery, there was one person who would understand and give him support and encouragement. For after all it was Centaine Courtney-Malcomess who had so carefully schooled her son in the acquisition and use of wealth and power.

'It could all come true, Mater. It could still happen, not exactly as we planned it, but it could still happen all the same.' Then a thought struck him, and a shadow passed across the bright light of his triumph.

He glanced down at the red folder that Manfred De La Rey, Minister of Police, had given him at the airstrip, just as he was about to climb up into the Mosquito, and which now lay on the co-pilot's seat beside him.

'There is only one problem we will have to deal with, if you accept our offer,' Manfred had said as he handed it over, 'and it is a serious problem. This is it.'

The folder contained a police Special Branch security report, and the name on the cover was:

TARA ISABELLA COURTNEY née
MALCOMESS

Tara Courtney made her round of the children's wing, calling in at each of the bedrooms. Nanny was just tucking Isabella under her pink satin eiderdown, and the child let out a cry of delight when she saw Tara.

'Mummy, Mummy, teddy has been naughty. I'm going to make him sleep on the shelf with my other dolls.'

Tara sat on her daughter's bed and hugged her while they discussed teddy's misdemeanours. Isabella was pink and warm and smelled of soap. Her hair was silky against Tara's cheek and it took an effort for Tara to kiss her and stand up.

'Time to go to sleep, Bella baby.'

The moment the lights went out Isabella let out such a shriek that Tara was stricken with alarm.

'What is it, baby?' She snapped on the lights again and rushed back to the bed.

'I've forgiven teddy. He can sleep with me after all.'

The teddy-bear was ceremoniously reinstated in Isabella's favour and she took him in a loving half-nelson and stuck her other thumb in her mouth.

'When is my daddy coming home?' she demanded drowsily around the thumb, but her eyes were closed and she was asleep before Tara reached the door.

Sean was sitting on Garrick's chest in the middle of the bedroom floor, tweaking the hair at his brother's temples with sadistic finesse. Tara separated them.

'Sean, you get back to your own room this instant, do you hear me? I have warned you a thousand times about bullying your brothers. Your father is going to hear all about this when he gets home.'

Garrick snuffled up his tears and came wheezing to his elder brother's defence.

'We were only playing, Mater. He wasn't bullying me.' But she could hear that he was on the verge of another asthma attack. She wavered. She really should not go out,

54

not with an attack threatening, but tonight was so important.

'I'll prepare his inhaler and tell Nanny to look in on him every hour until I get back,' she compromised.

Michael was reading, and barely looked up to receive her kiss. 'Lights out at nine o'clock. Promise me, darling.' She tried never to let it show, but he was always her favourite.

'I promise, Mater,' he murmured and under cover of the eiderdown carefully crossed his fingers.

On the way down the stairs she glanced at her wrist-watch. It was five minutes before eight. She was going to be late, and she stifled her maternal feelings of guilt and fled out to her old Packard.

Shasa detested the Packard, taking its blotched sun-faded paintwork and its shabby stained upholstery as an affront to the family dignity. He had given her a new Aston Martin on her last birthday, but she left it in the garage. The Packard suited her spartan image of herself as a caring liberal, and it blew a streamer of dirty smoke as she accelerated down the long driveway, taking a perverse pleasure in sending a pall of fine dust over Shasa's meticu-lously groomed vineyards. It was strange how even after all these years she felt herself a stranger at Weltevreden, and alien amongst its treasures and stuffy old-fashioned furnish-ings. If she lived here another fifty years it would never be her home, it was Centaine Courtney-Malcomess' home, the other woman's touch and memory lingered in every room that Shasa would never allow her to redecorate.

She escaped through the great ostentatious Anreith gateway into the real world of suffering and injustice, where the oppressed masses wept and struggled and cried out for succour and where she felt useful and relevant, where in the company of other pilgrims she could march forward to meet a future full of challenge and change.

The Broadhursts' home was in the middle-class suburb

of Pinelands, a modern ranch-type home with a flat roof and large picture windows, with ordinary functional mass-produced furniture and nylon wall-to-wall carpets. There were dog hairs on the chairs, well-thumbed intellectual books piled in odd corners or left open on the dining-room table, children's toys abandoned in the passageways, and cheap reproductions of Picasso and Modigliani hanging askew on the walls marked with grubby little fingerprints. Tara felt comfortable and welcome here, mercifully released from the fastidious splendour of Weltevreden.

Molly Broadhurst rushed out to meet her as she parked the Packard. She was dressed in a marvellously flamboyant caftan.

'You're late!' She kissed Tara heartily and dragged her through the disorder of the lounge to the music room at the rear.

The music room was an afterthought stuck on to the end of the house without any aesthetic considerations and was filled now with Molly's guests who had been invited to hear Moses Gama. Tara's spirits soared as she looked around her; they were all vibrant creative people, all of them spirited and articulate, filled with the excitment of living and a fine sense of justice and outrage and rebellion.

This was the type of gathering that Weltevreden would never see. Firstly, black people were included, students from the black University of Fort Hare and the fledgling University of the Western Cape, teachers and lawyers and even a black doctor, all of them political activists who, although denied a voice or a vote in the white parliament, were beginning to cry out with a passion that must be heard. There was the editor of the black magazine *Drum* and the local correspondent of the *Sowetan*, named after that sprawling black township.

Just to mingle socially with blacks made her feel breathlessly daring.

The whites in the room were no less extraordinary.

Some of them had been members of the Communist Party of South Africa before that organization had been disbanded a few years previously. There was a man called Harris whom she had met before at Molly's house. He had fought with the Irgun in Israel against the British and the Arabs, a tall fierce man who inspired a delicious fear in Tara. Molly hinted that he was an expert in guerrilla warfare and sabotage, and certainly he was always travelling secretly around the country or slipping across the border into neighbouring states on mysterious business.

Talking earnestly to Molly's husband was another lawyer from Johannesburg, Bram Fischer, who specialized in defending black clients charged under the myriad laws that were designed to muzzle and disarm them and restrict their movements. Molly said that Bram was reorganizing the old Communist Party into underground cells, and Tara fantasized that she might one day be invited to join one of these cells.

In the same group was Marcus Archer, another ex-Communist and an industrial psychologist from the Witwatersrand. He was responsible for the training of thousands of black workers for the gold-mining industry, and Molly said that he had helped to organize the black mineworkers' union. Molly had also whispered that he was a homosexual, and she had used an odd term for it that Tara had never heard before. 'He's gay, gay as a lark.' And because it was totally unacceptable to polite society, Tara found it fascinating.

'Oh, God, Molly,' Tara whispered. 'This is so exciting. These are all real people, they make me feel as though I am truly living at last.'

'There he is.' Molly smiled at this outburst and dragged Tara with her through the press of bodies.

Moses Gama leaned against the far wall faced by a half-circle of admirers, yet standing head and shoulders above them, and Molly pushed her way into the front row.

Tara found herself staring up at Moses Gama, and she thought that even in this brilliant company he stood out like a black panther in a pack of mangy alley cats. Though his head seemed carved from a block of black onyx, and his handsome Nilotic features were impassive, yet there was a force within him that seemed to fill all the room. It was like standing on the high slopes of a dark Vesuvius, knowing that at any instant it could boil over into cataclysmic eruption.

Moses Gama turned his head and looked at Tara. He did not smile, but a shadowy thing moved in the depths of his dark gaze.

'Mrs Courtney – I asked Molly to invite you.'

'Please don't call me that. My name is Tara.'

'We must talk later, Tara. Will you stay?'

She could not answer, she was too overcome at being singled out, but she nodded dumbly.

'If you are ready, Moses, we can begin,' Molly suggested, and taking him out of the group led him to the raised dais on which the piano stood.

'People! People! Your attention; please!' Molly clapped her hands, and the animated chatter died away. Everybody turned towards the dais. 'Moses Gama is one of the most talented and revered of the new generation of young black African leaders. He has been a member of the African National Congress since before the war, and a prime mover in the formation of the African Mineworkers' Union. Although the black trade unions are not officially recognized by the government of the day, yet the secret union of mineworkers is one of the most representative and powerful of all black associations, with more than a hundred thousand paid-up members. In 1950 Moses Gama was elected Secretary of the ANC, and he has worked tirelessly, selflessly and highly effectively in making the heart cry of our black citizens heard, even though they are denied a voice in their own destiny. For a short while Moses Gama was an appointed member of the government's Natives' Representative Council, that infamous attempt to appease black political aspirations, but it was he who resigned with the now celebrated remark, "I have been speaking into a toy telephone, with nobody listening at the other end."'

There was a burst of laughter and applause from the room, and then Molly turned to Moses Gama.

'I know that you have nothing to tell us that will comfort and soothe us – but, Moses Gama, in this room there are many hearts that beat with yours and are prepared to bleed with yours.'

Tara applauded until the palms of her hands were numb, and then leaned forward to listen eagerly as Moses Gama moved to the front of the dais.

He was dressed in a neat blue suit and a dark blue tie with a white shirt. Strangely, he was the most formally dressed man in a room full of baggy woollen sweaters and old tweed sports coats with leather patches on the elbows and gravy stains on the lapels. His suit was severely cut, draped elegantly from wide athletic shoulders, but he imparted to it a panache that made it seem that he wore the leopard-skin cloak of royalty and the blue heron feathers in his close-cropped mat of hair. His voice was deep and thrilling.

'My friends, there is one single ideal to which I cling with all my heart, and which I will defend with my very life, and that is that every African has a primary, inherent and inalienable right to the Africa which is his continent and his only motherland,' Moses Gama began, and Tara listened, enchanted, as he detailed how that inherent right had been denied the black man for three hundred years, and how in these last few years since the Nationalist government had come to power those denials were becoming formally entrenched in a monumental edifice of laws and ordinances and proclamations which was the policy of *apartheid* in practice.

'We have all heard it said that the whole concept of *apartheid* is so grotesque, so obviously lunatic, that it can never work. But I warn you, my friends, that the men who have conceived this crazy scheme are so fanatical, so obdurate, so convinced of their divine guidance, that they will force it to work. Already they have created a vast army of petty civil servants to administer this madness, and they have behind them the full resources of a land rich in gold and minerals. I warn you that they will not hesitate to squander that wealth in building up this ideological Frankenstein's monster of theirs. There is no price in material wealth and human suffering that is too high for them to contemplate.'

Moses Gama paused and looked down upon them, and it seemed to Tara that he personally felt every last agony of his people, and was filled with suffering beyond that which mortal men could bear.

'Unless they are opposed, my friends, they will create of this lovely land a desolation and an abomination; a land devoid of compassion, of justice, a land materially and spiritually bankrupt.'

Moses Gama spread his arms. 'These men call those of us who defy them traitors. Well, my friends, I call any man who does not oppose them a traitor – a traitor to Africa.'

He was silent then, glaring this accusation at them, and they were struck dumb for a moment, before they began to cheer him. Only Tara remained still in the uproar, staring up at him; she had no voice, and she was shivering as though there was malaria in her blood.

Moses' head sank until his chin was on his chest, and they thought he had finished. Then he raised that magnificent head again and spread his arms.

'Oppose them? How do we oppose them? I reply to you – we oppose them with all our strength and all our resolve and with all our hearts. If no price is too high for them to pay, then no price is too high for us. I tell you, my friends, there is nothing—' he paused for emphasis – '*nothing* I would not do to further the struggle. I am prepared both to die and to kill for it.'

The room was silent in the face of such deadly resolve. For those of them who were practitioners of elegant socialist dialectic, the effete intellectuals, such a declaration was menacing and disquieting, it had the sound of breaking bones in it and the stench of fresh-spilled blood.

'We are ready to make a beginning, my friends, and already our plans are far advanced. Starting in a few months' time we will conduct a nationwide campaign of defiance against these monstrous *apartheid* laws. We will burn the passes which we are ordered by act of parliament to carry, the hated *dompas* which is akin to the star that the Jews were forced to wear, the document that marks us as racial inferiors. We will make a bonfire of them and the smoke of their burning will sting and offend the nostrils of the civilized world. We will sit in the whites-only restaurants and cinemas, we will ride in the whites-only coaches of the railways, and swim from the whites-only beaches. We will cry out to the fascist police, "Come! Arrest us." And in our thousands we will overflow the white man's jails and block his law courts with our multitudes until the whole giant apparatus of *apartheid* breaks down under the strain.'

Tara lingered afterwards as he had asked her to, and when Molly had seen most of her guests leave, she came and took Tara's arm. 'Will you risk my spaghetti Bolognaise, Tara dear? As you know, I'm the worst cook in Africa, but you are a brave girl.'

Only a half-dozen of the guests had been invited to remain for a late dinner and they sat out on the patio. The mosquitoes whined around their heads and every once in a while a shift of the wind brought a sulphurous whiff from the sewerage works across the Black River. It did not seem to spoil their appetites and they tucked into Molly's notorious spaghetti bolognaise and washed it down with tumblers of cheap red wine. Tara found it a relief from the elaborate meals that were served at Weltevreden, accompanied always by the quasi-religious ceremony of tasting wines that cost a working man's monthly wage for the bottle. Here food and wine were merely fuel to power the mind and tongue, not for gloating over.

Tara sat beside Moses Gama. Although his appetite was hearty, he hardly touched the tumbler of wine. His table manners were African. He ate noisily with an open mouth, but strangely this did not offend Tara in the least. Somehow it confirmed his differentness, marked him as a man of his own people.

At first Moses gave most of his attention to the other guests, replying to the questions and comments that were called down the table to him. Then gradually he concentrated on Tara, at first including her in his general conversation, and at last, when he had finished eating, turning in his chair to face her fully and lowering his voice to exclude the others.

'I know your family,' he told her. 'Know them well, Mrs Centaine Courtney and more especially your husband, Shasa Courtney.'

Tara was startled. 'I have never heard them speak of you.'

'Why would they do so? In their eyes I was never important. They would have forgotten me long ago.'

'Where did you know them and when?'

'Twenty years ago. Your husband was still a child. I was a boss-boy, a supervisor in the H'ani Diamond Mine in South-west Africa.'

'The H'ani,' Tara nodded. 'Yes, the fountainhead of the Courtney fortune.'

'Shasa Courtney was sent by his mother to learn the workings of the mine. He and I were together for a few weeks, working side by side—' Moses broke off and smiled. 'We got along well, as well as a black man and a little white *baas* ever could, I suppose. We talked a great deal, and he gave me a book. Macaulay's *History of England*. I still have it. I recall how some of the things I said puzzled and disturbed him. He told me once, "Moses, that is politics. Blacks don't take part in politics. That's white men's business."' Moses chuckled at the memory, but Tara frowned.

'I can hear him say it,' she agreed. 'He hasn't changed much in twenty years,' and Moses stopped laughing.

'Your husband has become a powerful man. He has great wealth and influence.'

Tara shrugged. 'What good is power and wealth unless it is used with wisdom and compassion?'

'You have compassion, Tara,' he said softly. 'Even if I did not know of the work that you do for my people, I would sense it in you.'

Tara lowered her eyes from his smouldering regard.

'Wisdom.' His voice sank even lower. 'I think you have that also. It was wise not to speak of our last meeting in front of others.'

Tara's head came up and she stared at him. In the evening's excitement she had almost forgotten their encounter in the forbidden corridors of parliament.

'Why?' she whispered. 'Why were you there?'

'One day I may tell you,' he replied. 'When we have become friends.'

'We are friends,' she said, and he nodded.

'Yes, I think we are friends, but friendships have to be tried and proven. Now, tell me about your work, Tara.'

'It's so very little that I am able to do—' and she told him about the clinic and the feeding scheme for the children and the old people, unconscious of her own enthusiasm and antimation until he smiled again.

'I was right, you do have compassion, Tara, enormous compassion. I would like to see this work. Is it possible?'

'Oh, would you come – that would be marvellous!'

Molly brought him out to the clinic the following afternoon.

The clinic was on the southern edge of the black township of Nyanga – the name meant 'dawn' in the Xhosa language, but was hardly apt. Like most black townships it comprised row upon row of identical brick cottages with asbestos-sheet roofs separated by dusty lanes; although aesthetically ugly and uninspiring, the accommodation was adequate and offered reticulated water, mains sewerage and electricity. However, beyond the township proper, in the bushy dune country of the Cape Flats, had sprung up a shanty town that housed the overflow of black migrants from the impoverished rural areas, and Tara's clinic found its main clientele amongst these wretches.

Proudly Tara led Moses and Molly around the small building.

'Being the weekend, none of our volunteer doctors are here today,' she explained and Moses stopped to chat with the black nurses and with some of the mothers waiting patiently with their small children in the yard.

Afterwards she made coffee for all three of them in her tiny office and when Moses asked how the clinic was financed, Tara told him vaguely, 'Oh, we get a grant from the local provincial government—' but Molly Blackhurst cut in.

'Don't let her fool you – most of the running costs come out of her own pocket.'

'I cheat my husband on the housekeeping,' Tara laughed, dismissing it lightly.

'Would it be possible for us to drive around the squatter slums? I'd like to see them.' Moses looked at Molly, but she bit her lip and glanced at her wristwatch.

'Oh, damn, I have to get back,' and Tara intervened quickly.

'Don't worry, Molly. I can drive Moses around. You get on back and I will drop him off at your house later this evening.'

In the old Packard they bumped over the sandy tracks amongst the overgrown dunes, where the Port Jackson willow had been cleared to make way for hutments of rusty corrugated iron and cardboard and tattered plastic sheeting. Now and then they stopped and walked amongst the shanties. The south-easter was roaring in off the bay, filling the air with a mist of dust. They leaned against it as they walked.

The people knew Tara and smiled and called greetings to her as she passed, and the children ran to meet her and danced around her begging for the cheap boiled sweets she kept in her pocket.

'Where do they get water?' Moses asked, and she showed him how the older children had banded old oil drums with discarded car tyres. They filled the drums at a communal water tap at the boundary of the official township a mile away, and rolled the drums back to their hovels.

'They cut the Port Jackson willow for fuel,' Tara told him, 'but in winter the children are always full of colds and flu and pneumonia. You don't have to ask about about sewerage—' She sniffed at the thick odour of the shallow toilet pits, screened with strips of old burlap.

It was half dark when Tara parked the Packard at the back door of the clinic and switched off the engine. They sat quietly for a few minutes.

'What we have seen is no worse than a hundred other shanty towns, places where I have lived most of my life,' Moses said.

'I am sorry.'

'Why do you apologize?' Moses asked.

'I don't know, I just feel guilty.' She knew how inadequate it sounded and she opened the door of the Packard.

'There are some papers I must get from my office. I won't be a minute, and then I will drive you back to Molly's house.'

The clinic was deserted. The two nurses had locked up and gone home an hour before. Tara let herself in with her own key and went through the single consulting room to her own office. She glanced at herself in the mirror above the washstand in the corner as she washed her hands. She was flushed and her eyes sparkled. She was so accustomed to the squalor of the squatter camps that it had not depressed her as it once had; instead she felt tinglingly alive and strangely elated.

She stuffed the folder of correspondence and bills into her leather sling bag and locked the drawer of her desk, made sure the plug of the electric kettle was pulled out of the wall-socket and that the windows were closed, then switched off the lights and hurried out into the consulting room. She stopped with surprise. Moses Gama had followed her into the building and was sitting on the white draped examination bed against the far wall.

'Oh,' she recovered. 'Sorry I took so long—'

He shook his head, then stood up and crossed the tiled floor. He stopped, facing her. She felt awkward and uncertain as he studied her face solemnly.

'You are a remarkable woman,' he said in a deep quiet voice that she had not heard him use before. 'I have never met another white woman like you.'

She could think of no reply, and he went on softly, 'You are rich and privileged. You are gifted with everything that your life can offer you, and yet you come here. To this poverty and misery.'

He reached out and touched her arm. His palm and the inside of his fingers were a pale rose colour, contrasting vividly with the back of his hand and his dark muscular forearm, and his skin felt cool. She wondered if it were

66

really so, or if her own skin was hot. She felt hot, she felt a furnace glow deep within her. She looked down at his hand on her smooth pale arm. She had never been touched by a black man before, not deliberately, not lingeringly like this.

She let the strap of the sling bag slide off her shoulder and it fell to the tiled floor with a thud. She had been holding her own hands clasped in front of her hips in an instinctively defensive gesture but now she let them fall to her sides, and almost without conscious volition arched her back and pushed her lower body towards him. At the same time she raised her head and looked squarely into his eyes. Her lips parted and her breathing quickened. She saw it reflected in his own eyes and she said,

'Yes.'

He stroked her arm, up from the elbow to the shoulder, and she shuddered and closed her eyes. He touched her left breast and she did not pull away. His hand closed around her, she felt it fill his grip, and her flesh hardened, her flesh hardened, her nipple swelled and thrust out into his palm and he squeezed her. The feeling was so intense it was almost painful and she gasped as it rippled down her spine spreading like wavelets when a stone is thrown into a quiet pool.

Her arousal was so abrupt that she was unprepared. She had never considered herself a sensual person. Shasa was the only man she had ever known and it took all his skill and patience to quicken her body, but now at a touch her bones went soft with desire and her loins melted like wax in the flame and she could not breathe, so strong was her need of this man.

'The door,' she blurted. 'Lock the door.'

Then she saw that he had already barred the door, and she was grateful for it, for she felt that she could not have brooked the delay. He picked her up quickly and carried her to the bed. The sheet that covered it was spotless and so crisply starched that it crackled softly under her weight.

He was so huge that he terrified her, and though she had borne four children, she felt as though she was being split asunder as his blackness filled her, and then the terror passed to be replaced by a strange sense of sanctity. She was the sacrificial lamb, with this act she was redeeming all the sins of her own race, all the trespasses that they had committed against his people down the centuries; she was wiping away the guilt that had been her stigmata since as far back as she could remember.

When at the end he lay heavy upon her with his breathing roaring in her ears and the last wild convulsions racking his great black muscles, she clung to him with a joyous gratitude. For he had, at one and the same time, set her free from guilt and made her his slave for ever.

Subdued by the sadness of afterlove, and by the certain knowledge that her world was for ever altered, Tara was silent on the drive back to Molly's home. She parked a block before she reached it, and keeping the engine running she turned to examine his face in the reflection of the street lights.

'When will I see you again?' She asked the question that countless women in her position had asked before her.

'Do you wish to see me again?'

'More than anything else in my life.' She did not at that moment even think of her children. He was the only thing in her existence.

'It will be dangerous.'

'I know.'

'The penalties if we are discovered – disgrace, ostracism, imprisonment. Your life would be destroyed.'

'My life was a sham,' she said softly. 'Its destruction would be no great loss.'

He studied her features carefully, searching for insincerity. At last he was satisfied.

'I will send for you, when it is safe.'

'I will come immediately, whenever you call.'

'I must leave you now. Take me back.'

She parked at the side of Molly's house, in the shadow where they could not be observed from the road.

'Now the subterfuge and dissembling begins,' she thought calmly. 'I was right. It will never be the same again.'

He made no attempt to embrace her, it was not the African way. He stared at her, the whites of his eyes gleaming like ivory in the half dark.

'You realize that when you choose me you choose the struggle?' he asked.

'Yes, I know that.'

'You have become a warrior and you and your wants, even your life, are of no consequence. If you have to die for the struggle, I will not lift my hand to save you.'

She nodded. 'Yes, I know that.' The nobility of the concept filled her chest and made it difficult for her to breathe so her voice was laboured as she whispered, 'Greater love hath no man – I will make any sacrifice you ask of me.'

Moses went to the guest bedroom which Molly had allocated to him, and as he washed his face in the basin Marcus Archer slipped into the room without knocking, closed the door and leaned against it, watching Moses in the mirror.

'Well?' he asked at last, as though he was reluctant to hear the answer.

'Just as we planned it.' Moses dried his face on a clean towel.

'I hate the silly little bitch,'Marcus said softly.

'We agreed it was necessary.' Moses selected a fresh shirt from the valise on his bed.

'I know we agreed,' Marcus said. 'It was my suggestion, if you remember, but I do not have to like her for it.'

'She is an instrument. It is folly to let your personal feelings intrude.'

Marcus Archer nodded. In the end he hoped he could act like a true revolutionary, one of the steely hard men which the struggle needed, but his feelings for this man, Moses Gama, were stronger than all his political convictions.

He knew that it was completely one-sided. Over the years Moses Gama had used him as cynically and as calculatingly as he now planned to use the Courtney woman. His vast sexual appeal was to Moses Gama merely another weapon in his arsenal, another means of manipulating people. He could use it on men or women, young or old, no matter how attractive or unappealing, and Marcus admired him for the ability, and at the same time was devastated by it.

'We leave for the Witwatersrand tomorrow,' he said, as he pushed himself away from the door, for the moment controlling his jealousy. 'I have made the arrangements.'

'So soon?' Moses asked.

'I have made the arrangements. We will travel by car.'

It was one of the problems which dogged their work. It was difficult for a black man to travel about the huge subcontinent, liable as he was at any time to demands to show his *dompas* and to interrogation when the authority realized that he was far from the domicile shown on the pass without apparent reason, or that the pass had not been stamped by an employer.

Moses' association with Marcus and the nominal employment he provided with the Chamber of Mines gave him valuable cover when it was necessary to travel, but they always needed couriers. That was one of the functions that Tara Courtney would perform. In addition she was by birth and by marriage highly placed, and the information she could provide would be of the greatest value in the planning. Later, after she had proved herself, there would be other, more dangerous work.

I n the end, Shasa Courtney realized, it was his mother's advice which would tip the fine balance and decide whether he accepted or rejected the offer that had been made to him during the springbok hunt on the open plains of the Orange Free State.

Shasa would have been the first to despise any other man of his age who was still firmly enmeshed in the maternal apron strings, but he never considered that this applied to him. The fact that Centaine Courtney-Malcomess was his mother was merely incidental. What influenced him was that she was the shrewdest financial and political brain he had access to; she was also his business partner and his only true confidante. To make such an important decision without consulting her never even occurred to him.

He waited a week after his return to Cape Town to let his own feelings distil out, and for an opportunity to have Centaine alone, for he was in no doubt as to what his stepfather's reaction would be to the proposal. Blaine Malcomess was the Opposition representative on the parliamentary sub-committee examining the proposed establishment of an oil-from-coal project, part of the government's long-term plan to reduce the country's reliance on imported crude oil. The committee was going to take evidence on site, and for once Centaine was not accompanying her husband. That was the opportunity Shasa needed.

71

It was less than half an hour's drive from Weltevreden, across the Constantia Nek pass and down the other side of the mountains to the Atlantic seaboard where the home that Centaine had made for Blaine stood on five hundred acres of wild protea-covered mountainside that dropped steeply down to rocky headlands and white beaches. The original house, Rhodes Hill, had been built during Queen Victoria's reign by one of the old mining magnates from the Rand, but Centaine had stripped the interior and refurbished it completely.

She was waiting for Shasa on the verandah when he parked the Jaguar, and ran up the steps to embrace her.

'You're getting too thin,' she scolded him fondly. She had guessed from his telephone call that he wanted a serious discussion, and they had their own traditions. Centaine was dressed in an open-neck cotton blouse and slacks with comfortable hiking boots, and without discussing it she took his arm and they set out along the path that skirted her rose gardens and climbed the untended hillside.

The last part of the ascent was steep and the path rough, but Centaine took it without pause and came out on the summit ahead of him. Her breathing was hardly altered, and within a minute had returned to normal. 'She keeps herself in wonderful condition, Heaven alone knows what she spends on health cures and potions, and she exercises like a professional athlete,' Shasa thought as he grinned down at her proudly. He placed an arm around her small firm waist.

'Isn't it beautiful?' Centaine leaned lightly against him and looked out over the cold green Benguela current, as it swirled, decked in lacy foam, around Africa's heel, which like a medieval knight was spurred and armoured with black rock. 'This is one of my favourite places.'

'Whoever would have guessed it,' Shasa murmured, and led her to the flat lichen-covered rock that was her seat.

She perched up on it, hugging her knees and he sprawled on the bed of moss below her. They were both silent for a few moments, and Shasa wondered how often they had sat like this at this special place of hers, and how many heavy decisions they had taken here.

'Do you remember Manfred De La Rey?' he asked suddenly, but he was unprepared for her reaction. She started and looked down at him, colour draining from her cheeks, with an expression he could not fathom.

'Is something wrong, Mater?' He began to rise, but she gestured at him to remain seated.

'Why do you ask about him?' she demanded, but he did not reply directly.

'Isn't it strange how our paths seem to cross with his family? Ever since his father rescued us, when I was an infant and we were castaways living with the Bushmen in the Kalahari.'

'We needn't go over all that again,' Centaine stopped him, and her tone was brusque. Shasa realized he had been tactless. Manfred's father had robbed the H'ani Mine of almost a million pounds' worth of diamonds, an act of vengeance for fancied wrongs that he had convinced himself Centaine had inflicted on him. For that crime he had served almost fifteen years of a life sentence for robbery, and he had been pardoned only when the Nationalist government had come to power in 1948. At the same time the Nationalists had pardoned many other Afrikaners serving sentences for treason and sabotage and armed robbery, convicted by the Smuts' government when they had attempted to disrupt the country's war effort against Nazi Germany. However, the stolen diamonds had never been recovered, and their loss had almost destroyed the fortune that Centaine Courtney had built up with so much labour, sacrifice and heartache.

'Why do you mention Manfred De La Rey?' she repeated her question.

'I had an invitation from him to a meeting. A clandestine meeting – all very cloak and dagger.'

'Did you go?'

He nodded slowly. 'We met at a farm in the Free State, and there were two other cabinet ministers present.'

'Did you speak to Manfred alone?' she asked, and the tone of the question, the fact that she used his Christian name, caught Shasa's attention. Then he remembered the unexpected question that Manfred De La Rey had put to him.

'Has your mother ever spoken about me?' he had asked, and faced by Centaine's present reaction to his name, the question took on a new significance.

'Yes, Mater, I spoke to him alone.'

'Did he mention me?' Centaine demanded, and Shasa gave a little chuckle of puzzlement.

'He asked the same question – whether you ever spoke about him. Why are the two of you so interested in each other?'

Centaine's expression turned bleak, and he saw her close her mind to him. It was a mystery he would not solve by pursuing it openly, he would have to stalk it.

'They made me a proposition.' And he saw her interest reawaken.

'Manfred? A proposition? Tell me.'

'They want me to cross the floor.'

She nodded slowly, showing little surprise and not immediately rejecting the idea. He knew that if Blaine were here it would have been different. Blaine's sense of honour, his rigid principles, would have left no room for manoeuvre. Blaine was a Smuts man, heart and blood, and even though the old field-marshal had died of a broken heart soon after the Nationalists unseated him and took over the reins of power, still Blaine was for ever true to the old man's memory.

'I can guess why they want you,' Centaine said slowly. 'They need a top financial brain, an organizer and a businessman. It's the one thing they lack in their cabinet.'

He nodded. She had seen it instantly, and his enormous respect for her was confirmed yet again.

'What price are they willing to pay?' she demanded.

'A cabinet appointment – Minister of Mines and Industry.'

He saw her eyes go out of focus, and cross in a myopic stare as she gazed out to sea. He knew what that expression meant. Centaine was calculating, juggling with the future, and he waited patiently until her eyes snapped back into focus.

'Can you see any reason for refusing?' she asked.

'How about my political principles?'

'How do they differ from theirs?'

'I am not an Afrikaner.'

'That might be to your advantage. You will be their token Englishman. That will give you a special status. You will have a freer rein. They will be more reluctant to fire you than if you were one of their own.'

'I don't agree with their native policy, this *apartheid* thing of theirs, it's just financially unsound.'

'Good Lord, Shasa. You don't believe in equal political rights for blacks, do you? Not even Jannie Smuts wanted that. You don't want another Chaka ruling us, black judges and a black police force working for a black dictator?' She shuddered. 'We'd get pretty short shrift from them.'

'No, Mater, of course not. But this *apartheid* thing is merely a device for grabbing the whole pie. We have to give them a slice of it, we can't hog it all. That's a certain recipe for eventual bloody revolution.'

'Very well, *chéri*. If you are in the cabinet, you can see to it that they get a fair crack of the whip.'

He looked dubious, and made a side-show of selecting a cigarette from his gold case and lighting it.

'You have a special talent, Shasa,' Centaine went on persuasively. 'It's your duty to use it for the good of all.'

Still he hesitated, he wanted her to declare herself

fully. He had to know if she wanted this as much as he did.

'We can be honest with each other, *chéri*. This is what we have worked towards since you were a child. Take this job and do it well. After that who knows what else may follow?'

They were both silent then, they knew what they hoped would follow. They could not help themselves, it was their nature always to strive towards the highest pinnacle.

'What about Blaine?' Shasa said at last. 'How will he take it? I don't look forward to telling him.'

'I'll do that,' she promised. 'But you will have to tell Tara.'

'Tara,' he sighed. 'Now that will be a problem.'

They were silent again, until Centaine asked, 'How will you do it? If you cross the floor it will expose you to a blaze of hostile publicity.'

So it was agreed without further words, only the means remained to be discussed.

'At the next general election I will simply campaign in different colours,' Shasa said. 'They will give me a safe seat.'

'So we have a little time to arrange the details, then.'

They discussed them for another hour, planning with all the meticulous attention that had made them such a formidably successful team over the years, until Shasa looked up at her.

'Thank you,' he said simply. 'What would I ever do without you! You are tougher and cleverer than any man I know.'

'Get away with you,' she smiled. 'You know how I hate praise.' They both laughed at that absurdity.

'I'll walk you down, Mater.' But she shook her head.

'I've still got some thinking to do. Leave me here.'

She watched him go down the hill and her love and pride was so intense as to almost suffocate her.

'He is everything I ever wanted in a son, and he has fulfilled all my expectations, a thousand times over. Thank you, my son, thank you for the joy you have always given me.'

Then abruptly the words 'my son' triggered another reaction, and her mind darted back to the earlier part of their conversation.

'Do you remember Manfred De La Rey?' Shasa had asked her, but he could never know what the answer to that must be.

'Can a woman ever forget the child she bears?' she whispered the reply aloud, but her words were lost on the wind and on the sound of the green surf breaking on the rocky shore below the hill.

Every pew of the church was filled. The women's bonnets were colourful as a field of wild Namaqua daisies in the springtime, while the men's suits were sombre and severe. All their faces were upturned towards the magnificent carved pulpit of polished black stinkwood in which stood the Most Reverend Tromp Bierman, Moderator of the Dutch Reformed Church of South Africa.

Manfred De La Rey considered once again how much Uncle Tromp had aged in the years since the war. He had never fully recovered from the pneumonia he had contracted in the concentration camp at Koffiefontein, where that English-lover Jannie Smuts had incarcerated him with hundreds of other patriotic Afrikaners for the duration of the English war with Germany.

Uncle Tromp's beard was snow-white now, even more spectacular than the curly black bush it once had been. The hair on his head, also white, had been close-cropped to conceal its sparsity and it glittered like powdered glass on the high-domed pate, but his eyes were full of fire as he glowered at his congregation, and his voice that had earned him the sobriquet 'The Trumpet of God' had lost none of its power and rolled like a cannonade against the high-arched ceiling of the nave.

Uncle Tromp could still pack the pews, and Manfred nodded soberly but proudly as the thunderous outpouring burst over his head. He was not really listening to the words, merely enjoying the sense of continuity that filled him; the world was a safe good place when Uncle Tromp was in his pulpit. Then a man could trust in the God of the *Volk* which he evoked with so much certainty, and believe in the divine intervention which directed his life.

Manfred De La Rey sat in the front pew at the right side of the nave nearest the aisle. It was the most prestigious position in the congregation, and rightly so for Manfred was the most powerful and important man in the church. The pew was reserved for him and his family, and their names were gold-leafed on the hymn books that lay beside each seat.

Heidi, his wife, was a magnificent woman, tall and strong; her bare forearms below the puff sleeves were smooth and firm, her bosom large and shapely, her neck long and her thick golden hair plaited into ropes that were twisted up under the wide-brimmed black hat. Manfred had met her in Berlin when he had been the gold medallist light heavyweight boxer at the Olympic Games in 1936, and Adolf Hitler himself had attended their wedding. They had been separated during the war years, but afterwards Manfred had brought her out to Africa with their son, little Lothar.

Lothar was almost twelve years old now, a fine strong boy, blond as his mother, and upright as his father. He sat very straight in the family pew, his hair neatly slicked down with Brylcreem and the stiff white collar biting into his neck. Like his father, he would be an athlete, but he had chosen the game of rugby at which to excel. His three younger sisters, blonde and pretty in a fresh-faced healthy way, sat beyond him, their faces framed by the hoods of their traditional *voortrekker* bonnets and full-length skirts reaching to their ankles. Manfred liked them to wear national dress on Sundays.

Uncle Tromp ended with a salvo that thrilled his flock with the threat of hell-fire, and they rose to sing the final hymn. Sharing the hymn book with Heidi, Manfred examined her handsome Germanic features. She was a wife to be proud of, a good housekeeper and mother, a fine companion whom he could trust and confide in, and a glittering ornament to his political career. A woman like this could stand beside any man, even the Prime Minister of a powerful and prosperous nation. He let himself dwell on that secret thought. Yet everything was possible, he was a young man, the youngest by far in the cabinet, and he had never made a political mistake. Even his wartime activities gave him credit and prestige with his peers, although few people outside the inner circle knew of the full role he had played in the militant anti-British pro-Nazi secret army of the *Ossewa Brandwag*.

Already they were whispering that he was the coming man, and it was evident in the huge respect that was shown him as the service ended and the congregation left the church. Manfred stood, with Heidi beside him, on the lawns outside the church while one after another important and influential men came up to deliver social invitations, to ask a favour, to congratulate him on his speech introducing the new Criminal Law Amendment Bill in the House, or simply to pay their respects. It was almost twenty minutes before he was able to leave the church grounds.

The family walked home. It was only two blocks under the green oaks that lined the streets of Stellenbosch, the small university town which was the citadel of Afrikaner intellectualism and culture. The three girls walked ahead, Lothar followed them and Manfred with Heidi on his arm brought up the rear, stopping every few paces to acknowledge a greeting or exchange a few words with a neighbour or a friend or one of Manfred's constituents.

Manfred had purchased the house when they had arrived back from Germany after the war. Although it stood in a small garden, almost facing on to the street, it was a large house with spacious high-ceilinged rooms that suited the family well. Manfred had never seen any reason to change it, and he felt comfortable with Heidi's formal Teutonic furnishings. Now Heidi and the girls rushed through to help the servants in the kitchen, and Manfred went around the side of the house to the garage. He never used his official chauffeur-driven limousine at weekends, and he brought out his personal Chevrolet sedan and drove to fetch his father for the family Sunday luncheon.

The old man seldom attended church, especially when the Reverend Tromp Bierman was preaching. Lothar De La Rey lived alone on the small-holding that Manfred had bought for him on the outskirts of the town at the foot of the Helshoogte Pass. He was out in the peach orchard pottering with his beehives and Manfred paused by the gate to watch him with a mixture of pity and deep affection.

Lothar De La Rey had once been tall and straight as the grandson who now bore his name, but the arthritis he had contracted during the years in Pretoria Central Prison had bowed and twisted his body and turned his single remaining hand to a grotesque claw. His left arm was amputated above the elbow, too high to fit an artificial limb. He had lost it during the robbery that led to his imprisonment. He was dressed in dirty blue dungarees, with a stained brown hat on his head, the brim drooped over his eyes. One sleeve of the dungaree was pinned back.

Manfred opened the gate and went down into the peach orchard where the old man was stooping over one of the wooden hives.

'Good morning, Pa,' Manfred said softly. 'You aren't ready yet.'

His father straightened up and stared at him vaguely, and then started with surprise.

'Manie! Is it Sunday again already?'

'Come along, Pa. Let's get you tidied up. Heidi is cooking a roast of pork – you know how you love pork.'

He took the old man's hand, and led him unprotestingly up to the cottage.

'It's a mess, Pa.' Manfred looked around the tiny bedroom with distaste. The bed had obviously been slept in repeatedly without being remade, soiled clothing was strewn on the floor and used plates and mugs stood on the bedside table. 'What happened to the new maid Heidi found for you?'

'I didn't like her, cheeky brown devil,' Lothar muttered. 'Stealing the sugar, drinking my brandy. I fired her.'

Manfred went to the cupboard and found a clean white shirt. He helped the old man undress.

'When did you last bath, Pa?' he asked gently.

'Hey?' Lothar peered at him.

'It doesn't matter.' Manfred buttoned his father's shirt. 'Heidi will find another maid for you. You must try and keep her longer than a week this time.'

It wasn't the old man's fault, Manfred reminded himself. It was the prison that had affected his mind. He had been a proud free man, a soldier and a huntsman, a creature of the wild Kalahari Desert. You cannot cage a wild animal. Heidi had wanted to have the old man to live with them, and Manfred felt guilty that he had refused. It would have meant buying a larger home, but that was the least of it. Manfred could not afford to have Lothar dressed like a coloured labourer wandering vaguely around the house, coming into his study uninvited when he had important visitors with him, slobbering his food and making inane statements at the dinner table when he was entertaining. No, it was better for all of them, the old man especially, that he lived apart. Heidi would find another maid to take care of him, but he felt corrosive guilt as he took Lothar's arm and led him out to the Chevrolet.

He drove slowly, almost at a walking pace, steeling himself to do what he had been unable to do during the years since Lothar had been pardoned and freed from prison at Manfred's instigation.

'Do you remember how it was in the old days, Pa? When we fished together at Walvis Bay?' he asked, and the old man's eyes shone. The distant past was more real to him than the present, and he reminisced happily, without hesitation recalling incidents and the names of people and places from long ago.

'Tell me about my mother, Pa,' Manfred invited at last, and he hated himself for leading the old man into such a carefully prepared trap.

'Your mother was a beautiful woman,' Lothar nodded happily, repeating what he had told Manfred so many times since childhood. 'She had hair the colour of the desert dunes, with the early sun shining on them. A fine woman of noble German birth.'

'Pa,' Manfred said softly. 'You aren't telling me the truth, are you?' He spoke as though to a naughty child. 'The woman you call my mother, the woman who was your wife, died years before I was born. I have a copy of the death certificate signed by the English doctor in the concentration camp. She died of diphtheria, the white sore throat.'

He could not look at his father as he said it, but stared ahead through the windscreen, until he heard a soft choking sound beside him and with alarm turned quickly. Lothar was weeping, tears slid down his withered old cheeks.

'I'm sorry, Pa.' Manfred pulled the Chevrolet off the road and switched off the engine. 'I shouldn't have said that.' He pulled the white handkerchief from his pocket and handed it to his father.

Lothar wiped his face slowly, but his hand was steady, and his wandering mind seemed to have been concentrated by the shock.

'How long have you known that she was your real mother?' he asked, and his voice was firm and sure. Manfred's soul quailed, he had hoped to hear his father deny it.

'She came to see me when first I stood for parliament. She blackmailed me, for her other son's sake. I had him in my power. She threatened to expose the fact that I was her bastard son and destroy my candidacy if I acted against her other son. She dared me to ask you if it was not true, but I could not bring myself to do it.'

'It's true,' Lothar nodded. 'I'm sorry, my son. I lied to you only to protect you.'

'I know.' Manfred reached across and took the bony hand as the old man went on.

'When I found her in the desert, she was so young and helpless – and beautiful. I was young and lonely – it was just the two of us, and her infant, alone together in the desert. We fell in love.'

'You don't have to explain,' Manfred told him, but Lothar seemed not to hear him.

'One night two wild Bushmen came into our camp. I thought they were marauders, come to steal our horses and oxen. I followed them, and caught up with them at dawn. I shot them down before I was within range of their poison arrows. It was the way we dealt with those dangerous little yellow animals in those days.'

'Yes, Pa, I know.' Manfred had read the history of his people's conflict with and extermination of the Bushmen tribes.

'I did not know it then, but she had lived with these same two little Bushmen before I found her. They had

83

helped her survive the desert and tended her when she gave birth to her first child. She had come to love them, she even called them "old grandfather" and "old grandmother".' He shook his head wonderingly, still unable to comprehend this relationship of a white woman with savages. 'I did not know it, and I shot them without realizing what they meant to her. Her love for me changed to bitter hatred. I know now that her love could not have been very deep, perhaps it was only loneliness and gratitude and not love at all. After that she hated me, and the hatred extended to my child that she was carrying in her womb. To you, Manie. She made me take you away the moment you were born. She hated us both so deeply that she wanted never to set eyes on you. I cared for you after that.'

'You were my father and my mother.' Manfred bowed his head, ashamed and angry that he had forced the old man to relive those tragically cruel events. 'What you have told me explains so much that I could never understand.'

'Ja.' Lothar wiped fresh tears away with the white handkerchief. 'She hated me, but you see I still loved her. No matter how cruelly she treated me, I was obsessed with her. That was the reason why I committed the folly of the robbery. It was a madness and it cost me this arm.' He held up the empty sleeve. 'And my freedom. She is a hard woman. A woman without mercy. She will not hesitate to destroy anything or anybody who stands in her way. She is your mother, but be careful of her, Manie. Her hatred is a terrible thing.' The old man reached across and seized his son's arm, shaking it in his agitation. 'You must have nothing to do with her, Manie. She will destroy you as she has destroyed me. Promise me you will never have anything to do with her or her family.'

'I'm sorry, Pa,' Manfred shook his head. 'I am already tied to her through her son,' he hesitated to give voice to the next words, 'to my brother, to my half-brother, Shasa Courtney. It seems, Papa, that our bloodlines and our destinies are so closely tangled together that we can never be free of each other.'

'Oh, my son, my son,' Lothar De La Rey lamented. 'Be careful – please be careful.'

Manfred reached for the ignition key to start the engine, but paused before he touched it.

'Tell me, Pa. How do you feel for this woman now – for my mother?'

Lothar was silent for a moment before he answered. 'I hate her almost as much as I still love her.'

'It is strange that we can love and hate at the same time.' Manfred shook his head slightly with wonder. 'I hate her for what she has done to you. I hate her for all the things she stands for, and yet her blood calls to mine. At the end, when all else is put aside, Centaine Courtney is my mother and Shasa Courtney is my brother. Love or hatred – which will prevail, Papa?'

'I wish I could tell you, my son,' Lothar whispered miserably. 'I can only repeat what I have already told you. Be careful of them, Manie. Mother and son, they are dangerous adversaries.'

For almost twenty years Marcus Archer had owned the old farmhouse at Rivonia. He had purchased the five-acre small-holding before the area became fashionable. Now the fairways and greens of the Johannesburg Country Club, the most exclusive private club on the Witwatersrand, backed right up against Marcus' boundary. The trustees of the Country Club had offered him fifteen times his original purchase price, over £100,000, but Marcus steadfastly refused to sell.

On all the other large plots that comprised the Rivonia Estate, the prosperous new owners – entrepreneurs and stockbrokers and successful doctors – had built large pretentious homes, most of them in the low sprawling ranch-house style which was the rage, or with pink clay tile roofs, imaginative copies of Mexican *haciendas* or Mediterranean villas, and they had surrounded the main buildings with paddocks and stables, with tennis courts and swimming-pools and wide lawns that the winter highveld frosts burned the colour of cured tobacco leaves.

Marcus Archer had re-thatched the roof of the old farmhouse, whitewashed the walls, and planted frangipani and bougainvillaea and other flowering shrubs and let the grounds grow wild and unkempt, so that even from its own boundary fence the house was completely screened.

Although the area was now very much a bastion of the wealthy white elite, the Country Club employed a large staff of waiters and kitchen helpers and groundsmen and golf caddies, so black faces were not remarkable, as they might have been on the streets of some of the other wealthy white suburbs. Marcus' friends and political allies could come and go without arousing unwelcome interest. So Puck's Hill, as Marcus had recently renamed his farmhouse, gradually became the rallying ground for some of the most active of the African Nationalist movements, the leaders of black consciousness and their white compatriots, the remnants of the defunct Communist Party.

It was only natural, therefore, that Puck's Hill was chosen as the headquarters for the final planning and co-ordination of the black disobedience campaign that was about to begin. However, it was not a unified group that came together under Marcus Archer's roof, for although their stated final objective was the same, their separate visions of the future differed widely.

Firstly, there was the old guard of the African National Congress headed by Dr Xuma. They were the conservatives, committed to plodding negotiation with white civil servants within the unyielding established system.

'You people have been doing that since 1912 when the

ANC was formed,' Nelson Mandela glared at him. 'It is time to move on to confrontation, to force our will upon the Boers.'

Nelson Mandela was a young lawyer, practising on the Witwatersrand in partnership with another activist named Oliver Tambo. Together they were making a strong challenge for the leadership of the Young Turks in the Congress hierarchy.

'It is time for us to move on to direct action.' Nelson Mandela leaned forward in his chair and looked down the long kitchen table. The kitchen was the largest room in Puck's Hill, and all their meetings were held in it. 'We have drawn up a programme of boycott and strike and civil disobedience.' Mandela was speaking in English, and Moses Gama sitting near the end of the table watched him impassively, but all the time his mind was racing ahead of the speaker, assessing and evaluating. He as much as any of them present was aware of the undertones in the room. There was not a single black man present who did not cherish, somewhere in his soul, the dream of one day leading all the others, of one day being hailed as the paramount chief of all southern Africa.

Yet the fact that Mandela spoke in English pointed up the single most poignant fact that they had to face: they were all different. Mandela was a Tembu, Xuma was a Zulu, Moses Gama himself was an Ovambo, and there were half a dozen other tribes represented in the room.

'It would be a hundred times easier if we blacks were all one people,' Moses thought, and then despite himself he glanced uneasily at the Zulus, sitting together as a group across the table. They were the majority, not only in this room, but in the country as a whole. What if they somehow formed an alliance with the whites? It was a disquieting thought, but he put it firmly aside. The Zulus were the proudest, most independent of the warrior tribes. Before the white man came, they had conquered all their neighbouring peoples and held them subjugated. The Zulu King Chaka had called them his dogs. Because of their multitudes and their warrior tradition, it was almost certain that the first black President of South Africa would be a Zulu, or someone with very close ties to the Zulu nation. Ties of marriage – not for the first time Moses thought about that possibility with narrowed eyes; it was time he married anyway. He was almost forty-five years of age. A Zulu maiden of royal blood? He stored the idea for future consideration, and concentrated once again on what Nelson Mandela was saying.

The man had charisma and a presence, and he was articulate and persuasive, a rival – a very dangerous rival. Moses recognized that fact as he had often before. They were all rivals. However, the Youth League of the ANC was Nelson Mandela's power base, the hotheads, young men burning for action, and even now Mandela was proposing caution, tempering his call for action with reservations.

'There must be no gratuitous violence,' he was saying. 'No damage to private property, no danger to human life—' and although Moses Gama nodded wisely, he wondered how much appeal that would have with the rank and file of the Youth League. Would they not prefer the offer of a bloody and glorious victory? That was something else to be considered.

'We must show our people the way, we must demonstrate that we are all one in this enterprise,' Mandela was saying now, and Moses Gama smiled inwardly. The total membership of the ANC was seven thousand, while his secret union of mineworkers numbered almost ten times that figure. It would be as well to remind Mandela and the rest of them of his overwhelming support amongst the best paid and most strategically placed of all the black population. Moses turned slightly and looked at the man who sat beside him, and felt an untoward pang of affection. Hendrick Tabaka had been beside him like this for twenty years.

Swart Hendrick was a big man, as tall as Moses but wider across the shoulder, and heavier around the middle, with thick-muscled limbs. His head was round and bald as a cannonball and laced with scars from ancient fights and battles. His front teeth were missing, and Moses remembered how the white man who had done that to him had died.

He was Moses' half-brother, son of the same father, a chief of the Ovambo, but of a different mother. He was the one man in all the world whom Moses trusted, a trust not lightly given but earned over all of those twenty years. He was the only black man in this room who was not a rival, but was instead both comrade and loyal servant. Swart Hendrick nodded at him unsmilingly and Moses realized that Nelson Mandela had finished speaking and that they were all watching him, waiting for him to reply. He rose slowly to his feet, aware of the impression he was making, and he could see the respect in their expressions. Even his enemies in the room could not entirely conceal the awe which he inspired.

'Comrades,' he began. 'My brothers. I have listened to what my good brother Nelson Mandela has said and I agree with every word of it. There are just a few points which I feel I must add—' and he spoke for nearly an hour.

Firstly he proposed to them a detailed plan to call a series of wildcat strikes in the mines where the labour force was controlled by his unions.

'The strikes will be in sympathy with the defiance campaign, but we will not call a general strike which would give the Boers an excuse for heavy-handed action. We will bring out only a few mines at any one time, and then only for a limited period, before going back to work, just enough to thoroughly disrupt gold production and to exasperate management. We will nip at their heels like a terrier harassing a lion, ready to spring away the instant he turns. But it will be a warning. It will let them realize our strength, and what would happen if we called a general strike.'

He saw how they were impressed with his planning, and when he asked for a vote to confirm his proposal, he was given unanimous approval. It was another small victory, another addition to his prestige and influence within the group.

'In addition to the strike action, I would like to propose a boycott of all white-owned business on the Witwatersrand for the duration of the defiance campaign. The people will be allowed to buy their necessities of life from shops owned and run by black businessmen only.'

Hendrick Tabaka owned over fifty large general dealer stores in the black townships along the gold reef, and Moses Gama was his sleeping partner. He saw the others at the table baulk at the suggestion, and Mandela objected.

'It will cause undue hardship amongst our people,' he said. 'Many of them live in areas where they can trade only with white stores.'

'Then they must travel to areas where there are black-owned businesses, and it will do our people no harm to learn that the struggle demands sacrifices from all of us,' Moses answered him quietly.

'A boycott such as you propose would be impossible to enforce,' Mandela insisted, and this time Hendrick Tabaka replied to the objection.

'We will use the Buffaloes to make sure the people obey,' he growled, and now the more conservative members of the Council looked positively unhappy.

The Buffaloes were the union enforcers. Hendrick Tabaka was their commander and they had a reputation for swift, ruthless action. They were too close to being a private political army for the peace of mind of some of the other men in the room, and Moses Gama frowned slightly. It had been a mistake for Hendrick to mention his Buffaloes at all. Moses hid his chagrin when the vote to declare a boycott of white dealers on the Witwatersrand and enforce it strictly was defeated. It was a victory for Mandela and his moderates. So far the score was even, but Moses was not finished yet.

'There is one other matter I would like to bring up before we adjourn. I would like to consider what lies beyond the defiance campaign. What action do we take if the campaign is crushed by ruthless white police action, and followed by an onslaught on the black leaders and the promulgation of even more draconian laws of domination?' he asked. 'Will our response always be mild and subservient, will we always take off our caps and mutter, "Yes, my white *baas*! No, my white *baas*!"?'

He paused, and studied the others, seeing the disquiet he had expected in the faces of old Xuma and the conservatives, but he had not spoken for them. At the far end of the table there were two young men, still in their early twenties. They were observers from the executive of the Youth League of the ANC and Moses knew them both to be militants longing for fierce action. What he was about to say now was for them, and he knew they would take his words back to the other young warriors. It could begin the erosion of Nelson Mandela's support amongst the youth, and the transference of that support to a leader who was prepared to give them the blood and fire for which they hungered.

'I propose the formation of a military wing of the ANC,' Moses said, 'a fighting force of trained men, ready to die for the struggle. Let us call this army *Umkhonto we Sizwe*, the Spear of the Nation. Let us forge the spear secretly. Let us hone its edge to razor sharpness, keeping it hidden, but always ready to strike.' He used that deep thrilling tone of his, and he saw the two young men at the end of the table stir eagerly and their faces begin to glow with expectation.

'Let us choose our brightest and fiercest young men, and from them form the impis as our forefathers did.' He paused, and his expression became scornful. 'There are old men amongst us, and they are wise. I respect their grey hairs and their experience. But remember, comrades, the future belongs to the young. There is a time for fine words, and we have heard them spoken at our councils – often, too often. There is a time also for action, bold action and that is the world of the young.'

When at last Moses Gama sat down again he saw that he had moved them all deeply, each in his separate way. Old Xuma was shaking his grey pate, and his lips quivered. He knew his day had passed. Nelson Mandela and Oliver Tambo watched him impassively, but he saw the fury in their hearts beamed through their eyes. The battle lines had been drawn, and they had recognized their enemy. Yet, most important of all, he saw the expressions on the faces of the two Youth Leaguers. It was the look of men who had found a new star to follow.

'Since when have you conceived such a burning interest in archaeological anthropology?' Shasa Courtney asked as he shook out the pages of the *Cape Times*, and turned from the financial section to the sports pages at the rear.

'It was one of my majors,' Tara pointed out reasonably. 'May I pour you another cup of coffee?'

'Thank you, my dear.' He sipped the coffee before he spoke again. 'How long do you intend being away?'

'Professor Dart will be giving a series of four lectures on successive evenings, covering all the excavations from his original discovery of the Taung skull right up to the present time. He has been able to correlate the whole mass of material with one of these new electronic computers.'

Behind his newspaper Shasa smiled reflectively as he remembered Marylee from MIT and her IBM 701. He wouldn't mind another visit to Johannesburg himself in the near future.

'It's absolutely riveting stuff,' Tara was saying, 'and it all fits in with the new discoveries at Sterkfontein and Makapansgat. It really does seem that Southern Africa was the true cradle of mankind, and that Australopithecus is our direct ancestor.'

'So you will be away for at least four days?' Shasa interrupted. 'What about the children?'

'I have spoken to your mother. She will be happy to come across and stay at Weltevreden while I am away.'

'I won't be able to join you,' Shasa pointed out. 'The third reading of the new Criminal Law Amendment Bill is coming up, and all hands are needed in the House. I could have flown you up in the Mosquito – now you'll have to take the commercial flight on the Viscount.'

'What a pity,' Tara sighed. 'You would have enjoyed it. Professor Dart is a fascinating speaker.'

'You'll stay at the Carlton suite, of course. It's standing empty.'

'Molly has arranged for me to stay with a friend of hers at Rivonia.'

'One of her Bolshies, I presume.' Shasa frowned slightly. 'Try not to get yourself arrested again.' He had been waiting for an opportunity to talk about her political activities and he lowered the newspaper and looked at her thoughtfully, then realized it was not the correct moment and merely nodded. 'Your grass orphans and your widower will try to bumble along without you for a few days.'

'With your mother and sixteen servants at hand, I have no doubt you will survive,' she told him crisply, letting her irritation show through for an instant.

Marcus Archer met her at the airport. He was affable and amusing and while they listened to a Mozart programme on the car radio as they drove out to Rivonia Marcus discussed the composer's life and works. He knew much more about music than she did, but although she listened to his dissertation with pleasure and attention, she was nevertheless aware of his enmity. It was well concealed, but flashed out in a barbed remark or a spiced glance. He never mentioned Moses Gama's name, and nor did she. Molly had said he was a homosexual, the first she had ever encountered to her certain knowledge, and she wondered if they all hated women.

Puck's Hill was a delight, with its shaggy thatch and unkempt grounds, so different from Weltevreden's carefully manicured splendour.

'You'll find him at the end of the front stoep,' Marcus said, as he parked under one of the bluegums at the rear of the house. It was the first time he had referred to Moses, but even then he did not use his name. He wandered away and left her standing.

She had not known how to dress, though she imagined that he would not approve of slacks. So she had chosen a long loose skirt made of cheap but colourful trade print that she had purchased in Swaziland, and with it wore a simple green cotton blouse with sandals on her feet. Again, she had not been sure whether she should wear make-up, and she had compromised with a pale pink lipstick and just a touch of mascara. She thought she looked well enough in the mirror of the women's room at the airport as she combed her dense chestnut curls, but was suddenly stricken by the thought that he would find her pale skin insipid and unattractive.

Now standing alone in the sunshine, she was once again attacked by doubts and that terrible sense of inadequacy. If Marcus had been there, she would have begged him to drive her back to the airport, but he had disappeared and so she summoned up all her courage and walked slowly around the side of the whitewashed house.

She paused at the corner and looked down the long covered verandah. Moses Gama was sitting at a table at the far end with his back to her. The table was piled with books and writing materials. He was wearing a casual white shirt with open neck that contrasted with the marvellous anthracite of his skin. His head was bowed and he was writing rapidly on a block of notepaper.

Timidly she stepped up on to the verandah and although her approach was noiseless, he sensed her presence and turned abruptly when she was halfway down the verandah. He did not smile, but she thought she saw pleasure in his gaze as he stood up and came to meet her. He did not attempt to embrace her, or kiss her, and she was pleased, for it confirmed his differentness. Instead he led her to the second chair placed beside his table, and seated her in it.

'Are you well?' he asked. 'Are your children well?' The innate African courtesy, always the enquiry and then the offer of refreshment, 'Let me give you a cup of tea.' He poured from the tray already set on his cluttered desk, and she sipped with pleasure.

'Thank you for coming,' he said.

'I came as soon as I received your message from Molly, as I promised I would.'

'Will you always keep your promises to me?'

'Always,' she answered with simple sincerity, and he studied her face.

'Yes,' he nodded. 'I think you will.'

She could hold his gaze no longer, for it seemed to sear her soul and lay it bare. She looked down at the table top, at the closely written sheets of his handwriting.

'A manifesto,' he said, following her gaze. 'A blueprint for the future.'

He selected half a dozen sheets and handed them to her. She set aside her tea cup and took them from his hand, shivering slightly as their fingers touched. His skin was cool – that was one of the things that she remembered.

She read the sheets, her attention becoming fastened upon them more firmly the more she read, and when she finished them, she lifted her eyes to his face again.

'You have a poetry in your choice of words that makes the truth shine more luminously,' she whispered.

They sat on the cool verandah, while outside the brilliant highveld sun threw shadows black and crisp as paper cut-outs beneath the trees and the noonday swooned in the heat, and they talked.

There were no trivialities in their discussion, everything he said was thrilling and cogent, and he seemed to inspire her for her replies and her own observations she knew were measured and lucid and she saw she had aroused and held his interest. She no longer was aware of her small vanities of dress and cosmetics, all that mattered now were the words that they exchanged and the cocoon they wove out of them. With a start she realized that the day had slipped away unnoticed and the short African twilight was upon them. Marcus came to fetch her and show her to her sparsely furnished bedroom.

'We will leave for the museum in twenty minutes,' he told her.

In the lecture theatre of the Transvaal Museum the three of them sat near the back. There were half a dozen other blacks in the crowded audience, but Marcus sat between the two of them. A black man beside a white woman would have excited interest, and certain hostility. Tara found it difficult to concentrate on the eminent professor's address, and though she glanced in his direction only once or twice, it was Moses Gama who occupied all her thoughts.

Back at Puck's Hill they sat late in the cavernous kitchen, while Marcus hovered over the Aga stove, joining in their conversation while he produced a meal that even in her preoccupation Tara realized was as good as anything that had ever come out of the kitchens of Weltevreden.

It was after midnight when Marcus stood up abruptly.

'I will see you in the morning,' he said, and the look he gave Tara was once again spiced with venom. She could not understand how she had offended him, but soon it did not matter for Moses took her hand.

'Come,' he said softly, and she thought her legs might not support her weight.

Long afterwards she lay pressed to him, her body bathed in sweat and her nerves still spasming and twitching uncontrollably.

'Never,' she whispered, when she could speak again. 'I have never known anyone like you. You teach me things about myself that I never suspected. You are a magician, Moses Gama. How do you know so much about a woman?'

He chuckled softly. 'You know we are entitled to many wives. If a man cannot keep them all happy at the same time, then his life becomes a torment. He has to learn.'

'Do you have many wives?' she asked.

'Not yet,' he answered. 'But one day—'

'I will hate every one of them.'

'You disappoint me,' he said. 'Sexual jealousy is a silly European emotion. If I were to detect it in you, I would despise you.'

'Please,' she said quietly, 'never despise me.'

'Then never give me reason, woman,' he commanded, and she knew she was his to command.

She realized that the first day and night with him, spent alone and uninterrupted, was exceptional. She realized also that he must have set the time aside for her, and it must have been difficult to do so for there were others, hundreds of others, demanding his attention.

He was like one of the ancient African kings holding tribal court on the verandah of the old house. There were always men and women waiting patiently under the blue-gum trees in the yard for their turn to speak to him. They were of all types and ages, from simple uneducated folk newly arrived from the reserves in the country to sophisticated lawyers and businessmen in dark suits arriving at Puck's Hill in their own automobiles.

They had one thing in common only – the deference and respect they showed Moses Gama. Some of them clapped their hands in the traditional greeting and called him *Baba* or *Nkosi*, father or lord, others shook his hand in the European manner, but Moses greeted each of them in their own dialect. 'He must speak twenty languages,' Tara wondered.

Mostly he allowed Tara to sit quietly beside his table and he explained her presence with a quiet word.

'She is a friend – you may speak.'

However, twice he asked her to leave while he spoke to his more important visitors and once when a great black bull of a man, bald and scarred and gap-toothed, arrived in a shiny new Ford sedan, he excused them.

'This is Hendrick Tabaka, my brother,' he said, and the two of them left the verandah and strolled side by side in the sunlit garden just out of earshot of where Tara sat.

What she saw during those days impressed her immensely and confirmed her feelings of reverence for this man. Everything he did, every word he uttered, marked him as different, and the respect and adulation showered upon him by his fellow Africans proved that they also recognized that he was the giant of the future.

Tara felt awed that he had selected her for special attention, and yet already saddened by the certain knowledge that she could never have for herself alone any part of him. He belonged to his people, and she must be grateful for the precious grains of his time which she could glean for herself.

Even the evenings that followed, unlike that first evening, were crowded with people and events. Until long after midnight they sat at the table in the kitchen, sometimes as many as twenty of them at one time, smoking and laughing and eating and talking. Such talk, such ideas that lit the gloomy room and shimmered like angels' wings in the air around their heads. Then later, in the quiet dark hours, they made love and she felt as though her body no longer belonged to her but that he had taken it for his own, and devoured it like some darkly beloved predator.

She must have met a hundred new faces in those three short days and nights, and though some of them were hazy and made little lasting impression, it seemed as though she had become a member of a large diffuse new family, and because of the patronage of Moses Gama, she was immediately accepted and accorded complete unquestioning trust by both black and white.

On the last evening before her return to the dream world at Weltevreden, there was a guest beside her at the kitchen table to whom Tara took an instant unqualified liking. She was a young woman, at least ten years junior to Tara, barely into her twenties, but with an unusual maturity for one so young.

'My name is Victoria Dinizulu,' she introduced herself. 'My friends call me Vicky. I know you are Mrs Courtney.'

'Tara,' Tara corrected her quickly. Nobody had used her surname since she had left Cape Town and it sounded a jarring note in her own ears.

The girl smiled shyly in acknowledgement. She had the serene beauty of a black madonna, the classic moon face of the high-bred Zulu with huge almond eyes and full lips, her skin the colour of dark amber, her hair plaited into an intricate pattern of tiny curls over her skull.

'Are you related to the Courtneys of Zululand?' she asked Tara. 'Old General Sean Courtney and Sir Garrick Courtney of Theuniskraal, near Ladyburg?'

'Yes.' Tara tried not to show the shock she felt at the

mention of those names. 'Sir Garrick was my husband's grandfather. My own sons are named Sean and Garrick after them. Why do you ask, Vicky? Do you know the family well?'

'Oh yes, Mrs Courtney – Tara.' When she smiled, the Zulu girl's face seemed to glow like a dark moon. 'Long ago, during the last century, my grandfather fought at General Sean Courtney's side in the Zulu Wars against Cetewayo who stole the kingship of Zululand from my family. It was my grandfather, Mbejane, who should have been king. Instead he became General Courtney's servant.'

'Mbejane!' Tara cried. 'Oh, yes. Sir Garrick Courtney wrote about him in his *History of Zululand*. He was Sean Courtney's faithful retainer until his death. I remember they came up here to the goldfields of the reef together and later went on to what is now Rhodesia, hunting ivory.'

'You know all about that!' Vicky laughed with pleasure. 'My father used to tell me the same stories when I was a little girl. My father still lives near Theuniskraal. After my grandfather, Mbejane Dinizulu, died my father took his place as the old general's body servant. He even went to France with the general in 1916 and worked for him until the general was murdered. In his will the general left him a section of Theuniskraal for his lifetime and a pension of a thousand pounds a year. They are a fine family, the Courtneys. My old father still weeps whenever he mentions the general's name—' Vicky broke off and shook her head, suddenly perplexed and saddened. 'Life must have been so simple in those days, my grandfather and my father were hereditary chieftains and yet they were satisfied to spend their lives subservient to a white man, and strangely they loved that man and he, in his way, seemed to love them. I wonder sometimes if theirs was not the better way—'

'Do not even think that,' Tara almost hissed at her. 'The Courtneys have always been heartless robber barons, plundering and exploiting your people. Right and justice are on the side of your struggle. Never entertain the slightest doubt of that.'

'You are right,' Vicky agreed firmly. 'But sometimes it's nice to think of the friendship of the general and my grandfather. Perhaps one day we could be friends again, equal friends, both sides stronger for the friendship.'

'With every new oppression, with every new law passed, the prospect fades,' Tara said grimly, 'and I become more ashamed of my race.'

'I don't want to be sad and intense tonight, Tara. Let's talk about happy things. You said you have sons, Sean and Garrick, named after their ancestors. Tell me about them, please.'

However, the thought of the children and Shasa and Weltevreden made Tara feel guilty and uncomfortable, and as soon as she could she changed the subject again.

'Now tell me about yourself, Vicky,' she insisted. 'What are you doing in Johannesburg, so far from Zululand?'

'I work at Baragwanath Hospital,' Vicky told her.

Tara knew that was one of the largest hospitals in the world, certainly the largest in the southern hemisphere, with 2,400 beds and over 2,000 nurses and doctors, most of them black, for the hospital catered exclusively to black patients. All hospitals, like schools and transport and most other public facilities, were strictly segregated by law, true to the grand concept of *apartheid*.

Vicky Dinizulu was so modest about her own achievements that Tara had to draw out of her the fact that she was a qualified theatre sister.

'But you are so young, Vicky,' she protested.

'There are others younger,' the Zulu girl laughed. Her laughter had a pleasing musical lilt.

'She really is a lovely child,' Tara thought, smiling in sympathy, and then corrected herself. 'No, not a child – a clever and competent young woman.'

So Tara told her about her clinic at Nyanga, and the

problems of malnutrition and ignorance and poverty they encountered, and Vicky related some of her experiences and the solutions they had found to the terrible challenges that faced them in caring for the physical well-being of a peasant population trying to adapt to an urban existence.

'Oh, I have enjoyed talking to you,' Vicky blurted out at last. 'I don't know when I have ever spoken to a white woman like this before. So natural and relaxed and,' she hesitated, 'just like an elder sister or a dear friend.'

'A dear friend. Yes, I like that,' Tara agreed. 'And Puck's Hill is probably one of the few places in the whole of this country where we could meet and talk like this.'

Involuntarily both of them looked up towards the head of the long kitchen table. Moses Gama was watching them intently, and Tara felt her stomach flop over like a stranded fish. For a few moments there, she had been totally engrossed with the Zulu girl, but now her feelings for Moses Gama flooded back from full ebb. She forgot Vicky, until the girl spoke quietly beside her.

'He is a great man – our hope for the future.'

Tara glanced at her sideways. Vicky Dinizulu's face glowed with hero worship as she smiled shyly at Moses Gama, and jealousy struck Tara such a sickening blow in the pit of her stomach that for a moment she believed she was going to be physically ill.

The jealousy and terror of imminent separation persisted even after Tara was alone with Moses that night. When he made love to her she wanted to hold him within her for all eternity, knowing that this was the only time that he truly belonged to her. Too soon she felt the great dam burst and flood her and she cried out, pleading for it never to end, but her cry was incoherent and without sense, and then he was gone from within her and she was desolated.

She thought he had fallen asleep, and she lay and listened to his quiet breathing, holding him in the circle of her arms, but he was awake and he spoke suddenly, startling her.

'You were speaking to Victoria Dinizulu,' he said, and it took an effort for her to cast her mind back to the early part of the evening. 'What did you think of her?' he persisted.

'She is a lovely young woman. Intelligent and obviously dedicated. I like her very much.' She tried to be objective, but the sick jealous feeling was there deep in her belly.

'I had her invited,' Moses said. 'It was the first time I have met her.'

Tara wanted to ask, 'Why? Why did you invite her?' But she remained silent, dreading the reply. She knew her instincts had been correct.

'She is of the royal house of Zulu,' he said softly.

'Yes. She told me,' Tara whispered.

'She is well favoured, as I was told she was, and her mother had many sons. They breed many sons in the Dinizulu line. She will make a good wife.'

'Wife?' Tara breathed. She had not expected that.

'I need the alliance with the Zulus, they are the largest and most powerful tribe. I will begin the negotiations with her family immediately. I will send Hendrick to Ladyburg to see her father and make the arrangements. It will be difficult, he is one of the old school, dead set against mixed tribal marriages. It must be a wedding that will impress the tribe, and Hendrick will convince the old man of the wisdom of it.'

'But, but—' Tara found she was stuttering. 'You hardly know the girl. You spoke barely a dozen words to her all evening.'

'What does that have to do with it?' His tone was genuinely puzzled, and he rolled away from her and switched on the bedside light, dazzling her.

'Look at me!' he commanded, taking her by the chin

and lifting her face to the light, studying it for a moment and then removing his fingers as though he had touched something loathsome. 'I have misjudged you,' he said scornfully. 'I believed that you were an exceptional person. A true revolutionary, a dedicated friend of the black people of this land, ready to make any sacrifice. Instead I find a weak, jealous woman, riddled with bourgeois white prejudices.'

The mattress tipped under her as Moses stood up. He towered over the bed.

'I have been wasting my time,' he said, gathered his clothing, and still naked turned towards the door.

Tara threw herself across the room and clung to him, barring his way to the door.

'I'm sorry. I didn't mean it. Forgive me. Please forgive me,' she pleaded with him, and he stood cold and aloof and silent. She began to weep, her tears muffling her voice, until she was no longer making sense.

Slowly she slid down with her arms still encircling him, until she was on her knees hugging his legs.

'Please,' she sobbed. 'I will do anything. Just don't leave me. I will do anything, everything you tell me to do – only just don't send me away like this.'

'Get up,' he said at last, and when she stood before him like a penitent, he said softly, 'You have one more chance. Just one. Do you understand?' and she nodded wildly, still choking on her sobs, unable to answer him. She reached out hesitantly and when he did not pull away, took his hand and led him back to the bed.

As he mounted her again, he knew that at last she was ready, completely prepared. She would do anything and everything he commanded.

In the dawn she came awake to find him leaning over her staring into her face and immediately she relived the night's terror, the dreadful fear of his scorn and rejection. She felt weak and trembly, her tears very close, but he took her calmly and made love to her with a gentle consideration that reassured her and left her feeling whole and vital again. Then he spoke to her quietly.

'I am going to put my trust in you,' he told her, and her gratitude was so strong it left her breathless. 'I am going to accept you as one of us, one of the inner circle.'

She nodded, but could not speak, staring into his fierce black eyes.

'You know how we have conducted the struggle thus far,' he said, 'we have played by the white man's rules, but he made those rules, and he designed them so we could never win. Petitions and delegations, commissions of inquiry and representations – but in the end there are always more laws made against us, governing every facet of our lives, how we work, where we live, where we are allowed to travel, or eat or sleep or love—' He broke off with an exclamation of scorn. 'The time is coming when we will rewrite the rule book. First, the defiance campaign when we will deliberately flout the mass of laws which bind us, and after that—' Now his expression was savage. 'And after that the struggle will go on and become a great battle.'

She was silent beside him, studying his face.

'I believe there comes a time when a man confronted by great evil must take up the spear and become a warrior. He must rise up and strike it down.' He was watching her, waiting for a reply.

'Yes,' she nodded. 'You are right.'

'These are words, ideas, Tara,' he told her. 'But what of action? Are you ready for action?'

She nodded. 'I am ready.'

'Blood, Tara, not words. Killing and maiming and

burning. Tearing down and destroying. Can you face that, Tara?'

She was appalled, facing the reality at last, not merely the dizzy rhetoric. In her imagination she saw the flames roaring up through the great roof of Weltevreden and blood splashed on the walls shining wetly in the sunlight, while in the courtyard lay the broken bodies of children, of her own children, and she was on the very point of rejecting the images when he spoke again.

'Destroying what is evil, Tara, so that we may rebuild a good and just society.' His voice was low and compelling, it thrilled like a drug through her veins and the cruel images faded, she looked beyond them to the paradise, the earthly paradise they would build together.

'I am ready,' she said, and there was not a trace of a quaver in her voice.

There was an hour before Marcus would take her to the airport to catch the Viscount flight back to Cape Town. They sat at his table on the verandah, just the two of them, and Moses explained to her in detail what must be done.

'*Umkhonto we Sizwe,*' he told her. 'The Spear of the Nation.' The name shimmered and rang like polished steel in her brain.

'Firstly, you must withdraw from all overt liberal activities. You must abandon your clinic—'

'My clinic!' she exclaimed. 'Oh, Moses, my poor little ones, what will they do—' She broke off as she saw his expression.

'You care for the physical needs of a hundred,' he said. 'I'm concerned for the welfare of twenty million. Tell me which is more important.'

'You are right,' she whispered. 'Forgive me.'

'You will use the excuse of the defiance campaign to make a statement of your disillusion with the freedom movement and to announce your resignation from the Black Sash.'

106

'Oh, dear, what will Molly say?'

'Molly knows,' he assured her. 'Molly knows why you are doing it. She will help you in every way. Of course, the police Special Branch will continue to keep you under observation for a while, but when you give them nothing more for their files, they will lose interest and drop you.'

She nodded. 'I understand.'

'You must take more interest in your husband's political activities, cultivate his parliamentary associates. Your own father is the Deputy Leader of the Opposition, with access to the government ministers. You must become our eyes and our ears.'

'Yes, I can do all that.'

'Later, there will be other tasks for you. Many difficult and some even dangerous. Would you risk your life for the struggle, Tara?'

'For you, Moses Gama, I would do more. I would willingly lay down that life for you,' she replied, and when he saw that she meant it, he nodded with deep satisfaction.

'We will meet whenever we can,' he promised her. 'Whenever it is safe to do so.' And then he gave her the salute which would become the rallying cry of the defiance campaign, '*Mayibuye! Afrika!*'

And she replied, '*Mayibuye! Afrika!* Africa, let it persist!'

'I am an adulteress,' Tara thought, as she had each morning as she sat at the breakfast table during all the weeks that had passed since she had arrived back from Johannesburg. 'I am an adulteress.' And she thought it must show, like a brand upon her forehead for all the world to see. Yet Shasa had greeted her cheerfully on her return, apologizing for sending a driver to meet her at the airport and not coming in person, asking her if she had enjoyed her illicit interlude with Australopithecus. 'Thought you might have gone for someone a little younger. I mean a million years old is just a little long in the tooth, isn't it?' And since then their relationship had continued unaltered.

The children, with the exception of Michael, seemed not to have missed her at all. Centaine had run the household in her absence with her usual iron fist in a candy-flavoured glove, and after they had greeted Tara with dutiful but offhand kisses the children were full of what Nana had done and said, and Tara was painfully aware that she had neglected to bring any presents for them.

Only Michael was different. For the first few days he would not let her out of his sight, but traipsed around behind her, even insisting on spending his precious Saturday afternoon with her at the clinic while his two brothers went off to Newlands Rugby Ground with Shasa to watch Western Province playing the visiting All Blacks team from New Zealand.

Michael's company helped alleviate a little of the pain of making the first arrangements to close down the clinic. She had to ask her three black nursing sisters to start looking for other jobs. 'Of course, you'll be paid your salaries until you find other positions, and I will help you all I can—' But still she had to suffer the reproach in their eyes.

Now, almost a month later, she sat at Weltevreden's laden breakfast table on a Sunday morning in the dappled shade beneath the trellised vines of the terrace, while the servants in crisp white uniform fussed about them. Shasa read aloud extracts from the *Sunday Times* to which none of them listened, Sean and Garrick wrangled acrimoniously over who was the best full-back in the world, and Isabella clamoured for her daddy's attention. Michael was giving her a detailed account of the plot of the book he was reading, and she felt like an impostor, an actress playing a role for which she had not rehearsed her lines.

Shasa finally crumpled his newspaper and dropped it

beside his chair, acceding to Isabella's request to 'Take me on your lap, Daddy!', ignoring Tara's ritual protest, and demanded:

'All right, everybody, this meeting will come to order and address the serious question of what we are all going to do with this Sunday.' This precipitated a near riot which Isabella punctuated with shrill cries of 'Picnic! Picnic!' and finally picnic it was, after Shasa had used his casting vote in his daughter's favour.

Tara tried to excuse herself, but Michael was so close to tears that she relented and they all rode out together, with the servants and the picnic baskets following them in the little two-wheeled dog cart. Of course they could have gone by car, but the ride was half the fun.

Shasa had had the pool below the waterfall bricked out to make a natural swimming-pool and had built a thatched summer house on the bank. The great attraction was the long slide down the glassy-smooth rock of the waterfall on a red rubber inner tube, and the plunge over the final sheer drop into the green pool below, the entire journey accompanied by howls and shrieks of glee. It was sport that never palled and it kept the children busy all morning.

Shasa and Tara, in their bathing-suits, lolled on the grassy bank, basking in the hot bright sunlight. They used to come here often in the first days of their marriage, even before the pool was bricked and the summer house built. In fact Tara was certain that more than one of the children had been conceived on this grassy bank. Some of the warm feelings from those days persisted. Shasa opened a bottle of Riesling, and they were both more relaxed and friendly towards each other than they had been for years.

Shasa sensed his opportunity, fished the wine bottle out of the ice bucket and refilled Tara's glass before he said, 'My dear, I have something to tell you that is of great importance to both of us and may quite substantially change our lives.'

'He has found another woman,' she thought, half in dread, half in relief, so that she did not at first understand what he was telling her. Then suddenly the enormity of it crashed in upon her. Shasa was going to join them, he was going across to the Boers. He was throwing in his lot with the band of the most evil men that Africa had ever spawned. Those supreme architects of misery and suffering and oppression.

'I believe that I am being offered the opportunity to use my talents and my financial gift for the greater good of this land and its people,' he was saying, and she twirled the stem of the wineglass between her fingers and stared down into the pale golden liquid, not daring to lift her eyes and look at him in case he saw what she was thinking.

'I have considered it from every angle, and I have discussed it with Mater. I think I have a duty to the country, to the family and to myself. I believe that I have to do it, Tara.'

It was a terrible thing to feel the last blighted fruits of her love for him shrivel and fall away, and then almost instantly she felt free and light, the burden was gone and in its place came a rush of contrary emotion. It was so powerful that she could not put a name to it for a moment, and then she knew it was hatred.

She wondered that she had ever felt guilty on his account, she wondered even that she could ever have loved him. His voice droned on, justifying himself, attempting to excuse the inexcusable, and still she knew she dared not look up at him lest he see it in her eyes. She felt an almost irresistible need to scream at him, 'You are callous, selfish, evil, as they are!' and physically to attack him, to claw at his single eye with her nails, and it took all her will-power to sit still and quiet. She remembered what Moses had told her, and she clung to his words. They seemed the only sane things in all this madness.

Shasa finished the explanation that he had so carefully

prepared for her, and then waited for her reply. She sat on the plaid rug in the sun with her legs curled up under her, staring into the glass in her hands, and he looked at her as he had not done for years and saw that she was still beautiful. Her body was smooth and lightly tanned, her hair sparkled with ruby lights in the sun, and her big breasts that had always enchanted him seemed to have filled out again. He found himself attracted by her and excited as he had not been for a long time and he reached out gently and touched her cheek.

'Talk to me,' he invited. 'Tell me what you think about it.' And she lifted her chin and stared at him. For an instant he was chilled by her gaze, for it was as inscrutable and merciless as the stare of a lioness, but then Tara smiled slightly and shrugged, and he thought that he had been mistaken, it was not hatred he had seen in her eyes.

'You have decided already, Shasa. Why do you need my approval? I have never been able to prevent you doing anything you wanted to do before. Why would I presume to do that now?'

He was amazed and relieved, he had anticipated a bitter battle.

'I wanted you to know why,' he said. 'I want you to know that we both want the same thing – prosperity and dignity for everybody in this land. That we have different ways of trying to achieve it, and I believe that my way is more effective.'

'I repeat, why do you need my approval?'

'I need your cooperation,' he corrected her. 'For in a way this opportunity depends on you.'

'How?' she asked, and looked away from him to where the children were splashing and cavorting. Only Garrick was not in the water. Sean had ducked him, and now he sat shivering on the edge of the pool. His thin weedy body was blue with cold. He was fighting for breath, the rack of his ribs sticking out of his chest as he coughed and wheezed.

'Garry,' she called sharply. 'That's enough. Dry yourself and put on your jersey.'

'Oh, Ma,' he gasped a protest, and she flared at him.

'Do it this instant.' And when he went reluctantly to the summer house she turned back to Shasa.

'You want my cooperation?' She felt totally in control of herself. She would not let him see how she felt towards him and his monstrous intention. 'Tell me what you want me to do.'

'It will come as no surprise to you to hear that BOSS, the Bureau of State Security, has quite an extensive file on you.'

'In view of the fact that they have arrested me three times,' Tara smiled again, a tight humourless grimace, 'you are right, I'm not surprised.'

'Well, my dear, what it boils down to is that it would be impossible for me to hold cabinet rank while you were still raising Cain and committing mayhem with your sisters in the Black Sash.'

'You want me to give up my political work? But what about my record? I mean, I am an old hardened jailbird, you know.'

'Fortunately the security police regard you with a certain amused indulgence. I have seen a copy of your file. The assessment is that you are a dilettante, naïve and impressionable, and easily swayed by your more vicious associates.'

That insult was difficult to bear. Tara jumped to her feet and strode around the edge of the pool, seized Isabella by the wrist and dragged her from the pool.

'That's enough for you also, young lady.' She ignored Isabella's howls of protest and stripped off her bathing costume.

'You're hurting me,' Isabella wailed as Tara scrubbed her sodden hair with a rough dry towel and then wrapped her in it.

Isabella ran to her father, still snivelling and tripping over the tails of the towel.

'Mummy won't let me swim.' She crawled into his lap.

'Life is full of injustice.' Shasa hugged her, and she gave one last convulsive sob and then cuddled her damp curls against his shoulder.

'All right, I am an ineffectual dilettante.' Tara flopped down on the rug again. She had regained her composure and sat cross-legged facing him. 'But what if I refuse to give up? What if I continue to follow the dictates of my conscience?'

'Tara, don't try and force a confrontation,' he said softly.

'You always get what you want, don't you, Shasa?' She was goading him, but he shook his head, refusing the challenge.

'I want to discuss this logically and calmly,' he said, but she could not prevent herself flouting him, for the insult rankled.

'I would get the children – you must know that, your clever lawyers must have warned you of that.'

'God damn it, Tara, you know that's not what I had in mind,' Shasa said coldly, but he hugged the child closer and Isabella reached up and touched his chin.

'You are all scratchy,' she murmured happily, unaware of the tension. 'But I still love you, my daddy.'

'Yes, my angel, I love you also,' he said, and then to Tara, 'I wasn't threatening you.'

'Not yet,' she qualified. 'But that comes next, if I know you – and I should.'

'Can't we discuss this sensibly?'

'It's not necessary,' Tara capitulated suddenly. 'I had already made up my mind. I had already seen the futility of our little protests. I have known for some time that it was a waste of my life. I know I have neglected the children and during this last visit to Johannesburg I decided that I should take up my studies again and leave politics to the professionals. I had already decided to resign from the Sash and close down the clinic or hand it over to somebody else.'

He stared at her in amazement. He distrusted any victory too easily won.

'What do you want in return?' he asked.

'I want to go back to university and take a Ph.D. in archaeology,' she said crisply. 'And I want complete freedom to travel and pursue my studies.'

'You have a bargain,' he agreed readily, not even attempting to conceal his relief. 'You keep your nose clean politically, and you can go where and when you want.' And then despite himself his eyes dropped back to her breasts. He was right, they had filled out beautifully and bulged from the thin silken cups of her bikini. He felt a quick hot need of her.

She saw that look on his face. She knew it so well, and she was revolted by it. After what he had just told her, after the insults he casually offered her, after his betrayal of that which she held sacred and dear, she knew she could never take him again. She pulled up the top of her bikini and reached for her robe.

Shasa was delighted with their bargain, and though he seldom drank more than a glassful, this afternoon he finished the rest of the Riesling while he and the boys cooked their lunch on the barbecue pit.

Sean took his duties as assistant chef seriously. Only one or two of the chops landed up in the dirt, but as Sean explained to his younger brothers, 'Those are yours, and if you don't let your teeth touch, then you won't even feel the grit.'

At the table in the summer house Isabella helped Tara prepare the salads, dousing herself liberally with French dressing in the process, and when they sat down to eat Shasa had the children shrieking with laughter at his stories. Only Tara sat aloof from the general hilarity.

When the children were given permission to leave the

table with the injunction not to swim again for an hour while their food was digested, Tara asked him quietly, 'What time are you leaving tomorrow?'

'Early,' he replied. 'I have to be in Johannesburg before lunch. Lord Littleton is arriving on the Comet from London. I want to be there to meet him.'

'How long will you be away this time?'

'After the launching David and I will be going on tour,' he replied. He had wanted her to attend the launching party which would celebrate and publicize the opening of the subscription lists for shares in the new Silver River Mine. She had found an excuse but she noticed that he did not repeat the invitation now.

'So you'll be gone about ten days?' Every quarter Shasa and David made a tour of all the company's operations, from the new chemical factory at Chaka's Bay, and the paper pulp mills in the Eastern Transvaal to the H'ani Diamond Mine in the Kalahari Desert, which was the company's flagship.

'Perhaps a little longer,' Shasa demurred. 'I'll be in Johannesburg at least four days,' and he thought happily of Marylee from MIT and her IBM 701.

D avid Abrahams had persuaded Shasa to hand the Silver River launching over to one of those public relations consultants, a breed that had recently sprung up but which Shasa viewed with suspicion. Despite his original misgiving he was now reluctantly prepared to concede that it wasn't such a bad idea as he had first believed, even though it was going to cost over five thousand pounds.

They had flown out the editors of the London *Financial Times* and the *Wall Street Journal*, with their wives, and afterwards would be taking them on for five days in the

Kruger National Park with all expenses paid. All the local press and radio journalists were invited and as an unexpected bonus the television team that had come out from New York to do a series called 'Focus on Africa' for North American Broadcasting Studios had also accepted an invitation to attend the launching party.

In the entrance lobby of the Courtney Mining Co. offices they had set up a twenty-five-foot-high working replica of the mine headgear that would be erected above the Silver River main, and had surrounded it with an enormous display of wild proteas designed and executed by the same team which had won a gold medal at the Chelsea Flower Show in London the previous year. Appreciating that journalism is thirsty work, David had laid in one hundred cases of Moët & Chandon, although Shasa had vetoed the idea of a vintage *cru*.

'Even non-vintage is too damn good for them.' Shasa did not have a lofty view of the profession of journalism.

David had also hired the chorus line from the Royal Swazi Spa to provide a floor-show. The promise of a flash of bared bosom would be almost as big a draw as the champagne; to the South African censors the female nipple was every bit as dangerous as Karl Marx's *Communist Manifesto*.

On arrival every guest was handed a presentation pack which contained a glossy colour brochure, a certificate made out in his or her name for one £1 share in the Silver River Mining Co. and a genuine miniature bar of twenty-two carat South African gold, stamped with the company logo. David had sought Reserve Bank authority to have these bars struck by the South African Mint, and at almost thirty dollars each they had been a major part of the advertising budget, but the excitement they created and the subsequent publicity fully justified the expense.

Shasa made his address before the Moët & Chandon could soften the wits of his guests or the floor-show distract them. Speaking in public was something that Shasa had always enjoyed. Neither the fusillade of camera flashes nor the sultry brilliance of the arc lights set up by the NABS television camera team detracted from his enjoyment this evening.

Silver River was one of the major achievements of his career to date. He alone had recognized the chance that the gold reef spurred at depth from the main run of the Orange Free State series, and personally he had negotiated the drilling options. Only when the diamond drills had finally intercepted the narrow black band of the gold-bearing carbon leader almost a mile and a half below the surface of the arid plain had Shasa's decision been vindicated. The strike was rich beyond even his expectations, running at over twenty-six pennyweights of pure gold to the ton of reef.

Tonight was Shasa's night. It was his particular gift that he was able to extract from everything he did the last ounce of enjoyment, and he stood in the arc lights tall and debonair in his immaculately tailored evening dress, the black eye-patch giving him a rakish and dangerous air, so obviously at ease and in control of himself and the company he commanded, that he carried them all along with him effortlessly.

They laughed and applauded at the right places, and they listened with fascinated attention as he explained the scale of the investment that was called for and how it would help to strengthen the bonds of kinship that tied South Africa so securely to England and the British Commonwealth of Nations, and set up new lines of friendship with the investors of the United States of America from where he hoped almost thirty per cent of the necessary capital for the project would come.

When he ended to prolonged applause, Lord Littleton, as head of the underwriting bank, stood up to reply. He was lean and silver-haired, his evening dress just that touch archaic in cut, with wide cuffs to the trousers, as if to underline his aristocratic scorn of fashion. He told them of his bank's strong relationship with Courtney Mining and the intense interest that this new company had aroused in the City of London.

'From the very beginning we at Littleton Bank were pretty damned certain that we were going to earn our underwriting fees very easily. We knew that there would be very few unsubscribed shares for us to take up. So it gives me a deal of pleasure to stand before you here this evening and say, I told you so.' There was a buzz of comment and speculation which he raised a hand to silence. 'I am going to tell you something that not even Mr Shasa Courtney knows yet, and which I only learned myself an hour ago.' He reached into his pocket and brought out a telex flimsy which he waved at them.

'As you are aware, the subscription lists for shares in Silver River Mining opened this morning at 10 a.m. London time, two hours behind South African time. When my bank closed a few hours ago, they sent me this telex.' He placed gold-rimmed reading glasses on his nose. 'I quote: "Please convey congratulations to Mr Courtney and Courtney Mining and Finance as promoters of Silver River Mining Co. Stop. As of 4 p.m. London time today the Silver River issue was oversubscribed by four times. Ends Littleton Bank."'

David Abrahams seized Shasa's hand, the first to congratulate him. In the roar of applause they grinned at each other happily, until Shasa broke away and jumped down off the dais.

Centaine Courtney-Malcomess was in the first row of his audience and she sprang lightly to her feet to meet him. She was dressed in a sheath of gold lamé and wearing her full suite of diamonds, each stone carefully picked from thirty years' production of the H'ani Mine. Slim and glittering and lovely, she went to meet her son.

'Now we have it all, Mater,' he whispered as he hugged her.

'No, *Chéri*, we'll never have it all,' she whispered back. 'That would be dull. There is always something more to strive for.'

Blaine Malcomess was waiting to congratulate him, and Shasa turned to him with an arm still around Centaine's waist.

'Big night, Shasa.' Blaine took his hand. 'You deserve it all.'

'Thank you, sir.'

'What a pity Tara couldn't be here,' Blaine went on.

'I wanted her to come.' Shasa was immediately defensive. 'But as you know she decided she couldn't leave the children again so soon.'

The crowd surged around them, and they were laughing and replying to congratulations, but Shasa saw the public relations director hovering and eased his way through to her.

'Well, Mrs Anstey, you have done us proud.' He smiled at her with all his charm. She was tall and rather bony but with silky blonde hair that hung in a thick curtain over her bare shoulders.

'I always try to give full satisfaction.' Jill Anstey hooded her eyes and pouted slightly to give the remark an ambiguous slant. They had been teasing each other ever since they had met the previous day. 'But I'm afraid I have some more work for you, Mr Courtney. Will you bear with me just once more?'

'As often as you wish, Mrs Anstey.' Shasa played the game out, and she placed her hand on his forearm to lead him away, squeezing just a little more than was necessary.

'The television people from NABS want to do a five-minute interview with you, for inclusion in their "Africa in Focus" series. It could be a wonderful chance to speak directly to fifty million Americans.'

The TV team were setting up their equipment in the boardroom; the lights and cameras were being trained on the far end of the long room, where Centaine's portrait by Annigoni hung on the stinkwood panelling. There were three men in the camera crew, all young and casually dressed but clearly highly professional and competent, and with them was a girl.

'Who will do the interview?' Shasa asked, glancing around curiously.

'That's the director,' Jill Anstey said. 'And she'll talk to you.' It took him a moment to realize that she meant the girl, then he saw that without seeming to do so, the girl was directing the set-up, indicating a camera angle or a lighting change with a word or a gesture.

'She's just a child,' Shasa protested.

'Twenty-five and smart as a bunch of monkeys,' Jill Anstey warned him. 'Don't let the little-girl look fool you. She's a professional and a strong comer with a big following in the States. She did that incredible series of interviews with Jomo Kenyatta, the Mau Mau terrorist, not to mention the *Heartbreak Ridge* story in Korea. They say she'll get an Emmy for it.'

South Africa did not have a TV network, but Shasa had seen *Heartbreak Ridge* on BBC television during his last stay in London. It was a gritty, totally absorbing commentary on the Korean War, and Shasa found it hard to believe that this child had done that. She turned now and came directly to him, holding out her hand, frank and friendly, a fresh-faced *ingénue*.

'Hello, Mr Courtney, I'm Kitty Godolphin.' She had an enchanting Southern accent and there were fine golden freckles across her cheeks and her small pert nose, but then he saw that she had good bone structure and interesting planes to her face that would render her highly photogenic.

'Mr Courtney,' she said. 'You speak so well, I couldn't

resist trying to get a little more of you on film. I hope I haven't put you out too much.' She smiled at him, a sweet engaging smile, but he looked beyond it into eyes as hard as any diamonds from the H'ani Mine, eyes that were bright with a sharp cynical intelligence and ruthless ambition. That was unexpected and intriguing.

'Here's a show that will be worth the entrance fee,' he thought and glanced down. Her breasts were small, smaller than he usually chose, but they were unsupported and he could see their shape beneath her blouse. They were exquisite.

She led him to the leather chairs she had arranged to face each other under the lights.

'If you would sit on this side we'll get right into it. I'll do my introduction later. I don't want to keep you any longer than I have to.'

'As long as you like.'

'Oh, I know that you have a room full of important guests.' She glanced at her crew and one of them gave her a thumbs-up. She looked back at Shasa. 'The American public knows very little about South Africa,' she explained. 'What I am trying to do is capture a cross-section of your society and figure out how it all works. I will introduce you as a politician, mining tycoon and financier, and tell them about this fabulous new gold-mine of yours. Then we'll cut to you. OK?'

'OK!' He smiled easily. 'Let her roll.'

The clapper loader snapped the board in front of Shasa's face, somebody said 'Sound?' and somebody else replied, 'Rolling,' and then 'Action.'

'Mr Shasa Courtney, you have just told a meeting of your shareholders that your new gold-mine will probably be one of the five richest in South Africa, which makes it one of the richest in the world. Can you tell our viewers just how much of that fabulous wealth will be going back to people from whom it was stolen in the first place?' she asked with breath-taking candour. 'And I am, of course, referring to the black tribes who once owned the land.'

Shasa was off-balance for only the moment that it took him to realize that he was in a fight. Then he responded easily.

'The black tribes who once owned the land on which the Silver River Mine is situated were slaughtered, to the last man, woman and child, back in the 1820s by the impis of Kings Chaka and Mzilikazi, those two benevolent Zulu monarchs who between them managed to reduce the population of Southern Africa by fifty per cent,' he told her. 'When the white settlers moved northwards, they came upon a land denuded of all human life. The land they staked was open, they stole it from nobody. I bought the mineral rights from people who had clear undisputed title to it.' He saw a glint of respect in her eyes, but she was as quick as he had been. She had lost a point but she was ready to play the next.

'Historical facts are interesting, of course, but let's return to the present. Tell me, if you had been a man of colour, Mr Courtney, say black or an Asiatic businessman, would you have been allowed to purchase the concessions to the Silver River Mine?'

'That's a hypothetical question, Miss Godolphin.'

'I don't think so—' She cut off his escape. 'Am I wrong in thinking that the Group Areas Act recently promulgated by the parliament of which you are a sitting member, prevents non-white individuals and companies owned by blacks from purchasing land or mineral rights anywhere in their own land?'

'I voted against that legislation,' Shasa said grimly. 'But yes, the Group Areas Act would have prevented a coloured person acquiring the rights in the Silver River Mine,' he conceded. Too clever to labour a point well taken, she moved on swiftly.

'How many black people does the Courtney Mining and Finance Company employ in its numerous enterprises?' she asked with that sweet open smile.

'Altogether, through eighteen subsidiary companies, we provide work for some two thousand whites and thirty thousand blacks.'

'That is a marvellous achievement, and must make you very proud, Mr Courtney.' She was breathlessly girlish. 'And how many blacks do you have sitting on the boards of those eighteen companies?'

Again he had been wrong-footed, and he avoided the question. 'We make a point of paying well above the going rate for the job, and the other benefits we provide to our employees—' Kitty nodded brightly, letting him finish, quite happy that she could edit out all this extraneous material, but the moment he paused, she came in again:

'So there are no black directors on the Courtney companies' boards. Can you tell us how many black departmental managers you have appointed?'

Once long ago, hunting buffalo in the forests along the Zambezi River, Shasa had been attacked by a heat-maddened swarm of the big black African honey-bees. There had been no defence against them, and he had only escaped at last by diving into the crocodile-infested Zambezi River. He felt that same sense of angry helplessness now, as she buzzed around his head, effortlessly avoiding his attempts to swat her down and darting out to sting painfully almost at will.

'Thirty thousand black men working for you, and not a single director or manager amongst them!' she marvelled ingenuously. 'Can you suggest why that might be?'

'We have a predominantly tribal rural black society in this country and they come to the cities unskilled and untrained—'

'Oh, don't you have training programmes?'

Shasa accepted the opening. 'The Courtney group has a

123

massive training programme. Last year alone we spent two and a half million pounds on employee education and job training.'

'How long has this programme been in operation, Mr Courtney?'

'Seven years, ever since I became chairman.'

'And in seven years, after all that money spent on education, not one black of all those thousands has been promoted to managerial status? Is that because you have not found a single capable black, or is it because your job reservation policy and your strict colour bar prevent any black, no matter how good—'

He was driven back inexorably until in anger he went on the offensive. 'If you are looking for racial discrimination, why didn't you stay in America?' he asked her, smiling icily. 'I'm sure your own Martin Luther King would be able to help you more than I can.'

'There is bigotry in my country,' she nodded. 'We understand that, and we are changing it, educating our people and outlawing its practice, but from what I have seen, you are indoctrinating your children in this policy you call *apartheid* and enshrining it in a monumental fortress of laws like your Group Areas Act and your Population Registration Act which seeks to classify all men by the colour of their skin alone.'

'We differentiate,' Shasa conceded, 'but that does not mean that we discriminate.'

'That's a catchy slogan, Mr Courtney, but not original. I have already heard it from your Minister of Bantu Affairs, Dr Hendrik Frensch Verwoerd. However, I suggest to you that you do discriminate. If a man is denied the right to vote or to own land merely because his skin is dark, that in my book is discrimination.'

And before he could respond, she had switched again.

'How many black people do you number amongst your personal friends?' she asked engagingly, and the question transported Shasa instantly back across the years. He remembered as a lad standing his first shifts on the H'ani Mine and the man who had been his friend. The black boss-boy in charge of the weathering grounds on which the newly mined blue ore from the pit was laid out to soften and crumble to the point at which it could be carted to the mill.

He hadn't thought about him for years, yet he remembered his name without effort, Moses Gama, and he saw him in his mind's eye, tall and broad-shouldered, handsome as a young pharaoh with skin that glowed like old amber in the sunlight as they toiled side by side. He remembered their long rambling discussions, how they had read and argued together, drawn together by some unusual bond of the spirit. Shasa had lent him Macaulay's *History of England*, and when Moses Gama was fired from the H'ani Mine on the instigation of Centaine Courtney as a direct result of the unacceptably intimate friendly relationship between them, Shasa had asked him to keep the book. Now he felt again a faint echo of the sense of deprivation he had experienced at the time of their enforced parting.

'I have only a handful of personal friends,' he told her now. 'Ten thousand acquaintances, but only a very few friends—' He held up the fingers of his right hand. 'No more than that, and none of them happen to be black. Though once I had a black man as a friend, and I grieved when our ways parted.'

With the sure instinct which made her supreme in her craft, Kitty Godolphin recognized that he had given her a perfect peg on which to hang the interview.

'Once I had a black man as a friend,' she repeated softly. 'And I grieved when our ways parted. Thank you, Mr Courtney.' She turned to her camera man. 'OK, Hank, cut it and get the studio to print it tonight.'

She stood up quickly and Shasa towered over her.

'That was excellent. There is a great deal of material

125

there we can use,' she enthused. 'I am really grateful for your cooperation.'

Smiling urbanely Shasa leaned close to her. 'You are a devious little bitch, aren't you?' he said softly. 'A face like an angel and a heart of hell. You know it isn't like you made it sound, and you don't care. As long as you get a good story, you don't give a damn whether it's true or not or who it hurts, do you?'

Shasa turned from her and strode out of the boardroom. The floor-show had started and he went to the table at which Centaine and Blaine Malcomess were sitting, but the night had been spoiled for him.

He sat and glowered at the swirling dancers, not really seeing their long naked limbs and gleaming flesh but thinking furiously of Kitty Godolphin instead. Danger excited him, that was why he hunted lion and buffalo and flew his own Mosquito and played polo. Kitty Godolphin was dangerous. He was always attracted to intelligent and competent women, with strong personalities – and this one was devastatingly competent and made of pure silk and steel.

He thought about that lovely innocent face and child-like smile and the hard gleam of her eyes, and his fury was compounded by his desire to subjugate her, emotionally and physically, and the fact that he knew it would be difficult made the thought all the more obsessive. He found that he was physically aroused and that increased his anger.

He glanced up suddenly, and from across the room Jill Anstey, the public relations director, was watching him. The coloured lights played on the Slavic planes of her face and glinted on the platinum sheet of her hair. She slanted her eyes at him and ran the tip of her tongue over her lower lip.

'All right,' he thought. 'I have to take it out on somebody and you will do.' He inclined his head slightly, and Jill Anstey nodded and slipped out of the door behind her. Shasa murmured an apology to Centaine, then stood up and moved through the pounding music and semi-darkness towards the door through which Jill Anstey had disappeared.

Shasa got back to the Carlton Hotel at nine o'clock in the morning. Still in black tie and dinner jacket, he avoided the lobby and went up the back stairs from the underground garage. Centaine and Blaine were in the company suite, and Shasa had the smaller suite across the passage. He dreaded meeting either of them dressed as he was at this time in the morning, but he was lucky and got into his lounge uninterrupted.

Somebody had slipped an envelope under his door, and he picked it up without particular interest until he saw the Killarney Film Studios crest on the flap. Kitty Godolphin was working out of that studio and he grinned and split the flap with his thumbnail.

Dear Mr Courtney,
    The rushes are just great – you look better than Errol Flynn on film. If you want to see them, call me at the studio.

Kitty Godolphin

His anger had cooled and he was amused by her cheek, and though he had a full day ahead – lunch with Lord Littleton and meetings all afternoon – he phoned the studio.

'You just caught me,' Kitty told him. 'I was on my way out. You want to see the rushes? OK, can you get up here at six this evening?'

She was smiling that sweet childlike smile and mocking him with a malicious green sparkle in her eyes as she came down to the reception desk of the studio to shake his hand and lead him to her hired projection room in the complex.

'I knew I could rely on your masculine vanity to get you up here,' she assured him.

Her film crew were sprawled untidily over the front row of seats in the projection room, smoking Camels and drinking Cokes, but Hank, the camera man, had the film clip in the projector ready to run, and they watched it through in silence.

When the lights went up again, Shasa turned to Kitty and conceded.

'You are good – you made me look a real prick most of the time. And, of course, you can always lose the parts where I held my own on the cutting-room floor.'

'You don't like it?' she grinned, wrinkling her small nose so the freckles on it gleamed like tiny gold coins.

'You are a bushwhacker, shooting from cover, and I'm out there with my back wide open.'

'If you accuse me of faking it,' she challenged him, 'how about you taking me and showing me the way it really is. Show me the Courtney mines and factories and let me film them!'

So that was why she had called him. He smiled to himself, but asked, 'Have you got ten days?'

'I've got as long as it takes,' she assured him.

'All right, let's start with dinner tonight.'

'Great!' she enthused, and then turned to her crew. '*Mazeltov*, boys, Mr Courtney is standing us all dinner.'

'That's not exactly what I had in mind,' he murmured.

'Do tell?' She gave him her innocent little-girl look.

Kitty Godolphin was a rewarding companion. Her interest in everything he said or showed her was flattering and unfeigned. She watched his eyes or his lips as he spoke, and often leaned so close to listen that he could feel her breath on his face, but she never actually touched him.

For Shasa her appeal was heightened by her personal cleanliness. In the days they spent together, hot dusty days in the desert of the far west or in the eastern forests, tramping through pulp mills or fertilizer factories, watching the bulldozers strip the overburden from the coal deposits in billowing clouds of dust or baking in the depths of the great excavation of the H'ani Mine, Kitty was always fresh-faced and cool-looking. Even in the dust her eyes were clear and her small even teeth sparkled. When or where she had an opportunity to rinse her clothes he could never decide, but they were always clean and crisp and her breath when she leaned close to him was always sweet.

She was a professional. That impressed Shasa also. She would go to any lengths to get the film footage she wanted, taking no account of fatigue or personal danger. He had to forbid her riding on the outside of the mine cage on the H'ani main incline shaft to film the drop into the pit, but she went back later, while he was in a meeting with his mine manager, and got exactly the shot she wanted and then smiled away his fury when he found out. Her crew treated her with an ambivalence that amused Shasa. They held her in fond affection and were immensely protective of her, as though they were her elder brothers, and their pride in her achievements was unconcealed. However, at the same time they were much in awe of her ruthless search for excellence, to which they knew she would sacrifice them and anything else that got in her way. Her temper, although not often displayed, was merciless and vitriolic and when she gave an order, no matter how quietly or how sweet the smile that accompanied it, they jumped.

Shasa was also affected by the deep feelings which she had conceived for Africa, its land and its people.

'I thought America was the most beautiful country in all the world,' she said quietly one evening as they watched the sun set behind the great desolate mountains of the western deserts. 'But when I look at this, I have to wonder.'

Her curiosity took her into the compounds where the Courtney Company employees were housed, and she spent hours talking to the workers and their wives, filming it all, the questions and answers of black miners and white over-seers and shift bosses, their homes and the food they ate, their recreations and their worship, and at the end Shasa asked her, 'So how do you like the way I oppress them?'

'They live well,' she conceded.

'And they are happy,' he pushed her. 'Admit it. I hid nothing from you. They are happy.'

'They are happy like children,' she agreed. 'As long as they look up to you like big daddy. But just how long do you think you can keep fooling them? How long is it going to be before they look at you in your beautiful airplane flying back to parliament to make a few more laws for them to obey and say to themselves, "Hey, man! I'd like to try that also"?'

'For three hundred years under white government the people of this land have woven a social fabric which has held us all together. It works, and I would hate to see it torn asunder without knowing what will replace it.'

'How about democracy for a start?' she suggested. 'That's not a bad thing to replace it with – you know, *the will of the majority must prevail!*'

'You left out the best bit,' he flashed back at her. '*The interests of the minority must be safeguarded*. That doesn't work in Africa. The African knows and understands one principle: winner takes all – and let the minority go to the wall. That's what will happen to the white settlers in Kenya if the British capitulate to the Mau Mau killers.'

So they wrangled and sparred during the long hours of flying which took them over the enormous distances of the African continent. From one destination to the next, Shasa and Kitty went ahead in the Mosquito, and the helmet and oxygen mask were too large for her and made her appear even younger and more girlish. David Abrahams piloted the slower and more commodious company De Havilland Dove, the camera equipment and the crew flying with him, and even though most of Shasa's time on the ground was spent in meetings with his managers and administrative staff there was still much time that he could devote to the seduction of Kitty Godolphin.

Shasa was not accustomed to prolonged resistance from any female who warranted his concentrated attention. There might be a token flight, but always with coy glances over the shoulder, and usually they chose to hide from him in the nearest bedroom, absentmindedly forgetting to turn the key in the lock, and he expected it to go very much the same way with Kitty Godolphin.

Getting into her blue jeans was his first priority; convincing her that Africa was different from America and that they were doing the best job they could came second by a long way. At the end of the ten days he had succeeded in neither endeavour. Both Kitty's political convictions and her virtue remained intact.

Kitty's interest in him, however wide-eyed and intense, was totally impersonal and professional, and she gave the same attention to an Ovambo witchdoctor demonstrating how he cured abdominal cancer with a poultice of porcupine dung, or a muscled and tattooed white shift-boss explaining to her that a black worker should never be punched in the stomach as their spleens were always enlarged from malaria and could easily rupture – hitting them in the head was all right, he explained, because the African skull was solid bone anyway and you couldn't inflict serious damage that way.

'Mary Maria!' Kitty breathed. 'That was worth the trip in itself!'

So on the eleventh day of their odyssey, they flew out of the vastness of the Kalahari Desert, from the remote H'ani Diamond Mine on its mystic and brooding range of hills, into the town of Windhoek, capital of the old German colony of South-West Africa which had been mandated to South Africa in the Treaty of Versailles. It was a quaint little town, the German influence still very obvious in the architecture and the way of life of the inhabitants. Set in the hilly uplands above the arid littoral, the climate was pleasant, and the Kaiserhof Hotel, where Shasa kept another permanent suite, offered many of the creature comforts that they had lacked during the previous ten days.

Shasa and David spent the afternoon with their senior staff in the local office of the Courtney Company, which before its move to Johannesburg had been the head office, but which was still responsible for the logistics of the H'ani Mine. Kitty and her team, never wasting a moment, filmed the German colonial buildings and monuments and the picturesque Herero women on the streets. In 1904 this tribe of warriors had engaged the German administration in their worst colonial war which finally left eighty thousand Hereroes dead of famine and battle out of a total population of a hundred thousand. They were tall and magnificent-looking people and the women wore full-length Victorian skirts in butterfly colours and tall matching headdresses. Kitty was delighted with them, and late that afternoon came back to the hotel in ebullient mood.

Shasa had planned carefully, and had left David at the Courtney Company offices to finish the meeting. He was waiting to invite Kitty and her team through to the beer garden of the hotel where a traditional oom-pa-pa band in lederhosen and Alpine hats was belting out a medley of German drinking songs. The locally brewed Hansa Pilsner was every bit as good as the original of the Munich beerhalls, with a clear golden colour and thick creamy head. Shasa ordered the largest tankards, and Kitty drank level with her crew.

The mood turned festive until Shasa drew Kitty aside and under cover of the band told her quietly, 'I don't quite know how to break this to you, Kitty, but this will be our last evening together. I had my secretary book seats on the commercial flight for you and your boys to fly back to Johannesburg tomorrow morning.'

Kitty stared at him aghast. 'I don't understand. I thought we were flying down to your diamond concessions in the *Sperrgebiet*.' She pronounced it 'Spear Beat' in her enchanting accent. 'That was going to be the main act.'

'*Sperrgebiet* means "Forbidden Area",' Shasa told her sadly. 'And it means just that, Kitty, forbidden. Nobody goes in there without a permit from the government Inspector of Mines.'

'But I thought you had arranged a permit for us,' she protested.

'I tried. I telexed our local office to arrange it. The application was denied. The government doesn't want you in there, I'm afraid.'

'But why not?'

'There must be something going on in there that they don't want you to see or film.' He shrugged, and she was silent but he saw the play of fierce emotion across her innocent features and her eyes blazed green with anger and determination. He had early on discovered that the infallible means of making anything irresistibly attractive was to deny it to Kitty Godolphin. He knew that now she would lie, cheat or sell her soul to get into the *Sperrgebiet*.

'You could smuggle us in,' she suggested.

He shook his head. 'Not worth the risk. We might get away with it, but if I were caught it could mean a fine of £100,000 or five years in the slammer.'

She laid her hand on his arm, the first time she had deliberately touched him. 'Please, Shasa. I want so badly to film it.'

He shook his head sorrowfully. 'I'm sorry, Kitty, can't be done, I'm afraid,' and he stood up. 'Got to go up and change for dinner. You can break it to your crew while I'm away. Your flight back to Jo'burg leaves at ten o'clock tomorrow.'

It was obvious at the dinner-table that she hadn't warned

her crew of the change of plans, for they were still jovial and garrulous with good German beer.

For once Kitty took no part in the conversation, and she sat morosely at the end of the table, nibbling without interest at the hearty Teutonic fare and occasionally darting a sulky glance at Shasa. David skipped coffee to go and make his nightly phone call to Matty and the children, and Hank and his crew had been told of a local night spot with hot music and even hotter hostesses.

'Ten days with no feminine company except the boss,' Hank complained. 'My nerves need soothing.'

'Remember where you are,' Shasa warned him. 'In this country black velvet is royal game.'

'Some of the poontang I've seen today would be worth five years' hard labour,' Hank leered.

'Did you know that we have a South African version of Russian roulette?' Shasa asked him. 'What you do is take a coloured girl into a telephone booth. Then you phone the police Flying Squad and see who comes first.'

Kitty was the only one who didn't laugh, and Shasa stood up. 'I've got some papers to go over. We'll save the farewells until breakfast.'

In his suite he shaved and showered quickly, then slipped on a silk dressing-gown. As he went through to check that there was ice in the bar, there was a light tap on the door of the suite.

Kitty stood on the threshold looking tragic.

'Am I disturbing you?'

'No, of course not.' He held the door open and she crossed the lounge and stood staring out of the window.

'Can I get you a night-cap?' Shasa asked.

'What are you drinking?' she asked.

'A Rusty Nail.'

'I'll have one also – whatever it is.'

While he mixed Drambuie and malt whisky, she said, 'I

came to thank you for everything you've done for me these last ten days. It's going to be hard to say goodbye.'

He carried the glasses across to where she stood in the middle of the floor, but when he reached her she took both glasses from him and placed them on the coffee table. Then she stood on tiptoe, slid both arms around his neck and turned her face up for his kiss.

Her lips were soft and sweet as warm chocolate, and slowly she pushed her tongue deeply into his mouth. When at last their mouths parted with a little wet sucking sound, he stooped and hooked an arm around the back of her knees and lifted her against his chest. She clung to him, pressing her face against his throat as he carried her through to the bedroom.

She had the lean hips and flat belly of a boy, and her buttocks were white and round and hard as a pair of ostrich eggs. Like her face, her body seemed childlike and immature except for those tight little pear-shaped breasts and the startling burst of thick dark hair at the base of her belly, but when he touched her there he found to his surprise that it was fine as silk and soft as smoke.

Her love-making was so artful as to seem totally uncontrived and spontaneous. She had the trick of telling him exactly what he was doing to her in the coarsest barnyard terms, and the obscenities on that soft innocent-looking mouth were shockingly erotic. She took him to those heights that he had seldom scaled before, and left him completely satiated.

In the dawn glow she snuggled against him and whispered, 'I don't know how I am going to be able to bear being parted from you after this.'

He could see her face in the wall mirror across the room, although she was unaware of his scrutiny. 'Damn it – I can't let you go,' he whispered back. 'I don't care what it costs, I'm taking you down to the *Sperrgebiet* with me.'

In the mirror he watched her smile, a complacent and smug little smile. He had been correct, Kitty Godolphin used her sexual favours like trumps in a game of bridge.

At the airport her crew were packing their equipment into the Dove under David Abrahams' supervision when Shasa and Kitty drove up in the second company car, and Kitty jumped out and went to David.

'How are you going to work it, Davie?' she asked, and he looked puzzled.

'I don't understand the question.'

'You'll have to fake the flight plan, won't you?' Kitty insisted. Still mystified, David glanced at Shasa. Shasa shrugged and Kitty became exasperated.

'You know very well what I mean. How are you going to cover the fact that we are going into the *Sperrgebiet* without permits?'

'Without permits?' David echoed, and fished a handful of documents out of the zip pocket of his leather flying-jacket. 'Here are the permits. They were issued a week ago – all kosher and correct.'

Kitty wheeled and glared speechlessly at Shasa, but he refused to meet her eyes and instead ambled off to make his walk-around check of the Mosquito.

They didn't speak to each other again until Shasa had the Mosquito at twenty thousand feet, flying straight and level, then Kitty said into his earphones, 'You son of a bitch.' Her voice shook with fury.

'Kitty, my darling.' He turned and smiled at her over the oxygen mask, his single eye glinting happily. 'We both got what we wanted, and had a lot of fun in the process. What are you so mad about?'

She turned her face away and stared down at the magnificent lion-coloured mountains of the Khama's Hochtland. He left her to sulk. Some minutes later he heard an unusual stuttering sound in his headset, and he frowned and leaned forward to adjust the radio. Then, from the corner of his eye he saw that Kitty was hunched up in the seat shaking uncontrollably and that the stuttering sound was coming from her.

He touched her shoulder and she turned her face to him, it was swollen and crimson with suppressed laughter and tears of mirth were squeezing out of the corners of her eyes with the pressure. She couldn't hold it any longer, and she let out a snort.

'You crafty bastard,' she sobbed. 'Oh, you tricky monster—' and then she became incoherent as laughter overwhelmed her.

A long time later she wiped away her tears. 'We are going to get on just fine together, you and me,' she declared. 'Our minds work the same way.'

'Our bodies don't do too badly either,' he pointed out, and she unclipped her oxygen mask and leaned across to offer him her mouth again. Her tongue was sinuous and slippery as an eel.

Their time in the desert together passed too swiftly for Shasa, for since they had become lovers he found her a constant joy to be with. Her quick and curious mind stimulated his own, and through her observant eyes he saw old familiar things afresh.

Together they watched and filmed the elephantine yellow caterpillar tractors ripping the elevated terraces that had once been the ocean bed. He explained to Kitty how in the time when the crust of the earth was soft and the molten magma still burst through to the surface, the diamonds, conceived at great depth and heat and pressure, were carried up with this sulphurous outpouring.

In the endless rains of those ancient times the great rivers scoured the earth, running down to the sea, washing the diamonds down with them, until they collected in the pockets and irregularities of the seabed closest to the river mouth. As the emerging continent shrugged and shifted, so the old seabed was lifted above the surface. The rivers had long ago dried up or been diverted, and sediment covered the elevated terraces, concealing the diamond-bearing pockets. It had taken the genius of Twentyman-Jones to work out the old river courses. Using aerial photography and an inherent sixth sense, he had pinpointed the ancient terraces.

Kitty and her team filmed the process by which the sand and rubble churned up by the dozer blades was screened and sieved, and finally dry-blown with great multi-bladed fans, until only the precious stones – one part in tens of millions – remained.

In the desert nights the mine hutments, lacking air-conditioning, were too hot for sleep. Shasa made a nest of blankets out amongst the dunes, and with the faint peppery smell of the desert in their nostrils they made love under a blaze of stars.

On their last day Shasa commandeered one of the company jeeps and they drove out into a land of red dunes, the highest in all the world, sculptured by the incessant winds off the cold Benguela Current, their ridges crested like living reptiles as they writhed high against the pale desert sky.

Shasa pointed out to Kitty a herd of gemsbok, each antelope large as a pony, but with a marvellously patterned face mask of black and white and slender horns, straight and long as they were tall, that were the original unicorn of the fable. They were beautiful beasts, so adapted to their harsh country that they need never drink from surface water, but could survive only on the moisture they obtained from the silvery sun-scorched grasses. They watched them dissolve magically into the heat mirage, turning to squirming black tadpoles on the horizon before they disappeared.

'I was born here. Somewhere in these deserts,' Shasa

told her as they stood hand in hand on the crest of one of the dunes and looked down a thousand feet to where they had left the jeep in the gut of the sand mountains.

He told her how Centaine had carried him in her womb through this terrible terrain, lost and abandoned, with only two little Bushmen as her guides and companions, and how the Bushwoman, for whom the H'ani Mine was named, acted as midwife at his birth and named him Shasa – 'Good Water' – after the most precious substance in her world.

The beauty and the grandeur affected them both so they drew close together in the solitude, and by the end of that day Shasa was sure that he truly loved her and that he wanted to spend the rest of his life with her.

Together they watched the sun sink towards the red dunes and the sky turned to a screen of hot hammered bronze, dented with flecks of blue cloud as though by blows from a celestial blacksmith's hammer. As the sky cooled, the colours chameleoned into puce and orange and lofty purples until the sun sank behind the dunes – and at the instant it disappeared, a miracle occurred.

They both gasped in wonder as in a silent explosion the entire heavens flared into electric green. It lasted only as long as they held their breath, but in that time the sky was as green as the ocean depths or the ice in the gaping cracks of a high mountain glacier. Then it faded swiftly into the drab gun-metal of dusk, and Kitty turned to him with a silent question in her eyes.

'We saw it together,' Shasa said softly. 'The Bushmen call it the Green Python. A man can live a lifetime in the desert without seeing it. I have never witnessed it, not until this moment.'

'What does it mean?' Kitty asked.

'The Bushmen say it is the most fortunate of all good omens.' He reached out and took her hand. 'They say that those who see the Green Python will be specially blessed – and we saw it together.'

In the fading light they went down the slip face of the dune to where Shasa had parked the jeep. They sank almost knee-deep in the fluffy sun-warm sand, and laughing they clung to each other for support.

When they reached the jeep, Shasa took her by the shoulders, turned her to face him and told her, 'I don't want it to end, Kitty. Come with me. Marry me. I'll give you everything that life has to offer.'

She threw back her head to laugh in his face. 'Don't be daft, Shasa Courtney. What I want from life isn't yours to give,' she told him. 'This was fun, but it wasn't reality. We can be good friends for as long as you want, but our feet are set on different paths, and we aren't going in the same direction.'

The next day when they landed at Windhoek airport, a telegram addressed to her was pinned to the board in the crew room. Kitty read it swiftly. When she looked up she wasn't seeing Shasa any longer.

'There is another story breaking,' she said. 'I have to go.'

'When will I see you again?' Shasa asked, and she looked at him as though he were a complete stranger.

'I don't know,' she said, and she and her crew were on the commercial flight that left for Johannesburg an hour later.

Shasa was angry and humiliated. He had never offered to divorce Tara for any other woman – had never even contemplated it – and Kitty had laughed at him.

There were well-explored avenues down which he knew he could cure his anger; one was the hunt. For Shasa nothing else existed in the world when the hunter's passion thrilled in his blood, when a bull buffalo, big as a mountain and black as hell, came thundering down upon him, bloody saliva drooling from its raised muzzle, the polished points of its curved horns glinting, and murder in its small piglike eyes. However, this was the rainy season and the hunting grounds in the north would be muggy wet and malarial, and the grass high above a man's head. He could not hunt, so he turned to his other sure panacea, the pursuit of wealth.

Money held endless fascination for Shasa. Without that obsessive attraction he could not have accumulated such a vast store of it, for that required a devotion and dedication that few men are capable of. Those that lack it console themselves with old platitudes about it not buying happiness and being the root of all evil. As an adept, Shasa knew that money was neither good nor evil, but simply amoral. He knew that money had no conscience, but that it contained the most powerful potential for both good and evil. It was the man who possessed it who made the ultimate choice between them, and that choice was called power.

Even when he had believed himself to be totally absorbed with Kitty Godolphin, his instinct had been in play. Almost subconsciously he had noticed those tiny white specks way out on the green Benguela Current of the Atlantic. Kitty Godolphin had not been gone from his life for an hour before he stormed into the offices of Courtney Mining and Finance in Windhoek's main street and started demanding figures and documents, making telephone calls, summoning lawyers and accountants, calling in favours from men in high places in government, dispatching his minions to search the archives of the registrar and the local newspapers, assembling the tools of his trade, facts, figures and influence, and then losing himself happily in them, like an opium-eater with his pipe.

It was another five days before he was ready to bring it all together, and make the final weighing up. He had kept

David Abrahams with him, for David was an excellent sounding-board in a situation like this one, and Shasa liked to bounce ideas off him and catch the returns.

'So this is what it looks like,' Shasa began the summing up. There were five of them in the boardroom, sitting under the magnificent Pierneef murals that Centaine had commissioned when the artist was in his prime, Shasa and David, the local manager and the secretary of Courtney Mining, and the German lawyer based in Windhoek whom Shasa kept on permanent retainer.

'It looks like we have been asleep on our feet. In the last three years an industry has sprung up under our noses, an industry that last year alone netted twenty million pounds, four times the profits of the H'ani Mine, and we have let it happen.'

He glowered cyclops-eyed at his local manager for an explanation.

'We were aware of the recommencement of the fishing industry at Walvis Bay,' that unfortunate gentleman sought to explain. 'The application for pilchard trawling licences was gazetted, but I didn't think that fishing would match up with our other activities.'

'With due respect, Frank, that's the kind of decision I like to make myself. It's your job to pass on all information, of whatever nature, to me.' It was said quietly, but the three local men had no illusions as to the severity of the reprimand and they bowed their heads over their notepads. There was silence for ten seconds while Shasa let them suffer.

'Right, Frank,' Shasa ordered him. 'Tell us now what you should have told us four or five years ago.'

'Well, Mr Courtney, the pilchard-fishing industry was started in the early 1930s at Walvis Bay, and although initially successful it was overtaken by the Depression, and with the primitive trawling methods of those days was unable to survive. The factories closed down and became derelict.'

As Frank spoke, Shasa's mind went back to his childhood. He remembered his first visit to Walvis Bay and blinked with the realization that it had been twenty years ago. He and Centaine had driven down in her daffodil-coloured Daimler to call in the loan she had made to De La Rey's canning and fishing company and to close down the factory. Those were the desperate years of the Depression when the Courtney companies had survived only through his mother's pluck and determination – and ruthlessness.

He remembered how Lothar De La Rey, Manfred's father, had pleaded with his mother for an extension of the loan. When his trawlers lay against the wharf, loaded to the gunwales with their catch of silver pilchards, and the sheriff of the court, on Centaine's orders, had put his seals on the factory doors.

That was the day he had first met Manfred De La Rey. Manfred had been a bare-footed, cropped-head hulk of a lad, bigger and stronger than Shasa, burned dark by the sun, dressed in a navy-blue fisherman's jersey and khaki shorts that were smeared with dried fish-slime, while Shasa had worn immaculate grey slacks, white open-neck shirt and a college sweater with polished black shoes on his feet.

Two boys from different worlds, they had come face to face on the main fish wharf and their hostility had been instantaneous, their hackles rising like dogs, and within minutes, gibes and insults had turned to blows and they had flown at each other furiously, punching and wrestling down the wharf while the coloured trawlermen had egged them on delightedly. He remembered clearly even after all this time Manfred De La Rey's pale ferocious eyes glaring into his as they fell from the wharf on to the slippery, stinking cargo of dead pilchards, and he felt again the dreadful humiliation as Manfred had forced his head deeply into the quagmire of cold dead fish and he had begun to drown in their slime.

He jerked his mind back to the present, to hear his manager saying, 'So the position is now that the government has issued four factory licences to catch and process pilchards at Walvis Bay. The Department of Fisheries allocates an annual quota to each of the licensees, which is presently two hundred thousand tons.' Shasa contemplated the enormous profit potential of those quantities of fish. According to their published accounts, each of those four factories had averaged two million pounds profit in the last fiscal year. He knew he could improve on that, probably double it, but it didn't look as though he was going to get the chance.

'Approaches to both the Fisheries Department, and to higher authority' – Shasa had taken the administrator of the territory himself to dinner – 'have elicited the firm fact that no further licences will be issued. The only way to enter the industry would be to buy out one of the licensees.' Shasa smiled sardonically for he had already sounded out two of the companies. The owner of the first one had told Shasa in movingly eloquent terms to commit an unnatural sexual act on himself and the other had quoted a figure at which he might be prepared to negotiate which ended with a string of zeros that reached to the horizon. Despite his gloomy expression, it was the kind of situation in which Shasa revelled, seemingly hopeless, and yet with the promise of enormous rewards if he could find his way around the obstacles.

'I want a detailed breakdown of balance sheets on all four companies,' he ordered. 'Does anybody know the Director of Fisheries?'

'Yes, but he's straight up and down,' Frank warned him, knowing how Shasa's mind worked. 'His fists are tight

144

closed, and if we try to slip him a little gifty, he'll raise a stink they'll smell in the High Court in Bloemfontein.'

'Besides which the issue of licences is outside his jurisdiction,' the company secretary agreed with him. 'They are granted exclusively by the ministry in Pretoria, and there won't be any more. Four is the limit. That is the decision of the Minister himself.'

Five more days Shasa remained in Windhoek, covering every possible lead or chance with a total dedication to detail that was one of his strengths, but at the end of that time he was no closer to owning a factory licence at Walvis Bay than he had been when he had first spotted the little white trawlers out on the green ocean. The only thing he had achieved was to forget that malignant little sprite Kitty Godolphin for ten whole days.

However, when at last he admitted to himself that there was nothing more to be gained by staying on in Windhoek and he climbed into the pilot's seat of the Mosquito, Kitty Godolphin's memory mocked him from the empty seat beside him. On impulse, instead of laying a course direct to Cape Town, he detoured westwards, heading for the coast and Walvis Bay, determined to have one long look at the site before finally abandoning the idea.

There was something else besides Kitty's memory that plagued him as the Mosquito dropped down the escarpment towards the sea. It was a burr of doubt, a prickle of discomfort that he had overlooked something important in his investigations.

He saw the ocean ahead, wreathed in tendrils of fog where the cold current brushed the land. The high dunes writhed together like a nest of razor-backed vipers, the colour of ripe wheat and copper, and he banked the Mosquito and followed the endless beaches upon which the surf broke in regular snowy lines until he saw the horn of the bay spike into the restless ocean and the lighthouse on Pelican Point winked at him through the fog banks.

He throttled back the Rolls-Royce Merlins and went down, brushing the tops of the scattered fog banks and in the gaps he saw the trawler fleet at work. They were close in to the land, on the edge of the current line. Some of the boats had their nets full, and he saw the silver treasure glittering through the water as the trawlermen raised it slowly to the surface, while over them hung a shimmering white panoply of seabirds, greedy for the feast.

Then a mile away he picked out another boat hunting, cutting a foaming arabesque with its wake as it stalked yet another pilchard shoal.

Shasa pulled on flap and banked the Mosquito steeply, turning above the trawler to watch the hunt develop. He saw the shoal, a dark shadow as though a thousand gallons of ink had been spilled into the green waters, and he was amazed by its size, a hundred acres of solid fish, each individual no longer than his hand, but in their multitudes dwarfing leviathan.

'Millions of tons in one shoal,' he whispered. As he translated it into terms of wealth, the acquisitive passion flared up in him again. He watched the trawler beneath him throw its net around a tiny part of the gigantic shoal, and then he levelled out and flew at a hundred feet, skimming the fog banks, towards the maw of the bay. There were the four factory buildings, standing on the edge of the water, each with its own jetty thrusting out into the shallow waters, and black smoke billowing from the chimney stacks of the furnaces.

'Which one belonged to old De La Rey?' he wondered. On which of those flimsy structures had he fought with Manfred and ended with his ears and nose and mouth filled with fish slime? He grinned ruefully at the memory.

'But surely it was further north,' he puzzled, trying to cast his mind back twenty years. 'It wasn't down here so close to the hook of the bay.' He banked the Mosquito and flew back parallel to the beach, and then a mile ahead he saw the line of palings, rotted and black, running in an irregular line out into the waters of the bay, and on the beach the roofless old ruins of the factory.

'It's still there,' he realized, and instantly his skin prickled with excitement. 'It's still there, deserted and forgotten all these years.' He knew then what he had overlooked.

He made two more passes, so low that the blast of his propellers raised a miniature sandstorm from the tops of the dunes. On the seaward wall of the derelict factory whose corrugated iron covering was gnawed and streaked with red rust, he could still make out the faded lettering: SOUTH WEST AFRICAN CANNING AND FISHING CO. LTD.

He pushed on throttle and lifted the Mosquito's nose into a gentle climbing turn, bringing her out of the turn on course for Windhoek. Cape Town and his promise to his sons and Isabella to be home before the weekend were forgotten. David Abrahams had flown the Dove back to Johannesburg, leaving a few minutes before Shasa that morning, so there was nobody in Windhoek whom Shasa would trust to conduct the search. He went down to the registrar of deeds himself and an hour before the deed office closed for the weekend he found what he was looking for.

The licence to capture and process pilchards and all other pelagic fish was dated 20 September 1929 and signed by the administrator of the territory. It was made out in favour of one Lothar De La Rey of Windhoek, and there was no term of expiry. It was good now and for all time.

Shasa stroked the crackling, yellowing document, smoothing out the crumples in it lovingly, admiring the crimson revenue stamps and the administrator's fading signature. Here in these musty drawers it had lain for over twenty years – and he tried to put a value on this scrap of paper. A million pounds, certainly – five million pounds, perhaps. He chuckled triumphantly and took it to the deeds clerk to have a notorized copy made.

'It will cost you a pretty penny, sir,' the clerk sniffed. 'Ten and six for the copy and two pounds for the attestation.'

'It's a high price,' Shasa agreed, 'but I can just afford it.'

Lothar De La Rey came bounding up the wet black rocks, surefooted as a mountain goat, dressed only in a pair of black woollen bathing trunks. In one hand he carried a light fishing rod and in the other he held the trace on the end of which a small silver fish fluttered.

'I've got one, Pa,' he called excitedly, and Manfred De La Rey roused himself. He had been lost in thought; even on this, one of his rare vacations, his mind was still concentrated on the work of his ministry.

'Well done, Lothie.' He stood up and picked up the heavy bamboo surf rod that lay beside him. He watched his son gently unhook the small bait fish and hand it to him. He took it from him. It was cold and firm and slippery, and when he pressed the sharp point of his large hook through its flesh, the tiny dorsal fin along its back came erect and its struggles were frantic.

'Man, no old kob will be able to resist that.' Manfred held the live bait up for his son to admire. 'It looks so good, I could eat it myself.' He picked up the heavy rod.

For a minute he watched the surf break on the rocks below them, and then timing his moment he ran down to the edge, moving lightly for such a big man. The foam sucked at his ankles as he poised, and then swung the bamboo rod in a full whipping action. The cast was long and high, the live bait sparkled as it spun a parabola in the sunlight and then hit the green water a hundred yards out, beyond the first line of breakers.

Manfred ran back as the next wave dashed head-high at him. With the rod over his shoulder and line still streaming from the big Scarborough reel he beat the angry white surf and regained his seat high up on the rocks.

He thrust the butt of the rod into a crack in the rocks and jammed his old stained felt hat against the reel to hold it. Then he settled down on his cushion with his back to the rock and his son beside him.

'Good kob water,' he grunted. The sea was discoloured and cloudy, like home-made ginger beer, the perfect conditions for the quarry they were seeking.

'I promised Ma we would bring her a fish for pickling,' Lothar said.

'Never count your kob before it's in the pickle barrel,' Manfred counselled, and the boy laughed.

Manfred never touched him in front of others, not even in front of his mother and the girls, but he remembered the enormous pleasure it had given him when he was Lothar's age to have his own father's embrace, and so at times when they were alone together like this he would let his true feelings show. He let his arm slip down off the rock and fall around the boy's shoulders and Lothar froze with joy and for a minute did not dare to breathe. Then slowly he leaned closer to his father and in silence they watched the tip of the long rod nod in rhythm to the ocean.

'And so, Lothie, have you decided what you want to do with your life when you leave Paul Roos?' Paul Roos was the leading Afrikaans medium school in the Cape Province, the South African equivalent of Eton or Harrow for Afrikaners.

'Pa, I've been thinking.' Lothar was serious. 'I don't want to do law like you did, and I think medicine will be too difficult.'

Manfred nodded resignedly. He had come to terms with the fact that Lothar was not academically brilliant, but just a good average student. It was in all the other fields that he excelled. Already it was clear that his powers of leadership, his determination and courage, and his athletic prowess were all exceptional.

'I want to join the police,' the boy said hesitantly. 'When I finish at Paul Roos, I want to go to the police academy in Pretoria.'

Manfred sat quietly, trying to hide his surprise. It was probably the last thing he would have thought of himself.

At last he said. '*Ja*, why not! You'd do well there.' He nodded. 'It's a good life, a life of service to your country and your *Volk*.' The more he thought about it, the more he realized that Lothar was making a perfect choice – and of course, the fact that his father was Minister of Police wouldn't hurt the boy's career either. He hoped he would stick to it. '*Ja*,' he repeated, 'I like it.'

'Pa, I wanted to ask you—' Lothar started, and the tip of the rod jerked, bounced straight, and then arced over boldly. Manfred's old hat was thrown clear of the spinning reel as the line hissed from it in a blur.

Father and son leapt to their feet and Manfred seized the heavy bamboo and leaned back against it to set the hook.

'It's a monster,' he shouted, as he felt the weight of the fish, and the flow of line never checked, even when he thrust the palm of the leather mitten he wore against the flange of the reel to brake it. Within seconds blue smoke burned from the friction of reel and leather glove.

When it seemed that the last few turns of line would be stripped from the spindle of the reel, the fish stopped, and two hundred yards out there under the smoky grey waters it shook its head doggedly so the rod butt kicked against Manfred's belly.

With Lothar dancing at his side, howling encouragement and advice, Manfred winched in the fish, pumping the rod to recover a few turns of line at a time, until the reel was almost full again and he expected to see the quarry thrashing in the surf below the rocks. Then suddenly the fish made another long heavy run, and he had to begin the laborious back-straining task all over again.

At last they saw it, deep in the water below the rocks, its side shining like a great mirror as it caught the sun. With the rod bent taut as a longbow, Manfred forced it up until it flapped ponderously, washing back and forth in the suck and thrust of the waves, gleaming in marvellous iridescent shades of rose and pearl, its great jaws gaping with exhaustion.

'The gaff!' Manfred shouted. 'Now, Lothie, now!' and the boy sprang down to the water's edge with the long pole in his hands and buried the point of the gaff hook into the fish's shoulder, just behind the gills. A flush of blood stained the waters pink, and then Manfred threw down his rod and jumped down to help Lothar with the gaff pole.

Between them they dragged the fish, flapping and thumping, up the rocks above the high-water mark.

'He's a hundred pounds if he's an ounce,' Lothar exulted. 'Ma and the girls will be up till midnight pickling this one.'

Lothar carried the rods and the fishing box while Manfred slung the fish over his shoulder, a short loop of rope through its gills, and they trudged back around the curve of white beach. On the rocks of the next headland, Manfred lowered the fish for a few minutes to rest. Once he had been Olympic light heavyweight champion, but he had fleshed out since those days, his belly was softening and spreading and his breath was short.

'Too much time behind my desk,' he thought ruefully, and sank down on a black boulder. As he mopped his face he looked around him.

This place always gave him pleasure. It grieved him that he could find so little time in his busy life to come here. In their old student days he and Roelf Stander, his best friend, had fished and hunted on this wild unspoiled stretch of coast. It had belonged to Roelf's family for a hundred years, and Roelf would never have sold the smallest piece of it to anybody but Manfred.

In the end he had sold Manfred a hundred acres for one pound. 'I don't want to get rich on an old friend,' he had laughed away Manfred's offer of a thousand. 'Just let us have a clause in the contract of sale that I have a right of first option to buy it back at the same price at your death or whenever you want to sell.'

There beyond the headland on which they sat was the cottage that he and Heidi had built, white stucco walls and thatch, the only sign of human habitation. Roelf's own holiday house was hidden beyond the next headland, but within easy walking distance so they could be together whenever both families were on holiday at the same time.

There were so many memories here. He looked out to sea. That was where the German U-boat had surfaced when it had brought him back in the early days of the war. Roelf had been on the beach, waiting for him, and had rowed out in the darkness to fetch him and his equipment ashore. What mad exciting days those had been, the danger and the fighting, as they had struggled to raise the Afrikaner *Volk* in rebellion against the English-lover Jan Christiaan Smuts, and to declare South Africa a republic under the protection of Nazi Germany – and how very close they had come to success.

He smiled and his eyes glowed at the memory. He wished he could tell the boy about it. Lothie would understand. Young as he was, he would understand the Afrikaner dream of republic and he would be proud. However that was a story that could never be told. Manfred's attempt to assassinate Jan Smuts and precipitate the rebellion had failed. He had been forced to fly the country, and to languish for the rest of the war in a far-off land, while Roelf and the other patriots had been branded traitors and hustled into Jannie Smuts' internment camps, humiliated and reviled until the war ended.

How it had all changed. Now they were the lords of this land, although nobody outside the inner circle knew the part that Manfred De La Rey had played in those dangerous years. They were the overlords, and once again the dream of republic burned brightly, like a flame on the altar of Afrikaner aspirations.

His thoughts were broken up by the roar of a low-flying aircraft overhead, and Manfred looked up. It was a sleek blue and silver machine, turning away steeply to line up for the airstrip that lay just beyond the first line of hills. The airstrip had been built by the Public Works department when Manfred had achieved full ministerial rank. It was essential that he was in close contact with his department at all times, and from that landing-field an Air Force plane could fetch him within hours if he was needed in an emergency.

Manfred recognized this machine and knew who was flying it, but frowned with annoyance as he stood up and hefted the huge carcass of the fish again. He treasured the isolation of this place, and fiercely resented any unwarranted intrusion. He and Lothar set off on the last leg of the long haul back to the cottage.

Heidi and the girls saw them coming, and ran down the dunes to meet them and then surrounded Manfred, laughing and squealing their congratulations. He plodded up the soft dunes, with the girls skipping beside him, and hung the fish on the scaffold outside the kitchen door. While Heidi went to fetch her Kodak camera, Manfred stripped off his shirt which was stained with fish blood and stooped to the tap of the rainwater tank and washed the blood from his hand and the salt from his face.

As he straightened up again, with water dripping from his hair and running down his bare chest, he was abruptly aware of the presence of a stranger.

'Get me a towel, Ruda,' he snapped, and his eldest daughter ran to his bidding.

'I was not expecting you.' Manfred glowered at Shasa Courtney. 'My family and I like to be alone here.'

'Forgive me. I know I am intruding.' Shasa's shoes were floury with dust. It was a mile walk from the airstrip. 'I am sure you will understand when I explain that my business is urgent and private.'

Manfred scrubbed his face with the towel while he mastered his annoyance, and then, when Heidi came out with the camera in her hand, he introduced her gruffly.

Within minutes Shasa had charmed both Heidi and the girls into smiles, but Lothar stood behind his father and only came forward reluctantly to shake hands. He had learned from his father to be suspicious of Englishmen.

'What a tremendous kob,' Shasa admired the fish on the scaffold. 'One of the biggest I have seen in years. You don't often get them that size any more. Where did you catch it?'

Shasa insisted on taking the photographs of the whole family grouped around the fish. Manfred was still bare-chested, and Shasa noticed the old bluish puckered scar in the side of his chest. It looked like a gunshot wound, but there had been a war and many men bore scars of that nature now. Thinking of war wounds, he adjusted his own eye-patch self-consciously as he handed the camera back to Heidi.

'You will stay to lunch, *Meneer?*' she asked demurely.

'I don't want to be a nuisance.'

'You are welcome.' She was a handsome woman, with a large high bosom and wide fruitful hips. Her hair was dense and golden blonde, and she wore it in a thick plaited rope that hung almost to her waist, but Shasa saw Manfred De La Rey's expression and quickly transferred all his attention back to him.

'My wife is right. You are welcome.' Manfred's natural Afrikaner duty of hospitality left him no choice. 'Come, we will go to the front stoep until the women call for us to eat.'

Manfred fetched two bottles of beer from the ice-chest and they sat in deckchairs, side by side, and looked out over the dunes to the wind-flecked blue of the Indian Ocean.

'Do you remember where we first met, you and I?' Shasa broke the silence.

'*Ja*,' Manfred nodded. 'I remember very well.'

'I was back there two days ago.'

'Walvis Bay?'

'Yes. To the canning factory, the jetty where we fought,' Shasa hesitated, 'where you thumped me, and pushed my head into a mess of dead fish.'

Manfred smiled with satisfaction at the memory. '*Ja*, I remember.'

Shasa had to control his temper carefully. It still rankled and the man's smugness infuriated him, but the memory of his childhood victory had softened Manfred's mood as Shasa had intended it should.

'Strange how we were enemies then, and now we are allies,' Shasa persisted, and let him think about that for a while before he went on. 'I have most carefully considered the offer you made to me. Although it is difficult for a man to change sides, and many people will put the worst construction on my motives, I now see that it is my duty to my country to do what you suggest and to employ what talent I have for the good of the nation.'

'So you will accept the Prime Minister's offer?'

'Yes, you may tell the Prime Minister that I will join the government, but in my own time and my own way. I will not cross the floor of the House, but as soon as parliament is dissolved for the coming elections, I will resign from the United Party to stand for the National Party.'

'Good,' Manfred nodded. 'That is the honourable way.'

But there was no honourable way, Shasa realized, and was silent for a moment before he went on.

'I am grateful for your part in this, *Meneer*. I know that

you have been instrumental in affording me this opportunity. In view of what has happened between our families, it is an extraordinary gesture you have made.'

'There was nothing personal in my decision.' Manfred shook his head. 'It was simply a case of the best man for the job. I have not forgotten what your family has done to mine – and I never will.'

'I will not forget either,' Shasa said softly. 'I have inherited guilt – rightly or wrongly, I will never be sure. However, I would like to make some reparation to your father.'

'How would you do that, *Meneer?*' Manfred asked stiffly. 'How would you compensate a man for the loss of his arm and for all those years spent in prison? How will you pay a man for the damage to his soul that captivity has inflicted?'

'I can never fully compensate him,' Shasa agreed. 'However, suddenly and unexpectedly I have been given the opportunity to restore to your father a large part of that which was taken from him.'

'Go on,' Manfred invited. 'I am listening.'

'Your father was issued a fishing licence in 1929. I have searched the records. That licence is still valid.'

'What would the old man do with a fishing licence now? You don't understand – he is physically and mentally ruined.'

'The fishing industry out of Walvis Bay has revived and is booming. The number of licences has been severely limited. Your father's licence is worth a great deal of money.'

He saw the shift in Manfred's eyes, the little sparks of interest swiftly screened.

'You think my father should sell it?' he asked heavily. 'And by any chance would you be interested in buying it?' He smiled sarcastically.

Shasa nodded. 'Yes, of course I'd like to buy it, but that

might not be best for your father.' Manfred's smile withered, he hadn't expected that.

'What else could he do with it?'

'We could re-open the factory and work the licence together as partners. Your father puts up the licence, and I put up the capital and my business skills. Within a year or two, your father's share will almost certainly be worth a million pounds.'

Shasa watched him carefully as he said it. This was more, much more than a business offer. It was a testing. Shasa wanted to reach beyond the man's granite crust, that monumental armour of puritanical righteousness. He wanted to probe for weaknesses, to find any chinks that he could exploit later.

'A million pounds,' he repeated. 'Perhaps even a great deal more.' And he saw the sparks in the other man's fierce pale eyes again, just for an instant, the little yellow sparks of greed. The man was human after all. 'I can deal with him now,' Shasa thought, and to cover his relief he lifted his briefcase from the floor beside his deckchair and opened it on his lap.

'I have worked out a rough agreement—' he took out a sheaf of typed blue foolscap sheets ' – you could show it to your father, discuss it with him.'

Manfred took the sheets from him. '*Ja*, I will see him when I return home next week.'

'There is one small problem,' Shasa admitted. 'This licence was issued a long time ago. The government department may wish to repudiate it. It is their policy to allow only four licences—'

Manfred looked up from the contract. 'That will be no problem,' Manfred said, and Shasa lifted his beer tankard to hide his smile. They had just shared their first secret. Manfred De La Rey was going to use his influence for personal gain. Like a lost virginity, the next time would be easier.

Shasa had realized from the beginning that he would be an outsider in a cabinet of Afrikaner Nationalists. He desperately needed a trustworthy ally amongst them, and if that ally could be linked to him by shared financial blessings and a few off-colour secrets, then his loyalty would be secured. Shasa had just achieved this, with the promise of vast profits to himself to sweeten the bargain. A good day's work, he thought, as he closed the briefcase with a snap.

'Very good, *Meneer*. I'm grateful to you for having given me your time. Now I will leave you to enjoy what remains of your holiday undisturbed.'

Manfred looked up. '*Meneer*, my wife is preparing lunch for us. She will be very unhappy if you leave so soon.' At last his smile was genial. 'And this evening I will have a few good friends visit me for a *braaivleis*, a barbecue. There are plenty of spare beds. Stay the night. You can leave early tomorrow morning.'

'You are very kind.' Shasa sank back in his chair. The feeling between them had changed, but Shasa's intuition warned him there were hidden depths in their relationship which still had to be plumbed, and as he smiled into Manfred De La Rey's topaz-coloured eyes, he felt a sudden small chill, a cold wind through a chink in his memory. Those eyes haunted him. He was trying to remember something. It remained obscure but somehow strangely menacing. Could it have been from their childhood fight? he wondered. But he did not think so. The memory was closer than that, and more threatening. He almost grasped it, and then Manfred looked down at the contract again, almost as though he had sensed what Shasa was searching for, and the shape of the memory slipped away beyond Shasa's grasp.

Heidi De La Rey came out on to the verandah in her apron, but she had changed out of her faded old skirt and twisted her plaited hair up on top of her head.

'Lunch is ready – and I do hope you eat fish, Meneer Courtney.'

Shasa set out to charm the family during lunch. Heidi and the girls were easy. The boy Lothar was different, suspicious and withdrawn. However, Shasa had three sons of his own, and he drew him out with stories of flying and hunting big game, until despite himself the boy's eyes shone with interest and admiration.

When they rose from the table, Manfred nodded grudgingly. '*Ja, Meneer*, I must remember never to underestimate you.'

That evening a small group comprising a man and woman and four children came straggling over the dunes from the south, and Manfred's children rushed out to meet them and lead them up on to the verandah of the cottage.

Shasa stayed in the background throughout the noisy greetings of the two families. Theirs was obviously a close relationship of long standing.

Of course, Shasa recognized the head of the other family. He was a big man, even heavier in build than Manfred De La Rey. Like him, he had also been a member of the boxing team that had participated in the Berlin Olympic Games of 1936. He had been a senior lecturer in law at Stellenbosch University, but had recently resigned to become a junior partner in the firm of Van Schoor, De La Rey and Stander, the firm in which Manfred De La Rey had become the senior partner after the death of old Van Schoor some years before.

Apart from his law practice, Roelf Stander acted as Manfred's chief party organizer and had managed Manfred's 1948 campaign for him. Although not himself a member of parliament, he was a leg man of the National Party and Shasa knew that he was almost certainly a member of the *Broederbond*, the Brotherhood, that clandestine society of elite Afrikaners.

When Manfred De La Rey began to introduce them, Shasa saw that Roelf Stander recognized him and looked a little sheepish.

'I hope you aren't going to throw eggs at me again, *Meneer* Stander,' Shasa challenged him, and Roelf chuckled.

'Only if you make another bad speech, *Meneer* Courtney.'

During the 1948 election, in which Shasa had been defeated by Manfred De La Rey, this man had organized the gang of bully boys who had broken up Shasa's election meetings. Though Shasa was smiling now, his resentment was almost as fierce as it had been at the time. It had always been standard Nationalist tactics to break up the meetings of their opponents. Manfred De La Rey sensed the hostile feelings between them.

'We will soon be on the same side,' he said, as he stepped between them placatingly and placed a hand on each of their arms. 'Let me find a beer for both of you and we'll drink to letting bygones be bygones.'

The two of them turned away and quickly Shasa scrutinized Roelf Stander's wife. She was thin, almost to the point of starvation, and there was an air of resignation and weariness about her, so it took a moment for even Shasa's trained eye to see how pretty she must once have been, and how attractive she still was. She was returning his scrutiny, but dropped her eyes the moment they met Shasa's single eye.

Heidi De La Rey had not missed the exchange and now she took the woman's arm and led her forward.

'*Meneer* Courtney, this is my dear friend Sarah Stander.'

'*Aangename kennis*,' Shasa bowed slightly. 'Pleasant meeting, *Mevrou*.'

'How do you do, Squadron Leader,' the woman replied quietly, and Shasa blinked. He had not used his rank since the war. It was, of course, poor form to do so.

'Have we met?' he asked, for once off-balance and the woman shook her head quickly and turned to Heidi to speak about the children. Shasa was unable to pursue the matter, for at that moment Manfred handed him a beer and the three men carried their tankards down off the stoep to watch Lothar and the Standers' eldest boy, Jakobus, build the fire for the barbecue. Though the masculine conversation was informed and their views interesting – both Manfred and Roelf Stander were educated and highly intelligent men – Shasa found his thoughts returning to the thin pale woman who had used his Air Force rank. He wished for the opportunity to speak to her alone, but realized that was unlikely and dangerous. He knew very well how protective and jealous the Afrikaners were of their women, and how easy it would be to precipitate an ugly and damaging incident. So he kept away from Sarah Stander, but for the rest of the evening observed her carefully, and so gradually became aware of undercurrents of emotion in the relationships of the two families. The two men seemed very close and it was obvious that their friendship was of long standing, but with the women it was different. They were just too kind and considerate and appreciative of each other, the certain indications of deep-seated female antagonism. Shasa stored that revelation, for human relationships and weaknesses were essential tools of his trade, but it was only later in the evening that he made two other important discoveries.

He intercepted an unguarded look that Sarah Stander directed at Manfred De Le Rey while he was laughing with her husband, and Shasa recognized it instantly as a look of hatred, but that particularly corrosive type of hatred that a woman can conceive for a man whom she once loved. That hatred explained for Shasa the weariness and resignation that had almost ruined Sarah Stander's beauty. It explained also the resentment that the two women felt for each other. Heidi De La Rey must realize that Sarah had once loved her husband, and that beneath the hatred she probably still did. The play of feelings and emotions fascinated Shasa, he had learned so much of value and had achieved so much in a single day that he was well satisfied by the time that Roelf Stander called his family together.

'It's almost midnight, come on, everybody. We have a long walk home.'

Each of them had brought a flashlight, and there was a flurry of farewells, the girls and women exchanging kisses, while first Roelf Stander and then his son Jakobus came to shake Shasa's hand.

'Goodbye,' Jakobus said, with the innate good manners and respect for elders that every Afrikaner child is taught from birth. 'I would also like to hunt a black-maned lion one day.'

He was a tall well-favoured lad, two or three years older than Lothar; he had been as fascinated as Lothar by Shasa's hunting stories but there was something familiar about him that had niggled Shasa all evening. Lothar stood beside his friend, smiling politely, and suddenly it dawned on Shasa. The boys had the same eyes, the pale cat-eyes of the De La Reys. For a moment he was at a loss to explain it, and then it all fell into place. The hatred he had observed in Sarah Stander was explained. Manfred De La Rey was the father of her son.

Shasa stood beside Manfred on the top stair of the stoep and they watched the Stander family climb the dunes, the beams of their flashlights darting about erratically and the shrill voices of the children dwindling into the night, and he wondered if he could ever piece together the clues he had gleaned this evening and discover the full extent of Manfred De La Rey's vulnerability. One day it might be vital to do so.

It would be easy enough discreetly to search the records for the marriage date of Sarah Stander and compare it to the birth date of her eldest son, but how would he ever coax from her the true significance of her use of his military rank? She had called him 'Squadron Leader'. She knew him, that was certain, but how and where? Shasa smiled. He enjoyed a good mystery, Agatha Christie was one of his favourite authors. He would work on it.

Shasa woke with the grey of dawn lining the curtains over his bed, and a pair of bokmakierie shrikes singing one of their complicated duets from the scrub of the dunes. He stripped off the pyjamas Manfred had lent him and shrugged on the bathrobe, before he crept from the silent cottage and went down to the beach.

He swam naked, slashing over-arm through the cold green water and ducking under the successive lines of breaking white surf until he was clear; then he swam slowly parallel to the beach but five hundred yards off. The chances of shark attack were remote, but the possibility spiced his enjoyment. When it was time to go in he caught a breaking wave and rode it into the beach, and waded ashore, laughing with exhilaration and the joy of life.

He mounted quietly to the stoep of the cottage, not wanting to disturb the family, but a movement from the far end stopped him. Manfred sat in one of the deckchairs with a book in his hands. He was already shaved and dressed.

'Good morning, Meneer,' Shasa greeted him. 'Are you going fishing again today?'

'It's Sunday,' Manfred reminded him. 'I don't fish on a Sunday.'

'Ah, yes.' Shasa wondered why he felt guilty for having enjoyed his swim, then he recognized the antique leather-covered black book that Manfred was holding.

'The Bible,' he remarked, and Manfred nodded.

'*Ja*, I read a few pages before I begin each day, but on Sunday or when I have a particular problem to face, I like to read a full chapter.'

'I wonder how many chapters you read before you screwed your best friend's wife,' Shasa thought, but said aloud, 'Yes, the Book is a great comfort,' and tried not to feel a hypocrite as he went through to dress.

Heidi laid an enormous breakfast, everything from steak to pickled fish, but Shasa ate an apple and drank a cup of coffee before he excused himself.

'The forecast on the radio is for rain later. I want to get back to Cape Town before the weather closes in.'

'I will walk up to the airstrip with you.' Manfred stood up quickly.

Neither of them spoke until the track reached the ridge, and then Manfred asked suddenly, 'Your mother – how is she?'

'She is well. She always is, and she never seems to age.' Shasa watched his face, as he went on, 'You always ask about her. When did you last see her?'

'She is a remarkable woman,' Manfred said stolidly, avoiding the question.

'I have tried to make up in some way for the damage she has done your family,' Shasa persisted, and Manfred seemed not to have heard. Instead he stopped in the middle of the track, as if to admire the view, but his breathing was ragged. Shasa had set a fast pace up the hill.

'He's out of condition,' Shasa gloated. His own breathing was unruffled, and his body lean and hard.

'It's beautiful,' Manfred said, and only when he made a gesture that swept the wide horizon, did Shasa realize that he was talking about the land. He looked and saw that from the ocean to the blue mountains of the Langeberge inland, it was indeed beautiful.

'And the Lord said unto him, "This is the land which I sware unto Abraham, unto Isaac and unto Jacob, saying, I will give it unto thy seed",' Manfred quoted softly. 'The Lord has given it to us, and it is our sacred duty to keep it for our children. Nothing else is important compared to that duty.'

Shasa was silent. He had no argument with that sentiment, although the expression of it was embarrassingly theatrical.

'We have been given a paradise. We must resist with our lives all efforts to despoil it, or to change it,' Manfred went on. 'And there are many who will attempt just that. They are gathering against us already. In the days ahead we will need strong men.'

Again Shasa was silent, but now his agreement was tinged with scepticism. Manfred turned to him.

'I see you smile,' he said seriously. 'You see no threat to what we have built up here on the tip of Africa?'

'As you have said, this land is a paradise. Who would want to change it?' Shasa asked.

'How many Africans do you employ, *Meneer*?' Manfred seemed to change course.

'Almost thirty thousand altogether,' Shasa frowned with puzzlement.

'Then you will soon learn the poignancy of my warning,' Manfred grunted. 'There is a new generation of trouble-makers who have grown up amongst the native people. These are the bringers of darkness. They have no respect for the old orders of society which our forefathers so carefully built up and which have served us so faithfully for so long. No, they want to tear all that down. As the Marxist monsters destroyed the social fabric of Russia, so they seek to destroy all that the white man has built up in Africa.'

Shasa's tone was disparaging as he replied. 'The vast bulk of our black peoples are happy and law-abiding. They are disciplined and accustomed to authority, their own tribal laws are every bit as strict and circumscribing as the laws we impose. How many agitators are there amongst them, and how great is their influence? Not many and not much, would be my guess.'

'The world has changed more in the short time since the end of the war than it ever did in the hundred years before that.' Manfred had recovered his breath now, and he spoke forcefully and eloquently in his own language. 'The tribal laws which governed our black peoples are eroded as they leave the rural areas and flock to the cities in search of the sweet life. There they learn all the white man's vices, and they are ripened for the heresies of the bringers of darkness. The respect that they have for the white man and his government could easily turn to contempt, especially if they detect any weakness in us. The black man respects strength and despises weakness, and it is the plan of this new breed of black agitators to test our weaknesses and expose them.'

'How do you know this?' Shasa asked and then immediately was angry with himself. He did not usually deal in banal questions, but Manfred answered seriously.

'We have a comprehensive system of informers amongst the blacks, it is the only way a police force can do its job efficiently. We know that they are planning a massive campaign of defiance of the law, especially those laws that have been introduced in the last few years – the Group Areas Act and the Population Registration Act and the pass laws, the laws necessary to protect our complicated society from the evils of racial integration and miscegenation.'

'What form will this campaign take?'

'Deliberate disobedience, flouting of the law, boycotts of white businesses and wild-cat strikes in mining and industry.'

Shasa frowned as he made his calculation. The campaign would directly threaten his companies. 'Sabotage?' he asked. 'Destruction of property – are they planning that?'

166

Manfred shook his head. 'It seems not. The agitators are divided amongst themselves. They even include some whites, some of the old comrades from the Communist Party. There are a few amongst them who favour violent action and sabotage, but apparently the majority are prepared to go only as far as peaceful protest – for the moment.'

Shasa sighed with relief, and Manfred shook his head. 'Do not be too complacent, *Meneer*. If we fail to prevent them, if we show weakness now, then it will escalate against us. Look what is happening in Kenya and Malaya.'

'Why do you not simply round up the ringleaders now, before it happens?'

'We do not have such powers,' Manfred pointed out.

'Then you should damned well be given them.'

'*Ja*, we need them to do our job, and soon we will have them. But in the meantime we must let the snake put its head out of the hole before we chop it off.'

'When will the trouble begin?' Shasa demanded. 'I must make my arrangements to deal with the strikes and disturbances—'

'That is one thing we are not certain of, we do not think the ANC itself has as yet decided—'

'The ANC,' Shasa interjected. 'But surely they aren't behind this? They have been around for forty years or so, and they are dedicated to peaceful negotiations. The leaders are decent men.'

'They were,' Manfred corrected him. 'But the old leaders have been superseded by younger, more dangerous men. Men like Mandela and Tambo and others even more evil. As I said before, times change – we must change with them.'

'I had not realized that the threat was so real.'

'Few people do,' Manfred agreed. 'But I assure you, *Meneer*, that there is a nest of snakes breeding in our little paradise.'

They walked on in silence, down to the clay-surfaced

airstrip where Shasa's blue and silver Mosquito stood. While Shasa climbed into the cockpit and readied the machine for flight, Manfred stood quietly at the wingtip watching him. After Shasa had completed all his checks, he came back to Manfred.

'There is one certain way to defeat this enemy,' Shasa said. 'This new militant ANC.'

'What is that, *Meneer*?'

'To pre-empt their position. Take away from our black people the cause of complaint,' Shasa said.

Manfred was silent, but he stared at Shasa with those implacable yellow eyes. Then Manfred asked, picking his words carefully, 'Are you suggesting that we give the natives political rights, *Meneer*? Do you think that we should give in to the parrot cry of "One man, one vote" – is that what you believe, *Meneer*?' On Shasa's reply rested all Manfred's plans. He wondered if he could have been so wrong in his selection. Any man who believed that could never be a member of the National Party, let alone bear the responsibility of cabinet rank. His relief was intense as Shasa dismissed the idea contemptuously.

'Good Lord, no! That would be the end of us and white civilization in the land. Blacks don't need votes, they need a slice of the pie. We must encourage the emergence of a black middle class, they will be our buffer against the revolutionaries. I never saw a man yet with a full belly and a full wallet who wanted to change things.'

Manfred chuckled. 'That's good, I like it. You are correct, *Meneer*. We need massive wealth to pay for our concept of *apartheid*. It will be expensive, we accept that. That is why we have chosen you. We look to you to find the money to pay for our future.'

Shasa held out his hand and Manfred took it. 'On a personal level, *Meneer*, I am pleased to hear that your wife has taken notice of whatever you said to her. Reports from my Special Branch indicate that she has given up her liberal left-wing associations and is no longer taking any part in political protests.'

'I convinced her how futile they were,' Shasa smiled. 'She has decided to become an archaeologist instead of a Bolshevik.'

They laughed together, and Shasa climbed back into the cockpit. The engines started with a stuttering roar and a mist of blue smoke blew from the exhaust ports, clearing quickly. Shasa lifted a hand in salute and closed the canopy.

Manfred watched him taxi down to the end of the strip then come thundering back, and hurtle aloft in a flash of silver and blue. He shaded his eyes to watch the Mosquito bank away towards the south, and he felt again that strange almost mystic bond of blood and destiny to the man under the perspex canopy as Shasa waved in farewell. Though they had fought and hated each other, their separate people were bound together by a similar bond and at the same time held apart by religion and language and political beliefs.

'We are brothers, you and I,' he thought. 'And beyond the hatred lie the dictates of survival. If you join us, then other Englishmen may follow you, and neither of us can survive alone. Afrikaner and Englishman, we are so bound together that if one goes down, we both drown in the black ocean.'

'Garrick has to wear glasses,' Tara said, and poured fresh coffee into Shasa's cup.

'Glasses?' He looked up from his newspaper. 'What do you mean, glasses?'

'I mean eye glasses – spectacles. I took him to the optician while you were away. He is shortsighted.'

'But nobody in our family has ever worn glasses.' Shasa looked down the breakfast table at his son, and Garrick lowered his head guiltily. Until that moment he had not realized that he had disgraced the entire family. He had believed the humiliation of spectacles was his alone.

'Glasses.' Shasa's scorn was undisguised. 'While you are having him fitted with glasses, you might as well get them to fit a cork in the end of his whistle to stop him wetting his bed also.'

Sean let out a guffaw and dug an elbow into his brother's ribs, and Garrick was stung into self-defence. 'Gee, Dad, I haven't wet my bed since last Easter,' he declared furiously, red-faced with embarrassment and close to tears of humiliation.

Sean made circles with his thumbs and forefingers and peered through them at his brother.

'We will have to call you "Owly Wet Sheets",' he suggested, and as usual Michael came to his brother's defence.

'Owls are wise,' he pointed out reasonably. 'That's why Garry came top in his class this term. Where did you come in yours, Sean?' and Sean glared at him wordlessly. Michael always had a mild but stinging retort.

'All right, gentlemen.' Shasa returned to his newspaper. 'No bloodshed at the breakfast table, please.'

Isabella had been out of the limelight for long enough. Her father had given far too much of his attention to her brothers, and she hadn't yet received her dues. Her father had arrived home late the previous evening, long after she was in bed, and the traditional ceremony of home-coming had not been fully enacted. Certainly he had kissed and pampered her and told her how beautiful she was, but one vital aspect had been neglected, and though she knew it was bad manners to ask, she had contained herself long enough.

'Didn't you even bwing me a pwesent?' she piped, and Shasa lowered his newspaper again.

'A pwesent? Now what on earth is a pwesent?'

'Don't be a silly-billy, Daddy – you know what it is.'

'Bella, you know you mustn't beg for presents,' Tara chided.

'If I don't tell him, Daddy might just forget,' Isabella

pointed out reasonably, and made her special angel face at Shasa.

'My goodness gracious me.' Shasa snapped his fingers. 'I did almost forget!' And Isabella hopped her lace-clad bottom up and down on her high stool with excitement.

'You did! You did bring me one!'

'Finish your porridge first,' Tara insisted, and Isabella's spoon clanked industriously on china as she devoured the last of it and scraped the plate clean.

They all trooped though from the breakfast room to Shasa's study.

'I'm the likklest one. I get my pwesent first.' Isabella made up the rules of life as she went along.

'All right, likklest one. Step to the front of the line, please.'

Her face a masterpiece of concentration, Isabella stripped away the wrappings from her gift.

'A doll!' she squeaked and showered kisses upon its bland china face. 'Her name is Oleander, and I love her already.' Isabella was the owner of what was probably one of the world's definitive collections of dolls, but all additions were rapturously received.

When Sean and Garry were handed their long packages, they went still with awe. They knew what they were – they had both of them pleaded long and eloquently for this moment and now that it had arrived, they were reluctant to touch their gifts in case they disappeared in a puff of smoke. Michael hid his disappointment bravely; he had hoped for a book, so secretly he empathized with his mother when she cried with exasperation, 'Oh, Shasa, you haven't given them guns?'

All three rifles were identical. They were Winchester repeaters in .22 calibre, light enough for the boys to handle.

'This is the best present anybody ever gave me.' Sean lifted his weapon out of the cardboard box and stroked the walnut stock lovingly.

'Me too.' Garrick still couldn't bring himself to touch his. He knelt over the open package in the middle of the study floor, staring raptly at the weapon it contained.

'It's super, Dad,' said Michael, holding his rifle awkwardly and his smile was unconvincing.

'Don't use that word, Mickey,' Tara snapped. 'It's so American and vulgar.' But she was angry with Shasa, not Michael.

'Look.' Garry touched his rifle for the first time. 'My name – it's got my own name on it.' He stroked the engraving on the barrel with his fingertip, then looked up at his father with myopic adoration.

'I wish you'd brought them anything but guns,' Tara burst out. 'I asked you not to, Shasa. I hate them.'

'Well, my dear, they must have rifles if they are coming on a hunting safari with me.'

'A safari!' Sean shouted gleefully. 'When?'

'It's time you learned about the bush and the animals.' Shasa put his arm around Sean's shoulders. 'You can't live in Africa without knowing the difference between a scaly anteater and a chacma baboon.'

Garry snatched up his new rifle and went to stand as close to his father's side as he could, so that Shasa could also put his other arm around his shoulders – if he wanted to. However, Shasa was talking to Sean.

'We'll go up to the south-west in the June hols, take a couple of trucks from the H'ani Mine and drive through the desert until we reach the Okavango Swamps.'

'Shasa, I don't know how you can teach your own children to kill those beautiful animals. I really don't understand it,' Tara said bitterly.

'Hunting is a man's thing,' Shasa agreed. 'You don't have to understand – you don't even have to watch.'

'Can I come, Dad?' Garry asked diffidently, and Shasa glanced at him.

'You'll have to polish up your new specs, so you can see

172

what you're shooting at.' Then he relented. 'Of course you are coming, Garry,' and then he looked across at Michael, standing beside his mother. 'What about you, Mickey? Are you interested?'

Michael glanced apologetically at his mother before he replied softly. 'Gee, thanks Dad. It should be fun.'

'Your enthusiasm is touching,' Shasa grunted and then, 'Very well, gentlemen, all the rifles locked in the gun room, please. Nobody touches them again without my permission and my supervision. We'll have our first shooting practice this evening when I get back home.'

Shasa made a point of getting back to Weltevreden with two hours of daylight in hand, and he took the boys down to the range he had built over which to sight in his own hunting rifles. It was beyond the vineyards and far enough from the stables not to disturb the horses or any of the other livestock.

Sean, with the co-ordination of a born athlete, was a natural shot. The light rifle seemed immediately an extension of his body, and within minutes he had mastered the art of controlling his breathing and letting the shot squeeze away without effort. Michael was nearly as good, but his interest wasn't really in it and he lost concentration quickly.

Garry tried so hard that he was trembling, and his face was screwed up with effort. The horn-rimmed spectacles which Tara had fetched from the optician that morning kept sliding down his nose and misting over as he aimed, and it took ten shots for him finally to get one on the target.

'You don't have to pull the trigger so hard, Garry.' Shasa told him with resignation. 'It won't make the bullet go any further or any faster, I assure you.'

It was almost dark when the four of them got back to the house, and Shasa led them down to the gun room and showed them how to clean their weapons before locking them away.

'Sean and Mickey are ready to have a crack at the

pigeons,' Shasa announced, as they trooped upstairs to change for dinner. 'Garry, you will need a little more practice, a pigeon is more likely to die of old age than one of your bullets.'

Sean shouted with laughter. 'Kill them with old age, Garry.'

Michael did not join in. He was imagining one of the lovely blue and pink rock pigeons that nested on the ledge outside his bedroom window, dying in a drift of loose feathers, splattering ruby drops as it fluttered to earth. It made him feel physically sick, but he knew his father expected it of him.

That evening as usual the children came one at a time to say goodnight to Shasa as he was tying his black bow tie. Isabella was first.

'I'm not going to sleep a wink until you come home tonight, Daddy,' she warned him. 'I'm just going to lie all by myself in the dark.'

Sean came next. 'You are the best dad in the world,' he said as they shook hands. Kissing was for sissies.

'Will you let me have that in writing?' Shasa asked solemnly.

It was Michael who was always the most difficult to answer. 'Dad, do animals and birds hurt a lot when you shoot them?'

'Not if you learn to shoot straight,' Shasa assured him. 'But, Mickey, you have too much imagination. You can't go through life worrying about animals and other people all the time.'

'Why not, Dad?' Michael asked softly, and Shasa glanced at his wristwatch to cover his exasperation.

'We have to be at Kelvin Grove by eight. Do you mind if we go into that some other time, Mickey?'

Garrick came last. He stood shyly in the doorway of Shasa's dressing-room, but his voice shook with determination as he announced, 'I'm going to learn to be a crack

174

shot, like Sean. You'll be proud of me one day, Dad. I promise you.'

Garrick left his parents' wing and crossed to the nursery. Nanny stopped him at Isabella's door.

'She's asleep already, Master Garry.'

In Michael's room they discussed the promised safari, but Mickey's attention kept wandering back to the book in his hands, and after a few minutes Garry left him to it.

He looked into Sean's room cautiously, ready to take flight if his elder brother showed any signs of becoming playful. One of Sean's favourite expressions of fraternal affection was known as a chestnut and consisted of a painful knuckling of Garry's prominent ribcage. However, this evening Sean was hanging backwards over his bed, heels propped on the wall and the back of his head almost touching the floor, a Superman comic book held at arm's length above his face.

'Goodnight, Sean,' Garry said.

'Shazam!' said Sean without lowering the comic book.

Garrick retreated thankfully to his own room and locked the door. Then he went to stand before the mirror and regard the reflection of his new horn-rimmed spectacles.

'I hate them,' he whispered bitterly, and when he removed them they left red indentations on the bridge of his nose. He went down on his knees, removed the skirting board under the built-in wardrobe and reached into the secret recess beyond. Nobody, not even Sean, had discovered this hiding place.

Carefully he withdrew the precious package. It had cost him eight weeks of his accumulated pocket money, but was worth every penny. It had arrived in a plain wrapper with a personal letter from Mr Charles Atlas himself. 'Dear Garrick,' the letter had begun, and Garry had been overcome with the great man's condescension.

He laid out the course on his bed and stripped to his pyjama pants as he revised the lessons.

'Dynamic tension,' he whispered aloud, and he took up his stance before the mirror. As he began the sequence of exercises he kept time with the soft chant of, 'More and more in every way, I'm getting better every day.'

When he finished he was sweating heavily but he made an arm and studied it minutely.

'They *are* bigger,' he tried to put aside his doubts as he poked the little walnut of muscle that popped out of his straining biceps, 'they really are!'

He stowed the course back in its hidey-hole and replaced the skirting board. Then he took his raincoat from the wardrobe and spread it on the bare boards.

Garrick had read with admiration how Frederick Selous, the famous African hunter, had toughened himself as a boy by sleeping uncovered on the floor in winter. He switched out the light and settled down on the raincoat. It was going to be a long uncomfortable night, he knew from experience, already the floor boards were like iron, but the raincoat would prevent Sean detecting any nocturnal spillage when he made his morning inspection, and Garrick was certain that his asthma had improved since he had stopped sleeping on a soft mattress with a warm eiderdown over him.

'I'm getting better every day,' he whispered, closing his eyes tightly and willing himself to ignore the cold and the hardness of the floor. 'And then one day Dad will be proud of me – just like he is of Sean.'

'I thought your speech this evening was very good, even for you,' Tara told him, and Shasa glanced at her with surprise. She had not paid him a compliment for a long time now.

'Thank you, my dear.'

'I sometimes forget what a gifted person you are,' she went on. 'It's just that you make it seem so easy and natural.' He was so moved that he might have reached across to caress her, but she was leaning away from him and the Hooper coachwork of the Rolls was too wide for him to reach her.

'I must say, you look absolutely stunning this evening,' he compromised with a matching compliment, but as he had expected, she dismissed it with a grimace.

'Are you really going to take the boys on safari?'

'My dear, we have to let them make up their own minds about life. Sean will love it, but I'm not too sure about Mickey,' Shasa replied, and she noticed that he hadn't mentioned Garrick.

'Well, if you are determined, then I'm going to take advantage of the boys' absence. I have been invited to join the archaeological dig at the Sundi Caves.'

'But you are a novice,' he was surprised. 'That's an important site. Why would they invite you?'

'Because I offered to contribute two thousand pounds to the cost of the dig, that's why.'

'I see, this is straight blackmail.' He chuckled sardonically as he saw the reason for her flattery. 'All right, it's a deal. I'll give you a cheque tomorrow. How long will you be away?'

'I'm not sure.' But she thought, 'As long as I can be close to Moses Gama.'

The site at Sundi Caves was only an hour's drive from the house at Rivonia. She reached under the fur coat and touched her stomach. It would begin to show soon – she had to find excuses to keep away from the eyes of the family. Her father and Shasa would not notice, she was sure of that, but Centaine de Thiry Courtney-Malcomess had eyes like a hawk.

'I presume that my mother has agreed to care for Isabella while you are away,' Shasa was saying, and while she nodded, her heart was singing.

'Moses, I'm coming back to you – both of us are coming back, to you, my darling.'

Whenever Moses Gama came to Drake's Farm it was like a king returning to his own realm after a successful crusade. Within minutes of his arrival, the word was flashed almost telepathically through the vast sprawling black township, and a sense of expectancy hung over it, as palpable as the smoke from ten thousand cooking fires.

Moses usually arrived with his half-brother, Hendrick Tabaka, in the butcher's delivery van. Hendrick owned a chain of a dozen butcher's shops in the black townships along the Witwatersrand, so the sign-writing on the side of the van was authentic. In sky blue and crimson, it declared:

PHUZA MUHLE BUTCHERY
BEST MEAT AT BEST PRICES

From the vernacular 'Phuza Muhle' translated as 'Eat Well' and the van provided a perfect cover for Hendrick Tabaka wherever he went. Whether he was genuinely delivering slaughtered carcasses to his butcheries or goods to his general dealer stores, or was engaged in less conventional business – the distribution of illicitly brewed liquor, the notorious *skokiaan* or township dynamite, or ferrying his girls to their places of business nearer the compounds that housed the thousands of black contract workers of the gold-mines so that they could briefly assist them in relieving their monastic existence, or whether he was on the business of the African Mineworkers' Union, that close-knit and powerful brotherhood whose existence the white government refused to acknowledge – the blue and red van was the perfect vehicle. When he was at the wheel, Hendrick wore a peaked driver's cap and a khaki tunic with cheap brass buttons. He drove sedately and with meticulous attention to all the rules of the road, so that in twenty years he had never been stopped by the police.

When he drove the van into Drake's Farm, with Moses

178

Gama sitting in the passenger seat beside him, they were entering their own stronghold. This was where they had established themselves when together they had arrived from the wastelands of the Kalahari twenty years before. Although they were sons of the same father, they had been different in almost every way. Moses had been young and tall and marvellously handsome, while Hendrick was years older, a great bull of a man with a bald, scarred head and gapped and broken teeth.

Moses was clever and quick, self-educated to a high standard, charismatic and a leader of men, while Hendrick was the faithful lieutenant, accepting his younger brother's authority and carrying out his orders swiftly and ruthlessly. Though Moses Gama had conceived the idea of building up a business empire, it was Hendrick who had made the dream a reality. Once he was shown what to do, Hendrick Tabaka was as much a bulldog in tenacity as he was in appearance.

For Hendrick, what they had built between them, the business enterprises both illicit and legitimate, the trade union and its private army of enforcers known and dreaded throughout the compounds where the mineworkers lived and through the black townships as 'The Buffaloes', all these were an end in themselves. But for Moses Gama it was different. What they had achieved thus far was only the first stage on his quest for something so much greater that although he had explained it many times to Hendrick, his brother could not truly grasp the enormity of Moses Gama's vision.

In the twenty years since they had arrived here, Drake's Farm had changed entirely. In those early days it had been a small squatters' encampment, hanging like a parasite tick on the body of the huge complex of gold-mines that made up the central Witwatersrand. It had been a collection of squalid hovels, built of scrap lumber and wattle poles and old iron sheets, flattened paraffin cans and tarpaper on the bleak open veld, a place of open drains and cesspools, lacking reticulated water or electricity, without schools or clinics or police protection, not even recognized as human habitation by the white city fathers in Johannesburg's town hall.

It was only after the war that the Transvaal Divisional Council had decided to recognize reality and to expropriate the land from the absentee landowners. They had declared the entire three thousand acres an official township set aside for black occupation under the Group Areas Act. They had retained the original name, Drake's Farm, for its picturesque connotations to old Johannesburg, unlike the more mundane origin of the nearby Soweto, which was merely an acronym for South Western Townships. Soweto already housed over half a million blacks, while Drake's Farm was home to less than half that number.

The authorities had fenced off the new township and covered the greater part of it with monotonous lines of small three-roomed cottages, each identical except for the number stencilled on the cement brick front wall. Crowded close together and separated by narrow lanes with dusty untarred surfaces, the flat roofs in galvanized corrugated iron shone like ten thousand mirrors in the brilliant highveld sunlight.

In the centre of the township were the administrative buildings where, under a handful of white municipal supervisors, the black clerks collected the rents and regulated the basic services of reticulated water and refuse removal. Beyond this Orwellian vision of bleak and soulless order lay the original section of Drake's Farm, its hovels and shebeens and whorehouses – and it was here that Hendrick Tabaka still lived.

As he drove the delivery van slowly through the new section of the township, the people came out of their cottages to watch them pass. They were mostly women and children, for the men left each morning early, commuting to their employment in the city and returning only after nightfall. When they recognized Moses, the women clapped and ululated shrilly, the greeting for a tribal chief, and the children ran beside the van, dancing and laughing with excitement at being so close to the great man.

They drove slowly past the cemetery where the untidy mounds of earth were like a vast mole run. On some of the mounds crudely wrought crosses had been set while on the others raggedy flags fluttered in the wind and offerings of food and broken household utensils and weirdly carved totems had been placed to placate the spirits, Christian symbols side by side with those of the animists and witch-worshippers. They went down into the old township, into the higgledy-piggledy lanes, where the stalls of the witch-doctors stood side by side with those offering food and trade cloth and used clothes and stolen radios. Where the chickens and pigs rooted in the muddy ruts of the road and naked toddlers with only a string of beads around their fat little tummies defecated between the stalls and the young whores strutted their wares and the stink and the noise were wondrous.

This was a world no white men ever entered, and where even the black municipal police came only on invitation and under sufferance. It was Hendrick Tabaka's world, where his wives kept nine houses for him in the centre of the old quarter. They were sturdy well-built houses of burned brick, but the exteriors were left deliberately shabby and uncared for, so they blended into the general squalor. Hendrick had learned long ago not to draw attention to himself and his material possessions. Each of his nine wives had her own home, built in a circle around Hendrick's slightly more imposing house, and he had not limited himself to women of his own Ovambo tribe. His wives were Pondo and Xhosa and Fingo and Basuto, but not Zulu. Hendrick would never trust a Zulu in his bed.

They all came out to greet him and his famous brother

181

as Hendrick parked the van in the lean-to at the back of his own house. The obeisances of the women and their soft clapping of respect ushered the men into the living-room of Hendrick's house where two plush chairs covered with tanned leopard skins were set like thrones at the far end. When the brothers were seated the two youngest wives brought pitchers of millet beer, freshly brewed, thick as gruel, tart and effervescent and cold from the paraffin refrigerator, and when they had refreshed themselves, Hendrick's sons came in to greet their father and pay their respects to their uncle.

The sons were many, for Hendrick Tabaka was a lusty man and bred all his wives regularly each year. However, not all his elder sons were present today. Those of them whom Hendrick considered unworthy had been sent back to the country to tend the herds of cattle and goats that were part of Hendrick's wealth. The more promising boys worked in the butchery shops, the general dealers or the shebeens, while two of them, those especially gifted with intelligence, were law students at Fort Hare, the black university in the little town of Alice in the Eastern Cape.

Only Hendrick's younger boys were here to kneel respectfully before him, and of these there were two whom Moses Gama looked upon with particular pleasure. They were the twin sons of one of Hendrick's Xhosa wives, a woman of unusual accomplishments. Apart from being a dutiful wife and a breeder of sons, she was an accomplished dancer and singer, an amusing story-teller, a person of shrewd common sense and intelligence, and a noted *sangoma*, a healer and occult doctor with sometimes uncanny powers of prescience and divination. Her twins had inherited most of her gifts together with their father's robust physique and some of their uncle Moses' fine features.

At their birth, Hendrick had asked Moses to name them,

and he had chosen their names from his treasured copy of Macaulay's *History of England*. Of all his nephews they were his favourites, and he smiled now as they knelt before him. They were almost thirteen years old, Moses realized.

'I see you, Wellington Tabaka,' he greeted first the one and then the other. 'I see you, Raleigh Tabaka.'

They were not identical twins. Wellington was the taller lad, lighter-skinned, toffee-coloured against Raleigh's mulberry-stain black. His features had the same Nilotic cast as Moses' own, while Raleigh was more negroid, flat-nosed and thick-lipped, his body heavier and squatter.

'What books have you read since we last met?' Moses changed into English, forcing them to reply in the same language. 'Words are spears, they are weapons with which to defend yourself and with which to attack your enemies. English words have the sharpest blades, without them you will be warriors disarmed,' he had explained to them, and now he listened attentively to their halting replies in that language.

However, he noted the improvements in their command of the language and remarked on it. 'It is still not good enough, but you will learn to speak it better at Waterford,' and both boys looked uncomfortable. Moses had arranged for them to write the entrance examination for this elite multi-racial school across the border in the independent black kingdom of Swaziland, and the twins had both passed and been accepted and now were dreading the day not far away when they would be uprooted from this comfortable familiar world of theirs and packed off into the unknown. In South Africa all education was strictly segregated, and it was the declared policy of the Minister of Bantu Affairs, Dr Hendrik Verwoerd, not to educate black children to the point of discontentment. He had told parliament quite frankly that education for blacks should not conflict with the government policy of *apartheid* and should not be of such a standard as to evoke in the black pupil expectations

183

which could never be fulfilled. The annual expenditure by the state on each white pupil was £60 while that on a black student was £9 per annum. Those black parents who could afford it, the chiefs and small businessmen, sent their children out of the country to be educated, and Waterford was a favourite choice.

The twins escaped from the daunting presence of their father and uncle with relief, but their mother was waiting for them in the yard beside the blue and crimson van, and with a sharp inclination of her head ordered them into her own parlour.

The room was a sorceress's lair from which the twins were usually barred, and now they crept in with even more trepidation than they had entered their father's house. Against the far wall stood their mother's gods and goddesses carved in native woods and dressed in feathers and skins and beads, with eyes of ivory and mother-of-pearl, and bared teeth of dog and baboon. They were a terrifying assembly, and the twins shivered and dared not look directly upon them.

Before the family idols were arranged offerings of food and small coins, and from the other walls hung all the gruesome accoutrements of their mother's craft, gourds and clay pots of ointments and medicines, bundles of dried herbs, snake skins and mummified iguana lizards, bones and baboon skulls, glass jars of hippopotamus and lion fat, musk of crocodile, and other nameless substances which festered and bubbled and stank so foully that it made the teeth ache in their jaws.

'You wore the charms I gave you?' Kuzawa, their mother, asked. She was incongruously handsome in the midst of her unholy and hideous tools and medicines, full-faced and glossy-skinned with very white teeth and liquid, gazelle eyes. Her limbs were long and gleamed with secret and magical ointments and her breasts under the necklaces of ivory beads and charms were big and firm as wild Kalahari melons.

In response to her question, the twins nodded vehemently, too overcome to speak, and unbuttoned their shirts. The charms were hung around their necks, each on a thin leather thong. They were the horns of the little grey duiker, the open ends sealed with gum arabic, and Kuzawa had taken all the twelve years of their lives to assemble the magical potion that was contained in each of them. It was made up of samples of all the bodily excretions of Hendrick Tabaka, the father of the twins, his faeces and urine, his spittle and nasal mucus, his sweat and his semen, the wax from his ears and the blood from his veins, his tears and his vomit. With these, Kuzawa had mixed the dried skin from the soles of his feet, the clippings of his nails, the shavings of his beard and his pate and pubes, the lashes of his eyes plucked in his sleep, and the crusted scabs and pus from his wounds. Then she had added herbs and fats of wonderful efficacy, and spoken the words of power over them and finally, to make the charm infallible, she had paid a vast sum to one of the grave-robbers who specialized in such procurements to bring her the liver of an infant drowned at birth by its own mother.

All these ingredients she had sealed in the two little duiker horns, and the twins were never allowed into their father's presence except when they wore them hung around their necks. Now Kuzawa retrieved the two charms from her sons. They were far too precious to leave in the children's possession. She smiled as she weighed them in the smooth pink palms of her delicately shaped hands. They had been worth all the expense and the patience and the meticulous application of her skills to create.

'Did your father smile when he saw you?' she asked.

'He smiled like the rise of the sun,' Raleigh replied, and Kuzawa nodded happily.

'And were his words kind, did he make enquiry of you fondly?' she insisted.

'When he spoke to us he purred like a lion at meat,' Wellington whispered, still intimidated by his surroundings. 'And he asked us how we fared at school, and he commended us when we told him.'

'It is the charms that have ensured his favour,' Kuzawa smiled contentedly. 'As long as you wear them, your father will prefer you over all his other children.'

She took the two little buckhorns and went to kneel before the central carved figure in the array of idols, a fearsome image with a headdress of lion's mane that housed the spirit of her dead grandfather.

'Guard them well, O venerable ancestor,' she whispered, as she hung them around the neck of the image. 'Keep their powers strong until they are needed once again.'

They were safer there than in the deepest vault of the white man's banks. No human being, and only the most powerful of the dark ones, would dare challenge her grandfather's spirit for possession of the charms, for he was the ultimate guardian.

Now she turned back to the twins, took their hands and led them out of her lair into the family kitchen next door, putting aside the mantle of the witch and assuming that of the loving mother as she passed through the door and closed it behind her.

She fed the twins, bowls piled with fluffy white maize meal and butter beans and stew swimming with delicious fat, food that befitted the family of a rich and powerful man. And while they ate, she tended them lovingly, questioning and chaffing them, pressing more food upon them, her dark eyes glowing with pride, and finally reluctantly letting them go.

They fled from her, delirious with excitement, into the narrow fetid lanes of the old quarter. Here they were entirely at their ease. The men and women smiled and called greetings and pleasantries as they passed and laughed delightedly at their repartee for they were the favourites of all, and their father was Hendrick Tabaka.

Old Mama Nginga, fat and silver-haired, sitting at the front door of the shebeen that she ran for Hendrick, shouted after them, 'Where are you going, my little ones?'

'On secret business we cannot discuss,' Wellington shouted back, and Raleigh added:

'But next year our secret business will be with you, old mama. We will drink all your *skokiaan* and stab all your girls.'

Mama Nginga wobbled with delight, and the girls sitting in the windows shrieked with laughter. 'He is the cub of the lion, that one,' they told each other.

As they scurried through the lanes, they called out and from the hovels and the shanties of the old quarter and from the new brick cottages that the white government had built, their comrades hurried out to join them, until there were fifty or more lads of their own age following them. Some of them carried long bundles, carefully wrapped and bound up with rawhide thongs.

At the far end of the township the high fence had been cut, the gap concealed from casual scrutiny by a clump of scrub. The boys climbed through the gap and in the plantation of bluegums beyond they gathered in an excited jabbering cluster and stripped off the shabby Western European clothing they wore. They were uncircumcised, their penises although beginning to develop were still surmounted by the little wrinkled caps of skin. In a few years' time they would all of them go into the initiation class and endure the ordeal of the isolation and hardship, and the agony of the blade together. This, even more than their tribal blood, bound them together; all their lives they would be comrades of the circumcision knife.

They set aside their clothing carefully – any losses would have to be accounted for to angry parents – and then, naked, they gathered around the precious rolls and watched impatiently as they were opened by their acknowledged captains Wellington and Raleigh Tabaka, and each of them were issued with the uniform of the Xhosa warrior – not the true regalia, the cow-tails and rattles and headdress, those were for circumcised *amadoda* only. These were childish replicas, merely skins of dogs and cats, the strays and pariahs of the township, but they donned them as proudly as if they were genuine, and bound their upper arms and thighs and foreheads with strips of fur, and then took up their weapons.

Again these were not the warriors' long-bladed assegais, but were merely the traditional fighting-sticks. However, even in the hands of these children the long limber staves were formidable weapons. With a stick in each hand they were immediately transformed into shrieking demons. They brandished and swung the staves, using a practised wrist action that made them hiss and sing and whistle, they rattled them together, crossing them to form a guard against which the blows of their peers clattered, and they leapt and cavorted and danced, aiming blows at each other, until Raleigh Tabaka blew a sharp fluting command on his buckhorn whistle, and they fell in behind him in a compact, disciplined column.

He led them away. In a swaying stylized trot, fighting-sticks held high, singing and humming the battle chants of their tribe, they left the plantation and went out into the open undulating veld. The grass was knee-high and brown, and the chocolate-red earth showed through it in raw patches. The ground fell away gently to a narrow stream, its rocky bed enclosed by steep banks and then climbed again to meet the pale sapphire of the highveld sky.

Even as they started down the slope, the clean sweep of the far skyline was interrupted, a long line of waving headdresses showed above it, and then another band of lads appeared, clad like them in loincloths of skin, legs and arms and torsos bare. Carrying their fighting-sticks high, they paused along the crest, and as they saw each other, both bands gave tongue like hounds taking the scent.

'Zulu jackals,' howled Raleigh Tabaka, and his hatred was so intense that a fine sheen of sweat burst out upon his brow. For as long and as far back as his tribal memory reached, this had been the enemy; his hatred was in his blood, deep and atavistic. History did not record how often this scene had been repeated, how many thousands of times over the centuries armed impis of Xhosa and Zulu had faced each other thus; all that was remembered was the heat of the battle and the blood and the hatred.

Raleigh Tabaka leapt as high as the shoulder of his brother beside him, and screamed wildly, his treacherous voice breaking into a girlish squeak at the end.

'I am thirsty. Give me Zulu blood to drink!' and his warriors leapt and screamed.

'Give us Zulu blood!'

The threats and insults and challenges were flung back at them from the opposite ridge, carried to them on the wind. Then spontaneously both impis started down, singing and prancing into the shallow valley, until from the steep red banks they faced each other across the narrow streambed, and their captains strode forward to exchange more insults.

The Zulu *induna* was a lad the same age as the twins. He attended the same class as they did in the government secondary school in the township. His name was Joseph Dinizulu, and he was as tall as Wellington and as broad across the chest as Raleigh. His name and his strutting arrogance reminding the world that he was a princeling of the royal house of Zulu.

'Hey, you eaters of hyena dung,' he called. 'We smelt you from a thousand paces against the wind. The smell of Xhosa makes even the vultures puke.'

Raleigh leapt high, turning in the air and lifting the

skirts of his loincloth to expose his buttocks. 'I cleanse the air of the Zulu stench with a good clean fart!' he shouted. 'Sniff that, you jackal-lovers,' and he blew a raspberry so loud and long that the Zulus facing him hissed murderously and rattled their fighting-sticks.

'Your fathers were women, your mothers were monkeys,' Joseph Dinizulu cried, scratching his own armpits. 'Your grandfathers were baboons,' he imitated a simian lollop, 'and your grandmothers were—' Raleigh interrupted this recital of his ancestral line with a blast on the buckhorn whistle and leapt from the bank into the streambed. He landed on his feet, light as a cat, and with a bound was across. He went up the far bank so fast that Joseph Dinizulu, who had expected the exchange of pleasantries to last a little longer, fell back before his onslaught.

A dozen of the other Xhosa lads had responded to his whistle and followed him across, and Raleigh's furious attack had won a bridgehead for them on the far bank. They bunched up behind him with sticks hissing and singing, and drove into the centre of the opposing impi. The battle lust was on Raleigh Tabaka. He was invincible, his arms tireless, his hands and wrists so cunning that his sticks seemed to have separate life, finding the weak places in the guards of the Zulus who opposed him, thudding on flesh, cracking on bone, cutting open skin so that soon their sticks shone wet with blood and little droplets of it flew in the sunlight.

It seemed nothing could touch him, until abruptly something crashed into his ribs just below his raised right arm, and he gasped with pain and the sudden awareness of his own humanity. For a minute there he had been a warrior god, but suddenly he was a small boy, almost at the end of his strength, hurting very badly, and so tired that he could not mouth another challenge while before him danced Joseph Dinizulu, who seemed to have grown six inches in as many seconds. Again his fighting-stick whistled in, aimed at Raleigh's head, and only with a desperate defence he deflected it. Raleigh fell back a pace and looked around him.

He should have known better than to attack a Zulu so boldly. They were the most treacherous and sly of all adversaries, and the stratagem of encirclement was always their master-stroke. Chaka Zulu, the mad dog who had founded this tribe of wolves, had called the manoeuvre 'the Horns of the Bull'. The horns surrounded the enemy while the chest crushed him to death.

Joseph Dinizulu had not fallen back out of fear or surprise, it was his instinctive cunning, and Raleigh had led his dozen stalwarts into the Zulu trap. They were alone, none of the others had followed them across the stream. Over the heads of the encircling Zulus he could see them on the far bank, and Wellington Tabaka, his twin brother, stood at their head, silent and immobile.

'Wellington!' he screamed, his voice breaking with exhaustion and terror. 'Help us! We have the Zulu dog by the testicles. Come across and stab him in the chest!'

That was all he had time for. Joseph Dinizulu was on him again and each stroke of his seemed more powerful than the last. Raleigh's chest was agony, and then another blow crashed through his guard and caught him across the shoulder, paralysing his right arm to the fingertips, and the stick flew from his grasp.

'Wellington!' he screamed again. 'Help us!' and all around him his men were going down, some of them beaten to their knees, others simply dropping their sticks and cowering in the dust, screaming for mercy while the Zulu boys crowded in with their sticks rising and falling, the blows flogging into soft flesh, the Zulu war cries rising in jubilant chorus like hounds crowding in to rend the hares.

'Wellington!' He had one last glimpse of his brother across the stream and then a blow caught him on the forehead just above his eye, and he felt the skin split as warm blood poured down his face. Just before it blinded him he caught a last glimpse of Joseph Dinizulu's face, crazy with blood lust, and then his legs collapsed under him and he flopped face-first into the dirt, while the blows still thudded across his back and shoulders.

He must have lost consciousness for a moment, for when he rolled onto his side and wiped the blood from his eyes with the back of his hand he saw that the Zulus had crossed the stream in a phalanx and that the remnants of his impi were racing away in wild panic towards the bluegum plantation pursued by Dinizulu's men.

He tried to push himself upright, but his senses reeled and darkness filled his head, as he toppled once again. When next he came to he was surrounded by Zulus, jeering and mocking, covering him with insults. This time he managed to sit up, but then the tumult around him quieted and was replaced by an expectant hush. He looked up and Joseph Dinizulu pushed his way through the ranks and sneered down at him.

'Bark, Xhosa dog,' he ordered. 'Let us hear you bark and whine for mercy.'

Groggy, but defiant, Raleigh shook his head, and pain flared under his skull at the movement.

Joseph Dinizulu placed a bare foot on his chest and shoved hard. He was too weak to resist and he toppled over on his back. Joseph Dinizulu stood over him, and lifted the front of his loincloth. With his other hand he drew back his foreskin exposing the pink glans, and he directed a hissing stream of urine into Raleigh's face.

'Drink that, you Xhosa dog,' he laughed. It was hot and ammoniacal and burned like acid in the open wound on his scalp – and Raleigh's rage and humiliation and hatred filled all his soul.

'My brother, it is only very seldom that I try to dissuade you from something on which you have set your mind.' Hendrick Tabaka sat on the leopard-skin covering of his chair, leaning forward earnestly with his elbows on his knees. 'It is not the marriage in itself, you know how I have always urged you to take a wife, many wives, and get yourself sons – it is not the idea of a wife I disapprove of, it is this Zulu baggage that makes me lie awake at night. There are ten million other nubile young women in this land – why must you choose a Zulu? I would rather you took a black mamba into your bed.'

Moses Gama chuckled softly. 'Your concern for me proves your love.' Then he became serious. 'Zulu is the largest tribe in Southern Africa. Numbers alone would make them important, but add to that their aggressive and warlike spirit, and you will see that nothing will change in this land without Zulu. If I can form an alliance with that tribe, then all the dreams I have dreamed need not be in vain.'

Hendrick sighed, and grunted and shook his head.

'Come, Hendrick, you have spoken with them. Have you not?' Moses insisted, and reluctantly Hendrick nodded.

'I sat four days at the kraal of Sangane Dinizulu, son of Mbejane who was the son of Gubi, who was the son of Dingaan, who was the brother of Chaka Zulu himself. He deems himself a prince of Zulu, which he is at pains to point out means "The Heavens", and he lives in grand style on the land that his old master, General Sean Courtney, left him on the hills above Ladyburg, where he keeps many wives and three hundred head of fat cattle.'

'All this I know, my brother,' Moses interrupted. 'Tell me about the girl.'

Hendrick frowned. He liked to begin a story at the beginning and work through it, sparing no detail, until he reached the end.

'The girl,' he repeated. 'That old Zulu rogue whines that she is the moon of his night and the sun of his day, no daughter has ever been loved as he loves her – and he could never allow her to marry any man but a Zulu chief.' Hendrick sighed. 'Day after day I heard the virtues of this Zulu she-jackal recounted, how beautiful she is, how talented, how she is a nurse at the government hospital, how she comes from a long line of son-bearing wives—' Hendrick broke off and spat with disgust. 'It took three days before he mentioned what had been on his mind from the first minute – the *lobola*, the bride price,' and Hendrick threw up his hands in a gesture of exasperation. 'All Zulus are thieves and dung-eaters.'

'How much?' Moses asked with a smile. 'How much did he need to compensate him for a marriage outside the tribe?'

'Five hundred head of prime cattle, all cows in calf, none older than three years,' Hendrick scowled with outrage. 'All Zulus are thieves and he claims to be a prince, which makes him a prince of thieves.'

'Naturally you agreed to his first price?' Moses asked.

'Naturally I argued for two more days.'

'The final price?'

'Two hundred head,' Hendrick sighed. 'Forgive me, my brother. I tried, but the old dog of a Zulu was like a rock. It was his very lowest price for the moon of his night.'

Moses Gama leaned back in his chair, and thought about it. It was an enormous price. Prime cattle were worth £50 the head, but unlike his brother, Moses Gama had no yen for money other than as a means to procure an end.

'Ten thousand pounds?' he asked softly. 'Do we have that much?'

'It will hurt. I will ache for a year as though I have been whipped with a sjambok,' Hendrick grumbled. 'Do you realize just how much else a man could buy with ten thousand pounds, my brother? I could get you at least ten Xhosa maidens, pretty as sugar birds and plump as guinea fowl, each with her maidenhead attested by the most reliable midwife—'

'Ten Xhosa maidens would not bring the Zulu people within my reach,' Moses cut him off. 'I need Victoria Dinizulu.'

'The *lobola* is not the only price demanded,' Hendrick told him. 'There is more.'

'What else?'

'The girl is a Christian. If you take her, there will be no others. She will be your only wife, my brother, and listen to a man who has paid for wisdom in the heavy coin of experience. Three wives are the very minimum a man needs for contentment. Three wives are so busy competing with one another for their husband's favour that a man can relax. Two wives are better than one. However, a single wife, a one and only wife, can sour the food in your belly and frost your hair with silver. Let this Zulu wench go to someone who deserves her, another Zulu.'

'Tell her father that we will pay the price he asks and that we agree to his terms. Tell him also that if he is a prince, then we expect him to provide a marriage feast that befits a princess. We expect a marriage that will be the talk of Zululand from the Drakensberg Mountains to the ocean. I want every chieftain and elder of the tribe there to see me wed, I want every counseller and *induna*, I want the King of the Zulus himself to come and when they are all assembled, I will speak to them.'

'You might as well talk to a troop of baboons. A Zulu is too proud and too full of hatred to listen to sense.'

'You are wrong, Hendrick Tabaka.' Moses laid his hand on his brother's arm. 'We are not proud enough, nor do we hate enough. What pride we do have, the little hatred that we do have, is misspent and ill-directed. We waste it on each other, on other black men. If all the tribes of this land took all their pride and all their hatred and turned it on the white oppressor – then how could he resist us? This is what I will talk about when I speak at my wedding feast. This is what I have to teach the people. It is for this that we are forging *Umkhonto we Sizwe*, the Spear of the Nation.'

They were silent awhile. The depth of his brother's vision, the terrible power of his commitment, always awed Hendrick.

'It will be as you wish,' he agreed at last. 'When do you wish the wedding to take place?'

'On the full moon of mid-winter.' Moses did not hesitate. 'That will be the week before our campaign of defiance begins.'

Again they were silent, until Moses roused himself. 'It is settled, then. Is there anything else we should discuss before we take the evening meal?'

'Nothing.' Hendrick rose to his feet and was about to call his women to bring their food, when he remembered. 'Ah. There is one other thing. The white woman, the woman who was with you at Rivonia – do you know the one?'

Moses nodded. 'Yes, the Courtney woman.'

'That is the one. She has sent a message. She wishes to see you again.'

'Where is she?'

'She is close by, at a place called Sundi Caves. She has left a telephone number for you. She says it is an important matter.'

Moses Gama was clearly annoyed. 'I told her not to try and contact me,' he said. 'I warned her of the dangers.' He stood up and paced the floor. 'Unless she learns discipline and self-control, she will be of no value to the struggle. White women are like that, spoiled and disobedient and self-indulgent. She must be trained—'

Moses broke off and went to the window. Something in the yard had caught his attention, and he called out sharply.

'Wellington! Raleigh! Come here, both of you.'

A few seconds later the two boys shuffled self-consciously into the room, and stood just inside the door, hanging their heads guiltily.

'Raleigh, what has happened to you?' Hendrick demanded angrily. The twins had changed their furs and loincloths for their ordinary clothing, but the gash in Raleigh's forehead was still weeping through the wad of grubby rags he had strapped on it. There were speckles of blood on his shirt, and the swelling had closed one eye.

'*Baba!*' Wellington started to explain. 'It was not our fault. We were set upon by the Zulus.' And Raleigh darted a look of contempt at him before he contradicted his twin.

'We arranged a faction fight with them. It went well, until some of us ran away and left the others.' Raleigh raised his hand to his injured head. 'There are cowards even amongst the Xhosa,' he said, and again glanced at his twin. Wellington stood silent.

'Next time fight harder and show more cunning,' Hendrick Tabaka dismissed them and when they scurried from the room he turned to Moses. 'Do you see, my brother. Even with the children, what hope do you have of changing it?'

'The hope is with the children,' Moses told him. 'Like monkeys, you can train them to do anything. It is the old ones who are difficult to change.'

Tara Courtney parked her shabby old Packard on the edge of the mountain drive and stood for a few seconds looking down on the city of Cape Town spread below her. The south-easter was whipping the waters of Table Bay to cream.

She left the car and walked slowly along the verge, pretending to admire the flush of wild flowers which painted the rocky slope above her. At the head of the slope the grey rock bastion of the mountain rose sheer to the heavens, and she stopped walking and tilted her head back to look up at it. The clouds were driving over the top, creating the illusion that the wall of rock was falling.

Once again she darted a glance along the road up which she had driven. It was still empty. She was not being followed. The police must have finally lost interest in her. It was weeks since last she had been aware of being tailed.

Her aimless behaviour altered and she returned to the Packard and took a small picnic basket from the boot, then she walked quickly back to the concrete building that housed the lower cable station. She ran up the stairs and paid for a return ticket just as the attendant opened the doors at the end of the waiting room, and the small party of other passengers trooped out to the gondola and crowded into it.

The crimson car started with a jerk and they rose swiftly, dangling below the silvery thread of the cable. The other passengers were exclaiming with delight as the spreading panorama of ocean and rock and city opened below them, and Tara inspected them surreptitiously. Within a few minutes she was convinced that none of them were plain-clothes members of the Special Branch and she relaxed and turned her attention to the magnificent view.

The gondola was climbing steeply, rising almost verti-cally up the face of the cliff. The rock had weathered into almost geometrical cubes, so that they seemed to be the ancient building blocks of a giant's castle. They passed a party of rock-climbers roped together inching their way hand over hand up the sheer face. Tara imagined being out there, clinging to the rock with the empty drop sucking at her heels, and vertigo made her sway dizzily. She had to clutch the handrail to steady herself, and when the gondola docked at the top station on the brink of the thousand-foot-high cliff, she escaped from it thankfully.

In the little tearoom, built to resemble an Alpine Chalet,

Molly was waiting for her at one of the tables and she jumped up when she saw her friend.

Tara rushed to her and embraced her. 'Oh, Molly, my dear, dear, Molly, I have missed you so.'

After a few moments they drew apart, slightly embarrassed by their own display and the smiles of the other teashop customers.

'I don't want to sit still,' Tara told her. 'I'm just bursting with excitement. Come on, let's walk. I've brought some sandwiches and a thermos.'

They left the tearoom and wandered along the path that skirted the precipice. In mid-week there were very few hikers on the mountain, and before they had gone a hundred yards they were alone.

'Tell me about all my old friends in the Black Sash,' Tara ordered. 'I want to know everything you have been doing. How is Derek and how are the children? Who is running my clinic now? Have you been there recently? Oh, I so miss it all, all of you.'

'Steady on,' Molly laughed. 'One question at a time—' and she began to give Tara all the news. It took time, and while they chatted, they found a picnic spot and sat with their legs dangling over the cliff, drinking hot tea from the thermos, and with scraps of bread feeding the fluffy little hyrax, the rock rabbits that crept out of the crevices and cracks of the cliff.

At last they exhausted their stocks of news and gossip, and sat in companionable silence. Tara broke it at last.

'Molly, I'm going to have another baby.'

'Ah ha!' Molly giggled. 'So that's what has been keeping you busy.' She glanced at Tara's stomach.

'It doesn't show yet. Are you certain?'

'Oh, for Pete's sake, Molly. I'm hardly the simpering virgin, you know. Give me credit for the four I have already! Of course I'm certain.'

'When is it due?'

'January next year.'

'Shasa will be pleased. He dotes on the kids. In fact, apart from money, they are the only things I've ever seen Shasa Courtney sentimental about. Have you told him yet?'

Tara shook her head. 'No. You are the only one I've told. I came to you first.'

'I'm flattered. I wish you both joy.' Then she paused as she noticed Tara's expression and studied her more seriously.

'For Shasa there will be little joy in it, I'm afraid,' Tara said softly. 'It's not Shasa's baby.'

'Good Lord, Tara! You of all people—' Then she broke off, and thought about it. 'I'm going to ask another silly question, Tara, darling, but how do you know it isn't Shasa's effort?'

'Shasa and I – we haven't – well, you know – we haven't been man and wife since – oh, not for ages.'

'I see.' Despite her affection and friendship, Molly's eyes sparkled with interest. This was intriguing. 'But, Tara love, that isn't the end of the world. Rush home now and get Shasa's pants off. Men are such clots, dates don't mean much to them, and if he does start counting, you can always bribe the doctor to tell him it's a prem.'

'No, Molly, listen to me. If ever he saw the infant, he would know.'

'I don't understand.'

'Molly, I am carrying Moses Gama's baby.'

'Sweet Christ!' Molly whispered.

The strength of Molly's reaction brought home to Tara the full gravity of the predicament in which she found herself.

Molly was a militant liberal, as colour-blind as Tara was herself, and yet Molly was stunned by the idea of a white woman bearing a black man's infant. In this country miscegenation was an offence punishable by imprisonment, but that penalty was as nothing compared to the social outrage it would engender. She would become an outcast and a pariah.

'Oh dear,' Molly moderated her language. 'Oh dear, oh dear! My poor Tara, what a mess you are in. Does Moses know?'

'Not yet, but I hope to see him soon and I'll tell him.'

'You will have to get rid of it, of course. I have an address in Lourenço Marques. There is a Portuguese doctor there. We sent one of our girls from the orphanage to him. He's expensive, but clean and good, not like some dirty old crone in a back room with a knitting needle.'

'Oh, Molly, how could you think that of me? How could you believe I would murder my own baby?'

'You are going to keep it?' Molly gaped at her.

'Of course.'

'But, my dear, it will be—'

'Coloured,' Tara finished for her. 'Yes, I know, probably *café au lait* in colour and with crispy black hair and I will love it with all my heart. Just as I love the father.'

'I don't see how—'

'That's why I came to you.'

'I'll do whatever you want – just tell me what that is.'

'I want you to find me a coloured couple. Good decent people, preferably with children of their own, who will take care of the infant for me until I can arrange to take it myself. Of course, they will have all the money they need and more . . .' Her voiced trailed off and she stared at Molly imploringly.

Molly considered for a minute. 'I think I know the right couple. They are both school-teachers and they have four of their own, all girls. They'll do it for me – but, Tara, how are you going to hide it? It will begin to show soon, you were huge with Isabella. Shasa might not notice, he's so busy looking into his cheque book, but your mother-in-law is an absolute tartar. You couldn't get anything by her.'

'I've already made plans to cover that. I have convinced

Shasa that I have conceived a burning interest in archaeology to replace my political activities and I've got a job on the dig at Sundi Caves with the American archaeologist, Professor Marion Hurst, you know.'

'Yes, I've read two of her books.'

'I've told Shasa that I will only be away for two months, but once I'm out of his sight I'll just keep postponing my return. Centaine will look after the children, I've arranged that also, she loves doing it and, the Lord knows, the kids will benefit from it. She's a much better disciplinarian than I am. They'll be perfectly behaved angels by the time my beloved mother-in-law is finished with them.'

'You'll miss them,' Molly stated, and Tara nodded.

'Yes, of course, I shall miss them, but it's only another six months to go.'

'Where will you have the child?' Molly persisted.

'I don't know. I can't go to a recognized hospital or nursing home. Oh God, could you imagine the fuss if I produced a little brown bundle on their clean whites-only sheets, in their lovely clean whites-only maternity hospital. Anyway, there is plenty of time to arrange all that later. The first thing is to get away to Sundi, away from Centaine Courtney-Malcomess' malevolent eye.'

'Why Sundi, Tara, what made you choose Sundi?'

'Because I will be near to Moses.'

'Is it that important?' Molly stared at her mercilessly. 'Do you feel like that about him? It wasn't just a little experiment, just a little kinky fun to find out what it is really like with one of them?'

Tara shook her head.

'Are you sure, Tara? I mean I've had the same urge occasionally. I suppose it's natural to be curious, but I've never been caught at it.'

'Molly, I love him. If he asked me, I would lay down my life for him without a qualm.'

'My poor sweet Tara.' Tears started in Molly's eyes, and

she reached out with both arms. They hugged desperately and Molly whispered, 'He is far beyond your reach, my darling. You can never, never have him.'

'If I can have a little piece of him, for even a little while. That will be enough for me.'

Moses Gama parked the crimson and blue butcher's van in one of the visitors' bays and switched off the engine. In front of him stretched lawns on which a single small sprinkler was trying to atone for all the frosts and drought of the highveld winter, but the Kikuyu grass was seared and lifeless. Beyond the lawn was the long double-storeyed block of the Baragwanath nurses' home.

A small group of black nurses came up the pathway from the main hospital. They were in crisp white uniform, neat and efficient-looking, but when they drew level with the van and saw Moses at the wheel they dissolved into giggles, hiding their mouths with their hands in the instinctive gesture of subservience to the male.

'Young woman, I wish to speak to you.' Moses leaned out of the window of the van. 'Yes, you!' The chosen nurse was almost overcome with shyness. Her friends teased her as she approached Moses and paused timidly five paces from him.

'Do you know Sister Victoria Dinizulu?'

'*Eh he!*' the nurse affirmed.

'Where is she?'

'She is coming now. She is on the day shift with me.' The nurse looked around for escape, and instead picked out Victoria in the middle of the second group of white-clad figures coming up the path. 'There she is. Victoria! Come quickly!' the girl cried, and then fled, taking the steps up into the nurses' home two at a time. Victoria recognized him, and with a word to her friends, left them and cut across the dry brown lawns, coming directly to him. Moses climbed out of the van, and she looked up at him.

'I'm sorry. There was a terrible bus accident, we were working in theatre until the last case was attended to. I have kept you waiting.'

Moses nodded. 'It's not important. We have plenty of time still.'

'It will take me only a few minutes to change into street clothes,' she smiled up at him. Her teeth were perfect, so white that they seemed almost translucent, and her skin had the lustre of health and youth. 'I am so pleased to see you again – but I do have a very big bone to pick with you.' They were speaking English, and although hers was accented, she seemed confident in the language with a choice of words which matched his own fluency.

'Good,' he smiled gravely. 'We will have your bone for dinner – which will save me money.'

She laughed, a fine throaty chuckle. 'Don't go away, I will be back.' She turned and went into the nurses' home, and he watched her with pleasure as she climbed the steps. Her waist was so narrow that it accentuated the swell of her buttocks under the white uniform. Although her bosom was small, she was full-bottomed and broad-hipped; she would carry a child with ease. That kind of body was the model of Nguni beauty, and Moses was strongly reminded of the photographs he had seen of the *Venus de Milo*. Her carriage was erect, her neck long and straight, and although her hips swayed as though she danced to a distant music, her head and shoulders never moved. It was obvious that as a child she had taken her turn with the other young girls at carrying the brimming clay pots up from the water-hole, balancing the pot on her head without spilling a drop. That was how the Zulu girls acquired that marvellously regal posture.

With her round madonna face and huge dark eyes she

was one of the handsomest women he had ever seen, and while he waited, leaning against the bonnet of the van, he pondered how each race had its ideal of feminine beauty, and how widely they differed. That led him on to think of Tara Courtney, with her huge round breasts and narrow boyish hips, her long chestnut hair and soft insipid white skin. Moses grimaced, faintly repelled by the image, and yet both women were crucial to his ambitions, and his sensual response to them – attraction or revulsion – was completely irrelevant. All that mattered was their utility.

Victoria came back down the steps ten minutes later. She was wearing a vivid crimson dress. Bright colours suited her, they set off that glossy dark skin. She slid into the passenger's seat of the van beside him, and glanced at the cheap gold-plated watch on her wrist. 'Eleven minutes sixteen seconds. You cannot really complain,' she announced, and he smiled and started the engine.

'Now let us pick your thighbone of a dinosaur,' he suggested.

'*Tyrannosaurus rex*,' she corrected him. 'The most ferocious of the dinosaurs. But, no, we'll keep that for dinner as you suggested.'

Her banter amused him. It was unusual for an unmarried black girl to be so forthcoming and self-assured. Then he remembered her training and her life here at one of the world's largest and busiest hospitals. This wasn't a little country girl, empty-headed and giggling, and as if to make the point, Victoria fell into an easy discussion of General Dwight Eisenhower's prospects for election to the White House, and how that would affect the American civil rights struggle – and ultimately their own struggle here in Africa.

While they talked, the sun began to set and the city, with all its fine buildings and parks, fell behind them, until abruptly they entered the half world of Soweto township where half a million black people lived. The dusk was thick with the smell of wood-smoke from the cooking fires, and it turned the sunset a diabolical red, the colour of blood and oranges. The narrow unmade sidewalks were crowded with black commuters, each of them carrying a parcel or a shopping bag, all hurrying in the same direction, back to their homes after a long day that had begun before the sun with a tortuous journey by bus or train to their places of work in the outer world, and that now ended in darkness with the reverse journey which fatigue made even longer and more tedious.

The van slowed as the streets became more crowded, and then some of them recognized Moses and ran ahead of them, clearing the way.

'Moses Gama! It's Moses Gama, let him pass!' And as they went by, some of them shouted greetings.

'I see you, *Nkosi.*'

'I see you, *Baba!*' They called him father and lord.

When they reached the community centre which abutted the administration buildings the huge hall was overflowing, and they were forced to leave the van and go on foot for the last hundred yards.

However, the Buffaloes were there to escort them. Hendrick Tabaka's enforcers pushed a way through the solid pack of humanity, tempering this show of force with smiles and jokes so the crowd made way for them without resentment.

'It is Moses Gama, let him pass,' and Victoria hung on to his arm and laughed with the excitement of it.

As they went in through the main doors of the hall, she glanced up and saw the name above the door: H. F. VERWOERD COMMUNITY HALL.

It was fast becoming a custom for the Nationalist government to name all state buildings, airports, dams and other public works after political luminaries and mediocrities, but there was an unusual irony in naming the community hall of the largest black township after the white architect of the laws which they had gathered here to protest. Hendrik Frensch Verwoerd was the Minister of Bantu Affairs, and the principal architect of *apartheid*.

Inside the hall the noise was thunderous. A permit to use the hall for a political rally would have been denied by the township administration, so officially this had been billed and advertised as a rock 'n' roll concert by a band that gloried in the name of 'The Marmalade Mambas'.

They were on the stage now, four of them dressed in tight-fitting sequined suits that glittered in the flashing coloured lights. A bank of amplifiers sent the music crashing over the packed audience, like an aerial bombardment, and the dancers screamed back at them, swaying and writing to the rhythm like a single monstrous organism.

The Buffaloes opened a path for them across the dance floor and the dancers recognized Moses and shouted greetings, trying to touch him as he passed. Then the band became aware of his presence and broke off in the middle of the wild driving beat to give him a trumpet fanfare and a roll of drums.

Dozens of willing hands helped Moses up on to the stage, while Victoria remained below with her head at the level of his knees, trapped in the press of bodies that pressed forward to see and to hear Moses Gama. The band leader attempted to introduce him but even the power of the electronic amplifiers could not lift his voice above the tumultuous welcome that they gave Moses. From four thousand throats a savage sustained roar rose and went on and on without diminution. It broke over Moses Gama like a wild sea driven by a winter gale, and like a rock he stood unmoved by it.

Then he lifted his arms, and the sound died away swiftly until a suppressed and aching silence hung over that great press of humanity and into that silence Moses Gama roared.

'*Amandla!* Power!'

As a single voice they roared back at him, '*Amandla!*'

He shouted again, in that deep thrilling voice that rang

against the rafters and reached into the depths of their hearts.

'*Mayibuye!*'

They bellowed the reply back at him

'*Afrika!* Let Africa persist.'

And then they were silent again, expectant and wound up with excitement and tension, as Moses Gama began to speak.

'Let us talk of Africa,' he said.

'Let us talk of a rich and fruitful land with tiny barren pockets on which our people are forced to live.

'Let us speak of the children without schools and the mothers without hope.

'Let us speak of taxes and passes.

'Let us speak of famine and sickness.

'Let us speak of those who labour in the harsh sunlight, and in the depths of the dark earth.

'Let us speak of those who live in the compounds far from their families.

'Let us speak of hunger and tears and the hard laws of the Boers.'

For an hour he held them in his hands, and they listened in silence except for the groans and involuntary gasps of anguish, and the occasional growl of anger, and at the end Victoria found she was weeping. The tears flowed freely and unashamedly down her beautiful upturned moon face.

When Moses finished, he dropped his arms and lowered his chin upon his chest, exhausted and shaken by his own passion and a vast silence fell upon them. They were too moved to shout or to applaud.

In the silence Victoria suddenly flung herself on to the stage and faced them.

'*Nkosi Sikelel' iAfrika,*' she sang.

'God save Africa,' and immediately the band picked up the refrain, while from the body of the hall their magnificent African voices soared in haunting chorus. Moses Gama stepped up beside her and took her hand in his, and their voices blended.

At the end it took them almost twenty minutes to escape from the hall, their way was blocked by the thousands who wanted the experience to last, to touch them and to hear their voices and to be a part of the struggle.

In the course of one short evening the beautiful Zulu girl in the flaming crimson dress had become part of the almost mystic legend that surrounded Moses Gama. Those who were fortunate enough to be there that evening would tell those who had not, how she had looked like a queen as she stood and sang before them, a queen that befitted the tall black emperor at her side.

'I have never experienced anything like that,' Vicky told him, when at last they were alone again, and the little blue and crimson van was humming back along the main highway towards Johannesburg. 'The love they bear you is so powerful—' She broke off. 'I just can't describe it.'

'Sometimes it frightens me,' he agreed. 'They place such a heavy responsibility upon me.'

'I don't believe you know what fear is,' she said.

'I do.' He shook his head. 'I know it better than most.' And then he changed the subject. 'What time is it? We must find something to eat before curfew.'

'It's only nine o'clock.' Victoria looked surprised as she turned the dial of her wristwatch to catch the light of a street lamp. 'I thought it would be much later. I seem to have lived a lifetime in one short evening.'

Ahead of them a neon sign flickered: 'DOLLS' HOUSE DRIVE-IN. TASTY EATS.' Moses slowed and turned the van into the parking lot. He left Vicky for a few minutes to go to the counter of the replica dolls' house, then he returned with hamburgers and coffee in two paper mugs.

'Ah, that's good!' she mumbled through a mouthful of hamburger. 'I didn't realize I was so hungry.'

'Now what about this bone you threaten me with?' Moses asked, and he spoke in fluent Zulu.

'You speak Zulu!' She was amazed. 'I didn't know. When did you learn?' she demanded in the same language.

'I speak many languages,' he told her. 'If I want to reach all the people, there is no other way.' And he smiled. 'However, young woman, you don't change the subject so easily. Tell me about this bone.'

'Oh, I feel so stupid talking about it now, after all we have shared this evening . . .' She hesitated. 'I was going to ask you why you sent your brother to speak to my father before you had said anything to me. I'm not a country girl of the kraals, you know. I am a modern woman with a mind of my own.'

'Victoria, we should not discard the old traditions in our struggle for liberation. What I did was out of respect for you and for your father. I am sorry if it offended you.'

'I was a little ruffled,' she admitted.

'Will it help at all if I ask you now?' he smiled. 'You can still refuse. Before we go any further, think very deeply. If you marry me, you marry the cause. Our marriage will be part of the struggle of our people, and the road before us will be hard and dangerous, with never an end in sight.'

'I do not need to think,' she said softly. 'Tonight when I stood there before our people with your hand in mine, I knew that was the reason why I was born.'

He took both her hands in his and drew her gently towards him, but before their mouths could touch, the harsh white beam of a powerful spotlight shone into their faces. Startled, they drew apart, shielding their eyes with raised hands.

'Hey, what is this?' Moses exclaimed.

'Police!' a voice answered from the darkness beyond the open side window. 'Get out, both of you!'

They climbed out of the van, and Moses went around the bonnet to stand beside Victoria. He saw that while they had been engrossed with each other, a police pick-up had entered the parking lot and parked beside the restaurant building. Now four blue-uniformed constables with flashlights were checking the occupants of all the parked vehicles in the lot.

'Let me see your passes, both of you.' The constable in front of him was still shining the light in his eyes, but beyond it Moses could make out that he was very young.

Moses reached into his inner pocket, while Victoria searched in her purse, and they handed their pass booklets to the constable. He turned the beam of the flashlight on them and studied them minutely.

'It's almost curfew,' he said in Afrikaans, as he handed them back. 'You Bantu should be in your own locations at this time of night.'

'There is still an hour and a half until curfew,' Victoria replied sharply, and the constable's expression hardened.

'Don't take that tone with me, maid.' That term of address was insulting and again he shone the flashlight in her face. 'Just because you've got shoes on your feet and rouge on your face, doesn't mean you are a white woman. Just remember that.'

Moses took Victoria's arm and firmly steered her back to the van. 'We are leaving right away, officer,' he said placatingly, and once they were both in the van, he told Victoria, 'You will accomplish nothing by getting us both arrested. That is not the level at which we should conduct the struggle. That is just a callow little white boy with more authority than he knows how to carry.'

'Forgive me,' she said. 'I just get so angry. What were they looking for, anyway?'

'They were looking for white men with black girls, their Immorality Act to keep their precious white blood pure. Half their police force spends its time trying to peer into other people's bedrooms.' He started the van and turned onto the highway.

Neither of them spoke again until he parked in front of the Baragwanath nurses' home.

'I hope we will not be interrupted again,' Moses said quietly, and placing an arm around her shoulders turned her gently to face him.

Although she had seen how it was done on the cinema screen, and although the other girls in the hostel endlessly discussed what they referred to as 'Hollywood style', Victoria had never kissed a man. It was not part of Zulu custom or tradition. So she lifted her face to him with a mixture of trepidation and breathless expectation, and was amazed at the warmth and softness of his mouth. Swiftly the stiffness and tension went out of her neck and shoulders and she seemed to mould herself to him.

The work at Sundi Caves was even more interesting than Tara Courtney had expected it to be, and she adapted rapidly to the leisurely pace and life and intellectually stimulating companionship of the small specialist team of which she was now a part.

Tara shared a tent with two young students from the University of the Witwatersrand, and she found with mild surprise that the close proximity of other women in such spartan accommodation did not bother her. They were up long before dawn to escape the heat in the middle of the day, and after a quick and frugal breakfast Professor Hurst led them up to the site and allocated the day's labours. They rested and ate the main meal at noon, and then as the day cooled they returned to the site and worked on until the light failed. After that they had only enough energy for a hot shower, a light meal and the narrow camp beds.

The site was in a deep kloof. The rocky sides dropped steeply two hundred feet to the narrow riverbed in the gut.

The vegetation in the protected and sun-warmed valley was tropical, quite alien to that on the exposed grasslands that were scoured by wind and winter frosts. Tall candelabra aloes grew on the upper slopes, while further down it became even denser, and there were tree ferns and cycads, and huge strangler figs with bark like elephant hide, grey and wrinkled.

The caves themselves were a series of commodious open galleries that ran with the exposed strata. They were ideal for habitation by primitive man, located high up the slope and protected from the prevailing winds yet with a wide view out across the plain onto which the kloof debouched. They were close to water and readily defensible against all marauders, and the depth of the midden and accumulated detritus on the floor of the caves attested to the ages over which they had been occupied.

The roofs of the caves were darkened with the smoke of countless cooking fires and the inner walls were decorated with the engravings and childlike paintings of the ancient San peoples and their predecessors. All the signs of a major site with the presence of very early hominids were evident, and although the dig was still in its early stages and they had penetrated only the upper levels spirits and optimism were high and the whole feeling on the dig was of a close-knit community of persons bound by a common interest cooperating selflessly on a project of outstanding importance.

Tara particularly liked Marion Hurst, the American professor in charge of the excavations. She was a woman in her early fifties, with cropped grey hair, and a skin burned to the colour and consistency of saddle-leather by the suns of Arabia and Africa. They had become firm friends even before Tara discovered that she was married to a negro professor of anthropology at Cornell. That knowledge made their relationship secure, and relieved Tara of the necessity of any subterfuge.

One night she sat late with Marion in the shed they were using as a laboratory, and suddenly Tara found herself telling her about Moses Gama and her impossible love, even about the child she was carrying. The elder woman's sympathy was immediate and sincere.

'What iniquitous social order can keep people from loving others – of course, I knew all about these laws before I came here. That is why Tom stayed at home. Despite my personal feelings, the work here was just too important to pass up. However, you have my promise that I will do anything in my power to help the two of you.'

Yet Tara had been on the dig for five weeks without having heard from Moses Gama. She had written him a dozen letters and telephoned the Rivonia number, and the other number in Drake's Farm township. Moses was never there, and never responded to her urgent messages.

At last she could stand it no longer, and she borrowed Marion's pick-up truck and went into the city, almost an hour's drive with the first half of the journey over clay roads that were rutted and bumpy, and finally over wide black-top highways in a solid stream of heavy traffic, coming up from the coalfields at Witbank.

She parked the pick-up under the bluegum trees at the back of Puck's Hill and was suddenly afraid to see him again, terrified that it had all changed and he would send her away. It took all her courage to leave the cab of the pick-up and go around the big unkempt house to the front verandah.

At the far end there was a man sitting at the desk and her heart soared and then as swiftly plunged as he turned and saw her and stood up. It was Marcus Archer. He came down the long verandah towards her, and his smile was spiteful and vinegary.

'Surprise!' he said. 'The last person I expected to see.'

'Hello, Marcus. I was looking for Moses.'

'I know who you are looking for, dearie.'

'Is he here?'

Marcus shook his head. 'I haven't seen him for almost two weeks.'

'I have written and telephoned – he doesn't reply. I was worried.'

'Perhaps he doesn't reply because he doesn't want to see you.'

'Why do you dislike me so, Marcus?'

'Oh, my dear, whatever gave you that idea?' Marcus smiled archly.

'I'm sorry to have bothered you.' She began to turn away and then paused. Her expression hardened. 'Will you give him a message, when you see him?'

Marcus inclined his head, and for the first time she noticed the grey hairs in his ginger sideburns and the wrinkles in the corners of his eyes. He was much older than she had thought.

'Will you tell Moses that I came to find him, and that nothing has changed. That I meant every word I said.'

'Very well, dearie. I'll tell him.'

Tara went down the steps, but when she reached the bottom, he called after her.

'Tara.' And she looked up. He leaned on the railing of the verandah. 'You'll never have him. You know that, don't you? He will keep you only as long as he needs you. Then he will cast you aside. He will never belong to you.'

'Nor to you either, Marcus Archer,' she said softly, and he recoiled from her. 'He belongs to neither of us. He belongs to Africa and his people.' And she saw the desolation in his eyes. It gave her no satisfaction, and she went slowly back to the pick-up and drove away.

At Level Six in the main gallery of the Sundi Caves they exposed an extensive deposit of clay pottery fragments. There were no intact artefacts, and it was obviously a dumping site for the ancient potters. Nevertheless, the discovery was of crucial importance in dating the levels for the pottery was of a very early type.

Marion Hurst was excited by the find, and transmitted her excitement to all of them. By this time Tara had been promoted from the heavy work of grubbing in the dirt at the bottom of the trenches. She had displayed a natural aptitude for the puzzle game of fitting the fragments of bone and pottery together in their original form, and she now worked in the long prefabricated shed under Marion Hurst's direct supervision and was making herself an invaluable member of the team.

Tara found that while she was absorbed with the fragments, she could suppress the ache of longing and the turmoil of uncertainty and guilt. She knew that her neglect of her children and her family was unforgivable. Once a week she telephoned Rhodes Hill and spoke to her father and Centaine and to Isabella. The child seemed quite content, and in a strangely selfish way Tara resented the fact that she seemed not to pine for her mother but was accepting her grandmother as a happy substitute. Centaine was friendly and made no criticism of her continued absence, but Blaine Malcomess, her beloved father, was as usual bluntly outspoken.

'I don't know what you are trying to run away from, Tara, but believe me it never works. Your place is here with your husband and your children. Enough of this nonsense now. You know your duty, however unpleasant you may find it – it's still your duty.'

Of course, Shasa and the boys would soon be returning from their grand safari, and then she could procrastinate no longer. She would have to make a decision, and she was not even certain of the alternatives. Sometimes in the night, in those silent small hours when human energy and spirits are at their lowest ebb, she even considered following Molly's advice and aborting the child from her womb and turning her back on Moses, going back to the seductive and destructively soft life of Weltevreden.

'Oh, Moses, if only I could see you again. Just to speak to you for a few hours – then I would know what to do.'

She found herself withdrawing from the company of the other workers on the excavation. The cheerful carefree attitude of the two university students she shared her tent with began to irritate her. Their conversation was so naïve and childlike, even the music they played endlessly on a portable tape recorder was so loud and uncouth that it rasped her nerves.

With Marion's blessing she purchased a small bell tent of her own and erected it near the laboratory where she worked, so that when the others took their noonday siesta she could slip back to her work bench and forget all her insoluble problems in the totally absorbing task of fitting together the shattered scraps. Their antiquity seemed to soothe her and make the problems of the present seem trivial and unimportant.

It was here, at her bench, in the middle of a hot somnolent highveld afternoon, that the light from the open doorway was blocked suddenly, and she looked up frowning, wiping back the sweaty wisps of hair from her forehead with the back of her hand, and then her mouth went dry and her heart seemed to freeze for a long moment and then race wildly.

The sunlight was behind him, so his was a tall silhouette, broad-shouldered, slim-hipped and regal. She sobbed and sprang up from the bench and flew to him, wrapping her arms around his chest and pressing her face to his heart so that she could feel it beat against her cheek. She could not speak, and his voice was deep and gentle above her.

'I have been cruel to you. I should have come to you sooner.'

'No,' she whispered. 'It doesn't matter. Now that you are here, nothing else matters.'

He stayed only one night, and Marion Hurst protected them from the other members of the expedition so that they were alone in her small tent, isolated from the world and its turmoil. Tara did not sleep that night, each moment was far too precious to waste.

In the dawn he said to her. 'I must go again soon. There is something that you must do for me.'

'Anything!' she whispered.

'Our campaign of defiance begins soon. There will be terrible risk and sacrifice by thousands of our people, but for their sacrifice to be worthwhile it must be brought to the attention of the world.'

'What can I do?' she asked.

'By a most fortunate coincidence, there is an American television team in the country at this very moment. They are making a series called "Africa on Focus".'

'Yes, I know about them. They interviewed—' She broke off. She didn't want to mention Shasa, not now, not during this treasured interlude.

'They interviewed your husband,' he finished for her. 'Yes, I know. However, they have almost finished filming and I have heard that they plan to return to the United States within the next few days. We need them here. We need them to film and record our struggle. They must show it to the world – the spirit of our people, the indomitable will to rise above oppression and inhumanity.'

'How can I help?'

'I cannot reach the producer of this series on my own. I need a go-between. We have to prevent them leaving. We have to make certain they are here to film the defiance when it begins. You must speak to the woman in charge of the filming. Her name is Godolphin, Kitty Godolphin, and

218

she will be staying at the Sunnyside Hotel in Johannesburg for the next three days.'

'I will go to her today.'

'Tell her that the time is not yet agreed – but when it is, I will let her know, and she must be there with her camera.'

'I will see that she is,' Tara promised, and he rolled her gently on to her back and made love to her again. It seemed impossible, but for Tara every time was better than the last, and when he left her and rose from the camp bed she felt weak and soft and warm as molten wax.

'Moses,' she said softly, and he paused in buttoning the pale blue open-neck shirt.

'What is it?' he asked softly.

She had to tell him about the child she was carrying. She sat up, letting the rumpled sheet fall to her waist and her breasts, already heavy with her pregnancy, were dappled with tiny blue veins beneath the ivory smooth skin.

'Moses,' she repeated stupidly, trying to find the courage to say it, and he came to her.

'Tell me,' he commanded, and her courage failed her. She could not tell him, the risk that it would drive him away was too great.

'I just wanted to tell you how grateful I am that you have given me this opportunity to be of service to the struggle.'

It was much easier to contact Kitty Godolphin than she had expected it to be. She borrowed Marion's pick-up and drove five miles to the nearest village, and she telephoned from the public booth in the little single-roomed post office. The operator in the Sunnyside Hotel put her through to the room, and a firm young voice with a Louisiana lilt said, 'Kitty Godolphin. Who is this, please?'

'I'd rather not give my name, Miss Godolphin. But I

would like to meet you as soon as possible. I have a story for you, an important and dramatic story.'

'When and where do you want to meet?'

'It will take me two hours to reach your hotel.'

'I'll be waiting for you,' said Kitty Godolphin, and it was as easy as that.

Tara checked with Reception and the girl at the desk phoned through to Miss Godolphin's suite and then told her to go up.

A young girl, slim and pretty, in a tartan shirt and blue jeans opened the door to Tara's ring.

'Hello, is Miss Godolphin in? She's expecting me.'

The girl looked her over carefully, taking in her khaki bush skirt and mosquito boots, her tanned arms and face and the scarf tied around her thick auburn hair.

'I'm Kitty Godolphin,' said the girl, and Tara could not hide her surprise.

'OK, don't tell me. You expected an old bag. Come on in and tell me who you are.'

In the lounge Tara removed her sunglasses and faced her.

'My name is Tara Courtney. I understand you know my husband. Shasa Courtney, Chairman of Courtney Mining and Finance.'

She saw the shift in the other woman's expression, and the sudden hard gleam in those eyes that she had thought were frank and innocent.

'I meet a lot of people in my business, Mrs Courtney.'

Tara had not expected the hostility, and hurriedly she tried to forestall it.

'I'm sure you do—'

'Did you want to talk to me about your husband, lady? I don't have a lot of time to waste.' Kitty looked pointedly at her wristwatch. It was a man's Rolex and she wore it on the inside of her wrist like a soldier.

'No, I'm sorry. I didn't mean to give you that impression.

I have come here on behalf of someone else, someone who is unable to come to you himself.'

'Why not?' Kitty asked sharply, and Tara readjusted her early estimate of her. Despite her childlike appearance, she was as tough and sharp as any man Tara had ever met.

'Because he is being watched by the police Special Branch, and because what he is planning is dangerous and illegal.' Tara saw instantly that she had said the right things and had aroused the newswoman's instinct.

'Sit down, Mrs Courtney. Do you want some coffee?' She picked up the house phone and ordered from room service, then turned back to Tara.

'Now tell me. Who is this mysterious person?'

'You probably have never heard of him, but soon the whole world will know his name,' Tara said. 'It's Moses Gama.'

'Moses Gama, hell!' Kitty Godolphin exclaimed. 'For six weeks now I've been trying to catch up with him. I was beginning to think he was just a rumour, and that he didn't really exist. A Scarlet Pimpernel.'

'He exists,' Tara assured her.

'Can you get me an interview with him?' Kitty demanded, so anxious that she leaned across and grasped Tara's wrist impulsively. 'He's an Emmy score, that one. He is the one person in South Africa I really want to talk to.'

'I can do a whole lot better than that,' Tara promised her.

Shasa Courtney was determined that his sons would not grow up believing that the affluent white suburbs of Cape Town and Johannesburg were all of Africa. This safari was to show them the old Africa, primeval and eternal, and to establish for them a firm link with their history and their ancestors, to engender in them a sense of pride in what they were and in those who had gone before them.

He had set aside six whole weeks, the full period of the boys' school holidays, for this venture, and that had taken a great deal of planning and considerable heart-searching. The affairs of the company were so many-faceted and complex that he did not like leaving them, even in such capable hands as those of David Abrahams. The shaft-sinking at Silver River was going ahead apace, and they were down almost a thousand feet already while work on the plant was also far advanced. Apart from that, the first six pilchard trawlers for the factory at Walvis Bay were due for delivery in three weeks' time, and the canning plant was on the water from the suppliers in the United Kingdom. There was so much happening, so many problems that could demand his immediate decision.

Centaine was, of course, always on hand for David to consult with, but of late she had withdrawn more and more from the running of the company, and there were many eventualities that might arise that could only be dealt with by Shasa personally. Shasa weighed up the chances of this happening against what was necessary, in his view, for his sons' education and understanding of their place in Africa and their inherited duties and responsibilities, and decided he had to risk it. As a last resort he arranged a strict itinerary for the safari, of which both Centaine and David had a copy, so that they would know exactly where he was during every day of his absence, and a radio contact would be maintained with the H'ani Mine so that an aircraft could reach any of his camps in the deep bush within four or five hours.

'If you do call me out, then the reason had better be iron-clad,' Shasa warned David grimly. 'This is probably the only time in our lives that the boys and I will be able to do this.'

They left from the H'ani Mine the last week in May.

Shasa had taken the boys out of school a few days early, which in itself was enough to put everybody in the right mood and ensure a splendid beginning. He had commandeered four of the mine's trucks and made up a full team of safari boys, including drivers, camp servants, skinners, trackers, gun-bearers and the chef from the H'ani Mine Club. Of course, Shasa's own personal hunting vehicle was always kept in the mine workshops, tuned to perfection and ready to go at any time. It was an ex-Army jeep which had been customized and modified by the mine engineers without regard to expense. It had everything from long-range fuel tanks and gun racks to a short-wave radio set, and the seats were upholstered in genuine zebra skin while the paintwork was an artistic creation in bush camouflage. Proudly the boys clipped their Winchester .22 repeaters into the gun rack beside Shasa's big .375 Holland and Holland magnum, and dressed in their new khaki bush jackets scrambled into their seats in the jeep. As was the right of the eldest, Sean sat up front beside his father, with Michael and Garry in the open back.

'Anybody want to change his mind and stay at home?' Shasa asked as he started the jeep, and they took the question seriously, shaking their heads in unison, eyes shining and faces pale with excitement, too overcome to speak.

'Here we go, then,' Shasa said and they drove down the hill from the mine offices with the convoy of four trucks following them.

The uniformed mine guards opened the main gates and gave them a flashy salute, grinning widely as the jeep passed, and behind them the camp boys on the backs of the open trucks started to sing one of the traditional safari songs.

Weep, O you women, tonight you sleep alone
The long road calls us and we must go—

Their voices rose and fell to the eternal rhythm of Africa, full of its promise and mystery, echoing its grandeur and its savagery, setting the mood for the magical adventure into which Shasa took his sons.

They drove hard those first two days to get beyond the areas which had been spoiled by men's too frequent intrusions with rifle and four-wheel-drive vehicle, where the veld was almost bare of large game and those animals that they did see were in small herds that were running as soon as they heard the first hum of the jeep engine and were merely tiny specks in their own dust by the time they spotted them.

Sadly Shasa realized how much had changed since his earliest memory of this country. He had been Sean's age then and the herds of springbok and gemsbok had been on every side, great herds, trusting and confiding. There had been giraffe and lion, and small bands of Bushmen, those fascinating little yellow pygmies of the desert. Now, however, wild men and beast had all retreated before the inexorable advance of civilization deeper and deeper into the wilderness. Even now, Shasa could look ahead to the day when there would be no more wilderness, no more retreat for the wild things, when the roads and the railway lines would criss-cross the land and the endless villages and kraals would stand in the desolation they had created. The time when the trees were all cut down for firewood, and the grass was eaten to the roots by the goats and the top-soil turned to dust and blew on the wind. The vision filled him with sadness and a sense of despair, and he had to make a conscious effort to throw it off so as not to spoil the experience for his sons.

'I owe them this glimpse of the past. They must know a little of the Africa that once was, before it has all gone, so that they will understand something of its glory.' And he smiled and told them the stories, reaching back in his memory to bring out for them all his own experiences, and then going back further, to what he had learned from his own mother, and from his grandfather, trying to make clear to them the extent and depth of their family's involvement with this land, and they sat late around the camp fire that first night, listening avidly until, despite themselves, their eyelids drooped and their heads began to nod.

On they went, driving hard all day over rutted tracks, through desert scrub and grassland and then through mopani forest, not yet stopping to hunt, eating the food they had brought with them from the mine, though that night the servants muttered about fresh meat.

On the third day they left the rudimentary road they had been following since dawn. It was nothing more than a double track of tyres that had last been used months before, but now Shasa let it swing away towards the east and they went on northwards, breaking fresh ground, weaving through the open forest until abruptly they came out on the banks of a river, not one of the great African rivers like the Kavango, but one of its tributaries. Still, it was fifty feet wide, but green and deep, a formidable barrier that would have turned back any hunting safari before them that had come this far north.

Two weeks previously Shasa had reconnoitred this entire area from the air, flying the Mosquito low over the tree tops so that he could count the animals in each herd of game, and judge the size of the ivory tusks that each elephant carried. He had marked this branch of the river on his large-scale map, and had navigated the convoy back to this exact spot. He recognized it by the oxbow bend of the banks and the giant makuyu trees on the opposite side, with a fish-eagle nest in the upper branches.

They camped another two days on the southern river bank while every member of the safari, including the three boys and the fat Herero chef, helped to build the bridge. They cut the mopani poles in the forest, thick as a fat woman's thigh and forty feet long, and dragged them up with the jeep. Shasa kept guard against crocodiles, standing high on the bank with the .375 magnum under his arm while his naked gangs floated the poles out into the centre of the river and set them into the mud of the bottom. Then they lashed the cross-ties to them with ropes of mopani bark that still wept glutinous sap, red as blood.

When at last the bridge was complete, they unloaded the vehicles to lighten them, and one at a time Shasa drove them out on to the rickety structure. It swayed and creaked and rocked under them, but at last he had the jeep and all four trucks on the far bank.

'Now the safari truly begins,' he told the boys. They had entered a pocket of country, protected by its remoteness and its natural barriers of forest and river from men's over-exploitation, and from the air Shasa had seen the herds of buffalo thick as domestic cattle and the clouds of white egrets hovering over them.

That night he told the boys stories about the old elephant hunters – 'Karamojo' Bell, and Frederick Selous and Sean Courtney their own ancestor, Shasa's great-uncle and the namesake of his eldest son.

'They were tough men, all of them, incredible shots and natural athletes. They had to be to survive the hardships and the tropical disease. When he was a young man, Sean Courtney hunted on foot in the tsetse-fly belt of the Zambezi valley where the temperature reaches 115° at noon, and he could run forty miles in a day after the big tuskers. His eye was so sharp he could actually see the flight of his bullet.' The boys listened with total fascination, pleading with him to continue whenever he paused, until at last he told them, 'That's enough. You have to be up early tomorrow. Five o'clock in the morning. We are going to hunt for the first time.'

In the dark they drove slowly along the northern bank of the river in the open jeep, all of them bundled up against the cold for the frost lay thick in the open vleis and crunched under the jeep's tyres. In the first feeble light of dawn they found where a herd of buffalo had drunk during the night and then gone back into the heavy bush.

They left the jeep on the river bank, and stripped off their padded anoraks. Then Shasa put his two Ovambo trackers to the spoor and they followed the herd on foot. As they moved silently and swiftly through the dense second-growth mopani thickets, Shasa explained it all to the boys, speaking in a whisper and relying on hand signals to point out the different hoof prints of old bull and cow and calf, or to draw their attention to other smaller but equally fascinating animals and birds and insects in the forest around them.

A little before noon they finally came up with the herd. Over a hundred of the huge cow-like beasts, with their trumpet-shaped ears and the drooping horns that gave them such a lugubrious air. Most of them were lying in the mopani shade, ruminating quietly, although one or two of the herd bulls were dozing on their feet. The only movement was the lazy flick of their tails as the stinging flies swarmed over their flanks.

Shasa showed the boys how to work in close. Using the breeze and every stick of cover, freezing whenever one of the great horned heads swung in their direction, he took them within thirty feet of the biggest of the bulls. They could smell him, the hot rank bovine reek of him, and they could hear his breathing puffing through his wet drooling muzzle, hear his teeth grinding on his cud, so close they could see the bald patches of age on his shoulders and rump and the balls of dried mud from the wallow that clung in the stiff black hairs of his back and belly.

While they held their breaths in delicious terror and watched in total fascination, Shasa slowly raised the heavy rifle and aimed into the bull's thick neck, just forward of his massive shoulder.

'Bang!' he shouted, and the great bull plunged forward

wildly, crashing into the screen of thick mopani, and Shasa gathered his sons and drew them into the shelter of one of the grey tree trunks, keeping his arms around them while on all sides the panicking herd galloped, huge black shapes thundering by, the calves bawling and the old bulls grunting.

The sounds of their flight dwindled away into the forest though the dust of their passage hung misty in the air around them, and Shasa was laughing with the joy of it as he let his arms fall from their shoulders.

'Why did you do that?' Sean demanded furiously, turning his face up to his father. 'You could have shot him easily – why didn't you kill him?'

'We didn't come out here to kill,' Shasa explained. 'We came here to hunt.'

'But—' Sean's outrage turned to bewilderment ' – but what's the difference?'

'Ah! That's what you have to learn. That bull was a big one, but not big enough, and we have all the meat we need, so I let him go. That's lesson number one. Now, for lesson number two – none of you is going to kill anything until you know all about that animal, understand its habits and life cycle, and learn to respect it and hold it in high esteem. Then and only then.'

In camp that evening he gave them each two books, which he had had bound in leather with their own names on the cover: Roberts' *Mammals of South Africa* and his *Birds of South Africa*.

'I brought these especially for you, and I want you to study them,' he ordered. Sean looked appalled, he hated books and studying, but both Garry and Mickey hurried to their tent to begin the task.

Over the days that followed he questioned them on every animal and bird they saw. At first the questions were elementary, but he made them progressively more difficult and soon they could quote the biological names and give him full details of sizes and body weights of males and females, their calls and behaviour patterns, distribution and breeding, down to the smallest detail. Set an example by his younger brothers, even Sean mastered the difficult Latin names.

However, it was ten days before they were allowed to fire a shot and then it was only bird-hunting. Under strict supervision, they were allowed to hunt the fat brown francolin and speckled guinea fowl with their strange waxen yellow helmets in the scrub along the river. Then they had to clean and dress their kill and help the Herero chef to prepare and cook it.

'It's the best meal I've ever eaten,' Sean declared, and his brothers agreed with him enthusiastically through full mouths.

The next morning Shasa told them, 'We need fresh meat for the men.' In camp there were thirty mouths to feed, all with an enormous appetite for fresh meat. 'All right, Sean, what is the scientific name for impala?'

'*Aepyceros melampus*,' Sean gabbled eagerly. 'The Afrikaners call it *rooibok* and it weighs between 130 and 160 pounds.'

'That will do,' Shasa laughed. 'Go and get your rifle.'

In a patch of whistling thorn near the river, they found a solitary old ram, an outcast from the breeding herd. He had been mauled by a leopard and was limping badly on one foreleg, but he had a fine pair of lyre-shaped horns. Sean stalked the lovely red brown antelope just as Shasa had taught him, using the river bank and the wind to get within easy shot, even with the light rifle. However, when the boy knelt and raised the Winchester to his shoulder, Shasa slipped the safety-catch of his heavy weapon, ready to render the *coup de grâce*, if it was needed.

The impala dropped instantly, shot through the neck, dead before it heard the shot, and Shasa went to join his son at the kill.

As they shook hands, Shasa recognized in Sean the deep atavistic passion of the hunter. In some contemporary men that urge had cooled or been suppressed – in others it still burned brightly. Shasa and his eldest son were of that ilk, and now Shasa stopped and dipped his forefinger in the bright warm blood that trickled from the tiny wound in the ram's neck and then he traced his finger across Sean's forehead and down each cheek.

'Now you are blooded,' he said, and he wondered when that ceremony had first been performed, when the first man had painted his son's face with the blood of his first kill, and he knew instinctively that it had been back before recorded time, back when they still dressed in skins and lived in caves.

'Now you are a hunter,' he said, and his heart warmed to his son's proud and solemn expression. This was not a moment for laughter and chatter, it was something deep and significant, something beyond mere words. Sean had sensed that and Shasa was proud of him.

The following day they drew lots and it was Michael's turn to kill. Again Shasa wanted a solitary impala ram, so as not to alarm the breeding herd, but an animal with a good pair of horns as a trophy for the boy. It took them almost all that day of hunting before they found the right one.

Shasa and his two brothers watched from a distance as Michael made his stalk. It was a more difficult situation than Sean had been presented with, open grassland and a few scattered flat-top acacia thorns, but Michael made a stealthy approach on hands and knees, until he reached a low ant heap from which to make his shot.

Michael rose slowly and lifted the light rifle. The ram was still unaware, grazing head down thirty paces off, broadside on and offering the perfect shot for either spine or heart. Shasa was ready with the Holland and Holland to back him, should he wound the impala. Michael held his aim, and the seconds drew out. The ram raised its head and looked around warily, but Michael was absolutely still, the rifle to his shoulder, and the ram looked past him, not seeing him. Then it moved away unhurriedly, stopping once to crop a few mouthfuls. It disappeared into a clump of taller grass and without having fired, Michael slowly lowered his rifle.

Sean jumped to his feet, ready to rush out and challenge his brother, but Shasa restrained him with a hand on his shoulder. 'You and Garry go and wait for us back at the jeep,' he said.

Shasa walked out to where Michael was sitting on the ant heap with the unfired Winchester held across his lap. He sat down beside Michael and lit a cigarette. Neither of them said anything for almost ten minutes and then Michael whispered, 'He looked straight at me – and he had the most beautiful eyes.'

Shasa dropped the butt of his cigarette and ground it out under his heel. They were silent again, and then Michael blurted, 'Do I really *have* to kill something, Dad? Please don't make me.'

'No, Mickey,' Shasa put his arm around his shoulders. 'You don't have to kill anything. And in a different sort of way, I'm just as proud of you as I am of Sean.'

Then it was Garrick's turn. Again it was a solitary ram with a beautiful head of wide-curved horns and the stalk was through scattered bush and waist-high grass.

His spectacles glinting determinedly, Garry began his stalk under Shasa's patient supervision. However, he was still a long way out of range of the ram when there was a squawk and Garry disappeared into the earth. Only a small cloud of dust marked the spot where he had been. The impala raced away into the forest, and Shasa and the two boys ran out to where Garry had last been seen. They were guided by muffled cries of distress, and a disturbance in the grass. Only Garry's legs were still above ground, kicking helplessly in the air. Shasa seized them and heaved Garry out of the deep round hole in which he was wedged from the waist.

It was the entrance to an antbear burrow. Intent on his stalk, Garry had tripped over his own bootlace and tumbled headlong into the hole. The lenses of his spectacles were thick with dust and he had skinned his cheek and torn his bushjacket. These injuries were insignificant when compared to the damage to his pride. In the next three days Garry made as many attempts to stalk. All of these were detected by his intended victim long before he was within gunshot. Each time as he watched the antelope dash away, Garry's dejection was more abject and Sean's derision more raucous.

'Next time we will do it together,' Shasa consoled him, and the following day he coached Garry quietly through the stalk, carrying the rifle for him, pointing out the obstacles over which Garry would have tripped, and leading him the last ten yards by the hand until they were in a good position for the shot. Then he handed him the loaded rifle.

'In the neck,' he whispered. 'You can't miss.'

The ram had the best trophy horns they had seen yet, and he was twenty-five yards away. Garry lifted the rifle and peered through spectacles that were misted with the heat of excitement and his hands began to shake uncontrollably.

Watching Garry's face screwed up with tension, and seeing the erratic circles that the rifle barrel was describing, Shasa recognized the classic symptoms of 'buck fever' and reached out to prevent Garry firing. He was too late, and the ram jumped at the sharp crack of the shot, and then looked around with a puzzled expression. Neither Shasa nor the animal, and least of all Garry, knew where the bullet had gone.

'Garry!' Shasa tried to prevent him, but he fired again as wildly, and a puff of dust flicked from the earth halfway between them and the ram.

The impala went up into the air in a fluid and graceful leap, a flash of silken cinnamon-coloured skin and a glint of sweeping horns and then it was bounding away on those long delicate legs, so lightly it seemed not to touch the earth.

They walked back to the jeep in silence, Garry trailing a few paces behind his father, and his father, and his elder brother greeted him with a peal of merry laughter.

'Next time throw your specs at him, Garry.'

'I think you need a little more practice before you have another go at it,' Shasa told him tactfully. 'But don't worry. Buck fever is something that can attack anyone – even the oldest and most experienced.'

They moved camp, going deeper into the little Eden they had discovered. Now every day they came across elephant droppings, knee-high piles of fibrous yellow lumps the size of tennis balls, full of chewed bark and twigs and the stones of wild fruit in which the baboons and red-cheeked francolin delved delightedly for titbits.

Shasa showed the boys how to thrust a finger into the pile of dung to test for body heat and judge its freshness, and how to read the huge round pad-marks in the dust. To differentiate between bull and cow, between front and rear foot, to tell the direction of travel and to estimate the age of the animal. 'The tread is worn off the feet of the old ones – smooth as an old car tyre.'

Then, at last, they picked up the spoor of a huge old bull elephant, with smooth pad-marks the size of garbage-bin lids, and they left the jeep and followed him on foot for two days, sleeping on the spoor, eating the hard rations they carried. In the late afternoon of the second day, they caught up with the bull. He was in almost impenetrable jess bush through which they crept on hands and knees, and they were almost within touching distance when they made out the loom of the colossal grey body through the interlaced branches. Eleven foot high at the shoulder, he was grey as a storm cloud, and his belly rumbled like distant thunder. One at a time Shasa took the boys up closer to have a good look at him, and then they retreated out of the jess bush and left the outcast to his eternal wanderings.

'Why didn't you shoot him, Dad?' Garry stuttered. 'After following all that way?'

'Didn't you see? One tusk was broken off at the tip, and despite his bulk the other tusk was pretty small.'

They limped back over the miles on feet that were covered in blisters, and it took two rest days in camp for the boys to recover from a march that had been beyond their strength.

Often during the nights they were awakened and lay in their narrow camp beds, thrilling to the shrieking cries of the hyena scavenging the garbage dump beside the lean-to kitchen. They were accompanied by the soprano yelping bark of the little dog-like jackals. The boys learned to recognize all these and the other sounds of the night – the birds such as the night jar and the dikkop, the smaller mammals, the night ape, the genet and the civet, and the insects and reptiles that squealed and hummed and croaked in the reeds of the waterhole.

They bathed infrequently. In matters of hygiene Shasa was more easy-going than their mother and a thousand times more so than their grandmother, and they ate the delicious concoctions that the Herero chef dreamed up for them with plenty of sugar and condensed milk. School was far away and they were as happy as they had ever been with their father's complete and undivided attention and his wonderful stories and instruction.

'We haven't seen any signs of lions yet,' Shasa remarked at breakfast one morning. 'That's unusual. There are plenty of buffalo about, and the big cats usually keep close to the herds.'

Mention of lions gave the boys delightful cold shivers, and it was as though Shasa's words had conjured up the beast.

That afternoon, as the jeep bumped and weaved slowly through the long grass avoiding antbear holes and fallen logs, they came out on the edge of a long dry vlei, one of those grassy depressions of the African bush that during the rainy season become shallow lakes and at other times are treacherous swamps where a vehicle can easily bog down, or in the driest months are smooth treeless expanses resembling a well-kept polo ground. Shasa stopped the jeep in the tree line and searched the far side of the vlei, panning his binoculars slowly to pick up any game standing amongst the shadows of the tall grey mopani trees on the far side.

'Only a couple of bat-eared foxes,' he remarked, and passed the binoculars to the boys. They laughed at the antics of these quaint little animals, as they hunted grass-hoppers in the short green grass in the centre of the vlei.

'Hey, Dad!' Sean's tone changed. 'There is a big old baboon in the top of that tree.' He passed the binoculars back to his father.

'No,' Shasa said, without lowering the glasses. 'That's not a baboon. It's a human being!'

He spoke in the vernacular to the two Ovambo trackers in the back of the jeep, and there was a quick but heated discussion, everybody taking differing views.

'All right, let's go and take a look.' He drove the jeep

out into the open vlei, and before they were halfway across there was no longer any doubt. In the top branches of a high mopani crouched a child, a little black girl dressed only in a loincloth of cheap blue trade cotton.

'She's all alone,' Shasa exclaimed. 'Out here, fifty miles from the nearest village.'

Shasa sent the jeep roaring across the last few hundred yards then pulled up in a rolling cloud of dust and ran to the base of the mopani. He shouted up at the almost naked child. 'Come down!' and gestured to reinforce the command that she would certainly not understand. She neither moved nor raised her head from the branch on which she lay.

Shasa looked around him quickly. At the base of the tree lay a blanket roll which had been ripped open; the threadbare blankets had been shredded and torn. A skin bag had also been ripped and the dry maize meal it contained had poured into the dust, there was a black three-legged pot lying on its side, a crude axe with the blade rough-forged from a piece of scrap mild steel, and the shaft of a spear snapped off at the back of the head, but the point was missing.

A little further off were scattered a few rags on which blood stains had dried black as tar, and some other objects which were covered by a living cloak of big shimmering iridescent flies. As Shasa approached, the flies rose in a buzzing cloud, revealing the pathetic remains on which they had been feasting. There were two pairs of human hands and feet, gnawed off at the wrists and ankles, and then – horribly – the heads. A man and a woman, their necks chewed through and the exposed vertebrae crushed by great fangs. Both heads were intact, although the mouths and nostrils and empty eye-sockets were filled with the white rice pudding of eggs laid by the swarming flies. The grass was flattened over a wide area, crusted with dried blood, and the trodden dust was patterned with the unmistakable pug-marks of a fully grown male lion.

'The lion always leaves the head and hands and feet,' his Ovambo tracker said in a matter-of-fact voice, and Shasa nodded and turned to warn the boys to stay in the car. He was too late. They had followed him and were studying the grisly relics with varied expressions – Sean with ghoulish relish, Michael with nauseated horror and Garry with intense clinical interest.

Swiftly Shasa covered the severed heads with the torn blankets. He smelt that they were already in an advanced state of decomposition: they must have lain here many days. Then once again he turned his attention to the child in the branches high above them, calling urgently to her.

'She is dead,' said his tracker. 'These people have been dead four days at least. The little one has been in the tree all that time. She is surely dead.'

Shasa would not accept that. He removed his boots and safari jacket and climbed into the mopani. He went up cautiously, testing each hand-hold and every branch before committing his weight to it. To a height of ten feet above the ground the bark of the tree had been lacerated by claws. When the child was directly above him, almost within reach, Shasa called to her softly in Ovambo and then in Zulu.

'Hey, little one, can you hear me?'

There was no movement and he saw that her limbs were thin as sticks, and her skin ash-grey with that peculiar dusty look that in the African presages death. Shasa eased himself up the last few feet and reached up to touch her leg. The skin was warm, and he felt an unaccountable rush of relief. He had expected the soft cold touch of death. However, the child was unconscious and her dehydrated body was light as a bird as Shasa gently loosened her grip on the branch and lifted her against his chest. He climbed down slowly, shielding her from any jarring or rough movement and when he reached the ground carried her to the jeep and laid her in the shade.

The first-aid kit contained a comprehensive collection of medical equipment. Long ago, Shasa had been forced to minister to one of his gun-bearers mauled by a wounded buffalo and after that he never hunted without the kit, and he had learned to use all of it.

Swiftly he prepared a drip set and probed for the vein in the child's arm. The vein had collapsed, her pulse was weak and erratic, and he had to try again in the foot. This time he got the cannula in and administered a full bag of Ringers lactate, and while it was flowing he added 10 ccs of glucose solution to it. Only then did he attempt to make the child take water orally, and her swallowing reflex was still evident. A few drops at a time he got a full cup down her throat, and she showed the first signs of life, whimpering and stirring restlessly.

As he worked, he gave orders to his trackers over his shoulder. 'Take the spade, bury those people deep. It is strange that the hyena haven't found them yet, but make sure they don't do so later.'

One of the trackers held the child on his lap during the rough journey back to camp, protecting her from the jolts and heavy bumps. As soon as they arrived, Shasa strung the aerial of the short-wave radio to the highest tree in the grove, and after an hour of frustration finally made contact, not with the H'ani Mine, but with one of the Courtney Company's geological exploration units that was a hundred miles closer. Even then the contact was faint and scratchy and intermittent, but with many repetitions he got them to relay a message to the mine. They were to send an aircraft, with the mine doctor, to the landing strip at the police post at Rundu as soon as possible.

By this time, the little girl was conscious and talking to the Ovambo trackers in a weak piping voice that reminded

Shasa of the chirping of a nestling sparrow. She was speaking an obscure dialect of one of the river people from Angola in the north, but the Ovambo was married to a woman of her tribe and could translate for Shasa. The story she told was harrowing.

She and her parents had been on a journey to see her grandparents at the river village of Shakawe in the south, a trek on foot of hundreds of miles. Carrying all their worldly possessions, they had taken a short cut through this remote and deserted country when they had become aware that a lion was dogging them, following them through the forest – at first keeping its distance and then closing in.

Her father, an intrepid hunter, had realized the futility of stopping and trying to build some sort of shelter or of taking to the trees where the beast would besiege them. Instead he had tried to keep the lion off by shouting and clapping while he hurried to reach the river and the sanctuary of one of the fishing villages.

The child described the final attack when the animal, its thick ruff of black mane erect, had rushed in at the family, grunting and roaring. Her mother had only time enough to push the girl into the lowest branch of the mopani before the lion was on them. Her father had stood gallantly to meet it, and thrust his long spear into its shoulder, but the spear had snapped and the lion leapt upon him and tore out his bowels with a single swipe of curved yellow claws. Then it had sprung at the mother as she was attempting to climb into the mopani and hooked its claws into her back and dragged her down.

In her small birdlike voice the child described how the lion had eaten the corpses of her parents, down to the heads and feet and hands, while she watched from the upper branches. It had taken two days over the grisly feast, at intervals pausing to lick the spear wound in its shoulder. On the third day it had attempted to reach the child, ripping at the trunk of the mopani and roaring horribly. At last it had given up and wandered away into the forest, limping heavily with the wound. Even then the child had been too terrified to leave her perch and she had clung there until at last she had passed out with exhaustion and grief, exposure and fear.

While she was relating all this, the camp servants were refuelling the jeep and preparing supplies for the journey to Rundu. Shasa left as soon as this was done, taking the boys with him. He would not leave them in the camp while there was a wounded man-eating lion roaming in the vicinity.

They drove through the night, recrossing their jerry-built bridge and retracing their tracks until the following morning they intersected the main Rundu road, and that afternoon they finally arrived, dusty and exhausted, at the airstrip. The blue and silver Mosquito that Shasa had left at H'ani Mine was parked in the shade of the trees at the edge of the strip and the company pilot and the doctor were squatting under the wing, waiting patiently.

Shasa gave the child into the doctor's care, and went quickly through the pile of urgent documents and messages that the pilot had brought with him. He scribbled out orders and replies to these, and a long letter of instruction to David Abrahams. When the Mosquito took off again, the sick girl went with them. She would receive first-rate medical attention at the mine hospital, and Shasa would decide what to do with the little orphan once she was fully recovered.

The return to the safari camp was more leisurely than the outward journey, and over the next few days the excitement of the lion adventure was forgotten in the other absorbing concerns of safari life, not least of which was the business of Garry's first kill. Bad luck now combined with his lack of coordination and poor marksmanship to cheat him of this experience that he hungered for more than any other, while on the other hand Sean succeeded in providing meat for the camp at every attempt.

'What we are going to do is practise a little more on the pigeons,' Shasa decided, after one of Garry's least successful outings. In the evenings the flocks of fat green pigeons came flighting in to feast on the wild figs in the grove beside the waterhole.

Shasa took the boys down as soon as the sun lost its heat, and placed them in the hides they had built of saplings and dried grass, each hide far enough from the next and carefully sited so that there was no danger of a careless shot causing an accident. This afternoon Shasa put Sean into a hide at the near end of the glade, with Michael, who had once again declined to take an active part in the sport, to keep him company and pick up the fallen birds for him.

Then Shasa and Garry set off together for the far side of the grove. Shasa was leading with Garry following him as the game path twisted between the thick yellow trunks of the figs. Their bark was yellow and scaly as the skin of a giant reptile, and the bunches of figs grew directly on the trunks rather than on the tips of the branches. Beneath the trees the undergrowth was tangled and thick, and the game path was so twisted that they could see only a short distance ahead. The light was poor this late in the afternoon, with the branches meeting overhead.

Shasa came around another turn and the lion was in the game path, walking straight towards him only fifty paces away. In the instant he saw it, Shasa realized that it was the man-eater. It was a huge beast, the biggest he had ever seen in a lifetime of hunting. It stood higher than his waist, and its mane was coal-black, long and shaggy and dense, shading to blue grey down the beast's flanks and back.

It was an old lion, its flat face criss-crossed with scars. Its mouth was gaping, panting with pain as it limped towards him, and he saw that the spear wound in the shoulder had mortified, the raw flesh crimson as a rose petal and the fur around the wound wet and slicked down where the lion had been licking it. The flies swarmed to the wound, irritating and stinging, and the lion was in a vicious mood, sick with age and pain. It lifted its dark and shaggy head and Shasa looked into the pale yellow eyes and saw the agony and blind rage they contained.

'Garry!' he said urgently. 'Walk backwards! Don't run, but get out of here,' and without looking around he swung the sling of the rifle off his shoulder.

The lion dropped into a crouch, its long tail with the black bush of hair at the tip lashed back and forth like a metronome, as it gathered itself for the charge, and its yellow eyes fastened on Shasa, a focus for all its rage.

Shasa knew there would be time for only a single shot, for it would cover the ground between them in a blazing blur of speed. The light was too bad and the range was too far for that single shot to be conclusive, he would let it come in to where there could be no doubt, and the big 300-grain soft-nosed bullet from the Holland and Holland would shatter its skull and blow its brains to a mush.

The lion launched into its charge, keeping low to the earth, snaking in and grunting as it came, gut-shaking bursts of sound through the gaping jaws lined with long yellow fangs. Shasa braced himself and brought up the rifle, but before he could fire, there was the sharp crack of the little Winchester beside him and the lion collapsed in the middle of his charge, going down head first and cartwheeling, flopping over on its back to expose the soft butter-yellow fur of its belly, its limbs stretching and relaxing, the long curved talons in its huge paws slowly retracting into the pads, the pink tongue lolling out of its open jaws, and the rage dying out of those pale yellow eyes. From the tiny bullet hole between its eyes a thin serpent of blood crawled down to dribble from its brow into the dirt beneath it.

In astonishment Shasa lowered his rifle and looked round. Beside him stood Garry, his head at the level of Shasa's lowest rib, the little Winchester still at his shoulder, his face set and deadly pale, and his spectacles glinting in the gloom beneath the trees.

'You killed it,' Shasa said stupidly. 'You stood your ground and killed it.'

Shasa walked forward slowly and stooped over the carcass of the man-eater. He shook his head in amazement, and then looked back at his son. Garry had not yet lowered the rifle, but he was beginning now to tremble with delayed terror. Shasa dipped his finger into the blood that dribbled from the wound in the man-eater's forehead, then walked back to where Garry stood. He painted the ritual stripes on the boy's forehead and cheeks.

'Now you are a man and I'm proud of you,' he said. Slowly the colour flushed back into Garry's cheeks and his lips stopped trembling, and then his face began to glow. It was an expression of such pride and unutterable joy that Shasa felt his throat close up and tears sting his eyelids.

Every servant came from the camp to view the man-eater and to hear Shasa describe the details of the hunt. Then, by the light of the lanterns, they carried the carcass back. While the skinners went to work, the men sang of the hunter in Garry's honour.

Sean was torn between incredulous admiration and deepest envy of his brother, while Michael was fulsome in his praises. Garry refused to wash the dried lion's blood from his face when at last, well after midnight, Shasa finally ordered them to bed. At breakfast he still wore the crusted stripes of blood on his beaming grubby face and Michael read aloud the heroic poem he had written in Garry's honour. It began:

> With lungs to blast the skies with sound
> And breath hot as the blacksmith's forge

243

Eyes as yellow as the moon's full round
And the lust on human flesh to gorge –

Shasa hid a smile at the laboured rhyming, and at the end applauded as loudly as the end applauded as loudly as the rest of them. After breakfast they all trooped out to watch the skinners dressing out the lion skin, pegging it fur-side down in the shade, scraping away the yellow sub-cutaneous fat and rubbing in coarse salt and alum.

'Well, I still think it died of a heart attack.' Sean could suppress his envy no longer, and Garry rounded on him furiously.

'We all know what a clever dick you are. But when you shoot *your* first lion, then you can come and talk to me, smarty pants. All you are good for is a few little old impala!'

It was a long speech, delivered in white heat, and Garry never stumbled nor stuttered once. It was the first time Shasa had seen him stand up to Sean's casual bullying, and he waited for Sean to assert his authority. For seconds it hung in the balance, he could see Sean weighing it up, deciding whether to tweak the spikes of hair at Garry's temple or to give him a chestnut down the ribs. He could see also that Garry was ready for it, his fists clenched and his lips set in a pale determined line. Suddenly Sean grinned that charming smile.

'Only kidding,' he announced airily, and turned back to admire the tiny bullet-hole in the skull. 'Wow! Right between the eyes!' It was a peace offering.

Garry looked bemused and uncertain. It was the first time that he had forced Sean to back down, and he wasn't able immediately to grasp that he had succeeded.

Shasa stepped up and put his arm around Garry's shoulders. 'Do you know what I'm going to do, champ? I'm going to have the head fully mounted for the wall in your room, with eyes and everything,' he said.

For the first time, Shasa was aware that Garry had

developed hard little muscles in his shoulders and upper arms. He had always thought him a runt. Perhaps he had never truly looked at the child before.

Then suddenly it was over, and the servants were breaking camp and packing the tents and beds on to the trucks, and appallingly the prospect of the return to Weltevreden and school loomed ahead of them. Shasa tried to keep their spirits jaunty with stories and songs on the long drive back to H'ani Mine but with every mile the boys were more dejected.

On the last day when the hills which the Bushmen call the 'Place of All Life' floated on the horizon ahead of them, detached from the earth by the shimmering heat mirage, Shasa asked, 'Have you gentlemen decided what you are going to do when you leave school?' It was an attempt to cheer them up, more than a serious enquiry. 'What about you, Sean?'

'I want to do what we have been doing. I want to be a hunter, an elephant hunter like great-grand-uncle Sean.'

'Splendid!' Shasa agreed. 'Only problem I can see is that you are at least sixty years too late.'

'Well then,' said Sean, 'I'll be a soldier – I like shooting things.'

A shadow passed behind Shasa's eyes before he looked at Michael.

'What about you, Mickey?'

'I want to be a writer. I will work as a newspaper reporter and in my spare time I'll write poetry and great books.'

'You'll starve to death, Mickey,' Shasa laughed, and then he swivelled around to Garry who was leaning over the back of the driving seat.

'What about you, champ?'

'I'm going to do what you do, Dad.'

'And what is it I do?' Shasa demanded with interest.

'You are the Chairman of Courtney Mining and Finance, and you tell everybody else what to do. That's what I want to be one day, Chairman of Courtney Mining and Finance.'

Shasa stopped smiling and was silent for a moment, studying the child's determined expression, then he said lightly, 'Well then, it looks as though it's up to you and me to support the elephant hunter and the poet.' And he ran his hand over Garry's already unruly hair. It no longer required any effort to make an affectionate gesture towards his ugly duckling.

T hey came singing across the rolling grasslands of Zululand, and they were one hundred strong. All of them were members of the Buffaloes and Hendrick Tabaka had carefully picked them for this special honour guard. They were the best, and all of them were dressed in tribal regalia, feathers and furs and monkey-skin capes, kilts of cow-tails. They carried only fighting-sticks, for the strictest tradition forbade metal weapons of any kind on this day.

At the head of the column Moses Gama and Hendrick Tabaka trotted. They also had set aside their European clothing for the occasion, and of all their men they alone wore leopard-skin cloaks, as was their noble right. Half a mile behind them rose the dust of the cattle herd. This was the *lobola*, the marriage price, two hundred head of prime beasts, as had been agreed. The herd-boys were all of them sons of the leading warriors who had ridden in the cattle trucks with their charges during the three-hundred-mile journey from the Witwatersrand. In charge of the herd-boys were Wellington and Raleigh Tabaka and they had detrained the herd at Ladyburg railway station. Like their father, they had discarded their Western-style clothing for the occasion and were dressed in loincloths and armed with their fighting-sticks, and they danced and called to the cattle, keeping them in a tight bunch, both of them excited and filled with self-importance by the task they had been allotted.

Ahead of them rose the high escarpment beyond the little town of Ladyburg. The slopes were covered with dark forests of black wattle and all of it was Courtney land, from where the waterfall smoked with spray in the sunlight around the great curve of hills. All ten thousand acres of it belonged to Anna, Lady Courtney, the relict of Sir Garrick Courtney, and to Storm Anders, who was the daughter of General Sean Courtney. However, beyond the waterfall lay a hundred choice acres of land which had been left to Sangane Dinizulu in terms of the will of General Sean Courtney, for he had been a faithful and beloved retainer of the Courtney family as had his father Mbejane Dinizulu before him.

The road descended the escarpment in a series of hairpin bends, and when Moses Gama shaded his eyes and stared ahead, he saw another band of warriors coming down it to meet them. They were many more in number, perhaps five hundred strong. Like Moses' party they were dressed in full regimentals, with plumes of fur and feathers on their heads and war rattles on their wrists and ankles. The two parties halted at the foot of the escarpment, and from a hundred paces faced each other, though still they sang and stamped and brandished their weapons.

The shields of the Zulus were matched, selected from dappled cowhides of white and chocolate brown, and the brows of the warriors that carried them were bound with strips of the same dappled hide while their kilts and their plumes were cow-tails of purest white. They made a daunting and warlike show, all big men, their bodies gleaming with sweat in the sunlight, their eyes bloodshot with dust and excitement and the pots of millet beer they had already downed.

Facing them Moses felt his nerves crawl with a trace of the terror that these men had for two hundred years inspired in all the other tribes of Africa, and to suppress it he stamped and sang as loudly as his Buffaloes who pressed closely around him. On this his wedding day, Moses Gama had put aside all the manners and mores of the West, and slipped back easily into his African origins and his heart pumped and thrilled to the rhythms and the pulse of this harsh continent.

From the Zulu ranks opposite him sprang a champion, a magnificent figure of a man with the strip of leopard skin around his brow that declared his royal origins. He was one of Victoria Dinizulu's elder brothers, and Moses knew he was a qualified lawyer with a large practice at Eshowe, the Zululand capital, but today he was all African, fierce and threatening as he swirled in the *giya*, the challange dance.

He leapt and spun and shouted his own praises and those of his family, daring the world, challenging the men who faced him, while behind him his comrades drummed with their sticks on the rawhide shields, and the sound was like distant thunder, the last sound that a million victims had ever heard, the death-knell of Swazi and Xhosa, of Boer and Briton in the days when the impis of Chaka and Dingaan and Cetewayo had swept across the land, from Isandhlwana, the Hill of the Little Hand, where one thousand seven hundred British infantry were cut down in one of the worst military reverses that England had ever suffered in Africa, to the 'Place of Weeping' which the Boers named 'Weenen' for their grief for the women and children who died to that same dreadful drum roll when the impis came swarming down across the Tugela River, to a thousand other nameless and forgotten killing grounds where the lesser tribes had perished before the men of Zulu.

At last the Zulu champion staggered back into the ranks, streaked with sweat and dust, his chest heaving and froth upon his lips, and now it was Moses' turn to *giya*, and he danced out from amongst his Buffaloes, and leapt shoulder-high with his leopard skins swirling around him. His limbs shone like coal freshly cut from the face, and his eyes and teeth were white as mirrors flashing in the sunlight. His voice rang from the escarpment, magnified by the echoes, and though the men facing him could not understand the words the force and meaning of them was clear, his haughty disdain evident in every gesture. They growled and pressed forward, while his own Buffaloes were goaded by his example, their blood coming to the boil, ready to rush forward and join battle with their traditional foe, ready to perpetuate the bloody vendetta that had already run a hundred years.

At the very last moment, when violence and inevitable death were only a heartbeat away, and rage was as thick in the air as the static electricity of the wildest summer thunderstorm, Moses Gama stopped dancing abruptly, posing like a heroic statue before them – and so great was the force of his personality, so striking his presence, that the drumming of shields and the growl of battle rage died away.

Into the silence Moses Gama called in the Zulu language, 'I bring the marriage price!' and he held his stick aloft, a signal to the herd-boys who followed the marriage party.

Lowing and bawling, adding their dust to the dust of the dancers, the herd was driven forward and immediately the mood of the Zulus changed. For a thousand years, since they had come down from the far north, following the tsetse-fly-free corridors down the continent with their herds, the Nguni peoples from which the Zulu tribe would emerge under the black emperor Chaka had been cattle men. Their animals were their wealth and their treasure.

They loved cattle as other men love women and children. Almost from the day they could walk unaided the boys tended the herds, living with them in the veld from dawn to dusk every day, establishing with them a bond and almost mystic communion, protecting them from predators with their very lives, talking to them and handling them and coming to know them completely. It was said that King Chaka knew every individual beast in his royal herds, and that out of a hundred thousand head he would know immediately if one was missing and would ask for it with a complete description, and not hesitate to order his executioners with their knobkerries to dash out the brains of even the youngest herd-boy if there was even a suspicion of his negligence.

So it was a committee of strict and expert judges who put aside the dancing and posturing and boasting, and instead applied themselves to the serious business of appraising the bride price. Each animal was dragged from the herd, and amid a buzz of comment and speculation and argument, was minutely examined. Its limbs and trunk were palpated by dozens of hands simultaneously, its jaws were forced open to expose the teeth and tongue, its head twisted so that its ears and nostrils could be peered into, its udders stroked and weighed in the palm, its tail lifted to estimate its calf-bearing history and potential. Then finally, almost reluctantly, each animal was declared acceptable by old Sangane Dinizulu himself, the father of the bride. No matter how hard they tried, they could find no grounds for rejecting a single animal. The Ovambo and the Xhosa love their cattle every bit as much as the Zulu, and are as expert in their judgement. Moses and Hendrick had exercised all their skills in making their selection, for pride and honour were at stake.

It took many hours for every one of the two hundred animals to be examined while the bridegroom's party, still keeping aloof from the Zulus, squatted in the short grass on the side of the road, pretending indifference to the proceedings. The sun was hot and the dust aggravated the men's thirst, but no refreshment was offered while the scrutiny went on.

Then at last Sangane Dinizulu, his silver pate shining in the sun, but his body still upright and regal, called his herdboys. Joseph Dinizulu came forward. As the senior herdsman, the old man gave the herd into his care. Although his exhortations were severe and he scowled most ferociously, the old man's affection for his youngest son was ill-concealed, as was his delight at the quality of the stock which made up the marriage price. So when he turned and for the first time greeted his future son-in-law, he was having great difficulty in suppressing his smiles, they kept shooting out like beams of sunlight through cloud holes and were just as swiftly extinguished.

With dignity he embraced Moses Gama, and though he was a tall man, he had to reach up to do so. Then he stepped back and clapped his hands, calling to the small party of young women who were sitting a little way off.

Now they rose and helped each other to settle the enormous clay pots of beer upon each other's heads. Then they formed a line and came forward, singing and undulating their hips, although their heads remained steady and not a drop slopped over the rims of the pots. They were all unmarried girls, none of them wore the high clay headdress or the matron's leather cloak, and above their short beaded skirts their bodies were oiled and stark naked so their pert young breasts joggled and bounced to the rhythm of the song of welcome and the wedding guests murmured and smiled appreciatively. Although deep down old Sangane Dinizulu disapproved of marriage outside the tribe of Zulu, the *lobola* had been good and his future son-in-law was, by all accounts, a man of stature and importance. None could reasonably object to suitors of this calibre, and as there might be others like him in the bridegroom's party Sangane was not loath to show off his wares.

The girls knelt in front of the guests, hanging their heads and averting their eyes shyly. Giggling in response to the knowing looks and sly sallies of the men, they proffered the brimming beer-pots, and then withdrew swinging their hips so their skirts swirled up and pert young buttocks peeked provocatively from beneath them.

The beer-pots were so heavy that they required both hands to lift, and when they were lowered, there were thick white moustaches on the upper lips of the guests. Noisily they licked them away and the laughter became more relaxed and friendly.

When the beer-pots were empty, Sangane Dinizulu stood before them and made a short speech of welcome. Then they formed up again and started up the road that climbed the escarpment, but now Zulu ran shoulder to shoulder with Ovambo and Xhosa. Moses Gama had never believed he would see that happen. It was a beginning, he thought, a fine beginning, but there remained to be scaled a range of endeavour as high as the peaks of the Drakensberg Mountains which rose out of the blue distances before them as they topped the escarpment.

Sangane Dinizulu had set the pace up the slope, although he must be all of seventy years of age, and now he led the cavalcade of men and animals down to his kraal. It was sited on a grassy slope above the river. The huts of his many wives were arranged in a circle, beehives of smooth thatch each with an entrance so low that a man must stoop to enter. In the centre of the circle was the old man's hut. It also was a perfect beehive, but much grander than the others, and the thatch had been plaited into intricate patterns. It was the home of a chieftain of Zulu, a son of the heavens.

On the grassy slope was assembled a multitude, a

thousand or more of the most important men of the tribe with all their senior wives. Many of them had travelled for days to be here, and they squatted in clumps and clusters down the slope, each chieftain surrounded by his own retainers.

When the bridegroom's party came over the crest they rose as one man, shouting their greetings and drumming their shields, and Sangane Dinizulu led them down to the entrance of the kraal where he paused and spread his arms for silence. The wedding guests settled down again comfortably in the grass. Only the chieftains sat on their carved stools of office, and while the young girls carried the beer-pots amongst them Sangane Dinizulu made his wedding speech.

First he related the history of the tribe, and particularly of his own clan of Dinizulu. He recited their battle honours and the valiant deeds of his ancestors. These were many and it took a long time, but the guests were well content for the black beer-pots were replenished as swiftly as they were emptied, and although the old ones knew the history of the tribe as intimately as did Sangane Dinizulu, its repetition gave them endless satisfaction, as though it were an anchor in the restless sea of life. As long as the history and the customs persisted, the tribe was secure.

At last Sangane Dinizulu was done, and in a voice that was hoarse and scratchy, he ended, 'There are those amongst you who have queried the wisdom of a daughter of Zulu marrying with a man of another tribe. I respect these views, for I also have been consumed by doubts and have pondered long and seriously.'

Now the older heads in the congregation were nodding, and a few hostile glances were shot at the bridegroom's party, but Sangane Dinizulu went on.

'I had these same doubts when my daughter asked my permission to leave the hut of her mother and journey to *goldi*, the place of gold, and to work in the great hospital at

Baragwanath. Now I am persuaded that what she has done was right and proper. She is a daughter of which an old man can be proud. She is a woman of the future.'

He faced his peers calmly and resolutely, seeing the doubt in their eyes, but ignoring it.

'The man who will be her husband is not of Zulu – but he also is a man of the future. Most of you have heard his name. You know him as a man of force and power. I am persuaded that by giving him my daughter in marriage I am once again doing what is right – for my daughter and for the tribe.'

When the old man sat down on his stool they were silent, serious and withdrawn, and they looked uneasily towards the bridegroom where he squatted at the head of his party.

Moses Gama rose to his feet, and strode up the slope from where he could look down upon them. He was silhouetted against the sky, his height was emphasized and the royal leopard skin declared his lineage.

'O people of Zulu, I greet you.' That deep thrilling voice reached to everyone of them, carrying clearly in the silence, and they stirred and murmured with surprise as they realized that he was speaking fluent Zulu.

'I have come to take one of the most comely daughters of your tribe, but as part of the marriage price I bring you a dream and a promise,' he began, and they were attentive but puzzled. Slowly the mood changed as he went on to set out his vision for them, a unification of the tribes and a sloughing off of the white domination under which they had existed for three hundred years. The older men became more and more uneasy as they listened, they shook their heads and exchanged angry glances, some of them muttered aloud, an unusual discourtesy towards an important guest, but what he was suggesting was a destruction of the old ways, a denial of the customs and orders of society which had held together the fabric of their lives. In its place he was offering something strange and untested, a world turned upside down, a chaos in which old values and proven codes were discarded with nothing to replace them except wild words – and like all old men, they were afraid of change.

With the younger men it was different. They listened, and his words warmed them like the flames of the camp fire in the frosty winter night. One of them listened more intently than all the rest. Joseph Dinizulu was not yet fourteen years of age, but the blood of great Chaka charged his veins and pumped up his heart. These words, strange at first, began to sing in his head like one of the old fighting chants, and his breath came quicker as he heard Moses Gama end his bridal speech.

'So, people of Zulu, I come to give you back the land of your fathers. I come to give you the promise that once again a black man will rule in Africa, and that as surely as tomorrow's sun will rise, the future belongs to us.'

All of a sudden Joseph Dinizulu was struck by a sense of destiny.

'A black man will rule in Africa.'

For Joseph Dinizulu, as for many others there that day, the world would never be the same again.

Victoria Dinizulu waited in her mother's hut. She sat on the earthen floor with a tanned kaross of hyrax fur under her. She wore the traditional dress of a Zulu bride. The beadwork had been sewn by her mother and sisters, intricate and beautiful, each pattern carrying a hidden message. There were strings of coloured beads around her wrists and her ankles, and necklaces of beads, while her short skirt of leather strips was beaded and strings of beads were plaited into her hair and draped around her waist. In one respect only did her costume differ from that of the traditional Zulu bride: her breasts were covered, as they had been since puberty when she had been baptized into the Anglican Church. She wore a blouse of striped silk in gay colours which complemented the rest of her costume.

As she sat in the centre of the hut, she listened intently to the voice of her bridegroom from without. It carried clearly to her, though she had to shush the other girls when they whispered and giggled. Every word struck her with the force of an arrow, and she felt her love and duty for the man who uttered them swell until they threatened to choke her.

The interior of the hut was gloomy as an ancient cathedral for there were no windows, and the air was hazy with wood smoke that uncoiled lazily from the central fire and rose to the small hole in the summit of the belled roof. The cathedral atmosphere enhanced her mood of reverence, and when the voice of Moses Gama ceased, the silence seemed to enter her heart. No cheers or shouted agreement followed his speech. The men of Zulu were silent and disturbed by it. Victoria could feel it even where she sat in the darkened hut.

'It is time now,' her mother whispered, and lifted her to her feet. 'Go with God,' she whispered, for her mother was a Christian and had introduced her to that religion.

'Be a good wife to this man,' she instructed, and led her to the entrance of the hut.

She stepped outside, into the dazzling sunlight. This was the moment for which the guests had been waiting, and when they saw how beautiful she was, they roared like bulls and drummed their shields. Her father came to greet her and lead her to the carved ebony stool at the entrance of the kraal, so that the *cimeza* ceremony could begin.

The *cimeza* was the 'closing of the eyes' and Victoria sat with her eyes tightly closed as the representatives of the various clans came forward one at a time to place their gifts before her. Only then was Victoria allowed to open her eyes and exclaim in wonder at the generosity of the givers. There were gifts of pots and blankets and ornaments, marvellously woven beadwork, and envelopes of money.

Shrewdly old Sangane calculated the value of each as he stood behind her stool, and he was grinning with satisfaction when at last he gave the signal to his son Joseph to drive in the feast. He had set aside twelve fat steers for the slaughter, a gesture that proved him to be even more generous than the bearers of the wedding gifts, but then he was a great man and head of a noble clan. The chosen warriors came forward to slaughter the steers, and their mournful death bellows and the rank smell of fresh blood in the dust soon gave way to the aroma from the cooking fires that drifted blue smoke across the hillside.

At a gesture from old Sangane Moses Gama strode up the slope to the entrance of the kraal and Victoria rose to her feet to meet him. They faced each other and once again a silence fell. The guests were awed by this couple, the groom so tall and commanding, the bride beautiful and nubile.

Involuntarily they craned forward as Victoria unclipped the *ucu* string of beads from around her waist. This was the symbol of her virginity, and she knelt before Moses and, with both hands cupped in the formal and polite gesture, she offered him the beads. As he accepted her and her gift, a great shout went up from the guests. It was done, Moses Gama was her husband and her master at last.

Now the feasting and the beer-drinking could begin in earnest, and the raw red meat was heaped upon the coals and snatched off again barely singed, while the beer-pots passed from hand to hand and the young girls went swinging down the slope bearing fresh pots upon their heads.

Suddenly there was an uproar and a band of plumed

warriors came dashing up the slope towards where Victoria sat at the kraal entrance. They were her brothers and half-brothers and nephews, even Joseph Dinizulu was amongst them, and they shouted their war cries as they came to rescue their sister from this stranger who would take her from their midst.

However, the Buffaloes were ready for them, and with Hendrick at their head and sticks whistling and hissing, they rushed in to prevent the abduction. The women wailed and ululated and the fighting-sticks clattered and whacked on flesh, and the warriors howled and circled and charged at each other in a fine mist of dust.

It was for this that all metal weapons were strictly banned from the ceremony, for the fighting, which was at first playful, soon heated up and blood dripped and bones cracked before the abductors allowed themselves to be driven off. The blood was staunched with a handful of dust clapped on the wound, and both victors and vanquished had worked up a fine thirst and shouted to the girls to bring more beer. The uproar subsided for only a few minutes to be resumed almost immediately as from the top of the slope came the rumble of motor cars.

The children raced up the hill and began to clap and sing as two big motor cars appeared over the brow and came bumping slowly over the rough track that led to the kraal.

In the leading vehicle was a large white woman, with a red face as lined and craggy as that of a bulldog, and a wide-brimmed old-fashioned hat on her head from under which grey hair curled untidily.

'Who is she?' Moses demanded.

'Anna, Lady Courtney,' Victoria exclaimed. 'She was the one who encouraged me to leave here and go into the world.'

Impulsively Victoria ran forward to meet the vehicle,

and when Lady Courtney descended ponderously, she embraced her.

'So, my child, you have come back to us.' Lady Courtney's accent was still thick, though she had lived thirty-five years in Africa.

'Not for long.' Victoria laughed and Lady Courtney looked at her fondly. Once the child had served in the big house as one of her house maids, until her bright beauty and intelligence had convinced Lady Courtney that she was superior to such menial work.

'Where is this man who is taking you away?' she demanded, and Victoria took her hand.

'First you must greet my father, then I will introduce you to my husband.'

From the second motor car a middle-aged couple climbed down to be enthusiastically greeted by the crowd that pressed forward around them. The man was tall and dapper, with the bearing of a soldier. He was tanned by the sun and his eyes had the far-away look of the outdoor man. He twirled his moustaches and took his wife on his arm. She was almost as tall and even slimmer than he was, and despite the streaks of grey in her hair, she was still an unusually handsome woman.

Sangane Dinizulu came to greet them.

'I see you, Jamela!' His dignity was somewhat tempered by a happy grin of welcome, and Colonel Mark Anders answered him in perfectly colloquial Zulu.

'I see you, old man.' The term was one of respect. 'May all your cattle and all your wives grow fat and sleek.'

Sangane turned to his wife Storm, who was the daughter of old General Sean Courtney. 'I see you, *Nkosikazi*, you bring honour to my kraal.' The bond between the two families was like steel. It went back to another century and had been tested a thousand times.

'Oh, Sangane, I am so happy for you this day – and for

Victoria.' Storm left her husband and went quickly to embrace the Zulu girl.

'I wish you joy and many fine sons, Vicky,' she told her, and Victoria answered,

'I owe you and your family so much, *Nkosikazi*. I will never be able to repay you.'

'Don't ever try,' Storm told her with mock severity. 'I feel as though my own daughter is getting married today. Introduce us to your husband, Vicky.'

Now Moses Gama came towards them, and when Storm greeted him in Zulu, he replied gravely in English, 'How do you do, Mrs Anders. Victoria has spoken of you and your family very often.'

When at last he turned to Mark Anders, he proffered his right hand.

'How do you do, Colonel?' Mosses asked, and a wry smile flitted across his lips as he saw the white man hesitate momentarily before accepting the handshake. It was unusual for men to greet each other thus across the dividing line of colour, and despite his fluency in the language and his pretended affection for the Zulu people, Moses recognized this man.

Colonel Mark Anders was an anachronism, a son of the English Queen Victoria, a soldier who had fought in two world wars, and the warden of Chaka's Gate National Park which he had saved from the poachers and despoilers by dedication and sheer bloody-mindedness, and made into one of Africa's most celebrated wild-life sanctuaries. He loved the wild animals of Africa with a kind of paternal passion, protecting and cherishing them, and to only a slightly less degree his attitude towards the black tribes, especially the Zulus, was the same, paternalistic and condescending. By this definition he was the mortal enemy of Moses Gama, and as they looked into each other's eyes, they both recognized this fact.

'I have heard the lion roar from afar,' Mark Anders said in Zulu. 'Now I meet the beast face to face.'

'I have heard of you as well, Colonel,' Moses replied, pointedly speaking English.

'Victoria is a gentle child,' Mark Anders persisted in his use of Zulu. 'We all hope you will not teach her your fierce ways.'

'She will be a dutiful wife,' Moses said in English. 'She will do what I ask of her, I am sure.'

Storm had been following the exchange, sensing the innate hostility between the two men and now she intervened smoothly.

'If you are ready, Moses, we can all go down to Theuniskraal for the ceremony.'

Victoria and her mother had insisted on a Christian ceremony to reinforce traditional tribe wedding. Now Sangane and most of the other guests, who were pagan and ancestor-worshippers, remained at the kraal, while the diminished bridal party crowded into the two motor vehicles.

Theuniskraal was the home of Anna, Lady Courtney and the original seat of the Courtney family. It stood amongst its sprawling lawns and unruly gardens of palms and bougainvillaea and pride of India trees at the foot of the Ladyburg escarpment. It was a rambling old building of oddly assorted architectural styles, and beyond the gardens stretched endless fields of sugar cane, that dipped and undulated to the breeze like the swells of the ocean.

The wedding party trooped into the house to change into garb more suitable than beads and furs and feathers for the second ceremony while Lady Courtney and the family went to greet the Anglican priest in the marquee that had been set up on the front lawn.

When the bridegroom and his attendants came out on to the lawns half an hour later, they wore dark lounge suits and Victoria's elder brother, who had pranced and swirled his plumes in the *giya* just a few hours before, now wore his Law Association tie in an impeccable Windsor knot and aviator-style dark glasses against the glare of Theuniskraal's whitewashed walls, as he chatted affably with the Courtney family, while they waited for the bride.

Victoria's mother was decked out in one of Lady Courtney's cast-off caftans, for the two ladies were of similar build, and she was already sampling the fare that was laid out on the long trestle table in the marquee. Colonel Mark Anders and the Anglican priest stood a little aside from the main group; men of the same generation, they both found the proceedings disquieting and unnatural. It had taken all Storm's powers to persuade the priest to perform the ceremony, and then he had only agreed on condition that the wedding was not held in his own church in the village where his conservative white congregation might take offence.

'Damned if we weren't all a sight better off in the old days when everybody knew their place instead of trying to ape their betters,' Mark Anders grumbled, and the priest nodded.

'No sense in looking for trouble—' He broke off as Victoria came out on to the wide verandah. Storm Anders had helped her select her full-length white satin wedding dress with a wreath of tiny red tea roses holding the long veil in place around her brow. The contrast of red and white against her dark and glossy skin was striking and her joy was infectious. Even Mark Anders forgot his misgivings for the moment, as Lady Courtney at the piano struck up the wedding march.

At her father's kraal, Victoria's family had built a magnificent new hut for her nuptial night. Her brothers and half-brothers had cut the wattle saplings and the trunk for the central post and plaited the stripped green branches into the shape of the beehive. Then her mother and sisters and half-sisters had done the women's work of thatching, carefully combing the long grass stems and lacing the crisp bundles onto the wattle framework, packing and trimming and weaving them until the finished structure was smooth and symmetrical and the brushed grass stems shone like polished brass.

Everything the hut contained was new, from the three-legged pot to the lamp and the blankets and the magnificent kaross of hyrax and monkey skins which was the gift of Victoria's sisters, lovingly tanned and sewn by them into a veritable work of art.

At the cooking fire in the centre of the hut Victoria worked alone, preparing the first meal for her husband, while she listened to the shouted laughter of the guests outside in the night. The millet beer was mild. However, the women had brewed hundreds of gallons and the guests had been drinking since early morning.

Now she heard the bridegroom's party approaching the hut. There was singing and loud suggestive advice, cries of encouragement and rude exhortations to duty, and then Moses Gama stooped through the entrance. He straightened and stood tall over her, his head brushing the curved roof and outside the voices of his comrades retreated and dwindled.

Still kneeling, Victoria sat back on her heels and looked up at him. Now at last she had discarded her Western clothing and wore for the last time the short beaded skirt of the virgin. In the soft ruddy light of the fire her naked upper body had the dark patina of antique amber.

'You are very beautiful,' he said, for she was the very essence of Nguni womanhood. He came to her and took her hands and lifted her to her feet.

'I have prepared food for you,' she whispered huskily.

'There will be time later to eat.'

He led her to the piled kaross and she stood submissively while he untied the thong of her apron and then lifted her in his arms and laid her on the bed of soft fur.

As a girl she had played the games with the boys in the reed banks beside the waterhole, and out on the open grassy veld where she had gone with the other girls to gather firewood conveniently close to where the cattle were being herded. These games of touching and exploring, of rubbing and fondling, right up to the forbidden act of intromission, were sanctioned by tribal custom and smiled at by the elders, but none of them had fully prepared her for the power and skill of this man, or for the sheer magnificence of him. He reached deeply into her body and touched her very soul so that much later in the night she clung to him and whispered:

'Now I am more than just your wife, I am your slave to the end of my days.'

In the dawn her joy was blighted, and though her lovely moon face remained serene, she wept within when he told her, 'There will only be one more night – on the road back to Johannesburg. Then I must leave you.'

'For how long?' she asked.

'Until my work is done,' he replied, then his expression softened and he stroked her face. 'You knew that it must be so. I warned you that when you married me, you were marrying the struggle.'

'You warned me,' she agreed in a husky whisper. 'But there was no way that I could guess at the agony of your leaving.'

They rose early the following morning. Moses had acquired a secondhand Buick, old and shabby enough not to excite interest or envy, but one of Hendrick Tabaka's expert mechanics had overhauled the engine and tightened the suspension, leaving the exterior untouched. In it they would return to Johannesburg.

Though the sun had not yet risen, the entire kraal was astir, and Victoria's sisters had prepared breakfast for them. After they had eaten came the hard part of taking leave of her family. She knelt before her father.

'Go in peace, my daughter,' he told her fondly. 'We will think of you often. Bring your sons to visit us.'

Victoria's mother wept and keened as though it were a funeral, not a wedding, and Victoria could not comfort her although she embraced her and protested her love and duty until the other daughters took her away.

Then there were all her stepmothers and her half-brothers and half-sisters, and the uncles and aunts and cousins who had come from the furthest reaches of Zululand. Victoria had to make her farewells to all of them, though some partings were more poignant than others. One of these was her goodbye to Joseph Dinizulu, her favourite of all her relatives. Although he was a half-brother and seven years younger than she was, a special bond had always existed between them. The two of them were the brightest and most gifted of their generation in the family, and because Joseph lived at Drake's Farm with one of the elder brothers, they had been able to continue their friendship.

However, Joseph would not be returning to the Wit-watersrand. He had written the entrance exams and been accepted by the exclusive multi-racial school, Waterford, in Swaziland, and Anna, Lady Courtney would be paying his school fees. Ironically, this was the same school to which Hendrick Tabaka was sending his sons, Wellington and Raleigh. There would be opportunity for their rivalry to flourish.

'Promise me you will work hard, Joseph,' Vicky said. 'Learning makes a man strong.'

'I will be strong,' Joseph assured her. The elation that Moses Gama's speech had aroused in him still persisted. 'Can I come and visit you and your husband, Vicky? He is a man, the kind of man I will want to be one day.'

Vicky told Moses what the child had said. They were alone in the old Buick, all the wedding gifts and Vicky's possessions filling the boot and piled in the back seat, and they were leaving that great littoral amphitheatre of Natal, going up over the tail of the Drakensberg range onto the high veld of the Transvaal.

'The children are the future,' Moses nodded, staring ahead at the steep blue serpent of road that climbed the escarpment, past the green hill of Majuba where the Boers had thrashed the British in the first of many battles with them. 'The old men are beyond hope. You saw them at the wedding, how they kicked and baulked like unbroken oxen when I tried to show them the way – but the children, ah the children!' He smiled. 'They are like fresh clean sheets of paper. You can write on them what you will. The old men are stone-hard and impermeable, but the children are clay, eager clay waiting for the shaping hands of the potter.' He held up one of his hands. It was long and shapely, the hand of a surgeon or an artist, and the palm was a delicate shade of pink, smooth and not calloused by labour. 'Children lack any sense of morality, they are without fear, and death is beyond their conception. These are all things they acquire later, by the teaching of their elders. They make perfect soldiers for they question nothing and it takes no great physical strength to pull a trigger. If an enemy strikes them down they become the perfect martyrs. The bleeding corpse of a child strikes horror and remorse into even the hardest heart. Yes, the children are our key to the future.

Your Christ knew it when he said "Suffer the little children to come unto me".'

Victoria twisted on the leather bench seat of the Buick and stared at him.

'Your words are cruel and blasphemous,' she whispered, torn by her love for him and her instinctive rejection of what he had just said.

'And yet your reaction proves their truth,' he said.

'But . . .' she paused, reluctant to ask, and fearful to hear his reply. 'But are you saying that we should use our children—' She broke off, and an image of the paediatric section of the hospital came into her mind. She had spent the happiest months of all her training amongst the little ones. 'Are you suggesting that you would use the children in the front line of the struggle – as soldiers?'

'If a child cannot grow up a free man, then he might as well die as a child,' Moses Gama said. 'Victoria, you have heard me say this before. It is time now that you learn to believe it. There is nothing I would not do, no price I would not pay, for our victory. If I have to see a thousand little children dead so that a hundred thousand more may live to grow up free men, then for me the bargain is a fair one.'

Then, for the very first time in her life, Victoria Dinizulu was truly afraid.

That night they stayed at Hendrick Tabaka's house in Drake's Farm Township, and it was well after midnight before they could go to the small bedroom that had been set aside for them because there were many who demanded Moses' attention, men from the Buffaloes and the mineworkers' union, a messenger from the council of the ANC and a dozen petitioners and supplicants who came quietly as jackals to the lion when the word flashed through the township that Moses Gama had returned.

At all these meetings Victoria was present, although she never spoke and sat quietly in a corner of the room. At first the men were surprised and puzzled, darting quick glances across at her and reluctant to come to their business until Moses pressed them. None of them was accustomed to having women present when serious matters were discussed. However, none of them could bring themselves to protest, until the ANC messenger came into the room. He was invested with all the power and importance of the council he represented, and so he was the first to speak about Victoria's presence.

'There is a woman here,' he said.

'Yes,' Moses nodded. 'But not just a woman, she is my wife.'

'It is not fitting,' said the messenger. 'It is not the custom. This is men's business.'

'It is our purpose and our aim to tear down and burn the old customs and to build up the new. In that endeavour we will need the help of all our people. Not just the men, but the women and children also.'

There was a long silence while the messenger fidgeted under Moses' dark unrelenting stare.

'The woman can remain,' he capitulated at last.

'Yes,' Moses nodded. 'My wife will remain.'

Later in the darkness of their bedroom, in the narrowness of the single bed, Victoria pressed close to him, the soft plastic curves of her body conforming to his hardness, and she said:

'You have honoured me by making me a part of your struggle. Like the children, I want to be a soldier. I have thought about it and I have discovered what I can do.'

'Tell me,' he invited.

'The women. I can organize the women. I can begin with the nurses of the hospital, and then the other women

– all of them. We must take our part in the struggle beside the men.'

His arms tightened around her. 'You are a lioness,' he said. 'A beautiful Zulu lioness.'

'I can feel your heartbeat,' she whispered, 'and my own heart beats in exact time to it.'

In the morning Moses drove her to the nurses' home at the hospital. She stood at the top of the steps and did not go into the building. He watched her in the rear-view mirror as he drove away and she was still standing there when he turned into the traffic, heading back towards Johannesburg and the suburb of Rivonia.

He was one of the first to arrive at Puck's Hill that morning to attend the council meeting to which the previous night's messenger had summoned him.

Marcus Archer met Moses on the verandah, and his smile was vitriolic as he greeted him. 'They say a man is incomplete until he marries – and only then is he finished.'

There were two men already seated at the long table in the kitchen which had always been used as their council chamber. They were both white men.

Bram Fischer was the scion of an eminent Afrikaner family whose father had been a judge-president of the Orange Free State. Though he was an expert on mining law, and a QC at the Johannesburg bar, he had also been a member of the old Communist Party and was a member of the ANC, and lately his practice had become almost entirely the defence of those accused under the racial laws that the Nationalist government had enacted since 1948. Although he was a charming and erudite man with a real concern for his countrymen of all races, Moses was wary of him. He was a starry-eyed believer in the eventual miraculous triumph of good over evil, and firmly opposed the formation of *Umkhonto we Sizwe*, the military branch of the ANC. His pacifist influence on the rest of the Congress set a brake on Moses' aspirations.

The other white man was Joe Cicero, a Lithuanian immigrant. Moses could guess why he had come to Africa – and who had sent him. He was one of the eagles, fierce-hearted as Moses was himself, and an ally when the need for direct and even violent action was discussed. Moses went to sit beside him, across the table from Fischer. He would need Joe Cicero's support this day.

Marcus Archer, who loved to cook, set a plate of devilled kidneys and *œufs ranchero* in front of him, but before Moses had finished his breakfast the others began to arrive. Nelson Mandela and his faithful ally Tambo arrived together, followed quickly by Walter Sisulu and Mbeki and the others, until the long table was crowded and cluttered with papers and dirty plates, with coffee cups and ashtrays which were soon overflowing with crushed cigarette butts.

The air was thick with tobacco smoke and Marcus' cooking aromas, and the talk was charged and serious as they tried to decide and agree exactly what were the objects of the defiance campaign.

'We have to stir the awareness of our people, to shake them out of their dumb cowlike acceptance of oppression.' Mandela put the premier proposition, and across from him Moses leaned forward.

'More important, we must awaken the conscience of the rest of the world, for that is the direction from which our ultimate salvation will come.'

'Our own people—' Mandela began, but Moses interrupted him.

'Our own people are powerless without weapons and training. The forces of oppression ranged against us are too powerful. We cannot triumph without arms.'

'You reject the way of the peace, then?' Mandela asked. 'You presuppose that freedom can only be won at the point of the gun?'

'The revolution must be tempered and made strong in

the blood of the masses,' Moses affirmed. 'That is always the way.'

'Gentlemen! Gentlemen!' Bram Fischer held up his hand to stop them. 'Let us return to the main body of the discussion. We agree that by our campaign of defiance we hope to stir our own people out of their lethargy and to attract the attention of the rest of the world. Those are our two main objects. Let us now decide on our secondary objects.'

'To establish the ANC as the only true vehicle of liberation,' Moses suggested. 'At present we have less than seven thousand members, but by the end of the campaign we should aim to have enrolled one hundred thousand more.' To this there was general agreement, even Mandela and Tambo nodded, and when the vote was taken it was unanimous and they could go on to discuss the details of the campaign.

It was a massive undertaking, for it was planned that the campaign should be nationwide and that it should be conducted simultaneously in every one of the main centres of the Union of South Africa so as to place the utmost strain on the resources of the government and to test the response of the forces of law and order.

'We must fill their gaols until they burst. We must offer ourselves up for arrest in our thousands until the machinery of tyranny breaks down under the strain,' Mandela told them.

For three more days they sat in the kitchen at Puck's Hill, working out and agreeing every minute detail, preparing the lists of names and places, putting together the timetable of action, the logistics of transport and communication, establishing the lines of control from the central committee down through the provincial headquarters of the movement, and ultimately to the regional cadres in every black township and location.

It was an onerous task but at last there was only one detail left to decide – the day on which it would begin. Now they all looked to Albert Luthuli at the head of the table and he did not hesitate.

'June the 26th,' he said, and when there was a murmur of agreement, he went on, 'So be it, then. We all know our tasks.' And he gave them the salute of upraised thumbs. '*Amandla!* Power! *Ngawethu!*'

When Moses went out to where the old Buick was parked beneath the gum trees, the sunset was filling the western sky with furnace colours of hot orange and smouldering red, and Joe Cicero was waiting for him. He leaned against the silvery trunk of one of the bluegum trees, with his arms folded over his broad chest, a bearlike figure, short and squat and powerful.

He straightened up as Moses came towards him.

'Can you give me a lift in to Braamfontein, comrade?' he asked, and Moses opened the door of the Buick for him, and they drove in silence for ten minutes before Joe said quietly, 'It is strange that you and I have never spoken privately.' His accent was elusive, but the planes of his pale face above the short dark fringe of beard were flat and Slavic and his eyes were dark as tar pools.

'Why is it so strange?' Moses asked.

'We share common views,' Joe replied. 'We are both true sons of the revolution.'

'Are you certain of that?'

'I am certain,' Joe nodded. 'I have studied you and listened to you with approval and admiration. I believe that you are one of the steely men that the revolution needs, comrade.'

Moses did not reply. He kept his eyes on the road, and his expression impassive, letting the silence draw out, forcing the other man to break it.

'What are your feelings towards Mother Russia?' Joe asked softly at last, and Moses considered the question.

'Russia has never had colonies in Africa,' Moses answered carefully. 'I know that she gives support to the struggle in Malaya and Algeria and Kenya. I believe she is a true ally of the oppressed peoples of this world.'

Joe smiled and lit another Springbok cigarette from the flat maroon and white pack. He was a chain-smoker and his stubby fingers were stained dark brown.

'The road to freedom is steep and rocky,' he murmured. 'And the revolution is never secure. The proletariat must be protected from itself by the revolutionary guards.'

'Yes,' Moses agreed. 'I have read the works of both Marx and Lenin.'

'Then I was correct,' Joe Cicero murmured. 'You are a believer. We should be friends – good friends. There are difficult days ahead and there will be a need for steely men.' He reached over the back seat and picked up his attaché case. 'You can let me out at the central railway station, comrade,' he said.

It had been fully dark for two hours by the time Moses reached the camp in the gorge below the Sundi Caves and parked the Buick behind the Nissen hut that was the expedition's office and laboratory, and he went up the path to Tara Courtney's tent, stepping softly so as not to alarm her. He saw her silhouette against the canvas side. She was lying on her stretcher bed reading by the light of the petromax lantern, and he saw her start as he scratched on the canvas.

'Don't be afraid,' he called softly. 'It's me.'

And her reply was low but quivering with joy. 'Oh, God, I thought you'd never come.'

She was in a frenzy for him. Her other pregnancies had always left her feeling nauseous and bloated, and the thought of sexual contact during that time had been repugnant. But now, even though she was over three months pregnant, her wanting was a kind of madness. Moses seemed to sense her need, but did not try to match it. He lay naked upon his back on the stretcher, and he was like a pinnacle of black granite. Tara hurled herself upon him to impale herself. She was sobbing and uttering little cries and yelps. At once both clumsy and adroit, her body, not yet swollen by the child within her, thrashed and churned above him as he lay quiescent and unmoving, and she went on beyond physical endurance, beyond the limits of flesh, insatiable and desperate for him, until exhaustion at last overcame her and she rolled off him and lay panting weakly, her chestnut hair darkened by her own sweat and plastered to her forehead and neck, and there was a thin pink colouring of blood on the front of her thighs, so wild had been her passion.

Moses drew the sheet over her and held her until she had stopped shaking and her breathing had quietened, and then he said, 'It will begin soon – the date has been agreed.'

Tara was so transported that for a while she did not understand, and she shook her head stupidly.

'June the 26th,' Moses said. 'Across the land, in every city, all at the same time. Tomorrow I will be going to Port Elizabeth in the Eastern Cape to command the campaign there.'

That was hundreds of miles from Johannesburg, and she had come to be near him. With the melancholy of after-love upon her, Tara felt cheated and abused. She wanted to protest but with an effort checked herself.

'How long will you be away?'

'Weeks.'

'Oh, Moses!' she began, and then warned by his quick frown, she relapsed into silence.

'The American woman – the Godolphin woman. Have you contacted her? Without publicity the value of our efforts will be halved.'

'Yes.' Tara paused. She had been on the point of telling him that it was all arranged, that Kitty Godolphin would meet him any time he wanted, but she stopped herself. Instead of handing her over to Moses and standing aside, here was her chance to stay close to him.

'Yes, I have spoken to her. We met at her hotel, she is eager to meet you but she is out of town at the moment, in Swaziland.'

'That is no good,' Moses muttered. 'I had hoped to see her before I left.'

'I could bring her down to Port Elizabeth,' Tara cut in eagerly. 'She will be back in a day or two and I will bring her to you.'

'Can you get away from here?' he asked dubiously.

'Yes, of course. I will bring the television people down to you in my own car.'

Moses grunted uncertainly, and was silent while he thought about it, and then he nodded.

'Very well. I will explain how you will be able to contact me when you get there. I will be in the township of New Brighton, just outside the city.'

'Can I be with you, Moses? Can I stay with you?'

'You know that is impossible.' He was irritated by her persistence. 'No whites are allowed in the township without a pass.'

'The television team will not be able to help you much if we are kept out of the township,' Tara said quickly. 'We should be close to you to be of any use to the struggle.' Cunningly she had linked herself to Kitty Godolphin, and she held her breath as he thought about it.

'Perhaps,' he nodded, and she exhaled softly. He had accepted it. 'Yes. There might be a way. There is a mission hospital run by German nuns in the township. They are friends. You could stay there. I will arrange it.'

She tried not to let him see her triumph. She would be with him, that was all that was important. It was madness, but though her body was bruised and sore, already she wanted him again. It was not physical lust, it was more than that. It was the only way she could possess him, even for a few fleeting minutes. When she had him locked in her body, he belonged to her alone.

Tara was puzzled by Kitty Godolphin's attitude towards her. She was accustomed to people, both men and women, responding immediately to her own warm personality and good looks. Kitty was different, from the very beginning there had been a cold-eyed reserve and an innate hostility in her. Very swiftly Tara had seen beyond the angelic, little-girl image that Kitty so carefully projected, but even after she had recognized the tough and ruthless person beneath, she could find no logical reason for the woman's attitude. After all Tara was offering her an important assignment, and Kitty was examining the gift as though it were a live scorpion.

'I don't understand,' she protested, her voice and eyes snapping. 'You told me we could do the interview here in Johannesburg. Now you want me to traipse off into the deep sticks somewhere.'

'Moses Gama has to be there. Something important is about to take place—'

'What is so important?' Kitty demanded, fists on her lean denim-clad hips. 'What we agreed was important also.'

Most people, from leading politicians and international stars of sport and entertainment down to the lowest nonentity, were ready to risk slipping a spinal disc in their eagerness to appear for even the briefest moment on the little square screen. It was Kitty Godolphin's right, a semi-divine right, to decide who would be accorded that opportunity and who would be denied it. Moses Gama's cavalier behaviour was insulting. He had been chosen, and instead of displaying the gratitude which was Kitty Godolphin's due, he was setting conditions.

'Just what is so important that he cannot make the effort of common courtesy?' she repeated.

'I'm sorry, Miss Godolphin, I can't tell you that.'

'Well, then, I'm sorry also, Mrs Courtney, but you tell Moses Gama from me that he can go straight to hell without passing Go and without collecting his two hundred dollars.'

'You aren't serious!' Tara hadn't expected that.

'I have never been more serious in my life.' Kitty rolled her wrist to look at her Rolex. 'Now, if you will excuse me, I have more important matters to attend to.'

'All right,' Tara gave in at once. 'I will risk it. I'll tell you what is going to happen . . .' Tara paused while she considered the consequences, and then asked, 'You will keep it to yourself, what I am about to tell you?'

'Darling, if there is a good story in it, they wouldn't get it out of me with thumbscrew and hot irons – that is, not until I splash it across the screen myself.'

Tara told her in a rush of words, getting it out quickly before she could change her mind. 'It will be a chance to film him at work, to see him with his people, to watch him defying the forces of oppression and bigotry.'

She saw Kitty hesitating and knew that she had to think quickly.

'However, I should warn you, there may be danger. The confrontation could turn to violence and even bloodshed,' she said, and she had got it exactly right.

'Hank!' Kitty Godolphin shouted through to the lounge of her suite where the camera crew were strewn over the furniture like the survivors of a bomb blast, listening at full volume of the radio to the new rock 'n' roll sensation warning them to keep off his blue suede shoes.

'Hank!' Kitty raised her voice above Presley's. 'Get the cameras packed. We are going to a place called Port Elizabeth. If we can find where the hell it is.'

They drove through the night in Tara's Packard, and the suspension sagged under the weight of bodies and camera equipment. In his travels around the country Hank had discovered that cannabis grew as a weed around most of the villages in the reserves of Zululand and the Transkei. In an environment that the plant found agreeable, it reached the size of a small tree. Only a few of the older generation of black tribesmen smoked the dried leaves, and although it was proscribed as a noxious plant and listed as a dangerous drug, its use was so localized and restricted to the more primitive blacks in the remote areas – for no white person or educated African would lower himself to smoke it – that the authorities made little effort to prevent its cultivation and sale. Hank had found an endless supply of what he declared to be 'pure gold' for the payment of pennies.

'Man, a sack of this stuff on the streets of Los Angeles would fetch a hundred thousand dollars,' he murmured contentedly as he lit a hand-rolled cigarette and settled down on the back seat of the Packard. The heavy incense of the leaves filled the interior, and after a few draws Hank passed the cigarette to Kitty in the front seat. Kitty drew on the butt deeply and held the smoke in her lungs, as long as she was able, before blowing it out in a pale streamer against the windscreen. Then she offered the butt to Tara.

'I don't smoke tobacco,' Tara told her politely, and they all laughed.

'That ain't baccy, sweetheart,' Hank told her.

'What is it?'

'You call it *dagga* here.'

'*Dagga*.' Tara was shocked. She remembered that Centaine had fired one of her houseboys who smoked it.

'He dropped my Rosenthal tureen, the one that belonged

278

to Czar Nicholas,' Centaine had complained. 'Once they start on that stuff they become totally useless.'

'No thanks,' Tara said quickly, and thought how angry Shasa would be if he knew that she had been offered it. That thought gave her pause and she changed her mind. 'Oh, all right.' She took the butt, steering the Packard with one hand. 'What do I do?'

'Just suck it in and hold it down,' Kitty advised, 'and ride the glow.'

The smoke scratched her throat and burned her lungs, but the thought of Shasa's outrage gave her determination. She fought the urge to cough and held it down.

Slowly she felt herself relaxing, and a mild glow of euphoria made her body seem air-light and cleansed her mind. All the agonies of her soul became trivial and fell behind her.

'I feel good,' she murmured, and when they laughed, she laughed with them and drove on into the night.

In the early morning before it was fully light, they reached the coast, skirting the bay of Algoa where the Indian Ocean took a deep bite out of the continent, and the green waters were chopped to a white froth by the wind.

'Where do we go from here?' Kitty asked.

'The black township of New Brighton,' Tara told her. 'There is a mission run by German nuns, a teaching and nursing order, the Sisters of St Magdalene. They are expecting us. We aren't really allowed to stay in the township, but they have arranged it.'

Sister Nunziata was a handsome blonde woman, not much older than forty years. She had a clear scrubbed-looking skin and her manner was brisk and efficient. She wore the light grey cotton habit of the order, and a white shoulder-length veil.

'Mrs Courtney, I have been expecting you. Our mutual friend will be here later this morning. You will want to 'bathe and rest.' She led them to the cells that had been set aside for them and apologized for the simple comforts they contained. Kitty and Tara shared a cell. The floor was bare cement, the only decoration was a crucifix on the white-washed wall, and the springs of the iron bedsteads were covered with thin hard coir mattresses.

'She's just great,' Kitty enthused. 'I must get her on film. Nuns always make good footage.'

As soon as they had bathed and unpacked their equipment, Kitty had her crew out filming. She recorded a good interview with Sister Nunziata, her German accent lending interest to her statements, and then they filmed the black children in the schoolyard and the out-patients waiting outside the clinic.

Tara was awed by the girl's energy, her quick mind and glib tongue, and her eye for angle and subject as she directed the shooting. It made Tara feel superfluous, and her own lack of talent and creative skill irked her. She found herself resenting the other girl for having pointed up her inadequacies so graphically.

Then everything else was irrelevant. A nondescript old Buick sedan pulled into the mission yard and a tall figure climbed out and came towards them. Moses Gama wore a light blue open-neck shirt, the short sleeves exposed the sleek muscle in his upper arms and neck, and his tailored blue slacks were belted around his narrow waist. Tara didn't have to say anything, they all knew immediately who he was as Kitty Godolphin breathed softly beside her, 'My God, he is beautiful as a black panther.'

Tara's resentment of her flared into seething hatred. She wanted to rush to Moses and embrace him so that Kitty might know he was hers, but instead she stood dumbly while he stopped in front of Kitty and held out his right hand.

'Miss Godolphin? At last,' he said, and his voice brought out a rush of goose-bumps down Tara's arms.

The rest of the day was spent in reconnaisance and the filming of more background material, this time with Moses as the central figure in each shot. The New Brighton township was typical of the South African urban locations, rows of identical low-cost housing laid out in geometric squares of narrow roads, some of them paved and others rutted and filled with muddy puddles in which the pre-school children and toddlers, many of them naked or dressed only in ragged shorts, played raucously.

Kitty filmed Moses picking his way around the puddles, squatting to talk to the children, lifting a marvellously photogenic little black cherub in his arms and wiping his snotty nose.

'That's great stuff,' Kitty enthused. 'He's going to look magnificent on film.'

The children followed Moses, laughing and skipping behind him as though he were the Pied Piper, and the women attracted by the commotion came out of the squalid little cottages. When they recognized Moses and saw the cameras, they began to ululate and dance. They were natural actresses and completely without inhibition, and Kitty was everywhere, calling for shots and unusual camera angles, clearly delighted by the footage she was getting.

In the late afternoon the working men began to arrive back in the township by bus and train. Most of them were production-line workers in the vehicle assembly plants of Ford and General Motors, or factory-workers in the tyre companies of Goodyear and Firestone, for Port Elizabeth and its satellite town of Uitenhage formed the centre of the country's motor vehicle industry.

Moses walked the narrow streets with the camera following him, and he stopped to talk to the returning workers, while the camera recorded their complaints and problems, most of which were the practical everyday worries of making ends meet while remaining within the narrow lines demarcated by the forest of racial laws. Kitty could edit most of that out, but every one of them mentioned the 'show on demand' clause of the pass laws as the thing they hated and feared most. In every little vignette they filmed Moses Gama was the central heroic figure.

'By the time I've finished with him, he will be as famous as Martin Luther King,' Kitty enthused.

They joined the nuns for their frugal evening meal, and afterwards Kitty Godolphin was still not satisfied. Outside one of the cottages near the mission a family was cooking on an open fire, and Kitty had Moses join them, hunched over the fire in the night with the flames lighting his face, adding drama to his already massive presence as she filmed him while he spoke. In the background one of the women was singing a lullaby to the infant at her breast, and there were the murmurous sounds of the location, the soft cries of the children and the distant yapping of pariah dogs.

Moses Gama's words were poignant and moving, spoken in that deep thrilling voice, as he described the agony of his land and his people, so that Tara, listening to him in the darkness, found tears running down her face.

In the morning Kitty left her team at the mission, and without the camera the three of them, Kitty and Tara and Moses, drove in the Buick to the railway station that served the township and watched the black commuters swarm like hiving bees through the station entrance marked NON WHITES – NIE BLANKES, crowding onto the platform reserved for blacks, and as soon as the train pulled in flooding into the coaches set aside for them.

Through the other entrance, marked WHITES ONLY – BLANKES ALLEENLIK, a few white officials and others who had business in the township sauntered and unhurriedly entered the first-class coaches at the rear of the train where they sat on green leather-covered seats and gazed out through glass at the black swarm on the opposite platform with detached expressions as though they were viewing creatures of another species.

'I've got to try and get that,' Kitty muttered. 'I've got to get that reaction on film.' She was busily scribbling notes in her pad, sketching rough maps of the station layout and marking in camera sites and angles.

Before noon Moses excused himself. 'I have to meet the local organizers and make the final plans for tomorrow,' and he drove away in the Buick.

Tara took Kitty and the team down to the seaside at St George's Strand, and they filmed the bathers on the beaches lying under the signboards BLANKES ALLEENLIK – WHITES ONLY. School was out and tanned young people, the girls in bikinis and the boys with short haircuts and frank open faces, lolled on the white sand, or played beach games and surfed the rolling green waves.

When Kitty asked them, 'How would you feel if black people came to swim here?' some of them giggled nervously at a question they had never considered before:

'They aren't allowed to come here – they've got their own beaches.'

And at least one was indignant. 'They can't come here and look at our girls in bathing-costumes.' He was a beefy young man with sea salt caked in his sun-streaked hair and skin peeling from his sunburned nose.

'But wouldn't you look at the black girls in their bathing costumes?' Kitty asked innocently.

'*Sis*, man!' said the surfer, his handsome tanned features contorted with utter disgust at the suggestion.

'It's just too good to be true!' Kitty marvelled at her own fortune. 'I'll cut that in with some footage I've got of a beautiful black dancer in a Soweto night club.'

On the way back to the mission Kitty asked Tara to stop at the New Brighton railway station once again, for a final reconnaisance. They left the cameras in the Packard and two white-uniformed railway constables watched them with idle uninterest as they wandered around the almost deserted platforms that during the rush hours swarmed with thousands of black commuters. Quietly Kitty pointed out to her team the locations she had chosen earlier, and explained to them what shots she would be striving for.

That night Moses joined them for the evening meal in the mission refectory, and though the conversation was light and cheerful there was a hint of tension in their laughter. When Moses left, Tara went out with him to where the Buick was parked in the darkness behind the mission clinic.

'I want to be with you tonight,' she told him pathetically. 'I feel so alone without you.'

'That is not possible.'

'It's dark – we could go for a drive to the beach,' she pleaded.

'The police patrols are looking for just that sort of thing,' Moses told her. 'You would see yourself in the *Sunday Times* next weekend.'

'Make love to me here, please, Moses,' and he was angry.

'Your selfishness is that of a spoilt child – you think only of yourself and your own desires, even now when we are on the threshold of great events, you would take risks that could bring us down.'

Tara lay awake most of the night and listened to Kitty's peaceful breathing in the iron bed across the cell.

She fell asleep just before dawn, and awoke feeling nauseated and heavy, when Kitty leapt gaily out of bed in her pink-striped pyjamas, eager for the day.

'June 26th,' she cried. 'The big day at last!'

None of them took more than a cup of coffee for an early breakfast. Tara felt too sick and the others were too keyed up. Hank had checked his equipment the previous night, but now he went over it again before he loaded it into the Packard and they drove down to the railway station.

It was gloomy and the few street lights were still burning while under them the hordes of black commuters hurried.

However, by the time they reached the station the first rays of the sun struck the entrance and the light was perfect for filming. Tara noticed that a pair of police Black Maria vans were parked outside the main entrance and instead of the two young constables who had been on duty the previous day there were eight railway policemen in a group under the station clock. They were in blue uniform with black peaked caps and holstered sidearms on their polished leather Sam Browne belts. They all carried riot batons.

'They have been warned,' Tara exclaimed, as she parked across the street from the two vans. 'They are expecting trouble – just look at them.'

Kitty had twisted around and was giving last-minute instructions to Hank in the back seat, but when Tara glanced at her to assess her reaction to the waiting police, something about Kitty's expression and her inability to meet Tara's eyes made her pause.

'Kitty?' she insisted. 'These policemen. You don't seem—' She broke off as she remembered something. The previous afternoon on the way to the beach, Kitty had asked her to stop outside the Humewood post office because she wanted to send a telegram. However, from across the road looking through the post office window, Tara had seen her slip into one of the glass telephone booths. It had puzzled her at the time.

'You!' she gasped. 'It was you who warned the police!'

'Listen, darling,' Kitty snapped at her. 'These people want to get themselves arrested. That's the whole point. And I want film of them getting arrested. I did it for all our sakes—' She broke off and cocked her head. 'Listen!' she cried. 'Here they come!'

Faintly on the dawn there was the sound of singing, hundreds of voices together, and the group of policemen in the station entrance stirred and looked around apprehensively.

'OK, Hank,' Kitty snapped. 'Let's go!'

They jumped out of the Packard and hurried to the positions they had chosen, lugging their equipment.

The senior police officer with gold braid on his cap was a captain. Tara knew enough of police rank insignia from firsthand experience. He gave an order to his constables. Two of them began to cross the road towards the camera team.

'Shoot, Hank. Keep shooting!' Tara heard Kitty's voice, and the singing was louder now. The beautifully haunting refrain of *Nkosi Sikelel' iAfrika* carried by a thousand African voices made Tara shiver.

The two constables were halfway across the road when the first rank of protesters marched around the nearest row of shops and cottages and hurriedly the police captain called his constables back to his side.

They were twenty abreast, arms linked, filling the road from pavement to pavement, singing as they came on, and behind them followed a solid column of black humanity. Some of them were dressed in business suits, others in tattered cast-off clothing, some were silver-haired and others were in their teens. In the centre of the front rank, taller than the men around him, bare-headed and straight-backed as a soldier, marched Moses Gama.

Hank ran into the street with his sound technician following him. With the camera on his shoulder he retreated in front of Moses, capturing him on film, the sound man recording his voice as it soared in the anthem, full and magnificent, the very voice of Africa, and his features were lit with an almost religious fervour.

Hurriedly the police captain was drawing his men up across the whites-only entrance, and they were hefting their batons nervously, pale-faced in the early sunlight. The head of the column wheeled across the road and began to climb the steps, and the police captain stepped forward and spread his arms to halt them. Moses Gama held up one hand. The column came to a jerking shuffling halt, and the singing died away.

The police captain was a tall man with a pleasantly lined face. Tara could see him over their heads, and he was smiling. That was the thing that struck Tara. Faced with a thousand black protesters, he was still smiling.

'Come on now,' he raised his voice, like a schoolmaster addressing an unruly class. 'You know you can't do this, it's just nonsense, man. You are acting like a bunch of skollies, and I know you are good people.' He was still smiling as he picked a few of the leaders out of the front ranks. 'Mr Dhlouv and Mr Khandela – you are on the management committee, shame on you!' He waggled his finger, and the men he had spoken to hung their heads and grinned shamefacedly. The whole atmosphere of the march had begun to change. Here was the father figure, stern but benevolent, and they were the children, mischievous but at the bottom good-hearted and dutiful.

'Off you go, all of you. Go home and don't be silly now,' the captain called, and the column wavered. From the back ranks there was laughter, and a few of those who had been reluctant to join the march began to slip away. Behind the captain his constables were grinning with relief, and the crowd began to jostle as it broke up.

'Good Christ!' Kitty swore bitterly. 'It's all a goddamned anticlimax. I have wasted my time—'

Then onto the top steps of the railway station a tall figure stepped out of the ranks and his voice rang out over them, silencing them and freezing them where they stood. The laughter and the smiles died away.

'My people,' Moses Gama cried, 'this is your land. In it you have God's right to live in peace and dignity. This building belongs to all who live here – it is your right to enter, as much as any other person's that lives here. I am going in – who will follow me?'

A ragged, uncertain chorus of support came from the front ranks and Moses turned to face the police captain.

'We are going in, Captain. Arrest us or stand aside.'

At that moment a train, filled with black commuters, pulled into the platform and they hung out of the windows of the coaches and cheered and stamped.

'*Nkosi Sikelel' iAfrika!*' sang Moses Gama, and with his head held high he marched under the warning sign WHITES ONLY.

'You are breaking the law.' The captain raised his voice. 'Arrest that man.' And the thin rank of constables moved forward to obey.

Instantly a roar went up from the crowd behind him. 'Arrest me! Arrest me too!' And they surged forward, picking Moses up with them as though he were a surfer on a wave.

'Arrest me!' they chanted. 'Malan! Malan! Come and arrest us!'

The crowd burst through the entrance, and the white police constables were carried with them, struggling ineffectually in the press of bodies.

'Arrest me!' It had become a roar. '*Amandla! Amandla!*'

The captain was fighting to keep his feet, shouting to rally his men, but his voice was drowned out in the chant of 'Power! Power!' The captain's cap was knocked over his eyes and he was shoved backwards on to the platform. Hank, the cameraman, was in the midst of it, holding his Arriflex high and shooting out of hand. Around him the white faces of the constables bobbed like flotsam in a wild torrent of humanity. From the coaches the black passengers swarmed out to meet and mingle with the mob, and a single voice called out.

'*Jee!*' the battle cry that can drive an Nguni warrior into the berserker's passion, and '*Jee!*' a hundred voices answered him and '*Jee!*' again. There was the crash of breaking glass, one of the coach windows exploded as a shoulder thrust into it and '*Jee!*' they sang.

One of the white constables lost his footing and went sprawling backwards. Immediately he was trampled under foot and he screamed like a rabbit in a snare.

'*Jee!*' sang the men, transformed into warriors, the veneer of Western manners stripped away, and another window smashed. By now the platform was choked with a struggling mass of humanity. From the cab of the locomotive, the mob dragged the terrified engine-driver and his fireman. They jostled and pushed them, ringing them in.

'*Jee!*' they chanted, bouncing at the knees, working themselves up into the killing madness. Their eyes were glazing and engorging with blood, their faces turning into shining black masks.

'*Jee!*' they sang. '*Jee!*' and Moses Gama sang with them. Let the others call for restraint and passive resistance to the enemy, but all that was forgotten and now Moses Gama's blood seethed with all his pent-up hatred and '*Jee!*' he cried, and his skin crawled and itched with atavistic fury and his fighting heart swelled to fill his chest.

The police captain, still on his feet, had been driven back against the wall of the station-master's office. One epaulette had been torn from the shoulder of his uniform and he had lost his cap. There was a fleck of blood at the corner of his moustache where an elbow had struck him in the mouth, and he was struggling with the flap of the holster on his belt.

'Kill!' shouted a voice. '*Bulala!*' and it was taken up. Black hands clutched at the police captain's lapels, and he drew the service revolver from its holster and tried to raise it, but the crowd was packed too densely around him. He fired blindly from the hip.

The shot was a great blurt of sound, and somebody yelled with shock and pain, and the crowd around the captain backed away, leaving a young black man in an army-surplus greatcoat kneeling at his feet, moaning and clutching his stomach.

The captain, white-faced and panting, lifted the revolver and fired again into the air.

'Form up on me!' he shouted in a voice hoarse and breaking with terror and exertion. Another of his men was down on his knees, submerged in the milling crowd, but he managed to clear his revolver from its holster and he fired point-blank, emptying the chamber into the press around him.

Then they were running, blocking the entrance, jamming in it as they sought to escape the gunfire, and all the police constables were firing, some on their knees, all of them dishevelled and terrified, and the bullets told in the mass of bodies with loud, meaty thumps, like a housewife beating the dust from a hanging carpet. The air was thick with the smell of gunsmoke and dust and blood, of sweat and unwashed bodies and terror.

They were screaming and pushing, fighting their way out into the street again, leaving their fallen comrades crumpled on the platform in seeping puddles of blood, or crawling desperately after them dragging bullet-shattered limbs.

And the little group of policemen were running to help each other to their feet, bruised and bloodied in torn uniforms. They gathered up the engine-driver and his fireman and, staggering, supporting each other, drawn revolvers still in their hands, they crossed the platform stepping over the bodies and the puddles of blood and hurried down the steps to the two parked vans.

Across the road the crowd had reassembled and they screamed and shook their fists and chanted as the policemen scrambled into the vehicles and drove away at speed, and then the crowd swarmed into the roadway and hurled stones and abuse at the departing vans.

Tara had watched it all from the parked Packard, and now she sat paralysed with horror, listening to the animal growl of the crowd penetrated by the cries and groans of the wounded.

Moses Gama ran to her and shouted into the open window, 'Go and fetch Sister Nunziata. Tell her we need all the help we can get.'

Tara nodded dumbly and started the engine. Across the road she could see Kitty and Hank still filming. Hank was kneeling beside a wounded man, shooting into his tortured face, panning down onto the pool of blood in which he lay.

Tara pulled away, and the crowd in the road tried to stop her. Black faces, swollen with anger, mouthed at her through the Packard's windows and they beat with their fists on the roof, but she sounded her horn and kept driving.

'I have to get a doctor,' she shouted at them. 'Let me pass, let me through.'

She got through them, and when she looked in the rear-view mirror, she saw that in frustration and fury they were stoning the railway station, ripping up the pavement and hurling the heavy slabs through the windows. She saw a white face at one of the windows, and felt a pang for the station-master and his staff. They had barricaded themselves in the ticket office.

The crowd outside the building was solid, and as she drove towards the mission she passed a flood of black men and women rushing to join it. The women were ululating wildly, a sound that maddened their menfolk. Some of them ran into the road to try and stop Tara, but she jammed her palm down on the horn ring and swerved around them. She glanced up into her driving-mirror and one of them picked up a rock from the side of the road and hurled it after the car. The rock crashed against the metal of the cab and bounced away.

At the mission hospital they had heard the sound of

gunfire and the roar of the mob. Sister Nunziata, the white doctor, and her helpers were anxiously waiting on the verandah and Tara shouted up at her.

'You must come quickly to the station, Sister, the police have shot and wounded people – I think some of them are dead.'

They must have been expecting the call, for they had their medical bags on the verandah with them. While Tara backed and turned the Packard, Sister Nunziata and the doctor ran down the steps, carrying their black bags. They clambered into the cab of the mission's small blue Ford pick-up and turned towards the gate, cutting in front of Tara's Packard. Tara followed them, but by the time she had turned the Packard and driven out through the gates, the little blue pick-up was a hundred yards ahead of her. It turned the corner into the station road and even above the engine-beat Tara heard the roar of the mob.

When she swung through the corner the Ford was stopped only fifty paces ahead of her. It was completely surrounded by the crowd. The road from side to side was packed with screaming black men and women. Tara could not hear the words, there was no sense to their fury, it was incoherent and deafening. They were concentrating on the Ford, and took no notice of Tara in the Packard.

Those nearest to the Ford were beating on the metal cab, and rocking the vehicle on its suspension. The side door opened and Sister Nunziata stood on the running board, a little higher than the heads of the howling mob that pushed closely around her. She was trying to speak to them, holding up her hands and pleading with them to let her through to take care of the wounded.

Suddenly a stone was thrown. It arced up out of the crowd and hit the nun on the side of her head. She reeled as she stood, and there was a bright flash of blood on her white veil. Stunned, she raised her hand to her cheek and it came away bloody.

The sight of blood enraged them. A forest of black arms reached up to Sister Nunziata and dragged her down from the vehicle. For a while they fought over her, dragging her in the road and worrying her like a pack of hounds with the fox. Then suddenly Tara saw the flash of a knife, and sitting in the Packard she screamed and thrust her fingers into her mouth to silence herself.

The old crone who wielded the knife was a *sangoma*, a witchdoctor, and around her neck she wore the necklace of bones and feathers and animal skulls that were her insignia. The knife in her right hand had a handle of rhino horn and the hand-forged blade was nine inches long and wickedly curved. Four men caught the nun and threw her across the engine bonnet of the Ford while the old woman hopped up beside her. The men held Sister Nunziata pinioned, face up, while the crowd began to chant wildly, and the *sangoma* stooped over her.

With a single stroke of the curved blade she cut through the nun's grey habit and split her belly open from groin to rib cage. While Sister Nunziata writhed in the grip of the men who held her, the crone thrust her hand and naked arm into the wound. Tara watched in disbelief as she brought out something wet and glistening and purple, a soft amorphous thing. It was done so swiftly, so expertly, that for seconds Tara did not realize that it was Sister Nunziata's liver that the crone held in her bloody hands.

With a slash of the curved blade, the *sangoma* cut a lump from the still living organ and hopped to her feet. Balancing on the curved bonnet of the Ford she faced the crowd.

'I eat our white enemy,' she screeched; 'and thus I take his strength.' And the mob roared, a terrible sound, as the old woman thrust the purple lump into her toothless mouth and chewed upon it. She hacked another piece off the liver, and still chewing with open mouth, she threw it to the crowd below her.

'Eat your enemy!' she shrilled, and they fought for the bloody scraps like dogs.

'Be strong! Eat the liver of the hated ones!'

She threw them more and Tara covered her eyes and heaved convulsively. Acid vomit shot up her throat and she swallowed it down painfully.

Abruptly the driver's door of the Packard beside her was jerked open and rough hands seized Tara. She was dragged out into the road. The blood roar of the crowd deafened her, but terror armed her with superhuman strength, and she tore herself free of the clutching hands.

She was at the edge of the mob, and the attention of most of them was entirely on the ghastly drama around the Ford. The crowd had set the vehicle alight. Sister Nunziata's mutilated body lay on the bonnet like a sacrifice on a burning altar, while, trapped in the cab, the doctor thrashed around and beat at the flames with his bare hands, and the crowd chanted and danced around him like children around the bonfire on Guy Fawkes' night.

For that instant Tara was free, but there were men around her, shouting and reaching for her, their faces bestial, their eyes glazed and insensate. No longer human, they were driven into that killing madness in which there was no reason nor mercy. Swift as a bird Tara ducked under the outstretched arms and darted away. She found that she had broken out of the mob, and in front of her was a plot of wasteland strewn with old rusted car bodies and rubbish. She fled across it and behind her she heard her pursuers baying like a pack of hunting dogs.

At the end of the open land a sagging barbed-wire fence blocked her way, and she glanced back over her shoulder. A group of men still followed her, and two of them had outdistanced the others. They were both big and powerful-looking, running strongly on bare feet, their faces contorted in a cruel rictus of excitement. They came on silently.

Tara stooped into the space between the strands of the

wire. She was almost through when she felt the barbs catch in the flesh of her back, and pain arrested her. For a moment she struggled desperately, feeling her skin tear as she fought to free herself and blood trickled down her flanks – and then they seized her.

Now they shouted with wild laughter as they dragged her back through the fence, the barbs ripping at her clothing and her flesh. Her legs collapsed under her, and she pleaded with them.

'Please don't hurt me. I'm going to have a baby—'

They dragged her back across the waste plot, half on her knees, twisting and pleading in their grip – and then she saw the *sangoma* coming to meet them, hopping and capering like an ancient baboon, cackling through her toothless mouth, her bones and beads rattling around her scrawny neck and the curved knife in her blood-caked fingers.

Tara began to scream, and she felt her urine squirt uncontrollably down her legs. 'Please! Please don't!' she raved and terror was an icy blackness of her mind and body that crushed her to earth, and she closed her eyes and steeled herself to the stinging kiss of the blade.

Then in the mindless animal roar of the crowd, above the old crone's shrill laughter, there was another voice, a great lion's roar of anger and command that stilled all other sound. Tara opened her eyes and Moses Gama stood over her, a towering colossus, and his voice alone stopped them and drove them back. He lifted her in his arms and held her like a child. The crowd around the Packard opened before him as he carried her to it and placed her on the front seat and then slid behind the wheel.

As he started the engine and swung the Packard away in a hard U-turn the black smoke from the burning van poured over them and obscured the windscreen for a moment, and Tara smelled Sister Nunziata's flesh roasting.

This time she could not control herself and she flopped

forward, her head between her knees, and vomited on the floor of the Packard.

Manfred De La Rey had taken the chair at the top of the long table in the operations room in the basement of Marshall Square. He had come across from his own office suite in the Union Buildings in Pretoria to police headquarters at the centre of the storm, where he could be at hand to consider, with his senior officers, each fresh dispatch as it came in from the police provincial HQs around the country.

The entire wall facing Manfred's seat was a large-scale map of the subcontinent. Working in front of it were two junior police officers. They were placing magnetic markers on the map. Each of the small black discs had a name printed upon it and represented one of the almost five hundred ANC officials and organizers that had been so far identified by the Intelligence Department.

The discs were clustered most thickly along the great crescent of the Witwatersrand in the centre of the continent, although others were scattered across the entire map as the physical whereabouts of each person was confirmed by the police reports that were coming in every few seconds.

Amongst the rash of black markers were a very few red discs, less than fifty in all. These represented the known members of the Central Committee of the African National Congress.

Some of the names were those of Europeans; Harris, Marks, Fischer, and some were Asians like Naicker and Nana Sita, but the majority were African. Tambo and Sisulu and Mandela – they were all there. Mandela's red disc was placed on the city of Johannesburg, while Moroka was in the Eastern Cape and Albert Luthuli was in Zululand.

Manfred De La Rey was stony-faced as he stared at the map, and the senior police officers seated around him studiously avoided catching his eye or even looking directly at him. Manfred had a reputation of being the strongman of the cabinet. His colleagues privately referred to him as 'Panga Man' after the heavy chopping knife that was used in the cane fields and was the favourite weapon of the Mau Mau in Kenya.

Manfred looked the part. He was a big man. The hands that lay on the table before him were still, there was no fidgeting of nervousness or uncertainty, and they were big hard hands. His face was becoming craggy now, and his jowls and thick neck heightened the sense of power that emanated from him. His men were afraid of him.

'How many more?' he asked suddenly, and the colonel sitting opposite him, a man with the medal ribbons of valour on his chest, started like a schoolboy and quickly consulted his list.

'Four more to find – Mbeki, Mtolo, Mhlaba and Gama.' He read out the names on his list that remained unticked, and Manfred De La Rey relapsed into silence.

Despite his brooding stillness and forbidding expression, Manfred was pleased with the day's work. It was not yet noon on the first day and already they had pinpointed the whereabouts of most of the ringleaders. Altogether the ANC had planned the entire campaign with quite extra-ordinary precision and had exhibited unusual thoroughness and foresight in its execution, Manfred reflected. He had not expected them to be so efficient, the African was notoriously lackadaisical and happy-go-lucky – but then they had the advice and assistance of their white Communist comrades. The protests and demonstrations and strikes were widespread and effective. Manfred grunted aloud and the officers at the table looked up apprehensively, but dropped their eyes hurriedly when he frowned.

Manfred returned to his thoughts. No, not bad for a

bunch of kaffirs, even with a few white men to help them. Yet their naïvety and amateurishness showed in their almost total lack of security and secrecy. They had blabbed as though they were at a beer-drink. Full of their own importance they had boasted of their plans and made little effort to conceal the identities of the leaders and cover their movements. The police informers had had little difficulty in picking up the information.

There were, of course, exceptions and Manfred scowled as he considered the lists of leaders still unaccounted for. One name pricked like a burr, Moses Gama. He had made a study of the man's file. After Mandela, he was probably the most dangerous of them all.

'We must have him,' he told himself. 'We must get those two, Mandela and Gama.' And now he spoke aloud, barking the question: 'Where is Mandela?'

'At the moment he is addressing a meeting in the community hall at Drake's Farm township,' the colonel answered promptly, glancing up at the red marker on the map. 'He will be followed when he leaves, until we are ready to make the arrests.'

'No word of Gama yet?' Manfred asked impatiently, and the officer shook his head.

'Not yet, Minister, he was last seen here on the Witwatersrand nine days ago. He might have gone underground. We may have to move without him.'

'No,' Manfred snapped. 'I want him. I want Moses Gama.'

Manfred relapsed into silence, brooding and intense. He knew that he was caught in the cross-currents of history. He could feel the good winds blowing at his back, set fair to carry him away on his course. He knew also that at any moment those winds might drop, and the ebb of his tide might set in. It was dangerous – mortally dangerous but still he waited. His father and his ancestors had all been huntsmen. They had hunted the elephant and lion and he had heard them speak of the patience and the waiting that was part of the hunt. Now Manfred was a hunter as they had been, but his quarry, though every bit as dangerous, was infinitely more cunning.

He had set his snares with all the skill at his command. The banning orders, five hundred of them, were already made out. The men and women to whom they were addressed would be driven out from society into the wilderness. Prohibited from attending a gathering of more than three persons, physically confined to a single magisterial district, prohibited also from publishing a single written word and prevented from having their spoken word published by anyone else, their treacherous and treasonable voices would be effectively gagged. That was how he would deal with the lesser enemy, the smaller game of this hunt.

For the others, the fifty big game, the dangerous ones, he had other weapons ready. The warrants of arrest had been drawn up and the charges framed. Amongst them were high treason and furthering the aims of international Communism, conspiracy to overthrow the government by violent revolution, incitement to public violence – and these, if proven, led directly to the gallows tree. Complete success was there, almost within his grasp, but at any moment it could be snatched away.

At that moment a voice was raised so loudly in the operations room beyond the cubicle windows that they all looked up. Even Manfred swung his head towards the sound and narrowed his pale eyes. The officer who had spoken was sitting with his back to the window holding the telephone receiver to his ear, and scribbling on the notepad on the desk in front of him. Now he slammed the receiver back on to its bracket, ripped the top sheet off the pad and hurried into the map room.

'What is it?' demanded the super.

'We've got him, sir.' The man's voice was shrill with excitement. 'We've got Moses Gama. He is in Port

Elizabeth. Less than two hours ago he was at the head of a riot at the New Brighton railway station. The police were attacked, and were forced to open fire in self-defence. At least seven people have been killed, one of them a nun. She was horribly mutilated – there is even an unconfirmed report that she was cannibalized – and her body has been burned.'

'Are they sure it was him?' Manfred asked.

'No doubt, Minister. He was positively identified by an informer who knows him personally and the police captain has identified him by file and photograph.'

'All right,' Manfred De La Rey said. 'Now we can move.' He looked down at the Commissioner of Police at the far end of the long table. 'Do it, please, Commissioner,' he said, and picked up his dark fedora hat from the table. 'Report to me the moment you have them all locked up.'

He rode up in the lift to ground level and his chauffeur-driven limousine was waiting to take him back to his office in the Union Buildings. As he settled back against the leather-padded rear seat and the limousine pulled away, he smiled for the first time that morning.

'A nun,' he said aloud. 'And they ate her!' He shook his head with satisfaction. 'Let the bleeding hearts of the world read that and know what kind of savages we are dealing with.'

He felt the good winds of his fortune freshen, bearing him away towards those places which only recently he had allowed himself to dream of.

When they got back to the mission, Moses helped Tara out of the Packard. She was still pale and shaking like a woman with malaria. Her clothing was ripped and soiled with blood and dirt, and she could hardly stand unaided.

Kitty Godolphin and her camera crew had escaped the wrath of the mob by running across the railway tracks and hiding in a storm-water drain, then working their way in a wide circle back to the mission.

'We've got to get out of here,' Kitty yelled at Tara as she came out on to the verandah and saw Moses helping her up the steps. 'I've got the most incredible footage of my life. I can't trust it to anybody else. I want to get on the Pan Am flight from Jo'burg tomorrow morning and take the undeveloped cans to New York myself.' She was so excited that her voice shook wildly, and like Tara her denim jeans were torn and dusty. However, she was already packed and ready to leave, carrying the red canvas tote bag that was all her luggage.

'Did you film the nun?' Moses demanded. 'Did you film them killing Sister Nunziata?'

'Sure did, sweetheart!' Hank grinned. He was close behind Kitty. 'Got it all.'

'How many cans did you shoot?' Moses insisted.

'Four.' Hank was so excited he could not stand still. He was bouncing on his toes and snapping his fingers.

'Did you get the police shooting?'

'All of it, sweetheart, all of it.'

'Where is the film of the nun?' Moses demanded.

'Still in the camera.' Hank slapped the Arriflex that hung by his side. 'It's all here, baby. I had just changed film when they grabbed the nun and ripped her up.'

Moses left Tara leaning against the column of the verandah, and crossed to where Hank stood. He moved so casually that none of them realized what he was about to do. Kitty was still talking.

'If we leave right away, we can be in Jo'burg by tomorrow morning. The Pan Am flight leaves at eleven thirty—'

Moses had reached Hank's side. He seized the heavy camera, twisting the carrying strap so that Hank was pulled up on his toes helplessly, and he unclipped the round magazine of film from its seat on top of the camera body. Then he turned and smashed the magazine against the brick column of the verandah.

Kitty realized what he was doing and she flew at him like an angry cat, clawing for his eyes with her nails. 'My film,' she screeched. 'God damn you to hell, that's my film.'

Moses shoved her so violently that she collided with Hank, taking him off balance and they fell over each other, sprawling together on the verandah floor.

Moses hit the magazine again and this time the can burst open. The ribbon of glistening celluloid spilled out and cascaded over the retaining wall.

'You've ruined it,' Kitty screamed, coming to her feet and charging at him.

Moses tossed the empty can away, and caught Kitty's wrists, lifting her bodily off the ground and holding her effortlessly, though she struggled and kicked at him.

'You have the film of police brutality, the murder of innocent blacks,' he said. 'The rest of it you were not meant to witness. I will not let you show that to the world.' He pushed her away. 'You may take the Packard.'

Kitty glared at him, massaging her wrists where the skin was red from his grip and she spat like a cat.

'I won't forget that – one day you will pay for that, Moses Gama.' Her malignancy was chilling.

'Go,' Moses commanded. 'You have a plane to catch.'

For a moment she hesitated, and then she whirled, picked up her tote bag.

'Come on, Hank,' she called, and she ran down the stairs to the Packard and sprang into the driver's seat.

'You cock-sucking bastard,' Hank hissed at Moses as he passed. 'That was the best stuff I ever scored.'

'You've still got three cans,' Moses said softly. 'Be grateful for that.'

Moses watched them drive away in the Packard and then turned to Tara.

'We must move very fast now – the police will act at once. We have to get out of the township before they cordon it off. I am a marked man – we have to get clear.'

'What do you want me to do?' Tara asked.

'Come, I'll explain later,' Moses said and hustled her towards the Buick. 'First, we must get clear.'

Tara gave the salesman a cheque and waited in the tiny cubicle of his office that stank of cheap cigar smoke while he phoned her bank in Cape Town.

There was a crumpled newspaper on the cluttered desk, and she picked it up and read it avidly.

SEVEN DEAD IN P.E. RIOTS
NATIONWIDE DISTURBANCES
500 ACTIVISTS BANNED
MANDELA ARRESTED

Almost the entire newspaper was devoted to the defiance campaign and its consequences. At the bottom of the page, under the lurid accounts of the killing and the cannibalization of Sister Nunziata, there were accounts of the action taken by the ANC in other sectors of the country. Thousands had been arrested, and there were photographs of protesters being loaded into police vans, grinning cheerfully and giving the thumbs-up sign that had become the protester's salute.

The inner page of the newspaper gave the lists of almost

five hundred persons who had been banned, and explained the consequences of the banning orders – how they effectively terminated the public life of the victim.

There was also the much shorter list of persons who had been arrested for high treason and furthering the aims of the Communist Party, and Tara bit her lip when she saw Moses Gama's name. The police spokesman must have anticipated his arrest, but it was proof that the precautions Moses was taking were wise. High treason was a capital offence, and she had a mental picture of Moses, his head hooded, twisting and kicking from the gallows crossbeam. She shuddered and thrust the image aside, concentrating on the rest of the newspaper.

There were photographs, most of them murky and indistinct, of the leaders of the ANC, and she smiled humourlessly as she realized that these were the first fruits of the campaign. Up to this moment, not one in a hundred white South Africans had ever heard of Moses Gama, Nelson Mandela, or any of the other leaders, but now they had come bursting in on the national conscience. The world suddenly knew who they were.

The middle pages were mostly filled with public reaction to the campaign and to the government's countermeasures. It was too soon for the foreign reactions, but local opinion seemed almost unanimous: condemnation of the barbaric murder of Sister Nunziata, and high praise for police courage and the swift action of the Minister of Police in crushing the Communist-inspired plot.

The editor wrote:

We have not always been able to commend the actions and utterances of the Minister of Police. However, the need finds the man and we are thankful this day that a man of courage and strength stands between us and the forces of anarchy—

Tara's reading was interrupted by the used-car salesman. He bustled back into the tiny office to fawn on Tara and to gush.

'My dear Mrs Courtney, you must forgive me. I had no idea who you were, or I would never have subjected you to the humiliation of querying your cheque.'

He ushered her out to the yard, bowing and grinning ingratiatingly, and held open the door of the 1951-model black Cadillac for which Tara had just given her cheque for almost a thousand pounds.

Tara drove down the hill and parked on the Donkin overlooking the sea. The military and naval outfitters were only half a block down the main street and from their stocks she picked out a chauffeur's cap with a glossy patent-leather peak and a dove-grey tunic with brass buttons in Moses' size which the assistant packed in a brown paper bag.

Back in the new Cadillac she drove slowly down to the main railway station and parked opposite the entrance. She left the key in the ignition and slipped into the back seat. Within five minutes Moses came out. He was dressed in grubby blue overalls and the police constable at the railway entrance did not even glance at him. Moses sauntered down the sidewalk and as he drew level with the Cadillac Tara passed the paper bag through the open window.

Within ten minutes Moses was back, the overalls discarded, wearing the chauffeur's cap and smart new tunic over his dark slacks and black shoes. He climbed into the driver's seat and started the engine.

'You were right. There is a warrant out for your arrest,' she said softly.

'How do you know?'

'There is a newspaper on the seat.' She had folded it open at the report on his arrest. He read it swiftly, and then eased the Cadillac out into the traffic stream.

'What are you going to do, Moses? Will you give yourself up and stand trial?'

'The courtroom would be a platform from which to speak to the world,' he mused.

'And if you were convicted, the gallows would be an even more riveting pulpit,' she pointed out acidly, and he smiled at her in the rear-view mirror.

'We need martyrs – every cause must have martyrs.'

'My God, Moses, how can you speak like that? Every cause needs a leader. There are many who would make fine martyrs, but very few who can lead.'

He drove in silence for a while and then he said firmly, 'We will go to Johannesburg. I must talk to the others before I decide.'

'Most of the others have been arrested,' Tara pointed out.

'Not all.' He shook his head. 'I must talk to those who have escaped. How much money do you have?'

She opened her handbag and counted the notes she had in her purse.

'Over a hundred pounds.'

'More than enough,' he nodded. 'Be prepared to play the grand lady when the police stop us.'

They ran into the first road-block on the outskirts of the city at the Swartkops bridge. There was a line of cars and heavy vehicles and they moved forward slowly, stopping and starting, until two police constables signalled them over and a young police warrant officer came to the passenger window.

'Good afternoon, *Mevrou*.' He touched his cap. 'May we look in the boot of your car?'

'What is this about, officer?'

'The troubles, madam. We are looking for the trouble-makers who killed the nun and ate her.'

Tara leaned forward and spoke sharply to Moses. 'Open the boot for the policeman, Stephen.' And Moses climbed out and held the lid open while the constables made a cursory search. Not one of them looked at his face, the chauffeur's uniform had rendered him miraculously invisible.

'Thank you, lady.'

The warrant officer waved them through and Moses murmured, 'That was most unflattering. I thought I was a celebrity now.'

It was a long and arduous drive from the coast, but Moses drove sedately, careful not to give anyone an excuse to stop them and question them more carefully.

As he drove he tuned the Cadillac's wireless for the South African Broadcasting Corporation's hourly news bulletin. The reception was intermittent as the terrain varied, but they picked up one exciting item.

The Soviet Union supported by her allies had demanded an urgent debate in the United Nations' General Assembly on the situation in the country. This was the first time the UN had ever shown an interest in South Africa. For that alone all their sacrifice had been worthwhile. However, the rest of the news was disquieting. Over eight thousand protesters had been arrested and all the leaders banned or picked up, and a spokesman for the Minister of Police assured the country that the situation was firmly under control.

They drove on until after dark when they stopped at one of the small Orange Free State hotels that catered mainly for commercial travellers. When Tara asked for board and lodging for her chauffeur the request was taken as matter of course because all the travellers employed coloured drivers, and Moses was sent around the back to the servants' quarters in the hotel yard.

After the plain and unappetizing fare in the hotel dining room, Tara telephoned Weltevreden, and Sean answered on the second ring. They had returned from their hunting safari with Shasa the previous day, and were garrulous and excited. Each of the boys spoke to her in turn, so she was treated to three separate accounts of how Garrick had shot a man-eating lion. Then Isabella came on the line, and her sweet childish lisp tugged at Tara's heart, making her feel dreadfully guilty at her lack of maternal duty. Yet none of the children, Isabella included, seemed to have missed her in the least. Isabella was just as long-winded as her brothers in recounting all the things that she and Nana had done together, and the new dress that Nana had bought her and the doll that grandpa Blaine had brought back from England especially for her. None of them asked her how she was and when she was coming home to Weltevreden.

Shasa came on the line last, distant but friendly. 'We are all having a wonderful time – Garry shot a lion—'

'Oh God, Shasa, don't you tell me about it, I've already had three accounts of the poor beast's death.'

Within a few minutes they had run out of things to say to each other. 'Well then, old thing, take care of yourself. I see the uglies are cutting up rather rough on the Rand, but De La Rey has it well in hand,' Shasa ended. 'Don't get caught up in any unpleasantness.'

'I won't,' she promised. 'Now I'll let you go in to dinner.' Shasa liked to dine at eight o'clock sharp and it was four minutes before the hour. She knew he was already dressed and checking his watch. When she hung up she realized that he hadn't asked her where she was, what she was doing or when she was coming home.

'Saved me from having to lie,' she consoled herself.

From her bedroom she could look over the hotel yard, and the lights were on in the servants' quarters. Suddenly she was overwhelmed with loneliness. It was so chilling, that she seriously thought about creeping across the yard to be with him. It took an effort of will to thrust that madness aside, and instead she picked up the telephone again and asked the operator for the number at Puck's Hill.

A servant, with a marked African accent, answered and Tara's heart sank. It was vital that they find out whether the Rivonia house was still safe. They could be going into a police trap.

'Is *Nkosi* Marcus there?' she demanded.

'*Nkosi* Marcus no here, he go away, missus,' the servant told her. 'You Missus Tara?'

'Yes! Yes!' Although she did not remember a servant, he must have recognized her voice, and she was about to go on when Marcus Archer spoke in his normal voice.

'Forgive me, my dear, for the music-hall impression, but the sky has fallen in here. Everybody is in a panic – the pigs have moved much quicker than anybody expected. Joe and I are the only ones to survive, as far as I know. How is our good friend, have they got him?'

'He's safe. Can we come to Puck's Hill?'

'So far it seems as though they have overlooked us here, but do be careful, won't you? There are road-blocks everywhere.'

Tara slept very little and was up before dawn to begin the last leg of the journey. The hotel chef had made her a packet of corned-beef sandwiches and a thermos of hot tea, so they breakfasted as they drove. Any stop would increase their chances of discovery and arrest, and except to refuel they kept going and crossed the Vaal River before noon.

Tara had been seeking the right moment to tell Moses ever since she had returned to the Transvaal to be near him, but now she knew that there would never be a right moment and that within hours they would be at Puck's Hill. After that nothing was certain except that there would be confusion and great danger for all of them.

'Moses,' she addressed the back of his head in a resolute voice, 'I can't keep it from you any longer. I have to tell you now. I am bearing your child.'

She saw his head flinch slightly and then those dark mesmeric eyes were glowering at her in the driver's mirror.

'What will you do?' he asked. He had not asked if she were certain nor had he queried his paternity of the child. That was typical of him – and yet he had accepted no responsibility either. 'What will you do?'

'I am not sure yet. I will find a way to have it.'

'You must get rid of it.'

'No,' she cried vehemently. 'Never. He's mine. I will take care of him.'

He did not remark on her choice of the masculine pronoun.

'The child will be half-caste,' he told her. 'Are you prepared for that?'

'I will find a way,' she insisted.

'I cannot help you – not at all,' he went on remorselessly. 'You understand that.'

'Yes, you can,' she answered. 'You can tell me that you are pleased that I am carrying your son – and that you will love him, as I love his father.'

'Love?' he said. 'That is not an African word. There is no word for love in my vocabulary.'

'Oh, Moses, that is not true. You love your people.'

'I love them as a people entire, not as individuals. I would sacrifice any one of them for the good of the whole.'

'But our son, Moses. Something precious that we have made between us – don't you feel anything at all for him?'

She watched his eyes in the mirror and saw the pain in them.

'Yes,' he admitted. 'Of course I do. Yet I dare not acknowledge it. I must lock such feelings away lest they weaken my resolve and destroy us all.'

'Then I will love him for both of us,' she said softly.

As Marcus Archer had warned Tara, there were more road-blocks. As they drew closer to the great industrial and mining complex of the Witwatersrand they were stopped three times, the last at Halfway House, but each time the

310

chauffeur's uniform and Tara's white face and haughty manner protected him.

Tara had expected Johannesburg to be like a city under siege, but the road-blocks and the news posters on the street corners were the only indications of something unusual afoot. The headgear wheels of the mines they passed were spinning busily, and beyond the perimeter fences they saw the black miners in gumboots and shiny hard hats flocking to the shaft heads.

When they passed through downtown Johannesburg, the city streets were crowded as usual with shoppers of all races and their faces were cheerful and relaxed. Tara was disappointed. She was not sure what she had expected, but at least she had hoped for some visible sign that the people were on the march.

'You cannot expect too much,' Moses told her when she lamented that nothing had changed. 'The forces against us are obdurate as granite, and the resources they command are limitless. Yet it is a beginning – our first faltering step on the road to liberation.'

They drove past Puck's Hill slowly. It seemed deserted, and at least there were no signs of police activity. Moses parked the Cadillac in the wattle plantation at the back of the Country Club and left Tara while he went back on foot to make absolutely certain they were not running into a police trap.

He was back within half an hour. 'It's safe. Marcus is there,' he told her as he started the Cadillac and drove back.

Marcus was waiting for them on the verandah. He looked tired and worn, and he had aged dramatically in the short time since Tara had last seen him.

He led them into the long kitchen, and went back to the stove on which he was preparing a meal for them, and while he worked he told them everything that had happened in their absence.

'The police reaction was so massive and immediate that it must have been carefully prepared. We expected a delay while they caught up with the situation and gathered themselves. We expected to be able to exploit that delay, and call upon the masses to join us in the defiance campaign until it gathered its own momentum and became irresistible, but they were ready for us. There are not more than a dozen of the leaders at large now, Moses is one of the lucky ones, and without leaders the campaign is already beginning to grind to a halt.'

He glanced at Tara with a vindictive sparkle in his eye before he went on.

'However, there are still some pockets of resistance – our little Victoria is doing sterling work. She has organized the nurses at Baragwanath and brought them out as part of the campaign. She won't keep that up much longer – she'll be arrested or banned pretty damn soon, you can bet on that.'

'Vicky is a brave woman,' Moses agreed. 'She knows the risks, and she takes them willingly.'

He looked straight at Tara as he said it, as if daring her to voice her jealousy. She knew of his marriage, of course, but she had never spoken of it. She knew what the consequences would be, and now she dropped her eyes, unable to meet his challenge.

'We have underestimated this man De La Rey,' Moses said. 'He is a formidable opponent. We have achieved very little of what we hoped for.'

'Still, the United Nations is debating our plight,' Tara said quietly without looking up again.

'Debating,' Moses agreed scornfully. 'But it requires only a single veto from America or Britain or France, and no action will be taken. They will talk and talk while my people suffer.'

'Our people,' Marcus chided him. 'Our people, Moses.'

'My people,' Moses contradicted him harshly. 'The

others are all in prison. I am the only leader who remains. They are my people.' There was silence in the kitchen, except for the scrape of utensils on the plates as they ate, but Marcus was frowning and it was he who broke the silence.

'So what happens now?' he asked. 'Where will you go? You cannot stay here, the police may swoop at any moment. Where will you go?'

'Drake's Farm?' Moses mused.

'No.' Marcus shook his head. 'They know you too well there. The moment you arrive the whole township will know and there are police informers everywhere. It will be the same as turning yourself in at the nearest police station.'

They were silent again until Moses asked, 'Where is Joe Cicero? Have they taken him?'

'No,' Marcus answered. 'He has gone underground.'

'Can you contact him?'

'We have an arrangement. He will ring me here – if not tonight, then tomorrow.'

Moses looked across the table at Tara. 'Can I come with you to the expedition base at Sundi Caves? It's the only safe place I can think of at the moment.' And Tara's spirits bounded. She would have him for a little longer still.

Tara explained to Marion Hurst, not attempting to conceal Moses' identity nor the fact that he was a fugitive, and she was not surprised by the American woman's response.

'It's like Martin Luther King coming and asking me for sanctuary,' she declared. 'Of course I'll do whatever I can to help.'

As a cover, Marion gave Moses a job in the pottery section of the warehouse under the name of Stephen Khama, and he was absorbed immediately into the company of the expedition. Without asking questions the other members, both black and white, gathered around to shield him.

Despite Marcus Archer's assurances, it was almost a week before he was able to contact Joe Cicero, and another day before he could arrange for them to meet. The hardest possible way they had learned not to underestimate the vigilance of the police, while Joe Cicero had always been secretive and professional. Nobody was certain where he lived or how he maintained himself, his comings and goings were unannounced and unpredictable.

'I have always thought him to be theatrical and over-careful, but now I see the wisdom behind it,' Moses told Tara as they drove into the city. Moses was once more dressed in his chauffeur's uniform. 'From now on we must learn from the professionals, for those ranged against us are the hardest of professionals.'

Joe Cicero came out of the entrance of the Johannesburg railway station as Moses stopped the Cadillac for the red light at the pedestrian crossing, and he slipped unobtrusively into the back seat beside Tara. Moses pulled away, heading out in the direction of Doornfontein.

'I congratulate you on still being at large,' Joe told Moses wryly, as he lit a fresh cigarette from the butt of the last and glanced sideways at Tara. 'You are Tara Courtney,' and smiled at her surprise. 'What is your part in all this?'

'She is a friend,' Moses spoke for her. 'She is committed to us. You may speak freely in front of her.'

'I never speak freely,' Joe murmured. 'Only an idiot does that.' They were all silent then until Joe asked suddenly, 'And so, my friend, do you still believe that the revolution can be won without blood? Are you still one of the pacifists who would play the game by the rules that the oppressor makes and changes at will?'

'I have never been a pacifist,' Moses' voice rumbled. 'I have always been a warrior.'

'I rejoice to hear you say it, for it confirms what I have always believed.' Joe smiled a sly and inscrutable smile behind the fringe of dark beard. 'If I did not, I would not be sitting here now.' Then his tone altered. 'Make a U-turn here and take the Krugersdorp road!' he ordered.

The three of them were silent while Joe turned to scrutinize the following traffic. After a minute he seemed satisfied and relaxed in the back seat. Moses drove out of the built-up areas into the open grassy veld. The traffic around them thinned, and abruptly Joe Cicero leaned forward and pointed ahead to an empty lay-by on the side of the road.

'Pull in there,' he ordered, and as Moses parked the Cadillac he opened the door beside him. As he stepped out he jerked his head. 'Come!'

When Tara opened her own door to join them, Joe snapped, 'No, not you! Stay here!'

With Moses at his side he walked through the stand of scraggly black wattle into the open veld beyond, out of sight of the road.

'I told you the woman is trustworthy,' Moses said, and Joe shrugged.

'Perhaps. I do not take chances until it is necessary to do so.' And then he changed direction. 'I asked you once what you thought of Mother Russia.'

'And I replied that she was a friend of the oppressed peoples of the world.'

'She wishes to be your friend also,' Joe said simply.

'Do you mean me personally – Moses Gama?'

'Yes, you personally – Moses Gama.'

'How do you know this?'

'There are men in Moscow who have watched you carefully for many years. What they have seen they approve of. They offer you the hand of friendship.'

'I ask you again. How do you know this?'

'I am a colonel in the Russian KGB. I have been ordered to tell you this.'

Moses stared at him. It was moving so fast that he needed a respite to catch up.

315

'What does the offer of friendship entail?' he asked cautiously, buying time in which to think, and Joe Cicero nodded approvingly.

'It is good you ask the terms of our friendship. It confirms our estimate of you. That you are a careful man. You will be given the answer to that in due course. In the meantime be content with the fact that we have singled you out above all others.'

'Very well,' Moses agreed. 'But tell me why I have been chosen. There are other good men – Mandela is one of them.'

'Mandela was considered, but we do not believe he has the steel. We detect a softness in him. Our psychologists believe that he will flinch from the hard and bloody work of the revolution. We know also that he does not have the same high regard for Mother Russia that you do. He has even called her the new oppressor, the colonialist of the twentieth century.'

'What about the others?' Moses asked.

'There are no others,' Joe told him flatly. 'It was either you or Mandela. It is you. That is the decision.'

'They want my answer now?' Moses stared into the tar pits of his eyes, but they had a strangely lifeless dullness in them and Joe Cicero shook his head.

'They want to meet you, talk to you, make sure you understand the bargain. Then you will be trained and groomed for the task ahead.'

'Where will this meeting take place?'

Joe smiled and shrugged. 'In Moscow – where else?' And Moses did not let his amazement show on his face, though his hands clenched into fists at his sides.

'Moscow! How will I get there?'

'It has been arranged,' Joe assured him, and Moses lifted his head and stared at the tall thunderheads that rose in silver and blue splendour along the horizon. He was lost in thought for many minutes.

He felt his spirits grow light and take wing up towards those soaring thunder clouds. It had come – the moment for which he had worked and waited a lifetime. Destiny had cleared the field of all his rivals, and he had been chosen.

Like a victor's laurel they were offering a land and a crown.

'I will go to meet them,' he agreed softly.

'You will leave in two days' time. It will take me that long to make the final arrangements. In the meantime keep out of sight, do not attempt to take leave of any friends, do not tell anybody you are going – not even the Courtney woman or your new wife. I will get a message to you through Marcus Archer, and if he is arrested before then, I will contact you at the expedition base at Sundi Caves. Professor Hurst is a sympathizer.' Joe dropped the butt of his cigarette and while he ground it under his heel, he lit another. 'Now we will go back to the car.'

Victoria Gama stood at the top end of the sloping lawns of the Baragwanath nurses' home. She was still dressed in her uniform with the badges of a nursing sister sparkling on her tunic, but she looked very young and self-conscious as she faced the hundred or so off-duty nurses who were gathered on the lawns below her. The white matron had refused permission for them to meet in the dining-hall, so they were standing out under a sky full of towering thunderheads.

'My sisters!' She held out her hands towards them. 'We have a duty to our patients – to those in pain, to those suffering and dying, to those who turn to us in trust. However, I believe that we have a higher duty and more sacred commitment to all our people who for three hundred years have suffered under a fierce and unrelenting oppression—'

Victoria seemed to gather confidence as she spoke, and her sweet young voice had a music and rhythm that caught their attention. She had always been popular with the other nurses, and her winning personality, her capacity for hard work and her unselfish attitude had seen her emerge, not only as one of the most senior nursing staff for her age, but also as an example and a trend-setter amongst the younger nurses. There were women ten and fifteen years older than she was, who listened now to her with attention and who applauded her when she paused for breath. Their applause and approval bolstered Victoria and her voice took on a sharper tone.

'Across the land our leaders, in actions rather than pale words, are showing the oppressors that we will no longer remain passive and acquiescent. They are crying to the world for justice and humanity. What kind of women will we be if we stand aside and refuse to join them? How can we ignore the fact that our leaders are being arrested and harassed by the infernal laws—'

There was a stir in the crowd of uniformed nurses, and the faces which had been lifted towards Victoria turned away and the expressions of rapt concentration changed to consternation. From the edges of the crowd one or two of the nurses broke away and scuttled back up the steps of the nurses' home.

Three police vans had driven up to the gates, and the white matron and two of her senior staff had hurried out to confer with the police captain in charge of the contingent as he alighted from the leading vehicle. The matron's white tunic and skirt contrasted with the blue of the police uniforms, and she was pointing at Victoria and talking animatedly to the captain.

Victoria's voice faltered, and despite her resolve, she was afraid. It was an instinctive and corrosive fear. From her earliest remembered childhood the blue police uniforms had been symbols of unquestionable might and authority.

To defy them now went against all her instincts and the teaching of her father and all her elders.

'Do not challenge the white man,' they had taught her. 'For his wrath is more terrible than the summer fires that consume the veld. None can stand before it.'

Then she remembered Moses Gama, and her voice firmed; she beat down her fear and cried aloud, 'Look at yourselves, my sisters. See how you tremble and cast your eyes down at the sight of the oppressor. He has not yet spoken nor raised a hand to you, but you have become little children!'

The police captain left the group at the gate and came to the edge of the lawn. There he paused and raised a bull-horn to his lips.

'This is an illegal gathering on state-owned property.' His voice was magnified and distorted. 'You have five minutes to disperse and return to your quarters.' He raised his arm and ostentatiously checked his wristwatch. 'If you have not done so in that time—'

The nurses were scattering already, scampering away, not waiting for the officer to complete his warning, and Victoria found herself alone on the wide lawn. She wanted to run and hide also, but she thought about Moses Gama and her pride would not let her move.

The police officer lowered his loud-hailer and turned back to the white matron. They conferred again, and the officer showed her a sheaf of paper which he took from his dispatch case. The matron nodded and they both looked at Victoria again. Alone now, she still stood at the top of the lawn. Pride and fear held her rigid. She stood stiffly, unable to move as the police captain marched across to where she stood.

'Victoria Dinizulu?' he asked her in a normal conversational voice, so different from the hoarse booming of the loud-hailer.

Victoria nodded, and then remembered. 'No,' she

denied. 'I am Victoria Gama.' The police officer looked confused. He was very fair-skinned with a fine blond moustache. 'I was told you were Victoria Dinizulu – there has been a mess-up,' he muttered, and then he blushed with embarrassment and immediately Victoria felt sorry for him.

'I got married,' she explained. 'My maiden name was Victoria Dinizulu, but now I am Victoria Gama.'

'Oh, I see.' The captain looked relieved, and glanced down at the document in his hand. 'It's made out to Victoria Dinizulu. I suppose it's still all right, though.' He was uncertain again.

'It's not your fault,' Victoria consoled him. 'The wrong name, I mean. They can't blame you. You couldn't have known.'

'No, you're right.' The captain perked up visibly. 'It's not my fault. I'll just serve it on you anyway. They can sort it out back at HQ.'

'What is it?' Victoria asked curiously.

'It's a banning order,' the captain explained. He showed it to her. 'It's signed by the Minister of Police. I have to read it to you, then you have to sign it,' he explained and then he looked contrite. 'I'm sorry, it's my duty.'

'That is all right.' Vicky smiled at him. 'You have to do your duty.'

He looked down at the document again and began to read aloud:

TO VICTORIA THANDELA DINIZULU

Notice in terms of Section 9(i) of the Internal Security Act 1950 (Act 44 of 1950). Whereas I, Manfred De La Rey, Minister of Police, am satisfied that you are engaged in activities which endanger or are calculated to endanger the maintenance of public order –

The captain stumbled over the more complicated legal phraseology and mispronounced some of the English words. Vicky corrected him helpfully. The banning document was four typewritten pages, and the policeman reached the end of it with patent relief.

'You have to sign here.' He offered her the document.

'I don't have a pen.'

'Here, use mine.'

'Thank you,' said Victoria. 'You are very kind.'

She signed her name in the space provided and as she handed him back his pen, she had ceased to be a complete person. Her banning order prohibited her from being in the company of more than two other persons at any one time, except in the course of her daily work, of addressing any gathering or preparing any written article for publication. It confined her physically to the magisterial area of Johannesburg and required that she remain under house arrest for twelve hours of the day and also that she report daily to her local police station.

'I'm sorry,' the police captain repeated, as he screwed the top back on his pen. 'You seem a decent girl.'

'It's your job,' Victoria smiled back at him. 'Don't feel bad about it.'

Over the following days Victoria retreated into the strange half-world of isolation. During working hours she found that her peers and superiors avoided her, as though she were a carrier of plague. The matron moved her out of the room that she shared with two other nursing sisters and she was given a small single room on the unpopular southern side of the hostel which never received the sun in winter. In this room her meals were served to her on a tray as she was prohibited from using the dining-hall when more than two other persons were present. Each evening after coming off shift she made the two-mile walk down to the police station to sign the register, but this soon became a pleasant outing rather than a penance. She was able to smile and greet the people she passed on the street for they did not know she was a non-person and she enjoyed even that fleeting human contact.

Alone in her room she listened to her portable radio and read the books that Moses had given her, and thought about him. More than once she heard his name on the radio. Apparently a controversial film had been shown on the NABS television channel in the United States which had created a furore across the continent. It seemed that South Africa, which for most Americans was a territory remote as the moon and a thousand times less important, was suddenly a political topic. In the film Moses Gama had figured largely, and such was his presence and stature that he had been accepted abroad as the central figure in the African struggle. In the United Nations debate which had followed the television film, nearly every one of the speakers had referred to Moses Gama. Although the motion in the General Assembly calling for the condemnation of South Africa's racial discrimination had been vetoed in the Security Council by Great Britain, the debate had sent a ripple across the world and a cold shiver down the spine of the white government in the country.

South Africa had no television network, but on her portable radio Victoria listened to a pungent edition of *Current Affairs* on the state-controlled South African Broadcasting Corporation in which the campaign of defiance was described as the action of a radical minority, and Moses Gama was vilified as a Communist-inspired revolutionary criminal who was still at large, although a warrant had been issued for his arrest on a charge of high treason.

Cut off from all other sympathetic human contact, Victoria found herself pining for him with such desperate longing that she cried herself to sleep in her lonely room each night.

On the tenth day of her banning she was returning from her daily report to the police station, keeping to the edge of the pavement in that sensual gliding walk that the Nguni woman practises from childhood when she carries every load, from faggots of firewood to five-gallon clay pots of water, balanced upon her head. A light delivery van slowed down as it approached her from behind, and began to keep pace with her.

Victoria was accustomed to extravagant male attention, for she was the very essence of Nguni female beauty, and when the driver of the vehicle whistled softly, she did not glance in his direction but lifted her chin an inch and assumed a haughty expression.

The driver whistled again, more demandingly, and from the corner of her eye she saw the van was blue with the sign EXPRESS DRY CLEANERS – SIX HOUR SERVICE painted on the side. The driver was a big man, and although his cap was pulled low over his eyes, she sensed he was attractive and masterful. Despite herself her hips began to swing as she strode on, and her large perfectly round buttocks oscillated like the cheeks of a chipmunk chewing a nut.

'Victoria!' Her name was hissed, and the voice was unmistakable. She stopped dead and swung round to face him.

'You!' she whispered, and then glanced around her frantically.

For the moment the sidewalk was clear and only light traffic moved down the highway between rows of tall bluegum trees. Her eyes flashed back to his face, almost hungrily, and she whispered, 'Oh Moses, I didn't think you'd come.'

He leaned across the front seat of the van and opened the door nearest her, and she rushed across and threw herself into the moving van.

'Get down,' he ordered, and she crouched below the dashboard while he slammed the door closed and accelerated away.

'I couldn't believe it was you. I still don't – this van, where did you get it? Oh Moses, you'll never know how much – I heard your name on the radio, many times – so much has happened—' She found that she was gabbling almost hysterically. It had been so long since she had been able to talk freely, and it was as though the painful abscess of loneliness and longing had burst and all the poison was draining in the rush of words.

She began to tell him about the nurses' strike and the banning, and how Albertina Sisulu had contacted her and there was going to be a march by a hundred thousand women, to the government buildings at Pretoria, and she was going to defy her banning order to join the march.

'I want you to be proud of me. I want to be part of the struggle, for that is the only way I can truly be a part of you.'

Moses Gama drove in silence, smiling a little as he listened to her chatter. He wore blue overalls with the legend 'Express Dry Cleaners' embroidered across his back and the rear of the van was filled with racks of clothing that smelled strongly of cleaning solvent. She knew he had borrowed the van from Hendrick Tabaka.

After a few minutes Moses slowed the van and then turned off sharply on to a spur road which swiftly deteriorated into a rutted track, and then petered out entirely. He bumped the last few yards over tussocks of grass and then parked behind a ruined and roofless building, the windows from which the frames had been ripped out were like the eyes of a skull. Victoria straightened up from under the dashboard.

'I have heard about the nurses' strike and your banning,' he said softly as he switched off the engine. 'And yes, I am proud of you. Very proud. You are a wife fit for a chief.'

She hung her head shyly, and the pleasure his words gave her was almost unbearable. She had not truly realized how much she loved him while they had been separated, and now the full force of it rushed back upon her.

'And you are a chief,' she said. 'No, more than that – you are a king.'

'Victoria, I do not have much time,' he said. 'I should not have come here at all—'

'I would have shrivelled up if you had not – my soul was drought-stricken—' she burst out, but he laid his hand on her arm to still her.

'Listen to me, Victoria. I have come to tell you that I am going away. I have come to charge you to be strong while I am away.'

'Oh, my husband!' In her agitation she lapsed into Zulu. 'Where are you going?'

'I can tell you only that it is to a distant land.'

'Can I not journey by your side?' she pleaded.

'No.'

'Then I will send my heart to be your travelling companion, while the husk of me remains here to await your return. When will you come back, my husband?'

'I do not know, but it will be a long time.'

'For me every minute that you are gone will become a weary day,' she told him quietly, and he raised his hand and stroked her face gently.

'If there is anything you need you must go to Hendrick Tabaka. He is my brother, and I have placed you in his care.'

She nodded, unable to speak.

'There is only one thing I can tell you now. When I return I will take the world we know and turn it on its head. Nothing will ever be the same again.'

'I believe you,' she said simply.

'I must go now,' he told her. 'Our time together has come to an end.'

325

'My husband,' she murmured, casting down her eyes again. 'Let me be a wife to you one last time, for the nights are so long and cold when you are not beside me.'

He took a roll of canvas from the back of the van and spread it on the grass beside the parked van. Her naked body was set off by the white cloth as she lay upon it like a figure cast in dark bronze thrown down upon the snow.

At the end when he had spent himself and lay weak as a child upon her, she clasped his head tenderly to the soft warm swell of her bosom and she whispered to him, 'No matter how far and how long you travel, my love will burn away time and distance and I will be beside you, my husband.'

Tara was waiting for him, with the lantern lit, lying awake in the cottage tent when Moses returned to the camp. She sat up as he came through the fly. The blanket fell to her waist and she was naked. Her breasts were big and white and laced with tiny bluish veins around the swollen nipples – so different from those of the woman he had just left.

'Where have you been?' she demanded.

He ignored the question as he began to undress.

'You have been to see her, haven't you? Joe ordered you not to.'

Now he looked at her scornfully, and then deliberately rebuttoned the front of his overalls as he moved to leave the tent again.

'I'm sorry, Moses,' she cried, instantly terrified by the thought of his going. 'I didn't mean it, please stay. I won't talk like that again. I swear it, my darling. Please forgive me. I was upset, I have had such a terrible dream—' She threw aside the blanket and came up on her knees, reaching out both hands towards him. 'Please!' she entreated. 'Please come to me.'

For long seconds he stared at her and then began once more to unbutton his overalls. She clung to him desperately as he came into the bed.

'Oh, Moses – I had such a dream. I dreamed of Sister Nunziata again. Oh God, the look on their faces as they ate her flesh. They were like wolves, their mouths red and running with her blood. It was the most horrific thing, beyond my imagination. It made me want to despair for all the world.'

'No,' he said. His voice was low but it reverberated through her body as though she were the sounding box of a violin trembling to the power of the strings. 'No!' he said. 'It was beauty – stark beauty, shorn of all but the truth. What you witnessed was the rage of the people, and it was a holy thing. Before that I merely hoped, but after witnessing that I could truly believe. It was a consecration of our victory. They ate the flesh and drank the blood as you Christians do to seal a pact with history. When you have seen that sacred rage you have to believe in our eventual triumph.'

He sighed, his great muscular chest heaved in the circle of her arms and then he went to sleep. It was something to which she could never grow accustomed, the way he could sleep as though he had closed a door in his mind. She was left bereft and afraid, for she knew what lay ahead for her.

Joe Cicero came for Moses in the night. Moses had dressed like one of a thousand other contract workers from the goldmines in an Army-surplus greatcoat and woollen balaclava helmet that covered most of his face. He had no luggage, as Joe had instructed him, and when the ramshackle Ford pick-up parked across the road from them and flashed its lights once, Moses slipped out of the Cadillac and swiftly crossed to it. He did not say goodbye to Tara, they had taken their farewells long ago, and he did not look back to where she sat forlornly behind the wheel of the Cadillac.

As soon as Moses climbed into the rear of the Ford, it pulled away. The tail lights dwindled and were lost around the first curve of the road, and Tara was smothered by such a crushing load of despair that she did not believe she could survive it.

François Afrika was the headmaster of the Mannenberg coloured school on the Cape Flats. He was a little over forty years old, a plump and serious man with a *café au lait* complexion and thick very curly hair which he parted in the middle and plastered flat with Vaseline.

His wife Miriam was plump also, but much shorter and younger than he. She had taught history and English at the Mannenberg junior school until the headmaster had married her, and she had given him four children, all daughters. Miriam was president of the local chapter of the Women's Institute which she used as a convenient cover for her political activities. She had been arrested during the defiance campaign, but when that petered out she had not been charged and had been released under a banning order. Three months later, when the furore had died away completely, her banning order had not been renewed.

Molly Broadhurst had known her since before she had married François, and the couple were frequent visitors at Molly's home. Behind her thick spectacles Miriam wore a perpetual chubby smile. Her home in the grounds of the junior school was as clean as an operating theatre with crocheted antimacassars on the heavy maroon easy chairs, and a mirrorlike shine on the floors. Her daughters were always beautifully dressed with coloured ribbons in their pigtails and like Miriam were chubby and contented, a consequence of Miriam's cookery rather than her genes.

Tara met Miriam for the first time at Molly's home. Tara had come down by train from the expedition base at Sundi Caves two weeks before her baby was due. She had booked a private coupé compartment and kept the door locked throughout the entire journey to avoid being recognized. Molly had met her at Paarl station, for she had not wanted to risk being seen at the main Cape Town terminus. Shasa and her family still believed that she was working with Professor Hurst.

Miriam was all that Tara had hoped for, all that Molly had promised her, although she was not prepared for the maternity dress.

'You are pregnant also?' she demanded as they shook hands, and Miriam patted her stomach shyly.

'It's a cushion, Miss Tara, I couldn't just pop a baby out of nowhere, could I? I started with just a small lump as soon as Molly told me, and I've built it up slowly.'

Tara realized what inconvenience she had put her to, and now she embraced her impulsively. 'Oh, I can never tell you how grateful I am. Please don't call me Miss Tara. I'm your friend and plain Tara will do very well.'

'I'll look after your baby like it's my own, I promise you,' Miriam told her, and then saw Tara's expression and hastily qualified her assurance. 'But he will always be yours, Tara. You can come and see him whenever, and one day if you are able to take him – well, François and I won't stand in your way.'

'You are even nicer than Molly told me!' Tara hugged her. 'Come, I want to show you the clothes I've brought for our baby.'

'Oh, they are all blue,' Miriam exclaimed. 'You are so sure you are going to have a boy?'

'No question about it – I'm sure.'

'So was I,' Miriam chuckled. 'And look at me now – all girls! Though it's not too bad, they are good girls and they are all expecting this one to be a boy,' she patted her padded abdomen, 'and I know they are going to spoil him something terrible.'

Tara's baby was born in Molly Broadhurst's guest room. Dr Chetty Abrahamji who delivered it was an old friend of Molly's and had been a secret member of the Communist Party, one of its few Hindu members.

As soon as Tara went into labour, Molly telephoned Miriam Afrika, and she arrived with bag and bulging tummy and went in directly to see Tara.

'I'm so glad we have started at last,' she cried. 'I must admit that although it was a difficult pregnancy, it will be my quickest and easiest delivery.' She reached up under her own skirt and with a flourish produced the cushion. Tara laughed with her and then broke off as the next contraction seized her.

'Ouch!' she whispered. 'I wish mine was that easy. This one feels like a giant.'

Molly and Miriam took turns, sitting beside her and holding her hand when the contractions hit her, and the doctor stood at the foot of the bed exhorting her to, 'Push! Push!' By noon the following day Tara was exhausted, panting and racked, her hair sodden with sweat as though she had plunged into the sea.

'It's no good,' the doctor said softly. 'We'll have to move you into hospital and do a Caesar.'

'No! No!' Tara struggled up on an elbow, fierce with determination. 'Give me one more chance.'

When the next contraction came she bore down on it with such force that every muscle in her body locked and she thought the sinews in her loins must snap like rubber bands. Nothing happened, it was jammed solid, and she could feel the blockage like a great log stuck inside her.

'More!' Molly whispered in her ear. 'Harder – once more for the baby.' Tara bore down again with the strength of desperation and then screamed as she felt her flesh tear like tissue paper. There was a hot slippery rush between her thighs and relief so intense that her scream changed to a long drawn-out cry of joy, that joined with her infant's birth cry.

'Is it a boy?' she gasped, trying to sit up. 'Tell me – tell me quickly.'

'Yes,' Molly reassured her. 'It's a boy – just look at his whistle. Long as my finger. There's no doubt about that – he's a boy all right,' and Tara laughed out aloud.

He weighed nine and a half pounds with a head that was covered with pitch-black hair, thick and curly as the fleece of an Astrakhan lamb. He was the colour of hot toffee, and he had Moses Gama's fine Nilotic features. Tara had never seen anything so beautiful in all her life, none of her other babies had been anything like this.

'Let me hold him,' she croaked, hoarse with the terrible effort of his birth, and they placed the child still wet and slippery in her arms.

'I want to feed him,' she whispered. 'I must give him his first suck – then he will be mine for ever.' She squeezed out her nipple and pressed it between his lips and he fastened on it, snuffling and kicking spasmodically with pleasure.

'What is his name, Tara?' Miriam Afrika asked.

'We'll call him Benjamin,' Tara said. 'Benjamin Afrika. I like that – he is truly of Africa.'

Tara stayed with the infant five days. When finally she had to relinquish him, and Miriam drove away with him in her little Morris Minor, Tara felt as though part of her soul had been hacked away by the crudest surgery. If Molly had not been there to help her through, Tara knew she could not have borne it. As it was Molly had something for her.

'I've been saving it until now,' she told Tara. 'I knew how you would feel when you had to give up your baby. This will cheer you up a little.' She handed Tara an envelope, and Tara examined the handwritten address. 'I don't recognize the writing.' She looked mystified.

'I received it by a special courier – open it up. Go on!' Molly ordered impatiently, and Tara obeyed. There were four sheets of cheap writing paper. Tara turned to the last sheet and as she read the signature her expression altered.

'Moses!' she cried. 'Oh I can't believe it – after all these months. I had given up hope. I didn't even recognize his handwriting.' Tara clutched the letter to her breast.

'He wasn't allowed to write, Tara dear. He has been in a very strict training camp. He disobeyed orders and took a grave risk to get this note out to you.' Molly went to the door. 'I'll leave you in peace to read it. I know it will make up a little for your loss.'

Even after Molly had left her alone, Tara was reluctant to begin reading. She wanted to savour the pleasure of anticipation, but at last she could deny herself no longer.

Tara, my dearest,

I think of you every day in this place, where the work is very hard and demanding, and I wonder about you and our baby. Perhaps it has already been born, I do not know, and I wonder often if it is a boy or a little girl.

Although what I am doing is of the greatest importance for all of us – for the people of Africa, as well as for you and me – yet I find myself longing for you. The thought of you comes to me unexpectedly in the night and in the day and it is like a knife in my chest.

Tara could not read on, her eyes were awash with tears. 'Oh, Moses,' she bit her lip to prevent herself blubbering, 'I never knew you could feel like that for me.' She wiped her eyes with the back of her hand.

When I left you, I did not know where I was going, nor what awaited me here. Now everything is clear, and I know what the difficult tasks are that lie ahead of us. I know also that I will need your help. You will not refuse me, my wife? I call you 'wife' because that is how I feel towards you, now that you are carrying our child.

It was difficult for Tara to take it in. She had never expected him to give her this kind of recognition and now she felt humbled by it.

'There is nothing that I could ever refuse you,' she whispered aloud, and her eyes raced down the sheet. She turned it over quickly and Moses had written:

Once before I told you how valuable it would be if you used your family connections to keep us informed of affairs of state. Since then this has become more imperative. Your husband, Shasa Courtney, is going over to the side of the neo-Fascist oppressors. Although this fills you with hatred and contempt for him, yet it is a boon we could not have expected or prayed for. Our information is that he has been promised a place in the cabinet of that barbarous regime. If you were in his confidence, it would afford us a direct inside view and knowledge of all their plans and intentions. This would be so valuable that it would be impossible to put a price upon it.

'No,' she whispered, shaking her head, sensing what was coming, and it took courage for her to read on.

I ask you, for the sake of our land and our love, that when the child has been born and you are recovered from the birth, that you return to your husband's home at Weltevreden, ask his forgiveness for your absence, tell him that you cannot live without him and his children, and do all in your power to ingratiate yourself with him and to earn his confidence once more.

'I cannot do it,' Tara whispered, and then she thought of the children, and especially of Michael, and she felt herself wavering. 'Oh, Moses, you don't know what you are asking of me.' She covered her eyes with her hand. 'Please don't make me do it. I have only just won my freedom – don't force me to give it up again.' But the letter went on remorselessly:

> Every one of us will be called upon to make sacrifice in the struggle that lies ahead. Some of us may be required to lay down our very lives and I could well be one of those.

'No, not you, my darling, please not you!'

> However, for the loyal and true comrades there will be rewards, immediate rewards in addition to the ultimate victory of the struggle and the final liberation. If you can bring yourself to do as I ask you, then my friends here will arrange for you and me to be together – not where we have to hide our love, but in a free and foreign land where, for a happy interlude, we can enjoy our love to the utmost. Can you imagine that, my darling? Being able to spend the days and nights together, to walk in the streets hand in hand, to dine together in public and laugh openly together, to stand up unafraid and say what we think aloud, to kiss and do all the silly adorable things that lovers do, and to hold the child of our love between us—

It was too painful, she could not go on. When Molly found her weeping bitterly, she sat on the bed beside her and took her in her arms.

'What is it, Tara dear, tell me, tell old Molly.'

'I have to go back to Weltevreden,' she sobbed. 'Oh,

God, Molly, I thought I was rid of that place for ever, and now I have to go back.'

Tara's request for a formal meeting to discuss their matrimonial arrangements threw Shasa into a state of utmost consternation. He had been well enough satisfied by the informal understanding between them, by which he had complete freedom of action and control of the children, together with the respectability and protection of the marriage form. He had been happy to pay without comment the bills that Tara forwarded to him, and to see that her generous allowance was paid into her bank account promptly on the first of each month. He had even made good the occasional shortfall when the bank manager telephoned him to report that Tara had overdrawn. On one occasion there was a cheque made out to a second-hand motor dealer, for almost a thousand pounds. Shasa did not query it. Whatever it was, it was a bargain as far as he was concerned.

Now it looked as if all this was coming to an end, and Shasa immediately called a meeting of his principal advisers in the boardroom of Centaine House. Centaine herself was in the chair and Abraham Abrahams had flown down from Johannesburg, bringing with him the senior partner of a firm of renowned but very expensive divorce lawyers.

Centaine took over immediately. 'Let us consider the worst possible case,' she told them crisply. 'Tara will want the children and she'll want a settlement, plus a living allowance for herself and each of the children.' She glanced at Abe, who nodded his silver head, which set the rest of the legal counsel nodding like mandarin dolls, looking grave and learned, and secretly counting their fees, Shasa thought wryly.

'Damn it, the woman deserted me! I'll go to hell before I give her my children.'

'She will claim that you made it impossible for her to remain in the conjugal home,' Abe said, and then when he saw Shasa's thunderous expression, tried to soothe him. 'You must remember, Shasa, that she will probably be taking the best available legal advice herself.'

'Damned shyster lawyers!' said Shasa bitterly, and his counsel looked pained, but Shasa did not apologize nor qualify. 'I've already warned her I won't give her a divorce. My political career is at a very delicate stage. I cannot afford the scandal. Very soon I'll be contesting a general election.'

'You may not be able to refuse,' Abe murmured. 'Not if she has good grounds.'

'She hasn't any,' said Shasa virtuously. 'I've always been the considerate and generous husband.'

'Your generosity is famous,' Abe murmured drily. 'There is many an attractive young lady who could give you a testimonial on that score.'

'Really, Abe,' Centaine intervened. 'Shasa has always kept out of trouble with women—'

'Centaine, my dear. We are dealing with facts here – not maternal illusions. I am not a private detective and Shasa's private life is none of my concern. However, completely disinterested as I am, I am able to cite you at least six occasions in the last few years when Shasa has given Tara ample grounds—'

Shasa was making frantic signals down the table to shut Abe up, but Centaine leaned forward with an interested expression.

'Go ahead, Abe,' she ordered. 'Start citing!'

'In January two years ago the leading lady in the touring production of the musical *Oklahoma!*,' Abe began, and Shasa sank down in his chair and covered his eyes as though in prayer. 'A few weeks later the left-winger, ironically, in the visiting British women's hockey team.' So far Abe was avoiding mentioning names, but now he went on. 'Then there was the female TV producer from North American Broadcasting Studios, pert little vixen with a name like a fish – no, a dolphin, that's it, Kitty Godolphin. Do you want me to go on? There are a few more, but as I have said already, I'm not a private investigator. You can be sure that Tara will get herself a good one, and Shasa makes very little effort to cover his tracks.'

'That will do, Abe,' Centaine stopped him, and considered her son with disapproval and a certain grudging admiration.

'It's the de Thiry blood,' she thought. 'The family curse. Poor Shasa.' But she said sternly, 'It looks as though we do have a problem after all,' and she turned to the divorce lawyer.

'Let us accept that Tara has grounds of infidelity. What is the worst judgement we might expect against us?'

'It's very difficult, Mrs Courtney—'

'I'm not going to hold you to it,' Centaine told him brusquely. 'You don't have to equivocate. Just give me the worst case.'

'She could get custody, especially of the two younger children, and a large settlement.'

'How much?' Shasa demanded.

'Considering your circumstances, it could be—' the lawyer hesitated delicately ' – a million pounds, plus the trimmings, a house and allowance and a few other lesser items.'

Shasa sat up very straight in his chair. He whistled softly and then murmured, 'That is really taking seriously something that was merely poked in fun,' he said, and nobody laughed.

So Shasa took pains preparing for the reunion with Tara. He studied the written advice which Abe and the other lawyers had drawn up for him, and had his tactics firmly established. He knew what to say and what to avoid. He was to make no admissions and no promises, particularly regarding the children.

For the venue he chose the pool at the foot of the Constantia Berg, hoping that Tara would associate it with the happy hours they had spent there. He had his chef prepare an exquisite picnic hamper which contained all Tara's favourite delicacies, and he chose half a dozen bottles of his best wines from the cellar.

He took especial care with his appearance. He had his hair trimmed and picked out a new black silk eye-patch from the drawer that he kept full of them. He wore the after-shave she had given him and the cream-coloured wild silk suit which she had once remarked on favourably, with his Air Force scarf in the open neck of his blue shirt.

All the children were packed off to Rhodes Hill, into Centaine's care for the weekend, and he sent the chauffeur in the Rolls to fetch Tara from Molly Broadhurst's home where she was staying. The chauffeur brought her directly up to the pool and Shasa opened the door for her, and was surprised when she offered him her cheek for his kiss.

'You look so well, my dear,' he told her, and it was not entirely untrue. She had lost a lot of weight, her waist was once again wasped in and her bosom was magnificent. Despite the gravity of the moment Shasa felt his loins stir as he looked down that cleavage.

'Down, boy!' he admonished himself silently and looked away, concentrating on her face. Her skin had cleared, the rings below her eyes were barely discernible and her hair had been washed and set. Obviously she had taken the same pains with her appearance as he had.

'Where are the children?' she demanded immediately.

'Mater has them – so we could talk without interruption.'

'How are they, Shasa?'

'They are all just fine. Couldn't be better.' He wanted there to be no special pleading on that score.

'I do miss them terribly,' she said. The remark was ominous, and he did not reply. Instead he led her to the summerhouse and settled her on the couch facing the waterfall.

'It's so beautiful here.' She looked around her. 'It is my favourite spot on all of Weltevreden.' She took the wine-glass he handed her.

'Better days!' He gave her the toast. They clinked glasses and drank.

Then she set her glass down on the marble table-top and Shasa steeled himself to receive the opening shot of the engagement.

'I want to come back home,' she said, and he spilled white wine down the front of his silk suit, and then dabbed at it with the handkerchief from his breast pocket to give himself time to recover his balance.

In a perverse way he had been looking forward to the bargaining. He was a businessman, supremely confident in his ability to get the best trade. Furthermore, he had already adjusted to the idea of becoming a bachelor once more, and was beginning to look forward to the delights of that state, even if it cost him a million pounds. He felt the prickle of disappointment.

'I don't understand,' he said carefully.

'I miss the children. I want to be with them – and yet I don't want to take them away from you. They need a father as much as a mother.'

It was too easy. There had to be more than that, Shasa's bargaining instincts were sure.

'I have tried living alone,' she went on. 'And I don't like it. I want to come back.'

'So we just pick it up again where we dropped it?' he asked carefully, but she shook her head.

'That's impossible, we both know that.' She prevented further questions with a raised hand. 'Let me tell you what I want. I want to have all the benefits of my old life, access to my children, the prestige that goes with the name Courtney and the money not to have to stint—'

'You were always scornful of the position and the money before.' He could not prevent the jibe, but she took no offence.

'I had never had to do without it before,' she said simply. 'However, I want to be able to go away for a while when it becomes too much for me here – but I will not embarrass you politically or in any other way.' She paused. 'That's all of it.'

'And what do I get in return?' he asked.

'A mother for your children, and a public wife. I will preside at your dinner-parties, and make myself agreeable to your associates, I will even help you with your political electioneering, I used to be very good at that.'

'I thought that my politics disgusted you.'

'They do – but I will never let it show.'

'What about my conjugal rights, as they are delicately referred to by the lawyers?'

'No.' She shook her head. 'That will only complicate our relationship.' She thought of Moses. She could never be unfaithful to him, even if he had ordered it. 'No, but I have no objection to you going elsewhere. You have always been reasonably discreet. I know you will continue to be.'

He looked at her bosom and felt a twinge of regret, but the bargain she was offering amazed him. He had everything he wanted, and had saved himself a million pounds into the bargain.

'Is that all?' he asked. 'Are you sure?'

'Unless you can think of anything else we should discuss.'

He shook his head. 'Shall we shake hands on it – and open a bottle of the Widow?'

340

She smiled at him over the rim of her glass to conceal what she truly felt for him and his world, and she made a vow as she sipped the tingling yellow wine.

'You will pay, Shasa Courtney, you will pay for your bargain much more than you ever dreamed.'

For over a decade Tara had been the mistress of Weltevreden, so there was nothing difficult or alien in taking up that role again, except that now more than ever she felt that she was acting a part in a tedious and unconvincing play.

There were some differences, however. The guest list had altered subtly, and now included most of the top Nationalist politicians and party organizers, and more often than before the conversation at the dinner-table was in Afrikaans rather than English. Tara's knowledge of Afrikaans was adequate, it was after all a very simple language with a grammar so uncomplicated that the verbs were not even conjugated and much of the vocabulary was taken directly from English. However, she had some difficulty with the guttural inflections, and most of the time smiled sweetly and remained silent. She found that by doing so her presence was soon overlooked and she heard much more than she would have had she joined in the conversation.

A frequent visitor to Weltevreden now was the Minister of Police, Manfred De La Rey, and Tara found it ironical that she was expected to feed and entertain the one man who to her epitomized all that was evil and cruel in the oppressive regime that she hated with all her being. It was like sitting down to a meal with a man-eating leopard, even his eyes were pale and cruel as those of a great predatory cat.

Strangely, she found that despite her loathing, the man

fascinated her. It surprised her to find, once she had got over the initial shock of his presence, that he had a fine brain. Of course it was common knowledge that he had been a brilliant student in the law faculty of Stellenbosch University, and before standing for parliament he had built up a highly successful law practice in his own right. She knew also that no man who was not essentially brilliant was included in the Nationalist cabinet, yet his intelligence was sinister and ominous. She found herself listening to the most heinous concepts expressed with such logic and eloquent conviction that she had to shake herself out of his mesmeric influence, like a bird trying to break the spell of the cobra's swaying dance.

Manfred De La Rey's relationship to the Courtney family was another enigma to her. It was part of family lore how his father had robbed the H'ani Mine of a million pounds worth of diamonds, and how Blaine, her own father, and Centaine, before she was Blaine's wife, had pursued him into the desert and after a fierce battle captured him. Manfred's father had served fifteen years of a life sentence before being released under the amnesty that the Nationalists had granted to so many Afrikaner prisoners when they came to power in 1948.

The two families should have been bitter enemies, and indeed Tara detected definite traces of that hatred in the occasional tone of a remark and unguarded look that Manfred De La Rey and Shasa directed at each other, and there was a peculiarly brittle and artificial quality to the overtly friendly façade they showed, as though at any moment it might be stripped away and they would fly at each other's throats like fighting dogs.

On the other hand, Tara knew that Manfred was the one who had enticed Shasa into forsaking the ailing United Party and joining the Nationalists with the promise of ministerial rank, and that Shasa had made the De La Reys, father and son, major shareholders and directors in the new fish-canning company at Walvis Bay, a company which looked set to turn half a million pounds of profit in its very first year of operation.

The mystery of their relationship was made even more intriguing by Centaine. On the second occasion that Shasa invited Manfred De La Rey and his wife to dine at Weltevreden, Centaine had telephoned her a few days beforehand, and asked her bluntly if she and Blaine might join the party.

Although Tara had determined to see as little of Centaine as possible, and to do all in her power to reduce Centaine's influence over the children and the general running of the estate, Tara had been so taken aback by the direct request that she had not been able to think of an excuse.

'Of course, Mater,' she had agreed with false enthusiasm. 'I would have invited you and Daddy anyway, but I thought you might have found the evening tedious, and I know Daddy cannot abide De La Rey—'

'Whatever gave you that idea, Tara?' Centaine asked tartly. 'They are on opposite sides of the House, but Blaine has a healthy respect for De La Rey, and he concedes that De La Rey certainly handled the troubles firmly enough. His police did a magnificent job in clamping down on the ringleaders and preventing serious disruptions and further loss of life.'

Furious words filled Tara's mouth and she wanted to hurl them at her mother-in-law, but she gritted her teeth and took a deep breath, before she said sweetly, 'Well then, Mater, both Shasa and I will be looking forward to Friday night. Half-past seven for eight, and naturally the men will be wearing black tie.'

'Naturally,' said Centaine.

It had been a surprisingly mellow evening, when the explosive elements seated around the same table were considered, but it was a strict rule of Shasa's that shop party

343

politics were never discussed in Weltevreden's palatial dining-room. The men's conversation ranged from the projected All Blacks rugby tour to the recent angling capture of a six hundred pound blue-fin tunny in False Bay, the first of its kind. Manfred De La Rey and Blaine were both keen anglers and were excited by the prospect of such a magnificent prize.

Centaine was unusually quiet during the meal. Tara had placed her beside Manfred, but she listened attentively to everything that he said, and when they went through to the blue drawing-room at the end of the meal she stayed close to Manfred, and the two of them were soon oblivious of everyone else, lost in rapt but low-voiced discussion.

Manfred's statuesque blonde German wife, Heidi, had failed to enthral Tara with a long-winded complaint about the laziness and dishonesty of her coloured servants, and Tara escaped as soon as she could and took another cognac to her father on the long blue velvet sofa, and then settled beside him.

'Centaine says that you admire De La Rey,' she said quietly, and they both looked across at the other couple on the far side of the room.

'He's a formidable piece of work,' Blaine grunted. 'Hard as iron and sharp as an axe. Do you know even his own colleagues call him "Panga Man"?'

'Why does he fascinate Centaine so much? She rang me and demanded an invitation when she knew he would be here. She seems to have some sort of obsession with him. Why is that, Daddy, do you know?'

Blaine dropped his eyes and considered the firm grey ash on his cigar. What could he tell her? he wondered. He was one of probably only four people in the world who knew Manfred De La Rey was Centaine's bastard son. He remembered his own shock and horror when she had told him. Not even Shasa knew that he and Manfred were half-brothers, though Manfred knew, of course. Centaine had told him, when she used it as blackmail to prevent Manfred destroying Shasa's political career back in 1948.

It was all so complicated, and Blaine found himself disturbed as he had been so often over the years by the echoes of Centaine's follies and indiscretions before he had met her. Then he smiled ruefully. She was still a fiery and impetuous woman, and he wouldn't have had it any other way.

'I think she is interested in anything that affects Shasa's career. It's only natural she should be. De La Rey is Shasa's sponsor. It's as simple as that, my dear.'

'Yes, De La Rey is his sponsor,' Tara agreed. 'But what do you think, Daddy, about Shasa's turn of political coats?'

Despite her resolution to remain calm, she had raised her voice in agitation, and Shasa, who was in intimate conversation with the French Ambassador's chic and bold-eyed young second wife, heard his name across the room and glanced up in her direction. Tara dropped her voice quickly.

'What do you think of it, Daddy? Weren't you simply appalled?'

'I was at first,' Blaine admitted. 'But then I discussed it with Centaine and Shasa came to see me. We thrashed it out between us, and I had my say – but in the end I came to see his point of view. I don't agree with it, but I respect it. He believes that he can do the greatest good—' Tara heard her own father repeating all Shasa's trite and glib justifications and the sense of outrage overwhelmed her all over again. She found herself trembling with suppressed passion, and she wanted to scream out at them, Shasa and Centaine and her own father, but then she thought of Moses and the struggle and with an effort she was able to retain her self-control.

'I must remember everything,' she told herself. 'Everything that they say or do. Even the smallest detail might be of inestimable value to the struggle.'

So, faithfully, she reported it all to Molly Broadhurst. She slipped away from Weltevreden at least once a week on the pretence of visiting her dressmaker or her hairdresser. She and Molly met only after Tara had taken elaborate precautions to make sure she was not followed. Her instructions were to cut all her left-wing connections and to refrain at all times from political or socialistic comments in the presence of others. Molly was her only contact with the real world of the struggle, and she treasured every minute of their time together.

Miriam Afrika was always able to bring the baby to be with her during these interludes, and Tara held him in her arms and fed him his bottle as she made her report to Molly. Everything about little Benjamin fascinated her, from the tight curls of crisp black hair that covered his scalp, through the exquisite softness and colour shading of his skin – honey and old ivory – down to the soles of his tiny feet which were the palest, clearest, coral pink.

Then on one of her visits Molly had another letter for her from Moses, and even the joy of holding baby Benjamin paled beside that of those written words.

The letter had been written in Addis Ababa, the capital of Ethiopia. Moses was there to address a meeting of the heads of the black African states at the express invitation of the Emperor Haile Selassie, and he described to her the warm welcome that he had been given, and the offers of support, moral, financial and military, that had been pledged to the struggle in Anzania – that was the new name for South Africa. It was the first time she had heard it, and when she repeated it aloud, the sound of it stirred a deep patriotic response in her that she had never felt before. She read the rest of Moses' letter:

From here I will travel on to Algeria, where I will meet with Colonel Boumédienne, who is at this moment struggling against French imperialism, and whose great valour will surely bring freedom and happiness to his tragically oppressed land.

After that I will fly to New York, and it seems certain that I will be allowed to put our case to the General Assembly of the United Nations. All this is exciting, but I have even better news that affects you and our baby Benjamin.

If you continue the important work you are doing for the cause, our powerful friends are determined to give you a special reward. Some day the three of us – you and me and Benjamin – will be together in London. I cannot tell you how greatly I look forward to holding my son and to greeting you again.

I will write to you as soon as I have more definite news. In the meantime I entreat you to continue your valuable work for the cause, in particular you should make every effort to see that your husband is elected to the government front benches at the elections next month. This will make your position and value to the struggle unique.

For days after receiving this letter Tara's mood was so light and gay that both Shasa and Centaine remarked on it, and took it as a sign that she had finally accepted her responsibilities as the mistress of Weltevreden, and was prepared to honour the agreement that she had made with Shasa.

When the Prime Minister announced the date of the general election the country was immediately seized by the peculiar frenzy of excitement and intrigue which accompanies all major political activity in South Africa and the newspapers began their strident and partisan pronouncements.

Shasa's resignation from the United Party and his nomination as the Nationalist candidate for the constituency of South Boland was one of the highlights of the campaign. The English press castigated him, branding him a coward and a traitor, while the *Burger* and the *Transvaler*, those stalwarts of the Nationalist cause, hailed him as a far-seeing man of the future and looked forward to the day when all white South Africans, albeit under the firm hand of the National Party, marched shoulder to shoulder towards the golden republic which was the dream of all true South African patriots.

Kitty Godolphin had flown back from New York to cover the elections and to up-date her famous 'Focus on Africa' series that had won her another Emmy and had made her one of the highest paid of the new generation of young, pretty and waspish television commentators.

Shasa's political defection was the headline story when she landed at Jan Smuts Airport, and she telephoned him from the airport on his private line and got him in his office just as the board meeting he had been chairing broke up and he was about to leave Centaine House to fly up to the H'ani Mine for his monthly inspection.

'Hi!' she said gaily. 'It's me.'

'You bitch.' He recognized her voice instantly. 'After what you did to me, I should kick your bottom, wearing hobnailed boots and taking a full swing, at that.'

'Oh, did you see it? Wasn't it good? I thought I captured you perfectly.'

'Yes, I saw it last month on BBC while I was in London. You made me look like a cross between Captain Bligh and Simon Legree, although more pompous than either and a lot less loveable.'

'That's what I said – I got you perfectly.'

'I don't know why I am talking to you,' he chuckled despite himself.

'Because you are lusting after my miraculously beautiful body,' she suggested.

'I'd be wiser to make advances to a nest of hornets.'

'We aren't talking wisdom here, buddy boy, we are talking lust. The two are not compatible.' And Shasa had a poignant vision of her slim body and her perfect little breasts, and he felt slightly breathless.

'Where are you?' he asked.

'Johannesburg airport.'

'What are you doing this evening?' He made a quick calculation. He could postpone the H'ani Mine inspection, and it was four hours' flying time to Johannesburg in the Mosquito.

'I'm open to suggestions,' she told him, 'as long as the suggestions include an exclusive interview for NABS on your change of political status and your view of the up-coming elections and what they mean to the ordinary people of this country.'

'I should know better,' he said. 'But I'll be there in five hours. Don't go away.'

Shasa placed the receiver back on its cradle and stood for a moment wondering at himself. His change of plans would throw the entire company into consternation, for he had a tight schedule laid out for the weeks ahead, including the opening of his election campaign, but the woman had woven some sort of spell around him. Like a malignant sprite her memory had danced at the edge of his mind all these months, and now the thought of being with her filled him with that quivering expectation he had not known since he was a lad embarking on his very first sexual explorations.

The Mosquito was fuelled and parked on the hardstand ready for the flight to H'ani Mine. It took him ten minutes to calculate his new flight plan and file it with air traffic control and then he climbed up into the cockpit and, grinning like a schoolboy playing hookey, he cranked the Rolls-Royce Merlin engines.

It was dusk when he landed, but a company car was waiting for him and he drove directly to the Carlton Hotel in the centre of Johannesburg. Kitty was in the lobby as he came in through the revolving doors. She was fresh-faced as a teenager, long-legged and narrow-hipped in blue jeans, and she came to him with childlike enthusiasm and wrapped both arms around his neck to kiss him. Strangers in the lobby must have imagined Shasa was a father greeting his school-girl daughter, and they smiled indulgently.

'They let us into your suite,' she told him as she led him towards the elevator, skipping beside him to keep pace and hugging his arm in a pantomime of adoration. 'Hank had got his camera and lights set up already.'

'You aren't even giving me time to visit the heads,' Shasa protested, and she pulled a wry face.

'Let's get it over and done. Then we'll have more time for whatever you want to do afterwards.' She gave him a devilish grin, and he wagged his head in reluctant acquiescence.

It was deliberate, of course. Kitty was too professional to give him time to pull himself together and concentrate his mind. It was part of her technique to get her subject off-balance, while on the other hand she had been carefully preparing her own notes and questions during the five hours since they had spoken on the telephone.

She had rearranged the furniture in his suite, making one corner into an intimate nook and Hank had lit it and was standing by with his Arriflex. Shasa shook hands with him and exchanged a friendly greeting while Kitty poured him a massive whisky from the liquor cabinet.

'Take your jacket off,' she instructed as she handed it to him. 'I want you relaxed and casual.' She led him to the two facing chairs and while he sipped his whisky she lulled

350

him with an amusing account of the flight out which had been delayed by bad weather in London for eight hours. Then Hank gave her the signal and she said sweetly:

'Shasa Courtney, since the turn of this century your family has been a traditional ally of General Smuts. He was a personal friend of your grandfather, and your mother. He was a frequent guest in your house, and sponsored your own entry into the political arena. Now you have turned your back on the United Party which he led, and have deserted the fundamental principles of decency and fair play towards the coloured citizens of this country which were so much a part of General Smuts' philosophy. You have been called a deserter and a turncoat – and worse. Do you think that is a fair description, and if not, why not?'

The attack was so swift and savage that for a moment it checked him, but he had known what to expect, and he grinned. He knew he was going to enjoy this.

'General Smuts was a great man, but not quite as saintly towards the natives as you suppose. In all the time he was in power, their political status remained unchanged, and when they stepped out of line, he did not hesitate before sending in the troops and giving them a whiff of grape. Have you ever heard of the Bondelswart rebellion and the Bulhoek massacre?'

'You are suggesting that Smuts also oppressed the native people of this country?'

'No more than a strict headmaster oppresses his children. In the main, he never seriously addressed himself to the coloured question. He left that for a future generation to settle. We are that future generation.'

'All right, so what are you going to do about the black people of this country who outnumber you nearly four to one and have no political rights whatsoever in the land of their birth?'

'Firstly, we will try to avoid the trap of simplistic thinking.'

'Can you explain that?' Kitty frowned. She didn't want him to wriggle out of her grip by using vague terminology. 'Give us a concrete example of simplistic thinking.'

He nodded. 'You glibly use the terms black people and white people, dividing this population into two separate, if unequal, portions. That is dangerous. It might work in America. If all the American blacks were given white faces they would be simply Americans and think of themselves as that—'

'You are suggesting that this is not the case in Africa?'

'I am indeed,' Shasa agreed. 'If all the blacks in this country were given white faces, they would still think of themselves as Zulus and Xhosas and Vendas, and we would still be English and Afrikaners – very little would have altered.'

Kitty didn't like that, it was not what she wanted to tell her audiences.

'So, of course, you are ruling out the idea of a democracy in this country. You will never accept the policy of one man one vote, but will always aspire to white domination—'

Shasa cut in on her quickly. 'One man one vote would lead not to the black government you seem to foresee, but to a Zulu government, for the Zulus outnumber any other group. We would have a Zulu dictator, like good old King Chaka, and that would be a thrilling experience.'

'So what is your solution?' she demanded, hiding her irritation behind that little-girl smile. 'Is it white *baasskap*, white domination and savage oppression backed by an all-white army and police force—?'

'I don't know the solution,' he cut her off. 'It's something we have to work towards, but I expect it will be a system in which every tribal group, whether it be black, brown or white, can maintain its identity and its territorial integrity.'

'What a noble concept,' she agreed. 'But tell me when,

in the history of mankind, any group who enjoyed supreme political power over all others ever gave up that power without an armed struggle. Do you truly believe the white South Africans will be the first?'

'We'll have to make our own history,' Shasa matched her honeyed smile. 'But in the meantime the material existence of the black people in this country is five or six times better than any other on the African continent. More is spent on black education, black hospitals and black housing, per capita, than in any other African country.'

'How does the expenditure per capita on black education compare with expenditure on white education?' Kitty shot back at him. 'My information is that five times more is spent on the education of a white child, than on a black.'

'We will strive to correct that imbalance, as we build up the wealth of our nation, as the black peasant becomes more productive and makes more of a contribution to the taxation that pays for that education. At the moment the white section of the population pays ninety-five per cent of the taxes—'

That wasn't the way the interview was meant to go, and Kitty headed him off smoothly.

'And just how and when will the black people be consulted in these changes? Is it fair to say that nearly all blacks, and certainly all the educated and skilled blacks who are the natural leaders, totally reject the present political system which allows one-sixth of the population to decide the fate of the rest?'

They were still sparring when Hank lifted his head from the camera lens, and rolled his eyes.

'Out of film, Kitty, you told me twenty minutes tops. We have forty-five minutes in the can.'

'OK, Hank. My fault. I didn't realize we had such a garrulous bigot on the show.' She smiled at Shasa acidly. 'You can wrap it up, Hank, and I'll see you in the morning.

Nine o'clock at the studio.' She turned back to Shasa and they didn't even look up as Hank left the suite. 'So what did we decide?' she asked Shasa.

'That the problem is more complex than anybody, perhaps even we in government, realize.'

'Insoluble?' Kitty asked.

'Certainly – without delicacy and the utmost good will of everybody in the country, and our friends abroad.'

'Russia?' she teased him, and he shuddered.

'Britain,' he said.

'What about America?'

'No. Britain understands. America is too wrapped up in her own racial problems. They aren't interested in the dissolution of the British Empire. However, we have always stood by Britain – and now Britain will stand by us.'

'Your confidence in the gratitude of great nations is refreshing. However, I think you will find that in the next decade there will be an enormous rip-tide of concern over human rights emanating from the United States. At least I hope so – and North American Broadcasting Studios will be doing all in its power to build it up into a tidal wave.'

'Your job is to report reality, not to attempt to re-structure it,' Shasa told her. 'You are a reporter, not the God of Judgement.'

'If you believe that, you are naïve,' she smiled. 'We make and destroy kings.'

Shasa stared at her, as though he were seeing her for the first time. 'My God, you are in the power game, just like everybody else.'

'It's the only game in town, buddy boy.'

'You are amoral.'

'No more than you are.'

'Oh, yes you are. We are prepared to make our decisions and live with the consequences. You wreak your destruc-tion, then like a child with a broken toy, throw it aside and go on without a moment's remorse to some new cause that will sell more advertising time.'

He had made her angry. Her eyes slanted and narrowed into bright arrowheads and the freckles on her nose and cheeks glowed like specks of gold leaf. It roused him to see her come out from behind the screen, as hard and formidable as any adversary he had ever faced. He wanted to goad her further, to make her give way completely.

'You have made yourself the guru of Southern Africa on US television for one reason only. Not for concern over the fate of the black masses, but quite simply because you smell blood and violence in the air. You have sensed that this is where the action will be next and you want to be the one who captures it on film—'

'You bastard,' she hissed at him. 'I want peace and justice.'

'Peace and justice don't make good footage, Kitty my love. You are here to record the killing and the screaming – and if it doesn't happen soon enough, well that is easily fixed – you'll give it a little shove.'

She was out of her chair now, facing him, and her lips were frosty with rage.

'For the last hour you have been spouting the most vicious racial poison, and now you accuse me of injustice. You call me an *agent provocateur* for the violence that is coming.'

He raised an eyebrow, giving her the taunting supercilious smile which had enraged his opponents across the floor of the House, and it was too much for her to bear. She sprang at him, white-lipped and shaking with fury, and she clawed for his single mocking eye with both hands.

Shasa caught her wrists, and lifted her feet clear of the floor. She was shocked by his strength, but she lifted her knee sharply, driving for his groin. He turned slightly and caught the knee on the hard muscle of his thigh.

'Where did a nice girl learn a trick like that?' he asked, and twisted her arms behind her, took both her wrists in his left hand and then bowed over her. She pressed her lips together, and tried to turn her face away, but he found her mouth and while he kissed her, he opened her blouse and with his free hand took out her small breasts. Her nipples were standing out like ripe mulberries, she was as aroused as he was, but kicking and spitting with fury.

He swung her round and threw her face down over the thick padded arm of the buttoned leather chair, pinning her with a hand between her shoulder blades, and her bottom in the air. That's how they had administered the cane at Shasa's school, and now while she screamed and kicked he jerked the leather belt out of the loops of her jeans, and pulled her trousers and panties down as far as her ankles and stepped in close behind her. Her buttocks were white and round and they maddened him.

Though she fought and struggled without let-up, at the same time she lifted her hips slightly and arched her back to make it easier for him, and only when it happened did she stop fighting and push back hard against him, sobbing with the effort of keeping pace with him.

It was over very quickly for both of them, and she rolled over and pulled him down onto the chair and whispered raggedly into his mouth, 'Well, that's one hell of a way to settle an argument, I'll give you that much.'

Shasa ordered dinner served in the suite, grilled crayfish with a sauce Mornay, followed by a Chateaubriand, baked baby potatoes and fresh young asparagus. He sent the waiter away and served it himself for Kitty was clad only in one of the hotel's long towelling dressing gowns.

As he drew the cork on the bottle of Chambertin, he told her, 'I've put four days aside for us. In the last few weeks I have been fortunate enough to get my hands on fifty thousand acres of land across the Sabi River from the Kruger National Park. I've been after it for fifteen years. It belonged to the widow of one of the old Randlords and I had to wait for the old biddy to cross the great divide before it came on the market. It's marvellous unspoilt bush country, teeming with wild game, perfect place for a lost weekend, we'll fly down after breakfast tomorrow – nobody will know where we are.'

She laughed at him. 'You are out of your little mind, lover. I'm a working girl. At eleven o'clock tomorrow I've got an interview with the Leader of the Opposition, De Villiers Graaff, and I'm certainly not breezing off into the boondocks with you to stare at lions and tigers.'

'No tigers in Africa – you are the African expert, you should know that.' He was angry again. 'It's a case of false pretences. You got me all the way up here for nothing,' he accused.

'Nothing?' she chuckled again. 'You call that *nothing*?'

'I expected four days of it.'

'You overestimate the going price for an interview. All you get is the rest of the night, and then tomorrow it's back to work – for both of us.'

She was getting under his guard too often, Shasa realized. Last time he had proposed marriage to her, and the idea still had its appeal. She had moved him the way no woman had since he had first met Tara. It was partly her unattainability that made her so desirable. Shasa was accustomed to getting what he wanted, even if it was a hard and heartless little vixen with a childlike face and body.

He watched her eat the rare steak with the same sensual gusto as she made love. She was sitting cross-legged on the front edge of her chair and the hem of her dressing-gown had ridden up high on her thighs. She saw the direction of his gaze but made no effort to cover herself.

'Eat up,' she grinned at him. 'One thing at a time, lover.'

S hasa was chary of Tara's offer to assist his election campaign, and for the first two meetings left her at Weltevreden and drove out alone over Sir Lowry's Pass and the mountains.

South Boland, his new constituency, was an area of rich land, between the mountains and the sea, on the Cape's eastern littoral. The voters were almost entirely of Afrikaner extraction, and their families had held the land for three hundred years. They were wealthy farmers of wheat and sheep, Calvinist and conservative, but not as rabidly republican and anti-English as their cousins of the interior, the Free Staters and the Transvalers.

They received Shasa's first speeches with caution, and applauded him politely at the end. His opponent, the United Party candidate, was a blood Smuts man, like Blaine, who had been the incumbent until 1948 when he lost it to the Nationalists. Yet he still had a base of support in the district amongst the men who had known Smuts and had gone 'up north' to fight the Axis.

After Shasa's second meeting, the local Nationalist organizers were looking worried and scared.

'We are losing ground,' one of them told Shasa. 'The wives are suspicious of a man who campaigns without his own wife. They want to have a look at her.'

'You see, *Meneer* Courtney, you are a bit too good-looking. It's OK for the younger women who think you look like Errol Flynn, but the older women don't like it, and the men don't like the way the young women look at you. We have to show them you are a family man.'

'I'll bring my wife,' Shasa promised, but his spirits sank. What kind of impression would Tara create in this dour God-fearing community where many of the women still wore the *voortrekker* bonnets and the men believed a woman's place was either in the bed or in the kitchen?

'Another thing,' the chief party organizer went on tactfully. 'We need one of the top men, one of the cabinet ministers, to stand up on the platform with you. You see, *Meneer* Courtney, the people are having difficulty believing that you are a *ware* Nationalist. What with the English name and your family history.'

'We need somebody to make me look respectable, you mean?' Shasa hid his smile, and they all looked relieved.

'*Ja*, man! That's it!'

'What if I could get Minister De La Rey to come out for the meeting on Friday – and my wife, of course?'

'Hell, man!' they enthused. 'Minister De La Rey is perfect. The people like the way he handled the trouble. He is a good strong man. If you get him to come to talk to them, we'll have no more problems.'

Tara accepted the invitation without comment, and by an exercise in self-restraint Shasa refrained from giving her advice on how to dress or to conduct herself, and was delighted and grateful when she came on to the platform in the town hall of the little town of Caledon, dressed in a sober dark blue dress with her thick auburn hair neatly gathered into a bun behind her head.

Though pretty and smiling she was the picture of the good wife. Isabella sat up beside her with knee-length white socks and ribbons in her hair. A born actress, Isabella responded to the occasion by behaving like a candidate for holy orders. Shasa saw the organizers exchanging approving nods and relieved smiles.

Minister De La Rey, supported by his own blonde wife and large family, introduced Shasa with a fiery speech in which he made it very clear that the Nationalist government was not going to allow itself to be dictated to by foreign governments or Communist agitators, especially not if these agitators were black as well as Communist.

Manfred had a finely tuned style of oratory, and he thrust out his jaw and flashed those topaz-coloured eyes, he wagged his finger at them, and stood with arms defiantly akimbo when they stood up to applaud him at the end.

Shasa's style was different, relaxed and friendly, and when he tried his first joke they responded with genuine amusement. He followed it with assurances that the government would increase the already generous subsidy for farm products, especially wool and wheat, and that they would at the same time foster local industry and explore new overseas markets for the country's raw materials, particularly wool and wheat. He ended by telling them that many English-speakers were coming to realize that the salvation of the country lay in strong uncompromising government and predicted a substantial increase in the Nationalist majority.

This time there was no reservation in the tumultuous applause that followed his speech, and the votes of confidence in the government, the National Party and the Nationalist candidate for South Boland were all carried unanimously. The entire district, including the United Party supporters, turned up for the free barbecue on the local rugby grounds, to which Shasa invited them. Two whole oxen were roasted on the spit and were washed down with lakes of Castle beer and rivers of *mampoer*, the local peach brandy.

Tara sat with the women, looking meek and demure and speaking little, allowing the older women to develop pleasantly maternal feelings towards her, while Shasa circulated amongst their husbands, talking knowledgeably about such momentous subjects as scale on wheat and scab on sheep. The whole atmosphere was cosy and reassuring, and for the first time Shasa was able to appreciate the depth of planning by the party organizers, their dedication and commitment to the Nationalist cause, which resulted in this degree of mobilization of all its resources. The United Party could never match it, for the English-speakers were complacent and lethargic when it came to politics. It was the old English fault of wanting never to appear to try too hard. Politics was a kind of sport and every gentleman knew that sport should be played only by amateurs.

'No wonder we lost control,' Shasa thought. 'These chaps are professionals, and we just couldn't match them' – and then he checked himself. These were his organizers now, no longer the enemy. He had become a part of this slick, highly tuned political machine, and the knowledge was a little daunting.

At last, with Tara at his side, Shasa made a round of goodnights with a party organizer steering him tactfully to each of the most important local dignitaries, making sure that none of these was slighted, and everybody agreed that the family made a charming group.

They stayed overnight with the most prosperous of the local farmers, and the following morning, which was Sunday, attended the Dutch Reformed Church in the village. Shasa had not been in a church since Isabella was christened. He was not looking forward to it. This was another grand show, for Manfred De La Rey had prevailed upon his uncle, the Most Reverend Tromp Bierman, Moderator of the Church, to deliver the sermon. Uncle Tromp's sermons were famous throughout the Cape, and families thought nothing of travelling a hundred miles to listen to them.

'I never thought I would ever speak for a cursed *rooinek*,' he told Manfred. 'It is either advancing senility, or a sign of my great love for you, that I do so now.' Then he climbed into the pulpit, and with his great silver beard flashing like the surf of a stormy sea, he lashed the congregation with such force and fury that they quivered and squirmed with delicious terror for their souls.

At the end of the sermon, Uncle Tromp reduced the volume to remind them that there was an election coming up, and that a vote for the United Party was a vote for Satan himself. No matter how some of them felt about

Englishmen, they weren't voting for a man here, they were voting for the party upon which the Almighty had bestowed his blessing and into whose hands he had delivered the destiny of the *Volk*. He stopped just short of closing the gates of Heaven in the face of any of them who did not put their cross opposite the name of Courtney, but when he glared at them threateningly, there were very few who felt inclined to take a chance on his continued forbearance.

'Well, my dear, I can't thank you enough for your help,' Shasa told Tara, as they drove home over the high mountain passes of the Hottentots Holland. 'From here on it looks like a cakewalk.'

'It was interesting to watch our political system in action,' Tara murmured. 'All the other jockeys got down off their mounts and shooed you in.'

Polling day in South Boland was merely an endorsement of certain victory, and when the votes were counted it appeared that Shasa had wooed across at least five hundred erstwhile United Party voters, and, much to the delight of the Nationalist hierarchy, increased the majority most handsomely. As the results came in from around the rest of the country, it became apparent that the trend was universal. For the first time ever, substantial numbers of English-speakers were deserting Smuts' party. The Nationalists took 103 seats to the United Party's 53. The promise of strong, uncompromising government was bearing good fruits.

At Rhodes Hill Centaine gave an elaborate dinner dance for 150 important guests to celebrate Shasa's appointment to the new cabinet.

As they swirled together around the dance floor to the strains of 'The Blue Danube', Centaine told Shasa, 'Once again we have done the right thing at the right time, *chéri*. It can still come true – all of it.' And she sang softly the praise song that the old Bushman had composed at Shasa's birth:

His arrows will fly to the stars
And when men speak his name
It will be heard as far
And wherever he goes, he will find good water.

The clicking sounds of the Bushman language, like snapping twigs and footsteps in mud, raised nostalgic memories from the distant time when they had been together in the Kalahari.

Shasa enjoyed the Houses of Parliament. They were like an exclusive men's club. He liked the grandeur of white columns and lofty halls, the exotic tiles on the floors, the panelling and the green leather-covered benches. He often paused in the labyrinth of corridors to admire the paintings and the sculpted busts of famous men, Merriman and Louis Botha, Cecil Rhodes and Leander Starr Jameson, heroes and rogues, statesmen and adventurers. They had made this country's history – and then he reminded himself.

'History is a river that never ends. Today is history, and I am here at the fountainhead,' and he imagined his own portrait hanging there with the others one day. 'I'll have it commissioned at once,' he thought. 'While I am still in my prime. For the time being I'll hang it at Weltevreden, but I'll put a clause in my will.'

As a minister, he now had his own office in the House, the same suite of rooms that had been used by Cecil Rhodes when he was Prime Minister of the old Cape parliament before the House had been enlarged and extended. Shasa redecorated and furnished it at his own expense. Thesens, the timber firm from Knysna, installed the panelling. It was indigenous wild olive, marvellously grained and with a satiny lustre. He hung four of his finest Pierneef landscapes on the panelling, with a Van Wouw bronze of a Bushman hunter standing on the table beneath them. Although he was determined to keep the artwork authentically African, the carpet was the choicest green Wilton and his desk Louis XIV.

It felt strange to enter the chamber for the first time to take his place on the government front bench, a mirror image of his usual view. He ignored the hostile glances of his erstwhile colleagues, smiling only at Blaine's expressionless wink and while the Speaker of the House read the prayer, he measured the men to whom he had transferred his allegiance.

His reflections were interrupted as the Speaker of the House ended the prayer, and across the floor De Villiers Graaff, the tall, handsome Leader of the Opposition, rose to propose the traditional vote of no confidence, while the government members, smug and cocksure, still revelling in their heady election triumph, mocked him noisily with cries of 'Skande! Scandal!' and 'Siestog, man! Shame on you, man!'

Two days later Shasa rose to deliver his first speech from the government front benches and pandemonium seized the House. His former comrades howled their contempt and waved their order papers at him, stamping their feet and whistling with outrage, while his newly adopted party roared encouragement and support.

Tall and elegant, smiling with scorn, switching easily from English to Afrikaans, Shasa gradually quietened the benches opposite him with his low-key but riveting oratorial style, and once he had their attention he made them squirm uneasily as he dissected their party with an insider's surgical skill then held up their weaknesses and blemishes for them to contemplate.

When he sat down he left them severely discomforted, and the Prime Minister leaned forward in his seat to nod at him, an unprecedented public accolade, while most of the other ministers, even those northerners most hostile to his appointment, passed him notes of congratulation. Manfred De La Rey's note invited him to join a party of senior ministers for lunch in the members' dining-room. It was an auspicious beginning.

Blaine Malcomess and Centaine came out to Weltevreden for the weekend. As usual the family spent all of Saturday afternoon at the polo field. Blaine had recently resigned as captain of the South African team.

'It's obscene for a man over sixty to still be playing,' he had explained his decision to Shasa.

'You are better than most of us youngsters of forty, Blaine, and you know it.'

'Wouldn't it be pleasant to keep the captaincy in the family?' Blaine suggested.

'I've only got one eye.'

'Oh, tush, a man. You hit the ball as sweetly as you ever did. It's simply a matter of practice and more practice.'

'I don't have the time for that,' Shasa protested.

'There is time for everything in life that you really want.'

So Blaine forced him to practise, but deep down he knew that Shasa had lost interest in ball games and would never captain the national team. Oh, certainly he still rode like a centaur, his arm was strong and true and he had the courage of a lion when he was roused, but these days it needed stronger medicine to get his blood racing.

'It's a strange paradox that a man gifted with too many talents can fritter them all away without developing a single one to its full.' At that thought Blaine looked from Shasa to his sons.

As always Sean and Garrick had joined in the practice uninvited, and though they could not come close to matching the furious pace and skill of their elders, they were acting as pick-up men and passers for them.

Sean rode as his father had at that age and it gave Blaine a nostalgic pang to watch him. The horse was a part of him, the accord between rider and mount was total, his stick work was natural and unforced, but he lost interest quickly and made sloppy little errors, was more interested in teasing his brother and showing off and making eyes at the young girls in the stand than in perfecting his style.

Garrick was the opposite of his elder brother. He rode with enough sunlight shining between the saddle-leather and his bum to dazzle a blind man. However, his concentration was absolute, and he scowled murderously at the ball through his spectacles, using his stick with all the grace of a labourer digging a trench, but it was surprising how often he got a solid strike and how the bamboo-root ball flew when he did. Then Blaine was amazed by the sudden change in his physique. From the skinny little runt he had been not long before, he was almost grotesquely overdeveloped in shoulder and chest and upper arms for a child of his age. Yet when they went in for tea and dismounted, his still skinny legs gave him an unfortunate anthropoid appearance. When he removed his riding cap, his hair stuck up in unruly dark spikes, and while Sean sauntered across to make the girls giggle and blush, Garrick stayed close to his father. Again Blaine was surprised at how often Shasa spoke directly to the child, even demonstrating a fine point of grip by rearranging his fingers on the handle of the stick, and when he perfected it, Shasa punched his arm lightly and told him:

'That's it, champ. We'll get you into a green and gold jersey one day.'

Garrick's glow of gratification was touching to watch, and Blaine exchanged a glance with Centaine. Not long before, they had discussed Shasa's total lack of interest in the child, and the detrimental effect that it might have on him. Their fears for Garrick seemed to have been unfounded, Blaine conceded, it was the other two they should have been worrying about.

Michael was not riding today. He had hurt his wrist, a

mysterious injury which although excruciatingly painful showed no bruising nor swelling. It was astonishing how often that wrist, or his ankle or his knee, plagued him whenever there was the prospect of hard physical exercise in the offing. Blaine frowned as he glanced at him now, sitting beside Tara at the tea table under the oaks, both their heads bowed over a book of poetry. Neither of them had looked up once during all the shouting and galloping and ribald exchanges on the field. Blaine was a firm believer in the old adage that a young man should have a disciplined mind in a healthy body, and should be able to join robustly in the rough and tumble of life. He had spoken to Tara about him, but though she had promised to encourage Michael's participation in sport and games, Blaine had not noticed any evidence that she had done so.

There was a chorus of muted shrieks and giggles behind him, and Blaine glanced over his shoulder. Wherever Sean was these days there seemed always to be a flock of females. He attracted them the way a tree full of fruit brings a swarm of noisy mousebirds to it. Blaine had no idea who all these girls belonged to, some of them were the daughters of the estate managers and of Shasa's German wine-maker, the pretty blonde child was the American Consul's daughter and the two little dark ones were the French Ambassador's, but the others were unknown – probably the offspring of the half-dozen politicians and other members of the diplomatic corps who made up the usual guest-list for Saturday high tea at Weltevreden.

'Shouldn't really interfere,' Blaine grumbled to himself. 'But I think I'll have a word with Shasa. No good speaking to Tara. She's too soft by a long chalk.' Blaine glanced around and saw that Shasa had left the group at the tea table under the oaks and had moved down the pony lines. He was squatting with one of the grooms to examine the fore hock of his favourite pony, a powerful stallion he had named Kenyatta, because he was black and dangerous.

'Good opportunity,' Blaine grunted and went to join Shasa. They discussed taping the pony's leg, his only weak point, and then stood up.

'How's Sean making out at Bishops?' Blaine asked casually, and Shasa looked surprised.

'Tara been talking to you?' he asked. Sean had gone up to the senior school at the beginning of the year, after ending as head boy and captain of sport at his preparatory school.

'Having trouble?' Blaine asked.

'Going through a phase,' Shasa shrugged. 'He'll be all right. He has too much talent not to make good in the end.'

'What happened?'

'Nothing to worry about. He's become a bit of a rebel, and his grades have gone to hell. I gave him the sweet end of the riding-crop. Only language he speaks fluently. He'll be all right, Blaine, don't worry.'

'For some people it's all too easy,' Blaine remarked. 'They get into the habit of free-wheeling through life.' He saw Shasa bridle slightly, and realized he was taking the remark personally. Good, he thought, let him – and he went on deliberately, 'You should know, Shasa. You have the same weakness.'

'I suppose you do have the right to speak to me like that. The only man in the world who does,' Shasa mused. 'But don't expect me to enjoy it, Blaine.'

'I expect young Sean cannot accept criticism either,' Blaine said. 'He's the one I wanted to talk about, not you. How did we end up discussing you? However, since we are, let an old dog give a few words of caution to both of you. Firstly, don't dismiss Sean's behaviour too lightly, you may just find yourself with a serious problem one day, if you don't check it now. Some people have to have constant stimulation or else they get bored. I think Sean might be one of those. They become addicted to excitement and danger. Watch him, Shasa.'

'Thank you, Blaine,' Shasa nodded, but he was not grateful.

'As for you, Shasa. You have been playing life like a game.'

'That's all it is, surely,' Shasa agreed.

'If you truly believe that, then you have no right to take on the responsibility of cabinet rank,' Blaine said softly. 'No, Shasa. You have made yourself responsible for the welfare of sixteen million souls. It's no longer a game, but a sacred trust.'

They had stopped walking and turned to face each other.

'Think about that, Shasa,' Blaine said. 'I believe that there are dark and difficult days ahead, and you won't be playing for an increase in company dividends – you will be playing for the survival of a nation, and if you fail, it will mean the end of the world you know. You will not suffer alone—'

Blaine turned to Isabella as she ran to him.

'Grandpapa! Grandpapa!' she cried. 'I want to show you the new pony Daddy gave me,' and they both looked down at the beautiful child.

'No, Shasa, not you alone,' Blaine repeated, and took the child's hand.

'All right, Bella,' he said. 'Let's go down to the stables.'

S hasa had found that Blaine's words were like arrow-grass seeds. They scratched when they first attached themselves to your clothing, and then gradually worked themselves deeper until they penetrated the skin to cause real pain. Those words were still with him when he went into the cabinet room on Monday morning and took his place at the foot of the table, as befitted the most junior member of the gathering.

Before Blaine had spoken to him, Shasa had considered these meetings no more important than, say, a full board meeting of Courtney Mining and Finance. Naturally, he prepared himself as thoroughly, not only were his own notes exhaustive and cogent but he had assembled full portfolios on every other member of the cabinet. Blaine had helped him with this work, and the results had been fed into the company computer and were kept up to the minute. After a lifetime in politics, Blaine was a skilled analyst and he had been able to trace in the tenuous and concealed lines of loyalty and commitment that bound this group of important men together.

At the broadest level every single one of them, apart from Shasa, was a member of the *Broederbond* – the Brotherhood – that invidious secret society of eminent Afrikaners whose single object was to advance the interest of the Afrikaner above all others at every possible turn and at every level from that of national politics through business and the economy, on down to the levels of education and the civil service. No outsider could ever hope to fathom its ramifications, for it was protected by a curtain of silence which no Afrikaner dared to break. It united them all, no matter whether they were members of the Calvinist Dutch Reformed Church or of the even more extreme *Dopper* Church, the Hervormde Church which by Article No. 3 of its charter had ordained that heaven was reserved exclusively for members of the white race. The *Broederbond* united even the southerners, the Cape Nationalists, and those hard men from the north.

As Shasa rearranged his thick sheaf of notes, which he would not need since they were already committed to memory, he glanced down the table and saw how the two opposing forces in the cabinet had arranged themselves like the grouping of an army. Shasa was quite obviously arrayed with the southerners under Dr Theophilus Dönges, one of the most senior men, who had been a member of the cabinet since Dr Malan brought the party to power in 1948. He was leader of the party in the Cape, and Manfred De La Rey was one of his men. However, they were the smaller and least influential of the two groups. The northerners comprised both the Transvalers and the Orange Free Staters, and amongst them were the most formidable politicians in the land.

Strangely, in this assembly of impressive men, Shasa's attention went to a man who had been a member of the Senate as long as Shasa had himself been a member of the lower house. Before his appointment to the Senate in 1948, Verwoerd had been the editor of *Die Transvaler*, and before that he had been a professor at Stellenbosch University. Shasa knew that he had lectured to Manfred De La Rey when he was a student, and had exerted enormous influence upon him. However, they were in different camps now, Verwoerd was of the north. Since 1950 he had been Minister of Bantu Affairs, with godlike powers over the black population, and had made his name synonymous with the ideal of racial segregation at all levels of society.

For a man with such a monumental reputation for racial intolerance, the architect of the great edifice of *apartheid* which was being erected with intricate interlocking laws that dictated every aspect of the lives of the country's millions of black people, his appearance and manner were a pleasant surprise. His smile was kindly, almost benign, and he was quietly spoken but persuasive as he rose to address the cabinet and explain with the aid of a specially prepared map of South Africa his plans for the rearrangement of black population densities.

Tall and slightly round-shouldered, with his curly hair beginning to turn to silver, there could be little doubt of his utmost sincerity and belief in the absolute rightness of his conclusions. Shasa found himself being carried along on the plausible flood of his logic. Although his voice was pitched a little too high, and the tense note of his monologue grated on the ear, he carried them all on the strength, not only of his total conviction, but also of his personality. Even his opponents were filled with awe at his debating ability.

Only one small detail worried Shasa. Verwoerd's blue eyes were slitted, as though he were always looking into the sun, and though they were surrounded by a complex web of laughter lines, they were cold eyes, the eyes of a machine-gunner staring over the sights of his weapon.

Blaine's words came back to Shasa as he sat at the polished stinkwood table. 'No, Shasa, it's not a game. You have made yourself responsible for the welfare of sixteen million souls. It's no longer a game, but a sacred trust.'

But he remained expressionless as Verwoerd ended his presentation. 'Not one of us here today doubts that South Africa is a white man's country. My proposals will see to it that within the reserves the natives will have some measure of autonomy. However, as to the country as a whole, and the European areas in particular, we the white people are and shall remain the masters.'

There was a general murmur of agreement and approbation, and two of the others asked for clarification on minor points. There was no call to vote or to make any joint decision, for Verwoerd's lecture had been in the form of a report back from his department.

'I think that Dr Henk has covered this subject fully – unless anybody else has a question, we can go on to the next matter on the agenda.' The Prime Minister looked down the table at Shasa. The agenda read:

ITEM TWO: Projection by the Hon. Minister for Mines and Industry on the capital requirements of the private industrial sector over the next ten years and the proposal of means to satisfy such requirements.

This morning would be the first time Shasa would address the full cabinet, and he hoped he would muster only a small portion of Verwoerd's aplomb and persuasion.

His nervousness faded as soon as he rose to speak, for he had prepared in depth and detail. He began with an assessment of the foreign capital needs of the economy over the next decade, 'to carry us through to the end of the 1960s', and then set out to estimate the amounts available to them from their traditional markets within the British Commonwealth.

'As you see, this leaves us with a considerable shortfall, particularly in mining, the new oil-from-coal industry and the armaments sector. This is how I propose that shortfall should be met: in the first instance we have to look to the United States of America. That country is a potential source of capital that has barely been tapped—'

He held their attention completely as he described his department's plans to advertise the country as a prosperous market amongst the American business leaders, and to entice as many of them as he could to visit South Africa at the expense of his department. He also intended establishing associations with sympathetic and influential politicians and businessmen in the United States and the United Kingdom to promote the country's image, and to this end he had already contacted Lord Littleton, head of Littleton Merchant Bank, who had agreed to act as Chairman of the British South Africa Club. A similar association, the American South Africa Club, would be formed in the United States.

Shasa was encouraged by the obviously favourable reception of his presentation to continue with a matter he had not intended raising.

'We have just heard from Dr Verwoerd the proposal to build up self-governing black states within the country. I don't wish to tackle the political aspects of this scheme, but as a businessman I feel that I am competent to bring to your attention the final cost, in financial rather than human terms, of putting this into practice.'

Shasa went on swiftly to outline the massive obstacles in logistics and lost productivity that would result.

'We will have to duplicate a number of times the basic structures of the state in various parts of the country, and we must expect the bill for this to run into many billions of pounds. That money could more profitably be invested in wealth-producing undertakings—'

Across the table he saw Verwoerd's great charm ice over with a crust of hostility. Shasa knew he was autocratic and contemptuous of criticism, and he sensed that he was taking a risk by antagonizing a man who might one day wield ultimate power, but he went on doggedly.

'The proposal has another flaw. By decentralizing industry we will make it less effective and competitive. In a modern age when all countries are economically in competition with each other, we will be placing a handicap on ourselves.'

When he sat down he saw that though he might have convinced nobody, he had given them much to think about seriously and soberly, and when the meeting ended, one or two of the other ministers, most of them southerners, stayed to exchange a few words with him. Shasa sensed that he had enhanced his reputation and consolidated his place in the cabinet with that afternoon's work, and he drove back to Weltevreden feeling well pleased with himself.

He dropped his briefcase on the desk in his study and, hearing voices out on the terrace, went out into the late sunshine. The guest that Tara was entertaining was the headmaster of Bishops. Usually this worthy would summon the parents of recalcitrant pupils to appear before him as summarily as he did their offspring. This did not apply to the Courtney family. Centaine Courtney-Malcomess had been a governor of the school for almost thirty years, the only woman on the board. Her son had been head boy before the war and was now on the board with his mother, and both of them were major contributors to the College's coffers – amongst their gifts were the organ, the plate-glass windows in the new chapel, and the new kitchens to the main dining-hall. The headmaster had come to call upon Shasa, rather than the other way around. However, Tara was looking uneasy and stood up to greet Shasa with relief.

'Hello, Headmaster.' Shasa shook hands, but was not encouraged by the head's lugubrious expression.

'Headmaster wants to talk to you about Sean,' Tara explained. 'I think a man-to-man chat will be appropriate, so I will leave the two of you alone while I go and get a fresh pot of tea.'

She slipped away, and Shasa asked genially, 'Sun's over the yard arm. May I offer you a whisky, Headmaster?'

'No thank you, Mr Courtney.' That he had not used Shasa's Christian name was ominous, and Shasa adjusted his own expression to the correct degree of solemnity and took the chair beside him.

'Sean, hey? So what has that little hooligan been up to now?'

Tara opened the door to the dining-room quietly and crossed the floor to stand behind the drapes. She waited until the voices on the terrace were so intense and serious that she could be certain that Shasa would be there for the next hour at the least. She turned quickly and left the dining-room, closing the door behind her, and went swiftly down the wide marble-tiled passageway, past the library and the gun room. The door to Shasa's study was unlocked, the only doors ever locked at Weltevreden were those to the wine cellar.

Shasa's briefcase stood in the middle of his desk. She

opened it and saw the blue folder embossed with the coat of arms of the state which contained the typed minutes of that day's cabinet meeting. She knew that numbered copies were made and distributed to each minister at the end of the weekly meetings, and she had expected to find it in his case.

She lifted it out, careful not to disarrange anything else in the crocodile-skin attaché case, and carried it to the table beside the french doors. The light was better here, and in addition, by glancing around the drapes, she could see down the terrace to where Shasa and the headmaster were still deep in conversation under the trellis of vines.

Quickly she arranged the blue sheets on the table, and then focused the tiny camera that she took from the pocket of her skirt. It was the size of a cigarette-lighter. She was still unaccustomed to the mechanism, and her hands were shaking with nervousness. It was the first time she had done this.

Molly had given her the camera at their last meeting, and explained that their friends were so pleased by the quality of the information she was providing that they wanted to make her job easier for her. Her fingers felt like pork sausages as she manipulated the tiny knobs and snapped each of the sheets twice, to cover herself against possible mistakes of exposure or focus. Then she slipped the camera back into her pocket, before stacking the sheets in their folder and replacing it carefully in Shasa's briefcase in exactly the same way she had found it.

She was so nervous that her bladder felt as though it might burst and she had to run down the passage to the downstairs toilet. She only just reached it in time. Five minutes later she carried the silver Queen Anne teapot out on to the terrace. Usually this would have annoyed Shasa, who did not like her to usurp the servants' work, especially in front of guests. However, he was too engrossed in his discussion with the headmaster to notice.

'I find it difficult to believe that it is anything more than robust boyish spirits, Headmaster.' He was frowning as he sat forward in his chair, hands on his knees, to confront the schoolmaster.

'I have tried to look upon it that way.' The headmaster shook his head regretfully. 'In view of the special relationship that your family has to the school, I have been as lenient as I can be. However,' he paused meaningfully, 'we are not dealing simply with an isolated instance. Not simply one or two boyish pranks, but a state of mind, an entire behaviour pattern which is most alarming.' The headmaster broke off to accept the cup of tea that Tara passed across the table to him. 'Forgive me, Mrs Courtney, this is as painful to me as it must be to you.'

Tara said quietly, 'I can believe that. I know you look upon each of your boys as one of your own sons.' And she glanced at Shasa. 'My husband has been reluctant to come to terms with the problem.' She hid her smug satisfaction behind a sorrowful but brave little smile. Sean had always been Shasa's child, strong-willed and thoughtless of others. She had never understood nor accepted that cruel streak in him. She recalled his selfishness and lack of gratitude even before he could talk. As an infant when he had gorged himself at her breast, he would let her know he was satiated by biting her nipple with sufficient force to bruise her painfully. She had loved him, of course, but had found it hard to like him. As soon as he had learned to walk, he headed straight for his father, staggering after him like a puppy, and his first word had been 'Dada'. That hurt her, after she had carried him big and heavy in her belly and given him birth and suck, 'Dada'. Well, he was Shasa's child now and she sat back and watched him grapple with the problem, feeling a spiteful pleasure at his discomfort.

'He's a natural sportsman,' Shasa was saying, 'and a born leader. He has a good mind – I am convinced that he will pull himself together. I gave him a good thrashing after his school report at the end of last term, and I'll give him another this evening to get him in the right frame of mind.'

'With some boys the cane has no effect, or rather it has the opposite of the desired effect. Your Sean looks upon corporal punishment the way a soldier looks on his battle wounds, as a mark of his courage and fortitude.'

'I have always been against my husband beating the children,' Tara said, and Shasa flashed her a warning look, but the headmaster went on.

'I have also tried the cane on Sean, Mrs Courtney. He seems positively to welcome that punishment as though it affords him some special distinction.'

'But he is a good athlete,' Shasa repeated rather lamely.

'I see you choose, as I would, the term "athlete" rather than "sportsman",' the headmaster nodded. 'Sean is precocious and mature for his age. He is stronger than the other boys in his group and has no qualms in using his strength to win, not always in accordance with the rules of the game.' The headmaster looked at Shasa pointedly. 'He does have a good brain, but his school marks indicate that he is not prepared to use it in the classroom. Instead he applies his mind to less commendable enterprises.' The headmaster paused, sensing that this was not the moment to give a doting father concrete examples. He went on: 'He is also, as you have noted, a born leader. Unfortunately, he gathers about him the least desirable elements in the school, which he has formed into a gang with which he terrorizes the other boys, even those senior to him are afraid of him.'

'I find this difficult to accept.' Shasa was grim-faced.

'To be blunt, Mr Courtney: Sean seems to have a vindictive and vicious streak in him. I am, of course, looking for an improvement in him. However, if that is not soon forthcoming, I will have to make a serious decision over Sean's future at Bishops.'

'I had set my heart on him being head boy, as I was,' Shasa admitted, and the headmaster shook his head.

'Far from becoming head boy, Mr Courtney, unless Sean has pulled up his socks by the end of the year, I am, with the greatest reluctance, going to have to ask you to remove him from Bishops altogether.'

'My God!' Shasa breathed. 'You don't really mean that?'

'I'm sorry to say that I do.'

It was quite remarkable that Clare East had ever been employed by the headmaster of Bishops. The explanation was that the appointment was a temporary one, a mere six-month contract, to fill in after the unexpected resignation of the previous art master on the grounds of ill-health. The salary offered was such that it had attracted only two other applications, both patently unsuitable.

Clare had come to the interview with the headmaster dressed in clothes she had not worn for six years, not since she was twenty-one years of age. She had exhumed them from a forgotten cabin trunk for the occasion, a high-buttoned dress in drab green that conformed closely to the head's own ideas of suitable apparel for a school-mistress. Her long black hair she had plaited and twisted up severely behind her head, and the portfolio of her painting she had chosen to show him was composed of landscapes and seascapes and still lifes, subjects which had interested her at about the same time as she had bought the chaste woollen dress. At Bishops, art was not one of the mainstream subjects, but merely a catch-all for the pupils who showed little aptitude for the sciences.

Once Clare had charge of the art school, which was situated far enough from the main buildings as to offer her a certain freedom of behaviour, she reverted to her usual style of dress: wide loose skirts in vivid colours and flamboyant patterns, worn with Mexican-style blouses like those that Jane Russell had worn in *The Outlaw*. She had seen the movie five times while she was attending the London School of Arts, and modelled herself on Jane Russell, though of course Clare knew her own breasts were better than Russell's, just as big but higher and more pointed.

Her long hair she wore in a different style every day, and when she was teaching she always kicked off her sandals and strode around the art room barefooted, smoking thin black Portuguese cigarettes which one of her lovers brought her in packs of a thousand.

Sean had absolutely no interest in art. He had filtered down to this class by a process of natural rejection. Physics and chemistry demanded too much effort, and geography, the next lowest subject, was an even greater bore than paintbrushes.

Sean fell in love with Clare East the very moment that she walked into the art room. The first time she had paused at his easel to inspect the mess of colour he had smeared on his sheet of art paper, he realized that she was an inch shorter than he was, and when she reached up to correct one of his shaky outlines, he saw that she had not shaved her armpit. That bush of dark coarse hair, glistening with sweat, induced the hardest and most painful erection he had ever experienced.

He tried to impress her with manly strutting behaviour, and when that failed, he used an oath in her presence that he usually reserved for one of his polo ponies. Clare East sent him to the head with a note and the head gave him four strokes of his heavy Malacca cane, accompanying the beating with a few words of counsel.

'You will have to learn, young man, WHACK, that I will not allow you to compound atrocious behaviour, WHACK, with foul language, WHACK, especially in the presence of a lady, WHACK.'

'Thank you very much, Headmaster.' It was traditional to express gratitude for these ministrations, and to refrain from rubbing the injured area in the great man's presence. When Sean returned to the art room, his ardour, far from being cooled by the Malacca cane, was rather inflamed to unbearable proportions, but he realized he had to change tactics.

He discussed it with his henchman, Snotty Arbuthnot, and was only mildly discouraged by Snotty's advice. 'Forget it, man. Every fellow in school is whacking away thinking about Marsh Mallows—' the nickname was a reference to Clare East's bosom – 'but Tug saw her at the movies with some chap of at least thirty, with a moustache and his own car. They were smooching away like mad dogs in the back row. Why don't you go and see Poodle instead?'

Poodle was a sixteen-year-old from Rustenberg Girls' School, just across the railway line from Bishops. She was a young lady with a mission in life, to see as many boys across the borders of manhood as she could fit into her busy afternoons. Though Sean had never spoken to her, she had been a spectator at every one of his recent cricket matches and she had sent a message to him through a mutual friend suggesting a meeting in the pine forest on Rondebosch Common.

'She looks like a poodle,' Sean dismissed the suggestion scornfully, and resigned himself to distant adoration of Clare East, until one day he was searching her desk for those black Portuguese cigarettes for which he had developed a taste. Love did not mean he could not steal from her. In a locked drawer which he picked with a paper clip, he came across a stiff cardboard folder tied with green ribbons. The folder contained over twenty pencil drawings of nude male models, all of them signed and dated by Clare East, and after the first jealous shock, Sean realized that each drawing was of a different subject with only one common feature. While the models' faces had been roughed in, their genitals had been depicted in minute and loving detail, and all of them were fully tumescent.

381

What Sean had discovered was Clare's collection of scalps, or an equivalent thereof. Clare East had strong tastes, but even more than garlic and red wine she needed men in her diet. This was so evident in the secret folder that all Sean's deflated hopes were once more revived, and that night he commissioned Michael, for the sum of five shillings, to paint a portrait of Clare East in Sean's art book.

Michael was in the junior art class and was able to make his studies for the portrait without the model's knowledge, and the completed work surpassed even Sean's expectations. He submitted the portrait and at the end of the following session Clare dismissed the class with a rider, 'Oh Sean, will you please remain behind?'

When the art room was cleared, she opened his art book at the painting of herself.

'Did you do this, Sean?' she asked. 'It really is very good.' The question was innocent enough, but the difference between the portrait and Sean's own murky compositions was so evident that even he saw the danger of claiming authorship.

'I was going to tell you I did it,' he admitted openly, 'but I can't lie to you, Miss East. I paid my brother to do it for me.'

'Why, Sean?'

'I suppose because I like you so much,' he mumbled, and to her surprise she saw that he was actually blushing. Clare was touched. Up to that time she had actively disliked this boy. He was brash and cocky and a disruptive influence in her class. She was certain that it was he who was stealing her cigarettes.

This unsuspected sensitivity surprised her, and suddenly she realized that his bumptious behaviour had been to attract her attention. She relented towards him, and over the following days and weeks she showed Sean that she had forgiven him, by giving him small largesse – from a special smile to an extra few minutes of her time tidying up his creative efforts.

In return Sean began leaving gifts in her desk, thereby confirming her suspicion that he had been into it before. However, the theft of cigarettes stopped and she accepted the offerings of fruit and flowers without comment, just a smile and a nod as she passed his easel.

Then one Friday afternoon she opened her drawer and there lay a blue enamel box with 'Garrards' in gold lettering on the lid. She opened it with her back turned to the class, and she started uncontrollably and almost dropped the box as she realized that it contained a brooch of white gold. The centrepiece was a large star sapphire, and even Clare, who was no judge of gems, realized that it was an exquisite stone. It was surrounded by small diamonds set in a star pattern. Clare experienced a giddy rush of avarice. The brooch must certainly be worth many hundreds of pounds, more money than she had ever had in her hand at one time, more than a year's salary at her present parsimonious rate of pay.

Sean had taken the piece from his mother's dressing-table and hidden it in the thatch of the saddle room behind the stables until the furore had died down. All the house servants had been interrogated, first by Shasa, who was outraged by this breach of faith. Nothing, apart from liquor, had ever been stolen by his employees before. When his own investigations ran into a dead end, Shasa called in the police. Fortunately for Sean, it transpired that one of the junior maids had previously served a six-month sentence for theft from an employer. She was obviously guilty and the Wynberg magistrate gave her eighteen months, her offence compounded by her obstinate refusal to return the stolen brooch. Since she was now over twenty-one years, the maid was sent to the Pollsmoor Women's Prison.

Sean had waited another ten days for the incident to be forgotten before presenting the gift to the object of his passion. Clare East was mightily tempted. She realized that the brooch must have been stolen, but on the other hand she was, as usual for her, in serious financial difficulty. This was the only reason she had taken on her present employment. She looked back with nostalgic regret on the idle days of eating and drinking and painting and making love which had led her into her present embarrassed circumstances. The brooch would solve it all. She had no scruples of conscience, but a terror of being convicted of theft. She knew that her free and creative soul would wither behind the bars of a women's prison.

Surreptitiously she returned the brooch to her desk drawer and for the rest of that art period she was distracted and withdrawn. She chain-smoked cigarettes and kept well clear of the rear of the art room, where Sean made a fine picture of innocence as he applied himself with unusual industry to his easel. She did not have to tell him to remain behind when the bell rang at the end of the period. He came to where she sat at her desk.

'Did you like it?' he asked softly, and she opened the drawer and placed the enamel box in the centre of the desk between them.

'I cannot accept it, Sean,' she said. 'You know that very well.' She didn't want to ask him where he had obtained it. She didn't want to know, and involuntarily she reached out to touch the box for the last time. The enamel surface felt like a new-laid egg, smooth and warm to the touch.

'It's all right,' Sean said quietly. 'Nobody knows. They think somebody else took it. It's quite safe.'

Had the child seen through her so easily? She started at him. Was it one amoral soul recognizing another? It made her angry to be found out, to have her greed so exposed. She took her hand off the box and placed it in her lap.

She drew a breath, and steeled herself to repeat her refusal, but Sean stilled her by opening his art book and taking out three loose leaves. He placed them beside the blue enamel box, and she drew a hissing breath. They were her own drawings from her fun folder, signed by herself.

'I took these – sort of fair exchange,' Sean said, and she looked at him and truly saw him for the very first time.

He was young in years only. In the museum in Athens she had been enchanted by a marble statue of the great god Pan in his manifestation as a young boy. A beautiful child, but about him an ancient evil as enthralling as sin itself. Clare East was not a teacher by vocation, she felt no innate revulsion at the corruption of the young. It was simply that she had not thought of it before. With her hearty sexual appetite she had experienced almost everything else, including partners of her own sex, although those had been unsuccessful experiments long ago put behind her. Men she had known, in the biblical sense, in every possible variation of size and shape and colour. She took and discarded them with a kind of compulsive fervour, seeking always an elusive fulfilment which seemed to dance for ever just beyond her grasp. Often she was afraid, truly terrified, that she had reached the point of satiety, when her pleasure was irreparably blunted and jaded.

Now she was presented with a new and titillating perversion, enough to reawaken the lusty response that she had thought lost for ever. This child's loveliness contained a wickedness that left her breathless as she discovered it.

She had never been paid before, and this mannikin was offering her a prostitute's fee that was princely enough for a royal courtesan. She had never been blackmailed before, and he was threatening her with those unwise sketches. She knew what would happen if they ever fell into the hands of the school governors, and she did not doubt that he would carry out the unspoken threat. He had already hinted that he had placed blame for the theft of the sapphire brooch on an innocent party. Most tantalizing, she had never had a child before. She let her eyes run over him curiously. His skin was clear and firm, with the sweet gloss of youth on it. The hair on his forearms was silky, but his cheeks were bare. He was using a razor already, and he was taller than she was, a man's outline emerging from boyhood in his shoulders and narrow hips. His limbs were long and shapely, strange that she should never have noticed the muscle in his arms before. His eyes were green as emeralds, or of *crème de menthe* in a crystal glass, and there were tiny flecks of brown and gold surrounding the pupils. She saw those pupils dilate slightly as she leaned forward, deliberately letting the top of her blouse gape open to expose the swell and cleavage of her breasts. Carefully she picked up the enamel box.

'Thank you, Sean,' she whispered hoarsely. 'It's a magnificent gift and I shall treasure it.'

Sean picked up the lewd sketches and slipped them into his art book, hostage to the unspoken pact between them.

'Thank you, Miss East.' His voice was as rough as hers. 'I am so glad you like it.'

It was so exciting to see his agitation that her own loins melted and she felt the familiar pressure build up swiftly in her lower body. With calculated cruelty she stood up, dismissing him to the exquisite torture of anticipation. Instinctively she knew that he had planned it all. No further effort would be required from her, the boy's genius would provide the means and the moment, and it was part of the excitement, waiting to see what he would do.

She did not have long to wait, and though she had expected something unusual, she was surprised by the note he left on her desk.

Dear Miss East,

My son, Sean, tells me that you are having difficulty in procuring suitable lodgings. I do understand how difficult this can be, particularly in the summer when

386

the whole world seems to descend upon our little peninsula.

As it happens, I have a furnished cottage on the estate, which at the present time is standing empty. If you find it suitable, you are welcome to the use of it. The rental would be nominal. I should say a guinea a week would satisfy the estate bookkeeper, and you would find the cottage secluded and quiet with a lovely view over the Constantia Berg and False Bay, which will appeal to the artist.

Sean speaks highly of your work, and I look forward to seeing examples of it.

Very sincerely,
Tara Courtney

Clare East was paying five guineas a week for a single squalid room beside the railway tracks at the back of Rondebosch station. When she sold the sapphire brooch for three hundred pounds, which she suspected was a fraction of its real value, Clare had been determined to pay off her accumulated debts. However, as with so many of her good intentions, she closed her mind to the impulse, and instead blew most of the money on a secondhand Morris Minor.

She drove out to Weltevreden the following Saturday morning. Some instinct warned her not to attempt to conceal her Bohemian inclinations, and she and Tara recognized kindred spirits at the very first meeting. Tara sent a driver and one of the estate lorries to fetch her few sticks of furniture and her pile of finished canvases, and personally helped her move into the cottage.

As they worked together, Clare showed Tara a few of the canvases, beginning with the landscapes and seascapes. Tara's response was noncommittal, so once again, following her instinct, Clare stripped the cover off one of her abstracts, a cubist arrangement of blues and fiery reds, and held it up for Tara.

'Oh God, it's magnificent!' Tara murmured. 'So fierce and uncompromising. I love it.'

A few evenings later Tara came down the path through the pines, carrying a small basket. Clare was on the stoep of the cottage, sitting bare-footed and cross-legged on a leather cushion with a sketch-pad on her lap.

She looked up and grinned, 'I hoped you'd come,' and Tara flopped down beside her and took a bottle of Shasa's best estate wine, the fifteen-year-old vintage, out of the basket.

They chatted easily while Clare sketched, drinking the wine and watching the sunset over the mountains.

'It's good to find a friend,' Tara said impulsively. 'You can't imagine how lonely it is here sometimes.'

'With all the guests and visitors!' Clare chuckled at her.

'Those aren't real people,' Tara said. 'They are just talking dolls, stuffed with money and their own importance,' and she took a flat silver cigarette case out of the pocket of her skirt, and opened it. It contained rice papers and shredded yellow leaf.

'Do you?' she asked shyly.

'Darling, you have probably saved my life,' Clare exclaimed. 'Roll one for us this instant. I can't wait.'

They passed the joint back and forth, and in the course of their lazy conversation Clare remarked, 'I've been exploring. It's so beautiful here. A little earthly paradise.'

'Paradise can be an awful bore,' Tara smiled.

'I found a waterfall with a little summer house.'

'That's the picnic spot. None of the servants are allowed there, so if you want to swim in the buff, you don't have to worry. Nobody is going to surprise you.'

Clare had not seen Sean on the estate since she moved into the cottage. She had expected him to come panting to the door on the very first day, and was slightly piqued when he did not. Then after a few more days she was amused by his restraint, he had an instinct far beyond his years, the touch of the born philanderer, and she waited with a rising sense of anticipation for him to approach her. Then the delay began to gall her. She was unaccustomed to extended periods of celibacy, and her sleep started to become fitful and disturbed by erotic dreams.

The spring evenings lengthened and became balmy, and Clare took up Tara's suggestion to visit the pool below the waterfall. Each afternoon she hurried back to Weltevreden after school, and pulled a pair of shorts and a sleeveless blouse over her bikini before taking the short cut through the vineyards to the foot of the hills. Tara's assurances were well founded. The pool was always deserted except for the sugar birds amongst the proteas on the bank, and soon she discarded the bikini.

On her third visit, as she was standing under the waterfall letting her long dark hair flow down her body, she was suddenly aware that she was being watched. She sank down quickly, the water up to her chin, and looked around her apprehensively.

Sean sat on one of the wet black rocks at the head of the pool, almost within touching distance. The roar of the waterfall had muffled any sound of his approach. He was regarding her solemnly, and the resemblance to the youthful Pan god was enhanced in this wild and beautiful place. He was barefoot and wore only shorts and a cotton shirt. His lips were slightly parted and his teeth were white and perfect, a lock of dark hair had fallen over one eye and he lifted his hand and brushed it aside.

Slowly she raised herself until the water dropped to her waist, the foam swirled around her, and her body shone with wetness. She saw his eyes go to her breasts, and his tongue flicked between his teeth and he winced as if in pain. Matching his solemn expression, she crooked her finger and beckoned him. The noise of the waterfall prevented all speech.

He stood up and began to unbutton his shirt, and then paused. She saw that at last he was uncertain, and his confusion amused and excited her. She nodded encouragement and beckoned again. His expression firmed and he stripped off his shirt and threw it aside, then he unbuckled his belt and let his shorts drop around his ankles.

She drew breath sharply and felt the muscles on the inside of her thighs tense. She was not sure what she had expected, but protruding from a smoky haze of pubic hair he was long and white and rigid. Here, as in so many other ways, he was almost fully matured, the lingering signs of childhood on his body were all the more titillating for this.

He stood naked for only an instant and then dived head first into the pool, to surface beside her, water streaming down his face, grinning like an imp. Immediately she ducked away, and he chased her. He was a stronger swimmer than she was, moving in the water like a young otter, and he caught her in the middle of the pool.

They struggled together playfully, giggling and gasping, treading water, going under and bobbing up again. She was surprised by the hardness and strength of his body, and though she extended herself, he began to get the better of her. She was tiring and she slowed her movements and let him rub himself against her. Cold water and exertion had softened him, but she felt him grow again, his hips slipping over her belly, probing instinctively at her. She hooked an arm around his neck and pulled his face down between her breasts. His entire body arched and convulsed and for a moment she thought he had gone too far, and she reached down and squeezed him hard and painfully to stop him.

Then as he broke away, shocked by her assault, she turned and swam swiftly to the bank, dragged herself from the pool and ran wet and naked to the summer house. She snatched up her towel, wiped her face dry and, holding the towel in front of her, turned back to face him as he reached the door of the summer house behind her. He stood flushed and angry in the doorway, and they stared at each other, both of them panting heavily.

Then slowly she lowered the towel and tossed it over the couch. Swinging her hips deliberately she went to where he stood.

'All right, Master Sean. We know you are worse than useless with a paint brush. Let's see if there isn't anything else we can teach you.'

He was like a blank canvas on which she could trace her own designs, no matter how bizarre.

There were things from which her other lovers had recoiled, and other acts that she had only imagined and never had the courage to suggest to a partner. At last she felt free of all constraint. It was as though he could read her intentions. She had only to start some new experiment, guide him just part of the way, and he picked it up with a greedy relish that astonished her and carried it through to a conclusion that she had not always fully foreseen, and which sometimes left her stunned.

His strength and confidence increased with every one of their meetings. For the first time she had found something that did not swiftly pall. Gradually her existence seemed to centre around the summer house beside the pool, and she could not wait to reach it each evening. It required all her self-discipline to keep her hands off him in the art room. She could not trust herself to stand close to him, or to look at him directly during her classes.

Then he initiated a new series of dangerous games. He

would remain behind after class, for just a few minutes. It had to be very quick, but risk of discovery enhanced the thrill for both of them.

Once the janitor came in as they were busy and it was so close, so exciting, that she thought she had experienced heart failure at the climax. Sean was standing erect behind her desk, and she was kneeling in front of him. He had taken a handful of her hair and twisted it, holding her face against his lower body.

'I am looking for Miss East,' the janitor said from the doorway. He was a pensioner, almost seventy years of age but out of vanity he refused to wear spectacles. 'Is she here?' he demanded, peering at Sean myopically.

'Hello, Mr Brownlee. Miss East has gone up to the staff common room already,' Sean told him coolly, holding Clare by her hair so she could not pull away from him. The janitor muttered unintelligibly and turned to leave the art room, when to Clare's horror Sean called him back.

'Oh, Mr Brownlee, can I give her a message for you?' he asked, and he and the janitor talked for almost a minute that seemed like all the ages, while she, screened by the desk, was forced to continue.

She knew then, when she paused to think about it, that she was in over her head. She had seen glimpses of the cruelty and violence in him, and as the months passed his physical strength increased with all the sudden blooming of desert grass after rain. The last garlands of puppy fat around his torso were replaced by hard muscle and it seemed that before her eyes his chest broadened and took on a covering of springing dark curls.

Though sometimes she still challenged and fought him, each time he subdued her with greater ease, and then he would force her to perform one of the tricks to which she had originally introduced him, but which he had embroidered with little sadistic twists of his own.

She developed a taste for these humiliations, and she

began deliberately to provoke him, until at last she succeeded beyond her expectations. It was in her cottage – the first time they had met there because there was always the danger that Tara would drop in unexpectedly, but by now both of them were reckless.

Clare waited until he was fully ripe, his eyes glazing and his lips pulled back in a rictus of ecstasy, then she twisted and bucked, throwing him off her and she knelt before him and jeered with laughter.

He was angry, but she calmed him down. Then a few minutes later she did it again, and this time she squeezed him painfully, just as she had done that first evening at the pool.

Seconds later she lay dazed, only semi-conscious, sprawled half off the bed, both her eyes rapidly closing with plum-coloured swellings, her lips broken against her teeth, and blood dripping from her nose. Sean stood over her. His face was white as ice, the knuckles of his clenched fists grazed raw, still shaking with fury. He caught her by the tresses of her dark hair and knelt over her while he forced her to take him through her split and bleeding lips. After that there was no question but that he was her master.

Clare missed three days of school, while the worst of the swelling subsided and the bruises faded, and then wore dark sunglasses to her art class. When she passed Sean at his easel, she brushed herself against him like a cat, and he waited behind again after class.

Sean had gone long enough without boasting of his conquest, but Snotty Arbuthnot refused to believe him.

'You've got a screw loose if you think I swallow that,' he taunted. 'You think I'm as green as I'm cabbage-looking, man? You and Marsh Mallows – in your dreams, you mean!'

Sean had one alternative to beating him up. 'OK, then, I'll prove it to you.'

'Boy, it had better be good.'

'It will be,' Sean assured him grimly.

The following Saturday afternoon he placed Snotty amongst the protea bushes at the head of the waterfall, and for good measure, lent him the binoculars that his grandmother had given him for his fourteenth birthday.

'Let's take the cushions off the couch,' he suggested to Clare when she came into the summer house. 'We'll put them on the lawn, there on the bank. It will be warmer in the sun.' She agreed with alacrity.

Snotty Arbuthnot was still almost inarticulate when they met at the school gates the next day.

'Hell, man, I never dreamed that people did that. I mean, *unbelievable*, man! When she – you know – when she actually – well, I thought I was going to die on the spot.'

'Did I tell the truth?' Sean demanded. 'Or did I lie to you?'

'Man, it was super titanic. Boy, Sean, I was painting maps of Africa over my sheets all last night, I kid you not. Will you let me watch again – please, Sean, please?'

'Next time will cost you money,' Sean said. Even though performing to an audience had filled an exhibitionist need, Sean meant it as a refusal, but when Snotty asked without hesitation, 'How much, Sean? Just name your price!' Sean looked at him appraisingly.

It was Shasa's policy to keep his sons on very modest pocket-money, a policy that he had inherited from his own mother. 'They must learn the value of money,' was the family maxim.

Even Snotty whose father was only a surgeon received four times the pittance that was Sean's allowance. The protection racket that Sean ran amongst the juniors, an idea he had picked up from a George Raft movie at the Odeon, more than doubled his income. However, he was always lamentably short of hard cash, and Snotty could afford to pay.

'Two pounds,' Sean suggested. He knew that was exactly

his weekly pocket money, but Snotty smiled radiantly. 'You're on, man!'

However, it was only when Snotty actually placed the two crumpled notes in Sean's fist the following Saturday morning that Sean realized the full financial potential.

There was very little chance of Clare realizing that she was on stage. The protea bushes were dense, the noise of the waterfall covered the sound of any involuntary gasps or sniggers, and anyway, once she was started, Clare was deaf and blind to all else. Sean appointed Snotty his ticket salesman and organizer. The commission he received ensured Snotty's free admission to each Saturday performance. Reluctantly they decided to restrict admission to ten spectators at any one session, but even that meant a take of eighteen pounds every single week. It lasted almost three months, which was in itself a miracle, for after the first sell-out matinée the entire senior school was agog.

The word-of-mouth publicity was so good that Snotty was able to demand cash with reservation, and even so his booking sheet was full as far ahead as the beginning of the hols and half the fellows were saving so frantically to try and come up with two pounds that sales at the school tuck shop fell off dramatically. Snotty was trying to get Sean to agree to a midweek performance, or at least to an increase in the Saturday gate, when the first rumour reached the staff common room.

While passing the windows of one of the change rooms the history teacher had overheard two satisfied customers discussing the previous Saturday's performance. The headmaster was unable to bring himself to take the report seriously. The whole idea was patently preposterous. Nevertheless, he knew it was his duty to have a discreet word with Miss East, if only to warn her of the revolting tittle-tattle that was circulating.

He went down to the art room after school, late on Friday afternoon, a most inopportune moment. Clare had by this time abandoned all sense of discretion, for her it had become almost a self-destructive frenzy. She and Sean were in the paint store at the back of the art school, and it was some seconds before either of them realized that the headmaster was in the room with them.

For Shasa everything seemed to happen at once. Sean's expulsion from Bishops was a bombshell that ripped through Weltevreden. When it happened, Shasa was in Johannesburg, and they had to call him out of a meeting with the representatives of the Chamber of Mines to receive the headmaster's telephone call. On the open line the headmaster would give no details, and Shasa flew back to Cape Town immediately and drove directly from the airfield to the school.

Flabbergasted and seething with anger at the stark details the headmaster gave him, Shasa sent the Jaguar roaring around the lower slopes of Table Mountain towards Weltevreden.

From the first he had not approved of the woman who Tara had installed in the cottage. She was all the things he despised, with her great sloppy breasts and silly pretensions which she thought made her *avant-garde* and artistic. Her paintings were atrocious, daubed primary colours and child-ish perspectives, and she tried to conceal her lack of talent and taste behind Portuguese cigarettes, sandals and skirts of blindingly vivid designs. He decided to deal with her first.

However, she had fled, leaving the cottage in slovenly disarray. Thwarted, Shasa took his anger unabated up to the big house and shouted at Tara as he stormed into the hall.

'Where is the little blighter – I'm going to skin his backside for him.'

The other children, all three of them, were peeking over

the railing from the second-floor gallery, in a fine fever of vicarious terror. Isabella's eyes were as enormous as one of Walt Disney's fawns.

Shasa saw them and roared up the stair well. 'Back to your own rooms, this instant. That goes for you as well, young lady.' And they ducked and scampered. As an afterthought Shasa bellowed after them, 'And tell that brother of yours I want to see him in the gun room immediately.'

The three of them raced each other down the passage of the nursery wing, each of them determined to be the bearer of the dreaded summons. The gun room was the family equivalent of Tower Green where all executions took place.

Garrick got there first, and pounded on Sean's locked door.

'Pater wants you immediately,' he yelled.

'In the gun room—' Michael joined in, and Isabella who had been left far behind at the start, piped up breathlessly, 'He's going to skin your backside!' She was flushed and trembling with eagerness, and she hoped desperately that Sean would show her his bottom after Daddy had carried out his threat. She couldn't imagine what it would look like, and she wondered if Daddy would have the skin made into a floor mat like the skins of the zebras and lions in the gun room. It was probably the most exciting thing that had ever happened in her life.

In the entrance hall Tara was attempting to calm Shasa. She had seen him in a comparable rage only two or three times during their marriage, always when he fancied the family honour or reputation had been compromised. Her efforts were in vain, for he turned on her with his single eye glittering.

'Damn you, woman. This is mostly your fault. It was you who insisted on bringing that whore to live on Weltevreden.'

As Shasa stormed off to the gun room, his voice carried

clearly up the stairwell to where Sean was bracing himself to come down and face retribution. Up to that moment Sean had been so confused by the speed of events that he hadn't been thinking clearly. Now, as he descended the stairs, his mind was racing as he prepared his defence. He passed his mother, still standing in the middle of the chessboard black and white marble squares of the entrance hall floor, and she gave him a strained smile of encouragement.

'I tried to help, darling,' she whispered. They had never been close, but now for once Shasa's rage made them allies.

'Thank you, Mater.'

He knocked on the gun-room door, and opened it cautiously when his father roared. He closed it carefully behind him and advanced to the centre of the lion skin where he halted and stood to attention.

Beatings at Weltevreden followed an established ritual. The riding crops were laid out on the baize gun table, five of them of various lengths, weights and stinging potential. He knew his father would make a show of selecting the correct one for the occasion, and that today it would almost certainly be the long whippy whalebone. Involuntarily he looked to the over-stuffed leather chair beside the fireplace over which he would be asked to drape himself, reaching over to grip the legs of the chair on the far side. His father was an international polo player with wrists like steel springs, his strokes made even the headmaster's seem like a powder puff.

Then deliberately Sean closed his mind against fear and lifted his chin to stare calmly at his father. Shasa was standing in front of the fireplace, hands clasped beside his back, rocking on the balls of his feet.

'You have been fired from Bishops,' he said.

Although the headmaster had not specifically mentioned this fact to Sean himself during his extended diatribe, the news did not come as a complete surprise.

'Yes, sir,' he said.

'I find it hard to believe what I have been told about you. It is true that you were making a spectacle of yourself with this – this woman?'

'Yes, sir.'

'That you were letting your friends watch you?'

'Yes, sir.'

'And charging them money for the privilege?'

'Yes, sir.'

'A pound a head?'

'No, sir.'

'What do you mean – no sir?'

'Two pounds a head, sir.'

'You are a Courtney – what you do reflects directly on every member of this family. Do you realize that?'

'Yes, sir.'

'Don't keep saying that. In the name of all that is holy, how could you do it?'

'She started it, sir. I would have never even thought of it without her.'

Shasa stared at him, and suddenly his rage evaporated. He remembered himself at almost exactly the same age, standing chastened before Centaine. She had not beaten him, but had sent him to a lysol bath and a humiliating medical examination. He remembered the girl, a saucy little harlot only a year or two older than he was, with a shock of sunbleached hair and a sly smile – and he almost smiled himself. She had teased and provoked him, leading him on into folly, and yet he felt a strange nostalgic glow. His first real woman – he might forget a hundred others but never that one.

Sean had seen the anger fade out of his father's eye, and sensed that now was the moment to exploit the change of mood.

'I realize that I have brought scandal on the family, and I know that I have to take my medicine—' His father would like that, it was one of his sayings, 'Take your medicine like a man.' He saw the further softening of his father's regard. 'I know how stupid I have been, and before my punishment I would just like to say how sorry I am that I have made you ashamed of me.' This was not exactly true, and Sean instinctively knew it. His father was angry with him for being caught out, but deep down he was rather proud of his eldest son's now proven virility.

'The only excuse I have was that I couldn't help myself. She just drove me mad, sir. I couldn't think of anything else but – well, but what she wanted me to do with her.'

Shasa understood entirely. He was still having the same sort of problems at nearly forty – what was it that Centaine said? 'It's the de Thiry blood, we all have to live with it.' He coughed softly, moved by his son's honesty and openness. He was such a fine-looking boy, straight and tall and strong, so handsome and courageous, no wonder the woman had picked on him. He couldn't really be bad, Shasa thought, a bit of a devil perhaps, a little too cocksure, a little too eager for life – but not really bad. 'I mean, if boffing a pretty girl is mortal sin, there is no salvation for any of us,' he thought.

'I'm going to have to beat you, Sean,' he said aloud.

'Yes, sir, I know that.' Not a trace of fear, no whining. No, damn it, he was a good boy. A son to be proud of.

Shasa went to the gun table and picked up the long whalebone crop, the most formidable weapon in his arsenal, and without being ordered to do so, Sean marched to the armchair and adopted the prescribed position. The first stroke hissed in the air and cracked against his flesh, then suddenly Shasa grunted with disgust and threw the crop on to the gun table.

'The stick is for children – and you are no longer a child,' Shasa said. 'Stand up, man.'

Sean could hardly believe his luck. Although the single stroke had stung like a nest of scorpions, he kept an impassive face and made no effort to rub the seat of his pants.

'What are we going to do with you?' his father demanded, and Sean had the sense to remain silent.

'You have to finish matric,' Shasa stated flatly. 'We'll just have to find someone else to take you on.'

This was not as easy as Shasa had anticipated. He tried SACS and Rondebosch Boys and then Wynberg Boys. The headmasters all knew about Sean Courtney. He was, for a short while, the best-known schoolboy in the Cape of Good Hope.

In the end he was accepted by Costello's Academy, a cram school that operated out of a dilapidated Victorian mansion on the other side of Rondebosch Common, and was not particular about its admissions. Sean arrived for the first day and was gratified to find he was already a celebrity. Unlike the exclusive boys' school which he had recently left, there were girls in the classrooms and academic excellence and moral rectitude were not prerequisites for entrance to Costello's Academy.

Sean had found his spiritual home and he set about sorting out the most promising of his fellow scholars and organizing them into a gang which within a year was virtually running the cram school. His final selection included a half-dozen of the most comely and accommodating young ladies on the academy's roll. As both his father and erstwhile headmaster had noted, Sean was a born leader.

Manfred De La Rey stood to attention on the reviewing stand. He wore a severe dark pinstripe suit and a black Homburg hat, with a small spray of carnations and green fern in his buttonhole. This was the uniform of a Nationalist cabinet minister.

The police band was playing a traditional country air,

'*Die Kaapse Nooi*'—'The Cape Town girl', to a lively marching beat and the ranks of the police cadets stepped out vigorously, passing the stand with their FN rifles at the slope. As each platoon drew level with the dais, they gave Manfred the eyes right, and he returned the salute.

They made a grand show with their smart blue uniforms and sparkling brasswork catching the white highveld sunlight. These athletic young men, proud and eager, their perfect drill formations, their transparent dedication and patriotism, filled Manfred De La Rey with a vast sense of pride.

Manfred stood to attention while the formations wheeled past him and then formed up in review order on the open parade ground facing the stand. The band played a final ruffle of drums and then fell silent. Resplendent in full dress uniform and decorations, the police general stepped to the microphone and in a few crisp sentences introduced the minister, then fell back relinquishing the microphone to Manfred.

Manfred had taken especial care with the preparation of his speech, but before he began he could not prevent himself from glancing aside to where Heidi sat in the front row of honoured guests. This was her day also, and she looked like a blonde Valkyrie, her handsome Teutonic features set off by the wide-brimmed hat and its tall decoration of artificial roses. Few women would have the presence and stature to wear it without looking ridiculous, but on Heidi it was magnificent. She caught his eye and smiled at Manfred. 'What a woman,' he thought. 'She deserves to be First Lady in the land, and I will see that she is – one day. Perhaps sooner than she imagines.'

He turned back to the microphone and composed himself. He knew that he was a compelling orator, and he enjoyed the fact that thousands of eyes were concentrated upon him. He felt at ease up here on the dais, relaxed and in total control of himself and those below him.

'You have chosen a life of service to your *Volk* and to your country,' he began. He was speaking in Afrikaans and his reference to the *Volk* was quite natural. The intake of police recruits was almost exclusively from the Afrikaner section of the white community. Manfred De La Rey would not have had it any other way. It was desirable that control of the security forces should be vested solidly in the more responsible elements of the nation, those who understood most clearly the dangers and threats that faced them in the years ahead. Now he began to warn this dedicated body of young men of those dangers.

'It will require all our courage and fortitude to resist the dark forces which are arrayed against us. We must thank our Maker, the Lord God of our fathers, that in the covenant he made with our ancestors on the battlefield of Blood River he has guaranteed us his protection and guidance. It needs only that we remain constant and true, trusting him, worshipping him, for the way always to be made smooth for our feet to follow.'

He ended his address with the act of faith that had lifted the Afrikaner out of poverty and oppression to his rightful place in the land:

Believe in your God.
Believe in your *Volk*.
Believe in yourself.

His voice, magnified a hundred times, boomed across the parade ground, and he truly felt the divine and benevolent presence very close to him as he looked out upon their shining faces.

Now came the presentation. Out on the field there were shouted orders and the blue ranks came to attention. A pair of officers stepped forward to flank Manfred and one of them carried a velvet-lined tray on which were laid out the medals and awards.

Reading from the list in his hands the second officer called the recipients forward. One at a time they left the ranks, marching briskly, to halt before the imposing figure of Manfred De La Rey. He shook hands with each of them, and then pinned the medals upon their chests.

Then came the moment, and Manfred felt his pride suffocating him. The last of the award-winners was marching towards him across the parade ground, and this one was the tallest and smartest and straightest of them all. In the front rank of guests, Heidi was weeping silently with joy, and she dabbed unashamedly at her tears with a lace handkerchief.

Lothar De La Rey came to a halt in front of his father and stood to rigid attention. Neither of them smiled, their expressions were stern; they stared into each other's eyes, but between them flowed such a current of feeling that made words or smiles redundant.

With an effort Manfred broke that silent rapport, and turned to the police colonel beside him. He offered the sword to Manfred, and the engraved scabbard glistened in silver and gold as Manfred took it from him and turned back to his son.

'The sword of honour,' he said. 'May you wear it with distinction,' and he stepped up to Lothar and attached the beautiful weapon to the blanched belt at his son's waist. They shook hands, both of them solemn still, but the brief grip they exchanged expressed a lifetime of love and pride and filial duty.

They stood to attention, holding the salute, as the band played the national anthem:

> From the blue of our heavens
> From the depths of our seas—

And then the parade was breaking up, and young men were swarming forward to find their families in the throng, and there were excited female cries and laughter and long fervent embraces as they met.

Lothar De La Rey stood between his parents, with the sword hanging at his side, and while he shook the hands of an endless procession of well-wishers and made modest responses to their fulsome congratulations, neither Manfred nor Heidi could any longer contain their proud and happy smiles.

'Well done, Lothie!' One of Lothar's fellow cadets got through to him at last, and the two lads grinned as they shook hands, 'No doubt about who was the best man.'

'I was lucky,' Lothar laughed self-deprecatingly, and changed the subject. 'Have you been told your posting yet, Hannes?'

'Ja, man. I'm being sent down to Natal, somewhere on the coast. How about you, perhaps we'll be together?'

'No such luck,' Lothar shook his head. 'They are sending me to some little station in the black townships near Vereeniging – a place called Sharpeville.'

'Sharpeville? Bad luck, man.' Hannes shook his head with mock sympathy. 'I've never heard of it.'

'Nor had I. Nobody has ever heard of it,' said Lothar with resignation. 'And nobody ever will.'

On 24 August 1958 the Prime Minister, Johannes Gerhardus Strijdom, 'Lion of the Waterberg', succumbed to heart disease. He had only been at the head of government for four years, but his passing left a wide gap in the granite cliffs of Afrikanerdom, and like termites whose nest has been damaged, they rushed to repair it.

Within hours of the announcement of the Prime Minister's death, Manfred De La Rey was in Shasa's office, accompanied by two of the senior Cape back-benchers of the National Party.

'We have to try and keep the northerners out,' he announced bluntly. 'We have to get our man in.'

Shasa nodded cautiously. He was still regarded by most of the party as an outsider in the cabinet. His influence in the coming election of a new leader would not be decisive, but he was ready to watch and learn as Manfred laid out their strategy for him.

'They have already made Verwoerd their candidate,' he said. 'All right, he has been in the Senate most of his career and has little experience as an MP, but his reputation is that of a strong man and a clever one. They like the way he has handled the blacks. He has made the name Verwoerd and the word *apartheid* mean the same thing. The people know that under him there will be no mixing of races, that South Africa will always belong to the white man.'

'*Ja*,' agreed one of the others. 'But he is so brutal. There are ways of doing things, ways of saying things that don't offend people. Our own man is strong also. Dönges introduced the Group Areas Bill and the Separate Representation of Voters Bill – nobody can accuse him of being a *kafferboetie*, a nigger-lover. But he's got more style, more finesse.'

'The northerners don't want finesse. They don't want a genteel prime minister with sweet lips, they want a man of power, and Verwoerd is a talker, hell that man can talk and he's not afraid of work – and as we all know, anybody whom the English press hates so much can't be all bad.' They laughed, watching Shasa, waiting to see how he would take it. He was still an outsider, their tame *rooinek*, and he would not give them the satisfaction of seeing their raillery score. He smiled easily.

'Verwoerd is canny as an old bull baboon, and quick as a mamba. We'll have to work hard if we are to keep him out,' Shasa agreed.

They worked hard, all of them. Shasa was convinced

that despite his record of introducing racially inspired legislation to the House, Dönges was the most moderate and altruistic of the three men who allowed themselves to be persuaded to stand as candidates for the highest office in the land.

As Dr Hendrik Verwoerd himself said, as he accepted nomination, 'When a man receives a desperate call from his people, he does not have the right to refuse.'

On 2 September 1958, the caucus of the National Party met to choose the new leader. The caucus was made up of 178 Nationalist members of parliament and Nationalist senators voting together, and Verwoerd's short term in parliament that had seemed at first to be a weakness turned out to be an advantage. For years Hendrik Verwoerd had been the Leader of the Senate, and had dominated the upper house by the strength of his personality and the powers of his oratory. The senators, docile and compliant, men whose ranks had been enlarged to enable the governing party to force through distasteful legislation, voted for Verwoerd as a block.

Dönges survived the first ballot in which 'Blackie' Swart, the Free State's candidate, was eliminated, but on the second ballot, a straight contest between Verwoerd and Dönges, the northerners closed their ranks and swept Verwoerd into the premiership by ninety-eight votes to seventy-five.

That evening when, as prime minister, Hendrik Frensch Verwoerd broadcast to the nation, he did not try to conceal the fact that his election had been the will of Almighty God. 'He it is who has ordained that I should lead the people of South Africa in this new period of their lives.'

Blaine and Centaine had driven across from Rhodes Hill. It was a family tradition to gather in this room to listen to important broadcasts. Here they had heard speeches and announcements that had shifted the world they knew on its axis: declarations of war and peace, the news of the evil mushroom clouds planted in the skies above Japanese cities, the death of kings and beloved rulers, the accession of a queen, to all these and others they had listened together in the blue drawing-room of Weltevreden.

Now they sat quietly as the high-pitched, nervously strained but articulate voice of the new Prime Minister came to them, jarring when he repeated platitudes and well-worn themes.

'No one need doubt for a single moment that it will always be my aim to uphold the democratic institutions of our country, for they are the most treasured possessions of Western civilization,' Verwoerd told them, 'and the right of people with other convictions to express their views will be maintained.'

'Just as long as those views are passed by the government board of censors, the synod of the Dutch Reformed Church and the caucus of the National Party,' Blaine murmured, a sarcastic qualification for him, and Centaine nudged him.

'Do be quiet, Blaine, I want to listen.'

Verwoerd had moved on to another familiar subject, how the country's enemies had deliberately misconstrued his racial policies. It was not he who had coined the word *apartheid*, but other dedicated and brilliant minds had foreseen the necessity of allowing all the races of a complicated and fragmented society to develop towards their own separate potential. 'As the Minister of Bantu Affairs, since 1950 it has been my duty to give cohesion and substance to this policy, the only policy which will allow full opportunity for each and every group within its own racial community. In the years ahead, we will not deviate one inch from this course.'

Tara had been tapping her foot restlessly as she listened, but now she sprang to her feet. 'I'm sorry,' she blurted. 'I'm feeling a little queasy. I must get a breath of fresh air on the terrace—' and she hurried from the room. Centaine glanced sharply at Shasa, but he smiled and shrugged, was about to make a light comment, when the voice on the radio riveted them all once more.

'I come now to one of the most, if not the most sacred ideal of our people,' the high-pitched voice filled the room, 'and that is the formation of the Republic. I know how many of the English-speaking South Africans listening to me tonight are filled with a sense of loyalty to the British Crown. I know also that this divided loyalty has prevented them from always dealing with the real issues on their merits. The ideal of monarchy has too often been a divisive factor in our midst, separating Afrikaners and English-speakers when they should have been united. In a de-colonizing world, the black man and his newly fledged nations are beginning to emerge as a threat to the South Africa we know and love. Afrikaner and Englishman can no longer afford to stand apart, but must now link arms as allies, secure and strong in the ideal of a new white republic.'

'My God,' Blaine breathed, 'that's a new line. It used always to be the Afrikaner Republic exclusively, and nobody took it seriously, least of all the Afrikaners. But this time he is serious, and he has started something that is going to raise a stink. I remember all too well the contro-versy over the flag, back in the 1920s. That will seem like a love feast compared to the idea of a republic—' He broke off to listen as Verwoerd ended:

'Thus I give you my assurance that from now on the sacred ideal of Republic will be passionately pursued.'

When the Prime Minister finished speaking, Shasa crossed the room and switched off the radio; then he turned and stood with his hands thrust deeply into his pockets, and his shoulders hunched as he studied their faces. They were all of them subdued and shaken. For one hundred and fifty years the country had been British, and there was a pride and a vast sense of security in that state. Now it was to change, and they were afraid. Even Shasa felt strangely bereft and uncertain.

'He doesn't mean it. It's just another sop for his own people. They are always ranting about the republic,' Centaine said hopefully, but Blaine shook his head.

'We don't know this man very well yet. We only know what he wrote when he was editor of *Transvaler*, and we know with what vigour and determination he has set about segregating our society. There is one other thing we have learned about him. He is a man who means exactly what he says, and who will let nothing stand in his way.' He reached across and took Centaine's hand. 'No, my heart. You are wrong. He means it.'

They both looked up at Shasa, and Centaine asked for both of them, 'What will you do, *chéri*?'

'I am not sure that I will have any choice. They say he brooks no opposition, and I opposed him. I lobbied for Dönges. I may not be on the list when he announces his cabinet on Monday.'

'It will be hard to move to the back bench again,' Blaine remarked.

'Too hard,' Shasa nodded. 'And I will not do it.'

'Oh, *chéri*,' Centaine cried. 'You would not resign your seat – after all we have sacrificed, after all our hard work and hopes.'

'We'll know on Monday,' Shasa shrugged, trying not to let them see how bitterly disappointed he was. He had held true power for too short a time, just long enough to learn to enjoy the taste of it. He knew, furthermore, that there was so much he had to offer his country, so many of his efforts almost ready for harvesting. It would be hard to watch them wither and die with his own ambitions, before he had even tasted the first sweets, but Verwoerd would sack him from his cabinet. He could not doubt it for a moment.

'"If you can meet with triumph and disaster",' Centaine quoted, and then laughed gaily, with only the barest tremor in it. 'Now, chéri, let's open a bottle of champagne. It's the only way to treat those two impostors of Kipling's.'

Shasa entered his office in the House, and looked around it regretfully. It had been his for five years, and now he would have to pack up his books and paintings and furniture; the panelling and carpeting he would leave as a gift to the nation. He had hoped to make a larger bequest than that, and he grimaced and went to sit behind his desk for the last time and try to assess where he had erred and what he could have done if he had been allowed. The telephone on his desk rang, and he picked it up before his secretary in the outer office could reach it.

'This is the Prime Minister's secretary,' the voice told him, and for a moment he thought of the dead man and not his successor.

'The Prime Minister would like to see you as soon as is convenient.'

'I will come right away, of course,' Shasa replied, and as he replaced the receiver he thought, 'So he personally wants to have the pleasure of chopping me down.'

Verwoerd kept him waiting only ten minutes and then rose from behind his desk to apologize as Shasa entered his office. 'Forgive me. It has been a busy day,' and Shasa smiled at the understatement. His smile was not forced, for Verwoerd was displaying all his enormous charm, his voice soft and lulling, unlike the higher harsher tone of his public utterances, and he actually came around the desk and took Shasa's arm in an avuncular grip. 'But, of course, I had to speak to you, as I have spoken to all the members of my new cabinet.'

Shasa started so that he pulled his arm out of the other man's grip, and they turned to face each other.

'I am keeping the portfolio of Mines and Industry open, and of course there is no man better qualified for the job

411

than you. I have liked your presentations to the old cabinet. You know what you are talking about.'

'I cannot pretend not to be surprised, Prime Minister,' Shasa told him quietly, and Verwoerd chuckled.

'It is good to be unpredictable at times.'

'Why?' Shasa asked. 'Why me?' Verwoerd cocked his head on the side, a characteristic gesture of interrogation, but Shasa insisted, 'I know you value straight talk, Prime Minister, so I will say it. You have no reason to like me or to consider me an ally.'

'That is true,' Verwoerd agreed. 'But I don't need sycophants. I have enough of those already. What I have considered is that the job you are doing is vital to the eventual well-being of our land, and that there is no one who could do it better. I am sure we will learn to work together.'

'Is that all, Prime Minister?'

'You have mentioned that I like to talk straight. Very well, that is not all. You probably heard me begin my premiership with an appeal for a drawing together of the two sections of our white population, an appeal to Boer and Briton to forget old worn-out antipathy and side by side to build the Republic. How would it look if with the next breath I fired the only Englishman in my government?'

They both laughed, and then Shasa shook his head. 'On the matter of the Republic I will oppose you,' he warned, and for a moment saw through a chink the cold and monolithic ego of a man who would never bow to the contrary view, and then the chink was closed and Verwoerd chuckled.

'Then I will have to convince you that you are wrong. In the meantime you will be my conscience – what is the name of the character in the Disney story?'

'Which one?'

'The story of the puppet – Pinocchio, is it? What was the name of the cricket?'

'Jiminy Cricket,' Shasa told him.

'Yes, in the meantime you will be my Jiminy Cricket. Do you accept the task?'

'We both know it is my duty, Prime Minister.' As Shasa said it, he thought cynically, 'Isn't it remarkable that once ambition has dictated, duty so readily concurs?'

They were dining out that night, but Shasa went to Tara's room to tell her the news as soon as he had dressed.

She watched him in the mirror as he explained his reasons for accepting the appointment. Her expression was solemn but her voice had a brittle edge of contempt in it as she said, 'I am delighted for you. I know that is what you want, and I know that you will be so busy you will not even notice that I am gone.'

'Gone?' he demanded.

'Our bargain, Shasa. We agreed that I could go away for a while when I felt the need. Of course, I will return – that was also part of our bargain.'

He looked relieved. 'Where will you go – and for how long?'

'London,' she replied. 'And I should be away several months. I want to attend a course on archaeology at London University.' She tried to hide it from him, but she was wildly, deliriously excited. She had only heard from Molly that afternoon, just after the new cabinet had been announced. Molly had a message. Moses had at last sent for her, and she had already booked passage for Benjamin, Miriam and herself on the *Pendennis Castle* to Southampton. She would take the child to meet his father.

The mailship sailing was an exciting event in which the citizens of the mother city, of whatever station in life, could join gaily. The deck was crowded and noisy. Paper streamers

413

joined the tall ship to the quayside with a web of colour that fluttered in the south-easter. A coon band on the dock vied with the ship's band high up on the promenade deck, and the old Cape favourite 'Alabama' was answered by 'God Be With You Till We Meet Again'.

Shasa was not there. He had flown up to Walvis Bay to deal with some unforeseen problem at the canning factory. Nor was Sean, he was writing exams at Costello's Academy, but Blaine and Centaine brought the other three children down to the docks to see Tara off on her voyage.

They stood in a small family group, surrounded by the crowd, each of them holding a paper streamer and waving up at Tara on the first-class 'A' deck. As the gap between the quay and the ship's side opened, the foghorns boomed, and the paper streamers parted and floated down to settle on the dark waters of the inner harbour. The tugs pushed the great bows around until they lined up with the harbour entrance, and under the stern the gigantic propeller chopped the water into foam and drove her out into Table Bay.

Tara ran lightly up the companionway to her stateroom. She had protested only mildly when Shasa had insisted that she cancel her original bookings in tourist and travel first class. 'My dear, there are bound to be people we know on board. What would they think of my wife travelling steerage?'

'Not steerage, Shasa – tourist.'

'Everything below "A" deck is steerage,' he had replied, and now she was glad of his snobbery, for the stateroom was a private place where she could have Ben all to herself. It would have excited curiosity if she had been seen with a coloured child on the public deck. As Shasa had pointed out, there were watching eyes on board, and the reports would have flown back to Shasa like homing pigeons.

However, Miriam Afrika had good-naturedly agreed to wear a servant's livery and to act out the subterfuge of being Tara's maid during the voyage. Her husband had reluctantly let her go with Tara to England, despite the disruption to his own household. Tara had compensated him generously and Miriam had come aboard with the child registered as her own.

Tara hardly left her stateroom during the entire voyage, declining the captain's offer to join his table and shunning the cocktail parties and fancy-dress dance. She never tired of being with Moses' son, her love was a hunger that could never be appeased and even when, exhausted by her attentions, Benjamin fell asleep in his cot, Tara hovered over him constantly. 'I love you,' she whispered to him, 'best in the world after your daddy,' and she did not think of the other children, not even Michael. She ordered all their meals to be sent up to her suite, and ate with Benjamin, almost jealously taking over his care from Miriam. Only late at night with the greatest reluctance did she let her carry the child away to the tourist cabin on the deck below.

The days sped by swiftly and, at last, holding Benjamin's hand she stepped off the gangplank to the boat train in Southampton Docks for the ride up to London.

Again at Shasa's insistence, she had taken the suite at the Dorchester overlooking the Park that the family always used, with a single room at the back for Miriam and the baby for which she requested a separate bill and paid in cash out of her own pocket so that Shasa would have no record of it on her bank statement.

There was a message from Moses waiting for her at the porter's desk when she registered. She recognized the handwriting. She opened the envelope the moment she entered the suite, and felt the cold slide of disappointment. He wrote very formally:

Dear Tara,

I am sorry I was not able to meet you. However, it is necessary for me to attend important talks in Amsterdam with our friends. I will contact you immediately on my return.

Yours sincerely,
Moses Gama.

She was thrown into black despair by the tone of the letter and the dashing of her expectations. Without Miriam and the child she would have despaired. However, they passed the waiting days in the parks and Zoo, and in long walks along the river bank and through London's fascinating alleys and convoluted streets. She shopped for Benjamin at Marks & Spencer and C & A, avoiding Harrods and Selfridges, for those were Shasa's haunts.

Tara registered at the university for the course in African archaeology. She did not trust Shasa not to check that she had done so. In accordance with Shasa's other expectations she even dressed in her most demure twin set and pearls and took a cab up to Trafalgar Square to make a courtesy call on the High Commissioner at South Africa House. She could not avoid his invitation to lunch and had to show a bright face during a meal whose menu and wine-list and fellow guests could have been taken straight from a similar gathering at Weltevreden. She listened to the editor of the *Daily Telegraph*, who sat beside her, but kept glancing out of the windows at Nelson's tall column, and longed to be free as the cloud of pigeons that circled it. Her duty done, she escaped at last, only just in time to get back to the Dorchester and give Ben his bath.

She had bought him a plastic tugboat at Hamley's toy shop which was a great success, and Ben sat in the bath and chuckled with delight as the tugboat circled him.

Tara was laughing and drying her hands when Miriam came through from the lounge to the bathroom.

416

'There is somebody to see you, Tara.'

'Who is it?' Tara demanded without rising from where she knelt beside the bath.

'He wouldn't give his name.' Miriam kept a straight face. 'I will finish bathing Ben.'

Tara hesitated, she did not want to waste a minute away from her son. 'Oh all right,' she agreed, and with the towel in her hand she went through to the lounge, and stopped abruptly in the doorway.

The shock was so intense that her face drained of blood and she swayed giddily and had to snatch at the door jamb to steady herself.

'Moses,' she whispered, staring at him.

He wore a long tan-coloured trenchcoat, and the epauletted shoulders were spattered with rain drops. The coat seemed to accentuate his height and the breadth of his shoulders. She had forgotten the grandeur of his presence. He did not smile, but regarded her with that steady heart-checking stare of his.

'Moses,' she said again, and took a faltering step towards him. 'Oh, God, you'll never know how slowly the years have passed since last I saw you.'

'Tara.' His voice thrilled every fibre of her being. 'My wife,' and he held out his arms to her.

She flew to him and he enfolded her and held her close. She pressed her face to his chest and clung to him, inhaling the rich masculine smell of his body, as warm and exciting as the herby smell of the African noonday. For many seconds neither of them moved or spoke except for the involuntary tremors that shook Tara's body and the little moaning sound she made in her throat.

Then gently he held her off and took her face between his hands and lifted it to look into her eyes.

'I have thought about you every day,' he said, and suddenly she was weeping. The tears streamed down her cheeks, and into the corners of her mouth, so that when he kissed her, their metallic salt mingled with the slick taste of his saliva.

Miriam brought Benjamin out to them, clean and dry and dressed in his new blue pyjamas. He regarded his father solemnly.

'I greet you, my son,' Moses whispered. 'May you grow as strong and beautiful as the land of your birth,' and Tara thought that her heart might stop with the pride and sheer joy of seeing them together for the first time.

Though the colour of their skins differed, Benjamin was caramel and chocolate cream while Moses was amber and African bronze, Tara could see the resemblance in the shape of their heads and the set of jaw and brow. They had the same wide-spaced eyes, the same noses and lips, and to her they were the two most beautiful beings in her existence.

Tara kept the suite at the Dorchester, for she knew that Shasa would contact her there and that any invitations from South Africa House or correspondence from the university would be addressed to her at the hotel. But she moved into Moses' flat off the Bayswater Road.

The flat belonged to the Ethiopian Emperor, and was kept for the use of his diplomatic staff. However, Haile Selassie had placed it at Moses Gama's disposal for as long as he needed it. It was a large rambling apartment, with dark rooms and a strange mixture of furnishings, well-worn Western sofas and easy chairs with hand-woven woollen Ethiopian rugs and wall hangings. The ornaments were African artefacts, carved ebony statuettes, crossed two-handed broadswords, bronze Somali shields and Coptic Christian crosses and icons, in native silver studded with semi-precious stones.

They slept on the floor, in the African manner, on thin

hard mattresses filled with coir. Moses even used a small wooden head stool as a pillow, though Tara could not accustom herself to it. Benjamin slept with Miriam in the bedroom at the end of the passage.

Love-making was as naturally part of Moses Gama's life as eating or drinking or sleeping, and yet his skills and his consideration of her needs were an endless source of wonder and delight to her. She wanted more than anything else in life to bear him another child. She tried consciously to open the mouth of her womb, willing it to expand like a flower bud to accept his seed, and long after he had fallen asleep she lay with her thighs tightly crossed and her knees raised so as not to spill a precious drop, imagining herself a sponge for him, or a bellows to draw his substance up deeply into herself.

Yet the times they were alone were far too short for Tara, and it irked her that the flat seemed always filled with strangers. She hated to share Moses with them, wanting him all for herself. He understood this, and when she had been churlish and sulky in the presence of others, he reminded her sternly.

'I am the struggle, Tara. Nothing, nobody, comes ahead of that. Not even my own longings, not my life itself can come before my duty to the cause. If you take me, then you make that same sacrifice.'

To moderate the severity of his words, he lifted her in his arms and carried her to the mattress, and made love to her until she sobbed and rolled her head from side to side, delirious with the power and wonder of it, and then he told her, 'You have as much of me as any person will ever have. Accept that without complaint, and be grateful for it, for we never know when one of us may be called to sacrifice it all. Live now, Tara, live for our love this day, for there may never be a tomorrow.'

'Forgive me, Moses,' she whispered. 'I have been so small and petty. I will not disappoint you again.'

So she put aside her jealousy and joined in his work, and looked upon the men and women who came to the Bayswater Road no longer as strangers and interlopers, but as comrades – part of their life and the struggle. Then she could realize what a fascinating slice of humanity they represented. Most of them were Africans, tall Kikuyus from Kenya, Jomo Kenyatta's young men, the warriors of Mau Mau, once even the little man with a great heart and brain, Hastings Banda, spent an evening with them. There were Shonas and Shangaans from Rhodesia, Xhosas and Zulus from her own South Africa and even a few of Moses' own tribe from Ovamboland. They had formed a fledgling freedom association which they called South West Africa People's Organization, and they wanted Moses' patronage, which he gave them willingly. Tara found it difficult to think of Moses as belonging to a single tribe, all of Africa was his fief, he spoke most of their separate languages and understood their specific fears and aspirations. If ever the word 'African' described one man, that man was Moses Gama.

There were others who came to the flat in Bayswater Road; Hindus and Moslems and men of the north lands, from Ethiopia and Sudan and Mediterranean Africa, some of them still living under colonial tyranny, others newly liberated and eager to help their suffering fellow Africans.

There were white men and women also, speaking in the accents of Liverpool and the north country, of the coal mines or the mills; and other white men and women whose English was halting and laboured, but whose hearts were fierce, patriots from Poland and East Germany and the Soviet bloc, some from Mother Russia herself. All had a common love of freedom and hatred of the oppressor.

From the unlimited letter of credit that Shasa had given her to his London bank, Tara filled the flat with good food and liquor, taking a vindictive pleasure in paying out

Shasa's money for the very best fillet steak and choice lamb, for turbot and sole and lobster.

For the first time she derived pleasure from ordering burgundies and clarets of the best vintages and noblest estates, about which she had listened to Shasa lecturing his dinner guests so pompously. She laughed delightedly when she watched the enemies of all Shasa stood for, the ones called the 'bringers of darkness', quaffing his wines as though they were Coca-Cola.

She had not prepared food for a long time, the chef at Weltevreden would have been mortified if she had attempted to do so, and now she enjoyed working with some of the other women in the kitchen. The Hindu wives showed her how to make wondrous curries and the Arab women prepared lamb in a dozen exciting ways, so that every meal was a feast and an adventure. From the impecunious students to the heads of revolutionary governments and the leaders in exile of captive nations, they came to talk and plan, to eat and drink and exchange ideas even more heady than the wines that Tara poured for them.

Always Moses Gama was at the centre of the excitement. His vast brooding presence seemed to inspire and direct their energies, and Tara realized that he was making bonds, forging loyalties and friendships to carry the struggle onwards to the next plateau. She was immensely proud of him, and humbly proud of her own small part in the grand enterprise. For the very first time in her life she felt useful and important. Until the present time she had spent her life in trivial and meaningless activity. By making her a part of his work, Moses had made her a whole person at last. Impossible as it seemed, during those enchanted months her love for him was multiplied a hundredfold.

Sometimes they travelled together, when Moses was invited to speak to some important group, or to meet representatives of a foreign power. They went to Sheffield and Oxford to address elements from opposite ends of the political spectrum, the British Communist Party and the Association of Conservative Students. One weekend they flew to Paris to meet with officials from the French directorate of foreign affairs and a month later they even went to Moscow together. Tara travelled on her British passport and spent the days sightseeing with her Russian Intourist guide while Moses was closeted in secret talks in the offices of the fourth directorate overlooking the Gorky Prospekt.

When they returned to London, Moses and some of his exiled fellow South Africans organized a protest rally in Trafalgar Square directly opposite the imposing edifice of South Africa House, with its frieze of animal head sculptures and colonnaded front entrance. Tara could not join the demonstration, for Moses warned her that they would be photographed with telescopic lenses from the building, and forbade her to expose herself to the racist agents. She was far too valuable to the cause. Instead she struck upon a delightfully ironic twist, and telephoned the High Commissioner. He invited her to lunch again. She watched from his own office, sitting in one of his easy chairs in the magnificent stinkwood-panelled room, while below her in the square Moses stood beneath a banner APARTHEID IS A CRIME AGAINST HUMANITY and made a speech to five hundred demonstrators. Her only regret was that the wind and the traffic prevented her hearing his words. He repeated them to her that evening as they lay together on the hard mattress on the floor of their bedroom, and she thrilled to every single word.

One lovely English spring morning they walked arm in arm through Hyde Park, and Benjamin threw crumbs to the ducks in the Serpentine.

They watched the riders in Rotten Row, and admired the show of spring blooms in the gardens as they passed them on their way up to Speakers' Corner.

On the lawns the holiday crowds were taking advantage of the unseasonable sunshine, and many of the men were shirtless while the girls had pulled their skirts high on their thighs as they lolled on the grass. The lovers were entwined shamelessly, and Moses frowned. Public displays of this kind offended his African morality.

As they arrived at Speakers' Corner, they passed the militant homosexuals and Irish Republicans on their upturned milk crates and went to join the group of black speakers. Moses was instantly recognized, he had become a well-known figure in these circles, and half a dozen men and women hurried to meet him; all of them were coloured South African expatriates, and all of them were eager to give him the news.

'They have acquitted them—'

'They have set them all free—'

'Nokwe, Makgatho, Nelson Mandela – they are all free!'

'Judge Rumpff found every one of them not guilty of treason—'

Moses Gama stopped dead in his tracks and glowered at them as they surrounded him, dancing joyfully, and laughing in the pale English sunlight, these sons and daughters of Africa.

'I do not believe it,' Moses snarled angrily, and somebody shoved a crumpled copy of the *Observer* at him.

'Here! Read it! It's true.'

Moses snatched the newspaper from him. He read swiftly, scanning the front-page article. His face was set and bleak, and then abruptly he thrust the paper into his pocket and shouldered his way out of the group. He strode away down the tarmac pathway, a tall brooding figure and Tara had to run with Benjamin to catch up with him.

'Moses, wait for us.'

He did not even glance at her, but his fury was evident in the set of his shoulders and the fixed snarl on his lips.

'What is it, Moses, what has made you so angry? We

should rejoice that our friends are free. Please speak to me, Moses.'

'Don't you understand?' he demanded. 'Are you so witless that you do not see what has happened?'

'I don't – I'm sorry—'

'They have come out of this with enormous prestige, especially Mandela. I had thought that he would spend the rest of his life in prison, or better still, that they would have dropped him through the trap of the gallows.'

'Moses!' Tara was shocked. 'How can you speak like that? Nelson Mandela is your comrade.'

'Nelson Mandela is my rival to the death,' he told her flatly. 'There can only be one ruler in South Africa, either him or me.'

'I did not understand.'

'You understand very little, woman. It is not necessary that you should. All you must learn to do is obey me.'

She annoyed and irritated him with her perpetual moods and jealousies. He found it more difficult each day to accept her cloying adoration. Her soft pale flesh had begun to revolt him and each time it took more of an effort to feign passion. He longed for the day that he could be rid of her – but that day was not yet.

'I am sorry, Moses, if I have been stupid and made you angry.'

They walked on in silence, but when they came back to the Serpentine, Tara asked diffidently, 'What will you do now?'

'I have to lay claim to my rightful place as the leader of the people. I cannot allow Mandela to have a clear field.'

'What will you do?' she repeated.

'I must go back – back to South Africa.'

'Oh, no!' she gasped. 'You cannot do that. It is too dangerous, Moses. They will seize you the minute you set foot on South African soil.'

'No,' he shook his head. 'Not if I have your help. I will remain underground, but I will need you.'

'Of course. Whatever you want – but, my darling, what will you hope to achieve by taking such a dreadful risk?'

With an effort he put aside his anger, and looked down at her.

'Do you remember where we first met, the first time we spoke to each other?'

'In the corridors of the Houses of Parliament,' she answered promptly. 'I will never forget.'

He nodded. 'You asked me what I was doing there, and I replied that I would tell you one day. This is the day.'

He spoke for another hour, softly, persuasively, and as she listened her emotions rose and fell, alternating between a fierce joy and a pervading dread.

'Will you help me?' he asked at the end.

'Oh, I am so afraid for you.'

'Will you do it?'

'There is nothing I can deny you,' she whispered. 'Nothing.'

A week later Tara telephoned Centaine at Rhodes Hill and was surprised by the clarity of the connection. She spoke to each of the children in turn. Sean was monosyllabic and seemed relieved to surrender the telephone to Garry, who was solemn and pedantic, in his first year at business school. It was like talking to a little old man, and Garry's single topic of original news was the fact that his father had at last allowed him to start work part-time, as an office boy at Courtney Mining and Finance. 'Pater is paying me two pounds ten shillings a day,' he announced proudly. 'And soon I am to have my own office with my name on the door.'

When his turn came to speak to her, Michael read her a poem of his own, about the sea and the gulls. It was really very good, so her enthusiasm was genuine. 'I love you so much,' he whispered. 'Please come home soon.'

Isabella was petulant. 'What present are you going to bring me?' she demanded. 'Daddy bought me a gold locket with a real diamond—' and Tara was guiltily relieved when her daughter passed the telephone back to Centaine.

'Don't worry about Bella,' Centaine soothed her. 'We've had a little confrontation and mademoiselle's feathers are a wee bit ruffled.'

'I want to buy a coming-home present for Shasa,' Tara told her. 'I have found the most gorgeous medieval altar that has been converted into a chest. I thought it would be just perfect for his cabinet office at the House. Won't you measure the length of the wall on the right of his desk, under the Pierneef paintings – I want to be certain it will fit in there?'

Centaine sounded a little puzzled. It was unusual for Tara to show any interest in antique furniture. 'Of course I will measure it for you,' she agreed dubiously. 'But remember Shasa has very conservative tastes – I wouldn't choose anything too – ah . . .' She hesitated delicately, not wanting to denigrate her daughter-in-law's taste. 'Too obvious or flamboyant.'

'I'll phone you tomorrow evening.' Tara did not acknowledge the advice. 'You can read me the measurements then.'

Two days later Moses accompanied her when she returned to the antique dealer in Kensington High Street. Together they made meticulous measurements of both the exterior and interior of the altar. It was truly a splendid piece of work. The lid was inlaid with mosaic of semi-precious stones while effigies of the apostles guarded the four corners. They were carved in ivory and rare woods and decorated with gold leaf. The panels depicted scenes of

Christ's agony, from the scourging to the crucifixion. Only after careful examination did Moses nod with satisfaction.

'Yes, it will do very well.' Tara gave the dealer a bank draft for six thousand pounds.

'Price is Shasa's yardstick of artistic value,' she explained to Moses while they waited for his friends to come and collect the piece. 'At six thousand pounds he won't be able to refuse to have it in his office.'

The dealer was reluctant to hand the chest over to the three young black men who arrived in an old van in response to Moses' summons.

'It is a very fragile piece of craftsmanship,' he protested. 'I would feel a lot happier if you entrusted the packing and shipping to a firm of experts. I can recommend—'

'Please don't worry,' Tara reassured him. 'I accept full responsibility from now on.'

'It's such a beautiful thing,' the dealer said. 'I would simply curl up and die if it were even scratched.' He wrung his hands piteously as they carried it out and loaded it into the back of the van. A week later Tara flew back to Cape Town.

The day after the crate cleared Customs in Cape Town docks, Tara held a small, but select, surprise party in Shasa's cabinet office to present him with her gift. The Prime Minister was unable to attend, but three cabinet ministers came and with Blaine and Centaine and a dozen others crowded into Shasa's suite to drink Bollinger champagne and admire the gift.

Tara had removed the rosewood Georgian sofa table that had previously stood against the panelled wall, and replaced it with the chest. Shasa had some idea of what was in store. Centaine had dropped a discreet hint, and of course the charge had appeared on his latest statement from Lloyds Bank.

'Six thousand pounds!' Shasa had been appalled. 'That's the price of a new Rolls.' What on earth was the damned woman thinking of? It was ridiculous buying him extravagant gifts for which he paid himself; knowing Tara's tastes, he dreaded his first view of it.

It was covered by a Venetian lace cloth when Shasa entered his office, and he eyed it apprehensively as Tara said a few pretty words about how much she owed him, what a fine and generous husband and what a good father he was to her children.

Ceremoniously Tara lifted the lace cloth off the chest and there was an involuntary gasp of admiration from everyone in the room. The ivory figurines had mellowed to a soft buttery yellow and the gold leaf had the royal patina of age upon it. They crowded closer to examine it, and Shasa felt his unreasonable antipathy towards the gift cool swiftly. He would never have guessed that Tara could show such taste. Instead of the garish monstrosity he had expected, this was a truly great work of art, and if his instinct was correct, which it almost always was, it was also a first-class investment.

'I do hope you like it?' Tara asked him with unusual timidity.

'It's magnificent,' he told her heartily.

'You don't think it should be under the window?'

'I like it very well just where you put it,' he answered her, and then dropped his voice so nobody else could overhear. 'Sometimes you surprise me, my dear. I'm truly very touched by your thoughtfulness.'

'You too were kind and thoughtful to let me go to London,' she replied.

'I could skip the meeting this afternoon and get home early this evening,' he suggested, glancing down at her bosom.

'Oh, I wouldn't want you to do that,' she answered quickly, surprised by her own physical revulsion at the idea. 'I am certain to be exhausted by this afternoon. It's such a strain—'

'So our bargain still stands – to the letter?' he asked.

'I think that it is wiser that way,' she told him. 'Don't you?'

Moses flew from London directly to Delhi, and had a series of friendly meetings with Indira Gandhi, the President of the Indian Congress Party. She gave Moses the warmest encouragement and promises of help and recognition.

At Bombay he went on board a Liberian-registered tramp steamer with a Polish captain. Moses signed on as a deck-hand for the voyage to Lourenço Marques in Portuguese Mozambique. The tramp called in at Victoria in the Seychelles Islands to discharge a cargo of rice and then sailed direct for Africa.

In the harbour of Lourenço Marques Moses said goodbye to the jovial Polish skipper and slipped ashore in the company of five members of the crew who were bound for the notorious red-light area of the seaport. His contact was waiting for him in a dingy night club. The man was a senior member of the underground freedom organization which was just beginning its armed struggle against Portuguese colonial rule.

They ate the huge juicy Mozambique prawns for which the club was famous, and drank the tart green wine of Portugal while they discussed the advancement of the struggle and promised each other the support and assistance of comrades.

When they had eaten, the agent nodded to one of the bar girls and she came to the table and after a few minutes of arch conversation took Moses' hand and led him through the rear door of the bar to her room at the end of the yard.

The agent joined them there after a few minutes and while the girl kept watch at the door, to warn them of a surprise raid by the colonial police, the man handed Moses the travel documents he had prepared for him, a small bundle of second-hand clothing, and sufficient escudos to see him across the border and as far as the Witwatersrand gold-mines.

The next afternoon Moses joined a group of a hundred or more labourers at the railway station. Mozambique was an important source of labour for the gold-mines, and the wages earned by her citizens made a large contribution to the economy. Authentically dressed and in possession of genuine papers, Moses was indistinguishable from any other in the shuffling line of workers and he went aboard the third-class railway coach without even a glance from the uninterested white Portuguese official.

They left the coast in the late afternoon, climbed out of the muggy tropical heat and entered the hilly forests of the lowveld to approach the border post of Komatipoort early the following morning. As the coach rumbled slowly over the low iron bridge, it seemed to Moses that they were crossing not a river but a great ocean. He was filled with a strange blend of dismay and joy, of dread and anticipation. He was coming home – and yet home was a prison for him and his people.

It was strange to hear Afrikaans spoken again, guttural and harsh, but made even more ugly to Moses' ear because it was the language of oppression. The officials here were not the indolent and slovenly Portuguese. Dauntingly brisk and efficient, they examined his papers with sharp eyes, and questioned him brusquely in that hated language. However, Moses had already masked himself in the protective veneer of the African. His face was expressionless and his eyes blank, just a black face among millions of black faces, and they passed him through.

Swart Hendrick did not recognize him when he slouched into the general dealer's store in Drake's Farm township. He was dressed in ill-fitting hand-me-downs and wore an

430

old golfing cap pulled down over his eyes. Only when he straightened up to his full height and lifted the cap did Swart Hendrick start and exclaim in amazement, then seized his arm and, casting nervous glances over his shoulder, hustled his brother through into the little cubicle at the back of the store that he used as an office.

'They are watching this place,' he whispered agitatedly – 'Is your head full of fever, that you walk in here in plain daylight?' Only when they were safely in the locked office and he had recovered from the shock, did he embrace Moses. 'A part of my heart has been missing, but is now restored.'

He shouted over the rhino-board partition wall of his office, 'Raleigh, come here immediately, boy!' and his son came to peer in astonishment at his famous uncle and then kneel before him, lift one of Moses's feet and place it on his own head in the obeisance to a great chief. Smiling, Moses lifted him to his feet and embraced him, questioned him about his schooling and his studies and then let him respond to Swart Hendrick's order.

'Go to your mother. Tell her to prepare food. A whole chicken and plenty of maize meal porridge, and a gallon of strong tea with plenty of sugar. Your uncle is hungry.'

They stayed locked in Swart Hendrick's office until late that night, for there was much to discuss. Swart Hendrick made a full report of all their business enterprises, the state of the secret mineworkers' union, the organization of their Buffaloes, and then gave him all the news of their family and close friends.

When at last they left the office, and crossed to Swart Hendrick's house, he took Moses' arm and led him to the small bedroom which was always ready for his visits, and as he opened the door, Victoria rose from the low bed on which she had been sitting patiently. She came to him and, as the child had done, prostrated herself in front of him and placed his foot upon her head.

'You are my sun,' she whispered. 'Since you went away I have been in darkness.'

'I sent one of the Buffaloes to fetch her from the hospital,' Swart Hendrick explained.

'You did the right thing.' Moses stooped and lifted the Zulu girl to her feet, and she hung her head shyly.

'We will talk again in the morning.' Swart Hendrick closed the door quietly and Moses placed his forefinger under Vicky's chin and lifted it so he could look at her face.

She was even more beautiful than he remembered, an African madonna with a face like a dark moon. For a moment he thought of the woman he had left in London, and his senses cringed as he compared her humid white flesh, soft as putty, to this girl's glossy hide, firm and cool as polished onyx. His nostrils flared to her spicy African musk, so different from the other woman's thin sour odour which she tried to disguise with flowery perfumes. When Vicky looked up at him and smiled, the whites of her eyes and her perfect teeth were luminous and ivory bright in her lovely dark face.

When they had purged their first passion, they lay under the thick kaross of hyrax skins and talked the rest of the night away.

He listened to her boast of her exploits in his absence. She had marched to Pretoria with the other women to deliver a petition to the new Minister of Bantu Affairs, who had replaced Dr Verwoerd when he became Prime Minister.

The march had never reached the Union Buildings. The police had intercepted it, and arrested the organizers. She had spent three days and nights in prison, and she related her humiliations with such humour, giggling as she repeated the *Alice in Wonderland* exchanges between the magistrate and herself, that Moses chuckled with her. In the end, the charges of attending an unlawful assembly and incitement to public violence had been dropped, and Vicky and the other women had been released.

'But I am a battle-trained warrior now,' she laughed. 'I have bloodied my spear, like the Zulus of old King Chaka.'

'I am proud of you,' he told her. 'But the true battle is only just beginning—' and he told her a small part of what lay ahead for all them, and in the yellow flickering light of the lantern, she watched his face avidly and her eyes shone.

Before they at last drifted off into sleep the false dawn was framing the single small window, and Vicky murmured with her lips against his naked chest,

'How long will you stay this time, my lord?'

'Not as long as I wish I could.'

He stayed on three more days at Drake's Farm, and Vicky was with him every night.

Many visitors came when they heard that Moses Gama had returned and most of them were the fierce younger men of *Umkhonto we Sizwe*, the Spear of the Nation, the warriors eager for action.

Some of the older men of the Congress who came to talk with Moses left disturbed by what they had heard and even Swart Hendrick was worried. His brother had changed. He could not readily tell in what way he had changed, but the difference was there. Moses was more impatient and restless. The mundane details of business, and the day-to-day running of the Buffaloes and the trade union committees no longer seemed to hold his attention.

'It is as though he has fastened his eyes upon a distant hilltop, and cannot see anything in between. He speaks only of strange men in distant lands and what do they think or say that concerns us here?' he grumbled to the twins' mother, his only real confidante. 'He is scornful of the money we have made and saved, and says that after the revolution money will have no value. That everything will belong to the people—' Swart Hendrick broke off to think for a moment of his stores and his shebeens, the bakeries and herds of cattle in the reservations which belonged to him, the money in the Post Office savings book and in the white man's bank, and the cash that he kept hidden in many secret places – some of it even buried under the floor upon which he now sat and drank the good beer brewed by his favourite wife. 'I am not sure that I wish all things to belong to the people,' he muttered thoughtfully. 'The people are cattle, lazy and stupid, what have they done to deserve the things for which I have worked so long and hard?'

'Perhaps it is a fever. Perhaps your great brother has a worm in his bowel,' his favourite wife suggested. 'I will make a *muti* for him that will clear his guts and his skull.' Swart Hendrick shook his head sadly. He was not at all certain that even one of his wife's devastating laxatives would drive the dark schemes from his brother's head.

Of course, long ago he had talked and dreamed strange and wild things with his brother. Moses had been young and that was the way of young men, but now the frosts of wisdom were upon Hendrick's head, and his belly was round and full, and he had many sons and herds of cattle. He had not truly thought about it before, but he was a man contented. True, he was not free – but then he was not sure what free really meant. He loved and feared his brother very much, but he was not sure that he wanted to risk all he had for a word of uncertain meaning.

'We must burn down and destroy the whole monstrous system,' his brother said, but it occurred to Swart Hendrick that in the burning down might be included his stores and bakeries.

'We must goad the land, we must make it wild and ungovernable, like a great stallion, so that the oppressor is hurled to earth from its back,' his brother said, but Hendrick had an uncomfortable image of himself and his cosy existence taking that same painful toss.

'The rage of the people is a beautiful and sacred thing, we must let it run free,' Moses said, and Hendrick thought of the people running freely through his well-stocked premises. He had also witnessed the rage of the people in Durban during the Zulu rioting, and the very first concern of every man had been to provide himself with a new suit of clothing and a radio from the looted Indian stores.

'The police are the enemies of the people, they too will perish in the flames,' Moses said, and Hendrick remembered that when the faction fighting between the Zulus and the Xhosas had swept through Drake's Farm the previous November it was the police who had separated them and prevented many more than forty dead. They had also saved his stores from being looted in the uproar. Now Hendrick wondered just who would prevent them killing each other after the police had been burned, and just what day-to-day existence would be like in the townships when each man made his own laws.

However, Swart Hendrick was ashamed of his treacherous relief when three days later Moses left Drake's Farm and moved to the house at Rivonia. Indeed it was Swart Hendrick who had gently pointed out to his brother the danger of remaining when almost everybody in the township knew he had returned, and all day long there was a crowd of idlers in the street hoping for a glimpse of Moses Gama, the beloved leader. It was only a matter of time before the police heard about it through their informers.

The young warriors of *Umkhonto we Sizwe* willingly acted as Moses' scouts in the weeks that followed. They arranged the meetings, the small clandestine gatherings of the most fierce and bloody-minded amongst their own ranks. After Moses had spoken to them, the smouldering resentments which they felt towards the conservative and pacific leadership of the Congress was ready to burst into open rebellion.

Moses sought out and talked with some of the older members of Congress who, despite their age, were radical and impatient. He met secretly with the cell leaders of his own Buffaloes without the knowledge of Hendrick Tabaka, for he had sensed the change in his brother, the cooling of his political passions which had never boiled at the same white heat as Moses' own. For the first time in all the years he no longer trusted him entirely. Like an axe too long in use, Hendrick had lost the keen bright edge, and Moses knew that he must find another sharper weapon to replace him.

'The young ones must carry the battle forward,' he told Vicky Dinizulu. 'Raleigh, and yes, you also, Vicky. The struggle is passing into your hands.'

At each meeting he listened as long as he spoke, picking up the subtle shifts in the balance of power which had taken place in the years that he had been in foreign lands. It was only then that he realized how much ground he had lost, how far he had fallen behind Mandela in the councils of the African National Congress and the imagination of the people.

'It was a serious error on my part to go underground and leave the country,' he mused. 'If only I had stayed to take my place in the dock beside Mandela and the others—'

'The risk was too great,' Vicky made excuse for him. 'If there had been another judgement – if any of the Boer judges other than Rumpff had tried them, they might have gone to the gallows and if you had gone with them the cause would have died upon the rope with all of you. You cannot die, my husband, for without you we are children without a father.'

Moses growled angrily. 'And yet, Mandela stood in the dock and made it a showcase for his own personality. Millions who had never heard his name before saw his face

436

daily in their newspapers and his words became part of the language.' Moses shook his head. 'Simple words: *Amandla* and *Ngawethu*, he said, and everyone in the land listened.'

'They know your name also, and your words, my lord.'

Moses glared at her. 'I do not want you to try to placate me, woman. We both know that while they were in prison during the trial – and I was in exile – they formally handed over the leadership to Mandela. Even old Luthuli gave his blessing, and since his acquittal Mandela has embarked on a new initiative. I know that he has been travelling around the country, in fifty different disguises, consolidating that leadership. I must confront him, and wrest the leadership back from him very soon, or it will be too late and I will be forgotten and left behind.'

'What will you do, my lord? How will you unseat him? He is riding high now – what can we do?'

'Mandela has a weakness – he is too soft, too placatory towards the Boers. I must exploit that weakness.' He said it quietly, but there was such a fierce light in his eyes that Victoria shivered involuntarily, and then with an effort closed her mind against the dark images his words had conjured up.

'He is my husband,' she told herself, fervently. 'He is my lord, and whatever he says or does is the truth and the right.'

The confrontation took place in the kitchen at Puck's Hill. Outside the sky was pregnant with leaden thunder clouds, dark as bruises, that cast an unnatural gloom across the room and Marcus Archer switched on the electric lights that hung above the long table in their pseudo-antique brass fittings.

The thunder crashed like artillery and rolled heavily back and forth through the heavens. Outside the lightning flared in brilliant crackling white light and the rain poured from the eaves in a rippling silver curtain across the windows. They raised their voices against tumultuous nature so they were shouting at each other. They were the high command of *Umkhonto we Sizwe*, twelve men in all, all of them black except Joe Cicero and Marcus Archer – but only two of them counted, Moses Gama and Nelson Mandela. All the others were silent, relegated to the role of observers, while these two, like dominant black-maned lions, battled for the leadership of the pride.

'If I accept what you propose,' Nelson Mandela was standing, leaning forward with clenched fists on the table top, 'we will forfeit the sympathy of the world.'

'You have already accepted the principle of armed revolt that I have urged upon you all these years.' Moses leaned back in the wooden kitchen chair, balancing on its two back legs with his arms folded across his chest. 'You have resisted my call to battle, and instead you have wasted our strength in feeble demonstrations of defiance which the Boers crush down contemptuously.'

'Our campaigns have united the people,' Mandela cried. He had grown a short dark beard since Moses had last seen him. It gave him the air of a true revolutionary, and Moses admitted to himself that Mandela was a fine-looking man, tall and strong and brimming with confidence, a formidable adversary.

'They have also given you a good look at the inside of the white man's gaol,' Moses told him contemptuously. 'The time for those childish games has passed. It is time to strike ferociously at the enemy's heart.'

'You know we have agreed.' Mandela was still standing. 'You know we have reluctantly agreed to the use of force—'

Now Moses leapt to his feet so violently that his chair was flung crashing against the wall behind him.

'Reluctantly!' He leaned across the table until his eyes

were inches from Mandela's dark eyes. 'Yes, you are as reluctant as an old woman and timid as a virgin. What kind of violence is this you propose – dynamiting a few telegraph poles, blowing up a telephone exchange?' Moses' tone was withering with scorn. 'Next you will blow up a public shit house and expect the Boers to come cringing to you for terms. You are naïve, my friend, your eyes are full of stars and your head full of sunny dreams. These are hard men you are taking on and there is only one way you will get their attention. Make them bleed and rub their noses in the blood.'

'We will attack only inanimate targets,' Mandela said. 'There will be no taking of human life. We are not murderers.'

'We are warriors.' Moses dropped his voice, but that did not reduce its power. His words seemed to shimmer in the gloomy room. 'We are fighting for the freedom of our people. We cannot afford the scruples with which you seek to shackle us.'

The younger men at the foot of the table stirred with a restless eagerness, and Joe Cicero smiled slightly, but his eyes were fathomless and his smile was thin and cruel.

'Our violent acts should be symbolic,' Mandela tried to explain, but Moses rode over him.

'Symbols! We have no patience with symbolic acts. In Kenya the warriors of Mau Mau took the little children of the white settlers and held them up by their feet and chopped between their legs with razor-sharp pangas and threw the pieces into the pit toilets, and that is bringing the white men to the conference table. That is the type of symbol the white men understand.'

'We will never sink to such barbarism,' Nelson Mandela said firmly, and Moses leaned even closer to him, and their eyes locked. As they stared at each other, Moses was thinking swiftly. He had forced his opponent to make a stand, to commit himself irrevocably in front of the militants on the high command. Word of his refusal to engage in unlimited warfare would be swiftly passed to the Youth Leaguers and the young hawks, to the Buffaloes and the others who made up the foundation of Moses' personal support.

He would not push Mandela further now, that could only lose Moses some of his gains. He would not give Mandela the opportunity to explain that he might be willing to use harder measures in the future. He had made Mandela appear a pacifist in the eyes of the militants, and in contrast had shown them his own fierce heart.

He drew back disdainfully from Nelson Mandela and he gave a soft scornful chuckle, as he glanced at the young men at the end of the table and shook his head as though he had given up on a dull and stubborn child.

Then he sat down, crossed his arms over his chest and let his chin sink forward on his chest. He took no further part in the conference, remaining a massive brooding presence, by his very silence mocking Mandela's proposals for limited acts of sabotage on government property.

He had given them fine words, but Moses Gama knew that they would need deeds before they all accepted him as the true leader.

'I will give them a deed – such a deed that will leave not a doubt in their hearts,' he thought, and his expression was grim and determined.

The motorcycle was a gift from his father. It was a huge Harley Davidson with a seat like a cowboy saddle and the gear shift was on the side of the silver tank. Sean was not quite sure why Shasa had given it to him. His final results at Costello's Academy didn't merit such paternal generosity. Perhaps Shasa was relieved that he had managed to scrape through at all, and on the other hand perhaps he felt that encouragement was what Sean needed now, or again it might merely be an expression of Shasa's guilt feelings towards his eldest son. Sean didn't care to consider it too closely. It was a magnificent machine, all chrome and enamel and red glass diamond reflectors, flamboyant enough to catch the eye of any young lady, and Sean had wound it up to well over the ton on the straight stretch of road beyond the airport.

Now, however, the engine was burbling softly between his knees, and as they reached the crest of the hill he switched off the headlight and then as gravity took the heavy machine, he cut the engine. They free-wheeled down silently in darkness, and there were no street lights in this elegant suburb. The plots of land around each grand home were the size of small farms.

Near the foot of the hill Sean swung the Harley Davidson off the road. They bumped through a shallow ditch into a clump of trees. They climbed off and Sean pulled the motorcycle up on to its kick stand.

'OK?' he asked his companion. Rufus was not one of Sean's friends whom he could invite back to Weltevreden to meet the folks. Sean had only met him through their mutual love for motorcycles. He was smaller than Sean by at least four inches, and at first glance appeared to be a skinny runt of a lad with a grey complexion as though road grime and sump oil had soaked into his skin. He had nervously shy mannerisms, hanging his head and avoiding eye contact. It had taken some time for Sean to realize that Rufus's lean body was sinewy hard, that he was as quick and agile as a whippet, and that his whining voice and shifty eyes hid a sharp street-wise intelligence and a caustic and irreverent wit. It had not taken long after that for him to be promoted to the rank of principal lieutenant in Sean's gang.

Since graduating without particular distinction from Costello's Academy, his father had insisted that Sean enter articles with the object of one day becoming a member of the Institute of Chartered Accountants. The auditors of the Courtney Mining and Finance, Messrs Rifkin and Markovitch, had been prevailed upon, not without some misgivings on their part, to accept Sean as an articled clerk. This employment was not as dreary as Sean had at first imagined. He had no compunction in using the family name and his boundless charm to work himself into the plummiest audits, preferably of those companies which employed a large female staff, and none of the senior partners had courage enough to report to Shasa Courtney that his favourite son was on a free ride. The Courtney account was worth almost a quarter of a million pounds annually.

Sean was never more than an hour late for work in the morning, his hangover or his lack of sleep hidden by gold-framed aviator's glasses and his brilliant smile. A little judicious rest during the morning and some light banter with the typists and female clerks would set him up for a lunch at the Mount Nelson or Kelvin Grove which ended just in time for a swift return to the office to hand in an imaginative report to the senior partner, after which he was free for a game of squash or an hour's polo practice at Weltevreden.

He usually took dinner at home, it was cheaper than eating out, and although Shasa added substantially to the miserly salary paid by Messrs Rifkin and Markovitch, Sean was always in a financial crisis. After dinner he was free to shed his dinner jacket and black tie and change into a leather cycling jacket and steel-shod boots and then his other life beckoned, the life so different from his diurnal existence, a life of excitement and danger, full of colourful fascinating beings, of eager women and satisfying companions, of deliberate risks and wild adventures – like the one this evening.

Rufus unzipped his black leather jacket and grinned at

him. 'Ready, willing and able, as the actress said to the bishop.' Under the jacket he wore a black roll-neck sweater, black trousers and on his head a black cloth cap.

They didn't have to discuss what they were about to do. They had worked together on the same kind of job four times already, and all the planning had been gone over in detail. However, Rufus's grin was pale and tense in the starlight beneath the trees. This was their most ambitious project yet. Sean felt the delicious blend of fear and excitement like raw spirit in his blood tingling and charging him.

This was what he did it for, this feeling, this indescribable euphoria with which danger always charged him. This was just the first tickle of it, it would grow stronger, more possessing, as the danger increased. He often wondered just how high he could go, there must be a zenith beyond which it was not possible to rise, but unlike the sexual climax which was intense but so fleeting, Sean knew he had not even approached the ultimate thrill of danger. He wondered what it would be like, killing a man with his bare hands? Killing a woman the same way – but doing it as she reached her own climax beneath him? The very idea of that always gave him an aching erection, but until those opportunities presented themselves, he would savour the lesser moments such as these.

'Nail?' Rufus asked, offering him his cigarette tin, but Sean shook his head. He wanted nothing to blunt his enjoyment, not nicotine nor alcohol, he wanted to experience the utmost enjoyment of every instant.

'Smoke half of it and then follow me,' he ordered, and slipped away amongst the trees.

He followed the footpath along the low bank of the stream and then crossed at a shallow place, stepping lightly over the exposed rocks. The high diamond-mesh security fence was on the opposite bank, and he squatted below it. He didn't have to wait long. Within seconds a wolflike

443

shape appeared out of the darkness beyond the fence, and the moment it saw him the German shepherd rushed at him, hurling itself against the heavy-gauge wire fence.

'Hey, Prince,' Sean said quietly, leaning toward the animal, showing not the least sign of fear. 'Come on, boy, you know me.'

The dog recognized him at last. It had only barked once, not creating enough of an uproar to alert the household, and now Sean gently pushed his fingers through the diamond mesh, talking softly and soothingly. The dog sniffed his hand and its long tail began to wave back and forth in friendly salutation. Sean had a way with all living creatures, not only humans. The dog licked his fingers.

Sean whistled softly and Rufus scrambled up the bank behind him. Immediately the German shepherd stiffened and the hair on its back came erect. It growled throatily and Sean whispered, 'Don't be a fool, Prince. Rufus is a friend.'

It took another five minutes for Sean to introduce the two of them, but at last in response to Sean's urging, Rufus gingerly put his fingers through the mesh and the dog sniffed them carefully and wagged his tail.

'I'll go over first,' Sean said, and swarmed up the high fence. There were three strands of barbed wire at the top, but Sean flicked his body over, feet first, arching his back like a gymnast. He dropped lightly to earth and the dog rose on its hind legs and placed its front paws on his chest. Sean fondled his head, holding him while Rufus came over the barbed wire with even greater agility than Sean had.

'Let's go,' Sean whispered, and with the guard dog padding along beside them they went up towards the house, crouching as they ran and keeping to the shadow of the ornamental shrubs until they flattened against the wall, shrinking into the leafy ivy that covered the brickwork.

The house was a double-storeyed mansion, almost as imposing as Weltevreden. It belonged to another leading

Cape family, close friends of the Courtneys. Mark Weston had been at school with Shasa and in the same engineering class at university. His wife, Marjorie, was a contemporary of Tara Courtney's. They had two teenage daughters, the elder of which Sean had deprived of her virginity the previous year, and then dropped without another phone call.

The seventeen-year-old child had suffered a nervous breakdown, refusing to eat, threatening suicide and weeping endlessly until she had had to be taken out of school. Marjorie Weston had sent for Sean to try to remonstrate with him, and persuade him to let her daughter down gently. She had arranged the meeting without her daughter's knowledge, and while her husband was on one of his regular business trips to Johannesburg.

She took Sean to her sewing room on the ground floor and locked the door. It was Thursday afternoon, the servants' day off, and her younger daughter was at school while the eldest, Veronica, was in her bedroom upstairs palely pining.

Marjorie patted the sofa. 'Please come and sit next to me, Sean.' She was determined to keep the interview friendly. It was only when he was beside her that Marjorie realized how infernally goodlooking he was. Even more so than his father, and Marjorie had always had a strong fancy for Shasa Courtney.

She found that she was becoming a little breathless as she reasoned with Sean, but it was only when she placed her hand on his bare arm and felt the elastic muscle under the smooth young skin that she realized what was happening.

Sean had the philanderer's sure and certain instinct, perhaps he had inherited it from his father. He hadn't really thought about Veronica's mother that way. God! She was as old as his mother. However, since Clare East he had always had a taste for older women, and Marjorie Weston was slim and athletic from swimming and tennis and meticulously tanned to disguise the crow's feet at the corners of her eyes and the first signs of crêping at her throat; and where Veronica was vacuous and simpering, her mother was poised and mature, but with the same mauve-blue eyes that had first attracted him to the daughter and an even more carefully groomed mane of thick tawny hair.

As Sean became aware of her excitement, the flush of blood beneath her tan, the agitated breathing that made her bosom beneath the angora jersey and pearls work like a bellows and the subtle change in her body odour that the average male would not have noticed, but which to Sean was like an invitation on an embossed card, he found his own arousal was spiced by the perversity of the situation.

'A double,' he thought. 'Mother and daughter – now that's something different.'

He didn't have to plot further, he let his infallible instinct guide him.

'You are much more attractive than your daughters could ever be – the main reason I broke off with Ronny was I couldn't bear being near you without being able to do this—' and he leaned over her and kissed her with an open mouth.

Marjorie had believed herself to be in complete control of the situation right up until the moment she tasted his mouth. Neither of them spoke again until he was kneeling in front of her, holding her knees apart with both hands, and she was sprawled across the sofa with her pleated skirt rucked up around her waist. Then she panted brokenly, 'Oh Christ, I can't believe this is happening – I must be crazy.'

Now she sat at the foot of the stairs in her satin bathrobe. She was naked under the robe and every few seconds she shivered in a brief spasm. The night was warm, and the house was in darkness. The girls were asleep upstairs and Mark was away on one of his regular business

446

trips. This was the first chance at an assignation there had been in almost two weeks and she was shivering with anticipation. She had switched off the burglar alarms at nine o'clock as they had arranged – Sean was almost half an hour late. Perhaps something had happened and he wasn't coming after all. She hugged herself and shivered miserably at the thought, then she heard the light tap on the glass of the french windows leading on to the swimming-pool patio, and she leapt to her feet and raced across the darkened room. She found she was panting as she fumbled with the latch.

Sean stepped into the room and seized her. He was so tall and powerful that she turned to putty in his arms. No man had ever kissed her like this, so masterfully and yet so skilfully. She sometimes wondered who had taught him and then was consumed by jealousy at the thought. Her need of him was so intense that waves of giddy vertigo washed over her and without his arms to support her she was certain she would have sagged to the floor. Then he tugged at the knot that secured the belt of her robe. It came undone and he thrust his hand into the opening. She shifted her weight, setting her feet wider apart so he could reach her more easily, and she gave a stifled gasp as she felt him slip his forefinger into her and she pushed hard against his hand.

'Lovely,' Sean chuckled in her ear. 'Like the Zambezi River in flood.'

'Shh,' she whispered. 'You'll wake the girls.' Marjorie liked to think of herself as genteel and refined, yet his crude words increased her excitation to a fever. 'Lock the door,' she ordered him, her voice thick and shaking. 'Let's go upstairs.'

He released her and turned to the door. He pressed it closed until the catch snapped and then turned the key and in the same instant reversed the movement, leaving it unlocked.

'All right.' He turned back to Marjorie. 'All set.'

They kissed again, and she ran her hands frantically down the front of his body, feeling the throbbing hardness through the thin cloth. It was she who broke away at last.

'Oh, God, I can't wait any longer.' She took his hand and dragged him up the marble staircase. The girls' bedrooms were in the east wing and Marjorie locked the heavy mahogany door that secured the master suite. They were safe from discovery here, and at last she could let herself go completely.

Marjorie Weston had been married for over twenty years, and she had taken about the same number of lovers in that time. Some of them had merely been mad one-night frolics, others had been longer, more permanent liaisons. One had lasted for almost all these twenty years, an erratic on-and-off arrangement, passionate interludes interspersed with long periods of denial. However, none of her other lovers had been able to match this stripling in beauty and performance, in physical endurance and in devilish inventiveness, not even Shasa Courtney who was that other long-term lover. The son had the same intuitive understanding of her needs. He knew when to be rough and cruel and when to be loving and gentle, but in other ways he outstripped his father. She had never been able to exhaust him or even to force him to falter, and he had a streak of genuine brutality and inherent evil in him that could terrify her at times. Added to that was the almost incestuous delight of taking the son after having had the father.

Tonight Sean did not disappoint her. While she was driving hard towards her first climax of the evening he suddenly reached out to the bedside table and lifted the telephone receiver.

'Ring your husband,' he ordered, and thrust the instrument into her hand.

'God, are you mad!' she gasped. 'What would I say to him?'

'Do it!' he said, and she realized that if she refused, he would slap her across the face. He had done that before.

Still holding him between her thighs, she twisted awkwardly and dialled the Carlton Hotel in Johannesburg. When the hotel operator answered, she said, 'I wish to speak to Mr Mark Weston in Suite 1750.'

'You are going through,' the operator said, and Mark answered on the third ring.

'Hello, darling,' Marjorie said, and above her Sean began to move again. 'I couldn't sleep, so I thought I'd ring you. Sorry if I woke you.'

It became a contest, with Sean trying to force her to gasp or cry out, while she attempted to maintain a casual conversation with Mark. When he succeeded and she gave a little involuntary squeal, Mark asked sharply, 'What was that?'

'I made myself a cup of Milo and it was too hot. I burned my lip.'

She could see how it was exciting Sean also. His face was no longer beautiful but swollen and flushed so that his features seemed coarsened, and in her she felt him swell and harden, filling her to bursting point, until she could control herself no longer, and she broke off the telephone conversation abruptly. 'Goodnight, Mark, sleep well,' and slammed the receiver down on its cradle, just as the first scream came bursting up her throat.

Afterwards they lay still, both of them regaining their breath, but when he tried to roll off her she tightened the grip of her legs and held him hard. She knew that if she could keep him from sliding out, within minutes he would be ready again.

Outside on the front lawn, the dog barked once. 'Is someone there?' she asked.

'No. Prince is just being naughty,' Sean murmured, but he was listening intently, even though he knew that Rufus was too good to be heard, and they had planned every detail with care. Both he and Rufus knew exactly what they were after.

To commemorate the first month of their affair, Marjorie had bought Sean a set of Victorian dress studs and links in platinum and onyx and diamonds. She had invited him up to the house on a Thursday afternoon and led him through to Mark Weston's panelled study on the ground floor. While Sean watched, she checked the combination of the wall safe which was discreetly engraved on the corner of the silver-framed photograph of herself and the girls on Mark's desk, and then she had swung aside the false front of the section of the bookcase that concealed the safe and tumbled the combination of the lock.

She left the safe door ajar when she brought the gift to him. Sean had demonstrated his gratitude by pulling her skirts up and her peach-coloured satin bloomers down, then, sitting her on the edge of her husband's desk, he lifted her knees and placed her feet on each corner of the leather-bound blotter. Then while he stood in front of her and made love to her, he evaluated the contents of the safe over her shoulders.

Sean had heard his father talk about Mark Weston's collection of British and South African gold coins. It was apparently one of the ten most important in private hands anywhere in the world. In addition to the dozen thick leather-bound albums which contained the collection, the middle shelf of the safe held the ledgers and cash books for the running of the estate and household, and a small gentleman's jewel box, while the top shelf was crammed with wads of pristine banknotes still in the bank wrappers and a large canvas bag stencilled 'Standard Bank Ltd' which obviously contained silver. There could not have been less than £5,000 in notes and coins in the safe.

Sean had explained to Rufus exactly where to look for the safe combination, how to open the false front of the bookcase and what to expect when he did.

The knowledge that Rufus was at work downstairs and the danger of possible discovery stimulated Sean so that at one point Marjorie blurted, 'You aren't human – you are a machine.'

He left her at last, lying in the big bed like a wax doll that had melted in the sun, her limbs soft and plastic, the thick mane of her hair darkened and sodden with her own sweat and her mouth smeared out of shape by exhausted passions. Her sleep was catatonic.

Sean was still pent up and excited. He looked into Mark Weston's study on the way out. The front of the bookcase was open, the safe door wide, the ledgers and cash books tumbled untidily on the floor, and the excitement came on him again in a thick musky wave and he found he was once more fully tumescent.

It was dangerous to remain in the house another minute, and the knowledge made his arousal unbearable. He looked up the marble staircase again and only then did the idea come to him. Veronica's room was the second door down the east wing passage. She might scream if he woke her suddenly, she might hate him so that she would scream when she recognized him, but on the other hand she might not. The risk was lunatic, and Sean grinned in the darkness and started back up the marble staircase.

A silver blade of moonlight pierced the curtains and fell on Veronica's pale hair that swirled across the pillow. Sean leaned over her and covered her mouth with his hand. She came awake struggling and terrified.

'It's me,' he whispered. 'Don't be afraid, Ronny. It's me.'

Her struggles stilled, the fear faded from her huge mauve eyes, and she reached up for him with both arms. He lifted his hand off her mouth and she said, 'Oh, Sean, deep down I knew it. I knew you still loved me.'

Rufus was furious. 'I thought you had been caught,' he whined. 'What happened to you, man?'

'I was doing the hard work.' Sean kicked the Harley

451

Davidson and it roared into life. As he turned back onto the road he felt the weight of the saddle bags pull the machine off balance, but he met her easily and straightened up.

'Slow down, man,' Rufus leaned forward from the pillion to caution him. 'You'll wake the whole valley.' And Sean laughed in the wild rush of wind, drunk with excitement, and they went up over the crest at a hundred miles an hour.

Sean parked the Harley Davidson on the Kraaifontein road and they scrambled down the bank and squatted in the dry culvert beneath the road. By the light of an electric torch they shared the booty.

'You said there would be five grand,' Rufus whined accusingly. 'Man, there isn't more than a hundred.'

'Old man Weston must have paid his slaves.' Sean chuckled carelessly as he split the small bundle of bank notes, and pushed the larger pile towards Rufus. 'You need it more than me, kid.'

The jewel box contained cuff-links and studs, a diamond tie-pin that Sean judged to be fully five carats in weight, Masonic medallions, Mark Weston's miniature decorations on a bar – he had won an MC at El Alamein and a string of campaign medals – a Pathek Philippe dress watch in gold and a handful of other personal items.

Rufus ran over them with an experienced eye. 'The watch is engraved, all the other stuff is too hot to move, too dangerous, man. We'll have to dump it.'

They opened the coin albums. Five of them were filled with sovereigns. 'OK,' Rufus grunted. 'I can move that small stuff, but not these. They are red hot, burn your fingers.' With scorn he discarded the albums of heavy coins, the five-pound and five-guinea issues of Victoria and Elizabeth, Charles and the Georges.

After he dropped Rufus off at the illicit shebeen in the coloured District Six where Rufus had parked his own motorcycle, Sean rode out alone along the high winding road that skirts the sheer massif of Chapman's Peak. He parked the Harley on the edge of the cliff. The green Atlantic crashed against the rock five hundred feet below where he stood. One at a time Sean hurled the heavy gold coins out over the edge. He flicked them underhanded, so that they caught the dawn's uncertain light, and then were lost in the shadows of the cliff face as they fell, so he could not see them strike the surface of the water far below. When the last coin was gone, he tossed the empty albums after them and they fluttered as they caught the wind. Then he flung the gold wristwatch and the diamond pin out into the void. He kept the medals for last. It gave him a vindictive satisfaction to have screwed Mark Weston's wife and daughter, and then to throw his medals into the sea.

When he mounted the Harley Davidson and turned it back down the steep winding road, he pushed the goggles up on to his forehead and let the wind beat into his face and rake his eyes so that the tears streamed back across his cheeks. He rode hard, putting the glistening machine over as he went into the turns so that the footrest struck a shower of sparks from the road surface.

'Not much profit for a night's work,' he told himself, and the wind tore the words from his lips. 'But the thrills, oh, the thrills!'

When all his best efforts to interest Sean and Michael in the planetary system of the Court-ney companies had resulted in either lukewarm and deviously feigned enthusiasm or in outright uninterest, Shasa had gone through a series of emotions, beginning with puzzlement.

He tried hard to see how anyone, particularly a young

man of superior intellect, and even more particularly a son of his, could find the whole complex interlinking of wealth and opportunity, of challenge and reward, less than fascinating. At first he thought that he was to blame, that he had not explained it sufficiently, that he had somehow taken their response for granted and had through his own omissions, failed to quicken their attention.

To Shasa it was the very stuff of life itself. His first waking thought each morning, and his last before sleep each night, was for the welfare and sustenance of the company. So he tried again, more patiently, more exhaustively. It was like trying to explain colour to a blind man, and from puzzlement Shasa found himself becoming angry.

'Damn it, Mater,' he exploded, when he and Centaine were alone at her favourite place on the hillside above the Atlantic. 'They just don't seem to care.'

'What about Garry?' Centaine asked quietly.

'Oh, Garry!' Shasa chuckled disparagingly. 'Every time I turn around I trip over him. He is like a puppy.'

'I see you have given him his own office on the third floor,' Centaine observed mildly.

'The old broom cupboard,' Shasa said. 'It was a joke really, but the little blighter took it seriously. I didn't have the heart—'

'He takes most things seriously, does young Garrick,' Centaine observed. 'He's the only who does. He's quite a deep one.'

'Oh, come on, Mater! Garry?'

'He and I had a long chat the other day. You should do the same, it might surprise you. Did you know that he's in the top three in his year?'

'Yes, of course, I knew – but I mean, it's only his first year of business administration. One doesn't take that too seriously.'

'Doesn't one?' Centaine asked innocently, and Shasa was unusually silent for the next few minutes.

The following Friday Shasa looked into the cubbyhole at the end of the passage which served as Garry's office when he was temporarily employed by Courtney Mining during his college vacations. Garry leapt dutifully to his feet when he recognized his father and he pushed his spectacles up on the bridge of his nose.

'Hello, champ, what are you up to?' Shasa asked, glancing down at the forms that covered the desk.

'It's a control,' Garry was caught in a cross-fire – awe at his father's sudden interest in what he was doing and desperation to retain his attention and to obtain his approval.

'Did you know that we spent over a hundred pounds on stationery last month alone?' He was so anxious to impress his father that he stuttered again, something he only did when he was overexcited.

'Take a deep breath, champ.' Shasa eased into the tiny room. There was just room for the two of them. 'Speak slowly, and tell me about it.'

One of Garry's official duties was to order and issue the office stationery. The shelves behind his desk were filled with sheaves of typing paper and boxes of envelopes.

'According to my estimates we should be able to cut that below eighty pounds. We could save twenty pounds a month.'

'Show me.' Shasa perched on the corner of the desk and applied his mind to the problem. He treated it with as much respect as if they were discussing the development of a new gold-mine.

'You are quite right,' Shasa approved his figures. 'You have full authority to put your new control system into practice.' Shasa stood up. 'Well done,' he said, and Garry glowed with gratification. Shasa turned to the door so the lad wouldn't see his expression of amusement, and then he paused and looked back.

'Oh, by the way, I'm flying up to Walvis Bay tomorrow.

I'm meeting the architects and the engineers on site to discuss the extensions to the canning factory. Would you like to come along?'

Unable to trust his voice lest he stutter again, Garry nodded emphatically.

S hasa allowed Garry to fly. Garry had been granted his private pilot's licence two months previously, but he still needed a few hours for his twin-engine endorsement. A year older than Garry, Sean had been given his licence immediately he was eligible. Sean flew the way he rode and shot, naturally, gracefully, but carelessly. He was one of those pilots who flew by the grace of God and the seat of his pants. In contrast, Garry was painstaking and meticulous and therefore, Shasa admitted grudgingly, the better pilot. Garry filed a flight plan as though he was submitting a thesis for his doctorate, and his pre-flight checks went on so long that Shasa squirmed in the right-hand seat and only just contained himself from crying out, 'For God's sake, Garry, let's get on with it.'

Yet it was a mark of his trust that he allowed Garry to take the controls of the Mosquito at all. Shasa was prepared to take over at the first sign of trouble, but he was amply rewarded for his forbearance when he saw the sparkle of deep pleasure behind Garry's spectacles as he handled the lovely machine, lifting her up through the silver wreaths of cloud into a blue African sky where Shasa could share with him a rare feeling of total accord.

Once they arrived at Walvis Bay Shasa tended to forget that Garry was with him. He had become accustomed to his middle son's close attendance, and though he did not really think of it, it was becoming familiar and comforting to have him there. Garry seemed to anticipate his smallest need, whether it was a light for his cigarette or a piece of scrap paper and pencil on which to illustrate an idea to the architect. Yet Garry was quiet and unobtrusive, not given to inane questions and bumptious or facetious remarks.

The cannery was fast becoming one of the big winners in the Courtney stable of companies. For three seasons they had captured their full quota of pilchards, and then there had been an unusual development. In a private meeting Manfred De La Rey had suggested to Shasa that if the company were to issue a further ten thousand bonus shares in the name of a nominee in Pretoria, the consequences might be very much to everybody's advantage. Taking Manfred on trust, Shasa had issued the shares as suggested, and within two months there had been a review of their quota by the government Department of Land and Fisheries and that quota had been almost doubled to the two hundred thousand tons of pilchard that they were now permitted to capture annually.

'For three hundred years the Afrikaners have been left out of business,' Shasa smiled cynically as he received the glad tidings. 'But they are catching on fast. They are in the race now, and not too fussy about how they win. The Jews and the English had better look to their business laurels, here come the Nats.' And he set about planning and financing the extension to the cannery.

It was late afternoon before Shasa finished with the architects, but at this season there were still a few hours of daylight remaining.

'How about a swim at Pelican Point?' Shasa suggested to Garry, and they took one of the cannery Land-Rovers and drove along the hard wet sand at the edge of the bay. The waters of the bay stank of sulphur and fish offal, but behind it the high golden dunes and arid mountains rose in desolate grandeur, while out over the protected and silken waters the flamingo flocks were such a brilliant pink as to seem improbable and theatrical. Shasa drove fast around the curve of the bay with the wind ruffling their hair.

'So what, if anything, did you learn today?'

'I learned that if you want other people to talk too freely, you keep quiet and look sceptical,' Garry answered, and Shasa glanced at his son with a startled expression. That had always been a deliberate technique of his, but Shasa had never expected anyone so young and inexperienced to see through it. 'Without saying anything, you made the architect admit that he really hasn't worked out a solution to siting the boiler room yet,' Garry went on. 'And even I could see that his present proposal is an expensive compromise.'

'Is that so?' It had taken Shasa a full day of discussion to reach the same conclusion, but he wasn't going to say so. 'What would you do, then?'

'I don't know, Pater, not for sure,' Garry said. He had a pedantic manner of delivering an opinion which had at first irritated Shasa, but which now amused him, particularly as the opinions were usually worth listening to. 'But instead of simply sticking on another boiler, I would explore the possibility of installing the new Patterson process—'

'What do you know about the Patterson process?' Shasa demanded sharply. He had only heard about it himself very recently. Suddenly Shasa found himself arguing as though with an equal. Garry had read all the sales pamphlets and memorized the specifications and figures of the process, and had worked out for himself most of the advantages and disadvantages over the conventional method of preparation and canning.

They were still arguing as they rounded the sandy horn of the bay, and beyond the lighthouse the deserted beach, clean and white, stretched away in dwindling perspective to the horizon. Here the Atlantic waters were wild and green, cold and clean, foamy and effervescent with the rush of the surf.

They stripped off their clothes and, naked, swam out into the tumultuous seas, diving deep beneath each curling wave as it came hissing down upon them. At last they emerged, their bodies tinted blue with the cold, but laughing breathlessly with exhilaration.

As they stood beside the Land-Rover and towelled themselves, Shasa studied his son frankly. Even though sodden with salt water, Garry's hair stuck up in disorderly spikes and without his spectacles he had a bemused myopic look. His torso was massively developed, his chest was like a pickle barrel and he had grown such a coat of dark body hair that it almost obscured the ridges of muscle that covered his belly like chain mail.

'Looking at him, there is no way you would ever suspect that he was a Courtney. If I didn't know better, I would think that Tara had a little fling on the side.' Shasa was certain that Tara might be capable of many things, but never infidelity or promiscuity. 'There is nothing about him of his ancestry,' he thought, and then looked further and grinned suddenly.

'Well at least, Garry, you have inherited one of the Courtney gifts. You've got a wanger on you that would make old General Courtney himself turn in his grave with envy.'

Hurriedly Garry covered himself with his towel and reached into the Land-Rover for his underpants, but secretly he was pleased. Up until now he had always regarded that portion of his anatomy with suspicion. It seemed to be an alien creature with a will and existence of its own, determined to embarrass and humiliate him at the most unexpected or inappropriate moments, like that unforgettable occasion when he was standing in front of the commerce class at business school giving his dissertation and the girls in the front row started giggling, or when he was forced to retreat in confusion from the typing-pool at Centaine House because of the alien's sudden but very apparent interest in the surroundings. However, if his father spoke respectfully of it, and the shade of the legendary

459

general approved, then Garry was prepared to reconsider his own relationship with it and come to terms.

They flew on to the H'ani Mine the next morning. All three of the boys had done their stint at the H'ani. As indeed had Shasa so many years before, they had been required to work their way through every part of the mine's operation, from the drilling and blasting in the deep amphitheatre of the open pit, to the final separation rooms where at last the precious crystals were recovered from the crushed blue ground.

That forced labour had been more than sufficient for both Sean and Michael and neither of them had ever shown the least desire to return to the H'ani Mine again. Garry was the exception, he seemed to have developed the same love for these remote wild hills as both Shasa and Centaine shared. He asked to accompany his father here whenever Shasa's regular inspection tours were scheduled. In a few short years he had built up an expert knowledge of the mine's operation, and had at one time or another personally performed all of the tasks involved in the process of production. So on their last evening at the mine the two of them, Shasa and Garry, stood on the brink of the great pit and while the sun set over the desert behind them they stared down into its shadowy depths.

'It's strange to think that it all came out of there,' Garry said softly. 'Everything that you and Nana have built up. It makes one feel somehow humble, like when I am in church.' He was silent for a long moment and then went on. 'I love this place. I wish we could stay longer.'

To hear his own feeling echoed like this, moved Shasa deeply. Of his three sons, this was the only one who understood, who seemed capable of sharing with him the almost religious awe that this massive excavation and the wealth it produced evoked in him. This was the fountain-head, and only Garry had recognized it.

He placed his arm around Garry's shoulders and tried to

find words, but after a moment he simply said, 'I know how you feel, champ. But we have to get back home. I have to introduce my budget to the House on Monday.' It was not what he had wanted to say, but he sensed that Garry knew that, and as they picked their way down the rough pathway in the dusk, they were closer in spirit than they had ever been.

The budget for Shasa's Ministry of Mines and Industry had been almost doubled this year, and he knew that the Opposition were planning to give it a rough passage. They had never forgiven him for changing parties. So he was on his mettle as he rose to his feet and sought the Speaker's recognition, and then instinctively glanced up at the galleries.

Centaine was in the middle of the front row of the visitors' gallery. She was always there when she knew that either Shasa or Blaine was going to speak. She wore a small flat hat tilted forward over her eyes with a single yellow bird of paradise feather raked back at a jaunty angle, and she smiled and nodded encouragement as their eyes met.

Beside Centaine sat Tara. Now that was unusual. He couldn't remember when last she had come to listen to him.

'Our bargain doesn't include torture by boredom,' she had told him, but there she was looking surprisingly elegant in a dainty straw basher with a trailing pink ribbon around the crown and elbow-length white gloves. She touched the brim in a mocking salute, and Shasa lifted an eyebrow at her and then turned to the press gallery high above the Speaker's throne. The political correspondents from the English-speaking press were all there, pencils poised eagerly. Shasa was one of their favourite prey, but all their attacks seemed only to consolidate his position in the National

Party, and by their pettiness and subjectivity point up the efficiency and effectiveness with which he ran his ministry.

He loved the rough and tumble of parliamentary debate, and his single eye sparkled with battle lust as he took up his familiar slouch, both hands in his pockets, and launched into his presentation.

They were at him immediately, yapping and snapping at his heels, interjecting with expressions of disbelief and outrage, calling out 'Shame on you, sir!' and 'Scandal!' and Shasa's grin infuriated them and goaded them to excesses which he brushed aside with casual contempt, holding his own easily and then gradually overwhelming them and turning their own ridicule back upon them, while around him his colleagues grinned with admiration and encouraged his more devastating sallies with cries of 'Hoor, hoor! – Hear, hear!'

When the division was called, his party backed him solidly, and his budget was approved by the expected majority. It was a performance which had enhanced his stature and standing. He was no longer the junior member of the cabinet and Dr Verwoerd passed him a note.

'I was right to keep you on the team. Well done.'

In the front of the visitors' gallery Centaine caught his eye, and clasped both hands together in a boxer's victory flourish, yet somehow she made the gesture appear at once regal and ladylike. Shasa's smile faded as he realized that beside her Tara's seat was empty, she had left during the debate, and Shasa was surprised by his own feeling of disappointment. He would have liked her to witness his triumph.

The House was moving on to other business which did not concern him and on an impulse Shasa rose and left the chamber. He went up the wide staircase and down the long panelled passageway to his office suite. As he approached the front entrance to the suite, he checked suddenly and again on impulse turned at the corner of the passage and went down to the unobtrusive and unmarked doorway at the end.

This was the back door to his office, a convenient escape route from unwanted visitors which had been ordered by old Cecil John Rhodes himself as a by-pass of the front waiting-room, a means for special visitors to reach him and leave again unobserved. Shasa found it equally convenient. The Prime Minister used it occasionally, as did Manfred De La Rey, but the majority of other users were female, and their business with Shasa was seldom political.

Instead of rattling the key in the Yale lock, Shasa slipped it in silently and turned it gently, then pushed the door open sharply. On the inside the door was artfully blended into the panelling of his office and few people knew of its existence.

Tara was standing with her back towards him, bending over the altar chest. She did not know the door existed. Except for the gift of the chest, she had taken little interest in the decoration and furbishment of his office. It was a few seconds before she sensed that she was not alone, and then her reaction was extravagant. She jumped back from the chest and whirled to face him, and as she recognized Shasa, instead of showing relief, she paled with agitation and began to explain breathlessly.

'I was just looking at it – it's such a magnificent piece of work. Quite beautiful, I had forgotten how beautiful—'

One thing Shasa realized immediately, she was as guilty as if she had been caught red-handed in some dreadful crime, but he could not imagine what had made her react that way. She was quite entitled to be in his office, she had her own key to the front door, and she had given him the chest – she could admire it whenever she chose.

He remained silent and fastened his eye upon her accusingly, hoping to trick her into over-explaining, but she left the chest and moved across to the window behind his desk.

'You were doing very well on the floor,' she said. She was still a little breathless, but her colour had returned and she was recovering her composure. 'You always put on such a good show.'

'Is that why you left?' he asked, as he closed the door and pointedly crossed the room to the chest.

'Oh, you know how useless I am with figures, you quite lost me towards the end.'

Shasa studied the chest carefully. 'What was she up to?' he asked himself thoughtfully, but he could not see that anything was altered. The Van Wouw bronze sculpture of the Bushman was still in its place, so she could not have opened the lid.

'It's a marvellous piece,' he said, and stroked the effigy of St Luke at the corner.

'I had no idea there was a door in the panel.' Clearly Tara was trying to distract his attention from the chest, and her efforts merely piqued his curiosity. 'You gave me quite a turn.' Shasa refused to be led and ran his fingers over the inlaid lid.

'I should get Dr Findlay from the National Gallery to have a look at it,' Shasa mused. 'He's an expert on Medieval and Renaissance religious art.'

'Oh, I promised Tricia I would let her know when you arrived.' Tara sounded almost desperate. 'She's got an important message for you.' She crossed quickly to the interleading door and opened it. 'Tricia, Mr Courtney's here now.' Shasa's secretary popped her head into the inner office.

'Do you know a Colonel Louis Nel?' she asked. 'He's been trying to get hold of you all morning.'

'Nel?' Shasa was still studying the chest. 'Nel? No, I don't think so.'

'He says he knows you, sir. He says you worked together during the war.'

'Oh, good Lord, yes!' She had Shasa's full attention now.

'It was so long ago – but, yes, I know him well. He wasn't a colonel then.'

'He's Head of CID for the Cape of Good Hope now,' Tricia told him. 'And he wants you to telephone him as soon as you can. He says it's very urgent, he actually said "life and death".'

'Life and death, hey,' Shasa grinned. 'That probably means he wants to borrow money. Get him on the blower, please, Trish.'

He went to his desk, sat down and pulled the telephone towards him. He motioned Tara towards the couch, but she shook her head.

'I'm meeting Sally and Jenny for lunch,' and she sidled towards the door with a relieved expression. But he wasn't looking at her, he was staring out of the window over the oaks to the slopes of Signal Hill beyond, and he didn't even glance round as she slipped out of the room and closed the door quietly behind her.

Louis Nel's call had transported Shasa back almost twenty years in time. 'Was it that long ago?' he wondered. 'Yes, it was. My God, how quickly the years have passed.'

Shasa had been a young squadron leader, invalided back from the campaign in Abyssinia where he had lost his eye fighting the Duke of Aosta's army on the drive up to Addis Ababa. At a loose end, certain that his life was ruined and that he was a cripple and a burden on his family and friends, Shasa had gone into seclusion and started drinking heavily and letting himself slip into careless despondency. It had been Blaine Malcomess who had sought him out and given him a scornful and painful tongue-lashing, and then offered him a job helping track down and break up the *Ossewa Brandwag*, the Sentinels of the Wagon Train, a secret society of militant nationalist Afrikaners who were virulently opposed to Field-Marshal Jan Christiaan Smuts' pro-British war efforts.

Shasa had worked in cooperation with Louis Nel,

establishing the identity of the leading members of the pro-Nazi conspiracy and preparing the warrants for their arrest and internment. His investigations of the *Ossewa Brandwag*'s activities had put him in contact with a mysterious informer, a woman who had contacted him only by telephone and who took every precaution to conceal her identity. To this day Shasa did not know who she had been, or indeed if she were still alive.

This informer had revealed to him the OB theft of weapons from the government arms and munitions factory in Pretoria, and enabled them to deal a major blow to the subversive organization. Then the same informer had warned Shasa of the White Sword conspiracy. This was an audacious plot to assassinate Field-Marshal Smuts, and in the ensuing confusion to seize control of the armed forces, declare South Africa a republic, and throw in their lot with Adolf Hitler and the Axis powers.

Shasa had been able to foil the plot at the very last minute, but only by the most desperate efforts, and at the cost of his own grandfather's life. Sir Garrick Courtney had been shot by the assassin in mistaken identity, for the old man had physically resembled his good and dear friend, Field-Marshal Smuts.

Shasa had not thought about those dangerous days for many years. Now every detail came back vividly. He lived it all again as he waited for the telephone on his desk to ring; the reckless climb up the sheer side of Table Mountain as he tried to catch his grandfather and the Field-Marshal before they could reach the summit where the killer was waiting for them. He recalled his dreadful sense of helplessness as the rifle shot crashed and echoed against the rocky cliffs and he realized he was too late, the horror of finding his grandfather lying in the track with the ghastly bullet wound which had blown his chest open, and the old Field-Marshal kneeling beside him stricken with grief.

Shasa had chased the killer, using his intimate knowledge of the mountain to cut off his retreat against the top of the cliff. They fought chest to chest, fought for their very lives. White Sword had used his superior strength to break away and escape, but not before Shasa had put a bullet from his 6.5 mm Beretta into his chest. White Sword disappeared and the plot to overthrow Smuts' government collapsed, but the killer had never been brought to justice, and Shasa felt once again the agony of his grandfather's murder. He had loved the old man and named his second son after him.

The telephone rang at last and Shasa snatched it up.

'Louis?' he asked.

'Shasa!' Shasa recognized his voice immediately. 'It's been a long time.'

'It's good to speak to you.'

'Yes, but I wish I was the bearer of better news. I'm sorry.'

'What is it?' Shasa was immediately serious.

'Not on the telephone – can you come down to Caledon Square as soon as possible?'

'Ten minutes,' Shasa said, and hung up.

The headquarters of the CID was only a short walk from the House of Assembly and he stepped it out briskly. The episode with Tara and the chest was put out of his mind as he tried to imagine what bad news Louis Nel had for him.

The sergeant at the front desk had been alerted and he recognized Shasa immediately.

'The colonel is expecting you, Minister. I'll send someone to show you up to his office,' and he beckoned one of the uniformed constables.

Louis Nel was in his shirt-sleeves and he came to the door to welcome Shasa and lead him to one of the easy chairs.

'How about a drink?'

'Still too early for me.' Shasa shook his head, but he accepted the cigarette Louis offered him.

The policeman was lean as ever, but he had lost most of his hair and what remained was ice white. There were dark pouches beneath his eyes and after his welcoming smile his mouth settled back into a thin nervous line. He looked like a man who worried a lot, worked too hard and slept badly at night. He must be past retirement age, Shasa thought.

'How's the family – your wife?' Shasa asked. He had met her only once or twice and could not remember her name or what she looked like.

'We were divorced five years ago.'

'I'm sorry,' Shasa said, and Louis shrugged.

'It was bad at the time.' Then he leaned forward. 'Your family – you have three boys and a girl. That's right?'

'Ah! You have been doing a police number on me,' Shasa smiled, but Louis did not respond. His expression remained serious as he went on.

'Your eldest son – his name is Sean. That's right, isn't it?'

Shasa nodded, he was no longer smiling either, and he was seized by a sudden presentiment.

'You want to speak to me about Sean?' he asked softly.

Louis stood up abruptly and crossed to the window. He was looking down into the street as he answered.

'This is off the record, Shasa. Not the way we usually do things, but there are extraordinary factors here. Our past association, your present rank—' He turned back from the window. 'In the usual circumstances this would probably not have been brought to my notice at all, at least not at this stage of the investigation.'

The word 'investigation' startled Shasa, and he wanted Louis to give him the bad news and get it over with but he controlled his agitation and impatience and waited quietly.

'For some time now we have been troubled by a series of house-breakings in the better-class suburbs – you have surely read about them. The press are calling the thief the "Cape Raffles".'

'Of course,' Shasa nodded. 'Some of my friends, good friends, have been the victims – the Simpsons, the Westons. Mark Weston lost his collection of gold coins.'

'And Mrs Simpson lost her emeralds,' Louis Nel agreed. 'Some of those emeralds, the earrings, were recovered when we raided a fence in District Six. We were acting on a tip-off and we recovered an enormous quantity of stolen articles. We arrested the fence – he's a coloured chap who was running an electrical business in the front of his premises and receiving stolen goods through the back door. We have had him locked up for two weeks now, and he is beginning to co-operate. He gave us a list of names, and on it was one lovable little rogue named Rufus Constantine, ever heard of him?'

Shasa shook his head. 'How does this link up with my son?'

'I'm coming to that. This Constantine was apparently the one who passed the emeralds and some of the other booty. We picked him up and brought him in for questioning. He is a tough little monkey, but we found a way to open him up and make him sing to us. Unfortunately the tune wasn't very pretty.'

'Sean?' Shasa asked, and Louis nodded.

'I'm afraid so. Looks as though he was the leader of an organized gang.'

'It doesn't make sense. Not Sean.'

'Your son has built up quite a reputation.'

'He was a little wild at one time,' Shasa admitted, 'but he is settling down to his articles now, working hard. And why would he want to get involved in something like that? I mean, he doesn't need the money.'

'Articled clerks are not paid a great fortune.'

'I give him an allowance,' Shasa shook his head again. 'No, I don't believe it. What would he know about housebreaking?'

'Oh, no – he doesn't do it himself. He sets up the job and Rufus and his henchman do the dirty work.'

'Sets it up – what do you mean by that?'

'As a son of yours he is welcome in any home in the city, that is right, isn't it?'

'I suppose so.' Shasa was cautious.

'According to little Rufus, your son studies each prospective victim's home, decides on what valuables there are and pinpoints where they are kept – strong rooms, hidden drawers, wall safes and that sort of thing. Then he begins an affair with one of the family, the mother or a daughter, and uses his opportunities to let his accomplice into the home while he is entertaining the lady of his choice upstairs.'

Shasa stared at him wordlessly.

'By all accounts it works very well, and in more than one case the theft was not even reported to us – the ladies involved were more concerned with their reputations and their husband's wrath than with the loss of their jewellery.'

'Marge Weston?' Shasa asked. 'She was one of the ladies?'

'According to our information – yes, she was.'

Shasa whispered, 'The little bastard.' He was appalled, and totally convinced. It all fitted too neatly not to be true. Marge and Sean, his son and one of his mistresses, it was just not to be tolerated. 'This time he has gone too far.'

'Yes,' Louis agreed. 'Too far by a mile. Even as a first offender, he will probably get five or six years.'

All Shasa's attention snapped back to him. The shock to Shasa's pride and sense of propriety was such that he had not even begun to consider the legal implications, but now his righteous rage was snuffed out at the suggestion of his eldest son standing in the dock and being sentenced to long-term imprisonment.

'Have you prepared a docket yet?' he asked. 'Is there a warrant out?'

'Not yet.' Louis was speaking as carefully. 'We were only given this information a few hours ago.' He crossed to his desk and picked up the blue interrogation folder.

'What can I do?' Shasa asked quietly. 'Is there anything we can do?'

'I've done all I can,' Louis answered. 'I've done too much already. I could never justify holding up this information, nor could I justify informing you of an investigation in progress. I've already stretched my neck way out, Shasa. We go back a long way, and I'll never forget the work you did on White Sword – that's the only reason I took the chance . . .' He paused to take a deep breath, and Shasa, sensing there was more to come, remained silent. 'There is nothing else I can do. Nothing else anyone can do *at this level*.' He placed peculiar emphasis on the last three words, and then he added seemingly incongruously, 'I'm retiring next month, there'll be someone else in this office after that.'

'How long do I have?' Shasa asked, and he did not have to elaborate. They understood each other.

'I can sit on this file for another few hours, until five o'clock today, and then the investigation will have to go ahead.'

Shasa stood up. 'You are a good friend.'

'I'll walk you down,' Louis said, and they were alone in the lift before they spoke again. It had taken Shasa that long to master his perturbation.

'I hadn't thought about White Sword for years,' he changed the subject easily. 'Not until today. All that seems so far away and long ago, even though it was my own grandfather.'

471

'I've never forgotten it,' Louis Nel said softly. 'The man was a murderer. If he had succeeded, if you hadn't prevented it, all of us in this land would be a lot worse off than we are today.'

'I wonder what happened to White Sword – who he was and where he is now? Perhaps he is long dead, perhaps—'

'I don't think so – there is something that makes me doubt it. A few years ago I wanted to go over the White Sword file—'

The lift stopped at the ground floor and Louis broke off. He remained silent as they crossed the lobby and went out into the sunlight. On the front steps of the headquarters building, they faced each other.

'Yes?' Shasa asked. 'The file, the White Sword file?'

'There is no file,' Louis said softly.

'I don't understand.'

'No file,' Louis repeated. 'Not in police records or the Justice Department or the central records. Officially, White Sword never existed.'

Shasa stared at him. 'There must be a file – I mean, we worked on it, you and I. It was this thick—' Shasa held his thumb and forefinger apart. 'It can't have disappeared!'

'You can take my word for it. It has.' Louis held out his hand. 'Five o'clock,' he said gently. 'No later, but I will be in my office all day right up to five, if anyone wants to telephone me there.'

Shasa took his hand. 'I will never forget this.' He glanced at his wristwatch as he turned away. It was a few minutes before noon, and most fortunately he had a lunch date with Manfred De La Rey. He headed back up Parliament Lane, and the noon-day gun fired just as he went in through the main doors. Everybody in the main lobby, including the ushers, instinctively checked their watches at the distant clap of cannon shot.

Shasa turned towards the members' dining-room, but he

was far too early. Except for the white-uniformed waiters, it was deserted. In the members' bar he ordered a pink gin and waited impatiently, glancing every few seconds at his watch, but his appointment with Manfred was for twelve-thirty and it was no good going to search for him. He could be anywhere in the huge rambling building, so Shasa employed the time in cherishing and fanning his anger.

'The bastard!' he thought. 'I've allowed him to fool me all these years. All the signs were there, but I refused to accept them. He's dirty rotten, right to the core—' and then his indignation went off in a new direction. 'Marge Weston is old enough to be his mother, how many of my other women has he been boffing? Is nothing sacred to the little devil?'

Manfred De La Rey was a few minutes early. He came to the members' bar smiling and nodding and shaking hands, playing the genial politician, so that it took him a few minutes to cross the room. Shasa could barely contain his impatience, but he didn't want anyone to suspect his agitation.

Manfred asked for a beer. Shasa had never seen him take hard spirits, and only after he had taken his first sip did Shasa tell him quietly, 'I'm in trouble – serious trouble.'

Manfred's easy smile never faltered, he was too shrewd to betray his emotions to a room full of adversaries and potential rivals, but his eyes went cold and pale as those of a basilisk.

'Not here,' he said, and led Shasa through to the men's room. They stood shoulder to shoulder at the urinal and Shasa spoke softly but urgently, and when he finished, Manfred stood staring at the white ceramic trough for only a few seconds before he roused himself.

'What is the number?'

Shasa slipped him a card with Louis Nel's telephone number at CID headquarters.

473

'I'll have to use the security line from my office. Give me fifteen minutes. I will meet you back at the bar.' Manfred zipped his fly closed and strode out of the lavatory.

He was back in the members' bar within ten minutes, by which time Shasa was entertaining the four other members of the luncheon party, all of them influential back-benchers. When they finished their drinks, Shasa suggested, 'Shall we go through?' As they moved towards the dining-room Manfred took his upper arm in a firm grip, and leaned close to him, smiling as though conveying a pleasantry.

'I've squashed it, but he is to be out of the country within twenty-four hours, and I don't want him back. Is that a bargain?'

'I am grateful,' Shasa nodded, and his anger at his son was compounded by this obligation that had been forced upon him. It was a debt that he would have to repay, with interest.

Sean's Harley was parked down at the sports hall that Shasa had built as a joint Christmas present for all three boys two years previously. It contained a gymnasium and squash court, half-Olympic-size indoor swimming-pool and change rooms. As Shasa approached, he heard the explosive echo of the rubber ball from the courts and he went up to the spectators' gallery.

Sean was playing with one of his cronies. He wore white silk shorts but his chest was bare. There was a white sweat band around his forehead, and white tennis shoes on his feet. His body glistened with sweat and was tanned to a golden brown. He was impossibly beautiful, like a romantic painting of himself, and he moved with the unforced grace of a hunting leopard, driving the tiny black ball against the high white wall with such deceptive power that it resounded like a fusillade of rifle fire as it rebounded. He saw Shasa in the gallery and flashed him a dazzle of even white teeth and green eyes, so that despite his anger Shasa suffered a sudden pang at the idea of having to part from him.

In the change room Shasa dismissed his playing partner curtly: 'I want to speak to Sean – alone,' and as soon as he was gone he turned on his son. 'The police are on to you,' he said. 'They know all about you.' He waited for a reaction, but he was disappointed.

Sean towelled his face and neck. 'Sorry, Pater, you've lost me there. What is it they know?' He was cool and debonair, and Shasa exploded.

'Don't play your games with me, young man. What they know can put you behind bars for ten years.'

Sean lowered the towel and stood up from the bench. He was serious at last. 'How did they find out?'

'Rufus Constantine.'

'The little prick. I'll break his neck.' He wasn't going to deny it and Shasa's last hope that he was innocent faded.

'I'll break any necks that have to be broken,' Shasa snapped.

'So what are we going to do?' Sean asked, and Shasa was taken aback by his casual assumption.

'We?' he asked. 'What makes you think that I'm going to save your thieving hide?'

'Family honour,' Sean was matter-of-fact. 'You'll never let me go to court. The family would be on trial with me – you would never allow that.'

'That was part of your calculations?' Shasa asked, and when Sean shrugged, he added, 'You don't understand the words honour or decency.'

'Words,' Sean replied. 'Just words. I prefer actions.'

'God, I wish I could prove you wrong,' Shasa whispered. He was so furious now that he wanted the satisfaction of physical violence. 'I wish I could let you rot in some filthy cell.' His fists were clenched, and before he thought about it, he shifted into balance for the first blow, and instantly

Sean was on guard, his hands stiffening into blades crossed before his chest, and his eyes were fierce. Shasa had paid hundreds of pounds for his training by the finest instructors in Africa, and all of them had at last admitted that Sean was a natural fighter and that the pupil in each case outstripped the master. Delighted that Sean had at last found something that could hold his interest, Shasa had, before Sean began his articles, sent him to Japan for three months to study under a master of the martial arts.

Now, as he confronted his son, Shasa was suddenly aware of every one of his forty-one years, and that Sean was a man in full physical flower, a trained fighter and an athlete in perfect condition. He realized that Sean could toy with him and humiliate him, he could even read in Sean's expression that he was eager to do so. Shasa stepped back and unclenched his fists.

'Pack your bags,' he said quietly. 'You are leaving and you are not coming back.'

They flew north in the Mosquito, landing only to refuel in Johannesburg and then flying on to Messina on the border with Rhodesia. Shasa had a thirty per cent shareholding in the copper mine at Messina, so when he radioed ahead there was a Ford pick-up waiting for him at the airstrip.

Sean tossed his suitcase in the back of the truck and Shasa took the wheel. Shasa could have flown across the border to Salisbury or Lourenço Marques, but he wanted the break to be clean and definite. Sean crossing a border on foot would be symbolic and salutary. As he drove the last few miles through the dry hot bushveld to the bridge over the Limpopo River, Sean slumped down in the seat beside him, hands in his pockets and one foot up on the dashboard.

'I've been thinking,' he spoke in pleasant conversational tones. 'I've been thinking what I should do now, and I have decided to join one of the safari companies in Rhodesia or Kenya or Mozambique. Then when I've finished my apprenticeship, I'll apply for a hunting concession of my own. There is a fortune in it and it must be the best life in the world. Imagine hunting every day!'

Shasa had determined to remain withdrawn and stern, and up until now he had succeeded in speaking barely a word since leaving Cape Town, but at last Sean's total lack of remorse and his cheerfully selfish view of the future forced Shasa to abandon his good intentions.

'From what I hear, you wouldn't last a week without a woman,' he snapped, and Sean smiled.

'Don't worry about me, Pater. There will be bags of jig-jig, that's part of the perks – the clients are old and rich and they bring their daughters or their new young wives with them—'

'My God, Sean, you are completely amoral.'

'May I take that as a compliment, sir?'

'Your plans to apply for your own hunting concession and to run your own safari company – what do you intend using in lieu of money?'

Sean looked puzzled. 'You are one of the richest men in Africa. Just think – free hunting whenever you wanted it, Pater. That would be part of our deal.'

Despite himself, Shasa felt a prickle of temptation. In fact, he had already considered starting a safari operation and his estimates showed that Sean was correct. There was a fortune to be made in marketing the African wilderness and its unique wild life. The only thing that had prevented him doing it before was that he had never found a trustworthy man who understood the special requirements of a safari company to run it for him.

'Damn it—' he broke off that line of thought, 'I've spawned a devil's pup. He could sell a secondhand car to the judge who was passing the death sentence on him.' He felt his anger softened by reluctant admiration, but he spoke grimly. 'You don't seem to understand, Sean. This is the end of the road for you and me.'

As he said it they topped the rise. Ahead of them lay the Limpopo River, but despite Mr Rudyard Kipling, it was neither grey-green nor greasy and there was not a single fever tree on either bank. This was the dry season and though the river was half a mile wide the flow was reduced to a thin trickle down the centre of the bed. The long, low concrete bridge stretched northwards crossing the orange-coloured sand and straggly clumps of reeds.

They drove over the bridge in silence and Shasa stopped the pick-up at the barrier. The border post was a small square building with a corrugated-iron roof. Shasa kept the engine of the Ford running. Sean climbed out and lifted his suitcase out of the back of the truck, then crossed in front of the bonnet and came to Shasa's open window.

'No, Dad.' He leaned into the window. 'You and I will never reach the end of the road. I am part of you, and I love you too deeply for that ever to happen. You are the only person or thing I have ever loved.'

Shasa studied his face for any trace of insincerity, and when he found none, he reached up impulsively and embraced him. He had not meant this to happen, had been determined that it would not, but now he found himself reaching into the inside pocket of his jacket and bringing out the thick sheaf of banknotes and letters that he had carried with him, despite his best intentions to turn Sean loose without a penny.

'Here are a couple of pounds to tide you over,' he said, and his voice was gruff. 'And there are three letters of introduction to people in Salisbury who may be able to help you.'

Carelessly Sean stuffed them into his pocket and picked up his suitcase.

'Thanks, Pater. I don't deserve it.'

'No,' Shasa agreed. 'You don't – but don't worry too much about it. There won't be any more. That's it, Sean, finished. The first and only instalment of your inheritance.'

As always Sean's smile was a little miracle. It made Shasa doubt, despite all the evidence, that his son was thoroughly bad.

'I'll write, Pater. You'll see, one day we'll laugh about this – when we are together again.'

Lugging his suitcase Sean passed through the barrier, and after he disappeared into the customs hut, Shasa was left with an unbearable sense of futility. Was this how it ended after all the care and love over all the years?

Shasa was amused by the ease with which Isabella was able to overcome her lisp. Within two weeks of enrolling at Rustenberg Girls' Senior School, she was talking, and looking, like a little lady. Apparently the teachers and her fellow pupils had not been impressed by babytalk.

It was only when she was trying to wheedle her father that she still employed the lisp and the pout. She sat on the arm of his chair now and stroked the silver wings of hair above Shasa's ears.

'I have the most beautiful daddy in the world,' she crooned, and indeed the flashes of silver contrasted with the dense darkness of the rest of his hair and the tanned almost unlined skin of his face to enhance Shasa's looks. 'I have the kindest and most loving daddy in the world.'

'And I have the most scheming little vixen in the world for a daughter,' he said, and she laughed with delight, a sound that made his heart contract, and her breath in his face smelled milky and sweet as a newborn kitten, but he shored up his crumbling defences. 'I have a daughter who is only fourteen years old—'

'Fifteen,' she corrected him.

'Fourteen and a half,' he countered.

'Almost fifteen,' she insisted.

'A daughter under fifteen years of age, who is much too precious to allow out of my house after ten o'clock at night.'

'Oh, my big cuddly growly bear,' she whispered in his ear and hugged him hard, and as she rubbed her soft cheek against his, her breasts pressed against his arm.

Tara's breasts had always been large and shapely, he still found them immensely attractive. Isabella had inherited them from her. Over the last few months Shasa had watched with pride and interest their phenomenal growth, and now they were firm and warm against his arm.

'Are there going to be boys there?' he asked, and she sensed the first crack in his defence.

'Oh, I'm not interested in boys, Papa,' and she shut her eyes tight in case a thunderbolt came crashing down on her for such a fib. These days Isabella could think of little else but boys, they even occupied her dreams, and her interest in their anatomy was so intense that both Michael and Garry had forbidden her to come into their rooms while they were changing. Her candid and fascinated examination was too disconcerting.

'How will you get there and back? You don't expect your mother to wait up until midnight, do you? And I'll be in Jo'burg that night,' Shasa asked and she opened her eyes.

'Stephen can take me and bring me back.'

'Stephen?' Shasa asked sharply.

'Mommy's new chauffeur. He's so nice and awfully trustworthy – Mommy says so.'

Shasa wasn't aware that Tara had taken on a chauffeur. She usually drove herself, but that reprehensible old Packard of hers had finally given up the ghost when she was away at Sundi and he had prevailed on her to accept a new Chevvy station wagon. Presumably the chauffeur went with it. She should have consulted him – but they had drifted further and further apart over the last few years and seldom discussed domestic routine.

'No,' he said firmly. 'I won't have you driving around on your own at night.'

'I'll be with Stephen,' she pleaded, but he ignored the protest. He knew nothing about Stephen, except that he was male and black.

'I'll tell you what. If you can get a written guarantee from one of the other girls' parents – somebody I know – that they will get you there and back before midnight – well, then, all right, you may go.'

'Oh, Daddy! Daddy!' She showered soft warm kisses on his face, and then leapt up and did a little victory pirouette around his study. She had long willowy legs under the flaring skirt and a tight little bottom in lace panties.

'She is probably,' he thought, and then corrected himself, 'she is without doubt the most beautiful child in the entire world.'

Isabella stopped suddenly, and assumed a woebegone expression.

'Oh, Papa!' she cried in anguish.

'What is it now?' Shasa leaned back in his swivel chair and hid his smile.

'Both Patty and Lenora are going to have new dresses, and I shall look an awful frump.'

'A frump, forsooth! We cannot have that now, can we?' And she rushed to him.

'Does that mean I may have a new dress, Daddy darling?' She wound both arms around his neck again. The sound of a motor car coming up the drive interrupted their idyll.

'Here comes Mummy!' Isabella sprang from his lap and seizing his hand dragged him to the window. 'We can tell her about the party and the dress now, can't we, darling Daddy.'

The new Chevrolet with the high tailfins and great

chromed grille pulled up at the front steps, and the new chauffeur stepped out. He was an imposing man, tall and broad-shouldered in a dove-grey livery and cap with patent-leather peak. He opened the rear door, and Tara slipped out of her seat. As she passed him she tapped the chauffeur on the arm, an over-friendly gesture so typical of Tara's treatment of the servants which irritated Shasa as much as usual.

Tara came up the front stairs and disappeared from Shasa's view, while the chauffeur went back into the driver's seat and pulled away towards the garages. As he drove below the windows of the study, he glanced up. His face was half obscured by the peak of his cap, but there was something vaguely familiar about his jawline and the way his head was set on that corded neck and those powerful shoulders.

Shasa frowned, trying to place him, but the memory was an ancient one, or erroneous, and then behind him Isabella was calling in her special honeyed voice.

'Oh, Mummy, Daddy and I have something to tell you,' and Shasa turned from the window, steeling himself for Tara's familiar accusation of favouritism and indulgence.

T he hidden door to Shasa's parliamentary suite of offices provided the key to the problem that they had been working on over the weeks that Moses Gama had been in Cape Town.

It was simple enough for Moses to enter the parliament building itself, dressed in chauffeur's livery and carrying an armful of shopping – shoe boxes and hat boxes from the most expensive stores. He merely followed Tara as she swept past the doormen at the front entrance. There was virtually no security in operation, no register to sign, no lapel badges were necessary. A stranger might be asked to show a visitor's pass at the entrance, but as the wife of a cabinet minister Tara merited a respectful salute, and she made a point of getting to know the doormen. Sometimes she paused to ask after a sick child, or the janitor's arthritis, and with her sunny personality and her concerned condescension she was soon a favourite of the uniformed staff who guarded the entrance.

She did not take Moses in with her on every occasion, only when she was certain that there was no risk of meeting Shasa. She brought him often enough to establish his presence and his right to be there. When they reached Shasa's suite, Tara would order him to place the parcels in the inner office while she paused to chat with Shasa's secretary. Then, when Moses emerged from the office empty-handed, she would dismiss him lightly.

'Thank you, Stephen. You may go down now. I will need the car at eleven. Please bring it around to the front and wait for me.'

Then Moses would walk down the main staircase, standing respectfully aside for parliamentary messengers and members and cabinet members, once he even passed the Prime Minister on the stairs and he had to drop his gaze in case Verwoerd recognized the hatred in his eyes. It gave him a weird feeling of unreality to pass only an arm's length from the man who was the author of his people's misery, who more than any other represented all the forces of injustice and oppression. The man who had elevated racial discrimination to a quasi-religious philosophy.

Moses found he was trembling as he went on down the stairs, but he passed the doormen without a glance and the janitor in his cubicle barely lifted his eyes before concentrating once more on his newspaper. It was vital to Moses' plans that he should be able to leave the building unaccompanied, and constant repetition had made that possible. To the doormen he was almost invisible.

However, they had still not solved the problem of access

to Shasa's inner office. Moses might go in there long enough to deposit the armful of parcels, but he could not risk remaining longer, and especially he could not be in there behind a closed door, or alone with Tara. Tricia, Shasa's secretary, was alert and observant, and obsessively loyal to Shasa; like all Shasa's female employees she was more than just a little in love with him.

The discovery of the concealed rear door to the suite came as a blessing when they were almost desperately considering leaving the final preparation to Tara alone.

'Heavens, it was so simple, after all our worrying!' Tara laughed with relief, and the next time Shasa left for his inspection tour of the H'ani Mine, taking Garry with him as usual, she and Moses made one of their visits to parliament to test their arrangement.

After Moses had left her parcels in the inner office and in front of Tricia, Tara sent him away. 'I won't need the car until much later, Stephen, I'm having lunch with my father in the dining-room.'

Then as he left, closing the outer door behind him, Tara turned back to Tricia.

'I have a few letters to write. I'll use my husband's office. Please see that I'm not disturbed.'

Tricia looked dubious, she knew that Shasa was fussy about his desk and the contents of his drawers, but she could not think of any way to prevent Tara making use of it, and while she hesitated, Tara marched into Shasa's office, closed the door and firmly locked it behind her. Another precedent had been set.

On the outside there was a light tap, and it took her a moment to discover the inside lock, disguised as a light switch. She opened the panelled door a crack, Moses slipped through it into the office. She held her breath against the snap of the lock, and then turned eagerly to Moses.

'Both doors are locked,' she whispered, and she embraced him. 'Oh, Moses, Moses – it's been so long.'

Even though they spent so much time in each other's company, the moments of total privacy were rare and precious and she clung to him.

'Not now,' he whispered. 'There is work to do.'

Reluctantly she opened her embrace and let him go. He went to the window first, standing to one side as he drew the drapes so that he could not be seen from outside, and then he switched on the desk lamp and removed his uniform jacket, hanging it on the back of Shasa's chair, before crossing to the altar chest. He paused before it, putting Tara in mind of a worshipper, for his head was bowed and his hands clasped before him reverently. Then he roused himself and lifted the heavy bronze Van Wouw sculpture from the top of the chest. He carried it across the room and placed it on Shasa's desk. He went back and carefully opened the lid, wincing as the antique hinges squeaked.

The interior of the chest had been half-filled with the overflow from Shasa's bookshelves. Piles of old copies of *Hansard*, out-of-date White Papers and old parliamentary reports. Moses was annoyed at this unexpected obstacle.

'You must help me,' he whispered to Tara, and between them they began to unpack the chest.

'Keep everything in the same order,' Moses warned, as he passed the piles of publications to her. 'We will have to leave it exactly as it was.'

The chest was so deep that at the end Moses found it easier to climb into it and pass the last of the contents out to her. The carpet was covered with stacks of paper now, but the chest was empty.

'Let me have the tools,' Moses ordered. They were in one of the packets that Moses had carried up from the car, and she handed them to him.

'Don't make any noise,' she pleaded.

The chest was large enough to conceal him completely. She went to the door and listened for a moment. Tricia's typewriter was tapping away reassuringly. Then she went back to the chest and peered into it.

Moses was on his knees working on the floor of the chest with a screwdriver. The screws were authentically antique, taken from another old piece of furniture so that they were not obvious recent additions, and the floor panels of the chest were likewise aged oak and only close examination by an expert would have revealed that they were not original. Once the screws were loose, Moses lifted out the panels to reveal the compartment beneath. This was tightly packed with cotton waste and gently Moses worked it loose, and as he removed the top layer placed it in the package that had contained the tools.

Tara watched with awful fascination as the contents of the first secret compartment came into view. They were small rectangular blocks of some dark amorphous material, like sticky toffee or carpenter's putty, each covered with a translucent greaseproof wrapper and with a label marked in Russian Cyrillic script.

There were ten blocks in the top layer, but Tara knew that there must be two layers below that. Thirty blocks in all, each block weighed two pounds, which made a total of sixty pounds of plastic explosive. It looked mundane and harmless as some kitchen commodity, but Moses had warned her of its lethal power.

'A two-pound brick will destroy the span of a steel bridge, ten pounds would knock down the average house, sixty pounds—' he shrugged. 'It's enough to do the job ten times over.'

Once he had removed the packing and reassured himself of the contents, Moses replaced the panel and screwed it closed. Then he opened the centre panel of the floor. Again it was packed with cotton waste. As he removed it, he explained in a whisper, 'There are four different types of detonators to cover all possible needs. These,' he gingerly lifted a small flat tin the size of a cigarette pack out of its nest of cotton packing, 'these are electrical detonators that can be wired up to a series of batteries or to the mains. These,' he returned the tin to its slot and lifted the loose cotton to reveal a second larger tin, 'these are radio receiver detonators and are set off by a VHF transmission from this miniature transmitter.' It looked to Tara like one of the modern portable radios. Moses lifted it out of its nest. 'It needs only six torch batteries to activate it. Now these are simple acid time-fused detonators, primitive, and the time delay isn't very accurate, but this here is a trembler detonator. Once it is primed, the slightest movement or vibration will set it off. Only an expert will be able to defuse the charge once it is in place.'

Until this moment she had considered only the abstract dialectic of what they were doing, but now she was faced with the actuality. Here before her was the very stuff of violent death and destruction, the innocent appearance no less menacing than the coils of a sleeping mamba, and she found herself wavering.

'Moses,' she whispered. 'Nobody will be hurt. No human life, you said that – didn't you?'

'We have discussed that already.' His expression was cold and scornful, and she felt ashamed.

'Forgive me, please.'

Moses ignored her and unscrewed the third and last panel. This compartment contained an automatic pistol and four clips of ammunition. It took up little space and the rest of the compartment was packed with cotton waste which Moses removed.

'Give me the other packet,' he ordered, and when she passed it to him, he began to pack the contents into the empty recess. Firstly there was a compact tool kit which contained a keyhole saw and hand drill, drill bits and augers, a box of hearing-aid batteries for the detonator and torch batteries for the transmitter, a Penlite torch, a five-hundred-foot roll of thin electrical wire, diamond glass-cutters, putty, staples and tiny one-ounce tins of touch-up paint. Lastly there was a pack of hard rations, dried biscuit and cans of meat and vegetables.

'I wish you had let me give you something more appetizing.'

'It will be only two days,' Moses said, and she was reminded how little store he set by creature comforts.

Moses replaced the panel, but he did not tighten the retaining screws fully, so that they could be loosened by hand.

'All right, pass the books to me now.' He repacked the chest, replacing the bundles in the same order as he had found them, so that to a casual glance it would not be apparent that the contents of the chest had been disturbed. Carefully Moses closed the chest and replaced the bronze statue on the lid. Then he stood in front of the desk and surveyed the room carefully.

'I will need a place to hide.'

'The drapes,' Tara suggested, and he nodded.

'Not very original, but effective.' The curtains were embroidered brocade, cut full, and they reached to the floor.

'A key to that door – I'll need one.' He indicated the hidden door in the panelling.

'I will try—' Tara began and then broke off as there was a knock on the interleading door. For a moment he thought she might panic and he squeezed her arm to calm her.

'Who is it?' Tara called in a level voice.

'It's me, Mrs Courtney,' Tricia called respectfully. 'It's one o'clock and I'm going to take my lunch.'

'Go ahead, Tricia. I'll be a little longer, but I'll lock up when I leave.'

They heard the outer door close, and then Moses

488

released her arm. 'Go out and search her desk. See if she has a key to the back door.'

Tara was back within minutes with a small bunch of keys. She tried them in the lock and the third one turned the door in the panelling.

'The serial number is on it.' She scribbled a note of the number on Shasa's noteblock and ripped off the top sheet. 'I'll return the keys to Tricia's desk.'

When she came back, Moses was buttoning his uniform jacket, but she locked the door behind her.

'What I need now is a plan of the building. There must be one in the Public Works Department, and you must get me a copy. Tell Tricia to do it.'

'How?' she asked. 'What excuse can I give?'

'Tell her that you want to change the lighting in here,' he gestured at the chandelier in the roof. 'Tell her you must have an electrical plan of this section, showing the circuits and wall-fittings.'

'Yes, I can do that,' she agreed.

'Good. We are finished here for the time being. We can go now.'

'There is no hurry, Moses. Tricia will not be back for another hour.'

He looked down at her, and for a moment she thought she saw a flash of contempt, even disgust, in those dark brooding eyes, but she would not let herself believe that, and she pressed herself to him, hiding her face against his chest. Within seconds she felt the swelling and hardening of his loins through the cloth that separated their lower bodies, and her doubts were dispelled. She was certain that in his own strange African way he loved her still and she reached down to open his clothing and bring him out.

He was so thick that she could barely encompass him within the circle of her thumb and forefinger, and he was hot and hard as a shaft of black ironstone that had lain in the full glare of the sun at midday.

Tara sank down onto the thick silken rug, drawing him down on top of her.

Every day now increased the danger of discovery and both of them were aware of it.

'Will Shasa recognize you?' Tara asked Moses more than once. 'It is becoming more and more difficult to keep you from meeting him face to face. He asked about my new chauffeur a few days ago.'

Isabella had apparently drawn Shasa's attention to the new employee for her own selfish reasons, and Tara could cheerfully have thrashed her for it. But there had been the danger of establishing the importance of her new driver even more clearly in the child's devious mind, so she had let it pass without comment.

'Will he know you?' she insisted, and Moses considered it carefully.

'It was long ago, before the war. He was a child.' Moses shook his head. 'The circumstances were so different, the place so remote – and yet for a short while we were close. I believe we made a deep impression upon each other – if merely because of the unlikelihood of such a relationship, black man and white boy becoming familiar, developing an intimate friendship.' He sighed. 'It is certain, however, that at the time of the trial he must have read the intelligence reports and known of the warrant for my arrest, which, by the way, is still in force. Whether he would connect the wanted revolutionary criminal with his childhood friend, I do not know, but we cannot take that chance. We must do what has to be done as soon as possible.'

'It seems that Shasa has been out of town every weekend for the last five years.' Tara bit her lip with frustration. 'But now that I want him gone, he won't leave Weltevreden for a single day. First it's this damned polo business.' The

Argentinian polo team was touring the country, and Shasa was hosting their stay in Cape Town, while the polo fields of Weltevreden would be the venue for the first Test match of their visit. 'Then immediately after that it will be the British Prime Minister Harold Macmillan's visit. Shasa won't be leaving Cape Town before the end of the month at the very earliest.' She watched his face in the driving-mirror as he pondered it.

'There is risk either way,' he said softly. 'To delay is as dangerous as to act hastily. We must choose the exact moment.'

Neither of them spoke again until they reached the bus stop, and Moses parked the Chev on the opposite side of the road. Then he switched off the engine and asked:

'This polo match. When will it take place?'

'The Test match is on Friday afternoon.'

'Your husband will be playing?'

'The South African team will be announced in the middle of the week, but Shasa is almost certain to be on the team. He might even be chosen as captain.'

'Even if he is not, he will be the host. He must be there.'

'Yes,' Tara agreed.

'Friday – that will give me the whole weekend.' He made up his mind. 'We will do it then.' For a few moments Tara felt the suffocating desperation of somebody trapped in quicksand, sinking slowly, and yet there was an inevitability about it that made fear seem superfluous. There was no escape and she felt instead an enervating sense of acceptance.

'Here is the bus,' Moses said, and she heard the faintest tremor of excitement in his voice. It was one of the very few times that she had ever known his personal feelings to betray him.

As the bus drew up at the halt, she saw the woman and child standing on the platform at the rear. They were both peering eagerly at the parked Chev, and when Tara waved the child hopped down and started across the road. The bus pulled away and Miriam Afrika stayed on the platform at the back of the bus, staring back at them until it turned the next corner.

Benjamin came to meet them, his face bright with anticipation. He was growing into a likely lad, and Miriam always dressed him so well – clean white shirt, grey shorts and polished black shoes. His toffee-coloured skin had a scrubbed look and his crisp dark curls were trimmed into a neat cap.

'Isn't he just too gorgeous?' Tara breathed. 'Our son, Moses, our fine son.'

The boy opened the door and jumped in besides Moses. He looked up at him with a beaming smile and Moses embraced him briefly. Then Tara leaned over the seat and kissed him and gave him a brief but fierce hug. In public she had to limit any show of affection, and as he grew older, their relationship became more difficult and obscure.

The child still believed that Miriam Afrika was his mother, but he was almost six years old now, and a bright, intelligent and sensitive boy. She knew that he suspected some special relationship between the three of them. These clandestine meetings were too regular, and emotionally charged, for him not to suspect that something had remained to be fully explained to him.

Benjamin had been told merely that they were good friends of the family, but even at his tender age he would be aware of the social taboos that they were flouting, for his very existence must be permeated by the knowledge that white and black were somehow different and set apart from his own light brown, and sometimes he stared at Tara with a kind of wonder as though she were some fabulous creature from a fairy tale.

There was nothing Tara could think of that could fulfil her more than taking him in her arms and telling him, 'You are my baby, my own true baby, and I love you as much as

I love your father.' But she could not even let him sit on the seat beside her in case they were seen together.

They drove out across the Cape Flats towards Somerset West, but before they reached the village, Moses turned off onto a side track, through the dense stands of Port Jackson willow until they came out onto the long deserted curve of beach with the green waters of False Bay before them, and on each side the mountainous ramparts that formed the horns of the wide bay.

Moses parked the Chev and fetched the picnic basket from the boot, and then the three of them followed the footpath along the top of the beach until they reached their favourite spot. From here anyone approaching along the beach would be obvious from half a mile, while inland the exotic growth formed an almost impenetrable jungle. The only persons likely to venture this far along the lonely beach were surf fishermen casting into the tumbling waves for kob and steenbras, or lovers seeking seclusion. Here they felt safe.

Tara helped Benjamin change into his bathing-costume, and then all three of them went hand in hand to the enclosed rock pool where the child splashed and played like a spaniel puppy. When at last he was chilled through and tired, Tara towelled down his shivering body and dressed him again. Then he helped Moses build a fire amongst the dunes and grill the raw sausages and chops upon the coals.

After they had eaten, Benjamin wanted to swim again, but gently Tara forbade him. 'Not on a full stomach, darling.' So he went to search for shells along the tide-mark of the beach, and Tara and Moses sat on the crest of the dune and watched him. Tara was as happy and contented as she could ever remember being until Moses broke the silence.

'This is what we are working for,' he said. 'Dignity and a chance for happiness for all in this land.'

'Yes, Moses,' she whispered.

'It is worth any price.'

'Oh, yes,' she agreed fervently. 'Oh yes!'

'Part of the price is the execution of the architect of our misery,' he said sharply. 'I have kept this from you until now, but Verwoerd must die and all his henchmen with him. Destiny has appointed me his executioner – and his successor.'

Tara paled at his words, but they came as such a shock that she could not speak. Moses took her hand with a strange and unusual gentleness.

'For you, for me and for the child – that he may live with us in the sunshine of freedom.'

She tried to speak, but her voice faltered, and he waited patiently until she was able to enunciate.

'Moses, you promised!'

'No.' He shook his head. 'You persuaded yourself of that, and it was not the time to disillusion you.'

'Oh, God, Moses!' The enormity of it crashed in upon her. 'I thought you were going to blow up the empty building as a symbolic gesture, but all along you planned to—' She broke off, unable to complete the sentence, and he did not deny it.

'Moses – my husband Shasa, he will be on the bench beside Verwoerd.'

'Is he your husband?' Moses asked. 'Is he not one of them, one of the enemy?' She lowered her eyes to acknowledge the truth of this, and then suddenly she was agitated again.

'My father – he will be in the House.'

'Your father and your husband are part of your old life. You have left that behind you. Now, Tara, I am both your father and your husband, and the struggle is your new life.'

'Moses, isn't there some way they can be spared?' she pleaded.

He did not speak, but she saw the answer in his eyes and

she covered her face with both hands and began to weep. She wept silently, but the spasms of grief shook her whole body. Down on the beach the child's happy cries came to her faintly on the wind, and beside her Moses sat unmoving and without expression. After a while, she lifted her head and wiped the tears from her face with the palms of her hands.

'I'm sorry, Moses,' she whispered. 'I was weak, please forgive me. I was mourning my father, but now I am strong again, and ready to do whatever you require of me.'

The Test match against the visiting Argentinian polo team was the most exciting event that had taken place at Weltevreden in a decade or more.

As mistress of the estate, the planning and organization of the event should have fallen to Tara, but her lack of interest in the sport and her poor organizational skills were too much for Centaine Courtney-Malcomess to abide. She began by giving discreet advice and ended in exasperation by taking all responsibility out of her daughter-in-law's hands. The result was that the occasion was in every respect a towering success. After Centaine had chivvied the coloured greensman, and with Blaine's expert advice, the turf on the field was green and velvety, the going beneath it neither hard enough to jar the legs of the ponies nor soft enough to slow them down. The goalposts were painted in the colours of the teams, the pale blue and white of Argentina and orange, blue and white of South Africa, and two hundred flags in the same colours flew from the grandstand.

The stand itself was freshly painted, as were the fence pickets and the stables. A fence was erected to keep the general public out of the château's private grounds, but the new facilities designed by Centaine especially for the occasion included an extension to the grandstand, with public toilets below and an open-air restaurant that could seat two hundred guests. The extensions to the stables were sufficient for fifty ponies, and there were new quarters for the grooms. The Argentinians had brought their own, and they wore traditional gaucho costume with wide hats and their chaps decorated with silver coins.

Garry tore himself away from his new office at Centaine House, which was on the top floor, only three doors down from Shasa, and he spent two days at the stables watching and learning from these masters of horsecraft and the game of polo.

Michael had at last managed to secure an official assignment. He blissfully believed that the *Golden City Mail* in Johannesburg had appointed him their local correspondent on his own merits as a cub reporter. Centaine, who had made a discreet telephone call to the Chairman of Associated Newspapers of South Africa which owned the *Mail*, did nothing to disillusion him. Michael was to be paid five guineas for the day, plus a shilling a word for any copy of his actually printed by the newspaper. He interviewed every member of both teams, including the reserves, all the grooms, the umpire and referees. He drew up a full history and score card of all previous matches played between the two countries going back to the 1936 Olympic Games, and he worked out the pedigrees of all the ponies – but here he showed restraint by limiting the listing to only two generations. Even before the match day he had written enough to make *Gone with the Wind* look like a pamphlet. Then he insisted on telephoning this important copy through to a long-suffering sub at the newspaper offices, and the telephone charges far outstripped his five-guinea salary.

'Anyway, Mickey,' Shasa consoled him, 'if they print everything you have written at a shilling a word, you'll be a millionaire.'

The big disappointment for the family came on the Wednesday when the South African team was announced. Shasa was chosen to play in his usual position at Number Two but he was passed over for the captaincy. This went to Max Theunissen, a flamboyant, hard-riding millionaire farmer from Natal who was a long-time rival of Shasa's, ever since their first meeting on this same field as juniors many years before.

Shasa hid his disappointment behind a rueful grin. 'It means more to Max than it does to me,' he told Blaine, who was one of the selectors, and Blaine nodded.

'Yes,' he agreed. 'That's why we gave it to him, Shasa. Max values it.'

Isabella fell desperately in love with the Argentinian Number Four, a paragon of masculinity with olive skin, dark flashing eyes, thick wavy hair and dazzling white teeth.

She changed her frock three and four times a day, trying out all the most sophisticated of the clothes with which Shasa had filled her wardrobes. She even applied a very light coat of rouge and lipstick, not enough to catch Shasa's attention but just enough, she hoped, to pique José Jesús Gonçalves De Santos' interest. She exercised all her ingenuity in waylaying him, hanging around the stables endlessly and practising her most languid poses whenever he hove into view.

The object of her adoration was a man in his early thirties who was convinced that the Argentinian male was the world's greatest lover and that he, José Jesús Gonçalves De Santos, was the national champion. There were at least a dozen mature and willing ladies vying for his attention at any one time. He did not even notice the antics of this fourteen-year-old child, but Centaine did.

'You are making an exhibition of yourself, Bella,' she told her. 'From now on you are forbidden to go near the stables, and if I see one speck of make-up on your face again you may be certain your father will learn about it.'

Nobody went against Nana's orders, not even the boldest and most lovelorn, so Isabella was forced to abandon her fantasy of ambushing José in the hayloft above the stables and presenting him with her virginity. Isabella was not entirely certain what this entailed. Lenora had lent her a forbidden book which referred to it as 'a pearl beyond price'. Whatever it was, José Jesús could have her pearl and anything else he wanted.

However, Nana's strictures reduced her to trailing around after him at a discreet distance, and directing burning but long-range looks at him whenever he glanced in her direction.

Garry intercepted one of these passionate looks and was so alarmed by it that he demanded in a loud voice, and within earshot of her beloved, 'Are you sick, Bella? You keep looking like you are going to throw up.' It was the first time in her life that she truly hated her middle brother.

Centaine had planned for two thousand spectators. Polo was an elite sport with a limited following, and at two pounds each, tickets were expensive, but on the day the gate exceeded five thousand. This guaranteed the club a healthy profit but put a considerable strain on Centaine's logistics. All her reserves, which included Tara, were thrown in to deal with the overflow and to organize the additional food and drink required, and only when the teams rode out on to the field could Tara escape her mother-in-law's all-seeing eye and go up into the stand.

For the first chukka Shasa was riding a bay gelding whose hide was burnished until it shone like a mirror in the sunlight. In his green jersey piped with gold, and his snowy white breeches and glossy black boots, Tara had to admit to herself that Shasa looked magnificent. As he cantered below the stand he looked up and smiled, the black eye-patch gave an intriguing sinister nuance to his otherwise boyish and charming grin, and despite herself Tara responded, waving to him, until she realized that Shasa was not smiling at her but at someone below her in the stand. Feeling a little foolish, she stood on tiptoe and peered down to try and see who it was. The woman was tall with a narrow waist, but her face was obscured by the brim of a garden party hat decorated with roses. However, the arm she lifted to wave at Shasa was slim and tanned, with diamond engagement and gold wedding rings on the third finger of her shapely hand.

Tara turned away and removed her hat so that Centaine could not easily pick her out of the crowd, and she worked her way quickly but unobtrusively to the side exit of the stand. As she crossed the carpark and headed around the back of the stables, the first roaring cheer went up from the stand. Nobody would look for her for a couple of hours now, and she began to run. Moses had the Chev parked in the plantation of pines, near the guest cottages, and she pulled open the back door and tumbled into the seat.

'Nobody saw me leave,' she panted, and he started the engine and drove sedately down the long driveway and out through the Anreith gateway.

Tara checked her wristwatch; it was a few minutes past three o'clock, but it would take forty minutes to round the mountain and reach the city. They would reach the parliament building at four o'clock when the doormen were thinking about their tea-break. It was a Friday afternoon, and the House was in Committee of Supply, the kind of boring routine business which would leave the members nodding on the benches. In fact, Blaine and Shasa had tactfully arranged this schedule with the whips so that they, and quite a few of their peers, might sneak away to the polo without missing any important debate or division. Many of the other members must have made plans to leave early for the weekend, for the building was quiet and the lobby almost deserted.

Moses parked in the members' carpark and went around to the back of the station wagon to bring out the packages.

Then he followed Tara at a respectful distance as she climbed the front staircase. Nobody challenged them, it was all so easy, almost an anti-climax, and they went up to the second floor, past the press gallery entrance, where Tara had a glimpse of three junior reporters slumped dispiritedly on their benches as they listened to the Honourable Minister of Posts and Telegraphs droning out his self-congratulations on the exemplary fashion in which he had conducted his department during the previous fiscal year.

Tricia was sitting behind her desk in the outer office painting her fingernails with varnish, and she looked flustered and guilty as Tara walked in.

'Oh, Tricia, that is a pretty colour,' Tara said sweetly, and Tricia tried to look as though her fingers didn't belong to her, but the varnish was wet and she didn't quite know what to do with them.

'I've finished all the letters Mr Courtney left for me,' she tried to excuse herself, 'and it's been so quiet today, and I've got a date tonight – I just thought . . .' She petered out lamely.

'I've brought up some samples of curtain material,' Tara told her. 'I thought we'd change them when we installed the new light fittings. I would like it to be a surprise for Shasa, so don't mention it to him, if you can avoid it.'

'Of course not, Mrs Courtney.'

'I will be trying to work out the new colour scheme for the curtains, and I'll probably be here until long after five o'clock. If you've finished your work, why don't you go off early? I will take any phone calls.'

'Oh, I'd feel bad about that,' Tricia protested half-heartedly.

'Off you go!' Tara ordered firmly. 'I'll hold the fort. You enjoy your date – I hope you have a lovely evening.'

'It's so kind of you, Mrs Courtney. It really is.'

'Stephen, take those samples through and put them on

the couch, please,' Tara ordered without looking at Moses, and she lingered while Tricia cleared her desk with alacrity and headed for the door.

'Have a super weekend, Mrs Courtney – and thanks a lot.'

Tara locked the door after her and hurried through to the inner office.

'That was a bit of luck,' she whispered.

'We should give her some time to get clear,' Moses told her, and they sat side by side on the sofa.

Tara looked nervous and unhappy, but she kept silent for many minutes before she blurted out, 'Moses, about my father – and Shasa.'

'Yes?' he asked, but his voice was bleak, and she hesitated, twisting her fingers together nervously.

'Yes?' he insisted.

'No – you are right,' she sighed. 'It has to be done. I must be strong.'

'Yes, you must be strong,' he agreed. 'But now you must go, and leave me to do my work.'

She stood up. 'Kiss me please, Moses,' she whispered, and then after a moment broke from his embrace. 'Good luck,' she said softly.

She locked the outer door of the office and went down the staircase into the main lobby, and halfway down she was suddenly overwhelmed by a sense of doom. It was so strong that she felt the blood drain from her head and an icy sweat broke out on her forehead and upper lip. For a moment she felt dizzy, and had to clutch the banisters to prevent herself from falling. Then she forced herself to go on down and cross the lobby.

The janitor was staring at her strangely. She kept walking. He was leaving his cubicle and coming to intercept her. She felt panic come at her and she wanted to turn and run back up the stairs, to warn Moses that they had been discovered.

501

'Mrs Courtney.' The janitor stopped in front of her, blocking her path.

'What is it?' she faltered, trying to think up a plausible reply to his demands.

'I've got a small bet on the polo this afternoon, do you know how it's going?' She stared at him, and for a moment it did not make sense. She almost blurted out, 'Polo, what polo?' and then she caught herself and with an enormous effort of will and concentration chatted with the man for almost a minute before she could escape. In the carpark she could no longer control her panic and she ran to the Chev and flung herself behind the wheel sobbing for breath.

When he heard the key turn in the lock of the outer door, Moses went back into Shasa's office and drew the drapes over the windows.

Then he went to the bookshelves and studied the titles. He would not unpack the altar chest until the last moment. Tricia might return for something she had forgotten, there might be a routine check of the offices by the parliamentary staff. Shasa might even come in on the Saturday morning. Although Tara had assured him that Shasa would be fully occupied at Weltevreden with his guests over the whole weekend, Moses would take no chances. He would disturb nothing in the office until it was absolutely necessary.

He smiled as he saw Macaulay's *History of England* on the shelf. It was an expensive leather-bound edition, and it brought back vivid memories of the time when he and the man he was about to kill had been friends – of that time long ago when there had still been hope.

He passed on down the shelves until he reached a section in which Shasa obviously kept all those works with whose principles he differed, works ranging from *Mein Kampf* to Karl Marx with Socialism in between. Moses chose a volume of the collected works of Lenin and took it across to the desk. He settled down to read, confident that any unwanted visitor must give him sufficient time to reach his hiding-place behind the drapes.

He read until the dusk fell and the light failed in the room, then he took the blanket from the package he had brought up from the Chev and settled down on the sofa.

He woke early on Saturday morning, when the rock pigeons began crooning on the ledge outside the window, and let himself out of the panel door. He used the toilets at the end of the passage in the knowledge that it was going to be a long day, and took a cynical pleasure in defying the WHITES ONLY sign on the door.

Although the House did not sit on a Saturday, the main doors were open and there would still be some activity in the building, cleaners and staff, perhaps ministers using their offices. He could do nothing until the Sunday, when Calvinist principles forbade any work or unnecessary activity outside the body of the church. Again he spent the day reading, and at nightfall he ate from the supplies he had brought with him and disposed of the empty cans and wrappers in the rubbish bin in the toilets.

He slept fitfully and was fully awake before dawn on Sunday morning. He ate a frugal breakfast and changed into workman's overalls and tennis shoes from the package before he began a cautious reconnaissance of the House. The building was utterly silent and deserted. Looking down the stairs he saw that the front doors were barred and all the lights were extinguished. He moved about with more confidence, and tried the door to the press gallery. It was unlocked and he stood at the rail and looked down into the chamber where all the laws that had enmeshed and enslaved his people had been enacted and he felt his rage like a captive animal inside his chest, clamouring to be set free.

He left the gallery and went down the staircase into the

entrance lobby and approached the high main doors of the chamber. His footsteps echoed from the marble slabs. As he had expected, the doors were locked, but the locks were massive antiques. He knelt in front of them, and from his pocket took the folding wallet of locksmith's picks. His training in Russia had been exhaustively thorough and the lock resisted him for less than a minute. He opened one leaf of the door a crack and slipped through, closing it behind him.

Now he stood in the very cathedral of *apartheid*, and it seemed to him that the evil of it was a palpable thing that pressed in upon him with a physical weight and shortened his breathing. He moved slowly up the aisle towards the Speaker's throne with the massive coat of arms above it, and then he turned to the left, skirting the table on which the mace and dispatch boxes would lie, until he stood at the head of the Government front benches, at the seat of the Prime Minister, Dr Hendrik Frensch Verwoerd, and Moses' broad nostrils flared open as though he smelled the odour of the great beast.

With an effort he roused himself, setting aside his feelings and his passions, and became as objective as a workman. He examined the bench carefully, going down on his stomach to peer beneath it. Of course, he had studied every photograph of the chamber that he had been able to obtain, but these had been pathetically inadequate. Now he ran his hands over the green leather; the padding was indented by the weight of the men who had sat upon it, and at this close range it was scuffed and cracked with wear over the years. The bench frame was of massive mahogany, and when he groped up beneath the seat he found the heavy cross members that strengthened it. There were no surprises here, and he grunted with satisfaction.

He returned to Shasa's office, letting himself in through the panel door, and went immediately to unpack the altar chest. Once again he was careful to lay out the contents so that it could be repacked in exactly the same order. Then he climbed into the chest and lifted the floor panels.

The food he set aside for his evening meal, and he piled the blocks of plastic into the blanket. One of the advantages of this explosive was that it was inert and could endure the roughest handling. Without a detonator, it was completely safe.

He picked up the four corners of the blanket and slung it over his shoulder like a tent bag, and then hurriedly went down to the assembly chamber again. He stowed the blanket and its contents under a bench where it would escape casual discovery and went back to the office to fetch the tool kit. The third time he descended to the chamber, he locked the main doors behind him, so as to be able to work in total security.

He could not risk the noise of using an electric drill. He lay on his back beneath the Prime Minister's bench and began laboriously setting the staples into the mahogany above his face, boring the holes with the hand drill and then screwing in the threaded staples. He worked meticulously, pausing to measure and mark each hole, so it was almost an hour before he was ready to start placing the blocks of plastic. He arranged them in stacks of five, ten pounds of plastic in each stack, and wired them together. Then he wriggled back under the bench and secured each stack of five blocks in place. He threaded each tag end of wire through the loop of a separate staple and twisted them up tightly, then he reached for the next stack of bricks and set that in neatly against the last until the entire underside of the bench was lined with explosive.

Then he crawled out and checked his progress. There was a lip of mahogany below the leather cushion which completely hid the layer of blocks. Even when he squatted down as a person might do to retrieve a pen or fallen order paper from under the bench, he could not see a trace of his handiwork.

'That will do,' he murmured, and started to clean up.

Meticulously he brushed up every speck of sawdust from the drilling and the offcuts of wire, then he gathered his tools.

'Now we can test the transmitter,' he told himself and hurried upstairs to Shasa's office.

He inserted the new torch batteries in the transmitter and checked it. The test globe lit up brightly. He switched it off. Next he took the radio detonator from its cardboard box and placed the hearing-aid battery in its compartment. The detonator was the size of a matchbox, made of black Bakelite with a small toggle switch at one end. The switch had three positions: 'off', 'test' and 'receive'. A thin twist of wire prevented the switch accidentally being moved to 'on'. Moses switched it to 'test' and laid it on the sofa, then he went to the transmitter and flipped the 'on' switch. Immediately the tiny globe at one end of the detonator case lit up and there was a loud buzz, like a trapped bee inside the casing. It had received the signal from the transmitter. Moses switched off the transmitter and the buzz ceased and the globe extinguished.

'Now I must check if it will transmit from here to the assembly chamber.'

He left the transmitter on and descended once again to the chamber. Kneeling beside the Prime Minister's bench, he held the detonator in the palm of his hand and held his breath as he switched it to 'test'.

Nothing happened. He tried it three times more, but it would not receive the signal from the office upstairs. Clearly there was too much brick and reinforced concrete between the two pieces of equipment.

'It was going too easily,' he told himself ruefully. 'There had to be a snag somewhere,' and he sighed as he took the roll of wire from the tool kit. He had wanted to avoid stringing wire from the chamber to the office on the second floor; even though the wire was gossamer thin and the insulating cover was a matt brown, it would infinitely increase the risk of discovery.

'Nothing else for it,' he consoled himself.

He had already studied the electrical wiring plan of the building that Tara had procured from the Public Works Department, but he unrolled it and spread it on the bench beside him to refresh his memory as he worked.

There was a wall plug in the panelling behind the back benches of the government section. From the plan he saw that the conduit was laid behind the panelling and went up the wall into the roof. The diagram also showed the main fuse box in the janitor's office opposite the front door. The office was locked but he picked the lock without difficulty and threw the main switch.

Then he returned to the chamber, located the wall plug and removed the cover, exposing the wiring, and was relieved to find that it was colour-coded. That would make the job a lot easier.

So he left the chamber and went up to the second floor. There was a cleaner's cupboard in the men's toilet that contained a stepladder. The trap door that gave access to the roof was also in the men's toilet. He found it and set the stepladder below it. From the top of the ladder he removed the trap door and wriggled up through the square opening.

The space below the roof and the ceiling was dark and smelled of rats. He switched on his Penlite and began to pick his way through the forest of timber joists and roof posts. The dust had been undisturbed for years and rose in a languid cloud around his feet. He sneezed and covered his mouth and nose with a handkerchief as he went forward carefully, stepping from beam to beam, counting each pace to keep himself orientated.

Above the exposed section of wall that was certainly the top of the rear side wall of the chamber he found the electrical conduits. There were fifteen of them laid side by side. Some had been there a long time, while others were obviously new additions.

It took him a while to isolate the conduit that led down

to the chamber below, but when he unscrewed the joint in it, he recognized the coded wiring of the wall-socket that it contained. His relief was intense. He had anticipated a number of problems that he might have encountered at this stage, but now it would be a simple matter to get his own wire into the roof.

He uncoiled the long flexible electrician's spring that he had brought from his tools and fed the end of it into the open conduit tubing until he felt it encounter resistance. Then he began the tedious journey back through the roof, down the stepladder, along the passage, down the staircase and into the chamber.

He found the end of the electrician's spring protruding from the open wall-socket, and he attached the end of the coil of light detonator wire to it and laid out the rest of the wire so that it would feed smoothly into the conduit when he drew the spring in from the other end.

Back in the roof he recovered the spring and the end of the wire came up with it. Gently he drew in the rest of it, working overhand like a fisherman recovering his handline, until it came up firmly against the knot that held the far end to the bench in the chamber below. He coiled the wire neatly and left it, while he returned to the chamber. By this time his overalls were filthy with dust and cobwebs.

He untied the loose end of the wire from the bench and laid it out on the floor, leading it to the pack of plastic explosive under the front bench, making certain he had given himself sufficient slack. Then he worked carefully to conceal the exposed wire from casual detection. He threaded it under the green wall-to-wall carpeting and stapled it securely to the underside of the government benches. He filed a notch in the enamelled metal plate that covered the wall-socket and laid the wire into it while he screwed the cover back into place.

Then he went carefully over the floor and carpet to make certain he had left no trace of his work. Apart from the few inches of unobtrusive wire protruding from the wall socket, there was nothing to betray his preparations and he sat on Dr Verwoerd's bench to rest for a few minutes before beginning the final phase. He returned upstairs.

The most difficult and frustrating part of the entire job was placing himself in the roof directly above Shasa's office. Three times he had to climb down the ladder into the toilet and then pace out the angles of the passages and the exact location of the office suite before once more climbing back into the ceiling and attempting to follow the same route through the dust and the roof timbers.

Finally he was sure he was in the correct position and gingerly he bored a small hole through the ceiling between his feet. Light came up through the hole, but even when he knelt and placed his eye to the aperture, it was too small to see what lay below. He enlarged it slightly, but he still could see nothing, and yet again he had to make the journey back to the trap door and along the passage to Shasa's office.

Immediately he let himself into the office he saw that he had misjudged. The hole he had bored through the ceiling was directly above the desk, and in enlarging it he had cracked the plaster and dislodged a few fragments which had fallen on to the desk top. He realized that this could be a serious mistake. The hole was not large, but the network of hair cracks around it would be apparent to anyone studying the ceiling.

He thought about trying to cover or repair the damage, but knew that he would only aggravate it. He brushed the white crumbs of plaster off the desk, but this was all he could do. He would have to take comfort in the unlikelihood that anybody would look at the ceiling, and even if they did, that they would think nothing of the minute blemish. Angrily aware of his mistake, he did what he should have done originally and bored the next hole from below, standing on one of the bookshelves to reach the ceiling. Between the window drapes and the edge of the bookshelves, the hole was almost invisible to any but the most painstaking inspection. He went up into the roof and paid the end of the wire down through the second hole. When he returned to the office he found it dangling down the wall, the end of it lying in a tangle on the carpet in the corner.

He gathered and coiled the end and tucked it carefully behind the row of *Encyclopaedia Britannica* on the top shelf and then arranged the window drapes to cover the two or three inches that were visible protruding from the puncture in the ceiling. Once again he cleaned up, going over the shelf and floor for the last speck of plaster, and then, still not satisfied, returning to the desk. Another tiny crumb of white plaster had fallen and he wetted his finger with saliva and picked it up. Then he polished the desk top with his sleeve.

He left the office through the panel door, and went back over everything he had done. He closed the trap door in the roof of the toilet and brushed up the dust that he had dislodged. He replaced the cleaner's ladder in the closet and then returned for the last time to the chamber.

At last he was ready to wire up the detonator. He removed the wire safety device and switched the detonator on. He bored a hole in the soft centre block of explosive and placed the detonator into it. He taped it firmly in place, and then scraped the last inch of insulation from the gleaming copper wire and screwed that into the connector in the end of the black cylindrical detonator and crawled out from under the bench.

He gathered up his tools, made one last thorough check for any tell-tale evidence, and then, satisfied at last, he left the chamber, locking the main doors behind him and carefully polishing his sweaty fingerprints from the gleaming brass. Then he let himself into the janitor's office and switched on the current at the mains.

He retreated up the stairs for the last time and locked himself in Shasa's office before he checked his wristwatch.

It was almost half-past four. It had taken him all day, but he had worked with special care and he was well satisfied as he slumped down on the sofa. The strain on his nerves and the unremitting need for total concentration had been more wearying than any physical endeavour.

He rested awhile before repacking the altar chest. He stuffed his dirty overalls into the empty explosives compartment and placed the transmitter on top of them where he could reach it quickly. It would be a few minutes' work to retrieve it, connect it to the loose wire that was concealed behind the row of encyclopaedias, close the circuit and fire the detonator in the chamber below. He had calculated that Shasa's office was far enough from the centre of the blast, and that there were sufficient walls and cast concrete slabs between to cushion the effects of the explosion and ensure his own survival, but the chamber itself would be totally devastated. A good day's work indeed, and as the light in the room faded, he settled down on the sofa and pulled the blanket up over his shoulders.

At dawn he roused himself and made one last check of the office, glancing ruefully up at the insignificant spider-web of cracks in the ceiling. He gathered up his packages, then he let himself out through the panel door and went to the men's toilet.

He washed and shaved in one of the basins. Tara had provided a razor and hand towel in the packet of food. Then he donned his chauffeur's jacket and cap and locked himself in one of the toilets. He could not wait in Shasa's office for Tricia would come in at nine o'clock, nor could he leave until the House activity was in full swing and he could pass out through the front doors unremarked.

He sat on the toilet seat and waited. At nine o'clock he heard footsteps passing down the passage. Then somebody came in and used the cubicle next to his, grunting and farting noisily. At intervals over the next hour men came in, singly or in groups, to use the basins and urinals. However, in the middle of the morning there was a lull. Moses stood up, gathered his parcels, braced himself, let himself out of the cubicle, and briskly crossed to the door into the passage.

The passageway was empty and he started towards the head of the staircase, and then halfway there he chilled with horror and checked in mid-stride.

Two men came up the stairs, and into the passageway, directly towards Moses. Walking side by side, they were in earnest conversation and the shorter and elder of the two was gesticulating and grimacing with the vehemence of his explanation. The younger taller man beside him was listening intently, and his single eye gleamed with suppressed amusement.

Moses forced himself to walk on to meet them, and his expression fixed into that dumb patient mould with which the African conceals all emotion in the presence of his white master. As they approached each other, Moses stepped respectfully aside to let the two of them pass. He did not look directly at Shasa Courtney's face, but let his eyes slide by without making contact.

As they came level, Shasa burst out laughing at what his companion had told him.

'The silly old ass!' he exclaimed, and he glanced sideways at Moses. His laughter checked and a puzzled frown creased his forehead. Moses thought he was going to stop, but his companion seized his sleeve.

'Wait for the best bit – she wouldn't give him his pants until he—' He led Shasa on towards his own office, and without looking back or quickening his pace, Moses went on down the staircase and out through the front doors.

The Chev was parked in the lot at the top of the lane where he expected it to be. Moses placed his parcels in the back and then went round to the driver's door. As he slid in behind the steering-wheel, Tara leaned forward from the back seat and whispered:

'Oh, thank God, I was so worried about you.'

The arrival of Harold Macmillan and his entourage in Cape Town engendered real excitement and anticipation, not only in the mother city but throughout the entire country.

The British Prime Minister was on the final leg of an extensive journey down the length of Africa, where he had visited each of the British colonies and members of the Commonwealth on the continent, of which South Africa was the largest and richest and most prosperous.

His arrival meant different things for different sections of the white population. For the English-speaking community it was an affirmation of the close ties and deep commitment that they felt towards the old country. It reinforced the secure sense of being part of the wider body of the Commonwealth, and the certain knowledge that there still existed between their two countries, who had stood solidly beside each other for a century and more through terrible wars and economic crises, a bond of blood and suffering that could never be eroded. It gave them an opportunity to reaffirm their loyal devotion to the Queen.

For the Nationalist Afrikaners it meant something entirely different. They had fought two wars against the British crown, and though many Afrikaners had volunteered to fight beside Britain in two other wars – Delville Wood and El Alamein were only part of their battle honours – many others, including most members of the Nationalist cabinet, had vehemently opposed the declarations of war against Kaiser Wilhelm and Adolf Hitler. The Nationalist cabinet included members who had actively fought against the Union of South Africa's war efforts under Jan Smuts, and many now high in government, men like Manfred De La Rey, had been members of the *Ossewa Brandwag*. To these men the British Prime Minister's visit was an acknowledgement of their sovereign rights and their importance as rulers of the most advanced and prosperous nation on the continent of Africa.

During his stay Harold Macmillan was a guest at Groote Schuur, the official residence of the South African Prime Minister, and the climax of his visit was to be an address to both houses of the legislature of the Union of South Africa, the Senate and the House of Assembly, sitting together. On the evening of his arrival in Cape Town, the British Prime Minister was to be the guest of honour at a private dinner party to meet the ministers of Dr Verwoerd's cabinet, the leaders of the Opposition United Party and other dignitaries.

Tara hated these official functions with a passion, but Shasa was insistent. 'Part of our bargain, my dear. The invitation is specifically for Mr and Mrs, and you promised not to make an ass of me in public.'

In the end she even wore her diamonds, something she had not done in years, and Shasa was appreciative and complimentary.

'You really are a corker when you take the trouble to spruce up like that,' he told her, but she was silent and distracted on the drive around the southern slope of Table Mountain to Groote Schuur.

'Something is worrying you,' Shasa said as he steered the Rolls with one hand and lit a cigarette with his gold Ronson lighter.

'No,' she denied quickly. 'Just the prospect of saying the right things to a room full of strangers.'

The true reason for her concern was a long way from that. Three hours previously, while Moses drove her back from a meeting of the executive of the Women's Institute, he had told her quietly, 'The date and the time has been set.' He did not have to elaborate. Since she had picked him up outside the Parliament House just after ten o'clock the previous Monday, Tara had been haunted night and day by her terrible secret knowledge.

'When?' she whispered.

'During the Englishman's speech,' he said simply, and Tara winced. The logic of it was diabolical.

'Both houses sitting together,' Moses went on. 'All of them, all the slave-masters and the Englishman who is their accomplice and their protector. They will die together. It will be an explosion that will be heard in every corner of our world.'

Beside her Shasa snapped the cap of the Ronson and snuffed out the flame. 'It won't be all that unpleasant. I've arranged with protocol that you will be Lord Littleton's dinner partner – you get on rather well with him, don't you?'

'I didn't know he was here,' Tara said vaguely. This conversation seemed so petty and pointless in the face of the holocaust which she knew was coming.

'Special adviser on trade and finance to the British government.' Shasa slowed the Rolls and lowered his side window as he turned into the main gates of Groote Schuur and joined the line of limousines that were moving slowly down the driveway. He showed his invitation to the captain of the guard and received a respectful salute.

'Good evening, Minister. Please go straight on down to the front entrance.'

Groote Schuur was High Dutch for 'The Great Barn'. It had once been the home of Cecil John Rhodes, empire builder and adventurer, who had used it as his residence while he was Prime Minister of the old Cape Colony before the Act of Union in 1910 had united the separate provinces into the present Union of South Africa. Rhodes had left the huge house, restored after it was destroyed by fire, to the nation. It was a massive and graceless building, reflecting Rhodes' confessed taste for the barbaric, a mixture of different styles of architecture all of which Tara found offensive.

Yet the view from the lower slopes of Table Mountain

out over the Cape Flats was spectacular, a field of lights spreading out to the dark silhouette of the mountains that rose against the moon-bright sky. Tonight the bustle and excitement seemed to rejuvenate the ponderous edifice.

Every window blazed with light and the uniformed footmen were meeting the guests as they alighted from their limousines and ushering them up the broad front steps to join the reception line in the entrance lobby. Prime Minister Verwoerd and his wife Betsie were at the head of the line, but Tara was more interested in their guest.

She was surprised by Macmillan's height, almost as tall as Verwoerd, and by the close resemblance he bore to all the cartoons she had seen of him: the tufts of hair above his ears, the horsy teeth and the scrubby moustache. His handshake was firm and dry and his voice as he greeted her was soft and plummy, and then she and Shasa had passed on into the main drawing-room where the other dinner guests were assembling.

There was Lord Littleton coming to her, still wearing the genteelly shabby dinner jacket, the watered silk of the lapels tinged with the verdigris of age, but his smile was alight with genuine pleasure.

'Well, my dear, your presence makes the evening an occasion for me!' He kissed Tara's cheek and then turned to Shasa. 'Must tell you of our recent travels across Africa – fascinating,' and the three of them were chatting animatedly.

Tara's forebodings were for the moment forgotten, as she exclaimed, 'Now, milord, you cannot hold up the Congo as being typical of emerging Africa. Left to his own devices, Patrice Lumumba would be an example of what a black leader—'

'Lumumba is a rogue, and a convicted felon. Now Tshombe—' Shasa interrupted her and Tara rounded on him, 'Tshombe is a stooge and a quisling, a puppet of Belgian colonialism.'

'At least he isn't eating the opposition like Lumumba's lads are,' Littleton interjected mildly, and Tara turned back to him with the battle light in her eyes.

'That isn't worthy of somebody—' She broke off with an effort. Her orders were to avoid radical arguments and to maintain her role as a dutiful establishment wife.

'Oh, it's so boring,' she said. 'Let's talk about the London theatre. What is on at the moment?'

'Well, just before I left I saw *The Caretaker*, Pinter's new piece,' Littleton accepted the diversion, and Shasa glanced across the room. Manfred De La Rey was watching him with those intense pale eyes, and as he caught Shasa's eye he inclined his head sharply.

'Excuse me a moment,' Shasa murmured, but Littleton and Tara were so occupied with each other that they barely noticed him move away and join Manfred and his statuesque German wife.

Manfred always seemed ill at ease in tails, and the starched wing collar of his dress shirt bit into his thick neck and left a vivid red mark on the skin.

'So, my friend,' he teased Shasa. 'The dagos from South America thrashed you at your horse games, hey?'

Shasa's smile slipped a fraction. 'Eight to six is hardly a massacre,' he protested, but Manfred was not interested in his defence.

He took Shasa's arm and leaned closer to him, still smiling jovially as he said, 'There is some nasty work going on.'

'Ah!' Shasa smiled easily and nodded encouragement.

'Macmillan has refused to show Dr Henk a copy of the speech he is going to deliver tomorrow.'

'Ah!' This time Shasa had difficulty in maintaining the smile. If this was a fact, then the British Prime Minister was guilty of a flagrant breach of etiquette. It was common courtesy for him to allow Verwoerd to study his text so as to be able to prepare a reply.

'It's going to be an important speech,' Manfred went on.

'Yes,' Shasa agreed. 'Maud returned to London to consult with him and help him draw it up, they must have been polishing it up since then.' Sir John Maud was the British High Commissioner to South Africa. For him to be summoned to London underlined the gravity of the situation.

'You are friendly with Littleton,' Manfred said quietly. 'See if you can get anything out of him, even a hint as to what Macmillan is going to do.'

'I doubt he knows much,' Shasa was still smiling for the benefit of anybody watching them. 'But I'll let you know if I can find out anything.'

The dinner was served on the magnificent East India Company service, but was the usual bland and tepid offering of the civil service chefs whom Shasa was certain had served their apprenticeship on the railways. The white wines were sweet and insipid, but the red was a 1951 Weltevreden Cabernet Sauvignon. Shasa had influenced the choice by making a gift of his own *cru* for the banquet, and he judged it the equal of all but the very best Bordeaux. It was a pity that the white was so woefully bad. There was no reason for it, they had the climate and the soil. Weltevreden had always concentrated on the red but he made a resolution to improve his own production of whites, even if it meant bringing in another wine-master from Germany or France and buying another vineyard on the Stellenbosch side of the peninsula.

The speeches were mercifully short and inconsequential, a brief welcome from Verwoerd and a short appreciation from Macmillan, and the conversation at Shasa's end of the table never rose above such earth-shaking subjects as their recent defeat by the Argentinians on the polo field, Denis Compton's batting form and Stirling Moss's latest victory in the Mille Miglia. But as soon as the banquet ended Shasa sought out Littleton, who was still with Tara, drawing out the pleasure of her company to the last.

'Looking forward to tomorrow,' he told Littleton casually. 'I hear your Supermac is going to give us some fireworks.'

'Wherever did you hear that?' Littleton asked, but Shasa saw the sudden shift of his gaze and the guarded expression that froze his smile.

'Can we have a word?' Shasa asked quietly, and apologized to Tara. 'Excuse me, my dear.' He took Littleton's elbow and chatting amicably steered him through the glass doors on to the paved stoep under the trellised vines.

'What is going on, Peter?' He lowered his voice. 'Isn't there anything you can tell me?'

Their relationship was intimate and of long standing; such a direct appeal could not be ignored.

'I will be frank with you, Shasa,' Littleton said. 'Mac has something up his sleeve. I don't know what it is, but he is planning on creating a sensation. The press at home have been put on the alert. It's going to be a major policy statement, that is my best guess.'

'Will it alter things between us – preferential trade, for instance?' Shasa demanded.

'Trade?' Littleton chuckled. 'Of course not, nothing alters trade. More than that I can't tell you. We will all have to wait for tomorrow.'

Neither Tara nor Shasa spoke on the drive back to Weltevreden until the Rolls passed beneath the Anreith gateway and then Tara asked, her voice strained and jerky, 'What time is Macmillan making his speech tomorrow?'

'The special session will begin at eleven o'clock,' Shasa replied, but he was still thinking of what Littleton had told him.

'I wanted to be in the visitors' gallery. I asked Tricia to get me a ticket.'

'Oh, the session isn't being held in the chamber – not enough seating. It will be in the dining-room and I don't think they will allow visitors—' He broke off and stared at her. In the reflected light of the headlamps she had gone deathly pale.

'What is it, Tara?'

'The dining-room,' she breathed. 'Are you sure?'

'Of course I am. Is something wrong, my dear?'

'Yes – no! Nothing is wrong. Just a little heartburn, the dinner—'

'Pretty awful,' he agreed, and returned his attention to the road.

'The dining-room,' she thought, in near panic. 'I have to warn Moses. I have to warn him it cannot be tomorrow – all his arrangements will have been made for the escape. I have to let him know.'

Shasa dropped her at the front doors of the château and took the Rolls down to the garages. When he came back, she was in the blue drawing-room and the servants, who had as usual waited up for their return, were serving hot chocolate and biscuits. Shasa's valet helped him change into a maroon velvet smoking-jacket, and the housemaids hovered anxiously until Shasa dismissed them.

Tara had always opposed this custom. 'I could easily warm up the milk myself and you could put on a jacket without having another grown man to help you,' she complained when the servants had left the room. 'It's feudal and cruel to keep them up until all hours.'

'Nonsense, my dear.' Shasa poured himself a cognac to go with his chocolate. 'It's a tradition they value as much as we do – makes them feel indispensable and part of the family. Besides, chef would have a seizure if you were to mess with his kitchen.'

Then he slumped into his favourite armchair and became unusually serious. He began to talk to her as he had at the beginning of their marriage when they had still been in accord.

'There is something afoot that I don't like. Here we stand at the opening of a new decade, the 1960s. We have had nearly twelve years of Nationalist rule and none of my direst predictions have come to pass, but I feel a sense of unease. I have the feeling that our tide has been at full flood, but the turn is coming. I think that tomorrow may be the day when the ebb sets in—' He broke off, and grinned shamefacedly. 'Forgive me. As you know, I don't usually indulge in fantasy,' he said and sipped his chocolate and his cognac in silence.

Tara felt not the least sympathy for him. There was so much she wanted to say, so many recriminations to lay upon him, but she could not trust herself to speak. Once she began, she might lose control and divulge too much. She might not be able to prevent herself gloating on the dreadful retribution that awaited him and all those like him, and she did not want to prolong this *tête-à-tête*, she wanted to be free to go to Moses, to warn him that today was not the day he had planned for. So she rose. 'You know how I feel, we don't have to discuss it. I'm going to bed. Excuse me.'

'Yes, of course.' He stood up courteously. 'I'll be working for the next few hours. I have to go over my notes for my meeting with Littleton and his team tomorrow afternoon, so don't worry about me.'

Tara checked that Isabella was in her room and asleep, before she went to her suite and locked the door. She changed out of her long dress and jewellery into jeans and a dark sweater, then she made a cannabis cigarette, and while she smoked it she waited fifteen minutes by her watch for Shasa to settle down to his work. Then she switched off her lights. She dropped the cigarette butt into the toilet and flushed it away before she let herself into the passage once again, locking her suite against the unlikely chance that Shasa might come up to look for her. Then she went down the back stairs.

As she crossed the wide stoep, keeping against the wall, staying in the shadows and moving silently, a telephone rang in the library wing and she froze involuntarily, her heart jarring her ribs. Then she realized that the telephone must be Shasa's private line, and she was about to move on, when she heard his voice. Although the curtains were drawn, the windows of his study were open and she could see the shadow of his head against the drapes.

'Kitty!' he said. 'Kitty Godolphin, you little witch. I should have guessed that you'd be here.'

The name startled Tara, and brought back harrowing memories, but she could not resist the temptation to creep closer to the curtained window.

'You always follow the smell of blood, don't you?' Shasa said, and chuckled at her reply.

'Where are you? The Nellie.' The Mount Nelson was simply the best hotel in Cape Town. 'And what are you doing now – I mean right this moment? Yes, I know it's two o'clock in the morning, but any time is a good time – you told me that yourself a long time ago. It will take me half an hour to get there. Whatever else you do, don't start without me.' He hung up and she saw his shadow on the curtain as he stood up from his desk.

She ran to the end of the long stoep and jumped down into the hydrangea bed and crouched in the bushes. Within a few minutes Shasa came out of the side door. He had a dark overcoat over his smoking-jacket. He went down to the garages and drove away in the Jaguar. Even in his haste he drove slowly through the vineyards so as not to blow dust on his precious grapes, and, watching the headlights disappear, Tara hated him as much as she ever had. She thought that she should have grown accustomed to his philandering, but he was like a tom cat in rut – no woman was safe from him, and his moral outrage against Sean, his own son, for the same behaviour, had been ludicrous.

Kitty Godolphin – she cast her mind back to their first meeting and the television reporter's reaction to the mention of Shasa's name and now the reason for it became clear.

'Oh God, I hate him so. He is totally without conscience or pity. He deserves to die!' She said it aloud, and then clapped her hand over her mouth. 'I shouldn't have said it, but it is true! He deserves to die and I deserve to be free of him – free to go to Moses and my child.'

She rose out of the hydrangea bushes, brushed the clinging soil from her jeans and crossed the lawns quickly. The moon was in its first quarter, but bright enough to throw her shadow in front of her, and she entered the vineyard with relief and hurried down the rows of vines that were heavy with leaf and grape. She skirted the winery and the stables and reached the servants' cottages.

She had placed Moses in the room at the end of the second row of cottages and his window faced out on to the vineyard. She tapped on his window and his response was almost immediate; she knew he slept as lightly as a wild cat.

'It's me,' she whispered.

'Wait,' he said. 'I will open the door.'

He loomed in the doorway, naked except for a pair of white shorts, and his body shone in the moonlight like wet tar.

'You are foolish to come here,' he said, and taking her arm drew her into the single room. 'You are putting everything at risk.'

'Moses, please, listen to me. I had to tell you. It cannot be tomorrow.'

He stared at her contemptuously. 'You were never a true daughter of the revolution.'

'No, no, I am true, and I love you enough to do anything, but they have changed the arrangements. They will not use the chamber where you have set the charge. They will meet in the parliamentary dining-room.'

He stared at her a second longer, then he turned and went to the narrow built-in cupboard at the head of his bed and began to dress in his uniform.

'What are you going to do?' she asked.

'I have to warn the others – they also are in danger.'

'What others?' she asked. 'I did not know there were others.'

'You know only what you have to know,' he told her curtly. 'I must use the Chev – is it safe?'

'Yes, Shasa is not here. He has gone out. Can I come with you?'

'Are you mad?' he asked. 'If the police find a black man and a white woman together at this time of night—' He did not finish the sentence. 'You must go back to the house and make a phone call. Here is the number. A woman will answer, and you will say only, "Cheetah is coming – he will be there in thirty minutes." That is all you will say and then you will hang up.'

Moses threaded the Chev through the maze of narrow streets of District Six, the old Malay quarter. During the day this was a colourful and thriving community of small stores and businesses. General dealers and tailors and tinsmiths and halal butcheries occupied the ground-floor shops of the decrepit Victorian buildings, while from the cast-iron fretwork of the open balconies above hung a festival of drying laundry, and the convoluted streets were clamorous with the cries of steet vendors, the mournful horns of itinerant fishmongers and the laughter of children.

At nightfall the traders shuttered their premises and left the streets to the street gangs and the pimps and the prostitutes. Some of the more daring white revellers came here late at night, to listen to the jazz players in the crowded shebeens or to look for a pretty coloured girl – more for the thrill of danger and discovery than for any physical gratification.

Moses parked the Chev in a dark side street. On the

wall were the graffiti that declared this the territory of the Rude Boys, one of the most notorious of the street gangs, and he waited only a few seconds before the first gang member materialized out of the shadows, an urchin with the body of a child and the face of a vicious old man.

'Look after it well,' Moses flipped him a silver shilling. 'If the tyres are slashed when I come back, I'll do the same for your backside.' The child grinned at him evilly.

He climbed the dark and narrow staircase to the Vortex Club. A couple on the landing were copulating furtively but furiously against the wall as Moses squeezed past. The white man turned his face away but he never missed a beat.

At the door to the club somebody studied him briefly through the peephole and then let him enter. The long crowded room was hazy with tobacco smoke and the sweet smell of cannabis. The clientele included the full spectrum from gang members in zoot suits and wide ties to white men in dinner-jackets. Only the women were all coloured.

Dollar Brand and his Quartet were playing a sweet soulful jazz and everybody was still and attentive. Nobody even looked up as Moses slipped down the side wall to the door at the far end, but the man guarding it recognized Moses and stood aside for him to enter.

In the backroom there was only one man sitting at a round gambling table under a green shaded light. There was a cigarette smouldering between his fingers, and his face was pale as putty, his eyes implacable dark pits.

'You are foolhardy to call a meeting now,' said Joe Cicero, 'without good reason. All the preparations have been made. There is nothing more to discuss.'

'I have good reason,' said Moses, and sat down on the empty chair, facing him across the baize-covered table.

Joe Cicero listened without expression, but when Moses finished, he pushed the lank hair off his forehead with the back of his hand. Moses had learned to interpret that gesture as one of agitation.

'We cannot dismantle the escape route and then set it up again later. These things take time to arrange. The aircraft is already in position.'

It was an Aztec chartered from a company in Johannesburg, and the pilot was a lecturer in political philosophy at Witwatersrand University, the holder of a private pilot's licence and a secret member of the South African Communist Party.

'How long can he wait at the rendezvous?' Moses asked, and Cicero thought about it a moment.

'A week at the longest,' he replied.

The rendezvous was an unregistered airstrip on a large drought-stricken ranch in Namaqualand which was lying derelict, abandoned by the discouraged owner. From the airfield it was a four-hour flight to Bechuanaland, the British protectorate that lay against the north-western border of the Union of South Africa. Sanctuary had been arranged for Moses there, the beginning of the pipeline by which most political fugitives were channelled to the north.

'A week must be enough,' Moses said. 'Every hour increases the danger. At the very first occasion that we can be sure Verwoerd will take his seat again, I will do it.'

It was four o'clock in the morning before Moses left the Vortex Club and went down to where he had parked the Chev.

K itty Godolphin sat in the centre of the bed, naked and cross-legged with all the shameless candour of a child.

In the years Shasa had known her, she had changed very little physically. Her body had matured slightly, her breasts had more weight to them and the tips had darkened. He could no longer make out the rack of her ribs beneath the smooth pale skin, but her buttocks were still lean as a boy's and her limbs coltishly long and slim. Nor had she lost the air of guileless innocence, that aura of eternal youth which so contrasted with the cynical hardness of her gaze. She was telling him about the Congo. She had been there for the last five months and the material she had filmed would surely put her in line for her third Emmy and confirm her position as the most successful television journalist on the American networks. She was speaking in the breathless voice of an *ingénue*.

'They caught these three Simba agents and tried them under the mango trees outside the burnt-out hospital, but by the time they had sentenced them to death, the light was too bad for filming. I gave the commander my Rolex watch, and in return he postponed the executions until the sun was up the next morning so that Hank could film. It was the most incredible footage. The next morning they paraded the condemned men naked through the market-place and the local women bargained for the various parts of their bodies. The Baluba have always been cannibals. When they had sold all three of them, they took them down to the river and shot them, in the head, of course, so as not to damage the meat, and they butchered them there on the river bank and the women queued up to claim their portions.' She was trying to shock him, and it irritated Shasa that she had succeeded.

'Where do you stand, my love?' he asked bitterly. 'One day you are sympathetically interviewing Martin Luther King, and the next you are portraying all the grossest savagery of Africa.'

She laughed, that throaty chuckle that always roused him. 'And the very next day I am recording the British imperialist making bargains with your gang of bully boys while you stand with a foot on the neck of your slaves.'

'Damn it, Kitty. What are you – what are you trying to do?'

'Capture reality,' she told him simply.

'And when reality doesn't conform to your view of it, you bribe somebody with a Rolex watch to alter it.'

'I've made you mad.' She laughed delightedly, and he stood up from the bed and crossed to where he had thrown his clothes over the back of the chair. 'You look like a little boy when you sulk,' she called after him.

'It will be light in an hour. I have to get back home and change,' he said. 'I've got an appointment with my Imperialist slave-masters at eleven.'

'Of course, you've got to be there to hear Supermac tell you how much he wants to buy your gold and diamonds – and he doesn't care whether they are dripping with the sweat and blood—'

'All right, sweetness,' he cut her off. 'That's enough for one night.' He stepped into his trousers, and as he tucked in his shirt, he grinned at her. 'Why do I always pick screaming radical females?'

'You like the stimulation,' she suggested, but he shook his head, and reached for the velvet smoking-jacket.

'I prefer the loving – talking of which, when will I see you again?'

'Why, at eleven o'clock at the Houses of Parliament, of course. I'll try to get you in the shot, you are so photogenic, darling.'

He went to the bed and stooped over her to kiss that angelic smile on her lips. 'I can never understand what I see in you,' he said.

He was still thinking of her as he went down to the hotel carpark and wiped the dew off the windshield of the Jaguar. It was amazing how she had been able so effortlessly to hold his interest over all these years. No other woman, except Tara, had ever done that. It was silly how good he felt when he had been with her. She could still drive him wild with erotic desire, her tricks still worked on him, and afterwards he felt elated and wonderfully alive – and, yes, he enjoyed arguing with her.

'God, I haven't closed my eyes all night, yet I feel like a Derby winner. I wonder if I am still in love with the little bitch.'

He took the Jaguar down the long palm-lined drive from the Mount Nelson Hotel. Considering the proposition and recalling his proposal of marriage and her outright rejection, he went out through the hotel gates and took the main road that skirted the old Malay quarter of District Six. He resisted the temptation to shoot the red of the traffic lights at the foot of Roeland Street. It was highly unlikely there would be other traffic at this time of the morning, but he braked dutifully and was startled when another vehicle shot out of the narrow cross street and turned in front of his bonnet.

It was a sea-green Chevrolet station wagon, and he didn't have to check the number plate to know that it was Tara's. The headlights of the Jaguar shone into the cab of the Chev and for an instant he had a full view of the driver. It was Tara's new chauffeur. He had seen him twice before, once at Weltevreden and once in the House of Assembly, but this time the driver was bare-headed and Shasa could see the full shape of his head.

As he had on both the previous occasions, Shasa had a strong sense of recognition. He had definitely met or known this man before, but the memory was eroded by time and quickly extinguished by his annoyance. The chauffeur was not permitted to use the Chev for his own private purposes, and yet here he was in the small hours of the morning driving around as though the vehicle belonged to him.

The Chev pulled away swiftly. The chauffeur had obviously recognized Shasa and the speed was proof of his guilt. Shasa's first instinct was to give chase and confront the man, but the traffic light was still red against him and while he waited for it to change, he had time to reflect. He was in too good a mood to spoil it with unpleasantness, besides which any confrontation at four in the morning would be undignified, and would inevitably lead to questions about his own presence at the same hour on the fringes of the city's notorious red-light area. There would be a better time and place to deal with the driver, and Shasa let him go, but he had neither forgiven nor forgotten.

Shasa parked the Jaguar in the garage at Weltevreden, and the green Chev was in its place at the end of the line of cars, between Garry's MG and Shasa's customized Land-Rover. As he passed it, he laid his hand on the bonnet of the Chev and it was still hot, the metal ticking softly as it cooled. He nodded with satisfaction and went on up to the house, amused by the necessity to creep up to his own suite like a burglar.

He still felt light and happy at breakfast and he hummed as he loaded his plate with eggs and bacon from the silver chafing dish on the sideboard. He was the first one down but Garry was only a minute behind him.

'The boss should always be the first man on the job, and the last man off it,' he had taught Garry, and the boy had taken it to heart. 'No, no longer boy.' Shasa corrected himself, as he studied Garry. His son was only an inch shorter than he was, but wider across the shoulders and heavier in the chest. Down the full length of the corridor Shasa had often heard him grunting over his body-building weights. Even though he had just shaved, Garry's jaw was blue with beard that by evening would need the razor again, and despite the Brylcreem his hair was already springing up in unruly spikes.

He sat down beside Shasa, took a mouthful of his omelette and immediately began talking shop. 'He just isn't up to the job any more, Pater. We need a younger man in that position, especially with all the extra responsibility of the Silver River Mine coming on stream.'

'He has been with us twenty years, Garry,' Shasa said mildly.

'I'm not suggesting we shoot him, Dad. Just let him take his retirement. He *is* almost seventy.'

'Retirement will kill him.'

'If he stays it will kill us.'

'All right,' Shasa sighed. Garry was right, of course, the man had outlived his usefulness. 'But I will speak to him personally.'

'Thanks, Dad.' Garry's spectacles gleamed victoriously.

'Talking about the Silver River Mine, I have arranged for you to begin your stint up there just as soon as you have written your sup.'

Garry spent more time at Centaine House than in his lecture rooms at business school. As a consequence, he was carrying one subject for his Bachelor's degree in Commerce. He would write the supplementary examination the following week and Shasa was sending him up to work on the Silver River Mine for a year or two.

'After all, it has taken over from the old H'ani now as the Company flagship. I want you to move more and more into the centre of things.' He saw the glow of anticipation behind Garry's spectacles.

'Oh boy, am I looking forward to really starting work, after bashing the books all these dreary years.'

Michael came bursting breathlessly into the diningroom. 'Thank goodness, Pater, I thought I had missed you.'

'Slow down, Mickey,' Shasa cautioned him. 'You'll burst a blood vessel. Have some breakfast.'

'I'm not hungry this morning.' Michael sat down opposite his father. 'I wanted to talk to you.'

'Well, open fire, then,' Shasa invited.

'Not here,' Michael demurred. 'I rather hoped we could talk in the gun room,' and all three of them looked grave. The gun room was only used on the most portentous occasions, and a request for a meeting in the gun room was not to be taken lightly.

Shasa glanced at his watch. 'Mickey, Harold Macmillan is addressing both houses—'

'I know, Pater, but this won't take long. Please, sir.' The fact that Michael was calling him 'sir' underlined the seriousness of the request, but Shasa resented the deliberate timing.

Whenever Michael wanted to raise a contentious issue, he did so when Shasa's opportunity to respond was severely curtailed. The lad was as devious as his mother, whose child he indubitably was, spiritually as well as physically.

'Ten minutes, then,' Shasa agreed reluctantly. 'Will you excuse us please, Garry?' Shasa led the way down the passage and locked the gun-room door behind them.

'Very well.' He took his usual place in front of the fireplace. 'What is it, my boy?'

'I've got a job, Dad.' Michael was breathless again.

'A job. Yes, I know you have a part-time job as local stringer for the Mail. I enjoyed your report on the polo – in fact you read it to me. Very good it was,' Shasa grinned, 'all five lines of it.'

'No, sir, I've got a full-time job. I spoke to the editor of the Mail and they have offered me a job as a cub reporter. I start the first of next month.'

Shasa's grin faded into a scowl. 'Damn it, Mickey. You can't be serious – what about your education? You have two more years to go at university.'

'I am serious, sir. I will get my education on the paper.'

'No,' Shasa raised his voice. 'No, I forbid it. I won't have you leaving university before you are capped.'

'I'm sorry, sir. I've made up my mind.' Michael was pale and trembling, yet he had that obstinate set expression that infuriated Shasa even more than the words – but he controlled himself.

'You know the rules,' Shasa said. 'I've made them clear to all of you. If you do things my way, there is no limit to the help I will give you. If you go your own way, then you are on your own—' he took a breath, and then said it, surprised at how painful it was ' – like Sean.' God, how he still missed his eldest son.

'Yes, sir,' Michael nodded. 'I know the rules.'

'Well?'

'I have to do it, sir. There is nothing else I want to do with my life. I want to learn to write. I don't want to go against you, Pater, but I simply have to do it.'

'This is your mother's doing,' Shasa said coldly. 'She has put you up to this,' he accused, and Michael looked sheepish.

'Mater knows about it,' he admitted, 'but it's my decision alone, sir.'

'You understand that you will be forfeiting my support? You'll not receive another penny from me once you leave this house. You'll have to live on the salary of a cub reporter.'

'I understand, sir,' Michael nodded.

'All right, then, Michael. Off you go,' he said, and Michael looked stunned.

'Is that all, sir?'

'Unless you have some other announcement to make.'

'No, sir.' Michael's shoulders slumped. 'Except that I love you very much, Pater, and I appreciate all that you have done for me.'

'You have,' said Shasa, 'a most peculiar way of demonstrating that appreciation, if you don't mind me saying so.' He went to the door.

He was halfway into the city, racing the Jaguar down the new highway between the university and Groote Schuur, before he recovered from his affront at Michael's disloyalty, for that is how Shasa saw his son's decision. Now suddenly he began to think about newspapers again. Publicly he had always disparaged the strange suicidal impulse that gripped so many successful men in their middle years to own their own newspaper. It was notoriously difficult to milk a reasonable profit from a newspaper, but in secret Shasa had felt the sneaking temptation to indulge in the same rich man's folly.

'Not much profit,' he mused aloud, 'but the power! To be able to influence the minds of people!'

In South Africa the English press was hysterically anti-government, while the Afrikaans press was fawningly and abjectly the slave of the National Party. A thinking man could trust neither.

'What about an English-language paper that was aimed at the business community and politically uncommitted,' he wondered, as he had before. 'What if I were to buy one of the smaller weaker papers and build it up? After the Silver River Mine's next dividend is declared, we are going to be sitting on a pile of money.' Then he grinned. 'I must be getting senile, but at least I'll be able to guarantee a job for my drop-out journalist son!' And the idea of Michael as editor of a large influential newspaper had an increasing appeal, the longer he thought about it. 'Still, I wish the little blighter would get himself a decent education first,' he grumbled, but he had almost forgiven him for his treachery by the time he parked the Jaguar in the parking area reserved for cabinet ministers. 'Of course, I'll keep him on a decent allowance,' he decided. 'That threat was just a little bluff.'

A sense of excited expectation gripped the House as Shasa went up the stairs to the front entrance. The lobby was crowded with senators and members of parliament. The knots of dark-suited men formed and dissolved and reformed, in the intricate play of political cross-currents that fascinated Shasa. As an insider he could read the significance of who was talking to whom and why.

It took him almost twenty minutes to reach the foot of the staircase for as one of the prime actors he was drawn inexorably into the subtle theatre of power and favour. At last he escaped and with only minutes to spare hurried up the stairs and down the passage to his suite.

Tricia was hovering anxiously. 'Oh, Mr Courtney, everybody is looking for you. Lord Littleton telephoned and the Prime Minister's secretary left a message.' She was reading from her pad as she followed him into the inner office.

'Try to get the PM's secretary first, then Lord Littleton.' Shasa sat at his desk, and frowned as he noticed some chalky white specks on his blotter. He brushed them away irritably, and would have given Tricia an order to speak to the cleaners, but she was still reading from her pad and he had less than an hour to tackle the main items on her list before the joint sitting began.

He dealt with the queries that Verwoerd's secretary had for him. The answers were in his head and he did not have to refer to anybody in his department – and then Littleton was on the line. He wanted to discuss an addition to the agenda for their meeting that afternoon, and once they had agreed that, Shasa asked tactfully, 'Have you found out anything about the speeches this morning?'

'Afraid not, old man. I'm as much in the dark as you are.'

As Shasa reached across the desk to replace the receiver, he noticed another white speck of chalk on his blotter that had not been there a minute before; he was about to brush that away also, when he paused and looked up to see where it had come from. This time he scowled as he saw the small hole in his ceiling and the hair-line cracks around it. He pressed the switch on his intercom.

'Tricia, please come in here a moment.'

When she stood in the doorway, he pointed at the ceiling. 'What do you make of that?'

Tricia looked mystified and came to stand beside his chair. They both peered at the damage.

'Oh, I know,' Tricia looked relieved, 'but I'm not supposed to tell you.'

'Spit it out, woman!' Shasa ordered.

'Your wife, Mrs Courtney, said she was planning some renovations to your office as a surprise. I suppose she has asked Maintenance to do the work for her.'

'Damn!' Shasa didn't like surprises which interfered with the comfortable tenor of his existence. He liked his office the way it was and he didn't want anybody, particularly anyone of Tara's *avant-garde* taste, interfering with something that worked extremely well as it was.

'I think she is planning to change the curtains also,' Tricia added innocently. She didn't like Tara Courtney. She considered her shallow, insincere and scheming. She didn't approve of her disrespectful attitude to Shasa, and she wasn't above sowing a few seeds of dissension. If Shasa was free, there was just a chance, a very small and remote chance that he might see her clearly and realize just how much she, Tricia, felt for him, 'And she was talking about altering the light fittings,' she added.

Shasa jumped up from his desk and went to touch his curtains. He and Centaine had studied at least a hundred samples of fabric before choosing this one. Protectively he rearranged the drapes, and then he noticed the second hole in the ceiling and the thin insulated wire that protruded from it. He had difficulty controlling his fury in front of his secretary.

'You get on to Maintenance,' he instructed. 'Talk to Odendaal himself, not one of his workmen, and you tell him I want to know exactly what is going on. Tell him whatever it is, it's damned shoddy workmanship and that there is plaster all over my desk.'

'I'll do that this morning,' Tricia promised, and then, placatingly, 'It's ten minutes to, Mr Courtney – you don't want to be late.'

Manfred De La Rey was just leaving his own office as Shasa came down the passage, and they fell in side by side.

'Have you found out anything?'

'No – have you?'

Manfred shook his head. 'It's too late anyway – nothing we can do now.'

Shasa saw Blaine Malcomess at the door of the dining-room and went to greet him. They filed into the panelled dining-room together.

'How is Mater?'

'Centaine is fine – looking forward to seeing you for dinner tomorrow evening.' Centaine was holding a dinner party in Littleton's honour out at Rhodes Hill. 'I left her giving the chef a nervous breakdown.' They laughed together and then found their seats in the front row of chairs. As a minister and Deputy Leader of the Opposition, they both warranted reserved seats.

Shasa swivelled in his seat and looked to the back of the large hall where the press cameras had been set up. He picked out Kitty Godolphin, looking tiny and girlish beside her camera crew, and she winked at him mischievously. Then the two Prime Ministers were taking their places at the top table and Shasa leaned across to Manfred De La Rey and murmured, 'I hope this isn't all a hoo-ha over nothing – and that Supermac has really got something of interest to tell us.'

Manfred shrugged. 'Let's hope it isn't too exciting either,' he said. 'Sometimes it's safer to be bored—' but he broke off as the Speaker of the House called for silence and rose to introduce the Prime Minister of Great Britain, and the packed room, filled with the most powerful men in the land, settled into attentive and expectant silence.

Even when Macmillan, tall and urbane and strangely benign in expression, rose to his feet, Shasa had no sense of being at the anvil while history was being forged and he crossed his arms over his chest and lowered his chin in the attitude of listening and concentration in which he fol-lowed all debate and argument.

Macmillan spoke in an unemotional voice, but with

weight and lucidity, and his text had all the indications of having been carefully prepared, meticulously polished and rehearsed.

'The most striking of all the impressions I have formed since I left London a month ago,' he said, 'is the strength of this African national consciousness. In different places it may take different forms, but it is happening everywhere. The wind of change is blowing through the continent. Whether we like it or not, this growth of national consciousness is a political fact. We must all accept it as a fact. Our national policies must take account of it.'

Shasa sat up straight and unfolded his arms, and around him there was a similar stirring of incredulity. It was only then that Shasa realized with a clairvoyant flash that the world he knew had altered its shape, that in the fabric of life that had held together their diverse nation for almost three hundred years, the first rent had been torn by a few simple words, a rent that could never be repaired. While he attempted to grasp the full extent of the damage, Macmillan was going on in those plummy measured tones.

'Of course, you understand this as well as anyone. You are sprung from Europe, the home of nationalism.' Cunningly, Macmillan was including them in his new sweeping view of Africa. 'Indeed, in the history of our times yours will be recorded as the first of the African nationalisms.'

Shasa glanced at Verwoerd beside the British Prime Minister and he could see that he was agitated and alarmed. He had been caught unawares by Macmillan's stratagem of withholding his text from him.

'As a fellow member of the Commonwealth, it is our earnest desire to give South Africa our support and encouragement, but I hope you won't mind me saying frankly that there are some aspects of your policies which make it impossible for us to do this without being false to our own deep convictions about the political destinies of free men.'

Macmillan was announcing nothing less than a parting

of ways and Shasa was devastated by the idea. He wanted to leap to his feet and shout, 'But I am British also – you cannot do this to us.' He looked around him almost pleadingly and saw his own deep distress echoed on the faces of Blaine and most of the other English members of the House.

Macmillan's words had devastated them.

Shasa's mood persisted over the remainder of that day and the next. The atmosphere at the meetings with Littleton and his advisers was one of mourning, and though Littleton himself was apologetic and conciliatory, they all knew that the damage was real and irreparable. The fact was undeniable. Britain was dropping them. She might go on trading with them, but at arm's length. Britain had chosen sides.

Late on the Friday a special session of the House was announced for the following Monday, when Verwoerd would make his accounting to his parliament and his people. They had the weekend to brood over their fate. Macmillan's speech even cast a shadow over Centaine's dinner party on the Friday evening, and Centaine took it as a personal insult.

'The man's timing is atrocious,' she confided to Shasa. 'The day before my party! Perfidious Albion!'

'You French have never trusted the British,' Shasa teased her, his first attempt at humour in forty-eight hours.

'Now I know why,' Centaine retorted. 'Look at the man – typically English. He hides expediency in a cloak of high moral indignation. He does what is best for England and makes himself a saint while he does it.'

It was left for Blaine Malcomess to sum up after the women had left the men to their port and cigars in Rhodes Hill's magnificent dining-room.

'Why are we so incredulous?' he asked. 'Why do we feel it so impossible that Britain would reject us, simply because we fought two wars for her?' He shook his head. 'No, the caravan moves on and so must we. We must ignore the gloating of the London press, we must ignore their delight in this unprecedented rebuke and repudiation of all of us, the Nationalists and those that strenuously oppose them. From now on we will be increasingly alone, and we must learn to stand on our own feet.'

Shasa nodded. 'Macmillan's speech was a huge political gain for Verwoerd. There is only one way for us to go now. The bridge has been chopped down behind us. No retreat is possible. We have to go along with Verwoerd. South Africa will be a republic before the year is out, mark my words, and after that—' Shasa drew on his cigar while he considered ' – and after that only God and the Devil know for certain.'

'At times it seems that God and fate take a direct hand in our petty affairs,' Tara said softly. 'But for a tiny detail, the choice of the dining-room rather than the chamber, we might have destroyed the man who had brought us a message of hope.'

'For once it does seem that your Christian God favours us.' Moses watched her in the driving-mirror as he drove the Chevrolet through the Monday rush-hour traffic. 'Our timing has been perfect. At the moment when the British Government, supported by the British press and the nation, has recognized our rights, the political destinies of free men, as Macmillan put it, we will deliver our first hard blow for the promised freedom.'

'I am afraid, Moses, afraid for you and for all of us.'

'The time for fear has passed,' he told her. 'Now is the time for courage and resolution, for it is not oppression and slavery that breeds revolution. The lesson is clear. Revolution rises out of the promise of better things. For three hundred years we have borne oppression in weary resig-

540

nation, but now this Englishman has shown us a glimpse of the future and it is golden with promise. He has given our people hope, and after today, after we have struck down the most evil man in Africa's dark and tormented history, when Verwoerd is dead, the future will at last belong to us.' He had spoken softly, but with that peculiar intensity that made her blood thrill through her veins and pound in her eardrums. She felt the elation, but also the sorrow and the fear.

'Many men will die with him,' she whispered. 'My father. Is there no way he can be spared, Moses?'

He did not reply, but she saw the reflection of his gaze in the mirror and she could not bear the scorn. She dropped her own eyes and murmured.

'I'm sorry – I will be strong. I will not speak of it again.' But her mind was racing. There must be some way to keep her father out of the chamber at the fateful moment, but it would have to be compelling. As Deputy Leader of the Opposition, he must attend such solemn business as Verwoerd's speech. Moses disturbed her thoughts.

'I want you to repeat your duties to me,' he said.

'We have gone over it so often,' she protested weakly.

'There must be no misunderstanding.' His tone was fierce. 'Do as I tell you.'

'Once the House is in session – so that we are certain Shasa will not intercept us – we will go up to his suite in the usual way,' she began, and he nodded confirmation as she went over the arrangements, correcting her when she omitted a detail. 'I will leave the office at exactly ten thirty and go to the visitors' gallery. We must be certain that Verwoerd is there.'

'Do you have your pass?'

'Yes.' Tara opened her handbag and showed him. 'As soon as Verwoerd rises to begin his address, I will return to the office, using the panel door. By that time you will have . . .' Her voice faltered.

'Go on,' he ordered harshly.

'You will have connected the detonator. I will confirm that Verwoerd is in his seat, and you will . . .' Again her voice dried up.

'I will do what has to be done,' he finished for her and then went on, 'After the explosion there will be a period of total panic and confusion – with enormous damage to the ground floor. There will be no control, no organized police or security effort. That period will last sufficiently long for us to go downstairs and leave the building unchallenged, just as most other survivors will be doing.'

'When you leave the country, can I come with you, Moses?' she pleaded.

'No.' He shook his head firmly. 'I must travel swiftly and you would impede us and put us in danger. You will be safer here. It will only be for a short time. After the assassination of the white slave-masters, our people will rise. The young comrades of *Umkhonto we Sizwe* are in position and ready to call the nation to revolution. Millions of our people will spontaneously fill the streets. When they have seized power, I will return. Then you will have a place of high honour by my side.'

It was amazing how naïvely she accepted his assurances, he thought grimly. Only a besotted woman could doubt that afterwards the security police would take her away, and her interrogation would be brutal. It did not matter. It did not matter if they tried and hanged her. Her husband would be dead with Verwoerd and Tara Courtney's usefulness would be at an end. One day, when the people's democratic government of the African National Congress ruled the land, they would name a street or a square after her, the white woman martyr, but now she was expendable.

'Give me your promise, Moses,' she begged him.

His voice was a deep reassuring rumble. 'You have done well, everything I have required of you. You and your son will have a place at my side just as soon as that is possible. I give you my promise.'

'Oh, Moses, I love you,' she whispered. 'I shall always love you.' Then she sat back in her seat and adopted the role of cool white madam, as Moses turned the Chevrolet out of Parliament Lane into the members' carpark and the constable at the gate saw the sticker on the windshield and saluted respectfully.

Moses parked in the reserved bay and switched off the engine. They had fifteen minutes to wait before the House went into session.

'Ten minutes to, Mr Courtney,' Tricia called Shasa on the intercom. 'You had better start going down, if you don't want to miss the opening of the PM's speech.'

'Thank you, Tricia.' Shasa had been totally absorbed with his own work. Verwoerd had asked him to draw up a full report on the country's ability to respond to an embargo on sales of military equipment to South Africa by her Western erstwhile allies. Apparently Macmillan had hinted at this possibility to Verwoerd, a veiled threat in private conversation just before his departure. Verwoerd wanted the report before the month's end, which was typical of the man, and Shasa would have difficulty meeting that deadline.

'Oh, by the way, Mr Courtney,' Tricia stopped him breaking off the connection. 'I spoke to Odendaal.'

'Odendaal?' It took Shasa a moment to make the mental switch.

'Yes, about the work on your ceiling.'

'Oh, I hope you gave him a flea in the ear. What did he say?'

'He says there has been no work done in your office, and no request from your wife or anybody else for rewiring of any kind.'

'That's decidedly odd,' Shasa looked up at the damage, 'because somebody has definitely been fiddling around in here. If it wasn't Odendaal, then have you any idea who it might be, Tricia?'

'No, Mr Courtney.'

'Nobody been in here to your knowledge?' Shasa insisted.

'Nobody, sir, except of course your wife and her driver.'

'All right, thank you, Tricia.' Shasa stood up and fetched his jacket from the dumb valet in the corner. While he shrugged into it, he studied the hole above his desk and the length of wire that had been drawn out of the corner beside the bookcase and the end tucked behind the row of encyclopaedias. Until Tricia mentioned it, he had forgotten his irritation in the face of other more dire considerations, but now he thought about the little mystery with full attention.

He crossed to the mirror and while he reshaped the knot of his tie and adjusted his black eye-patch he pondered the additional enigma of Tara's new chauffeur. Tricia's remark had reminded him of it. He still hadn't taken the man to task for his unauthorized private use of the Chev. 'Damn – where have I seen him before?' he wondered, and with one last glance at the ceiling, he left the office. He was still thinking about the driver as he went down the corridor. Manfred De La Rey was waiting for him at the head of the stairs. He was smiling and quietly triumphant, and Shasa realized that he had not spoken to him in private since the shock of Macmillan's speech.

'So,' Manfred greeted him, 'Britannia has cut the apron strings, my friend.'

'Do you remember how once you called me *Soutpiel*?' Shasa asked.

'*Ja.*' Manfred chuckled. '"Salt Prick" – with one foot in Cape Town and the other in London and the best part of you dangling in the Atlantic Ocean. *Ja*, I remember.'

'Well, from now on I will have both feet in Cape Town,' Shasa told him. It was not until that moment, when the fact of Britain's rejection had sunk in, that Shasa realized for the first time that above all other things he was first and foremost a South African.

'Good,' Manfred nodded. 'So at last you understand that although we may not always like each other or agree, circumstances have made us brothers in this land. One cannot survive without the other, and in the end we have only each other to turn to.'

They went down into the chamber and took their seats on the green leather benches, side by side.

When the Assembly rose to pray, to ask God's blessing on their deliberations, Shasa looked across the floor at Blaine Malcomess and felt a familiar rush of affection for him. Silver-haired but tanned and handsome with those protruding ears and big strong nose, Blaine had been a tower in his life for as long as he cared to remember. In his new mood of patriotism – and, yes, of defiance of Britain's rejection – he was glad of the knowledge that this would draw them still closer together. It would narrow the political differences between them, just as it had brought Afrikaner and Englishman closer.

As the prayer ended, he sat down and turned his attention to Dr Hendrik Frensch Verwoerd as he rose to make his address. Verwoerd was a strong, articulate speaker and a brilliant debater. His address was sure to be long and carefully reasoned. Shasa knew they were in for fine entertainment and he crossed his arms, leaned against the padded back rest with anticipation and closed his eyes.

Then before Verwoerd could say his first word, Shasa opened his eyes and sat up straight on his bench. In that moment when he had cleared his mind of all recent worry, while he was relaxed and receptive, the ancient memory had flashed in upon him – full blown. He remembered where and when he had last seen Tara's new chauffeur.

'Moses Gama,' he said aloud, but his words were lost in the applause that greeted the Prime Minister.

T ara gave the doorman at the main entrance to parliament a cheery smile, and was surprised at herself. She felt cocooned in a layer of unreality, as though she watched an actress playing her role.

She heard the muffled applause from the chamber as she swept up the stairs with Moses following her at a respectful distance in his chauffeur's uniform and burdened by an armful of parcels. They had done this so often, and Tara smiled again as they passed one of the secretaries in the corridor. She tapped on the door to Shasa's suite and without waiting for an answer swept into the outer office. Tricia rose from her desk.

'Oh, good morning, Mrs Courtney. You'll be late for the PM's address. You'd better hurry.'

'Stephen, you can just leave the parcels.' Tara stopped in front of Tricia as Moses closed the outer door.

'Oh, by the way. Somebody has been working on the ceiling of your husband's office,' Tricia came around the desk, as though to lead the way to Shasa's office. 'We wondered if you knew anything—'

Moses placed the armful of parcels on a chair, and with his hands free turned to Tricia as she came level with him. He whipped one arm around her neck and with his other hand covered her mouth. Tricia was powerless in his grip, but her eyes flew wide with shock.

'There are ropes and a gag in the top packet,' Moses spoke softly to Tara. 'Get them.'

Tara stood paralysed. 'You said nothing about this,' she blurted.

'Get them.' His voice was still low, but it crackled with impatience and Tara sprang to obey.

'Tie her hands behind her,' Moses ordered, and while Tara fumbled at the knots, he stuffed a clean, white folded cloth into the terrified girl's mouth and taped it in place.

'Stay in here,' he ordered Tara, 'in case somebody comes in,' and he bundled Tricia through into the inner office and forced her down on her stomach behind the desk. Swiftly he checked Tara's knots. They were loose and sloppy. He retied them and then bound Tricia's ankles as securely.

'Come in here,' he called, and Tara was flustered and stammering as she rushed in.

'Moses, you haven't hurt her?'

'Stop that!' he told her. 'You have important work to do and you are behaving like a hysterical child.'

She closed her eyes, clenched her fists and took a deep breath. 'I'm sorry.' She opened her eyes. 'I realize that it was necessary. I didn't think. I am all right now.'

Moses had already crossed to the corner of the bookshelf and he reached up and brought down the roll of wire from behind the encyclopaedias. He paid it out across the carpet as he moved back to the desk.

'Good,' he said. 'Now go to your seat in the gallery. Wait five minutes after Verwoerd begins to speak and then come back here. Do not run, do not even hurry. Do everything calmly and deliberately.'

'I understand.' Tara crossed to the mirror and opened her handbag. Quickly she ran a comb through her hair and retouched her lipstick.

Moses had gone to the altar chest and lifted the heavy bronze Bushman statue. He placed it on the carpet and lifted the lid of the chest. Tara hesitated, watching him anxiously.

'Why are you waiting?' he asked. 'Go, woman, and do your duty.'

'Yes, Moses.' She hurried to the door of the outer office.

'Lock both doors behind you,' he ordered.

'Yes, Moses,' she whispered.

As Tara went down the corridor, she was searching in her handbag again, and she found her leather-bound notepad with the miniature gold-plated pencil in the spine loops. At the head of the stairs she paused, and used the banisters to steady the notepad while she scribbled hastily on a blank page.

> Daddy,
>   Centaine has been seriously injured in a motorcar accident. She is asking for you. Please come quickly.
>
>   Tara

She tore the page out of the notebook and folded it. It was the one appeal to which she knew her father would respond and she wrote his name on the folded note.

Instead of going directly to the visitors' gallery, she hurried down the wide staircase into the lobby and ran to one of the uniformed parliamentary messengers who was standing outside the main doors to the chamber.

'You have to get this message to Colonel Malcomess,' she told him.

'I don't like to go in now, Dr Verwoerd is speaking,' the messenger demurred, but she thrust the note into his hand.

'It's terribly urgent,' she pleaded and her distress was evident. 'His wife is dying. Please – please.'

'I'll do what I can.' The messenger accepted the note, and Tara ran back up the stairs. She showed her pass to the doorman at the entrance to the visitors' gallery and squeezed past him.

The gallery was crowded. Somebody had taken Tara's seat, but she edged forward and craned to look down into the chamber. Dr Verwoerd was on his feet, talking in Afrikaans. His silvery curls were neatly cropped and his eyes slitted with concentration as he used both hands to emphasize his words.

'The question that this person from Britain put to us was not addressed to the South African monarchists, nor was it addressed to the South African republicans. It was to all of us that he spoke.' Verwoerd paused. 'The question he asked was simply this. Does the white man survive in Africa or does he perish?'

He had electrified the chamber. There was not a movement nor a shift of eyes from his face – until the uniformed parliamentary messenger slipped unobtrusively down the front row of Opposition benches and stopped beside Blaine.

Even then he had to touch Blaine's shoulder to draw his attention, and Blaine accepted the note without seeming to realize what he was doing. He nodded at the messenger, and, with the folded scrap of paper unread in his fingers, once more focused all his attention on Verwoerd where he stood below the Speaker's throne.

'Read it, Daddy!' Tara whispered aloud. 'Please read it.'

In all that multitude Shasa was the only one who was not mesmerized by Verwoerd's oratory. His thoughts were a jumbled torrent, one racing after another, overtaking and mingling as they followed without logical sequence.

'*Moses Gama!*' It was scarcely believable that the memory had taken so long to return to him, even over the years and in spite of changes that time had wrought in both of them. They had once been good friends, and the man had made a deep impression on Shasa at a formative period of his life.

Then again, Shasa had heard the name much more

recently; it had been on the list of wanted revolutionaries during the 1952 troubles. While the others, Mandela and Sobukwe and the rest, had stood trial, Moses Gama had disappeared, and the warrant for his arrest was outstanding. Moses Gama was still a criminal at large, and a dangerous revolutionary.

'Tara!' His mind darted aside. She had selected Gama as her chauffeur and, given her political leanings, it was impossible that she didn't know who he was. Suddenly Shasa knew that Tara's meek repudiation of her previous left-wing companions and her new conciliatory behaviour had all been a sham. She had not changed at all. This man Moses Gama was more dangerous than all and any of her previous effete companions. Shasa had been hoodwinked. In fact she must have moved even further to the left, crossing the delicate line between legitimate political opposition and criminal involvement. Shasa almost rose to his feet, and then remembered where he was. Verwoerd was speaking already.

'The need to do justice to all does not mean only that the black men must be nurtured and protected. It means justice and protection for the white men in Africa also—'

Shasa glanced up at the visitors' gallery and there was a stranger sitting in Tara's seat. Where was Tara? She must be in his office – and the association of ideas led him on.

Moses Gama had been in his office. Shasa had seen him in the corridor and Tricia had told him, 'Only Mrs Courtney and her driver.' Moses Gama had been in his office and somebody had drilled the ceiling and laid electrical wires. It had not been Odendaal or Maintenance. It hadn't been anyone who had authority to do so.

'We are not newcomers to Africa. Our forefathers were here before the first black man,' Verwoerd was saying. 'Three hundred years ago, when our ancestors set out into the interior of this land, it was an empty wilderness. The black tribes were still far to the north, making their way slowly southwards. The land was empty and our forefathers claimed it and worked it. Later they built the cities and laid the railways and sank the mine-shafts. Alone, the black man was incapable of doing any of these things. Even more than the black tribes we are men of Africa and our right to be here is as God-given and inalienable as is theirs.'

Shasa heard the words but made no sense of them – Moses Gama, probably with the help and connivance of Tara, had laid electrical wires in his office and – suddenly, he gasped aloud. The altar chest. Tara had placed the chest in his office, like the Trojan Horse.

Wild with anxiety now, he swivelled his whole body towards the visitors' gallery, and this time he saw Tara. She was squeezed against one wall and even at this distance Shasa could see that she was pale and distraught. She was watching someone or something on the Opposition side of the chamber, and Shasa followed her gaze.

Blaine Malcomess was oblivious of all else as he followed the Prime Minister's speech. Shasa saw the messenger reach him and hand him the note.

Shasa looked back at the gallery and Tara was still concentrated on her father. After all the years Shasa could read her expression, and he had never seen her so worried and concerned, even when one of the children was gravely ill.

Then her face cleared with patent relief and Shasa glanced back at Blaine. He had unfolded the note and was reading it. Suddenly Blaine leapt to his feet and hurried towards the main doors.

Tara had summoned her father – that much was obvious. Shasa stared at her, trying to divine her purpose. Almost as though she sensed his gaze, Tara looked directly at him, and her relief crumbled into horror and wild guilt. She turned and fled from the visitors' gallery, pushing aside those who stood in her way.

A second longer Shasa stared after her. Tara had enticed

her father out of the chamber, and her concern could only have been so intense had she believed he was in some kind of dire danger. This was followed by guilt and horror as she realized that Shasa was watching her. It was clear to Shasa then that something terrible was about to happen. Moses Gama and Tara – there was danger, mortal danger – and Tara was trying to save her father. The danger was pressing and imminent – the wires in his office, the chest, Blaine and Tara and Moses Gama. He knew they were all interwoven and that he had little time in which to act.

Shasa jumped to his feet and strode down the aisle. Verwoerd frowned and checked his speech, watching him, while all around the chamber heads turned. Shasa quickened his stride. Manfred De La Rey reached out to touch him as he passed his bench, but without a glance at him Shasa brushed past his outstretched hand and went on.

As he hurried out into the lobby Shasa saw Blaine Malcomess near the front door talking agitatedly to the janitor. As soon as he saw Shasa he said, 'Thank God!' and came towards him across the chequered marble floor.

Shasa turned away from him and looked up the staircase. From the top Tara stared down at him, white-faced and terrified, held by some unnatural passion.

'Tara!' Shasa called and started towards the foot of the staircase, but she whirled and disappeared around the angle of the corridor.

Shasa flew at the stairs, taking them three at a time.

'What's happening, Shasa?' Blaine called after him, but Shasa did not answer.

He came out of the staircase still at a run, and as he rounded the corner Tara was halfway down the corridor ahead of him. He did not waste time by shouting at her, and instead flung himself forward, and sprinted after her. As she ran, Tara glanced over her shoulder and saw him swiftly overtaking her.

'Moses!' she screamed. 'Look out, Moses!'

It was futile, the panelled walls of Shasa's office were too thick and soundproof for her warning to reach him, and her cry confirmed all Shasa's worst suspicions.

Instead of running straight on towards the front door of his suite as Shasa expected, Tara jinked suddenly into the side passage, ducking under Shasa's outstretched arm and he tried to turn with her but he was off balance as she disappeared into his blind spot.

Shasa ran into the corner of the wall, crashing into it head-first, taking it on the brow above his blind eye. The silk patch cushioned the impact slightly, but still the skin split and blood poured down his cheek. Although he was stunned, Shasa managed to keep his feet. He staggered in a full circle, still dazed. Blaine was following him, his face flushed with effort and concern as he ran down the corridor.

'What the hell is going on, Shasa?' he roared.

Shasa turned from him, and saw Tara at the door to the back entrance of his office. She had a key, but she was in such a state that her hands were shaking too wildly to insert it in the lock.

Shasa gathered himself, shaking the darkness out of his head, and the droplets of his blood splattered the wall beside him. Then he launched himself after Tara. She saw him coming and dropped the key, it tinkled at her feet, and she clenched her fists and beat with them on the closed door.

'Moses!' she screamed. 'Moses!'

As Shasa reached her the door was jerked open from the inside, and Moses Gama stood in the threshold. The two men confronted each other over Tara's head until Tara ran forward.

'Moses, I tried to warn you,' she screamed and threw both arms around him.

In that instant Shasa looked beyond the pair and saw that the altar chest stood open, its contents piled on the carpet. The coil of wire that he had found behind the encyclopaedias had been laid across the floor to his desk and connected to some kind of compact electrical apparatus. Shasa had never seen one before, but he knew instinctively that it was a detonation device and that it was ready to fire. On the desk top beside it lay an automatic pistol. As a firearms enthusiast and collector, he recognized it as a Tokarev 7.62 mm, the standard Russian military issue. On the floor behind his desk Tricia lay on her side. She was gagged and bound at wrists and ankles, but she was wriggling desperately and giving little muffled cries.

Shasa lunged forward to tackle Moses Gama, but the black man gathered Tara in his arms and hurled her into Shasa's chest. The two of them reeled backwards against the jamb of the door. Moses spun around and leapt to the desk, as Shasa tried to get free of Tara. She was clinging to him and moaning.

'No! No! He must do it.'

Shasa broke her grip and flung her aside, but across the room Moses was standing over the electrical transmitter. He pressed a switch and a bulb on the panel of the casing glared redly.

Shasa knew that he could not reach Moses across the floor before he fired the device, but his mind was racing ahead of his limbs and body. He saw the wire strung out across the carpet, almost at his feet, and he stooped and took a twist of it around his right hand and heaved back against it with all his strength.

The end of the wire was firmly attached to the transmitter, and as Shasa hauled on it the device was jerked out of Moses' hands and flew off the desk top to clatter across the floor, midway between the two of them.

They both leapt for it at the same instant, but Moses was by a fraction of a second the quickest, and his hands scrabbled on the transmitter. Shasa was in full stride, and he did not check. He leaned forward, and transferred all the weight and power of his body into his hips, swinging his right leg into the kick he aimed at Moses' head.

The kick caught Moses in the side of the temple, and snapped his head over. The transmitter tumbled from his grip and he was flung over backwards, rolling until he crashed into the desk.

Shasa followed him and aimed another flying kick at his head, but Moses caught his foot on his raised forearm and seized his ankle. He twisted violently, lifting the ankle and Shasa was caught on one foot with his weight backwards, and he fell heavily.

Moses pulled himself up the side of the desk and reached out for the Tokarev pistol, and Shasa scrambled after him on hands and knees. As Moses swung the pistol around, Shasa lunged at him again and grabbed his wrist with both hands. They wrestled over the floor, rolling and kicking and grunting, fighting for the Tokarev.

Tara had recovered and now she ran into the room and picked up the fallen transmitter. She stood helplessly with it in her hands.

'Moses, what must I do?' she cried.

Moses grunted with a supreme effort as he rolled on top of Shasa. 'The yellow button. Push the yellow button!'

At that instant Blaine Malcomess ran in through the open door. 'Stop her, Blaine!' Shasa yelled. 'They are going to blow—' Moses' elbow hit him in the mouth and cut off the words.

While the two of them still struggled on the floor, Blaine held out both hands to his daughter.

'Here, give that to me, Tara.'

'Don't touch me, Daddy.' She backed away from him, but she was trying to locate the yellow button, groping for it while she stared at her father. 'Don't try and stop me, Daddy.'

'Blaine,' Shasa gasped, but broke off as Moses attempted

once more to wrench his pistol arm out of Shasa's grip. The corded black muscles in Moses' arm bulged and writhed with the effort, and Shasa made a choking sound in his throat as he tried to hold him.

The muzzle blast of the pistol lit the room like a flash bulb and there was the immediate sharp stink of burnt powder.

Blaine Malcomess, his arms outstretched towards Tara, spun around as the bullet hit him and he went reeling into the bookcase. He stood there for a moment with the blood starting to spread in a dark tide down the front of his white shirt and then he sagged slowly onto his knees.

'Daddy!' Tara dropped the transmitter and ran to him. She fell on her knees beside him.

Shock had weakened Shasa's grip for an instant and Moses twisted free and jumped to his feet, but as he lunged for the transmitter, Shasa was after him. He caught Moses from behind as he stooped over the transmitter and with one arm around his throat pulled him away from it. In his efforts to break the throttling grip, Moses dropped the pistol and clawed at Shasa's arm with both hands. They grappled wildly, twisting and grunting, and the transmitter lay at their feet.

Shasa shifted his weight, lifted one foot and drove his heel into the panel of the transmitter; the panel crackled as it was stove in, but the red bulb still burned.

Moses was galvanized to fresh effort by the damage to the transmitter, and he almost tore himself free of Shasa's grip, twisting to face him, but Shasa put out all his strength and they stood chest to chest, gasping and heaving, spittle and sweat and droplets of blood from Shasa's head wound smearing both their faces.

Again Shasa had him off balance for a moment, and he aimed another kick at the transmitter. He landed solidly and it went skidding across the floor and crashed into the wall beyond the desk. The plastic case split open at the impact, the wire tore loose from the terminal and the red bulb flickered and then extinguished.

Moses gave a wild despairing cry and sent Shasa flying backwards over the desk. As he lay sprawled across the desk top, Moses scooped up the pistol from the carpet and staggered to the open doorway. There he turned and raised the Tokarev and aimed at Shasa.

'You!' he gasped. 'You!' but his hands were shaking and the pistol wavered. He fired and the bullet thudded into the desk top beside Shasa's head, tearing up a blur of splinters.

Before Moses could fire again, Manfred De Le Rey bulked in the doorway behind him. He had seen Shasa's agitation and followed him up from the chamber.

He took in the situation at first glance, and he reacted instantly. He swung the big hard fist that had won him an Olympic gold medal, and it crashed into the side of Moses Gama's neck below the ear.

The pistol fell from Moses' hand and he toppled forward unconscious on top of it.

Shasa dragged himself off the desk and tottered across to Blaine.

'Here,' he whispered, as he dropped to his knees beside him. 'Let me have a look.'

Tara was blubbering incoherently. 'Daddy, I'm sorry. I didn't mean this to happen. I only did what I thought was right.'

Shasa tried to pull her away, but she clung to Blaine, blood on her hands and down the front of her dress.

'Let him alone,' Shasa said, but she was hysterical now, and tugged at her father so that his head jerked from side to side loosely. 'Daddy, speak to me, Daddy.'

Shasa leaned back and slapped her hard, knocking her head across.

'Leave him, you murderous bitch,' he hissed at her, and she crawled away from him, her face beginning to redden and swell from the blow. Shasa ignored her and gently opened the jacket of Blaine's dark suit.

Shasa was a hunter, and he recognized the bright clear colour of arterial blood seething with tiny bubbles from the torn lungs.

'No,' he whispered. 'Please, no!'

Only then he realized that Blaine was watching his face, reading in it his own death.

'Your mother—' he said, and the wind of his lungs puffed through the bullet hole in his chest. 'Tell Centaine—' He could not go on.

'Don't talk,' Shasa said. 'We will get a doctor.' He shouted over his shoulder at Manfred who was already on the telephone, 'Hurry, man. Hurry!'

But Blaine gripped his sleeve, tugging it urgently. 'Love—' He choked on his own blood. 'Tell her – love – tell her I love her.' He got it out at last, and panted as the blood gurgled in his chest – and then he gathered himself for his last great effort.

'Shasa,' he said. 'Shasa, my son – my only son.'

The noble silver head fell forward, and Shasa held it to his chest, hugging him as he had never been able to before.

Then still holding him, Shasa wept for the man who had been his friend and his father. The tears squeezed out of his empty eyesocket and trickled from under the silk eye-patch down his face to mingle with his own blood and drip from his chin.

When Tara crawled forward on her knees, and reached out to touch her father's corpse, Shasa lifted his head and looked at her.

'Don't touch him,' he said softly. 'Don't you dare soil him with your touch.' There was such a look in his single eye, such contempt and hatred in his face, that she recoiled from him and covered her face with both hands. Still on her knees, she began to sob hysterically. The sound of it rallied Shasa. Gently he laid Blaine on his back and closed his eyes with his fingertips.

In the doorway Moses groaned and shuddered, and Manfred slammed the telephone back on its cradle and crossed to him. He stood over him, with those huge fists clenched and asked, 'Who is he?'

'Moses Gama.' Shasa stood up, and Manfred grunted.

'So, we have been looking for him for years. What was he doing?'

'I'm not sure.' Shasa went to where Tricia lay and stooped over her. 'But I think he has laid explosives somewhere in the House. That is the transmitter. We'd better clear the place and have the Army bomb-disposal—' He didn't have to finish, for at that moment there was the sound of running men in the corridor and three of the security guards burst into the suite.

Manfred took over immediately, snapping orders at them. 'Get the handcuffs on that black bastard.' He pointed at Moses. 'And then I want the building cleared.'

Shasa freed Tricia, leaving the gag until last, but the instant her mouth was clear Tricia pointed at Tara where she still knelt sobbing beside Blaine's corpse.

'She—' Shasa did not let her finish. He seized her wrist and jerked Tricia to her feet.

'Quiet!' he snarled at her, and his fury silenced the girl for a moment. He dragged her through into the outer office and closed the door.

'Listen to me, Tricia.' He faced her, still holding both her wrists.

'But she was with him.' Tricia was trembling. 'It was her—'

'Listen to me.' Shasa shook her into silence. 'I know. I know all about it. But I want you to do something for me. Something for which I will always be grateful. Will you do it?'

Tricia sobered and stared at him. She saw the blood and the tears on his face and thought her heart might break for him. Shasa took the handkerchief from his top pocket and wiped his face.

'For me, Tricia. Please,' he repeated and she gulped noisily and nodded.

'If I can,' she agreed.

'Don't say anything about my wife's part in this until the police take a formal statement from you. That won't be until much later. Then you can tell them everything.'

'Why?' she asked.

'For me and for my children. Please, Tricia.'

Again she nodded and he kissed her forehead. 'You are a good brave girl,' he said and left her.

He went back into the inner office. The security police were grouped around Moses Gama. He was manacled but he lifted his head and stared at Shasa for a moment. It was a smouldering gaze, dark and filled with outrage. Then they led him away.

The office was crowded and noisy. White-uniformed ambulance attendants were bringing a stretcher through the doorway. A doctor, a member of parliament summoned from the chamber, was working over Blaine as he lay on his back, but now he stood up, shook his head and gestured at the stretcher bearers to take Blaine's body. The uniformed guards, supervised by Manfred De La Rey, were already gathering up the pieces of the smashed transmitter and beginning to trace the wire to its source.

Tara was sitting in the chair behind his desk, weeping silently into her hands. Shasa went past her to the wall safe hidden behind one of the paintings.

He tumbled the combination and swung open the steel door, screening it with his own body. Shasa always kept two or three thousand pounds in banknotes against an emergency. He stuffed the wads into his pockets, and then quickly he sorted through the stack of family passports until he found Tara's. He relocked the safe, went to where she sat and pulled her to her feet.

'Shasa, I didn't—'

'Keep quiet,' he hissed at her, and Manfred De La Rey glanced at him across the office.

'She's had a terrible shock,' Shasa said. 'I'm taking her home.'

'Come back here as soon as you can,' Manfred nodded. 'We'll need a statement.'

Still gripping her arm, Shasa marched her out of the office and down the corridor. The fire alarm bells were ringing throughout the building and members and visitors and staff were streaming out through the front doors. Shasa joined them, and as soon as they were out in the sunlight he led Tara to the Jaguar.

'Where are we going?' Tara asked, as they drove away. She sat very small and subdued in her corner of the bucket seat.

'If you talk to me again, I may lose control,' he warned her tightly. 'I may not be able to stop myself strangling you.'

She did not speak again until they reached Youngsfield Airport, and Shasa pushed her up into the cockpit of the silver and blue Mosquito.

'Where are we going?' she repeated, but he ignored her as he went through the start-up procedures and taxied out to the end of the runway. He did not speak until they had climbed to cruise altitude and were flying straight and level.

'The evening flight for London leaves Johannesburg at seven o'clock. As soon as we are in radio contact, I will reserve your seat,' he told her. 'We will get there with an hour or so to spare.'

'I don't understand,' she whispered into her oxygen mask. 'Are you helping me to escape? I don't understand why.'

'For my mother, firstly. I don't want her to know that you murdered her husband – it would destroy her.'

'Shasa, I didn't—' She was weeping again, but he felt no twinge of compassion.

'Shut up,' he said. 'I don't want to listen to your blubbering. You will never know the depths of my feelings for you. Hatred and contempt are gentle words that do not describe them.' He drew a breath. Then went on, 'After my mother, I am doing it for my children. I don't want them to live their lives with the knowledge of what their mother truly was. That is too much for a young man or woman to be burdened with.'

Then they were both silent, and Shasa allowed the terrible grief of Blaine's death, which up until then he had suppressed, to rise up and engulf him. In the seat beside him Tara was mourning her father also, spasms of weeping shook her shoulders. Her face above the mask was chalky and her eyes were like wounds.

As strong as his grief was Shasa's hatred. After an hour's flying, he spoke again.

'If you ever return to this country again, I will see you hanged. That is my solemn promise. I will be divorcing you for desertion as soon as possible. There will be no question of alimony or maintenance or child custody. You will have no rights nor privileges of any kind. As far as we are concerned, it will be as though you have never existed. I expect you will be able to claim political asylum somewhere, even if it is in Mother Russia.'

Again he was silent, gathering himself, regaining full control.

'You will not even be at your father's funeral, but every minute of every day his memory will stalk you. That is the only punishment I am able to inflict upon you – God grant it is enough. If He is just, your guilt will slowly drive you mad. I pray for that.'

She did not reply, but turned her face away. Later, when

they were on approach to Johannesburg, descending through ten thousand feet, with the skyscrapers and the white mine dumps glowing in the late sunlight ahead of them, Shasa asked:

'You were sleeping with him, weren't you?'

Instinctively, she knew it was the last chance she would ever have to inflict pain upon him, and she turned in the seat to watch his face as she replied.

'Yes, I love him – and we are lovers.' She saw him wince, but she wanted to hurt him more and she went on. 'Apart from my father's death, there is nothing I regret. Nothing I have done of which I am ashamed. On the contrary, I am proud to have known and loved a man like Moses Gama – proud of what I have done for him and for my country.'

'Think of him kicking and choking on the rope, and be proud of that also,' Shasa said quietly, and landed. He taxied the Mosquito to the terminal buildings and they climbed down onto the tarmac and faced each other. There was a bruise on her face where he had struck her, and the icy highveld wind pulled at their clothing and ruffled their hair. He handed her the little bundle of bank notes and her passport.

'Your seat on the London flight is reserved. There is enough here to pay for it and to take you where you want to go.' His voice broke as his rage and his sorrow took control of him again. 'To hell or the gallows, if my wish for you comes true. I hope never to see or hear of you again.'

He turned away from her, but she called after him.

'We were always enemies, Shasa Courtney, even in the best times. And we will be enemies to the very end. Despite your wish, you will hear of me again. I promise you that much.'

He climbed into the Mosquito and it was minutes before he had himself sufficiently in hand to start the engines. When he looked out through the windshield again, she was gone.

Centaine would not let them bury Blaine. She could not bear the thought of him lying in the earth, swelling and putrefying.

Mathilda Janine, Blaine's younger daughter, came down from Johannesburg with David Abrahams, her husband, in the company Dove, and they sat with the family in the front row of the memorial chapel at the crematorium. Over a thousand mourners attended the service and both Dr Verwoerd and Sir De Villiers Graaff, the Leader of the Opposition, were amongst them.

Centaine kept the little urn of Blaine's ashes on the table beside her bed for almost a month, before she could get up her courage. Then she summoned Shasa, and the two of them climbed the hill to her favourite rock.

'Blaine and I used to come here so often,' she whispered. 'This will be the place where I shall come when I need to know that he is still close to me.'

She was nearly sixty years old, and when Shasa studied her with compassion, he saw that for the first time she truly looked that old. She was letting the grey grow out in the thick bush of her hair and he saw that soon there would be more of it than the black. Grief had dulled her gaze and weighed down the corners of her mouth, and that clear youthful skin which she so carefully cherished, seemed overnight to have seamed and puckered.

'Do it for me, please Shasa,' she said, and handed him the urn.

Shasa opened it and stepped out of the lee of the rock, into the full force of the south-easter. The wind fluttered his shirt like a trapped bird, and he turned to look back at her.

Centaine nodded encouragement, and he held the urn high and upended it. The ashes streamed away like dust in the wind, and when the urn was empty, Shasa turned to her once more.

'Break it!' she commanded, and he hurled the vessel

against the rock face. It shattered, and she gasped and swayed on her feet.

Shasa ran to her and held her in his arms.

'Death is the only adversary I know I shall never overcome. Perhaps that is why I hate it so,' she whispered.

He led her to her seat on the rock and they were silent for a long while, staring out over the wind-speckled Atlantic, and then Centaine said, 'I know you have been protecting me. Now tell me about Tara. What was her part in this?'

So he told her, and when he finished Centaine said, 'You have made yourself an accessory to murder. Was it worth it?'

'Yes. I think so,' he answered without hesitation. 'Could any of us have survived her trial if I had allowed her to be arrested and charged?'

'Will there be consequences?'

Shasa shook his head. 'Manfred – he will protect us again. Just as he did with Sean.'

Shasa saw her pain at the mention of Sean's name. Like him she had never recovered from it, but now she said quietly, 'Sean was one thing, but this is murder and treason and attempting to assassinate a head of state. It is fostering bloody revolution and attempting by force to overthrow a government. Can Manfred protect us from that? And if he can, why should he?'

'I don't know the answers to that, Mater.' Shasa looked at her searchingly. 'I thought that perhaps you did.'

'What do you mean?' she asked, and he thought that he might have taken her unawares, for there was fear and confusion in her eyes for an instant. Blaine's death had slowed her and weakened her. Before that, she would never have betrayed herself so readily.

'In protecting us, me in particular, Manfred is protecting himself and his political ambitions,' Shasa reasoned it out carefully. 'For if I am destroyed, then – I am his *protégé* –

his own career would be blighted. But there is more than that. More than I can fathom.'

Centaine did not reply, but she turned her head away and looked out to sea.

'It's as though Manfred De La Rey feels some strange loyalty to us, or a debt that he must repay – or even a sense of deep guilt towards our family. Is that possible, Mater? Is there something that I do not know of that would put him under an obligation to us? Have you withheld something from me all these years?'

He watched her struggle with herself, and at one moment it seemed she might burst out with some long-hidden truth, or with a terrible secret that she had carried too long alone. Then he saw her expression firm and it was almost possible to watch the strength and force which had been drained from her since Blaine's death flow back into her.

It was a little miracle. Age seemed to fall away from her. Her eyes brightened and her carriage of head and shoulders was once more erect and perky. Even the lines and creases around her eyes and mouth seemed to smooth away.

'Whatever gave you that idea?' she asked crisply, and stood up. 'I've been moping and pining far too long. Blaine would never have approved of that.' She took Shasa's arm. 'Come along. I've still got a life to live and work to do.'

Halfway down the hill, she asked suddenly, 'When does the trial of Moses Gama begin?'

'The tenth of next month.'

'Do you know he once worked for us, this Moses Gama?'

'Yes, Mater. I remembered him. That was how I was able to stop him.'

'He was a terrible troublemaker even in those days. We must do all we can to ensure that he pays the extreme penalty. That is the least we can do for Blaine's memory.'

'I don't understand why you are saddling me with this little scrubber,' Desmond Blake protested acidly. He had been twenty-two years on the newspaper and before the gin bottle had taken over he had been the best courtroom and political journalist on the staff of the *Golden City Mail*. The quantities of gin which he absorbed had not only placed a ceiling on his career but had greyed and prematurely lined his face, ruined his liver and soured his disposition without, however, clouding his insight into the criminal mind nor spoiling his political acumen.

'Well, he is a bright lad,' his editor explained reasonably.

'This is the biggest, most sensational trial of our century,' Desmond Blake said, 'and you want me to drag a cub reporter with me, a puking infant who couldn't even cover a local flower show or a mayoral tea party.'

'I think he has a lot of potential – I just want you to take him in hand and show him the ropes.'

'Bullshit!' said Desmond Blake. 'Now tell me the real reason.'

'All right.' The editor showed his exasperation. 'The real reason is that his grandmother is Centaine Courtney and his father is Shasa Courtney, and Courtney Mining and Finance have acquired thirty-five per cent of the shareholding of our parent company over the past months, and if you know nothing else you should know that nobody bucks Centaine Courtney, not if they want to remain in business. Now take the kid with you and stop bitching. I haven't got time to argue any more – I've got a paper to get out.'

Desmond Blake threw up both hands in despair, and as he rose to leave the office his editor added one last unsubtle threat.

'Just look at it this way. Des. It will be good job insurance, especially for an ageing newshound who needs the price of a bottle of gin a day. Just think of the kid as the boss's son.'

Desmond wandered lugubriously down the length of the city room. He knew the boy by sight. Somebody had pointed him out as a sprig of the Courtney empire and wondered aloud what the hell he was doing here instead of on the polo field.

Desmond stopped beside the corner desk which Michael was sharing with two other juniors.

'Your name is Michael Courtney?' he asked, and the boy leapt to his feet.

'Yes, sir.' Michael was overcome at being directly addressed by somebody who had his own column and by-line.

'Shit!' said Desmond bitterly. 'Nothing is more depressing than the shining face of youth and enthusiasm. Come along, boy.'

'Where are we going?' Michael snatched up his jacket eagerly.

'To the George, boy. I need a double to give me the strength to go through with this little lark.'

At the bar of the George, he studied Michael over the rim of his glass.

'Your first lesson, boy—' He took a swallow of gin and tonic. 'Nothing is ever what it seems to be. Nobody is ever what he says he is. Engrave that on your heart. Your second lesson. Stick to your orange juice. They don't call this stuff mother's ruin for nothing. Your third lesson. Always pay for the drinks with a smile.' He took another swig. 'So you are from Cape Town, are you? Well that's just fine, because that is where we are going, you and me. We are going to see a man condemned to die.'

Vicky Gama took the bus from Baragwanath Hospital to Drake's Farm. It went only as far as the administration building and the new government school. She had to walk the last mile through the narrow dusty lanes between the rows of raw brick cottages. She walked slowly, for although her pregnancy was only four months advanced she was beginning to tire easily.

Hendrick Tabaka was in the crowded general dealer's shop, watching the tills, but he came to Vicky immediately and she greeted him with the respect due to her husband's eldest brother. He led her through to his office, and called for one of his sons to bring her a comfortable chair.

Vicky recognized Raleigh Tabaka, and smiled at him as he placed her chair. 'You have grown into a fine young man, Raleigh. Have you finished your schooling now?'

'*Yebo, sissie.*' Raleigh returned her greeting with polite reserve, for even though she was the wife of his uncle, she was a Zulu. His father had taught him to distrust all Zulus. 'I help my father now, *sissie*. I learn the business from him and soon I will manage one of the shops on my own.'

Hendrick Tabaka smiled proudly at his favourite son. 'He learns fast, and I have great faith in the boy.' He endorsed what Raleigh had said. 'I am sending him soon to our shop at Sharpeville near Vereeniging to learn the bakery business.'

'Where is your twin brother, Wellington?' Vicky asked, and immediately Hendrick Tabaka frowned heavily and waved at Raleigh to leave the office. As soon as they were alone, he answered her question angrily. 'The white priests have captured Wellington's heart. They have seduced him from the gods of his tribe and his ancestors and taken him to the service of the white man's God. This strange Jesus God with three heads. It grieves me deeply, for I had hoped that Wellington, like Raleigh, would be the son of my old age. Now he studies to be a priest, and I have lost him.'

He sat down at the tiny cluttered table that served him

as a desk and studied his own hands for a moment. Then he raised that bald cannonball head, the scalp criss-crossed with ridged scars from old battles.

'So, wife of my brother, we live in a time of great sorrow. Moses Gama has been taken by the white men's police, and we cannot doubt what they will do with him. Even in my sorrow, I must recall that I warned him that this would happen. A wise man does not throw stones at the sleeping lion.'

'Moses Gama did what he knew was his duty. He lived out the deed for which he was born,' Vicky said quietly. 'He struck a blow for all of us – you and me and our children.' She touched her belly where beneath the white nurse's uniform the first bulge of her pregnancy showed. 'And now he needs our help.'

'Tell me how I can help.' Hendrick inclined his head. 'For he was not only my brother, but my chief as well.'

'We need money to hire a lawyer to defend him in the white man's court. I have been to see Marcus Archer and the others of the ANC at the house in Rivonia. They will not help us. They say that Moses acted without their agreement or approval. They say that it was agreed not to endanger human life. They say that if they give us money to help in the defence, the police will trace it to them. They say many other things – everything but the truth.'

'What is the truth, my sister?' Hendrick asked.

And suddenly Vicky's voice was quivering with fury. 'The truth is that they hate him. The truth is that they are afraid of him. The truth is that they are jealous of him. Moses has done what none of them would have dared. He has aimed a spear at the heart of the white tyrant, and though the blow failed, now all the world knows that it was struck. Not only in this land, but beyond the sea, all the world knows now who is the leader of our people.'

'That is true,' Hendrick nodded. 'His name is on every man's lips.'

'We must save him, Hendrick my brother. We must do everything we can to save him.'

Hendrick rose and went to the small cupboard in the corner. He dragged it aside to reveal the door of an ancient Chatwood safe built into the wall behind it.

When he opened the green steel door, the safe was packed with wads of banknotes.

'This belongs to Moses. It is his share. Take what you need,' said Hendrick Tabaka.

The Supreme Court of the Cape Province of South Africa stands on one side of the gardens that Jan van Riebeeck, the first Governor of the Cape, laid out in the 1650s to provision the ships of the Dutch East India Company. On the opposite side of the beautiful gardens stand the Houses of Parliament that Moses Gama had attempted to destroy. So he was to be tried within a quarter of a mile of the scene of the crime of which he stood accused.

The case aroused the most intense international interest and the film crews and journalists began flying into Cape Town a week before it was set down to commence.

Vicky Gama arrived by train after the thousand-mile journey down the continent from the Witwatersrand. She travelled with the white lawyer who would defend Moses and more than fifty of the more radical members of the African National Congress, most of them, like herself, under thirty years of age, and many of them secret members of Moses Gama's *Umkhonto we Sizwe* military wing of the party. Amongst these was Vicky's half-brother, Joseph Dinizulu, now a young man of almost twenty-one studying to be a lawyer at the black university of Fort Hare. The money given to Vicky by Hendrick Tabaka paid for all of them.

Molly Broadhurst met them at the Cape Town station. Vicky, Joseph and the defence lawyer would be staying at her home in Pinelands during the trial, and she had arranged accommodation for all the others in the black townships of Langa and Guguletu.

Desmond Blake and Michael Courtney flew down together from Johannesburg on the commercial flight, and while Desmond put a severe strain on the bar service Michael pored over the notebook in which he was roughing out a schedule of all the research into the history of the ANC and the background of Moses Gama and his tribe that he felt they would need.

Centaine Courtney-Malcomess was at the airport to meet the flight. Much to Michael's embarrassment, she had two servants to carry Michael's single valise out to the daffodil-yellow Daimler that, as usual, she was driving herself. Since Tara had left, Centaine had once more taken over the running of Weltevreden.

'The paper has booked rooms for us at the Atlantic Hotel, Nana,' Michael protested, after he had dutifully embraced his grandmother. 'It's very convenient for the law courts and the national library.'

'Nonsense,' said Centaine firmly. 'The Atlantic is a bug-run and Weltevreden is your home.'

'Father said I wouldn't be welcome back.'

'Your father has missed you even more than I have.'

Shasa sat Michael beside him at dinner, and even Isabella was almost totally excluded from their conversation. Shasa was so impressed by his youngest son's sudden new maturity that the following morning he instructed his broker to purchase another hundred thousand shares in the holding company that owned the *Golden City Mail*.

Manfred and Heidi dined at Weltevreden the evening before the trial began and while they drank pre-prandial cocktails Manfred expressed the concern that Shasa and Centaine shared.

'What the prosecution and the court must avoid is allowing the proceedings to deteriorate into a trial not of a murderer and a terrorist, but of our social system and our way of life. The vultures of the international press are already assembled eager to show us in the worst possible light, and as usual to distort and misrepresent our policy of *apartheid*. I only wish we had some control over the courts and the press.'

'You know I can't agree with you on that one.' Shasa shifted in his chair. 'The complete independence of our press and the impartiality of our judicial system gives us credibility in the eyes of the rest of the world.'

'Don't lecture me. I am a lawyer,' Manfred pointed out stiffly.

It was strange how despite their enforced and mutually beneficial relationship, they were never truly friends and antagonism was always ready to surface between them. Now it took some little time for the tension to ease, and for them to adopt once more an outward show of cordiality. Only then could Manfred tell Shasa, 'We have finally agreed with the prosecution not to raise in court the matter of your wife's involvement with the accused. Apart from the difficulty of beginning extradition proceedings with Britain – she would almost certainly ask for political asylum – there is the consideration of her relationship with Gama. Black man and white woman—' Manfred's expression was one of deep disgust. 'It is repugnant to all decent principles. Raising the subject would not further the prosecution, but would simply give the yellow press something more to drool over. No, it will do none of us any good at all.' Manfred put special emphasis on this last sentence. It was all that needed to be said, but Shasa did not let it pass.

'I owe you a great deal – for my son, Sean, and now my wife.'

'*Ja*, you owe me a great deal,' Manfred nodded. 'Perhaps I will ask you for something in return one day.'

'I hope so,' said Shasa. 'I do not like having outstanding debts.'

Outside the Supreme Court both pavements were filled with people. They were standing shoulder to shoulder and overflowing into the street, complicating the efforts of the traffic wardens and impeding the flow of traffic until it was reduced to a crawl.

A newspaper poster, GUY FAWKES KILLER TRIAL BEGINS TODAY, hung drunkenly from one of the lampposts until it was knocked down by the push of the crowd and trodden underfoot.

The throng was thickest at the colonnaded entrance to the Supreme Court and each time one of the players in the drama arrived the journalists and photographers surged forward. The State Prosecutor smiled and waved to them like a film star, but most of the others, intimidated by the crowds and the exploding flash bulbs and shouted questions, scurried for the entrance and the protection of the police guards.

Only minutes before the court was due to go into session, a chartered bus turned into the slow-moving stream of traffic and came down towards the entrance. The sound of singing grew louder as it approached, the lovely haunting chorus of African voices rising and sinking and weaving the intricate tapestry of sound that thrilled the ears and raised the gooseflesh on the skins of the listeners.

When the bus finally halted in front of the Supreme Court, a young Zulu woman stepped down into the street. She wore a flowing caftan of green and yellow and black, the colours of the African National Congress, and her head was bound in a turban of the same colours.

Her pregnancy had given Vicky a fullness of body that enhanced her natural fine looks. There was no trace left of the shy little country girl. She carried her head high, and moved with all the confidence and style of an African Evita.

The press camera men recognized instantly that they were being presented with an unusual opportunity and they rushed forward with their equipment to capture her dark beauty, and the sound of her voice as she sang the thrilling hymn to freedom.

'*Nkosi Sikelel' iAfrika* – God Save Africa.'

Behind her, holding hands, and singing, came all the others, some of them white like Molly Broadhurst and some of them Indians and coloured like Miriam and Ben Afrika, but most of them pure African. They streamed up the steps into the courthouse to fill the section of the gallery of the courtroom reserved for non-whites and to overflow into the corridors outside.

The rest of the court was packed with the press and the curious, while a separate section had been set aside for observers from the diplomatic corps. Every one of the embassies was represented.

At every entrance to the court were police guards wearing sidearms, and four policemen of warrant officer rank were drawn up around the dock. The prisoner was a killer and a dangerous revolutionary. They were taking no chances.

Yet when he stepped up into the dock, Moses Gama seemed none of these things. He had lost weight during his imprisonment, but this merely enhanced his great height and the wide angularity of his shoulders. His cheeks were hollow, and the bones of his face and forehead were more prominent, but he stood proudly as ever with his chin up and that dark messianic glow in his eyes.

His presence was so overpowering that he seemed to take possession of the room; the gasp and hum of curiosity as he stood before them was subdued by an almost tangible sense of awe. In the back of the gallery Vicky Dinizulu sprang to her feet and began to sing, and those around her came in with the chorus. As he listened to her beautiful ringing voice, Moses Gama inclined his head slightly, but he did not smile or give any other sign of recognition.

Vicky's freedom song was interrupted by a cry of '*Stilte in die hof! Opstaan!* Silence in the court! Stand up!'

The Judge-President of the Cape, wearing the scarlet robes which indicated that this was a criminal trial, took his seat on the bench beneath the carved canopy.

Justice André Villiers was a big man with a flamboyant courtroom style. He had a reputation for being a connoisseur of food, good wine and pretty girls. He was also noted for handing down savage sentences for crimes of violence.

Now he slumped massively on the bench and glowered around his court as the charge sheet was read, but his gaze checked momentarily as it reached each female, the length of the pause proportional to the prettiness of the recipient. On Kitty Godolphin he spent at least two seconds and when she smiled her angelic little-girl smile at him, he hooded his eyes slightly before passing on.

There were four main charges on the sheet against Moses Gama, two of attempted murder, and one each of high treason and murder. Every one of these was a capital offence but Moses Gama showed no emotion as he listened to them read out.

Judge Villiers broke the expectant silence that followed the reading. 'How do you plead to these charges?'

Moses leaned forward, both clenched fists on the rail of the dock and his voice was low and full of scorn, but it carried to every corner of the crowded court.

'Verwoerd and his brutal government should be in this dock,' he said. 'I plead not guilty.'

Moses sat down and did not raise his eyes while the judge enquired who appeared for the crown, and the prosecutor introduced himself to the court, but when Mr Justice Villiers asked:

'Who appears for the defence?' before the advocate whom Vicky and Hendrick Tabaka had retained could reply, Moses sprang to his feet again.

'I do,' he cried. 'I am on trial here for the aspirations of the African people. No other can speak for me. I am the leader of my people, I will answer for myself and for them.'

There was such consternation in the court now, such uproar that for a few moments the judge pounded his gavel in vain, demanding silence, and when it was at last obtained, he threatened them.

'If there is another such demonstration of contempt for this court, I will not hesitate to have it cleared.'

He turned back to Moses Gama to reason with him and try to persuade him to accept legal representation, but Moses forestalled him.

'I wish to move immediately that you, Judge Villiers, recuse yourself from this case,' he challenged, and the scarlet-robed judge blinked and was for a moment stunned into silence.

Then he smiled grimly at the prisoner's effrontery and asked, 'On what grounds do you make this application?'

'On the grounds that you, as a white judge, are incapable of being impartial and fair to me, a black man, forced to submit to the immoral laws of a parliament in which I have no representation.'

The judge shook his head, half in exasperation and half in admiration. 'I am going to deny your application for recusal,' he said. 'And I am going to urge you to accept the very able services of the counsel who has been appointed to represent you.'

'I accept neither his services, nor the competence of this court to condemn me. For all the world knows that is what you propose. I accept only the verdict of my poor enslaved people and of the free nations out there. Let them and history decide my innocence or guilt.'

The press were electrified, some of them so enchanted that they made no effort to write down his words. None of them would ever forget them. For Michael Courtney sitting in the back row of the press section, it was a revelation. He had lived with Africans all his life, his family employed them by the tens of thousands, but until this moment he had never met a black man of such dignity and awe-inspiring presence.

Judge Villiers sagged down in his seat. He always maintained his place firmly in the centre-stage of his court, overshadowing everybody in it with the ruthless authority of a born actor. Here he sensed he had met an equal. The entire attention of everybody in the court was captivated by Moses Gama.

'Very well,' Judge Villiers said at last. 'Mr Prosecutor, you may proceed to present the case for the crown.'

The prosecutor was a master of his profession and he had an infallible case. He worked it up with meticulous attention to detail, with logic and with skill.

One at a time he submitted his exhibits to the court. The wiring and the electrical detonator, the Tokarev pistol and spare magazines. Although it was considered too dangerous to allow the blocks of plastic explosives and the detonators into the courtroom, photographs were submitted and accepted. The altar chest was too large to bring into court, and again photographs were accepted by Judge Villiers. Then there were the gruesome photographs of Shasa's office, with Blaine's covered body against the bookcases and his blood splashed over the carpet, and the wreckage of broken furniture and scattered papers. Centaine turned her face away as the photographs were handed in and Shasa squeezed her arm and tried to shield her from the curious glances.

After all the exhibits had been tabled, the prosecutor

called his first witness. 'I call the Honourable Minister of Mines and Industry, Mr Shasa Courtney.'

Shasa was on the witness stand for the rest of that day and all of the following morning, describing in detail how he had discovered and thwarted the bombing.

The prosecutor took him back to his first childhood meeting with Moses Gama, and as Shasa described their relationship, Moses raised his head and for the first time since he had taken the stand looked directly into Shasa's face. In vain Shasa searched for the slightest trace of that sympathy they had once shared, but there was none. Moses Gama's stare was baleful and unwavering.

When at last the prosecutor had finished with Shasa, he turned to the accused. 'Your witness,' he said, and Justice Villiers roused himself.

'Do you wish to cross-examine the witness?'

Moses shook his head and looked away, but the judge insisted. 'This will be your last opportunity to query or refute the witness's evidence. I urge you to make full use of it.'

Moses crossed his arms over his chest, and closed his eyes as though in sleep, and from the non-white section of the court there were hoots of laughter and the stamping of feet.

Justice Villiers raised his voice, 'I will not warn you again,' and there was silence in the face of his anger.

Over the next four days the prosecutor placed his witnesses on the stand.

Tricia, Shasa's secretary, explained how Moses had gained entrance to the office suite in the guise of a chauffeur and how on the day of the murder Moses had seized and bound her. How she had watched him fire the fatal shot that killed Colonel Malcomess.

'Do you wish to cross-examine the witness?' Judge Villiers asked, and once again Moses shook his head.

Manfred De La Rey gave his evidence and described how he had found Moses Gama with the pistol in his hand and Blaine Malcomess lying on the floor dying. How he had heard him cry, 'You! You!' and saw him deliberately fire the pistol at Shasa Courtney.

'Do you wish to cross-examine the witness?' the judge asked, and this time Moses did not even look up.

An electrical engineer described the captured equipment and identified the transmitter as being of Russian origin. An explosives expert told the court of the destructive power of the plastic explosives placed beneath the Government benches.

'In my opinion it would have been sufficient to destroy totally the entire chamber and the adjoining rooms. It would certainly have killed every person in the main chamber, and most of those in the lobby and the surrounding offices.'

After each witness had finished his evidence Moses again refused to cross-examine. At the end of the fourth day the crown had presented its case, and Judge Villiers adjourned the court with one last appeal to the prisoner.

'When the court reconvenes on Monday, you will be required to answer the charges against you. I must once more impress upon you the grave nature of the accusations, and point out to you that your very life is at stake. Yet again I urge you to accept the services of legal counsel.'

Moses Gama smiled at him with contempt.

Dinner at Weltevreden that evening was a sombre affair. The only one who was unaffected by the day's events was Garry, who had flown down in the Mosquito from the Silver River Mine for the weekend.

While the rest of the family sat in silence, each of them brooding on the events of these last days and their own particular part in them, Garry was enthusiastically selling to Centaine and Shasa his latest plan for reducing costs at the mine.

'Accidents cost us money in lost production. I'll admit that in the last two years our safety record has been about average for the industry as a whole, but if we could cut down our fatalities to one per hundred thousand shifts or better, we could reduce our overall production costs by over twelve per cent. That is twenty million pounds a year. On top of that we would get the added bonus of worker satisfaction and cooperation. I have put all the figures through the computer.' Garry's eyes behind his spectacles glittered as he mentioned that piece of equipment. Shasa had reports from Dave Abrahams and the general manager of the Silver River that Garry sometimes sat all night at one of the terminals of the new IBM computer that the company had at last installed.

'The lad knows his way around the machine as well, if not better, than any of our full-time operators. He can almost make it sit up and whistle "God Save the Queen".' David Abrahams had not attempted to conceal his admiration and Shasa had remarked deprecatingly, to conceal his paternal pride, 'That will be a redundant accomplishment by next year, when we become a republic.'

'Oh, Garry, you are being an utter bore,' Isabella interrupted him at last. 'All that business about tonnages and pennyweights – at the dinner table, what's more. No wonder you can't find a girlfriend.'

'For once I think Bella is right,' Centaine said quietly from the end of the table. 'That's enough for one night, Garry. I just cannot concentrate at the moment. I think this has been one of the worst weeks of my entire life, having to watch that monster, with Blaine's blood on his hands, sitting there defying us and making a mockery of our system of justice. He threatens to tear down the whole structure of government, to plunge us all into anarchy and the same savagery of Africa which rent the land before we whites arrived. Then he smirks at us from the dock. I hate him. I have never hated anything or anybody as much as I hate him. I pray each night that they hang him.'

Unexpectedly it was Michael who replied. 'Yes, we hate him, Nana. We hate him because we are afraid of him, and we are afraid of him because we do not understand him or his people.'

They all stared at him in astonishment.

'Of course we understand him,' Centaine said. 'We have lived in Africa all our lives. We understand them as nobody else does.'

'I don't think so, Nana. I think if we had truly understood and listened to what this man had to say, Blaine would be alive today. I think he could have been an ally and not our deadly enemy. I think Moses Gama could have been a useful and highly respected citizen, and not a prisoner on trial for his life.'

'What strange ideas you have picked up on that newspaper of yours! He murdered your grandfather,' Centaine said, and shot a glance down the table at Shasa. Shasa interpreted it fluently and it meant, 'We have another problem on our hands here,' but Michael was going on obliviously.

'Moses Gama will die on the gallows – I think we all know that. But his words and his ideas will live on. I know now why I had to be a journalist. I know what I have to do. I have to explain those ideas to the people of this land, to show them that they are just and fair, and not dangerous at all. In those ideas are the hopes for our survival as a nation.'

'It is a good thing I sent the servants out,' Centaine interrupted him. 'I never thought to hear words like those spoken in the dining-room of Weltevreden.'

Vicky Gama waited for over an hour in the visitors' room at Roeland Street prison while the warders examined the contents of the package she had brought for Moses and made up their minds whether or not to allow her to hand it to the prisoner.

'It is only clothing,' Vicky pointed out reasonably.

'These aren't ordinary clothes,' the senior warden protested.

'They are the traditional robes of my husband's tribe. He is entitled to wear them.'

In the end the prison governor was called in to arbitrate and when he finally gave his permission, Vicky complained, 'Your men have been deliberately rude and obstructive to me.'

He smiled at her sarcastically. 'I wonder how you will treat us, madam, if you and your brothers in the ANC ever seize power. I wonder if you will allow us even the courtesy of a trial or whether you will slaughter us in the streets, as your husband tried to do.'

When Vicky was at last allowed to hand the parcel to Moses under the watchful eye of four warders, he asked her, 'Whose idea was this?'

'It was mine but Hendrick paid for the skins and his wives sewed them.'

'You are a clever woman,' Moses commended her, 'and a dutiful wife.'

'You, my lord, are a great chief, and it is fitting that you should wear the robes of your office.'

Moses held up the full-length cloak of leopard skins, heavy and glossy golden, studded with the sable rosettes.

'You have understood,' he nodded. 'You have seen the necessity of using the white man's courtroom as a stage from which to shout our craving for freedom to the world.'

Vicky lowered her eyes and her voice. 'My lord, you must not die. If you die, then the great part of our dream of

583

freedom dies with you. Will you not defend yourself, for my sake and for the sake of our people?'

'No, I will not die,' he assured her. 'The great nations of the world will not let that happen. Britain has already made her position clear and America cannot afford to let them execute me. Her own nation is racked by the struggle of the American coloured people – she cannot afford to let me go to my death.'

'I do not trust the altruism of great nations,' Vicky said softly.

'Then trust in their own self-interest,' Moses Gama told her. 'And trust in me.'

When Moses Gama rose before the court in the golden and black robes of leopard skin, he seemed a reincarnation of one of the ancient black kings. He riveted them.

'I call no witnesses,' Gama told them gravely. 'All I will do is to make a statement from the dock. That is as far as I am prepared to co-operate in this mockery of justice.'

'My lord,' the prosecutor was on his feet immediately. 'I must point out to the court—'

'Thank you!' Judge Villiers interrupted him in frigid tones. 'I do not need to be told how to conduct this trial,' and the prosecutor sank back into his seat, still making inarticulate sounds of protest.

Heavily the scarlet-robed justice turned his attention back to Moses Gama.

'What counsel for the prosecution is trying to tell me is that I should make it clear to you that if you do not enter the witness stand and take the oath, if you do not submit to cross-examination, then what you have to say will have little relevance to the proceedings.'

'An oath to your white man's God, in this courtroom

with a white judge and a white prosecutor, with white prosecution witnesses and white policemen at the doors. I do not deign to submit to that kind of justice.'

Judge Villiers shook his head with a woeful expression and turned both his hands palms up. 'Very well, you have been warned of the consequences. Proceed with your statement.'

Moses Gama was silent for a long time, and then he began softly.

'There was once a small boy who wandered with joy through a beautiful land, who drank from the sweet clear rivers, who listened with pleasure to the song of the bird and studied the antics of the springbok and pangolin and all the marvellous wild things, a small boy who tended his father's herds, and sat at night by the fire and listened to the tales of the great heroes of his people, of Bambata and Sekhukhuni and mighty Chaka.

'This boy believed himself to be one of a peaceful people who owned the land on which they lived and were free to move wherever they wished in confidence and joy. Then one day when the boy was nine years of age a curious being came to the kraal at which the boy lived, a creature with a red face and a lordly manner, and the boy saw that the people were afraid, even his father and his grandfather who were chieftains of the tribe, were afraid as the boy had never seen them afraid before.'

There was no sound nor movement in the crowded courtroom as Moses Gama described his loss of innocence and how he had learned the bitter truths of his existence. He described his bewilderment as the universe he knew was proved an illusion. He told them of his first journey into the outside world, where he learned that as a man with a black skin there were places where his existence was circumscribed and limited.

When he went to the white man's towns, he found that he could not walk the streets after curfew without a pass, that he could not live outside the areas that had been set aside for his people on the outskirts of that town, but most important to him he found that he could not attend the white man's schools. He learned that in nearly every public building there was a separate entrance for him to use, that there were skills he was not allowed to acquire, and that in almost every way he was considered different and inferior, condemned by the pigmentation of his skin always to remain on the bottom rung of existence.

Yet he knew that he was a man like other men, with the same hopes and desires. He knew that his heart beat as fiercely and that his body was as strong, and his brain was as bright and quick as any other. He decided that the way to rise above the station in life that had been allotted him was to use that brain rather than employ his body like a beast of burden as most of his people were forced to do.

He turned to the white man's books and was astonished to find that the heroes of his people were described as savages and cattle-thieves and treacherous rebels. That even the most sympathetic and charitable of the authors he read referred to his people as children, unable to reason or think for themselves, children who must be sternly protected but prevented from taking part in the decisions which governed their lives.

He described to them how at last he had realized that it was all some monstrous lie. That he was not different, that because his skin was black he was not unclean or contaminated or childlike. He knew then for what purpose he had been put upon this earth.

'I came to know that the struggle against injustice was my life,' he said simply. 'I knew that I had to make the white men who ruled me and my people understand.'

He explained how each of his attempts to get the white men to listen had failed. How all his people's efforts had resulted only in more savage and draconian laws, in fiercer oppressions.

'In the end I had to accept that there was only one course left to me. That was to take up arms and to strike at the head of the serpent whose venom was poisoning and destroying my people.'

He was silent and his audience who had listened in complete and rigid silence for most of the morning, sighed and stirred, but as soon as Moses Gama spread his arms they were completely attentive once more.

'Every man has a right and a sacred duty to protect his family and his nation from the tyrant, to fight against injustice and slavery. When he does so he becomes a warrior and not a criminal. I challenge this judge and this white man's court to treat me as a soldier and a prisoner of war. For that is what I am.'

Moses Gama drew his leopard skins about him and sat down, leaving them all shaken and silenced.

Judge Villiers had sat through the entire address with his chin couched in his hand, his eyes hooded with concentration, but now he let his hand drop and he leaned forward to glower at the prisoner.

'You claim to be the leader of your people.'

'I do,' Moses replied.

'A leader is chosen or elected. How were you chosen?'

'When an oppressed people has no voice, then their leaders come forward of their own accord to speak for them,' Moses told him.

'So you are a self-proclaimed leader,' the judge said quietly. 'And your decision to declare war on our society was taken alone. Is that correct?'

'We are involved in a colonial war of liberation,' Moses Gama replied. 'Like our brothers in Algeria and Kenya.'

'You approved of the methods of the Mau Mau, then?' Judge Villiers asked.

'Their cause was just – their methods, whatever they might have been, were therefore just.'

'The end justifies the means – any means?'

'The struggle for liberation is all, in the name of liberty any deed is sanctified.'

'The slaughter and multiation of innocents, of women and children. These are also justified?'

'If one innocent should die that a thousand might go free, then it is justified.'

'Tell me, Moses Gama, do you believe in democracy – in the concept of "One man, one vote"?'

'I believe that every man should have one vote to elect the leaders of the nation.'

'And after the leaders are chosen, what should happen?'

'I believe that the people should submit to the wisdom of their chosen leaders.'

'A one-party state – with a president for life?'

'That is the African way,' Moses Gama agreed.

'It is also the way of the Marxists,' Judge Villiers observed drily. 'Tell me, Moses Gama, what makes a black totalitarian government superior to a white totalitarian government?'

'The wishes of the majority of the people.'

'And the sanction of your people, of which only you are aware, makes you a holy crusader – above the laws of civilized man?'

'In this land there are no such laws, for the men who make the laws are barbarians,' said Moses Gama softly, and Judge Villiers had no more questions to put to him.

Twenty-four hours later Mr Justice André Villiers delivered his judgement to a hushed and expectant court.

'The basis of the case brought by the crown against the accused rests upon the consideration of how an individual reacts to what he perceives as an injustice. It raises the question of the individual's right or duty to resist those laws which he considers unjust or evil. I have had to consider what loyalty a person owes to a government which was elected by a process from which he was totally excluded, a government which has furthermore embarked upon a programme of legislation that will deliberately alienate that person from most of the major rights, privileges and benefits of the society of which he is a member—' For almost an hour Judge Villiers enlarged on and examined this proposition, then he summed up. 'I have therefore reached the conclusion that no duty of loyalty exists towards a state in which the individual is denied the basic democratic right of representation. Accordingly, on the charge of high treason I find the accused not guilty.'

There was a throaty roar from the body of the court and in the non-white section of the gallery they were dancing and singing. For almost a full minute Judge Villiers watched them, and those members of the court who knew him well were amazed by his forbearance. But the judge's features were crumpled with an unusual compassion and terrible sadness as he took up his gavel to quieten them.

In the silence he spoke again. 'I come now to the other charges against the accused. Those of murder and attempted murder. The crown has, with the help of the most eminent and trustworthy witnesses, made out a case which the accused has not attempted to challenge. I accept that the accused placed a large body of explosive in the assembly chamber of the South African parliament with the intention of detonating that charge during a speech by the Prime Minister and thereby inflicting the greatest possible damage and death. I accept also that when his plot was discovered, he slew Colonel Blaine Malcomess and immediately thereafter attempted to murder Minister Courtney.' The judge paused and turned his head towards Moses Gama, who sat impassively in the dock, still wearing his leopard-skin robes of chieftainship.

'The accused has offered the defence that he is a soldier

in a war of liberation and is therefore not subject to the civil law. While I have already expressed my sympathy for and understanding of the accused's aspirations and those of the black people whom he claims to represent, I cannot entertain his demand that he be treated as a prisoner of war. He is a private individual who, while fully aware of the consequences of his actions, set out on the dark road of violence, determined to inflict the greatest possible destruction in the most indiscriminate fashion. It is therefore without any hesitation whatsoever that I find the accused guilty of murder and two charges of attempted murder.'

There was no sound in the courtroom as Judge Villiers went on softly, 'The prisoner will rise for sentence.'

Slowly Moses Gama came to his full height and he regarded Judge Villiers with an imperial stare.

'Is there anything you wish to say before sentence is passed upon you?' the judge asked.

'This is not justice. We both know that – and history will record it so.'

'Is there anything further you wish to say?'

When Moses shook his head, Judge Villiers intoned, 'Having found you guilty on the three main charges, I have carefully considered whether any extenuating circumstances exist in your case – and at last having determined that there are none, I have no alternative but to impose upon you the maximum penalty which the law decrees. On all the remaining charges, taken jointly and severally, I sentence you, Moses Gama, to death by hanging.'

The silence persisted for a moment longer and then from the rear of the court a woman's voice rose in keening ululation, the harrowing wail of African mourning. It was taken up immediately by all the other black women in the courtroom and Judge Villiers made no attempt to silence it.

In the dock Moses Gama raised a clenched fist above his head.

'*Amandla!*' he roared, and his people answered him with a single voice: '*Ngawethu! Mayibuye! Afrika!*'

Manfred De La Rey sat high in the grandstand, in one of the special boxes reserved for the most important spectators. Every single seat in the stand had been sold weeks before and the standing areas around the field were crammed to capacity. This great concourse of humanity had assembled to watch one of the major events of the sporting calendar, the clash between the Western Province and Northern Transvaal rugby football teams. At stake was the Currie Cup, a trophy for which every province of South Africa competed annually in a knock-out tournament. The fanatical partisanship which this contest evoked went far beyond that of mere sporting competition.

Manfred smiled sardonically as he looked around him. The Englishman Macmillan had said that theirs was the first of the African nationalisms. If that was correct, then this was one of their most important tribal rituals, one that united and reaffirmed the Afrikaners as a cohesive entity. No outsider could grasp the significance of the game of rugby football in their culture. True it had been developed at a British public school almost one hundred and fifty years ago, but then, Manfred thought wryly, it was too good for the *rooinekke* and it took an Afrikaner to understand the game and play it to its full potential.

Then again to call it a game was the same as calling politics or war a game. It was more, a thousand times more. To sit here amongst his own, to be a part of this immense spirit of Afrikanerdom, gave him the same sort of religious awe that he felt when he stood within the congregation of the Dutch Reformed Church, or when he was part of the throng that gathered before the massive Voortrekker Monument that stood on the hills above the city of Pretoria. On the day of the Covenant with God, his people gathered there each year to celebrate the victory that the Almighty had given them over the Zulu King Dingaan at the battle of Blood River.

As was fitting on such an occasion as this, Manfred wore his green blazer piped in gold with the flying Springbok emblem on the pocket and the legend 'Boxing 1936' below it. No matter that the buttons could no longer fasten across his dignified girth, he wore it with pride.

His pride was infinitely magnified when he looked down on the field. The turf was seared by the frosts of early winter but the highveld sunlight gave everything a lucid quality so that Manfred could make out every detail of his son's beloved features as he stood out near the centre of the field.

Lothar De La Rey's magnificent torso was not obscured by the blue woollen jersey that he wore, rather it was emphasized by the thin stuff, so that the lean hard muscle in his belly and chest stood proud. His bare legs were sturdy, but at the same time long and shapely, and the cap of close-cropped hair, coppery blond, burned like fire in the bright highveld sunshine.

Slowly Lothar bowed his head, as though to pray, and a hush fell over the packed grandstand. There was no breath of sound from even one of the forty thousand throats, and Lothar's dark brows clenched in complete concentration.

Slowly he lifted his arms, spreading them like the wings of a falcon on the edge of flight, until they were at the level of his shoulders, a strangely graceful gesture, and he raised his body on tiptoe so that the great muscles of his thighs tightened and changed shape – and then he began to run.

He ran with the bounding motion of that hunting cat, the cheetah, lifting his knees high and driving his whole body forward. Behind him the turf was scarred by the power of his studded boots, and in the immense silence of the arena his grunting breaths, timed to the long elastic strides, carried to where Manfred sat.

The leather ball, shiny brown and ovate, was balanced on one point, and as Lothar bore down on where it stood on the green turf, his pace quickened yet his body remained in perfect balance. The kick was a continuation of that long driving stride, his right leg whipped straight at the exact instant that his toe struck the ball and his weight was so far forward that his leg swung on up in an arcing parabola until his foot, with his toe extended like that of a ballet dancer, was high above his head, while both his arms were flung forward to maintain that graceful balance. The ball was grossly deformed by the brutal impact of the kick, but in flight it snapped back into shape, and rose in a flat hard trajectory towards the two tall white goalposts at the end of the field. It neither tumbled nor wobbled, but flew with a stable motion, as steady in the air as a flighted arrow.

However, a hoarse and anxious sigh went up from the watchers, as they realized that it was aimed too far to the right. Although the power of that mighty right leg had driven it high above the level of the cross bar, it was going to miss the goalposts on the right and Manfred came to his feet with forty thousand others and groaned in helpless agony.

A miss would mean ignominious defeat, but if the ball passed between the white uprights, it would be victory, sweet and famous, by a single point.

The ball rose higher still, up out of the sheltered arena, and it caught the wind. Lothar had studied the flags on the roof of the grandstand before he began his run, and now the wind swung the ball in gently, but not enough, oh, sweet God, not nearly enough. Then gradually the ball lost impetus and power as it reached the zenith of its trajectory, and as it slowed, so the wind took charge, curving it ever more sharply to the left, and Manfred's groan turned to a roar of delight as it fell through the very centre of the goalposts, grazing the white cross bar, and the referee's shrill long-drawn-out whistle signalled the end of the match.

Beside Manfred his boyhood friend, Roelf Stander, was pounding his back in congratulation.

'Man, I tell you, he is going to be a Springbok for sure, just like his Pa.'

On the field Lothar was surrounded by his team mates who were fighting for a chance to embrace him, while from the stands a wave of spectators was sweeping across the field to lionize him.

'Come, let's go down to the dressing-room.' Manfred took his companion's arm, but it was not that easy. They were stopped every few paces by the well-wishers and Manfred smiled and shook their hands and accepted their congratulations. Although this was part of his life, and his very soul fed on the adulation and enormous respect which every one of them, even the richest and most famous of them, showed towards him, yet today it irked Manfred to be kept from his son.

When at last they reached the dressing-room, the crowd that filled the corridor outside opened miraculously before them, and where others were turned away, they were respectfully ushered through into the steamy noisy room that stank of sweaty clothing and stale urine and hot masculine bodies.

Lothar was in the centre of the crowd of naked young men, singing and wrestling in rough camaraderie, but when he saw his father he broke away and came to him immediately, dressed only in a pair of grass-stained shorts with his magnificent young body glossy with sweat and a brown beer bottle clutched in one hand. His face was rapturous with pride and the sense of his own achievement.

'My son—' Manfred held out his right hand and Lothar seized it joyously.

'My son—' Manfred repeated, but his voice failed him

and his vision misted over with pride. He jerked his son's hand, pulling him against his own chest, and held him hard, hugging him unashamedly, even while Lothar's sweat stained his shirt and his team mates howled with delight.

The three of them, Manfred, Roelf Stander and Lothar, drove home in the new ministerial Cadillac. They were happy as schoolboys, grinning and joshing each other and singing the bawdy old rugby songs. When they stopped at the traffic lights before entering the main traffic stream at Jan Smuts Drive that would take them the thirty miles across the grassy undulating highveld to Pretoria there were two small black urchins darting and dodging perilously amongst the vehicles, and one of them peered through the side window of the Cadillac at Manfred, grinning cockily and holding up a copy of the *Mail* from the bundle of newspapers he carried under his arm.

Manfred was about to dismiss him with an impatient gesture, for the *Mail* was an English rag. Then he saw the headlines APPEAL FAILS: GUY FAWKES KILLER TO HANG and he rolled down his side window and flipped the child a coin.

He passed the paper to Roelf Stander with the terse command, 'Read it to me!' and drove on.

This morning the appeal of Moses Gama against his conviction for murder and attempted murder by the Cape Division of the Supreme Court was dismissed by a full bench of the Appellate Division in Bloemfontein and the date set for the execution by hanging was confirmed.

'*Ja, goed.*' Although Manfred scowled with concentration as he listened, his relief was intense. Over the months the media and the public had come to accept the Gama case as something intimately linked to Manfred De La Rey. The fact that he had personally made the arrest and that he was Minister of Police had combined so that the prosecution of the case had become, in the public imagination, a measure of the strength and efficiency of the police force and of Manfred's *kragdadigheid*, his own personal power.

More than any other quality the Afrikaner *Volk* demanded strength and determination in its leaders. This case, with its terrifying message of black peril and bloody revolution, had invoked the most intense feelings of insecurity throughout the land. People wanted to be reassured that their safety and the security of the state were in strong hands. Manfred, with his sure political instincts, had realized that the dice of his future were being cast.

Unfortunately, there had been a complication in what should have been a straightforward matter of justice and swift retribution. The fact that the judge of the Supreme Court had dismissed the charge of high treason and had made some controversial and ill-considered remarks about the individual's duty of loyalty to a state in which he was denied direct representation had been taken up by the foreign press and the case had captured the attention of left-wing liberals and Bolsheviks around the Western world. In America the bearded hippies and Commie university students had formed 'Save Moses Gama' committees and had picketed the White House and the South African Embassy in Washington, while even in England there had been demonstrations in Trafalgar Square outside South Africa House by Communist-inspired and financed gangs of black expatriates and some white riff-raff. The British Prime Minister had summoned the South African High Commissioner for consultations and President Eisenhower had instructed his ambassador in Pretoria to call upon Hendrik Verwoerd and appeal for mercy for the condemned man.

The South African government had stood firm in its rejection of these appeals. Their position was that the matter was one for the judiciary and that they would not interfere with the course of justice. However, their lordships of the Appellate Division were occasionally known to indulge in unwise demonstrations of compassion or obscure legal dialectic, in fits of independent thinking which accorded ill with the hard task of the police and the aspirations of the Afrikaner *Volk*.

This time, mercifully, they had been spared one of their lordships' quirky decisions and in that little green-painted room in Pretoria Central Prison the noose now waited for Moses Gama, and he would crash through the trap to the eternity into which he had planned to send the leaders of the nation.

'*Ja, goed!* Now read the editorial!' Manfred ordered Roelf Stander. The *Golden City Mail* was one of the English-language newspapers, and even for that section of the press the views it held were liberal. Manfred would never have bought it for preference, but having done so he was now prepared to dilute his grim satisfaction at the Appeal Court's verdict, with the irritation of listening to the left-wing erudition of the *Mail's* editorial staff.

Roelf Stander rustled the news sheet and cleared his throat.

'"A Martyr is Born",' he read, and Manfred gave a growl of anger.

When Moses Gama dies at the end of the hangman's rope, he will become the most significant martyr in the history of the black African struggle for liberation.

Moses Gama's elevation will not be on account of his moving eloquence nor of the awe-inspiring power of his presence. Rather it will be for the simple reason that he has posed a question so grave and so fateful that by its very nature the answer to it can never be given by a single national court of law. The answer rests instead in the heart of mankind itself. For that question is aimed at the very foundation of man's existence upon this earth. Simply stated, it is this: is a man who is deprived of any peaceful or lawful means of asserting his basic human rights justified in turning, in the last resort, to violence?

Manfred snorted. 'Enough of that. I should not have bothered to have you read it out. It is so predictable. If the black savages cut the throats of our children and ate their raw livers, there would still be those *rooinekke* who would chastize us for not having provided salt for the feast! We will not listen to any more of that. Turn to the sports page. Let us hear what they have to say about Lothie and his *manne*, though I doubt that those *souties* can tell the difference between a stick of biltong and a rugby ball.'

When the Cadillac pulled up the long drive to Manfred's official residence in the elite suburb of Waterkloof there was a large gathering of family and friends at the swimming-pool at the far end of the wide green lawns, and the younger ones came running to meet them and to embrace Lothar as soon as he stepped out of the Cadillac.

'We listened on the radio,' they cried, as they clamoured for a turn to hug and kiss him. 'Oh, Lothie, you were wonderful.' Each of his sisters took one of his arms, while their friends and the Stander girls crowded as close as they could to him as they escorted him down to the pool where the older women waited to congratulate him.

Lothar went to his mother first, and while they embraced Manfred watched them with an indulgent smile of pride. What a fine-looking family he had. Heidi was still a magnificent woman and no man could ask for a more dutiful wife. Not once in all the years had he ever regretted his choice.

'My friends, my family, all my loved ones,' Manfred raised his voice, and they turned to him and fell into silent expectation. Manfred was a compelling speaker, and as a nation they were susceptible to oratory and fine words, for they were constantly exposed to them, from pulpit and political platform, from the cradle to the grave.

'When I look at this young man who is my son, at this fine young South African, and those of our young people like him, then I know that I need not worry for the future of our *Volk*,' Manfred proclaimed in the sonorous tones to which his listeners responded instinctively, and they applauded and cried '*Hoor, hoor!*' each time he paused.

Amongst the listeners there was one at least who was not entirely captivated by his artistry. Although Sarah Stander smiled and nodded, she could feel her stomach churn and her throat burn with the acid of her rejected love.

Sitting in this lovely garden, watching the man she had loved beyond life itself, the man to whom she would have dedicated every moment of her existence, the man to whom she had given her girlish body and the tender blossom of her virginity, the man whose seed she had taken joyously into her womb, she felt that ancient, now rancid passion change its shape and texture to become hard and bitter hatred. She listened to Manfred extolling his wife, and she knew that she should have been that woman, those praises should have been for her alone. She should have been at his side to share his triumphs and his achievements.

She watched Manfred embrace Lothar and with his arm around his shoulders commend his firstborn to them all, smiling with pride as he recited his virtues, and Sarah Stander hated them both, father and son, for Lothar De La Rey was not his firstborn.

She turned her head and saw Jakobus standing on the periphery, shy and self-effacing, but every bit as handsome as the big golden-headed athlete. Jakobus, her own son, had the dark brows and pale topaz-coloured eyes of the De La Reys. If Manfred were not blind, he would see that. Jakobus was as tall as Lothar, but was not possessed of his half-brother's raw-boned frame and layers of rippling muscle. He had an appealing fragility of body, and his features were not so dashingly masculine. Instead, he had the face of a poet, sensitive and gentle.

Sarah's own expression went dreamy and soft as she remembered his conception. She had been little more than a child, but her love had been that of a mature woman, as she crept through the silent old house to the room in which Manfred slept. She had loved him all her life, but in the morning he was leaving, sailing away to a far-off land, to Germany as a member of the Olympic team, and she had been troubled for weeks with a deep premonition of losing him for ever. She had wanted in some way to ensure against that insupportable loss, to try to make certain of his return, so she had given him everything that she had, her heart and her soul and her barely matured body, trusting him to return them to her.

Instead he had met the German woman and had married her. Sarah could still vividly recall the cablegram from Germany that had announced his dreadful betrayal, and her own devastation when she read the fateful words. Part of her had shrivelled and died on that day, part of her soul had been missing ever since.

Manfred De La Rey was still speaking, and he had them laughing now with some silly joke, but he looked towards her and saw that she was serious. Perhaps he read something of her thoughts in her eyes for his own gaze flicked across to where Jakobus stood and then back to her and for an instant she sensed an unusual emotion – regret or guilt – within him.

She wondered not for the first time if he knew about Jakobus. Surely he must at least have suspected it. Her marriage to Roelf had been so hasty, so unheralded, and the birth of Kobus had followed so swiftly. Then the physical resemblance of son to father was so strong, surely Manfred knew it.

Roelf knew, of course. He had loved her without hope

until Manfred rejected her, and he had used her pregnancy to gain her consent. Since then he had been a good and dutiful husband and his love and concern for her had never faltered but he was not Manfred De La Rey. He was not, nor could he ever be, a man as Manfred De La Rey was a man. He had never had Manfred's force and power, his drive and personality and ruthlessness, and she could never love him as she loved Manfred.

'Yes,' she admitted to herself, 'I have always loved Manfred, and I will love him to the end of my life, but my hatred of him is as strong as my love and with time it will grow stronger still. It is all that I have to sustain me.'

Manfred was ending his speech now, talking about Lothar's promotion. Of course, Sarah thought bitterly, his promotion would not have been so rapid if his father had not been the Minister of Police and he had not had such skill with a rugby ball. Her own Kobus could expect no such preferment. Everything he achieved would be with his own talent and by his own efforts. She and Roelf could do little for him. Roelf's influence was minimal, and even the university fees for Jakobus' education were a serious drain on their family finances. She had been forced to face the fact that Roelf would never go much further than he was now. His entry into legal practice had been a mistake and a failure. By the time he had accepted that fact and returned to the academic life as a lecturer in law, he had lost so much seniority that it would be many years, if ever, before he was given the chair of law. No, there was not much they could do to help Kobus – but then, of course, none of the family, not even Kobus himself, knew what he wanted from life. He was a brilliant student, but he totally lacked direction or purpose, and he had always been a secretive lad. It was so difficult to draw him out. Once or twice Sarah had succeeded in doing so, but she had been frightened by the strange and radical views he expressed. Perhaps it was best not to explore her son's mind too deeply, she thought, and smiled across at him just as, at last, Manfred stopped singing his own son's praises.

Jakobus came to her side now. 'Can I get you another orange juice, Mama? Your glass is empty.'

'No, thank you, Kobus. Stay with me for a while. I see so little of you these days.'

The men had charged their beer tankards and led by Manfred trooped towards the barbecue fires on the far side of the pool. Amid laughter and raillery Manfred and Lothar were tying candy-striped aprons around their waists and arming themselves with long-handled forks.

On a side table there was a huge array of platters piled with raw meat, lamb chops and *sosaties* on long skewers, German sausages and great thick steaks, enough to feed an army of starving giants and, Sarah calculated sourly, costing almost her husband's monthly salary.

Since Manfred and his one-armed demented father had mysteriously acquired shares in that fishing company in South West Africa he had become not only famous and powerful, but enormously rich as well. Heidi had a mink coat now and Manfred had purchased a large farm in the rich maize-producing belt of the Orange Free State. It was every Afrikaner's dream to own a farm, and Sarah felt her envy flare as she thought about it. All that should have been hers. She had been deprived of what was rightly hers by that German whore. The word shocked her, but she repeated it silently – whore!

He was mine, whore, and you stole him from me.

Jakobus was talking to her, but she found it difficult to follow what he was saying. Her attention kept stealing back to Manfred De La Rey. Every time his great laugh boomed out she felt her heart contract and she watched him from the corners of her eyes.

Manifred was holding court; even dressed in that silly apron and with a cooking fork in his hand, he was still the focus of all attention and respect. Every few minutes more guests arrived to join the gathering, most of them important and powerful men, but all of them gathered slavishly around Manfred and deferred to him.

'We should understand why he did it,' Jakobus was saying, and Sarah forced herself to concentrate on her son.

'Who did it, dear?' she asked vaguely.

'Mama, you haven't been listening to a word,' Jakobus smiled gently. 'You really are a little scatterbrain sometimes.' Sarah always felt vaguely uncomfortable when he spoke to her in such a familiar fashion, none of her friends' children would show such disrespect.

'I was talking about Moses Gama,' Jakobus went on, and at the mention of that name everybody within earshot turned towards the two of them.

'They are going to hang that black thunder, at last,' somebody said, and everybody agreed immediately.

'Ja, about time.'

'We have to teach them a lesson – you show mercy to a kaffir and he takes it as weakness.'

'Only one thing they understand—'

'I think it will be a mistake to hang him,' Jakobus said clearly, and there was a stunned silence.

'Kobie! Kobie!' Sarah tugged at her son's arm. 'Not now, darling. People don't like that sort of talk.'

'That is because they never hear it – and they don't understand it,' Jakobus explained reasonably, but some of them turned away deliberately while a middle-aged cousin of Manfred's said truculently, 'Come on, Sarie, can't you stop your brat talking like a Commie.'

'Please, Kobie,' she used the diminutive as a special appeal, 'for my sake.'

Manfred De La Rey had become aware of the disturbance and the flare of hostility amongst his guests, and now he looked across the fires on which the steaks were sizzling and he frowned.

'Don't you see, Mama, we have to talk about it. If we

don't, people will never hear any other point of view. None of them even read the English newspapers.'

'Kobie, you will anger your Uncle Manie,' Sarah pleaded. 'Please stop it now.'

'We Afrikaners are cut off in this little make-believe world of ours. We think that if we make enough laws the black people will cease to exist, except as our servants—'

Manfred had come across from the fires now, and his face was dark with anger.

'Jakobus Stander,' he rumbled softly. 'Your father and your mother are my oldest and dearest friends, but do not trespass on the hospitality of this house. I will not have wild and treasonable ideas bandied about in front of my family and friends. Behave yourself, or leave immediately.'

For a moment it seemed the boy might defy him. Then he dropped his gaze and mumbled. 'I'm sorry, *Oom* Manie.' But when Manfred turned and strode back to the barbecue fire, he said just loud enough for Sarah to hear, 'You see, they won't listen. They don't want to hear. They are afraid of the truth. How can you make a blind man see?'

Manfred De La Rey was still inwardly seething with anger at the youth's ill-manners, but outwardly he was his usual bluff self as he resumed his self-imposed duties over the cooking fires, and led the jovial banter of his male guests. Gradually his irritation subsided, and he had almost put aside Moses Gama and the long shadow that he had thrown over them all, when his youngest daughter came running down from the long low ranch-type house.

'Papa, Papa, there is a telephone call for you.'

'I can't come now, *skatjie*,' Manfred called. 'We don't want our guests to starve. Take a message.'

'It's *Oom* Danie,' his daughter insisted, 'and he says he must talk to you now. It's very important.'

Manfred sighed and grumbled good-naturedly as he

untied his apron, and handed his fork to Roelf Stander. 'Don't let them burn!' and he strode up to the house.

'Ja!' he barked into the telephone.

'I don't like to disturb you, Manie.'

'Then why do you do it?' Manfred demanded. Danie Leroux was a senior police general, and one of his most able officers.

'It's this man Gama.'

'Let the black bastard hang. That is what he wants.'

'No! He wants to do a deal.'

'Send someone else to speak to him, I do not want to waste my time.'

'He will only talk to you, and we believe he has something important he will be able to tell you.'

Manfred thought for a moment. His instinct was to dismiss the request out of hand, but he let reason dictate to him.

'All right,' he agreed heavily. 'I will meet him.' There would also be a perverse pleasure in confronting a vanquished foe. 'But he is going to hang – nothing will stop that,' he warned quietly.

The prison authority had confiscated the leopard-skin robes of chieftainship, and Moses Gama wore the prison-issue suiting of coarse unbleached calico.

The long unremitting strain of awaiting the outcome of his appeal had told heavily. For the first time Vicky noticed the frosting of white in his cap of dark crinkling hair, and his features were gaunt, his eyes sunken in dark bruised-looking hollows. Her compassion for him threatened to overwhelm her, and she wished that she could reach out and touch him, but the steel mesh screen separated them.

'This is the last time I am allowed to visit you,' she whispered, 'and they will only let me stay for fifteen minutes.'

'That will be long enough, for there is not much to say, now that the sentence has been confirmed.'

'Oh, Moses, we were wrong to believe that the British and the Americans would save you.'

'They tried,' he said quietly.

'But they did not try very hard, and now what will I do without you. What will the child I am carrying do without a father?'

'You are a daughter of Zulu, you will be strong.'

'I will try, Moses my husband,' she whispered. 'But what of your people? They are also children without a father. What will become of them?'

She saw the old fierce fire burn in his eyes. She had feared it had been for ever extinguished, and she felt a brief and bitter joy to know it was still alight.

'The others will seek to take your place now. Those of the Congress who hate and envy you. When you die they will use your sacrifice to serve their own ambitions.'

She saw that she had reached him again, and that he was angry. She sought to inflame his anger to give him reason and strength to go on living.

'If you die, your enemies will use your dead body as a stepping-stone to climb to the place you have left empty.'

'Why do you torment me, woman?' he asked.

'Because I do not want you to die, because I want you to live – for me, for our child, and for your people.'

'That cannot be,' he said. 'The hard Boers will not yield, not even to the demands of the great powers. Unless you can find wings for me to fly over these walls, then I must go to my fate. There is no other way.'

'There is a way,' Vicky told him. 'There is a way for you to survive – and for you to put down the enemy who seek to usurp your place as the leader of the black nations.'

He stared at her as she went on.

'When the day comes that we sweep the Boers into the sea, and open the doors of the prisons, you will emerge to take your rightful place at the head of the revolution.'

'What is this way, woman? What is this hope that you hold out to me?'

He listened without expression as she propounded it to him, and when she had finished, he said gravely, 'It is true that the lioness is fiercer and crueller than the lion.'

'Will you do it, my lord – not for your own sake, but for all us weak ones who need you so?'

'I will think on it,' he conceded.

'There is so little time,' she warned.

The black ministerial Cadillac was delayed only briefly at the gates to the prison, for they were expecting Manfred De La Rey. As the steel gates swung open, the driver accelerated through into the main courtyard and turned into the parking slot that had been kept free. The prison commissioner and two of his senior staff were waiting, and they hurried forward as soon as Manfred climbed out of the rear door.

Briefly Manfred shook hands with the commissioner and said, 'I wish to see the prisoner immediately.'

'Of course, Minister, it has been arranged. He is waiting for you.'

'Lead the way.'

Manfred's heavy footfalls echoed along the dreary green-painted corridors, while the senior warders scurried ahead to unlock the interleading doors of each section and relock them as Manfred and the prison commissioner passed through. It was a long walk, but they came at last to the condemned block.

'How many awaiting execution?' Manfred demanded.

'Eleven,' the commissioner replied. The figure was not unusually high, Manfred reflected. Africa is a violent land and the gallows play a central role in the administration of justice.

'I do not want to be overheard, even by those soon to die.'

'It has been arranged,' the commissioner assured him. 'Gama is being kept separate from the others.'

The warders opened one last steel door and at the end of a short passage was a barred cell. Manfred went through but when the commissioner would have followed, Manfred stopped him.

'Wait here!' he ordered. 'Lock the door after me and open it again only when I ring.'

As the door clanged shut Manfred walked on to the end of the passage.

The cell was small, seven foot by seven, and almost bare. There was a toilet bowl against the side wall and a single iron bunk fixed to the opposite wall. Moses Gama sat on the edge of the bunk and he looked up at Manfred. Then slowly he came to his feet and crossed the cell to face him through the green-painted bars.

Neither man spoke. They stared at each other. Though only the bars separated them, they were a universe and an eternity apart. Though their gazes locked, there was no contact between their minds, and the hostility was a barrier between them more obdurate and irreconcilable than the steel bars.

'Yes?' Manfred asked at last. The temptation to gloat over a vanquished adversary was strong, but he withstood it. 'You asked to see me?'

'I have a proposal to put to you,' Moses Gama said.

'You wish to bargain for your life?' Manfred corrected him, and when Moses was silent, he smiled. 'So it seems that you are no different from other men, Moses Gama. You are neither a saint nor even the noble martyr that some say you are. You are no better than other men, no better than any of us. In the end your loyalty is to yourself alone. You are weak as other men are weak, and like them, you are afraid.'

'Do you wish to listen to my proposal?' Moses asked, without a sign of having heard the taunts.

'I will hear what you have to say,' Manfred agreed. 'That is why I came here.'

'I will deliver them to you,' Moses said, and Manfred understood immediately.

'By "them" you mean those who also claim to be the leaders of your people? The ones who compete with your own claim to that position?'

Moses nodded and Manfred chuckled and shook his head with admiration.

'I will give you the names and the evidence. I will give you the times and the places.' Moses was still expressionless. 'You have underestimated the threat that they are to you, you have underestimated the support they can muster, here and abroad. I will give you that knowledge.'

'And in return?' Manfred asked.

'My freedom,' said Moses simply.

'*Magtig!*' The blasphemy was a measure of Manfred's astonishment. 'You have the effrontery of a white man.' He turned away so that Moses could not see his face while he considered the magnitude of the offer.

Moses Gama was wrong. Manfred was fully aware of the threat, and he had a broad knowledge of the extent and the ramifications of the conspiracy. He understood that the world he knew was under terrible siege. The Englishman had spoken of the winds of change – they were blowing not only upon the African continent, but across the world. Everything he held dear, from the existence of his family to that of his *Volk* and the safety of the land that God had delivered unto them, was under attack by the forces of darkness.

Here he was being offered the opportunity to deal those forces a telling blow. He knew then what his duty was.

'I cannot give you your freedom,' he said quietly. 'That is too much – but you knew that when you demanded it, didn't you?' Moses did not answer him, and Manfred went on, 'This is the bargain I will offer you. I will give you your life. A reprieve, but you will never leave prison again. That is the best I can do.'

The silence went on so long that Manfred thought he had refused and he began to turn away when Moses spoke again.

'I accept.'

Manfred turned back to him, not allowing his triumph to show.

'I will want all the names, all the evidence,' he insisted.

'You will have it all,' Moses assured him. 'When I have my reprieve.'

'No,' Manfred said quietly. 'I set the terms. You will have your reprieve when you have earned it. Until then you will get only a stay of execution. Even for that I will need you to name a name so that I can convince my compatriots of the wisdom of our bargain.'

Moses was silent, glowering at him through the bars.

'Give me a name,' Manfred insisted. 'Give me something to take to the Prime Minister.'

'I will do better than that,' Moses agreed. 'I will give you two names. Heed them well. They are – Mandela and Rivonia.'

MMichael Courtney was in the city room of the *Mail* when the news that the Appellate Division had denied Moses Gama's appeal and confirmed the date of his execution came clattering out on the tape. He let the paper strip run through his fingers, reading it with total concentration, and when the message ended, he went to his desk and sat in front of his typewriter.

He lit a cigarette and sat quietly, staring out of the window over the tops of the scraggly trees in Joubert Park. He had a pile of work in his basket and a dozen reference books on his desk. Desmond Blake had slipped out of the office to go down to the George to top up his gin tank and left Michael to finish the article on the American elections. Eisenhower was nearing the end of his final term and the editor wanted a pen portrait of the presidential candidates. Michael was working on his biographical notes of John Kennedy, but having difficulty choosing the salient facts from the vast amount that had been written about the young Democratic candidate, apart from those that everybody knew, that he was a Catholic and a New Dealer and that he had been born in 1917.

America seemed very far away that morning, and the election of an American president inconsequential in comparison with what he had just read on the tape.

As part of his self-education and training, Michael made a practice each day of selecting an item of important news and writing a two-thousand-word mock editorial upon it. These exercises were for his own sake, the results private and jealously guarded. He showed them to no one, especially not Desmond Blake whose biting sarcasm and whose willingness to plagiarize Michael had learned to fear. He kept these articles in a folder in the locked bottom drawer of his desk.

Usually Michael worked on these exercises in his own time, staying on for an hour or so in the evening or sitting up late at night in the little bed-sitter he rented in

Hillbrow, pecking them out on his rickety old secondhand Remington.

However, this morning he had been so moved by the failure of Gama's appeal that he could not concentrate on the Kennedy story. The image of the imperial-looking black man in his leopard-skin robes kept recurring before Michael's eyes, and his words kept echoing in Michael's ears.

Suddenly he reached forward and ripped the half-completed page out of his machine. Then he swiftly rolled a clean sheet into it. He didn't have to think, his fingers flew across the keys, and the words sprang up before his eyes: 'A Martyr is Born.'

He rolled the cigarette to the side of his mouth and squinted against the spiral of blue smoke, and the words came in short staccato bursts. He did not have to search for facts or dates or figures. They were all there, crisp and bright in his head. He never paused. He never had to weigh one word against another. The precise word was there on the page almost of its own volition.

When he finished it half an hour later, he knew that it was the best thing he had ever written. He read it through once, shaken by the power of his own words, and then he stood up. He felt restless and nervous. The effort of creation rather than calming or exhausting him had excited him. He had to get outside.

He left the sheet in the typewriter and took his jacket off the back of his chair. The sub glanced up at him enquiringly.

'Going to find Des,' he called. In the newsroom there was a conspiracy to protect Desmond Blake from himself and the gin bottle and the sub nodded agreement and returned to his work.

Once he was out of the building, Michael walked fast, pushing his way through the crowds on the sidewalks, stepping out hard with both hands thrust into his pockets.

He didn't look where he was going, but it didn't surprise him when at last he found himself in the main concourse of the Johannesburg railway station.

He fetched a paper cup of coffee from the kiosk near the ticket office and took it to his usual seat on one of the benches. He lit a cigarette and raised his eyes towards the domed glass ceiling. The Pierneef murals were placed so high that very few of the thousands of commuters who passed through the concourse each day ever noticed them.

For Michael they were the essence of the continent, a distillation of all of Africa's immensity and infinite beauty. Like a celestial choir, they sang aloud all that he was trying to convey in clumsy stumbling sentences. He felt at peace when at last he left the massive stone building.

He found Des Blake on his usual stool at the end of the bar counter at the George.

'Are you your brother's keeper?' Des Blake enquired loftily, but his words were slurred. It took a great deal of gin to make Des Blake slur.

'The sub is asking for you,' Michael lied.

He wondered why he felt any concern for the man, or why any of them bothered to protect him – but then one of the other senior journalists had given him the answer to that. 'He was once a great newspaperman, and we have to look after our own.'

Des was having difficulty fitting a cigarette into his ivory holder. Michael did it for him, and as he held a match he said, 'Come on, Mr Blake. They are waiting for you.'

'Courtney, I think I should warn you now. You haven't got what it takes, I'm afraid. You'll never cut the mustard, boy. You are just a poor little rich man's son. You'll never be a newspaperman's anus.'

'Come along, Mr Blake,' said Michael wearily, and took his arm to help him down off the stool.

The first thing Michael noticed when he reached his desk again was that the sheet of paper was missing from his

613

typewriter. It was only in the last few months, since he had been assigned to work with Des Blake, that he had been given his own desk and machine, and he was fiercely jealous and protective of them.

The idea of anyone fiddling with his typewriter, let alone taking work out of it, infuriated him. He looked around him furiously, seeking a target for his anger, but every single person in the long, crowded noisy room was senior to him. The effort it cost him to contain his outrage left him shaking. He lit another cigarette, the last one in his pack, and even in his agitation he realized that that made it twenty since breakfast.

'Courtney!' the sub called across to him, raising his voice above the rattle of typewriters. 'You took your time. Mr Herbstein wants you in his office right away.'

Michael's rage subsided miraculously. He had never been in the editor's office before, Mr Herbstein had once said good morning to him in the lift but that was all.

The walk down the newsroom seemed the longest of his life, and though nobody even glanced up as he passed, Michael was certain that they were secretly sniggering at him and gloating on his dilemma.

He knocked on the frosted-glass panel of the editor's door and there was a bellow from inside.

Timidly Michael pushed the door open and peered round it. Leon Herbstein was on the telephone, a burly man in a sloppy hand-knitted cardigan with thick horn-rimmed spectacles and a shock of thick curly hair shot through with strands of grey. Impatiently he waved Michael into the room and then ignored him while he finished his conversation on the telephone.

At last he slammed down the receiver and swivelled his chair to regard the young man who was standing uneasily in front of his desk.

Ten days before, Leon Herbstein had received a quite unexpected invitation to a luncheon in the executive dining-room of the Courtney Mining and Finance Company's new head office building. There had been ten other guests present, all of them leaders of commerce and industry, but Herbstein had found himself in the right-hand seat beside his host.

Leon Herbstein had never had any great admiration for Shasa Courtney. He was suspicious of vast wealth, and the two Courtneys – mother and son – had a formidable reputation for shrewd and ruthless business practices. Then again, Shasa Courtney had forsaken the United Party of which Leon Herbstein was an ardent supporter, and had gone across to the Nationalists. Leon Herbstein had never forgotten the violent anti-Semitism which had attended the birth of the National Party, and he considered the policy of *apartheid* as simply another manifestation of the same grotesque racial bigotry.

As far as he was concerned, Shasa Courtney was one of the enemy. However, he sat down at his luncheon table quite unprepared for the man's easy and insidious charm and his quick and subtle mind. Shasa devoted most of his attention to Leon Herbstein, and by the end of the meal the editor had considerably moderated his feelings towards the Courtneys. At least he was convinced that Shasa Courtney truly had the best interests of all the people at heart, that he was especially concerned with improving the lot of the black and underprivileged sections, and that he was wielding an important moderating influence in the high councils of the National Party.

In addition, he left the Courtney building with a heightened respect for Shasa Courtney's subtlety. Not once had Shasa mentioned the fact that he and his companies now owned 42 per cent of the stock of Associated Newspapers of South Africa or that his son was employed as a junior journalist on the *Mail*. It hadn't been necessary, both men had been acutely aware of these facts while they talked.

Up to that time Leon Herbstein had felt a natural antagonism towards Michael Courtney. Placing him in the care of Des Blake had been all the preference he had shown to the lad. However, after that luncheon he had begun to study him with more attention. It didn't take an old dog long to attribute the improvement in much of the copy that Des Blake had been turning out recently to the groundwork that Michael Courtney was doing for him. From then onwards, whenever he passed Michael's desk, Herbstein made a point of quickly and surreptitiously checking what work was in his machine or in the copy basket.

Herbstein had the journalist's trick of being able to assimilate a full typed sheet at a single glance, and he was grimly amused to notice how often Des Blake's column was based on the draft by his young assistant, and how often the original was better than the final copy.

Now he studied Michael closely as he stood awkwardly before his desk. Despite the fact that he had cropped his hair in one of those appalling brush cuts that the youth were affecting these days and wore a vividly patterned bow tie, he was a likeable-looking lad, with a strong determined jawline and clear, intelligent eyes. Perhaps he was too thin for his height, and a little gawky, but he had quite noticeably matured and gained in self-assurance during the short period he had been at the *Mail*.

Suddenly Leon realized that he was being cruel, and that his scrutiny was subjecting the lad to unnecessary agony. He picked up the sheet of typescript that lay in front of him, and slid it across his untidy desk.

'Did you write that?' he demanded gruffly, and Michael snatched up the sheet protectively.

'I didn't mean anybody to read it,' he whispered, and then remembered who he was talking to and threw in a lame, 'sir.'

'Strange.' Leon Herbstein shook his head. 'I always

believed we were in the business of writing so that others could read.'

'I was just practising.' Michael held the sheet behind his back.

'I made some corrections,' Herbstein told him, and Michael jerked the page out from behind him and scanned it anxiously.

'Your third paragraph is redundant, and "scar" is a better word than "cicatrice" – otherwise we'll run it as you wrote it.'

'I don't understand, sir,' Michael blurted.

'You've saved me the trouble of writing tomorrow's editorial.' Herbstein reached across and took the page from Michael's limp fingers, tossed it into his Out basket and then concentrated all his attention on his own work.

Michael stood gaping at the top of his head. It took him ten seconds to realize that he had been dismissed and he backed towards the door and closed it carefully behind him. His legs just carried him to his desk, and then collapsed under him. He sat down heavily in his swivel chair and reached for his cigarette pack. It was empty and he crumpled it and dropped it into his wastepaper basket.

Only then did the full significance of what had happened hit him and he felt cold and slightly nauseated.

'The editorial,' he whispered, and his hands began to tremble.

Across the desk Desmond Blake belched softly and demanded, 'Where are the notes on that American what's-'is-name fellow?'

'I haven't finished it yet, Mr Blake.'

'Listen, kid. I warned you. You'll have to extract your digit from your fundamental orifice if you want to get anywhere around here.'

Michael set his alarm clock for five o'clock the next morning and went downstairs with his raincoat over his pyjamas. He was waiting on the street corner with the newspaper urchins when the bundles of newsprint were tossed onto the pavement from the back of the *Mail's* delivery van.

He ran back up the stairs clutching a copy of the paper and locked the door to his bed-sitter. It took all his courage to open it at the editorial page. He was actually shaking with terror that Mr Herbstein might have changed his mind, or that it was all some monstrous practical joke.

There under the *Mail's* crest at the very top of the editorial page was his headline: A MARTYR IS BORN.

He read it through quickly, and then started again and read it aloud, mouthing each word, rolling it over his tongue like a noble and precious wine. He propped the paper, open at the editorial, beside the mirror while he shaved, and then carried it down to the Greek fast-food café where he had his breakfast each morning and showed it to Mr Costa, who called his wife out of the kitchen.

'Hey, Michael, you a big shot now.' Mrs Costa embraced him, smelling of fried bacon and garlic. 'You a big-shot newspaperman now.'

She let him use the telephone in the back room and he gave the operator the number at Weltevreden. Centaine answered on the second ring.

'Mickey!' she cried delightedly. 'Where are you? Are you in Cape Town?'

He calmed her down and then read it to her. There was a long silence. 'The editorial, Mickey. You aren't making this up, are you? I'll never forgive you if you are.'

Once he had reassured her, Centaine told him, 'I can't remember ever being so excited about anything in years. I'm going to call your father, you must tell him yourself.'

Shasa came on the line, and Michael read it to him. 'You wrote that?' Shasa asked. 'Pretty hot stuff, Mickey. Of course I don't agree with your conclusions – Gama must hang. However, you almost convinced me otherwise, but we can debate that when next we are together. In the

618

meantime, congratulations, my boy. Perhaps you did make the right decision after all.'

Michael found that he was a minor celebrity in the newsroom, even the sub stopped by his desk to congratulate him and discuss the article for a few moments, and the pretty little blonde on the reception desk who had never before been aware of his existence smiled and greeted him by name.

'Listen, kid,' said Desmond Blake. 'One little fart doesn't make a whole sewage farm. In future I don't want you pushing copy over my head. Every bit of shit you write comes across my desk, get it?'

'I'm sorry, Mr Blake. I didn't—'

'Yeah! Yeah! I know, you didn't mean it. Just don't go getting a big head. Remember whose assistant you are.'

The news of Moses Gama's reprieve threw the newsroom into a state of pandemonium that didn't subside for almost a week. Michael was drawn in, and some of his days ended at midnight when the presses began their run and began when the first papers hit the streets the next morning.

However, he found that the excitement seemed to release limitless reserves of energy in him and he never felt tired. He learned to work quickly and accurately and his way with words gradually assumed a deftness and polish that was apparent even to himself.

Two weeks after the reprieve the editor called him into his office. He had learned not to knock, any waste of time irritated Leon Herbstein and made him bellow aggressively. Michael went straight on in, but he had not yet entirely mastered the pose of world-weary cynicism which he knew was the hallmark of the veteran journalist, and he was all radiant eagerness as he asked, 'Yes, Mr Herbstein?'

'OK, Mickey, I've got something for you.' Every time Mr Herbstein used his Christian name, Michael still thrilled with delicious shock.

'We are getting a lot of requests from readers and

overseas correspondents. With all the interest in the Gama case, people want to know more about the black political movements. They want to know the difference between the Pan-Africanist Congress and the African National Congress, they want to know who's who – who the hell are Tambo and Sisulu, Mandela and Moses Gama and what do they stand for? All that sort of stuff. You seem to be interested in black politics and enjoy digging around in the archives – besides I can't spare one of my top men on this sort of background stuff. So get on with it.' Herbstein switched his attention back to the work on his desk, but Michael by now had sufficient confidence to stand his ground.

'Am I still working under Mr Blake?' he asked. He had learned by this time if you called him 'sir' it just made Leon Herbstein mad.

Herbstein shook his head but did not even look up. 'You are on your own. Send everything to me. No hurry, any time in the next five minutes will do nicely.'

Michael soon discovered that the *Mail*'s archives were inadequate, and served merely to initiate him into the complexity and daunting size of the project he had been set. However, from them he was at least able to draw up a list of the various black political groups and related associations such as the officially unrecognized black trade unions, and from there to compile a list of their own leaders and officials.

He cleared one wall of his bed-sitting room and put up a board on which he pinned all this information, using different-coloured cards for each grouping and press photographs of the principal black leaders. All this achieved was to convince him of how little was known about the black movements by even the most well-informed of the white section of the nation.

The public library added very little to his understanding. Most of the books on the subject had been written ten or more years before and simply traced the African National Congress from those distant days of its inception in 1912 and the names mentioned were all of men now dead or in their dotage.

Then he had his first inspiration. One of the *Mail's* sister publications under the banner of Associated Newspapers of South Africa was a weekly magazine called *Assegai*, after the broad-bladed war spear that the impis of Chaka the Zulu conqueror had wielded. The magazine was aimed at the educated and more affluent section of the black community. Its editorial policy was dictated by the white directors of Associated Newspapers but amongst the articles and photographs of African football stars and torch singers, of black American athletes and film actors, an occasional article slipped through of a fiercely radical slant.

Michael borrowed a company car and went out to see the editor of *Assegai* in the vast black location of Drake's Farm. The editor was a graduate of the black university of Fort Hare, a Xhosa named Solomon Nduli. He was polite but cool, and they had chatted for half an hour before a barbed remark let Michael know that he had been recognized as a spy for the security police, and that he would learn nothing of value.

A week later the *Mail* published the first of Michael's articles in its Saturday magazine edition. It was a comparison of the two leading African political organizations: the Pan-Africanist Congress, which was a jealously exclusive body to which only pure-blooded African blacks were admitted and whose views were extremely radical, and the much larger African National Congress which, although predominantly black, also included whites and Asians and mixed-blood members such as the Cape coloureds, and whose objectives were essentially conciliatory.

The article was accurate, obviously carefully researched, but, most important, the tone was sympathetic, and it carried the by-line 'by Michael Courtney'.

The following day Solomon Nduli called Michael at the offices of the *Mail*, and suggested another meeting. His first words when they shook hands were, 'I'm sorry. I think I misjudged you. What do you want to know?'

Solomon took Michael into a strange world that he had never realized existed – the world of the black townships. He arranged for him to meet Robert Sobukwe, and Michael was appalled by the depth of the resentment the black leader of the Pan-Africanist Congress expressed, particularly for the pass laws, by his enormous impatience to effect an upheaval of the entire society, and by the thinly veiled violence in the man.

'I will try to arrange for you to meet Mandela,' Solomon promised, 'although, as you know, he is underground now, and wanted by the police. But there are others you must talk to.'

He took Michael to Baragwanath Hospital and introduced him to the wife of Moses Gama, the lovely young Zulu woman he had seen at the trial in Cape Town. Victoria was heavily pregnant, but with a calm dignity that impressed Michael deeply until he sensed the same terrible resentment and latent violence in her that he had found in Robert Sobukwe.

The next day Solomon took him back to Drake's Farm to meet a man named Hendrick Tabaka, a man who seemed to own most of the small businesses in the location and looked like a heavyweight wrestler with a head like a cannonball criss-crossed with scars.

He appeared to Michael to represent the opposite end of the black protest consciousness. 'I have my family and my business,' he told Michael, 'and I will protect them from anybody, black or white.' And Michael was reminded of a view that his father had often expressed, but to which Michael had not given much consideration before this. 'We must give the black people a piece of the pie,' Shasa Courtney had said. 'Give them something of their own. The truly dangerous man is one with nothing to lose.'

Michael gave the second article in the series the title 'Rage' and in it he tried to describe the deep and bitter resentment that he had encountered on his journeys into the half-world of the townships. He ended the article with the words:

Despite this deep sense of outrage, I never found the least indication of hatred towards the white person as an individual by any of the black leaders with whom I was able to speak. Their resentment seemed to me to be directed only at the Nationalist government's policy of *apartheid* while the vast treasure of mutual goodwill built up over three hundred years between the races seems to be entirely undiminished by it.

He delivered the article to Leon Herbstein on the Thursday and found himself immediately embroiled in an editorial review of it that lasted until almost eight o'clock that evening. Leon Herbstein called in his assistant and his deputy editor, and their views were divided between publishing with only minor alterations and not publishing at all, for fear of bringing down the wrath of the Publications Control Board, the government censors who had the power to ban the *Mail* and put it out of business.

'But it's all true,' Michael protested. 'I have substantiated every single fact I have quoted. It's true and it's important – that is all that really matters.' And the three older journalists looked at him pityingly.

'All right, Mickey,' Leon Herbstein dismissed him at last. 'You can go on home. I will let you know the final decision in due course.'

As Michael moved dispiritedly towards the door, the deputy editor nodded at him. 'Publish or not, Mickey, it is a damned good effort. You can be proud of it.'

When Michael got back to his apartment he found somebody sitting on a canvas holdall outside his front door. Only when the person stood up did he recognize the massively developed shoulders, the glinting steel-rimmed spectacles and spiky hairstyle.

'Garry,' he shouted joyously, and rushed to embrace his elder brother.

They sat side by side on the bed and talked excitedly, interrupting each other and laughing and exclaiming at each other's news.

'What are you doing in Jo'burg?' Michael demanded at last.

'I've come up from Silver River just for the weekend. I want to get at the new computer mainframe in head office, and there are a few things I want to check at the land surveyor's office. So I thought, what the hell – why spend money on a hotel when Mickey has a flat? So I brought my sleeping-bag. Can I doss on your floor.'

'The bed pulls out into a double,' Mickey told him happily. 'You don't have to sleep on the floor.'

They went down to Costa's restaurant and Garry bought a pack of chicken curry and half a dozen Cokes. They ate the food out of the pack, sharing a spoon to save washing up, and they talked until long after midnight. They had always been very close to each other. Even though he was younger, Michael had been a staunch ally during those dreadful childhood years of Garry's bed-wetting and stuttering and Sean's casually savage bullying. Then again Michael had not truly realized how lonely he had been in this strange city until this moment, and now there were so many nostalgic memories and so much unrequited need for affection to assuage, so many subjects of earth-shattering importance to discuss. They sat up into the small hours dealing with money and work and sex and the rest of it.

Garry was stunned to learn that Michael earned thirty-seven pounds ten shillings a month.

'How much does this kennel cost you a month?' he demanded.

'Twenty pounds,' Michael told him.

'That leaves you seventeen pounds ten a month to eat and exist. They should be arrested for slave labour.'

'It's not as bad as that – Pater gives me an allowance to make do. How much do you earn, Garry?' Michael demanded, and Garry looked guilty.

'I get my board and lodging and all my meals at the mine, single quarters, and I am paid a hundred a month as an executive trainee.'

'Son of a gun!' Michael was deeply impressed. 'What do you do with all that?'

It was Garry's turn to look amazed. 'Save it, of course. I've got over two thousand in the bank already.'

'But what are you going to do with all that?' Michael insisted. 'What are you going to spend it on?'

'Money isn't for spending,' Garry explained. 'Money is for saving – that is, if you want to be rich.'

'And you want to be rich?' Michael asked.

'What else is there?' Garry was genuinely puzzled by the question.

'What about doing an important job the best way you can? Isn't that something to strive for, even better than getting rich?'

'Oh, sure!' said Garry with vast relief. 'But then, of course, you won't get rich unless you do just that.'

It was almost two in the morning when Michael at last switched off the bedside lamp and they settled down nose to toes, until Garry asked in the darkness the question he had not been able to ask until then.

'Mickey, have you heard from Mater at all?'

Michael was silent for so long that he went on impetuously. 'I have tried to speak to Dad about her, but he just clams up and won't say a word. Same with Nana, except she went a little further. She said, "Don't mention that woman's name in Weltevreden again. She was responsible for Blaine's murder." I thought you might know where she is.'

'She's in London,' Michael said softly. 'She writes to me every week.'

'When is she coming back, Mickey?'

'Never,' Michael said. 'She and Pater are getting a divorce.'

'Why, Mickey, what happened that she had to leave like that, without even saying goodbye?'

'I don't know. She won't say. I wrote and asked her, but she wouldn't tell me.'

Garry thought he had gone to sleep, but after a long silence Michael said so softly that he barely caught the words, 'I miss her, Garry. Oh, God, how much I miss her.'

'Me too,' said Garry dutifully, but each week that passed was so filled with excitement and new experience that for Garry her memory had already faded and blurred.

The next morning Leon Herbstein called Mickey into his office.

'OK, Mickey,' he said. 'We are going to run the "Rage" article as you wrote it.' Only then did Michael realize how important that decision had been to him. For the rest of that day his jubilation was tempered by that reflection. Why was his feeling of relief so powerful? Was it the personal achievement, the thought of seeing his name in print again? It was part of that, he was honest with himself, but there was something else even deeper and more substantial. The truth. He had written the truth and the truth had prevailed. He had been exonerated.

Michael went down early the next morning and brought a copy of the *Mail* up to the bed-sitter. He woke Garry up and read the 'Rage' feature to him. Garry had only come in a few hours before dawn. He had spent most of the night in the computer room at the new Courtney Mining building in Diagonal Street. David Abrahams, on Shasa's discreet suggestion, had arranged for him to have a free hand with the equipment when it was not being used on company business. This morning Garry was red-eyed with exhaustion and his jowls were covered with a dense dark pelt of new beard. However, he sat up in his pyjamas and listened with attention while Michael read to him, and when he had finished Garry put on his spectacles and sat solemnly reading it through for himself while Michael brewed coffee on the gas-ring in the corner.

'It's funny, isn't it,' Garry said at last. 'How we just take them for granted. They are there, working the shifts at the Silver River or harvesting the grapes at Weltevreden, or waiting on table. But you never think of them as actually having feelings and desires and thoughts the same as we do – not until you read something like this.'

'Thank you, Garry,' Michael said softly.

'What for?'

'That's the greatest compliment anybody has ever paid me,' Michael said.

He saw very little more of Garry that weekend. Garry spent the Saturday morning at the deeds registry until that office closed at noon and then went on up to the Courtney building to take over the computer as soon as the company programmers went off for their weekend.

He let himself back into the flat at three the next morning and climbed into the bottom end of Michael's bed. When they both awoke late on the Sunday morning, Michael suggested, 'Let's go out to Zoo Lake. It's a hot day and the girls will be out in their sundresses.' He offered the bait deliberately for he was desperate for Garry's company, lonely and suffering from a sense of anti-climax after all the worry and uncertainty previous to the printing of the 'Rage' article and the subsequent apparent lack of any reaction to it.

'Hey, Mickey, I'd love to come with you – but I want to do something on the computer. It's Sunday, I'll have it to myself all day.' Garry looked mysterious and self-satisfied. 'You see, I'm on to something, Mickey. Something incredible, and I can't stop now.'

Alone Michael caught the bus out to Zoo Lake. He spent the day sitting on the lawns reading and watching the girls. It only made him feel even more lonely and insignificant. When he got back to his dreary little flatlet, Garry's bag was gone and there was a message written with soap on his shaving mirror: 'Going back to Silver River. Might see you next weekend. G.'

When Michael walked into the *Mail's* offices on the Monday morning he found that those members of the newspaper's staff who had arrived ahead of him were gathered in a silent nervous cluster in the middle of the newsroom while half a dozen strangers were going through the filing cabinets and rifling the papers and books on the desks. They had already assembled a dozen large cardboard cartons of various papers, and these were stacked in the aisle between the desks.

'What is happening?' Michael asked innocently, and his sub gave him a warning glance as he explained.

'These are police officers of the security branch.'

'Who are you?' The plain-clothes officer who was in charge of the detail came across to Michael, and when he gave his name the officer checked his list.

'Ah, yes – you are the one we want. Come with me.' He led Michael down to Leon Herbstein's office and went in without knocking.

There was another stranger with Herbstein. 'Yes, what is it?' he snapped, and the security policeman answered diffidently.

'This is the one, Captain.'

The stranger frowned at Michael, but before he could speak Leon Herbstein interrupted quickly.

'It's all right, Michael. The police have come to serve a banning order on the Saturday edition with the 'Rage' article in it, and they have a warrant to search the offices. They also want to talk to you, but it's nothing to worry about.'

'Don't be too sure of that,' said the police captain heavily. 'Are you the one who wrote that piece of Commie propaganda?'

'I wrote the "Rage" article,' Michael said clearly, but Leon Herbstein cut in.

'However, as the editor of the *Golden City Mail* it was my decision to print it, and I accept full responsibility for the article.'

The captain ignored him and studied Michael for a moment before going on. 'Man, you are just a kid. What do you know, anyway?'

'I object to that, Captain,' Herbstein told him angrily. 'Mr Courtney is an accredited journalist—'

'*Ja*,' the captain nodded, 'I expect that he is.' But he went on addressing Michael, 'What about you? Do you object to coming down to Marshall Square police headquarters to help us with our investigations?'

Michael glanced at Herbstein and he said immediately, 'You don't have to go, Michael. They don't have a warrant for your arrest.'

'What do you want from me, Captain?' Michael hedged.

'We want to know who told you all that treasonable stuff you wrote about.'

'I can't disclose my sources,' Michael said quietly.

'I can always get a warrant if you refuse to cooperate,' the captain warned him ominously.

'I'll come with you,' Michael agreed. 'But I won't disclose my sources. That's not ethical.'

'I'll be down there with a lawyer right away, Michael,' Herbstein promised. 'You don't have to worry, the *Mail* will back you all the way.'

'All right. Let's go,' said the police captain.

Leon Herbstein accompanied Michael down the

newsroom and as they passed the cartons of impounded literature the captain observed gloatingly, 'Man, you've got a pile of banned stuff there, Karl Marx and Trotsky even – that's really poisonous rubbish.'

'It's research material,' said Leon Herbstein.

'Ja, try telling that to the magistrate,' the captain chortled.

As soon as the doors of the elevator closed on the captain and Michael, Herbstein trotted heavily back to his office and snatched up the telephone.

'I want an urgent call to Mr Shasa Courtney in Cape Town. Try his home at Weltevreden, his office in Centaine House and his ministerial office at the Houses of Parliament.'

He got through to Shasa in his parliamentary suite and Shasa listened in silence while Herbstein explained to him what had happened.

'All right,' Shasa said crisply at the end of it. 'You get the Associated Newspapers lawyers down to Marshall Square immediately, then ring David Abrahams at Courtney Mining and tell him what has happened. Tell him I want a massive reaction, everything we have got. Tell him also that I will be flying up immediately in the company jet. I want a limousine at the airport to meet me, and I will go to see the Minister of Police at the Union Buildings in Pretoria the minute I arrive.'

Even Leon Herbstein, who had seen it all before, was impressed by the mobilization of the vast resources of the Courtney empire.

At ten o'clock that evening Michael Courtney was released from interrogation on the direct orders of the Minister of Police and when he walked out of the front entrance of Marshall Square headquarters he was flanked by half a dozen lawyers of formidable reputation who had been retained by Courtney Mining and Associated Newspapers.

At the pavement Shasa Courtney was waiting in the

back seat of the black Cadillac limousine. As Michael climbed in beside him, he said grimly, 'It is possible, Mickey, to be a bit too bloody clever for your own good. Just what the hell are you trying to do? Burn down everything we have worked for all our lives?'

'What I wrote was the truth. I thought you, of all people, would understand, Pater.'

'What you wrote, my boy, is incitement. Taken by the wrong people and used on simple ignorant black folk, your words could help to open a Pandora's box of horrors. I want no more of that sort of thing from you, do you hear me, Michael?'

'I hear you, Pater,' Michael said softly. 'But I can't promise to obey you. I'm sorry, but I have to live with my own conscience.'

'You are as bad as your bloody mother,' said Shasa. He had sworn twice in as many minutes, the first time in his life that Michael had ever heard his father use coarse language. That and the mention of his mother, also the first time Shasa had done so since she left, silenced Michael completely. They drove without speaking to the Carlton Hotel. Shasa only spoke again when they were in his permanent suite.

'All right, Mickey,' he said with resignation. 'I take that back. I can't demand that you live your life on my terms. Follow your conscience, if you must, but don't expect me to come rushing in to save you from the consequences of your actions every time.'

'I have never expected that, sir,' Michael said carefully. 'And I won't in future either.' He paused and swallowed hard. 'But all the same, sir, I want to thank you for what you did. You have always been so good to me.'

'Oh, Mickey, Mickey!' Shasa cried, shaking his head sorrowfully. 'If only I could give you the experience I earned with so much pain. If only you didn't have to make exactly the same mistakes I made at your age.'

'I am always grateful for your advice, Pater,' Michael tried to placate him.

'All right, then, here's a piece for nothing,' Shasa told him. 'When you meet an invincible enemy you don't rush headlong at him, swinging with both fists. That way you merely get your head broken. What you do is you sneak around behind him and kick him in the backside, then run like hell.'

'I'll remember that, sir,' Michael grinned, and Shasa put his arm around his shoulders. 'I know you smoke like a bush fire, but can I offer you a drink, my boy?'

'I'll have a beer, sir.'

The next day Michael drove out to visit Solomon Nduli at Drake's Farm. He wanted to have his views on the 'Rage' article, and tell him of the consequences he had suffered at Marshall Square.

That was not necessary. Solomon Nduli somehow knew every detail of his detention and interrogation and Michael found he was a celebrity in the offices of *Assegai* magazine. Nearly every one of the black journalists and magazine staff wanted to shake his hand and congratulate him on the article.

As soon as they were alone in his office, Solomon told him excitedly, 'Nelson Mandela has read your piece and he wants to meet you.'

'But he is wanted by the police – he's on the run.'

'After what you wrote, he trusts you,' Solomon said, 'and so does Robert Sobukwe. He also wants to see you again.' Then he noticed Michael's expression, and the excitement went out of him as he asked quietly, 'Unless you think it's too dangerous for you.'

Michael hesitated for only a moment. 'No, of course not. I want to meet them both. Very much.'

Solomon Nduli said nothing. He simply reached across the desk and clasped Michael's shoulder. It was strange what a pleasurable sensation that grip gave Michael, the first comradely gesture he had ever received from a black man.

S hasa banked the HS125 twin-engined jet to give himself a better view of the Silver River Mine a thousand feet below.

The headgear was of modern design, not the traditional scaffolding of steel girders with the great steel wheels of the haulage exposed. It was instead a graceful unbroken tower of concrete, tall as a ten-storey building, and around it the other buildings of the mine complex, the crushing works and uranium extraction plant and the gold refinery, had been laid out with equal aesthetic consideration. The administration block was surrounded by green lawns and flowering gardens, and beyond that there was an eighteen-hole golf course, a cricket pitch and a rugby field for the white miners. An Olympic-size swimming-pool adjoined the mine club and single quarters. On the opposite side of the property stood the compound for the black mineworkers. Here again Shasa had ordered that the traditional rows of barracks be replaced by neat cottages for the senior black staff and the bachelor quarters were spacious and pleasant, more like motels than institutions to house and feed the five thousand tribesmen who had been recruited from as far afield as Nyasaland in the north and Portuguese Mozambique in the east. There were also soccer fields and cinemas and a shopping complex for the black employees, and between the buildings were green lawns and trees.

The Silver River was a wet mine and each day millions of gallons of water were pumped out of the deep workings and these were used to beautify the property. Shasa had reason to be proud.

Although the main shaft had intersected the gold-bearing reef at great depth – more than a mile below the surface – still the ore was so rich that it could be brought to the surface for enormous profit. What's more, the price could not be pegged at $35 per ounce for much longer. Shasa was convinced that it would double and even treble.

'Our guardian angel,' Shasa smiled to himself as he levelled the wings of the HS125, and began his preparations for the landing.

'Of all the blessings that have been heaped upon this land, gold is the greatest. It has stood us through the bad times, and made the good times glorious. It is our treasure and more, for when all else fails, when our enemies and the fates conspire to bring us down, gold glows with its bright particular lustre to protect us. A guardian angel indeed.'

Although the company pilot in the right-hand seat watched critically, for Shasa had only converted to jets within the last twelve months, Shasa brought the swift machine in to the long blue tarmac strip with casual ease. The HS125 was painted in silver and blue with the stylized diamond logo on the fuselage, just as the old Mosquito had been. It was a magnificent machine. With its seating for eight passengers and its blazing speed, it was infinitely more practical than the Mosquito, but Shasa still occasionally mourned her loss. He had flown over five thousand hours in the old Mosquito before at last donating her to the airforce museum, where, restored to her combat camouflage and armaments, she was one of the prime exhibits.

Shasa rolled the glistening new jet down to the hangar at the far end of the strip, and a reception committee was out to meet him headed by the general manager of the Silver River, all of them holding their ears against the shrill wail of the engines.

The general manager shook Shasa's hand and said immediately, 'Your son asked me to apologize that he wasn't able to meet you, Mr Courtney. He is underground at the moment, but asked me to tell you he will come up to the guest house as soon as he gets off shift.' The general manager, emboldened by Shasa's smile of paternal approval, risked a pleasantry. 'It must run in the family, but it's difficult to get the little blighter to stop working, we almost have to tie him down.'

There were two guest houses, one for other important visitors to the mine, and this one set aside exclusively for Shasa and Centaine. It was so sybaritic and had cost so much that embarrassing questions had been put to Shasa at the annual general meeting of the company by a group of dissident shareholders. Shasa was totally unrepentant. 'How can I work properly if I'm not allowed at least some basic comforts? A roof over my head – is that too much to ask?'

The guest house had its own squash court and heated indoor pool, cinema, conference room, kitchens and wine cellar. The design was by one of Frank Lloyd Wright's most brilliant pupils and Hicks had come out from London to do the interior. It housed the overflow of Shasa's art collection and Persian carpets from Weltevreden, and the mature trees in the landscaped garden had been selected from all over the country to be replanted here. Shasa felt very much at home in this little *pied-à-terre*.

The underground engineer and the chief electrical engineer were already waiting in the conference room and Shasa went straight in and was at work within ten minutes of landing the jet. By eight o'clock that evening he had exhausted his engineers and he let them go.

Garry was waiting next door in Shasa's private study, filling in the time playing with the computer terminal, but he leapt up as Shasa walked in.

'Dad, I'm so glad I've found you. I've been trying to catch up with you for days – I'm running out of time.' He was stuttering again. These days he only did that when he was wildly over-excited.

'Slow down, Garry. Take a deep breath,' Shasa advised

him, but the words kept tumbling out, and Garry seized his father's hand and led him to the computer to illustrate what he was trying to put across.

'You know what Nana has always said, and what you are always telling me about land being the only lasting asset, well—' Garry's powerful spatulate fingers rippled over the computer keys. Shasa watched with curiosity as Garry presented his case, but when he realized what the boy was driving at, he quickly lost interest and concentration.

However, he listened to it all before he asked quietly, 'So you have paid for the option with your own money?'

'I have it signed, here!' Garry brandished the document. 'It cost me all my savings, over two thousand pounds just for a one-week option.'

'Let me recap, then,' Shasa suggested. 'You have spent two thousand pounds to acquire a one-week option on a section of agricultural ground on the northern outskirts of Johannesburg which you intend to develop as a residential township, complete with a shopping complex, theatres, cinemas and all the trimmings—'

'There is at least twenty million pounds of profit in the development – at the very least.' Garry manipulated the computer keyboard and pointed to the rippling green figures. 'Just look at that, Dad!'

'Garry! Garry!' Shasa sighed. 'I think you have just lost your two thousand pounds, but the experience will be worth it in the long run. Of course there is twenty million profit in it the long run. Everybody knows that, and everybody wants a piece of that action. It's just for that reason that there is such strict control on township development. It takes at least five years to get government approval for a new township, and there are hundreds of pitfalls along the way. It's a highly complex and specialized field of investment, and the outlay is enormous – millions of pounds at risk. Don't you see, Garry? Your piece of land is probably not the best available, there will be a dozen other projects ahead of yours and township development just isn't one of the areas which we deal in—' Shasa broke off and stared at his son. Garry was flapping his hands and stuttering so badly that Shasa had to warn him again, 'Big breath.'

Garry gasped and his barrel chest expanded until his shirt buttons strained. It came out quite clearly.

'I already have approval,' he said.

'That takes years – I've explained.' Shasa was brusque. He began to rise. 'We should change for dinner. Come on.'

'Dad, you don't understand,' Garry insisted. 'Approval has already been granted.'

Shasa sat down slowly. 'What did you say?' he asked quietly.

'Township approval was granted in 1891 by the *Volksraad* of the old Transvaal Republic. It was signed by President Kruger himself, but it is still perfectly legal and binding. It was just forgotten, that is all.'

'I don't believe it.' Shasa shook his head. 'How on earth did you get on to this, Garry?'

'I was reading a couple of old books about the early days of the Witwatersrand and the gold-mines. I thought that if I was going to learn mining, the very least I could do was bone up on the history of the industry,' Garry explained. 'And in one of the books there was a mention of one of the old Rand lords and his grandiose idea of building a paradise city for the very rich away from the coarse and rowdy centre of Johannesburg. The author mentioned that he had actually bought a six-thousand-acre farm and had it surveyed and that approval had been granted by the *Volksraad*, and then the whole idea had been abandoned.'

'What did you do then?'

'I went to the archives and looked up the proceedings of the *Volksraad* for the years 1889 to 1891 and there it was – the approval. Then I researched the title deeds of the property at the deeds registry and went out to the farm itself. It's called Baviaansfontein and it's owned by two brothers, both in their seventies. Nice old fellows, we got on well and they showed me their horses and cattle, and invited me to lunch. They thought the option was a big joke, but when I showed them my two thousand pounds, they had never seen so much money in one pile in their lives.' Garry grinned. 'Here are copies of the title deeds and the original township approval.' Garry handed them to his father and Shasa read through slowly, even moving his lips like a semi-literate so as to savour every word of the ancient documents.

'When does your option expire?' he asked at last, without looking up.

'Noon on Thursday. We will have to act fast.'

'Did you take out the option in the name of Courtney Mining?' Shasa asked.

'No. In my own name, but of course, I did it for you and the company.'

'You thought this out alone,' Shasa said carefully. 'You researched it yourself, dug up the original approval, negotiated the option with the owners, paid for it with two thousand of your own hard-earned cash. You did all the work and took all the risks and now you want to hand it over to someone else. That isn't very bright, is it?'

'I don't want to hand it over to just anybody – to you, Dad. Everything I do is for you, you know that.'

'Well, that changes as of now,' said Shasa briskly. 'I will personally lend you the two hundred thousand purchase price and we will fly up to Johannesburg first thing tomorrow to clinch the deal. Once you own the land, Courtney Mining will begin negotiating with you the terms of a joint venture to develop it.'

The negotiations started tough, and then as Garry got his first taste of blood, they grew tougher.

'My God, I've sired a monster,' Shasa complained, to

hide his pride in his offspring's bargaining technique. 'Come on, son, leave something in it for us.'

To mollify his father a little Garry announced a change in the name of the property. In future it would be known as Shasaville. When they at last signed the final agreement, Shasa opened a bottle of champagne and said, 'Congratulations, my boy.'

That approbation was worth more to Garry than all the townships and every grain of gold on the Witwatersrand.

Lothar De La Rey was one of the youngest police captains on the force, and this was not entirely on account of his father's position and influence. From the time he had been awarded the sword of honour at police college he had distinguished himself in every field that was considered important by the higher command. He had studied for and passed all his promotion examinations with distinction. A great emphasis was placed on athletic endeavour and rugby football was the major sport in the police curriculum. It was now almost certain that Lothar would be chosen as an international during the forthcoming tour by the New Zealand All Blacks. He was well liked both by his senior officers and his peers, and his service record was embellished by an unbroken string of excellent ratings. Added to this he had shown an unusual aptitude for police work. Neither the plodding monotony of investigation nor the routine of patrol wearied him, and in those sudden eruptions of dangerous and violent action Lothar had displayed resourcefulness and courage.

He had four citations on his service record, all of them for successful confrontation with dangerous criminals. He was also the holder of the Police Medal for Gallantry, which he had been awarded after he had shot and killed two notorious drug dealers during a foot-chase through the black township at night, and a single-handed shoot-out from which he had emerged unscathed.

Added to all this was the assessment by his superiors that while he was amenable to discipline, he also had the highly developed qualities of command and leadership. Both these were very much Afrikaner characteristics. During the North African campaign against Rommel, General Montgomery, when told that there was a shortage of officer material, had replied, 'Nonsense, we've got thousands of South Africans. Each of them is a natural leader – from childhood they are accustomed to giving orders to the natives.'

Lothar had been stationed at the Sharpeville police station since graduating from Police College and had come to know the area intimately. Gradually he had built up his own network of informers, the basis of all good police work, and through these prostitutes and shebeen owners and petty criminals he was able to anticipate much of the serious crime and to identify the organizers and perpetrators even before the offence was committed.

The higher command of the police force was well aware that the young police captain with illustrious family connections was in a large measure responsible for the fact that the police in the Sharpeville location had over the past few years built up a reputation of being one of the most vigorous and active units in the heavily populated industrial triangle that lies between Johannesburg, Pretoria and Vereeniging.

In comparison to greater Soweto, Alexandra or even Drake's Farm, Sharpeville was a small black township. It housed a mere forty thousand or so of all ages, and yet the police raids for illicit liquor and pass offenders were almost daily routine, and the lists of arrests and convictions by which the efficiency of any station is judged were out of all proportion to its size. Much of this industry and dedication to duty was quite correctly attributed to the energy of the young second-in-command.

Sharpeville is an adjunct to the town of Vereeniging where in 1902 the British Commander Lord Kitchener and the leaders of the Boer commandos negotiated the peace treaty which brought to an end the long-drawn-out and tragic South African War. Vereeniging is situated on the Vaal River fifty miles south of Johannesburg and its reasons for existing are the coal and iron deposits which are exploited by ISCOR, the giant state-owned Iron and Steel Corporation.

At the turn of the century the black workers in the steel industry were originally housed in the Top Location, but as conditions there became totally inadequate and outmoded a new location was set aside for them in the early 1940s and named after John Sharpe, the mayor for the time being of the town of Vereeniging. As the new dwellings in Sharpeville became available, the population was moved down from Top Location, and although the rents were as high as £2 7s 6d per month, the translocations were effected gradually and peaceably.

Sharpeville was, in fact, a model township, and though the cottages were the usual box shape, they were all serviced with water-borne sewerage and electricity, and there were all the other amenities including a cinema, shopping areas and sports facilities, together with their very own police station.

In the midst of one of the most comprehensive pieces of social engineering of the twentieth century – which was the policy of *apartheid* in practice – Sharpeville was a remarkable area of calm. All around, hundreds of thousands of people were being moved and regimented and reclassified in accordance with those monumental slabs of legislation, the Group Areas Act and the Population Registration Act. All around the fledgling leaders of black consciousness and liberation were preaching and exhorting and organizing, but Sharpeville seemed untouched by it all. The white city fathers of Vereeniging pointed out with quite justifiable satisfaction that the Communist agitators had been given short shrift in the Sharpeville location and that their black people were law-abiding and peaceful. The figures for serious crime were amongst the lowest in the industrialized section of the Transvaal, and offenders were taken care of with commendable expedition. Even the rent-defaulters were evicted from the location in summary fashion, and the local police force was always cooperative and conscientious.

When the law was extended to make it obligatory for black women to carry passes, as well as their menfolk, and when throughout most of the country this innovation was strenuously resisted, the ladies of Sharpeville presented themselves at the police station in such numbers and in such cooperative spirit that most of them had to be turned away with the injunction to 'come back later'.

In early March of 1960 Lothar De La Rey drove his official Land-Rover through this stable and law-abiding community, following the wide road across the open space in front of the police station. The cluster of police buildings, in the same austere and utilitarian design as the others in the location, were surrounded by a wire mesh fence about eight feet high, but the main gates were standing open and unguarded.

Lothar drove through and parked the Land-Rover below the flagpole on which the orange, blue and white national flag floated on a breeze that carried the faint chemical stink of the blast furnaces at the ISCOR plant. In the charge office he was immediately the centre of attention as his men came to congratulate him on the kick that had won the Currie Cup.

'Green and gold next,' the duty sergeant predicted as he

shook Lothar's hand, referring to the colours of the national rugby team jersey.

Lothar accepted their admiration with just the right degree of modesty, and then put an end to this breach of discipline and routine.

'All right, back to work everybody,' he ordered, and went to check the charge book. Where a charge office in Soweto might expect to have three or four murders and a dozen or so rape cases, there had been a single 'schedule one' crime committed in Sharpeville during the previous twenty-four hours and Lothar nodded with satisfaction and went through to report to his station commander.

In the doorway he came to attention and saluted, and the older man nodded and indicated the chair opposite him.

'Come in, Lothie. Sit down!'

He rocked his chair on to its back legs and watched Lothar as he removed his uniform cap and gloves.

'*Bakgat* game on Friday,' he congratulated him. 'Thank you for the tickets. Hell, man, that last kick of yours!'

He felt a stab of envy as he examined his number two. *Liewe land!* Beloved Land, but he looked like a soldier, so tall and straight! The commander glanced down at his own slack guts, and then back at the way the lad wore his uniform on those wide shoulders. You had only to look at him to see his class. It had taken the commander until the age of forty to gain the rank of captain, and he was resigned to the fact that he would go on pension at the same rank – but this one. No what! He would probably be a general before he was forty.

'Well, Lothie,' he said heavily. 'I'm going to miss you.' He smiled at the gleam in those alert but strangely pale yellow eyes. '*Ja*, my young friend,' he nodded, 'your transfer – you leave us at the end of May.'

Lothar leaned back in his chair and smiled. He suspected

that his own father had been instrumental in keeping him so long on this station, but although it had been increasingly irksome to waste time in this little backwater, his father knew best and Lothar was grateful for the experience he had gained here. He knew that a policeman only really learns his job on the beat, and he had put in his time. He knew he was a good policeman, and he had proved it to them all. Anybody who might be tempted to attribute his future promotions to his father's influence had only to look at his service record. It was all there. He had paid his dues in full, but now it was time to move on.

'Where are they sending me, sir?'

'You lucky young dog.' The commander shook his head with mock envy. 'You are going to CID headquarters at Marshall Square.'

It was the plum. The most sought-after, the most prestigious posting that any young officer could hope for. CID headquarters was right at the very nerve centre and heart of the entire force. Lothar knew that from there it would be swift and sure. He would have his general's stars while he was still a young man, and with them the maturity and reputation to make his entry into politics smooth and certain. He could retire from the force on the pension of a general, and devote the rest of his life to his country and his *Volk*. He had it all planned. Each step was clear to Lothar. When Dr Verwoerd went, he knew that his father would be a strong contender to take over the premiership. Perhaps one day there would be a second Minister of Police with the name of De La Rey, and after that another De La Rey at the head of the nation. He knew what he wanted, what road he had to follow, and he knew also that his feet were securely upon that road.

'You are being given your chance, Lothie,' the commander echoed his own thoughts. 'If you take it, you will go far – very far.'

'However far it is, sir, I will always remember the help and encouragement you have given me here at Sharpeville.'

'Enough of that. You have a couple of months before you go.' The commander was suddenly embarrassed. Neither of them were men who readily displayed their emotions. 'Let's get down to work. What about the raid tonight? How many men are you going to use?'

Lothar had the headlights of the Land-Rover switched off, and he drove slowly for the four-cylinder petrol engine had a distinctive beat that his quarry would pick up at a distance if the vehicle was driven hard.

There was a sergeant beside him, and five constables in the rear of the Land-Rover, all of them armed with riot batons. In addition, the sergeant had an automatic twelve-gauge Greener shotgun and Lothar wore his sidearm on his Sam Browne belt. They were lightly armed, for this was merely a liquor raid.

Sale of alcohol to blacks was strictly controlled, and was restricted to the brewing of the traditional cereal-based beer by state-controlled beer-halls. The consumption of spirits and wines by blacks was forbidden, but this prohibition caused illicit shebeens to flourish. The profits were too high to be passed by. The liquor was either stolen or purchased from white bottle stores or manufactured by the shebeen owners themselves. These home brews were powerful concoctions known generally as *skokiaan*, and according to the recipe of the individual distiller could contain anything from methylated spirits to the corpses of poisonous snakes and aborted infants. It was not uncommon for the customers of the shebeens to end up permanently blinded, or demented, or occasionally dead.

Tonight Lothar's team was setting out to raid a newly established shebeen which had been in business for only a few weeks. Lothar's information was that it was controlled by a black gang called 'The Buffaloes'.

Of course, Lothar was fully aware of the size and scope of the Buffaloes' operations. They were without doubt the largest and most powerful underworld association on the Witwatersrand. It was not known who headed the gang but there had been hints that it was connected to the African Mineworkers' Union and to one of the black political organizations. Certainly it was most active on the gold-mining properties closer to Johannesburg, and in the large black townships such as Soweto and Drake's Farm.

Until now they had not been bothered by the Buffaloes here in Sharpeville, and for this reason the setting up of a controlled shebeen was alarming. It might herald a deter-mined infiltration of the area which would almost certainly be followed by a campaign to politicize the local black population, with the resulting protest rallies and boycotts of the bus line and white-owned businesses, and all the other trouble whipped up by the agitators of the African National Congress and the newly formed Pan-Africanist Congress.

Lothar was determined to crush it before it spread like a bush fire through his whole area. Above the soft burble of the engine, out there in the darkness he heard a sharp double-fluted whistle and almost immediately it was repeated at a distance, down near the end of the avenue of quiet cottages.

'*Magtig!*' Lothar swore softly but bitterly. 'They've spot-ted us!' The whistles were the warnings of the shebeen lookouts.

He switched on the headlights and gunned the Land-Rover. They went hurtling down the narrow street.

The shebeen was at the end of the block, in the last cottage hard up against the boundary fence with a stretch of open veld beyond. As the headlights swept across the front of the cottage, he saw half a dozen dark figures pelting away from it, and others were fighting each other to get out of the front door and leaping from the windows.

Lothar swung the Land-Rover up over the pavement, through the tiny garden, and braked it into a deliberate and skilfully executed broadside, blocking the front door.

'Let's go!' he yelled, and his men flung the doors open and sprang out.

They grabbed the bewildered shebeen drinkers who were trapped between the Land-Rover and the cottage wall. As one of them began to resist, he dropped to a practised swing of a riot baton and the limp body was bundled into the back of the vehicle.

Lothar sprinted around the side of the cottage, and caught a woman in his arms as she jumped through the window. He turned her upside down in the air and held on to one ankle as he reached out and seized the arm of the next man through the window. In a single swift motion he handcuffed the two of them together, wrist to ankle, and left them floundering and falling over each other like a pair of trussed hens.

Lothar reached the back door of the cottage, and made his first mistake. He seized the handle and jerked the door open. The man had been waiting on the inside, poised and ready, and as the door began to open he hurled his full weight upon it and the edge of it crashed into Lothar's chest. The wind was driven from his lungs, and hissed up his throat as he went over backwards down the steps, sprawling on the hard sun-baked earth, and the man leaped clean over him.

Lothar caught a glimpse of him against the light, and saw that he was young and well built, lithe and quick as a black cat. Then he was racing away into the darkness, heading for the boundary fence that backed up to the cottage.

Lothar rolled over onto his knees and came to his feet. Even with the start the fugitive had, there was nobody who could outrun Lothar in a fair match. He was at the peak of fitness, after months of rigorous training for the Currie Cup match and the national trials, but as he started forward the agony of his empty lungs made him double over and wheeze for breath.

Ahead of him the fleeing figure ducked through a hole in the mesh of the fence, and Lothar fell to his knees and snapped open the holster at his side. Three months before, he had been runner-up in the police pistol championships at Bloemfontein, but now his aim was unsteady with agony and the dark figure was merging with the night, quartering away from him. Lothar fired twice but after each long bright muzzle flash there was no thumping impact of bullet into flesh and the runner was swallowed up by darkness. Lothar slid the weapon back into his holster, and fought to fill his lungs – his humiliation was more painful than his injury. Lothar was unaccustomed to failure.

He forced himself to get to his feet. None of his men should see him grovelling, and after only a minute, and even though his lungs were still on fire, he went back and dragged his two captives to their feet with unnecessary violence. The woman was stark naked. Obviously she had been entertaining a client in the back bedroom, but now she was wailing tragically.

'Shut your mouth, you black cow,' he told her, and shoved her through the back door of the cottage.

The kitchen had been used as the bar. There were cases of liquor stacked to the ceiling, and the table was piled with a high pyramid of empty tumblers.

In the front room the floor was covered with broken glass and spilled liquor, evidence of the haste with which it had been vacated, and Lothar wondered how so many customers had fitted into a room that size. He had seen at least twenty escape into the night.

He shoved the naked prostitute towards one of his black constables. 'Take care of her,' he ordered, and the man grinned lasciviously and tweaked one of her tawny melon-round breasts.

'None of that,' Lothar warned him. He was still angry at the one who had got away, and the constable saw his face and sobered. He led the woman through into the bedroom to find her clothing.

Lothar's other men were coming in, each of them leading two or three sorry-looking captives.

'Check their passes,' Lothar ordered, and turned to his sergeant. 'All right, Cronje, let's get rid of this stuff.'

Lothar watched as the cases of liquor were carried out and stacked in front of the cottage. Two of his constables opened them and smashed the bottles against the edge of the kerb. The sweet fruity smell of cheap brandy filled the night and the gutter ran with the amber-brown liquid.

When the last bottle had been destroyed, Lothar nodded at his sergeant. 'Right, Cronje, take them up to the station.' And while the prisoners were loaded into the two police trucks that had followed his Land-Rover, Lothar went back into the cottage to check that his men had not overlooked anything of importance.

In the back room with its tumbled bed and stained sheets, he opened the single cupboard and distastefully used the point of his riot baton to rummage through it.

Beneath the pile of clothing at the bottom of the cupboard was a small cardboard carton. Lothar pulled it out and tore open the lid. It was filled with a neat stack of single-leaf pamphlets, and idly he glanced at the top one until its impact struck him. He snatched up the sheet and turned it to the light from the bare bulb in the ceiling.

This is the *Poqo* of which it is said, 'Take up your spear in your right hand, my beloved people, for the foreigners are looting your land.'

Poqo was the military branch of the Pan-Africanist Congress. The word *Poqo* meant pure and untainted, for none other than pure-blooded African Bantu could become

649

members, and Lothar knew it for an organization of young fanatics already responsible for a number of vicious and brutal murders. In the little town of Paarl in the Cape *Poqo* had marched hundreds strong upon the police station and when driven back had vented their fury upon the civilian population, massacring two white women, one a girl of seventeen years. In the Transkei they had attacked a road-party encampment and murdered the white supervisor and his family in the most atrocious manner. Lothar had seen the police photographs and his skin crawled at the memory. *Poqo* was a name to fear and Lothar read the rest of the pamphlet with full attention.

On Monday we are going to face the police. All the people of Sharpeville will be as one on that day. No man or woman will go to his place of work. No man or woman will leave the township by bus or train or taxi. All the people will gather as one and march to the police station. We are going to protest at the pass law which is a terrible burden, too heavy for us to carry. We will make the white police fear us.

Any man or woman who does not march with us on Monday will be hunted down. On that day all the people will be as one.

Poqo has said this thing. Hear it and obey it.

Lothar read the crudely printed pamphlet through again, and then he murmured, 'So it has come at last.' He picked out the sentence which had offended him most, 'We will make the white police fear us,' and he read it aloud.

'So! We will see about that!' And he shouted for his sergeant to take the carton of subversive leaflets out to the truck.

There was an inevitability in Raleigh Tabaka's life. The great river of his existence carried him along with it so that he was powerless to break free of it or even swim against the current.

His mother, as one of the most adept of the tribal *sangomas* of Xhosa, had first instilled in him the deep awareness of his African self. She had showed him the mysteries and the secrets, and read the future for him in the casting of the bones.

'One day you will lead your people, Raleigh Tabaka,' she prophesied. 'You will become one of the great chiefs of Xhosa and your name will be spoken with those of Makana and Ndlame – all these things I see in the bones.'

When his father, Hendrick Tabaka, sent him and his twin brother Wellington across the border to the multi-racial school in Swaziland, his Africanism had been con-firmed and underscored, for his fellow pupils had been the sons of chiefs and black leaders from countries like Basuto-land and Bechuanaland. These were countries where black tribes ruled themselves, free of the white man's heavy paternal fluences, and he listened with awe as they spoke of how their families lived on equal terms with the whites around them.

This came as a total revelation to Raleigh. In his existence the whites were a breed apart, to be feared and avoided, for they wielded an unchallenged power over him and all his people.

At Waterford he learned that this was not the law of the universe. There were white pupils, and although it was at first strange, he ate at the same table as they did, from the same plates and with the same utensils, and slept in a bed alongside them in the school dormitory, and sat on the toilet seat still warm from a white boy's bottom and vacated it to another little white boy waiting impatiently outside the door for him to finish. In his own country none of these things were allowed, and when he went home for the holidays he read the notices with his eyes wide open – the notices that said WHITES ONLY – *BLANKES ALLEENLIK*. From the windows of the train he saw the beautiful farms and the fat cattle that the white men owned, and the bare eroded earth of the tribal reservations, and when he reached home at Drake's Farm he saw that his father's house, which he remembered as a palace, was in reality a hovel – and the resentment began to gnaw at his soul and the wounds it left festered.

Before Raleigh left to go to school, his Uncle Moses Gama used to visit his father. From infancy he had been in awe of his uncle, for power burned from him like one of those great veld fires which consumed the land and towered into the heavens in a column of dense smoke and ash and sparks.

Even though Moses Gama had been absent from Drake's Farm for so many years, his memory had never been allowed to grow dim, and Hendrick had read aloud to the family the letters that he had received from him in distant lands.

So when at last Raleigh matriculated and left Waterford to return to Drake's Farm and begin work in his father's businesses, he announced that he wanted to take his place in the ranks of the young warriors.

'After you have been to initiation camp,' his father promised him, 'I will introduce you to *Umkhonto we Sizwe*'!

Raleigh's initiation set the final stamp on his special sense of Africanism. With his brother Wellington and six other young men of his initiation class, he left Drake's Farm and travelled by train in the bare third-class carriage to the little magisterial town of Queenstown which was the centre of the Xhosa tribal territories.

It had all been arranged by his mother, and the elders of the tribe met them at Queenstown station. In a rickety old truck they were driven out to a kraal on the banks of the great Fish River and delivered into the care of the tribal custodian, an old man whose duty it was to preserve and safeguard the history and customs of the tribe.

Ndlame, the old man, ordered them to strip off their clothing and to hand over all the possessions they had brought with them. These were thrown on a bonfire on the river bank, as a symbol of childhood left behind them. He took them naked into the river to bathe, and, then still glistening wet, he led them up the far bank to the circumcision hut where the tribal witchdoctors waited.

When the other initiates hung back fearfully, Raleigh went boldly to the head of the column and was the first to stoop through the low entrance to the hut. The interior was thick with smoke from the dung fire and the witch-doctors, in their skins and feathers and fantastic head-dresses, were weird and terrifying figures.

Raleigh was smitten with terror, for the pain which he had dreaded all his childhood and for the forces of the supernatural which lurked in the gloomy recesses of the hut, yet he forced himself to run forward and leap over the smouldering fire.

As he landed on the far side the witchdoctors sprang upon him and forced him into a kneeling position, holding his head so he was forced to watch as one of them seized his penis and drew out the rubbery collar of his foreskin to its full length. In ancient times the circumciser would have used a hand-forged blade, but now it was a Gillette razor blade.

As they intoned the invocation to the tribal gods, Raleigh's foreskin was cut away, leaving his glans soft and pink and vulnerable. His blood spattered on to the dung floor between his knees, but he uttered not a sound.

Ndlame helped him rise, and he staggered out into the sunlight and fell upon the river bank, riding the terrible burning pain, but the shrieks of the other boys and the sounds of their wild struggles carried clearly to where he lay. He recognized his brother Wellington's cries of pain as the shrillest and loudest of them all.

Raleigh knew that their foreskins would be gathered up by the witchdoctors, salted and dried and added to the tribal totem. A part of them would remain for ever with the custodians and no matter how far they wandered the witchdoctors could call them back with the foreskin curse.

When all the other initiates had suffered the circumciser's knife, Ndlame led them down to the water's edge and showed them how to wash and bind their wounds with medicinal leaves and herbs, and to strap their penises against their stomachs. 'For if the Mamba looks down, he will bleed again,' he warned them.

They smeared their bodies with a mixture of clay and ash. Even the hair on their heads was crusted with the dead-white ritual paint, so that they looked like albino ghosts. Their only clothing was skirts of grass and they built their huts in the deepest and most secret parts of the forest, for no woman might look upon them. They prepared their own food, plain maize cakes without any relish, and meat was forbidden them during the three moons of the initiation. Their only possession was their food bowl of clay.

One of the boys developed an infection of his circumcision wound, the stinking green pus ran from it like milk from a cow's teat, and the fever consumed him so his skin was almost painfully hot to the touch. The herbs and potions that Ndlame applied were of no avail. He died on the fourth day and they buried him in the forest and Ndlame took his food bowl away. It would be thrown through the front door of his mother's hut by one of the witchdoctors, without a word being spoken, and she would know that her son had not been acceptable to the tribal gods.

Each day from before dawn's light until after sunset, Ndlame gave them instruction and taught them their duties as members of the tribe, as husbands and as fathers. They learned to endure pain and hardship with stoicism. They learned discipline and duty to their tribe, the ways of the wild animals and plants, how to survive in the wilderness, and how to please their wives and raise their children.

When the wounds of the circumcision blade had healed, Ndlame bound up their members each night in the special knot called the Red Dog, to prevent them spilling their seed in the sacred initiation huts. Each morning Ndlame inspected the knots carefully to ensure that they had not been loosened to enjoy the forbidden pleasure of masturbation.

When the three moons had passed, Ndlame led them back to the river and they washed away the white initiation clay and anointed their bodies with a mixture of fat and red ochre, and Ndlame gave them each a red blanket, symbol of manhood, with which they covered themselves. In procession, singing the manhood songs which they had practised, they went to where the tribe waited at the edge of the forest.

Their parents had gifts for them, clothing and new shoes and money, and the girls giggled and ogled them boldly, for they were men now and able at last to take a wife, as many wives as they could afford, for the *lobola*, the marriage fee, was heavy.

The two brothers, accompanied by their mother, journeyed back to Drake's Farm, Wellington to take leave of their father, for he was going on to take holy orders, and Raleigh to remain at his father's side, to learn the multifarious facets of Hendrick Tabaka's business activities and eventually to take the helm and become the comfort and mainstay of Hendrick's old age.

These were fascinating and disturbing months and years for Raleigh. Until this time he had never guessed at his father's wealth and power, but gradually it was revealed to him. The pages in the ledger turned for him one at a time. He learned of his father's general dealer stores, and the butcheries and bakeries in all the black townships spread throughout the great industrial triangle of the Transvaal that was based on the gold-mines and the iron deposits and the coalfields. Then he went on to learn about the cattle herds and rural general dealer's stores in the tribal reservations owned by his father and cared for by his myriad brothers, about the shebeens and the whores that operated behind the front of legitimate business, and finally he learned about the Buffaloes, that ubiquitous and shadowy association of many men from all the various tribes, whose chief was his own father.

He realized at last just how rich and powerful his father was, and yet how because he was a black man, he could not display his importance and could wield his power only covertly and clandestinely. Raleigh felt his anger stir, as it did whenever he saw those signs WHITES ONLY – *BLANKES ALLEENLIK* and saw the white men pass in their shiny automobiles, or when he stood outside the universities and hospitals which were closed to him.

He spoke to his father about these things that troubled him and Hendrick Tabaka chuckled and shook his head. 'Rage makes a man sick, my son. It spoils his appetite for life and keeps him from sleep at night. We cannot change our world, so we must look for the good things in life and enjoy those to the full. The white man is strong, you cannot imagine how strong, you have not seen even the strength of his little finger. If you take up the spear against him, he will destroy you and all the good things we have – and if the gods and the lightnings intervened and by chance you destroyed the white man, think what would follow him. There would come a darkness and a time without law and protection that would be a hundred times worse than the white man's oppressions. We would be consumed by the rage of our own people, and we would not have even the consolation of these few sweet things. If you open your ears and your eyes, my son, you will hear how the young people call us collaborators and how they talk of a redistribution of wealth, and you will see the envy in their eyes. The dream you have, my son, is a dangerous dream.'

'And yet I must dream it, my father,' said Raleigh, and then, one unforgettable day, his uncle, Moses Gama, returned from foreign lands and took him to meet other young men who shared the same dream.

So during the day Raleigh worked at his father's business and in the evenings he met with the other young comrades of *Umkhonto we Sizwe*. At first they only talked, but the words were sweeter and headier than the smoke of the *dagga* pipes of the old men.

Then Raleigh joined the comrades who were enforcing the decrees of the African National Congress, the boycotts and the strikes and the work stoppages. He went to Evaton location with a small task force to enforce the bus boycott and they attacked the black workers in the bus queues who were trying to get to their places of employment or who were going to shop for their families, and they beat them with *sjamboks*, the long leather quirts, and with their fighting-sticks.

On the first day of the attacks, Raleigh was determined to demonstrate his zeal to his comrades and he used his fighting-stick with all the skill which he had learned as a child in faction fights with the boys of the other tribes.

There was a woman in the queue for the bus who defied Raleigh's order to go home, and she spat at him and his comrades and called them *tsotsies* and *skelms*, gangsters and rogues. She was a woman in middle age, large and matronly, with cheeks so plump and shiny that they looked as though they had been rubbed up with black shoe polish, and with such a queenly manner that at first the young comrades of *Umkhonto we Sizwe* were abashed by her scorn and might have withdrawn.

Then Raleigh saw that this was his opportunity to prove his ardour and he leaped forward and confronted the woman. 'Go home, old woman,' he warned her. 'We are no longer dogs to eat the white man's shit.'

'You are a little uncircumcised boy with filth on your tongue,' she began, but Raleigh would not let her continue. He swung the long supple fighting-stick, and it split her shiny black cheek as cleanly as the cut of an axe, so for an instant Raleigh saw the bone gleam in the depths of the wound before the swift crimson flood obscured it. The big woman screamed and fell to her knees, and Raleigh felt a strange sensation of power and purpose, a euphoria of patriotic duty. For a moment the woman kneeling before him became the focus of all his frustration and his rage.

The woman saw it in his eyes and held up both arms over her head to ward off the next blow. Raleigh struck again, with all his strength and skill, using his wrist so that the fighting-stick whined in the air and the blow landed on the woman's elbow. Her arms were wreathed in layers of deep fat. It hung in dewlaps from her upper arms and in bracelets about her wrists, but it could not cushion the power behind that whistling stick. The joint of her elbow shattered, and her forearm dropped and twisted at an impossible angle as it hung helplessly at her side.

The woman screamed again, this time the sound was so filled with outrage and agony that it goaded the other young warriors and they fell upon the bus passengers with such fury that the terminus was strewn with the wailing and sobbing injured and the concrete floor was washed sticky red.

When the ambulances came with sirens wailing to collect the casualties, the comrades of *Umkhonto we Sizwe* pelted them with stones and half bricks and Raleigh led a small group of the bolder ones who ran out into the street and turned one of the stranded ambulances on its side, and when the petrol poured from the tank, Raleigh lit a match and tossed it on to the spread pool.

The explosive ignition singed his eyelashes and burned

away the front of his hair, but that evening when they got back to Drake's Farm, Raleigh was the hero of the band of warriors, and they gave him the praise-name of *Cheza*, which means 'the Burner'.

As Raleigh was accepted into the middle ranks of the Youth League of the ANC and *Umkhonto we Sizwe*, so he gradually understood the cross-currents of power within them and the internal politics of the rival groups of moderates and radicals – those who thought that freedom could be negotiated and those who believed that it must be won with the blade of the spear, those who thought that the treasures so patiently built up over the years – the mines and the factories and the railways – should be preserved and those who believed that it should all be destroyed and rebuilt again in the name of freedom by the pure ones.

Raleigh found himself inclining more and more towards the purists, the hard fighting men, the exclusive Bantu elite, and when he heard the name *Poqo* for the first time he thrilled to the sound and sense of it. It described exactly his own feelings and desires – the pure, the only ones.

He was present in the house in Drake's Farm when Moses Gama spoke to them and promised them that the long wait was almost at an end.

'I will take this land by its heels and set it upon its head,' Moses Gama told the group of intense loyal young warriors. 'I will give you a deed, a sign that every man and woman will understand instantly. It will bring the tribes into the streets in their millions and their rage will be a beautiful thing, so pure and strong that nobody, not even the hard Boers, will be able to resist.'

Soon Raleigh came to sense in Moses Gama a divinity that set him above all other humans, and he was filled with a religious love for him and a deep and utter commitment. When the news reached Raleigh that Moses Gama had been caught by the white police as he was on the point of blowing up the Houses of Parliament and destroying all the evil contained in that iniquitous institution, Raleigh was almost prostrated by his grief, and yet set on fire by Moses Gama's courage and example.

Over the weeks and months that followed Raleigh was exasperated and angered by the calls for moderation from the high councils of the ANC, and by the dispirited and meek acceptance of Moses Gama's imprisonment and trial. He wanted to vent his wrath upon the world, and when the Pan-Africanist Congress broke away from the ANC Raleigh followed where his heart led.

Robert Sobukwe, the leader of the Pan-Africanist Congress, sent for him. 'I have heard good words of you,' he told Raleigh. 'And I know the man who is your uncle, the father of us all who languishes in the white man's prison. It is our duty – for we are the pure ones – to bring our message to every black man in the land. There is much work to do, and this is the task I have set for you alone, Raleigh Tabaka.' He led Raleigh to a large-scale map of the Transvaal. 'This area has been left untouched by the ANC.' He placed his hand over the sweep of townships and coalfields and industry around the town of Vereeniging. 'This is where I want you to begin the work.'

Within a week Raleigh had conditioned his father to the idea that he should move to the Vereeniging area to take charge of the family interests there, the three stores in Evaton and the butchery and bakery in Sharpeville, and his father liked the idea the more he thought about it, and he agreed.

'I will give you the names of the men who command the Buffaloes down there. We can begin moving the shebeens into the Sharpeville area. So far we have not put our cattle to graze on those pastures, and the grass there is tall and green.'

Raleigh moved slowly at first. He was a stranger in Sharpeville and he had to consolidate his position.

However, he was a strong and comely young man, and he spoke fluently all the major languages of the townships. This was not an unusual achievement, there were many who spoke all the four related languages of the Nguni group of peoples, the Zulus, the Xhosas, the Swazi and the Ndebele, which make up almost seventy per cent of the black tribes of South Africa and whose speech is characterized by elaborate clicking and clucking sounds.

Many others, like Raleigh, were also conversant with the other two languages which are spoken by almost the entire remainder of the black population, the Sotho and the Tswana.

Language was no barrier, and Raleigh had the additional advantage of being placed in charge of his father's business interest in the area, and therefore was accorded almost immediate recognition and respect. Sooner or later every single resident of Sharpeville would come to either Tabaka's bakery or butcher shop and be impressed by the articulate and sympathetic young man who listened to their worries and troubles and extended them credit to buy the white bread and fizzy drinks and tobacco; these were the staple diet of the townships where much of the old way of life was abandoned and forgotten, where the soured milk and maize meal were difficult to procure and where rickets made the children lethargic, bent their bones and turned their hair fine and wispy and dyed a peculiar bronze colour.

They told Raleigh their little troubles, like the cost of renting the township houses and the hardship of commuting such distances to their place of work that it was necessary to rise long before the sun. And then they told Raleigh their greater worries, of being evicted from their homes and of the harassment by the police who were always raiding for liquor and pass offences and prostitution and to enforce the influx control laws. But always it came down to the passes, the little booklets that ruled their lives. The police were always there to ask 'Where is your pass? Show me your pass book.' The *dompas*, they called them, 'the damned pass', in which were stamped all their details of birth and residence and right to reside; no black person could get a job unless he or she produced the damned pass book.

From all the people who came to the shops, Raleigh chose the young vital ones, the brave ones with rage in their hearts, and they met discreetly at first in the storeroom at the back of the bakery, sitting on the bread baskets and the piles of flour bags, talking the night through.

Then they moved more openly, speaking to the older people and the children in the schools, going about as disciples to teach and explain. Raleigh used the funds of the butchery to buy a secondhand duplicator, and he typed the pamphlets on the pink wax sheets and ran them off on the machine.

They were crude little pamphlets, with botchy typing errors and obvious corrections and each one began with the salutation, 'This is *Poqo* of which it is said—' and ended with the stern injunction, '*Poqo* has said this thing. Hear it and obey it.' The young men whom Raleigh had recruited distributed these and read them to those who could not read for themselves.

At first Raleigh allowed only men to come to the meetings in the back room of the bakery store, for they were purists and it was the traditional role of the men to herd the cattle and hunt the game and defend the tribe, while the women thatched the huts and tilled the earth for maize and sorghum and carried the children on their backs.

Then the word was passed down from the high command of *Poqo* and PAC that the women were also part of the struggle. So Raleigh spoke with his young men and one evening a girl came to their Friday-night meeting in the bakery storeroom.

She was a Xhosa and she was tall and strong with beautiful swelling buttocks and a round sweet face like one of the wild veld flowers. While Raleigh spoke she listened silently. She did not move or fidget or interrupt and her huge dark eyes never left Raleigh's face.

Raleigh felt that he was inspired that night, and though he never looked directly at the girl and seemed to address himself to the young warriors, it was to her he spoke and his voice was deep and sure and his own words reverberated in his skull and he listened to them with the same wonder as the others did.

When he finished speaking at last, they all sat in silence for a long time and then one of the young men turned to the girl and said, 'Amelia—' that was the first time ever that Raleigh heard her name, 'Amelia, will you sing for us?'

She did not simper or hang her head or make modest protestations. She simply opened her mouth, and sound poured out of her, glorious sound that made the skin on Raleigh's forearms and at the back of his neck tingle.

He watched her mouth while she sang. Her lips were soft and broad, shaped like two leaves of the wild peach tree, with a dark iridescence that shaded to soft pink on the inside of her mouth, and when she reached for an impossibly sweet high note, he saw that her teeth were perfect white as bone that had lain for a season in the veld, polished by the wind and bleached by the African sun.

The words of the song were strange to him, but like the voice that sang them, they thrilled Raleigh:

> When the roll of heroes is called,
> Will my name be on it?
> I dream of that day when I will
> Sit with Moses Gama,
> And we will talk of the passing of the Boers.

She went away with the young men who had brought her, and that night Raleigh dreamed of her. She stood

663

beside the pool in the great Fish River in which he had washed away the white clay paint of his childhood and she wore the short beaded kilt and her breasts and her legs were bare. Her legs were long and her breasts were round and hard as black marble and she smiled at him with those even white teeth, and when Raleigh awoke his seed was splashed upon the blanket which covered him.

Three days later she came to the bakery to buy bread and Raleigh saw her through the peephole above his desk through which he could watch all that was happening in the front of the store and he went through to the counter and greeted her gravely.

'I see you, Amelia.'

She smiled at him and replied, 'I see you also, Raleigh Tabaka,' and it seemed that she sang his name, for she gave it a music that he had never heard in it before.

She purchased two loaves of white bread, but Raleigh lingered over the sale, wrapping each loaf carefully and counting the pennies of her change as though they were gold sovereigns.

'What is your full name?' he asked her.

'I am called Amelia Sigela.'

'Where is your father's kraal, Amelia Sigela?'

'My father is dead, and I live with my father's sister.'

She was a teacher at the Sharpeville primary school and she was twenty years old. When she left with her bread wrapped in newspaper and her buttocks swinging and jostling each other beneath the yellow European-style skirt, Raleigh returned to his desk in the cubicle of his office and sat for a long time staring at the wall.

On Friday Amelia Sigela came again to the meeting in the back room of the bakery and at the end she sang for them once more. This time Raleigh knew the words and he sang with her. He had a good deep baritone but she gilded it and wreathed it in the glory of her startling soprano and when the meeting broke up, Raleigh walked back with her through the dark streets to her aunt's house in the avenue beyond the school.

They lingered at the door and he touched her arm. It was warm and silky beneath his fingers. On the Sunday when he took the train back to Drake's Farm to make his weekly report to his father, he told his mother about Amelia Sigela and the two of them went through to the sacred room where his mother kept the family gods.

His mother sacrificed a black chicken and spoke to the carved idols, particularly to the totem of Raleigh's maternal great-grandfather, and he replied in a voice that only Raleigh's mother could hear. She listened gravely, nodding at what he said, and later, while they ate the sacrificial chicken with rice and herbs, she promised, 'I will speak to your father on your behalf.'

The following Friday after the meeting, Raleigh walked home with Amelia again, but this time as they passed the school where she taught, he drew her into the shadow of the buildings and they stood against the wall very close together. She made no attempt to pull away when he stroked her cheek, so he told her:

'My father is sending an emissary to your aunt to agree a marriage price.' Amelia was silent and he went on, 'However, I will ask him not to do so, if you do not wish it.'

'I wish it very much,' she whispered, and slowly and voluptuously she rubbed herself against him like a cat.

The *lobola*, the marriage price, was twenty head of cattle, worth a great deal of money, and Hendrick Tabaka told his son, 'You must work for it, just like other young men are forced to do.'

It would take Raleigh three years to accumulate enough to buy the cattle, but when he told Amelia, she smiled and told him, 'Each day will make me want you more. Think then how great will be my want after three years, and think how sweet will be that moment when the wanting is assuaged.'

Every afternoon, when school was out, Amelia came to the bakery and quite naturally she took to working behind the counter selling the bread and the round brown buns. Then when Raleigh closed the shop, she cooked his evening meal for him, and when he had eaten, they walked back to her aunt's house together.

Amelia slept in a tiny room hardly bigger than a closet, across the passage from her aunt. They left the interleading doors open and Raleigh lay on Amelia's bed with her and under the blanket they played the sweet games that custom and tribal law sanctioned all engaged couples to play. Raleigh was allowed to explore delicately and with his fingertips hunt for the little pink bud of flesh hidden between soft furry lips that old Ndlame had told him about at initiation camp. The Xhosa girls are not circumcised like the women of some of the other tribes, but they are taught the arts of pleasing men, and when he could stand it no longer, she took him and held him between her crossed thighs, avoiding only the final penetration that was reserved by tribal lore for their wedding night, and skilfully she milked him of his seed. Strangely, it seemed that every time she did this, rather than depleting him, she replenished the well of his love for her until it was overflowing.

Then the time came when Raleigh judged it expedient to begin infiltrating the Buffaloes into the township. With Hendrick Tabaka's blessing and under Raleigh's supervision they opened their first shebeen in a cottage at the far end of the township, hard up against the boundary fence.

The shebeen was run by two of the Buffaloes from Drake's Farm who had done this type of work for Hendrick Tabaka before. They knew all the little tricks like adulterating the liquor to make it go further and having one or two girls in the back room for the men that liquor had made amorous.

However, Raleigh warned them about the local police force, who had an ugly reputation, and about one of the white officers in particular, a man with pale predatory eyes that had given him his nickname *Ngwi* the leopard. He was a hard cruel man who had shot to death four men in the time he had been in Sharpeville, two of them members of the Buffaloes who had been supplying the township with *dagga*.

At first they were cautious and wary, vetting their customers carefully and placing lookouts on all approaches to the shebeen, but then as the weeks passed, with business improving each night, they relaxed a little. There was very little competition. Other shebeens had been closed down swiftly, and the customers were so thirsty that the Buffaloes could charge three and four times the usual rate.

Raleigh brought the liquor stocks into the township in his little blue Ford pick-up, the crates hidden beneath sacks of flour and sheep carcasses. He spent as little time as possible at the shebeen, for every minute was dangerous. He would drop off the supplies, collect the empty bottles and the cash and be gone within a half an hour. He never drove the pick-up directly to the front door of the cottage, but parked it in the dark veld beyond the boundary fence and the two Buffaloes would come through the hole in the wire mesh and help him carry the crates of cheap brandy.

After a while Raleigh realized that the shebeen offered another good distribution point for the *Poqo* pamphlets that he printed on the duplicator. He usually kept a stock of these in the cottage and the two Buffaloes who ran the shebeen and the girls who worked in the back room had orders to give one to each of their customers.

In early March, not long after the glad tidings of Moses Gama's reprieve and the mitigation of his death sentence to life imprisonment, Sobukwe sent for Raleigh. The rendezvous was in a house in the vast black township of Soweto. It was not one of the boxlike flat-roofed cottages, but was rather a large modern bungalow situated in the elite section of the township known as 'Beverly Hills'. It had a tiled roof, its own swimming-pool, garaging for two vehicles and large plate-glass windows overlooking the pool.

When Raleigh arrived in the blue pick-up, he found that he was not the only invited guest and there were a dozen or so other vehicles parked along the kerb. Sobukwe had invited all his middle-ranking field officers to this briefing and over forty of them crowded into the sitting-room of the bungalow.

'Comrades,' Sobukwe addressed them. 'We are ready to flex our muscles. You have worked hard and it is time to gather in some of the fruits of your labours. In all the places where the Pan-Africanist Congress is strong – not only here on the Witwatersrand but across the country – we are going to make the white police fear our power. We are going to hold a mass protest demonstration against the pass laws—'

Listening to Sobukwe speak, Raleigh was reminded of the power and personality of his own imprisoned uncle, Moses Gama, and he was proud to be part of this magnificent company. As Sobukwe unfolded his plans Raleigh made a silent but fervent resolution that at Sharpeville, the area for which he was responsible, the demonstration would be impressive and solid.

He related every detail of the meeting, and every word that Sobukwe had spoken, to Amelia. Her lovely round face seemed to glow with excitement as she listened and she helped him print the sheets announcing the demonstration and to pack them into the old liquor cartons in lots of five hundred.

On the Friday before the planned demonstration Raleigh ran a shipment of liquor down to the Buffaloes' shebeen, and he took a carton of pamphlets with him. The Buffaloes were waiting for him in the darkness beside the track, and one of them flashed a torch to guide the pick-up into the scraggy patch of black wattle, and they unloaded the liquor and trudged across to the township fence.

In the cottage Raleigh counted the empty bottles and

the full ones and checked these figures against the cash in the canvas bank bag. It tallied and he gave a brief word of commendation to the two Buffaloes, and looked into the front room which was packed with cheerful noisy drinkers.

Then when the door to the nearest bedroom opened and a big Basuto iron-worker came out, grinning and buttoning the front of his blue overalls, Raleigh squeezed past him into the back room. The girl was straightening the sheets on the bed. She was bending over with her back to Raleigh and she was naked, but she looked over her shoulder and smiled when she recognized him. Raleigh was popular with all the girls. She had the money ready for him, and Raleigh counted it in front of her. There was no means of checking her, but over the years Hendrick Tabaka had developed an instinct for a cheating girl, and when Raleigh delivered the money to him he would know if she were holding out.

Raleigh gave her a box of pamphlets and she sat beside him on the bed while he read one of them to her.

'I will be there on Monday,' she promised. 'And I will tell all my men these things and give them each a paper.' She placed the box in the bottom of the cupboard and then came back to Raleigh and took his hand.

'Stay a little while,' she invited him. 'I will straighten your back for you.'

She was a pretty plump little thing and Raleigh was tempted. Amelia was a traditional Nguni maiden, and she did not suffer the curse of Western-style jealousy. In fact, she had urged him to accept the offers of the other girls. 'If I am not allowed to sharpen your spear, let the joy-girls keep it bright for the time when I am at last allowed to feel its kiss.'

'Come,' the girl urged Raleigh now, and stroked him through the cloth of his trousers. 'See how the cobra awakes,' she laughed. 'Let me wring his neck!'

Raleigh took one step back towards the bed, laughing

with her – then suddenly he froze and the laugh was cut off abruptly. Out in the darkness he had heard the whistle of the lookouts.

'Police,' he snapped. 'The Leopard—' and there was the sudden distinctive rumble of a Land-Rover being driven hard and headlights flashed across the cheap curtaining that covered the window.

Raleigh sprang to the door. In the front room the drinkers were fighting to escape through the door and windows, and the table, covered with glasses and empty bottles, was overturned and glass shattered. Raleigh shouldered panic-stricken bodies out of his way and reached the kitchen door. It was locked but he opened it with his own key and slipped through, locking it again behind him.

He switched off the lights and stole across to the back door and placed his hand on the door knob. He would not make the mistake of running out into the yard. The Leopard was notoriously quick with his pistol. Raleigh waited in the darkness, and he heard the screams and the scuffling, the crack of the riot batons on flesh and bone and the grunting of the men who swung them and he steeled himself.

Just beyond the door, he heard light running footsteps and suddenly the door handle was seized from the far side and violently twisted. As the man on the outside tried to pull the door open, Raleigh held it, and the other man heaved and swore, leaning back on it with all his weight.

Raleigh let the handle go, and reversed his resistance, throwing his body against the cheap pine door so that it burst open. He felt it crash into human flesh and he had a glimpse of the brown-uniformed figure hurtling backwards down the stairs. Then he used his own momentum to leap up and outwards, clearing the police officer like a steeple-chaser, and he went bounding away towards the hole in the mesh fence.

As he ducked through it he glanced back and saw the police officer on his knees. Though his features were contracted and swollen with pain and anger, Raleigh recognized him. It was *Ngwi*, the killer of men, and the blue service revolver glinted in his hand as it cleared the holster at his side.

Fear sped Raleigh's feet as he darted away into the darkness, but he jinked and twisted as he ran. Something passed close to his head with a snapping report that hurt his eardrums and made him flinch his head wildly and he jinked again. Behind him was another thudding report but he did not hear the second bullet and he saw the dark shape of the Ford ahead of him.

He tumbled into the front seat and started the engine. Without switching on the headlights he bumped over the verge onto the track and accelerated away into the darkness.

He found that he still had the canvas bag of money clutched in his left hand, and his relief was intense. His father would be incensed at the loss of the liquor stocks, but his anger would have been multiplied many times if Raleigh had lost the money as well.

Solomon Nduli telephoned Michael Courtney at his desk in the newsroom. 'I have something for you,' he told Michael. 'Can you come out to the *Assegai* offices right away?'

'It's after five already,' Michael protested, 'and it's Friday night. I won't be able to get a pass to enter the township.'

'Come,' Solomon insisted. 'I will wait for you at the main gate.'

He was as good as his promise, a tall, gangly figure in steel-rimmed glasses, waiting under the street lamp near the main gates, and as soon as he slipped into the front seat of the company car, Michael passed him his cigarette pack.

'Light one for me, as well,' he told Solomon. 'I brought

some sardine and onion sandwiches and a couple of bottles of beer. They are on the back seat.' There was no public place in Johannesburg, or in the entire land for that matter, where two men of different colour could sit and drink or eat together. Michael drove slowly and aimlessly through the streets while they ate and talked.

'The PAC are planning their first big act since they broke away from the ANC,' Solomon told Michael through a mouthful of sardine and onion. 'In some areas they have built up strong support. In the Cape and the rural tribal areas, even in some parts of the Transvaal. They have pulled in all the young militants who are unhappy with the pacifism of the old men. They want to follow Moses Gama's example, and take on the Nationalists in a head-on fight.'

'That's crazy,' Michael said. 'You can't fight Sten guns and Saracen armoured cars with half bricks.'

'Yes, it's crazy, but then some of the young people would prefer to die on their feet than live on their knees.'

They were together for an hour, talking all that time, and then at last Michael drove him back to the main gates of Drake's Farm.

'So that's it then, my friend.' Solomon opened the car door. 'If you want the best story on Monday, I would suggest you go down to the Vereeniging area. The PAC and *Poqo* have made that their stronghold on the Witwatersrand.'

'Evaton?' Michael asked.

'Yes, Evaton will be one of the places to watch,' Solomon Nduli agreed. 'But the PAC have a new man in Sharpeville.'

'Sharpeville?' Michael asked. 'Where is that? I've never heard of it.'

'Only twelve miles from Evaton.'

'I'll find it on my road map.'

'You might think it worth the trouble to go there,' Solomon encouraged Michael. 'This PAC organizer in

Sharpeville is one of the party's young lions. He will put on a good show, you can count on that.'

M anfred De La Rey asked quietly. 'So, how many reinforcements can we spare for the stations in the Vaal area?'

General Danie Leroux shook his head and smoothed back the wings of silver hair at his temples with both hands. 'We have only three days to move in reinforcements from the outlying areas and most of those will be needed in the Cape. It will mean stripping the outlying stations and leaving them very vulnerable.'

'How many?' Manfred insisted.

'Five or six hundred men for the Vaal,' Danie Leroux said with obvious reluctance.

'That will not be enough,' Manfred growled. 'So we will reinforce all stations lightly, but hold most of our forces in mobile reserve and react swiftly to the first hint of trouble.' He turned his full attention to the map that covered the operations table in the control room of police headquarters in Marshall Square. 'Which are the main danger centres on the Vaal?'

'Evaton,' Danie Leroux replied without hesitation. 'It's always one of the trouble spots, and then Van Der Bijl Park.'

'What about Sharpeville?' Manfred asked, and held up the crudely printed pamphlet that he had tightly rolled in his right hand. 'What about this?'

The general did not reply immediately, but he pretended to study the operations map as he composed his reply. He was well aware that the subversive pamphlets had been discovered by Captain Lothar De La Rey, and he knew how the Minister felt about his son. Indeed Danie Leroux shared the general high opinion of Lothar, so he did not want to belittle him in any way or to offend his minister.

'There may well be disturbances in the Sharpeville area,' he conceded. 'But it is a small township and has always been very peaceful. We can expect our men there to behave well and I do not see any immediate danger. I suggest we send twenty or thirty men to reinforce Sharpeville, and concentrate our main efforts on the larger townships with violent histories of boycotts and strikes.'

'Very well,' Manfred agreed at last. 'But I want you to maintain at least forty per cent of our reinforcements in reserve, so that they can be moved quickly to any area that flares up unexpectedly.'

'What about arms?' Danie Leroux asked. 'I am about to authorize the issue of automatic weapons to all units.' He turned the statement into a query and Manfred nodded.

'Ja, we must be ready for the worst. There is a feeling amongst our enemies that we are on the verge of capitulation. Even our own people are becoming frightened and confused.' His voice dropped, but his tone was fiercer and more determined. 'We have to change that. We have to crush these people who wish to tear down and destroy all we stand for and give this land over to bloodshed and anarchy.'

T he centres of support for the PAC were widely scattered across the land, from the eastern tribal areas of the Ciskei and the Transkei to the southern part of the great industrial triangle along the Vaal River, and a thousand miles south of that in the black township of Langa and Nyanga that housed the greater part of the migrant worker force that serviced the mother city of Cape Town.

In all these areas Sunday 20 March 1960 was a day of

feverish effort and planning, and of a peculiar expectancy. It was as though everybody at last believed that this new decade would be one of immense change.

The radicals were filled with a feeling of infinite hope, however irrational, and with a certainty that the Nationalist government was on the verge of collapse. They felt that the world was with them, that the age of colonialism had blown away on the winds of change, and that after a decade of massive political mobilization by the black leaders the time of liberation was at last at hand. All it needed now was one last shove, and the walls of *apartheid* would crash to earth, crushing under them the evil architect Verwoerd and his builders who had raised them up.

Raleigh Tabaka felt that marvellous euphoria as he and his men moved through the township, going from cottage to cottage with the same message: 'Tomorrow we will be as one people. No one will go to work. There will be no buses and those who try to walk to the town will be met by the *Poqo* on the road. The names of all who defy the PAC will be taken and they will be punished. Tomorrow we are going to make the white police fear us.'

They worked all that day, and by evening every person, man and woman, in the township had been warned to stay away from work and to assemble in the open space near the new police station early on the Monday morning.

'We are going to make the white police fear us. We want everybody to be there. If you do not come, we will find you.'

Amelia had worked as hard and unremittingly as Raleigh had done, but like him she was still fresh, unwearied and excited as they ate a quick and simple meal in the back room of the bakery.

'Tomorrow we will see the sun of freedom rise,' Raleigh told her as he wiped his bowl with a crust of bread. 'But we cannot afford to sleep. There is still much work to do this night.' Then he took her hand and told her, 'Our children will be born free, and we will live our life together like men, and not like animals.' And he led her out into the darkening township to continue the preparations for the great day that lay ahead.

They met in groups on the street corners, all the eager young ones, and Raleigh and Amelia moved amongst them delegating their duties for the morrow, selecting those who would picket the road leading from Sharpeville to Vereeniging.

'You will let no one pass. Nobody must leave the township,' Raleigh told them. 'All the people must be as one when we march on the police station tomorrow morning.'

'You must tell the people not to fear,' Raleigh urged them. 'Tell them that the white police cannot touch them and that there will be a most important speech from the white government concerning the abolition of the pass laws. Tell the people they must be joyful and unafraid and that they must sing the freedom songs that PAC has taught them.'

After midnight Raleigh assembled his most loyal and reliable men, including the two Buffaloes from the shebeen, and they went to the homes of all the black bus drivers and taxi drivers in the township and pulled them from their beds.

'Nobody will leave Sharpeville tomorrow,' they told them. 'But we do not trust you not to obey your white bosses. We will guard you until the march begins. Instead of driving your buses and taxis tomorrow and taking our people away, you will march with them to the police station. We will see to it that you do. Come with us now.'

As the false dawn flushed the eastern sky, Raleigh himself scaled a telephone pole at the boundary fence and cut the wires. When he slid down again he laughed, as he told Amelia, 'Now our friend the Leopard will not find it so easy to call in other police to help him.'

Captain Lothar De La Rey parked his Land-Rover and left it in a sanitary lane in a patch of shadow out of the street lights and he moved quietly to the corner and stood alone.

He listened to the night. In the years he had served at Sharpeville he had learned to judge the pulse and the mood of the township. He let his feelings and his instincts take over from reason, and almost immediately he was aware of the feral excitement and sense of expectation which had the township in its grip. It was quiet until you listened, as Lothar was listening now. He heard the dogs. They were restless, some close, others at a distance, yapping and barking, and there was an urgency in them. They were seeing and scenting groups and single figures in the shadows. Men hurrying on secret errands.

Then he heard the other sounds, soft as insect sounds in the night. The whistle of lookouts on the watch for his patrols and the recognition signals of the street gangs. In one of the dark cottages nearby a man coughed nervously, unable to sleep, and in another a child whimpered fretfully and was instantly hushed by a woman's soft voice.

Lothar moved quietly through the shadows, listening and watching. Even without the warning of the pamphlets, he would have known that tonight the township was awake and strung up.

Lothar was not an imaginative or romantic young man, but as he scouted the dark streets he suddenly had a clear mental picture of his ancestors performing this same dire task. He saw them bearded and dressed in drab homespun, armed with the long muzzle-loaders, leaving the security of the laagered wagons, going out alone into the African night to scout for the enemy, the *swartgevaar*, the black danger. Spying out the bivouac where the black impis lay upon their war shields, waiting for the dawn to rush in upon the wagons. His nerves crawled at those atavistic memories, and he seemed to hear the battle chant of the tribes in the night and the drumming of assegai on rawhide shield, the stamp of bare feet and the crash of war rattles on wrist and ankle as they came in upon the wagons for the dawn attack.

In his imagination the cry of the restless infant in the nearby cottage became the death screams of the little Boer children at Weenen, where the black impis had come sweeping down from the hills to massacre all in the Boer encampment.

He shivered in the night as he realized that though so much had changed, as much had remained the same. The black danger was still there, growing each day stronger and more ominous. He had seen the confident challenging look of the young bucks as they swaggered through the streets and heard the warlike names they had adopted, the Spear of the Nation and the Pure Ones. Tonight, more than ever, he was aware of the danger and he knew where his duty lay.

He went back to the Land-Rover and drove slowly through the streets. Time and again he glimpsed small groups of dark figures, but when he turned the spotlight upon them, they melted away into the night. Everywhere he went he heard the warning whistles out there in the darkness, and his nerves tightened and tingled. When he met his own foot-patrolling constables, they also were nervous and ill at ease.

When the dawn turned the eastern sky pale yellow and dimmed out the street lamps he drove back through the streets. At this time in the morning they should have been filled with hurrying commuters, but now they were empty and silent.

Lothar reached the bus terminus, and it too was almost deserted. Only a few young men in small groups lounged at the railings. There were no buses, and the pickets stared at the police Land-Rover openly and insolently as Lothar drove slowly past.

As he skirted the boundary fence, passing close to the

main gates, he exclaimed suddenly and braked the Land-Rover. From one of the telephone poles the cables trailed limply to the earth. Lothar left the vehicle and went to examine the damage. He lifted the loose end of the dangling copper wire, and saw immediately that it had been cut cleanly. He let it drop and walked slowly back to the Land-Rover.

Before he climbed into the driver's seat, he glanced at his wristwatch. It was ten minutes past five o'clock. Officially he would be off duty at six, but he would not leave his post today. He knew his duty. He knew it would be a long and dangerous day and he steeled himself to meet it.

That Monday morning, 21 March 1960, a thousand miles away in the Cape townships of Langa and Nyanga the crowds began assembling. It was raining. That cold drizzling Cape north-wester blew from the sea, dampening the ardour of the majority, but by 6 a.m. there was a crowd of almost ten thousand gathered outside the Langa bachelor quarters, ready to begin the march on the police station.

The police anticipated them. During the weekend they had been heavily reinforced and all officers and senior warrant officers issued with Sten guns. Now a Saracen armoured car in drab green battle paint entered the head of the wide road in which the crowd had assembled, and a police officer addressed them over the loudspeaker system. He told them that all public meetings had been banned and that a march on the police station would be treated as an attack.

The black leaders came forward and negotiated with the police, and at last agreed to disperse the crowd, but warned that nobody would go to work that day and there would be another mass meeting at 6 p.m. that evening. When the evening meeting began to assemble, the police arrived in Saracen armoured cars, and ordered the crowd to disperse. When they stood their ground, the police baton-charged them. The crowd retaliated by stoning the police and in a mass rushed forward to attack them. The police commander gave the command to fire and the Sten guns buzzed in automatic fire and the crowd fled, leaving two of their number dead upon the field.

From then on weeks of rioting and stoning and marches racked the Cape peninsula, culminating in a massed march of tens of thousands of blacks. This time they reached the police headquarters at Caledon Square, but dispersed quietly after their leaders had been promised an interview with the Minister of Justice. When the leaders arrived for this interview they were arrested on orders of Manfred De La Rey, the Minister of Police, and because police reserves had by this time been stretched almost to breaking point soldiers and sailors of the defence force were rushed in to supplement the local police units and within three days the black townships were cordoned off securely.

In the Cape the struggle was over.

I n Van Der Bijl Park ten miles from Vereeniging and in Evaton, both notorious centres of radical and violent black political resistance, the crowds began to gather at first light on Monday 21 March.

By nine o'clock the marchers, thousands strong, set out in procession for their local police stations. However, they did not get very far. Here, as in the Cape, the police had been reinforced and the Saracen armoured cars met them on the road and the loud-hailers boomed out the orders to disperse. The orderly columns of marchers bogged down in the quicksands of uncertainty and ineffectual leadership and the police vehicles moved down on them ponderously, forcing them back, and finally broke up their formations with baton charges.

Then abruptly the sky was filled with a terrible rushing sound and every black face was turned upwards. A flight of Sabre jet fighter aircraft of the South African Air Force flashed overhead, only a hundred feet above the heads of the crowd. They had never seen modern jet fighters in such low-level flight and the sight and the sound of the mighty engines was unnerving. The crowds began to break up, and their leaders lost heart. The demonstrations were over almost before they had begun.

Robert Sobukwe himself marched to Orlando police station in greater Soweto. It was five miles from his house in Mofolo, and although small groups of men joined him along the way, they were less than a hundred strong when they reached the police station and offered themselves for arrest under the pass laws.

In most other centres there were no marches, and no arrests. At Hercules police station in Pretoria six men arrived passless and demanded to be arrested. A jocular police officer obligingly took their names and then sent them home.

In most of the Transvaal it was undramatic and anti-climactic – but then there was Sharpeville.

R aleigh Tabaka had not slept all night, he had not even lain down to rest but had been on his feet exhorting and encouraging and organizing.

Now at six o'clock in the morning he was at the bus depot. The gates were still locked, and in the yard the long ungainly vehicles stood in silent rows while a group of three anxious-looking supervisors waited inside the gates for the drivers to arrive. The buses should have commenced their first run at 4.30 a.m. and by now there was no possibility that they could honour their schedules.

From the direction of the township a single figure jogged down the deserted road and behind the depot gate the bus company supervisors brightened and moved forward to open the gate for him. The man hurrying towards them wore the brown peaked driver's cap, with the brass insignia of the bus company on the headband.

'Ha,' Raleigh said grimly. 'We have missed one of them,' and he signalled his men to intercept the black-leg driver.

The driver saw the young men ahead of him and he stopped abruptly.

Raleigh sauntered up to him smiling and asked, 'Where are you going, my uncle?'

The man did not reply but glanced around him nervously.

'You were not going to drive your bus, were you?' Raleigh insisted. 'You have heard the words of PAC of which all men have taken heed, have you not?'

'I have children to feed,' the man muttered sullenly. 'And I have worked twenty-five years without missing a day.'

Raleigh shook his head sorrowfully. 'You are a fool, old man. I forgive you for that – you cannot be blamed for the worm in your skull that has devoured your brains. But you are also a traitor to your people. For this I cannot forgive you.' And he nodded to his young men. They seized the driver and dragged him into the bushes beside the road.

The driver fought back, but they were young and strong and many in number and he went down screaming under the blows and after a while, when he was quiet, they left him lying in the dusty dry grass. Raleigh felt no pity or remorse as he walked away. The man was a traitor, and he should count himself fortunate if he survived his punishment to tell his children of his treachery.

At the bus terminus Raleigh's pickets assured him that only a few commuters had attempted to defy the boycott, but they had scurried away as soon as they had seen the waiting pickets.

'Besides,' one of them told Raleigh, 'not a single bus has arrived.'

'You have all begun this day well. Now let us move on to greet the sun of our freedom as it dawns.'

They gathered in the other pickets as they marched, and Amelia was waiting with her children and the other school staff at the corner of the school yard. She saw Raleigh and ran laughing to join him. The children giggled and shrieked with excitement, delighted with this unexpected release from the drudgery of the schoolroom, and they skipped behind Raleigh and his young pickets as they went on.

From each cottage they passed the people swarmed out and when they saw the laughing children, they were infected by the gaiety and excitement. Amongst them by now there were grey heads, and young mothers with their infants strapped to their backs, older women in aprons leading a child on each hand, and men in the overalls of the steel company or the more formal attire of clerks and messengers and shop assistants, and the black petty civil servants who assisted in the administration of the *apartheid* laws. Soon the road behind Raleigh and his comrades was a river of humanity.

As they approached the open common ground they saw that there was already a huge concourse of people gathered there, and from every road leading onto the common more came swarming each minute.

'Five thousand?' Raleigh asked Amelia, and she squeezed his hand and danced with excitement.

'More,' she said. 'There must be more, ten thousand – even fifteen thousand. Oh, Raleigh, I am so proud and happy. Look at our people – isn't it a fine sight to see them all here?' She turned and looked up at him adoringly. 'And I am so proud of you, Raleigh. Without you these poor people would never realize their misery, would never have the will to do anything to change their lot, but look at them now.'

As Raleigh moved forward the people recognized him and made way for him, and they shouted his name and called him 'brother' and 'comrade'.

At the end of the open common was a pile of old bricks and builders' rubble and Raleigh made his way towards it, and when he reached it he climbed up on top of it and raised his arms for silence.

'My people, I bring you the word of Robert Sobukwe who is the father of PAC, and he charges you thus – Remember Moses Gama! Remember all the pain and hardships of your empty lives! Remember the poverty and the oppression!'

A roar went up from them and they raised their clenched fists or gave the thumbs-up sign and they shouted '*Amandla*' and '*Gama*'. It was some time before Raleigh could speak again, but he told them, 'We are going to burn our passes.' He brandished his own booklet as he went on. 'We are going to make fires and burn the *dompas*. Then we are going to march as one people to the police station and ask them to arrest us. Then Robert Sobukwe will come to speak for us—' this was a momentary inspiration of Raleigh's, and he went on happily, 'then the police will see that we are men, and they will fear us. Never again will they force us to show the *dompas*, and we will be free men as our ancestors were free men before the white man came to this land.' He almost believed it as he said it. It all seemed so logical and simple.

So they lit the fires, dozens of them across the common, starting them with dry grass and crumpled sheets of newspaper, and then they clustered around them and threw their pass books into the flames. The women began swaying their hips and shuffling their feet, and the men danced with them and the children scampered around between their legs and they all sang the freedom songs.

It was past eight o'clock before the marshals could get them moving, and then the mass of humanity began to uncoil like a huge serpent and crawl away towards the police station.

Michael Courtney had watched the Evaton demonstration fizzle out ignominiously, and from a public telephone booth he phoned the Van Der Bijl Park police station to learn that after a police baton-charge on the marchers all was now quiet there also. When he tried to telephone the Sharpeville police he could not get through, although he wasted almost ten shillings in the coin slot and spent forty frustrating minutes in the telephone booth. In the end he gave up in disgust and went back to the small Morris station wagon which Nana had given him for his last birthday present.

He set off back towards Johannesburg, steeling himself for Leon Herbstein's sarcasm. 'So you got a fine story of the riot that didn't take place. Congratulations, Mickey, I knew I could rely on you.'

Michael grimaced and lit another cigarette to console himself, but as he reached the junction with the main road he saw the sign 'Vereeniging 10 miles' and a smaller sign below it 'Sharpeville Township', and instead of turning towards Johannesburg, he turned south and the Morris buzzed merrily down the strangely open and uncrowded roadway.

Lothar De La Rey kept a toilet kit in his desk, complete with razor and toothbrush. When he got back to the station he washed and shaved in the hand basin in the men's toilet and he felt refreshed, although the sense of ominous disquiet that he had experienced during his night patrol still remained with him.

The sergeant at the charge office saluted him as he entered.

'Good morning, sir, are you signing off duty?' but Lothar shook his head.

'Has the *kommandant* come on duty yet?'

'He came in ten minutes ago.'

'Have you had any telephone calls since midnight, sergeant?'

'Now you come to mention it, sir, no, we haven't. That's funny, isn't it?'

'Not so funny – the lines have been cut. You should have seen that in the station log,' Lothar snapped at him and went through to the station commander's office.

He listened gravely to Lothar's report. '*Ja*, Lothie. You did good work. I'm not happy about this business. I've had a bad feeling ever since you found those damned pamphlets. They should have given us more men here, not just twenty raw recruits. They should have given us experienced men, instead of sending them to Evaton and the other stations.'

'I have called in the foot patrols,' Lothar told him crisply. He did not want to listen to complaints about the decisions of his superiors. He knew there were good reasons for everything. 'I suggest we hold all our men here at the station. Concentrate our forces.'

'*Ja*, I agree,' said the commander.

'What about weapons? Should I open the armoury?'

'*Ja*, Lothie. I think you can go ahead.'

'And I'd like to talk to the men before I go out on patrol again.'

'All right, Lothie. You tell them we have everything in hand. They must just obey orders and it will be all right.'

Lothar saluted and strode back into the charge office.

'Sergeant, I want an issue of arms to all white members.'

'Sten guns?' The man looked surprised.

'And four spare magazines per man,' Lothar nodded. 'I will sign the order into the station log.'

The sergeant handed him the keys and together they went through to the strong room, unlocked and swung open the heavy steel Chubb door. The Sten guns stood in their racks against the side wall. Cheap little weapons of pressed steel manufacture, they looked like toys, but the 9 mm parabellum cartridges they fired would kill a man as efficiently as the finest crafted Purdey or square-bridged Mauser.

The reinforcements were almost entirely from the police college, fresh-faced and crew-cut, eager boys who looked up at the decorated captain with awe as he told them, 'We are expecting trouble. That's why you are here. You have been issued Stens – that alone is a responsibility that each of you must take seriously. Wait for orders, do not act without them. But once you have them, respond swiftly.'

He took one of his constables with him, and drove down to the main township gates with his Sten gun on the seat beside him. It was well after six o'clock by then, but the streets were still quiet. He passed fewer than fifty people, all of them hurrying in the same direction. The Post Office repair truck was waiting at the gate, and Lothar escorted it down to where the telephone wires had been severed. He waited while a linesman scaled the pole and spliced the wires, and then he escorted the truck back to the gates. Before he reached the broad avenue that led up to the station gates, Lothar pulled to the side of the road and switched off the engine.

The constable in the back seat shifted in his seat and began to say something, but Lothar snapped at him, 'Quiet!' and the man froze. They sat in silence for several seconds, before Lothar frowned.

There was a sound like the sea heard from afar, a gentle susurration, and he opened the door of the Land-Rover and stepped out. The whisper was like the wind in tall grass, and there was a faint vibration that he seemed to feel in the soles of his feet.

Lothar jumped back into the Land-Rover and drove swiftly to the next road junction, and turned down it towards the open commonage and the school. The sound grew until he could hear it above the beat of the engine. He turned the next corner and tramped so hard on the brakes that the Land-Rover shuddered and skidded to a halt.

Ahead of him from side to side the road was blocked solid with humanity. They were shoulder to shoulder, rank upon rank, thousand upon thousands, and when they saw the police vehicle ahead of them a great shout of 'Amandla' went up, and they surged forward.

For a moment Lothar was paralysed by shock. He was not one of those unusual creatures who never felt fear. He had known fear intimately, on the clamorous field when standing to meet the concerted rush of muscled bodies across the turf as well as in the silent streets of the township as he hunted dangerous unscrupulous men in the night. He had conquered those fears and found a strange exhilaration in the feat. But this was a new thing.

This was not human, this was a monster he faced now. A creature with ten thousand throats and twenty thousand

legs, a sprawling insensate monster that roared a meaningless word and had no ears to hear nor mind to reason. It
was the mob and Lothar was afraid. His instinct was to
swing the Land-Rover around and race back to the security
of the station. In fact, he had already slammed the gear
lever into reverse before he had control of himself.

He left the engine running and opened the side door,
and the constable in the back seat blasphemed and his
voice was thick with terror. 'Sodding Christ, let's get out of
here.'

It served to steel Lothar, and he felt contempt for his
own weakness. As he had done so many times before, he
strangled his fear and climbed onto the bonnet of the Land-
Rover.

Deliberately he had left the Sten gun on the front seat
and he did not even unbutton the holster on his belt. A
single firearm was useless against this sprawling monster.

He held up his arms and shouted, 'Stop! You people
must go back. That is a police order.' But his words were
drowned in the multitudinous voice of the monster, and it
came on apace. The men in the front rank started to run
towards him and those behind shouted and pressed forward
faster.

'Go back,' Lothar roared, but there was not the slightest
check in the ranks and they were close now. He could see
the expressions on the faces of the men in front, they were
grinning, but Lothar knew how swiftly the African mood
can change, how close below the smiles lies the violence of
the African heart. He knew he could not stop them, they
were too close, too excited, and he was aware that his
presence had inflamed them, the mere sight of his uniform
was enough.

He jumped down and into the cab, reversed the Land-
Rover and then accelerated forward, swinging the wheel
into a full lock, and he pulled away as the leaders were
within arm's reach.

He pushed the accelerator flat against the floorboards. It was almost two miles back to the station. As he made a quick calculation on how long it would take the march to reach it, he was already rehearsing the orders he would give and working out additional precautions to secure the station.

Suddenly there was another vehicle in the road ahead of him. He had not expected that, and as he swerved to avoid it he saw it was a Morris with lacquered wooden struts supporting the station wagon body. The driver was a young white man.

Lothar slowed and pulled his side window open. 'Where the hell do you think you're going?' he shouted, and the driver leaned out of the window and smiled politely.

'Good morning, Captain.'

'Have you got a permit to be here?'

'Yes, do you want to see it?'

'No, hell,' Lothar told him. 'The permit is cancelled. You are ordered to leave the township immediately, do you hear?'

'Yes, Captain, I hear.'

'There might be trouble,' Lothar insisted. 'You are in danger. I order you to leave immediately for your own safety.'

'Right away,' Michael Courtney agreed, and Lothar accelerated away swiftly.

Michael watched him in the rear-view mirror until he was out of sight, and then he lit a cigarette and drove sedately on in the direction from which the police vehicle had come in such desperate haste. The police captain's agitation had confirmed that he was heading in the right direction and Michael smiled with satisfaction as he heard the distant sounds of many voices.

At the end of the avenue he turned towards the sound, and then pulled in to the side of the road and switched off the engine. He sat behind the wheel and stared ahead at the huge crowd that poured down the street towards him. He was unafraid, detached – an observer not a participant – and as the crowd came on he was studying it avidly, anxious not to miss a single detail, already forming the sentences to describe it and scribbling them in his notebook.

'Young people in the vanguard, many children amongst them, all of them smiling and laughing and singing—'

They saw Michael in the parked Morris and they called to him and gave him the thumbs-up signal.

'The good will of these people always amazes me,' he wrote. 'Their cheerfulness and the lack of personal antipathy towards us ruling whites—'

There was a handsome young man in the van of the march, he walked a few paces ahead of the rest. He had a long confident stride so the girl beside him had to skip to keep up with him. She held his hand and her teeth were even and very white in her lovely dark moon face. She smiled at Michael and waved as she passed him.

The crowd split and flowed past on each side of the parked Morris. Some of the children paused to press their faces against the windows, peering in at Michael, and when he grinned and pulled a face at them they shrieked with laughter and scampered on. Once or two of the marchers slapped the roof of the Morris with open palms, but it was rather a cheerful greeting than a hostile act and they scarcely paused but marched on after the young leaders.

For many minutes the crowd flowed past and then only the stragglers, the latecomers, cripples and the elderly with stiff hampered gait were going by, and Michael started the engine of the Morris and U-turned across the street.

In low gear he followed the crowd at a walking pace, driving with one hand while he scribbled notes in the open pad on his lap.

'Estimate between six and seven thousand at this stage, but others joining all the time. Old man on crutches with his wife supporting him, a toddler dressed only in a short vest showing his little bum. A woman with a portable radio balanced on her head playing rock 'n' roll music as she dances along. Many peasant types, probably illegals, still wearing blankets and barefooted. The singing is beautifully harmonized. Also many well-dressed and obviously educated types, some wearing government uniforms, postmen and bus drivers, and workers in overalls of the steel and coal companies. For once, a call has gone out that has reached all of them, not just the politicized minority. A sense of excited and naïve expectation that is palpable. Now the song changes – beginning at the head of the march, but the others pick it up swiftly. They are all singing, doleful and tragic, not necessary to understand the words. This is a lament—'

At the head of the march Amelia sang with such fervour that the tears burst spontaneously from her huge dark eyes and glistened down her cheeks:

> The road is long
> Our burden is heavy
> How long must we go on –

The mood of gaiety changed, and the music of many thousand voices soared in a great anguished cry.

> How long must we suffer?
> How long? How long?

Amelia held hard to Raleigh's hand and sang with all her being and her very soul, and they turned the last corner. Ahead of them at the end of the long avenue was the diamond-meshed fence that surrounded the police station.

Then in the hard china blue of the highveld sky above the corrugated-iron roof of the police station, a cluster of tiny dark specks appeard. At first they seemed to be a flock of birds, but they swelled in size with miraculous speed as they approached, shining in the early rays of the morning sun with a silent menace.

The head of the march stopped and those behind pressed up behind and then halted also. All their faces turned up towards the menacing machines that bore down upon them, with gaping shark mouths and outstretched pinions, so swiftly that they outran their own engine noise.

The leading Sabre jet dropped lower still, skimming the roof of the police station, and the rest of the formation followed it down. The singing faltered into silence, and was followed by the first wails of terror and uncertainty. One after another the great airborne machines hurtled over their heads. It seemed they were low enough to reach up and touch, and the ear-splitting whine of their engines was a physical assault that drove the people to their knees. Some of them crouched in the dusty roadway, others threw themselves flat and covered their heads, while still others turned and tried to run back, but they were blocked by the ranks behind them and the march disintegrated into a confused struggling mass. The men were shouting and the women wailed and some of the children were shrieking and weeping with terror.

The silver jets climbed out and banked steeply, coming around in formation for the next pass; their engines screamed and the shock waves of their passing rumbled across the sky.

Raleigh and Amelia were amongst the few who had stood their ground, and now Raleigh shouted, 'Do not be afraid, my friends. They cannot harm you.'

Amelia took her lead from him and she called to her children, 'They will not hurt you, my little ones. They are pretty as birds. Just look how they shine in the sun!' And the children stifled their terror and a few of them giggled uncertainly.

'Here they come again!' Raleigh shouted. 'Wave to them

693

like this.' And he cavorted and laughed, and the other young people quickly imitated him and the people began to laugh with them. This time as the machines thundered over their heads, only a few of the old women fell over and grovelled in the road, but most of them merely cringed and flinched and then laughed uproariously with relief when the machines were past.

Under the urging of Raleigh and his marshals, the march began slowly to disentangle itself and move forward again, and when the jet fighters made their third pass, they looked up and waved at the helmeted heads under the transparent canopies. This time the aircraft did not bank and come around. Instead they winged away into the blue and the terrible sound of their engines dwindled and the people began to sing again and to embrace each other as they marched, celebrating their courage and their victory.

'Today you will all be free,' Raleigh shouted, and those close enough to hear him believed him, and turned to shout to those farther back.

'Today we will all be free!'

Ahead of them the gates of the police station yard were closed and locked, but they saw the ranks of men drawn up beyond the wire. The uniforms were dark khaki and the morning sun sparkled on the badges and on the ugly stubby blue weapons that the white police carried.

Lothar De La Rey stood on the front steps leading up to the charge office, under the lamp with the words POLICE – *POLISIE* engraved upon the blue glass, and steeled himself not to duck as the formation of jet fighters flashed low over the station roof.

He watched the distant mob pulse and contract like some giant black amoeba as the aircraft harassed them, and then regain its shape and come on steadily. He heard the singing swell up in chorus and he could make out the features of those in the front ranks.

The sergeant beside him swore softly. 'My God, just look at those black bastards, there must be thousands of them,' and Lothar recognized in the man's tone his own horror and trepidation.

What they were looking upon was the nightmare of the Afrikaner people that had recurred for almost two centuries, ever since their ancestors moving up slowly from the south through a lovely land populated only by wild game had met suddenly upon the banks of the great Fish River the cohorts of this dark multitude.

He felt his nerves crawl like poisonous insects upon his skin as the tribal memories of his people assaulted him. Here they were once more, the tiny handful of white men at the barricades, and there before them was the black barbaric host. It was as it had always been, but the horror of his situation was not in the least diluted by the knowledge that it had all happened before. Rather it was made more poignant, and the natural reaction of defence more compelling.

However, the fear and loathing in the sergeant's voice braced Lothar against his own weakness, and he tore his gaze from the approaching horde and looked to his own men. He saw how pale they were, how deathly still they stood and how very young so many of them were – but then it was the Afrikaner tradition that the boys had always taken their places at the laager barricades even before they were as tall as the long muzzle-loading weapons they carried.

Lothar forced himself to move, to walk slowly down the line in front of his men, making certain that no trace of his own fear was evident in expression or gesture.

'They don't mean trouble,' he said, 'they have their women and children with them. The Bantu always hide the women if they mean to fight.' His voice was level and without emotion. 'The reinforcements are on their way,' he told them. 'We will have three hundred men here within the hour. Just stay calm and obey orders.' He smiled encouragement at a cadet whose eyes were too big for his pale face, whose ears stuck out from under his cap, and who chewed his lower lip nervously as he stared out through the wire. 'You haven't been given orders to load, *Jong*. Get that magazine off your weapon,' he ordered quietly and the boy unclipped the long, straight magazine from the side of his Sten gun without once taking his eyes from the singing, dancing horde in front of them.

Lothar walked back down the line with a deliberate tread, not once glancing at the oncoming mob, nodding encouragement at each of his men as he came level or distracting them with a quiet word. But once he reached his post on the station steps again he could no longer contain himself and he turned to face the gate and only with difficulty prevented himself exclaiming out loud.

They filled the entire roadway from side to side and end to end and still they came on, more and more of them pouring out of the side road like a Karoo river in flash flood.

'Stay at your posts, men,' he called. 'Do nothing without orders!' And they stood stolidly in the bright morning sunlight while the leaders of the march reached the locked gates and pressed against them, gripping the wire and peering through the mesh, chanting and grinning as behind them the rest of the huge unwieldy column spread out along the perimeter. Like water contained by a dam wall, compressed by their own multitudes, they were building up rank upon rank until they completely surrounded the station yard, hemming in the small party of uniformed men. And still they came on, those at the back joining the dense throng at the main gates until the station was a tiny rectangular island in a noisy restless black sea.

Then the men at the gates called for silence and

gradually the chanting and laughter and general uproar died away.

'We want to speak with your officers,' called a young black man in the front rank at the closed gates. He had his fingers hooked through the mesh and the crowd behind him pushed him so hard against the wire that the high gates shook and trembled.

The station commander came out of the charge office, and as he went down the steps Lothar fell in a pace behind him. Together they crossed the yard and halted in front of the gate.

'This is an illegal gathering,' the commander addressed the young man who had called out to them. 'You must disperse immediately.' He was speaking in Afrikaans.

'It is much worse than that, officer,' the young man smiled at him happily. He was replying in English, a calculated provocation. 'You see, none of us are carrying our pass books. We have burned them.'

'What is your name, you?' the commander demanded in Afrikaans.

'My name is Raleigh Tabaka and I am the branch secretary of the Pan-Africanist Congress, and I demand that you arrest me and all these others,' Raleigh told him in fluent English. 'Open the gates, policeman, and take us into your prison cells.'

'I am going to give you five minutes to disperse,' the commander told him menacingly.

'Or what?' Raleigh Tabaka asked. 'What will you do if we do not obey you?' and behind him the crowd began to chant.

'Arrest us! We have burned the *dompas*. Arrest us!'

There was an interruption and a burst of ironic cheers and hooted laughter from the rear of the crowd, and Lothar jumped up on the bonnet of the nearest police Land-Rover to see over their heads.

A small convoy of three troop carriers filled with uniformed constables had driven out of the side road and was now slowly forcing its way through the crowd. The densely packed ranks gave way only reluctantly before the tall covered trucks, but Lothar felt a rush of relief.

He jumped down from the Land-Rover and ordered a squad of his men to the gates. As the convoy came on the people beat upon the steel sides of the trucks with their bare fists and jeered and hooted and gave the ANC salute. A fine mist of dust rose around the trucks and the thousands of milling shuffling feet of the crowd.

Lothar's men forced the gates open against the pressure of black bodies and as the trucks drove through, they swung them shut, and hurriedly locked them again as the crowd surged forward against them.

Lothar left the commander to haggle and bluster with the leaders of the crowd and he went to deploy the reinforcements along the perimeter of the yard. The new men were all armed and Lothar posted the older, more steady-looking of them on top of trucks from where they had a sweeping field of fire over all four sides of the fence.

'Stay calm,' he kept repeating. 'Everything is under control. Just obey your orders.'

He hurried back to the gateway as soon as he had placed the reinforcements, and the commander was still arguing with the black leaders through the wire.

'We will not leave here until either you arrest us, or the pass laws are abolished.'

'Don't be stupid, man,' the commander snapped. 'You know neither of those things is possible.'

'Then we will stay,' Raleigh Tabaka told him and the crowd behind him chanted:

'Arrest us! Arrest us! Now!'

'I have placed the new men in position,' Lothar reported in a low voice. 'We have nearly two hundred now.'

'God grant it will be enough if they turn nasty,' the

commander muttered and glanced uneasily along the line of uniformed men. It seemed puny and insignificant against the mass that confronted them through the wire.

'I have argued with you long enough.' He turned back to the men behind the gate. 'You must take these people away now. That is a police order.'

'We stay,' Raleigh Tabaka told him pleasantly.

As the morning wore on, so the heat increased and Lothar could feel the tension and the fear in his men rising with the heat and the thirst and the dust and the chanting. Every few minutes a disturbance in the crowd made it eddy and push like a whirlpool in the flow of a river, and each time the fence shook and swayed and the white men fingered their guns and fidgeted in the baking sun. Twice more during the morning reinforcements arrived and the crowd let them through until there were almost three hundred armed police in the compound. But instead of dispersing, the crowd continued to grow as every last person who had hidden away in the township cottages, expecting trouble, finally succumbed to curiosity and crept out to join the multitude.

After each new arrival of trucks there was another round of argument and futile orders to disperse, and in the heat and the impatience of waiting, the mood of the crowd gradually changed. There were no more smiles and the singing had a different tone to it as they began to hum the fierce fighting songs. Rumours flashed through the throng – Robert Sobukwe was coming to speak to them, Verwoerd had ordered the passes to be abolished and Moses Gama to be released from jail, and they cheered and sang and then growled and surged back and forth as each rumour was denied.

The sun made its noon, blazing down upon them, and the smell of the crowd was the musky African odour, alien and yet dreadfully familiar.

The white men who had stood to arms all that morning

were reaching the point of nervous exhaustion and each time the crowd surged against the frail wire fence they made little jumpy movements and one or two of them without orders loaded their Sten guns and lifted them into the high port position. Lothar noticed this and went down the line, ordering them to unload and uncock their weapons.

'We have to do something soon, sir,' he told his commander. 'We can't go on like this – someone or something is going to snap.' It was in the air, strong as the odour of hot African bodies, and Lothar felt it in himself. He had not slept that night, and he was haggard and he felt brittle and jagged as a blade of obsidian.

'What do you suggest, De La Rey?' the commander barked irritably, just as edgy and tense. 'We must do something, you say. *Ja*, I agree – but what?'

'We should take the ringleaders out of the mob.' Lothar pointed at Raleigh Tabaka, who was still at the gate. It was almost five hours since he had taken up his station there. 'That black swine there is holding them together. If we pick him and the other ringleaders out, the rest of them will soon lose interest.'

'What is the time?' the commander asked, and although it seemed irrelevant, Lothar glanced at his watch.

'Almost one o'clock.'

'There must be more reinforcements on the way,' the commander said. 'We will wait another fifteen minutes and then we will do as you suggest.'

'Look there,' Lothar snapped and pointed to the left.

Some of the younger men in the crowd had armed themselves with stones and bricks, and from the rear other missiles, chunks of paving slab and rocks, were being passed over the heads of the crowd to those in the front ranks.

'*Ja*, we have to break this up now,' the commander agreed, 'or else there will be serious trouble.'

Lothar turned and called a curt order to the constables

nearest him. 'You men, load your weapons and move up to the gate with me.'

He saw that some of the other men further down the line had taken his words as a general order to load, and there was the snicker of metal on metal as the magazines were clamped on to the Sten guns and the cocking handles jerked back. Lothar debated with himself for a moment whether he should countermand, but time was vital. He knew he had to get the leaders out of the crowd, for violence was only seconds away. Some of the black youths in front of the crowd were already shaking the mesh and heaving against it.

With his men behind him he marched to the gate and pointed at Raleigh Tabaka. 'You,' he shouted. 'I want to speak to you.' He reached through the square opening beside the gate lock and seized the front of Raleigh's shirt.

'I want you out of there,' he snarled, and Raleigh pulled back against his grip, jostling the men behind him.

Amelia screamed and clawed at Lothar's wrist. 'Leave him! You must not hurt him.'

The young men around them saw what was happening and hurled themselves against the wire.

'*Jee!*' they cried, that long, deep, drawn-out war cry that no Nguni warrior can resist. It made their blood smoke with the fighting madness, and it was taken up as others echoed them.

'*Jee!*'

The section of the crowd behind where Raleigh struggled with Lothar De La Rey heaved forward, throwing themselves upon the fence, humming the war cry, and the fence buckled and began to topple.

'Get back!' Lothar shouted at his men, but the back ranks of the crowd surged forward to see what was happening in front – and the fence went.

It came crashing over, and though Lothar jumped back, one of the metal posts hit him a glancing blow and he was knocked to his knees. The crowd was no longer contained, and the ranks behind pushed those in front so they came bursting into the yard, trampling over Lothar as he struggled to get to his feet.

From one side a brick came sailing out of the crowd in a high parabola. It struck the windscreen of one of the parked trucks, and shattered it in a shower of diamond-bright chips.

The women were screaming, and falling under the feet of those who were borne forward by the pressure from behind, and men were fighting to get back behind the wire as others thrust them forward, uttering that murderous war cry *'Jee!'* that brought on the madness.

Lothar was sprawled under the rushing tide, struggling to regain his feet, while a hail of stones and bricks came over the wire. Lothar rolled to his feet, and only because he was a superb athlete he kept his balance as the rush of frenzied bodies carried him backwards.

There was a loud and jarring sound close behind him that Lothar did not at first recognize. It sounded as though a steel rod had been drawn rapidly across a sheet of corrugated iron. Then he heard the other terrible sounds, the multiple impact of bullets into living flesh, like ripe melons bursting open from blows with a heavy club, and he shouted, 'No! Oh good Christ, no!' But the Sten guns rushed and tore the air with a sound like sheets of silk being ripped through, drowning out his despairing protest, and he wanted to shout again, 'Cease fire!' but his throat had closed and he was suffocating with horror and terror.

He made another strenuous effort to give the order, and his throat strained to enunciate the words, but no sound came and his hands moved without his conscious volition, lifting the Sten gun from his side, jerking back the cocking handle to feed a round into the breech. In front of him the crowd was breaking and turning, the pressure of human bodies against him was relieved, so he could mount the sub-machine-gun to waist height.

He tried to stop himself, but it was all a nightmare over which he had no control, the weapon in his hands shuddered and buzzed like a chain saw. In a few fleeting seconds the magazine of thirty rounds was empty, but Lothar had traversed the Sten gun like a reaper swinging a scythe, and now the bloody harvest lay before him in the dust twitching and kicking and moaning.

Only then did he realize fully what he had done, and his voice returned.

'Cease fire!' he screamed and struck out at the men around him to reinforce the order. 'Cease fire! Stop it! Stop it!'

Some of the younger recruits were reloading to fire again, and he ran amongst them striking out with the empty Sten to prevent them. A man on the roof of one of the troop carriers lifted his weapon and fired another burst and Lothar leapt onto the cab and knocked up the barrel so that the last spray of bullets went high into the dusty air.

From his vantage point on the cab of the truck, Lothar looked out over the sagging fence across the open ground where the dead and the wounded lay, and his spirit quailed.

'Oh, God forgive me. What have we done?' he choked. 'Oh, what have we done?'

In the middle of the morning Michael Courtney took a chance, for there seemed to be a lull in the activity around the police station. It was, of course, difficult to make out exactly what was happening. He could see only the backs of the rear ranks of the crowd, and over their heads the top of the wire fence and the iron roof of the station. However, the situation seemed for the moment to be quiet and apart from a little desultory singing the crowd was passive and patient.

He jumped into the Morris and drove back down the avenue to the primary school. The buildings were deserted, and without any qualms he tried the door which was marked 'Headmaster' and it was unlocked. There was a telephone on the cheap deal desk. He got through to the *Mail* offices on the first try, and Leon Herbstein was in his office.

'I've got a story,' Michael said, and read out his copy. When he finished he told Leon, 'If I were you, I'd send a staff photographer down here. There is a good chance of some dramatic pictures.'

'Give me the directions how to find you.' Leon acquiesced immediately, and Michael drove back to the police station just as another convoy of police reinforcements pushed through the crowd and entered the station gates.

The morning wore on and Michael ran out of cigarettes, a minor tragedy. He was also hot and thirsty and wondered what it was like standing in that mob out there, hour after hour.

He could sense the mood of the crowd changing. They were no longer cheerful and expectant. There was a sense of frustration, of having been cheated and duped, for Sobukwe had not arrived, nor had the white police made the promised announcement to abolish the *dompas*.

The singing started again, but in a harsh and aggressive tone. There were scuffles and disturbances in the crowd, and over their heads Michael saw the armed police take up positions on the cabs of the trucks parked beyond the wire.

The staff photographer from the *Mail* arrived, a young black journalist who was able to enter the township without a permit. He parked his small brown Humber beside the Morris and Michael cadged a cigarette from him and then quickly briefed him on what was happening, and sent him

704

forward to mingle with the back rows of the crowd and get to work.

A little after noon, some of the youths broke away from the crowd and began to search the verges of the road and the nearest gardens for missiles. They pulled up the bricks that bordered the flower-beds and broke chunks off the concrete paving slabs, then hurried back to join the crowd, carrying those crude weapons. This was an ominous development, and Michael climbed up on the bonnet of his beloved Morris, careless of the paintwork which he usually cherished and polished every morning.

Although he was over a hundred and fifty yards from the station gate, he now had a better view over the heads of the crowd, and he watched the growing agitation and restlessness until the police on the vehicle cabs, the only ones he could see, raised and began loading and cocking their weapons. They were obviously responding to an order and Michael felt a peculiar little chill of anxiety.

Suddenly there was a violent disturbance in the densest part of the crowd directly in front of the main gates. The mass of people surged and heaved and there was an uproar of protesting shouts and cries. Those in the rear of the crowd, closest to where Michael stood, pushed forward to see what was going on, and suddenly there was a metallic rending sound.

Michael saw the tops of the gates begin to move, toppling and bending under the strain, and as they went over there was a scattered volley of thrown rocks and bricks, and then, like the waters of a broken dam, the crowd rushed forward.

Michael had never heard the sound of sub-machine-gun fire before. So he did not recognize it, but he had heard a bullet striking flesh during that childhood safari on which his father had taken the brothers.

The sound was unmistakable, a meaty thumping, almost like a housewife beating a dusty carpet. However, he couldn't believe it, not until he saw the policemen on the cabs of the vehicles. Even in his horror he noticed how the weapons they held jumped and spurted tiny petals of fire an instant before the sound reached him.

The crowd broke and ran at the first buzzing bursts of fire. They spread out like ripples across a pond, streaming back past where Michael stood, and incredibly some of them were laughing, as though they had not realized what was happening, as though it were all some silly game.

In front of the broken gates the bodies were strewn most thickly, nearly all of them face down and with their heads pointing outwards, in the direction they were running as they were struck down, but there were others further out and the guns were still clamouring and people were still falling right beside where Michael stood, and the area around the police station was clear, so that through the dust he could see the figures of the uniformed police beyond the sagging wire. Some of them were reloading and others were still firing.

Michael heard the flitting sound of bullets passing close beside his head, but he was too mesmerized and shocked to duck or even to flinch.

Twenty paces away a young couple ran back past him. He recognized them as the pair who had headed the procession earlier, the tall good-looking lad and the pretty moon-faced girl. They were still holding hands, the boy dragging the girl along with him, but as they passed Michael the girl broke free and doubled back to where a child was standing bewildered and lost amongst the carnage.

As the girl stooped to pick up the child, the bullets hit her. She was thrown back abruptly as though she had reached the end of an invisible leash, but she stayed on her feet for a few seconds longer, and Michael saw the bullets come out through her back at the level of her lowest ribs. For a brief moment they raised little tented peaks in the

706

cloth of her blouse, and then erupted in pink smoky puffs of blood and tissue.

The girl pirouetted and began to sag. As she turned, Michael saw the two entry wounds in her chest, dark studs on the white cloth, and she collapsed on to her knees.

Her companion ran back to try and support her, but she slipped through his hands and fell forward on her face. The boy dropped down beside her and lifted her in his arms, and Michael saw his expression. He had never before seen such desolation and human suffering in another being.

R aleigh held Amelia in his arms. Her head drooped against his shoulder like that of a sleepy child and he could feel her blood soaking into his clothing. It was hot as spilled coffee and it smelled sickly sweet in the heat.

Raleigh groped in his pocket and found his handkerchief. Gently he wiped the dust from her cheeks and from the corners of her mouth, for she had fallen with her face against the earth.

He was crooning to her softly, 'Wake up, my little moon. Let me hear your sweet voice—'

Her eyes were open and he turned her head slightly to look into them. 'It is me, Amelia, it is Raleigh – don't you see me?' But even as he stared into her widely distended pupils a milky sheen spread over them, dulling out their dark beauty.

He hugged her harder, pressing her unresisting head against his chest and he began to rock her, humming softly to her as though she were an infant, and he looked out across the field.

The bodies were strewn about like overripe fruit fallen from the bough. Some of them were moving, an arm straightened or a hand unclenched, an old man began to crawl past where Raleigh knelt, dragging a shattered leg behind him.

Then the police officers were coming out through the sagging gates. They wandered about the field in a dazed uncertain manner, still carrying their empty weapons dangling from limp hands, stopping to kneel briefly beside one of the bodies, and then standing again and walking on.

One of them approached. As he came closer Raleigh recognized the blond captain who had seized him at the gate. He had lost his cap and the top button was missing from his tunic. His crew-cut hair was darkened with sweat, and droplets of sweat stood on his waxen pale forehead. He stopped a few paces off and looked at Raleigh. Although his hair was blond, his eyebrows were dark and thick and his eyes were yellow as those of a leopard. Raleigh knew then how he had earned his nickname. Those pale eyes were underscored with smudges of fatigue and horror, dark as old bruises, and his lips were dry and cracked.

They stared at each other – the black man kneeling in the dust with the dead woman in his arms and the uniformed white man with the empty Sten gun in his hands.

'I didn't mean it to happen—' said Lothar De La Rey and his voice croaked, 'I'm sorry.'

Raleigh did not answer, gave no sign of having heard or understood and Lothar turned away and walked back, picking his way amongst the dead and the maimed, back into the laager of wire mesh.

The blood on Raleigh's clothing began to cool, and when he touched Amelia's cheek again he felt the warmth going out of it also. Gently he closed her eyelids, and then he unbuttoned the front of her blouse. There was very little bleeding from the two entry wounds. They were just below her pointed virgin breasts, small dark mouths in her smooth amber-coloured skin, set only inches apart. Raleigh ran two fingers of his right hand into those bloody mouths, and there was residual warmth in her torn flesh.

'With my fingers in your dead body,' he whispered. 'With the fingers of my right hand in your wounds, I swear an oath, my love. You will be avenged. I swear it on our love, upon my life and upon your death. You will be avenged.'

I n the days of anxiety and turmoil following the massacre of Sharpeville, Verwoerd and his Minister of Police acted with resolution and strength.

A state of emergency was declared in almost half of South Africa's magisterial districts. Both the PAC and ANC were banned and those of their supporters suspected of incitement and intimidation were arrested and detained under the emergency regulations. Some estimates put the figure of detainees as high as eighteen thousand.

In early April at the meeting of the full cabinet to discuss the emergency, Shasa Courtney risked his political future by rising to address a plea to Dr Verwoerd for the abolition of the pass book system. He had prepared his speech with care, and the genuine concern he felt for the importance of the subject made him even more than usually eloquent. As he spoke he became gradually aware that he was winning the support of some of the other senior members of the cabinet.

'In a single stroke we will be removing the main cause of black dissatisfaction, and depriving the revolutionary agitators of their most valuable weapon,' he pointed out.

Three other senior ministers followed Shasa, each voicing their support for the abolition of the *dompas*, but from the top of the long table Verwoerd glowered at them, becoming every minute more angry until at last he jumped to his feet.

'The idea is completely out of the question. The reference books are there for an essential purpose: to control the influx of blacks into the urban areas.'

Within a few minutes he had brutally bludgeoned the proposal to death, and made it clear that to try to resurrect it would be political suicide for any member of the cabinet, no matter how senior.

Within days Dr Hendrik Verwoerd was himself on the brink of the chasm. He visited Johannesburg to open the Rand Easter Show. He made a reassuring speech to the huge audience that filled the arena of the country's largest agricultural and industrial show, and as he sat down, to thunderous applause, a white man of insignificant appearance made his way between the tiers of seats and in full view of everybody drew a pistol and holding it to Dr Verwoerd's head fired two shots.

With blood pouring down his face Verwoerd collapsed, and security guards overpowered his assailant. Both bullets, fired at point-blank range, had penetrated the Prime Minister's skull, and yet his most remarkable tenacity and will to survive, combined with the expert medical attention he received, saved him.

In little more than a month he had left hospital and had once more taken up his duties as the head of state. The assassination attempt seemed to have been without motive or reason, and the assailant was judged insane and placed in an asylum. By the time Dr Verwoerd had fully recovered from the attempt on his life calm had been restored to the country as a whole, and Manfred De La Rey's police were in total control once more.

Naturally the reaction of the international community towards the slaughter and the subsequent measures to regain control was heavily critical. America led the rest in her condemnations, and within months had instituted an embargo on the sale of arms to South Africa. More damaging than the reaction of foreign governments was the crash on the Johannesburg stock exchange, the collapse of property values and the attempted flight of capital out of the country. Strict exchange-control regulations were swiftly imposed to forestall this.

Manfred De La Rey had come out of it all with his power and position greatly enhanced. He had acted the way his people expected him to, with strength and forthright determination. There was no doubt at all now that he was one of the senior members of the cabinet and in the direct line of succession to Hendrik Verwoerd. He had smashed the Pan-Africanist Congress and the ANC. Their leaders were in total disarray and all of them were in hiding or had fled the country.

With the safety of the state secured, Dr Verwoerd could at last turn his full attention to the momentous business of realizing the golden dream of Afrikanerdom – the Republic.

The referendum was held in October 1960, and so great were the feelings, for and against, engendered by the prospect of breaking with the British crown that there was a ninety per cent poll. Cunningly, Verwoerd had decreed that a simple majority, and not the usual two-thirds majority, would suffice, and on the day he got his majority: 850,000 to 775,000. The Afrikaner response was an hysteria of joy, of speeches and wild rejoicing.

In March the following year Verwoerd and his entourage went to London to attend the conference of the Commonwealth prime ministers. He came out of the meeting to tell the world, 'In the light of opinions expressed by other member governments of the Commonwealth regarding South Africa's race policies, and in the light of future plans regarding the race policies of the South African Government, I told the other prime ministers that I was withdrawing my country's application for continued membership of the Commonwealth after attaining the status of a republic.'

From Pretoria Manfred De La Rey cabled Verwoerd, 'You have preserved the dignity and pride of your country, and the nation owes you eternal gratitude.'

Verwoerd returned home to the adulation and hero worship of his people. In the heady euphoria, very few, even amongst the English-speaking opposition, realized just how many doors Verwoerd had locked and barred behind him and just how cold and bleak the winds that Macmillan had predicted would blow across the southern tip of Africa in the coming years.

With the Republic safely launched Verwoerd could at last select his praetorian guard to protect it and hold it strong. Erasmus, the erstwhile Minister of Justice who had acted neither as ruthlessly nor as resolutely as was expected during the emergency, was packed off as the ambassador of the new Republic to Rome, and Verwoerd presented two new ministers to his cabinet.

The new Minister of Defence was the member for the constituency of George in the Cape, P. W. Botha, while Erasmus's replacement as Minister of Justice was Balthazar Johannes Vorster. Shasa Courtney knew Vorster well, and as he listened to him make his first address to the cabinet he reflected how much like Manfred De La Rey the man was.

They were almost the same age and, like Manfred, Vorster had been a member of the extreme right-wing anti-Smuts pro-Nazi *Ossewa Brandwag* during the war. Whereas it was generally accepted that Manfred had remained in Germany during the war years – although he was very mysterious and secretive about that period of his life – John Vorster had been interned in Smuts' Koffiefontein concentration camp for the duration.

Both Vorster and De La Rey had been educated at

Stellenbosch University, the citadel of Afrikanerdom, and their political careers had run closely parallel courses. Although Manfred had won his seat in parliament in the historic 1948 elections, John Vorster in the same elections had gained the distinction of being the only candidate in South African history to lose by a mere two votes. Later, in 1953, he vindicated himself by winning the same Brakpan seat with a majority of seven hundred.

Now that the two of them were seated at the long table in the cabinet room, their physical resemblance was striking. They were both heavy rugged-looking men, with bulldog features, both obdurate, unflinching and tough, the epitome of the hard Boer.

Vorster confirmed this for Shasa as he began to speak, leaning forward aggressively, confident and articulate. 'I believe we are in a fight to the death with the forces of Communism, and that we cannot defeat subversion or thwart revolution by closely observing the Queensberry rules. We have to put aside the old precepts of *habeas corpus*, and arm ourselves with new legislation that will enable us to pre-empt the enemy, to pick out their leaders and put them away where they can do little harm. This is not a new concept, gentlemen.'

Vorster smiled down the table and Shasa was struck by the way in which his dour features lit up with that impish smile.

'You all know where I spent the war years, without the benefit of trial. Let me tell you right now – it worked. It kept me out of mischief and that's what I intend to do with those who would destroy this land – keep them out of mischief. I want power to detain any person whom I know to be an enemy of the state, without trial, for a period of up to ninety days.'

It was a masterly performance and Shasa felt some trepidation in having to follow it, especially when he could not be so sanguine in his own view of the future.

'At the moment I have two major concerns,' he told his colleagues seriously. 'The first is the arms embargo placed upon us by the Americans. I believe that other countries are soon going to bow to American pressure and extend the embargo. One day we might even have the ridiculous situation where Great Britain will refuse to sell us the arms we need for our own defence.' Some of the others at the table fidgeted and looked incredulous. Shasa assured them: 'We cannot afford to underestimate this hysteria of America for what they call civil rights. Remember that they sent troops to help force blacks into white schools.' The memory of that appalled them all and there were no further signs of disbelief as Shasa went on. 'A nation who can do that will do anything. My aim is to make this country totally self-sufficient in conventional armaments within five years.'

'Is that possible?' Verwoerd asked sharply.

'I believe so.' Shasa nodded. 'Fortunately, this eventuality has been anticipated. You yourself warned me of the possibility of an arms embargo when you appointed me, Prime Minister.'

Verwoerd nodded and Shasa repeated, 'This is my aim; self-sufficient in conventional weapons in five years—' Shasa paused dramatically. 'And nuclear capable in ten years.'

This was stretching their credulity and there were interjections and sharp questions, so that Shasa held up his hands and spoke firmly.

'I am deadly serious, gentlemen. We can do it! Given certain circumstances.'

'Money,' said Hendrik Verwoerd, and Shasa nodded.

'Yes, Prime Minister, money. Which brings me to my second major consideration.' Shasa drew a deep breath, and steeled himself to broach an unpalatable truth. 'Since the Sharpeville shootings, we have had a crippling flight of capital from the country. Cecil Rhodes was wont to say that the Jews were his birds of good omen. When the Jews came, an enterprise or a country was assured of success, and when the Jews left you could expect the worst. Well the sad truth, gentlemen, is that our Jews are leaving. We have to entice them to stay and bring back those who have already left.'

Again there was restlessness around the table. The National Party had been conceived on that wave of anti-Semitism between the world wars, and although it had abated since then, traces of it still existed.

'These are the facts, gentlemen.' Shasa ignored their discomfort. 'Since Sharpeville, the value of property has collapsed to half what it was before the shooting, and the stock market is at its lowest since the dark days of Dunkirk. The businessmen and investors of the world are convinced that this government is tottering and on the point of capitulating to the forces of Communism and darkness. They see us as being engulfed in despondency and anarchy, with black mobs burning and looting and white civilization about to go up in flames.' They laughed derisively and John Vorster made a bitter interjection.

'I have just explained what steps we will take.'

'Yes.' Shasa cut him off quickly. 'We know that the foreign view is distorted. We know that we still have a strong and stable government, that the country is prosperous and productive and that the vast majority of our people, both black and white, are law-abiding and content. We know that we have our guardian angel, gold, to protect us. But we have to convince the rest of the world.'

'Do you think that's possible, man?' Manfred asked quickly.

'Yes, with a full-scale and concerted campaign to give the truth of the situation to the businessmen of the world,' Shasa said. 'I have recruited most of our own leaders in industry and commerce to assist. We will go out at our own expense to explain the truth. We will invite them here – journalists, businessmen and friends – to see for themselves how tranquil and how under control the country truly is, and just how rich are the opportunities.'

Shasa spoke for another thirty minutes and when he ended, his own fervour and sincerity had exhausted him; but then he saw how he had finally convinced his colleagues and he knew the results were worth the effort. He was convinced that from the horror of Sharpeville he could mount a fresh endeavour that would carry them to greater heights of prosperity and strength.

Shasa had always been resilient, with extraordinary recuperative powers. Even in his Air Force days, when he brought the squadron in from a sortie over the Italian lines and the others had sat around the mess, stunned and shattered by the experience, he had been the first to recover and to start the repartee and boisterous horseplay. Shasa left the cabinet room drained and exhausted but by the time he had driven the vintage Jaguar SS around the mountain and through the Anreith gate of Weltevreden, he was sitting up straight in the bucket seat, feeling confident and jaunty again.

The harvest was long past and the labourers were in the vineyards pruning the vines. Shasa parked the Jaguar and went down between the rows of bare leafless plants to talk to them and give them encouragement. Many of these men and women had been on Weltevreden since Shasa had been a child, and the younger ones had been born here. Shasa looked upon them as an extension of his family and they in turn regarded him as their patriarch. He spent half an hour with them listening to their small problems and worries, and settling most with a few words of assurance, then he broke off and left them abruptly as a figure on horseback came down the far side of the vineyard at full gallop.

From the corner of the stone wall Shasa watched Isabella gather her mount, and he stiffened as he realized what she was going to do. The mare was not yet fully schooled and

Shasa had never trusted her temperament. The wall was of yellow Table Mountain sandstone, five foot high.

'No, Bella!' he whispered. 'No, baby!'

But she turned the mare and drove her at the wall, and the horse reacted gamely. Her quarters bunched and the great muscles rippled below the glossy hide. Isabella lifted her and they went up.

Shasa held his breath, but even in his suspense he could appreciate what a magnificent sight they made, horse and rider, thoroughbreds both – the mare with her forelegs folded up under her chest and her ears pricked forward, soaring away from the earth, and Isabella leaning back in the saddle, her back arched and her young body supple and lovely, long legs and fine thrusting breasts, red mouth laughing and her hair flying free, sparkling with ruby lights in the late yellow sunlight.

Then they were over and Shasa exhaled sharply. Isabella swung the mare down to where he stood at the corner.

'You promised to ride with me, Pater,' she scolded him. Shasa's instinct was to reprimand her for that jump, but he prevented himself. He knew she would probably respond by pulling the mare's head around and taking the jump again from this side. He wondered just when he had lost control of her, and then grinned ruefully as he answered himself. 'About ten minutes after she was born.'

The mare was dancing in a circle and Isabella flung her hair back with a toss of her head.

'I waited almost an hour for you,' she said.

'Affairs of state—' Shasa began.

'That's no excuse, Pater. A promise is a promise.'

'It's still not too late,' he pointed out, and she laughed as she challenged him.

'I'll race that old banger of yours down to the stables!' And she booted the mare into a gallop.

'Not fair,' he called after her. 'You have too much start,'

but she turned in the saddle and stuck her tongue out at him. He ran to the Jag, but she cut across North Field and was dismounted by the time he drove into the stableyard.

She tossed her reins to a groom and ran to embrace him. Isabella had a variety of kisses, but this type, lingering and loving, with a little bit of ear-nuzzling at the end, was reserved for when she badly wanted something from him, something that she knew he was going to try to refuse.

While he pulled on his riding boots she sat close beside him on the bench and told him a funny story about her sociology professor at varsity.

'This huge shaggy St Bernard wandered into the lecture theatre and Prof. Jacobs was quick as a flash. Better that the dogs should come to learning, he said, than learning should go to the dogs.' She was a natural mimic. As they left the saddle room, she hugged his arm.

'Oh, Daddy, if only I could find a boy like you, but they're all so utterly dreary.'

'Long may they remain that way,' he wished fervently.

He made a cup with his hands for her to mount, but she laughed at him and sprang to the saddle easily on those long lovely legs.

'Come on, slowcoach. It'll be dark soon.'

Shasa enjoyed being alone with her. She enchanted him with her mercurial changes of mood and subject. She had a quick mind and quirky sense of humour to go with her extraordinary face and body, but she alarmed him when she showed flashes of that restless refusal to concentrate for long on a single topic. Sean had been like that, needing constant stimulation to hold his interest, easily bored by anything that could not keep the same breathless pace that he set. Shasa was amazed that Isabella had lasted out a year of university studies, but he was resigned to the fact that she wasn't going to graduate. Every time they discussed it, she was more disparaging of the academic life. Make-believe, she called it. Kid's stuff. And when he replied, 'Well, Bella, you are still a kid,' she bridled at him.

'Oh, Daddy, you don't understand!'

'Don't I? Don't you think I was your age once?'

'I suppose so – but that was in biblical times, for God's sake.'

'Ladies don't swear,' he remonstrated automatically.

She attracted admirers in slavish droves, and treated them with callous indifference for a while and then dropped them with almost feline cruelty, and all the time the restlessness in her was more apparent.

'I should have been stricter with her right from the beginning,' he decided grimly, and then grinned. 'What the hell, she's my only indulgence – and she'll be gone soon enough.'

'Do you know that when you smile like that you are the sexiest man in the world?' she interrupted his thoughts.

'What do you know about sexiness, young lady?' he demanded gruffly to cover his gratification, and she tossed her head at him.

'Wouldn't you like to know?'

'No, thank you,' he refused hastily. 'I'd probably have a hernia on the spot.'

'My poor old Daddy.' She edged the mare over until their knees touched and she leaned across to hug him.

'All right, Bella,' he smiled. 'You'd better tell me what you want. Your heavy artillery has demolished my defences entirely.'

'Oh, Daddy, you make me seem so scheming. I'll race you down to the polo grounds.'

He let her lead, holding his stallion's nose just behind her stirrup all the way down the hill. Nonetheless, she was flushed with triumph as she pulled in the mare and turned back to him.

'I had a letter from Mater,' she said.

For a moment Shasa didn't realize what she had said, then his smile iced over and he glanced at his gold Rolex wristwatch.

'We'd better be getting back.'

'I want to talk about my mother. We haven't talked about her since the divorce.'

'There isn't anything to discuss. She's out of our lives.'

'No.' Isabella shook her head. 'She wants to see me – me and Mickey. She wants us to go to London and visit her.'

'No,' he said fiercely.

'She's my mother.'

'She signed away all claim to that title.'

'I want to see her – she wants to see me.'

'We'll talk about it some other time.'

'I want to talk about it now. Why won't you let me go?'

'Your mother did things which put her beyond the pale. She would exert an influence of evil upon you.'

'Nobody influences me – unless I want them to,' she said. 'And what did Mother do anyway? Nobody has ever explained that.'

'She committed an act of calculated treachery. She betrayed us all – her husband, her father, her family, her children and her country.'

'I don't believe it.' Isabella shook her head. 'Mater was always so concerned for everybody.'

'I cannot, and will not, give you all the details, Bella. Just believe me when I tell you that if I had not spirited her out of the country, she would have stood trial as an accessory to the murder of her own father and for the crime of high treason.'

They rode up to the stables in silence, but as they entered the yard and dismounted, Isabella said quietly, 'She should have the chance to explain it to me herself.'

'I can forbid you to go, Bella, you are still a minor. But you know I won't do that. I'll simply ask you not to go to London to see that woman.'

'I'm sorry, Daddy. Mickey is going, and I am going with him.' She saw his expression, and went to him quickly. 'Please try to understand. I love you, but I love her too. I have to go.'

They drove up to the house in the Jaguar without speaking again, but as he parked the car and switched off the ignition, Shasa asked, 'When?'

'We haven't decided yet.'

'I tell you what. We'll go together some time and perhaps we could go on to Switzerland for a week's skiing or Italy to do some sight-seeing. We might even stop in Paris to get you a new frock. Lord knows, you are short of clothes.'

'My dear father, you are a crafty old dog, aren't you?'

They were still laughing as they went arm in arm up the front steps of Weltevreden. Centaine came out of her study door across the lobby. When she saw them she snatched the gold-rimmed reading glasses off her nose – she hated even the family to see her wearing them – and she demanded, 'What are you two so merry about? Bella is wearing her triumphant expression. What has she talked you into this time?'

Centaine didn't wait for an answer, but pointed to the huge banana-shaped package almost ten foot long, wrapped in thick layers of brown hessian, that lay in the middle of the chequered marble floor.

'Shasa, this arrived for you this morning and it has been cluttering up the house all day. Please get rid of it, whatever it is.'

Centaine had lived on alone at Rhodes Hill for almost a year after Blaine's death before Shasa had been able to persuade her to close the house up and return to Weltevreden.

Now she ran a strict routine to which they were all expected to conform.

'Now what on earth is this?' Shasa tentatively attempted to lift one end of the long package, and then grunted. 'It's made of lead, whatever it is.'

'Hold on, Pater,' Garry called from the top of the staircase. 'You'll bust something.' He came bounding down the stairs, three at a time. 'I'll do that for you – where do you want it?'

'The gun room will do. Thanks, Garry.'

Garry enjoyed showing off his strength and he lifted the heavy package easily, and manoeuvred it down the passageway, then through the gun-room door and laid it on the lion skin in front of the fireplace.

'Do you want me to open it?' he asked, and without waiting for an answer went to work on it.

Isabella perched on the desk, determined not to miss anything, and none of them spoke until Garry had stripped away the last sheet of hessian and stood back.

'It's magnificent,' Shasa breathed. 'I have never seen anything quite like that in my life before.' It was a single tusk of curved ivory, almost ten foot long, as thick as a pretty girl's waist at one end and tapering to a blunt point at the other.

'It must weigh almost a hundred and fifty pounds,' Garry said. 'But just look at the workmanship.'

Shasa knew that the ivory workers of Zanzibar were the only ones who could do something like this. The entire length of the tusk had been carved with hunting scenes of exquisite detail and the finest execution.

'It's beautiful.' Even Isabella was impressed. 'Who sent it to you?'

'There is an envelope—' Shasa pointed to the litter of discarded wrappings, and Garry picked it out and passed it to him.

The envelope contained a single sheet of notepaper.

722

                              In camp on the Tana River
                                                 Kenya.
Dear Dad,
     Happy birthday – I'll be thinking of you on the day.
This is my best jumbo to date – 146lbs before the
carving.
     Why don't you come hunting with me?

                                                 Love,
                                                 Sean

     With the note in one hand, Shasa squatted beside the
tusk and stroked the creamy smooth surface. The carvings
depicted a herd of elephant, hundreds of them in a single
herd. From old bulls and breeding cows to tiny calves, they
fled in a long spiral frieze around the ivory shaft, diminishing in elegant perspective towards the point. The herd was
harassed and attacked by hunters along its length, beginning with men in lion skins armed with bows and poisoned
arrows, or with broad-bladed elephant spears; towards the
end of this primeval cavalcade the hunters were on horseback and wielding modern firearms. The path of the herd
was strewn with great fallen carcasses, and it was beautiful
and real and tragic.
     However, it was neither the beauty nor the tragedy that
thickened Shasa's voice as he said, 'Will you two leave me
alone, please.' He did not look around at them, he did not
want them to see his face.
     For once Isabella did not argue, but took Garry's hand
and led him from the room.
     'He hasn't forgotten my birthday,' Shasa murmured, as
he stroked the ivory. 'Not once since he left.' He coughed
and stood up abruptly, jerked the handkerchief from his
breast pocket and blew his nose loudly and then wiped his
eyes.
     'And I haven't even written to him, I haven't even
replied to one of his letters.' He stuffed the handkerchief

                              723

back into his pocket and went to stand at the window, staring out over the lawns where the peacocks strutted. 'The stupid cruel thing is that he has always been my favourite of the three of them. Oh, God, I'd give anything to see him again.'

T he rain was icy grey, drifting like smoke over the thick forests of bamboo that cloaked the crests of the Aberdare Mountains.

The four of them moved in single file with the Ndorobo tracker on the point, following the spoor in the forest earth that beneath the litter of fallen bamboo leaves was the colour and consistency of molten chocolate.

Sean Courtney took the second position, covering the tracker and poised to make any quick decision. He was the youngest of the three white men but command had quite naturally devolved upon him. Nobody had contested it.

The third man in the line, Alistair Sparks, was the youngest son of a Kenyan settler family. Although he possessed enormous powers of endurance, was a fine natural shot and a consummate bushman, he was lazy and evasive and needed to be pushed to exercise all his skills to the full.

Raymond Harris was on the drag at number four. He was almost fifty years old, full of malaria and gin, but in his time had been one of the legendary white hunters of East Africa. He had taught Sean everything he knew, until the pupil had excelled the master. Now Raymond was content to bring up the rear and let Sean and Matatu, the tracker, get them into position for the kill.

Matatu was naked except for his filthy tattered loincloth and the rain made tiny rivulets down his glossy black hide. He worked the spoor with the same instinct and super-human sense of sight, smell and hearing, as one of the wild animals of the forest. They had been following these tracks for two days already, stopping only when the light failed completely each night, and taking up the chase again with the first flush of dawn.

The spoor was running sweet and hot. Sean was probably as good a tracker as a white man could be and he judged that they were only four or five hours behind and gaining swiftly. The quarry had angled up the steep slope of this nameless peak, heading to cross the ridge just below the main crest. Sean caught glimpses of the top through the dense vault of bamboo over their heads and the blown streamers of misty rain.

Suddenly Matatu stopped dead, and Sean popped his tongue to warn the others and froze with his thumb on the safety-catch of the big double-barrelled Gibbs.

After a moment Matatu turned abruptly aside, dropping the spoor, and went sliding as swiftly and silently as a dark serpent down the slope, away from the line and direction of the quarry.

Five years before, when Sean had first taken Matatu into his service, he might have protested and tried to force him to stay with the run of the spoor, but now he followed without argument, and although he was going at his best hunting speed he just managed to hold the tracker in sight.

Sean was dressed in a cloak of colobus monkey skins and he wore Somali sandals of elephant hide on his feet and a shaggy cap of monkey skin covered his obviously Caucasian hair. His arms, legs and face were blackened with a mixture of rancid hippo fat and soot, and he had not bathed in two weeks. He looked and smelled like the men he was hunting.

There were five Mau Mau in the band that they were pursuing, all of them members of the notorious gang run by the self-styled General Kimathi. Five days previously they had attacked one of the coffee shambas near Nyeri in the foothills of the mountain range. They had disembowelled the white overseer and stuffed his severed genitals into his mouth, and they had chopped off his wife's limbs with the heavy-bladed pangas, beginning at wrist and ankle and working gradually towards the trunk of her body, until they hacked through the great joints in her shoulders and groin.

Sean and his group of scouts had reached the shamba almost twelve hours after the gang had fled. They had left the Land-Rover and taken the spoor on foot.

Matatu took them directly down the slope. The narrow river at the bottom was a tumultuous silver torrent. Sean stripped off his furs and sandals and went into it naked. The cold chilled his bones until they ached and the roaring waters swirled over his head but he carried the line across and then brought the others safely over.

Matatu was the last across, carrying Sean's clothing and his rifle, and immediately he was off again, like a wraith of the forest. Sean followed him with the agony of cold shuddering through his body and the sodden furs a heavy burden to add to the rifle and his pack.

A herd of buffalo crashed away through the forest ahead of them, and the bovine stink lingered in their nostrils long after they were gone. Once Sean had a glimpse of a huge antelope, ginger red with vertical white stripes down its heavy body and a head of magnificent spiral horns. It was a bongo. He would have charged one of his rich American clients $1000 for a shot at that rarest and most elusive of all antelopes, but it ghosted away into the bamboo and Matatu led them on without apparent purpose or direction, the spoor three hours cold behind them.

Then Matatu skirted one of the rare forest clearings and stopped again. He glanced back over his naked shoulder and grinned at Sean with the patent adoration of a hunting dog who acknowledges the most important being in its universe.

Sean stepped up beside him and looked down at the spoor. He would never know how Matatu did it. He had tried to make him explain, but the wizened little gnome had merely laughed with embarrassment and hung his head.

It was a kind of magic that went beyond the mere art of observation and deduction. What Matatu had just done was to drop the spoor when it was sweet and hot, and go off at an improbable tangent, running blind through trackless bamboo and over wild peaks, to meet the spoor again with the unerring instinct of a migrating swallow, having cut the corner and gained three hours on the quarry.

Sean squeezed his shoulder and the Ndorobo wriggled his whole body with pleasure.

They were less than an hour behind the gang now, but the rain and the mist were bringing on the night prematurely. Sean signalled Matatu on. Not one of them had spoken a single word all that day.

The men they were chasing were becoming careless. In the beginning they had anti-tracked and covered spoor, doubled and jinked so cunningly that even Matatu had puzzled to unravel the sign and get away on the run of it – but now they were feeling confident and secure. They had broken off the succulent bamboo shoots to chew as they marched, leaving glaring wounds on the plants, and they had trodden deeply, heeling with fatigue, leaving signs that Matatu could follow like a tarmac road. One of the fugitives had even defecated on the track, not bothering to cover his faeces, and they were still steaming with his body warmth. Matatu grinned at Sean over his shoulder and made the fluttery hand signal which said 'Very close'.

Sean eased open the action of the double-barrelled Gibbs, without allowing the sidelock to click. He slid the brass-cased cartridges out of the breeches, and replaced them with two others from the leather ammunition pouch beneath his monkey-skin cape. The .577 cartridges were thicker than a man's thumb and the clumsy, blunt-nosed bullet heads were jacketed in copper and capped with soft blue lead so they could mushroom through living tissue, tearing open a wide channel and inflicting terrible damage. This little ritual of changing his cartridges was one of

Sean's superstitions – he always did it just before he closed with dangerous game. He closed the rifle as gently and silently as he had opened it and glanced back at the two men behind him.

The whites of Alistair's eyes gleamed in his blackened face. He carried the Bren gun. Sean had not been able to wean him from it. Despite its unwieldy long barrel and great weight, Alistair loved the automatic weapon. 'When I'm after Mickey Mouse I like to be able to turn the air blue with lead,' he explained with that lazy grin. 'Nobody is going to get a chance to stuff my knackers down my throat, matey!'

At the rear Ray Harris gave Sean the thumbs-up signal, but the sweat and rain had cut pale runnels through the soot and fat on his face, and even through the camouflage Sean could see how haggard he was with fear and fatigue. 'The old man is getting past it,' Sean thought dispassionately. 'Have to put him out to grass soon.'

Ray carried the Stirling sub-machine-gun. Sean suspected it was because he could no longer manage the weight of a more substantial weapon. 'In the bamboo it's point-blank,' Ray excused his choice, and Sean had not bothered to argue or to point out that the tiny 9 mm bullets would be deflected by the frailest twig, and smothered in the dense vegetation of the Aberdares – while the big 600-grain slug from his own Gibbs would plough straight through branch and stem and still blow the guts out of the Mickey Mouse on the other side, while the stubby 20-inch barrels were perfect for close work in the bamboo, and he could swing them without risking hooking up in the brush.

Sean clicked his tongue softly and Matatu went away on the spoor in that soft-footed, ungainly lope which he could keep up day and night without tiring. They crossed another heavily bambooed ridge and in the valley beyond Matatu stopped again. It was so dark by now that Sean had to move up beside him, and go down on one knee to examine the sign. It took him almost a minute to make sense of it, even after Matatu had pointed out the other set of tracks coming in from the right.

Sean gestured Ray to move up and laid his lips to his ear. 'They have joined another party of Mickey Mice – probably from the base camp. Eight of them, three women, so we have thirteen in a bunch now. A lovely lucky number.'

But as he spoke the light was going, and the rain started again, spilling softly out of the purple-black sky. Within five hundred yards Matatu stopped for the last time and Sean could just make out the pale palm of his right hand as he made the wash-out signal. Night had blanketed the spoor.

The white men each found a treetrunk to prop themselves against, spreading out in a defensive circle facing outwards. Sean took Matatu under the monkey-skin cloak with him as though he were a tired gun dog. The little man's skinny body was as cold and wet as a trout taken from a mountain stream and he smelled of herbs and leaf mould and wild things. They ate the hard salted dry buffalo meat and cold maize cakes from their belt pouches and slept fitfully in each other's warmth while the raindrops pattered down on the fur over their heads.

Matatu touched Sean's cheek and he was instantly awake in the utter darkness, slipping the safety-catch of the Gibbs that lay across his lap. He sat rigid, listening and alert.

Beside him Matatu snuffled the air and after a moment Sean did the same. 'Woodsmoke?' he whispered, and both of them came to their feet. In the darkness, Sean moved to where Alistair and Ray were lying and got them up. They went forward in the night, holding the belt of the man ahead to keep in contact. The whiffs of smoke were intermittent but stronger.

It took almost two hours for Matatu to locate the Mau

Mau encampment precisely, using his sense of smell and hearing, and at the end the faint glow of a patch of camp-fire coals. Although the bamboo dripped all around, they could hear them – a soft cough, a strangled snore, the gabble of a woman in a nightmare – and Sean and Matatu moved them into position.

It took another hour; but in the utter darkness before the true dawn Alistair was lying up the slope, forty feet from the dying camp fire. Raymond was amongst the rocks on the bank of the stream on the far side, and Sean lay with Matatu in the dense scrub beside the path that led into the camp.

Sean had the barrel of the Gibbs across his left forearm and his right hand on the pistol grip with the safety-catch under his thumb. He had spread the fur cloak over both himself and Matatu, but neither of them even drowsed. They were keyed up to the finest pitch. Sean could feel the little Ndorobo trembling with eagerness where their bodies touched. He was like a bird dog with the scent of the grouse in his nostrils.

The dawn came stealthily. First Sean realized that he could see his own hand on the rifle in front of his face, and then the short thick barrels appeared before his eyes. He looked beyond them and made out a tendril of smoke from the fire rising out of the Stygian forest towards the lighter pitch of darkness that was the sky through the canopy of bamboo.

The light came on more swiftly, and he saw that there were two crude shelters, one on each side of the fire, low lean-tos not more than waist high, and he thought he saw a movement in one of them, perhaps a recumbent figure rolling over and pulling up a skin blanket over his head.

Again somebody coughed, a thick phlegmy sound. The camp was waking. Sean glanced up the slope and then down into the stream bed. He could see the soft sheen of the water-polished boulders – but nothing of the other two hunters.

The light hardened. Sean closed his eyes for a moment and then opened them again. He could see sharply the support of the roof of the nearest shelter, and dimly beyond it a human shape wrapped in a fur blanket.

'Shooting light in two minutes,' he thought. The others would know it also. All three of them had waited like this in countless dawns beside the rotting carcass of pig or antelope for the leopard to come to the bait. They could judge that magical moment when the sights were crisp enough to make the sure killing shot. This dawn they would wait for Sean before they came in with the Bren and the Stirling.

Again Sean closed his eyes and when he opened them again the figure in the nearest shelter was sitting up and looking towards him. For a gut-swooping instant he thought he had been spotted and he almost fired. Then he checked himself as the head turned away from him.

Abruptly the figure threw the fur blanket aside and stood up, crouching under the low roof of the shelter.

Sean saw it was a woman, one of the Mau Mau camp followers, but for Sean just as cruel and depraved as any of her menfolk. She stepped out into the open beside the dead fire wearing only a short kilt of some pale material. Her breasts were high and pointed and her skin smooth and glossy as newly mined anthracite in the soft dawn light.

She came directly towards where Sean lay, and though her gait was still clumsy and unsteady with sleep, he saw that she was young and comely. A few more paces and she would stumble over him, but then she stopped again and yawned and her teeth were very white, gleaming in the soft grey light.

She lifted her kilt around her waist and squatted facing Sean, spreading her knees and bowing her head slightly to watch herself as she began to urinate. Her water splashed noisily and the sharp ammoniacal tang of it made Sean's nostrils flare.

She was so close that he did not have to lift the Gibbs to his shoulder. He shot her in the stomach. The heavy rifle bounded in his grip and the bullet picked the girl up and while she was in the air it broke her in half, blowing a hole through her spine into which her own head would have fitted, and she folded up, loose and floppy as a suit of discarded clothing as she fell back onto the muddy forest floor.

Sean fired the second barrel as one of the other Mau Mau bolted out of the nearest shelter. The Gibbs made a sound like the slamming of a great steel door, and the man was hurled back into the shelter with half his chest torn away.

Sean had two more cartridges held between the fingers of his left hand, and as he opened the breech of the Gibbs the spent brass cases pinged away over his shoulder and he slid the fresh cartridges into the empty breeches and closed the rifle again in the same movement.

The Bren and the Stirling were firing now. Their muzzle flashes were bright and pretty as fairy lights in the gloom, twinkling and sparkling, and the bullets went *frip! frip! frip!* amongst the leaves and sang shrilly as they ricocheted into the forest.

Sean shot again and the Gibbs cannoned down another naked figure, knocking him flat against the soft earth as though he had been run down by a locomotive. And again he shot, but this one was a snap shot and the Mau Mau jinked just as the Gibbs thundered. The bullet hit him in the shoulder joint and blew his right arm off so it hung by a tatter of torn flesh and flapped against his side as he spun around. Raymond's Stirling buzzed and cut him down.

Sean reloaded and shot left and right, clean kills with

each barrel and by the time he had reloaded again the camp was silent, and the Bren and the Stirling had ceased firing.

Nothing moved. All three men were deadly natural shots, and the range was point-blank. Sean waited a full five minutes. Only a fool walked directly up to dangerous game no matter how dead it appeared to be. Then he rose cautiously to his knees with the rifle at high port across his chest.

The last Mau Mau broke. He had been feigning dead in the far shelter, and he had judged his moment finely, waiting until the attackers relaxed and began to move. He flushed like a jack rabbit and shot into the bamboo on the far side of the clearing. Alistair's Bren was blanketed by the wall of the nearest shelter but he fired nevertheless and the bullets futilely thrashed the hut. From the river bank Ray had a clearer shot, but he was a fraction of a second slow, the cold had brought out the malaria in his blood and his hand shook. The bamboo absorbed the light 9 mm bullets as though he had fired into a haystack.

For the first ten paces the running Mau Mau was screened from Sean's view by the wall of the nearest hut, and then Sean caught only a flickering glimpse of him as he dived into the bamboo, but already Sean was on him, swinging the stubby double barrels as though he were taking a right-hand passing shot on a driven francolin. Although he could no longer see his quarry in the dense bamboo, he continued his swing on the line of the man's run, instinctively leading him. The Gibbs gave its angry bellow and red flame blazed from the muzzle.

The huge bullet smashed into the wall of bamboo, and at Sean's side Matatu shouted gleefully, 'Piga! Hit!' as he heard the bullet tell distinctly on living flesh.

'Take the blood spoor!' Sean commanded and the little Ndorobo loped across the clearing. But it was not necessary:

the Mau Mau lay where he had dropped. The bullet had ploughed through bamboo, leaf and stem, without being deflected an inch from its track.

Ray and Alistair came into the camp, weapons ready, and picked over the bodies. One of the other Mau Mau women was still breathing, though bloody bubbles seethed on her lips, and Ray shot her in the temple with the Stirling.

'Make sure none of them got away,' Sean ordered Matatu in Swahili.

The little Ndorobo made a quick circuit of the encampment to check for out-going spoor, and then came back grinning. 'All here.' He gloated. 'All dead.' Sean tossed the Gibbs to him and drew the ivory-handled hunting-knife from the sheath on his belt.

'Damn it, laddie,' Ray Harris protested as Sean walked back to where the body of the first girl lay. 'You are the bloody end, man.' He had seen Sean do this before and although Ray Harris was a hard, callous man who for thirty years had made his living out of blood and gunfire, still he gagged as Sean squatted over the corpse and stropped the blade on the palm of his hand.

'You are getting soft, old man.' Sean grinned at him. 'You know they make beautiful tobacco pouches,' he said, and took the dead girl's breast in his hand, pulling the skin taut for the stroke of the knife blade.

S hasa found Garry in the boardroom. He was always there twenty minutes before any of the other directors arrived, arranging his piles of computer print-out sheets and other notes around him and going over his facts and figures for one last time before the meeting began. Shasa and Centaine had argued before appointing Garry to the board of Courtney Mining.

'You can ruin a pony by pushing him too hard too soon.'

'We aren't talking about a polo pony,' Centaine had replied tartly. 'And it's not a case of pushing. He's got the bit between his teeth, to continue your chosen metaphor, Shasa, and if we try and hold him back we will either discourage him or drive him out on his own. Now is the time to give him a bit of slack rein.'

'But you made me wait much longer.'

'You were a late-blooming rose, and the war and all that business held you up. At Garry's age you were still flying Hurricanes and chasing around Abyssinia.'

So Garry had gone on the board, and like everything else in his life he had taken it very seriously indeed. Now he looked up as his father confronted him down the length of the boardroom.

'I heard you have been borrowing money on your own bat,' Shasa accused.

Garry removed his spectacles, polished them diligently, held them up to the light and then replaced them on his large Courtney nose, all to gain time in which to compose his reply.

'Only one person knows about that. The manager of the Adderly Street branch of Standard Bank. He could lose his job if he blabbed about my personal business.'

'You forget that both Nana and I are on the board of the Standard Bank. All loans of over a million pounds come up before us for approval.'

'Rand,' Garry corrected his father pedantically. 'Two million rand – the pound is history.'

'Thanks,' Shasa said grimly. 'I'll try to move with the times. Now how about this two million rand you have borrowed?'

'A straightforward transaction, Dad. I put up my shares in the Shasaville township as collateral, and the bank lent me two million rand.'

'What are you going to do with it? That's a small fortune.' Shasa was one of the few men in the country who would qualify that amount with that particular adjective, and Garry looked mildly relieved.

'As a matter of fact, I have used half a million to buy up fifty-one per cent of the issued shareholding of Alpha Centauri Estates, and loaned the company another half million to get it out of trouble.'

'Alpha Centauri?' Shasa looked mystified.

'The company owns some of the prime property on the Witwatersrand and here in the Cape Peninsula. It was worth almost twenty-six million before the crash at Sharpeville.'

'And now it's worth zero,' Shasa suggested, and before Garry could protest, 'What have you done with the other million?'

'Gold shares – Anglos and Vaal Reefs. At the fire sale prices I paid for them they are returning almost twenty-six per cent. The dividends will pay the interest on the entire bank loan.'

Shasa sat down in his seat at the head of the boardroom table and studied his son carefully. He should have been conditioned by now, but Garry still managed to surprise Shasa. It was an imaginative but neatly logical coup, and if it had not been his own son, Shasa would have been impressed. As it was, he felt duty bound to find flaws in it.

'What about your Shasaville shares – you are taking an awful chance?'

Garry looked puzzled. 'I don't have to explain it to you, Pater. You taught me. Shasaville is tied up. We can't sell or develop aggressively until land values recover, so I've used my shares to take full advantage of the crash.'

'What if land values never recover?' Shasa demanded relentlessly.

'If they don't, it will mean the country is finished anyway. I will lose my share of nothing which is nothing. If they do recover, I will be in profit by twenty or thirty million.'

Shasa picked at that for a while and then changed his angle of attack. 'Why didn't you come to me to borrow the money, instead of going behind my back?'

Garry grinned at him and tried to smooth down the crest of wiry black hair that stuck up on his crown. 'Because you would have given me a list of five hundred reasons why not, just as you are doing now. Besides, I wanted to do this one on my own. I wanted to prove to you that I'm not a kid any more.'

Shasa twiddled the gold pen on the pad in front of him and when he could think of no other criticism, he grumbled, 'You don't want to get too damned clever for your own good. There is a line between good business sense and outright gambling.'

'How do you tell the difference?' Garry asked. For a moment Shasa thought he was being facetious and then he realized that as usual Garry was deadly serious. He was leaning forward eagerly waiting for his father to explain, and he really wanted to know.

Shasa was saved by the entry of the other senior directors: Centaine on the arm of Dr Twentyman-Jones and David Abrahams arguing amiably but respectfully with his father, and thankfully he let the subject drop. Once or twice during the meeting he glanced down the table at Garry, who was following all the discussion with a rapt expression, the light from the picture window reflecting a miniature image of the crest of Table Mountain in the lenses of his spectacles. When all the business on the agenda had been completed and Centaine had started to rise to lead them through to the executive dining-room, Shasa arrested them.

'Madame Courtney and gentlemen, one additional piece of business. Mr Garry Courtney and I have been discussing the general state of the property market. We both feel that property and equities are very much undervalued at the moment and that the company should take advantage of

737

this fact, but I'd like him to tell you in his own words and to put forward certain proposals. Would you oblige us please, Mr Courtney?'

It was Shasa's own way of giving the lad a jolt and cutting him back a little. In the six months since his elevation, Garry had never been called upon to address the full board and now Shasa dropped it on him without warning and sat back with vindictive relish in his wing-backed leather chairman's throne and folded his arms.

At the bottom of the table Garry blushed furiously, and glanced longingly at the stinkwood door, his only escape, before giving the traditional salutation to his fellow directors.

'Ma-Ma-dame Courtney and ge-ge-gentlemen.' He stopped and threw his father a pitiful look of appeal, but when he received a stern uncompromising frown in return, he took a deep breath and launched into it. He stumbled once or twice, but when first Abe Abrahams and then Centaine shot cutting questions at him, he forgot about his stutter and talked for forty-five minutes.

At the end they were silent for a while, and then David Abrahams said, 'I should like to propose that we appoint Mr Garrick Courtney to prepare a list of specific proposals to follow up the presentation that he has just made to this meeting, and to report back to us at an extraordinary meeting early next week, at a time convenient to all members of the board.'

Centaine seconded, and it was adopted unanimously, and then David Abrahams ended, 'I should like the minutes to record the board's gratitude to Mr Courtney for his lucid address and to thank him for bringing these considerations to the board's attention.'

The glow of achievement and recognition lasted Garry all the way down in the elevator to the basement garage where his MG stood in his private parking bay beside Shasa's Jaguar. It stayed with him all the way down

Adderley Street to the lonely skyscraper of the Sanlam building which stood on the open ground of the foreshore that had been reclaimed from the sea. Even going up in the lift to the twentieth floor of the Sanlam building he still felt tall and important and decisive. Only when he entered the reception area of Gantry, Carmichael and Associates did the vital glow begin to fade, and his stiff van Heusen collar bit painfully into the corded muscles of his bull neck.

The two pretty young girls at the desk showed him the full amount of deference due to one of the partnership's important clients, but by this time Garry was too nervous to take advantage of the chair he was offered and he wandered around the lobby pretending to admire the tall vases of proteas while surreptitiously checking his image in the floor-to-ceiling mirrors behind the floral display.

He had paid forty guineas off the peg for the double-breasted suit in his favourite Prince of Wales check, but the swell of his chest muscles made the lapels flare unevenly and the material rucked up around his biceps. He yanked at the cuffs in an attempt to smooth the sleeves, and then abandoned that effort and instead concentrated on trying to press his hair flat with the heel of his palm. He started guiltily as he saw in the mirror the door to the partners' sanctum open and Holly Carmichael come striding into the reception lobby.

As Garry turned to face her, all his recent bravado and confidence collapsed around him and he gawked at her. It was impossible but she was even more poised and chic than the vivid image of her he had carried with him since their last meeting.

Today she was wearing a blue and white striped Chanel suit with a pleated skirt that swirled around her calves, allowing just a flash of her perfect rounded knees as she came towards him. Her lightly tanned legs in sheer nylon had the patina of polished ivory, and her ankles and her wrists in the cuffs of the Chanel suit were elegantly turned, her feet and hands narrow and yet perfectly proportioned to her long willowy limbs.

She was smiling and Garry felt the same sensual vertigo that he sometimes experienced after bench-pressing five times his own bodyweight of iron. Her teeth were opalescent, and as her mouth formed his name and smiled he watched it with breathless fascination.

She was as tall as he was, but he knew he could lift her with one hand and he quivered at the almost sacrilegious thought of taking this divine creature in his hands.

'Mr Courtney, I hope we haven't kept you waiting.' She took his arm, and led him towards her office. He felt like a performing bear on a chain beside her grace and lightness. The light touch of her fingers on his arm burned like a branding iron.

Her hair was streaked with a shading of all the colours of blonde from platinum to dark burnt honey, and it fell in a lustrous cascade to just above the padded shoulders of the Chanel suit, and every time she moved her head he caught the perfume of those shining tresses and his stomach muscles contracted.

Her fingers were still on his biceps and she was talking directly into his face, still smiling. Her breath smelled like a flower and her mouth was so beautiful and soft and red that he felt guilty looking at it, as though he were spying on some secret and intimate part of her body. He tore his eyes from her mouth and raised them to her eyes. His heart jumped against his ribs like a maniac in a padded cell for one eye was sky blue and the other violet flecked with gold. It gave her face a striking asymmetry, not exactly a squint but a disconcerting myopic imbalance and Garry's legs felt as weak as if he had run ten miles.

'I have something for you at last,' Holly Carmichael said, and led him into her office.

The long room reflected her own extraordinary style, which had attracted Garry to her work long before he had met her. He had first seen an example of it in the *Institute of Architects Yearbook*. Holly Carmichael had won the 1961 Award of the Institute for a beach house on the dunes overlooking Plettenburg Bay that she had designed as a holiday home for one of the Witwatersrand insurance magnates. She used wood and stone and material in a blend that was at the same time modern and classical, that married space and shape in a natural harmony that excited the eye and yet gave solace to the soul.

Her office was decorated in soft mulberry and ethereal blue, functional and yet both restful and unmistakably feminine. The delicate pastel drawings on all four walls were her own work.

In the centre of the floor on a low table stood a miniature-scale reproduction of the Shasaville estate, as she visualized it after development was complete. Holly led Garry to it and stood back while he circled it slowly, studying it from every angle.

She watched the change come over him.

All the gawkiness was gone. Even the shape of his body seemed to change. It was imbued with the same kind of massive grace as that of the bull in the arena tensing for the charge.

Holly researched the background of all her clients, in order to better anticipate their requirements. With this one she had taken special care. The word in the marketplace was that, despite appearances, Garrick Courtney was a formidable presence and had already demonstrated his acumen and courage by procuring the Shasaville title and a controlling interest in Alpha Centauri Estates.

Her accountant had drawn up an approximate list of his assets which included, along with his property interests, considerable equity in blue-chip gold companies and the Courtney mining shares which he had acquired from his family when he was appointed to the board of that company.

More significant was the prevailing view that both Centaine and Shasa Courtney had given up on his brothers, and decided that Garrick Courtney was their hope for the future. He was the heir apparent to the Courtney millions and nobody knew the sum total of those – two hundred million, five hundred million – not inconceivably a billion rand. Holly Carmichael shivered slightly at the thought.

As she watched him now she saw not a large bumbling young man in steel-rimmed spectacles, who made an expensive suit of fine wool look like a bag of laundry, and whose hair stood up in a startled tuft at the crown. She saw power.

Power fascinated Holly Carmichael, power in all its forms – wealth, reputation, influence and physical power. She shivered slightly as she recalled the feel of the muscle under his sleeve.

Holly was thirty-two years of age, almost ten years senior to him, and her divorce would count heavily against her. Both Centaine and Shasa Courtney were conservative and old-fashioned.

'They'll have to be good to stop me,' she told herself. 'I get what I want – and this is what I want, but it's not going to be a push-over.'

Then she considered the effect she had on Garry Courtney. She knew he was besotted with her. The first part would be easy. Without any effort at all she had already enmeshed him, she could enslave him as readily. After that would come the difficult part. She thought of Centaine Courtney and all she had heard about her, and she shivered again, this time with neither pleasure nor excitement.

Garry stopped in front of her. Although their eyes were on a level, he now seemed to tower over her as he glowered at her. A moment before she had felt herself perfectly in control, now suddenly she was uncertain.

'I've seen what you can do when you really try,' he said.

'I want you to try for me. I don't want second best. I don't want this.'

Holly stared at him in amazement. She had not even contemplated his rejection, certainly not in such brutal terms. Her shock persisted a moment longer and then was replaced with anger.

'If that is your estimate of my work, Mr Courtney, I suggest you find yourself another architect,' she told him in a cold fury and he didn't even flinch.

'Come here,' he ordered. 'Look at it from this angle. You've stuck that roof on the shopping centre without any regard to the view from the houses on this slope of the hill. And look here. You could have used the fair-ways of the golf course to enhance the aspect of these flagship properties instead of shutting them off the way you have.'

He had taken hold of her arm, and though she knew he was not expending even a small part of his strength, still the potential she could feel in his fingers frightened her a little. She no longer felt confident and patronizing as he pointed out the flaws in her design. While he spoke she knew that he was right. Instinctively she had been aware of the defects he was now exposing, but she had not taken the trouble to find the solutions to them. She had not expected somebody so young and inexperienced to be so discriminating – she had treated him like a doting boy who would accept anything she offered. Her anger was directed at herself as much as at him.

He finished his criticism at last and she said softly, 'I'll return your deposit and we can tear up the contract.'

'You signed the contract and accepted the deposit, Mrs Carmichael. Now I want you to deliver. I want something beautiful and startling and right. I want something that only you can give me.'

She had no answer, and his manner changed, he became peculiarly gentle and solicitous.

'I didn't mean to insult you. I think at the least you are the very best, and I want you to prove me right – please.'

She turned away from him and went to her drawing-board at the end of the room, slipped out of her jacket and tossed it over the desk and picked up one of her pencils.

With the pencil poised over the blank sheet, she said, 'It seems that I've got a lot of lost ground to make up. Here we go—' and she drew the first bold, decisive line across the sheet. 'At least we know now what we don't want. Let's find out what we do want. Let's start with the shopping centre.'

He came to stand behind her and watched in silence for almost twenty minutes before she glanced back at him with the violet eye glinting through the veil of shining blonde hair. She didn't have to ask the question.

'Yes,' he nodded.

'Don't go away,' she said. 'When you are near I can feel your mood and judge your response.'

He took off his jacket and threw it beside hers over the desk top, and he stood beside her in his shirtsleeves with his hands thrust into his trouser pockets and his shoulders hunched. He remained absolutely still, his concentration monumental, and yet his presence seemed to inspire her to tap the mystical springs of her talent. At last she saw in her mind how it should have been and she began to rough it out, her pencil flying and flicking over the sheet.

When the day faded, he went to close the curtains and switch on the overhead lights. It was after eight when she at last threw down her pencil and turned to him. 'That's the feeling I want to give it. You were right – the first attempt wasn't worthy.'

'Yes, I was right in one other respect. You are the very best.' He picked up his jacket and shrugged it over his massive shoulders, and she felt a tingle of dismay. She didn't want him to go yet, she knew when he did she would feel exhausted and spent. The effort of creation had drained her resources.

'You can't send me home to begin cooking at this hour,' she said. 'That would be the sadistic act of a truly cruel taskmaster.'

Suddenly all his confidence evaporated, and he blushed and mumbled something inaudible. She knew she would have to take charge from here.

'The least you can do is feed the slave. How about offering me dinner, Mr Courtney?'

She created her usual stir of masculine interest as she preceded Garry into the restaurant, and she was glad he had noticed. She was surprised by the aplomb with which he discussed the wine list with the *maître* until she remembered that Weltevreden was one of the leading wineries of the Cape of Good Hope.

During dinner their conversation was serious, and she was relieved not to have to endure the usual banalities of a first date. They discussed the Sharpeville crisis and its implications, social and economic, and she was amazed at the depth of his political insight until she remembered that his father was a minister in Verwoerd's cabinet. He had a ringside seat.

'If it wasn't for that Prince of Wales check suit and those ghastly steel-framed spectacles,' she thought, 'and the crest of hair that makes him look like Woody Woodpecker—'

When he asked her to dance she had misgivings. They were the only couple on the tiny circular floor, and there were a dozen people in the room she knew. However, the moment he put his arm around her waist she relaxed. Despite his bulk he was agile and light on his feet with an excellent sense of timing, and she began to enjoy herself, until abruptly his dancing style changed and he held her differently. For a while she was puzzled. She attempted to maintain the close contact of hips which had enabled her to anticipate his moves, and only then she became aware of his arousal. She was at first amused and then despite herself intrigued. Like the rest of him it was massive and hard. She played a little game of brushing lightly against him and withdrawing, all the while chatting casually and feigning total ignorance of his predicament. Afterwards he drove her in the MG to where her own car was parked. She hadn't ridden in an open sports car since her varsity days and the wind in her hair gave her a nostalgic thrill.

He insisted on following her Mercedes back to Bantry Bay to see her safely home and they said goodnight on the pavement outside her apartment block. She considered inviting him up for coffee, but her sure instinct warned her to protect the shining image of her that he so obviously had conceived.

Instead she told him, 'I'll have some more drawings for you to look at by the end of next week.'

This time she put everything of her talent into the preliminary sketches, and she knew they were good. He came to her office again and they worked over them until late and then dined together. It was Thursday night and the restaurant was half empty. They had the dance floor to themselves and this time she worked her hips lightly and cunningly against him as they moved.

When she said goodnight outside her apartment block, she asked, 'I suppose you will be at the Met on Saturday?'

The Metropolitan Handicap was the premier race on the Cape turf calendar.

'I don't race,' Garry replied reluctantly. 'We are polo people, and Nana, my grandmother, doesn't approve of me—' he stopped himself as he realized how callow that sounded, and he ended, ' – well, somehow I've just never got around to racing.'

'Well, it's about time you did,' she said firmly. 'And I need a partner for Saturday – that's if you don't object.'

Garry sang all the way home to Weltevreden, bellowing happily into the rushing night air as he drove the MG through the curves and dips of the mountain road.

It took Garry a while to understand that the actual racing was not the main attraction of the meeting. It was secondary to the fashion show and the complicated social interaction of the racegoers.

Amongst the bizarre and outrageous creations that some of the women wore, Holly's floating blue silk and the wide-brimmed hat with a single real pink rose on the brim were elegant and understated, and drew envious glances from the other women. Garry discovered that he knew nearly everybody in the members' enclosure; many of them were friends of his family, and Holly introduced him to those he did not know. They all reacted to the Courtney name, and Holly was subtly attentive, drawing him into conversation with these strangers until he felt at ease.

They made a remarkable couple, 'Beauty and the Beast', as one of the unkind wags suggested, and a buzz of gossip followed them around the ring: 'Holly has been out cradle-snatching', and 'Centaine will have her burned at the stake'.

Garry was totally oblivious to the stir they were creating, and once the horses were brought into the ring for the first race he was in his element. Horses were part of the life at Weltevreden. Shasa had carried him on the saddle before he could walk, and he had a natural eye for horseflesh.

The first race was a maiden handicap, and the betting was wide open as none of these two-year-olds had raced before. Garry singled out a black colt in the parade. 'I like his chest and legs,' he told Holly and she checked his number on the card.

'Rhapsody,' she said. 'There has never been a good horse with an ugly name – and he's trained by Miller and ridden by Tiger Wright.'

'I don't know about that, but I do know that he is in peak condition and he wants to work,' Garry told her. 'Just look at him sweating already.'

'Let's have a bet on him,' Holly suggested, and Garry looked dubious. The family strictures against gambling echoed in his ears, but he didn't want to offend Holly or appear childish in her eyes.

'What do I do?' he asked.

'You see those gangsters standing up there?' She pointed at the line of bookmakers. 'You pick any one of them, give him your money and say, "Rhapsody to win." She handed Gerry a ten-rand note. 'Let's dib ten each.'

Garry was appalled. Ten rand was a great deal of money. It was one thing to borrow two million on a legitimate business scheme, but quite another thing to hand ten to a stranger in a loud suit with a cigar. Reluctantly he produced his wallet.

Rhapsody was in the ruck at the turn, but as they came clear of the bend, Tiger Wright steered him wide and then asked him to run. The colt jumped away and caught the leaders in front of the stand where Holly was hopping up and down and holding her hat on with one hand. He was two lengths clear at the post and Holly threw both arms around Garry's neck and kissed him in front of ten thousand beady eyes.

As Garry handed over her share of their winnings, she said, 'Oh, wouldn't it be fun to own one's very own racehorse.'

He phoned her apartment at six o'clock the following morning.

'Garry?' she mumbled. 'It's Sunday. You can't do this to me – not at six o'clock.'

'This time I've got something to show you,' he said, and his enthusiasm was so infectious that she agreed weakly.

'Give me an hour to wake up properly.'

He drove her down to the curving beach of False Bay

beyond Muizenberg and parked at the top of the dunes. Forty horses with their apprentice jockeys and grooms were cantering along the edge of soft white sand or wading bareback in the curling green surf. Garry led her down to the group of four men who were supervising the training and introduced her.

'This is Mr Miller.' The trainer and his assistants looked at Holly approvingly. She wore a pink scarf around her forehead but her thick blonde hair fell freely down the back of her neck and the short marine peajacket emphasized the length and shape of her legs in the ski pants and calf boots.

The trainer whistled to one of his apprentices and only when he turned the colt out of the circle of horses did Holly recognize it.

'Rhapsody,' she cried.

'Congratulations, Mrs Carmichael,' the trainer said. 'He's going to do us all proud.'

'I don't understand.' She was bewildered.

'Well,' Garry explained, 'you said it would be fun to own your own horse, and it is your birthday on the twelfth of next month. Happy birthday.'

She started at him in confusion, wondering how he knew that date and how she was going to tell him that she couldn't possibly accept such an extravagant gift. But Garry was so rosy with self-satisfaction, waiting to be thanked and applauded, that she thought, 'And why not – just this once! The hell with conventions!'

She kissed him for the second time, while the others stood around and grinned knowingly.

In the MG on the way home she told him. 'Garry, I cannot possibly accept Rhapsody. It's much too generous of you.' His disappointment was transparent and pathetic. 'But,' she went on, 'I could accept half of him. You keep the other half and we will race him together, as partners. We could even register our own racing colours.' She was amazed at her own genius. A living creature owned jointly would cement the bond between them. 'Let all the Court-neys rant and rave. This one is mine,' she promised herself.

When they reached her apartment, she told him, 'Park there, next to the Mercedes.' And she took his arm and led him to the elevator.

Like her office, the apartment was an expression of her artistry and sense of form and colour. The balcony was high above the rocks, and the surf crashed and sucked back and forth below them so that it seemed they stood on the prow of an ocean liner.

Holly brought a bottle of champagne and two tulip glasses from the kitchen. 'Open it!' she ordered and held the glasses while he spilled the creaming wine into them.

'Here's to Rhapsody,' she gave him the toast.

While she made a huge bowl of salad for their brunch, she instructed him in the art of mixing a dressing for it.

They drank the rest of the champagne with the salad and then sprawled on the thick carpet of her living-room floor, surrounded by books of silk samples as they discussed their racing colours, and finally decided on a vivid fuchsia pink.

'It will look beautiful against Rhapsody's glossy black skin.' She looked up at him. He was kneeling beside her, and her instinct told her that this was the precise moment.

She rolled slowly on to her back and hooded those bi-coloured eyes invitingly, but still he hesitated and she had to reach up with one hand and draw his head down to hers, and then his strength shocked her.

She felt helpless as an infant in his embrace, but after a while when she was certain that he would not hurt her, she began to enjoy the sensation of physical helplessness in the storm of his kisses and let him take control for a while until she sensed that he needed guidance once again.

She bit him on the cheek and when he released her and started back in surprise and consternation, she broke from his grip and darted to the bedroom door. As she looked back he was still kneeling in the centre of the floor, staring after her in confusion, and she laughed and left the door open.

He came in like a bull at the cape, but she stopped him dead with another kiss and, holding his mouth with hers, unbuttoned his shirt and slipped her hand into the opening. She was unprepared for the thick pelt of springing dark hair that covered his chest, and her own reaction to it. All her other men had been smooth and soft. She believed that was her preference, but now her sexual arousal was instantaneous and her loins swam with excitement.

She dominated him with her lips and fingertips, not allowing him to move while she undressed him and then, as the last of his clothing fell around his ankles, she exclaimed aloud, 'Oh dear God!' and then caught his wrist to prevent him covering himself with his hands.

None of her other men had been like this, and for a moment she felt uncertain of her ability to cope with him. Then her wanting overwhelmed any doubts and she led him to the bed. She made him lie there while she undressed in front of him, and every time he tried to cover himself she ordered him, 'No! I like to look at you.'

He was so different, all muscle and hair: his concave belly was rippled with muscle like the sand on a wind-swept beach and his limbs were clad in muscle. She wanted to begin, but she wanted even more to ensure that this would be something that he would never forget, that would make him hers for all his life.

'Don't move,' she whispered, and naked she stooped over him. She let her breasts swing forward and her nipples just brush the curls on his chest, and she touched the tip of her tongue to the corner of his eye and then ran it down slowly to his mouth.

'I have never done this before,' he whispered hoarsely. 'I don't know how.'

'Shh, my darling, don't talk,' she whispered into his mouth, but the idea of his virginity elated her.

'He's mine,' she told herself triumphantly. 'After today he will be mine for ever!' And she ran her tongue down across his chin, down over his throat, until she felt him thrust up hard and thick between her dangling breasts and then she reached down and took him in both hands.

It was darkening in the room when at last they lay exhausted. Outside the sun had sunk into the Atlantic and left the evening sky infuriated by its going. Garry lay with his cheek cushioned on her breasts. Like an unweaned child he could not get enough of them. Holly was proud of her bosom and his fascination with it amused and flattered her. She smiled contentedly as he nuzzled against her.

His spectacles lay on the bedside table and she studied his face in the half light. She liked the big virile nose and the determined line of his jaw, but the steel-framed spectacles had to go, she decided, those and the Prince of Wales checks which emphasized the squatness of his body. On Monday her first concern would be to find out from Ian Gantry, her partner, the name of his personal tailor. She had already chosen the pattern – crisp grey or distinguished blue, with a vertical chalk stripe that would make him taller and slimmer. His reconstruction would be one of her most challenging and rewarding projects and she looked forward to it.

'You are wonderful,' Garry murmured. 'I've never met anybody like you in my life.' Holly smiled again and stroked his thick dark hair. It sprang up under her fingers.

'You've got a double crown,' she told him softly. 'That means you are lucky and brave.'

'I didn't know that,' he said, which was not surprising, as Holly had invented it as she said it.

'Oh yes,' she assured him. 'But it also means that we have to grow our hair a little fuller over the crown, otherwise it will stand up in a tuft like this.'

'I didn't know that either.' Garry reached up and felt his tuft. 'I'll try that, but you'll have to tell me how long to let it grow – I don't want to look like a hippy.'

'Of course.'

'You are wonderful,' he repeated. 'I mean, totally wonderful.'

'The woman is obviously a gold-digger,' Centaine said firmly.

'We can't be sure of that, Mater,' Shasa demurred. 'I have heard that she is a damned good architect.'

'That has absolutely nothing to do with it. She is old enough to be his mother. She is after one thing, and one thing only. We'll have to put a stop to this immediately. Otherwise it could get out of hand. It's the talk of the town, all my friends are gloating. They were at Kelvin Grove on Saturday, smooching all over the dance floor.'

'Oh, I think it will blow over,' Shasa suggested. 'Just so long as we take no notice.'

'Garry hasn't slept at Weltevreden for a week. The woman is as blatant and shameless—' Centaine broke off and shook her head. 'You'll have to speak to her.'

'Me?' Shasa raised an eyebrow.

'You are good with females. I'd be sure to lose my temper with the hussy.'

Shasa sighed, although secretly he welcomed the excuse to have a look at this Holly Carmichael. He couldn't imagine what Garry's taste in women would be. The lad had never given any indications before. Shasa imagined sensible shoes and horn-rimmed glasses, fat and fortyish, serious and erudite – and he shuddered. 'All right, Mater, I'll warn her off, and if that doesn't work we can always send Garry down to the vet to be fixed.'

'I wish you wouldn't joke about something as worrying as this,' said Centaine severely.

Although Holly had been expecting it for almost a month, when the call finally came the shock of it was unmitigated. Shasa Courtney had addressed the Businesswomen's Club the previous year, so she recognized his voice instantly, and was glad that it was he rather than Centaine Courtney she had to contend with.

'Mrs Carmichael, my son Garry has shown me some of your preliminary sketches for the Shasaville township. As you know, Courtney Mining and Finance are considerable shareholders in the project. Although Garry is responsible for the development, I hoped we could meet to exchange a few ideas.'

She had suggested her own office, but Shasa neatly thwarted her attempt to choose the field of battle and sent a chauffeur to bring her out to Weltevreden in the Rolls. She realized that she was being deliberately placed in surroundings which were intended to overpower her, and show her up in the splendour of a world in which there was no place for her. So she went to endless pains with her dress and appearance, and as she was ushered into Shasa Courtney's study she saw him start and knew that first blood was hers. She made the room with all its treasures seem as though it had been designed around her, and Shasa Courtney's cool supercilious smile faded as he came to take her hand.

'What a magnificent Turner,' she said. 'I always think he must have been an early riser. The sunlight only has that golden lustre in the early morning.' His expression changed again as he realized there was depth below her striking exterior.

They circled the room, ostensibly admiring the other paintings, fencing elegantly, testing each other for weakness and finding none, until Shasa deliberately broke the pattern with a direct personal compliment to fluster her.

'You have the most remarkable eyes,' he said, and

watched her keenly to see how she would react. She counter-attacked instantly.

'Garry calls them amethyst and sapphire.' She had wrongfooted him neatly. He had expected her to avoid that name until he raised it.

'Yes, I understand the two of you have been working closely.'

He went to the ivory-inlaid table on which glasses and decanters had been set out.

'May I offer you one of our sherries? We are very proud of them.'

He brought her the glass and looked into those extraordinary eyes. 'The little devil,' he thought ruefully. 'He has done it again. Who would have expected Garry to come up with something like this!'

She sipped the wine. 'I like it,' she said. 'It's dry as flint without any astringency.'

He inclined his head slightly to acknowledge the accuracy of her judgement.

'I can see that it would be fruitless to attempt to obfuscate. I didn't ask you here to discuss the Shasaville project.'

'That's good,' she said. 'Because I didn't even bother to bring the latest drawings.'

He laughed delightedly. 'Let's sit down and get comfortable.'

She chose the Louis XIV chair with Aubusson embroidered upholstery because she had seen the twin to it in the Victoria and Albert Museum, and she crossed one ankle over the other and watched him struggle to get his eyes back up again.

'I had fully intended to buy you off,' he said. 'I realize, after having met you, that would have been a mistake.'

She said nothing, but watched him over the rim of the glass, and her foot swung like a metronome, with the same ominous rhythm.

'I wondered what price to set,' he went on. 'And the figure of one hundred thousand came to mind.'

The foot kept swinging and despite himself Shasa glanced down at her calf and exquisitely turned ankle.

'Of course, that was ludicrous,' he went on, still watching her foot in the Italian leather court shoe. 'I realize now that I should have considered at least half a million.'

He was trying to find her price, and he looked back at her face, searching for the first glint of avarice, but it was hard to concentrate. Sapphire and amethyst, forsooth, Garry's hormones must be boiling out of his ears – and Shasa felt a stab of envy.

'Naturally, I was thinking in pounds sterling. I haven't adjusted to this rand business yet.'

'How fortunate, Mr Courtney,' she said, 'that you decided not to insult us both. This way we can be friends. I'd prefer that.'

All right, that didn't work out the way he had planned. He set down his sherry glass. 'Garry is still a child,' he changed tack.

She shook her head. 'He's a man. It just needed somebody to convince him of that. It wasn't difficult to do.'

'He doesn't know his own mind.'

'He is one of the most definite and determined men I have ever met. He knows exactly what he wants and he will do anything to get it.' She waited a moment to let the challenge contained in those words become clearer, then she repeated softly, 'Anything.'

'Yes,' he agreed softly. 'That's a Courtney family trait. We will do anything to get what we want – or to destroy anything that stands in our way.' He paused, just as she had done and then repeated quietly, 'Anything.'

'You had three sons, Shasa Courtney. You have one left. Are you willing to take that chance?'

He reared back in his chair and stared at her. She was unprepared for the agony that she saw in his expression and for a moment she thought she had gone too far. Then he subsided slowly.

'You fight hard and dirty,' he acknowledged sadly.

'When it is worthwhile.' She knew it was dangerous with an opponent of this calibre, but she felt sorry for him. 'And for me this is worthwhile.'

'For you, yes, I can see that – but for Garry?'

'I think I owe you complete honesty. At the beginning it was a little bit of daring. I was intrigued by his youth – that in itself can be devastatingly appealing. And by the other obvious attractions which you have hinted at.'

'The Courtney empire and his place in it.'

'Yes. I would have been less than human if that hadn't interested me. That's the way it started, but almost immediately it began to change.'

'In what way?'

'I began to understand his enormous potential, and my own influence in developing it fully. Haven't you noticed any change in him in the three months since we have been together? Can you truly tell me my influence on him has been detrimental?'

Despite himself Shasa smiled. 'The pinstripe suits and the hornrimmed glasses. They are a vast improvement, I'll admit.'

'Those are only the unimportant outward signs of the important inward changes. In three months Garry has become a mature and confident man, he has discovered many of his own strengths and talents and virtues, not the least of which is a warm and loving disposition. With my help he will discover all the others.'

'So you see yourself in the role of architect still, building a marble palace out of clay bricks.'

'Don't mock him.' She was angry, protective and

defensive as a lioness. 'He is probably the best of all the Courtneys and I am probably the best thing that will ever happen to him in his life.'

He stared at her, and exclaimed with wonder as it dawned upon him. 'You love him – you really love him.'

'So you understand at last.'

She stood up and turned towards the door.

'Holly,' he said, and the unexpected use of her first name arrested her. She wavered, still pale with anger, and he went on softly, 'I didn't understand, forgive me. I think Garry is a fortunate young man to have found you.' He held out his hand. 'You said we might be friends – is that still possible?'

Table Bay was wide open to the north-westerly gales that bore in off the wintry grey Atlantic. The ferry took the short steep seas on her bows and lurched over the crests, throwing the spray as high as the stubby masthead.

It was the first time Vicky had ever been at sea and the motion terrified her as nothing on earth had ever done. She clutched the child to her, and stared straight ahead, but it was difficult to maintain her balance on the hard wooden bench, and thick spray dashed against the porthole and poured over the glass in a wavering mirage that distorted her view. The island looked like some dreadful creature swimming to meet them, and she recalled all the legends of her tribe of the monsters that came out of the sea and devoured any human being found upon the shore.

She was glad that Joseph was with her. Her half-brother had grown into a fine young man. He reminded her of the faded photograph of her grandfather, Mbejane Dinizulu, that her mother kept on the wall of her hut. Joseph had the same broad forehead and wide-spread eyes, and although his nose was not flattened but high-bridged, his clean-shaven chin was rounded and full.

He had just completed his law degree at the black University of Fort Hare, but before he underwent his consecration into the hereditary role of Zulu chieftainship Vicky had prevailed upon him to accompany her upon the long journey down the length of the sub-continent. As soon as he returned to the district of Ladyburg in Zululand he would begin his training for the chieftainship. This was not the initiation to which the young men of the Xhosa and the other tribes were forced to submit. Joseph would not suffer the brutal mutilation of ritual circumcision. King Chaka had abolished that custom. He had not tolerated the time that his young warriors wasted in recuperation, which could better be spent in military training.

Joseph stood beside Vicky, balancing easily to the ferry's agitated plunges, and he placed his hand upon her shoulder to reassure her. 'Not much longer,' he murmured. 'We will soon be there.'

Vicky shook her head vehemently, and clutched her son more securely to her bosom. The cold sweat broke out upon her forehead, and waves of nausea assailed her, but she fought them back.

'I am the daughter of a chief,' she told herself. 'And the wife of a king. I will not surrender to womanly weakness.'

The ferry ran out of the gale into the calm waters in the lee of the island, and Vicky drew a long ragged breath and stood up. Her legs were unsteady, and Joseph helped her to the rail.

They stood side by side and stared at the bleak and infamous silhouette of Robben Island. The name derived from the Dutch word for seal, and the colonies of these animals that the first explorers had discovered upon its barren rocks.

When the fishing and sealing industries based upon the

island failed it was used as a leper colony and a place of banishment for political prisoners, most of them black. Even Makana, the prophet and warrior, who had led the first Xhosa onslaughts against the white settlers across the great Fish River, had been sent here after his capture, and here he had died in 1820, drowned in the roaring seas that beat upon the island as he tried to escape. For fifty years his people had refused to believe he was dead, and to this day his name was a rallying cry for the tribe.

One hundred and forty-three years later, there was another prophet and warrior imprisoned upon the island, and Vicky stared out across the narrowing strip of water at the low square unlovely structure, the new high-security prison for dangerous political prisoners where Moses Gama was now incarcerated. After his stay of execution, Moses had remained on death row at Pretoria Central Prison for almost two years, until finally mitigation of the death sentence to life imprisonment at hard labour had been officially granted by the state president and he had been transferred to the island. Moses was allowed one visit every six months, and Vicky was bringing his son to see him.

The journey had not been easy, for Vicky herself was the subject of a banning order. She had shown herself an enemy of the state by her appearances at Moses' trial, dressed in the colours of the African National Congress, and by her inflammatory utterances which were widely reported by the news media.

Even to leave the township of Drake's Farm to which the banning order confined her she had to obtain a travel permit from the local magistrate. This document set out precisely the terms upon which she was allowed to travel, the exact time which she was required to leave her cottage, the route and means of transport she must take, the duration of her visit to her husband and the route she must take upon her return journey.

The ferry manoeuvred in towards the jetty and there were uniformed warders to seize the mooring ropes as they were thrown across. Joseph took the boy's hand from her and with his free hand helped Vicky across the narrow gap. They stood together on the wooden boards of the jetty and looked around uncertainly. The warders ignored them as they went on with the business of docking and unloading the ferry.

It was ten minutes before one of them called across to them, 'All right, come this way,' and they followed him up the paved road towards the security block.

The first glimpse that Vicky had of her husband after six months appalled her.

'You are so thin,' she cried.

'I have not been eating very well.' He sat down on the stool facing her through the mesh of the screen. They had developed a cryptic code during the four visits she had been allowed at Pretoria Central, and not eating well meant that he was on another hunger strike.

He smiled at her and his face was skull-like so that his lips had retracted and his teeth were too big for his face. When he placed his hands on the shelf in front of him his wrists protruded from the cuffs of his khaki prison uniform and they were bone covered with a thin layer of skin.

'Let me see my son,' he said, and she drew Matthew to her.

'Greet your father,' she told the boy, and he stared solemnly at Moses through the grille. The gaunt stranger on the other side of the wire had never picked him up or held him on his lap, had never kissed or fondled him, had never even touched him. The mesh was always between them.

A warder sat beside Moses to see that the visiting rules were strictly observed. The time allowed was one hour, sixty minutes exactly, and only family matters could be discussed – no news of the day, no discussion of prison conditions and especially nothing with a political flavour to it.

One hour of family matters, but they used their code. 'I am sure that my appetite will return once I have news of the family,' Moses told her, 'on paper.' So she knew that he was hunger-striking to be allowed to read the newspapers. Therefore he would not have heard the news about Nelson Mandela.

'The elders have asked *Gundwane* to visit them,' she told him. *Gundwane* was their code name for Mandela. It meant 'cane rat' and the elders were the authorities. He nodded to show that he understood that Mandela had at last been arrested, and he smiled tautly. The information he had given to Manfred De La Rey had been used effectively.

'How are the family members on the farm?' he asked.

'All is well, and they are planting their crops,' Vicky told him, and he understood that the *Umkhonto we Sizwe* teams working out of Puck's Hill had begun their campaign of terror bombings. 'Perhaps you will all be reunited sooner than we think,' she suggested.

'Let us hope so,' Moses agreed. A reunion would mean that the Puck's Hill team would join him here on the island, or take the shorter road to the gallows.

The hour passed too swiftly, and the warder was standing up. 'Time up. Say your goodbyes.'

'I leave my heart with you, my husband,' Vicky told him, and watched the warder lead him away. He did not look back at her, and his gait dragged like that of an exhausted old man.

'It is only the starvation,' she told Joseph as they walked back to the ferry. 'He is still courageous as a lion, but weak from lack of food.'

'He is finished,' Joseph contradicted her quietly. 'The Boers have beaten him. He will never breathe the air of freedom again. He will never see the outside of his prison again.'

'For all of us, born black, this whole country is a prison,' Vicky said fiercely, and Joseph did not reply until they were once more aboard the ferry and running back before the gale, towards the flat-topped mountain whose lower slopes were flecked with white walls and shining glass.

'Moses Gama chose the wrong road,' Joseph said. 'He tried to assault the walls of the white fortress. He tried to burn it down, not realizing that even if he had succeeded all he would have inherited would have been ashes.'

'And you, Joseph Dinizulu,' Vicky flashed at him scornfully, 'you are wiser?'

'Perhaps not, but at least I will learn from the mistakes of Moses Gama and Nelson Mandela. I will not spend my life rotting in a white man's prison.'

'How will you assault the white man's fortress, my clever little brother?'

'I will cross the lowered drawbridge,' he said. 'I will go in through the open gates, and one day the castle and its treasures will be mine, even if I have to share a little of them with the white man. No, my angry little sister, I will not destroy those treasures with bombs and flames. I will inherit them.'

'You are mad, Joseph Dinizulu.' She stared at him, and he smiled complacently at her.

'We shall see who is mad and who is sane,' he said. 'But remember this, little sister, that without the white man we would still be living in grass huts. Look to the north and see the misery of those countries which have driven out the whites. No, my sister, I will keep the white man here – but one day he will work for me, not I for him.'

'Forget your anger, my son.' Hendrick Tabaka leaned forward and placed his right hand on Raleigh's shoulder. 'Your anger will destroy you. Your enemy is too strong. See what has happened to Moses Gama, my own brother. See what is the fate of Nelson Mandela. They went out to fight the lion with bare hands.'

'Others are still fighting,' Raleigh pointed out. 'The warriors of *Umkhonto we Sizwe* are still fighting. Every day we hear of their brave deeds. Every day their bombs explode.'

'They are throwing pebbles at a mountain,' Hendrick said sadly. 'Every time they explode a little bomb against the pylon of a power line, Vorster and De La Rey arm another thousand police and write another hundred banning orders.' Hendrick shook his head. 'Forget your anger, my son, there is a fine life for you at my side. If you follow Moses Gama and Mandela, you will end the way they have ended – but I can offer you wealth and power. Take a wife, Raleigh, a good fat wife and give her many sons, forget the madness and take your place at my side.'

'I had a wife, my father, and I left her at Sharpeville,' Raleigh said. 'But before I left her, I made a vow. With my fingers deep in her bloody wounds, I made a vow.'

'Vows are easy to make,' Hendrick whispered, and Raleigh saw how age had played like a blowtorch across his features, withering and searing and melting the bold lines of his cheekbones and jaw. 'But vows are difficult to live with. Your brother Wellington has also made a vow to the white man's god. He will live like a eunuch for the rest of his life, without ever knowing the comfort of a woman's body. I fear for you, Raleigh, fruit of my loins. I fear that your own vow will be a heavy burden for all your life.' He sighed again. 'But since I cannot persuade you, what can I do to ease the rocky pathway for you?'

'You know that many of the young people are leaving this country?' Raleigh asked.

'Not only the young ones,' Hendrick nodded. 'Some of the high command have gone also. Oliver Tambo has fled and Mbeki and Joe Modise with many others.'

'They have gone to set the first phase of the revolution afoot.' Raleigh's eyes began to shine with excitement. 'Lenin himself taught us that we cannot move immediately to the Communist revolution. We must achieve the phase of national liberation first. We have to create a broad front of liberals and churchmen and students and workers under the leadership of the vanguard party. Oliver Tambo has gone to create that vanguard party – the anti-*apartheid* movement in exile – and I want to be part of that spearhead of the revolution.'

'You wish to leave the country of your birth?' Hendrick stared at him in bewilderment. 'You wish to leave me and your family?'

'It is my duty, Father. If the evils of this system are ever to be destroyed, we will need the help of that world out there, of all the united nations of the world.'

'You are dreaming, my son,' Hendrick told him. 'Already that world, in which you place so much trust and hope, has forgotten Sharpeville. Once again money from the foreign nations, from America and Britain and France, is pouring into this country. Every day the country prospers—'

'America has refused to supply arms.'

'Yes,' Hendrick chuckled ruefully. 'And the Boers are making their own. You cannot win, my son, so stay with me.'

'I must go, my Father. Forgive me, but I have no choice. I must go, but I need your help.'

'What do you want me to do?'

'There is a man, a white man, who is helping the young ones to escape.'

Hendrick nodded. 'Joe Cicero.'

'I want to meet him, Father.'

'It will take a little time, for he is a secret man, this Joe Cicero.'

It took almost two weeks. They met on a municipal bus that Raleigh boarded at the central depot in Vereeniging. He wore a blue beret, as he had been instructed, and sat in the second row of seats from the back.

The man who took the seat directly behind him lit a cigarette and as the bus pulled away, said softly, 'Raleigh Tabaka.'

Raleigh turned to look into a pair of eyes like puddles of spilled engine oil.

'Do not look at me,' Joe Cicero said. 'But listen carefully to what I tell you—'

Three weeks later Raleigh Tabaka, carrying a duffel bag and authentic seaman's papers, went up the gangplank of a Dutch freighter that was carrying a cargo of wool to the port of Liverpool. He never saw the continent disappear below the watery horizon for he was already below decks at work in the ship's engine room.

Sean did the deal at breakfast on the last day of the safari. The client owned seventeen large leather tanneries in as many different states and half the real estate in Tucson, Arizona. His name was Ed Liner and he was seventy-two years of age.

'Son, I don't know why I want to buy myself a safari company. I'm getting a little long in the tooth for this big game stuff,' he grumbled.

'That's bullshit, Ed,' Sean told him. 'You nearly walked me off my feet after that big jumbo, and the trackers all call you *Bwana* One-Shot.'

Ed Liner looked pleased with himself. He was a wiry little man with a ruff of snowy hair around his brown-freckled pate.

'Give me the facts again,' he invited. 'One last time.'

Sean had been working on him for three weeks, since the first day of the safari, and he knew Ed had the figures by heart, but he repeated them now.

'The concession is five hundred square miles, with a forty-mile frontage on the south bank of Lake Kariba—' As he listened, Ed Liner stroked his wife as though he were caressing a pet kitten.

She was his third wife and she was just two years younger than Sean, but fifty years younger than her husband. She had been a dancer at the Golden Egg in Vegas, and she had a dancer's legs and carriage, with big innocent blue eyes and a curling cloud of blonde hair.

She watched Sean with a vicious little curl to her cupid-bow lips as he made his pitch. Sean had been working on her just as assiduously as he had on her husband, thus far with as little success.

'All you've got, honey,' she had told Sean, 'is a pretty face and a hungry dick. The woods are full of those. Daddy Eddie has got fifty million bucks. It's no contest, sonny boy.'

The camp table was set under a magnificent wild fig tree on the banks of the Mara River. It was a bright African morning. The plain beyond the river was golden with winter grass, and studded with flat-topped acacia trees. The herds of wildebeest were dark shadows on the gold and a giraffe was feeding from the upper branches of the nearest acacia, his long graceful neck swaying against the brittle blue of the sky, his hide paved with bold rectangles of red brown. From upriver there came the bellowing sardonic laughter of a bull hippo, while from the branches of the fig tree above them the golden weaver birds dangled upside down from their woven basket nests, fluttering and shrilling to entice the drab brown females to move in and take up residence. Legend had it that both Hemingway and Ruark had camped at this very spot and breakfasted beneath this same wild fig.

'What do you think, Sugar Sticks?' Ed Liner ran his bony brown fingers down the inside of his wife's thigh. She wore wide-legged khaki culottes and from where Sean sat he could see a little red-blonde pubic curl peeking out from under the elastic of her panties. 'Do you think we should give old Sean here a half million bucks to set up our very own safari outfit down in the Zambezi valley of Rhodesia?'

'You know best, Daddy Eddie.' She affected a cute little-girl voice, and she batted her long eyelashes at him and turned so that her bosom strained the buttons of her khaki shirt.

'Just think of it,' Sean invited. 'Your very own hunting concession, to do with as you want.' He watched her carefully as he went on. 'You could shoot the full quota all yourself if you wanted, as many animals as you wanted.' Despite her curls and pouting lips, Lana Liner had a vicious a sadistic streak as any man Sean had ever hunted with. While Ed had chosen only to take the lion and elephant that he had paid for, Lana had killed every single animal she was entitled to, and then had killed those her husband had refused.

She was a passable shot, and derived as much pleasure from cutting down one of the dainty little Thompson's gazelle with her .300 Weatherby magnum as she had when she dropped her black-maned Masai lion with a perfect heart shot. He had seen the sexual radiance in her immediately after each kill, heard her rapid breathing and seen the pulse beat in her throat with excitement, and his philanderer's instinct had assured him that Lana Liner was vulnerable to him only in those few minutes after she had seen the bullet strike and the blood flash.

'As much hunting as you want, whenever you want it,' Sean tempted her, and saw the excitement in her baby blue eyes.

She ran the tip of her tongue over her scarlet lips and

said in her breathless little-girl voice, 'Why don't you buy it for my birthday, Daddy Eddie.'

'Goddamm!' Ed laughed. 'Why not! OK, son, you've got yourself a deal. We'll call it Lana Safaris. I'll get my lawyers to draw up the papers soon as we get home to Tucson.'

Sean clapped his hands, and shouted at the kitchen tent. 'Maramba! *Letta* champagne *hapa. Pacey! Pacey!*' and the camp waiter in his long white kanza and red pill-box fez brought the green bottle on its silver tray, dewed with cold from the refrigerator.

They drank the wine and laughed in the morning sunlight, and shook hands and discussed the new venture until the gunbearer brought the hunting car around with the rifles in the racks and Matatu, the Ndorobo tracker, perched up on the back and grinning like a monkey.

'I've had enough,' Ed said. 'Guess I'll get packed up and ready to meet the charter plane when it comes in this afternoon.' Then he saw the pout of disappointment on Lana's red lips. 'You go off with Sean, Sugar Sticks,' he told her. 'Have a good hunt, but don't be late back. The charter flight is due to arrive at three, and we must get back to Nairobi before dark.'

Sean drove with Lana in the seat beside him. He had cut the sleeves out of his shirt to leave his upper arms bare, and they were sleek and glossy with muscle. Dark chest hair curled out of the V-neck of the shirt, and he wore his shining dark hair in a page-boy almost to his shoulders, but bound up around the forehead with a patterned silk bandana to keep it out of his eyes.

When he grinned at her, he was almost impossibly handsome, but there was a vindictive twist to his smile as he said, 'Ready for a bit of sport, sport?' And she said, 'Just as long as I get to do the shooting, sonny boy.'

They followed the track along the river bank, heading

back towards the hills. The Land-Rover was stripped and the windshield removed, and Matatu and the gunbearer in the raised back seat scanned the edges of the riverine bush and searched the track for sign of passage during the night.

Alarmed by the engine beat, a bushbuck family came dancing up the bank from the river, heading for the dense cover with the ewe and the lamb leading, followed by the ram, striped and spotted with cream on a dark chocolate ground, his corkscrew horns held high.

'I want him,' Lana cried and reached over her shoulder for the Weatherby.

'Leave him,' Sean snapped. 'He won't go fifteen inches and you've got a better trophy already.'

She pouted at him sulkily, and he ignored her as the bushbuck scampered into the bush. Sean hit four-wheel drive and angled the Land-Rover down the bank of one of the Mara's tributaries, splashed and jolted through water as deep as the hubs and then roared up the far bank.

A small herd of Burchell's zebra cantered away ahead of them, stiff black manes erect, their vivid stripes shaded to nondescript grey at a distance, uttering their abrupt honking bark. Lana eyed them hungrily, but she had already shot the twenty zebra allowed on both her and Ed's licences.

The track swung back towards the river and through trees they had a view across the wide plains. The Masai Mara, which meant 'the great spotted place of the Masai', and the grassland were blotched with herds of game and clumps of acacia.

'*Bwana*,' Matatu cried, and at the same instant Sean saw the sign. He braked the Land-Rover and with Matatu beside him went to examine the splashes of khaki-green dung and the huge round bovine prints in the soft earth of the track. The dung was loose and wet, and Matatu thrust his forefinger into one of the pats to test for body heat.

'They drank at the river an hour before dawn,' he said.

Sean walked back to the Land-Rover and stood close to

Lana, almost touching her as he said, 'Three old bulls. They crossed three hours ago, but they are feeding and we could catch them within an hour. I think they are the same three we saw the day before yesterday.' They had spotted the dark shapes in the dusk, from the opposite bank of the wide Mara river, but with insufficient daylight left for them to circle upstream to the ford and take up the chase. 'If they are the same old mud bulls, one of them is a fifty-incher, and there aren't many of them that size around any more. Do you want to have a go?'

She jumped down from the Land-Rover, and reached for the Weatherby in the gun rack.

'Not that popgun, Sugar Sticks,' Sean warned her. 'Those are big mean old buff out there. Take Ed's Winchester.' The .458 threw a bullet more than twice as heavy as the 200-grain Nosler that the Weatherby fired.

'I shoot better with my own piece than with Ed's cannon,' Lana said. 'And only Ed is allowed to call me Sugar Sticks.'

'Ed is paying me a thousand dollars a day for the best advice on Harley Street. Take the .458, and is it all right if I call you Treacle Pins, then?'

'You can go screw, sonny boy,' Lana said and her baby voice gave the obscenity a strangely lascivious twist.

'That's exactly what I had in mind, Treacle Pins, but let's go kill a buff first.'

She tossed the Weatherby to her gunbearer, and strode away from him with her hard round buttocks oscillating in the khaki culottes. 'Just like the cheeks of a squirrel chewing a nut,' Sean thought happily, and took the big double-barrelled Gibbs down from the rack.

The spoor was gross, three big bull buffalo weighing over a ton each and scarring the earth with brazen hoofs and grazing as they went. Matatu wanted to run away with it, but Sean checked him. He didn't want to bring Lana up to the chase shaking and panting with fatigue, so they went out on it at an extended walk, going hard but keeping within the girl's capabilities.

In the open acacia forest they reached the spot where the bulls had ceased feeding and bunched up, then struck determinedly towards the blue silhouette of distant hills, and Sean explained to Lana in a whisper, 'This is where they were when the sun rose. As soon as it was light, they headed for the thick stuff. I know where they will lie up, we'll catch them with another half hour.'

Around them the forest closed in, and acacia gave way to the dense claustrophobic thorn and green jess. Visibility ahead dropped to a hundred and then fifty feet, and they had to crouch beneath the interlacing branches. The heat built up, and the dappled light was deceptive, filling the forest with strange shapes and menacing shadow. The stink of the buffalo seemed to steam around them in the heat, a rank gamy smell, and they found the flattened beds and smeared yellow dung where the bulls had lain down for the first time, and then stood up and moved on.

Ahead of them Matatu made the open-handed sign for 'Very close', and Sean opened the breech of the Gibbs and changed the big brass .577 Kynoch cartridges for two others from his bullet pouch. He kept the original pair between the fingers of his left hand, ready for an instant reload. He could fire those four cartridges in half the time it would take even the most skilled rifleman to fire four from a magazine rifle. It was so silent and still in the jess that they could hear each other breathe, and the blood pounding in their own ears.

Suddenly there was a clatter, and they all froze. Sean recognized the sound. Somewhere just ahead of them a buffalo had shaken his great black head to drive away the plaguing flies, and one of his curved horns had struck a branch. Sean sank on to his knees signalling Lana to come up beside him, and together they crawled forward.

Suddenly and unexpectedly they came to a hole in the

jess, a tiny clearing twenty paces across, and the earth was trodden like a cattle kraal and littered with pancakes of old black dung.

They lay on the edge of the clearing and peered across into the tangled vegetation on the far side. The sunlight into the clearing dazzled them, and the shadow beyond it was confused and obscure.

Then the bull shook his head again, and Sean saw them. They were lying in a bunch, a mountainous mass of blackness in the shadows, and their heads overlapped so that the heavy bosses and curls of horn formed an inextricable puzzle. Though they were less than thirty paces away, it was impossible to separate one animal from the others, or one set of horns from the bunch.

Slowly Sean turned his head and laid his lips against Lana's ear. 'I am going to get them up,' he whispered. 'Be ready to take the shot as I call it.'

She was sweating and trembling. He could smell her fear and excitement, and it excited him also. He felt his loins thicken and stiffen, and for a moment he savoured the sensation, pressing his hips against the earth as though he had her body under him. Then deliberately he knocked the brass cartridges in his left hand against the steel barrels of the Gibbs. The sharp metallic sound was shocking in the silence.

Across the clearing the three bulls lumbered to their feet, and faced the sound. Their heads were lifted, drooling wet muzzles held high and the bosses of rough horn, black as ironstone, joined above their vicious piggy little eyes, the tips curving down and up again to the wide points, and their ears flared like trumpets.

'The middle one,' Sean said softly. 'Rake him through the chest.'

He stiffened in anticipation of her shot, and then glanced sideways. The barrel of the Weatherby was describing small erratic circles as Lana tried to hold her aim, and it flashed upon Sean that she had forgotten to change the power of her variable telescopic sight. She was looking at a bull buffalo from thirty paces through a lens of ten multiplications. It was like looking at a battleship through a microscope: all she was seeing was a black shapeless mass.

'Don't shoot!' he whispered urgently but the Weatherby erupted in a long blazing muzzle-flash across the clearing, and the big bull lurched and tossed his head, grunting to the strike of shot. Sean saw the dried mud puff from his scabby black skin, low down in the joint of his right shoulder, and as the bull spun away into the jess, Sean swung the Gibbs on him to take the back-up shot. But one of the other buffalo turned across the wounded animal, screening him for the instant that it took for him to crash away into the jess, and Sean lifted the Gibbs without firing.

They lay side by side and listened to the thunderous rush of bodies dwindle into the jess.

'I couldn't see clearly,' Lana said in her childish piping treble.

'You had the scope on full power, you silly bitch.'

'But I hit him!'

'Yes, Treacle Breeches, you hit him – more's the pity. You broke his right front leg.' Sean stood up and whistled for Matatu. In a few quick words of Swahili he explained the predicament, and the little Ndorobo looked at Lana reproachfully.

'Stay here with your gunbearer,' Sean ordered Lana. 'We'll go and finish the business.'

'I'm going with you.' Lana shook her head.

'This is what I'm paid for,' Sean told her. 'Cleaning up the mess. Stay here and let me do my job.'

'No,' she said. 'It's my buff. I'll finish it.'

'I haven't got time to argue,' Sean said bitterly. 'Come on then, but do as you are told.' And he waved Matatu forward to pick up the blood spoor.

There were bone splinters and hair where the bull had stood.

'You smashed the big bone,' Sean told her. 'It's a racing certainty that the bullet broke up. At that range it was probably still going 3,500 feet per second when it hit – even a Nosler bullet can't stand that.'

The bull was bleeding profusely. Bright blood had sprayed the jess as he blundered through, and blood had formed a dark gelatinous puddle where he stood for the first time to listen for his pursuers. The other two bulls had deserted him and Sean grunted with satisfaction. That would prevent confusion, shooting at the wrong animal in the mix-up.

Lana kept close beside him. She had removed the scope from the Weatherby and left it with the gunbearer, and now she carried the rifle at high port across her chest.

Abruptly they stepped into another narrow clearing, and Matatu squeaked and bolted back between Sean and the girl as the bull broke from the far side of the clearing and came down on them in a bizarre crabbing sideways gait. His nose was up, and the long mournful droop of his horns gave him a funereal menace. His broken leg flapped loosely, hampering his gait, so he rocked and plunged, and bright blood was forced in a spurting stream from the wound by the movement.

'Shoot!' said Sean. 'Aim at his nose!' But without looking at her he sensed her terror, and her first movement as she turned to run.

'Come on, you yellow bitch. Stand and shoot it out,' he snarled at her. 'This is what you wanted – now do it.'

The Weatherby whiplashed, and flame and thunder tore across the clearing. The buffalo flinched at the shot, and black flinty chips flew from the boss of his horns.

'High!' Sean called. 'Shoot him on the nose.' And she shot again, and hit the horn a second time and the bull kept coming.

'Shoot!' Sean called, watching the great armoured head over the express sights of the Gibbs. 'Come on, bitch, kill him!'

'I can't,' she screamed. 'He's too close!' The bull filled all their existence, a mountain of black hide and muscle and lethal horn, so close that at last he dropped his head to toss and gore them, to rip and trample and crush them under the anvil of his crenellated boss.

As the massive horns went down, Sean shot him through the brain and the bull rolled forward over his own head. Sean pulled Lana out from under the flying hoofs as the bull somersaulted. She had dropped the rifle and now she clung to him helplessly, shaking, her red mouth slack and smeared with terror.

'Matatu!' Sean called quietly, holding her to his chest, and the little Ndorobo reappeared at his side like a genie. 'Take the gunbearer with you,' Sean ordered. 'Go back to the Land-Rover and bring it back here, but do not hurry.'

Matatu grinned lewdly and ducked his head. He had an enormous respect for his *Bwana*'s virility and he knew what Sean was going to do. He only wondered that it had taken so long for the *Bwana* to straighten this pale albino creature's back for her. He disappeared into the jess like a black shadow and Sean turned the girl's face up to his own and thrust his tongue deeply into the wet red wound of her mouth.

She moaned and clung to him, and with his free hand he unbuckled her belt and jerked down the culottes. They fell in a tangle around her ankles and she kicked them away. He hooked his thumbs into the waistband of her panties and tore them off her, then he pushed her down on top of the hot and bleeding carcass of the buffalo. She fell with her legs sprawled open and the muscles of the dead animal were still twitching and contracting from the brain shot, and the sweet coppery smell of blood mingled with the rank wild stink of game and dust.

Sean stood over her and tore open the front of his breeches and she looked up at him with the terror still clouding her eyes.

'Oh you bastard,' she sobbed. 'You filthy rotten bastard.'

Sean dropped on his knees between her long loose limbs and cupped his hands under her hard little buttocks. As he lifted her lower body he saw that her fluffy blonde mount was already as sodden as the fur of a drowned kitten.

They drove back to camp with the body of the dead bull crammed into the back of the Land-Rover, the great horned head dangling over the side, and Matatu and the gunbearer perched upon it, singing the hunter's song.

Lana never said a word all the way back. Ed Liner was waiting for them under the dining tent, but his welcoming grin faded as Lana threw her torn panties on the table in front of him and piped in her little-girl voice, 'You know what naughty old Sean did, Daddy Eddie? He raped your little girl, that's what he did – he held her down and stuck his big dirty thing into her.'

Sean saw the fury and hatred in the old man's faded eyes, and he groaned inwardly. 'The bitch,' he thought. 'The sneaky little bitch. You loved it. You screamed for more.'

Half an hour later Lana and Ed were in the red and silver Beechcraft Baron when it took off from the narrow bush strip. As it banked away on course for Nairobi, Sean glanced down at his own trouser front.

'Well, OK, King Kong,' he murmured. 'I hope you are satisfied, that just cost us fifty thousand dollars an inch.' He turned back to the Land-Rover still shaking his head sadly as he picked up the bundle of mail that the pilot of the Beechcraft had brought down from the office in Nairobi. There was a yellow cable envelope on top of the pile and he opened it first.

'I am marrying Holly Carmichael on 5th August. Please be my best man. Love. Garry.'

Sean read it through twice, and Lana and Ed Liner were forgotten.

'I'd love to see what kind of bag would marry Garry,' he chuckled. 'Pity I can't go home—' He broke off and thought about it. 'But why not! Why the hell not! Living dangerously is half the fun.'

Shasa Courtney sat at his desk in the study at Weltevreden, studying the Turner on the opposite wall as he composed the next paragraph in his mind.

He was drafting his Chairman's Report for the cabinet select committee of Armscor. The armaments company had been set up by special act of parliament, and the strict secrecy of its operations was ensured by that act.

When President Eisenhower had initiated the arms embargo against South Africa as a punitive reaction to the Sharpeville massacre and the racial policies of the Verwoerd government, the country's annual expenditure on weapons manufacture had been a mere £300,000. Four years later they had an annual budget of half a billion.

'Dear old Ike did us a big favour.' Shasa smiled now. 'The law of unforeseen consequences in action again, sanctions always backfire. Now our biggest worry is to find a testing ground for our own atomic bomb.'

He addressed himself once more to that section of his report, and wrote:

Taking into consideration the foregoing, I am of the opinion that we should adopt the third option, i.e. underground testing. With this in view, the corporation has already conducted investigations to determine the most suitable geological areas. (See attached geological survey reports.)

The shot holes will be drilled by a commercial

diamond drilling company to a depth of four thousand feet to obviate contamination of the underground water supplies.

There was a knock on the door and Shasa looked up in angry disbelief. The entire household knew that he was not to be disturbed, and there was no reason nor excuse for this intrusion.

'Who is it?' he barked, and the door was opened without his permission.

For a moment he did not recognize the person who stepped into the study. The long hair and deep tan, the flamboyant costume – the gilet of kudu skin, and the bright silk scarf knotted at the throat, the mosquito boots and cartridge belt were all unfamiliar. Shasa stood up uncertainly.

'Sean?' he asked. 'No, I don't believe this is happening.' He wanted to be angry and outraged. 'Damn it, Sean, I warned you never . . .' but he could not go on, his joy was too intense and his voice petered out.

'Hello, Dad.' Sean came striding towards him, and he was taller and more handsome and self-assured than Shasa remembered. Shasa abhorred all manner of theatrics and affectation of dress, but Sean wore his costume with such panache that it appeared natural and correct.

'What the hell are you doing here?' Shasa found his voice at last, but there was no rancour in his question.

'I came as soon as I got Garry's cable.'

'Garry cabled you?'

'Best man – he wanted me to be his best man, and I didn't even have a chance to change.' He stopped in front of Shasa, and for a moment they studied each other.

'You are looking good, Pater,' Sean smiled, and his teeth were white as bone against the tan.

'Sean, my boy.' Shasa lifted his hands, and Sean seized him in a bear hug.

'I thought about you every single day—' Sean's voice was tight and his cheek was pressed to Shasa's cheek. 'God, how I missed you, Dad.'

Shasa knew instinctively that it was a lie, but he was delighted that Sean had bothered to tell the lie.

'I've missed you, too, my boy,' he whispered. 'Not every day, but often enough to hurt like hell. Welcome back to Weltevreden.' And Sean kissed him. They had not kissed since Sean was a child, that sort of sentimental display was not Shasa's usual style, but now the pleasure of it was almost unbearable.

Sean sat at Centaine's right hand at dinner that evening. His dinner jacket was a little tight around the chest and smelled of moth balls, but the servants, overjoyed to have him home, had pressed razor edges into the crease of his trousers and steamed out the silk lapels. He had shampooed his hair, and oddly the thick glossy locks seemed to enhance rather than detract from his over-powering masculinity.

Isabella, taken by surprise like everybody else, had come drifting downstairs, dressed for dinner with her shoulders and back bare, but her cool and distant poise had evaporated as she saw Sean. She squealed and rushed at him.

'It's been so boring since you went away!'

She wouldn't let go of his arm until they went in to dinner, and even now she leaned forward to watch his lips as he talked, her forgotten soup cooling, avid to take in every word. When Shasa at the end of the table made a remark about Kenyan barbers and Sean's hair style, she rushed to her eldest brother's defence.

'I love his hair like that. You are so antediluvian sometimes, Papa. He's beautiful. I swear if Sean ever cuts a single hair on his beautiful head, I will take vows of silence and chastity on the spot.'

'A consummation devoutly to be wished,' murmured her father.

Centaine, although less effusive, was as delighted as any

of them to have Sean home again. Of course, she knew every detail of the circumstances in which he had left. She and Shasa were the only ones in the family who did, but that had been almost six years ago, and things could change in that time. It was difficult to believe that anybody who looked like that, even more beautiful than her own beloved Shasa, and who was possessed of such charm and natural grace, could be entirely bad. She consoled herself that although he had made a few mistakes when he was a child, he was now a man. Centaine had seldom seen more of a man, and she listened as attentively as the rest of them to his stories and laughed as merrily at his sallies.

Garry kept repeating, 'I didn't really believe you'd come. I sent that cable on an impulse. I wasn't even sure of your address.' And then to Holly, who was sitting beside Sean at the long table, 'Isn't he wonderful, Holly – isn't he everything I told you?'

Holly smiled and murmured polite agreement, and twisted slightly in her chair to prevent Sean pointing up the story he was telling by placing his hand on her thigh again. She glanced around the table, and caught Michael's eye. He was the only one who was not following Sean's tale with total concentration. Holly had only met Michael for the first time the previous day, when he arrived from Johannesburg for the wedding, but the two of them had found an immediate rapport, which had swiftly deepened as Holly had discovered Michael's protective concern and affection for Garry.

Now Michael raised an eyebrow at Holly, and smiled an apology at her. He had seen his elder brother looking at her, he had seen through Sean's devices to attract her attention, and had even seen her start and pale as Sean touched her beneath the table. He would talk to Sean after dinner, and quietly warn him off, for Garry himself would never see what was happening. He was too besotted by his elder brother's return. It was up to Michael – it had always been his duty to protect Garry from Sean. In the meantime he smiled reassurance at Holly, and Sean intercepted the look and interpreted it accurately. He showed no reaction. His expression was frank and open and his voice sparkling and full of humour as he finished the story and the others all laughed, all except Michael and Holly.

'You are so funny,' Isabella sang. 'I just hate you for being my brother. If only I could find another boy who looked like you.'

'There's not one of them good enough for you, Bella,' Sean said, but he was watching Michael, and as the laughter subsided, he asked lightly, 'And so, Mickey, how is life on that Commie newspaper of yours? Is it true that you are going to change its name to the *ANC Times*, or is it the *Mandela Mail* or the *Moses Gama Gazette*?'

Michael laid down his knife and fork and met Sean's gaze squarely.

'The policy of the *Golden City Mail* is to defend the helpless, to attempt to secure a decent dignified existence for all, and to tell the truth as we see it – at any cost.'

'I don't know about that, Mickey,' Sean grinned at him. 'But a couple of times out there in the bush I've wished that I had a copy of the *Golden City Mail* with me – yes, sir, every time I run out of toilet paper, I wish I had your column right there.'

'Sean!' Shasa said sharply, and his indulgent expression faded for the first time since Sean's arrival. 'There are ladies present.'

'Nana.' Sean turned to Centaine. 'You have read Mickey's column, haven't you? Don't tell me you agree with those bright pink sentiments of his?'

'That's enough,' Shasa said sternly. 'This is a reunion and a celebration.'

'I'm sorry, Pater.' Sean was mock contrite. 'You are right. Let's talk about fun things. Let me tell Mickey about the Mau Mau in Kenya, and what they did to the white kids.

Then he can tell me about his Commie ANC friends here, and what he wants them to do to our kids.'

'Sean, that's not fair,' Michael said softly. 'I am not a Communist, and I have never advocated Communism or the use of force—'

'That's not what you wrote in yesterday's edition. I had the great and glorious privilege of reading your column on the plane down from Jo'burg.'

'What I actually wrote, Sean, was that Vorster and De La Rey between them are making the mistake of labelling as Communist everything that our black population sees as desirable – civil rights, universal franchise, trade unions and black political organizations such as the ANC. By naming these as Communist-inspired they are making the idea of Communism highly attractive to our blacks.'

'We've just got a black government in Kenya, with a convicted terrorist and murderer as the new head of state. That's why I'm getting out and moving to Rhodesia. And here is my own beloved brother paving the way for another black Marxist government of rabble-rousers and bomb-throwers right here in the good old Republic. Tell me, which of the terrorists do you fancy for president, Mickey, Mandela or Moses Gama?'

'I won't warn either of you again,' Shasa told them ominously. 'I will not abide politics at the dinner table.'

'Daddy is right,' Isabella joined in. 'You are both being so utterly dreary – and just when I was beginning to really enjoy myself.'

'And that's enough from the peanut gallery also,' Centaine picked out Isabella. 'Eat your food, please, Mademoiselle, you are all skin and bones as it is.' But she was studying Sean.

'He has been home six hours and already we are all at each other's throats,' she thought. 'He still has a talent for controversy. We must be wary of him – I wonder why he really came home.'

She found out very soon after dinner, when Sean asked to see her and Shasa in the gun room.

After Shasa had poured a tiny glass of Chartreuse for her, and balloon snifters of Hennessy for Sean and himself, they all settled down in the leather chairs. The men went through the ritual of preparing their cigars, cutting the tips and warming and finally lighting them with the cedarwood tapers.

'All right, Sean,' Shasa said. 'What did you want to talk to us about?'

'You know how we discussed the safari business, Pater, just before I left?' Shasa noticed how he showed no contrition as he mentioned his enforced departure. 'Well, I've had six years of experience now, and I won't offend you with false modesty. I'm one of the top hunters in the business. I've a list of over fifty clients who want to hunt with me again. I have their telephone numbers, you can ring them and ask them.'

'All right, I will,' Shasa said. 'But go on.'

'Ian Smith's government in Rhodesia is developing the safari business there. One of the concessions they are putting up for auction in two months' time is a plum.' Shasa and Centaine listened in attentive silence, and when Sean finished almost an hour later, they exchanged a significant glance. They understood each other perfectly after thirty years of working so closely, and they did not have to speak to agree that Sean had made a virtuoso performance. He was a good salesman, and his figures added up to the promise of rich profits, but Shasa saw the little shadow at the back of his mother's dark eyes.

'Just one thing perturbs me a little, Sean. After all these years you come breezing in again – and the first thing you do is ask for half a million dollars.'

Sean stood up and strolled across the gun room. The carved tusk hung above the stone fireplace, the central position in the room, pride of place amongst all Shasa's own hunting trophies.

Sean studied it for a moment, and then turned back slowly to face them.

'You never wrote to me once in all those years, Pater. That's all right, I understand why. But don't accuse me of not caring. I thought about you and Nana every day I was away.' It was cleverly done. He did not mention the tusk on the wall, and Centaine could have sworn there were genuine tears just at the back of his marvellously green clear eyes. She felt her doubts soften and begin to dissolve.

'My God, how can any woman resist him,' she thought. 'Even his own grandmother!' She looked across at Shasa and was amazed to see that Sean had shamed him. Neatly and adroitly he had shifted guilt and Shasa had to cough and clear his throat before he could speak.

'I must admit it sounds interesting,' he said gruffly. 'But you'll have to speak to Garry.'

'Garry?' Sean asked in surprise.

'Garry is the director in charge of new projects and investments,' Shasa told him and Sean smiled.

He had just knocked together two of the toughest, shrewdest heads in the business. Garry would be a piece of cake.

Holly Carmichael's father was the Presbyterian minister of a small parish in Scotland, and he and his wife flew out to Africa quite determined to see their daughter decently married, and to pay for the privilege.

Centaine took him for a ride around the estate and explained kindly that only by being very selective could she restrict her guest list to under a thousand. 'Those are just family friends, and our most important business and political associates. Of course it does not include the workers here on Weltevreden or the employees of Courtney Mining and Finance who will be accorded their own separate festivities.'

The Reverend Carmichael looked stricken.

'Madam, I love my daughter – but a clergyman's stipend—'

'I don't really like to mention it,' Centaine went on smoothly, 'but it is Holly's second marriage – and you have already done your duty with the first. I would be grateful if you would consent to perform the ceremony, and let me take care of the other small details.' With one deft stroke Centaine had procured a clergyman to marry her grandson, for despite veiled offers to install stained-glass windows and restore church roofs, both the local Church of England and Anglican priests had refused to perform the offices. At the same time she had achieved a free hand with the wedding arrangements.

'It will be,' she promised herself, 'the wedding of the decade.'

The old slave church on the estate had been rethatched and restored for the occasion, and the bougainvillaea blossom of exactly the shade that Holly had chosen for her dress was flown down from the Eastern Transvaal in the company aircraft to decorate it. The rest of the ceremony and the following celebrations were arranged on the same scale and with similar attention to detail with all the resources of Weltevreden and the Courtney group of companies to carry them through.

The church could seat only 150, and twenty of those were the coloured family retainers from the estate who had known and cared for Garry since the day of his birth. The other thousand guests waited in the marquee on the polo field and the ceremony was relayed to them over the public address system.

The road down the hill from the church to the polo field was lined with the other estate workers whose seniority and length of service were insufficient to procure them a seat in the church. They had stripped Centaine's rose garden of blooms and they showered Garry and his new bride with rose petals as they led the procession down the hill in the open carriage, and the women danced and sang and tried to touch Holly for luck as she went by.

In his grey topper Garry stood taller than Holly and his bulk of shoulder and chest made her seem light as a cloud of pink mist beside him, so lovely that the guests gasped and hummed with admiration as he brought her into the marquee on his arm.

The best man's speech was one of the highlights of the afternoon. Sean had them roaring and squealing with laughter and clapping his most amusing sallies, although Holly frowned and reached for Garry's hand under the table when Sean made oblique references to Garry's stutter and his Charles Atlas course.

Sean was the first to dance with Holly after she and Garry had circled the floor in the wedding waltz. He held her close as they turned together and murmured, 'Silly girl, you could have had the pick of the litter, but, never fear, it's still not too late.'

'I did and it is,' she replied, and her smile was cold and thorny. 'Now why don't you go off and give my bridesmaids the benefit of your charms. The poor things are panting like puppy dogs.'

Sean turned the rebuff with a light laugh and handed her over to Michael for the rest of the dance. While he snapped his fingers at one of the waiters to bring him another glass of champagne, he surveyed the tent from the vantage point of the raised dais, picking out the interesting females, making his selections not only on the basis of their looks but on their apparent availability. Those who sensed his scrutiny and blushed or simpered or boldly returned his regard went immediately to the head of his list.

In passing he noticed that Isabella had finally got around Nana, and was wearing one of those mini-skirts that were all the rage. The hem finished just below the creases of her cheeky little buttocks, and with the impartial eye of the connoisseur he saw that her legs were quite extraordinary, and that every man, no matter what his age, glanced down at them as she circled the dance floor.

Thinking of Nana, he looked around for her quickly. Her seat at the high table was empty. Then he found her. She was near the back of the tent, sitting at a table with a big burly man who had his back turned to Sean. They were in earnest conversation, and his grandmother's intensity interested him. He knew that Centaine never wasted effort on the trivialities. The man must be important. As he thought that, the man turned slightly and Sean recognized him. His heart skipped guiltily. It was the Minister of Police, Manfred De La Rey. He was the one who had quashed the charges against Sean, in return for his guarantee to leave the country and never return.

Sean's instinct was to slip away without drawing De La Rey's attention to himself and then he grinned at his own stupidity. He had just stood up and made a dashing speech in front of them all. 'How's that for drawing attention?' he thought, and then grinned again at his own daring. 'Living dangerously is half the fun,' he reminded himself, and jumped down off the dais without spilling a drop of champagne and deliberately sauntered across the tent towards his grandmother and her companion.

Centaine saw him coming and placed her hand on Manfred's sleeve. 'Careful, here he comes now.' It had just taken all her influence, a recital of all the debts and secrets between them, to protect Sean, and now here was the impudent young devil flaunting himself in front of Manfred.

She tried to warn him off with a frown, but Sean stooped

and kissed her cheek. 'You are a genius, Nana, there has never been a party like this. The planning and the eye to detail – we are all proud of you!'

He hugged her and though she pushed him off haughtily, saying, 'Now don't be a big booby,' her frown was displaced by the ghost of a smile. 'Damn it, he's got the cheek of all the Courtneys,' she thought proudly, and then turned to Manfred.

'You don't know my grandson. Sean, this is Minister De La Rey.'

'I've heard of you,' Manfred growled without offering to shake hands. 'I've heard a great deal about you.' And with relief Centaine turned to the couple who were returning to the table from the dance floor. 'And this is Mrs De La Rey and her son Lothar – all old friends of the family. Heidi, may I present my grandson Sean.'

Sean bowed over her hand, and Heidi considered him thoughtfully and said in her lisping German accent. 'He is the only one of your grandchildren I have not met, Centaine. A fine boy.'

Sean turned to Lothar and held out his hand. 'Hello. I'm Sean – and if I didn't know who you were, I'd be the only one in the country. Your play against the Lions on the last tour was magical, that boot of yours is worth a million rand.'

The two young men sat down on a pair of empty chairs and were immediately engrossed in a discussion of rugby football and the recent visit of the British team. Although she continued her conversation with Manfred, Centaine watched her two grandsons covertly. Apart from their youth and self-assurance, they were so different in appearance, one blond and Germanic, the other dark and romantic, yet she sensed that they were in other ways very similar. Strong men, untroubled by unnecessary scruples, men who knew what they wanted and how to go about getting it. Perhaps they inherited that from her, she smiled to herself, and perhaps like her they were hard and unrelenting adversaries, prepared to destroy anything that stood in their way.

Centaine had the trick of listening to two conversations at once and she heard Lothar De La Rey say, 'Mind you, I've heard about you also and what you did in Kenya. Didn't you get a citation for the George Cross for cleaning up the last of the Mau Mau gangs?'

Sean laughed. 'My timing was wrong. The Brits couldn't give me a gong for shooting Mickey Mice at the same time as they were handing the country over to Kenyatta. Not really cricket, you know, old boy. But how did you find out about that?'

'It's my job to know these things,' Lothar told him, and Sean nodded.

'Yes, of course, you are in the police. Aren't you a major or something?'

'As of last week, a colonel in the Bureau of State Security.'

'Congratulations.'

'You know, anything you could tell us about Mau Mau will be useful. I mean the real first-hand stuff about anti-terrorist work. You see, I think we might have the same problem here one of these days.'

'Well, the worst was over by the time I got there, but yes, of course – anything I can do. I'm going back up north in a few weeks, to Rhodesia. But if I can help—'

'Rhodesia.' Lothar dropped his voice so that Centaine could no longer hear. 'That's interesting. We'd like to know what's going on there also. Yes, I think it is vital that we get together before you leave. A man like you in place could be of really crucial help to us—' Lothar broke off. His expression changed and he stood up hurriedly, looking over Sean's shoulders.

Following his gaze Sean looked around and Isabella stood close behind him. She draped one hand languidly over Sean's shoulder, and leaned one hip against him, but she was watching Lothar.

'This is Bella, my baby sister,' Sean told Lothar, and Isabella murmured, 'Not such a baby any more, big brother.' She had not taken her eyes off Lothar's face.

She had first noticed him in the church during the ceremony and recognized him immediately. He was one of the most famous athletes in the country, a national heart-throb. Sean's conversation with him had given her the opportunity she had been waiting for.

Despite the fact that her voice was cool and her manner aloof and distant, Sean felt her tremble against him and he grinned inwardly. 'Your ovaries are going off like fire crackers, little sister.' But he said, 'Why don't you sit down and bring a little sunlight into our drab existence, Bella?'

She ignored him and spoke directly to Lothar. 'Do you spend all your time dressed up in a rugby jersey, pushing people around in scrums and kicking little balls? Or somewhere along the line did you learn to dance, Lothar De La Rey?'

'Ouch!' Sean murmured. Even for a Courtney, that was pretty direct. And Lothar inclined his head and asked gravely, 'May I have the pleasure of this dance, Isabella Courtney?'

They made one circuit of the floor without speaking and then Lothar said, 'If you were my woman, I would not allow you to wear a skirt like that.'

'Why? Don't you like my legs?' she asked.

'I like your legs very much indeed,' he replied. 'But if you were my woman, I would not like other men to look at them the way they are doing now.'

'You are a prude, Lothar De La Rey.'

'Perhaps, Isabella Courtney, but I believe there is a time and a place for everything.'

She pushed a little closer to him and thought happily to

herself, 'So let's find that time and place, you big gorgeous hunk of brawn.'

Morosely Manfred watched his son on the dance floor and his wife leaned across and echoed his thoughts.

'That hussy is throwing herself at Lothie. Just look at her, showing everything she has. I wish I could go and pull her away from him.'

'I wouldn't do that, *skat*,' Manfred advised soberly. 'Nothing could make her more attractive to him than our disapproval. But don't worry, Heidi. We have brought him up the right way. He might have a little man's sport with her, but that's not the kind of girl he will bring home.' He stood up heavily. 'Trust our boy, Heidi. But now you must forgive me. I must talk to Shasa Courtney – it's very important.'

Shasa, in full morning dress, a white carnation in his buttonhole, the black patch over one eye and a long black cheroot between his teeth, was in deep conversation with the groom, but when he saw Manfred approaching and recognized the seriousness of his mien, he slapped Garry's shoulder lightly and said, 'I think it's a good bet, but you listen to what Sean has to say. Make up your own mind, then come and discuss it with me,' and then he left Garry and came to meet Manfred.

'We must talk – privately,' Manfred greeted him.

'Now?' Shasa looked incredulous, but Manfred insisted.

'It will not take long.'

'Let's go up to the house.' Shasa took his arm, and chatting amiably led him to the exit, as though they were going off to the men's room together. As soon as they were outside the marquee, they headed for the carpark behind the grandstand.

Manfred prowled around Shasa's gun room, restlessly peering at the framed photographs of hunting safaris, at the mounted animal heads and the racks of sporting rifles and shotguns in their glass-fronted cabinet, while Shasa slouched in one of the armchairs and watched him patiently, letting him take his time, puffing on the black cheroot.

'Is this room secure? We cannot be overheard?' Manfred asked, and Shasa nodded.

'Perfectly secure. I do much of my private business here – besides which, the house is deserted. Every last servant is down at the polo field.'

'*Ja, nee, goed!*' Manfred came to take the armchair facing Shasa.

'You cannot go off to England as you planned,' he said, and Shasa laughed.

'Why on earth not?'

'I will tell you why,' Manfred assured him, but made no attempt to do so. Instead he asked, 'Did you ever see a film called *The Manchurian Candidate?*' He pronounced it in the Afrikaans fashion 'fi-lim'.

For a moment Shasa was surprised by the irrelevance of the question. Then he replied, 'No, I didn't get around to the movie, but I did read the book by Richard Condon. Rather enjoyed it, to tell the truth.'

'Do you remember the story-line?'

'Yes. It was about a plot to assassinate one of the American presidential candidates.'

'That's right,' Manfred nodded. 'The assassin was hypnotized and programmed to respond to the sight of a playing card, one of the aces, I think.'

'Ace of spades,' Shasa agreed. 'The death card. He would respond like an automaton to any command he received after he had seen the ace. In a hypnotic trance he was ordered to carry out the assassination.'

'Do you think the idea was credible? Do you think a

man could be completely subjected to the hypnotic suggestion of another?'

'I don't know,' Shasa admitted. 'The Koreans and the Russians are supposed to have perfected the technique of brain-washing. Perhaps it is possible, in special circumstances, with a particularly susceptible subject – I don't know.'

Manfred sat in silence for so long that Shasa began to fidget. Then he spoke curtly, 'Our jobs are in danger,' he said, and Shasa went very still. '*Ja.*' Manfred nodded heavily. 'Verwoerd is thinking of reshuffling the cabinet. You and I will be sacked.'

'You have done a difficult job,' Shasa said softly. 'And you have done it as well as was humanly possible. The storm is over, the country is calm and stable.'

Manfred sighed. '*Ja,* you also. In a few short years since Sharpeville, you have helped rally the economy. Foreign investment is pouring in, thanks to your efforts. The value of property is higher than it was before the crisis. You have done an excellent job building up the armaments industry. Very soon our own atomic bomb – but we are going to be sacked. My information is always reliable.'

'Why?' Shasa asked, and Manfred shrugged.

'Verwoerd took two bullets in the head. Who knows what damage that caused.'

'He shows no signs of any permanent damage. He is just as logical, rational and decisive after the operation to remove the bullets.'

'Do you think so?' Manfred asked. 'Do you think his obsession with race is logical and rational?'

'Verwoerd was always obsessed with racial matters.'

'No, my friend, that is not so,' Manfred contradicted him. 'He didn't want the Ministry of Bantu Affairs when Malan first offered it to him. Race meant nothing to him. He was concerned only with the growth and survival of Afrikaner nationalism.'

'He certainly threw himself into it body and soul, when he did take the job,' Shasa smiled.

'*Ja*, that's true, but then he saw *apartheid* as uplifting to the blacks, a chance to conduct their own affairs, and become masters of their own destiny. He saw it as exactly similar to the partition of India and Pakistan. He was concerned with racial differences, but he was not a racist. Not in the beginning.'

'Perhaps.' Shasa was dubious.

'Since those bullets in the head he has changed,' Manfred said. 'Before that he was strong-willed and certain of his own infallibility, but since then he will brook not the slightest criticism or even a hint that anything he says or does might be wrong. Race has become an obsession, to the point of lunacy – this business with the coloured English cricketer, what is his name again?'

'Basil D'Oliviera – and he is South African. He plays for England because he can't play for South Africa.'

'*Ja*, it's madness. Now Verwoerd even refuses to have a black servant to tend him. He would not attend the film version of *Othello* because Laurence Olivier had painted his face black. He has lost all sense of proportion. He is going to undo all the hard, painstaking work we have done to restore calm and properity. He is going to destroy this country – and he is going to destroy us personally, you and me, because we have stood up to some of his wilder excesses in cabinet. You even suggested he permanently abolish the pass laws – he has never forgiven you for that. He calls you a liberal.'

'All right, but I can't believe he would take the Ministry of Police away from you.'

'That is what he plans. He wants to give it all to John Vorster – combine Justice and Police into a single portfolio and call it "Law and Order", or some such other title.'

Shasa stood up and went to the cabinet at the end of the room. He poured two large cognacs and Manfred did not protest when he placed one of them on the table at his elbow.

'You know, Shasa, for a long time now I have had a dream. I've never told anybody about it, not even Heidi, but I will tell you. I dreamed that one day I would be the Prime Minister, and that you, Shasa Courtney, would be the state President of this country of ours. The two of us, Englishman and Afrikaner, side by side as South Africans.'

They sat quietly and thought about it, and Shasa found himself becoming angry at being cheated of that honour. Then Manfred went off at another tangent.

'Do you know that even though the Americans are refusing to sell us arms we still cooperate very closely with their CIA on all matters of intelligence that affect our mutual interests in Southern Africa?' Manfred asked, and although Shasa could not fathom this new change of direction, he nodded.

'Yes, of course, I know that.'

'The Americans have just interrogated a Russian defector in West Berlin. They passed on some of the intelligence to us. There is a Manchurian Candidate in place, and his target is Verwoerd.'

Shasa gaped at him. 'Who is the assassin?'

'No.' Manfred held up his hands. 'They don't know. Even though the Russian was highly placed, he did not know. All he could tell the Americans was that the assassin has access to the Prime Minister, and he will be used soon, very soon.' He picked up the cognac glass, and swirled the oily brown liquid around the crystal bowl. 'There was one other small clue. The assassin has a history of mental illness, and he is a foreigner, not born in this country.'

'With that information it should be possible to identify him,' Shasa mused. 'You could check every single person who has access to the PM.'

'Perhaps,' Manfred agreed. 'But what we must decide – here in secret, just the two of us – is, do we really want to find the Manchurian Candidate and stop him? Would it be in the best interest of our country to prevent the assassination?'

Shasa spilled the cognac down the lapels of his morning jacket, but he did not seem to notice. Aghast, he was staring at Manfred. After a long pause, he set down his glass, drew a silk handkerchief from his inner pocket and began to mop the spilled liquor.

'Who else knows about this?' he asked, concentrating on his cleaning, not looking up.

'One of my senior officers. He is the liaison with the military attaché at the American Embassy, who is the CIA man here.'

'No one else?'

'Only me – and now you.'

'Your officer is trustworthy?'

'Completely.'

At last Shasa looked up. 'Yes, now I see why I should cancel my trip to London. If something should happen to Verwoerd, it would be essential for me to be here when his successor is chosen.'

He lifted his glass in a salute, and after a moment Manfred returned the gesture. They drank the silent toast, watching each other's eyes over the rims of the crystal glasses.

There were only two couples left on the dance floor, and except for the band and the servants who were cleaning up and stacking the chairs, the marquee was empty.

At last the coloured band-master descended from the stand and approached Sean diffidently. 'Master, it's after two o'clock already.' Sean glared at him over the head of the girl he was dancing with, and the man quailed. 'Please,

Master, we've been playing since lunchtime, nearly fourteen hours.'

Sean's thunderous expression changed dramatically into that radiant boyish smile of his. 'Off you go, then! You have been just great – and this is for you and your boys.' He tucked a crumpled wad of banknotes into the bandleader's top pocket, and called to the other couple.

'Come on, gang. We are off to Navvies.'

Isabella had her face pressed to Lothar's shirt front, but she looked up brightly.

'Oh, goody! she cried. 'I've never been there. Nana says it's sordid and disreputable. Let's go!'

Sean had borrowed Garry's MG and Isabella raced him in her new Alfa Romeo, and managed to keep up with him through the curves of the mountain drive. They were neck and neck as they tore down Buitenkant Street to the notorious Navigator's Den in the Bo-kaap area near the docks.

Sean had purloined two bottles of whisky from the bar in the marquee, and his partner was draped around his neck.

'Let's carouse,' he suggested, and pushed his way through the cluster of seamen and prostitutes who crowded the entrance to the nightclub.

The interior was so dark that they could only barely make out the band, and the music was so loud that they had to sit close and yell at each other.

'You are a marvellous brother,' Isabella shouted and leaned across to kiss Sean. 'You don't preach to me.'

'It's your life, Bella baby, you enjoy it – and call me if anybody tries to stop you.'

She perched on Lothar's knee and nuzzled his neck. Sean's partner had collapsed, and he laid her out full length on the padded bench, with her head in his lap, while he and Lothar sat with their shoulders touching and talked seriously. The music blanketed their voices, so that from further than a few feet nobody could overhear them.

'Do you know that you still have a rather prominent billing in the police files?' Lothar asked.

'It does not come as any great surprise,' Sean admitted.

'You don't mind taking a chance, do you?' Lothar smiled. 'I like your nerve.'

'From what I know and see, I'd say that you are a fairly nerveless customer yourself,' Sean grinned back at him.

'I could make sure that your file disappeared,' Lothar offered.

'In exchange for a little something or other, no doubt?'

'Naturally,' Lothar agreed. 'You get nothing for nothing.'

'And all you get for a pinch of dung is a cloud of flies,' Sean laughed, and refilled the whisky glasses. 'What do you want from me?'

'If you were to act as an intelligence agent for the Bureau of State Security – our man in Rhodesia – we might forget about your little indiscretions.'

'Why not?' Sean agreed instantly. 'Anything for a laugh and living dangerously is half the fun.'

'Do stop being so boring, you two,' Isabella cried, stroking Lothar's cheek. 'Come and dance with me.'

Sean's partner sat up groggily and blurted, 'I'm going to be sick.'

'Emergency,' said Sean. He hauled her to her feet and hustled her through to the tiny women's room.

There were two other females fussing over the single wash hand basin, and they squealed demurely.

'Don't worry about us, ladies.' Sean pushed his partner into the cubicle and aimed her at the toilet bowl. Noisily she got shot of what was troubling her and then straightened up and grinned at him shakily. Tenderly he wiped her mouth with a wad of toilet paper.

'How are you feeling?'

'I feel better now.'

'Good, let's go somewhere and ball.'

'OK,' she said, perking up miraculously. 'That's what I've been waiting for the whole evening.'

Sean stopped beside Lothar and Isabella on the crowded floor.

'We are cutting out of here – something just came up, if you will pardon the expression.'

'I'll call you at Weltevreden some time tomorrow,' Lothar said. 'Just to arrange the details.'

'Don't make it too early,' Sean advised and grinned at his sister. 'See you later, Bella Bunny.'

'For God's sake, don't say "Be good!"' Isabella pleaded.

'Perish the thought.' Sean picked up his partner and carried her down the stairs.

Isabella made one more circuit of the floor, just to let Sean get clear, then she murmured, 'That's enough dancing for one night – let's go.'

Lother had never seen a woman drive with Isabella's skill and flair. He relaxed in the passenger seat and watched her. Despite the long day and its excesses, she was still dewy fresh as a rose petal and her eyes were clear and sparkling.

She was the first English girl he had ever been with, and her free and forthright manner at once appalled and intrigued him. With their strict Calvinist upbringing Afrikaner girls would never make themselves so available or behave with such abandon. Yet although she shocked him more than a little, she was without any doubt the most strikingly lovely girl he had ever met.

Isabella drove straight through the intersection of Paradise Road and Rhodes Drive.

'You've missed the turn to Weltevreden,' he pointed out, and she gave him a brief impish grin.

'That's not where we are going. From here you are in my hands, Lothar De La Rey.'

They followed the coastal road from Muizenberg around the bay, through the deserted streets of Simonstown, the British naval base, and then on towards the tip of the continent.

Where the road skirted a high cliff above the sea, Isabella pulled the Alfa off the road and cut the engine.

'Come on,' she ordered, took his hand and led him to the edge of the cliff. The dawn was turning the eastern sky to lemon and orange, and far beneath them the cliffs were folded upon themselves to form a sheltered bay. 'It's so beautiful here,' Isabella whispered. 'One of my favourite places.'

'Where are we?' Lothar asked.

'It's called Smitswinkel Bay,' she told him, and led him by the hand to the start of the steep pathway that descended the cliff.

At the bottom a narrow horse-shoe of silver sand surrounded the bay, and above the beach a few locked and shuttered shacks were crammed against the foot of the cliff. The dawn light filtered down, soft and pearly, and the waters of the bay glowed with the misty sheen of moonstones.

Isabella kicked off her shoes and walked down to the water's edge, and then without looking round at him she slipped her dress off her shoulders and let it drop to the sand. Beneath it she wore only a pair of silk and lace panties. For a long moment she stood staring out across the bay and her back was long and shaped like the neck of lovely vase, the beads of her spine just showed beneath skin that was pale and lustrous as mother-of-pearl. Then she stooped to pull the panties down to her ankles, and stepped out of them.

She was naked and Lothar's breathing caught in his throat as he watched her walk slowly down to the water's edge, her hips rolling in time to the lazy pulse of the ocean. She walked out until she was waist-deep and she lowered herself until only her head was above the surface. Then she turned and looked back at him. The challenge and the invitation were as clear as if she had called them aloud.

Lothar undressed as unhurriedly as she had done. Naked, he walked into the bay and she rose to meet him, the waters streaming from her bare shoulders down her breasts, and she lifted her arms and placed them around his neck.

She teased him with her tongue, letting him explore the warmth and softness of her mouth, and she gave a little purring chuckle as she felt how much he wanted her.

The sound goaded him and he lifted her in his arms and carried her out beyond her depth. She was forced to cling to him, and her body was weightless. He handled her like a doll and she offered no resistance. His strength seemed limitless – it made her feel helpless and vulnerable, but she was grateful for his patience. To hurry now would spoil it all. She wanted this to be something far beyond the frenzied groping and often painful thrusting that was all she had been offered by the three or four college lads she had allowed this far.

She learned quickly that he could tease as well as she could, and he let her float around him, light as the buoyant kelp in the gentle swell of the ocean while he stood four-square and refused to make the final assault. In the end it was she who succumbed to impatience.

In contrast to the cool water that eddied around her, he was like a flaming brand buried deep in her body. She could not believe the hardness and the heat, and she cried aloud with incredible delight. None of the others had been anything like this. From now on this was all that counted, this was what she had been searching for all along.

Still clinging together they waded ashore, and by now it was full morning. They bundled up their clothes and still naked she led him to the last shack in the row. While she searched for the key in her purse, he asked, 'Who does this belong to?'

'It's one of Daddy's hiding places. I only discovered it quite by chance and he doesn't know that I have a key.'

She got the door open and led him into the single room.

'Towels,' she said, and opened one of the cupboards. They made a game out of drying each other, but the light-hearted mood changed quickly to serious intent, and she dragged him to the bunk against the wall.

'Where I come from the man does the asking,' he chuckled.

'You are an old-fashioned chauvinist prude,' she told him.

As she clambered up onto the bunk he saw that her bottom was still bright pink from the cold waters of the bay; he found that peculiarly endearing and he was suddenly overwhelmed by a sense of tenderness towards her.

'You are so gentle,' she whispered. 'So strong and yet so gentle.'

It was mid-morning before they felt hungry, and dressed only in one of her father's old fishing jerseys, Isabella raided the larder for their breakfast.

'How do you fancy smoked oysters and asparagus with your baked beans?'

'Won't your father miss you?' he asked as he opened the cans.

'Oh, Daddy is a push-over. He will believe anything I tell him. It's my grandmother we have to watch out for, but I've arranged with one of my girlfriends to cover for us.'

'Ah, so you knew where we were going to end up?' he asked.

'Of course.' She rolled her eyes at him. 'Didn't you?'

They sat cross-legged on the bunk with the plates on their laps and Isabella tasted the mixture. 'It's ghastly,' she gave her opinion, 'if I wasn't starving I wouldn't touch it.'

'Of course, you will see your mother while you are in London?' he asked, and the loaded spoon stopped halfway to Isabella's mouth.

'How did you know I was going to London – and how did you know my mother was there?'

'I probably know more about your mother than you do,' Lothar told her, and she replaced the spoon on her plate and stared at him.

'For instance?' she challenged.

'Well, for instance, your mother is a rabid enemy of this country. She is a member of the banned ANC and of the anti-*apartheid* group. She associates regularly with members of the South African Communist Party. In London she runs a safe house for political refugees and escaped terrorists.'

'My mother?' Isabella shook her head.

'Your mother was deeply implicated in the plot to blow up the Houses of Parliament and assassinate most of the members of the House, including the Prime Minister – and your father and my father.'

Isabella was still shaking her head, but he went on expressionlessly, watching her with those golden leopard eyes.

'She was directly responsible for the death of her own father, your grandfather, Colonel Blaine Malcomess. She was an accomplice of Moses Gama who is now serving a life sentence for terrorism and murder, and if she had not escaped she would probably be in jail with him.'

'No,' said Isabella softly. 'I don't believe it.'

She was amazed and distressed by the change in him. Minutes before he had been so gentle, now he was hard and cruel, wounding her with words as he went on, 'For instance, did you know that your mother was Moses Gama's lover, and that she bore him a son? Your half-brother is an attractive coffee colour.'

'No!' Isabella recoiled, shaking her head in disbelief. 'How do you know all this?'

'From the signed confession of Moses Gama, the man himself. I can arrange for you to see a copy, but that is not really necessary. You will almost certainly meet your bastard half-brother in London. He is living there with your mother. His name is Benjamin Afrika.'

Isabella jumped up and carried her plate to the kitchen-ette. She dumped the food into the garbage bin and without looking around, she asked, 'Why are you telling me all this?'

'So that you will know your duty.'

'I don't understand.' She still would not look at him.

'We believe your mother and her associates are planning some sort of violent action against this country. We are not sure what it is. Any information on their activities would be invaluable.'

Isabella turned slowly and stared at him. Her face was pale and stricken.

'You want me to spy on my own mother?'

'We simply would like to know the names of the people you meet in her company while you are in London.'

She was not listening. She cut in on what he was saying.

'You planned this. You picked me out, not because you thought I was attractive or sweet or desirable. You deliber-ately set out to seduce me, just for this.'

'You are beautiful, not attractive. You are magnificent, not sweet,' he said.

'And you are a bastard, a ruthless heartless bastard.'

He stood up and went to where his clothes hung behind the door.

'What are you going to do?' she demanded.

'Get dressed and go,' he told her.

'Why?'

'You called me a bastard.'

'You are.' Her eyes were glutted with tears. 'An irresist-ible bastard. Don't go, Lothar, please don't go.'

Isabella was relieved when her father told her that he was unable to fly to London with her and Michael. Meeting her mother again after all these years, and after what Lothar had told her, would be difficult enough, without her father there to complicate matters and confuse her feelings. She had, indeed, tried to beg off going to London herself. She wanted to be close to Lothar, but he had been the one who insisted she make the trip.

'I will be back in Johannesburg and we wouldn't see much of each other anyway,' he told her. 'And besides that you have your duty and you have given me your word.'

'I know Daddy would give me a PR job with the company in Jo'burg. I could get a flat and we could see lots of each other, I mean lots and lots!'

'When you come back from London,' he promised.

There were representatives from South Africa House and the London office of Courtney Mining to meet Isabella and Michael at Heathrow and a company limousine to take them to the Dorchester.

'Pater always overdoes it by a mile,' Michael remarked, embarrassed by the reception. 'We could have taken a taxi.'

'No point in being a Courtney, unless you get to enjoy it,' Isabella disagreed.

When Isabella was shown up to her suite, which looked out over Hyde Park, there was an enormous bouquet of flowers waiting for her with a note:

Sorry I can't be with you, darling. Next time we will paint the town bright scarlet together.

Your old Dad.

Even before the porter had brought her bags up, Isabella dialled the number that Tara had given her and she was answered on the third ring.

'This is the Lord Kitchener Hotel, may I help you?'

It was strangely nostalgic to be greeted by an African accent in a strange city.

'May I speak to Mrs Malcomess, please?'

In her letter Tara had warned her that she had reverted to her maiden name after the divorce.

'Hello, Mater.' Isabella tried to sound natural when Tara came on the line, but Tara's delight was unrestrained.

'Oh, Bella darling, where are you? Is Mickey with you? How soon can you get here? You have got the address, haven't you? It's so easy to find.'

Isabella tried to match Michael's enthusiasm and excitement as they drove through the streets of London and the taxi-driver pointed out the landmarks they passed, but she was in a funk at the prospect of seeing her mother again.

It was one of those rather seedy little tourist hotels in a side street off the Cromwell Road. Only part of the neon sign was lit. THE ORD KITCH, it flashed in electric blue, and on the glass of the front door were plastered the emblems of the AA and *Routiers* and a blaze of credit card stickers.

Tara rushed out through the glass doors while they were still paying off the taxi. She embraced Michael first, which gave Isabella a few moments to study her mother.

She had put on weight, her backside in the faded blue jeans was huge, and her bosom hung shapelessly in the baggy man's sweater.

'She's an old bag.' Isabella was appalled. Even though Tara had never gone to any pains with her appearance, she had always had an air of freshness and neatness. But now her hair had turned grey, and she had obviously made a half-hearted attempt to henna it back to its original colour, and then given up. The grey was streaked brassy ginger and violent mulberry red, and it was twisted up into a careless

807

bun at the nape of her neck from which particoloured wisps had escaped.

Her features had sagged almost to obscure the bone structure which had been one of her most striking assets, and though her eyes were still large and bright the skin around them had creased and bagged.

At last she released Michael, and turned to Isabella.

'My darling little girl, I would hardly have recognized you. What a lovely young woman you have become.'

They embraced. Isabella recalled how her mother had smelled, it was one of her pleasant childhood memories, but this woman smelled of some cheap and flowery perfume, of cigarette smoke and boiled cabbage, and – Isabella could barely credit her own senses – of underclothing that had been worn too long without changing.

She broke off the embrace, but Tara kept hold of her arm, and with Michael on the other side of her led them into the Lord Kitchener Hotel. The receptionist was a black lad, and Isabella recognized his voice as the one who had answered her phone call.

'Phineas is from Cape Town also,' Tara introduced them. 'He is one of our other runaways. He left after the troubles in '61 and, like the rest of us, he won't be going home yet. Now let me show you around the Lordy—' She laughed. 'That's what my permanent guests call it, the Lordy. I thought of changing the name, it's so colonial and Empire—'

Tara chattered on happily as she led them around the hotel. The carpets in the passages were threadbare, and the rooms had washbasins, but shared the toilet and bathroom at the end of each passage.

Tara introduced them to any of her guests they met in the corridors or public rooms. 'These are my son and daughter from Cape Town,' and they shook hands with German and French tourists who spoke no English, Pakistanis and Chinese, black Kenyans and coloured South Africans.

'Where are you staying?' Tara wanted to know.

'At the Dorchester.'

'Of course.' Tara rolled her eyes. 'Fifty guineas a day, paid for by the sweat of the workers in the Courtney mines. That is what your father would have chosen. Why don't you and Mickey move in here? I have two nice rooms on the top floor free at the moment. You would meet so many interesing people, and we'd see so much more of each other.'

Isabella shuddered at the thought of sharing the toilet at the end of the passage and jumped in before Michael could agree.

'Daddy would be furious, he has prepaid for us – and now we know our way, it's only a short taxi ride.'

'Taxis,' Tara sniffed. 'Why not take the bus or the underground like any ordinary person?'

Isabella stared at her speechlessly. Didn't she understand that they weren't ordinary people? They were Courtneys. She was about to say so, when Michael sensed her intention and intervened smoothly.

'Of course you are quite right. You'll have to tell us what number bus to take and where to get off, Mater.'

'Mickey, darling, please don't call me Mater any longer. It's so terribly bourgeois. Call me either Mummy or Tara, but not that.'

'All right. It will be a little bit strange at first, but OK. I'll call you Tara.'

'It's almost lunch time,' Tara announced blithely. 'I asked cook to make a bread-and-butter pudding, I know it's one of your favourites, Mickey.'

'I'm not awfully hungry, Mater – Tara,' Isabella announced. 'And it must be jet-lag or something, but—'

Michael pinched her sharply. 'That's lovely, Tara. We'd love to stay for lunch.'

'I just have to look into the kitchen – make sure it's all under control – come along.'

As they entered the kitchen a child came running to Tara. He must have been helping the Irish cook, for his hands were white with flour to the elbows. Tara hugged him, happily heedless of the flour that rubbed off on her sweater.

A mat of short woolly curls covered his pate, and his skin was a clear light toffee colour. His eyes were huge and dark, and he had appealing gamin features. He reminded Isabella of any one of the dozens of children of the estate workers on Weltevreden. She smiled at him, and he gave back a cocky but friendly grin.

'This is Benjamin,' Tara said. 'And these, Benjamin, are your brother and sister – Mickey and Isabella.'

Isabella stared at the child. She had tried to discount and forget all that Lothar had told her, and in some measure she had succeeded. But now it all came rushing back, the words roaring in her ears like flood waters.

'Your half-brother is an attractive coffee colour,' Lothar had told her and she wanted to scream, 'How could you, Mater, how could you do this to us?' But Michael had recovered from his obvious surprise, and now he held out his hand towards the child and said,

'Hi there, Ben. It's fine that we are brothers – but how about you and me being friends also?'

'Hey, man – I like that,' Benjamin agreed instantly. To add to Isabella's dismay and confusion, he spoke in a broad South London accent.

Isabella spoke barely a dozen words during lunch. The pea soup was thickened with flour that had not cooked through and it stuck to the roof of her mouth. The boiled silverside lay limply in its own watery gravy, and the cabbage was cooked pink.

They sat at the table with Phineas, the receptionist, and five other of Tara's guests, all black South African expatriates, and the boisterous conversation was almost entirely conducted in left-wing jargon. The government of which Isabella's beloved father was a minister was always referred to as the 'racist regime' and Michael joined cheerfully in the discussion about the redistribution of wealth and the return of the land to those who worked it after the revolution had succeeded and the People's Democratic Republic of Azania had been established. Isabella wanted to scream at him, 'Damn you, Mickey, they are talking about Weltevreden and the Silver River Mine. These are terrorists and revolutionaries – and their sole purpose is to destroy us and our world.'

When the bread-and-butter pudding was served, she could take it no longer.

'I'm sorry, Tara,' she whispered. 'I have a splitting headache, and I simply have to get back to the Dorchester and lie down.' She was so pale and discomforted that Tara made only a token protest and genuine noises of concern. Isabella refused to let Michael escort her. 'I won't spoil your fun. You haven't seen Mater – Tara – in ages. I'll just grab a taxi.'

Perhaps it really was fatigue that had weakened her, but in the cab she found herself weeping with chagrin and shame and fury.

'Damn her! Damn her to hell,' she whispered. 'She has disgraced and dishonoured all of us, Daddy and Nana and me and all the family.'

As soon as she reached her room she locked her door, threw herself on the bed and reached for the telephone.

'Exchange, I want to put a call through to Johannesburg in South Africa—' She read the number out of her address book.

The delay was less than half an hour and then a marvellously homey Afrikaans accent said, 'This is Police Headquarters, Bureau of State Security.'

'I want to speak to Colonel Lothar De La Rey.'

'De La Rey.'

Despite the thousands of miles that separated them, his voice was crisp and clear, and in her imagination she saw him again naked on the beach in the dawn, like a statue of a Greek athlete but with those glowing golden eyes, and she whispered, 'Oh, God, Lothie, I've missed you. I want to come home. I hate it here.'

He spoke quietly, reassuring and consoling her, and when she had calmed he ordered her, 'Tell me about it.'

'You were right. Everything you said was true – even to her little brown bastard, and the people are all revolutionaries and terrorists. What do you want me to do, Lothie? I'll do anything you tell me.'

'I want you to stay there, and stick it out for the full two weeks. You can telephone me every day, but you must stay on. Promise me, Bella.'

'All right – but, God, I miss you and home.'

'Listen, Bella. I want you to go to South Africa House the first opportunity you have. Don't let anybody know, not even your brother Michael. Ask for Colonel Van Vuuren, the military attaché. He will show you photographs and ask you to identify the people you meet.'

'All right, Lothie – but I've told you twice already how much I miss you, while you, you swine, haven't said a word.'

'I have thought about you every day since you left,' Lothar said. 'You're beautiful and funny and you make me laugh.'

'Don't stop,' Isabella pleaded. 'Just keep talking like that.'

Adrian Van Vuuren was a burly avuncular man, who looked more like a friendly Free State farmer than a Secret Service man. He took her up to the ambassador's office and introduced her to His Excellency, who knew Shasa well, and they chatted for a few minutes. His Excellency invited

812

Isabella to the races at Ascot the coming Saturday but Colonel Van Vuuren intervened apologetically.

'Miss Courtney is doing a little job for us at present, Your Excellency. It might not be wise to make too much public display of her connections to the embassy.'

'Very well,' the ambassador agreed reluctantly. 'But you will come to lunch with us, Miss Courtney – not often we have such a pretty girl at our gatherings.'

Van Vuuren gave her the short tour of the embassy and its art treasures, which ended in his office on the third floor.

'Now, my dear, we have some work for you.'

A pile of albums was stacked on his desk, each full of head-and-shoulder photographs of men and women. They sat side by side and Van Vuuren flicked through the pages, picking out the mug shots of the people she had met at the Lord Kitchener Hotel.

'You make it easier for us by knowing their names,' Van Vuuren remarked, and turned to a photograph of Phineas, the hotel receptionist.

'Yes, that's him,' Isabella confirmed, and Van Vuuren looked up his details in a separate ledger. 'Phineas Mophoso. Born 1941. Member of PAC. Convicted of public violence 16 May 1961. Violated bail conditions. Illegal emigration late 1961. Present location believed UK.'

'Small fry,' Van Vuuren grunted, 'but small fry often shoal with big fish.' He offered to provide an embassy car to drive Isabella back to the Dorchester.

'Thank you, but I'll walk.'

She had tea alone at Fortnum & Masons and when she got back to the hotel Michael was frantic with worry.

'For Heaven's sake, Mickey. I'm not a baby. I can look after myself. I just felt like exploring on my own.'

'Mater is giving a party for us at the Lord Kitchener this evening. She wants us there before six.'

'You mean Tara, not Mater – and the Lordy, not the Lord Kitchener. Don't be so bourgeois and colonial, Mickey darling.'

At least fifty people crowded into the residents' lounge of the Lordy for Tara's party, and she provided unlimited quantities of draught bitter and Spanish red wine to wash down the Irish cook's unforgettable snacks. Michael entered into the spirit of the occasion. He was at all times the centre of an arguing gesticulating group. Isabella backed herself into a corner of the lounge and with a remote and icy *hauteur* discouraged any familiar approach from the other guests, while at the same time memorizing their names and faces as Tara introduced them.

After the first hour the smoky claustrophobic atmosphere, and the volume of conversation lubricated by Tara's Spanish plonk, became oppressive and Isabella's eyes felt gritty and a dull ache started in her temples. Tara had disappeared and Michael was still enjoying himself.

'That's my patriotic duty for tonight,' she decided, and sidled towards the door taking care not to alert Michael to her departure.

As she passed the deserted reception desk, she heard voices from behind the frosted glass door of Tara's tiny office, and she had an attack of conscience.

'I can't just go off without thanking Mater,' she decided. 'It was an awful party, but she went to a lot of trouble and I am one of the guests of honour.'

She slipped behind the desk, and was about to tap on the panel of the door when she heard her mother say, 'But, comrade, I didn't expect you to arrive tonight.' The words were commonplace, but the tone in which Tara said them was not. She was more than agitated – she was afraid, deadly afraid.

A man's voice replied, but it was so low and hoarse that Isabella could not catch the words, and then Tara said, 'But they are my own children. It's perfectly safe.'

This time the man's reply was sharper. 'Nothing is ever safe,' he said. 'They are also your husband's children, and your husband is a member of the Fascist racist regime. We will leave now and return later after they have gone.'

Isabella acted instinctively. She darted back into the lobby and out through the glass front doors of the hotel. The narrow street was lined with parked vehicles, one of them a dark delivery van tall enough to screen her. She hid behind it.

After a few minutes, two men followed her out of the front entrance of the hotel. They both wore dark raincoats but their heads were bare. They set off briskly, walking side by side towards the Cromwell Road and as they came level with where she leaned against the side of the van, the street light lit their faces.

The man nearest to her was black, with a strong, resolute face, broad nose and thick African lips. His companion was white and much older. His flesh was pale as putty and had the same soft amorphous look. His hair was black and lank and lifeless. It hung on to his forehead, and his eyes were dark and fathomless as pools of coal tar – and Isabella understood why her mother had been afraid. This was a man who inspired fear.

Colonel Van Vuuren sat beside her at his desk with the pile of albums in front of them. 'He is a white man. That makes life a lot easier for all of us,' he said as he selected one of the albums.

'These are all white,' he explained. 'We have got them all in here. Even the ones safely behind bars, like Bram Fischer.'

She found his photograph on the third page.

'That's the one.'

'Are you sure?' Van Vuuren asked. 'It's not a very good photo.'

It must have been taken as he was climbing into a vehicle, for the background was a city street. He was glancing back, most of his body obscured by the open door of the vehicle, and movement had blurred his features slightly.

'Yes. That's him all right,' Isabella repeated. 'I could never mistake those eyes.'

Van Vuuren referred to the separate ledger. 'The photograph was taken in East Berlin by the American CIA two years ago. He is a wily bird, that's the only picture we have. His name is Joe Cicero. He is the Secretary General of the South African Communist Party and a colonel in the Russian KGB. He is a chief of staff of the military wing of the banned ANC, the *Umkhonto we Sizwe*.' Van Vuuren smiled. 'And so, my dear, the big fish has arrived. Now we must try and identify his companion. That will not be so easy.'

It took almost two hours. Isabella paged through the albums slowly. When she finished one pile, Van Vuuren's assistent brought in another armful of albums and she began again. Van Vuuren sat patiently beside her, sending out for coffee and encouraging her with a smile and a word when she flagged.

'Yes.' Isabella straightened up at last. 'This is the one.'

'You have been wonderful. Thank you.' Van Vuuren reached for the ledger and turned to the *curriculum vitae of* the man in the photograph.

'Raleigh Tabaka,' he read out. 'Secretary of the Vaal branch of PAC and member of *Poqo*. Organizer of the attack on the Sharpeville police station. Disappeared three years ago, before he could be detained. Since then there have been rumours that he was seen in training camps in Morocco and East Germany. He is rated as a trained and dangerous terrorist. Two big fish together. Now, if we could just find what they are up to!'

Tara Courtney waited up long after her party had broken up. The last guests had staggered through the glass doors, and Michael had kissed her goodnight and gone off to try and pick up a late cruising taxi in the Cromwell Road.

Since first she had met him, Joe Cicero had been associated with danger and suffering and loss. There was always an aura of mystery and a passionless evil surrounding him. He terrified her. The man with him she had met for the first time that night. Joe Cicero had introduced him only as Raleigh, but Tara's heart had gone out to him immediately. Although he was much younger, he reminded her so strongly of her own Moses. He had the same smouldering intensity and compelling presence, the same dark majesty of bearing and command.

They came back a little after two in the morning, and Tara let them in and led them through to her own bedroom in the back area of the hotel.

'Raleigh will stay with you for the next two or three weeks. Then he will return to South Africa. You will provide everything he asks for, particularly the information.'

'Yes, comrade,' Tara whispered. Although she was the registered owner and licensed proprietress of the hotel, the money for the purchase had been provided by Joe Cicero and she took her orders directly from him.

'Raleigh is the nephew of Moses Gama,' Joe said, watching her carefully with those expressionless black eyes as she turned to the younger man.

'Oh, Raleigh, I didn't realize. It is almost as though we are one family. Moses is the father of my son, Benjamin.'

'Yes,' Raleigh, answered. 'I know that. This is the reason that I am able to give you the object of my mission to South Africa. Your dedication is proven and unquestioned. I am going back to Africa to free your husband and my uncle, Moses Gama, from the prison of the Fascist racist

Verwoerd regime to lead the democratic revolution of our people.'

Her joy dawned slowly with her understanding. Then she went to Raleigh Tabaka and as she embraced him she was weeping with happiness.

'I will give anything to help you succeed,' she whispered through her tears. 'Even my life.'

Jakobus Stander had only two classes on a Friday morning, and the last one ended at 11.30. He left the grounds of the University of the Witwatersrand immediately afterwards and caught the bus down to Hillbrow. It was a ride of only fifteen minutes and he reached his flat a little after midday.

The suitcase was still on the low coffee table where he had placed it the night before, after he had finished working on it. It was a cheap brown case made of imitation leather with a pressed metal lock.

He stood staring at it with pale topaz-coloured eyes. Except for the eyes, he was an unremarkable young man. Although he was tall, he was too thin and the grey flannel trousers hung loosely around his waist. His hair was long, flecked with dandruff, hanging over the back of his collar, and the elbows of his baggy brown corduroy jacket were patched with leather. Rather than a tie he wore a turtle-neck jersey with the collar rolled over. It was the self-consciously shabby uniform of the left-wing intellectual, adopted by even the Professor of the Department of Sociology in which Jakobus was a senior lecturer.

Without removing the jacket, he sat down on the narrow bed and stared at the suitcase.

'I am one of the only ones left,' he thought. 'It's all up to me now. They have taken Baruch and Randy and Berny – I am all alone.'

There had been less than fifty of them even in the best times. A small band of true patriots, champions of the proletariat, almost all of them white and young, members of the young liberals or students and faculty members involved in radical student politics at the English-speaking universities of Cape Town and the Witwatersrand. Kobus had been the only Afrikaner in their ranks.

At first they had called themselves the National Committee of Liberation, and their methods had been more sophisticated than *Umkhonto we Sizwe* and the Rivonia group. They had used dynamite and electrical timing devices, and their successes had been many and heartening. They had destroyed power substations and railway switching systems, even a reservoir dam, and in the triumphant mood of those early days they had restyled themselves the African Resistance Movement.

In the end they had been destroyed in exactly the same manner as Mandela and his Rivonia group, by the inefficiency of their own security and the inability of the members who were captured by the security police to withstand interrogation.

He was one of the only ones left, but he knew that his hours of freedom were numbered. The security police had taken Berny two days ago and by now he would have talked. Berny was not made of heroic stuff, a small pale and nervous creature, too soft-hearted for the cause. Jakobus had argued against his recruitment, but that was too late now. The Bureau of State Security had Berny, and Berny knew his name. There was very little time left, but still he procrastinated. He looked at his wristwatch. It was almost one o'clock. His mother would be home by now, preparing his father's lunch. He lifted the telephone.

Sarah Stander stood over the kitchen stove. She felt tired and dispirited, but she seemed always to be tired these days. The telephone rang and she turned down the hot plate of the stove, and wiped her hands on her apron as she went through to her husband's study.

The room was lined with shelves of dusty law books that had once been a promise of hope to her, a symbol of success and advancement, but now seemed rather to be the fetters that bound Roelf and her in penury and mediocrity.

She lifted the phone. 'Hello. This is *Mevrou* Stander.'

'Mama,' Jakobus replied, and she gave a little coo of joy.

'My boy – where are you?' But at his reply her spirits plunged again.

'In the flat in Johannesburg, Mama.' That was a thousand miles away, and her longing to see him devastated her.

'I hoped you were—'

'Mama,' he cut her off. 'I had to speak to you. I had to explain. Something terrible is going to happen. I wanted to tell you – I don't want you to be angry with me, I don't want you to hate me.'

'Never!' she cried. 'I love you too much, my boy—'

'I don't want Papa and you to feel bad. What I do is not your fault. Please understand and forgive me.'

'Kobus, my son, what is it? I don't understand what you are saying.'

'I can't tell you, Mama. Soon you will understand. I love you and Papa – please remember that.'

'Kobus,' she cried. 'Kobus!' but the earpiece clicked and then there was only the hum of a broken connection.

Frantically she rang the exchange and asked to be reconnected but it took fifteen minutes before the operator called her back.

'There is no reply from your Johannesburg number.'

Sarah was distraught. She roamed around her kitchen, the midday meal forgotten, twisting her apron in her fingers, trying desperately to think of some way of reaching her son. When her husband came in through the front door she rushed down the passageway and threw her arms around his neck, and she gabbled out her fears.

'Manie!' Roelf said. 'I will telephone him. He can send one of his men around to Kobus's flat.'

'Why didn't I think of that?' Sarah sobbed.

The secretary in Manfred's ministry told them he was not available and would not be in again until Monday morning.

'What will we do now?' Roelf was as worried as she was.

'Lothie.' Sarah brightened. 'He is in the police in Johannesburg. Ring Lothie, he will know what to do.'

J akobus Stander broke the connection to his mother, and jumped to his feet. He knew he must act quickly and decisively now. Already he had wasted too much time, they would be coming for him soon.

He picked up the suitcase and left the flat, locking the door behind him. He rode down in the lift, still holding the heavy suitcase, even though the handle cut into his fingers. There were two girls in the lift with him. They ignored him and chattered to each other all the way down. He watched them surreptitiously. 'It may be you,' he thought. 'It could be anybody.'

The girls barged out of the lift ahead of him, and he followed slowly, walking lopsidedly because of the weight of the brown suitcase.

He caught the bus at the corner and took the seat nearest the door, placing the suitcase on the seat beside him, but retaining his grip on the handle all the way.

The bus stopped outside the side entrance of the Johannesburg railway station, and Jakobus was the first passenger to alight. Lugging the suitcase, he started towards the station entrance, and then his steps began to drag and his mouth went dry with terror. There was a constable of the railway police at the entrance, and as Jakobus hesitated he looked directly at him. Jakobus wanted to drop the suitcase and run back to the bus which was pulling away behind him, but the press of other passengers bore him forward like a dead leaf in a stream.

He did not want to catch the constable's eye. He trudged forward, head bowed, concentrating on the heels of the fat woman in white shoes just ahead of him. He looked up as he came level with the station portals, and the constable was walking away from him, his hands clasped lightly behind his back. Jakobus's legs felt rubbery and his relief was so intense that he thought he was going to be ill. He fought down his nausea and kept on going with the stream of commuters.

At the centre of the concourse under the high arched skylight of glass there was a goldfish pond surrounded by wooden benches. Although most of the benches were crowded with travellers snatching a few minutes' rest between trains or awaiting the arrival of friends, there was room for Jakobus at the end of one of them.

He sat down and placed the suitcase between his feet. He was sweating heavily and he had difficulty in breathing. Waves of nausea kept welling up from the pit of his guts and there was a bitter sick taste at the back of his throat.

He wiped his face with his handkerchief and kept swallowing hard until gradually he had control of himself again. Then he looked around him. The other benches were still crowded. In the centre of the one facing him there was a mother with two daughters. The youngest one was still in napkins, she sat on her mother's lap with a dummy in her mouth. The elder girl had skinny sun-browned legs and arms and frilly petticoats under her short skirt. She leaned against her mother's side and sucked a lollipop on a stick. Her mouth was dyed bright red by the sticky candy.

All around Jakobus passed a continual stream of

humanity, coming and going down the broad staircase that led up to the street. Like columns of ants, they spread out to reach the separate platforms, and the loudspeakers boomed out information on arriving and departing trains, and the hiss and huff of escaping steam from the locomotives echoed against the high arches of glass above where Jakobus sat.

He looked down at the suitcase between his feet. He had drilled a needle hole through the imitation leather. A strand of piano wire emerged from the aperture, and he had fixed a brass curtain ring to the end of it, and taped the ring to the brown leather beside the handle.

Now he picked at the tape with his fingernail and peeled it away. He stuck his forefinger through the brass ring and gently pulled the wire taut. There was a muted click from the interior of the suitcase and he started guiltily and looked around him again. The little girl with the lollipop stuck in her cheek had been watching him. She gave him a sticky smile and shyly cuddled closer to her mother's side.

Using his heels and the back of his legs, Jakobus pushed the suitcase slowly under the bench on which he was seated. Then he stood up and walked briskly across to the men's toilets on the far side of the concourse. He stood in front of one of the porcelain urinals and checked his wristwatch. It was ten minutes after two. He zipped up his fly and walked out of the men's room.

The mother and the two little girls were still sitting where he had left them, and the brown suitcase lay under the bench opposite. As he passed the child recognized him and smiled again. He did not return the smile but went up the staircase into the street. He walked down to the Langham Hotel at the corner and went into the men's bar. He ordered a cold Castle beer and drank it slowly, standing at the bar, checking his wristwatch every few minutes. He wondered if the mother and the two little girls had left, or if they were still sitting on the bench.

The ferocity of the explosion shocked him. He was almost a block away but it knocked over his glass and the dregs of the beer ran across the bar top. There was consternation throughout the bar room. Men were swearing with surprise and astonishment and rushing to the door.

Jakobus followed them out into the street. The traffic had stopped, and people were swarming out of the buildings to block the pavements. From the station entrance a cloud of dust and smoke billowed and through it staggered vague shadowy figures, powdered with dust, their clothing hanging off them in rags. Somewhere a woman began to scream, and all around him there were shouted questions.

'What is it? What happened?'

Jakobus turned and walked away. He heard the sirens of the police cars and the fire engines coming closer, but he did not look back.

'No, *Tannie* Sarie, I haven't seen Kobus since we last met at Waterkloof.' Lothar De La Rey tried to be patient. The Standers were old friends of his parents, and he had spent many happy childhood holidays at the cottage on the Stander farm at the seaside. That was before *Oom* Roelf Stander had been forced to sell the farm. 'Yes, yes, *Tannie*. I know, but Kobus and I live in different worlds now – I know how worried you must be. Yes, of course.'

Lothar was taking the call in his private office in the headquarters complex of Marshall Square, and he glanced at his wristwatch as he listened to Sarah Stander's plaintive voice. It was just before two o'clock.

'What time was it when he telephoned you?' Lothar asked, and listened to her reply. 'That was an hour ago. Where did he say he was speaking from? All right, *Tannie*, what is his address in Hillbrow?' He scribbled it on the pad in front of him. 'Now tell me, *Tannie*, what was it exactly he said. Something terrible and you must forgive him? Yes, that doesn't sound very good, I agree. Suicide? No, *Tannie* Sarie, I'm sure he didn't mean that, but I will send one of my men to check his flat, why don't you ring the university in the meantime?'

One of the other telephones on his desk squealed and he ignored it. 'What did they say at the university?' he asked. 'All right, *Tannie*, I will telephone you and *Oom* Roelf just as soon as I have any news.' By now all three of his telephones were shrilling, and Captain Lourens, his assistant, was signalling him frantically from the door of his office.

'Yes, I understand, *Tannie* Sarie. Yes, I promise I will telephone you. But I must ring off now.' Lothar replaced the receiver and looked up at Lourens.

'*Ja*, what is it, man?'

'An explosion at the main railway station. It looks like another bomb.'

Lothar jumped to his feet and snatched up his jacket. 'Casualties?' he demanded.

'There are bodies and blood all over the place.'

'The bloody swines,' Lothar said bitterly.

The street was cordoned off. They left the police car at the barrier and Lothar, who was in plain clothes, showed his identification and the sergeant saluted him. There were five ambulances parked outside the station entrance with their lights flashing.

At the head of the staircase leading down into the main concourse Lothar paused. The damage was terrible. The glass in the arched skylights had been blown out and it coated the marble floors, glittering like a field of ice crystals.

The restaurant had been turned into a first-aid station and the white-jacketed doctors and ambulance crews were at work. The stretcher-bearers were carrying their grisly loads up the staircase to the waiting vehicles.

The officer in charge of the investigation was a major from Marshall Square. He had his men searching the wreckage already, working methodically in an extended line across the concourse. He recognized Lothar and beckoned to him. The glass crunched under Lothar's feet as he crossed to join him.

'How many dead?' he asked without any preamble.

'We have been incredibly lucky, Colonel. About forty injured, mostly by flying glass, but only one dead.'

He reached down and pulled back the plastic sheet that was spread at his feet.

Under it lay a little girl in a short dress with a frilly lace petticoat. Both her legs and one arm had been blown away, and the dress was soaked with her blood.

'Her mother lost both eyes, and her little sister will lose one arm,' the major said, and Lothar saw that the child's face was miraculously unscathed. She seemed to be sleeping. Her mouth was bright red with sticky sugar and in her remaining hand she still clutched the stick of a half-eaten lollipop.

'Lourens,' Lothar said quietly to his assistant. 'Ring Records. Use the telephone in the restaurant. Tell them I want a computer run on my desk when I get back to the square. I want the name of every known white radical on the list. It had to be a white man in this section of the station.'

He watched Lourens cross the concourse and then he looked down at the tiny body under the plastic sheet.

'I'm going to get the bastard who did this,' he whispered. 'This one isn't going to get away.'

His staff were waiting for him when he got back to the office forty minutes later. They had already vetted the computerized list and checked the names of those in detention, in exile or those whose whereabouts could be assumed to be outside the Witwatersrand area.

There remained 396 suspects unaccounted for. They were listed in alphabetical order and it was almost four o'clock before they had worked down to the 'S' section. As Lothar folded over the last sheet of the print-out the name seemed to leap from the page at him:

STANDER, JAKOBUS PETRUS

In the same moment Sarah Stander's plaintive voice echoed in his ears.

'Stander,' he said crisply. 'This one is a new addition.' He had last checked the list twenty-four hours before. It was one of the most important tools of his trade, the names upon it so familiar that he could conjure up each face clearly in his mind's eye. Kobus' name had not been there on his last reading.

Captain Lourens picked up the internal telephone to Records, and spoke to the files clerk on the section, then he turned back to Lothar as he hung up the receiver.

'Stander's name comes from the interrogation of a member of the African Resistance Movement, Bernard Fisher. He was arrested on the 5th, two days ago. Stander is a lecturer at Wits University.'

'I know who he is.' Lothar strode out of the operations room into his private office and ripped the top sheet off his notepad. 'And I know where he is.' He drew the .38 police special from his shoulder holster and checked the load as he gave his orders. 'I want four units of the Flying Squad and a break-in team with flak jackets and shotguns – and I want photographs of the bomb victims, the girl—'

The flat was on the fifth floor at the end of a long open gallery. Lothar placed men on every stairwell and both fire escapes, at the lift station and in the main lobby. He and Lourens went up with the break-in team, and they all moved stealthily into position.

With the police special cocked in his right hand, his back against the wall, clear of the door, he reached out and rang the bell.

There was no reply. He rang again, and they waited tensely. The silence drew out. Lothar reached out to ring a third time, when there were light hesitant footsteps beyond the glass panel door.

'Who is it?' a breathless voice called.

'Kobus – it's me, Lothie.'

'*Liewe Here!* Sweet God!' and the sound of running footsteps receded into the flat.

'Go!' said Lothar and the hammer man from the break-in team stepped up to the door with the ten-pound sledgehammer. The lock burst open at the first stroke and the door crashed back against its hinges.

Lothar was the first one in. The lounge was deserted and he ran straight through into the bedroom.

Behind him Lourens shouted, '*Pasop!* Look out! He might be armed!' But Lothar wanted to stop him reaching a window and jumping.

The bathroom door was locked and he heard running water beyond it. He took the door with his shoulder, and the panel splintered. His own momentum carried him on into the bathroom.

Jakobus was leaning over the washbasin, shaking tablets from a bottle into the palm of his hand and cramming them into his mouth. His cheeks bulged, and he was gagging and swallowing.

Lothar brought the barrel of the revolver down on the wrist that held the bottle, and the bottle shattered into the basin. He caught Jakobus by his long hair and forced him to his knees. He wedged open his jaws with thumb and forefinger and with the fingers of his other hand hooked the crushed damp porridge of tablets out of his mouth.

'I want an ambulance team with a stomach pump up

here,' he yelled at Lourens. 'And get an analysis of that bottle – its label and contents.'

Jakobus was struggling and Lothar hit him open-handed, back and across the face. Jakobus whimpered and subsided, and Lothar thrust his forefinger deeply down his throat.

Gasping and choking and retching, Jakobus started struggling again, but Lothar held him easily. He worked his forefinger around in his throat, keeping on even when hot vomit spurted up over his hand. Satisfied at last he let Jakobus lie in a puddle of his own vomit while he rinsed his hands in the basin.

He dried his hands and seized Jakobus by the back of his shirt. He hauled him to his feet, dragged him through into the lounge and flung him into one of the armchairs.

Lourens and the forensic team were already working over the apartment.

'Did you get the photographs?' Lothar asked, and Lourens handed him a buff envelope.

Jakobus sat huddled in the chair. His shirt was fouled with vomit, and his nose and eyes were red and running. The corner of his mouth was torn where Lothar had forced it open, and he was trembling violently.

Lothar sorted through the contents of the envelope and then he laid a glossy black and white print on the coffee table in front of Jakobus.

Jakobus stared at it. It was a photograph of the truncated body of the child, nestled in a pool of her own blood with the lollipop in her hand. He began to weep. He sobbed and choked and turned his head away. Lothar moved around behind his chair and caught the back of his neck, forced his head back.

'Look at it!' he ordered.

'I didn't mean it,' Jakobus whispered brokenly. 'I didn't mean it to happen.'

The cold white fury faded from Lothar's brain, and he

released Jakobus's head and stepped back from him uncertainly. Those were the words he had used. 'I didn't mean it to happen.' The exact words he had used as he had stood over the black boy with the dead girl's head cradled in his lap and the raw wounds running red into the dust of Sharpeville.

Suddenly Lothar felt weary and sickened. He wanted to go away by himself. Lourens could take over from here, but he braced himself to fight off the despair.

He laid his hand on Jakobus's shoulder, and the touch was strangely gentle and compassionate.

'Ja, Kobus, we never mean it to happen – but still they die. Now it is your turn, Kobus, your turn to die. Come, let's go.'

T he arrest was made six hours after the bomb blast, and even the English press was lavish in its praise of the efficiency of the police investigation. Every front page across the nation carried photographs of Colonel Lothar De La Rey.

Six weeks later, in the Johannesburg Supreme Court, Jakobus Stander pleaded guilty to the charge of murder and was sentenced to death. Two weeks later his appeal was denied by the Appellate Division in Bloemfontein and sentence of death was confirmed. Lothar De La Rey's promotion to brigadier was announced within days of the Appellate Division's decision.

R aleigh Tabaka arrived in Cape Town while the Stander trial was still in progress. He came back the way he had left, as a crewman on a Liberian-registered tramp steamer.

His papers, although issued in the name of Goodwill Mhlazini, were genuine and he passed quickly through customs and immigration and with his bag over his shoulder walked up the foreshore to the main Cape Town railway station.

When he reached the Witwatersrand the following evening, he caught the bus out to Drake's Farm and went to the cottage where Victoria Gama was staying. Vicky opened the door and she had the child by the hand. There was the smell of cooking from the little kitchenette in the back.

She started violently as she saw him. 'Raleigh, come in quickly.' She drew him into the cottage and bolted the door.

'You shouldn't have come here. You know that I am banned. They watch this place,' she told him as she went quickly to the windows and drew the curtains. Then she came back to where he stood in the centre of the room and studied him.

'You have changed,' she said softly. 'You are a man now.' The training and the discipline of the camps had left their mark. He stood straight and alert, and he seemed to exude an intensity and a force that reminded her of Moses Gama.

'He has become one of the lions,' she thought, and she asked, 'Why have you come here, Raleigh, and how can I help you?'

'I have come to free Moses Gama from the prison of the Boers – and I will tell you how you can help me.'

Victoria gave a little cry of joy, and clutched the child closer to her. 'Tell me what to do,' she pleaded.

He would not stay to eat the evening meal with Victoria, would not even sit down on one of the cheap deal chairs.

'When is your next visit to Moses?' he asked in a low but powerful voice.

'In eight days' time,' Victoria told him, and he nodded.

'Yes, I knew it was soon. That was part of our planning. Now, here is what you must do—'

When the prison launch ran out from Cape Town harbour, carrying Victoria and the child to exercise their six-monthly visiting rights, Raleigh Tabaka was on the deck of one of the crayfish trawlers that was moored alongside the repair wharf in the outer harbour. Raleigh was dressed like one of the trawlermen in a blue jersey, yellow plastic overalls and sea boots. He pretended to be working on the pile of crayfish pots on the foredeck, but he studied the ferry as it passed close alongside before it made the turn out through the entrance to the breakwater. He made out Victoria's regal figure in the stern. She was wearing her caftan in yellow, green and black, the colours of the ANC which always infuriated the jailers.

When the ferry had cleared the harbour and was set on course towards the low whale-backed profile of Robben Island far out in the bay, Raleigh walked back along the deck of the eighty-foot trawler to the wheelhouse.

The skipper of the trawler was a burly coloured man, dressed like Raleigh in jersey and waterproofs. Raleigh had met his son at the Lord Kitchener Hotel in London, an activist who had taken part in the Langa uprising and had fled the country immediately afterwards.

'Thank you, comrade,' Raleigh said, and the skipper came to the door of the wheelhouse and took the black pipe from between his even white teeth.

'Did you find out what you wanted?'

'Yes, comrade.'

'When will you need me for the next part?'

'Within ten days,' Raleigh replied.

'You must give me at least twenty-four hours' warning. I

have to get a permit from the Fisheries Department to work in the bay.'

Raleigh nodded. 'I have planned for that.' He turned his head to look forward towards the trawler's bows. 'Is your boat strong enough?' he asked.

'You let me worry about that,' the skipper chuckled. 'A boat that can live in the South Atlantic winter gales is strong enough for anything.' He handed Raleigh the small canvas airline bag that contained his street clothes. 'We will meet again soon then, my friend?'

'You can be sure of that, comrade,' Raleigh said quietly and went up the gangplank onto the wharf.

Raleigh changed out of his trawlerman's gear in the public toilet near the harbour gates, and then went across to the carpark behind the customs house. Ramsami's old Toyota was parked up against the fence, and Raleigh climbed into the back seat.

Sammy Ramsami looked up from the copy of *The Cape Times* he was reading. He was a good-looking young Hindu lawyer who specialized in political cases. For the previous four years he had represented Vicky Gama in her neverending legal battle with authority, and he had accompanied her from the Transvaal on this visit to her husband.

'Did you get what you wanted?' he asked, and Raleigh grunted noncommittally.

'I don't want to know what this is all about,' Sammy Ramsami said, and Raleigh smiled coldly.

'Don't worry, comrade, you will not be burdened with that knowledge.'

They did not speak again, not for the next four hours while they waited for Vicky to return from the island. She came at last, tall and stately in her brilliant caftan and turban, the child beside her, and the coloured stevedores working on the dock recognized her and cheered her as she passed.

She came to the Toyota and climbed into the front seat with the child on her lap.

'He is on another hunger strike,' she said. 'He has lost so much weight he looks like a skeleton.'

'That will make our work a lot easier,' said Sammy Ramsami and he started the Toyota.

At nine o'clock the next morning Ramsami presented an urgent application to the Supreme Court for an order that a private physician be allowed access to the prisoner Moses Gama, and as grounds to support his application he presented the sworn affidavits of Victoria Dinizulu Gama and the local representative of the International Red Cross as to the deterioration in the prisoner's physical and mental condition.

The judge in chambers issued an order calling on the Minister of Justice to show cause within twenty-four hours why the access order should not be granted. The state attorney general opposed the application strenuously, but after listening to Mr Samuel Ramsami's submission, the judge granted the order.

The physician named in the order was Dr Chetty Abrahamji, the same man who had delivered Tara Courtney's son. He was a consulting physician at Groote Schuur Hospital. In company with the government district physician, Dr Abrahamji made the ferry trip out to Robben Island where for three hours he examined the prisoner in the prison clinic.

At the end of the examination he told the state doctor, 'I don't like this at all. The patient is very much under weight, complaining of indigestion and chronic constipation. I don't have to spell out what those presentations suggest.'

'Those symptoms have been caused by the fact that the prisoner has been on a hunger strike. In fact I have been considering attempting to force-feed.'

'No, Doctor,' Abrahamji interrupted him. 'I see the

symptoms as much more significant. I am ordering a CAT scan.'

'There are no facilities available for a CAT scan on the island.'

'Then he will have to be moved to Groote Schuur for the examination.'

Once again the state attorney general opposed the order for the prisoner to be moved from Robben Island to Groote Schuur Hospital, but the judge was influenced by Dr Abrahamji's written report and impressed by his verbal evidence and once again granted the order.

Moses Gama was brought to the mainland amid the strictest conditions of secrecy and security. No previous warning of the move was given to any person outside those directly involved, to prevent the organization of any form of demonstration by liberal political bodies, and to frustrate the intense desire of the press to obtain a photograph of this patriarch of black aspirations.

It was necessary, however, to give Dr Abrahamji twenty-four hours' advance notice to enable him to reserve the use of the test equipment at the hospital, and the police moved into the area of the hospital the evening before the transfer. They cleared the corridors and rooms through which the prisoner would move of all but essential hospital staff, and searched them for explosives or any indication of illegal preparations.

From the public telephone booth in the main hospital administration block Dr Abrahamji rang Raleigh Tabaka at Molly Broadhurst's house in Pinelands.

'I am expecting company at two o'clock tomorrow afternoon,' he said simply.

'Your guest must not leave you until after nightfall,' Raleigh replied.

'That can be arranged,' Abrahamji agreed, and hung up.

The prison ferry came in through the harbour entrance at one o'clock in the afternoon. The deadlights of the cabin portholes were closed, and there were armed prison warders on deck, fore and aft, and their vigilance was apparent, even from where Raleigh was working on the foredeck of the trawler.

The ferry sailed across the harbour to 'A' berth, its usual mooring. There was an armoured prison van waiting on the dock, with four motor-cycle police in uniform and a grey police Land-Rover. Through the riot screens on the cab of the Land-Rover Raleigh could make out the shape of helmets and the short thick barrels of automatic shotguns held at port arms.

As the ferry touched the wharf, the prison van reversed up and the rear doors swung open. The armed warders seated on the padded benches in the body of the truck jumped down to meet the prisoner. Raleigh had just a glimpse of a tall gaunt figure in plain prison khaki uniform as he was hustled up the gangplank and into the waiting van, but even across the width of the harbour basin he could see that Moses Gama's hair was now pure silvery white, and that he was manacled at the wrists and that heavy leg-irons hampered his gait.

The doors of the van slammed shut. The motor-cycle escort closed information around it and the Land-Rover followed closely behind it as it sped away towards the main dock gates.

Raleigh left the trawler and Molly Broadhurst was waiting for him beyond the main gates. They drove up the lower slopes of Table Mountain to where the hospital stood, a massive complex of white walls and red clay tiles below the stone pines and open meadows of Rhodes Estate and the tall grey rock buttresses of the mountain itself. Raleigh made a careful note of the time required for the journey from the docks to the hospital.

They drove slowly up the busy road to the main entrance of the hospital. The police Land-Rover, motor-cycles and armoured van were lined up in the public carpark beyond the entrance to the out-patients section. The warders had doffed their riot helmets and were standing around the vehicles in relaxed attitudes.

'How will Abrahamji keep him there until dark?' Molly wanted to know.

'I did not ask,' Raleigh replied. 'I expect he will keep on demanding further tests, or will deliberately sabotage the machinery – I don't know.'

Raleigh turned the car in a circle in front of the main entrance and they drove back down the hill.

'You are sure there is no other way to leave the hospital grounds?' Raleigh asked.

'Quite sure,' Molly replied. 'The van must pass here. Drop me at the bus stop. It will be a long wait and at least I will have a bench to sit on.'

Raleigh pulled into the kerb. 'You have the number of the telephone on the dock, and coins?' She nodded.

'Where is your nearest telephone from here?' he insisted.

'I have checked it all carefully. There is a public phone booth at the corner.' She pointed. 'It will take two minutes for me to reach it, and if it is out of order or occupied, there is another telephone in the café across the street. I have already made friends with the proprietor.'

Raleigh left her at the bus stop and drove back to the centre of town. He left Molly's car in the side street they had agreed upon so that it would not be found at the docks or anywhere in the vicinity and he walked back down the Heerengracht showing his seaman's papers at the gate.

The skipper of the trawler was in the wheelhouse and he handed Raleigh a mug of heavily sweetened coffee which he sipped as they went over the final arrangements.

'Are my men ready?' Raleigh asked as he stood up, and the skipper shrugged. 'That is your business, not mine.'

They were in the bottom of the trawler's deep hold

where the heat in the unventilated space was oppressive. Robert and Changi were stripped to vests and jogging shorts. They jumped up as Raleigh came down the ladder.

'So far it goes well,' Raleigh assured them. They were old companions from the PAC *Poqo* days, and Changi had been at Sharpeville on the terrible day that Amelia died.

'Are you ready?' Raleigh asked him.

'We can check,' Changi suggested. 'Once more will not hurt us.'

The inflatable Zodiac boat that stood on the floor of the hold was the seventeen-foot six-inch model that could carry ten adults with ease. The fifty-horsepower Evinrude outboard motor could push it at thirty knots. The cover of the engine had been painted matt black.

The rig had been stolen by Robert and Changi working together from the yard of a boat dealer two days before, and could not be traced back to any of them.

'The engine?' Raleigh demanded.

'Robert has checked and serviced it.'

'I even changed the gear-box oil,' Robert agreed. 'She runs beautifully.'

'Tanks?'

'Both full,' Robert said. 'We have a range of a hundred miles or better.'

'Wet-suits?'

'Check,' Changi said. 'And thermal blankets for the leader.'

'Tools?' Raleigh asked, and Changi opened the padded flotation bag and laid out the tools on the deck, checking each as Raleigh called them from his list.

'Good,' Raleigh agreed at last. 'You can rest now. Nothing more to do.'

Raleigh climbed up out of the hold. It was still too early. He glanced at his wristwatch. Not yet four o'clock, but he left the trawler and went down the dock to the public telephone booth at the end.

He telephoned directory enquiries and asked for a fictitious number in Johannesburg, just to make certain the line was in order. Then he sat on the edge of the wharf with his legs dangling and watched the seagulls squabbling over the offal and refuse that floated on the harbour waters.

It was fully dark by seven-forty but it was another twenty minutes before the telephone in the booth rang and Raleigh jumped up.

'They are on their way.' Molly's voice was soft and muffled.

'Thank you, comrade,' Raleigh said. 'Go home now.'

He hurried back down the wharf and the trawler skipper had seen him coming. As Raleigh jumped down on to the dock the two deckhands threw off the lines. The big caterpillar motor blustered and the trawler surged away from the dock and headed out through the entrance.

Raleigh swarmed down into the hold where Robert and Changi were already in their wet-suits. They had Raleigh's suit laid out for him and they helped him into it.

'Ready?' one of the deckhands called down from above.

'Send it down,' Raleigh shouted back, and they watched the arm of the derrick swing out over the hold, silhouetted against the stars, and the line came down from the boom.

The three of them worked swiftly, hooking the Zodiac on, but before they had finished the beat of the trawler's engine died away and the motion of the hull in the water changed as the vessel's way died and she began to drift.

Raleigh led them up the ladder on to the deck. The night was moonless, but the stars were bright and clear. The light breeze was from the south-east, so there was unlikely to be a change in this fair weather. All the trawler's navigational lights and the lights in the wheelhouse were extinguished.

Cape Town was ablaze with lights. The mountain was floodlit, a great ghostly silver hulk under the stars, while behind them the lights on Robben Island twinkled low on the black sea. Raleigh judged that they were about half-way between the city and the island.

The skipper was waiting for him on deck.

'We must move fast now,' he said.

Robert and Changi climbed into the Zodiac. Their wet-suits were black, the rubber sides of the boat were black and the engine cover of the Evinrude was black. They would be almost invisible on the black waters.

'Thank you, comrade,' Raleigh said and offered the skipper his hand.

'*Amandla!*' said the skipper as he gripped it. 'Power!' and Raleigh took his place in the bows of the Zodiac.

The winch clattered and the Zodiac rose swaying, swung out over the side, and then fell swiftly to the surface of the water.

'Start up,' Raleigh instructed, and Robert whipped the starter cord and the engine fired and caught with the first pull.

'Case off,' Raleigh ordered, and Changi unhooked the line from the boom, while Robert manoeuvred the Zodiac alongside the trawler and tied on to the light line from the rail. He let the engine idle for five minutes to warm it thoroughly and then cut it.

The two vessels lay silently linked together and the minutes passed torturously.

Suddenly the skipper called down. 'I have them in sight.'

'Are you certain?' Raleigh cupped his hands around his mouth to reply.

'I've seen that ferry every day of my life.' The skipper was leaning over the rail. 'Start your motor and cast off.'

The Evinrude roared into life and the Zodiac dropped back astern of the trawler. Now Raleigh could make out the ferry. It was coming almost directly towards them; both the green and red navigational lights showed.

The trawler moved forward, a wash of white water churning out from under her stern. She was still completely blacked out, and her speed built up rapidly. The skipper had assured Raleigh that she was capable of fourteen knots. She turned in a wide arc across the black surface and headed straight for the approaching ferry at speed.

Robert ran the Zodiac out to one side, and dropped back slightly, shearing off two hundred feet from the larger vessel.

The ferry held its course. Clearly it hadn't spotted the darkened ship bearing down out of the night. Raleigh stood up in the bows of the Zodiac, steadying himself with two turns of the painter around his wrist, and he watched the two vessels come together. The ferry was half the length of the steel-hulled trawler and it lay much lower in the water.

At the very last moment somebody on board the ferry shouted and then the bows of the trawler crashed into her, taking her just forward of the beam. Raleigh had warned the skipper not to damage the cabin and risk harming the occupants.

The trawler checked and the bows rose high as she trod the smaller vessel down, and then the ferry rolled over in a flurry of foam and breaking water. The trawler drove over her, broke free of her swamped hull, and went dashing away into the darkness. Within a hundred yards she had disappeared.

'The chains will pull him under,' Raleigh shouted. 'Work quickly!' He fitted his face plate over his mouth and nose.

Robert sent the Zodiac roaring alongside the sinking ferry. She had turned turtle and her bottom was painted with orange antifouling. Her lights were still burning beneath the water and there were three or four swimming warders thrashing around, trying to get a grip on the sides.

Raleigh and Changi, each carrying a short jemmy bar, slid over the side and dived under the trawler's submerged transom.

Raleigh jammed the point of the jemmy into the lock of the cabin door and with a single heave tore it away. The door slid back and a burst of trapped air exploded in silver bubbles around his head.

The cabin was flooded, but the lights were still burning, lighting the interior like a goldfish bowl, and a confusion of bodies, clad in the serge uniform of the Prison Service, were struggling and kicking and swirling around the cabin. Amongst them Raleigh picked out the khaki cotton drill tunic of a prisoner. He seized a handful of it and pulled Moses Gama clear.

Changi took Moses Gama's other arm and they swam him between them out from under the heaving transom and up to the surface. It had taken less than sixty seconds since the trawler had rammed, and Robert gunned the Zodiac up to them the moment they surfaced. He reached down and caught hold of Moses Gama's arm, the two men in the water heaved from under him and he rolled over the side of the Zodiac on to the floor boards.

Raleigh and Changi seized the loops of rope on the Zodiac's side to pull themselves up and the moment they were on board Robert gunned the Evinrude and they shot away from the foundering vessel. The splashing and cries of distress faded behind them as Robert turned the Zodiac back towards the shore. The long deserted stretch of Woodstock beach showed as a pale line of sand and surf in the starlight ahead.

Raleigh stripped off his face plate and leaned solicitously over the figure on the deck. He lifted him into a sitting position, and Moses Gama coughed painfully.

'I see you, my uncle,' Raleigh said softly.

'Raleigh?' Moses' voice was rough with the salt water he had swallowed. 'Is it you, Raleigh?'

'We will be ashore in ten minutes, my uncle.' Raleigh tucked one of the thermal blankets around Moses' shoulders. 'All the plans for your escape have been carefully laid. Everything's ready for you, my uncle. Soon now you will be where nobody can touch you.'

Robert ran the rubber inflatable in through the surf at full throttle and they shot up the sand, clear of the water. As they came to a standstill, they lifted Moses Gama out of the Zodiac and ran with him up the beach, carrying him between them so his chained feet barely touched the sand.

There was a small closed van parked amongst the dunes and Raleigh jerked the rear doors open and they lifted Moses into the back and laid him on the mattress that covered the floorboards. Changi jumped in beside him and Raleigh slammed the rear doors closed. Robert would take the Zodiac out and sink it.

Raleigh stripped off the jacket of his wet suit. The key to the van was on a loop of nylon line around his neck. He opened the driver's door and slid behind the wheel. The van was facing back along the track. The track joined the road that skirted the industrial area of Paarden Eiland and Raleigh drove sedately along it, towards the black township of Langa.

The official Cape Town residence of the Minister of Police was one of those clustered around the Prime Minister's residence at Groote Schuur. The cumbersome physical division of the legislative and excutive arms of government between the cities of Cape Town and Pretoria made for costly duplications. During the annual session of parliament in Cape Town all the ministers and the entire diplomatic corps were forced to move down from Pretoria a thousand miles to the north, and official residences had to be maintained in both cities at enormous expense.

Manfred De La Rey's ministerial residence was an elegant Edwardian mansion set in acres of its own private lawns and gardens. As Roelf Stander parked his shabby little second-hand Morris in front of this imposing building, it seemed oddly out of place.

Sarah Stander had been desperately trying to arrange a private meeting with Manfred ever since her son had been convicted and sentenced to death. However, Manfred had been in Pretoria, or at his ranch in the Free State, or opening a memorial to the women who had died in the British concentration camps during the Boer War, or addressing the National Party caucus, and therefore unable to see her.

Sarah had persisted, telephoning his office at parliament every day, telephoning Heidi at home and pleading with her, until at last Manfred had agreed to see her at seven o'clock in the morning before he left for parliament.

Sarah and Roelf had driven in the Morris from Stellenbosch, leaving before sun-up so as not to be late for the appointment. When the coloured butler showed them through to the dining-room, Manfred and Heidi were seated at the breakfast table.

Heidi sprang up and came to kiss Sarah's cheek.

'I am sorry we have not seen you for so long, Sarie.'

'Yes,' Sarah agreed bitterly. 'I also am sorry – but as you explained to me, Manie has been too busy for us.'

Manfred stood up from the head of the table. He was in his shirt-sleeves and the linen table napkin was tucked into the top of his dark suit trousers.

'Roelf,' he smiled, and they shook hands like old friends.

'Thank you for agreeing to see us, Manie,' Roelf said humbly. 'I know how busy you are these days.' The years had not been kind to Roelf Stander, he had greyed and shrunk and Manfred felt a secret satisfaction as he studied him.

'Sit down, Roelf.' Manfred led him to a place at the breakfast table. 'Heidi has ordered breakfast for you – will you start with porridge?'

He seated Roelf and then reluctantly turned back to Sarah. She was still standing beside Heidi.

'Hello, Sarie,' he said. She had been such a pretty little thing. They had grown from childhood together. There were still the remains of that girlhood beauty in her eyes and the shape of her face. The memory of the love they had once shared rushed back to him, and he felt the sweet nostalgic yearning for his youth. He had a vivid image of her lying naked on a bed of pine needles in the forest high up on the slopes of the Hottentots Holland mountains on the day that they had become lovers.

He searched in his heart for a vestige of what he had felt for her then, but he found none. Any love that once had flowered between them had been smothered by the knowledge of her treachery. For more than two decades he had delayed his revenge, contenting himself with slowly undermining and reducing this woman to her present state, waiting for exactly the right moment to extract the final retribution. It had come – and he savoured the moment.

'Hello, Manie,' she whispered, and she thought, 'He has been so cruel. He has filled my life with pain that has been difficult to bear. Now all I ask from him is my son's life – surely he will not deny me that also.'

'So, why have you come to see me?' Manie asked, and Heidi led Sarah to a seat at the table. She took the silver teapot from the coloured servant and told him, 'Thank you, Gamat, you can leave us now. Please close the door.' And she poured steaming coffee into Sarah's cup.

'Yes, Sarie,' she agreed. 'Tell us why you have come to see us.'

'You know why I have come to you,' Sarah said. 'It is Kobus.'

A deathly stillness held them all over the slow passage of the seconds, and then Manfred sighed.

'Ja,' he said. 'Kobus. Why do you come to me about Kobus?'

845

'I want you to help him, Manie.'

'Kobus has been tried and convicted of a sickening act of senseless brutality,' Manfred said slowly. 'The highest court in the land has decreed that he must die on the gallows. How can I help Kobus?'

'The same way you helped that black terrorist, Moses Gama.' Sarah was pale and the coffee cup clattered as she tried to set it down on the saucer. 'You saved his life – now save the life of my son.'

'The state president exercised leniency in Gama's case—'

'No, Manie,' Sarah interrupted. 'It was you that changed it. I know – you have the power to save Kobus.'

'No.' He shook his head. 'I haven't got that sort of power. Kobus is a murderer. The worst kind of killer – one without compassion or remorse. I cannot help him.'

'You can. I know you can, Manie. Please, I beg of you, save my son.'

'I cannot.' Manfred's expression set. His mouth hardened into a straight unrelenting line. 'I will not.'

'You must, Manie. You have no choice – you must save him.'

'Why do you say that?' He was becoming angry. 'There is nothing I *must* do.'

'You must save him, Manie, because he is your son also. He is the child of our love, Manie, you have no choice. You must save him.'

Manfred sprang to his feet and placed his hand protectively on Heidi's shoulder. 'You come into my house and insult me and my wife.' His voice shook with the force of his anger. 'You come here with wild stories and accusations.'

Roelf Stander had sat quietly through it all, but now he lifted his head and spoke softly. 'It is true, Manie. Every word she tells you is true. I knew she was carrying your

846

child when I married her. She told me frankly. You had deserted her – you had married Heidi and I loved her.'

'You know it is true,' Sarah whispered. 'You have always known, Manie. You cannot have looked into Kobus' eyes without knowing. Both your sons have your yellow eyes, Manie, Lothar and Kobus – both of them. You know he is your son.'

Manfred sank back on to his chair. In the silence Heidi reached across and deliberately took his hand. That reassuring touch seemed to rally him.

'Even if that were true, there is nothing I would do. No matter whose son he is, justice must run its course. A life for a life. He must pay the penalty for his deed.'

'Manie, please. You must help us—' Sarah was weeping now, and the tears at last spilled down her pale cheeks. She tried to throw herself at Manfred's feet, but Roelf caught her and held her. She struggled weakly in his arms, but he held her and looked at Manfred.

'In the name of our friendship, Manie, everything we have done and shared – won't you help us?' he pleaded.

'I am sorry for you, Roelf.' Manfred stood up again. 'You must take your wife home now.'

Roelf drew Sarah gently towards the door, but before they reached it Sarah pulled out of his hands and faced Manfred again.

'Why?' she cried in anguish. 'I know you can – why will you not help us?'

'Because of you White Sword failed,' he said softly. 'That is why I will not help you.'

She was struck dumb by the words, and Manfred turned to Roelf. 'Take her away now,' he ordered. 'I have finished with her at last.'

During the long journey back to Stellenbosch Sarah huddled in the passenger seat and sobbed brokenly. Only when Roelf parked the Morris outside their cottage did she straighten up, and her voice and her face were ruined with grief.

'I hate him,' she repeated. 'Oh God, how I hate him.'

'I spoke to David Abrahams this morning,' Isabella said, leaning forward in the saddle to pat the mare's neck so that her father couldn't see her face. 'He offered me a job at the Johannesburg office.'

'Correction,' said Shasa. 'You telephoned David and told him that Johannesburg needed a PRO at a salary of two thousand a month plus dress allowance plus five-day week and a company car – and I believe you even stipulated the make, Porsche 911, wasn't it? David called me the minute you hung up.'

'Oh, Daddy, don't be so technical.' Isabella tossed her head defiantly. 'You wouldn't want me to dress in rags and starve up there, would you?'

'What I would want is for you to stay here where I can keep an eye on you.' Shasa felt the leaden weight of impending loss in his chest as he looked at her. She was the spice of his life, and she had only been back from London a month or so. Now she wanted to be off again. His instinct was to fight to keep her, but Centaine had advised, 'Let them go gently, and there is a chance they will come back to you.'

'It isn't Siberia or the Outer Hebrides, Daddy. Do be practical. It's just up the road.'

'A thousand miles up the road,' Shasa agreed. 'And much closer to the rugby stadium at Loftus Versveld.'

'I don't know what you mean.' It was very seldom Shasa could catch her off-balance, and vindictively he relished her agitation.

'Rugby football,' he explained. 'Great sweaty oafs beating their bony heads together.'

She recovered splendidly. 'Pater, if this has anything to do with Lothar De La Rey, I would just like to point out that he is one of the greatest athletes of our time and the youngest brigadier in the history of the police force – and that he means absolutely nothing to me at all.'

'Your indifference is monumental. I am greatly relieved.'

'Does that mean I can accept David's job offer?'

Shasa sighed and the loneliness descended upon him like a winter's evening. 'How can I stop you, Bella?'

She let out a triumphant squeal and leaned out of the saddle to wrap those long tanned arms around his neck, and Shasa's stallion danced under him with aristocratic affront.

Isabella chattered merrily all the way back to the château.

'One thing I forgot to mention to David was a housing allowance. Flats are so awfully expensive in Joey's. I couldn't find anything suitable on the pittance he is paying me.' Shasa shook his head with admiration.

The grooms were waiting in the kitchen yard to take the horses, and still in their jodhpurs and riding boots they went through to the breakfast room with Isabella hanging lovingly on her father's arm.

Centaine was at the sideboard, helping herself to scrambled eggs from the chafing dish. She was still in her gardening clothes and had been amongst her roses since dawn. Now she looked at Isabella inquiringly – and Isabella gave her a happy wink.

'Damn it,' Shasa intercepted the exchange. 'I've been set up. It's a conspiracy.'

'Of course I told Nana first.' Isabella hugged his arm. 'I always start at the top.'

'When she was little I always threatened to hand her over to a policeman if she was naughty,' Centaine said complacently as she carried her plate to the breakfast table. 'I hope this policeman can cope with her.'

'He's not a policeman,' Isabella protested. 'He's a brigadier.'

Shasa ladled eggs and fried tomato onto his plate and went to his place at the head of the table. The morning paper was folded neatly on his side plate, and he shook it open at the front page as he sat down. The main news was the proposed meeting between the British Prime Minister, Harold Wilson, and Ian Smith to settle the Rhodesian issue. Now he saw that the suggested venue was a British warship at sea. Israel and Jordan were still disputing the Hebron Valley, and closer to home the Robben Island ferry had capsized during the night with the certain loss of at least two lives, while eight others were missing.

The telephone on the sideboard rang and Centaine looked up from buttering her toast. 'That will be Garry,' she said. 'He rang twice while you were out riding.'

'It's only eight o'clock in the morning,' Shasa protested, but he went to answer the telephone. 'Hello, Garry, where are you?'

Garry sounded surprised. 'At the office, of course.'

'What's the problem?'

'Swimming-pools,' Garry answered. 'I have a chance to get the franchise for a new process of making cheap swimming-pools. It's called Gunite. Holly and I saw it when we were on honeymoon in the States.'

'Good Lord, only the very rich can afford private swimming-pools,' Shasa protested.

'Everybody will buy my swimming-pools – every home in the country will have one by the time I'm finished.'

Garry's enthusiasm was infectious.

'It works, Pater. I've seen it, and the figures add up perfectly. Only trouble is I have to give an answer by noon today. Someone else is interested.'

'How much?' Shasa asked.

'Four million initially – that's for the franchise and

plant. Another four million over two years for running costs, then we will be into profit.'

'All right,' Shasa said. 'Go ahead.'

'Thanks, Pater. Thanks for trusting me.'

'Well, you haven't let me down yet. How is Holly?'

'She's fine. She's right here with me.'

'At the office at eight in the morning?' Shasa laughed.

'Of course.' Again Garry sounded surprised. 'We are a team. The swimming-pools were her idea.'

'Give her my love,' Shasa said and hung up.

As he went back to his seat, Centaine said, 'It's the Prime Minister's budget vote this afternoon. I thought I'd drop in.'

'It should be interesting,' Shasa agreed. 'I think Verwoerd is going to make a major policy speech about the country's international position. I have a committee meeting on armaments this morning, but why don't you meet me for lunch and you can listen to Doctor Henk's speech from the public gallery afterwards. I'll ask Tricia to get you a ticket.'

Tricia was waiting for him anxiously when an hour later Shasa walked into his parliamentary suite.

'The Minister of Police wants to see you most urgently, Mr Courtney. He asked me to let him know the moment you arrived. He said he'd come to your office.'

'Very well.' Shasa glanced at his appointment book on her desk. 'Let him know I'm here and then get a ticket for my mother for the public gallery this afternoon. Is there anything else?'

'Nothing important.' Tricia picked up the in-house telephone to ring the Minister of Police's office and then paused. 'There has been a strange woman ringing you this morning. She called three times. She wouldn't give her name and she asked for Squadron Leader Courtney. Funny, isn't it?'

'All right, let me know if she calls again.' Shasa was frowning as he went through to his own office. The use of his old Air Force rank was strangely disquieting. He went to his desk and began work on the mail and the memoranda that Tricia had placed on his blotter, but almost immediately the buzzer rang on his intercom.

'Minister De La Rey is here, sir.'

'Ask him to come right in, Tricia.'

Shasa rose and went to meet Manfred, but as they shook hands he could see that Manfred was a worried man.

'Did you read the news report about the sinking of the ferry?' Manfred did not even return his greeting but came immediately to business.

'I noticed it, but didn't read it all.'

'Moses Gama was on the boat when it sank,' Manfred said.

'Good Lord.' Shasa glanced involuntarily at the ivory and gold-leaf altar chest which still stood against the wall of his office. 'Is he safe?'

'He is missing,' Manfred said. 'He may have drowned, or he may be alive. Either way we are in a very serious predicament.'

'Escaped?' Shasa asked.

'One of the survivors, a prison officer, says that there were two vessels at the accident scene, a large ship without lights that collided with the ferry and another smaller craft that arrived seconds after the ferry capsized. In the darkness it was impossible to see any details. It is a distinct possibility that Gama was spirited away.'

'If he drowned, we will be accused of murdering him,' Shasa said softly, 'with disastrous international repercussions.'

'And if he is at large, we will face the possibility of a popular uprising of the blacks similar to Lange and Sharpeville.'

'What are you doing about it?' Shasa asked.

'The entire police force is on full alert. One of our best men, my own son Lothar, is flying down from the Witwatersrand in an Air Force jet to take charge of the investigation. He will land within the next few minutes. Navy divers are already attempting to salvage the wreckage of the ferry.'

For another ten minutes they discussed all the implications of the wreck, and then Manfred moved to the door.

'I will keep you informed as we get further news.'

Shasa followed him into the outer office, and as they passed Tricia's desk she stood up.

'Oh, Mr Courtney, that woman called again while you were with Minister De La Rey.' Manfred and Shasa both paused, and Tricia went on, 'She asked for Squadron Leader Courtney again, sir, and when I told her you were in conference, she said she had news for you about White Sword. She said you'd understand.

'White Sword!' Shasa froze and stared at her. 'Did she leave a number?'

'No, sir, but she said that you must meet her at the Cape Town railway station at five-thirty this afternoon. Platform four.'

'How will I know who she is?'

'She says she knows you by sight. You are merely to wait on the platform, she will come to you.'

Shasa was so preoccupied with the message that he did not notice Manfred De La Rey's reaction to the code name 'White Sword'. All colour had drained from Manfred's craggy features, and his upper lip and jowls were covered by a sheen of perspiration. Without another word he turned and strode out into the corridor.

The name 'White Sword' kept plaguing Shasa all through the Armscor meeting. They were discussing the new air-to-ground missiles for the Air Force but Shasa found it difficult to concentrate. He was plagued by the memory of his grandfather, that good and gentle man whom Shasa had loved and who had been murdered by White Sword. His death had been one of the fiercest tragedies of his young life, and the rage that he had felt at the brutal killing came back to him afresh.

'White Sword,' he thought. 'If I can find out who you are, even after all these years, you will pay, and the interest will be more onerous for the time the debt has stood.'

Manfred De La Rey went directly to his office at the end of the corridor after he had left Shasa. His secretary spoke to him as he passed her desk but he did not seem to hear her.

He locked the door to his own office, but did not sit at the massive mahogany desk. He prowled the floor restlessly, his eyes unseeing and his heavy jaws chewing like a bulldog with a bone. He took the handkerchief from his jacket pocket and wiped his chin and then paused to examine his face in the wall mirror behind his desk. He was so pale that his cheeks had a bluish sheen, and his eyes were savage as those of a wounded leopard caught in a trap.

'White Sword,' he whispered aloud. It was twenty-five years since he had used that code name, but he remembered standing on the bridge of the German U-boat, coming in towards the land in darkness, with his hair and great bushy beard dyed black, staring out at the signal fires on the beach where Roelf Stander waited for him.

Roelf Stander had been with him through all the dangerous days and the wild endeavours. They had planned many of their operations in the kitchen of the Stander cottage in the little village of Stellenbosch. It was there in that kitchen that he had given them the details of the action that would be the signal for the glorious uprising of Afrikaner patriots. And at all those meetings Sarah Stander had been present, a quiet unobtrusive presence, serving coffee and food, never speaking – but listening. It was only many years later that Manfred had been able to guess at how well she had listened.

In 1948, when the Afrikaners had at last won at the ballot box the power which they had failed to seize at the point of the sword, Manfred's hard and loyal work had been rewarded with a deputy minister's post in the Department of Justice.

One of his first acts had been to send for the files of the unsolved attempt on the life of Jan Smuts, and the murder of Sir Garrick Courtney. Before he destroyed the files he read them through carefully, and he learned that they had been betrayed. There had been a traitor in their gallant band of patriots – a woman who had telephoned the Smuts police officers to warn them of the assassination.

He had guessed at the woman's identity, but had never extracted his full retribution, waiting for the moment to ripen, savouring the thought of revenge over the decades, watching the traitor's misery, watching her growing old and bitter, while frustrating her husband's efforts to succeed in law and politics, in the guise of mentor and adviser, steering him into folly and disaster until Roelf Stander had lost all his sustenance, his property and his will to carry on. All that time Manfred had waited for the perfect moment for the final revenge stroke – and at last it had arrived. Sarah Stander had come to him to plead for the life of the bastard he had placed in her womb – and he had denied her. The pleasure of it had been exquisite, made more poignant by the years he had waited for it.

Now the woman had turned vindictive. He had not anticipated that. He had expected the blow to break and destroy her. Only the greatest good fortune had given him forewarning of this new betrayal she planned.

He turned from the mirror and sat down at his desk. He

reached determinedly for the telephone and told his secretary, 'I want Colonel Bester in the Bureau of State Security.'

Bester was one of his most trusted officers.

'Bester,' he barked. 'I want a detention order drawn up urgently. I will sign it myself, and I want it executed immediately.'

'Yes, Minister. Can you give me the name of the detainee?'

'Sarah Stander,' Manfred said. 'Her address is 16 Eike Laan, Stellenbosch. If the arresting officers cannot find her there, she should be on platform four of the Cape Town railway station at five-thirty p.m. this afternoon. The woman must speak to no one before she is arrested – your men must make certain of that.'

As Manfred hung up he smiled grimly. Under the law he had the power to arrest and detain any person for ninety days, and to hold that person completely *incommunicado*. A great deal could happen in ninety days. Things could change, a person might even die. It was all taken care of. The woman could cause no further trouble.

The telephone on his desk rang, and Manfred snatched it up, expecting it to be Bester again.

'Yes, what is it?'

'Pa, it's me – Lothie.'

'Yes, Lothie. Where are you?'

'Caledon Square. I landed twenty minutes ago, and I have taken over the investigation. There is news, Pa. The divers have found the ferry. There is no sign of the prisoner's body but the cabin door has been forced open. We must assume that he escaped. Worse than that, somebody engineered his escape.'

'Find him,' Manfred said softly. 'You must find Moses Gama. If we don't, the consequences could be disastrous.'

'I know,' Lothar said. 'We will find him. We have to find him.'

Centaine refused to eat the food in the parliamentary dining-room. 'It's not that I am fussy, *chéri*, in the desert I ate live locusts and meat that had lain four days in the sun, but—' She and Shasa walked down through the gardens, across the top end of town to the Café Royal on Greenmarket Square, where the first oysters of the season had arrived from Knysna lagoon.

Centaine sprinkled lemon juice and tabasco sauce, scooped a gently pulsating mouthful from the half shell and sighed with pleasure.

'And now, *chéri*,' she dabbed the juice from her lips, 'tell me why you are so far away that you do not laugh at even my best efforts.'

'I'm sorry, Mater.' Shasa signalled to the waiter to top up his champagne glass. 'I had a strange phone call this morning – and I haven't been able to concentrate on anything else. Do you remember White Sword?'

'How can you ask?' Centaine laid down her fork. 'Sir Garry was more dear to me than my own father. Tell me all about it.'

They spoke of nothing else for the rest of lunch, exploring together ancient memories of that terrible day on which a noble and generous man had died, a man who had been precious to them both.

At last Shasa called for the bill. 'It's half past one already. We will have to hurry to reach the House before it beings. I don't want to miss any part of Verwoerd's speech.'

At sixty-six years of age Centaine was still active and agile, and Shasa was not forced to moderate his stride for her. They were still talking animatedly as they passed St George's Cathedral and turned into the gardens.

Ahead of them two men sat on one of the park benches, and there was something about them that caught Shasa's attention even at a distance of a hundred yards. The taller of the pair was a swarthy complexioned man who wore the uniform of a parliamentary messenger. He sat very stiffly upright and stared straight ahead of him with a fixed expression.

The man beside him was also dark-haired but his face was colourless as putty and the dead black hair fell forward on to his forehead. He was leaning close to the parliamentary messenger, speaking into his ear as though imparting a secret, but the messenger's face was expressionless and he showed not the least reaction to the other man's words.

As they came level with the bench, Shasa leaned forward to see past Centaine, and at less than five paces looked directly into the pale face of the smaller of the men. His eyes were black and implacable as pools of liquid tar, but as Shasa studied him, the man deliberately turned his face away. Yet his lips kept moving, talking so softly to the man in the parliamentary uniform that Shasa could not catch even a murmur of his voice.

Centaine tugged at his sleeve. 'Chéri, you are not listening to me.'

'I'm sorry, Mater,' Shasa apologized absentmindedly.

'I wonder why this woman chose the railway station,' Centaine repeated.

'I suppose she feels safer in a public place,' Shasa hazarded, and glanced back over his shoulder. The two men were still on the bench, but even in his preoccupation with other things the passionless malevolence that Shasa had seen in that tar-black gaze made him shiver as though an icy wind had blown upon the back of his neck.

As they turned into the lane that led to the massive edifice of parliament, Shasa felt suddenly confused and uncertain. There was too much happening all around him over which he had no control. It was a sensation to which he was not accustomed.

Joe Cicero whispered the formula softly. 'You can feel the worm in your belly.'

'Yes,' the man beside him replied, staring straight ahead. Only his lips moved as he made the reply, 'I can feel the worm.'

'The worm asks if you have the knife.'

'Yes, I have the knife,' said the man. His father had been a Greek and he had been born illegitimate in Portuguese Mozambique of a mulatto woman. His mixed blood was not apparent. It seemed merely as though he was of Mediterranean extraction. Only Europeans were employed as messengers in the South African parliament.

'You can feel the worm in your belly,' Joe Cicero reinforced the man's conditioning.

'Yes, I can feel the worm.'

Eight times in the past few years he had been in mental institutions. It was while he was in the last of these that he had been selected and the conditioning of his mind accomplished.

'The worm asks if you know where to find the devil,' Joe Cicero told him. The man's name was Demetrio Tsafendas and he had been introduced into South Africa the previous year, once his conditioning was completed.

'Yes,' said Tsafendas. 'I know where to find the devil.'

'The worm in your belly orders you to go straight to where the devil is,' Joe Cicero said softly. 'The worm in your belly orders you to kill the devil.' Tsafendas stood up. He moved like an automaton. 'The worm orders you to go now!'

Tsafendas started towards the parliament building with an even, unhurried tread.

Joe Cicero watched him go. It was done. All the pieces had been placed with great care. At last the first boulder had started to roll down the hillside. It would gather others as it built up speed and momentum. Soon it would be a mighty avalanche and the shape of the mountain would be changed for ever.

Joe Cicero stood up and walked away.

The first person Shasa saw as he and Centaine walked up the front steps to the parliament entrance was Kitty Godolphin and his heart surged with excitement and unexpected pleasure. He hadn't seen her since that illicit interlude in the south of France eighteen months before. Shasa had chartered a luxury yacht and they had cruised as far as Capri. When they parted, she had promised to write – but she never kept her promises and here she was again with no warning, smiling that sweet girlish smile with the devilment in her eyes, coming to greet him as innocently and naturally as though their last kiss had been hours before.

'What are you doing here?' he demanded without any preliminaries, and Kitty said to Centaine, 'Hello, Mrs Courtney. How did such a nice cultured lady ever end up with such an ill-mannered son?'

Centaine laughed, she liked Kitty. Shasa thought that it was a case of kindred spirits. Kitty explained, 'I was in Rhodesia to get a profile on Ian Smith before he meets Harold Wilson, and I made a side trip for the speech that Verwoered is giving today, and of course to visit with you.'

They chatted for a few minutes, then Centaine excused herself. 'I must get a good seat in the gallery.'

As she moved away Shasa asked Kitty softly, 'When can I see you?'

'This evening?' Kitty suggested.

'Yes – oh no, damn it.' He remembered his rendezvous with the White Sword informer. 'Where are you staying?'

'The Nellie as usual.'

'Can I call you there later?'

'Sure,' she smiled. 'Unless I get any better offers.'

'You little bitch! Why don't you marry me?'

'I'm too good for you, buster.' It had become one of their stock jokes. 'But I don't mind an order of small beer and chips on the side. See you later.'

Shasa watched her climb the staircase towards the press gallery. Over all the years he had known her, she seemed not to have aged a day. She still had the body of a girl, and the light spring of youth in her step. He pushed back the sudden cold gloom of loneliness that threatened to engulf him and walked into the chamber.

The benches were filling. Shasa saw that the Prime Minister was in his seat at the head of the Government benches. He was talking to Frank Waring, the Minister of Sport, and the only other Englishman in the cabinet.

Verwoerd looked fit and vigorous. It seemed impossible that he had taken two revolver bullets through his skull and had come back with such power to dominate his own party and the entire chamber this way. He seemed to have an infinite capacity for survival and, of course, Shasa grinned cynically, the luck of the devil himself.

Shasa started towards his own seat, and Manfred De La Rey jumped up and came to intercept him.

He seized Shasa's arm and leaned close to him. 'The divers have raised the ferry. Gama's body is not in it and the door to the cabin has been forced. It looks as though the bastard has got clean away. But we have every exit from the country guarded and my men will get him. He cannot get away. I think the Prime Minister is going to make the announcement of his disappearance during his speech this afternoon.'

Shasa and Manfred began walking towards their seats on the front bench, when somebody bumped so roughly against Shasa that he exclaimed and glanced around. It was the uniformed messenger that Shasa had noticed on the park bench.

'Be careful, fellow,' Shasa snapped at him as he recovered his balance, but the man did not seem to hear.

Although his expression was vacant and his eyes staring and unseeing, the messenger walked with a quick determined step, brushing past Manfred and heading towards the Opposition benches on the left side of the Speaker's throne.

'Damned rude,' Shasa said, pausing to watch him.

Suddenly the messenger seemed to change his mind, he veered across the chamber and hurried towards where Dr Verwoerd was sitting. The Prime Minister saw him coming and looked up expectantly, supposing that the man had a message for him. Nobody else in the chamber seemed to be taking any notice of the messenger's erratic behaviour, but Shasa was watching with puzzlement.

As the messenger stood over Dr Verwoerd, he swept his dark uniform jacket open and Shasa saw the silver flash of steel.

'Good Christ!' he exclaimed. 'He's got a knife.'

The messenger lifted the blade and struck once, and strangely the Prime Minister was smiling, as though he did not realize what was happening. The blade came free and the silver was misted pink with blood.

Shasa started forward, but Manfred still had hold of his arm. 'The Manchurian Candidate,' he hissed and Shasa froze.

Standing over the Prime Minister, the assassin struck again and then again. With each blow the blood spurted down his white shirt front and Dr Verwoerd lifted his hands in a pathetic gesture of appeal.

At last the men closest to him realized what was happening and they leapt upon the assailant. A knot of struggling men swarmed over him, but the man was fighting back with a kind of demonic strength.

'Where is the Devil?' he shouted wildly. 'I'll get the Devil.'

They bore him to the green carpet and pinned him there.

Dr Verwoerd still sat in his seat staring down at his own chest from which the bright flood poured. Then he pulled the lapels of his jacket closed as though to hide the terrible sight of his own blood, and with a sigh slid forward and crumpled on to the carpeted floor of the chamber.

Shasa and Manfred De La Rey were in Shasa's parliamentary office when Tricia brought the news through.

'Gentlemen, the party whip has just telephoned. Dr Verwoerd has been declared dead on arrival at the Volks Hospital.'

Shasa went to the liquor cabinet behind his desk and poured two glasses of cognac.

They watched each other's eyes as they drank silently, and then Shasa lowered his glass and said, 'We must start at once to draw up a list of those we can rely on to support you. I think John Vorster is the man you will have to beat for the premiership, and his people will already be busy.'

They worked together through the afternoon preparing their lists, placing ticks and crosses and queries against the names. Telephoning, wheedling and extorting, arranging meetings, making promises and commitments, trading and compromising, and as the afternoon wore on a stream of important visitors, allies, passed through Shasa's suite.

While they worked, Shasa watched Manfred, and wondered again how fate had chosen such strange travelling companions as they were. It seemed that they had nothing in common except that one most vital trait – burning unrelenting ambition and hunger for power.

Well, it was at their fingertips now, almost within their grasp, and Manfred was a man possessed. The effect of his enormous force of character was apparent on the men who came up to Shasa's office suite. One by one they were swept along by it, and one by one they swore their allegiance to him.

Slowly it dawned upon Shasa that it was no longer a possibility – or even a probability. They were going to win. He knew in his guts and his heart. It was theirs – the premiership and the presidency between them. They were going to win.

In the heady excitement of it all the afternoon passed swiftly, the grandfather clock in the corner of Shasa's office chimed the hours softly, such a familiar sound that he hardly noticed it until it struck five and he started and jumped to his feet, confirming the time with his wristwatch.

'It's five o'clock.' He started towards the door.

'Where are you going? I need you here,' Manfred called after him. 'Come back, Shasa.'

'I'll be back,' Shasa answered, and ran into the outer office.

There were men waiting there, important men. They stood up to greet him, and Tricia called, 'Mr Courtney—'

'Not now.' Shasa ran past them. 'I'll back soon.'

It would be quicker on foot than trying to take the Jaguar through the five o'clock rush-hour traffic, and Shasa began to run.

He realized that the woman informer was so nervous and afraid that she would probably not linger at the rendezvous. He had to get there before the appointed time. As he ran he reviled himself for having forgotten such an important appointment, but it was all confusion and uncertainty.

He raced down the sidewalk, crowded with office workers relieved of the tedium of their day who poured out of the buildings. Shasa pushed and shoved, and weaved and ducked. Some of those he barged into shouted angrily after him.

He sprinted through the columns of slowly moving vehicles, and ran into the Adderley Street entrance of the railway station. The clock above the main concourse stood at five thirty-seven. He was already late, and platform four was at the far end of the building.

Wildly he raced down the concourse, and barged on to the quay. He slowed to a hurried walk, and made his way down the platform, examining the faces of the commuters waiting there. They stared back at him incuriously, and he glanced up at the platform clock: five-forty. Ten minutes late. She had come and gone. He had missed her.

He stood in the centre of the platform and looked despairingly around him, not certain what to do next. Overhead the public address system squawked, 'Train from Stellenbosch and the Cape Flats arriving platform four.'

That was it, of course. Shasa felt a vast relief. The train was late. She must be on the train, that was why she had chosen this place and time.

Shasa craned his head anxiously as the carriages rumbled slowly into the platform and, with a squeal and hiss of vacuum brakes, came to a halt. The doors were thrown open and passengers spewed out of them, beginning to move in a solid column towards the platform exit.

Shasa jumped up on the nearest bench, the better to see and to be seen.

'Mr Courtney.' A woman's voice. Her voice – he recognized it, even after all the years. 'Mr Courtney.'

He stood on tiptoe, trying to see over the heads of the passengers.

'Mr Courtney!' There she was, caught up in the crowd, trying to push her way through to him, and waving frantically to attract his attention.

He recognized her instantly. The shock immobilized him for a few seconds as he stared as he stared at her. It was the Stander woman, the one he had met briefly at Manfred's holiday cottage when he had flown there to make the cannery deal with him. That was years ago, but he remembered that she had called him Squadron Leader. He should have pieced it together at that time. How foolish and unperceptive he had been. Shasa was still standing on the bench staring at her, when suddenly something else caught his attention.

Two men were roughly pushing their way through the crowds of passengers. Two big men in dark ill-fitting suits and the fedora hats that were somehow the mark of the plain-clothes Security Police. Clearly they were making for the Stander woman.

At the same moment as Shasa, she saw the two detectives and her face went white with terror.

'Mr Courtney!' she screamed. 'Quickly – they are after me.' She broke out of the crowd and began to run towards Shasa. 'Hurry, please hurry.'

Shasa jumped down from the bench and ran to meet her, but there was an old woman carrying an armful of parcels in his way. He almost knocked her down, and in the moments it took to untangle himself, the two detectives had caught up with Sarah Stander, and seized her from either side.

'Please!' She gave a despairing scream, then with wild, improbable strength broke free of her captors, and ran the last few paces to Shasa.

'Here!' She thrust an envelope into Shasa's hand. 'Here it is.'

The two security officers had recovered swiftly and bounded after her. One of them seized both her arms from behind and dragged her away. The other came to confront Shasa.

'We are police officers. We have a warrant for the arrest of the woman.' He was panting with his efforts. 'She gave something to you. I saw it. You must hand it over to me.'

'My good man!' Shasa drew himself up and gave the detective his most haughty stare. 'Do you have any idea just who you are speaking to?'

'Minister Courtney!' The man recognized him then, and his confusion was comic. 'I'm sorry, sir. I didn't know—'

'What is your name, rank and serial number?' Shasa snapped.

'Lieutenant Van Outshoorn No. 138643.' Instinctively the man stood to attention.

'You can be sure you will hear more of this, Lieutenant,' Shasa warned him frostily. 'Now carry on with your other duties.' Shasa turned on his heel and strode away down the platform, tucking the envelope into his inner pocket, leaving the detective staring after him in dismay.

He did not open the envelope until he reached his office again. Tricia was still waiting for him.

'I was so worried when you ran out like that,' she cried. Good, loyal Tricia.

'It's all right,' he reassured her. 'It all worked out fine. Where is Minister De La Rey?'

'He left soon after you, sir. He said he would be at home at Groote Schuur. You could reach him there if you needed him.'

'Thank you, Tricia. You may go home now.'

Shasa went through to his own office and locked the door. He went to his desk and sat down in his studded leather chair. He took the envelope from his inner pocket and laid it in front of him on the desk blotter, and he studied it.

It was of cheap coarse paper, and his name was written in a round girlish hand. The ink had smeared and run.

'Meneer Courtney.'

Shasa was suddenly reluctant to touch it again. He had a premonition of some terrible revelation which would turn the even tenor of his existence into strife and turmoil.

He picked up the Georgian silver paper knife from his desk set and tested the point with his thumb. He turned the envelope over and slid the point of the knife under the flap. The envelope contained a sheet of ruled notepaper with a single line of writing in the same girlish script.

Shasa stared at it. There was no sense of shock. Deep in his subconscious he must have known the truth all along. It was the eyes, of course, the yellow topaz eyes of White Sword that had stared into his own on the day his grandfather died.

There was not even a moment of doubt, no twinge of incredulity. He had even seen the scar, the ancient gunshot wound in Manfred's body, the mark of the bullet he had fired at White Sword, and every other detail fitted perfectly.

'Manfred De La Rey is White Sword.'

From the moment they had first met that childhood day upon the fishing jetty at Walvis Bay, the fates had stalked them, driving them inexorably towards their destiny.

'We were born to destroy each other,' Shasa said softly, and reached for the telephone.

It rang three times before it was answered.

'De La Rey.'

'It's me,' Shasa said.

'*Ja*. I have been waiting.' Manfred's voice was weary and resigned, in bitter contrast to the powerful tones in which he had exhorted and rallied his supporters just a short while before. 'The woman reached you. My men have informed me.'

'The woman must be set free,' Shasa told him.

'It has been done already. On my orders.'

'We must meet.'

'*Ja*. It is necessary.'

'Where?' Shasa asked. 'When?'

'I will come to Weltevreden,' Manfred said, and Shasa was taken too much by surprise to respond. 'But there is one condition.'

'What is your condition?' Shasa asked warily.

'Your mother must be there when we meet.'

'My mother?' This time Shasa could not contain his amazement.

'Yes, your mother – Centaine Courtney.'

'I don't understand – what has my mother got to do with this business?'

'Everything,' said Manfred heavily. 'She has everything to do with it.'

When Kitty Godolphin got back to her suite that evening, she was in a mood of jubilation. Under her direction, Hank's camera had captured the dramatic moments as the bloodstained body of Dr Verwoerd was carried from the chamber to the waiting ambulance, and she had recorded the panic and confusion, the spontaneous unrehearsed words and expressions of his friends and his bitter enemies.

The moment she entered the suite, she booked a call through to her news editor at NABS in New York to warn him of the priceless footage she had obtained. Then she poured herself a gin and tonic and sat impatiently beside the telephone waiting for her call to come through.

She lifted it as it rang.

'Kitty Godolphin,' she said.

'Miss Godolphin.' A strange voice, speaking with a deep melodious African accent, greeted her. 'Moses Gama sends you his greetings.'

'Moses Gama is serving a life sentence in a high security prison,' Kitty replied brusquely. 'Don't waste my time, please.'

'Last night Moses Gama was rescued by warriors of the *Umkhonto we Sizwe* from the Robben Island prison ferry,' said the voice, and Kitty felt the flesh of her cheeks and lips go numb with the shock of it. She had read the reports of the ferry sinking. 'Moses Gama is in a safe place. He wishes to speak to the world through you. If you agree to meet him, you will be allowed to use your camera to record his message.'

For a full three seconds she could not answer. Her voice had failed her but her mind was racing. 'This is the big one,' she thought. 'This is the one that comes only once in a lifetime of work and striving.' She cleared her throat and said, 'I will come.'

'A dark blue van will arrive at the ballroom entrance to the hotel in ten minutes from now. The driver will flick his lights twice. You are to enter the rear doors of the van immediately, without speaking to any person.'

The vehicle was a small Toyota delivery van, and Kitty and Hank with the sound and camera equipment were cramped in the interior so that it was difficult to move, but Kitty crawled forward until she could speak to the driver.

'Where are we going?'

The driver glanced at her in the rear-view mirror. He was a young black man of striking appearance, not handsome but with a powerful African face.

'We are going into the townships. There will be police patrols and road-blocks. The police are everywhere searching for Moses Gama. It will be dangerous, so you must do exactly as I tell you.'

For almost an hour they were in the van, driving through darkened back streets, sometimes stopping and waiting in silence until a shadowy figure came out of the night to whisper a few words to the driver of the van, then going on again until at last they parked for the last time.

'From here we walk,' their guide told them, and led them down the alleys and secret routes of the gangs and comrades, slipping past the rows of township cottages, twice hiding while police Land-Rovers cruised past, and finally entering the back door of one of the thousands of identical undistinguished cottages.

Moses Gama sat at a table in the tiny back kitchen.

Kitty recognized him instantly although his hair was now almost completely silver and his great frame was skeletally wasted. He wore a white open-neck shirt and dark blue slacks, and as he rose to greet her, she saw that though he had aged and his body was ravaged, the commanding presence and his messianic dark gaze were as powerful as when she had first met him.

'I am grateful that you have come,' he told her gravely. 'But we have very little time. The Fascist police follow closely as a pack of wolves. I have to leave here within a short while.'

Hank was already at work, setting up his camera and lights, and he nodded to Kitty. She saw that the gritty reality of the surrounding, the bare walls and plain unadorned wooden furniture, would add drama to the setting, and Moses' silver hair and enfeebled condition would touch the hearts of her audience.

She had prepared a few questions in her mind, but they were unnecessary. Moses Gama looked at the camera and spoke with a sincerity and depth that was devastating.

'There are no prison walls thick enough to hold the longing of my people for freedom,' he said. 'There is no grave deep enough to keep the truth from you.'

He spoke for ten minutes and Kitty Godolphin who was old in experience and hardened in the ways of a naughty world was weeping unashamedly as he ended, 'The struggle is my life. The battle belongs to us. We will prevail, my people. *Amandla! Ngawethu!*'

Kitty went up to him and embraced him. 'You make me feel very humble,' she said.

'You are a friend,' he replied. 'Go in peace, my daughter.'

'Come.' Raleigh Tabaka took Kitty's arm and led her away. 'You have stayed too long already. You must leave now. This man's name is Robert. He will lead you.'

Robert was waiting at the kitchen door of the cottage.

'Follow me,' he ordered, and led them across the bare

dusty backyard, through the shadows to the corner of the road. There he stopped unexpectedly.

'What happens now?' Kitty asked in a whisper. 'Why are we waiting here?'

'Be patient,' Robert said. 'You will learn the reason soon.'

Suddenly Kitty was aware that they were not alone. There were others waiting like them in the shadows. She could hear them now, the murmur of voices, quiet but expectant. She could see them as her eyes adjusted to the night, many figures, in small groups, huddled beside the hedges or in the shelter of the buildings.

Dozens, no hundreds of people, men and women, and every moment their numbers increased as more came out of the night shadows, gathering round the cottage that contained Moses Gama, as though his presence was a beacon, a flame that, like moths, they could not resist.

'What is happening?' Kitty asked softly.

'You will see,' Robert replied. 'Have your camera ready.'

The people were beginning to leave the shadows, creeping closer to the cottage, and a voice called out, '*Baba!* Your children are here. Speak to us, Father.'

And another cried. 'Moses Gama, we are ready. Lead us!'

And then they began to sing, softly at first, '*Nkosi Sikelel' iAfrika* – God save Africa!' and the voices joined and began to harmonize, those beautiful African voices, thrilling and wonderful.

Then there was another sound, distant at first, but swiftly growing closer, the sobbing undulating wail of police sirens.

'Have your camera ready,' said Robert again.

As soon as the American woman and her cameraman had left the cottage, Moses Gama began to rise from the table.

'It is done,' he said. 'Now we can leave.'

'Not yet, my uncle,' Raleigh Tabaka stopped him. 'There is something else that we must do first.'

'It is dangerous to delay,' Moses insisted. 'We have been in this place too long. The police have informers everywhere.'

'Yes, my uncle. The police informers are everywhere.' Raleigh put a peculiar emphasis on his agreement. 'But before you go on to the place where the police cannot touch you, we must talk.'

Raleigh came to stand at the front of the table facing his uncle.

'This was planned with great care. This afternoon the white monster Verwoerd was assassinated in the racist parliament.'

Moses started. 'You did not tell me this,' he protested, but Raleigh went on quietly, 'The plan was that in the confusion after Verwoerd's assassination you would emerge to lead a spontaneous rising of our people.'

'Why was I not told of this?' Moses asked fiercely.

'Patience, my uncle. Hear me out. The men who planned this are from a cold bleak land in the north, they do not understand the African soul. They do not understand that our people will not rise until their mood is ready, until their rage is ripe. That time is not yet. It will take many more years of patient work to bring their rage to full fruit. Only then can we gather the harvest. The white police are still too strong. They would crush us by raising their little finger and the world would stand by and watch us die as they watched the rebellion in Hungary die.'

'I do not understand,' Moses said. 'Why have you gone this far if you did not intend to travel to the end of the road?'

'The revolution needs martyrs as well as leaders. The mood and temper of the world must be roused, for without them we can never succeed. Martyrs and leaders, my uncle.'

'I am the chosen leader of our people,' Moses Gama said simply.

'No, my uncle.' Raleigh shook his head. 'You have proved unworthy. You have sold out your people. In exchange for your life, you delivered the revolution into the hands of the enemy. You gave Nelson Mandela and the heroes of Rivonia to the foe. Once I believed you were a god, but now I know that you are a traitor.'

Moses Gama stared at him silently.

'I am glad you do not deny this, my uncle. Your guilt is proven beyond any doubt. By your action you have forfeited any claim to the leadership. Nelson Mandela alone has the greatness for that role. However, my uncle, the revolution needs martyrs.'

From the pocket of his jacket Raleigh Tabaka took something wrapped in a clean white cloth. He laid it on the table. Slowly he opened the bundle, taking care not to touch what it contained.

They both stared at the revolver.

'This pistol is police issue. Only hours ago it was stolen from a local police arsenal. The serial number is still on the police register. It is loaded with police-issue ammunition.'

Raleigh folded the cloth around the grip of the pistol. 'It still has the fingerprints of the police officers upon it,' he said.

Carrying the pistol he went round the table to stand behind Moses Gama's chair and placed the muzzle of the pistol at the back of his neck.

From outside the cottage they heard the singing begin.

'God save Africa.' Raleigh repeated the words. 'You are fortunate, my uncle. You have a chance to redeem yourself. You are going to a place where nobody can ever touch you again, and your name will live for ever, pure and unsullied. "The great martyr of Africa who died for his people."'

Moses Gama did not move or speak, and Raleigh went on softly, 'The people have been told you are here. They are gathered outside in their hundreds. They will bear witness to your greatness. Your name will live for ever.'

Then above the singing they heard the police sirens coming closer, wailing and sobbing.

'The brutal Fascist police have also been told that you are here,' Raleigh said softly.

The sound of the sirens built up and then there were the roar of engines, the squeal of brakes, the slamming of Land-Rover doors, the shouted commands, the pounding footsteps, and the crash of the front door being smashed in with sledgehammers.

As Brigadier Lothar De La Rey led his men in through the front door of the cottage, Raleigh Tabaka said softly, 'Go in peace, my uncle,' and he shot Moses Gama in the back of the head.

The heavy bullet threw Moses forward, his shattered head slammed face down upon the table, the contents of his skull and chips of white bone splattered against the wall and over the kitchen floor.

Raleigh dropped the police pistol onto the table and slipped out into the dark yard. He joined the watching throng in the street outside, mingling with them, waiting with them until the covered body was carried out of the front door of the cottage on a stretcher. Then he shouted in a strong clear voice, 'The police have murdered our leader. They have killed Moses Gama.'

As the cry was taken up by a hundred other voices, and the women began the haunting ululation of mourning, Raleigh Tabaka turned and walked away into the darkness.

A servant opened the front door of Weltevreden to Manfred De La Rey.

'The master is expecting you,' he said respectfully. 'Please come with me.'

He led Manfred to the gun room and closed the double mahogany doors behind him.

Manfred stood on the threshold. There was a log fire burning in the hearth of the stone fireplace and Shasa Courtney stood before it. He was wearing a dinner jacket and black tie and a new black silk patch over his eye. He was tall and debonair with silver wings of hair at his temples, but his expression was merciless.

Centaine Courtney sat at the desk below the gun racks. She also wore evening dress, a brocaded Chinese silk in her favourite shade of yellow with a necklace of magnificent yellow diamonds from the H'ani Mine. Her arms and shoulders were bare and in the muted light her skin seemed flawless and smooth as a young girl's.

'White Sword,' Shasa greeted him softly.

'*Ja*,' Manfred nodded. 'But that was long ago – in another war.'

'You killed an innocent man. A noble old man.'

'The bullet was intended for another – for a traitor, an Afrikaner who had delivered his people to the British yoke.'

'You were a terrorist then, as Gama and Mandela are terrorists now. Why should your punishment be any different from theirs?'

'Our cause was just – and God was on our side,' Manfred replied.

'How many innocents have died for what other men call "just causes"? How many atrocities have been committed in God's name?'

'You cannot provoke me.' Manfred shook his head. 'What I attempted was right and proper.'

'We shall see whether or not the courts of this land

agree with you,' Shasa said, and looked across the room to Centaine. 'Please ring the number on the pad in front of you, Mater. Ask for Colonel Bothma of CID. I have already asked him to be available to come here.'

Centaine made no move, and her expression, as she studied Manfred De La Rey, was tragic.

'Please do it, Mater,' Shasa insisted.

'No,' Manfred intervened. 'She cannot do it – and nor can you.'

'Why do you believe that?'

'Tell him, Mother,' said Manfred.

Shasa frowned quickly and angrily, but Centaine held up her hand to stop him speaking.

'It is true,' she whispered. 'Manfred is as much my son as you are, Shasa. I gave birth to him in the desert. Although his father took him still wet and blind from my child bed, although I did not see him again for almost thirteen years, he is still my son.'

In the silence one of the logs in the fireplace fell in a soft shower of ash and it sounded like an avalanche.

'Your grandfather has been dead for twenty years and more, Shasa. Do you want to break my heart by sending your brother to the gallows?'

'My duty – my honour,' Shasa faltered.

'Manfred was as merciful once. He had it in his power to destroy your political career before it began. At my request and in the knowledge that you were brothers, he spared you.' Centaine was speaking softly, but remorselessly. 'Can you do less?'

'But – he is only your bastard,' Shasa blurted.

'You are my bastard also, Shasa. Your father was killed on our wedding day, before the ceremony. That was the fact that Manfred could have used to destroy you. He had you in his power – as he is now in your power. What will you do, Shasa?'

Shasa turned away from her, and stood with his head bowed staring into the fireplace. When he spoke at last, his voice was racked with pain.

'The friendship – the brotherhood even – all of it is an illusion,' he said. 'It is you, Mater, whom I must honour.'

No one replied to him, and he turned back to Manfred.

'You will inform the caucus of the National Party that you are not available for the premiership and you will retire from public life,' he said quietly, and saw Manfred flinch and the ruination of his dreams in the agony of his expression. 'That is the only punishment I can inflict upon you, but perhaps it is more painful and lingering than the gallows. Do you accept it?'

'You are destroying yourself at the same time,' Manfred told him. 'Without me the presidency is beyond your grasp.'

'That is my punishment,' Shasa agreed. 'I accept it. Do you accept yours?'

'I accept,' said Manfred De La Rey. He turned to the double mahogany doors, flung them open and strode from the room.

Shasa stared after him. Only when they heard his car pull away down the long driveway did he turn back to Centaine. She was weeping as she had wept on the day that he brought her the news of Blaine Malcomess' death.

'My son,' she whispered. 'My sons.' And he went to comfort her.

A week after the death of Dr Hendrik Verwoerd, the caucus of the National Party elected Balthazar Johannes Vorster to the premiership of South Africa.

He owed his elevation to the awe-inspiring reputation that he had built for himself while he was Minister of Justice. He was a strong man in the mould of his predecessor and in his acceptance speech he stated boldly, 'My role is to walk fearlessly along the road already pointed out by Hendrik Verwoerd.'

Three days after his election he sent for Shasa Courtney.

'I wanted personally to thank you for your hard work and loyalty over the years, but now I think it is time for you to take a well-earned rest. I would like you to go as the South African Ambassador to the Court of St James in London. I know that with you there South Africa House will be in good hands.'

It was the classic dismissal, but Shasa knew that the golden rule for politicians is never to refuse office.

'Thank you, Prime Minister,' he replied.

Thirty thousand mourners attended the funeral of Moses Gama in Drake's Farm township.

Raleigh Tabaka organized the funeral and was the captain of the honour guard of *Umkhonto we Sizwe* that stood at the graveside and gave the ANC salute as the coffin was lowered into the earth.

Vicky Dinizulu Gama, dressed in her flowing caftan of yellow and green and black, defied her banning order to make a speech to the mourners.

Fierce and strikingly beautiful, she told them, 'We must devise a death for the collaborators and sell-outs that is so grotesquely horrible that not one of our people will ever dare to turn traitor upon us.'

The sorrow of the multitudes was so terrible that when a young woman amongst them was pointed out as a police informer they stripped her naked and whipped and beat her until she fell unconscious. Then they doused her with petrol and set her alight and kicked her while she burned. Afterwards the children urinated on her charred corpse. The police dispersed the mourners with tear gas and baton-charges.

Kitty Godolphin filmed it all, and when the footage was cut in with the Moses Gama interview and the graphic footage from the scene of his brutal slaying by the police, it was amongst the most gripping and horrifying ever shown on American television.

When Kitty Godolphin was promoted to head of NABS News, she became the highest-paid female editor in American television.

B efore taking up his post as ambassador in London, Shasa went on a four-week safari in the Zambezi valley with his eldest son. The Courtney Safaris hunting concession covered five hundred square miles of wonderful game-rich wilderness, and Matatu led Shasa to lion and buffalo and a magnificent old bull elephant.

The Rhodesian bush war was becoming deadly earnest. Sean had been awarded the Silver Cross of Rhodesia for gallantry and around the camp fire he described how he had won it.

'Matatu and I were following a big bull jumbo when we cut the spoor of twelve ZANU gooks. We dropped the jumbo and tracked the terrs. It was pissing with rain and the cloud was on the treetops so the fire force couldn't get in to back us up. The terrs were getting close to the Zambezi so we pushed up on them. The first warning we had that they had set an ambush for us was when we saw the fairy lights in the grass just ahead of us.

'Matatu was leading and he took the first burst in the belly. That made me fairly bitter and I went after the gooks with the old .577. It was five miles to the river and they ran like the clappers of hell, but I polished off the last two in the water before they could reach the Zambian side. When I turned around, there was Matatu standing right behind me. The little bugger had backed me up for five miles with his tripes hanging out of the hole in his guts.'

Across the camp fire the little Ndorobo's face had brightened as he heard his name mentioned, and Sean told him in Swahili, 'Show the *Bwana Makuba* your new belly button.'

Obligingly Matatu hoisted his tattered shirt tails and displayed for Shasa the fearsome scars the AK47 bullets had left on his stomach.

'You are a stupid little bugger,' Sean told him severely, 'running around with a hole in your guts, instead of lying down and dying like you should have. You are bloody stupid, Matatu.'

Matatu's whole body wriggled with pleasure. 'Bleddy stupid bugger,' he agreed proudly. He knew that this was the highest accolade to which he could possibly aspire, uttered as it was by the god-head of his entire firmament.

While Shasa was still packing his books and paintings for the journey to London, Garry and Holly moved into Weltevreden.

'I'll be over there for at least three years,' Shasa said. 'And when I come back we can talk again, but I shall probably get myself a flat in town. On my own the old place is just too big for me.'

Holly was pregnant, and prevailed on Centaine to stay on to help her 'just until the baby is born'.

'Holly is the only woman that Mater can stand within half a mile of her on a permanent basis,' Shasa remarked to Garry as the two ladies of Weltevreden began planning the redecoration of the nursery wing together.

I sabella's love affair with Lothar De La Rey survived in stormy seas and wild winds during the months of the enquiry into the death of Moses Gama.

The commission of inquiry exonerated Brigadier Lothar De La Rey with a verdict of 'No Guilt'. The local English-language as well as the international press jeered cynically at this verdict and an emergency meeting of the General Assembly of the United Nations passed a resolution calling for comprehensive mandatory sanctions on South Africa, which was predictably vetoed in the Security Council. However, amongst his own people, Lothar's reputation was greatly enhanced and the Afrikaans press lauded him as its chosen hero.

Not a week after the commission made its findings public, Isabella woke in the bedroom of her luxurious Sandton flat to find Lothar already fully dressed, standing over the bed and watching her with an expression of such deep regret that she sat up quickly, fully awake, and let the pink satin sheets fall to her waist.

'What is it, Lothie?' she cried. 'Why are you leaving so early? Why are you looking at me like that?'

'There will be a by-election in the Doornberg constituency. It's one of our safe seats. The party organizers have offered it to me, and I have accepted. I'm resigning my police commission and going into politics.'

'Oh, that's wonderful,' Isabella cried, and reached out to

him with both arms. 'I was reared on politics. We will make a great team, Lothie. I'll be an amazing help to you – you'll see!'

Lothar lifted his eyes from her naked breasts, but made no move to touch her, and she let her arms drop.

'What is it?' Her expression changed.

'I'm going back to my own people, Bella,' he said quietly. 'Back to my *Volk* and my God. I know what I want. I want one day to succeed where my father failed. I want the position he almost achieved, but I need a wife who is one of my own people. A good Afrikaner girl. I have already chosen her. I am going to her now. So we must say goodbye, Bella. Thank you. I will never forget you, but it is over now.'

'Get out,' she said. 'Get out – and don't come back.'

He hesitated and her voice rose to a scream, 'Get out, you bastard. Get out!'

He went to the bedroom door and closed it softly behind him, and Isabella snatched the water jug from the bedside table and hurled it at the door. It shattered and she threw herself face down on the bed and began to weep.

She cried all that day, and at nightfall went into the bathroom and filled the bath with hot water. Lothar had left a packet of razor blades on the shelf next to her douche bag, and she unwrapped one of them slowly and held it up in front of her eyes. It looked terrifyingly evil, and the light glinted on the edge, but she lowered it until it touched the skin of her wrist. It stung like a scorpion and she jerked her wrist away.

'No, Lothar De La Rey, I won't give you the satisfaction,' she said angrily, and dropped the blade into the toilet bowl and went back into the bedroom. She picked up the phone.

When she heard her father's voice, Isabella trembled with the shock of what she had almost done.

'I want to come home, Daddy,' she whispered.

'I'll send the jet for you,' Shasa said without hesitation. 'No, hell, I'll fly up to fetch you myself.'

She was waiting on the tarmac and she ran into his arms. Halfway back to Cape Town he touched her cheek and said, 'I'll need an official hostess at Highveld.' That was the ambassador's residence in London. 'I'm even prepared to renegotiate your salary.'

'Oh, Daddy,' she said. 'Why aren't all the men in the world like you!'

J akobus Stander was hanged in the Pretoria Central prison. Sarah Stander and her husband were waiting outside when the death notice was posted on the main gates of the prison.

The night that they returned to the cottage in Stellenbosch Sarah rose once Roelf was asleep and in the bathroom she took a massive overdose of barbiturates.

She was dead in the bed beside him when Roelf Stander woke the following morning.

M anfred and Heidi went to live on their farm in the Free State where Manfred raised pedigree merino sheep.

At the agricultural show in Bloemfontein Manfred won a blue ribbon for the champion ram on show three years in succession.

Always fleshly, Manfred put on a great deal of weight, eating out of boredom more than appetite. Only Heidi knew how he chaffed at inactivity, how much he longed to walk once again the corridors of power, and how pointless and frustrating he felt his existence had become.

He suffered his heart attack while wandering alone in the veld and shepherds found his body the next morning lying where he had fallen. Centaine flew up in the company jet to his funeral. She was the only member of the Courtney family present when Manfred was buried with full honours in Heroes' Acre, surrounded by the graves of many other outstanding Afrikaners, including Dr Hendrik Verwoerd.

When Shasa Courtney was driven back from Buckingham Palace in the ambassadorial limousine after presenting his credentials to Her Majesty Queen Elizabeth II, the streets were wet with the grey London drizzle.

Despite the weather, the demonstrators were waiting for him in Trafalgar Square with their placards: THE SPIRIT OF MOSES GAMA LIVES ON and *APARTHEID* IS A CRIME AGAINST HUMANITY.

As Shasa alighted from the limousine in front of the embassy, the demonstrators tried to push forward, but a line of blue-uniformed London bobbies linked arms to hold them back.

'Shasa Courtney!' Halfway across the sidewalk Shasa stopped dead in his tracks at the familiar voice, and he looked around.

He did not recognize her at first, then he saw her in the front rank of the demonstration and he turned back. He struck a tall elegant figure in his court dress and top hat. He stopped in front of her and spoke to one of the constables.

'Thank you, officer, but I know this lady, you may let her through.' Then, as she ducked under the constable's outstretched arm, he greeted her, 'Hello, Tara.'

He found it difficult to believe how she had changed.

She was a blowsy middle-aged drab, only her eyes were still beautiful as they blazed at him.

'Moses Gama lives on. The monsters of *apartheid* can murder our heroes, but the battle is ours. In the end we will inherit the earth.' Her voice was a screech.

'Yes, Tara,' he replied. 'There are heroes and there are monsters, but most of us are ordinary mortals caught up in events too turbulent for any of us. Perhaps when the battle is over, all we will inherit will be the ashes of a once beautiful land.'

He turned away from her and walked into the entrance of the embassy without looking back.

Author's Note

Once again I have taken some small liberties with the timetables of history, in particular the dates on which the *Umkhonto we Sizwe* and *Poqo* movements began, Nelson Mandela was acquitted in his first treason trial, and Harold Macmillan made his 'Winds of Change' speech.

I hope that you, the reader, will forgive me for the sake of the narrative.

Wilbur Smith

SHOUT AT THE DEVIL

Foreword

I will not deny that this story was suggested to me by the action in World War I, when the German mercantile raider *Königsberg* was sunk in the Kikunya channel of the Rufiji delta by ships of the Royal Navy.

However, I will most emphatically deny that the rogues and scoundrels depicted in my tale bear the slightest resemblance to any members of the company of men that operated to the destruction of *Königsberg*. In particular, I would strongly resist the suggestion that Flynn Patrick O'Flynn is based on the character of the gallant Colonel 'Jungle Man' Pretorius, who actually went aboard *Königsberg*, disguised as a native bearer, and paced out the ranges for the guns of His Majesty's warships *Severn* and *Mersey*.

I would like to express my thanks to Lieutenant-Commander Mathers (R.N. retired) for his assistance in my researches.

PART ONE

PART ONE

Flynn Patrick O'Flynn was an ivory poacher by profession, and modestly he admitted that he was the best on the east coast of Africa.

Rachid El Keb was an exporter of precious stones, of women for the harems and great houses of Arabia and India, and of illicit ivory. This he admitted only to his trusted clients; to the rest he was a rich and respectable owner of coastal shipping.

In an afternoon during the monsoon of 1912, drawn together by their mutual interest in pachyderms, Flynn and Rachid sat in the back room of El Keb's shop in the Arab quarter of Zanzibar, and drank tea from tiny brass thimbles. The hot tea made Flynn O'Flynn perspire even more than usual. It was so humid hot in the room that the flies sat in languid stupor upon the low ceiling.

'Listen, Kebby, you lend me just one of those stinking little ships of yours and I'll fill her so high with tusks, she'll damn nigh sink.'

'Ah!' replied El Keb carefully, and went on waving the palm-leaf fan in his own face – a face that resembled that of a suspicious parrot with a straggly, goatee beard.

'Have I ever let you down yet?' Flynn demanded aggressively, and a drop of sweat fell from the tip of his nose onto his already damp shirt.

'Ah!' El Keb repeated.

'This scheme has a flair. It has the touch of greatness to it. This scheme . . .' Flynn paused to find a suitable adjective, '. . . this scheme is Napoleonic. It is Caesarian!'

'Ah!' El Keb said again, and refilled his tea cup. Lifting

3

it delicately between thumb and forefinger, he sipped before speaking. 'It is necessary only that I should risk the total destruction of a sixty-foot dhow worth . . .' prudently he inflated the figure, '. . . two thousand English pounds?'

'Against an almost certain recovery of twenty thousand,' Flynn cut in quickly, and El Keb smiled a little, almost dreamily.

'You'd put the profits so high?' he asked.

'That's the lowest figure. Good God, Kebby! There hasn't been a shot fired in the Rufiji basin for twenty years. You know damn well it's the Kaiser's private hunting reserve. The Jumbo are so thick in there I could round them up and drive them in like sheep.' Involuntarily Flynn's right forefinger crooked and twitched as though it were already curled around a trigger.

'Madness,' whispered El Keb, with the gold gloat softening the shape of his lips. 'You'd sail into the Rufiji river from the sea, hoist the Union Jack on one of the islands in the delta and fill the dhow with German ivory. Madness.'

'The Germans have formally annexed none of those islands. I'd be in and out again before Berlin had sent their first cable to London. With ten of my gun-boys hunting, we'd fill the dhow in two weeks.'

'The Germans would have a gunboat there in a week. They've got the *Blücher* lying at Dar es Salaam under steam, heavy cruiser with nine-inch guns.'

'We'd be under protection of the British flag. They couldn't dare touch us – not on the high seas – not with things the way they are now between England and Germany.'

'Mr O'Flynn, I was led to believe you were a citizen of the United States of America.'

'You damn right I am.' Flynn sat up a little straighter, a little more proudly.

'You'd need a British captain for the dhow,' El Keb mused, and stroked his beard thoughtfully.

'Jesus, Kebby, you didn't think I was fool enough to sail that cow in myself?' Flynn looked pained. 'I'll find someone else to do that, and to sail her out again through the Imperial German navy. Me, I'm going to walk in from my base camp in Portuguese Mozambique and go out the same way.'

'Forgive me.' El Keb smiled again. 'I underestimated you.' He stood up quickly. The splendour of the great jewelled dagger at his waist was somewhat spoiled by the unwashed white of his ankle-length robe. 'Mr O'Flynn, I think I have just the man to captain your dhow for you. But first it is necessary to alter his financial circumstances so that he might be willing to accept employment.'

– 2 –

The leather purse of gold sovereigns had been the pivot on which the gentle confusion of Sebastian Oldsmith's life turned. It had been presented to him by his father when Sebastian had announced to the family his intention of sailing to Australia to make his fortune in the wool trade. It had comforted him during the voyage from Liverpool to the Cape of Good Hope where the captain had unceremoniously deposited him after Sebastian's misalliance with the daughter of the gentleman who was proceeding to Sydney to take up his appointment as Governor of New South Wales.

In gradually dwindling quantity the sovereigns had remained with him through the series of misfortunes that ended in Zanzibar, when he awoke from heat-drugged sleep in a shoddy room to find that the leather purse and its contents were gone, and with them were gone the letters of introduction from his father to certain prominent wool-brokers of Sydney.

It occurred to Sebastian as he sat on the edge of his bed that the letters had little real value in Zanzibar, and with increasing bewilderment, he reviewed the events that had blown him so far off his intended course. Slowly his forehead creased in the effort of thought. It was the high, intelligent forehead of a philosopher crowned by a splendid mass of shiny black curls; his eyes were dark brown, his nose long and straight, his jaw firm, and his mouth sensitive. In his twenty-second year, Sebastian had the face of a young Oxford don; which proves, perhaps, how misleading looks can be. Those who knew him well would have been surprised that Sebastian, in setting out for Australia, had come as close to it as Zanzibar.

Abandoning the mental exercise that was already giving him a slight headache, Sebastian stood up from the bed and, with the skirt of his nightshirt flapping around his calves, began his third minute search of the hotel room. Although the purse had been under his mattress when he went to sleep the preceding evening, this time Sebastian emptied the water jug and peered into it hopefully. He unpacked his valise and shook out each shirt. He crawled under the bed, lifted the coconut matting and probed every hole in the rotten flooring before giving way to despair.

Shaved, the bed-bug bites on his person anointed with saliva, and dressed in the grey three-piece suit which was showing signs of travel fatigue, he brushed his derby hat and placed it carefully over his curls, picked up his cane in one hand, and lugging his valise in the other, he went down the stairs into the hot noisy lobby of the Hotel Royal.

'I say,' he greeted the little Arab at the desk with the most cheerful smile he could muster. 'I say, I seem to have lost my money.'

6

A silence fell upon the room. The waiters carrying trays out to the hotel veranda slowed and stopped, heads turned towards Sebastian with the same hostile curiosity as if he had announced that he was suffering from a mild attack of leprosy.

'Stolen, I should imagine,' Sebastian went on, grinning. 'Nasty bit of luck, really.'

The silence exploded as the bead curtains from the office were thrown open and the Hindu proprietor erupted into the room with a loud cry of, 'Mr Oldsmith, what about your bill?'

'Oh, the bill. Yes, well, let's not get excited. I mean, it won't help, now, will it?'

And the proprietor proceeded to become very excited indeed. His cries of anguish and indignation carried to the veranda where a dozen persons were already beginning the daily fight against heat and thirst. They crowded into the lobby to watch with interest.

'Ten days you owe. Nearly one hundred rupees.'

'Yes, it's jolly unfortunate, I know.' Sebastian was grinning desperately, when a new voice added itself to the uproar.

'Now just hold on a shake.' Together Sebastian and the Hindu turned to the big red-faced, middle-aged man with the pleasantly mixed American and Irish accent. 'Did I hear you called Mr Oldsmith?'

'That is correct, sir.' Sebastian knew instinctively that here was an ally.

'An unusual name. You wouldn't be related to Mister Francis Oldsmith, wool merchant of Liverpool, England?' Flynn O'Flynn enquired politely. He had perused Sebastian's letters of introduction passed on to him by Rachid El Keb.

'Good Lord!' Sebastian cried with joy. 'Do you know my pater?'

7

'Do I know Francis Oldsmith?' Flynn laughed easily, and then checked himself. His acquaintance was limited to the letterheads. 'Well, I don't exactly know him person to person, you understand, but I think I can say I know *of* him. Used to be in the wool business myself once.' Flynn turned genially to the hotel proprietor and breathed on him a mixture of gin fumes and good-fellowship. 'One hundred rupees was the sum you mentioned.'

'That's the sum, Mr O'Flynn.' The proprietor was easily soothed.

'Mr Oldsmith and I will be having a drink on the veranda. You can bring the receipt to us there.' Flynn placed two sovereigns on the counter; sovereigns that had so recently reposed beneath Sebastian's mattress.

With his boots propped on the low veranda wall, Sebastian regarded the harbour over the rim of his glass. Sebastian was not a drinking man but in view of Flynn O'Flynn's guardianship he could not be churlish and refuse hospitality. The number of craft in the bay suddenly multiplied miraculously before his eyes. Where a moment before one stubby little dhow had been tacking in through the entrance, there were now three identical boats sailing in formation. Sebastian closed one eye and by focusing determinedly, he reduced the three back to one. Mildly elated with his success, he turned his attention to his new friend and business partner who had pressed such large quantities of gin upon him.

'Mr O'Flynn,' he said with deliberation, slurring the words slightly.

'Forget that mister, Bassie, call me Flynn. Just plain Flynn, the same as in gin.'

'Flynn,' said Sebastian. 'There isn't anything – well, there isn't anything funny about this?'

'How do you mean *funny*, boy?'

'I mean' – and Sebastian blushed slightly. 'There isn't anything illegal, is there?'

'Bassie.' Flynn shook his head sorrowfully. 'What do you take me for, Bassie? You think I'm a crook or something, boy?'

'Oh, no, of course not, Flynn,' and Sebastian blushed a shade deeper. 'I just thought – well, all these elephants we're going to shoot. They must belong to somebody. Aren't they German elephants?'

'Bassie, I want to show you something.' Flynn set down his glass and groping in the inside pocket of his wilted tropical suit, he produced an envelope. 'Read that, boy!'

The address at the head of the sheet of cheap notepaper was 'The Kaiserhof. Berlin. Dated June 10, 1912', and the body of the letter read:

Dear Mr Flynn O'Flynn,
    I am worried about all those elephants down in the Rufiji basin eating up all the grass and smashing up all the trees and things, so if you've got time, would you go down there and shoot some of them as they're eating up all the grass and smashing up all the trees and things.
                    Yours sincerely,
                    Kaiser Willem III.
                    Emperor of Germany.

A vague uneasiness formed through the clouds of gin in Sebastian's skull. 'Why did he write to you?'

'Because he knows I'm the best goddamned elephant hunter in the world.'

'You'd expect him to use better English, wouldn't you?' Sebastian murmured.

'What's wrong with his English?' Flynn demanded truculently. He had spent some time in composing the letter.

'Well, I mean that bit about eating up all the grass – he said that twice.'

'Well, you got to remember he's a German. They don't write English too good.'

'Of course! I hadn't thought of that.' Sebastian looked relieved and lifted his glass. 'Well, good hunting!'

'I'll drink to that,' and Flynn emptied his glass.

– 3 –

Sebastian stood with both hands gripping the wooden rail of the dhow and stared out across a dozen miles of water at the loom of the African mainland. The monsoon wind had ruffled the sea to a dark indigo and it flipped spray from the white-caps into Sebastian's face. Overlaying the clean salt of the ocean was the taint of the mangrove swamps, an evil smell as though an animal had died in its own cage. Sebastian sniffed it with distaste as he searched the low, green line of the coast for the entrance to the maze of the Rufiji delta.

Frowning, he tried to reconstruct the Admiralty chart in his mind. The Rufiji river came to the sea through a dozen channels spread over forty miles, and in doing so, carved fifty, maybe a hundred, islands out of the mainland.

Tidal water washed fifteen miles upstream, past the mangroves to where the vast grass swampland began. It was there in the swampland that the elephant herds had taken shelter from the guns and arrows of the ivory hunters, protected by Imperial decree and by a formidable terrain.

The murderous-looking ruffian who captained the dhow uttered a string of sing-song orders, and Sebastian turned to watch the complicated manoeuvre of tacking the ungainly craft. Half-naked seamen dropped out of the rigging like over-ripe brown fruit and swarmed around the sixty-foot teak boom. Bare feet padding on the filthy deck, they ran the boom back and forward again. The dhow creaked like an old man with arthritis, came round wearily on to the wind, and butted its nose in towards the land. The new motion, combined with the swamp smell and the smell of freshly-stirred bilges, moved something deep within Sebastian. His grip upon the rail increased, and new sweat popped out like little blisters on his brow. He leaned forward, and, to shouts of encouragement from the crew, made another sacrifice to the sea gods. He was still draped worshipfully across the rail as the dhow wallowed and slid in the turbulent waters of the entrance, and then passed into the calm of the southernmost channel of the Rufiji basin.

Four days later, Sebastian sat cross-legged with the dhow captain on a thick Bokhara carpet spread upon the deck, and they explained to each other in sign language that neither of them had the vaguest idea where they were. The dhow was anchored in a narrow water-way hemmed in by the twisted and deformed trunks of the mangroves. The sensation of being lost was not new to Sebastian and he accepted it with resignation, but the dhow captain, who could run from Aden to Calcutta and back to Zanzibar with the certainty of a man visiting his own outhouse, was not so stoical. He lifted his eyes to the heavens and called upon Allah to intercede with the djinn who guarded this stinking labyrinth, who made the waters flow in strange, unnatural ways, who changed the shape of each island, and thrust mud banks in their path. Driven on by his own eloquence, he leapt to the rail and screamed defiance into the brooding mangroves until flocks of ibis rose and milled in the heat mists above the dhow. Then he flung himself down on the carpet and fixed Sebastian with a stare of sullen malevolence.

'It's not really my fault, you know.' Sebastian wriggled

with embarrassment under the stare. Then once again he produced his Admiralty chart, spread it on the deck, and placed his finger on the island which Flynn O'Flynn had ringed in blue pencil as the rendezvous. 'I mean, it *is* rather your cup of tea, finding the place. After all, you *are* the navigator, aren't you?'

The captain spat fiercely on his deck, and Sebastian flushed.

'Now that sort of thing isn't going to get us anywhere. Let's try and behave like gentlemen.'

This time the captain hawked it up from deep down in his throat and spat a lump of yellow phlegm into the blue pencil circle on Sebastian's map, then he rose to his feet and stalked away to where his crew squatted in a group under the poop.

In the short dusk, while the mosquitoes whined in a thin mist about Sebastian's head, he listened to the Arabic muttering and saw the glances that were directed at him down the length of the dhow. So when the night closed over the ship like a bank of black steam, he took up a defensive position on the foredeck and waited for them to come. As a weapon he had his cane of solid ebony. He laid it across his lap and sat against the rail until the darkness was complete, then, silently, he changed his position and crouched beside one of the water barrels that was lashed to the base of the mast.

They were a long time coming. Half the night had wasted away before he heard the stealthy scuff of bare feet on the planking. The absolute blackness of the night was filled with the din of the swamp; the boom and tonk of frogs, the muted buzz of insects and the occasional snort and splash of a hippo, so that Sebastian had difficulty in deciding how many they had sent against him. Crouching by the water barrel he strained his eyes unavailingly into the utter blackness and tuned his hearing to filter out the

12

swamp noises and catch only those soft little sounds that death made as it came down the deck towards him.

Although Sebastian had never scaled any academic heights, he had boxed light heavyweight for Rugby, and fast-bowled for Sussex the previous cricket season when he had led the county bowling averages. So, although he was afraid now, Sebastian had a sublime confidence in his own physical prowess and it was not the kind of fear that filled his belly with oily warmth, nor turned his ego to jelly, but rather, it keyed him to a point where every muscle in his body quivered on the edge of exploding. Crouching in the night he groped for the cane that he had laid on the deck beside him. His hands fell on the bulky sackful of green coconuts that made up part of the dhow's deck cargo. They were carried to supplement, with their milk, the meagre supply of fresh water on board. Quickly Sebastian tore open the fastenings of the sack and hefted one of the hard round fruits.

'Not quite as handy as a cricket ball, but—' murmured Sebastian and came to his feet. Using the short run up he delivered the fast ball with which he had shattered the Yorkshire first innings the previous year. It had the same effect on the Arab first innings. The coconut whirred and cracked against the skull of one of the approaching assassins and the rest retired in confusion.

'Now send the men,' roared Sebastian and bowled a short lifter that hastened the retreat.

He selected another coconut and was about to deliver that also when there was a flash and a report from aft, and something howled over Sebastian's head. Hastily he ducked behind the sack of coconuts.

'My God, they've got a gun up there!' Sebastian remembered then the ancient muzzle-loading Jezail he had seen the captain polishing lovingly on their first day out from Zanzibar, and he felt his anger rising in earnest.

13

He jumped to his feet and hurled his next coconut with fury.

'Fight fair, you dirty swine!' he yelled.

There was a delay while the dhow captain went through the complicated process of loading his piece. Then a cannon report, a burst of flame, and another potleg howled over Sebastian's head.

Through the dark hours before dawn the lively exchange of jeers and curses, of coconuts and potlegs continued. Sebastian more than held his own for he scored four howls of pain and a yelp, while the dhow captain succeeded only in shooting away a great deal of his own standing rigging. But as the light of the new day increased, so Sebastian's advantage waned. The Arab captain's shooting improved to such an extent that Sebastian spent most of his time crouching behind the sack of coconuts. Sebastian was nearly exhausted. His right arm and shoulder ached unmercifully, and he could hear the first stealthy advance of the Arab crew as they crept down towards his hide. In daylight they could surround him and use their numbers to drag him down.

While he rested for the final effort, Sebastian looked out at the morning. It was a red dawn, angry and beautiful through the swamp mists so the water glowed with a pink sheen and the mangroves stood very dark around the ship.

Something splashed farther up the channel, a water bird perhaps. Sebastian looked for it without interest, and heard it splash again and then again. He stirred and sat up a little straighter. The sound was too regular for that of a bird or a fish.

Then around the bend in the channel, from behind the wall of mangroves, driven on by urgent paddles, shot a dugout canoe. Standing in the bow with a double-barrelled elephant gun under his arm and a clay pipe sticking out of his red face, was Flynn O'Flynn.

14

'What the hell's going on here?' he roared. 'Are you fighting a goddamned war? I've been waiting a week for you lot!'

'Look out, Flynn!' Sebastian yelled a warning. 'That swine has got a gun!'

The Arab captain had jumped to his feet and was looking around uncertainly. Long ago he had regretted his impulse to rid himself of the Englishman and escape from this evil swamp, and now his misgivings were truly justified. Having committed himself, however, there was only one course open to him. He lifted the Jezail to his shoulder and aimed at O'Flynn in the canoe. The discharge blew a long grey spurt of powder from the muzzle, and the potleg lifted a burst of spray from the surface of the water beyond the canoe. The echoes of the shot were drowned by the bellow of O'Flynn's rifle. He fired without moving the pipe from his mouth and the narrow dug-out rocked dangerously with the recoil.

The heavy bullet picked up the Arab captain's scrawny body, his robe fluttered like a piece of old paper and his turban flew from his head and unwound in mid-air as he was flung clear of the rail to drop with a tall splash alongside. He floated face down, trapped air ballooning his robe about him and then he drifted away slowly on the sluggish current. His crew, stunned and silent, stood by the rail and watched him depart.

Dismissing the neat execution as though it had never happened, O'Flynn glared up at Sebastian and roared, 'You're a week late. I haven't been able to do a goddamned thing until you got here. Now let's get the flag up and start doing some work!'

4

The formal annexation of Flynn O'Flynn's island took place in the relative cool of the following morning. It had taken some hours for Flynn to convince Sebastian of the necessity of occupying the island for the British crown, and he succeeded only by casting Sebastian in the role of empire builder. He made some flattering comparisons between Clive of India and Sebastian Oldsmith of Liverpool.

The next problem was the choice of a name. This stirred up a little Anglo-American enmity, with Flynn O'Flynn campaigning aggressively for 'New Boston'. Sebastian was horrified, his patriotic ardour burned brightly.

'Now hold on a jiffy, old chap,' he protested.

'What's wrong with it? You just tell me what's wrong with it!'

'Well, first of all this is going to be one of His Britannic Majesty's possessions, you know.'

'New Boston,' O'Flynn repeated. 'That sounds good. That sounds real good.'

Sebastian shuddered. 'I think it would be – well, not quite suitable. I mean, Boston was the place where they had that tea thing, you know.'

The argument raged more savagely as Flynn lowered the level in the gin bottle, until finally Sebastian stood up from the carpet on the floor of the dhow cabin, his eyes blazing with patriotic outrage. 'If you would care to step outside, sir,' he enunciated with care as he stood over the older man, 'we can settle this matter.' The dignity of the challenge was spoiled by the low roof of the cabin which made it necessary for Sebastian to stoop.

'Man, I'd eat you without spitting out the bones.'

'That, sir, is your opinion. But I must warn you I was highly thought of in the light heavyweight division.'

'Oh, goddamn it.' Flynn shook his head wearily and capitulated. 'What difference does it make what we call the mother-loving place. Sit down, for God's sake. Here! Let's drink to whatever you want to call it.'

Sebastian sat on the carpet and accepted the mug that Flynn handed him. 'We shall call it—' he paused dramatically, 'we shall call it New Liverpool,' and he lifted the mug.

'You know,' said Flynn, 'for a limey, you aren't a bad guy,' and the rest of the night was devoted to celebrating the birth of the new colony.

In the dawn the empire builders were paddled ashore in the dug-out by two of Flynn's gun-bearers.

The canoe ran aground on the narrow muddy beach of New Liverpool, and the sudden halt threw both of them off-balance. They collapsed gently together on to the floor of the dug-out, and had to be assisted ashore by the paddlers.

Sebastian was formally dressed for the occasion but had buttoned his waistcoat awry and he kept tugging at it as he peered about him.

Now at high tide, New Liverpool was about a thousand yards long and half as broad. At the highest point it rose not more than ten feet above the level of the Rufiji river. Fifteen miles from the mouth the water was only slightly tainted with salt and the mangrove trees had thinned out and given way to tall matted elephant grass and slender bottle palms.

Flynn's gun-bearers and porters had cleared a small opening above the beach, and had erected a dozen grass huts around one of the palm trees. It was a dead palm, its crown leaves long gone, and Flynn pointed an unsteady finger at it.

'Flag pole,' he said indistinctly, took Sebastian's elbow and led him towards it.

Tugging at his waistcoat with one hand and clutching the bundled Union Jack that Flynn had provided in the other, Sebastian felt a surge of emotion within him as he looked up at the slender column of the palm tree.

'Leave me,' he mumbled and shook off Flynn's guiding hand. 'We got to do this right. Solemn occasion – very solemn.'

'Have a drink.' Flynn offered him the gin bottle, and when Sebastian waved it away, he lifted it to his own lips.

'Shouldn't drink on parade.' Sebastian frowned at him. 'Bad form.'

Flynn coughed at the vicious sting of the liquor and smote himself on the chest with his free hand.

'Should draw the men up in a hollow square,' Sebastian went on. 'Ready to salute the flag.'

'Jesus, man, get on with it,' grumbled Flynn.

'Got to do it right.'

'Oh, hell,' Flynn shrugged with resignation, then issued a string of orders in Swahili.

Puzzled and amused, Flynn's fifteen retainers gathered in a ragged circle about the flag pole. They were a curious band, gathered from half a dozen tribes, dressed in an assortment of cast-off Western clothing, half of them armed with ancient double-barrelled elephant rifles from which Flynn had carefully filed the serial numbers so they could never be traced back to him.

'Fine body of men,' Sebastian beamed at them in alcoholic goodwill, unconsciously using the words of a Brigadier who had inspected Sebastian's cadet parade at Rugby.

'Let's get this show on the road,' Flynn suggested.

'My friends,' Sebastian obliged, 'we are gathered here today . . .' It was a longish speech but Flynn weathered it by nipping away quietly at the gin bottle, and at last Sebastian ended with his voice ringing and tears of great emotion prickling his eyelids, '. . . In the sight of God and man, I hereby declare this island part of the glorious Empire of His Majesty, George V, King of England, Emperor of India, Protector of the Faith . . .' His voice wavered as he tried to remember the correct form, and he ended lamely, '. . . and all that sort of thing.'

A silence fell on the assembly and Sebastian fidgeted with embarrassment. 'What do I do now?' he enquired of Flynn O'Flynn in a stage whisper.

'Get that goddamned flag up.'

'Ah, the flag!' Sebastian exclaimed with relief, and then uncertainly, 'How?'

Flynn considered this at length. 'I guess you have to climb up the palm tree.'

With shrill cries of encouragement from the gun-bearers, and with Flynn shoving and cursing from below, the Governor of New Liverpool managed to scale the flag pole to a height of about fifteen feet. There he secured the flag and descended again so swiftly he tore the buttons off the front of his waistcoat, and twisted his ankle. He was borne away to one of the grass huts singing, 'God save our Gracious King' in a voice broken with gin, pain and patriotism.

For the rest of their stay on the island, the Union Jack flew at half mast above the encampment.

Carried initially by two Wakamba fishermen, it took fully ten days for the word of the annexation to reach the outpost of the German Empire one hundred miles away at Mahenge.

5

Mahenge was in the bush country above the coastal lowlands. It consisted, in its entirety, of four trading posts owned by Indian shopkeepers – and the German boma.

The German boma was a large stone building, thatched, set about with wide verandas over which purple bougainvillea climbed in profusion. Behind it stood the barracks and parade ground of the African Askari, and before it a lonely flag pole from which streamed the black, red and yellow of the empire. A speck in the vastness of the African bush, seat of government for an area the size of France. An area that spread south to the Rovuma river and the border of Portuguese Mozambique, east to the Indian Ocean, and west to the uplands of Sao Hill and Mbeya.

From this stronghold the German Commissioner (Southern Province) wielded the limitless powers of a medieval robber baron. One of the Kaiser's arms, or, more realistically, one of his little fingers, he was answerable only to Governor Schee in Dar es Salaam. But Dar es Salaam was many torturous miles away, and Governor Schee was a busy man not to be troubled with trivialities. Just as long as the Herr Commissioner Herman Fleischer collected the taxes, he was free to collect them in his own sweet way; though very few of the indigenous inhabitants of the southern province would have described Herman Fleischer's ways as sweet.

At the time that the messenger, carrying the news of the British annexation of New Liverpool, trotted up over the last skyline and saw through the acacia thorn trees ahead of him the tiny clustered buildings of Mahenge, Herr Fleischer was finishing his midday meal.

A man of large appetite, his luncheon consisted of

approximately two pounds of *Eisbein*, as much pickled cabbage, and a dozen potatoes, all swimming in thick gravy. Having aroused his taste-buds, he then went on to the sausage. The sausage came by weekly fast-runner from Dodoma in the north, and was manufactured by a man of genius, a Westphalian immigrant who made sausages with the taste of the Black Forest in them. The sausage, and the Hansa beer cooling in its earthernware jug, aroused in Herr Fleischer a delicious nostalgia. He ate not quietly but steadily, and, these quantities of food confined within the thick grey corduroy of his tunic and breeches, built up a pressure that squeezed the perspiration from his face and neck, forcing him to pause and mop up at regular intervals.

When he sighed at last and sagged back in his chair, the leather thongs squeaked a little under him. A bubble of trapped gas found its way up through the sausage and passed in genteel eruption between his lips. Tasting it, he sighed again in happiness and squinted out from the deep shade of the veranda into the flat shimmering glare of the sunlight.

Then he saw the messenger coming. The man reached the steps of the veranda and squatted down in the sun with his loin-cloth drawn up modestly between his legs. His body was washed shiny black with sweat but his legs were powdered with fine dust to the knees, and his chest swelled and subsided as he drank the thin hot air. His eyes were downcast, he could not look directly at the Bwana Mkuba until his presence was formally acknowledged.

Herman Fleischer watched him broodingly, his mood evaporating for he had been looking forward to his afternoon siesta – and the messenger had spoiled that. He looked away at the low cloud above the hills in the south and sipped his beer. Then he selected a cheroot from the box before him and lit it. The cheroot burned slowly and evenly, restoring a little of his good humour. He smoked it short before flicking the stub over the veranda wall.

'Speak,' he grunted, and the messenger lifted his eyes, and gasped with wonder and awe at the beauty and dignity of the Commissioner's person. Although this was ritual admiration, it never failed to stir a faint pleasure in Herr Fleischer.

'I see you, Bwana Mkuba – Great Lord,' and Fleischer inclined his head slightly. 'I bring you greetings from Kalani, headman of Batja, on the Rufiji. You are his father, and he crawls on his belly before you. Your hair of yellow, and the great fatness of your body, blind him with beauty.'

Herr Fleischer stirred restlessly in his chair. References to his corpulence, however well-intentioned, always annoyed him. 'Speak,' he repeated.

'Kalani says thus: "Ten suns ago, a ship came into the delta of the Rufiji, and stopped by the Island of the Dogs, Inja. On the island, the men of this ship have built houses, and above the houses, they have placed on a dead palm tree the cloth of the Insingeese which is of blue and white and red, having many crosses within crosses."'

Herr Fleischer struggled upright in his chair and stared at the messenger. The pink of his complexion slowly became cross-veined with red and purple.

'Kalani says also: "Since their coming the voices of their guns have never ceased to speak along the Rufiji river, and there has been a great killing of elephants so that in the noonday the sky is dark with the birds that come for the meat."'

Herr Fleischer was thrashing around in his chair, speech was locked in his throat and his face had swollen so it threatened to burst like an over-ripe fruit.

'Kalani says further: "Two white men are on the island. One is a man who is very thin and young and is therefore of no account. The other white man Kalani has seen only at a great distance but by the redness of this man's face, and by his bulk, he knows in his heart it is Fini."'

At the name Herr Fleischer became articulate, if not coherent – he bellowed like a bull in rut. The messenger winced, such a bellow from the Bwana Mkuba usually preceded a multiple hanging.

'Sergeant!' The next bellow had form, and Herr Fleischer was on his feet, struggling to clinch the buckle of his belt.

'Rasch!' he roared again. O'Flynn was in German territory again; O'Flynn was stealing German ivory once more – and compounding the insult by flying the Union Jack over the Kaiser's domain.

'Sergeant, where the thunder of God are you?' With incredible speed for a fat man Herr Fleischer raced down the long length of the veranda. For three years now, ever since his arrival in Mahenge, the name of Flynn O'Flynn had been enough to ruin his appetite, and produce in him a condition very close to epilepsy.

Around the corner of the veranda appeared the sergeant of the Askari, and Herr Fleischer braked just in time to avert collision.

'A storm patrol,' bellowed the Commissioner, blowing a cloud of spittle in his agitation. 'Twenty men. Full field packs, and one hundred pounds of ammunition. We leave in an hour.'

The sergeant saluted and doubled away across the parade ground. A minute later a bugle began singing with desperate urgency.

Slowly, through the black mists of rage, reason returned to Herman Fleischer. He stood with shoulders hunched, breathing heavily through his mouth, and mentally digested the full import of Kalani's message.

This was not just another of O'Flynn's will-o'-the-wisp forays across the Rovuma from Mozambique. This time he had sailed brazenly into the Rufiji delta, with a full-scale expedition, and hoisted the British flag. A queasy sensation, not attributable to the pickled pork, settled on Herr Fleischer's stomach. He knew the makings of an international incident when he saw one.

This, perhaps, was the goad that would launch the fatherland on the road to its true destiny. He gulped with excitement. They had flapped that hated flag in the Kaiser's face just once too often. This was history being made, and Herman Fleischer stood in the centre of it.

Trembling a little, he hurried into his office, and began drafting the report to Governor Schee that might plunge the world into a holocaust from which the German people would rise as the rulers of creation.

An hour later, he rode out of the boma on a white donkey with his slouch uniform hat set well forward on his head to shield his eyes from the glare. Behind him his black Askari marched with their rifles at the slope. Smart in their pillbox kepis with the backflaps hanging to the shoulder, khaki uniforms freshly pressed, and putteed legs rising and falling in unison, they made as gallant a show as any commander could wish.

A day and a half march would bring them to the confluence of the Kilombero and Rufiji rivers where the Commissioner's steam launch was moored.

As the buildings of Mahenge vanished behind him, Herr Fleischer relaxed and let his ample backside conform to the shape of the saddle.

– 6 –

'Now, have you got it straight?' Flynn asked without conviction. The past eight days of hunting together had given him no confidence in Sebastian's ability to carry out a simple set of instructions without introducing some remarkable variation of his own. 'You go down the river to the island, and you load the ivory onto the dhow. Then you come back here with all the canoes to pick up the next batch.' Flynn paused to allow his words to absorb into the spongy tissue of Sebastian's head before he went on. 'And for Chrissake don't forget the gin.'

'Right you are, old chap.' With eight days' growth of black beard, and the skin peeling from the tip of his sunburned nose, Sebastian was beginning to fit the role of ivory poacher. The wide-brimmed terai hat that Flynn had loaned him came down to his ears, and the razor edges of the elephant grass had shredded his trouser legs and stripped the polish from his boots. His wrists and the soft skin behind his ears were puffy and speckled with spots of angry red where the mosquitoes had drunk deep, but he had lost a little weight in the heat and the ceaseless walking, so now he was lean and hard-looking.

They stood together under a monkey-bean tree on the bank of the Rufiji, while at the water's edge the bearers were loading the last tusks into the canoes. There was a purple-greenish smell hanging over them in the steamy heat, a smell which Sebastian hardly noticed now – for the last eight days had seen a great killing of elephant and the stink of green ivory was as familiar to him as the smell of the sea to a mariner.

'By the time you get back tomorrow morning the boys will have brought in the last of the ivory. We'll have a full dhow-load and you can set off for Zanzibar.'

'What about you? Are you staying on here?'

'Not bloody likely. I'll light out for my base camp in Mozambique.'

'Wouldn't it be easier for you to come along on the dhow? It's nearly two hundred miles to walk.' Sebastian was solicitous; in these last days he had conceived a burning admiration for Flynn.

'Well, you see, it's like this . . .' Flynn hesitated. This was no time to trouble Sebastian with talk of German gunboats waiting off the mouth of the Rufiji. 'I have to get back to my camp, because . . .' Suddenly inspiration came to Flynn O'Flynn. 'Because my poor little daughter is there all alone.'

'You've got a daughter?' Sebastian was taken by surprise.

'You damn right I have.' Flynn experienced a sudden rush of paternal affection and duty. 'And the poor little thing is there all alone.'

'Well, when will I see you again?' The thought of parting from Flynn, of being left to try and find his own way to Australia saddened Sebastian.

'Well,' Flynn was tactful. 'I hadn't really given that much thought.' This was a lie. Flynn had thought about it ceaselessly for the last eight days. He was eagerly anticipating waving farewell to Sebastian Oldsmith for all time.

'Couldn't we . . .' Sebastian blushed a little under his sun-reddened cheeks. 'Couldn't we sort of team up together? I could work for you, sort of as an apprentice?'

The idea made Flynn wince. He almost panicked at the thought of Sebastian permanently trailing along behind him and discharging his rifle at random intervals. 'Well now, Bassie boy,' he clasped a thick arm around Sebastian's shoulders, 'first you sail that old dhow back to Zanzibar and old Kebby El Keb will pay you out your share. Then you write to me, hey? How about that? You write me, and we'll work something out.'

Sebastian grinned happily. 'I'd like that, Flynn. I'd truly like that.'

'All right, then, off you go. And don't forget the gin.'

With Sebastian standing in the bows of the lead canoe, the double-barrelled rifle clutched in his hands, and the terai hat pulled down firmly over his ears, the little flotilla of heavily laden canoes pulled out from the bank and caught

26

the current. Paddles dipped and gleamed in the evening sunlight as they arrowed away towards the first bend downstream.

Still standing unsteadily in the frail craft, Sebastian looked back and waved his rifle at Flynn on the bank.

'For Chrissake, be careful with that goddamn piece,' Flynn bellowed too late. The rifle fired, and the recoil toppled Sebastian sprawling onto the pile of ivory behind him. The canoe rocked dangerously while the paddlers struggled to keep it from capsizing, and then disappeared around the bend.

Twelve hours later, the canoes reappeared around the same bend, and headed towards the lone monkey-bean tree on the bank. The canoes rode lightly, empty of ivory, and the paddlers were singing one of the old river chants.

Freshly shaved, wearing a clean shirt and his other pair of boots, a case of Flynn's liquor between his knees, Sebastian peered eagerly ahead for his first glimpse of the big American.

A fine blue tendril of camp-fire smoke smeared out across the river, but there were no figures waving a welcome from the bank. Suddenly Sebastian frowned as he realized that the silhouette of the monkey-bean tree had altered. He wrinkled his eyes, peering ahead uncertainly.

Behind him rang the first cry of alarm from his boatmen. 'Allemand!' And the canoe swerved under him.

He glanced back and saw the other canoes wheel away in tight circles aimed downstream, the boatmen jabbering in terror as they leaned forward to thrust against the paddles.

His own canoe was in swift pursuit of the others as they darted beyond the bend.

'Hey!' Sebastian shouted at the sweat-shiny backs of his paddlers. 'What do you think you're doing?'

They gave him no answer but the muscles beneath their black skins bunched and rippled in their frantic efforts to drive the canoe faster.

'Stop that immediately!' Sebastian yelled at them. 'Take me back, dash it all. Take me to the camp.'

In desperation Sebastian lifted the rifle and aimed at the nearest man. 'I'm not joking,' he yelled again. The native glanced over his shoulder into the gaping twin muzzles and his face, already twisted with fear, now convulsed into a mask of terror. They had all developed a healthy reverence for the way Sebastian handled that rifle.

The man stopped paddling, and one by one the others followed his example. Sitting frozen under the hypnotic eyes of Sebastian's rifle.

'Back!' said Sebastian and gestured eloquently upstream. Reluctantly the man nearest him dipped his paddle and the canoe turned broadside across the current. 'Back!' Sebastian repeated and the men dipped again.

Slowly, warily, the single canoe crept upstream towards the monkey-bean tree and the grotesque new fruit that hung from its branches.

The hull slid in onto the firm mud and Sebastian stepped ashore.

'Out!' he ordered the boatmen and gestured again. He wanted them well away from the canoe for he knew that, otherwise, the moment his back was turned they would set off downstream again with renewed enthusiasm. 'Out!' and he herded them up the steep bank into Flynn O'Flynn's camp.

The two bearers who had died of gunshot wounds lay beside the smouldering fire. But the four men in the monkey-bean tree had been less fortunate. The ropes had cut deeply into the flesh of their necks and their faces were swollen, mouths wide in the last breath that had never been taken. On the lolling tongues the flies crawled like metallic green bees.

'Cut them down!' Sebastian roused himself from the

nausea that was bubbling queasily up from his stomach. The boatmen stood paralysed and Sebastian felt anger now mixed with his revulsion. Roughly he shoved one of the men towards the tree. 'Cut them down,' he repeated, and thrust the handle of his hunting knife into the man's hand. Sebastian turned away as the native shinned up into the fork of the tree with the knife blade clamped between his teeth. Behind him he heard the heavy meaty thuds as the dead men dropped from the tree. Again his stomach heaved, and he concentrated on his search of the trampled grass around the camp.

'Flynn!' he called softly. 'Flynn. I say Flynn! Where are you?' There were the prints of hobnailed boots in the soft earth, and at one place he stooped and picked up the shiny brass cylinder of an empty cartridge case. Stamped into the metal of the base around the detonator cap were the words *Mauser Fabriken. 7 mm.*

'Flynn!' more urgently now as the horror of it came home to him. 'Flynn!' and he heard the grass rustle near him. He swung towards it, half raising the rifle.

'Master!' and Sebastian felt disappointment swoop in his chest.

'Mohammed. Is that you, Mohammed?' and he recognized the wizened little figure with the eternal fez perched on the woolly head as it emerged. Flynn's chief gun-boy, the only one with a little English.

'Mohammed,' with relief, and then quickly, 'Fini? Where is Fini?'

'They shot him, master. The Askari came in the early morning before the sun. Fini was washing. They shot him and he fell into the water.'

'Where? Show me where.'

Below the camp, a few yards from where the canoe was drawn up, they found the pathetic little bundle of Flynn's clothing. Beside it was a half-consumed cake of cheap soap

29

and a metal hand-mirror. There were the deep imprints of naked feet in the mud, and Mohammed stooped and broke off one of the green reeds at the water's edge. Wordlessly he handed it to Sebastian. A drop of blood had dried black on the leaf, and it crumbled as Sebastian touched it with his thumb-nail.

'We must find him. He might still be alive. Call the others. We'll search the banks downstream.'

In an agony of loss, Sebastian picked up Flynn's soiled shirt and crumpled it in his fist.

– 7 –

Flynn shucked off his pants and the filthy bush-shirt. Shivering briefly in the chill of dawn, he hugged himself and massaged his upper arms while he peered into the shallow water, searching the bottom for the tell-tale chicken-wire pattern that would mean a crocodile was buried in the mud waiting for him.

His body was porcelain-white where clothing had protected it from the sun, but his arms were chocolate-brown, and a deep vee of the same brown dipped down from his throat onto his chest. Above it the battered red face was creased and puffy with sleep, and his long, greying hair was tangled and matted. He belched thunderously, and grimaced at the taste of old gin and pipe tobacco, then, satisfied that no reptile lay in ambush, he stepped into the water and lowered his massive hams to sit waist-deep. Snorting, he scooped water with his cupped hands over his head, then lumbered out onto the bank again. Sixty seconds is a long time to stay in a river like the Rufiji, for the crocodiles come quickly to the sound of splashing.

Naked, dripping, hair plastered down across his face, Flynn began to soap himself, working up a thick lather at his crotch and tenderly massaging his abundant genitalia, he washed away the sloth of sleep and his appetite stirred. He called up at the camp, 'Mohammed, beloved of Allah and son of his prophet, shake your black arse out of the sack and get the coffee brewing.' Then as an afterthought, he added, 'And put a little gin in it.'

Soapsuds filled Flynn's armpits, and coated the melancholy sag of his belly when Mohammed came down the bank to him. Mohammed was balancing a large enamel mug from which curled little wisps of aromatic steam, and Flynn grinned at him, and spoke in Swahili. 'Thou art kind and merciful; this charity will be writ against your name in the Book of Paradise.'

He reached for the mug but before his fingers touched it, there was a fusillade of gun-fire above them and a bullet hit Flynn high up in the thigh. It spun him sideways so he sprawled half in mud and half in water.

Lying stunned with the shock, he heard the rush of Askari into the camp, heard their shouted triumph as they clubbed with the gun-butt those who had survived the first volley. Flynn wriggled into a sitting position.

Mohammed was coming to him anxiously.

'Run,' grunted Flynn. 'Run, damn you.'

'Lord . . .'

'Get out of here.' Savagely Flynn lashed out at him, and Mohammed recoiled. 'The rope, you fool. They'll give you the rope and wrap you in a pigskin.'

A second longer Mohammed hesitated, then he ducked and scampered into the reeds.

'Find Fini,' roared a bull voice in German. 'Find the white man.'

Flynn realized then that it was a stray bullet that had hit him – perhaps even a ricochet. His leg was numb from the hip down, but he dragged himself into the water. He could not run, so he must swim.

31

'Where is he? Find him!' raged the voice, and suddenly the grass on the bank burst open and Flynn looked up.

For the first time they confronted each other. These two who had played murderous hide-and-seek for three long years across ten thousand square miles of bush.

'Ja!' Fleischer's jubilant bellow as he swung and sighted the pistol at the man in the water below him. 'This time!' aiming carefully, steadying the Luger with both hands.

The brittle snapping sound of the shot, and the slap of the bullet into the water a foot from Flynn's head were followed by Fleischer's snarl of disappointment.

Filling his lungs, Flynn ducked below the surface. Frog-kicking with his good leg, trailing the wounded one, he turned with the current and swam. He swam until his trapped breath threatened to explode his chest, and coloured lights flashed and twinkled behind his clenched eyelids. Then he clawed to the surface. On the bank Fleischer was waiting for him with a dozen of his Askari. 'There he is!' as Flynn blew like a whale thirty yards downstream. Gun-fire crackled and the water whipped and leaped and creamed around Flynn's head.

'Shoot straight!' Howling in frustration and blazing wildly with the Luger, Fleischer watched the head disappear and Flynn's fat white buttocks break the surface for an instant as he dived. Sobbing with anger and exertion, Fleischer turned his fury on the Askari around him. 'Pigs! Stupid black pig dogs!' And he swung the empty pistol against the nearest head, knocking the man to his knees. Intent on avoiding the flailing pistol, none of them were ready when Flynn surfaced for the second time. A desultory volley kicked fountains no closer than ten feet to Flynn's bobbing head, and he dived again.

'Come on! Chase him!' Herding his Askari ahead of him, Fleischer trotted along the bank in pursuit. Twenty yards of good going, then they came to the first swamp hole and waded through it to be confronted by a solid barrier of elephant grass. They plunged into it and were swallowed so they no longer had sight of the river.

'Schnell! Schnell! He'll get away,' gasped Fleischer and the thick stems wrapped his ankles so that he fell headlong in the mud. Two of his Askari dragged him up and they staggered on until the thicket of tall grass ended, and they stood on the elbow of the river bend with a clear view a thousand yards downstream.

Disturbed by the gun-fire, the birds were up, milling in confused flight above the reed-beds. Their alarm cries blended into a harsh chorus that spoiled the peace of the brooding dawn. They were the only living things in sight. From bank to far bank, the curved expanse of water was broken only by a few floating islands of papyrus grass; rafts of matted vegetation cut loose by the current and floating unhurriedly down towards the sea.

Panting, Herman Fleischer shook off the supporting hands of his two Askari and searched desperately for a glimpse of Flynn's bobbing head. 'Where did he go?' His fingers trembled as he fitted a new clip of ammunition into the Luger. 'Where did he go?' he demanded again, but none of his Askari drew attention to himself by venturing a reply.

'He must be on this side!' The Rufiji was half a mile wide here, Flynn could not have crossed it in the few minutes since they had last seen him. 'Search the bank!' Fleischer ordered. 'Find him!'

With relief the sergeant of his Askari turned on his men, quickly splitting them into two parties and sending them up and downstream to scour the water's edge.

Slowly Fleischer returned the pistol to its holster and fastened the flap, then he took a handkerchief from his pocket and mopped at his face and neck.

'Come on!' he snapped at his sergeant, and set off back towards the camp.

When he reached it, his men had already set out the folding table and chair. New life had been stirred into Flynn's camp-fire, and the Askari cook was preparing breakfast.

Sitting at the table with the front of his tunic open, spooning up oatmeal porridge and wild honey, Fleischer was soothed into a better humour by the food, and by the thorough manner in which the execution of the four captives was conducted.

When the last of them had stopped twitching and kicking and hung quietly with his comrades in the monkey-bean tree, Herman wiped up the bacon grease in his plate with a hunk of black bread and popped it into his mouth. The cook removed the plate and replaced it with a mug of steaming coffee at the exact moment when the two parties of searchers straggled into the clearing to report that a few drops of blood at the water's edge was the only sign they had found of Flynn O'Flynn.

'Ja,' Herman nodded, 'the crocodiles have eaten him.' He sipped appreciatively at his coffee mug before he gave his next orders. 'Sergeant, take this up to the launch.' He pointed at the stack of ivory on the edge of the clearing. 'Then we will go down to the Island of the Dogs and find this other white man with his English flag.'

– 8 –

There was only the entry wound, a dark red hole from which watery blood still oozed slowly. Flynn could have thrust his thumb into it but instead he groped gently around the back of his leg and located the lump in his flesh where the spent slug had come to rest just below the skin.

'God damn it, God damn it to hell,' he whispered in pain, and in anger, at the unlikely chance which had deflected the ricochet downwards to where he had stood below the bank, deflecting it with just sufficient velocity to lodge the bullet in his thigh instead of delivering a clean in-and-out wound.

Slowly he straightened his leg, testing it for broken bone. At the movement, the matt of drifting papyrus on which he lay rocked slightly.

'Might have touched the bone, but it's still in one piece,' he grunted with relief, and felt the first giddy swing of weakness in his head. In his ears was the faint rushing sound of a waterfall heard far off. 'Lost a bit of the old juice,' and from the wound a fresh trickle of bright blood broke and mingled with the water-drops to snake down his leg and drip into the dry matted papyrus. 'Got to stop that,' he whispered.

He was naked, his body still wet from the river. No belt or cloth to use as a tourniquet but he must staunch the bleeding. His fingers clumsy with the weakness of the wound, he tore a bunch of the long sword blade leaves from the reeds around him and began twisting them into a rope. Binding it around his leg above the wound, he pulled it tight and knotted it. The dribble of blood slowed and almost stopped before Flynn sank back and closed his eyes.

Beneath him the island swung and undulated with the eddy of the current and the wavelets pushed up by the rising morning wind. It was a soothing motion, and he was tired – terribly, achingly, tired. He slept.

The pain and the cessation of motion woke him at last. The pain was a dull persistent throb, a pulse that beat through his leg and groin and his lower belly. Groggily he pulled himself on to his elbows and looked down on his own body. The leg was swollen, bluish-looking from the constriction of the grass rope. He stared at it dully, without comprehension, for a full minute before memory flooded back.

'Gangrene!' he spoke aloud, and tore at the knot. The rope fell away and he gasped at the agony of new blood flowing into the leg, clenching his fists and grinding his teeth against it. The pain slowed and settled into a steady beat, and he breathed again, wheezy as a man with asthma.

Then the change of his circumstances came through to the conscious level of his mind and he peered around short-sightedly. The river had carried him down into the man-grove swamps again, down into the maze of little islands and water-ways of the delta. His raft of papyrus had been washed in and stranded against a mud bank by the falling tide. The mud stank of rotting vegetation and sulphur. Near him a gathering of big green river crabs were clicking and bubbling over the body of a dead fish, their little eye-stalks raised in perpetual surprise. At Flynn's movement they sidled away towards the water with their red-tipped claws raised defensively.

Water! Instantly Flynn was aware of the gummy saliva that glued his tongue to the roof of his mouth. Reddened by the harsh sunlight, heated by the first fever of his wound, his body was a furnace that craved moisture.

Flynn moved and instantly cried out in pain. His leg had stiffened while he slept. It was now a heavy anchor, shackling him helplessly to the papyrus raft. He tried again, easing himself backwards on his hands and his buttocks, dragging the leg after him. Each breath was a sob in his dry throat, each movement a white-hot lance into his thigh. But he must drink, he had to drink. Inch by inch, he worked his way to the edge of the raft and slid from it on to the mud bank.

The water had receded with the tide, and he was still

fifty paces from the edge. With the motion of a man swimming on his back, he moved across the slimy evil-smelling mud, and his leg slithered after him. It was beginning to bleed again, not copiously but a bright wine-drop at a time.

He reached the water at last, and rolled onto his side with the bad leg uppermost in an attempt to keep the wound out of the mud. On one elbow he buried his face in the water, drinking greedily. The water was warm, tainted with sea salt, and musky with rotted mangroves so it tasted like animal urine. But he gulped it noisily with his mouth and his nostrils and his eyes below the surface. At last he must breathe, and he lifted his head, panting for breath, coughing so the water shot up his throat, out through his nose and dimmed his vision with tears. Gradually his breathing steadied and his eyes cleared. Before he bowed his head to drink again, he glanced out across the channel and saw it coming.

It was on the surface, still a hundred yards away but swimming fast, driving towards him with the great tail churning the water. A big one – at least fifteen feet of it – showing like the rough bark of a pine log, leaving a wide wake across the surface as it came.

And Flynn screamed, just once, but shrill and high and achingly clear. Forgetting the wound in his panic, he tried to get to his feet, pushing himself up with his hands – but the leg pinned him. He screamed again, in pain and in fear.

Belly down, he wriggled in frantic haste from the shallow water back onto the mud bank, dragging himself across the glutinous slime, clawing and threshing towards the papyrus raft where it lay stranded among the mangrove roots fifty yards away. Expecting each moment to hear the slithering rush of the huge reptile across the mud behind him, he reached the first of the mangroves and rolled on his side, looking back, coated with black mud, his face working in his terror and the sound of it spilling in an incoherent babble through his lips.

The crocodile was at the edge of the mud bank, still in the river. Only its head showed above the surface and the little piggy bright eyes watched him unwinkingly, each set on its knot of horny scale.

Desperately Flynn looked about him. The mud bank was a tiny island with this grove of a dozen mangroves set in the centre of it. The trunks of the mangroves were twice as thick as a man's chest, but without branches for the first ten feet of their height; smooth bark slimy with mud and encrusted with little colonies of fresh-water mussels. Unwounded Flynn would not have been able to climb any of them – with his leg those branches above him were doubly inaccessible.

Wildly now he searched for a weapon – anything, no matter how puny – to defend himself. But there was nothing. Not a branch of driftwood, not a rock – only the thick black sheet of mud around him.

He looked back at the crocodile. It had not moved. His first feeble hope that it might not come out onto the mud bank withered almost before it was born. It would come. Cowardly, loathsome creature it was – but in time it would gather its courage. It had smelled his blood; it knew him to be wounded, helpless. It would come.

Painfully Flynn leaned his back against the roots of mangrove, and his terror settled down to a steady, pulsing fear – as steady as the pain in his leg. During the frantic flight across the bank, stiff mud had plugged the bullet hole and stopped the bleeding. But it does not matter now, Flynn thought, nothing matters. Only the creature out there, waiting while its appetite overcomes its timidity, swamps its reluctance to leave its natural element. It might take five minutes, or half a day – but, inevitably, it will come.

There was a tiny ripple around its snout, the first sign of its movement, and the long scaly head inched in towards the edge. Flynn stiffened.

The back showed, its scales like the patterned teeth of a file, and beyond it, the tail with the coxcomb double crest. Cautiously, on its short bowed legs, it waddled through the shallows. Wet and shiny, as broad across the back as a percheron stallion, more than a ton of cold, armoured flesh, it emerged from the water. Sinking elbow-deep into the soft mud, so its belly left a slide mark behind it. Grinning savagely, but with the jagged, irregular teeth lying yellow and long on its lips, and the small eyes watching him.

It came so slowly that Flynn lay passively against the tree, mesmerized by the deliberate waddling approach.

When it was half-way across the bank, it stopped – crouching, grinning – and he smelled it. The heavy odour of stale fish and musk on the warm air.

'Get away!' Flynn yelled at it, and it stood unmoving, unblinking. 'Get away!' He snatched up a handful of mud and hurled it. It crouched a little lower on its stubby legs and the fat crested tail stiffened, arching slightly.

Sobbing now, Flynn threw another handful of mud. The long grinning jaws opened an inch, then shut again. He heard the click as its teeth met, and it charged. Incredibly fast through the mud, grinning still, it slithered towards him.

This time Flynn's voice was a lunatic babble of horror and he writhed helplessly against the mangrove roots.

The deep booming note of the gun seemed not part of reality, but the crocodile reared up on its tail, drowning the echoes of the shot with its own hissing bellow, and above the next boom of the gun, Flynn heard the bullet strike the scaly body with a thump.

Mud sprayed as the reptile rolled in convulsions, and then, lifting itself high on its legs, it lumbered in ungainly flight towards the water. Again and again the heavy rifle fired, but the crocodile never faltered in its rush, and the surface of the water exploded like blown glass as it launched itself from the bank and was gone in the spreading ripples.

Standing in the bows of the canoe with the smoking rifle in his hands, while the paddlers drove in towards the bank, Sebastian Oldsmith shouted anxiously, 'Flynn, Flynn – did it get you? Are you all right?'

Flynn's reply was a croak. 'Bassie. Oh, Bassie boy, for the first time in my life I'm real pleased to see you,' and he sagged only half conscious against the mangrove roots.

– 9 –

The sun burned down on the dhow where it lay at anchor off the Island of the Dogs, yet a steady breeze came down the narrow waterway between the mangroves and plucked at the furled sail on the boom.

With a rope sling under his armpits, they lifted Flynn from the canoe and swung him, legs dangling, over the bulwark. Sebastian was ready to receive him and lower him gently to the deck.

'Get that goddamn sail up, and let's get the hell out of the river,' gasped Flynn.

'I must tend to your leg.'

'That can wait. We've got to get out into the open sea. The Germans have got a steam launch. They'll be looking for us. We can expect them to drop in on us at any minute.'

'They can't touch us – we're under the protection of the flag,' Sebastian protested.

'Listen, you stupid, bloody limey,' Flynn's voice was a squawk of pain and impatience. 'That murdering Hun will give us a rope dance with or without the flag. Don't argue, get that sail up!'

They laid him on a blanket in the shadow of the high poop before Sebastian hurried forward to release the Arab crew from the hold. They came up shiny with sweat and blinking in the dazzle of the sun. It took perhaps fifteen seconds for Mohammed to explain to them the urgency of the situation, and this invoked a few seconds of paralysed horror before they scattered to their stations. Four of them were hauling ineffectively at the anchor rope, but the great lump of coral was buried in the gluey mud of the bottom. Sebastian pushed them aside impatiently and with one knife stroke, severed the rope.

The crew, with the enthusiastic assistance of Flynn's bearers and gun-boys, ran up the faded and patched old sail. The wind caught it and bellied it. The deck canted slightly and two Arabs ran back to the tiller. From under the bows came the faint giggle of water, and from the stern spread a wide oily wake. With a cluster of the Arabs and bearers calling directions in the bows to the steersman at the rudder, the ancient dhow pointed downstream and ambled towards the sea.

When Sebastian went back to Flynn, he found old Mohammed squatting anxiously beside him and watching, as Flynn drank from the square bottle. Already a quarter of its contents had disappeared.

Flynn lowered the gin bottle, and breathed heavily through his mouth. 'Tastes like honey,' he gasped.

'Let's look at that leg.' Sebastian stooped over Flynn's naked, mud-besmeared body. 'My God, what a mess! Mohammed, get a basin of water and try and find some clean cloth.'

With the coming of evening, the breeze gathered strength, kicking up a chop on the widening water-ways of the delta. All afternoon the little dhow had butted against the run of the tide, but now began the ebb and it helped push her down towards the sea.

'With any luck we'll reach the mouth before sunset.' Sebastian was sitting beside Flynn's blanket-wrapped form under the poop. Flynn grunted. He was weak with pain, and groggy with gin. 'If we don't, we'll have to moor somewhere for the night. Can't risk the channel in the dark.' He received no reply from Flynn and himself fell silent.

Except for the gurgle of the bow-wave and the singsong chant of the pilot, a lazy silence blanketed the dhow. Most of the crew and the bearers were strewn in sleep about the deck, although two of them worked quietly over the open galley as they prepared the evening meal.

The heavy miasma of the swamps blended poorly with the stench of the bilges and the cargo of green ivory in the holds. It seemed to act as a drug, increasing Sebastian's fatigue. His head sagged forward on his chest and his hands slipped from the rifle in his lap. He slept.

The magpie chatter of the crew, and Mohammed's urgent hands on his shoulder, shook him awake. He came to his feet and gazed blearily around him. 'What is it? What is the trouble, Mohammed?'

For answer, Mohammed shouted the crew into silence, and turned back to Sebastian. 'Listen, master.'

Sebastian shook the remnants of sleep from his head, then cocked it slightly. 'I can't hear...' He stopped, an expression of uncertainty on his face.

Very faintly in the still of the evening he heard it, a faint huffing rhythm, as though a train passed in the distance. 'Yes,' he said, still uncertain. 'What is it?'

'The toot-toot boat, she comes.'

Sebastian stared at him without comprehension.

'The Allemand. The Germans.' Mohammed's hands fluttered with agitation. 'They follow us. They chase. They catch. They . . .' He clutched his own throat with both hands and rolled his eyes. His tongue protruded from the corner of his mouth.

Flynn's entire retinue was gathered in a mob around Sebastian, and at Mohammed's graphic little charade, they burst once more into a frightened chorus. Every eye was on Sebastian, waiting for his lead, and he felt confused, uncertain. Instinctively he turned to Flynn. Flynn lay on his back, his mouth open, snoring. Quickly Sebastian knelt beside him. 'Flynn! Flynn!' Flynn opened his eyes but they were focused beyond Sebastian's face. 'The Germans are coming.'

'The Campbells are coming. Hurrah! Hurrah!' muttered Flynn and closed his eyes again. His usually red face was flushed hot-scarlet with fever.

'What must I do?' pleaded Sebastian.

'Drink it!' advised Flynn. 'Never hesitate. Drink it!' his eyes still closed, his voice slurred.

'Please, Flynn. Please tell me.'

'Tell you?' muttered Flynn in delirium. 'Sure! Have you heard the one about the camel and the missionary?'

Sebastian jumped to his feet and looked wildly about him. The sun was low, perhaps another two hours to nightfall. *If only we can hold them off until then.* 'Mohammed. Get the gun-boys up into the stern,' he snapped, and Mohammed, recognizing the new crispness in his voice, turned on the mob about him to relay the order.

The ten gun-boys scattered to gather their weapons and

then crowded up on to the poop. Sebastian followed them, gazing anxiously back along the channel. He could see two thousand yards to the bend behind them and the channel was empty, but he was sure the sound of the steam engine was louder.

'Spread them along the rail,' he ordered Mohammed. He was thinking hard now; always a difficult task for Sebastian. Stubborn as a mule, his mind began to sulk as soon as he flogged it. He wrinkled his high scholar's forehead and his next thought emerged slowly. 'A barricade,' he said. The thin planking of the bulwark would offer little protection against the high-powered Mausers. 'Mohammed, get the others to carry up everything they can find, and pile it here to shield the steersmen and the gun-boys. Bring everything – water barrels, the sacks of coconuts, those old fishing-nets.'

While they hurried to obey the order, Sebastian stood in frowning concentration, prodding the mass within his skull and finding it as responsive as a lump of freshly kneaded dough. He tried to estimate the relative speeds of the dhow and a modern steam launch. Perhaps they were moving at half the speed of their pursuers. With a sliding sensation, he decided that even in this wind, sail could not hope to out-run a propeller-driven craft.

The word *propeller*, and the chance that at that moment he was forced to move aside to allow four of the men to drag an untidy bundle of old fishing-nets past, eased the next idea to the surface of his mind.

Humbled by the brilliance of his idea, he clung to it desperately, lest it somehow sink once more below the surface to be lost. 'Mohammed . . .' he stammered in his excitement. 'Mohammed, those nets . . .' He looked back again along the wide channel, and saw it still empty. He looked ahead and saw the next bend coming towards them; already the helmsman was chanting the orders preparatory to tacking the dhow. 'Those nets. I want to lay them across the channel.'

Mohammed stared at him aghast, his wizened face crinkling deeper in disbelief.

'Cut off the corks. Leave every fourth one.' Sebastian grabbed his shoulders and shook him in agitation. 'I want the net to sag. I don't want them to spot it too soon.'

They were almost up to the bend now, and Sebastian pointed ahead. 'We'll lay it just around the corner.'

'Why, master?' pleaded Mohammed. 'We must run. They are close now.'

'The propeller,' Sebastian shouted in his face. He made a churning motion with his hands. 'I want to snag the propeller.'

A moment longer Mohammed stared at him, then he began to grin, exposing his bald gums.

While they worked in frantic haste the muffled engine beat from upstream grew steadily louder, more insistent.

The dhow wallowed and balked at the efforts of the helmsman to work her across the channel. Her head kept falling away before the wind, threatening to snarl the net in her own rudder, but slowly the line of bobbing corks spread from the mangroves on one side towards the far bank, while in grim concentration Sebastian and a group led by Mohammed paid the net out over the stern. Every few minutes they lifted their faces to glance at the bend upstream, expecting to see the German launch appear and hear the crackle of Mauser fire.

Gradually the dhow edged in towards the north bank, sowing the row of corks behind her, and abruptly Sebastian realized that the net was too short – too short by fifty yards. There would be a gap in their defence. If the launch cut the bend fine, hugging the bank as it came, then they were lost.

Already the note of its engine was so close that he could hear the metallic whine of the drive shaft.

Now also there was a new problem. How to anchor the loose end of the net? To let it float free would allow the current to wash it away, and open the gap still further.

'Mohammed. Fetch one of the tusks. The biggest one you can find. Quickly. Go quickly.'

Mohammed scampered away and returned immediately, the two bearers with him staggering under the weight of the long curved shaft of ivory.

His hands clumsy with haste, Sebastian lashed the end rope of the net to the tusk. Then grunting with the effort, he and Mohammed hoisted it to the side rail, and pushed it overboard. As it splashed, Sebastian shouted at the helmsman, 'Go!' and pointed downstream. Thankfully the Arab wrenched the tiller across. The dhow spun on her heel and pointed once more towards the sea.

Silently, anxiously, Sebastian and his gun-boys lined the stern and gazed back at the bend of the channel. In the fists of each of them were clutched the short-barrelled elephant rifles, and their faces were set intently.

The chug of the steam engine rose louder and still louder.

'Shout as soon as it shows,' Sebastian ordered. 'Shoot as fast as you can. Keep them looking at us, so they don't see the net.'

And the launch came around the bend; flying a ribbon of grey smoke from its single stack and the bold red, yellow and black flag of the Empire at its bows. A neat little craft, forty-footer, low in the waist, small deckhouse aft, gleaming white in the sunlight, and the white moustache of the bow wave curled about her bows.

'Shoot!' bellowed Sebastian as he saw the Askari clustered on the foredeck. 'Shoot!' and his voice was lost in the concerted blast of the heavy-calibre rifles around him. One of the Askari was flung backwards against the deckhouse, his arms spread wide as he hung there a moment in the attitude of crucifixion before subsiding gently on to the deck. His comrades scattered and dropped into cover behind the steel bulwark. A single figure was left alone on the deck; a massive figure in the light grey uniform of the German colonial service, with his wide-brimmed slouch hat, and gold gleaming at the shoulders of his tunic.

Sebastian took him in the notch of his rear sight, held the bead on his chest, and jerked the trigger. The rifle jumped joyously against his shoulder, and he saw a fountain of spray leap from the surface of the river a hundred yards beyond the launch. Sebastian fired again, closing his eyes in anticipation of the savage recoil of the rifle. When he opened them, the German officer was still on his feet, shooting back at Sebastian with a pistol in his outstretched right hand. He was making better practice than Sebastian. The fluting hum of his fire whipped about Sebastian's head, or smacked into the planking of the dhow.

Hastily Sebastian ducked behind the water barrel and clawed a pair of cartridges from his belt. Sharper, higher than the dull booming of the elephant rifles, climbed the brittle crackle of the Mauser fire as the Askari joined in.

Cautiously Sebastian lifted his eyes above the water barrel. The launch was cutting the bend fine, and with a sudden swoop of dismay, he knew it was going to clear the fishnet by twenty feet. He dropped his rifle on to the deck and jumped to his feet. A Mauser bullet missed his ear by so little that it nearly burst his eardrum. Instinctively he ducked, then checked the movement and instead ran to the helmsman. 'Get out of the way!' he yelled in his excitement and his fear. Roughly he shoved the man aside and, grasping the tiller, pushed it across. Perilously close to the jibe, the dhow veered across the channel, opening the angle between it and the launch. Looking back Sebastian saw the fat German officer turn and shout an order towards the wheelhouse.

Almost immediately the bows of the launch swung, following the dhow's manoeuvre, and Sebastian felt triumph flare in his chest. Now directly in the path of the launch lay the line of tiny black dots that marked the net.

His deep-drawn breath trapped in his lungs, Sebastian watched the launch sweep over the net. His grip on the tiller tightened until his knuckles threatened to push out through the skin, and then he expelled his breath in a howl of joy and relief.

For the line of corks was suddenly plucked below the surface, leaving the small disturbance of ripples where each had stood. For ten seconds the launch sped on, then abruptly the even sound of her passage altered, a harsh clattering intruded, and her bows swung suddenly as she slowed.

The gap between the two craft widened. Sebastian saw the German officer drag a frightened Askari from the wheel-house and club him unmercifully about the head, but the squeals of Teutonic fury were muted by the swiftly increasing distance, and then drowned by the tumultuous clamour of his own crew, as they pranced and danced about the deck.

The Arab helmsman hopped up on to the water barrel and hoisted the skirts of his dirty grey robe to expose his naked posterior at the launch in calculated mockery.

– 11 –

Long after the dhow had sailed sedately first out of rifle range, and then out of sight, Herman Fleischer gave himself over completely to the epilepsy of frustrated anger. He raved about the tiny deck, lashing out with ham-sized fists while his Askari skittled around him trying to keep out of range. Repeatedly he returned to the unconscious form of his helmsman to kick him as he lay. At last his fury burned itself down to the level where it allowed him to trundle aft and hang over the stern rail peering down at the sodden bundle of netting which was wrapped around the propeller.

'Sergeant!' His voice was hoarse with strain. 'Get two men with knives over the side to cut that away!'

And a stillness fell upon them all. Every man tried to shrink himself down into insignificance, so that the choice might not fall on him. Two volunteers were selected, divested of their uniforms and hustled to the stern, despite their terrified entreaties.

'Tell them to hurry,' grunted Herman, and went to his folding chair. His personal boy placed the evening meal with its attendant pitcher of beer on the table before him and Herman fell to.

Once from the stern there was a squeak and a splash, following by a furious burst of rifle fire. Herman frowned and looked up from his plate.

'A crocodile has taken one of the men,' his sergeant reported in agitation.

'Well, put another one over,' said Herman and returned with unabated relish to his meal. This last batch of sausage was particularly tasty.

The netting had wound so tightly about the blades and shaft of the propeller, that it was an hour after midnight when the last of it was hacked away by lantern light.

The drive shaft had twisted slightly and run one of its bearings, so even at quarter speed there was a fearsome clattering and threshing sound from the stern as the launch limped slowly down the channel towards the sea.

In the grey and pallid pink of dawn they crept past the last island of mangroves and the launch lifted her head to the sluggish thrust of the Indian Ocean. It was a windless morning of flat calm, and Herman peered without hope into

49

the misty half light that obscured the ocean's far horizon. He had come this far only on the slight chance that the dhow might have gone aground on a mud bank during her night run down the river.

'Stop!' he shouted at his battered helmsman. Immediately the agonized clatter of the propeller ceased, and the launch rose and fell uneasily on the long oily swells.

So they had got clear away then. He could not risk his damaged launch on the open sea. He must go back, and leave the dhow and its ivory and its many candidates for the rope, to head unmolested for that pest-hole of rogues and pirates on Zanzibar Island.

Moodily he looked out across the sea and mourned that cargo of ivory. There had been perhaps a million Reichsmarks of it aboard, of which his unofficial handling fee would have been considerable.

Also he mourned the departure of the Englishman. He had never hanged one before.

He sighed and tried to comfort himself with the thought of that damned American, now well digested in the maw of a crocodile, but truly it would have been more satisfying to see him kick and spin on the rope.

He sighed again. Ah, well! At least he would no longer have the perpetual worry of Flynn O'Flynn's presence on his border, nor would he have to suffer the nagging of Governor Schee and his endless demands for O'Flynn's head.

Now it was breakfast time. He was about to turn away when something out there in the lightening dawn caught his attention.

A long low shape, its outline becoming crisper as he watched. There were cries from his Askari as they saw it also, huge in the dawn. The stark square turrets with their slim gun-barrels, the tall triple stacks and the neat geometrical patterns of its rigging.

'The *Blücher*!' roared Herman in savage elation. 'The *Blücher*, by God!' He recognized the cruiser, for he had seen her not six months before, lying in Dar es Salaam harbour. 'Sergeant, bring the signal pistol!' He was capering with excitement. In reply to Herman's hasty message, Governor Schee must have sent the *Blücher* racing southwards to blockade the Rufiji mouth. 'Start the engine. Schnell! Run out to her,' he shouted at the helmsman as he slid one of the fat Verey cartridges into the gaping breech of the pistol, snapped it closed and pointed the muzzle to the sky.

Beside the tall bulk of the cruiser the launch was as tiny as a floating leaf, and Herman looked up with apprehension at the frail rope ladder he was expected to climb. His Askari assisted him across the narrow strip of water between the two vessels and he hung for a desperate minute until his feet found the rungs and he began his ponderous ascent. Sweating profusely he was helped on to the deck by two seamen and faced an honour guard of a dozen or more. Heading them was a young lieutenant in crisp, smart tropical whites.

Herman shrugged off the helping hands, drew himself to attention with a click of heels. 'Commissioner Fleischer.' His voice shaky with exertion.

'Lieutenant Kyller.' The officer clicked and saluted.

'I must see your captain immediately. A matter of extreme urgency.'

Kapitän zur See Count Otto von Kleine inclined his head gravely as he greeted Herman. He was a tall, thin man, who wore a neat, pointed blond beard with just a few threads of grey to give it dignity. 'The English have landed a full-scale expeditionary force in the Rufiji delta, supported by capital ships? This is correct?' he asked immediately.

'The report was exaggerated.' Herman regretted bitterly the impetuous wording of his message to the Governor; he had been fired with patriotic ardour at the time. 'In fact, it was only . . . ah,' he hesitated, 'one vessel.'

'Of what strength? What is her armament?' demanded von Kleine.

'Well, it was an unarmed vessel.'

And von Kleine frowned. 'Of what type?'

Herman flushed with embarrassment. 'An Arab dhow. Of about twenty-two metres.'

'But this is impossible. Ridiculous. The Kaiser has delivered an ultimatum to the British Consul in Berlin. He has issued mobilization orders to five divisions.' The captain spun on his heel and began to pace restlessly about his bridge, clapping his hands together in agitation. 'What was the purpose of this British invasion? Where is this . . . this dhow? What explanation must I send to Berlin?'

'I have since learned that the expedition was led by a notorious ivory poacher named O'Flynn. He was shot resisting arrest by my Askari, but his accessory, an unknown Englishman, escaped down the river last night in the dhow.'

'Where will they be headed?' The captain stopped pacing and glared at Herman.

'Zanzibar.'

'This is stupidity, utter stupidity. We will be a laughing stock! A battle cruiser to catch a pair of common criminals!'

'But, Captain, you must pursue them.'

'To what purpose?'

'If they escape to tell their story, the dignity of the Emperor will be lowered throughout the length of Africa. Think if the British Press were to hear of this! Also, these men are dangerous criminals.'

'But I cannot board a foreign ship on the high seas. Especially if she flies the Union Jack. It would be an act of war – an act of piracy.'

'But, Captain, if she were to sink with all hands, sink without a trace?'

And Captain von Kleine nodded thoughtfully. Then abruptly he snapped his fingers and turned to his pilot. 'Plot me a course for Zanzibar Island.'

– 13 –

They lay becalmed below a sky of brazen cobalt, and every hour of the calm allowed the Mozambique current to push the little dhow another three miles off its course. Aimlessly she swung her head to meet each of the long swells, and then let it fall away into the troughs.

For the twentieth time since dawn, Sebastian climbed up on to the poop-deck and surveyed the endless waters, searching for a ruffle on the glassy surface that would herald the wind. But there was never any sign of it. He looked towards the west, but the blue line of the coast had long since sunk below the horizon.

'I'm an old dog, *Fisi*,' bellowed Flynn from the lower deck. 'Hear me laugh,' and he imitated faithfully the yammering cry of an hyena. All day Flynn had regaled the company with snatches of song and animal imitations. Yet his delirium was interspaced with periods of lucidity. 'I reckon this time old Fleischer got me good, Bassie. There's a sack of poison forming round that bullet. I can feel it there. A fat, hot sack of it. Reckon we've got to dig for it pretty soon. Reckon if we can't make it back to Zanzibar pretty soon, we're going to have to dig for it.' Then his mind escaped once more into the hot land of delirium.

'My little girl, I'll bring you a pretty ribbon. There, don't cry. A pretty ribbon for a pretty girl.' His voice syrupy, then suddenly harsh. 'You cheeky little bitch. You're just like that goddamned mother of yours. Don't know why I don't chase you out,' this last followed immediately by the hyena imitation again.

Now Sebastian turned away from the poop rail and looked down on Flynn. Beside him the faithful Mohammed was dipping strips of cloth in a bucket of sea water, wringing them out and then laying them on Flynn's flushed forehead in a futile attempt to reduce the fever.

Sebastian sighed. His responsibilities lay heavily. The command of the expedition had devolved squarely upon him. And yet, there was a sneaky sensation of pleasure, of pride in his execution of that command to the present. He went back and replayed in his mind the episode of the fish-net, remembering the quick decision that had altered the launch's course and lured it into the trap. He smiled at the memory, and the smile was not his usual self-effacing grin, but something harder. When he turned away to pace the narrow deck there was more spring in his step, and he set his shoulders square.

Again he stopped by the rail and looked towards the west. There was a cloud on the horizon, a tiny dark figure of it. And he watched it with hope that it might herald the start of the afternoon sea breeze. Yet it seemed unnatural. As he watched, it moved. He could swear it moved. Now

54

his whole attention was fastened upon it. Realization began to flicker in him, building up until it was certainty.

A ship. By God, a ship!

He ran to the poop ladder, and slid down into the waist, across it to the mast.

The crew and the bearers watched him with awakening interest. Some of them got to their feet.

Sebastian jumped on to the boom, balancing there a moment before he started to shin up the mast. Using the mainsail hoops like the rungs of a ladder, he reached the masthead and clung there, peering eagerly into the west.

There she was – no doubt about it. He could see the tips of the triple stacks, each with its feather of dark smoke, and he began to cheer.

Below him the rail was lined with his men, all peering out in the direction they took from him. Sebastian slid down the mast, the friction burning his hands in his haste. His feet hit the deck and he ran to Flynn. 'A ship. A big ship coming up fast.' Flynn rolled his head and looked at him vaguely. 'Listen to me, Flynn. There'll be a doctor aboard. We'll get you to a port in no time.'

'That's good, Bassie.' Flynn's brain clicked back into focus. 'You've done real good.'

She came up over the horizon with astonishing rapidity, and her silhouette changed as she altered course towards them. But not before Sebastian had seen the gun turrets.

'A warship!' he shouted. To his mind this proved her British – only one nation ruled the waves. 'They've seen us!' He waved his hands above his head.

Bows on, each second growing in size, grey and big, she bore down upon the little dhow.

Gradually the cheering of the crew faltered and subsided into an uneasy silence. Magnified by the still, hot air, huge on the velvety gloss of the ocean, lifting a bow wave of pearling white, the warship came on. No check in her speed, the ensign at her masthead streaming away from them so they could not see the colours.

'What are they going to do?' Sebastian asked aloud, and was answered by Flynn's voice. Sebastian glanced around. Balancing on his good leg with one arm draped around Mohammed's neck, Flynn was hopping across the deck towards him.

'I'll tell you what they're going to do! They're going to hit us smack-bang up the arse!' Flynn roared. 'That's the *Blücher*! That's a German cruiser!'

'They can't do that!' Sebastian protested.

'You'd like to bet? She's coming straight from the Rufiji delta – and my guess is she's had a chat with Fleischer. He's probably aboard her.' Flynn swayed against Mohammed, gasping with the pain of his leg before he went on. 'They're going to ram us, and then machine-gun anyone still floating.'

'We've got to make a life raft.'

'No time, Bassie. Look at her come!'

Less than five miles away, but swiftly narrowing the distance, the *Blücher*'s tall bows knifed towards them. Wildly Sebastian looked around the crowded deck, and he saw the pile of cork floats they had cut from the fish nets.

Drawing his knife, he ran to one of the sacks of coconuts and cut the twine that closed the mouth. He slipped the knife back into its sheath, stooped, and up-ended the sack, spilling coconuts on to the deck. Then with the empty sack in his hand he ran to the pile of floats and dropped on his knees. In frantic haste he shovelled them into the sack, half filling it before he looked up again. The *Blücher* was two miles away, a tall tower of murderous grey steel.

With a length of rope Sebastian tied the sack closed and dragged it to where Flynn stood supported by Mohammed.

'What are you doing?' Flynn demanded.

'Fixing you up! Lift your arms!' Flynn obeyed and

56

Sebastian tied the free end of the rope around his chest at the level of his armpits. He paused to unlace and kick off his boots before speaking again. 'Mohammed, you stay with him. Hang on to the sack and don't let go.' He left them, trotting on bare feet to find his rifle propped against the poop. Buckling on his cartridge belt, he hurried back to the rail.

Sebastian Oldsmith was about to engage a nine-inch battle cruiser with a double-barrelled Gibbs .500.

She was close now, hanging over them like a high cliff of steel. Even Sebastian could not miss a battle cruiser at two hundred yards, and the heavy bullets clanged against the armoured hull, ringing loudly above the hissing rush of the bow wave.

While he reloaded, Sebastian looked up at the line of heads in the bows of the *Blücher*; grinning faces below the white caps with their little swallow-tailed black ribbons. 'You bloody swine,' he shouted at them. Hatred stronger than he had ever dreamed possible choked his voice. 'You filthy, bloody swine.' He lifted the rifle and fired without effect, and the *Blücher* hit the dhow.

It struck with a crash and the crackling roar of rending timber. It crushed her side and cut through in the screaming of dying men and the squeal of planking against steel.

It trod the dhow under, breaking her back, forcing her far below the surface. At the initial shock, Sebastian was hurled overboard, the rifle thrown from his hands. He struck the armoured plate of the cruiser a glancing blow and then dropped into the sea beside her. The thrust of the bow wave tumbled him aside, else he would have been dragged along the hull and his body shredded against the steel plate.

He surfaced just in time to suck a lungful of air before the turbulence of the great screws caught him and plucked him under again, driving him deep so the pressure stabbed like red-hot needles in his eardrums. He felt himself swirled end over end, buffeted, shaken vigorously as the water tore at his body.

Colour flashed and zigzagged behind his closed eyelids. There was a suffocating pain in his chest and his lungs pumped, urgently craving air, but he sealed his lips and kicked out with his legs, clawing at the water with his hands.

The churning wake of the cruiser released its grip upon him, and he was shot to the surface with such force that he broke clear to the waist before dropping back to drink air greedily. He unbuckled the heavy cartridge belt and let it sink before he looked about him.

The surface of the sea was scattered with floating debris, and a few bobbing human heads. Near him a section of torn planking rose in a burst of trapped air bubbles. Sebastian struck out for it and clung there, his legs hanging in the clear green water.

'Flynn,' he gasped. 'Flynn, where are you?'

A quarter of a mile away, the *Blücher* was circling slowly, long and menacing and shark-like, and he stared at it in hatred and in fear.

'Master!' Mohammed's voice behind him.

Sebastian turned quickly and saw the black face and the red face beside the floating sack of corks a hundred yards away. 'Flynn!'

'Good-bye, Bassie,' Flynn called. 'The old Hun is coming back to finish us off. Look! They've got machine guns set up on the bridge. See you on the other side, boy.'

Quickly Sebastian looked back at the cruiser and saw the clusters of white uniforms on the angle of her bridge. 'Ja, there are still some of them alive.' Through borrowed binoculars, Fleischer scanned the littered area of the wreck. 'You will use the Maxims, of course, Captain? It will be quicker than picking them off with rifles.'

Captain von Kleine did not answer. He stood tall on his

bridge, slightly round-shouldered, staring out at the wreckage with his hands clasped behind him. 'There is something sad in the death of a ship,' he murmured. 'Even such a dirty little one as this.' Suddenly he straightened his shoulders and turned to Fleischer. 'Your launch is waiting for you at the mouth of the Rufiji. I will take you there, Commissioner.'

'But first the business of the survivors.'

Von Kleine's expression hardened. 'Commissioner, I sank that dhow in what I believed to be my duty. But now I am not sure that my judgement was not clouded by anger. I will not trespass further on my conscience by machine-gunning swimming civilians.'

'You will then pick them up. I must arrest them and give them trial.'

'I am not a policeman,' he paused and his expression softened a little. 'That one who fired the rifle at us. I think he must be a brave man. He is a criminal, perhaps, but I am not so old in the ways of the world that I do not love courage merely for its own sake. I would not like to know I have saved this man for the noose. Let the sea be the judge and the executioner.' He turned to his lieutenant. 'Kyller, prepare to drop one of the life rafts.' The lieutenant stared at him in disbelief. 'You heard me?'

'Yes, my Captain.'

'Then do it.' Ignoring Fleischer's squawks of protest, von Kleine crossed to the pilot. 'Alter course to pass the survivors at a distance of fifty metres.'

'Here she comes.' Flynn grinned tightly, without humour, and watched the cruiser swing ponderously towards them.

The cries of the swimmers around him, pleading mercy, were plaintive as the voices of sea birds – tiny on the immensity of the ocean.

'Flynn. Look at the bridge!' Sebastian's voice floated across to him. 'See him there. The grey uniform.'

Tears from the sting of sea salt in his wound, and the distortion of fever had blurred Flynn's vision, yet he could make out the spot of grey among the speckling of white uniforms on the bridge of the cruiser.

'Who is it?'

'You were right. It's Fleischer,' Sebastian shouted back, and Flynn began to curse.

'Hey, you filthy, fat butcher,' he bellowed, trying to drag himself up onto the floating sack of corks. 'Hey, you whore's chamber pot.' His voice carried above the murmur of the cruiser's engines running at dead-slow. 'Come on, you blood-smeared little pig.'

The tall hull of the cruiser was close now, so close he could see the bulky figure in grey turn to the tall white-uniformed officer beside him, gesticulating in what was clearly entreaty.

The officer turned away, and moved to the rail of the bridge. He leaned out and waved to a group of seamen on the deck below him.

'That's right. Tell them to shoot. Let's get it over with. Tell them . . .'

A large square object was lifted over the rail by the gang below the bridge. It dropped and fell with a splash alongside.

Flynn's voice dried up, and he watched in disbelief as the white-clad officer lifted his right arm in a gesture that might have been a salute. The beat of the cruiser's engines mounted as it increased speed, and she swung away towards the west.

Flynn O'Flynn began to laugh, the cackling hysteria of relief and delirium. He rolled off the sack of corks and his head dropped forward, so the warm green water smothered his laughter. Mohammed took a handful of the grey hair and lifted his face to prevent him drowning.

Sebastian reached the raft, and grasped the rope that hung in loops around its sides. He paused to regain his breath before hauling himself up to lie gasping, the blood-warm sea-water streaming from his sodden clothing, and watched the shape of the battle cruiser recede into the west.

'Master! Help me!'

The voice roused him and he sat up. Mohammed was struggling, dragging Flynn and the sack through the water. Among the floating wreckage a dozen others of the crew and the bearers were flapping their way towards the raft; the weaker swimmers were already failing, their cries becoming more pitiful, and their splashing more frenzied.

There were oars roped to the slatted deck of the raft. Quickly Sebastian cut one loose with his hunting knife and began rowing towards the pair. His progress was slow, for the raft was an ungainly bitch that balked and swung away from the thrust of the oar.

An Arab crewman reached the raft and scrambled aboard, then another, and another. Each of them freed an oar and helped with the rowing. They passed the body of one of the bearers floating just below the surface, both its legs cut off above the knees and the bones sticking out of the ragged meat of the stumps. This was not the only one – there was other human flotsam among the scattered wreckage, and the pinky-brown stains that drifted away on the current attracted the sharks.

The Arab beside Sebastian saw the first one and called out, pointing with the oar.

It came hunting, its fin waggling from side to side as it tacked up against the current, so that they could sense its excitement, the cold, unthinking excitement of Euselachii hunger. Below the surface, distorted and dark, showed the tapering length of its body. Not a big one. Perhaps nine feet in length and four hundred pounds in weight, but big enough to chop a leg with one bite. No longer guided by the drift of blood-taste, picking up the vibrations of the swimmers, it straightened and came in on its first run.

'Shark!' Sebastian yelled at Flynn and Mohammed where they floundered ten yards away. And both of them panicked; no longer making for the raft, they tried to clamber on to the sack of corks. Terror has no logic. Their only concern was to lift their dangling legs from the water, but the sack was too small, too unstable and their panic attracted the shark's attention. It veered towards them, showing the full height of its curved triangular fin, each sweep of its tail breaking the surface as it drove in.

'This way,' shouted Sebastian. 'Come to the raft!' He was hacking at the water with the oar, while beside him the Arabs worked in equal dedication. 'This way, Flynn. For God's sake, this way.'

His voice penetrated their panic, and once more they struck out for the raft. But the shark was closing fast, long and dappled by sunlight through the surface ripple.

The sack was still tied to Flynn's body, and its resistance to the water slowed them as it dragged behind. The shark swerved and made its first pass; it seemed to hump up out of the water, and its mouth opened. The upper jaw bulged out, the lower jaw gaped, and the multiple rows of teeth came erect like the quills of a porcupine, *and it hit the sack*. Locking its jaws into the coarse jute material, worrying it, still humped out of the water, shaking its blunt head clumsily, scattering a spray of water drops that flew like shattered glass in the sun.

'Grab here!' commanded Sebastian, leaning out to offer the blade of the oar to the pair in the water. They clutched at it with the strength of fear, and Sebastian drew them in.

But the sack and the shark were still attached to Flynn, its threshing threatening to break Flynn's hold on the life-line around the raft.

Dropping to his knees, Sebastian fumbled the knife from its sheath and sawed at the rope. It parted. The shark, still worrying the sack, worked away from the raft and Sebastian helped the Arabs to drag first Flynn, and then Mohammed, over the side.

They were not finished yet. There were still half a dozen men in the water.

Realizing its error at last, the shark relinquished its hold on the sack. It backed away. For a moment it hung motionless, puzzled, then it circled out towards the nearest sound of splashing. One of the gun-boys, clawing at the water in exhausted dog-paddle. The shark hit him in the side, and pulled him under. Moments later he reappeared, his mouth an open pink cave as he screamed, the water about him clouded dark red-brown by his own blood. Again he was pulled under as the shark hit his legs, but again he floated. This time face down, wriggling feebly, and the shark circled him, dashing in to chop off a mouthful of his flesh, backing away to gulp it down before coming in again.

Then there was another shark, two more, ten, so many that Sebastian could not count them, as they circled and dived in ecstatic greed, until the sea around the raft trembled and swirled in agitation.

Sebastian and his Arabs managed to drag two more of the crew into the raft and they had a third half out of the water when a six-foot white-pointer shot up from the depths, and fastened on his thigh with such violence that it almost jerked all of them overboard. But they steadied themselves and held on to the man's arms, frozen in this gruesome tug-of-war, while the shark worried the leg, so dog-like in its determination that Sebastian expected it to growl.

Little Mohammed staggered to his feet, snatched up an oar and swung it against the pointed snout with all his strength. They had dragged the shark's head from the water, and the oar fell on it with a series of rubbery thumps, but the shark held on. Fresh, bright blood squirted and trickled from the leg in its jaws, running down the shark's glistening snake-like head into the open slits of its gill covers.

'Hold him!' gasped Sebastian, and drew his knife. The raft rocking crazily under him, he leaned over the man's outstretched body and drove the knife blade into the shark's expressionless little eye. It popped in a burst of clear fluid, and the shark stiffened and trembled. Sebastian withdrew the blade and stabbed into the other eye. With a convulsive gulp the shark opened its jaws and slid back into the sea to meander blindly away.

There were no more swimmers. The little group on the raft huddled together and watched the shark pack milling hungrily, seeming to sniff at the tainted water as they gathered the last morsels of meat.

The shark victim hosed the deck with his severed femoral artery and died before any of them could rouse themselves to apply a tourniquet.

'Push him over,' grunted Flynn.

'No,' Sebastian shook his head.

'Chrissake, we're crowded enough as it is. Chuck the poor bastard over.'

'Later on, not now.' Sebastian could not stand to watch the sharks squabble over the corpse.

'Mohammed, get a couple of your lads on the oars. I want to pick up as many of those coconuts as we can.'

By the time darkness stopped them, they had retrieved fifty-two of the floating coconuts, sufficient to keep the seven of them thirst-free for a week.

It was cold that night. They crowded together for warmth

and watched the underwater pyrotechnics, as the shark pack circled the raft in phosphorescent splendour.

– 15 –

'Yᴏu've got to cut for it,' Flynn whispered, and he shivered with cold in the burning heat of the midday sun.

'I don't know anything about it,' Sebastian protested, yet he could see that Flynn was dying.

'No more do I. But this is certain – you've got to do it soon . . .' Flynn's eyes had sunk into plum-coloured cavities and the smell of his breath was that of something long dead.

Staring at the leg, Sebastian had difficulty controlling his nausea. It was swollen fat and purple. The bullet hole was covered with a crusty black scab, but Sebastian caught a whiff of the putrefaction under it – and this time his nausea came up acid-sweet into the back of his throat. He swallowed it.

'You've got to do it, Bassie boy.'

Sebastian nodded, and tentatively laid his hand on the leg. Immediately he jerked his fingers away, surprised by the heat of the skin.

'You've got to do it,' urged Flynn. 'Feel for the slug. It's not deep. Just under the skin.'

He felt the lump. It moved under his fingers, the size of a green acorn in the taut hot flesh.

'It's going to hurt like Billy-o.' Sebastian's voice was hoarse.

The rowers were resting on their oars, watching with frank curiosity, while the raft eddied and swung in the drift of the Mozambique current. Above them the sail that Sebastian had rigged from salvaged planking and canvas flapped wearily, throwing a shadow across the leg.

'Mohammed, you and one other to hold the master's shoulders. Two others to keep his legs still.'

Flynn lay quiescent, pinioned beneath them on the slats of the deck.

Sebastian knelt over him, gathering his resolve. The knife he had sharpened against the metal edge of the raft, and then scrubbed clean with coconut fibre and seawater. He had sluiced the leg also, and washed his hands until the skin tingled. Beside him on the deck stood half a coconut shell containing perhaps an ounce of evaporated salt scraped from the deck and the sail, ready to pack into the open wound. 'Ready?' he whispered.

'Ready,' grunted Flynn, and Sebastian located the lump of the bullet and drew the edge of the blade across it timidly. Flynn gasped, but human skin was tougher than Sebastian allowed. It did not part.

'Goddamn you!' Flynn was sweating already. 'Don't play with it. Cut, man, cut!'

This time Sebastian slashed, and the flesh split open under the blade. He dropped the knife and drew back in horror as the infection bubbled up through the lips of the knife wound. It looked like yellow custard mixed with prune juice – and the smell of it filled his nostrils and his throat.

'Go for the slug. Go for it with your fingers.' Flynn writhed beneath the men who held him. 'Hurry. Hurry. I can't take much more.'

Steeling himself, closing his throat against the vomit that threatened to vent at any moment, Sebastian slipped his little finger into the slit. Hooking with it for the bullet, finding it, easing it up although tissue clung to it reluctantly, until it popped from the wound and dropped on to the deck. A fresh gush of warm poison followed it out, flowing over Sebastian's hand, and he crawled to the edge of the raft, choking and gagging.

16

'If only we had some red cloth.' Flynn sat against the rickety mast. He was still very weak but four days ago the fever had broken with the release of the poison.

'What would you do with it?' Sebastian asked.

'Catch me one of those dolphins. Man, I'm so god-damned hungry I'd eat it raw.'

A four-day diet of coconut pulp and milk had left all their bellies grumbling.

'Why red?'

'They go for red. Make a lure.'

'You haven't any hooks or line.'

'Tie it to a bit of twine from the sack and tease them up to the surface – then harpoon one with your knife tied to an oar.'

Sebastian was silent, peering thoughtfully over the side at the deep flashes of gold where the shoal of dolphin played under the raft. 'It's got to be red, hey?' he asked, and Flynn looked at him sharply.

'Yeah. It's got to be red.'

'Well . . .' Sebastian hesitated, and then flushed with embarrassment under his tropical sunburn.

'What's wrong with you?'

Still blushing, Sebastian stood up and loosened his belt – then, shyly as a bride on her wedding night, he drew down his pants.

'My God,' breathed Flynn in shock, as he held up his hand to shield his eyes.

'Hau! Hau!' was the chorus of admiration from the crew.

'Got them at Harrods,' said Sebastian with becoming modesty.

Red, Flynn had asked for – but Sebastian's underpants were the brightest, most beautiful red; the most vivid sunset and roses red, he could have imagined. They hung in oriental splendour to Sebastian's knees.

'Pure silk,' said Sebastian, fingering the cloth. 'Ten shillings a pair.'

'Whoa now! Come on, little fishy. Come on there,' Flynn whispered as he lay on his belly, head and shoulders over the edge of the raft. On its thread of twine, the scrap of red danced deep in the green water. A long, slithering flash of gold shot towards it, and Flynn jerked the twine away at the last instant. The dolphin swirled and darted back. Again Flynn jerked the twine. Chameleon lines and dots of excitement showed against the gold of the dolphin's body. 'That's it, fishy. Chase it.' The other fish of the shoal joined hunt, forming a sparkling planetary system of movement around the lure. 'Get ready!'

'I'm ready.' Sebastian stood over him, poised like a javelin thrower. In the excitement he had forgotten to don his pants and his shirt-tails flapped around his thighs in a most undignified manner. But his legs were long and finely muscled, the legs of an athlete. 'Get back!' he snapped at the crew who were crowded around him so that the raft was listing dangerously. 'Get back – give me room,' and he hefted the oar with the long hunting knife lashed to the tip.

'Here they come.' Flynn's voice trembled with excitement as he worked the scrap of red cloth upwards, and the shoal followed it. 'Now!' he shouted as a single fish broke the surface – four feet of flashing gold, and Sebastian lunged. The steady hand and eye that had once clean-bowled the great Frank Woolley directed the oar. Sebastian hit the dolphin an inch behind the eye, and the blade slipped through to lacerate the gills.

For a few seconds the oar came alive in his hands as the

dolphin twitched and fought on the blade, but there were no barbs to hold in the flesh, and the fish slipped from the knife.

'God damn it to hell!' bellowed Flynn.

'Dash it all!' echoed Sebastian.

But ten feet down the dolphin was mortally wounded; it jigged and whipped like a golden kite in a high wind while the rest of the shoal scattered.

Sebastian dropped the oar and began stripping his shirt.

'What are you doing?' demanded Flynn.

'Going after it.'

'You're mad. Sharks!'

'I'm so hungry, I'll eat a shark also,' and he dived over the side. Thirty seconds later he surfaced, blowing like a grampus but grinning triumphantly, with the dead dolphin clasped lovingly to his bosom.

They ate strips of raw fish seasoned with evaporated salt, squatting around the mutilated carcass of the dolphin.

'Well, I've paid a guinea for worse meals than this,' said Sebastian, and belched softly. 'Oh, I beg your pardon.'

'Granted,' Flynn grunted with his mouth full of fish; and then eyeing Sebastian's nudity with a world-weary eye, 'Stop boasting and put your pants on before you trip over it.'

Flynn O'Flynn was slowly, very slowly, revising his estimate of Sebastian Oldsmith.

17

The rowers had long since lost any enthusiasm they might have had for the task. They kept at it only in response to offers of bodily violence by Flynn – and the example set by Sebastian, who worked tirelessly. The thin layer of fat that had sheathed Sebastian's muscles was long since consumed, and his sun-baked body was a Michelangelo sculpture as he leaned and dug and pulled the oar.

Six days they had dragged the raft across the southward push of the current. Six days of sun-blazing calm, with the sea flattening, until now in the late afternoon, it looked like an endless sheet of smooth green velvet.

'No,' said Mohammed. 'That means, *The two porcupines make love under the blanket.*'

'Oh!' Sebastian repeated the phrase without interrupting the rhythm of his rowing. Sebastian was a dogged pupil of Swahili, making up in determination what he lacked in brilliance. Mohammed was proud of him, and opposed any attempt by the other members of the crew to usurp his position as chief tutor.

'That's all right about the porcupines shagging themselves to a standstill,' grunted Flynn. 'But what does this mean . . . ?' and he spoke in Swahili.

'It means, *Big winds will blow across the sea,*' interpreted Sebastian, and glowed with achievement.

'And I'm not joking either.' Flynn stood up, crouching to favour his bad leg, and shaded his eyes to peer into the east. 'You see that line of cloud?'

Laying aside the oar, Sebastian stood beside him and flexed the aching muscles of his back and shoulders. Immediately all activity ceased among the other rowers.

'Keep going, me beauties!' growled Flynn, and reluctantly they obeyed. Flynn turned back to Sebastian. 'You see it?'

'Yes.' It was drawn like a kohl line across the eyelid of a Hindu woman, smeared black along the horizon.

'Well, Bassie, there's the wind you've been griping about. But, my friend, I think it's a little more than you bargained for.'

In the darkness they heard it coming from far away, a muted sibilance in the night. One by one, the fat stars were blotted out in the east as dark cloud spread out to fill half the midnight sky.

A single gust hit the raft and flogged the makeshift sail with a clap like a shotgun, and the sleepers woke and sat up.

'Hang on to those fancy underpants,' muttered Flynn, 'or you'll get them blown right up your backside.'

Another gust, another lull, but already there was the boisterous slapping of small waves against the sides of the raft.

'I'd better get that sail down.'

'You had, and all,' agreed Flynn, 'and while you're at it, use the rope to fix life-lines for us.' In haste, spurred on by the rising hiss of the wind, they lashed themselves to the slats of the deck.

The main force of the wind spun the raft like a top, splattering them with spray; the spray was icy cold in the warm rush of the wind. The wind was steady now and the raft moved uneasily – the jerky motion of an animal restless at the prick of spurs.

'At least it will push us towards the land,' Sebastian shouted across at Flynn.

'Bassie, boy, you think of the cutest things,' and the first

71

wave came aboard, smothering Flynn's voice, breaking over their prostrate bodies, and then streaming out through the slatted deck. The raft wallowed in dismay, then gathered itself to meet the next rush of the sea.

Under the steady fury of the wind, the sea came up more swiftly than Sebastian believed was possible. Within minutes the waves were breaking over the raft with such weight as to squeeze the breath from their lungs, submerging them completely, driving the raft under before its buoyancy reasserted itself and lifted it, canting crazily, and they could gasp for air in the smother of spray.

Waiting for the lulls, Sebastian inched his way across the deck until he reached Flynn. 'How are you bearing up?' he bellowed.

'Great, just great,' and another wave drove them under.

'Your leg?' spluttered Sebastian as they came up.

'For Chrissake, stop yapping,' and they went under again.

It was completely dark, no star, no sliver of moon, but each line of breaking water glowed in dull, phosphorescent malevolence as it dashed down upon them, warning them to suck air and cling with cramped fingers hooked into the slats.

For all eternity Sebastian lived in darkness, battered by the wind and the wild, flying water. The aching chill of his body dulled out into numbness. Slowly his mind emptied of conscious thought, so when a bigger wave scoured them, he heard the tearing sound of deck slats pulling loose, and the lost wail as one of the Arabs was washed away into the night sea – but the sound had no meaning to him.

Twice he vomited sea water that he had swallowed, but it had no taste in his mouth, and he let it run heedlessly down his chin and warm on to his chest, to be washed away by the next torrential wave.

His eyes burned without pain from the harsh rake of windflung spray, and he blinked them owlishly at each advancing wave. It seemed, in time, that he could see more clearly, and he turned his head slowly. Beside him, Flynn's face was a leprous blotch in the darkness. This puzzled him, and he lay and thought about it but no solution came, until he looked beyond the next wave, and saw the faint promise of a new day show pale through the black massed cloud-banks.

He tried to speak, but no sound came for his throat was swollen closed with the salt, and his tongue was tingling numb. Again, he tried. 'Dawn coming,' he croaked, but beside him Flynn lay like a corpse frozen in rigor mortis.

Slowly the light grew over that mad, grey sea but the scudding black cloud-banks tried desperately to oppose its coming.

Now the seas were more awesome in their raging insanity. Each mountain of glassy grey rose high above the raft, shielding it for a few seconds from the whip of the wind, its crest blowing off like the plume of an Etruscan helmet, before it slid down, collapsing upon itself in the tumbling roar of breaking water.

Each time, the men on the raft shrank flat on the deck, and waited in bovine acceptance to be smothered again beneath the white deluge.

Once, the raft rode high and clear in a freak flat of the storm, and Sebastian looked about him. The canvas and rope, the coconuts and the other pathetic accumulation of their possessions were all gone. The sea had ripped away many of the deck slats so that the metal floats of the raft were exposed; it had torn the very clothing from them so they were clad in sodden tatters. Of the seven men who had ridden the raft the previous day, only he and Flynn, Mohammed and one more, were left – the other three were gone, gobbled up by the hungry sea.

Then the storm struck again, so that the raft reeled and reared to the point of capsizing.

Sebastian sensed it first in the altered action of the waves; they were steeper, marching closer together. Then, through the clamour of the storm, a new sound, like that of a cannon fired at irregular intervals with varying charges of gunpowder. He realized suddenly that he had been hearing this sound for some time, but only now had it penetrated the stupor of his fatigue.

He lifted his head, and every nerve of his being shrieked in protest at the effort. He looked about, but the sea stood up around him like a series of grey walls that limited his vision to a circle of fifty yards. Yet that discordant boom, boom, boom, was louder now and more insistent.

In the short, choppy waves, a side-break caught the raft and tossed it high – lifting him so he could see the land; so close that the palm trees showed sharply, bending their stems to the wind and threshing their long fronds in panic. He saw the beach, grey-white in the gloom and, beyond it, far beyond it, rose the watery blue of the high ground.

These things had small comfort for him when he saw the reef. It bared its black teeth at him, snarling through the white water that burst like cannon-fire upon it before cascading on into the comparative quiet of the lagoon. The raft was riding down towards it.

'Flynn,' he croaked. 'Flynn, listen to me!' but the older man did not move, His eyes were fixed open and only the movement of his chest, as he breathed, proved him still alive. 'Flynn.' Sebastian released one of his clawed hands from its grip on the wooden slatting. 'Flynn!' he said, and struck him across the cheek.

74

'Flynn!' The head turned towards Sebastian, the eyes blinked, the mouth opened, but no voice spoke.

Another wave broke over the raft. This time the cold, malicious rush of it stirred Sebastian, roused a little of his failing strength. He shook the water from his head. 'Land,' he whispered. 'Land,' and Flynn stared at him dully.

Two lines of surf away, the reef showed its ragged back again. Clinging with only one hand to the slatting, Sebastian fumbled the knife from its sheath and hacked clumsily at the life-line that bound him to the deck. It parted. He reached over and cut Flynn's line, sawing frantically at the wet hemp. That done, he slid back on his belly until he reached Mohammed and freed him also. The little African stared at him with bloodshot eyes from his wrinkled monkey face.

'Swim,' whispered Sebastian. 'Must swim,' and resheathing the knife, he tried to crawl over Mohammed to reach the Arab but the next wave caught the raft, rearing up under it as it felt the push of the land, rearing so steeply that this time the raft was overturned and they were thrown from it into the seething turmoil of the reef.

Sebastian hit the water flat, and was hardly under before he had surfaced again. Beside him, close enough to touch, Flynn emerged. In the strength born of the fear of death, Flynn caught at Sebastian, locking both arms around his chest. The same wave that had capsized them had poured over the reef and covered it completely, so that where the coral fangs had been was now only a frothy area of disturbed water. In it bobbed the debris of the raft, shattered into pieces against the reef. The mutilated corpse of the Arab was still roped to a piece of the wreckage. Flynn and Sebastian were locked like lovers in each other's arms and the next wave, following close upon the first, lifted them, and shot them forward over the submerged reef.

In one great swoop that left their guts behind them, they were carried over the coral which could have minced them into jelly, and tumbled into the quiet lagoon. With them went little Mohammed, and what remained of the raft.

The lagoon was covered by a thick scum of wind spume, creamy as the head of a good beer. So when the three of them staggered waist-deep towards the beach, supporting each other with arms around shoulders, they were coated with white froth. It made them look like a party of drunken snowmen returning home after a long night out.

– 18 –

Mohammed squatted with a pile of madafu, the shiny green coconuts, beside him. The beach was littered with them, for the storm had stripped the trees. He worked in feverish haste with Sebastian's hunting knife, his face frosted with dried salt, mumbling to himself through cracked and swollen lips, shaving down through the white, fibrous material of the shell until he exposed the hollow centre filled with its white custard and effervescent milk. At this point the madafu was snatched from his hands by either Flynn or Sebastian. His despair growing deeper, he watched for a second the two white men drinking with heads thrown back, throats pulsing as they swallowed, spilled milk trickling from the corners of their mouths, eyes closed tight in their intense pleasure; then he picked up another nut and got to work on it. He opened a dozen before he was able to satiate the other two, and he held the next nut to his own mouth and whimpered with eagerness.

Then they slept. Bellies filled with the sweet, rich milk, they sagged backwards on the sand and slept the rest of that day and that night, and when they woke, the wind had dropped, although the sea still burst like an artillery bombardment on the reef.

'Now,' said Flynn, 'where, in the name of the devil and all his angels, are we?' Neither Sebastian nor Mohammed answered him. 'We were six days on the raft. We could have drifted hundreds of miles south before the storm pushed us in.' He frowned as he considered the problem. 'We might even have reached Portuguese Mozambique. We could be as far as the Zambezi river.'

Flynn focused his attention on Mohammed. 'Go!' he said. 'Search for a river, or a mountain that you know. Better still, find a village where we can get food – and bearers.'

'I'll go also,' Sebastian volunteered.

'You wouldn't know the difference between the Zambezi and the Mississippi,' Flynn grunted impatiently. 'You'd be lost after the first hundred yards.'

Mohammed was gone for two days and a half, but Sebastian and Flynn ate well in his absence.

Under a sun shelter of palm fronds they feasted three times a day on crab and sand-clams, and big green rock-lobster which Sebastian fished from the lagoon, baking them in their shells over the fire that Flynn coaxed from two dry sticks.

On the first night the entertainment was provided by Flynn. For some years now, Flynn's intake of gin had averaged a daily two bottles. The abrupt cessation of supply resulted in a delayed but classic visitation of *delirium tremens*. He spent half the night hobbling up and down the beach brandishing a branch of driftwood and hurling obscenities at the phantoms that had come to plague him. There was one purple cobra in particular which pursued him doggedly, and it was only after Flynn had beaten it noisily to death behind a palm tree, that he allowed Sebastian to lead him back to the shelter and seat him beside the camp-fire. Then he got the shakes. He shook like a man on a jack-hammer. His teeth rattled together with such violence that Sebastian was sure they must shatter. Gradually, however, the shakes subsided and by the following noon he was able to eat three large rock-lobsters and then collapse into a death-like sleep.

He woke in the late evening, looking as well as Sebastian had ever seen him, to greet the returning Mohammed and the dozen tall Angoni tribesmen who accompanied him. They returned Flynn's greeting with respect. From Beira to Dar es Salaam, the name 'Fini' was held in universal awe by the indigenous peoples. Legend credited him with powers far above the natural order. His exploits, his skill with the rifle, his volcanic temper and his seeming immunity from death and retribution, had formed the foundation of a belief that Flynn had carefully fostered. They said in whispers around the night fires when the women and the children were not listening that 'Fini' was in truth a reincarnation of the Monomatapa. They said further that in the intervening period between his death as the Great King and his latest birth as 'Fini', he had been first a monstrous crocodile, and then *Mowana Lisa*, the most notorious man-eating lion in the history of East Africa, a predator responsible for at least three hundred human killings. The day, twenty-five years previously, that Flynn had stepped ashore at Port Amelia was the exact day that *Mowana Lisa* had been shot dead by the Portuguese Chef D'Post at Sofala. All men knew these things – and only an idiot would take chances with 'Fini' – hence the respect with which they greeted him now.

Flynn recognized one of the men. 'Luti,' he roared, 'you scab on an hyena's backside!'

Luti smiled broadly, and bobbed his head in pleasure at being singled out by Flynn.

'Mohammed,' Flynn turned to his man. 'Where did you find him? Are we near his village?'

'We are a day's march away.'

'In which direction?'

'North.'

'Then we are in Portuguese territory!' exalted Flynn. 'We must have drifted down past the Rovuma river.'

The Rovuma river was the frontier between Portuguese Mozambique and German East Africa. Once in Portuguese territory, Flynn was immune from the wrath of the Germans. All their efforts at extraditing him from the Portuguese had proved unsuccessful, for Flynn had a working agreement with the Chef D'Post, Mozambique, and through him with the Governor in Lourenço Marques. In a manner of speaking, these two officials were sleeping partners in Flynn's business, and were entitled to a quarterly financial statement of Flynn's activities, and an agreed percentage of the profits.

'You can relax, Bassie boy. Old Fleischer can't touch us now. And in three or four days we'll be home.'

The first leg of the journey took them to Luti's village. Lolling in their maschilles, hammock-like litters slung beneath a long pole and carried by four of Luti's men at a synchronized jog trot, Flynn and Sebastian were borne smoothly out of the coastal lowland into the hills and bush country.

The litter-bearers sang as they ran, and their deep melodious voices, coupled with the swinging motion of the maschille, lulled Sebastian into a mood of deep contentment. Occasionally he dozed. Where the path was wide enough to allow the maschilles to travel side by side, he lay and chatted with Flynn, at other times he watched the changing country and the animal life along the way. It was better than London Zoo.

Each time Sebastian saw something new, he called across for Flynn to identify it.

In every glade and clearing were herds of the golden-brown impala; delicate little creatures that watched them in wide-eyed curiosity as they passed.

Troops of guinea-fowl, like a dark cloud shadow on the earth, scratched and chittered on the banks of every stream.

Heavy, yellow eland, with their stubby horns and swinging dewlaps, trotting in Indian file, formed a regal frieze along the edge of the bush.

Sable and roan antelope; purple-brown waterbuck, with a perfect circle of white branded on their rumps; buffalo, big and black and ugly; giraffe, dainty little klip-springer, standing like chamois on the tumbled granite boulders of a kopje. The whole land seethed and skittered with life.

There were trees so strange in shape and size and foliage that Sebastian could hardly credit them as existing. Swollen baobabs, fifty feet in circumference, standing awkwardly as prehistoric monsters, fat pods filled with cream of tartar hanging from their deformed branches. There were forests of msasa trees, leaves not green as leaves should be, but rose and chocolate and red. Fever trees sixty feet high, with bright yellow trunks, shedding their bark like the brittle parchment of a snake's skin. Groves of mopani, whose massed foliage glittered a shiny, metallic green in the sun; and in the jungle growth along the river banks, the lianas climbed up like long, grey worms and hung in loops and festoons among the wild fig and the buffalo-bean vines and the tree ferns.

'Why haven't we seen any sign of elephant?' Sebastian asked.

'Me and my boys worked this territory over about six months ago,' Flynn explained. 'I guess they just moved on a little – probably up north across the Rovuma.'

In the late afternoon they descended a stony path into a valley, and for the first time Sebastian saw the permanent habitations of man. In irregular shaped plots, the bottom land of the valley was cultivated, and the rich black soil threw up lush green stands of millet, while on the banks of the little stream stood Luti's village; shaggy grass huts, shaped like beehives, each with a circular mud-walled granary standing on stilts beside it. The huts were arranged in a rough circle around an open space where the earth was packed hard by the passage of bare feet.

The entire population turned out to welcome Flynn: three hundred souls, from hobbling old white heads with grinning toothless gums, down to infants held on mothers' naked hips, who did not interrupt their feeding but clung like fat black limpets with hands and mouth to the breast.

Through the crowd that ululated and clapped hands in welcome, Flynn and Sebastian were carried to the chief's hut and there they descended from the maschilles.

Flynn and the old chief greeted each other affectionately; Flynn because of favours received and because of future favours yet to be asked for, and the chief because of Flynn's reputation and the fact that wherever Flynn travelled, he usually left behind him large quantities of good, red meat.

'You come to hunt elephant?' the chief asked, looking hopefully for Flynn's rifle.

'No.' Flynn shook his head. 'I return from a journey to a far place.'

'From where?'

In answer, Flynn looked significantly at the sky and repeated, 'From a far place.'

There was an awed murmur from the crowd and the chief nodded sagely. It was clear to all of them that 'Fini' must have been to visit and commune with his *alter ego*, Monomatapa.

'Will you stay long at our village?' again hopefully.

'I will stay tonight only. I leave again in the dawn.'

'Ah!' Disappointment. 'We had hoped to welcome you with a dance. Since we heard of your coming, we have prepared.'

'No,' Flynn repeated. He knew a dance could last three or four days.

'There is a great brewing of palm wine which is only now ready for drinking,' the chief tried again, and this time his argument hit Flynn like a charging rhinoceros. Flynn had been many days without liquor.

'My friend,' said Flynn, and he could feel the saliva spurting out from under his tongue in anticipation. 'I cannot stay to dance with you but I will drink a small gourd of palm wine to show my love for you and your village.' Then turning to Sebastian he warned, 'I wouldn't touch this stuff, Bassie, if I were you – it's real poison.'

'Right,' agreed Sebastian. 'I'm going down to the river to wash.'

'You do that,' and Flynn lifted the first gourd of palm wine lovingly to his lips.

Sebastian's progress to the river resembled a Roman triumph. The entire village lined the bank to watch his necessarily limited ablutions with avid interest, and a buzz of awe went up when he disrobed to his underpants.

'Bwana Manali,' they chorused. 'Lord of the Red Cloth,' and the name stuck.

As a farewell gift the headman presented Flynn with four gourds of palm wine, and begged him to return soon – bringing his rifle with him.

They marched hard all that day and when they camped at nightfall, Flynn was semi-paralysed with palm wine, while Sebastian shivered and his teeth chattered uncontrollably.

From the swamps of the Rufiji delta, Sebastian had brought with him a souvenir of his visit – his first full go of malaria.

They reached Lalapanzi the following day, a few hours

82

before the crisis of Sebastian's fever. Lalapanzi was Flynn's base camp and the name meant 'Lie Down', or more accurately, 'The Place of Rest'.

It was in the hills on a tiny tributary of the great Rovuma river, a hundred miles from the Indian Ocean, but only ten miles from German territory across the river. Flynn believed in living close to his principal place of business.

Had Sebastian been in full possession of his senses, and not wandering in the hot shadow land of malaria, he would have been surprised by the camp at Lalapanzi. It was not what anybody who knew Flynn O'Flynn would have expected.

Behind a palisade of split bamboo to protect the lawns and gardens from the attentions of the duiker and steenbok and kudu, it glowed like a green jewel in the sombre brown of the hills. Much hard work and patience must have gone into damming the stream, and digging the irrigation furrows, which suckled the lawns and flower-beds and the vegetable garden. Three indigenous fig trees dwarfed the buildings, crimson frangipani burst like fireworks against the green kikuyu grass, beds of bright barberton daisies ringed the gentle terraces that fell away to the stream, and a bougain-villaea creeper smothered the main building in a profusion of dark green and purple.

Behind the long bungalow, with its wide, open veranda, stood half a dozen circular rondavels, all neatly capped with golden thatch and gleaming painfully white, with burned limestone paint, in the sunlight.

The whole had about it an air of feminine order and neatness. Only a woman, and a determined one at that, could have devoted so much time and pain to building up such a speck of prettiness in the midst of brown rock and harsh thorn veld.

She stood on the veranda in the shade like a valkyrie, tall and sun-browned and angry. The full-length dress of faded blue was crisp with new ironing, and the neat mends in the fabric invisible except at close range. Gathered close about her waist, her skirt ballooned out over her woman's hips and fell to her ankles, slyly concealing the long straight legs beneath. Folded across her stomach, her arms were an amber brown frame for the proud double bulge of her bosom, and the thick braid of black hair that hung to her waist twitched like the tail of an angry lioness. A face too young for the marks of hardship and loneliness that were chiselled into it was harder now by the expression of distaste it wore as she watched Flynn and Sebastian arriving.

They lolled in their maschilles, unshaven, dressed in filthy rags, hair matted with sweat and dust; Flynn full of palm wine, and Sebastian full of fever – although it was impossible to distinguish the symptoms of their separate disorders.

'May I ask where you've been these last two months, Flynn Patrick O'Flynn?' Although she tried to speak like a man, yet her voice had a lift and a ring to it.

'You may not ask, daughter!' Flynn shouted back defiantly.

'You're drunk again!'

'And if I am?' roared Flynn. 'You're as bad as that mother of yours (may her soul rest in peace), always going on and on. Never a civil word of welcome for your old Daddy, who's been away trying to earn an honest crust.'

The girl's eyes switched to the maschille that carried Sebastian, and narrowed in mounting outrage. 'Sweet merciful heavens, and what's this you've brought home with you now?'

Sebastian grinned inanely, and tried valiantly to sit up as Flynn introduced him. 'That is Sebastian Oldsmith. My very dear friend, Sebastian Oldsmith.'

'He's also drunk!'

'Listen, Rosa. You show some respect.' Flynn struggled to climb from his maschille.

'He's drunk,' Rosa repeated grimly. 'Drunk as a pig. You can take him straight back and leave him where you found him. He's not coming in this house.' She turned away, pausing only a moment at the front door to add, 'That goes for you also, Flynn O'Flynn. I'll be waiting with the shotgun. You just put one foot on the veranda before you're sober – and I'll blow it clean off.'

'Rosa – wait – he isn't drunk, please,' wailed Flynn, but the fly-screen door had slammed closed behind her.

Flynn teetered uncertainly at the foot of the veranda stairs; for a moment it looked as though he might be foolhardy enough to put his daughter's threat to the test, but he was not that drunk.

'Women,' he mourned. 'The good Lord protect us,' and he led his little caravan around the back of the bungalow to the farthest of the rondavel huts. This room was sparsely furnished in anticipation of Flynn's regular periods of exile from the main building.

– 19 –

Rosa O'Flynn closed the front door behind her and leaned back against it wearily. Slowly her chin sagged down to her chest, and she closed her eyes to imprison the itchy tears beneath the lids, but one of them squeezed through and quivered like a fat, glistening grape on her lashes, before falling to splash on the stone floor.

'Oh, Daddy, Daddy,' she whispered. It was an expression of those months of aching loneliness. The long, slow slide of days when she had searched desperately for work to fill her hands and her mind. The nights when, locked alone in her room with a loaded shotgun beside the bed, she had lain and listened to the sounds of the African bush beyond the window, afraid then of everything, even the four devoted African servants sleeping soundly with their families in their little compound behind the bungalow.

Waiting, waiting for Flynn to return. Lifting her head in the noonday and standing listening, hoping to hear the singing of his bearers as they came down the valley. And each hour the fear and the resentment building up within her. Fear that he might not come, and resentment that he left her for so long.

Now he had come. He had come drunk and filthy, with some oafish ruffian as a companion, and all her loneliness and fear had vented itself in that shrewish outburst. She straightened and pushed herself away from the door. Listlessly she walked through the shady cool rooms of the bungalow, spread with a rich profusion of animal skins and rough native-made furniture, until she reached her own room and sank down on the bed.

Beneath her unhappiness was a restlessness, a formless, undirected longing for something she did not understand. It was a new thing; only in these last few years had she become aware of it. Before that she had gloried in the companionship of her father, never having experienced and, therefore, never missing the society of others. She had taken it as the natural order of things that much of her time must be spent completely alone with only the wife of old Mohammed to replace her natural mother – the young Portuguese girl who had died in the struggle to give life to Rosa.

She knew the land as a slum child knows the city. It was her land and she loved it.

Now all of it was changing, she was uncertain, without bearings in this sea of new emotion. Lonely, irritable – and afraid.

A timid knocking on the back door of the bungalow roused her, and she felt a leap of hope within her. Her anger at Flynn had long ago abated – now he had made the first overture she would welcome him to the bungalow without sacrifice of pride.

Quickly she bathed her face in the china wash-basin beside her bed, and patted her hair into order before the mirror, before going through to answer the knock.

Old Mohammed stood outside, shuffling his feet and grinning ingratiatingly. He stood in almost as great an awe of Rosa's temper as that of Flynn himself. It was with relief, therefore, that he saw her smile.

'Mohammed, you old rascal,' and he bobbed his head with pleasure.

'You are well, Little Long Hair?'

'I am well, Mohammed – and I can see you are also.'

'The Lord Fini asks that you send blankets and quinine.'

'Why?' Rosa frowned quickly. 'Is the fever on him?'

'Not on him, but on Manali, his friend.'

'Is he bad?'

'He is very bad.'

The rich hostility that her first glimpse of Sebastian had invoked in Rosa, wavered a little. She felt the woman in her irresistibly drawn towards anything wounded or sick, even such an uncouth and filthy specimen as she had seen Sebastian to be.

'I will come,' she decided aloud, while silently qualifying her surrender by deciding that under no circumstances would she let him in the house. Sick or healthy, he would stay out there in the rondavel.

Armed with a pitcher of boiled drinking water, and a bottle of quinine tablets, closely attended by Mohammed carrying an armful of cheap trade blankets, she crossed to the rondavel and entered.

She entered it at an unpropitious moment. For Flynn

had spent the last ten minutes exhuming the bottle he had so carefully buried some months before beneath the earthen floor of the rondavel. Being a man of foresight, he had caches of gin scattered in unlikely places around the camp, and now, in delicious anticipation, he was carefully wiping damp earth from the neck of the bottle with the tail of his shirt. So engrossed with this labour he was not aware of Rosa's presence until the bottle was snatched from his hands, and thrown through the open side window to pop and tinkle as it burst.

'Now what did you do that for?' Flynn was hurt as deeply as a mother deprived of her infant.

'For the good of your soul.' Icily Rosa turned from him to the inert figure on the bed, and her nose wrinkled as she caught the whiff of unwashed body and fever. 'Where did you find this one?' she asked without expecting an answer.

– 20 –

Five grains of quinine washed down Sebastian's throat with scalding tea, heated stones were packed around his body, and half a dozen blankets swaddled him to begin the sweat.

The malarial parasite has a thiry-six-hour life cycle, and now at the crisis, Rosa was attempting to raise his body temperature sufficiently to interrupt the cycle and break the fever. Heat radiated from the bed, filling the single room of the rondavel as though it were a kitchen. Only Sebastian's head showed from the pile of blankets, and his face was flushed a dusky brick colour. Although sweat spurted from every pore of his skin and ran back in heavy drops to soak his hair and his pillow, yet his teeth rattled together and he shivered so that the camp-bed shook.

Rosa sat beside his bed and watched him. Occasionally

she leaned forward with a cloth in her hand and wiped the perspiration from his eyes and upper lip. Her expression had softened and become almost broody. One of Sebastian's curls had plastered itself wetly across his forehead, and, with her finger-tips, Rosa combed it back. She repeated the gesture, and then did it again, stroking her fingers through his damp hair, instinctively gentling and soothing him.

He opened his eyes, and Rosa snatched her hand away guiltily. His eyes were misty grey, unfocused as a newborn puppy's, and Rosa felt something squirm in her stomach.

'Please don't stop.' His voice was slurred with the fever, but even so Rosa was surprised at the timbre and inflection. It was the first time she had heard him speak and it was not the voice of a ruffian. Hesitating a moment, she glanced at the door of the hut to make sure they were alone before she reached forward to touch his face.

'You are kind – good and kind.'

'Sshh!' she admonished him.

'Thank you.'

'Sshh! Close your eyes.'

His eyes flickered down and he sighed, a gusty, broken sound.

The crisis came like a big wind and shook him as though he were a tree in its path. His body temperature rocketed, and he tossed and writhed in the camp-bed, trying to throw off the weight of blankets upon him, so that Rosa called for Mohammed's wife to help her restrain him. His perspiration soaked through the thin mattress and dripped to form a puddle on the earth floor beneath the bed, and he cried out in the fantasy of his fever.

Then, miraculously, the crisis was past, and he slumped into relaxation. He lay still and exhausted so that only the shallow flutter of his breathing showed there was life in him. Rosa could feel his skin cooling under her hand, and she saw the yellowish tinge with which the fever had coloured it.

'The first time it is always bad.' Mohammed's wife released her grip on the blanket-wrapped legs.

'Yes,' said Rosa. 'Now bring the basin. We must wash him and change his blankets, Nanny.'

She had worked many times with men who were sick or badly hurt; the servants and the bearers and the gun-boys, and, of course, with her father. But now, as Nanny peeled back the blankets and Rosa swabbed Sebastian's unconscious body with the moist cloth, she felt an inexplicable tension within her – a sense of dread mingled with tight excitement. She could feel new blood warming her cheeks, and she leaned forward, so that Nanny could not see her face as she worked.

The skin of his chest and upper arms was creamy-smooth as polished alabaster, where the sun had not stained it. Beneath her fingers it had an elastic hardness, a rubbery sensuality and warmth that disturbed her. When she realized suddenly that she was no longer wiping with the flannel but using it to caress the shape of hard muscle beneath the pale skin, she checked herself and made her actions brusque and businesslike.

They dried his upper body, and Nanny reached to jerk the blankets down below Sebastian's waist.

'Wait!' It came out of Rosa as a cry, and Nanny paused with her hand on the bedclothes and her head held at an angle, quizzical, birdlike. Her wizened old features crinkled in sly amusement.

'Wait,' Rosa repeated in confusion. 'First help me get the night-shirt on him,' and she snatched up one of Flynn's freshly ironed but threadbare old night-shirts from the chair beside the bed.

'It cannot bite you, Little Long Hair,' the old woman teased her gently. 'It has no teeth.'

'You just stop that kind of talk,' snapped Rosa with unnecessary violence. 'Help me sit him up.'

Between them they lifted Sebastian and slipped the night-shirt down over his head, before lowering him to the pillow again.

'And now?' Nanny asked innocently. For answer, Rosa handed her the flannel, and turned to stare fixedly out of the rondavel window. Behind her she heard the rustle of blankets and then Nanny's voice.

'Hau! Hau!' The age-old expression of deep admiration, followed by a cackle of delighted laughter, as Nanny saw the back of Rosa's neck turning bright pink with embarrassment.

Nanny had smuggled Flynn's cut-throat razor out of the bungalow, and was supervising critically as Rosa stroked it gingerly over Sebastian's soapy cheeks. There was no sound medical reason why a malaria patient should be shaved immediately after emerging from the crisis, but Rosa had advanced the theory that it would make him feel more comfortable and Nanny had agreed enthusiastically. Both of them were enjoying themselves with all the sober delight of two small girls playing with a doll.

Despite Nanny's cautionary clucks and sharp hisses of in-drawn breath, Rosa succeeded in removing the hair that covered Sebastian's face like the black pelt of an otter without inflicting any serious wounds. There was a nick on the chin and another below the left nostril, but neither of these bled more than a drop or two.

Rosa rinsed the razor and then narrowed her eyes thoughtfully as she surveyed her handiwork, and that thing squirmed in her stomach again. 'I think,' she muttered, 'we should move him into the main bungalow. It will be more comfortable.'

'I will call the servants to carry him,' said Nanny.

– 21 –

Flynn O'Flynn was a busy man during the period of Sebastian's convalescence. His band of followers had been seriously depleted during the recent exchange with Herman Fleischer on the Rufiji, so to replace his losses, he press-ganged all the maschille-bearers who had carried them home from Luti's village. These he put through a preliminary course of training and at the end of four days selected a dozen of the most promising, to become gun-boys. The remainder he despatched homeward despite their protests; they would dearly have loved to stay for the glamour and reward that they were certain would be heaped upon their more fortunate fellows.

Thereafter the chosen few were entered upon the second part of their training. Securely locked in one of the rondavels behind the bungalow, Flynn kept the tools of his trade. It was an impressive arsenal.

Rack upon rack of cheap Martini Henry .450 rifles, a score of W. D. Lee-Metfords that had survived the Anglo-Boer war, a lesser number of German Mausers salvaged from his encounters with Askari across the Rovuma, and a very few of the expensive hand-made doubles by Gibbs and Messrs Greener of London. Not a single weapon had a serial number on it. Above these, neatly stacked on the wooden shelves, were bulk packages of cartridges, wrapped and soldered in lead foil – enough of them to fight a small battle.

The room reeked with the slick, mineral smell of gun oil.

Flynn issued his recruits with Mausers, and set about instructing them in the art of handling a rifle. Again he weeded out those who showed no aptitude and he was left finally with eight men who could hit an elephant at fifty paces. This group passed into the third and last period of training.

Many years previously, Mohammed had been recruited into the German Askari. He had even won a medal during the Salito rebellion of 1904, and from there had risen to the rank of sergeant and overseer of the officers' mess. During a visit by the army auditor to Mbeya, where Mohammed was at that time stationed, there had been discovered a stock discrepancy of some twenty dozen bottles of schnapps, and a hole in the mess funds amounting to a little over a thousand Reichsmarks. This was a hanging matter, and Mohammed had resigned without ceremony from the Imperial Army and reached the Portuguese border by a series of forced marches. In Portuguese territory he had met Flynn, and solicited and received employment from him. However, he was still an authority on German army drill procedure and retained a command of the language.

The recruits were handed over to him, for it was part of Flynn's plans that they be able to masquerade as a squad of German Askari. For days thereafter the camp at Lalapanzi reverberated to Mohammed's Teutonic cries, as he goose-stepped about the lawns at the head of his band of nearly naked troopers, with his fez set squarely on the grey wool of his head.

This left Flynn free to make further preparations. Seated on the stoep of the bungalow, he pored sweatily over his correspondence for many days. First there was a letter to:

His Excellency, The Governor,
    German Administration of East Africa,
        Dar Es Salaam.

Sir,
    I enclose my account for damages, as follows, here-with:

1 Dhow (Market value)	£1,500.—.—.
10 Rifles	£200.—.—.
Various stores and provisions etcetera (too numerous to list)	£100.—.—.
Injury, suffering and hardships (estimated)	£200.—.—.
TOTAL	£2,000.—.—.

This claim arises from the sinking of the above-said dhow off the mouth of the Rufiji, 10th July, 1912, which was an act of piracy by your gunboat, the *Blücher*.

I would appreciate payment in gold, on or before 25th September, 1912, otherwise I will take the necessary steps to collect same personally.

    Yours sincerely,
        Flynn Patrick O'Flynn, Esq.,
            (Citizen of The United States of America).

After much heavy thought, Flynn had decided not to include a claim for the ivory as he was not too certain of its legality. Best not to mention it.

He had considered signing himself 'United States Ambassador to Africa', but had discarded the idea on the grounds that Governor Schee knew damned well that he was no such thing. However, there was no harm in reminding him of Flynn's nationality – it might make the old rogue

94

hesitate before hanging Flynn out of hand if ever he got his hooks into him.

Satisfied that the only response to his demands would be a significant increase in Governor Schee's blood pressure, Flynn proceeded with his preparations to make good his threat of collecting the debt *personally*.

Flynn used this word lightly – he had long ago selected a representative debt collector in the form of Sebastian Oldsmith. It now remained to have him suitably outfitted for the occasion, and, armed with a tape-measure from Rosa's work-basket, Flynn visited Sebastian's sick bed. These days, visiting Sebastian was much like trying to arrange an interview with the Pope. Sebastian was securely under the maternal protection of Rosa O'Flynn.

Flynn knocked discreetly on the door of the guest bedroom, paused for a count of five, and entered.

'What do you want?' Rosa greeted him affectionately. She was sitting on the foot of Sebastian's bed.

'Hello, hello,' said Flynn, and then again lamely, 'Hello.'

'I suppose you're looking for a drinking companion,' accused Rosa.

'Good Lord, no!' Flynn was genuinely horrified by the accusation. What with Rosa's depredations his stock of gin was running perilously low, and he had no intention of sharing it with anyone. 'I just called in to see how he was doing.' Flynn transferred his attention to Sebastian. 'How you feeling, old Bassie boy?'

'Much better, thank you.' In fact, Sebastian was looking very chirpy indeed. Freshly shaved, dressed in one of Flynn's best night-shirts, he lay like a Roman emperor on clean sheets. On the low table beside his bed stood a vase of frangipani blooms, and there were other floral tributes standing about the room – all of them cut and carefully arranged by Rosa O'Flynn.

He was steadily putting on weight again as Rosa and Nanny stuffed food into him and colour was starting to drive the yellowish fever stains from his skin. Flynn felt a prickle of irritation at the way Sebastian was being pampered like a stud stallion, while Flynn himself was barely tolerated in his own home.

The metaphor which had come naturally into Flynn's mind now sparked a further train of thought, and a sharper prickle of irritation. *Stud stallion!* Flynn looked at Rosa with attention, and noticed that the dress she wore was the white one with gauzy sleeves, that had belonged to her mother – a garment that Rosa usually kept securely locked away, a garment she had worn perhaps twice before in her life. Furthermore, her feet, which were usually bare about the house, were now neatly clad in store-bought patent leather, and, by Jesus, she was wearing a sprig of bougainvillaea tucked into the shiny black slick of her hair. The tip of her long braid, which was usually tied carelessly with a thong of leather, flaunted a silk ribbon.

Now, Flynn O'Flynn was not a sentimental man but suddenly he recognized in his daughter a strange new glow, and a demure air that had never been there before, and within himself he became aware of an unusual sensation, so unfamiliar that he did not recognize it as paternal jealousy. He did, however, recognize that the sooner he sent Sebastian on his way, the safer it would be.

'Well, that's fine, Bassie,' he boomed genially. 'That's just fine. Now, I'm sending bearers down to Beira to pick up supplies, and I just thought they might as well get some clothes for you while they were there.'

'Well, thank you very much, Flynn.' Sebastian was touched by the kindness of his friend.

'Might as well do it properly.' Flynn produced his tape-measure with a flourish. 'We'll send your measurements down to old Parbhoo and he can tailor-make some stuff for you.'

'I say, that *is* jolly decent of you.'

And completely out of character, thought Rosa O'Flynn as she watched her father carefully noting the length of Sebastian's legs and arms, and the girth of his neck, chest and waist.

'The boots and the hat will be a problem,' Flynn mused aloud when he had finished. 'But I'll find something.'

'And what do you mean by that, Flynn O'Flynn?' Rosa demanded suspiciously.

'Nothing, just nothing at all.' Hurriedly Flynn gathered his notes and his tape, and fled from further interrogation.

Some time later, Mohammed and the bearers returned from the shopping expedition to Beira, and he and Flynn immediately closeted themselves in secret conclave in the arsenal.

'Did you get it?' demanded Flynn eagerly.

'Five boxes of gin I left in the cave behind the waterfall at the top of the valley,' whispered Mohammed, and Flynn sighed with relief. 'But one bottle I brought with me.' Mohammed produced it from under his tunic. Flynn took it from him and drew the cork with his teeth, before spilling a little into the enamel mug that was standing ready.

'And the other purchases?'

'It was difficult – especially the hat.'

'But did you get it?' Flynn demanded.

'It was a direct intervention of Allah.' Mohammed refused to be hurried. 'In the harbour was a German ship, stopped at Beira on its way north to Dar es Salaam. On the boat were three German officers. I saw them walking upon the deck.' Mohammed paused and cleared his throat portentously. 'That night a man who is my friend rowed me out to the ship, and I visited the cabin of one of the soldiers.'

'Where is it?' Flynn could not hold his patience. Mohammed stood up, went to the door of the rondavel and called to one of the bearers. He returned and set a bundle on the table in front of Flynn. Grinning proudly, he waited while Flynn unwrapped the bundle.

'Good God Almighty,' breathed Flynn.

'Is it not beautiful?'

'Call Manali. Tell him to come here immediately.'

Ten minutes later Sebastian, whom Rosa had at last reluctantly placed on the list of walking wounded, entered the rondavel, to be greeted effusively by Flynn. 'Sit down, Bassie boy. I've got a present for you.'

Reluctantly, Sebastian obeyed, eyeing the covered object on the table. Flynn stood over it and whisked away the cloth. Then, with the same ceremony as the Archbishop of Canterbury placing the crown, he lifted the helmet above Sebastian's head and lowered it reverently.

On the summit a golden eagle cocked its wings on the point of flight and opened its beak in a silent squawk of menace, the black enamel of the helmet shone with a polished gloss, and the golden chain drooped heavily under Sebastian's chin.

It was indeed a thing of beauty. A thing of such presence that it completely overwhelmed Sebastian, enveloping his head to the bridge of his nose so that his eyes were just visible below the jutting brim.

'A few sizes too large,' Flynn conceded. 'But we can stuff some cloth into the crown to keep it up.' He backed away a few paces and cocked his head on one side as he examined the effect. 'Bassie boy, you'll slay them.'

'What's this for?' Sebastian asked in concern from under the steel helmet.

'You'll see. Just hold on a shake.' Flynn turned to Mohammed who was cooing with admiration in the doorway. 'The clothes?' he asked, and Mohammed beckoned imperiously to the bearers to bring in the boxes they had carried all the way from Beira.

Parbhoo, the Indian tailor, had obviously laboured with dedication and enthusiasm. The task set him by Flynn had touched the soul of the creative artist in him.

Ten minutes later, Sebastian stood self-consciously in the centre of the rondavel while Flynn and Mohammed circled him slowly, exclaiming with delight and self-congratulation.

Below the massive helmet, which was now propped high with a wad of cloth between steel and scalp, Sebastian was dressed in the sky-blue tunic and riding breeches. The cuffs of the jacket were ringed with yellow silk – a stripe of the same material ran down the outside of the breeches – and the high collar was covered with embroidered metal thread. Complete with spurs, the tall black boots pinched his toes so painfully that Sebastian stood pigeon-toed and blushed with bewilderment. 'I say, Flynn,' he pleaded, 'what's all this about?'

'Bassie boy.' Flynn laid a hand fondly on his shoulder. 'You're going to go in there and collect hut tax for . . .' he almost said *me*, but altered it quickly to '. . . us.'

'What is hut tax?'

'Hut tax is the annual sum of five shillings, paid by the headmen to the German Governor for each hut in his village.' Flynn led Sebastian to the chair and seated him as gently as though he were pregnant. He lifted a hand to still Sebastian's further enquiries and protests. 'Yes, I know you don't understand. But I'll explain it to you carefully. Just keep your mouth shut and listen.' He sat down opposite Sebastian and leaned forward earnestly. 'Now! The Germans owe us for the dhow and that, like we agreed – right?'

Sebastian nodded, and the helmet slid forward over his eyes. He pushed it back.

'Well, you are going to go across the river with the gun-bearers dressed as Askari. You are going to visit each of the villages before the real tax-collector gets there and picks up the money that they owe us. Do you follow me so far?'

'Are you coming with me?'

'Now, how can I do that? Me with my leg not properly healed yet?' Flynn protested impatiently. 'Besides that, every headman on the other side knows who I am. Not one of them has ever laid eyes on you before. You just tell them you're a new officer – straight out from Germany. One look at that uniform, and they'll pay up sharpish.'

'What happens if the real tax-inspector has already been?'

'They don't start collecting until September usually – and then they start in the north and work down this way. You'll have plenty of time.'

Frowning below the rim of the helmet, Sebastian brought forward a series of objections – each one progressively weaker than its predecessor, and, one by one, Flynn annihilated them. Finally there was a long silence while Sebastian's brain ground to a standstill.

'Well?' Flynn asked. 'Are you going to do it?'

And the question was answered from an unexpected quarter in feminine, but not dulcet tones. 'He is certainly *not* going to do it!'

Guiltily as small boys caught smoking in the school latrines, Flynn and Sebastian wheeled to face the door which had carelessly been left ajar.

Rosa's suspicions had been aroused by all the surreptitious activity around the rondavel, and when she had seen Sebastian join in, she had not the slightest qualms about listening outside the window. Her active intervention was not on ethical grounds. Rosa O'Flynn had acquired a rather elastic definition of honesty from her father. Like him, she believed that German property belonged to anybody who could get their hands on it. The fact that Sebastian was involved in a scheme based on dubious moral foundations in no way lowered her opinion of him – rather, in a sneaking sort of way, it heightened her estimate of him as a potential breadwinner. To date, this was the only area in which she had held misgivings about Sebastian Oldsmith.

From experience she knew that those of her father's business enterprises in which Flynn was not eager to participate personally always involved a great deal of risk. The thought of Sebastian Oldsmith dressed in a sky-blue uniform, marching across the Rovuma and never coming back, roused in her the same instincts as those of a lioness shortly to be deprived of her cubs.

'He is certainly *not* going to do it,' she repeated, and then to Sebastian. 'Do you hear me? I forbid it. I forbid it absolutely.'

This was the wrong approach.

Sebastian had, in turn, acquired from his father very Victorian views on the rights and privileges of women. Mr Oldsmith, the senior, was a courteous domestic tyrant, a man whose infallibility had never been challenged by his wife. A man who regarded sex deviates, Bolsheviks, trade union organizers, and suffragettes, in that descending order of repugnance.

Sebastian's mother, a meek little lady with a perpetually harassed expression, would no more have contemplated *absolutely forbidding* Mr Oldsmith a course of action, than she would have contemplated denying the existence of God. Her belief in the divine rights of man had extended to her sons. From a very tender age Sebastian had grown accustomed to worshipful obedience, not only from his mother but also from his large flock of sisters.

Rosa's present attitude and manner of speech came as a shock. It took him but a few seconds to recover and then he rose to his feet and adjusted the helmet. 'I beg your pardon?' he asked coldly.

'You heard me,' snapped Rosa. 'I'm not going to allow this.'

Sebastian nodded thoughtfully, and then hastily grabbed at the helmet as it threatened to spoil his dignity by blind-folding him again. Ignoring Rosa he turned to Flynn. 'I will leave as soon as possible – tomorrow?'

'It will take a couple more days to get organized,' Flynn demurred.

'Very well then.' Sebastian stalked from the room, and the sunlight lit his uniform with dazzling splendour.

With a triumphant guffaw, Flynn reached for the enamel mug at his elbow. 'You made a mess of that one,' he gloated, and then his expression changed to unease.

Standing in the doorway, Rosa O'Flynn's shoulders had sagged, the angry line of her lips drooped.

'Oh, come on now!' gruffed Flynn.

'He won't come back. You know what you are doing to him. You're sending him in there to die.'

'Don't talk silly. He's a big boy, he can look after himself.'

'Oh, I hate you. Both of you – I hate you both!' and she was gone, running across the yard to the bungalow.

– 22 –

In a red dawn Flynn and Sebastian stood together on the stoep of the bungalow, talking together quietly.

'Now listen, Bassie. I reckon the best thing you can do is send back the collection from each village, as you make it. No sense in carrying all that money round with you.' Tactfully Flynn refrained from pointing out that by following this procedure, in the event of Sebastian running into trouble half-way through the expedition, the profits to that time would be safeguarded.

Sebastian was not really listening – he was more preoccupied with the whereabouts of Rosa O'Flynn. He had seen very little of her in the last few days.

'Now you listen to old Mohammed. He knows which are the biggest villages. Let him do the talking – those headmen are the biggest bunch of rogues you'll ever meet. They'll all plead poverty and famine, so you've got to be tough. Do you hear me? Tough, Bassie, tough!!'

'Tough,' agreed Sebastian absent-mindedly, glancing surreptitiously into the windows of the bungalow for a glimpse of Rosa.

'Now another thing,' Flynn went on. 'Remember to keep moving fast. March until nightfall. Make your cooking fire, eat, and then march again in the dark before you camp. Never sleep at your first camp, that's asking for trouble. Then get away again before first light in the morning.' There were many other instructions, and Sebastian listened to them without attention. 'Remember the sound of gunfire carries for miles. Don't use your rifle except in emergency, and if you do fire a shot, then don't hang about afterwards. Now the route I've planned for you will never take you more than twenty miles beyond the Rovuma. At the first sign of trouble, you run for the river. If any of your men get hurt, leave them. Don't play hero, leave them and run like hell for the river.'

'Very well,' muttered Sebastian unhappily. The prospect of leaving Lalapanzi was becoming less attractive each minute. Where on earth was she?

'Now remember, don't let those headmen talk you out of anything. You might even have to . . .' Here Flynn paused to find the least offensive phraseology, '. . . you might even have to hang one or two of them.'

'Good God, Flynn. You're not serious.' Sebastian's full attention jerked back to Flynn.

'Ha! Ha!' Flynn laughed away the suggestion. 'I was joking, of course. But . . .' he went on wistfully, 'the Germans do it, and it gets results, you know.'

'Well, I'd better be on my way.' Sebastian changed the subject ostentatiously and picked up his helmet. He placed it upon his head and descended the steps to where his Askari, with rifles at the slope, were drawn up on the lawn. All of them, including Mohammed, were dressed in authentic uniform, complete with puttees and the little pillbox kepis. Sebastian had prudently refrained from asking Flynn how he had obtained these uniforms. The answer was evident in the neatly patched circular punctures in most of the tunics, and the faint brownish stain around each mend.

In single file, the blazing eagle on Sebastian's headpiece leading like a beacon, they marched past the massive solitary figure of Flynn O'Flynn on the veranda. Mohammed called for a salute and the response was enthusiastic, but ragged. Sebastian tripped on his spurs and with an effort, regained his equilibrium and plodded on gamely.

Shading his eyes against the glare, Flynn watched the gallant little column wind away down the valley towards the Rovuma river. Flynn's voice was without conviction as he spoke aloud, 'I hope to God he doesn't mess this one up.'

– 23 –

Once out of sight of the bungalow, Sebastian halted the column. Sitting beside the footpath, he sighed with relief as he removed the weight of the metal helmet from his head and replaced it with a sombrero of plaited grass, then he eased the spurred boots from his already aching feet, and slipped on a pair of rawhide sandals. He handed the discarded equipment to his personal bearer, stood up, and in his best Swahili ordered the march to continue.

Three miles down the valley the footpath crossed the stream above a tiny waterfall. It was a place of shade where great trees reached out towards each other across the narrow watercourse. Clear water trickled and gurgled between a tumble of lichen-covered boulders, before jumping like white lace in the sunlight down the slippery black slope of the falls.

Sebastian paused on the bank and allowed his men to proceed. He watched them hop from boulder to boulder, the bearers balancing their loads without effort, and then scramble up the far bank and disappear into the dense river bush. He listened to their voices becoming fainter with distance, and suddenly he was sad and alone.

Instinctively he turned and looked back up the valley towards Lalapanzi, and the sense of loss was a great emptiness inside him. The urge to return burned up so strongly, that he took a step back along the path before he could check himself.

He stood irresolute. The voices of his men were very faint now, muted by the dense vegetation, overlaid by the drowsy droning of insects, the wind murmur in the top branches of the trees, and the purl of falling water.

Then the soft rustle beside him, and he turned to it quickly. She stood near him and the sunlight through the leaves threw a golden dapple on her, giving a sense of unreality, a fairy quality, to her presence.

'I wanted to give you something to take with you, a farewell present for you to remember,' she said softly. 'But there was nothing I could think of,' and she came forward, reached up to him with her arms and her mouth, and she kissed him.

Sebastian Oldsmith crossed the Rovuma river in a mood of dreamy goodwill towards all men.

Mohammed was worried about him. He suspected that Sebastian had suffered a malarial relapse and he watched him carefully for evidence of further symptoms.

Mohammed at the head of the column of Askari and bearers had reached the crossing place on the Rovuma, before he realized that Sebastian was missing. In wild concern he had taken two armed Askari with him and hurried back along the path through the thorn scrub and broken rock – expecting at any moment to find a pride of lions growling over Sebastian's dismembered corpse. They had almost reached the waterfall when they met Sebastian ambling benignly along the path towards them, an expression of ethereal contentment lighting his classic features. His magnificent uniform was not a little rumpled; there were fresh grass stains on the knees and elbows, and dead leaves and bits of dried grass clung to the expensive material. From this Mohammed deduced that Sebastian had either fallen, or in sickness had lain down to rest.

'Manali,' Mohammed cried in concern. 'Are you well?'

'Never better – never in all my life,' Sebastian assured him.

'You have been lying down,' Mohammed accused.

'Son of a gun,' Sebastian borrowed from the vocabulary of Flynn O'Flynn. 'Son of a gun, you can say that again – and then repeat it!' and he clapped Mohammed between the shoulder blades with such well-intentioned violence that it almost floored him. Since then, Sebastian had not spoken again, but every few minutes he would smile and shake his head in wonder. Mohammed was truly worried.

They crossed the Rovuma in hired canoes and camped

that night on the far bank. Twice during the night Mohammed awoke, slipped out of his blanket, and crept across to Sebastian to check his condition. Each time Sebastian was sleeping easily and the silver moonlight showed just a suggestion of a smile on his lips.

In the middle of the next morning, Mohammed halted the column in thick cover and came back from the head to confer with Sebastian. 'The village of M'topo lies just beyond,' he pointed ahead. 'You can see the smoke from the fires.'

There was a greyish smear of it above the trees, and faintly a dog began yapping.

'Good. Let's go.' Sebastian had donned his eagle helmet and was struggling into his boots.

'First I will send the Askari to surround the village.'

'Why?' Sebastian looked up in surprise.

'Otherwise there will be nobody there when we arrive.' During his service with the German Imperial Army, Mohammed had been on tax expeditions before.

'Well – if you think it necessary,' Sebastian agreed dubiously.

Half an hour later Sebastian swaggered in burlesque of a German officer into the village of M'topo, and was dismayed by the reception he received. The lamentations of two hundred human beings made a hideous chorus for his entry. Some of them were on their knees and all of them were wringing their hands, smiting their breasts or showing other signs of deep distress. At the far end of the village M'topo, the headman, waited under guard by Mohammed and two of his Askari.

M'topo was an old man, with a cap of pure white wool, and an emaciated body covered with a parchment of dry skin. One eye was glazed over with tropical ophthalmia, and he was clearly very agitated. 'I crawl on my belly before you, Splendid and Merciful Lord,' he greeted Sebastian, and prostrated himself in the dust.

'I say, that isn't necessary, you know,' murmured Sebastian.

'My poor village welcomes you,' whimpered M'topo. Bitterly he recriminated himself for thus being taken unawares. He had not expected the tax expedition for another two months, and had taken no pains with the disposal of his wealth. Buried under the earthen floor of his hut was nearly a thousand silver Portuguese escudos and half again as many golden Deutschmarks. The traffic of his villagers in dried fish, netted in the Rovuma river, was highly organized and lucrative.

Now he dragged himself pitifully to his old knees and signalled two of his wives to bring forward stools and gourds of palm wine.

'It has been a year of great pestilence, disease and famine,' M'topo began his prepared speech, when Sebastian was seated and refreshed. The rest of it took fifteen minutes to deliver, and Sebastian's Swahili was now strong enough for him to follow the argument. He was deeply touched. Under the spell of palm wine and his new rosy outlook on life, he felt his heart going out to the old man.

While M'topo spoke, the other villagers had dispersed quietly and barricaded themselves in their huts. It was best not to draw attention to oneself when candidates for the rope were being selected. Now a mournful silence hung over the village, broken only by the mewling of an infant and the squabbling of a pair of mangy mongrels, contesting the ownership of a piece of offal.

'Manali,' impatiently Mohammed interrupted the old man's catalogue of misfortune. 'Let me search his hut.'

'Wait,' Sebastian stopped him. He had been looking about, and beneath the single baobab tree in the centre of the village he had noticed a dozen or so crude litters. Now he stood up and walked across to them.

When he saw what they contained, his throat contracted with horror. In each litter lay a human skeleton, the bones still covered with a thin layer of living flesh and skin. Naked men and women mixed indiscriminately, but their bodies so wasted that it was almost impossible to tell their sex. The pelvic girdles were gaunt basins of bone, elbows and knees great deformed knobs distorting the stick-like limbs, each rib standing out in clear definition, the faces were skulls whose lips had shrunk to expose the teeth in a perpetual sardonic grin. But the real horror was contained in the sunken eye cavities; the lids were fixed wide open – and the eyeballs glared like red marbles. There was no pupil nor iris, just those polished orbs the colour of blood.

Sebastian stepped back hurriedly, feeling his belly heave and the taste of it in his throat. Not trusting himself to speak, he beckoned for M'topo to come to him, and pointed at the bodies in the litters.

M'topo glanced at them without interest. They were so much part of the ordinary scene that for many days he had not consciously been aware of their existence. The village was situated on the edge of a tsetse fly belt, and since his childhood there had always been the sleeping sickness cases lying under the baobab tree, deep in the coma which precedes death. He could not understand Sebastian's concern.

'When . . . ?' Sebastian's voice faltered, and he swallowed before going on. 'When did these people last eat?' he asked.

'Not for a long time.' M'topo was puzzled by the question. Everybody knew that once the sleeping time came they never ate again.

Sebastian had heard of people dying of starvation. It happened in places like India, but here he was confronted with the actual fact. A revulsion of feeling swept over him.

This was irrefutable proof that all M'topo had told him was true. This was famine as he had not believed really could exist – and he had been trying to extort money from these people!

Sebastian walked slowly back to his stool and sank down upon it. He removed the heavy helmet from his head, held it in his lap and sat staring miserably at his own feet. He was helpless with guilt and compassion.

Flynn O'Flynn had reluctantly provided Sebastian with one hundred escudos as travelling expenses to meet any emergency that might arise before he could make his first collection. Some of this had been expended on the hire of canoes to cross the Rovuma, but there was still eighty escudos left.

From his hip-pocket, Sebastian produced the tobacco pouch containing the money and counted out half of it. 'M'topo,' his voice was subdued. 'Take this money. Buy food for them.'

'Manali,' screeched Mohammed in protest. 'Manali. Do not do it.'

'Shut up!' Sebastian snapped at him, and prodded the handful of coins towards M'topo. 'Take it!'

M'topo stared at him as though he offered a live scorpion. It was as unnatural as though a man-eating lion had walked up and rubbed itself against his leg.

'Take it,' Sebastian insisted impatiently, and in disbelief, M'topo extended his cupped hands.

'Mohammed,' Sebastian stood up and replaced his helmet, 'we'll move on immediately to the next village.'

Long after Sebastian's column had disappeared into the bush again, old M'topo squatted alone, clutching the coins, too stunned to move. At last he roused himself and shouted for one of his sons.

'Go quickly to the village of Saali, who is my brother. Tell him that a madman comes to him. A German lord who comes to collect the hut tax and stays to offer gifts. Tell him . . .' here his voice broke as though he could not believe what he was about to say,' . . . tell him that this lord should be shown the ones who sleep, and that the madness will then come upon him, and he will give you forty escudos of the Portuguese. And, furthermore, there will be no hangings.'

'Saali, my uncle, will not believe these things.'

'No,' M'topo admitted. 'It is true that he will not believe. But tell him anyway.'

– 25 –

Saali received the message from his elder brother, and it induced in him a state of terror bordering on paralysis. M'topo, he knew, had a vicious sense of humour – and there was between them that matter of the woman Gita, a luscious little fourteen-year-old who had deserted the village of M'topo within two days of taking up her duties as M'topo's junior wife, on the grounds that he was impotent and smelled like an hyena. She was now a notable addition to Saali's household. Saali was convinced that the true interpretation of his brother's message was that the new German commissioner was a rampaging lion who would not be content with merely hanging a few of the old men but who might extend his attentions to Saali himself. Even should he escape the noose, he would be left destitute; his carefully accumulated hoard of silver, his six fine tusks of ivory, his goat herd, his dozen bags of white salt, the bar of copper, his two European-made axes, the bolts of trade cloth – all of his treasures gone! It required an heroic effort to rouse himself from the stupor of despair and make his few futile preparations for flight.

Mohammed's Askari caught him as he was heading for

the bush at a trot, and when they led him back to meet Sebastian Oldsmith, the tears that coursed freely down his cheeks and dripped on to his chest were genuine.

Sebastian was very susceptible to tears. Despite the protests of Mohammed, Sebastian pressed upon Saali twenty silver escudos. It took Saali about twenty minutes to recover from the shock, at the end of which time he, in turn, shocked Sebastian profoundly by offering him on a temporary basis the unrestricted services of the girl, Gita. This young lady was witness to the offer made by her husband, and was obviously whole-heartedly in favour of it.

Sebastian set off again hurriedly, with his retinue straggling along behind him in a state of deep depression. Mohammed now had a bad case of the mutters.

Drums tap-tap-tapped, runners scurried along the network of footpaths that crossed and criss-crossed the bush; from hilltop to hilltop men called one to the other in the high-pitched wail that carries for miles. The news spread. Village after village buzzed with incredulous excitement, and then the inhabitants flocked out to meet the mad German commissioner.

By this time Sebastian was thoroughly enjoying himself. He was carried away with the pleasure of giving, delighted with these simple lovable people who welcomed him sincerely and pressed humble little gifts upon him. Here a scrawny fowl, there a dozen half-incubated eggs, a basin of sweet potatoes, a gourd of palm wine.

But Santa Claus's bag, or, more accurately, his tobacco pouch, was soon empty – and Sebastian was at a loss for some way to help alleviate the misery and poverty he saw in each village. He considered issuing indulgences from future tax . . . *the bearer is hereby excused from the payment of hut tax for five years* . . . but realized that this was a lethal

112

gift. He shuddered at what Herman Fleischer might do to anybody he caught in possession of one of these.

Finally he struck on the solution. These people were starving. He would give them food. He would give them meat.

In fact, this was one of the most desirable commodities Sebastian could have offered. Despite the abundance of wild life, the great herds of game that spread across the plains and hills, these people were starved for protein. The primitive hunting methods they employed were so ineffectual, that the killing of a single animal was an event that happened infrequently, and then almost by accident. When the carcass was shared out among two or three hundred hungry mouths, there was only a few ounces of meat for each. Men and women would risk their lives in attempting to drive a pride of lions from their kill, for just a few mouthfuls of this precious stuff.

Sebastian's Askari joined in the sport with delight. Even old Mohammed perked up a little. Unfortunately, their marksmanship was about the same standard as Sebastian's own, and a day's hunting usually resulted in the expenditure of thirty or forty rounds of Mauser ammunition, and a bag of sometimes as little as one half-grown zebra. But there were good days also, like the memorable occasion when a herd of buffalo virtually committed suicide by running down on the line of Askari. In the resulting chaos one of Sebastian's men was shot dead by his comrades, but eight full-grown buffalo followed him to the happy hunting grounds.

So Sebastian's tax tour proceeded triumphantly, leaving behind a trail of empty cartridge cases, racks of meat drying in the sun, full bellies, and smiling faces.

26

Three months after crossing the Rovuma river, Sebastian found himself back at the village of his good friend, M'topo. He had by-passed Saali's in order to avoid the offended Gita.

Sitting alone in the night within the hut that M'topo placed at his disposal, Sebastian was having his first misgivings. On the morrow, he would begin the return to Lalapanzi, where Flynn O'Flynn was waiting for him. Sebastian was acutely aware that from Flynn's point of view the expedition had not been a success – and Flynn would have a great deal to say on the subject. Once more Sebastian puzzled on the fates which took his best intentions, and manipulated them in such a manner that they became completely unrecognizable from the original.

Then his thoughts kicked off at a tangent. Soon, the day after tomorrow, if all went well, he would be back with Rosa. The deep yearning that had been his constant companion these last three months throbbed through Sebastian's whole body. Staring into the wood-fire on the hearth of the hut, it seemed as though the embers formed a picture of her face, and in his memory he heard her voice again.

'Come back, Sebastian. Come back soon.'

And he whispered the words aloud, watching her face in the fire. Gloating on each detail of it. He saw her smile, and her nose wrinkled a little, the dark eyes slanted upwards at the corners.

'Come back, Sebastian.'

The need of her was a physical pain so intense that he could hardly breathe, and his imagination reconstructed every detail of their parting beside the waterfall. Each subtle change and inflection of her voice, the very sound of her breathing, and the bitter salt taste of her tears upon his lips.

He felt again the touch of her hands, her mouth – and through the wood-smoke that filled the hut, his nostrils flared at the warm woman smell of her body.

'I'm coming, Rosa. I'm coming back,' he whispered, and stood up restlessly from beside the fire. At that moment his attention was jerked back to the present by a soft scratching at the door of the hut.

'Lord. Lord.' He recognized old M'topo's hoarse croaking. 'What is it?'

'We seek your protection.'

'What is the trouble?' Sebastian crossed to the door and lifted the cross-bar. 'What is it?'

In the moonlight M'topo stood with a skin blanket draped around his frail shoulders. Behind him a dozen of the villagers huddled in trepidation.

'The elephant are in our gardens. They will destroy them before morning. There will be nothing, not a single stalk of millet left standing.' He swung away and stood with his head cocked. 'Listen, you may hear them now.'

It was an eerie sound in the night, the high-pitched elephant squeal, and Sebastian's skin crawled. He could feel the hair on his forearms become erect.

'There are two of them.' M'topo's voice was a scratchy whisper. 'Two old bulls. We know them well. They came last season and laid waste our corn. They killed one of my sons who tried to drive them off.' In entreaty, the old man clawed hold of Sebastian's arm and tugged at it. 'Avenge my son, lord. Avenge my son for me, and save our millet that the children will not go hungry again this year.'

Sebastian responded to the appeal in the same manner that St George would have done.

In haste he buttoned his tunic and went to fetch his rifle. On his return he found his entire command armed to the teeth, and as eager for the hunt as a pack of foxhounds. Mohammed waited at their head.

'Lord Manali, we are ready.'

'Now, steady on, old chap.' Sebastian had no intention of sharing the glory. 'This is my shauri. Too many cooks, what?'

M'topo stood by, wringing his hands with impatience, listening alternately first to the distant sounds of the garden raiders feeding contentedly in his lands, and then to the undignified wrangling between Sebastian and his Askari, until at last he could bear it no longer. 'Lord, already half the millet is eaten. In an hour it will all be gone.'

'You're right,' Sebastian agreed, and turned angrily on his men. 'Shut up, all of you. Shut up!'

They were unaccustomed to this tone of command from Sebastian, and it surprised them into silence.

'Only Mohammed shall accompany me. The rest of you go to your huts and stay there.'

It was a working compromise, Sebastian now had Mohammed as an ally. Mohammed turned on his comrades and scattered them before falling in beside Sebastian.

'Let us go.'

At the head of the main gardens, high on its stilts of poles, stood a rickety platform. This was the watch-tower from which, night and day, a guard was kept over the ripening millet. It was now deserted, the two young guards had left hurriedly at the first sight of the garden raiders. Kudu or waterbuck were one thing, a pair of bad-tempered old elephant bulls were another matter entirely.

Sebastian and Mohammed reached the watch-tower and paused beneath it. Quite clearly now they could hear the rustling and ripping sound of the millet stalks being torn up and trampled.

'Wait here,' whispered Sebastian, slinging his rifle over his shoulder, as he turned to the ladder beside him. He climbed slowly and silently to the platform, and from it, looked out over the gardens.

The moon was so brilliant as to throw sharply defined shadows below the tower and the trees. Its light was a soft silver that distorted distance and size, reducing all things to a cold, homogeneous grey.

Beyond the clearing the forest rose like frozen smoke clouds, while the field of standing millet moved in the small night wind, rippling like the surface of a lake.

Humped big and darker grey, standing high above the millet, two great islands in the soft sea of vegetation, the old bulls grazed slowly. Although the nearest elephant was two hundred paces from the tower, the moon was so bright that Sebastian could see clearly as he reached forward with his trunk, coiled it about a clump of the leafy stalks and plucked them easily. Then swaying gently, rocking his massive bulk lazily from side to side, he beat the millet against his lifted foreleg to shake the clinging earth from the roots before lifting it and stuffing it into his mouth. The tattered banners of his ears flapped gently, an untidy tangle of millet leaves hanging from his lips between the long curved shafts of ivory, he moved on, feeding and trampling so that behind him he left a wide path of devastation.

On the open platform of the tower, Sebastian felt his stomach contracting, convulsing itself into a hard ball, and his hands on the rifle were unsteady; his breathing whistled softly in his own ears as the elephant thrill came upon him. Watching those two huge beasts, he found himself held motionless with an almost mystic sense of awe; a realization of his own insignificance, his presumption in going out against them, armed with this puny weapon of steel and wood. But beneath his reluctance was the tingle of tight nerves – that strange blend of fear and eagerness – the age-old lust of the hunter. He roused himself and climbed down to where Mohammed waited.

Through the standing corn that reached above their heads, stepping with care between the rows so that they disturb not a single leaf, they moved in towards the centre of the garden. Ears and eyes tuned to their finest limit, breathing controlled so that it did not match the wild pump of his heart, Sebastian homed in on the crackle and rustle made by the nearest bull.

Even though the millet screened him, he could feel the weak wash of the wind move his hair softly, and the first whiff of elephant smell hit him like an open-handed blow in the face. He stooped so suddenly that Mohammed almost bumped into him from behind. They stood crouching, peering ahead into the moving wall of vegetation. Sebastian felt Mohammed lean forward beside him, and heard his whisper breathed softer than the sound of the wind. 'Very close now.'

Sebastian nodded, and then swallowed jerkily. He could hear clearly the soft slithering scrape of leaves brushing against the rough hide of the old bull. It was feeding down towards them. They were standing directly in the path of its leisurely approach, at any moment now – at any moment!

Standing with the rifle lifted protectively, sweat starting to prickle his forehead and upper lip in the cool of the night, his eyes watering with the intensity of his gaze, Sebastian was suddenly aware of massive movement ahead of him. A solid shape through the bank of dancing leaves, and he looked up. High above him it loomed, black and big so that the night sky was blotted out by the spread of its ears, so near that he stood beneath the forward thrust of its tusks, and he could see the trunk uncoil like a fat grey python and grope forward blindly towards him; and beneath it the mouth gaped a little, spilling leaves at the corners.

He lifted the rifle, pointing it upwards without aiming, almost touching the elephant's hanging lower lip with the muzzle, and he fired. The shot was a blunt burst of sound in the night.

The bullet angled up through the pink palate of the animal's mouth, up through the spongy bone of the skull; mushrooming and exploding, it tore into the fist-sized cell that contained the brain, and burst it into a grey jelly.

Had it passed four inches to either side; had it been deflected by one of the larger bones, Sebastian would have died before he had time to work the bolt of the Mauser, for he stood directly below the outstretched tusks and trunk. But the old bull reeled backwards from the shot, his trunk falling flabbily against his chest, his forelegs spreading, and his head unbalanced by long tusks sagged forwards, knees collapsed suddenly under him, and he fell so heavily that they heard the thump in the village half a mile away.

'Son of a gun!' gasped Sebastian, staring in disbelief at the dead mountain of flesh. 'I did it. Son of a gun, I did it!' Jubilation, a delirious release from fear and tension, mounted giddily within him. He lifted an arm to hit Mohammed across the back, but he froze in that attitude.

Like the shriek of steam escaping from a burst boiler, the other bull squealed in the moonlight nearby. And they heard the crackling rush of his run in the corn.

'He's coming!' Sebastian looked frantically about him for the sound had no direction.

'No,' squawked Mohammed. 'He turns against the wind. First he seeks for the smell of us, and then he will come.' He grabbed Sebastian's arm and clung to him, while they listened to the elephant circling to get down-wind of them.

'Perhaps he will run,' whispered Sebastian.

'Not this one. He is old and evil-tempered, and he has killed men before. Now he will hunt us.' Mohammed pulled at Sebastian's arm. 'We must get out into the open. In this stuff we will have no chance, he will be on top of us before we see him.'

They started to run. There is no more piquant sauce for fear than flying feet. Once he starts to run, even a brave man becomes a coward. Within twenty paces, both of them were in headlong flight towards the village. They ran without regard for stealth, fighting their way through the tangle of leaves and stalks, panting wildly. The noise of their flight blanketed the sounds made by the elephant, so they lost all idea of his whereabouts. This sharpened the spurs of terror that drove them, for at any moment he might loom over them.

At last they stumbled out into the open, and paused, panting, sweating heavily, heads swinging from side to side as they tried to place the second bull.

'There!' shouted Mohammed. 'He comes,' and they heard the shrill pig-squealing, the noisy rush of his charge through the millet.

'Run!' yelled Sebastian, still in the grip of panic, and they ran.

Around a freshly lit bonfire at the edge of the village, waited the rejected Askari and a hundred of M'topo's men. They waited in anxiety for they had heard the shot and the fall of the first bull – but since then, the squealing and shouting and crashing had left them in some doubt as to what was happening in the gardens.

This doubt was quickly dispelled as Mohammed, closely followed by Sebastian, came down the path towards them, giving a fair imitation of two dogs whose backsides had been dipped in turpentine. A hundred yards behind them the bank of standing millet burst open, and the second bull came out in full charge.

Immense in the firelight, hump-back, shambling in the deceptive speed of his run, streaming his huge ears, each squeal of rage enough to burst the eardrums – he bore down on the village.

'Get out! Run!' Sebastian's shouted warning was as

wheezy as it was unnecessary. The waiting crowd was no longer waiting, it scattered like a shoal of sardines at the approach of a barracuda.

Men threw aside their blankets and ran naked; they fell over each other and ran headlong into trees. Two of them ran straight through the middle of the bonfire and emerged on the other side trailing sparks with live coals sticking to their feet. In a wailing hubbub they swept back through the village, and from each hut women with infants bundled under their arms, or slung over their backs, scurried out to join the terrified torrent of humanity.

Still making good time, Sebastian and Mohammed were passing the weaker runners among the villagers, while from behind, the elephant was gaining rapidly on all of them.

With the force and velocity of a great boulder rolling down a steep hillside, the bull reached the first hut of the village and ran into it. The flimsy structure of grass and light poles exploded, bursting asunder without diminishing the fury of the animal's charge. A second hut disintegrated, then a third, before the elephant caught the first human straggler.

She was an old woman, tottering on thin legs, the empty pouches of her breasts flopping against her wrinkled belly, a long monotonous wail of fear keening from the toothless pit of her mouth as she ran.

The bull uncoiled his trunk from his chest, lifted it high above the woman and struck her across the shoulder. The force of the blow crumpled her, bones snapped in her chest like old dry sticks, and she died before she hit the ground.

The next was a girl. Groggy with sleep, yet her naked body was silver-smooth and graceful in the moonlight, as she emerged from a hut into the path of the bull's charge. Lightly the thick trunk enfolded her, and then with an effortless flick threw her forty feet into the air.

She screamed, and the sound of the scream knifed through Sebastian's panic. He glanced over his shoulder in time to see the girl thrown high in the night sky. Her limbs were spread-eagled and she spun in the air like a cartwheel before she dropped back to earth – falling heavily so that the scream was cut off abruptly. Sebastian stopped running.

Deliberately the elephant knelt over the girl's feebly squirming body, and driving down with his tusks, impaled her through the chest. She hung from the shaft of ivory, squashed and broken, no longer recognizable as human, until the elephant shook his head irritably and threw her off.

It needed a sight as horrible as this to rally Sebastian's shattered nerves – to summon the reserves of his manhood from the far places that fear had scattered them. The rifle was still in his hands, but he was shaking with fear and exertion; sweat had drenched his tunic and plastered his curly hair on to his forehead, and his breath sawed hoarsely in his throat. He stood irresolute, fighting the driving urge to run again.

The bull came on, and now his one tusk was painted glistening black with the girl's blood, and gouts of the same stuff were splattered across his bulging forehead and the bridge of his trunk. It was this that changed Sebastian's fear first to disgust, and then to anger.

He lifted the rifle and it weaved unsteadily in his hands. He sighted along the barrel and suddenly his vision snapped into sharp focus and his nerves stilled their clamour. He was a man again.

Coldly he moved the blob of the foresight on to the bull's head, holding it on the deep lateral crease at the root of the trunk, and he squeezed the trigger. The butt jumped solidly into his shoulder, the report stung his eardrums, but he saw the bullet strike exactly where he had aimed it – a spurt of dust from the crust of dried mud that caked the animal's head and the skin around it, twitched, the eyelids quivered shut for an instant, then blinked open again.

Without lowering the rifle Sebastian jerked the bolt open, and the empty case ejected crisply, pinging away into the dust. He levered another cartridge into the breach and held his aim into the massive head. Again he fired and the elephant staggered drunkenly. The ears which had been cocked half back, now fanned open and the head swung vaguely in his direction.

He fired again, and the bull winced as the bullet lanced into the bone and gristle of his head, then he turned and came for Sebastian – but there was a slackness, a lack of determination in his charge. Aiming now for the chest, handling the rifle with cold method, Sebastian fired again and again, leaning forward against the recoil of the rifle, sighting every shot with care, knowing that each of them was raking the chest cavity, tearing through lung and heart and liver.

And the bull broke his run into a shuffling, uncertain walk, losing direction, turning away from Sebastian to stand broadside, the barrel of his chest heaving against the agony of his torn vitals.

Sebastian lowered the rifle and with steady fingers pressed fresh cartridges down into the empty magazine. The bull groaned softly and from the tip of his trunk, blood hosed up from the haemorrhaging lungs.

Without pity, cold in his anger, Sebastian lifted the reloaded rifle, and aimed for the dark cavity that nestled in the centre of the huge ear. The bullet struck with the sharp thwack of an axe swung against a tree trunk, and the elephant sagged and fell forward to the brain shot. His weight drove his tusks into the earth, burying them to the lip.

27

Four tons of meat delivered fresh to the very centre of the village was good value. The price paid was not exorbitant, M'topo decided. Three huts could be rebuilt in two days, and only four acres of millet had been destroyed. Furthermore, of the women who had died, one was very old and the other, although she was almost eighteen years old, had never conceived. There was good reason, therefore, to believe she was barren and not a great loss to the community.

Warmed by the early sun, M'topo was a satisfied man. With Sebastian beside him, he sat on his carved wooden stool and grinned widely as he watched the fun.

Two dozen of his men, armed with short-handled, long-bladed spears, and divested of all clothing, were to act as butchers. They were gathered beside the mountainous carcass arguing good-naturedly as they waited for Mohammed and his four assistants to remove the tusks. Around them, in a wider circle, waited the rest of the villagers, and while they waited, they sang. A drum hammered out the rhythm for them, and the clap of hands and the stamp of feet confirmed it. The masculine bass was a foundation from which the clear, sweet soprano of the women soared, and sank, and soared again.

Beneath Mohammed's patiently chipping axe, first the one tusk and then the other were freed from the bone that held them, and, with two Askari staggering under the weight, they were carried to where Sebastian sat, and laid with ceremony at his feet.

It occurred to Sebastian that four big tusks carried home to Lalapanzi might in some measure mollify Flynn O'Flynn. They would at least cover the costs of the expedition. The thought cheered him up considerably, and he turned to M'topo. 'Old one, you may take the meat.'

'Lord.' In gratitude, M'topo clapped his hands at the level of his chest, and then turned to squawk an order at the waiting butchers.

A roar of excitement and meat hunger went up from the crowd as one of them scrambled up on to the carcass, and drove his spear though the thick grey hide behind the last rib. Then walking backwards, he drew it down towards the haunch and the razor steel sliced deep. Two others made the lateral incisions, opening a square flap – a trapdoor into the belly cavity from which the fat coils of the viscera bulged, pink and blue and glossy wet in the early morning sunlight. In mounting eagerness, four others dragged from the square hole the contents of the belly, and then, while Sebastian stared in disbelief, they wriggled into the opening and disappeared. He could hear their muffled shouts reverberating within the carcass as they competed for the prize of the liver. Within minutes one of them reappeared, clutching against his chest a slippery lump of tattered, purple liver. Like a maggot, he came squirming out of the wound, painted over-all with a thick coating of dark red blood. It had matted in the woolly cap of his hair, and turned his face into a gruesome mask from which only his teeth and his eyes gleamed white. Carrying the mutilated liver, laughing in triumph, he ran through the crowd to where Sebastian sat.

The offering embarrassed Sebastian. More than that, it made his gorge rise, and he felt his stomach heave as it was thrust almost into his lap.

'Eat,' M'topo encouraged him. 'It will make you strong. It will sharpen the spear of your manhood. Ten, twenty women will not tire you.'

It was M'topo's opinion that Sebastian needed this type

of tonic. He had heard from his brother Saali, and from the chiefs along the river, about Sebastian's lack of initiative.

'Like this.' M'topo cut a hunk of the liver and popped it into his mouth. He chewed heartily, and the juice wet his lips as he grinned in appreciation. 'Very good.' He thrust a piece into Sebastian's face. 'Eat.'

'No.' Sebastian's gorge pressed heavily on the back of his throat, and he stood up hurriedly. M'topo shrugged, and ate it himself. Then he shouted to the butchers to continue their work.

In a miraculously short space of time the huge carcass disintegrated under the blades of the spears and machetes. It was a labour in which the entire village joined. With a dozen strokes of the knife, a butcher would free a large hunk of flesh and throw it down to one of the women. She, in turn, would hack it into smaller pieces and pass these on to the children. Squealing with excitement, they would run with them to the hastily erected drying racks, deposit them and come scampering back for more.

Sebastian had recovered from his initial revulsion and now he laughed to see how every mouth was busy, chewing as they worked and yet at the same time managing to emit a surprising volume of noise.

Among the milling feet the dogs snarled and yipped, and gulped the scraps. Without interrupting their feeding, they dodged the casual kicks and blows that were aimed at them.

Into the midst of this cosy, domestic scene entered Commissioner Herman Fleischer with ten armed Askari.

28

Herman Fleischer was tired and there were blisters on his feet from the series of forced marches that had brought him to M'topo's village.

A month before he had left his headquarters at Mahenge to begin the annual tax tour of his area. As was his custom, he had started in the northern province, and it had been an unusually successful expedition. The wooden chest with the rampant black eagle painted on its lid had grown heavier with each day's journey. Herman had amused himself by calculating how many more years service in Africa would be necessary before he could resign and return home to Plaven and settle down on the estate he planned to buy. Three more years as fruitful as this, he decided, would be sufficient. It was a bitter shame that he had not been able to capture O'Flynn's dhow on the Rufiji thirteen months previously – that would have advanced his date of departure by a full twelve months. Thinking about it stirred his residual anger at that episode, and he placated it by doubling the hut tax on the next village he visited. This raised such a howl of protest from the village headman that Herman nodded at his sergeant of Askari, who began ostentatiously to unpack the rope from his saddlebag.

'O fat and beautiful bull elephant,' the headman changed his mind hastily. 'If you will wait but a little while, I will bring the money to you. There is a new hut, without lice or fleas, in which you may rest your lovely body, and I will send a young girl to you with beer for your thirst.'

'Good,' agreed Herman. 'While I rest, my Askari will stay with you.' He nodded at the sergeant to bind the chief, then waddled away to the hut.

The headman sent two of his sons to dig beneath a

certain tree in the forest, and they returned an hour later with mournful faces, carrying a heavy skin bag.

Contentedly Herman Fleischer signed an official receipt for ninety per cent of the contents of the bag – Fleischer allowed himself a ten per cent handling fee – and the headman, who could not read a word of German, accepted it with relief.

'I will stay tonight in your village,' Herman announced. 'Send the same girl to cook my food.'

The runner from the south arrived in the night, and disturbed Herman Fleischer at a most inopportune moment. The news he carried was even more disturbing. From his description of the new German commissioner who was doing Herman's job for him in the southern province, and shooting up the countryside in the process, Herman immediately recognized the young Englishman whom he had last seen on the deck of a dhow in the Rufiji delta.

Leaving the bulk of his retinue, including the bearers of the tax chest, to follow him at their best speed, Herman mounted at midnight on his white donkey and, taking ten Askari with him, he rode southwards on a storm patrol.

Five nights later, in those still dark hours that precede the dawn, Herman was camped near the Rovuma river when he was awakened by his sergeant.

'What is it?' Grumpy with fatigue, Herman sat up and lifted the side of his mosquito net.

'We heard the sound of gun-fire. A single shot.'

'Where?' He was instantly awake, and reaching for his boots.

'From the south, towards the village of M'topo on the Rovuma.'

Fully dressed now, Herman waited anxiously, straining his ears against the small sounds of the African night. 'Are you sure . . . ?' he began as he turned to his sergeant, but he did not finish. Faintly, but unmistakable in the darkness, they heard the pop, pop, pop of a distant rifle – a pause and then another shot.

'Break camp,' bellowed Herman. 'Rasch! You black heathen. Rasch!'

The sun was well up by the time they reached M'topo's village. They came upon it suddenly through the gardens of tall millet that screened their approach. Herman Fleischer paused to throw out his Askari in a line of skirmishers before closing in on the cluster of huts, but when he reached the fringe, he stopped once more in surprise at the extraordinary spectacle which was being enacted in the open square of the village.

The dense knot of half-naked black people that swarmed over the remains of the elephant was perfectly oblivious of Herman's presence until at last he filled his lungs, and then emptied them again in a roar that carried over the hubbub of shouts and laughter. Instantly a vast silence fell upon the gathering, every head turned towards Herman and from each head eyes bulged in horrific disbelief.

'Bwana Intambu,' a small voice broke the silence at last. 'Lord of the rope.' They knew him well.

'What . . . ?' Herman began, and then gasped in outrage as he noticed in the crowd a black man he had never seen before, dressed in the full uniform of German Askari. 'You!' he shouted, pointing an accusing finger, but the man whirled and ducked away behind the screen of blood-smeared black bodies. 'Stop him!' Herman fumbled with the flap of his holster.

Movement caught his eye and he turned to see another pseudo-Askari running away between the huts. 'There's another one! Stop him! Sergeant, Sergeant, get your men here!'

The initial shock that had held them frozen was now past, and the crowd broke and scattered. Once again, Herman Fleischer gasped in outrage as he saw, for the first time, a figure sitting on a carved native stool on the far side of the square. A figure in an outlandish uniform of bright but travel-stained blue, frogged with gold, his legs clad in high jackboots, and on his head the dress helmet of an illustrious Prussian regiment.

'Englishman!' Despite the disguise, Herman recognized him. He had finally succeeded in unbuttoning the flap of his holster, and now he withdrew his Luger. 'Englishman!' He repeated the insult and lifted the pistol.

With the quickness of mind for which he was noted, Sebastian sat bewildered by this unforeseen turn of events, but when Herman showed him the working end of the Luger, he realized that it was time to take his leave, and he attempted to leap nimbly to his feet. However, the spurs on his boots became entangled once more and he went backwards over the stool. The bullet hissed harmlessly through the empty space where he would have been standing.

'God damn!' Herman fired again, and the bullet kicked a burst of splinters out of the heavy wooden stool behind which Sebastian was lying. This second failure aroused in Herman Fleischer the blinding rage which spoiled his aim for the next two shots he fired, as Sebastian went on hands and knees around the corner of the nearest hut.

Behind the hut, Sebastian jumped to his feet and set off at a run. His main concern was to get out of the village and into the bush. In his ears echoed Flynn O'Flynn's advice.

'Make for the river. Go straight for the river.'

And he was so occupied with it that, when he charged around the side of the next hut, he could not check himself in time to avoid collision with one of Herman Fleischer's Askari, who was coming in the opposite direction. Both of them went down together in an untidy heap, and the steel helmet fell forward over Sebastian's eyes. As he struggled into a sitting position, he removed the helmet and found the man's woolly black head in front of him. It was ideally placed and Sebastian was holding the heavy helmet above it. With the strength of both his arms, he brought the helmet down again, and it clanged loudly against the Askari's skull. With a grunt the Askari sagged backwards and lay quietly in the dust. Sebastian placed the helmet over his sleeping face, picked up the man's rifle from beside him and got to his feet once more.

He stood crouching in the shelter of the hut while he tried to make sense of the chaos around him. Through the pandemonium set up by the panic-stricken villagers, who were milling about with all the purpose of a flock of sheep attacked by wolves, Sebastian could hear the bellowed commands of Herman Fleischer, and the answering shouts of the German Askari. Rifle-fire cracked and whined, to be answered by renewed outbursts of screaming.

Sebastian's first impulse was to hide in one of the huts but he realized this would be futile. At the best it would only delay his capture.

No, he must get out of the village. But the thought of covering the hundred yards of open ground to the shelter of the nearest trees, while a dozen Askari shot at him, was most unattractive.

At this moment Sebastian became aware of an unpleasant warmth in his feet, and he looked down to find that he was standing in the live ashes of a cooking fire. The leather of his jackboots was already beginning to char and smoke. He stepped back hurriedly, and the smell of burning leather acted as a laxative for the constipation of his brain.

From the hut beside him he snatched a handful of thatch and stooped to thrust it into the fire. The dry grass burst into flame, and Sebastian held the torch to the wall of the hut. Instantly fire bloomed and shot upwards. With the torch in his hand, Sebastian ducked across the narrow opening to the next hut and set fire to that also.

'Son of a gun!' exulted Sebastian as great oily billows of

smoke obscured the sun and limited his field of vision to ten paces.

Slowly he moved forward in the rolling cloud of smoke, setting fire to each hut he passed, and delighted in the frustrated bellows of Germanic rage he heard behind him. Occasionally ghostly figures scampered past him in the acrid half-darkness but none of them paid him the slightest attention, and each time Sebastian relaxed the pressure of his forefinger on the trigger of the Mauser, and moved on.

He reached the last hut and paused there to gather himself for the final sprint across open ground to the edge of the millet garden. Through the eddying bank of smoke, the mass of dark green vegetation from which he had fled in terror not many hours before, now seemed as welcoming as the arms of his mother.

Movement near him in the smoke, and he swung the Mauser to cover it; he saw the square outline of a kepi and the sparkle of metal buttons, and his finger tightened on the trigger.

'Manali!'

'Mohammed! Good God, I nearly killed you.' Sebastian threw up the rifle barrel as he recognized him.

'Quickly! They are close behind me.' Mohammed snatched at his arm and dragged him forward. The jack-boots pinched his toes and thumped like the hooves of a galloping buffalo as Sebastian ran. From the huts behind them a voice shouted urgently and, immediately afterwards, came the vicious crack of a Mauser and the shrill whinny of the ricochet.

Sebastian had a lead of ten paces on Mohammed as he plunged into the bank of leaves and millet stalks.

29

'What should we do now, Manali?' Mohammed asked, and the expression on the faces of the two other men echoed the question with pathetic trust. A benevolent chance had reunited Sebastian with the remnants of his command. During the flight through the millet gardens, with random rifle-fire clipping the leaves about their heads, Sebastian had literally fallen over these two. At the time they were engaged in pressing their bellies and their faces hard against the earth, and it had taken a number of lusty kicks with the jackboot to get them up and moving.

Since then Sebastian, mindful of Flynn's advice, had cautiously and circuitously led them down to the landing-place on the bank of the Rovuma. He arrived to find that Fleischer's Askari, by using the direct route and without the necessity of concealing themselves, had arrived before him. From the cover of the reed-banks Sebastian watched dejectedly, as they used an axe to knock the bottoms out of the dug-out canoes that were drawn up on the little white beach.

'Can we swim across?' he asked Mohammed in a whisper, and Mohammed's face crumpled with horror, as he considered the suggestion. Both of them peered out through the reeds across a quarter of a mile of deep water that flowed so fast, its surface was dimpled with tiny whirlpools.

'No,' said Mohammed with finality.

'Too far?' asked Sebastian hopelessly.

'Too far. Too fast. Too deep. Too many crocodiles,' agreed Mohammed, and in an unspoken but mutual desire to get away from the river and the Askari, they crawled out of the reed-bank and crept away inland.

In the late afternoon they were lying up in a bushy gully

about two miles from the river and an equal distance from M'topo's village.

'What should we do now, Manali?' Mohammed repeated his question, and Sebastian cleared his throat before answering.

'Well . . .' he said and paused while his wide brow wrinkled in the agony of creative thought. Then it came to him with all the splendour of a sunrise. 'We'll just jolly well have to find some other way of getting across the river.' He said it with the air of a man well pleased with his own perspicacity. 'What do you suggest, Mohammed?'

A little surprised to find the ball returned so neatly into his own court, Mohammed remained silent.

'A raft?' hazarded Sebastian. The lack of tools, material and opportunity to build one was so obvious, that Mohammed did not deign to reply. He shook his head.

'No,' agreed Sebastian. 'Perhaps you are right.' Again the classic beauty of his features was marred by a scowl of concentration. At last he demanded, 'There are other villages along the river?'

'Yes,' Mohammed conceded. 'But the Askari will visit each of them and destroy the canoes. Also they will tell the headmen who we are, and threaten them with the rope.'

'But they cannot cover the whole river. It has a frontier of five or six hundred miles. We'll just keep walking until we find a canoe. It may take us a long time but we'll find one eventually.'

'If the Askari don't catch us first.'

'They'll expect us to stay close to the border. We'll make a detour well inland, and march for five or six days before we come back to the river again. We'll rest now and move tonight.'

*

134

Heading on a diagonal line of march away from the Rovuma and deeper into German territory, moving north-west along a well defined footpath, the four of them kept walking all that night. As the slow hours passed so the pace flagged and twice Sebastian noticed one or other of his men wander off the path at an angle until suddenly they started and looked about in surprise, before hurrying back to join the others. It puzzled him and he meant to ask them what they were doing, but he was tired and the effort of speech was too great. An hour later he found the reason for their behaviour.

Plodding along, with the movement of his legs becoming completely automatic, Sebastian was slowly overcome by a state of gentle well-being. He surrendered to it and let the warm, dark mists of oblivion wash over his mind.

The sting of a thorn branch across his cheek jerked him back to consciousness and he looked about in bewilderment. Ten yards away on his flank, Mohammed and the two gun-boys walked along the path in single file, their faces turned towards him with expressions of mild interest in the moonlight. It took some moments for Sebastian to realize that he had fallen asleep on his feet. Feeling a complete ass, he trotted back to take his place at the head of the line.

When the fat silver moon sank below the trees, they kept going by the faint glow of reflected light, but slowly that waned until the footpath hardly showed at their feet. Sebastian decided that dawn could be only an hour away and it was time to halt. He stopped and was about to speak when Mohammed's clutching hand on his shoulder prevented him.

'Manali!' There was a tone in Mohammed's whisper that cautioned him, and Sebastian felt his nerves jerk taut.

'What is it?' he breathed, protectively unslinging the Mauser.

'Look. There – ahead of us.'

Screwing up his eyes Sebastian searched the blackness ahead, and it was a long time before the faint ruddiness in the solid blanket of darkness registered itself upon the exhausted retinas of his eyes. 'Yes!' he whispered. 'What is it?'

'A fire,' breathed Mohammed. 'There is someone camped across the path in front of us.'

'Askari?' asked Sebastian.

'Perhaps.'

Peering at the ruby puddle of dying coals, Sebastian felt the hair on the back of his neck stir and come erect with alarm. He was fully awake now. 'We must go around them.'

'No. They will see our spoor in the dust of the path and they will follow us,' Mohammed demurred.

'What then?'

'First let me see how many there are.'

Without waiting for Sebastian's permission, Mohammed slipped away and disappeared into the night like a leopard. Five anxious minutes Sebastian waited. Once he thought he heard a scuffling sound but he was not certain. Mohammed's shape materialized again beside him. 'Ten of them,' he reported. 'Two Askari and eight bearers. One of the Askari sat guard by the fire. He saw me, so I killed him.'

'Good God!' Sebastian's voice rose higher. 'You did what?'

'I killed him. But do not speak so loud.'

'How?'

'With my knife.'

'Why?'

'Lest he kill me first.'

'And the other?'

'Him also.'

'You killed both of them?' Sebastian was appalled.

'Yes, and took their rifles. Now it is safe to go on. But the bearers have with them many cases. It comes to me that this party follows after Bwana Intambu, the German commissioner, and that they carry with them all his goods.'

'But you shouldn't have killed them,' protested Sebastian. 'You could have just tied them up or something.'

'Manali, you argue like a woman,' Mohammed snapped impatiently, and then went on with his original line of thought. 'Among the cases is one that by its size I think is the box for the tax money. The one Askari slept with his back against it as though to give it special care.'

'The tax money?'

'Yes.'

'Well, son of a gun!' Sebastian's scruples dissolved and in the darkness his expression was suddenly transformed into that of a small boy on Christmas morning.

They woke the German bearers by standing over them and prodding them with the rifle barrels. Then they hustled them out of their blankets and herded them into a small group, bewildered and shivering miserably in the chill of dawn. Wood was heaped on the fire; it burned up brightly, and by its light Sebastian examined the booty.

The one Askari had bled profusely from the throat on to the small wooden chest. Mohammed took him by the heels and dragged him out of the way, then used his blanket to wipe the chest clean.

'Manali,' he said with reverence. 'See the big lock. See the bird of the Kaiser painted on the lid . . .' He stooped over the chest and took a grip on the handles, '. . . but most of all, feel the weight of it!'

Amongst the other equipment around the fire, Mohammed found a thick coil of one-inch manila rope. A commodity which was essential equipment on any of Herman Fleischer's safaris. With it, Mohammed roped the bearers together, at waist level, allowing enough line between each of them to make concerted movement possible but preventing individual flight.

'Why are you doing that?' Sebastian asked with interest, through a mouthful of blood sausage and black bread. Most of the other boxes were filled with food, and Sebastian was breakfasting well and heartily.

'So they cannot escape.'

'We're not taking them with us – are we?'

'Who else will carry all this?' Mohammed asked patiently.

Five days later Sebastian was seated in the bows of a long dug-out canoe, with the charred soles of his boots set firmly on the chest that lay in the bilges. He was eating with relish a thick sandwich of polony and picked onions, wearing a change of clean underwear and socks that were a few sizes too large, and there was clutched in his left hand an open bottle of Hansa beer – all these with the courtesy of Commissioner Fleischer.

The paddlers were singing with unforced gaiety, for the hiring fee that Sebastian had paid them would buy each of them a new wife at least.

Hugging the bank of the Rovuma on the Portuguese side, driven on by willing paddles and the eager current, in twelve hours they covered the distance that it had taken Sebastian and his heavily-laden bearers five days on foot.

The canoe deposited Sebastian's party at the landing opposite M'topo's village, only ten miles from Lalapanzi. They walked that distance without resting and arrived after nightfall.

30

The windows of the bungalow were darkened, and the whole camp slept. After cautioning them to silence, Sebastian drew his depleted band up on the front lawn with the tax chest set prominently in front of them. He was proud of his success and wanted to achieve the appropriate mood for his home-coming. Having set the stage, he went up on to the stoep of the bungalow and tip-toed towards the front door with the intention of awakening the household by hammering upon it dramatically.

However, there was a chair on the stoep, and Sebastian tripped over it. He fell heavily. The chair clattered and the rifle slipped from his shoulder and rang on the stone flags.

Before Sebastian could recover his feet, the door was flung open and through it appeared Flynn O'Flynn in his night-shirt and armed with a double-barrelled shotgun. 'Caught you, you bastard!' he roared and lifted the shotgun.

Sebastian heard the click of the safety-catch and scrambled to his knees. 'Don't shoot! Flynn, it's me.'

The shotgun wavered a little. 'Who are you – and what do you want?'

'It's me – Sebastian.'

'Bassie?' Flynn lowered the shotgun uncertainly. 'It can't be. Stand up, let's have a look at you.'

Sebastian obeyed with alacrity.

'Good God,' Flynn swore in amazement. 'It is you. Good God! We heard that Fleischer caught you at M'topo's village a week ago. We heard he'd nobbled you for keeps!' He came forward with his right hand extended in welcome. 'You made it, did you? Well done, Bassie boy.'

Before Sebastian could accept Flynn's hand, Rosa came through the doorway, brushed past Flynn, and almost knocked Sebastian down again. With her arms locked around his chest and her cheek pressed to his unshaven cheek, she kept repeating, 'You're safe! Oh Sebastian, you're safe.'

Acutely aware of the fact that Rosa wore nothing under the thin night-gown, and that everywhere he put his hands they came in contact with thinly-veiled warm flesh, Sebastian grinned sheepishly at Flynn over her shoulder.

'Excuse me,' he said.

His first two kisses were off target for she was moving around a lot. One caught her on the ear, the next on her eyebrow, but the third was right between the lips.

When at last they were forced to separate or suffocate, Rosa gasped, 'I thought you were dead.'

'All right, missie,' growled Flynn. 'You can go and put some clothes on now.'

Breakfast at Lalapanzi that morning was a festive affair. Flynn took advantage of his daughter's weakened condition and brought a bottle of gin to the table. Her protests were half-hearted, and later with her own hands she poured a little into Sebastian's tea to brace it.

They ate on the stoep in golden sunshine that filtered through the bougainvillaea creeper. A flock of glossy starlings hopped and chirruped on the lawns, and an oriel sang from the wild fig-trees. All nature conspired to make Sebastian's victory feast a success, while Rosa and Nanny did their best from the kitchen – drawing upon the remains of Herman Fleischer's supplies that Sebastian had brought home with him.

Flynn O'Flynn's eyes were bloodshot and underhung with plum-coloured pouches, for he had been up all night counting the contents of the German tax chest and working out his accounts by the light of a hurricane lamp. Nevertheless, he was in a merry mood made merrier by the cups of fortified tea on which he was breakfasting. He joined warmly in the chorus of praise and felicitation to Sebastian Old-smith that was being sung by Rosa O'Flynn.

'You turned up one for the book, so help me, Bassie,' he chortled at the end of the meal. 'I'd just love to hear how Fleischer is going to explain this one to Governor Schee. Oh, I'd love to be there when he tells him about the tax money – son of a gun, it'll nigh kill them both.'

'While you're on the subject of money,' Rosa smiled at Flynn, 'have you worked out how much Sebastian's share comes to, Daddy?' Rosa only used Flynn's paternal title when she was extremely well-disposed towards him.

'That I have,' admitted Flynn, and the sudden shiftiness of his eyes aroused Rosa's suspicions. Her lips pursed a little.

'And how much is it?' she asked in the syrupy tone which Flynn recognized as the equivalent of the blood roar of a wounded lioness.

'Sure now, and who wants to be spoiling a lovely day with the talking of business?' Under pressure, Flynn exaggerated the brogue in his voice in the hope that Rosa would find it beguiling. A forlorn hope.

'How much?' demanded Rosa, and he told her.

There was a sickly silence. Sebastian paled under his sunburn and opened his mouth to protest. On the strength of his half share, he had the previous night made to Rosa O'Flynn a serious proposal, which she had accepted.

'Leave this to me, Sebastian,' she whispered and laid a restraining hand on his knee as she turned back to her father. 'You'll let us have a look at the accounts, won't you?' Still syrupy sweet.

'Sure and I will. They're all straight and square.'

The document that Flynn O'Flynn produced under the main heading, 'Joint Venture Between F. O'Flynn, Esq.,

S. Oldsmith, Esq., and Others. German East Africa. Period May 15, 1913, to August 21, 1913,' showed that he belonged to an unorthodox school of accountancy.

The contents of the tax chest had been converted to English sterling at the rates laid down by *Pear's Almanac* for 1893. Flynn set great store by this particular publication.

From the gross proceeds of £4,652. 18s. 6d., Flynn had deducted his own fifty per cent share and the ten per cent of the other partners – the Portuguese Chef D'Post and the Governor of Mozambique. From the balance he had then deducted the losses incurred on the Rufiji expedition (for which see separate account addressed to German East African Administration). From there he had gone on to charge the expenses of the second expedition, not forgetting such items as:

To L. Parbhoo (Tailor)	£15.10.—.
To One German Dress Helmet (say)	£ 5.10.—.
To Five Uniforms (Askari)	
£ 2.10.—. each	£12.10.—.
To Five Mauser Rifles £10.—.—. each	£50.—.—.
To Six Hundred and Twenty-Five	
Rounds 7mm Ammunition	£22.10.—.
To Advance re travelling expenses,	
One Hundred Escudos made to S.	
Oldsmith, Esq.	£ 1. 5.—.

Finally, Sebastian's half share of the net losses amounted to a little under twenty pounds.

'Don't worry,' Flynn assured him magnanimously. 'I don't expect you to pay it now – we'll just deduct it from your share of the profits of the next expedition.'

'But, Flynn, I thought you said – well, I mean, you told me I had a half share.'

'And so you have, Bassie, and so you have.'

'You said we were equal partners.'

'You must have misunderstood me, boy. I said a half share – and that means after expenses. It's just a great pity there was such a large accumulated loss to bring forward.'

While they discussed this, Rosa was busy with a stub of indelible pencil on the reverse side of Flynn's account. Two minutes later she thrust the result across the breakfast table at Flynn. She said, 'And that's the way I work it out.'

Rosa O'Flynn was a student of the 'One-for-you-one-for-me' school, and her reckonings were much simpler than those of her father.

With a cry of anguish, Flynn O'Flynn lodged objection. 'You don't understand business.'

'But I recognize crookery when I see it,' Rosa flashed back.

'You'd call your old father a crook?'

'Yes.'

'I've a damn good mind to take the kiboko to you. You're not too big and uppity that I can't warm your tail up good.'

'You just try it!' said Rosa, and Flynn backpedalled.

'Anyway, what would Bassie do with all that money? It's not good for a youngster. It would spoil him.'

'He'd marry me with it. That's what he'd do with it.'

Flynn made a noise as though there were a fish-bone stuck in his throat, his face mottled over with emotion and he swung ominously in Sebastian's direction. 'So!' he rasped. 'I thought so!'

'Now steady on, old chap,' Sebastian tried to soothe him.

'You come into my home and act like the king of bloody England. You try to fraudulently embezzle my money – but that's not enough! Oh no! That's not a bloody 'nough. You've also got to start tampering with my daughter just to round things off.'

'Don't be coarse,' said Rosa.

'That's rich – *don't be coarse*, she says, and just what exactly have you two been up to behind my back?'

Sebastian stood up from the breakfast table with dignity. 'I will not have you speak so of a lady in my presence, sir. Especially of the lady who has done me the great honour of consenting to become my wife.' He begun unbuttoning his jacket. 'Will you step into the garden with me, and give me satisfaction?'

'Come along, then.' As Flynn lumbered out of his chair he made as if to pass Sebastian, but at that moment Sebastian's arms were behind him, still bound by the sleeves of his jacket as he attempted to shrug it off. Flynn side-stepped swiftly, paused a moment as he took his aim, and then drove his left fist into Sebastian's stomach.

'Oof!' said Sebastian, and leaned forward involuntarily to meet Flynn's other fist as it came up from the level of his knees. It took Sebastian between the eyes, and he changed direction abruptly and ran backwards across the veranda. The low wooden railing caught him behind the knees and he toppled slowly into the flower-beds below the stoep.

'You've killed him,' wailed Rosa, and picked up the heavy china tea-pot.

'I hope so,' said Flynn, and ducked as the pot flew towards his head, passed over it and burst against the wall of the stoep, spraying tea and steam.

There was an ominous stirring among Rosa's flowers, and presently Sebastian's head emerged with blue hydrangea petals festively strewn in his hair and the skin around both eyes fast swelling and chameleoning to a creditable match with the petals. 'I say, Flynn. That wasn't fair,' he announced.

'He wasn't looking,' Rosa accused. 'You hit him before he was ready.'

'Well, he's looking now,' roared Flynn and went down

the veranda stairs like a charging hippopotamus. From the hydrangeas, Sebastian rose to meet him and took up the classic stance of the ring fighter. 'Marquis of Queensberry rules?' he cautioned as Flynn closed in.

Flynn signified his rejection of the Marquis's code by kicking Sebastian on the shin. Sebastian yelped and hopped one-legged out of the flower-bed, while Flynn pursued him with a further series of lusty kicks. Placing his boot twice in succession into Sebastian's posterior, the third kick, however, missed and the force behind it was sufficient to throw Flynn on to his back. He sprawled on the lawn, and the pause while he scrambled to his knees gave Sebastian respite to ready himself for the next round.

Both his eyes had puffed and he was experiencing discomfort from his rear end; nevertheless, he stood once again with his left arm extended and the right crossed over his chest. Glancing beyond Flynn, Sebastian saw his fiancée descending from the veranda. She was armed with a bread-knife.

'Rosa!' Sebastian was alarmed. It was clear that Rosa would not stop at patricide to protect her love. 'Rosa! What are you doing with that knife?'

'I'm going to stick him with it!'

'You'll do no such thing,' said Sebastian, but Flynn did not have the same faith in his daughter's restraint. Very hurriedly, he moved into a defensive position behind Sebastian. From there he listened with attention to the argument between Sebastian and Rosa. It took a full minute for Sebastian to persuade Rosa that her assistance was not necessary and that he was capable of handling the situation on his own. Reluctantly, Rosa retreated to the veranda.

'Thanks, Bassie,' said Flynn, and kicked him in his already bruised behind. It was extremely painful.

Very few people had ever seen Sebastian Oldsmith lose

his temper. The last time it had happened was eight years previously; the two sixth-formers who had invoked it by forcing Sebastian's head into a toilet bowl and flushing the cistern, were both hospitalized for a short period.

This time there were more witnesses. Attracted by the cries and crash of breaking crockery, Flynn's entire following, including Mohammed and his Askari, had arrived from the compound and were assembled at the top of the lawn. They watched in breathless wonder.

From the grandstand of the veranda, Rosa, her eyes sparkling with the strange feminine ferocity that arises in even the mildest women when their man fights for them, exhorted Sebastian to even greater violence.

Like all great storms, it did not last long, and when it was over the silence was appalling. Flynn lay stretched full-length on the lawn. His eyes closed, his breathing snored softly in his throat, bursting from his nose in a froth of red bubbles.

Mohammed and five of his men carried him towards the bungalow. He lay massive on their shoulders with the bulge of his belly rising and falling softly, and an expression of unusual peace on his bloody face.

Standing alone on the lawn, Sebastian's features were contorted with savagery and his whole body shook as though he was in high fever. Then, watching them carry the huge, inert body, suddenly Sebastian's mood was past. His expression changed first to concern, and then to gentle dismay. 'I say . . .' his voice was husky and he took a pace after them. 'You shouldn't have kicked me.' His hands opened helplessly, and he lifted them in a gesture of appeal. 'You shouldn't have done it.'

Rosa came down from the veranda and walked slowly towards him. She stopped and looked up at him, half in awe, half in glowing pride. 'You were magnificent,' she whispered. 'Like a lion.' She reached up with both arms around his neck, and before she kissed him she spoke again. 'I love you,' she said.

Sebastian had very little luggage to take with him. He was wearing everything he possessed. Rosa on the other hand had boxes of it, enough to give full employment to the dozen bearers that were assembled on the lawn in front of the bungalow.

'Well,' murmured Sebastian, 'I suppose we should start moving.'

'Yes,' whispered Rosa, and looked at the gardens of Lalapanzi. Although she had suggested this departure, now that the time had come she was uncertain. This place had been her home since childhood. Here she had spun a cocoon that had shielded and protected her, and now that the time had come to emerge from it, she was afraid. She took Sebastian's arm, drawing strength from him.

'Don't you want to say good-bye to your father?' Sebastian looked down at her with the tender protectiveness that was such a new and delightful sensation for him.

Rosa hesitated a moment, and then realized that it would take very little to weaken her resolve. Her dutiful affection for Flynn, which at the moment was submerged beneath the tide of anger and resentment, could easily re-emerge should Flynn employ a little of his celebrated blarney. 'No,' she said.

'I suppose it's best,' Sebastian agreed. He glanced guiltily towards the bungalow where Flynn was, presumably, still lying in state – attended by the faithful Mohammed. 'But do you think he'll be all right? I mean, I did hit him rather hard, you know.'

'He'll be all right,' Rosa said without conviction, and tugged at his sleeve. Together they moved to take their places at the head of the little column of bearers.

Kneeling on the floor of the bedroom, below the window sill, peering with one swollen eye through a slit in the curtain, Flynn saw this decisive move. 'My God,' he whispered in concern. 'The young idiots are really leaving.'

Rosa O'Flynn was his last link with that frail little Portuguese girl. The one person in his life that Flynn had truly loved. Now that he was about to lose her also, Flynn was suddenly aware of his feeling for his daughter. The prospect of never seeing her again filled him with dismay.

As for Sebastian Oldsmith, here no sentiment clouded his reasoning. Sebastian was a valuable business asset. Through him, Flynn could put into operation a number of schemes that he had shelved as involving disproportionate personal risk. In these last few years Flynn had become increasingly aware of the depreciation that time and large quantities of raw spirit had wrought in his eyes and legs and nerves. Sebastian Oldsmith had eyes like a fish eagle, legs like a prize fighter, and no nerves at all that Flynn could discern. Flynn needed him.

Flynn opened his mouth and groaned. It was the throaty death rattle of an old bull buffalo. Peering through the curtain, Flynn grinned as he saw the young couple freeze, and stand tense and still in the sunlight. Their faces were turned towards the bungalow, and in spite of himself, Flynn had to admit they made a handsome pair; Sebastian tall above her with the body of a gladiator and the face of a poet; Rosa small beside him but with the full bosom and wide hips of womanhood. The slippery black cascade of her hair glowed in the sun, and her dark eyes were big with concern.

Flynn groaned again but softly this time. A breathless, husky sound, the last breath of a dying man, and instantly Rosa and Sebastian were running towards the bungalow. Her skirts gathered up above her knees, long legs flying, Rosa led Sebastian up onto the veranda.

Flynn had just sufficient time to return to his bed and compose his limbs and his face into the attitude of one fast sinking towards the abyss.

'Daddy!' Rosa leaned over him, and Flynn opened his eyes uncertainly. For a moment he did not seem to recognize her, then he whispered, 'My little girl,' so faintly she hardly caught the words.

'Oh, Daddy, what is it?' She knelt beside him.

'My heart.' His hand crawled up like a hairy spider across his belly and clutched weakly at his hairy chest. 'Like a knife. A hot knife.'

There was a terrible silence in the room, and then Flynn spoke again. 'I wanted to ... give you my ... my blessing. I wish happiness for you ... wherever you go.' The effort of speech was too much, and for a while he lay gasping. 'Think of your old Daddy sometimes. Say a prayer for him.'

A fat, tiny tear broke from the corner of Rosa's eye and slid down her cheek.

'Bassie, my boy.' Slowly Flynn's eyes sought him, found him, and focused with difficulty. 'Don't blame yourself for this. I was an old man anyway – I've had my life.' He panted a little and then went on painfully. 'Look after her. Look after my little Rosa. You are my son now. I've never had a son.'

'I didn't know ... I had no idea that your heart ... Flynn, I'm dreadfully sorry. Forgive me.'

Flynn smiled, a brave little smile that just touched his lips. He lifted his hand weakly and held it out towards Sebastian. While Sebastian clasped his hand, Flynn considered offering him the money that had been the cause of the dispute as a dying man's gift but he manfully restrained himself from such extravagance. Instead he whispered, 'I would like to have seen my grandson, but no matter. Goodbye, my boy.'

'You'll see him, Flynn. I promise you that. We'll stay, won't we, Rosa? We'll stay with him.'

'Yes, we'll stay,' said Rosa. 'We won't leave you, Daddy.'

'My children.' Flynn sank back and closed his eyes. Thank God, he hadn't offered the money. A peaceful little smile hovered around his mouth. 'You've made an old man very happy.'

– 31 –

Flynn made a strong come-back from the edge of death, so strong, in fact, that it aroused Rosa's suspicions. However, she let it pass for she was happy to have avoided the necessity of leaving Lalapanzi. In addition, there was another matter which was taking up a lot of her attention.

Since she had said good-bye to Sebastian at the start of his tax tour, Rosa had been aware of the cessation of certain womanly functions of her body. She consulted Nanny who, in turn, consulted the local nungane who, in his turn, opened the belly of a chicken, and consulted its entrails. His findings were conclusive, and Nanny reported back to Rosa, without disclosing the source of her information, for Little Long Hair had an almost blasphemous lack of faith in the occult.

Delighted, Rosa took Sebastian for a walk down the valley, and when they reached the waterfall where it had all begun, she stood on tip-toe, put both arms around his neck and whispered in his ear. She had to repeat herself for her voice was muffled with breathless laughter.

'You're joking,' gasped Sebastian, and then blushed bright crimson.

'I'm not, you know.'

'Good grief,' said Sebastian; and then, groping for something more expressive, 'Son of a gun!'

'Aren't you pleased?' Rosa pouted playfully. 'I did it for you.'

'But we aren't even married.'

'That can be arranged.'

'And quickly, too,' agreed Sebastian. He grabbed her wrist. 'Come on!'

'Sebastian, remember my condition.'

'Good grief, I'm sorry.'

He took her back to Lalapanzi, handing her over the rough ground with as much care as though she was a case of sweating gelignite.

'What's the big hurry?' asked Flynn jovially at dinner that evening. 'I've got a little job for Bassie first. I want him to slip across the river . . .'

'No, you don't,' said Rosa. 'We are going to see the priest at Beira.'

'It would only take Bassie a couple of weeks. Then we could talk about it when he gets back.'

'We are going to Beira – tomorrow!'

'What's the rush?' Flynn asked again.

'Well, the truth is, Flynn, old boy . . .' Wriggling in his chair, colouring up vividly, Sebastian relapsed into silence.

'The truth is I'm going to have a baby,' Rosa finished for him.

'You're *what*?!' Flynn stared at her in horror.

'You said that you wanted to see your grandchild,' Rosa pointed out.

'But I didn't mean you to start work on it right away,' roared Flynn, and he rounded on Sebastian. 'You dirty young bugger!'

'Father, your heart!' Rosa restrained him. 'Anyway, don't pick on Sebastian, I did my share as well.'

'You shameless . . . You brazen little . . .'

Rosa reached behind the seat cushion where Flynn had hidden the gin bottle. 'Have a little of this – it will help calm you.'

They left for Beira the following morning. Rosa was carried in a maschille with Sebastian trotting beside it in anxious attendance, ready to help ease the litter over the fords and rough places, and to curse any of the bearers who stumbled.

When they left Lalapanzi, Flynn O'Flynn brought up the rear of the column, lying in his maschille with a square-faced bottle for company, scowling and muttering darkly about 'fornication' and 'sin'.

But both Rosa and Sebastian ignored him, and when they camped that night the two of them sat across the camp-fire from him, and whispered and laughed secretly together. They pitched their voices at such a tantalizing level that even by straining his ears, Flynn could not overhear their conversation. It infuriated him to such an extent that finally he made a loud remark about '. . . beating the hell out of the person who had repaid his hospitality by violating his daughter.'

Rosa said that she would give anything to see him try it *again*. In her opinion it would be better than a visit to the circus. And Flynn gathered his dignity and his gin bottle and stalked away to where Mohammed had laid out his bedding under a lean-to of thorn bushes.

During the dark hours before dawn they were visited by an old lion. He came with a rush from the darkness beyond the fire-light, grunting like an angry boar, the great black bush of his mane erect, snaking with incredible speed towards the huddle of blanket-wrapped figures about the fire.

Flynn was the only one not asleep. He had waited all night, watching Sebastian's reclining figure; just waiting for him to move across to the temporary thorn-bush shelter that gave Rosa privacy. Lying beside Flynn was his shotgun, double-loaded with big loopers, lion shot, and he had every intention of using it.

When the lion charged into the camp, Flynn sat up quickly and fired both barrels of the shotgun at point-blank range into the man-eater's head and chest, killing it instantly. But the momentum of its rush bowled it forward, sent it sliding full into Sebastian, and both of them rolled into the camp-fire.

Sebastian awoke to lion noises, and gun-fire, and the violent collision of a big body into his, and red-hot coals sticking to various parts of his anatomy. With a single bound, and a wild cry, he threw off his blanket, came to his feet, and went into such a lively song and dance routine, yodelling and high-kicking, and striking out at his imaginary assailants that Flynn was reduced to a jelly of helpless laughter.

The laughter, and the praise and thanks showered on him by Sebastian, Rosa, and the bearers, cleared the air.

'You saved my life,' said Sebastian soulfully.

'Oh Daddy, you're wonderful,' said Rosa. 'Thank you. Thank you,' and she hugged him.

The mantle of the hero felt snug and comfortable on Flynn's shoulders. He became almost human – and the improvement continued as each day's march brought them closer to the little Portuguese port of Beira, for Flynn greatly enjoyed his rare visits to civilization.

The last night they camped a mile from the outskirts of the town, and after a private conference with Flynn, old Mohammed went ahead armed with a small purse of escudos to make the arrangements for Flynn's formal entry on the morrow.

Flynn was up with the dawn, and while he shaved with care, and dressed in clean moleskin jacket and trousers, one of the bearers polished his boots with hippo fat, and two others scaled the tall bottle palm tree near the camp and cut fronds from its head.

All things being ready, Flynn ascended his maschille and lay back elegantly on the leopard-skin rugs. On each side of Flynn a bearer took his position, armed with a palm-frond, and began to fan him gently. Behind Flynn, in single file, followed other servants bearing tusks of ivory and the still-green lion skin. Behind this, with instructions from Flynn not to draw undue attention to themselves, followed Sebastian and Rosa, and the baggage bearers.

With a languid gesture such as might have been used by Nero to signal the start of a Roman circus, Flynn gave the order to move.

Along the rough road through the thick coastal bush, they came at last to Beira and entered the main street in procession.

'Good Lord,' Sebastian expressed his surprise when he saw the reception that awaited them, 'where did they all come from?'

Both sides of the street were lined with cheering crowds, mainly natives, but with here and there a Portuguese or an Indian trader come out of his shop to find the cause of the disturbance.

'Fini!' chanted the crowd, clapping their hands in unison. 'Bwana Mkuba! Great Lord! Slayer of elephant. Killer of lions!'

'I didn't realize that Flynn was so well regarded.' Sebastian was impressed.

'Most of them have never heard of him,' Rosa disillusioned him. 'He sent Mohammed in last night to gather a claque of about a hundred or so. Pays them one escudo each to come and cheer – they make so much noise that the entire population turns out to see what is going on. They fall for it every time.'

'What on earth does he go to so much trouble for?'

'Because he enjoys it. Just look at him!'

Lying in his maschille, graciously acknowledging the applause, Flynn was very obviously loving every minute of it.

The head of the procession reached the only hotel in Beira and halted. Madame da Souza, the portly, well-moustached widow who was the proprietress of the hotel, rushed down to welcome Flynn with a smacking kiss and usher him ceremoniously through the shabby portals. Flynn was the kind of customer she had always dreamed about.

When Rosa and Sebastian at last fought their way through the crowd into the hotel, Flynn was already seated at the bar counter and half way through a tall glass of Laurentia beer. The man sitting on the stool beside his was the Governor of Mozambique's aide-de-camp, who had come to deliver His Excellency's invitation for Flynn O'Flynn to dine at Government House that evening. It was settlement day in the partnership of 'Flynn O'Flynn and Others'. His Excellency José De Clare Don Felezardo da Silva Marques had received from Governor Schee, in Dar es Salaam, an agitated report, in the form of an official protest and an extradition demand, of the success of the partnership's operations during the last few months – and His Excellency was delighted to see Flynn.

In fact, so pleased was His Excellency with the progress of the partnership's affairs, that he exercised his authority to waive the formalities required by law to precede a marriage under Portuguese jurisdiction. This saved a week, and the afternoon after their arrival in Beira, Rosa and Sebastian stood before the altar in the stucco and thatch cathedral, while Sebastian tried with little success to remember enough of his schoolroom Latin to understand just what he was getting himself into.

The wedding veil, which had belonged to Rosa's mother, was yellowed by many years of storage under tropical conditions, but it served well enough to keep off the flies which were always bad during the hot season in Beira.

Towards the end of the long ceremony, Flynn was so overcome by the heat, the gin he had taken at lunch, and an unusually fine flood of Irish feeling, that he began snuffling loudly. While he mopped at his eyes and nose with a grubby handkerchief, the Governor's aide-de-camp patted his shoulder soothingly and murmured encouragement.

The priest declared them husband and wife, and the congregation launched into a faltering rendition of the *Te Deum*. His voice quivering with emotion and alcohol, Flynn kept repeating, 'My little girl, my poor little girl.' Rosa lifted her veil and turned to Sebastian who immediately forgot his misgivings as to the form of the ceremony, and enfolded her enthusiastically in his arms.

Still maintaining his chorus of 'My little girl,' Flynn was led away by the aide-de-camp to the hotel where the proprietress had prepared the wedding feast. In deference to Flynn O'Flynn's mood this started on a sombre note but as the champagne, which Madame da Souza had specially bottled the previous evening, started to do its work, so the tempo changed. Among his other actions, Flynn gave Sebastian a wedding present of ten pounds and poured a full glass of beer over the aide-de-camp's head.

When, later that evening, Rosa and Sebastian slipped away to the bridal suite above the bar, Flynn was giving lusty tongue in the chorus of 'They are jolly good fellows', Madame da Souza was seated on his lap, and overflowing it in all directions. Every time Flynn pinched her posterior, great gusts of laughter made her shake like a stranded jellyfish.

Later the pleasure of Rosa and Sebastian's wedding-bed was disturbed by the fact that, in the bar-room directly below them, Flynn O'Flynn was shooting the bottles off the shelves with a double-barrelled elephant rifle. Every direct hit was greeted by thunderous applause from the other guests. Madame da Souza, still palpitating with laughter, sat in a corner of the bar-room dutifully making such entries in her notebook as, 'One bottle of Grandio London Dry Gin 14.50 escudos; one bottle Grandio French Cognac Five Star 14.50 escudos; one bottle Grandio Scotch whisky 30.00 escudos; I magnum Grandio French Champagne 75.90 escudos.' 'Grandio' was the brand-name of the house, and signified that the liquor each bottle contained had been brewed and bottled on the premises under the personal supervision of Madame da Souza.

Once the newly-wed couple realized that the uproar from the room below was sufficient to mask the protests of their rickety brass bedstead, they no longer grudged Flynn his amusements.

For everyone involved it was a night of great pleasure, a night to be looked back upon with nostalgia and wistful smiles.

– 32 –

Even at Flynn's prodigious rate of expenditure, his share of the profits from Sebastian's tax expedition lasted another two weeks.

During this period Rosa and Sebastian spent a little of their time wandering hand in hand through the streets and bazaars of Beira, or sitting, still hand in hand, on the beach and watching the sea. Their happiness radiated from them so strongly that it affected anyone who came within fifty feet of them. A worried stranger hurrying towards them along the narrow little street with his face creased in a frown would come under the spell; his pace would slacken, his step losing its urgency, the frown would smooth away to be replaced by an indulgent grin as he passed them. But mostly they remained closeted in the bridal suite above the bar – entering it in the early afternoon and not reappearing until nearly noon the following day.

Neither Rosa nor Sebastian had imagined such happiness could exist.

At the expiry of the two weeks Flynn was waiting for them in the bar-room as they came down to lunch. He hurried out to join them as they passed the door. 'Greetings! Greetings!' He threw an arm around each of their shoulders. 'And how are you this morning?' He listened without attention as Sebastian replied at length on how well he felt, how well Rosa was, and how well both of them had slept. 'Sure! Sure!' Flynn interrupted his rhapsodizing. 'Listen, Bassie, my boy, you remember that £10 I gave you?'

'Yes.' Sebastian was immediately wary.

'Let me have it back, will you?'

'I've spent it, Flynn.'

'You've *what?*' bellowed Flynn.

'I've spent it.'

'Good God Almighty! All of it? You've squandered ten pounds in as many days?' Flynn was horrified by his son-in-law's extravagance and Sebastian, who had honestly believed the money was his to do with as he wished, was very apologetic.

They left for Lalapanzi that afternoon. Madame da Souza had accepted Flynn's note of hand for the balance outstanding on her bill.

At the head of the column Flynn, broke to the wide, and

nursing a burning hangover, was in evil temper. The line of bearers behind him, bedraggled and bilious from two weeks spent in the flesh-pots, were in similar straits. At the rear of the doleful little caravan, Rosa and Sebastian chirruped and cooed together – an island of sunshine in the sea of gloom.

The months passed quickly at Lalapanzi during the monsoon of 1913. Gradually, as its girth increased, Rosa's belly became the centre of Lalapanzi. The pivot upon which the whole community turned. The debates in the servants' quarters, led by Nanny, the accepted authority, dealt almost exclusively with the contents thereof. All of them were hot for a man-child, although secretly Nanny cherished a treacherous hope that it might be another Little Long Hair.

Even Flynn, during the long months of enforced inactivity while the driving monsoon rains turned the land into a quagmire and the rivers into seething brown torrents, felt his grand-paternal instincts stirred. Unlike Nanny, he had no doubts as to the unborn child's sex, and he decided to name it Patrick Flynn O'Flynn Oldsmith.

He conveyed his decision to Sebastian while the two of them were hunting for the pot in the kopjes above the homestead.

By dint of diligent application and practice, Sebastian's marksmanship had improved beyond all reasonable expectation. He had just demonstrated it. They were jump-shooting in thick cat-bush among the broken rock and twisted ravines of the kopjes. Constant rain had softened the ground and enabled them to move silently down-wind along one of the ravines. Flynn was fifty yards out on Sebastian's right, moving heavily but deceptively fast through the sodden grass and undergrowth.

The kudu were lying in dense cover below the lip of the ravine. Two young bulls, bluish-gold in colour, striped with thin chalk lines across the body, pendulent dewlaps heavily fringed with yellow hair, two and a half twists in each of the corkscrew horns – big as polo ponies but heavier. They broke left across the ravine when Flynn jumped them from their hide, and the intervening bush denied him a shot.

'Breaking your way, Bassie,' Flynn shouted and Sebastian took two swift paces around the bush in front of him, shook the clinging raindrops from his lashes, and slipped the safety-catch. He heard the tap of big horn against a branch, and the first bull came out of the ravine at full run across his front. Yet it seemed to float, unreal, intangible, through the blue-grey rain mist. It blended ghostlike into the background of dark rain-soaked vegetation, and the clumps of bush and the tree trunks between them made it an almost impossible shot. In the instant that the bull flashed across a gap between two clumps of buffalo thorn, Sebastian's bullet broke its neck a hand's width in front of the shoulder.

At the sound of the shot, the second bull swerved in dead run, gathered its forelegs beneath its chest and went up in a high, driving leap over the thorn bush that stood in its path. Sebastian traversed his rifle smoothly without taking the butt from his shoulder, his right hand flicked the bolt open and closed, and he fired as a continuation of the movement.

The heavy bullet caught the kudu in mid-air and threw it sideways. Kicking and thrashing, it struck the ground and rolled down the bank of the ravine.

Whooping like a Red Indian, Mohammed galloped past Sebastian, brandishing a long knife, racing to reach the second bull and cut its throat before it died so that the dictates of the Koran might be observed.

Flynn ambled across to Sebastian. 'Nice shooting, Bassie boy. Salted and dried and pickled, there's meat there for a month.'

And Sebastian grinned in modest recognition of the

compliment. Together they walked across to watch Mohammed and his gang begin paunching and quartering the big animals.

With the skill of a master tactician, Flynn chose this moment to inform Sebastian of the name he had selected for his grandson. He was not prepared for the fierce opposition he encountered from Sebastian. It seemed that Sebastian had expected to name the child Francis Sebastian Oldsmith. Flynn laughed easily, and then in his most reasonable and persuasive brogue he started pointing out to Sebastian just how cruel it would be to saddle the child with a name like that.

It was a lance in the pride of the Oldsmiths, and Sebastian rose to the defence. By the time they returned to Lalapanzi, the discussion needed about six hot words to reach the stage of single combat.

Rosa heard them coming. Flynn's bellow carried across the lawns. 'I'll not have my grandson called a pewling, milksop name like that!'

'Francis is the name of kings and warriors and gentle-men!' cried Sebastian.

'My aching buttocks, it is!'

Rosa came out on to the wide veranda and stood there with her arms folded over the beautiful bulge that housed the cause of the controversy.

They saw her and started an undignified race across the lawns, each trying to reach her first to enlist her support for their respective causes.

She listened to the pleadings, a small and secret smile upon her lips, and then said with finality, 'Her name will be Maria Rosa Oldsmith.'

Some time later Flynn and Sebastian were together on the veranda.

Ten days before the last rains of the season had come roaring in from the Indian Ocean and broken upon the unyielding shield of the continent. Now the land was drying out; the rivers regaining their sanity and returning, chastened, to the confines of their banks. New grass lifted from the red earth to welcome the return of the sun. For this brief period the whole land was alive and green; even the gnarled and crabbed thorn trees wore a pale fuzz of tender leaves. Behind each pair of guinea-fowl that clinked and scratched on the bottom lawns of Lalapanzi, there paraded a file of dappled chicks. Early that morning a herd of eland had moved along the skyline across the valley, and beside each cow had trotted a calf. Everywhere was new life, or the expectation of new life.

'Now, stop worrying!' said Flynn, as his impatient pacing brought him level with Sebastian's chair.

'I'm not worrying,' Sebastian said mildly. 'Everything will be all right.'

'How do you know that?' challenged Flynn.

'Well . . .'

'You know the child could be stillborn, or something.' Flynn shook his finger in Sebastian's face. 'It could have six fingers on each hand – how about that? I heard about one that was born with . . .'

While Flynn related a long list of horrors, Sebastian's expression of proud and eager anticipation crumbled slowly. He rose from his chair and fell into step beside Flynn. 'Have you got any gin left?' he asked hoarsely, glancing at the shuttered windows of Rosa's bedroom. Flynn produced the bottle from the inside pocket of his jacket.

An hour later, Sebastian was hunched forward in his chair, clutching a half-full tumbler of gin with both hands. He stared into it miserably. 'I don't know what I'd do if it was born with . . .' He could not go on. He shuddered and lifted the tumbler to his lips. At that instant a long, petulant wail issued from the closed bedroom. Sebastian leapt as though he had been bayoneted from behind, and spilled the gin down his shirt. His next leap was in the direction of the bedroom, a direction Flynn had also chosen. They collided heavily and then set off together at a gallop along the veranda. They reached the locked door and hammered upon it for admission. But Nanny, who had evicted them in the first instance, still adamantly refused to lift the locking bar or to give them any information as to the progress of the birthing. Her decision was endorsed by Rosa.

'Don't you dare let them in until everything is ready,' she whispered huskily, and roused herself from the stupor of exhaustion, to help Nanny with washing and wrapping the infant.

When at last everything was ready, she lay propped on the pillows with her child held against her chest, and nodded to Nanny. 'Open the door,' she said.

The delay had confirmed Flynn's worst suspicions. The door flew open, and he and Sebastian fell into the room, wild with anxiety.

'Oh, thank God, Rosa. You're still alive!' Sebastian reached the bed and fell on his knees beside it.

'You check his feet,' instructed Flynn. 'I'll do his hands and head,' and before Rosa could prevent him, he had lifted the infant out of her arms.

'His fingers are all right. Two arms, one head,' Flynn muttered above Rosa's protests and the infant's muffled squawls of indignation.

'This end is fine. Just fine!' Sebastian spoke in rising relief and delight. 'He's beautiful, Flynn!' And he lifted the shawl that swaddled the child's body. His expression cracked and his voice choked. 'Oh, my God!'

'What's wrong?' Flynn asked sharply.

'You were right, Flynn. He's deformed.'

'What? Where?'

'There!' Sebastian pointed. 'He hasn't got a what-ye-ma-call-it,' and they both stared in horror.

It was many long seconds before they realized simultaneously that the tiny cleft was no deformity but very much as nature had intended it.

'It's a girl!' said Flynn in dismay.

'A girl!' echoed Sebastian, and quickly pulled down the shawl to preserve his daughter's modesty.

'It's a girl,' Rosa smiled, wan and happy.

'It's a girl,' cackled Nanny in triumph.

Maria Rosa Oldsmith had arrived without fuss and with the minimum of inconvenience to her mother, so that Rosa was on her feet again within twenty-four hours. All her other activities were conducted with the same consideration and dispatch. She cried once every four hours; a single angry howl which was cut off the instant the breast was thrust into her mouth. Her bowel movements were equally regular and of the correct volume and consistency, and the rest of her days and nights were devoted almost entirely to sleeping.

She was beautiful; without the parboiled, purple look of most new-borns; without the squashed-in pug features or the vague, squinty eyes.

From the curly cap of silk hair to the tips of her pink toes, she was perfection.

It took Flynn two days to recover from the disappointment of having been cheated out of a grandson. He sulked in the arsenal or sat solitary at the end of the veranda. On the second evening Rosa pitched her voice just high enough to carry the length of the veranda.

'Don't you think Maria looks just like Daddy – the same mouth and nose? Look at her eyes.'

Sebastian opened his mouth to deny the resemblance

emphatically but closed it again, as Rosa kicked him painfully on the ankle.

'She is the image of him. There's no doubting who her grandfather is.'

'Well, I suppose . . . If you look closely,' Sebastian agreed unhappily.

At the end of the veranda, Flynn sat with his head cocked in an attitude of attention. Half an hour later Flynn had sidled up to the cradle and was studying the contents thoughtfully. By the following evening he had moved his chair alongside and was leading the discussion with such remarks as, 'There is quite a strong family resemblance. Look at those eyes – no doubt who her Granddaddy is!'

He interspersed his observations with warnings and instructions, 'Don't get so close, Bassie. You're breathing germs all over her.' 'Rosa, this child needs another blanket. When did she have her last feed?'

It was not long before he started bringing pressure to bear on Sebastian.

'You've got responsibilities now. Have you thought about that?'

'How do you mean, Flynn?'

'Just answer me this. What have you got in this world?'

'Rosa and Maria,' Sebastian answered promptly.

'Fine. That's just great! And how are you going to feed them and clothe them and . . . and look after them?'

Sebastian expressed himself well satisfied with the existing arrangements.

'I bet you are! It isn't costing you a thing. But I reckon it's about time you got up off your bum and did something.'

'Like what?'

'Like going and shooting some ivory.'

Three days later, armed and equipped for a full-scale poaching expedition, Sebastian led a column of gun-boys and bearers down the valley towards the Rovuma river.

Fourteen hours later, in the dusk of evening, he led them back.

'What in the name of all that's holy, are you doing back here?' Flynn demanded.

'I had this premonition.' Sebastian was sheepish.

'What premonition?'

'That I should come back,' muttered Sebastian.

He left again two days later. This time he actually crossed the Rovuma before the premonition overpowered him once more, and he came back to Rosa and Maria.

'Well,' Flynn sighed with resignation. 'I reckon I'll just have to go along with you and make sure you do it.' He shook his head. 'You've been a big disappointment to me, Bassie.' The biggest disappointment being the fact that he had hoped to have his granddaughter to himself for a few weeks.

'Mohammed,' he bellowed. 'Get my gear packed.'

– 33 –

Flynn sent his scouts across the river and when they reported back that the far bank was clear of German patrols, Flynn made the crossing.

This expedition was a far cry from Sebastian's amiable and aimless wandering in German territory. Flynn was a professional. They crossed in the night. They crossed in strictest silence and landed two miles downstream from M'topo's village. There was no lingering on the beach, but an urgent night march that began immediately and went on in grim silence until an hour before dawn; a march that took them fifteen miles inland from the river, and ended in a grove of elephant thorn, carefully chosen for the kopjes and ravines around it that afforded multiple avenues of escape in each direction.

Sebastian was impressed by the elaborate precautions that Flynn took before going into camp; the jinking and counter-marching, the careful sweeping of their spoor with brushes of dry grass, and the placing of sentries on the kopje above the camp.

During the ten days they waited there, not a single branch was broken from a tree, not a single axe-stroke swung to leave a tell-tale white blaze on the dark bush. The tiny night fire fed with dry trash and dead wood was carefully screened, and before dawn was smothered with sand so that not a wisp of smoke was left to mark them in the day.

Voices were never raised above conversational tones, and even the clatter of a bucket brought such a swift and ferocious reprimand from Flynn, that on all of them was a nervous awareness, an expectancy of danger, a tuning of the minds and bodies to action.

On the eighth night the scouts that Flynn had thrown out began drifting back to the camp. They came in with all the stealth and secrecy of night animals and huddled over the fire to tell what they had seen.

'. . . Last night three old bulls drank at the water-hole of the sick hyena. They carried teeth so, and so, and so . . .' showing the arm to measure the length of ivory, '. . . apart from them, ten cows left their feet in the mud, six of them with young calves. Yesterday, at the place where the hill of Inhosana breaks and turns its arms, I saw where another herd had crossed, moving towards the dawn; five young bulls, twenty-three cows and . . .'

The reports were jumbled, unintelligible to Sebastian who did not carry a map of the land in his head. But Flynn, sitting beside the fire listening, fitted the fragments together and built them into an exact picture of how the game was moving. He saw that the big bulls were still separated from the breeding herds – that they lingered on the high ground while the cows had started moving back towards the swamps from which the floods had driven them, anxious to take their young away from the dangers that the savannah forests would offer once the dry season set in.

He noted the estimates of thickness and length of tusk. Immature ivory was hardly worth carrying home, good only for carving into billiard balls and piano keys. The market was glutted with it.

But on the other hand, a prime tusk, over one hundred pounds in weight, seven foot long and twice the thickness of a fat woman's thigh, would fetch fifty shillings a pound avoirdupois.

An animal carrying such a tusk in each side of his face was worth four or five hundred pounds in good, gold sovereigns.

One by one Flynn discarded the possible areas in which he would hunt. This year there were no elephant in the M'bahora hills. There was good reason for this; thirty piles of great sun-bleached bones lay scattered along the ridge, marking the path that Flynn's rifles had followed two years before. The memory of gun-fire was too fresh and the herds shunned that place.

There were no elephant on the Tabora escarpment. A blight had struck the groves of mapundu trees, and withered the fruit before it could ripen. Dearly the elephant loved mapundu berries and they had gone elsewhere to find them.

They had gone up to the Sania Heights, to Kilombera, and to the Salito hills.

Salito was an easy day's march from the German boma at Mahenge. Flynn struck it from his mental list.

As each of the scouts finished his report, Flynn asked the question which would influence his final decision.

'What of *Plough the Earth*?'

And they said, 'We saw nothing. We heard nothing.'

The last scout came in two days after the others. He looked sheepish and more than a little guilty.

'Where the hell have you been?' Flynn demanded, and the gun-boy had his excuse ready.

'Knowing that the great Lord Fini would ask of certain matters, I turned aside in my journey to the village of Yetu, who is my uncle. My uncle is a fundi. No wild thing walks, no lion kills, no elephant breaks a branch from a tree but my uncle knows of it. Thus I went to ask him of these things.'

'Thy uncle is a famous fundi, he is also a famous breeder of daughters,' Flynn remarked drily. 'He breeds daughters the way the moon breeds stars.'

'Indeed, my uncle Yetu is a man of fame.' Hurriedly the scout went on to turn Flynn aside from this line of discussion. 'My uncle sends his greetings to the Lord Fini and bids me speak thus: "This season there are many fine elephants on the Sania Heights. They walk by twos and threes. With my own eyes I have seen twelve which show ivory as long as the shaft of a throwing spear, and I have seen signs of as many more." My uncle bids me speak further: "There is one among them of which the Lord Fini knows for he has asked of him many times. This one is a bull among great bulls. One who moves in such majesty that men have named him *Plough the Earth*."'

'You do not bring a story from the honey-bird to cool my anger against you?' Flynn demanded harshly. 'Did you dream of *Plough the Earth* while you were ploughing the bellies of your uncle's many daughters?' His eagerness was soured by scepticism. Too many times he had followed wild stories in his pursuit of the great bull. He leaned forward across the fire to watch the gun-bearer's eyes as he replied, 'It is true, lord.' Flynn watched him carefully but found no hint of guile in his face. Flynn grunted, rocked back on his hams, and lowered his gaze to the small flames of the camp-fire.

For his first ten years in Africa, Flynn had heard the legend of the elephant whose tusks were of such length that their points touched the ground and left a double furrow along his spoor. He had smiled at this story as he had at the story of the rhinoceros who fifty years before had killed an Arab slaver, and now wore around his horn a massive gold bangle studded with precious stones. They said the bangle had lodged there as he gored the Arab. There were a thousand other romantic tales come out of Africa; from Solomon's treasure to the legend of the elephants' graveyard, and Flynn believed none of them.

Then he saw a myth come alive. One evening, camped near the Zambezi in Portuguese territory, he had taken a bird-gun and walked along the bank hoping for a brace of sand-grouse. Two miles from the camp he had seen a flight of birds coming in to the water, flying fast as racing pigeons, whistling in on backswept wings, and he had ducked into a thick bank of reeds and watched them come.

As they banked steeply overhead, dropping towards the sand-banks of the river, Flynn jumped to his feet and fired left and right, folding the lead bird and the second, so they crumpled in mid-air and tumbled, leaving a pale flurry of feathers to mark their fall.

But Flynn never saw the birds hit the ground. For, while the double blast of the shotgun still echoed along the river, the reed-bed below where he stood swayed and crashed and burst open, then an elephant came out into the open.

It was a bull elephant that stood fourteen feet high at the shoulder. An elephant so old that his ears were shredded to half their original size. The hide that covered his body hung in folds and deep wrinkles, baggy at the knees and the throat. The tuft of his tail long ago worn bald. The rheumy tears of great age staining his seared and dusty cheeks.

He came out of the reed-bed in a shambling, hump-backed run, and his head was tilted at an awkward, unnatural angle.

Flynn could hardly credit his vision when he saw the

reason why the old bull cocked his head back in that fashion. From each side of the head extended two identical shafts of ivory, perfectly matched, straight as the columns of a Greek temple, with not an inch of taper from lip to bluntly rounded tip. They were stained to the colour of tobacco juice, fourteen long feet of ivory that would have touched the ground, if the elephant had carried his head relaxed.

As Flynn stood frozen in disbelief, the bull passed him by a mere fifty yards and lumbered on into the forest.

It took Flynn thirty minutes to get back to camp and exchange the bird-gun for the double-barrelled Gibbs, snatch up a water bottle, shout for his gun-boys, and return to the river.

He put Mohammed to the spoor. At first there were only the round pad marks in the dusty earth, smooth pad marks the size of a dustbin lid; the graining on the old bull's hooves had long been worn away. Then after five miles of flight there were other marks to follow. On each side of the spoor a double line scuffed through dead leaves and grass and soft earth where the tips of the tusks touched, and Flynn learned why the old bull was called *Plough the Earth*.

They lost the spoor on the third day in the rain, but a dozen times in the years since then, Flynn had followed and lost those double furrows, and once, through his binoculars, he had seen the old bull again, standing dozing beneath a grove of marula trees at a distance of three miles, his eroded old head propped up by the mythical tusks. When Flynn reached the spot on which he had seen the bull, it was deserted.

In all his life Flynn had never wanted anything with such obsessive passion as he wanted those tusks.

Now he sat silently staring into the camp-fire, remembering all these things, and the lust within him was tighter and more compelling than he had ever felt for a woman.

At last he looked up at the scout and said huskily, 'Tomorrow, with the first light, we will go to the village of Yetu, at Sania.'

A fly settled on Herman Fleischer's cheek and rubbed its front feet together in delight, as it savoured the prospect of drinking from the droplet of sweat that quivered precariously at the level of his ear lobe.

The Askari standing behind Herman's chair flicked the zebra tail switch with such skill, that not one of the long black hairs touched the Commissioner's face, and the fly darted away to take its place in the circuit that orbited around Herman's head.

Herman hardly noticed the interruption. He was sunk down in the chair, glowering at the two old men who squatted on the dusty parade ground below the veranda. The silence was a blanket that lay on them all in the stupefying heat. The two headmen waited patiently. They had spoken, and now they waited for the Bwana Mkuba to reply.

'How many have been killed?' Herman asked at last, and the senior of the two headmen answered.

'Lord, as many as the fingers of both your hands. But these are the ones of which we are certain, there may be others.'

Herman's concern was not for the dead, but their numbers would be a measure of the seriousness of the situation. Ritual murder was the first stage on the road to rebellion. It started with a dozen men meeting in the moonlight, dressed in cloaks of leopard skin, with designs of white clay painted on their faces. With the crude iron claws strapped to their hands, they would ceremoniously mutilate a young girl, and then devour certain parts of her body. This was harmless entertainment in Herman's view, but when it happened more frequently, it generated in the district a mood of abject terror. This was the climate of revolt. Then the leopard priests would walk through the villages in the night, walk openly in procession with the torches burning, and the men who lay shivering within the barricaded huts would listen to the chanted instructions from the macabre little procession – and they would obey.

It had happened ten years earlier at Salito. The priests had ordered them to resist the tax expedition that year. They had slaughtered the visiting Commissioner and twenty of his Askari, and they cut the bodies into small pieces with which they festooned the thorn trees.

Three months later a battalion of German infantry had disembarked at Dar es Salaam and marched to Salito. They burned the villages and they shot everything – men, women, children, chickens, dogs and goats. The final casualty list could only be estimated, but the officer commanding the battalion boasted that they had killed two thousand human beings. He was probably exaggerating. Nevertheless, the Salito hills were still devoid of human life and habitation to this day. The whole episode was irritating and costly – and Herman Fleischer wanted no repetition of it during his term of office.

On the principle that prevention was better than cure, he decided to go down and conduct a few ritual sacrifices of his own. He humped himself forward in his chair, and spoke to his sergeant of Askari.

'Twenty men. We will leave for the village of Yetu, at Sania, tomorrow before dawn. Do not forget the ropes.'

On the Sania Heights, in the heat of the day, an elephant stood under the wide branches of a wild fig-tree. He was asleep on his feet but his head was propped up by two long columns of stained ivory. He slept as an old man sleeps, fitfully, never sinking very deep below the level of consciousness. Occasionally the tattered grey ears flapped, and each time a fine haze of flies rose around his head. They hung in the hot air and then settled again. The rims of the elephant's ears were raw where the flies had eaten down through the thick skin. The flies were everywhere. The humid green shade beneath the wild fig was murmurous with the sound of their wings.

Across the divide of the Sania Heights, four miles from the spot where the old bull slept, three men were moving up one of the bush-choked gulleys towards the ridge.

Mohammed was leading. He moved fast, half-crouched to peer at the ground, glancing up occasionally to anticipate the run of the spoor he was following. He stopped at a place where a grove of mapundu trees had carpeted the ground beneath them with a stinking, jellified mass of rotten berries. He looked back at the two white men and indicated the marks in the earth, and the pyramid of bright yellow dung that lay upon it. 'He stopped here for the first time in the heat, but it was not to his liking, and he has gone on.'

Flynn was sweating. It ran down his flushed jowls and dripped on to his already sodden shirt. 'Yes,' he nodded and a small cloud-burst of sweat scattered from his head at the movement. 'He will have crossed the ridge.'

'What makes you so certain?' Sebastian spoke in the same sepulchral whisper as the others.

'The cool evening breeze will come from the east – he will cross to the other side of the ridge to wait for it.' Flynn spoke with irritation and wiped his face on the short sleeve of his shirt. 'Now, you just remember, Bassie. This is my elephant, you understand that? You try for it and, so help me God, I'll shoot you dead.'

Flynn nodded to Mohammed and they moved on up the slope, following the spoor that meandered between outcrops of grey granite and scrub.

The crest of the ridge was well defined, sharp as the spine of a starving ox. They paused below it, squatting to rest in the coarse brown grass. Flynn opened the binocular case that hung on his chest, lifted out the instrument and began to polish the lens with a scrap of cloth.

'Stay here!' Flynn ordered the other two, then on his belly he wriggled up towards the skyline. Using the cover of a tree stump, he lifted his head cautiously and peered over.

Below him the Sania Heights fell away at a gentle slope, fifteen hundred feet and ten miles to the plain below. The slope was broken and crenellated, riven into a thousand gulleys and ravines, covered over-all with a mantle of coarse brown scrub and dotted with clumps of bigger trees.

Flynn settled himself comfortably on his elbows and lifted the binoculars to his eyes. Systematically he began to examine each of the groves below him.

'Yes!' he whispered aloud, wriggling a little on his belly, staring at the picture puzzle beneath the spread branches of the tree, a mile away. In the shade there were shapes that made no sense, a mass too diffuse to be the trunk of the tree.

He lowered the glasses and wiped away the sweat that clung in his eyebrows. He closed his eyes to rest them from the glare, then he opened them again and lifted the glasses.

For two long minutes he stared before suddenly the puzzle made sense. The bull was standing half away from him, merging with the trunk of the wild fig, the head and half the body obscured by the lower branches of the tree – and what he had taken to be the stem of a lesser tree was, in fact, a tusk of ivory.

A spasm of excitement closed on his chest.

'Yes!' he said. 'Yes!'

Flynn planned his stalk with care, taking every precaution against the intervention of fate that twenty years of elephant hunting had taught him.

He had gone back to where Sebastian and Mohammed waited.

'He's there,' he told them.

'Can I come with you?' Sebastian pleaded.

'In a barrel you can,' snarled Flynn as he sat and pulled off his heavy boots to replace them with the light sandals that Mohammed produced from the pack. 'You stay here until you hear my shot. You so much as stick your nose over the ridge before that – and, so help me God, I'll shoot it off.'

While Mohammed knelt in front of Flynn and strapped the leather pads to his knees to protect them as he crawled over rock and thorn, Flynn fortified himself from the gin bottle. As he recorked it, he glowered at Sebastian again. 'That's a promise!' he said.

At the top of the ridge Flynn paused again with only his eyes lifted over the skyline, while he plotted his stalk, fixing in his memory a procession of landmarks – an ant-hill, an outcrop of white quartz, a tree festooned with weaver birds' nests – so that as he reached each of these he would know his exact position in relation to that of the elephant.

Then with the rifle cradled across the crook of his elbows he slid on his belly to begin the stalk.

Now, an hour after he had left the ridge, he saw before him through the grass a slab of granite like a headstone in an ancient cemetery. It stood square and weathered brown, and it was the end of the stalk.

He had marked it from the ridge as the point from which

he would fire. It stood fifty yards from the wild fig-tree, at a right angle from the old bull's position. It would give him cover as he rose to his knees to make the shot.

Anxious now, suddenly overcome with a premonition of disaster – sensing that somehow the cup would be dashed from his lips, the maid plucked from under him before the moment of fulfilment, Flynn started forward. Slithering towards the granite headstone, his face set hard in nervous anticipation, he reached the rock.

He rolled carefully on to his side and, holding the heavy rifle against his chest, he slipped the catch across and eased the rifle open, so that the click of the mechanism was muted. From the belt around his waist he selected two fat cartridges and examined the brass casings for tarnish or denting; with relief he saw the fingers that held them were steadier. He slipped the cartridges into the blank eyes of the breeches, and they slid home against the seatings with a soft metallic plong. And now his breathing was faintly ragged at the end of each inhalation. He closed the rifle, and with his thumb pushed the safety-catch forward into the 'fire' position.

His shoulder against the rough, sun-heated granite, he drew up his legs against his belly and rolled gently on to his knees. With his head bowed low and the rifle in his lap, he knelt behind the rock, and for the first time in an hour he lifted his head. He brought it up with inching deliberation. Slowly the crystalline texture of the granite passed before his eyes, then suddenly he looked across fifty yards of open ground at his elephant.

It stood broadside to him but the head was hidden by the leaves and branches of the wild fig. The brain shot was impossible from here. His eyes moved down on to the shoulder and he saw the outline of the bone beneath the thick grey skin. He picked out the point of the elbow and his eyes moved back into the barrel of the chest. He could visualize the heart pulsing softly there beneath the ribs, pink and soft and vital, throbbing like a giant sea anemone.

He lifted the rifle, and laid it across the rock in front of him. He looked along the barrels, and saw the blade of dry grass that was wound around the bead of the foresight, obscuring it. He lowered the rifle and with his thumb-nail picked away the shred of grass. Again he lifted and sighted.

The black blob of the foresight lay snugly in the deep, wide vee of the backsight; he moved the gun, riding the bead down across the old bull's shoulder then back on to the chest. It lay there ready to kill, and he took up the slack in the trigger, gently, lovingly, with his forefinger.

The shout was faint, a tiny sound in the drowsy immensity of the hot African air. It came from the high ground above him.

'Flynn!' and again, 'Flynn!'

In an explosive burst of movement under the wild fig-tree, the old bull swung his body with unbelievable speed, his great tusks riding high. He went away from Flynn at an awkward shambling run, his flight covered by the trunk of the fig-tree.

For stunned seconds, Flynn crouched behind the boulder, and with each second the chances of a shot dwindled. Flynn jumped to his feet and ran out to one side of the fig-tree, opening his field of fire for a snap shot at the bull as he fled, a try for the spine where it curved down between the massive haunches to the tuftless tail.

Spiked agony stabbed up through the ball of his lightly shod foot, as he trod squarely on a three-inch buffalo thorn. Red-tipped, wickedly barbed, it buried its full length in his flesh, and he stumbled to his knees crying a protest at the pain.

Two hundred yards away, the old bull disappeared into one of the wooded ravines, and was gone.

'Flynn! Flynn!'

Sobbing in pain and frustration, his injured foot twisted up into his lap, Flynn sat in the grass and waited for Sebastian Oldsmith to come down to him.

'I'll let him get real close,' Flynn told himself. Sebastian was approaching with the long awkward strides of a man running downhill. He had lost his hat and the black tangled curls danced on his head at each stride. He was still shouting.

'I'll give it to him in the belly,' Flynn decided. 'Both barrels!' and he groped for the rifle that lay beside him.

Sebastian saw him and swerved in his run.

Flynn hefted the rifle. 'I warned him. I said I'd do it,' and his right hand settled around the pistol grip of the rifle, his forefinger instinctively hooking forward for the trigger.

'Flynn! Germans! A whole army of them. Just over the hill. Coming this way.'

'Christ!' said Flynn, immediately abandoning his homicidal intentions.

– 35 –

Lifting himself in the stirrups, Herman Fleischer reached behind to massage himself. His buttocks were of a plump, almost feminine, quantity and quality. After five hours in the saddle Herman longed to rest them. He had just crossed the ridge of the Sania Heights on his donkey, and it was cool here beneath the outspread branches of the wild fig-tree. He flirted with the temptation, decided to indulge himself, and turned to give the order to the troop of twenty Askari who stood behind him. All of them were watching him avidly, anticipating the order that would allow them to throw themselves down and relax.

'Lazy dogs!' thought Herman as he scowled at them. He

turned away from them, settled his aching posterior gently on to the saddle and growled. 'Akwende! Let us go!' His heels thumped against the flanks of his donkey and it started forward at a trot.

From a crotch in the trunk of the fig-tree ten feet above Herman's head, Flynn O'Flynn viewed his departure over the double barrels of his rifle. He watched the patrol wind away down the slope and drop from sight over a fold in the ground before he put up the gun.

'Phew! That was close.' Sebastian's voice came from the leafy mass above Flynn.

'If he'd touched one foot to the ground, I'd have blown his bloody head off,' said Flynn. He sounded as though he regretted missing the opportunity. 'All right, Bassie, get me down out of this frigging tree.'

Fully dressed, except for his boots, Flynn sat against the base of the fig-tree and proffered his right foot to Sebastian. '. . . I had him right there in my sights.'

'Who?' asked Sebastian.

'The elephant, you idiot. For the first time I had him cold. And then . . . Yeow! What the hell are you doing?'

'I'm trying to get the thorn out, Flynn.'

'Feels like you're trying to knock it in with a hammer.'

'I can't get a grip on it.'

'Use your teeth. That's the only way,' Flynn instructed, and Sebastian paled a little at the thought. He considered Flynn's foot. It was a large foot; corns on the toes, flakes of loose skin and other darker matter between them. Sebastian could smell it at a range of three feet. 'Couldn't you reach it with your own teeth, Flynn?' he hedged.

'You think I'm a goddamned contortionist?'

'Mohammed?' Sebastian's eyes lit up with relief as he turned on the little gun-bearer. In answer to the question Mohammed drew back his lips in a death's head grin, exposing his smooth, pink toothless gums. 'Yes,' agreed

180

Sebastian. 'I see what you mean.' He returned his gaze to the foot, and studied it with sickened fascination. His adam's apple bobbed as he swallowed.

'Get on with it,' said Flynn, and Sebastian stooped. There was a howl from Flynn, and Sebastian straightened up with the wet thorn gripped in his teeth. He spat it out explosively, and Mohammed handed him the gin bottle. Sebastian gargled from it loudly but when he lifted the bottle to his lips again, Flynn laid a restraining hand on his forearm. 'Now don't overdo it, Bassie boy,' he remonstrated mildly, retrieved the bottle and placed it to his own mouth. It seemed to refuel Flynn's anger, for when he removed the bottle his voice had fire in it. 'That goddamn sneaking, sausage-eating slug. He spoiled the only chance I've ever had at that elephant.' He paused to breathe heavily. 'I'd like to do something really nasty to him, like . . . like . . .' he searched for some atrocity to commit upon Herman Fleischer, and suddenly he found one. 'My God!' he said, and his scowl changed to a lovely smile. 'That's it!'

'What?' Sebastian was alarmed. He was certain that he would be selected as the vehicle of Flynn's revenge. 'What?' he repeated.

'We will go . . .' said Flynn, '. . . to Mahenge!'

'Good Lord, that's the German headquarters!'

'Yes,' said Flynn. 'With no Commissioner and no Askari to guard it! They've just passed us, heading in the opposite direction.'

36

They hit Mahenge two hours before dawn, in that time of utter darkness when mankind's vitality is at its lowest ebb. The defence put up by the corporal and five Askari whom Fleischer had left to guard his headquarters was hardly heroic. In fact, they were only half awakened by the lusty and indiscriminate use of Flynn's boot, and by the time they were fully conscious, they found themselves securely locked behind the bars of the jail-house. There was only one casualty. It was, of course, Sebastian Oldsmith, who, in the excitement, ran into a half-open door. It was fortunate, as Flynn pointed out, that he struck the door with his head, otherwise he might have done himself injury. But as it was, he had recovered sufficiently by sunrise to watch the orgy of looting and vandalism in which Flynn and his gun-bearers indulged themselves.

They began in the office of the Commissioner. Built into the thick adobe wall of the room was an enormous iron safe.

'We will open that first,' decreed Flynn as he eyed it greedily. 'See if you can find some tools.'

Sebastian remembered the blacksmith shop at the end of the parade ground. He returned from there laden with sledge-hammers and crow-bars.

Two hours later they were sweating and swearing in an atmosphere heavy with plaster dust. They had torn the safe from the wall, and it lay in the centre of the floor. Three of Flynn's gun-boys were beating on it with sledge-hammers in a steadily diminishing display of enthusiasm, while Sebastian worked with a crow-bar at the hinge joints. He had succeeded in inflicting a few bright scratches upon the metal. Flynn was seated on the Commissioner's desk, steadily working himself into a fury of frustration; for the last hour his contribution to the assault on the safe had been limited to consuming half a bottle of schnapps that he had found in a drawer of the desk.

'It's no use, Flynn.' Sebastian's curls were slick with perspiration, and he licked at the blisters on the palms of his hands. 'We will just have to forget about it.'

'Stand back!' roared Flynn. 'I'll shoot the goddamned thing open.' He rose from the desk wild-eyed, his double-barrelled Gibbs clutched in his hands.

'Wait!' shouted Sebastian and he and the gun-bearers scattered for cover.

The detonations of the heavy rifle were thunderous in the confined space of the office; gun-smoke mingled with the plaster dust, and the bullets ricocheted off the metal of the safe, leaving long smears of lead upon it, before whining away to embed themselves in the floor, wall and furniture.

This act of violence seemed to placate Flynn. He lost interest in the safe. 'Let's go and find something to eat,' he said mildly, and they trooped through to the kitchens.

Once Flynn had shot away the lock, Herman Fleischer's larder proved to be an Aladdin's cave of delight. The roof was hung with hams and polonies and sausages, there were barrels of pickled meats, stacks of fat round cheeses, cases of Hansa beer, cases of cognac, pyramids of canned truffles, asparagus tips, pâté, shrimps, mushrooms, olives in oil, and other rarities.

They stared at this profusion in awe, and then moved forward together. Each man to his own particular tastes, they fell upon Herman Fleischer's treasure house. The gun-boys rolled out a cask of pickled pork, Sebastian started with his hunting knife on the cans, while Flynn devoted himself to the case of Steinhager in the corner.

It took two hours of dedicated eating and drinking for them to reach saturation point.

'We'd better get ready to move on now,' Sebastian belched softly, and Flynn nodded owlish agreement, the movement spilling a little Steinhager down his bush jacket. He wiped at it with his hand and then licked his fingers.

'Yep! Best we are gone before Fleischer gets home.' He looked at Mohammed. 'Make up full loads of food for each of the bearers. What you can't carry away we'll dump in the latrine buckets.' He stood up carefully. 'I'll just have a look round, and make sure we haven't missed anything important,' and he went out through the door with unsteady dignity.

In Fleischer's office he stood for a minute regarding the invulnerable safe balefully. It was certainly much too heavy to carry away, and abandoning the notion with regret, he looked around for some outlet for his frustration.

There was a portrait of the Kaiser on the entrance wall, a colour print showing the Emperor in full dress, mounted on a magnificent cavalry charger. Flynn picked up an indelible pencil from the desk and walked across to the picture. With a dozen strokes of the pencil he drastically altered the relationship between horse and rider. Then, beginning to chuckle, he printed on the whitewashed wall below the picture, 'The Kaiser loves horses.'

This struck him as being such a pearl of wit, that he had to summon Sebastian and show it to him. 'That's what you call being subtle, Bassie, boy. All good jokes are subtle.'

It seemed to Sebastian that Flynn's graffiti were as subtle as the charge of an enraged rhinoceros but he laughed dutifully. This encouraged Flynn to a further essay in humour. He had two of the gun bearers carry in a bucket from the latrines, and under his supervision, they propped it above the half-open door of Herman Fleischer's bedroom.

An hour later, heavily laden with booty, the raiding party left Mahenge and began the first of a series of forced marches aimed at the Rovuma river.

37

In a state of mental confusion induced by a superfluity of adrenalin in the bloodstream, Herman Fleischer wandered through his ransacked boma. As he discovered each new outrage he regarded it with slitted eyes and laboured breathing. But first it was necessary to effect a jail-break in reverse in order to free his own captive Askari. When they emerged through the hole in the prison wall, Herman curtly ordered his sergeant to administer twenty strokes of the kiboko to each of them, as a token rebuke for their inefficiency. He stood by and drew a little comfort from the solid slap of the kiboko on bare flesh and the shrieks of the recipient.

However, the calming effect of the floggings evaporated when Herman entered the kitchen area of his establishment, and found that his larder of painstakingly accumulated foodstuffs was now empty. This nearly broke his spirit. His jowls quivered with self-pity, and from under his tongue saliva oozed in melancholic nostalgia. It would take a month to replace the sausages alone, heaven knew how long to replace the cheeses imported from the fatherland.

From the larder he went through to his office and found Flynn's subtleties. Herman's sense of humour was not equal to the occasion.

'Pig-swine, English bastard,' he muttered dejectedly, and a dark wave of despair and fatigue washed over him as he realized the futility of setting out in pursuit of the raiders. With two days start he could never hope to catch them before they reached the Rovuma. If only Governor Schee, who was so forthcoming with criticism, would allow him to cross the river one night with his Askari and visit the community at Lalapanzi. There would be no one left the following morning to make complaint to the Portuguese Government about breach of sovereignty.

Herman sighed. He was tired and depressed. He would go to his bed now and rest a while before supervising the tidying up of his headquarters. He left the office and plodded heavily along the stoep to his private quarters, and pushed open the door of his bedroom.

His bedroom temporarily uninhabitable, Herman reposed that night on the open stoep. But his sleep was disturbed by a dream in which he pursued Flynn O'Flynn across an endless plain without ever narrowing the gap between them, while above him circled two huge birds – one with the austere face of Governor Schee, and the other with the face of the young English bandit – at regular intervals these two voided their bowels on him. After the previous afternoon's experience the olfactory hallucinations which formed part of the dream were horribly realistic.

He was tactfully awakened by one of his household servants, and struggled up in bed with an ache behind his eyes and a foul taste in his mouth.

'What is it?' he growled.

'There is a bearer from Dodoma who brings a book with the red mark of the Bwana Mkuba upon it.'

Herman groaned. An envelope with Governor Schee's seal affixed to it usually meant trouble. Surely he could not so speedily have learned about Flynn O'Flynn's latest escapade.

'Bring coffee!'

'Lord, there is no coffee. It was all stolen,' and Herman groaned again.

'Very well. Bring the messenger.' He would have to endure the ordeal of Governor Schee's rebukes without the fortifying therapy of a cup of coffee. He broke the seal and began to read:

> 4th August, 1914.
> The Residency,
> Dar es Salaam.

To The Commissioner (Southern Province)
At: Mahenge.
Sir,

It is my duty to inform you that a state of war now exists between the Empire and the Governments of England, France, Russia, and Portugal.

You are hereby appointed temporary Military Commander of the Southern Province of German East Africa, with orders to take whatever steps you deem necessary for the protection of our borders, and the confusion of the enemy.

In due course a military force, now being assembled at Dar es Salaam, will be despatched to your area. But I fear that there will be a delay before this can be achieved.

In the meantime, you must operate with the force presently at your disposal.

There was more, much more, but Herman Fleischer read the detailed instructions with perfunctory attention. His headache was forgotten, the taste in his mouth unnoticed in the fierce surge of warrior passions that arose within him.

His chubby features puckered with smiles, he looked up from the letter and spoke aloud. 'Ja, O'Flynn, now I will pay you for the bucket.'

He turned back to the first page of the letter, and his mouth formed the words as he read '. . . whatever steps you deem necessary for the protection of our borders, and the confusion of the enemy.'

At last. At last he had the order for which he had pleaded so many times. He shouted for his sergeant.

38

'Perhaps they will come home tonight.' Rosa Oldsmith looked up from the child's smock she was embroidering.

'Tonight, or tomorrow, or the next day,' Nanny replied philosophically. 'There is no profit in guessing at the coming or going of men. They all have worms in their heads,' and she began again to rock the cradle, squatting beside it on the leopard-skin rugs like an animated mummy. The child snuffled a little in its sleep.

'I'm sure it will be tonight. I can feel it – something good is going to happen.' Rosa laid aside her sewing and crossed to the door that led out on to the stoep. In the last few minutes the sun had gone down below the trees, and the land was ghostly quiet in the brief African dusk.

Rosa went out on to the stoep, and hugging her arms across her chest at the chill of evening, she stared out down the darkening length of the valley. She stood there, waiting restlessly, and as the day passed swiftly into darkness, so her mood changed from anticipation to a formless foreboding.

Quietly, but with an edge to her voice, she called back into the room, 'Light the lamps please, Nanny.'

Behind her she heard the sounds of metal on glass, then the flare of a sulphur match, and a feeble yellow square of light was thrown out on to the veranda to fall around her feet.

The first puff of the night wind was cold on her bare arms. She felt the prickle of goose-flesh and she shivered unexpectedly.

'Come inside, Little Long Hair,' Nanny ordered. 'The night is for mosquitoes and leopards – and other things.'

But Rosa lingered, straining her eyes into the darkness until she could no longer see the shape of the fig-trees at the bottom of the lawn. Then abruptly she turned away and went into the bungalow. She closed the door and slid the bolt across.

Later she woke. There was no moon outside and the room was dark. Beside her bed she could hear the soft, piglet sounds that little Maria made in her sleep.

Again the disquieting mood of the early evening returned to her and she lay still in her bed, waiting and listening in the utter blackness, and the darkness bore down upon her so that she felt herself shrinking, receding, becoming remote from reality, small and lonely in the night.

In fear then she lifted the mosquito netting and groped for the cradle. The baby whimpered as she lifted her and brought her into the bed beside her, but Rosa's arms quietened her and soon she slept against the breast, and the warmth of the tiny body stilled Rosa's own agitation.

The shouting woke her, and she opened her eyes with a surge of joy, for the shouts would be Sebastian's bearers. Before she was fully awake she had thrown aside the bedclothes, struggled out from under the mosquito netting, and was standing in her night-dress with the baby clasped to her chest.

It was then that she realized that the room was no longer in darkness. From the window into the yard it was lit by a red-gold glow that flared, and flickered, and faded.

The last tarnish of sleep was cleaned from her brain, so she could hear that the shouts from outside were not those of welcome, and on a lower key, there were other sounds – a whispering, rustling, and popping, that she could not identify.

She crossed to the window, moving slowly, with dread for what she might find, but before she reached it a scream froze her. It came from the kitchen yard, a scream that quivered on the air long after it had ended, a scream of terror and of pain.

'Merciful God!' she whispered, and forced herself to peer out.

The servants' quarters and the outhouses were on fire. From the thatch of each the flames stood up in writhing yellow columns, lighting the darkness.

There were men in the yard, many men, and all of them wore the khaki uniform of German Askari. Each of them carried a rifle, and the bayonet blades glittered in the glare of the flames.

'They have crossed the river – No, oh please God, no!' and Rosa hugged the baby to her, crouching down below the window sill.

The scream rang out again, but weaker now, and she saw a knot of four Askari crowded around something that squirmed in the dust of the yard. She heard their laughter, the excited laughter of men who kill for fun, as they stabbed down on the squirming thing with their bayonets.

At that moment another of the servants broke from the burning outbuildings and ran for the darkness beyond the circle of the flames. Shouting again, the Askari left the dying man and chased the other. They turned him like a pack of trained greyhounds coursing a gazelle, laughing and shouting in their excitement, and drove him back into the daylight glare of the flames.

Bewildered, surrounded, the servant stopped and looked wildly about him, his face convulsed with terror. Then the Askari swarmed over him, clubbing and hacking with their rifles.

'Oh, oh God, no.' Rosa's whisper sobbed in her throat, but she could not drag her eyes away.

Suddenly in the uproar she heard a new voice, a bull-bellow of authority. She could not understand the words for they were shouted in German but from around the angle of the bungalow appeared a white man, a massive figure in the blue corduroy uniform of the German Colonial Service, with a slouch hat pulled low down on his head, and a pistol brandished in one hand. From the description that Sebastian had given her, she recognized the German Commissioner.

'Stop them!' Rosa did not speak aloud, the appeal was in her mind only. 'Please, stop them burning and killing.'

The white man was railing at his Askari, his face turned towards where Rosa crouched and she saw it was round and pink like that of an overweight baby. In the fire-light it glistened with a fine sheen of sweat.

'Stop them. Please stop them,' Rosa pleaded silently, but under the Commissioner's direction three of the Askari ran to where, in the excitement of the chase, they had dropped their torches of dry grass. While they lit them from the flaming outbuildings, the other Askari left the corpses of the two servants and spread out in a circle around the bungalow, facing inwards, with their rifles held at high port. Most of the bayonets were dulled with blood.

'I want Fini and the Singese – not bearers and gun-boys – I want the white men! Burn them out!' shouted Fleischer, but Rosa recognized only her father's name. She wanted to cry out that he was not here, that it was only her and the child.

The three Askari were running in towards the bungalow now, sparks and fire smeared back from the torches they carried. In turn each man checked his run, poised himself like a javelin thrower, then hurled his torch in a high, smoking arc towards the bungalow. Rosa heard them thump, thump, on to the thatched roof above her.

'I must get my baby away, before the fire catches,' and

she hurried across the room, out into the passage. It was dark here and she groped along the wall until she found the entrance to the main room. At the front door she fumbled with the bolts, and opened it a crack. Peering through to the fire-lit lawns beyond the stoep, she saw the dark forms of Askari waiting there also, and she drew back.

'The side windows of the kitchen,' she told herself. 'They're closest to the bush. That's the best chance,' and she stumbled back into the passage.

Above her now there was a sound like high wind and water, a rushing sound blending with the crackle of burning thatch, and the first taint of smoke stung her nostrils.

'If only I can reach the bush,' she whispered desperately, and the child in her arms began to cry.

'Hush, my darling, hush now,' but her voice was scratchy with fear. Maria seemed to sense it; her petulant whimperings changed to lusty high-pitched yells and she struggled in Rosa's grasp.

From the side windows of the kitchen Rosa saw the familiar waiting figures of the Askari hovering at the edge of the fire-light. She felt despair catch her stomach in a cold grip and squeeze the resolve from her. Suddenly her legs were weak under her and her whole body was shaking.

From within the bungalow behind her there came a thunderous roar as part of the burning roof collapsed. A blast of scalding air blew through the kitchen and the tall column of sparks and flames thrown up by the collapse lit the surroundings even more vividly. It showed another figure beyond the line of Askari, scampering in from the edge of the bush like a little black monkey, and Rosa heard Nanny's voice.

'Little Long Hair! Little Long Hair.' A plaintive, ancient wail.

Nanny had escaped into the bush during the first minutes

of the attack. She had lain there watching until the roof of
the bungalow fell in – then she could no longer contain
herself. Insensible of her own danger, caring for nothing
except her precious charges, she was coming back.

The Askari saw her also. Their rigid, well-spaced line
crumpled as all of them ran to head her off. Suddenly the
ground between Rosa and the edge of the bush was clear.
Now there was a chance – just the smallest chance that she
could get the child away. She flung the window open and
dropped through it to the earth.

One moment she hesitated and glanced towards the
confusion of running men away on her right hand. In that
moment she saw one of the Askari catch up with the old
woman and lunge forward with his bayonet. Nanny reeled
from the force of the blow in her back. Involuntarily her
arms were flung wide open, and for a fleeting second Rosa
saw the point of the bayonet appear miraculously from the
centre of her chest, as it impaled her.

Then Rosa was running towards the wall of bush and
scrub fifty yards ahead of her, while Maria howled in her
arms. The sound attracted the attention of the Askari. One
of them shouted a warning, and then the whole pack was
after her in full tongue.

Rosa's senses were overwrought by her terror, so finely
tuned that it seemed the passage of time was lagging.
Weighed down by the child, each pace she took dragged on
for ever, as though she waded through waist-deep water.
The long night-dress around her legs hampered her, and
there was rough stone and thorn beneath her bare feet. The
wall of bush ahead of her seemed to come no closer, and
she ran with the cold hand of fear squeezing her chest and
cramping her breathing.

Then into her line of vision from the side came a man,
an Askari, a big man bounding towards her with the long

loping gallop of a bull baboon, cutting across her line of flight, his open mouth an obscene pink pit in the shiny black of his face.

Rosa screamed and swung away from him. Now she was running parallel to the edge of the bush and behind her she heard the slap of feet upon the earth, closing fast, and the babbling chorus of the pursuit.

A hand snatched at her shoulder, and she twisted away from it, feeling the stuff of her night-gown tear beneath the clutching fingers.

Blind with terror she stumbled a dozen paces back towards the burning homestead. She felt the vast waves of heat from it in her face and through her thin clothing – and then a rifle butt struck her in the small of the back, and a bright burst of agony paralysed her legs. She dropped to her knees, still holding Maria.

They ringed her in, a palisade of human bodies and gloating, blood-crazed faces.

The big one who had felled her with the rifle butt stooped over her and before she recognized his intention, he had snatched Maria from her arms and stepped back again.

He stood laughing, holding the child by her ankles, letting her swing head downwards, so her tiny face was suffused with blood, scarlet in the light of the flames.

'No, please, no!' Rosa crawled painfully towards the man. 'Give her back to me. My baby. Please give her back,' and she lifted her arms towards him.

The Askari dangled the child tantalizingly in front of her, retreating slowly as she crawled towards him. The others were laughing, hoarse sensual laughter, crowding around her, faces contorted with enjoyment, and polished ebony black with the sweat of excitement, as they jostled each other for a better view of the sport.

Then with a wild yell, the Askari swung Maria high,

whirled her twice above his head as he pivoted to face the bungalow – and threw Maria up towards the burning roof.

The tiny body flew with the looseness of a rag doll through the air, her night-dress fluttered as she dropped and struck the roof, rolled awkwardly down the slope of it with her clothing blooming into instant flame, until she reached a weak spot in the burning thatch. It sucked Maria in like a fiery mouth and blew a belch of sparks as it swallowed her. At that instant Rosa heard the voice of her child for the last time. It was a sound she was never to forget.

For a moment the men about her were hushed, and then as though wind blew through trees, they moved a little with a sound that was half sigh, half moan.

Still kneeling, facing the burning building which was now a pyre, Rosa slumped forward and lifted her hands to cover her face as though in prayer.

The Askari who had thrown the child snatched up his rifle from where it lay at his feet and stood over her. He lifted it above his head the way a harpooner holds his steel with the point of the bayonet aimed at the base of Rosa's neck where her hair had fallen open to expose the pale skin.

In the moment that the Askari paused to take his aim, Herman Fleischer shot him in the back of the head with the Luger.

'Mad dog!' the Commissioner shouted at the Askari's corpse. 'I told you to take them alive.'

Then, breathing like an asthma case from the exertion of his run to intervene, he turned to Rosa.

'Fräulein, my apologies,' he doffed the slouch hat with ponderous courtesy, and spoke in German that Rosa did not understand. 'We do not make war on women and babies.'

She did not look up at him. She was crying quietly into her cupped hands.

39

'Early in the year for a bush fire,' Flynn muttered. He sat with an enamel mug cupped in his hands and blew steam from the hot coffee. His blanket had slid down to his waist.

Across the camp-fire from him Sebastian was also sitting in a muddle of bedding, and cooling his own pre-dawn mug of coffee. At Flynn's words he looked up from his labour, and out into the dark south.

False dawn had paled the sky just enough to define the hills below it as an undulating mass that seemed much closer than it was. That way lay Lalapanzi – and Rosa and Maria.

Without real interest Sebastian saw the radiated glow at one point along the spine of the ridge; a fan of pink light no larger than a thumb-nail.

'Not a very big one,' he said.

'No,' agreed Flynn. 'Hope she doesn't spread though,' and he gulped noisily at his mug.

As Sebastian watched it idly, the glow diminished, shrinking into insignificance at the coming of the sun, and above it the stars paled out also.

'We'd best get moving. It's a long day's march and we've wasted enough time on this trip already.'

'You're a regular bloody fire-eater when it comes to getting your home comforts.' Flynn feigned disinterest, yet secretly the thought of returning to his grand-daughter had strong appeal. He hurried the coffee a little and scalded his tongue.

Sebastian was right. They had wasted a lot of time on the return trip from the Mahenge raid.

First, there was a detour to avoid a party of German Askari that one of the native headmen had warned them was at M'topo's village. They had trekked upstream for three days before finding a safe crossing, and a village willing to hire canoes.

Then there was the brush with the hippo which had cost them almost a week. As was usual practice, the four hired canoes, loaded to within a few inches of freeboard with Flynn, Sebastian, their retinue and loot, had slipped across the Rovuma and were hugging the Portuguese bank as they headed downstream towards the landing opposite M'topo's village when the hippo had disputed their passage.

She was an old cow hippo who a few hours earlier had given birth to her calf in a tiny island of reeds, separated from the south bank by twenty feet of lily-padded water. When the four canoes entered this channel in line astern with the paddlers chanting happily, she took it as a direct threat to her offspring and she threw a tantrum.

Two tons of hippo in a tantrum has the destructive force of a localized hurricane. Surfacing violently from under the leading canoe, she had thrown Sebastian, two gun-boys, four paddlers, and all their equipment, ten feet in the air. The canoe, rotted with beetle, had snapped in half and sunk immediately.

The mother hippo had then treated the three following canoes with the same consideration, and within the space of a few minutes, the canal was clogged with floating debris, and struggling, panic-stricken men. Fortunately they were no more than ten feet from the bank. Sebastian was first ashore. None of them, however, was very far behind him, and they all took off like the start of a cross-country race over the veld, when the hippo emerged from the river and signified that, not satisfied with wrecking the flotilla, she intended chopping a few of them in half with her guillotine jaws.

A hundred yards later she abandoned the pursuit, and trotted back to the water, wiggling her little ears and snorting in triumph. Half a mile farther on the survivors had stopped running.

They camped there that night without food, bedding or weapons, and the following morning, after a heated council of war, Sebastian was elected to return to the river and ascertain whether the hippo was still in control of the channel. He came back at high speed to report that she was.

Three more days they waited for the hippo and her calf to move away. During this time they suffered the miseries of cold nights and hungry days, but the greatest misery was inflicted on Flynn O'Flynn whose case of gin was under eight feet of water – and by the third morning he was threatening *delirium tremens* again. Just before Sebastian set off for his morning reconnaissance of the channel, Flynn informed him agitatedly that there were three blue scorpions sitting on his head. After the initial alarm, Sebastian went through the motions of removing the imaginary scorpions and stamping them to death, and Flynn was satisfied.

Sebastian returned from the river with the news that the hippo and her calf had evacuated the island, and it was now possible to begin salvage operations.

Protesting mildly and talking about crocodiles, Sebastian was stripped naked and coaxed into the water. On his first dive, he retrieved the precious case of gin.

'Bless you, my boy,' Flynn murmured fervently as he eased the cork out of a bottle.

By the following morning Sebastian had recovered nearly all their equipment and booty, without being eaten by crocodiles, and they set off for Lalapanzi on foot.

Now they were in their last camp before Lalapanzi, and Sebastian felt his impatience rising. He wanted to get home to Rosa and baby Maria. He should be home by evening.

'Come on, Flynn. Let's go.' He flicked the coffee grounds from his mug, threw aside his blanket, and shouted to

Mohammed and the bearers who were huddled around the other fire.

'Safari! Let us march.'

Nine hours later, with the daylight dying around him, he breasted the last rise and paused at the top.

All that day eagerness had lengthened his stride, and he had left Flynn and the column of heavily laden bearers far behind.

Now he stood alone, and stared without comprehension at the smoke-blackened ruins of Lalapanzi from which a few thin tendrils of smoke still drifted.

'Rosa!' Her name was a harsh bellow of fear, and he ran wildly.

'Rosa!' he shouted as he crossed the scorched and trampled lawns.

'Rosa! Rosa! Rosa!' the echo from the kopje above the homestead shouted back.

'Rosa!' He saw something amongst the bushes at the edge of the lawn, and he ran to it. Old Nanny lying dead with the blood dried black on the floral stuff of her night-gown.

'Rosa!' He ran back towards the bungalow. The ash swirled in a warm mist around his legs as he crossed the stoep.

'Rosa!' His voice rang hollowly through the roofless shell of the house, as he stumbled over the fallen beams that littered the main room. The reek of burned cloth and hair and wood almost choked him, so that his voice was husky as he called again.

'Rosa!'

He found her in the burnt-out kitchen block and he thought she was dead. She was slumped against the cracked and blackened wall. Her night-gown was torn and scorched, and the snarled skeins of hair, that hid her face, were powdered with white wood ash.

'My darling. Oh, my darling.' He knelt beside her, and timidly touched her shoulder. Her flesh was warm and alive beneath his fingers, and he felt relief leap up into his throat, blocking it so he could not speak again. Instead, he brushed the tangle of hair from her face and looked at it.

Beneath the charcoal smears of dirt her skin was pale as grey marble. Her eyes, tight closed, were heavily underscored with blue, and rimmed with crusty red.

He touched her lips with the tips of his fingers, and she opened her eyes, But they looked beyond him; unseeing, dead eyes. They frightened him. He did not want to look into them, and he drew her head towards his shoulder.

There was no resistance in her. She lay against him quietly, and he pressed his face into her hair. Her hair was impregnated with the smell of smoke.

'Are you hurt?' he asked her in a whisper, not wanting to hear the answer. But she made no answer, lying inert in his arms.

'Tell me, Rosa. Speak to me. Where is Maria?'

At the mention of the child's name, she reacted for the first time. She began to tremble.

'Where is she?' more urgency in his voice now.

She rolled her head against his shoulder and looked across the floor of the room. He followed the direction of her gaze.

Near the far wall an area of the floor had been swept clear of debris and ash. Rosa had done it with her bare hands while the ash was still hot. Her fingers were blistered and burned raw in places, and her arms were black to the elbows. Lying in the centre of this cleared space was a small, charred thing.

'Maria?' Sebastian whispered, and Rosa shuddered against him.

'Oh, God,' he said, and lifted Rosa. Carrying her against his chest, he staggered from the ruins of the bungalow out into the cool, sweet evening air, but in his nostrils lingered the smell of smoke and burned flesh. He wanted to escape from it. He ran blindly along the path and Rosa lay unresisting in his arms.

– 40 –

The following day Flynn buried their dead on the kopje above Lalapanzi. He placed a thick slab of granite over the small grave that stood apart from the others, and when it was done he sent a bearer to the camp to fetch Rosa and Sebastian.

When they came, they found him standing alone by Maria's grave under the marula trees. His face was puffy and purply red. The thinning grey hair hung limply over his ears and forehead, like the wet feathers of an old rooster. His body looked as though it was melting. It sagged at the shoulders and the belly. Sweat had soaked through his clothing across the shoulders, and at the armpits and crotch. He was sick with drink and sorrow.

Sebastian stood beside Rosa, and the three of them took their silent farewell of the child.

'There is nothing else to do now,' Sebastian spoke huskily.

'Yes,' said Flynn. He stooped slowly and took a handful of the new earth from the grave. 'Yes, there is.' He crumbled the earth between his fingers. 'We still have to find the man who did this – and kill him.'

Beside Sebastian, Rosa straightened up. She turned to Sebastian, lifted her chin, and spoke for the first time since he had come home.

'Kill him!' she repeated softly.

PART TWO

With his hands clasped behind his back, and his chin thrust forward aggressively, Rear-Admiral Sir Percy Howe sucked in his lower lip and nibbled it reflectively. 'What was our last substantiated sighting on *Blücher*?' he asked at last.

'A month ago, sir. Two days before the outbreak of war. Sighting reported by S.S. *Tygerberg*. Latitude 0°27″N. Longitude 52°16″E. Headed south-west; estimated speed, eighteen knots.'

'And a hell of a lot of good that does us,' Sir Percy interrupted his flag-captain and glared at the vast Admiralty plot of the Indian Ocean. 'She could be back in Bremerhaven by now.'

'She could be, sir,' the flag-captain nodded, and Sir Percy glanced at him and permitted himself a wintry smile.

'But you don't believe that, do you, Henry?'

'No, sir, I don't. During the last thirty days, eight merchantmen have disappeared between Aden and Lourenço Marques. Nearly a quarter of a million tons of shipping. That's the *Blücher*'s work.'

'Yes, it's the *Blücher*, all right,' agreed the Admiral, and reached across the plot to pick up the black counter labelled '*Blücher*', that lay on the wide green expanse of the Indian Ocean.

A respectful silence held the personnel of the plotting room South Atlantic and Indian Oceans while they waited for the great man to reach his decision. It was a long time coming. He stood bouncing the '*Blücher*' in the palm of his right hand, his grey eyebrows erect like the spines of a hedgehog's back, as his forehead creased in thought. A full minute they waited.

'Refresh my memory of her class and commission.' Like most successful men Sir Percy would not hurry a decision when there was time to think, and the duty lieutenant who had anticipated his request, stepped forward with the German Imperial Navy list open at the correct page.

'"*Blücher*. Commissioned August 16, 1905. 'B' Class heavy cruiser. Main armament, eight nine-inch guns. Secondary armament, six six-inch guns."'

The lieutenant finished his reading and waited quietly.

'Who is her captain?' Sir Percy asked, and the lieutenant consulted an addendum to the list.

'"Otto von Kleine (Count). Previously commanded the light cruiser *Sturm Vogel*."'

'Yes,' said Sir Percy. 'I've heard of him,' and he replaced the counter on the plot, keeping his hand on it. 'A dangerous man to have here, south of Suez,' and he pushed the counter up towards the Red Sea and the entrance to the canal, where the tiny red shipping lanes amalgamated into a thick artery, ' – or here,' and he pushed it down towards the Cape of Good Hope, around which were curved the same red threads that joined London to Australia and India. Sir Percy lifted his hand from the black counter and left it sitting menacingly upon the shipping lanes.

'What force have we deployed against him so far?' and in answer the flag-captain picked up a wooden pointer and touched in turn the red counters that were scattered about the Indian Ocean.

'*Pegasus* and *Renounce* in the north. *Eagle* and *Plunger* sweeping the southern waters, sir.'

'What further force can we spare, Henry?'

'Well, sir, *Orion* and *Bloodhound* are at Simonstown,' and he touched the nose of the African continent with the pointer.

'*Orion* – that's Manderson, isn't it?'

206

'Yes, sir.'

'And who has *Bloodhound?*'

'Little, sir.'

'Good,' Sir Percy nodded with satisfaction. 'A six-inch cruiser and a destroyer should be able to deal with *Blücher*,' and he smiled again. 'Especially with a hellion like Charles Little handling the *Bloodhound*. I played golf with him last summer – he damn nigh drove the sixteenth green at St Andrews!'

The flag-captain glanced at the Admiral and, on the strength of the destroyer captain's reputation, decided to permit himself an inanity. 'The young ladies of Cape Town will mourn his departure, sir.'

'We must hope that Kapitän zur See Otto von Kleine will mourn his arrival,' chuckled Sir Percy.

'Daddy likes you very much.'

'Your father is a man of exquisite good taste,' Commander the Honourable Charles Little conceded gallantly, and rolled his head to smile at the young lady who lay beside him on a rug, in the dappled shade beneath the pine trees.

'Can't you ever be serious?'

'Helen, my sweet, at times I can be deadly serious.'

'Oh, you!' and his companion blushed prettily as she remembered certain of Charles's recent actions, which would make her father hastily revise his judgement.

'I value your father's good opinion, but my chief concern is that you endorse it.'

The girl sat up slowly and while she stared at him her hands were busy, brushing the pine needles from the glorious tangle of her hair, readjusting the fastenings of her blouse, spreading the skirts of her riding-habit to cover sweet legs clad in dark, tall polished leather boots.

She stared at Charles Little and ached with the strength

of her want. It was not a sensual need she felt, but an over-powering obsession to have this man as her very own. To own him in the same way as she already owned diamonds, and furs, and silk, and horses, and peacocks, and other beautiful things.

His body sprawled out on the rug with all the unconscious grace of a reclining leopard. A secret little smile tugged at the corners of his lips and his eyelids drooped to mask the sparkle of his eyes. His recent exertions had dampened the hair that flopped forward onto his forehead.

There was something satanical about him, an air of wickedness, and Helen decided it was the slant of the eyebrows and the way his ears lay flat against his temples, but were pointed like those of a satyr, yet they were pink and smooth as those of an infant.

'I think you have devil's ears,' she said, and then she blushed again, and scrambled to her feet avoiding Charles's arm that reached out for her. 'Enough of that!' she giggled and ran to the thoroughbred hunter that was tied near them in the forest. 'Come on,' she called as she mounted.

Charles stood up lazily and stretched. He tucked the tail of his shirt into his breeches, folded the rug on which they had lain, and went to his own horse.

At the edge of the pine forest, they checked their mounts and sat looking down over the Constantia valley.

'Isn't it beautiful?' she said.

'It is indeed,' he agreed.

'I meant the view.'

'And so did I.' Twice in the six days he had known her, she had led him up this mountain and subjected him to the temptation. Below them lay six thousand acres of the richest land in all of Africa.

'When my brother Hubert was killed there was no one left to carry it on. Just my sister and I – and we are only girls. Poor Daddy isn't so well any more – he finds it such a strain.'

Charles let his eyes move lazily from the great squat buttress of Table Mountain on their left, across the lush basin of vineyards below them, and then on to where the glittering wedge of False Bay drove into the mountains.

'Doesn't the homestead look lovely from here?' Helen drew his attention to the massive Dutch-gabled residence, with its attendant outbuildings grouped in servility behind it.

'I am truly impressed by the magnificence of the stud fee,' Charles murmured, purposefully slurring the last two words, and the girl glanced at him in surprise, beginning to bridle.

'I beg your pardon?'

'It is truly magnificent scenery,' he amended. Her persistent efforts at ensnaring him were beginning to bore Charles. He had teased and avoided more artful huntresses.

'Charles,' she whispered. 'How would you like to live here. I mean, forever?'

And Charles was shocked. This little provincial had no understanding whatsoever of the rules governing the game of flirtation. He was so shocked that he threw back his head and laughed.

When Charles laughed it sent shivers of delight through every woman within a hundred yards. It was a merry sound with underlying tones of sensuality. His teeth were very white against the sea-tan of his face, and the muscles of his chest and upper arms tensed into bold relief beneath the silk shirt he wore.

Helen was the only witness of this particular performance, and she was helpless as a sparrow in a hurricane. Eagerly she leaned across the space between their horses and touched his arm. 'You would like it, Charles. Wouldn't you?'

She did not know that Charles Little had a private income of twenty thousand pounds a year, that when his father died he would inherit the title Viscount Sutherton and the estates that went with it. She did not know that one of those estates would swallow her father's own three times over; nor did she know that Charles had passed by willing young ladies with twice her looks, ten times her fortune, and a hundred times her breeding.

'You would, Charles. I know you would!'

So young, so vulnerable, that he stopped the flippant reply before it reached his lips.

'Helen,' he took her hand. 'I am a sea creature. We move with the wind and the waves,' and he lifted her hand to his lips.

A while she sat, feeling the warm pressure of his lips upon her flesh, and the burn of tears behind her eyes. Then she snatched her hand away, and wheeled her horse. She lifted the leather riding-crop and slashed the glossy black shoulder between her knees. Startled, the stallion jumped forward into a dead run back along the road towards the Constantia valley.

Charles shook his head and grimaced with regret. He had not meant to hurt her. It had been an escapade, something to fill the waiting days while *Bloodhound* went through the final stages of her refit. But Charles had learned to harden himself to the ending of his adventures – to the tears and tragedy.

'Shame on you, you heartless cad,' he said aloud, and touching his mount with his heels ambled in pursuit of the galloping stallion.

He caught up with the stallion in the stable yards. A groom was walking it, and there were darker sweat patches on its coat, and the barrel of its chest still heaved with laboured breathing.

Helen was nowhere in sight, but her father stood at the

stable gates – a big man, with a square-cut black beard picked out with grey.

'Enjoy your ride?'

'Thank you, Mr Uys.' Charles was noncommittal, and the older man glanced significantly at the blown stallion before going on.

'There's one of your sailors been waiting for you for an hour.'

'Where is he?' Charles's manner altered abruptly, became instantly businesslike.

'Here, sir.' From the deep shade of the stable doorway, a young seaman stepped out into the bright sunlight.

'What is it, man?' Impatiently Charles acknowledged his salute.

'Captain Manderson's compliments, sir, and you're to report aboard H.M.S. *Orion* with all possible speed. There's a motor car waiting to take you to the base, sir.'

'An untimely summons, Commander.' Uys gave his opinion lounging against the worked stone gateway. 'I fear we will see no more of you for a long time.'

But Charles was not listening. His body seemed to quiver with suppressed excitement, the way a good gundog reacts to the scent of the bird. 'Sailing orders,' he whispered, ' – at last. At last!'

There was a heavy south-east swell battering Cape Point, so the sea spray wreathed the beam of the lighthouse on the cliffs above. A flight of malgas came in so high towards the land that they caught the last of the sun, and glowed pink above the dark water.

Bloodhound cleared Cape Hangklip and took the press of the South Atlantic on her shoulder, staggered from it with a welter of white water running waist-deep past her foredeck gun-turrets. Then in retaliation she hurled herself at the

211

next swell, and Charles Little on her bridge exulted at the vital movement of the deck beneath his feet.

'Bring her round to oh-five-oh.'

'Oh-five-oh, sir,' repeated his navigating lieutenant.

'Revolutions for seventeen knots, pilot.'

Almost immediately the beat of the engines changed, and her action through the water became more abandoned.

Charles crossed to the angle of the flimsy little bridge and looked back into the dark, mountain-lined maw of False Bay. Two miles astern the shape of H.M.S. *Orion* melted into the dying light.

'Come along, old girl. Do try and keep up,' murmured Charles Little with the scorn that a destroyer man feels for any vessel that cannot cruise at twenty knots. Then he looked beyond *Orion* at the land. Below the massif of Table Mountain, near the head of the Constantia valley a single pin prick of light showed.

'There'll be fog tonight, sir,' the pilot spoke at Charles's elbow, and Charles turned without regret to peer over the bows into the gathering night.

'Yes, a good night for pirates.'

– 42 –

The fog condensed on the grey metal of the bridge, so the footplates were slippery underfoot. It soaked into the overcoats of the men huddled against the rail, and it dewed in minute pearls on the eyebrows and beard of Kapitän zur See Otto von Kleine. It gave him an air of derring-do, the reckless look of a scholarly pirate.

Every few seconds Lieutenant Kyller glanced anxiously at his captain, wondering when the order to turn would come. He hated this business of creeping inshore in the fog, with a flood tide pushing them towards a hostile coast.

'Stop all engines,' said von Kleine, and Kyller repeated the order to the helm with alacrity. The muted throbbing died beneath their feet, and afterwards the fog-blanketed air was heavy with a sepulchral hush.

'Ask masthead what he makes of the land.' Von Kleine spoke without turning his head, and after a pause Kyller reported back.

'Masthead is in the fog. No visibility.' He paused. 'Foredeck reports fifty fathoms shoaling rapidly.'

And von Kleine nodded. The sounding tended to confirm his estimate that they were sitting five miles off the breakwater of Durban harbour. When the morning wind swept the fog aside he hoped to see the low coastal hills of Natal ahead of him, terraced with gardens and whitewashed buildings – but most of all he hoped to see at least six British merchantmen anchored off the beach waiting their turn to enter the congested harbour, plump and sleepy under the protection of the shore batteries; unaware just how feeble was the protection afforded by half a dozen obsolete ten-pounders manned by old men and boys of the militia.

German naval intelligence had submitted a very detailed report of the defences and conditions prevailing in Durban. After careful perusal of this report, von Kleine had decided that he could trade certain betrayal of his exact position to the English for such a rich prize. There was little actual risk involved. One pass across the entrance of the harbour at high speed, a single broadside for each of the anchored merchantmen, and he could be over the horizon again before the shore gunners had loaded their weapons.

The risk, of course, was in showing *Blücher* to the entire population of Durban city and thereby supplying the Royal Navy with its first accurate sighting since the declaration of war. Within minutes of his first broadside, the British squadrons, which were hunting him, would be racing in from all directions to block each of his escape routes. He hoped to counter this by swinging away towards the south, down into that watery wilderness of wind and ice below latitude 40°, to the rendezvous with *Esther*, his supply ship. Then on to Australia or South America, as the opportunity arose.

He turned to glance at the chronometer above the ship's compass. Sunrise in three minutes, then they could expect the morning wind.

'Masthead reports the fog dispersing, sir.'

Von Kleine aroused himself, and looked out into the fog banks. They were moving now, twisting upon themselves in agitation at the warmth of the sun. 'All engines slow ahead together,' he said.

'Masthead,' warbled one of the voice-pipes in the battery in front of Kyller. 'Land bearing green four-oh. Range, ten thousand metres. A big headland.'

That would be the bluff above Durban, that massive whale-backed mountain that sheltered the harbour. But in the fog von Kleine had misjudged his approach; he was twice as far from the shore as he had intended.

'All engines full ahead together. New course. Oh-oh-six.' He waited for the order to be relayed to the helm before strolling across to the voice-pipes. 'Guns. Captain.'

'Guns,' the voice from far away acknowledged.

'I will be opening fire with high explosives in about ten minutes. The target will be massed merchant shipping on an approximate mark of three hundred degrees. Range, five thousand metres. You may fire as soon as you bear.'

'Mark three hundred degrees. Range, five thousand metres. Sir,' repeated the pipe, and von Kleine snapped the voice-tube cover shut and returned to his original position, facing forward with his hands clasped loosely behind his back.

Below him the gun-turrets revolved ponderously and the long barrels lifted slightly, pointing out into the mist with impassive menace.

A burst of dazzling sunshine struck the bridge so fiercely that Kyller lifted his hand to shield his eyes, but it was gone instantly as the *Blücher* dashed into another clammy cold bank of fog. Then as though they had passed through a curtain on to a brilliantly lit stage, they came out into a gay summer's morning.

Behind them the fog rolled away in a sodden grey wall from horizon to horizon. Ahead rose the green hills of Africa, rimmed with white beach and surf and speckled with thousands of whiter flecks that were the buildings of Durban town. The scaffolding of the cranes along the harbour wall looked like derelict sets of gallows.

Humped on the smooth green mirror of water between them and the shore, lay four ungainly shapes looking like a troop of basking hippo. The British merchantmen.

'Four only,' muttered von Kleine in chagrin. 'I had hoped for more.'

The forty-foot barrels of the nine-inch guns moved restlessly, seeming to sniff for their prey, and the *Blücher* raced on, lifting a hissing white wave at her bows, vibrating and shuddering to the thrust of her engines as they built up to full speed.

'Masthead,' the voice-tube beside Kyller squawked urgently.

'Bridge,' said Kyller but the reply was lost in the deafening detonation of the first broadside, the long thunderous roll of heavy gun-fire. He jumped involuntarily, taken unawares, and then quickly lifted the binoculars from his chest to train them on the British merchantmen.

All attention, every eye on the bridge was concentrated ahead, waiting for the fall of shot upon the doomed vessels.

In the comparative silence that followed the bellow of the broadside, a shriek from the masthead voice-pipe carried clearly.

'Warships! Enemy warships dead astern!'

'Starboard ten.' Von Kleine raised his voice a little louder than was his wont, and still under full power, *Blücher* swerved away from the land, leaning out from the turn, with her wake curved like an ostrich plume on the surface of the sea behind her, and ran for the shelter of the fog banks, leaving the rich prize of cargo shipping unscathed. On her bridge von Kleine and his officers were staring aft, the merchantmen forgotten as they searched for this new threat.

'Two warships.' The masthead look-out was elaborating his sighting report. 'A destroyer and a cruiser. Bearing ninety degrees. Range, five-oh-seven-oh. Destroyer leading.'

In the spherical field of von Kleine's binoculars the neat little triangle of the leading destroyer's superstructure popped up above the horizon. The cruiser was not yet in sight from the bridge.

'If they'd been an hour later,' lamented Kyller, 'we'd have finished the business and . . .'

'What does masthead see of the cruiser?' von Kleine interrupted him impatiently. He had no time to mourn this chance of fate – his only concern was to evaluate the force that was pursuing him, and then make the decision whether to run, or to turn back and engage them immediately.

'Cruiser is a medium, six or nine-inch. Either "O" class, or an "R". She's four miles behind her escort. Both ships still out of range.'

The destroyer was of no consequence; he could run down on her and blast her into a burning wreck, before her feeble little 4.7-inch guns were able to drop a shell within a mile of *Blücher*, but the cruiser was another matter entirely. To tackle her, *Blücher* would be engaging with her own class;

victory would only be won after a severe mauling, and she was six thousand miles from the nearest friendly port where she could effect major repairs.

There was a further consideration. These two British ships might be the vanguard of a battle squadron. If he turned now and challenged action, engaged the cruiser in a single ship action, he might suddenly find himself pitted against imponderable odds. There could very well be another cruiser, or two, or three – even a battleship, below the southern horizon.

His duty and his orders dictated instant flight, avoiding action, and so prolonging *Blücher*'s fighting life.

'Enemy are streaming their colours, sir,' Kyller reported.

Von Kleine lifted his binoculars again. At the destroyer's masthead flew the tiny spots of white and red. This time he must leave the challenge to combat unanswered. 'Very well,' he said, and turned away to his stool in the corner of the bridge. He slumped into it and hunched his shoulders in thought. There were many interesting problems to occupy him, not least of them was how long he could run at full speed towards the north while his boilers devoured coal ravenously, and each minute widened the gap between *Blücher* and *Esther*.

He swivelled his stool and looked back over his stern. The destroyer was visible to the unaided eye now, and von Kleine frowned at it in irritation. She would yap at his heels like a terrier, clinging to him and shouting his course and speed across the ether to the hungry British squadrons, that must even now be closing with him from every direction. For days now he could expect to see her sitting in his wake.

'Come on! Come on!' Charles Little slapped his hand impatiently against the padded arm of his stool as he watched *Orion*.

For a night and a day he had watched her gaining on *Blücher* but so infinitesimally slowly that it required his range finder to confirm the gain every thirty minutes.

Orion's bows were unnaturally high, and the waves she lifted with the passage of her hull through the water were the white wings of a seagull in the tropical sunlight; for Manderson, her captain, had pumped out her forward fresh-water tanks and fired away half the shell and explosive propellant from her forward magazines. Every man whose presence in the front half of the ship was not essential to her operation had been ordered aft to stand on the open deck as human ballast – all this in an effort to lift *Orion*'s bows and to coax another inch of speed from the cruiser.

Now she faced the most dangerous hour of her life, for she was creeping within extreme range of *Blücher*'s terrible nine-inch armament, and, taking into account the discrepancy in their speeds, it would be another hour before she could bring her own six-inch guns to bear. During that time she would be under fire from *Blücher*'s after turrets and would have no answer to them.

It was heart-breaking for Charles to watch the chase, for *Bloodhound* had not once been asked to extend herself. Below there was a reserve of speed that would allow her to close with *Blücher* in fifty minutes of steaming – always provided she was not smashed into a fiery shambles long before.

Thus the three vessels fled towards the ever-receding northern horizon. The two long shapes of the cruisers flying arrow straight, solid columns of reeking smoke pouring from the triple funnels to besmear the gay, glittering surface of the sea with a long double bank of black that dispersed only slowly on the easterly breeze; while, like a water beetle, the diminutive *Bloodhound* circled out to the side of *Blücher* from where, when the time came, she could spot the fall of *Orion*'s shells more accurately and signal the corrections to her. But always *Bloodhound* tactfully kept outside the fifteen-mile radius which marked the length of *Blücher*'s talons.

'We can expect *Blücher* to open fire at any moment now, sir,' the navigating lieutenant commented as he straightened up from the sextant, over which he had been measuring the angle subtended by the two cruisers.

Charles nodded in agreement. 'Yes. Von Kleine must try for a few lucky hits, even at that range.'

'This isn't going to be very pretty to watch.'

'We'll just have to sit tight, keep our fingers crossed, and hope old *Orion* can—' He stopped abruptly, and then jumped up from his stool. 'Hello! *Blücher*'s up to something!'

The silhouette of the German cruiser had altered drastically in the last few seconds. The gap between her funnels widened and now Charles could see the humped menace of her forward turrets.

'By God, she's altering course! The bloody bastard is bringing all his turrets to bear!'

Lieutenant Kyller studied his captain's face. In sleep there was an air of serenity about the man. It reminded Kyller of a painting he had seen in the cathedral at Nürnberg, a portrait of Saint Luke by Holbein. The same fine bone structure, the golden-blond beard and moustache that framed the mobile and sensitive lips. He pushed the idea aside and leaned forward. Gently he touched von Kleine's shoulder.

'Captain. My Captain,' and von Kleine opened his eyes. They were smoky blue with sleep but his voice was crisp.

'What is it, Kyller?'

'The gunnery officer reports the enemy will be within range in fifteen minutes.'

Von Kleine swivelled his stool and looked quickly about his ship. Above him the smoke poured from every funnel, and from the mouth of each stack a volcano of sparks and shimmering heat blew steadily. The paint had blistered and peeled from the metal of the funnels and they glowed red hot, even in the sunlight. *Blücher* was straining herself far beyond the limits her makers had set. God alone knew what injury this constant running at full speed was doing her, and von Kleine winced as he felt her tremble in protest beneath him.

He turned his eyes astern. The British cruiser was hull up on the horizon now. The difference in their speeds must be a small fraction of a knot, but *Blücher*'s superiority in fire power was enormous.

For a moment he allowed himself to ponder the arrogance of a nation that constantly, almost by choice, matched their men and ships against unnatural odds. Always they sent terriers to fight against wolfhounds. Then he smiled, you had to be English or mad, to understand the English.

He glanced out to starboard. The British destroyer had worked out on to his flank. It could do little harm from there.

'Very well, Kyller . . .' He stood as he spoke.

'Bridge – Engine Room,' the voice-tube squealed.

'Engine Room – Bridge.' Kyller turned to it.

'Our port main bearing is running red hot. I must shut down our port engine!'

The words struck von Kleine like a bucket of iced water thrown down his back. He leaped to the voice-tube.

'This is the Captain. I must have full power for another hour!'

'I can't do it, sir. Another fifteen minutes and the main drive shaft will seize up. God knows what damage it will do.'

For five seconds von Kleine hunched silently over the voice-tube. His mind raced. On one engine *Blücher* would lose ten knots on her speed. The enemy would be able to manoeuvre about him freely – possibly hold off until nightfall and then . . . He must attack immediately; turn on them and press his attack home with all his armament.

'Give me full power for as long as you can,' he snapped, and then turning to the gunnery officer's tube, 'This is the Captain. I am turning four points to starboard, and will keep the enemy directly on our starboard beam for the next fifteen minutes. After that I will be forced to reduce speed. Open fire when you bear.' Von Kleine snapped the cover closed and turned to his yeoman of signals. 'Hoist the battle ensign!'

He spoke softly, without heat, but there were lights in his eyes like those in a blue sapphire.

– 44 –

'There she goes!' whispered Charles Little without lowering his glasses. Upon the black turrets of *Blücher* the gun-fire gleamed and sparkled without sound. Quickly he traversed his glasses across the surface of the sea until he found *Orion*. She was plunging in eagerly, narrowing the gap very rapidly between herself and *Blücher*. In another seven minutes she would be able to return the German's fire.

Suddenly, a quarter of a mile ahead of her, there rose from the sea a series of tall columns, stately as the columns of a Greek temple, slender and beautiful, shining like white marble in the sun. Then slowly they dropped back.

'Short,' grunted the navigating lieutenant.

'Her guns are still cold,' Charles commented. 'Please God let old *Orion* get within range.'

Again *Blücher*'s shells fell short, and short again, but each time they were closer to the low bulk of *Orion*, and the next broadside dropped all around her, partially screening her with spray, and *Orion* started to zigzag.

'Another three minutes,' the navigating lieutenant spoke with tension making his voice husky.

At regular intervals of fifteen seconds the German salvos fell around *Orion* – once within fifty feet of her bows so that as she tore into the standing columns of spray, they blew back over her and mingled with the black smoke of her funnels.

'Come on, old girl! Go in and get her. Go on! Go on!' Charles was gripping the rail in front of him and cheering like a maniac, all the dignity of his rank and his thirty-five years gone in the tense excitement of the battle. It had infected all of them on the bridge of the destroyer, and they capered and shouted with him.

'There she blows!' howled the lieutenant.

'She's opened fire!'

'Go it, *Orion*, go it!'

On *Orion*'s forward turrets gun-fire sparkled, then again and again. The harsh roll of the broadsides carried to them against the light wind.

'Short,' groaned Charles. 'She's still out of range.'

'Short again!'

'Still short.'

Each time the call of shot was signalled by the chief yeoman at the Aldis lamp, and briefly acknowledged from *Orion*'s bridge-works.

'Oh my God,' moaned Charles.

'She's hit!' echoed his lieutenant.

A flat yellow glare, like sheet lightning on a summer's day, lit *Orion's* afterdeck, and almost immediately a ball of yellowish grey smoke enveloped her. Through it Charles saw her after-funnel sag drunkenly and hang back at an unnatural angle.

'She's holding on!'

Orion emerged from the shell smoke and dragged it after her like a funeral cloak, but her speed seemed unabated, and the regular salvos burned briefly and brightly on her forward turrets.

'Now she's hitting,' exulted the lieutenant, and Charles turned quickly to see shell-fire burst on *Blücher*, and his wide grin split his face.

'Kill her! Kill her!' he roared, knowing that though *Blücher* was better armed yet she was as vulnerable as *Orion*. Her plating was egg-shell thin and the six-inch shells that crashed through it would be doing her terrible damage.

Now the two cruisers were pounding each other. The range was closing so rapidly that soon they must hit with every broadside. This was a contest from which only one ship, or neither of them, would emerge.

Charles was trying to estimate the damage that had been inflicted upon *Blücher* during the last few minutes. She was on fire forward. Sulphur-yellow flames poured from her, her upperworks were riven into a grotesque sculpture of destruction, and a pall of smoke enveloped her, so her profile was shadowy and vague, yet every fifteen seconds her turrets lit with those deadly little flashes.

Charles turned to assess the relative damage that *Orion* had suffered. He found and held her with his binoculars – and at that moment *Orion* ceased to exist.

Her boilers, pierced by high explosive shell, burst and tore her in half. A cloud of white steam spurted five hundred feet into the air, completely blanketing her. The steam hung for thirty seconds, then sagged wearily, and rolled aside. *Orion* was gone. A wide circle of oil slick and floating debris marked her grave. The speed of her charge had run her clean under.

On the bridge of *Bloodhound*, the cheering strangled into deathly silence. The silence was not spoiled but rather accentuated by the mournful note of the wind in her rigging and the muted throb of her engines.

– 45 –

For eight long hours Charles Little had ridden his anger and his hatred, using the curb to hold it on the right side of madness, resisting the consuming and suicidal urge to hurl his ship at the German cruiser and die as *Orion* had died.

Immediately after the sinking of *Orion*, the *Blücher* had reduced speed sharply and turned due south. With her fires still raging, she had limped along like a gun-shot lion. The battle ensigns at her masthead were tattered by shrapnel and blackened by smoke.

As soon as she had passed, *Bloodhound* altered course and cruised slowly over the area of water that was still rainbowed by floating oil and speckled with wreckage. There were no survivors from *Orion*; all of them had died with her.

Bloodhound turned and trailed after the crippled German cruiser, and the hatred that emanated from the destroyer was of such strength that it should have reached out across the sea as a physical force and destroyed *Blücher*.

But as Charles Little stood at the rail of his bridge, he saw the smoke and flame upon *Blücher*'s decks reduce perceptibly every minute as her damage control teams fought it to a standstill. The last wisp of smoke from her shrivelled.

'Fire's out,' said the pilot, and Charles made no answer. He had hoped that the flames would eat their way into one of *Blücher*'s magazines and blow her into the same oblivion into which she had sent *Orion*.

'But she isn't making more than six knots. *Orion* must have hit her in the engine room.' Hopefully the navigating lieutenant went on, 'My bet is that she's got major damage below. At this speed we can expect *Pegasus* and *Renounce* to catch up with us by midday tomorrow. The *Blücher* will stand no chance!'

'Yes,' agreed Charles softly.

Summoned by *Bloodhound*'s frantic radio transmissions, *Pegasus* and *Renounce*, the two heavy cruisers of the northern squadron, were racing down the East African coast, cutting through the five hundred miles of water that separated them.

– 46 –

'Kyller. Ask the chief how he's making out.' Von Kleine was fretting beneath the calm set of his features. Night was closing, and in the darkness, even the frail little English destroyer was a danger to him. There was danger all around, danger must each minute be approaching from every quarter of the sea. He must have power on his port side engine before nightfall; it was a matter of survival; he must have speed to carry him south through the hunting packs of the British – south to where *Esther* waited to give him succour, to replace the shell he had fired away, to replenish his coal bunkers which were now dangerously depleted. Then once more *Blücher* would be a force to reckon with. But first he must have speed.

'Captain.' Kyller was beside him again. 'Commander Lochtkamper reports they have cleared the oil line to the main bearing. They have stripped the bearing and there is no damage to the shaft. He is fitting new half shells. The work is well advanced, sir.'

The words conjured up for von Kleine a picture of half-naked men, smeared to the elbows with black grease, sweating in the confined heat of the drive shaft tunnel as they worked. 'How much longer?' he asked.

'He promised full power on both engines within two hours, sir.'

Von Kleine sighed with relief, and glanced over his stern at the British destroyer that was shadowing him. He began to smile.

'I hope, my friend, that you are a brave man. I hope that when you see me increase speed, you will not be able to control your disappointment. I hope tonight you will try with your torpedoes, so that I can crush you, for your eyes always on me are a dangerous embarrassment.' He spoke so softly that his lips barely moved, then he turned back to Kyller. 'I want all the battle lights checked and reported.'

'Aye, aye, sir.'

Von Kleine crossed to the voice-tubes. 'Gunnery officer,' he said. 'I want "X" turret guns loaded with star shell and trained to maximum elevation . . .' He went on listing his preparations for night action and then he ended, '. . . stand all your gun crews down. Let them eat and rest. From dusk action stations onwards they will be held in the first degree of readiness.'

'Commander, sir!'

The urgent call startled Commander Charles Little, and he spilled his mug of cocoa. This was the first period of rest he had allowed himself all day, and now it was interrupted within ten minutes. 'What is it?' He flung open the door of the chart room, and ran out on to the bridge.

'*Blücher* is increasing speed rapidly.'

'No!' It was too cruel a blow, and the exclamation of protest was wrung from Charles. He darted to the voice-pipe.

'Gunnery officer. Report your target.'

A moment's delay, and then the reply. 'Bearing mark, green oh-oh. Range, one-five-oh-five-oh. Speed, seventeen knots.'

It was true. *Blücher* was under full power again, with all her guns still operable. *Orion* had died in vain.

Charles wiped his mouth with the open palm of his hand, and felt the brittle stubble of his new beard rasp under his fingers. Beneath the tan, his face was sickly pale with strain and fatigue. There were smears of dark blue beneath his eyes, and in their corners were tiny lumps of yellow mucus. His eyes were bloodshot, and the wisp of hair that escaped from under the brim of his cap was matted on to his forehead by the salt spray, as he peered into the gathering dusk.

The fighting madness which had threatened all that day to overwhelm him, rose slowly from the depth of his belly and his loins. He no longer struggled to suppress it.

'Turn two points to starboard, pilot. All engines full ahead together.' The engine telegraph clanged, and *Bloodhound* pivoted like a polo pony. It would take her thirty minutes to work up to full speed, and by that time it would be dark.

'Sound action stations.' Charles wanted to attack in the hour of darkness before the moon came up. Through the ship the alarm bells thrilled, and without taking his eyes from the dark dot on the darkening horizon, Charles listened to the reports coming into the bridge, until the one for which he waited, 'Torpedo party closed up, sir!'

Now he turned and went to the voice-tube. 'Torps,' he said, 'I hope to give you a chance at *Blücher* with both port

227

and starboard tubes. I am going to take you in as close as possible.'

The men grouped around Charles on the bridge listened to him say 'as close as possible', and knew that he had pronounced sentence of death upon them.

Henry Sargent, the navigating lieutenant, was afraid. Stealthily he groped in the pocket of his overcoat until he found the little silver crucifix that Lynette had given him. It was warm from his own body heat. He held it tightly.

He remembered it hanging between her breasts on its silver chain, and the way she had lifted both hands to the back of her neck as she unclasped it. The chain had caught in the shiny cascade of hair as she had tried to free it, kneeling on the bed facing him. He had leaned forward to help her, and she had clung to him, pressing the warm smooth bulge of her pregnant stomach against him.

'God protect you, my darling husband,' she had whispered. 'Please God bring you back safely to us.'

And now he was afraid for her and the daughter he had never seen.

'Hold your course, damn you!' he snapped at Herbert Cryer, the helmsman.

'Aye, aye, sir,' Herbert Cryer replied with just a trace of injured innocence in his tone. No man could hold *Bloodhound* true when she hurled herself from swell to swell with such abandoned violence, she must yaw and throw her head that fraction before the helm could correct her. The reprimand was unjustified, uttered in fear and tension. 'Give it a flipping break, mate,' Herbert retorted silently. 'You're not the only one who is going to catch it. Tighten up the old arsehole like a bloody officer and a ruddy gentleman.'

In these wordless exchanges of repartee with his officers, Herbert Cryer was never bested. They were wonderful release for resentments and pent-up emotion, and now because he was also afraid, he became silently lyrical.

'Climb-aboard-Romeo's one-way express to flipping glory.' Commander Little's reputation with the ladies had resulted in him being irreverently but affectionately baptized by his crew. 'Come along with us. We're off to shout at the devil, while Charlie kisses his daughter.'

Herbert glanced sideways at his commander and grinned. Fear made the grin wolfish, and Charles Little saw it and misinterpreted it. He read it as a mark of the same berserk fury that possessed him. The two of them grinned at each other for an instant in complete misunderstanding, before Herbert refocused his attention on *Bloodhound*'s next wild crabbing lunge.

Charles was afraid as well. He was afraid of finding a weakness in himself – but this was the fear that had walked at his right hand all his life, close beside him, whispering to him, 'Harder, try harder. You must do it better, you must do it quicker, or bigger than they do, or they'll laugh at you. You mustn't fail – not in one thing, not for one moment, you mustn't fail. You mustn't fail!' This fear was the eternal companion and partner in every venture on which he embarked.

It had stood beside the thirteen-year-old Charles in a duck blind, while he fired a twelve-gauge shotgun, and wept slow fat tears of agony every time the recoil smashed into his bruised bicep and shoulder.

It had stooped over him as he lay in the mud hugging a broken collar bone. 'Get up!' it hissed at him. 'Get up!' It had forced him to his feet and led him back to the unbroken colt to mount again, and again, and again.

So conditioned was he to respond to its voice that when it crouched beside him now, twisted and misshapen on the footplates of the bridge, its presence almost tangible, and croaked so Charles alone could hear it, 'Prove it!' Prove it!'

there was only one course open to Charles Little; a peregrine stooping at a golden eagle, he took his ship in against the *Blücher*.

– 47 –

'The turn to starboard was a feint.' Otto von Kleine spoke with certainty, staring out to where the dusk had obliterated the frail silhouette of the English destroyer. 'Even now he is turning again to cross our stern. He will attack on our port side.'

'Captain, it could be the double bluff,' Kyller answered dubiously.

'No.' Von Kleine shook his golden beard. 'He must try to outline us against the last of the light from the sunset. He will attack from the east.' A moment longer he frowned in thought, as he anticipated his opponent's moves across the chessboard of the ocean. 'Kyller, plot me his course, assuming a speed of twenty-five knots, a turn four points to port three minutes after our last sighting, a run of fifteen miles across our stern, and then a turn of four points to starboard. If we hold our present course and speed, where will he be in relation to us, in ninety minutes' time?'

Working quickly, Kyller completed the problem. Von Kleine had been mentally checking every step of the calculation. 'Yes,' he agreed with Kyller's solution, and already he had formulated the orders for change of course and speed to place *Bloodhound* in ambush.

48

U nder full power, *Bloodhound* threw a bow-wave ten feet high, and a wake that boiled out for a quarter of a mile behind her, a long, faintly phosphorescent smear in the darkness.

Aboard *Blücher* a hundred pairs of eyes were straining out into the night, watching for that phosphorescence. Behind the battle lights on her upperworks men waited, in the dimly-lit turrets men waited, on the open bridge, at the masthead, deep in her belly, the crew of *Blücher* waited.

Von Kleine had reduced speed to lessen his own wake, and turned away from the land at an angle of forty-five degrees. He wanted to catch the Englishman on his starboard beam, out of torpedo range.

He stood peering out across the dark sea, with the fur-lined collar of his overcoat drawn up to his ears. The night was cool. The sea was a black immensity, vast as the sky that was lined in glowing ivory by the whorls and smears of the star patterns.

A dozen men saw it at the same instant; pale, ethereal, seeming to float upon the darkness of the sea like a plume of iridescent mist – the wake of the Englishman.

'Star shell!' Von Kleine snapped the order to the waiting guns. He was alarmed by the English destroyer's proximity. He had hoped to spot her at greater range.

High above the ocean, the star shells burst blue-white, so intensely bright as to sear the retina of the eye that looked directly at them. Beneath them the surface of the sea was polished ebony, sculptured and scooped with the pattern of the swells. The two ships were starkly and crisply lit, steaming on converging courses, already so close to each other that the mile-long, solid white beams of their battle lights jumped out to join, fumbling together like the hands of hesitant lovers.

In almost the same second both ships opened fire, but the banging of *Bloodhound*'s little 4.7-inch guns was lost in the bellow of the cruiser's broadside.

Blücher was firing over open sights with her guns depressed until the long barrels were horizontal to the surface of the sea. Her first salvo was aimed a fraction high, and the huge shells howled over *Bloodhound*'s open bridge.

The wind of their passage, the fierce draught of disrupted air they threw out, caught Charles Little and sent him reeling against the compass pinnacle. He felt the ribs below his armpit crack.

The command he shouted at the helm was hoarse with pain.

'Turn four points to port! Steer for the enemy!' and *Bloodhound* spun like a ballet dancer, and charged straight at *Blücher*.

The cruiser's next broadside was high again but now her secondary armament had joined in, and a four-pound shell from one of the quick-firing pom-poms burst on the director tower above *Bloodhound*'s bridge. It swept the exposed area with a buzzing hailstorm of shrapnel.

It killed the navigating lieutenant instantly, cutting away the top of his head as though it were the shell of a soft-boiled egg. He fell on the deck and splattered the footplates with the warm custard of his brains.

A piece of the red-hot shell casing, the size of a thumb-nail, entered the point of Herbert Cryer's right elbow and shattered the bone to splinters. He gasped at the shock and sprawled against the wheel.

'Hold her. Hold her true!' The order from Commander Little was blurred as the speech of a spastic. Herbert Cryer pulled himself up and with his left hand spun the wheel to meet *Bloodhound*'s wild swing, but with his right arm hanging useless, his steering was clumsy and awkward.

'Steady her, man. Hold her steady!' Again that thick slurring voice, and Cryer was aware of Charles Little beside him, his hands on the helm, helping to hold *Bloodhound*'s frantic head.

'Aye, aye, sir.' Cryer glanced at his commander and gasped again. This time in horror. Razor-sharp steel had sliced off Charles Little's ear, then gone on to cut his cheek away, and expose the bone of his jaw and the white teeth that lined it. A flap of tattered flesh hung down on to his chest, and from a dozen severed blood vessels dark blood dripped and spurted and dribbled.

The two of them crouched wounded over the wheel, with the dead men at their feet, and aimed *Bloodhound* at the long low bulk of the German cruiser.

Now in the daylight glare of the star shells, the sea around them was thrashed and whipped into seething life by the cacophony of *Blücher*'s guns. Tall towers of white water rose briefly and majestically about them, then dropped back to leave the surface troubled and restless with foam.

And *Bloodhound* drove on until suddenly it seemed she had run into a cliff of solid granite. Beneath their feet, she jarred and bucked violently. A nine-inch shell had taken her full in the bows.

'Port full rudder.' Charles Little's voice was sloshy sounding, wet with the blood that filled his mouth, and together they spun the wheel to full left lock.

But *Bloodhound* was dying. The shell had split her bows wide open, torn her plating and fanned it open like the petals of a macabre orchid. The black night sea rushed through her. Already her bows were sinking, slumping wearily, lifting her stern so the rudder no longer had full purchase. But even in death she was trying desperately to obey. Slowly she swung, inchingly, achingly, she swung.

Charles Little left the helm and tottered towards the starboard rail. His legs were numb and heavy under him, and the weakness of his lost blood drummed in his ears. He reached the rail and clung there, peering down on the torpedo tubes that stood on the deck below him.

The tubes looked like a rack of fat cigars, and with weary jubilation Charles saw that there were men still tending them, crouching behind the sheet of armour plate, waiting for *Bloodhound* to turn and bring *Blücher* on to her starboard beam.

'Turn, old girl. Come on! That's it! Turn!' Charles croaked through the blood.

Another shell struck *Bloodhound*, and she heaved in mortal agony. Perhaps this movement, combined with a chance push of the sea swell, was enough to swing her those last few degrees.

There, full in the track of the torpedo tubes, lit by her own star shells and the gun-fire from her turrets, a scant thousand yards across the black water, lay the German cruiser.

Charles heard the whoosh, whoosh, whoosh, whoosh, of the tubes as they fired. He saw the long sharklike shapes of the torpedoes leap out from the deck and strike the water, saw the four white wakes arrowing away in formation, and behind him he heard the torpedo officer's triumphant shout, distorted by the voice-pipe.

'All four fired, and running true!'

Charles never saw his torpedoes strike, for one of *Blücher*'s nine-inch shells hit the bridgework three feet below him. For one brief unholy instant, he stood in the centre of a furnace as hot as the flames of the sun.

49

Otto von Kleine watched the English destroyer explode. Towering orange flames erupted from her, and a solid ball of black smoke spun upon itself, blooming on the dark ocean like a flower from the gardens of hell. The surface of the sea around her was dimpled by the fall of thrown debris and the cruiser's shells – for all of *Blücher*'s guns were still blazing.

'Cease fire,' he said, without taking his eyes from the awesome pageant of destruction that he had created.

Another salvo of star shell burst above, and von Kleine lifted his hand to his eyes and pressed his thumb and forefinger into the closed lids, shielding them from the stabbing brilliance of the light. It was finished, and he was tired.

He was tired, drained of nervous and physical energy, overwhelmed by the backwash of fatigue that followed these last two days and nights of ceaseless strain. And he was sad – sad for the brave men he had killed, and the terrible destruction he had wrought.

Still holding his eyes, he opened his mouth to give the order that would send *Blücher* once more thrashing southward, but before the words reached his lips, a wild shout from the look-out interrupted him.

'Torpedoes! Close on the starboard beam!'

Long seconds von Kleine hesitated. He had let his brain relax, let the numbness wash over it. The battle was over, and he had dropped back from the high pinnacle of alertness on which he had balanced these last desperate hours. It needed a conscious physical effort to call up his reserves, and during those seconds, the torpedoes fired by *Bloodhound* in her death throes were knifing in to revenge her.

At last von Kleine snapped the bonds of inertia that

bound his mind. He leaped to the starboard rail of the bridge, and saw in the light of the star shells the pale phosphorescent trails of the four torpedoes. Against the dark water they looked like the tails of meteors on a night sky.

'Full port rudder. All engines full astern together!' he shouted, his voice pitched high with consternation.

He felt his ship swerve beneath him, thrown violently over as the great propellers clawed at the sea to hold her from crossing the path of the torpedoes.

Hopelessly he stood and reviled himself. *I should have anticipated this. I should have known the destroyer had fired.*

Helplessly he stood and watched the four white lines drawn swiftly across the surface towards him.

In the last moments he felt a fierce upward surge of hope. Three of the English torpedoes would miss. That was certain. They would cross *Blücher*'s bows as she side-stepped. And the fourth torpedo it was just possible would miss also.

His fingers upon the bridge rail clenched, until it felt as though they must press into the metal. His breath jammed in his throat and choked him.

Ponderously, *Blücher* swung her bows away. If he had given the order for the turn only five seconds earlier . . .

The torpedo struck *Blücher* five feet below the surface, on the very tip of her curved keel.

The explosion shot a mountain of white water one hundred and fifty feet into the air. It slammed *Blücher* back onto her haunches with such violence that Otto von Kleine and his officers were thrown heavily to the steel deck.

Von Kleine scrabbled to his knees and looked forward. A fine veil of spray, like pearl dust in the light of the star shells, hung over *Blücher*. As he watched, it subsided slowly.

*

All that night they struggled to keep *Blücher* afloat.

They sealed off her bows with the five-inch steel doors in the watertight bulkhead, and behind those doors they locked thirty German seamen whose battle stations were in the bows. At intervals during the frenzied activity of the night, von Kleine had visions of those men floating face-down in the flooded compartments.

While the pumps clanged throughout the ship to free her of the hundreds of tons of sea-water that washed through her, von Kleine left the bridge and, with his engineer commander and damage control officer, they listed the injuries that *Blücher* had received.

In the dawn they assembled grimly in the chart-room behind the bridge, and assessed their plight.

'What power can you give me, Lochtkamper?' von Kleine demanded of his engineer.

'I can give you as much as you ask.' A reddish-purple bruise covered half the engineer's face where he had been thrown against a steam cock-valve when the torpedo struck. 'But anything over five knots will carry away the watertight bulkheads forward. They will take the full brunt of the sea.'

Von Kleine swivelled his stool, and looked at the damage control officer. 'What repairs can you effect at sea?'

'None, sir. We have braced and propped the watertight bulkhead. We have patched and jammed the holes made by the British cruiser's guns. But I can do nothing about the underwater damage without a dry dock – or calm water where I can put divers over the side. We must enter a port.'

Von Kleine leaned back on his stool and closed his eyes to think.

The only friendly port within six thousand miles was Dar es Salaam, the capital of German East Africa, but he knew the British were blockading it. He discarded it from his list of possible refuges.

An island? Zanzibar? – The Seychelles? – Mauritius? – All hostile territories with no anchorage safe from bombardment by a British squadron.

A river mouth? The Zambezi? No, that was in Portuguese territory, navigable for only the first few miles of its length.

Suddenly he opened his eyes. There was one ideal haven situated in German territory, navigable even by a ship of *Blücher*'s tonnage for twenty miles. It was guarded from overland approach by formidable terrain, yet he could call upon the German Commissioner for stores and labour and protection.

'Kyller,' he said. 'Plot me a course for the Kikunya mouth of the Rufiji delta.'

Five days later the *Blücher* crawled painfully as a crippled centipede into the northernmost channel of the Rufiji delta. She was blackened with battle smoke, her rigging hung in tatters, and at a thousand places shell splinters had pierced her upperworks. Her bows were swollen and distorted, and the sea washed through her forward compartments and then boiled and spilled out of the ghastly rents in her plating.

As she passed between the forests of mangroves that lined the channel, they seemed to enfold her like welcoming arms.

Overside she lowered two picket boats and these darted ahead of her like busy little water beetles as they sounded the channel, and searched for a secure anchorage. Gradually *Blücher* wriggled and twisted her way deeper and deeper into the wilderness of the delta. At a place where the flood waters of the Rufiji had cut a deep bay between two islands, and formed a natural jetty on both sides, the *Blücher* came to rest.

50

Herman Fleischer wiped his face and neck with a hand towel and then looked at the sodden material. God, how he hated the Rufiji basin. As soon as he entered its humid and malodorous heat, a thousand tiny taps opened under his skin and out gushed the juices of his body.

The prospect of an extended stay aroused in him a dark resentment for all things, but especially to this young snob who stood beside him on the foredeck of the steam launch. Herman darted a glance at him now. Cool he looked, as though he were sauntering down Unter den Linden in June. The shimmering white of his tropical uniform was unwrinkled and dry, not like the thick corduroy that bunched damply at Herman's armpits and crotch. Mother of a dog, it would start the rash again; he could feel it beginning to itch and he scratched at it moodily, then checked his hand as he saw the lieutenant smile.

'How far are we from *Blücher*?' and then as an afterthought he used the lieutenant's surname without rank, 'How far, Kyller?' It was as well to keep reminding the man that as the equivalent of a full colonel, he far outranked him.

'Around the next bend, Commissioner.' Kyller's voice carried the lazy inflection that made Fleischer think of champagne and opera houses, of skiing parties, and boar hunts. 'I hope that Captain von Kleine has made adequate preparation to defend her against enemy attack?'

'She is safe.' For the first time there was a brittle undertone to Kyller's reply, and Fleischer pounced on it. He sensed an advantage. For the last two days, ever since Kyller had met him at the confluence of the Ruhaha river, Herman had been needling him to find a weakness.

'Tell me, Kyller,' he dropped his voice to an intimate,

confidential level. 'This is in strict confidence, of course, but do you really feel that Captain von Kleine is able to handle this situation? I mean, do you feel that someone else might have been able to reach a more satisfactory result?' Ah! Yes! That was it! Look at him flush, look at the anger stain those cool brown cheeks. For the first time the advantage was with Herman Fleischer.

'Commissioner Fleischer,' Kyller spoke softly but Herman exulted to hear his tone. 'Captain von Kleine is the most skilful, efficient, and courageous officer under which I have had the honour to serve. He is, furthermore, a gentleman.'

'So?' Herman grunted. 'Then why is this paragon hiding in the Rufiji basin with his buttocks shot full of holes?' Then he threw back his head and guffawed in triumph.

'At another time, sir, and in different circumstances, I would ask you to withdraw those words.' Kyller turned from him and walked to the forward rail. He stood there staring ahead, while the launch chugged around another bend in the river, opening the same dreary vista of dark water and mangrove forest. Kyller spoke without turning his head. 'There is the *Blücher*,' he said.

There was nothing but the sweep of water and the massed fuzzy heads of the mangroves below a hump of higher ground upon the bank. The laughter faded from Herman's chubby face as he searched, then a small scowl replaced it as he realized that the lieutenant was baiting him. There was certainly no battle cruiser anchored in the water-way. 'Lieutenant . . .' he began angrily, then checked himself. The high ground was divided by a narrow channel, not more than a hundred yards wide, fenced in by the mangrove forest, but the channel was blocked by a shapeless and ungainly mound of vegetation. He stared at it uncomprehendingly until suddenly beneath the netting that was festooned with branches of mangroves, he saw the blurred outline of turrets and superstructure.

The camouflage had been laid with fascinating ingenuity. From a distance of three hundred yards the *Blücher* was invisible.

– 51 –

The bubbles came up slowly through the dark water as though it had the same viscosity as warm honey. They burst on the surface in a boiling white rash.

Captain von Kleine leaned across the foredeck rail of the *Blücher* and peered at the disturbance below him, with the absorption of a man attempting to read his own future in the murky mirror of the Rufiji waters. For almost two hours he had waited like this, drawing quietly on a succession of little black cheroots, occasionally easing his body into a more comfortable position.

Although his body was at rest, his brain was busy, endlessly reviewing his preparations and his plans. His preparations were complete, he had mentally listed them and found no omissions.

A party of six seamen had been despatched fifteen miles downstream by picket boat to the entrance of the delta. They were encamped on a hummock of high ground above the channel to watch the sea for the British blockade squadron.

As *Blücher* crept up the channel she had sown the last of her globular multi-horned mines behind her. No British ship could follow her.

Remote as the chances of overland attack seemed, yet von Kleine had set up a system of defence around the *Blücher*. Half his seamen were ashore now, spread in a network to guard each of the possible approaches. Fields of fire had been cut through the mangroves for his Maxim guns. Crude fortifications of log and earth had been built and manned, communication lines set up, and he was ready.

After long discussions with his medical officer, von Kleine had issued orders to protect the health of his men. Orders for the purification of water, the disposal of sanitation and waste, for the issue of five grains of quinine daily to each man, and fifty other safeguards to health and morale.

He had ordered an inventory made of stocks of food and supplies, and he was satisfied that with care he could subsist for a further four months. Thereafter he would be reduced to fishing and hunting, and foraging.

He had despatched Kyller upstream to make contact with the German Commissioner, and solicit his full cooperation.

Four days had been spent in hiding the *Blücher* under her camouflage, in setting up a complete workshop on the foredeck under sun awnings, so that the engineers could work in comparative comfort.

Now at last they had begun a full underwater appraisal of *Blücher*'s wounds.

Behind him he heard the petty officer pass an order to the team at the winch. 'Bring him up – slowly.'

The donkey engine spluttered into life, and the winch clattered and whined shrilly. Von Kleine stirred against the rail and focused his full attention on the water below him.

The heavy line and airpipe reeled in smoothly, then suddenly the surface bulged and the body of the diver was lifted dangling on the line. Black in shiny wet rubber, the three brass-bound cyclopean eyes of his helmet glaring, grotesque as a sea monster, he was swung inboard and lowered to the deck.

Two seamen hurried forward and unscrewed the bolts at the neck, lifted off the heavy helmet, and exposed the head of the engineering commander, Lochtkamper. The heavy face, flat and lined as that of a mastiff, was made heavier than usual by the thoughtful frown it now wore. He looked across at his captain and shook his head slightly.

'Come to my cabin when you are ready, Commander,' said von Kleine, and walked away.

'A small glass of cognac?' von Kleine suggested.

'I'd like that, sir.' Commander Lochtkamper looked out of place in the elegance of the cabin. The hands that accepted the glass were big, knuckles scarred and enlarged by constant violent contact with metal, the skin etched deeply with oil and engine filth. When he sank into the chair at his captain's invitation, his legs seemed to have too many knees.

'Well?' asked von Kleine, and Lochtkamper launched into his report. He spoke for ten minutes and von Kleine followed him slowly through the maze of technicalities where strange and irrelevant obscenities grew along the way. In moments of deep concentration such as these Lochtkamper fell back on the gutter idiom of his native Hamburg, and von Kleine was unable to suppress a smile when he learned that the copulatory torpedo had committed a perversion on one of the main frames, springing the plating whose morals were definitely suspect. The damage sounded like that suffered in a brothel during a Saturday night brawl.

'Can you repair it?' von Kleine asked at last.

'It will mean cutting away all the obscenely damaged plating, lifting it to the deck, recutting it, welding and shaping it. But we will still be short of at least eight hundred obscene square feet of plate, sir.'

'A commodity not readily obtainable in the delta of the Rufiji river,' von Kleine mused.

'No, sir.'

'How long will it take you – if I can get the plating for you?'

'Two months, perhaps.'

'When can you start?'

'Now, sir.'

'Do it then,' said von Kleine, and Lochtkamper drained his glass, smacked his lips, and stood up. 'Very good cognac, sir,' he complimented his captain, and shambled out of the cabin.

– 52 –

Staring upward at the massive warship, Herman Fleischer surveyed the battle damage with the uncomprehending curiosity of a landsman. He saw the gaping ulcers where *Orion*'s shells had struck, the black blight where the flames had raged through her, the irregular rash with which the splinters had pierced and peppered her upperworks, and then he dropped his eyes to the bows. Work cradles were suspended a few feet above the water, and upon them clutters of seamen were illuminated by the crackling blue glare of the welding torches.

'God in heaven, what a beating!' He spoke with sadistic relish.

Kyller ignored the remark. He was directing the native helmsman of the launch to the landing ladder that had been rigged down the side of *Blücher*. Not even the presence of this sweaty peasant, Fleischer, could spoil his pleasure in this moment of homecoming. To Ernst Kyller, the *Blücher* was home in the deep sense of the word; it contained all that he valued in life, including the man for whom he bore a devotion surpassing the natural duty of a son to his father.

He was savouring the anticipation of von Kleine's smile and words of commendation for another task well done.

'Ah, Kyller!' Von Kleine rose from behind his desk and moved around it to greet his lieutenant.

'Back so soon? Did you find Fleischer?'

'He is waiting outside, sir.'

'Good, good. Bring him in.'

Herman Fleischer paused in the companion-way and blinked suspiciously around the cabin. His mind was automatically converting the furnishings into Reichsmarks, the rugs were silk Teheran in blue and gold and red, the chairs were in dark buttoned leather, all the heavy furniture, including the panelling, was polished mahogany. The light fittings were worked in brass, the glasses in the liquor cabinet were sparkling diamond crystal flanked by a platoon of bottles that wore the uniforms of the great houses of Champagne and Alsace and the Rhine. There was a portrait in oils opposite the desk of two women, both beautiful golden women, clearly mother and daughter. The portholes were curtained with forest-green velvet, corded and tasselled in gold.

Herman decided that the Count must be a rich man. He had a proper respect for wealth, and it showed in the way he stepped forward, drew himself up, brought his heels together sharply, and then creased his bulging belly in a bow.

'Captain. I came as soon as I received your message.'

'I am grateful, Commissioner.' Von Kleine returned the salutation. 'You will take refreshment?'

'A glass of beer, and ...' Herman hesitated, he was certain that somewhere aboard *Blücher* there must be a treasure trove of rare foods, '... a bite to eat. I have not eaten since noon.'

It was now the middle of the afternoon. Von Kleine saw

nothing unusual in a two-hour period of abstinence, yet he passed the word for his steward while he opened a bottle of beer for his guest.

'I must congratulate you on your victory over the two English warships, Captain. Magnificent, truly magnificent!'

Lying back in one of the leather chairs Fleischer was engaged in mopping his face and neck, and Kyller grinned cynically as he listened to this new tune.

'A victory that was dearly bought,' murmured von Kleine, bringing the glass to Fleischer's chair. 'And now I need your help.'

'Of course! You need only ask.'

Von Kleine went to his desk, sat down and drew towards him a sheaf of notes. From their chamois leather case, he produced a pair of gold-rimmed spectacles and placed them on his nose.

'Commissioner . . .' he started, but at that moment he completely lost Fleischer's attention. For with a discreet knock the Captain's steward returned with a large, heavily laden carving-plate. He placed it on the table beside Fleischer's chair.

'Sweet Mother of God!' whispered Herman, his eyes glittering, and a fresh sweat of excitement breaking out on his upper lip.

'Smoked salmon!'

Neither von Kleine nor Kyller had ever been privileged to watch Herman eat before. They did so now in awed silence. This was a specialist working with skill and dedication. After a while von Kleine made another effort to attract Herman's attention by coughing and rustling his sheaf of notes, but the Commissioner's snufflings and small moans of sensual pleasure continued. Von Kleine glanced at his lieutenant and lifted a golden eyebrow, Kyller half smiled in embarrassment. It was like watching a man in orgasm, so intimate that von Kleine was obliged to light a cheroot and concentrate his attention on the portrait of his wife and daughter across the cabin.

A gusty sigh signalled Herman's climax, and von Kleine looked at him again. He sagged back in the chair, a vague and dreamy smile playing over the ruddy curves of his face. The plate was empty, and with the sweet sorrow of a man remembering a lost love, Herman dabbed a forefinger on to the last shred of pink flesh and lifted it to his mouth.

'That was the best salmon I have ever tasted.'

'I am pleased that you found it so.' Von Kleine's voice crackled a little. He felt slightly nauseated by the exhibition.

'I wonder if I might trouble you for another glass of beer, Captain.'

Von Kleine nodded at Kyller, and the lieutenant went to refill Fleischer's glass.

'Commissioner. I need at least eight hundred square feet of $1\frac{1}{2}$-inch steel plate delivered to me here. I want it within six weeks,' von Kleine said, and Herman Fleischer laughed. He laughed the way a man laughs at a children's tale of fairies and witches, then suddenly he noticed von Kleine's eyes . . . and he stopped abruptly.

'Lying in Dar es Salaam harbour under British blockade is the steamer *Rheinlander*.' Von Kleine went on speaking softly and clearly. 'You will proceed there as fast as you can. I will send one of my engineers with you. He will beach the *Rheinlander* and dismantle her hull. You will then arrange to convey the plating to me here.'

'Dar es Salaam is one hundred kilometres away.' Herman was aghast.

'According to the Admiralty chart it is seventy-five kilometres,' von Kleine corrected him.

'The plating will weigh many tons!' he cried.

'In German East Africa there are many hundreds of thousands of indigenes. I doubt not that you will be able to persuade them to serve as porters.'

'The route is impossible . . . and what is more, there is a band of enemy guerrillas operating in the area north of here. Guerrillas led by those same bandits that you allowed to escape from the dhow, off the mouth of this river.' In agitation Fleischer had risen from his chair and now he pointed a fat accusing forefinger at von Kleine. 'You allowed them to escape. Now they are ravaging the whole province. If I try to bring a heavily laden, slow moving caravan of porters down from Dar es Salaam, word will reach them before I have marched five kilometres. It's madness – I won't do it!'

'It seems then, that you have a choice.' Von Kleine smiled with his mouth only. 'The English marauders, or a firing party on the afterdeck of this ship.'

'What do you mean?' howled Fleischer.

'I mean that my request is no longer a request, it is now an order. If you defy it, I will immediately convene a court martial.'

Von Kleine drew his gold watch and checked the time.

'We should be able to dispose of the formalities and shoot you before dark. What do you think, Kyller?'

'It will be cutting things fine, sir. But I think we could manage it.'

– 53 –

When the Governor of Mozambique had offered Flynn a captaincy in the army of Portugal, there had been an ugly scene. Flynn felt strongly that he deserved at least the rank of colonel. He had suggested terminating their business relationship. The Governor had countered with an offer of major – and signalled to his aide-de-camp to refill Flynn's glass. Flynn had accepted both offers, but the one under protest. That was seven months ago, a few short weeks after the massacre at Lalapanzi.

Since then Flynn's army, a mixed bag of a hundred native troops, officered by himself, Sebastian and Rosa Oldsmith, had been operating almost continually in German territory.

There had been a raid on the Songea railway siding where Flynn had burned five hundred tons of sugar, and nearly a thousand of millet that was in the warehouses awaiting shipment to Dar es Salaam, supplies badly needed by Governor Schee and Colonel Lettow von Vorbeck who were assembling an army in the coastal area.

There had been another brilliant success when they had ambushed and wiped out a band of thirty Askari at a river crossing. Flynn released the three hundred native recruits that the Askari were escorting, and advised them to get the hell back to their villages and forsake any ambitions of military glory – using the corpses of the Askari that littered the banks of the ford as tangible argument.

Apart from cutting every telegraph line, and blowing up the railway tracks they came across, three other raids had met with mixed results. Twice they had captured supply columns of bearers carrying in provisions to the massing German forces. Each time they had been forced to run as German reinforcements came up to drive them off. The third effort had been an abject failure, the ignominy of it being compounded by the fact that they had almost had the person of Commissioner Fleischer in their grasp.

Carried on the swift feet of the runners who were part of Flynn's intelligence system came the news that Herman Fleischer and a party of Askari had left Mahenge boma and marched to the confluence of the Ruhaha and Rufiji rivers. There they had gone aboard the steam launch and disappeared into the fastness of the Rufiji delta on a mysterious errand.

'What goes up must come down,' Flynn pointed out to Sebastian. 'And what goes down the Rufiji must come up again. We will go to the Ruhaha and wait for Herr Fleischer to return.'

For once there was no argument from either Sebastian or Rosa. Between the three of them it was understood without discussion that Flynn's army existed chiefly to act as the vehicle of retribution. They had made a vow over the grave of the child, and now they fought not so much from a sense of duty or patriotism, but from a burning desire for revenge. They wanted the life of Herman Fleischer in part payment for that of Maria Oldsmith.

They set out for the Ruhaha river. As happened so often these days, Rosa marched at the head of the column. There was only the long braid of dark hair hanging down her back to show she was a woman, for she was dressed in bush jacket and long khaki cotton trousers that concealed the feminine fullness of her hips. She stepped out long-legged, and from her shoulder the loaded Mauser hung on its strap and bumped lightly against her flank at each pace.

The change in her was so startling as to leave Sebastian bewildered. The new hard line of her mouth, her eyes that gave off the dark hot glow of a fanatic, the voice that had lost the underlying ripple of laughter. She spoke seldom, but when she did, both Flynn and Sebastian were forced to hear her with respect. Sometimes listening to that flat deadly tone Sebastian could feel a prickle of horror under his skin.

They reached the landing-place and the jetty on the Ruhaha river and waited for the launch to return. It came three days later, heralding its approach by the soft chugging of its engine. When it came round the river bend, pushing briskly against the current, headed for the wooden jetty, they were lying in wait for it.

'There he is!' Sebastian's voice was thick with emotion as he recognized the plump grey-clad figure in the bows.

'The swine, oh, the bloody swine!' and he jerked the bolt of his rifle open then snapped it shut.

'Wait!' Rosa's hand closed on his wrist before he could lift the butt to his shoulder.

'I can get him from here!' protested Sebastian.

'No. I want him to see us. I want to tell him first. I want him to know why he must die.'

The launch swung in broadside to the current, losing its way, until it came in gently to nudge the jetty. Two of the Askari jumped ashore, laying back on the lines to hold her while the Commissioner disembarked.

Fleischer stood on the jetty for a minute, looking back down the river. This action should have warned Flynn, but he did not see its significance. Then the Commissioner shrugged slightly and trudged up the jetty towards the boat-house.

'Tell your men to drop their weapons into the river,' said Flynn in his best German as he stood up from the patch of reeds beside the jetty.

Herman Fleischer froze in mid-stride, but his belly quivered and his head turned slowly towards Flynn. His blue eyes seemed to spread until they filled his face, and he made a clucking noise in his throat.

'Tell them quickly, or I will shoot you through the stomach,' said Flynn, and Fleischer found his voice. He relayed Flynn's order to the Askari, and there were a series of splashes around the launch as it was obeyed.

Movement in the corner of his eye made Fleischer swing his head, and he was face to face with Rosa Oldsmith. Beyond her in a half circle stood Sebastian and a dozen armed Africans, but some instinct warned Fleischer that the woman was the danger. There was a merciless quality about her, some undefinable air of deadly purpose. It was to her he addressed his question.

'What do you want?' His voice was husky with apprehension.

'What did he say?' Rosa asked her father.

'He wants to know what you want.'

'Ask him if he remembers me.'

As he heard the question, Fleischer remembered her in her night-dress, kneeling in the fire-light, and with the memory came real fear.

'It was a mistake,' he whispered. 'The child! I did not order it.'

'Tell him . . .' said Rosa, 'tell him that I am going to kill him.' And her hands moved deliberately on the Mauser, slipping the safety-catch across, but her eyes never left his face.

'It was a mistake,' Herman repeated and he stepped backwards, lifting his hands to ward off the bullet that he knew must come.

At that moment Sebastian shouted behind Rosa, just one word.

'Look!'

Around the bend of the Ruhaha river, only two hundred yards from where they stood, another launch swept into view. It came silently, swiftly and at its stubby masthead flew the ensign of the German navy. There were men in crisp white uniforms clustered around the Maxim machine gun in its bows.

Flynn's party stared at it in complete disbelief. Its presence was as unbelievable as that of the Loch Ness monster in the Serpentine or a man-eating lion in St Paul's Cathedral, and in the long seconds that they stood paralysed the launch closed in quickly on the jetty.

Herman Fleischer broke the spell. He opened his mouth

and from the barrel of his chest issued a bellow that rang clearly across the water.

'Kyller, they are Englishmen!'

Then he moved, with three light steps he danced sideways, incredibly quickly he moved his gross body from under the threatening muzzle of Rosa's rifle and dived from the jetty into the dark green swirl of water below the boards.

The splash of his dive was immediately followed by the tack, tack, tack of the launch's machine gun – and the air was filled with the swishing crack of a hundred whips. The launch drove straight in towards them with the Maxim blazing on its prow. Around Flynn, and Rosa and Sebastian the earth erupted in a rapid series of dust fountains, a ricochet howled dementedly, one of the gun-boys spun on his heels in a brief dervish dance and then sprawled down the bank, with his rifle clattering on the wooden boards of the jetty, and the frozen party on the bank exploded into violent movement. Flynn and his black troopers ducked and dodged away up the bank, but Rosa ran forward. She reached the edge of the jetty unscathed through the hail-storm of Maxim fire, there she checked and aimed the Mauser at the wallowing body of Herman Fleischer in the water below her.

'You killed my baby!' Rosa shrieked, and Fleischer looked up at her and knew he was about to die. A Maxim bullet struck the metal of the rifle, tearing it from Rosa's hands, and she staggered off balance, her arms windmilling as she tottered on the edge of the jetty.

Sebastian reached her as she fell. He caught her and swung her up on to his shoulder, whirled with her and bounded away up the bank, running with all the reserves of his strength unlocked by the key of his terror.

With ten of the gun-boys Sebastian took the rearguard; for that day and the next they skirmished back along the line of the retreat, briefly holding each natural defensive point until the Germans brought up the Maxim gun. Then they dropped back, retreating slowly while Flynn and Rosa made a straight run of it. In the second night Sebastian broke contact with the pursuers and fled north towards the rendezvous at the stream below the ruins of Lalapanzi.

Forty-eight hours later he reached it. In the moonlight he staggered into the camp, and Rosa threw off her blankets and came running to him with a low joyous cry of greeting. She knelt before him, unlaced and gently drew off each of his boots. While Sebastian gulped the mug of coffee and hot gin that Flynn brewed for him, Rosa bathed and tended the blisters that had burst on his feet. Then she dried her hands, stood and picked up her blankets.

'Come,' she said, and together they walked away along the bank of the stream. Behind a curtain of hanging creepers, on a nest of dry grass and blankets, while the jewelled night sky glowed above them, they gave each other the comfort of their bodies for the first time since the death of the child. Afterwards they slept entwined until the low sun woke them. Then they rose and went down the bank together naked into the stream. The water was cold when she splashed him, and she giggled like a little girl and ran through the shallows across the sandbank with the water bursting in a sparkling spray around her legs, drops of it glittering like sequins on her skin, her waist was the neck of a Venetian vase flaring down into full double rounds on her lower body.

He chased and caught her and they fell together and knelt facing each other, spluttering and laughing, and with each gust of laughter her bosom jumped and bounced. Sebastian leaned forward with the laughter drying in his throat and cupped them in his hands.

Instantly her own laughter ceased, she looked at him a

moment, then suddenly her face hardened and she struck his hands away.

'No!' she hissed at him, and jumping to her feet she waded to where her clothing lay on the bank. Swiftly she covered her femininity, and as she strapped the heavy bandolier of ammunition around her body the last soft memory of their loving was gone from her face.

– 54 –

It was that stinking Rufiji water, Herman Fleischer decided, and moved painfully in his maschille as another cramp took him.

The hot hand of dysentery that closed on his stomach added to his mood of dark resentment. His present discomfort was directly linked to the arrival of *Blücher* in his territory, the indignities he had experienced at the hands of her captain, the danger he had run into in his brush with the English bandits at the start of this expedition, and since then the constant gruelling work and ever-present fear of another attack, the nagging of the engineer whom von Kleine had placed over him – he hated everything to do with that cursed warship, he hated every man aboard her.

The jogging motion of the maschille bearers stirred the contents of his belly, making it gurgle and squeak. He would have to stop again, and he looked ahead for a suitable place in which to find privacy.

Ahead of him the caravan of porters was toiling along the shallow bottom of a valley between two sparsely wooded ridges of shale and broken rock.

The column was spread out in an untidy straggle half a mile long, for it comprised just under a thousand men.

In the van a hundred of them, stripped to loin-cloths

and shiny with sweat, were wielding their long pangas on the scrub. The blades glinting as they rose and fell, the thudding of the blows muted in the lazy heat of afternoon. Working under the supervision of Gunther Raube, the young engineering officer from *Blücher*, they were cutting out the narrow track, widening it for the passage of the bulky objects that followed.

Dwarfing the men that swarmed around them, these four objects rolled slowly along, rocking and swaying over patches of uneven ground. Now and then halting as they came up against a tree stump or an outcrop of rock, before the animal exertions of two hundred black men could get them rolling again.

Three weeks previously they had beached the freighter *Rheinlander* in Dar es Salaam harbour and dismantled eight slabs of her plating. Then from the metal frames of her hull, Raube had shaped eight enormous wheel rims, fourteen feet in diameter; into each of these he had welded a sheet of $1\frac{1}{2}$-inch plating ten foot square. Using the freighter's bollards as axles, he had linked these eight discs in four pairs. Thus each of these contraptions looked like the wheel and axle assembly of a gigantic Roman chariot.

Herman Fleischer had made a swift recruitment tour, and secured nine hundred able-bodied volunteers from the town of Dar es Salaam and its outlying villages. These nine hundred were now engaged in trundling the four sets of wheels southward towards the Rufiji delta. While they worked, Herman's Askari stood by with loaded Mausers to discourage any of the volunteers from succumbing to an attack of homesickness; a malady which was fast reaching epidemic proportions, aggravated as it was by shoulders rubbed raw by contact with harsh sun-heated metal, and by palms whose outer layers of skin had been smeared away on the rough hemp ropes. They had been two weeks at their labours and they were still thirty torturous miles from the river.

Herman Fleischer squirmed again in his maschille as the amoebic dysentery gnawed at his guts.

'Mother of a pig!' he moaned, and then shouted at the bearers, 'Quickly, take me to those trees.' He pointed to a clump of wild ebony that smothered one of the side draws of the valley.

With alacrity, the maschille bearers swung off the path and trotted up the draw. Within the screen of wild ebony they paused while the Commissioner alighted from the hammock and hurried into the deepest recess of the bush to be alone. Then they drew themselves down with a communal sigh and gave themselves up to a session of African callisthenics.

When the Commissioner came out of retreat he was hungry. It was cool and restful in the shade, an ideal place to take his mid-afternoon snack. Raube would have to fend for himself for an hour or so. Herman nodded to his personal servant to set up the camp table and open the food box. His mouth was full of sausage when the first rifle shot clapped dully in the dusty dry air.

– 55 –

'Where is he? He must be here. The scouts said he was here. Can you see him?' Rosa Oldsmith spoke through lips that were chapped dry by sun and wind, white flakes of skin had come loose from the raw red patches of sunburn on her nose, and her eyes were bloodshot from the dust and the glare.

She lay on her stomach behind a bank of shale and coarse grass with the Mauser probing out in front of her.

'Can you see him?' she demanded again impatiently, turning her head towards her father.

Flynn grunted noncommittally, holding the binoculars to his eyes, panning them slowly down the length of the valley then back again to the head of the strange caravan.

'There is a white man there,' he said.

'Is it Fleischer, is it?'

'No,' doubtfully Flynn gave the negative. 'No, I don't think so.'

'Look for him. He must be there somewhere.'

'I wonder what the hell those things are.'

Flynn concentrated on the four huge sets of wheels. The lens of the binoculars magnified the heat distortion through the still air, making them change shape and size so that one second they were insignificant and the next they were monstrous.

'Look for Fleischer. Damn those things, look for Fleischer,' Rosa snapped at him.

'He's not with them.'

'He must be. He must be there.' Rosa rolled on her side and reached out to snatch the binoculars from Flynn's hands. Eagerly she scanned the long column that moved slowly towards them up the valley.

'He must be there. Please God, he must be there,' she whispered her hatred through cracked dry lips.

'We will have to attack soon. They are nearly in position now.'

'We must find Fleischer.' Desperately Rosa searched, her knuckles showing white through sun-brown skin as she clutched the binoculars.

'We can't let it go much longer. Sebastian is in position, he will be expecting my signal.'

'Wait! You must wait.'

'No. We can't let them get closer.' Flynn half lifted his body, and called softly.

'Mohammed! Are you ready?'

'We are ready.' The reply came from farther down the slope where the line of riflemen lay.

'Remember my words, oh, thou chosen of Allah. Kill the Askari first and the others will run.'

'Your words ring in my ears with the brightness and the beauty of golden bells,' Mohammed replied.

'Up yours!' said Flynn and unbuttoned the pocket flap of his tunic. He fumbled out the hand-mirror and held it slanted to catch the sun, deflecting a bright splinter of light towards the far slope of the valley. From the jumble of rock and bush there was an immediate answering flash as Sebastian acknowledged the signal.

'Ah!' Flynn breathed theatrical relief, 'I was afraid our Bassie might have fallen asleep over there.' And he picked up the Mauser from the rock in front of him.

'Wait,' pleaded Rosa. 'Please wait.'

'We can't. You know we can't – if Fleischer is down there then we'll get him. If he isn't, then waiting any longer isn't going to help us.'

'You don't care,' she accused. 'You have forgotten about Maria already.'

'No,' said Flynn. 'No, I haven't forgotten,' and he cuddled the Mauser into his shoulder. There was an Askari he had been watching. A big man who moved ahead of the column. Even at this range Flynn sensed that this man was dangerous. He moved with a leopard's slouching awareness, head cocked and alert.

Flynn picked him up in the notch of the rear sight and rode the pip down his body, aiming low to compensate for the downhill shot, taking him in the belly. He gathered the slack in the trigger, squeezing it up gently. The Mauser cracked viciously and the recoil jumped back into his shoulder.

Incredulously Flynn saw the bullet throw a jump of dust from the slope below the Askari. A clean miss at four hundred yards from a carefully aimed shot – By Christ, he was getting old.

Frantically he worked the bolt of the rifle, but already the Askari had ducked for cover, unslinging his rifle as he disappeared into a bank of grey thorn bush, and Flynn's next shot ripped ineffectively into the coarse dry vegetation.

'Damn it to hell!' howled Flynn, and his voice was small in the storm of gun-fire that blew around him. From both slopes all his riflemen were shooting down into the solid pack of humanity that clogged the valley floor.

For startled seconds the mass of native bearers stood quiescent under the lash of the Mausers, each man frozen in the attitude in which the attack had caught him; bent to the giant wheels, leaning forward against the ropes, panga raised to strike at a branch, or merely standing watching while others worked. Every head lifted to stare up at the slopes from which Flynn's hidden rifles menaced them, then with a sound like a rising wind a single voice climbed in a wail of terror, to be lost almost instantly in the babble from a thousand throats.

Without regard for Flynn's orders to single out only the armed Askari, his men were firing blindly into the mass of men around the wheels, bullets striking with a meaty thump, thump, thump, or whining from rock to inflict the ghastly secondary wounds of a ricochet.

Then the bearers broke. Flowing back like flood water along the valley, carrying the Askari whose khaki uniforms bobbed with them like driftwood in the torrent.

Beside Flynn in the donga, Rosa was firing also. Her hands on the rifle incongruously feminine, fingers long and sensitive working the bolt as though it were the shuttle of a loom, weaving death, her eyes slitted behind the gunsight, her lips barely moving as they formed the name which had become her battle hymn.

'Maria! Maria!' With each shot she said it softly.

As he fumbled a fresh clip of cartridges from his bandolier, Flynn glanced sideways at her. Even in this moment of hot excitement Flynn felt the prickle of disquiet as he saw his daughter's face. There was a madness in her eyes, the madness of grief too long sustained, the madness of hatred too carefully nourished.

His rifle was loaded and he switched his attention back to the valley. The scene had changed. From the rush of fear-crazed bearers, the German, whom Flynn had earlier watched through the binoculars, was rallying a defence. With him was the big Askari, the one that Flynn had missed with his first shot. These two stood to hold the guards who were being carried away on the rush of panic-stricken bearers, stopping them, turning them back, pushing and shoving them into defensive cover around the four huge wheels. Now they were returning the fire of Flynn's men.

'Mohammed! Get that man! The white man – get him!' roared Flynn, and fired twice, missing with each shot. But his bullets passed so close that the German dodged back behind the metal shield of the nearest wheel.

'That's done it,' lamented Flynn, as his hopes of quick success faded. 'They're getting settled in down there. We are going to have to prise them loose.'

The prospect was unattractive. Flynn had found from experience that while every man in his motley band was a hero when firing from ambush, and a master in the art of strategic retreat, yet their weak suit was frontal assault, or any other manoeuvre that involved exposure to the enemy. Of the hundred under his command, there were a dozen whom he could rely on to obey an order to attack. Flynn was understandably reluctant to issue such an order, for there are few situations more humiliating than bellowing, 'Charge!' – then having everybody look at you with a 'Who, me? You must be joking!' expression.

Now he steeled himself to do it, aware that with every second the battle madness of his men was cooling and being replaced by sanity and caution. He filled his lungs and opened his mouth, but Rosa saved him.

She rolled and lifted her knees, coming on to her feet with one fluid motion whose continuation was a catlike leap that carried her over the shale bank and into the open. Boyish, big-hipped, but graceful – the rifle across her hip, firing. Long hair streaming, long legs flying, she went down the slope.

'Rosa!' roared Flynn in consternation, and jumped up to chase her in an ungainly lumbering run like the charge of an old bull buffalo.

'Fini!' shouted Mohammed, and scampered after his master.

'My goodness!' Sebastian gasped where he lay on the opposite side of the valley. 'It's Rosa!' and in a completely reflex response he found himself on his feet and bounding down the rocky slope.

'Akwende!' yelled the man beside him, carried away in his excitement, and before any of them had time to think, fifty of them were up and following. After the first half-dozen paces they were committed, for once they had started to run down the steep incline they could not stop without falling flat on their faces, they could only accelerate.

Down both slopes of the valley, scrambling, sliding on loose stone, pell-mell through thorn bush, screaming, shouting, they poured down on the cluster of Askari around the wheels.

From opposite sides, Rosa and Sebastian were first to reach the perimeter of the German position. Their momentum carried them unscathed through the first line of the defenders, and then with the empty rifle in her hands Rosa ran chest to chest against the big Askari who rose from behind a boulder to meet her. She shrieked as he caught her, and the sound exploded within Sebastian's brain in a red burst of fury.

Twenty yards away Rosa struggled with the man, but she was helpless as a baby in his arms. He lifted her, changing his grip on her body, snatching her up above his head, steadying himself to hurl her down on to the pointed rock behind which he had hidden. There was such animal power in the bunched muscles of his arms, in the thick sweat-slimy neck, in the muscular straddled legs, that Sebastian knew that when he dashed Rosa against the rock he would kill her. Her spine, her ribs must shatter with the force of it; the soft vital organs within her trunk must bruise or burst.

Sebastian went for him. Brushing from his path two lesser men of the bewildered defenders, clubbing the Mauser in his hands because he could not fire for fear of hitting Rosa, silently saving his breath for physical effort, he crossed the distance that separated them and reached them in the moment that the Askari began the first downward movement of his arms.

'Aah!' A gusty grunt was forced up Sebastian's throat by the force with which he swung the rifle, he used it like an axe, swinging it low with the full weight of his body behind it. The blade of the butt hit the Askari across the small of his back, and within his body cavity the kidneys popped like over-ripe satsuma plums. He was dying as he toppled backwards. As he hit the ground Rosa fell on top of him, his body cushioning her fall.

Sebastian dropped the rifle and stooped to gather her in his arms, crouching over her protectively.

Around them Flynn led his men boiling over the defenders, swamping them, knocking the rifles from their hands and dragging them to their feet, laughing in awe of their own courageous assault, chattering in excitement and relief.

Sebastian was on the point of straightening up and lifting Rosa to her feet, he glanced around quickly to assure himself that all danger was past – and his breathing jammed in his throat.

Ten paces away, kneeling in the shadow of one of the huge steel wheels was the white officer. He was a young man, swarthy for a German, but with pale green eyes. The tropical white of his uniform was patchy with damp sweat stains, and smeared with dust; his cap was pushed back, the gold braid on its peak sparkling with incongruous gaiety, for beneath it the face was taut and angry, the mouth pulled tight by the clenched jaws.

There was a Luger pistol clutched in his right hand. He lifted it and aimed.

'No!' croaked Sebastian, clumsily trying to shield Rosa with his own body, but he knew the German was going to fire.

'Mädchen!' cried Sebastian in his schoolboy German. 'Nein shutzen dis ein Mädchen!' and he saw the change in the young officer's expression, the pale green glitter of his eyes softening as he responded automatically to the appeal to his chivalry. Yet still the Luger was levelled, and over it Sebastian and the officer stared at each other. All this in seconds, but the delay was enough. While the officer still hesitated, suddenly it was too late, for Flynn stood over him and pressed the muzzle of his rifle into the back of the German's neck.

'Drop it, me beauty. Else I'll shoot your tonsils clean out through your Adam's apple.'

Strewn along the floor of the valley were the loads dropped by the native bearers, in their anxiety to leave for far places and fairer climes. Many of the packs had burst open and all had been trampled in the rush, so the contents littered the ground and discarded clothing flapped in the lower branches of the thorn trees.

Flynn's men were looting, a pastime in which they demonstrated a marked aptitude and industry. Busy as jackals around a lion's kill they gleaned the spoils and bickered over them.

The German officer sat quietly against the metal wheel. In front of him stood Rosa; she had in her hand the Luger pistol. The two of them watched each other steadily and expressionlessly. To one side Flynn squatted and pored over the contents of the German's pockets. Beside him Sebastian was ready to give his assistance.

'He's a naval officer,' said Sebastian, looking at the German with interest. 'He's got an anchor on his cap badge.'

'Do me a favour, Bassie,' pleaded Flynn.

'Of course.' Sebastian was ever anxious to please.

'Shut up!' said Flynn, without looking up from the contents of the officer's wallet which he had piled on the ground in front of him. In his dealings with Flynn, Sebastian had built up a thick layer of scar tissue around his sensitivity. He went on without a change of tone or expression.

'I wonder what on earth a naval officer is doing in the middle of the bush – pushing these funny contraptions around.' Sebastian examined the wheel with interest, before addressing himself to the German. 'Bitte, was it das?' He pointed at the wheel. The young officer did not even glance at him. He was watching Rosa with almost hypnotic concentration.

Sebastian repeated his question and when he found that he was again ignored he shrugged slightly, and leaned across to lift a sheet of paper from the small pile in front of Flynn.

'Leave it,' Flynn slapped his hand away. 'I'm reading.'

'Can I look at this, then?' He touched a photograph.

'Don't lose it,' cautioned Flynn, and Sebastian held it in his lap and examined it. It showed three young men in white overalls and naval peaked caps. They were smiling broadly into the camera with their arms linked together. In the background loomed the superstructure of a warship, the gun-turrets showed clearly. One of the men in the photograph was their prisoner who now sat against the wheel.

Sebastian reversed the square of heavy cardboard and read the inscription on the back of it.

'"Bremerhaven. 6 Aug. 1911."'

Both Flynn and Sebastian were absorbed in their studies, and Rosa and the German were alone. Completely alone, isolated by an intimate relationship.

Gunther Raube was fascinated. Staring into the girl's face, he had never known this sensation of mingled dread and elation which she invoked within him. Though her expression was flat and neutral, he could sense in her a hunger and a promise. He knew that they were bound together by something he did not understand, between them there was something very important to happen. It excited him, he felt it crawling like a living thing in his loins, ghost-walking along his spine, and his breathing was cramped and painful. Yet there was fear with it, fear that was as cloying as warm olive oil in his belly.

'What is it?' he whispered huskily as a lover. 'I do not understand. Tell me.'

And he sensed that she could not understand his language, but his tone made something move in her eyes.

They darkened like cloud shadow on a green sea, and he saw she was beautiful. With a pang he thought how close he had been to firing the Luger she now held in her hand.

I might have killed her, and he wanted to reach out and touch her. Slowly he leaned forward, and Rosa shot him in the centre of his chest. The impact of the bullet threw him back against the metal frame of the wheel. He lay there looking at her.

Deliberately, each shot spaced, she emptied the magazine of the pistol. The Luger jumped and steadied and jumped again in her hand. Each blurt of gun-fire shockingly loud, and the wounds appeared like magic on the white front of his shirt, beginning to weep blood as he slumped sideways, and he lay with his eyes still fastened on her face as he died.

The pistol clicked empty and she let it drop from her hand.

– 57 –

Sir Percy held the square of cardboard at arm's length to read the inscription on the back of it.

'"Bremerhaven. 6 Aug. 1911,"' he said. Across the desk from him his flag-captain sat uncomfortably on the edge of the hard-backed H.M. issue chair. His right hand reached for his pocket, checked, then withdrew guiltily.

'For God's sake, Henry. Smoke that damned thing if you must,' grunted Sir Percy.

'Thank you, sir.' Gratefully Captain Henry Green completed the reach for his pocket, brought out a gnarled briar and began stuffing it with tobacco.

Laying aside the photograph, Sir Percy took up the bedraggled sheet of paper and studied the crude hand-drawn circles upon it, reading the descriptions that were linked by arrows to the circles. This sample of primitive art had been laboriously drawn by Flynn Patrick O'Flynn as an addendum to his report.

'You say this lot came in the diplomatic bag from the Embassy in Lourenço Marques?'

'That's right, sir.'

'Who is this fellow . . .' Sir Percy checked the name, 'Flynn Patrick O'Flynn?'

'It seems that he is a major in the Portuguese army, sir.'

'With a name like that?'

'You find these Irishmen everywhere, sir.' The captain smiled. 'He commands a group of scouts who raid across the border into German territory. They have built up something of a reputation for derring-do.'

Sir Percy grunted again, dropped the paper, clasped his hands behind his head and stared across the room at the portrait of Lord Nelson.

'All right, Henry. Let's hear what you make of it.'

The captain held a flaring match to the bowl of his pipe and sucked noisily, waved the match to extinguish it, and spoke through wreaths of smoke.

'The photograph first. It shows three German engineering officers on the foredeck of a cruiser. The one in the centre was the man killed by the scouts.' He puffed again. 'Intelligence reports that the cruiser is a "B" class. Nine-inch guns in raked turrets.'

'"B" class?' asked Sir Percy. 'They only launched two vessels of that class.'

'*Battenberg* and *Blücher*, sir.'

'*Blücher*!' said Sir Percy softly.

'*Blücher*!' agreed Henry Green. 'Presumed destroyed in a surface action with His Majesty's ships *Bloodhound* and *Orion* off the east coast of Africa between 16 and 20 September.'

'Go on.'

'Well, this officer could have been a survivor from *Blücher* who was lucky enough to come ashore in German East Africa – and is now serving with von Vorbeck's army.'

'Still dressed in full naval uniform, trundling strange round objects about the continent?' asked Sir Percy sceptically.

'An unusual duty, I agree, sir.'

'Now what do you make of these things?' With one finger Sir Percy prodded Flynn's diagram in front of him.

'Wheels,' said Green.

'For what?'

'Transporting material.'

'What material?'

'Steel plate.'

'Now who would want steel plate on the east coast of Africa?' mused Sir Percy.

'Perhaps the captain of a damaged battle cruiser.'

'Let's go down into the plotting room.' Sir Percy heaved his bulk out of the chair, and headed for the door.

His shoulders hunched, massive jaw jutting, Admiral Howe brooded over the plot of the Indian Ocean.

'Where was this column intercepted?' he asked.

'Here, sir.' Green touched the vast map with the pointer. 'About fifteen miles south-east of Kibiti. It was moving southwards towards . . .' He did not finish the statement but let the tip of the marker slide down on to the complexity of islands that clustered about the mouth of the long black snake that was the Rufiji river.

'Admiralty plot for East Africa, please.' Sir Percy turned to the lieutenant in charge of the plot, and the lieutenant selected Volume II of the blue-jacketed books that lined the shelf on the far wall.

'What are the sailing directions for the Rufiji mouth?' demanded the Admiral, and the lieutenant began to read.

'*Ras Pombwe to Kikunya mouth, including Mto Rufiji and Rufiji delta (Latitude 8° 17″S, Longitude 39° 20″E). For fifty* miles the coast is a maze of low, swampy, mangrove-covered islands, intersected by creeks comprising the delta of Mto Rufiji. During the rainy season the whole area of the delta is frequently inundated.

'The coast of the delta is broken by ten large mouths, eight of which are connected at all times with Mto Rufiji.'

Sir Percy interrupted peevishly, 'What is all this *Mto* business?'

'Arabic word for "river", sir.'

'Well, why don't they say so? Carry on.'

'With the exception of *Simba Uranga mouth* and *Kikunya mouth*, all other entrances are heavily shoaled and navigable only by craft drawing one metre or less.'

'Concentrate on those two then,' grunted Sir Percy, and the lieutenant turned the page.

'*Simba Uranga mouth*. Used by coasting vessels engaged in the timber trade. There is no defined bar and, in 1911, the channel was reported by the German Admiralty as having a low river level mean of ten fathoms.

'The channel is bifurcated by a wedge-shaped island, *Rufiji-ya-wake*, and both arms afford secure anchorage to vessels of large burden. However, holding ground is bad and securing to trees on the bank is more satisfactory. Floating islands of grass and weed are common.'

'All right!' Sir Percy halted the recitation, and every person in the plotting room looked expectantly at him. Sir Percy was glowering at the plot, breathing heavily through his nose. 'Where is *Blücher*'s plaque?' he demanded harshly.

The lieutenant went to the locker behind him, and came back with the black wooden disc he had removed from the plot two months previously. Sir Percy took it from him, and rubbed it slowly between thumb and forefinger. There was complete silence in the room.

Slowly Sir Percy leaned forward across the map and placed the disc with a click upon the glass top. They all

270

stared at it. It sat sinister as a black cancer where the green land met the blue ocean.

'Communications!' grunted Sir Percy and the yeoman of signals stepped forward with his pad ready.

'Despatch to Commodore Commanding Indian Ocean. Captain Joyce. H.M.S. *Renounce*. Maximum Priority. Message reads: Intelligence reports indicate high probability . . .'

– 58 –

'You know something, Captain Joyce, this is bloody good gin.' Flynn O'Flynn pointed the base of the glass at the ceiling, and in his eagerness to engulf the liquid, he did the same for the slice of lemon that the steward had placed in his glass. He gurgled like an airlocked geyser, his face changed swiftly to a deeper shade of red, then he expelled the lemon and with it a fine spray of gin and Indian tonic in a burst of explosive coughing.

'Are you all right?' Anxiously Captain Joyce leapt across the cabin and began pounding Flynn between the shoulderblades. He had visions of his key tool in the coming operation being asphyxiated before they had started.

'Pips!' gasped Flynn. 'Goddamned lemon pips.'

'Steward!' Captain Joyce called over his shoulder without interrupting the tattoo he was playing on Flynn's back. 'Bring the major a glass of water. Hurry!'

'Water?' wheezed Flynn in horror and the shock was sufficient to diminish the strength of his paroxysm.

The steward, who from experience could recognize a drinking man when he saw one, rose nobly to the occasion. He hurried across the cabin with a glass in his hand. A mouthful of the raw spirit effected a near miraculous cure, Flynn lay back in his chair, his face still bright purple but his breathing easing, and Joyce withdrew to the far side of the cabin to inhale with relief the moist warm tropical air that oozed sluggishly through the open porthole. After a close range whiff of Flynn's body smell, it was as sweet as a bunch of tulips.

Flynn had been in the field for six weeks, and during that time it had not occurred to him to change his clothing. He smelled like a Roquefort cheese.

There was a pause while everybody recovered their breath, then Joyce picked up where he had left off.

'I was saying, Major, how good it was of you to return so promptly to meet me here.'

'I came the moment I received your message. The runner was waiting for us in M'topo's village. I left my command camped south of the Rovuma, and pushed through in forced marches. A hundred and fifty miles in three days! Not bad going, hey?'

'Damn good show!' agreed Joyce, and looked across at the other two men in the cabin for confirmation. With the Portuguese Governor's aide-de-camp was a young army lieutenant. Neither of them could understand a word of English. The aide-de-camp was wearing a politely non-committal expression, and the lieutenant had loosened the top button of his tunic and was lolling on the cabin's day couch with a little black cigarette drooping from his lips. Yet he contrived to look as gracefully insolent as a matador.

'The English captain asks that you recommend me to the Governor for the Star of St Peter.' Flynn translated Captain Joyce's speech to the aide-de-camp. Flynn wanted a medal. He had been hounding the Governor for one these last six months.

'Will you please tell the English captain that I would be delighted to convey his written citation to the Governor.' The aide-de-camp smiled blandly. Through their business association he knew better than to take Flynn's translation literally. Flynn scowled at him, and Joyce sensed the strain in the cabin. He went on quickly.

'I asked you to meet me here to discuss a matter of very great importance.' He paused. 'Two months ago your scouts attacked a German supply column near the village of Kibiti.'

'That's right.' Flynn sat up in his chair. 'A hell of a fight. We fought like madmen. Hand-to-hand stuff.'

'Quite,' Joyce agreed quickly. 'Quite so. With this column was a German naval officer . . .'

'I didn't do it,' interjected Flynn with alarm. 'It wasn't me. He was trying to escape. You can't pin that one on me.'

Joyce looked startled.

'I beg your pardon.'

'He was shot trying to escape – and you try and prove different,' Flynn challenged him hotly.

'Yes, I know. I have a copy of your report. A pity. A great pity. We would dearly have liked to interrogate the man.'

'You calling me a liar?'

'Good Lord, Major O'Flynn. Nothing is further from my mind.' Joyce was finding that conversation with Flynn O'Flynn was similar to feeling your way blindfolded through a hawthorn bush. 'Your glass is empty, may I offer you a drink?'

Flynn's mouth was open to emit further truculent denials, but the offer of hospitality took him unawares and he subsided.

'Thank you. It's damn good gin, haven't tasted anything like it in years. I don't suppose you could spare a case or two?'

Again Joyce was startled.

'I'm sure the wardroom secretary will be able to arrange something for you.'

'Bloody good stuff,' said Flynn, and sipped at his recharged glass. Joyce decided on a different approach.

'Major O'Flynn, have you heard of a German warship, a cruiser, named *Blücher?*'

'Have I, hell!' bellowed Flynn with such vehemence that Joyce was left in no doubt that he had struck another jarring note. 'The bastard sank me!'

These words conjured up in the eye of Captain Joyce's mind a brief but macabre picture of a Flynn floating on his back, while a battle cruiser fired on him with nine-inch guns.

'Sank you?' asked Joyce.

'Rammed me! There I was sailing along in this dhow peaceful as anything when up she comes and – bang, right up the arse.'

'I see,' murmured Joyce. 'Was it intentional?'

'You bloody tooting it was.'

'Why?'

'Well . . .' started Flynn, and then changed his mind. 'It's a long story.'

'Where did this happen?'

'About fifty miles off the mouth of the Rufiji river.'

'The Rufiji?' Joyce leaned forward eagerly. 'Do you know it? Do you know the Rufiji delta?'

'Do I know the Rufiji delta?' chucked Flynn. 'I know it like you know the way to your own Thunder Box. I used to do a lot of business there before the war.'

'Excellent! Wonderful!' Joyce could not restrain himself from pursing his lips and whistling the first two bars of 'Tipperary'. From him this was expression of unadulterated joy.

'Yeah? What's so wonderful about that?' Flynn was immediately suspicious.

'Major O'Flynn. On the basis of your report, Naval Intelligence considers it highly probable that the *Blücher* is anchored somewhere in the Rufiji delta.'

'Who are you kidding? The *Blücher* was sunk months ago – everybody knows that.'

'Presumed sunk. She, and the two British warships that pursued her, disappeared off the face of the earth – or more correctly the ocean. Certain pieces of floating wreckage were recovered that indicated that a battle had been fought by the three ships. It was thought that all three had gone down.' Joyce paused and smoothed the grey wings of hair along his temples. 'But now it seems certain that *Blücher* was badly damaged during the engagement, and that she was holed up in the delta.'

'Those wheels! Steel plating for repairs!'

'Precisely, Major, precisely. But . . .' Joyce smiled at Flynn, '. . . thanks to you, they did not get the plating through.'

'Yes, they did.' Flynn growled a denial.

'They did?' demanded Joyce harshly.

'Yeah. We left them lying in the veld. My spies told me that after we had gone the Germans sent another party of bearers up and took them away.'

'Why didn't you prevent it?'

'What the hell for? They've got no value,' Flynn retorted.

'The enemy's insistence must have demonstrated their value.'

'Yeah. The enemy were so insistent they sent up a couple of Maxim guns with the second party. In my book the more Maxims there are guarding something, the less value it is.'

'Well, why didn't you destroy them while you had the chance?'

'Listen, friend, how do you reckon to destroy twenty tons of steel – swallow it perhaps?'

'Do you realize just what a threat this ship will be once it is seaworthy?' Joyce hesitated. 'I tell you now in strict confidence that there will be an invasion of German East

Africa in the very near future. Can you imagine the havoc if *Blücher* were to slip out of the Rufiji and get among the troop convoys?'

'Yeah – all of us have got troubles.'

'Major.' The captain's voice was hoarse with the effort of checking his temper. 'Major. I want you to do a reconnaissance and locate the *Blücher* for us.'

'Is that so?' boomed Flynn. 'You want me to go galloping round in the delta when there's a Maxim behind every mangrove tree. It might take a year to search that delta, you've got no idea what it's like in there.'

'That won't be necessary.' Joyce swivelled his chair, he nodded at the Portuguese lieutenant. 'This officer is an aviator.'

'What's that mean?'

'He is a flyer.'

'Yeah? Is that so good? I did a bit of sleeping around when I was young – still get it up now and then.'

Joyce coughed.

'He flies an aircraft. A flying-machine.'

'Oh!' said Flynn. He was impressed. 'Jeez! Is that so?' He looked at the Portuguese lieutenant with respect.

'With the co-operation of the Portuguese army I intend conducting an aerial reconnaissance of the Rufiji delta.'

'You mean flying over it in a flying-machine?'

'Precisely.'

'That's a bloody good idea.' Flynn was enthusiastic.

'When can you be ready?'

'What for?'

'For the reconnaissance.'

'Now just hold on a shake, friend!' Flynn was aghast. 'You not getting me into one of those flying things.'

Two hours later they were still arguing on the bridge of H.M.S. *Renounce*, as Joyce conned her back towards the land to deposit Flynn and the two Portuguese on the beach from which his launch had picked them up that morning. The British cruiser steamed over a sea that was oil-slick calm and purple blue, and the land lay as a dark irregular line on the horizon.

'It is essential that someone who knows the delta flies with the pilot. He has just arrived from Portugal, besides which he will be fully occupied in piloting the machine. He must have an observer.' Joyce was trying again.

Flynn had lost all interest in the discussion, he was now occupied with weightier matters.

'Captain,' he started, and Joyce recognized the new tone of his voice and turned to him hopefully.

'Captain, that other business. What about it?'

'I'm sorry – I don't follow you.'

'That gin you promised me, what about it?'

Captain Arthur Joyce R.N. was a man of gentle mien. His face was smooth and unlined, his mouth full but grave, his eyes thoughtful, the streaks of silver grey at his temples gave him dignity. There was only one pointer to his true temperament, his eyebrows grew in one solid continuous line across his face; they were as thick and furry across the bridge of his nose as they were above his eyes. Despite his appearance he was a man of dark and violent temper. Ten years on his own bridge, wielding the limitless power and authority of a Royal Naval Captain had not mellowed him, but had taught him how to use the curb on his temper. Since early that morning when he had first shaken Flynn O'Flynn's large hairy paw, Arthur Joyce had been exercising every bit of restraint he possessed – now he had exhausted it all.

Flynn found himself standing speechless beneath the full blaze of Captain Joyce's anger. In a staccato, low-pitched speech, Arthur Joyce told him his opinion of Flynn's courage, character, reliability, drinking habits and sense of personal hygiene.

277

Flynn was shocked and deeply hurt.

'Listen . . .' he said.

'YOU listen,' said Joyce. 'Nothing will give me more pleasure than to see you leave this ship. And when you do so you can rest content in the knowledge that a full report of your conduct will go to my superiors – with copies to the Governor of Mozambique, and the Portuguese War Office.'

'Hold on!' cried Flynn. Not only was he going to leave the cruiser without the gin, but he could imagine that the wording of Joyce's report would ensure that he never got that medal. They might even withdraw his commission. In this moment of terrible stress the solution came to him.

'There is one man. *Only* one man who knows the delta better than I do. He's young, plenty of guts – and he's got eyes like a hawk.'

Joyce glared at him, breathing hard as he fought to check the headlong run of his rage.

'Who?' he demanded.

'My own son,' intoned Flynn, it sounded better than son-in-law.

'Will he do it?'

'He'll do it. I'll see to that,' Flynn assured him.

– 59 –

'It's as safe as a horse and cart,' boomed Flynn, he liked the simile, and repeated it.

'How safe is a horse and cart when it's up in the clouds?' asked Sebastian, without lowering his eyes from the sky.

'I'm disappointed in you, Bassie. Most young fellows would jump at this chance.' Flynn was literally in excellent spirits. Joyce had come through with three cases of best Beefeater gin. He sat on one of the gasoline drums that lay beneath the shade of the palm trees above the beach, around him in various attitudes of relaxation lay twenty of his scouts, for it was a drowsy, warm and windless morning. A bright sun burned down from a clear sky, and the white sand was dazzling against the dark green of the sea. The low surf sighed softly against the beach, and half a mile out, a cloud of seabirds were milling and diving on a shoal of bait-fish. Their cries blending with the sound of the sea.

Even though they were a hundred miles north of the Rovuma mouth, deep in German territory, a holiday atmosphere prevailed. Heightened by anticipation of the imminent arrival of the flying-machine they were enjoying themselves – all of them except Sebastian and Rosa. They were holding each other's hands and looking into the southern sky.

'You must find it for us.' Rosa's voice was low, but not low enough to cover her intensity. For the last ten days, since Flynn had returned from his meeting with Joyce on board the *Renounce*, she had spoken of little else but the German warship. It had become another cup to catch the hatred that overflowed from her.

'I'll try,' said Sebastian.

'You must,' she said. 'You must.'

'Should be able to get a good view from up there. Like standing on a mountain – only with no mountain under you,' said Sebastian and he felt his skin crawl at the thought.

'Listen!' said Rosa.

'What?'

'Ssh!'

And he heard it, an insect drone that swelled and sank and swelled again. They heard it under the trees also, and some of them came out into the sun and stood peering towards the south.

Suddenly in the sky there was a flash of reflected sunlight off metal or glass, and a shout went up from the watchers.

It came in towards them, low on wobbly wings, the clatter of its engine rising to a crescendo, its shadow racing ahead of it along the white beach. The group of native scouts exploded in panic-stricken retreat, Sebastian dropped on his face in the sand, only Rosa stood unmoving as it roared a few feet over her head, and then rose and banked away in a curve out over the sea.

Sebastian stood up and sheepishly brushed sand from his bush-jacket, as the aircraft levelled in and sank down on to the hard-packed sand near the water's edge. The beat of its engine faded to a spluttering burble, and it waddled slowly towards them, the backwash of the propeller sending a misty plume of sand scudding out behind. The wings looked as though they were about to fall off.

'All right,' bellowed Flynn at his men who were standing well back in the palm grove. 'Get these drums down there.'

The pilot switched off the motor, and the silence was stunning. He climbed stiffly out of the cockpit on to the lower wing, dumpy and awkward in his thick leather jacket, helmet and goggles. He jumped down on to the beach and shrugged out of the jacket, pulled off the helmet and was revealed as the suave young Portuguese lieutenant.

'Da Silva,' he said offering his right hand as Sebastian ran forward to greet him. 'Hernandez da Silva.'

While Flynn and Sebastian supervised the refuelling of the aircraft, Rosa sat with the pilot under the palms, while he breakfasted on garlic polony and a bottle of white wine that he had brought with him – suitably exotic food for a dashing knight of the air.

Although his mouth was busy, the pilot's eyes were free and he used them on Rosa. Even at a distance of fifty yards Sebastian became aware with mounting disquiet that Rosa was suddenly a woman again. Where before there had been a lifted chin and the straight-forward masculine gaze; now there were downcast eyes broken with quick bright glances and secret smiles, now there were soft rose colours that glowed and faded beneath the sun-browned skin of her cheeks and neck. She touched her hair with a finger, pushing a strand back behind her ear. She tugged at the front of her bush-jacket to straighten it, then drew her long khaki-clad legs up sideways beneath her as she sat in the sand. The pilot's eyes followed the movement. He wiped the neck of the wine bottle on his sleeve, and then with a flourish offered it to Rosa.

Rosa murmured her thanks and accepted the bottle to sip at it delicately. With the freckles across her cheeks and the skin peeling from her nose she looked as fresh and as innocent as a little girl, Sebastian thought.

The Portuguese lieutenant on the other hand looked neither fresh nor innocent. He was handsome, if you liked the slimy continental type with that slightly jaded tom cat look. Sebastian decided that there was something obscenely erotic about that little black moustache, that lay upon his upper lip and accentuated the cherry-pink lips beneath.

Watching him take the bottle back from Rosa and lift it towards her in salutation before drinking, Sebastian was overcome with two strong desires. One was to take the wine bottle and thrust it down the lieutenant's throat, the other was to get him into the flying-machine and away from Rosa just as quickly as was possible.

'Paci. Paci,' he growled at Mohammed's gang who were slopping gasoline into the funnel on the upper wing. 'Get a move on, for cat's sake!'

'Get your clobber into this thing, Bassie, and stop giving orders – you know it just confuses everybody.'

'I don't know where to put it – you'd better tell that greaser to come and show me. I can't speak his language.'

'Put it in the front cockpit – the observer's cockpit.'

'Tell that damned Portuguese to come here.' Sebastian dug in stubbornly. 'Tell him to leave Rosa alone and come here.'

Rosa followed the pilot to the aircraft and the expression of awed respect on her face, as she listened to him throwing out orders in Portuguese, infuriated Sebastian. The ritual of starting the aircraft completed, it stood clattering and quivering on the beach, and the pilot waved imperiously at Sebastian from the cockpit to come aboard.

Instead he went to Rosa and took her possessively in his arms.

'Do you love me?' he asked.

'What?' she shouted above the bellow of the engine.

'Do you love me?' he roared.

'Of course I do, you fool,' she shouted back and smiled up into his face before going up on tip-toe to kiss him while the slipstream of the propeller howled around them. Her embrace had passion in it that had not been there these many months, and Sebastian wondered sickly how much of it had been engendered by an outside agency.

'You can do that when you get back.' Flynn prised him loose from Rosa's grip, and boosted him up into the cockpit. The machine jerked forward and Sebastian clutched desperately to retain his balance, then glanced back. Rosa was waving and smiling, he was not certain if the smile was directed at him or at the helmeted head in the cockpit behind him, but his jealousy was swamped by the primeval instinct of survival.

Clutching with both hands at the sides of the cockpit, even his toes curling in their boots as though to grip the floorboards of the cockpit, Sebastian stared ahead.

The beach disappeared beneath the fuselage in a solid white blur; the palm trees whipped past on one side, the sea on the other; the wind tore at his face and tears streamed back along his cheeks, the machine bumped and bucked and jounced, and then leaped upwards under him, dropped back to bounce once more and then was airborne. The earth fell away gently beneath them as they soared, and Sebastian's spirits soared with them. His misgivings melted away.

Sebastian remembered at last to pull the goggles down over his eyes to protect them from the stinging wind, and godlike he looked down through them at a world that was small and tranquil.

When at last he looked back over his shoulder at the pilot, this strange and wonderful shared experience of immortality had lifted him above the petty passions of mere men, and they smiled at each other.

The pilot pointed out over the right wing tip, and Sebastian followed the direction of his arm.

Far, far out on the crenellated blue blanket of the sea, tiny beneath vast fluffy piles of thunderhead cloud, he saw the grey shape of the British cruiser *Renounce* with the pale white feather of its wake fanning on the surface of the ocean behind it.

He nodded and smiled at his companion. Again the pilot pointed, this time ahead.

Still misty in the blue haze of distance, haphazard as the unfitted pieces of a jigsaw puzzle, the islands of the Rufiji delta were spilled and scattered between ocean and mainland.

In the rackety little cockpit, Sebastian squatted over his pack and took from it binoculars, pencil and map-case.

It was hot. Moist itchy hot. Even in the shade beneath the festooned camouflage-nets the decks of *Blücher* were smothered with hot sticky waves of swamp air. The sweat that oozed and trickled down the glistening bodies of the half-naked men who slaved on her foredeck gave them no relief, for the air was too humid to evaporate the moisture. They moved like sleep-walkers, with slow mechanical determination, manhandling the thick sheet of steel plate into its slings beneath the high arm of the crane.

Even the flow of obscenity from the lips of Lochtkamper, the engineering commander, had dried up like a spring in drought season. He worked with his men, like them stripped to the waist, and the tattoos on his upper arms and across his chest heaved and bulged as they rode on an undulating sea of muscles.

'Rest,' he grunted; and they straightened up from their labour, mouths gaping as they sucked in the stale air, massaging aching backs, glowering at the sheet of steel with true hatred.

'Captain.' Lochtkamper became aware of von Kleine for the first time. He stood against the forward gun-turret, tall in full whites, the blond beard half concealing the cross of black enamel and silver that hung at his throat. Lochtkamper crossed to him.

'It goes well?' von Kleine asked, and the engineer shook his head.

'Not as well as I had hoped.' He wiped one huge hand across his forehead, leaving a smudge of grease and rust scale on his own face. 'Slow,' he said. 'Too slow.'

'You have encountered difficulties?'

'Everywhere,' growled the engineer, and he looked

around at the heat mist and the mangroves, at the sluggish black waters and the mud banks. 'Nothing works here – the welding equipment, the winch engines, even the men – everything sickens in this obscene heat.'

'How much longer?'

'I do not know, Captain. I truly do not know.'

Von Kleine would not press him. If any man could get *Blücher* seaworthy, it would be this man. When Lochtkamper slept at all, it was here on the foredeck, curled like a dog on a mattress thrown on the planking. He slept a few exhausted hours amid the whine and groan of the winches, the blue hissing glare of the welding torches and the drum splitting hammering of the riveters, then he was up again bullying, leading, coaxing and threatening.

'Another three weeks,' Lochtkamper estimated reluctantly. 'A month at the most – if all goes as it does now.'

They were both silent, standing together, two men from different worlds drawn together by a common goal, united by respect for each other's ability.

A mile up the channel, movement caught their attention. It was one of the launches returning to the cruiser, yet it looked like a hayrick under its bulky cargo. It came slowly against the sluggish current, sitting so low in the water that only a few inches of freeboard showed, while its load was a great shaggy hump on which sat a dozen black men.

Von Kleine and Lochtkamper watched it approaching.

'I still do not know about that obscene wood, Captain.' Lochtkamper shook his big untidy head again. 'It is so soft, so much ash, it could clog the furnace.'

'There is nothing else we can do,' von Kleine reminded him.

When *Blücher* entered the Rufiji, her coal-bunkers were almost empty. There was enough fuel for perhaps four thousand miles of steaming. Hardly enough to carry her in a straight run down into latitude 45° south, where her mother ship, *Esther*, waited to refuel her, and fill her magazines with shell.

There was not the faintest chance of obtaining coal. Instead von Kleine had set Commissioner Fleischer and his thousand native porters to cutting cordwood from the forests, that grew at the apex of the delta. It was a duty that Commissioner Fleischer had opposed with every argument and excuse he could muster. He felt that in delivering safely to Captain von Kleine the steel plating from Dar es Salaam, he had discharged any obligation that he might have towards the *Blücher*. His eloquence availed him not at all – Lochtkamper had fashioned two hundred primitive axe heads from the steel plate, and von Kleine had sent Lieutenant Kyller up-river with Fleischer to help him keep his enthusiasm for wood-cutting burning brightly.

For three weeks now, the *Blücher*'s launches had been plying steadily back and forth. Up to the present they had delivered some five hundred tons of timber. The problem was finding storage for this unwieldy cargo once the coal-bunkers were filled.

'We will have to begin deck loading the cordwood soon,' von Kleine muttered, and Lochtkamper opened his mouth to reply when the alarm bells began to clamour an emergency, and the loudhailer boomed.

'Captain to the bridge. Captain to the bridge.'

Von Kleine turned and ran.

On the companion ladder he collided with one of his lieutenants. They caught at each other for balance and the lieutenant shouted into von Kleine's face.

'Captain – an aircraft. Flying low. Coming this way. Portuguese markings.'

'Damn it to hell!' Von Kleine pushed past him, and bounded up the ladder. He burst on to the bridge, panting.

'Where is it?' he shouted.

The officer of the watch dropped his binoculars and turned to von Kleine with relief.

'There it is, sir!' He pointed through a hole in the tangled screen of camouflage that hung like a veranda roof over the bridge.

Von Kleine snatched the binoculars from him and, as he trained them on the distant winged shape in the mist haze above the mangroves, he issued his orders.

'Warn the men ashore. Everybody under cover,' he barked. 'All guns trained to maximum elevation. Pom-poms loaded with shrapnel. Machine-gun crews closed up – but no firing until my orders.'

He held the aircraft in the round field of the field glasses.

'Portuguese, all right,' he grunted; the green and red insignia showed clearly against the brown body of the aircraft.

'She's searching . . .' The aircraft was sweeping back and forth, banking over and turning back at the end of each leg of her search pattern, like a farmer ploughing a field. Von Kleine could make out the head and shoulders of a man crouched forward in the squat round nose of the aircraft. '. . . Now we'll find out how effective is our camouflage.'

So the enemy have guessed at last. They must have reported the convoy of steel plate – or perhaps the chopping of the cordwood has alerted them, he thought, watching the aircraft tacking slowly towards him. *We could not hope to go undetected for ever – but I did not expect them to send an aircraft.*

Then suddenly the thought struck him so hard that he gasped with the danger of it. He whirled and ran to the forward rail of the bridge and peered out through the camouflage net.

Still half a mile distant, trundling slowly down the centre of the channel with the wide rippling V of her wake spread on the current behind her, clumsy as a pregnant hippo with her load of cordwood, the launch was aimed straight at *Blücher*. From the air she would be as conspicuous as a fat tick on a white sheet.

'The launch . . .' shouted von Kleine, '. . . hail her. Order her to run for the bank – get her under cover.'

But he knew it was useless. By the time she was within hail, it would be too late. He thought of ordering his forward turrets to fire on the launch and sink her – but discarded the idea immediately, the fall of shell would immediately draw the enemy's attention.

Impatiently he stood gripping the rail of the bridge, and mouthing his anger and his frustration at the approaching launch.

– 61 –

Sebastian hung over the edge of the cockpit. The wind buffeted him, flapping his jacket wildly about his body, whipping his hair into a black tangle. With his usual dexterity Sebastian had managed to drop the binoculars overboard. They were the property of Flynn Patrick O'Flynn, and Sebastian knew that he would be expected to pay for them. This spoiled Sebastian's enjoyment of the flight to some extent, he already owed Flynn a little over three hundred pounds. Rosa would have something to say also. However, the loss of the binoculars was no handicap, the aircraft was flying too low and was so unstable that the unaided eye was much more effective.

From a height of five hundred feet the mangrove forest looked like a fluffy overstuffed mattress, a sickly fever green in colour, with the channels and the water-ways between them dark gun-metal veins that flashed the sunlight back like a heliograph. The clouds of white egrets that rose in alarm as the aircraft approached looked like drifts of torn paper scraps. A fish eagle hung suspended in silent flight ahead of them, the wide span of its wings flared at the tips like the fingers of a hand. It dipped away, sliding past the aircraft's wing tip so close that Sebastian saw the fierce yellow eyes in its white hooded head.

Sebastian laughed with delight, and then grabbed at the side of the cockpit to steady himself, as the machine rocked violently under him. This was the pilot's method of attracting Sebastian's attention, and Sebastian wished he would think up some other way of doing it.

He looked back angrily shouting in the howl of wind and engine.

'Watch it! You stupid dago.'

Da Silva was gesticulating wildly, his pink mouth working under the black moustache, his eyes wild behind the panes of his goggles, his right hand stabbing urgently out over the starboard wing.

Sebastian saw it immediately on the wide water-way, the launch was so glaringly conspicuous that he wondered why he had not seen it before, then he recalled that his attention had been concentrated on the terrain directly beneath the aircraft – and he excused himself.

Yet there was little to justify da Silva's excitement, he thought. This was no battle cruiser, it was a tiny vessel of perhaps twenty-five feet. Quickly he ran his eyes down the channel, following it to the open sea in the blue distance. It was empty.

He glanced back at the pilot and shook his head. But da Silva's excitement had, if anything, increased. He was making another frenzied hand-signal that Sebastian could not understand. To save argument Sebastian nodded in agreement, and instantly the machine dropped away under him so that Sebastian's belly was left behind and he clutched desperately at the side of the cockpit once more.

In a shallow turning dive, da Silva took the machine

down and then levelled out with the landing-wheels almost brushing the tops of the mangroves. They rushed towards the channel, and as the last mangroves whipped away under them da Silva eased the nose down still farther and they dropped to within a few feet of the surface of the water. It was a display of fine flying that was completely wasted on Sebastian. He was cursing da Silva quietly, his eyes starting from their sockets.

A mile ahead of them across the open water bobbed the overladen launch. It was only a few feet below their own level, and they raced towards it with the wash of the propeller blowing a squall of ripples across the surface behind them.

'My God!' The blasphemy was wrung from Sebastian in his distress. 'He's going to fly right into it!'

It was an opinion that seemed to be shared by the crew of the launch. As the machine roared in on them, they began to abandon ship. Sebastian saw two men leap from the high piled load of timber and hit the water with small white splashes.

At the last second da Silva lifted the plane and they hopped over the launch. For a fleeting instant Sebastian stared at a range of fifteen feet into the face of the German naval officer who crouched down over the tiller bar at the stern of the launch. They were then past and climbing sharply, banking and turning back.

Sebastian saw the launch had rounded to, and that her crew were clambering aboard and splashing around her sides. Once more the aircraft dropped towards the channel, but da Silva had throttled back and the engine was burbling under half power. He levelled out fifty feet above the water, and flew sedately, keeping away from the launch and well towards the northern side of the channel.

'What are you doing?' Sebastian mouthed the question

at da Silva. In reply the pilot made a sweeping gesture with his right hand at the thick bank of mangroves alongside.

Puzzled, Sebastian stared into the mangroves. What was the fool doing, surely he didn't think that . . .

There was a hump of high ground on the bank, a hump that rose perhaps one hundred and fifty feet above the level of the river. They came up to it.

Like a hunter following a wounded buffalo, moving carelessly through thin scattered bush which could not possibly give cover to such a large animal, and then suddenly coming face to face with it – so close, that he sees the minute detail of crenellation on the massive bosses of the horns, sees the blood dripping from moist black nostrils, and the dull furnace glare of the piggy little eyes – in the same fashion Sebastian found the *Blücher*.

She was so close he could see the pattern of rivets on her plating, the joints in the planking of her foredeck, the individual strands of the canopy of camouflage netting spread over her. He saw the men on her bridge, and the gun-crews behind the pom-poms and the Maxim machine guns on the balconies of her upperworks. From her squatting turrets her big guns gaped at him with hungry mouths, revolving to follow the flight of the machine.

She was monstrous, grey and sinister among the mangroves, crouching in her lair, and Sebastian cried aloud in surprise and alarm, a sound without shape or coherence, and at the same moment the engine of the aeroplane bellowed in full power, as da Silva thrust the throttle wide and hauled the joystick back into his crotch.

As the aircraft rocketed upwards, the deck of the *Blücher* erupted in a thunderous volcano of flame. Flame flew in great bell-shaped ejaculations from the muzzles of her nine-inch guns. Flame spat viciously from the multi-barrelled pom-poms and the machine guns on her upperworks.

Around the little aircraft the air boiled and hissed, disrupted, churned into violent turbulence by the passage of the big shells.

Something struck the plane, and she was whirled upwards like a burning leaf from a garden bonfire. Wing over wing she rolled, her engine surging wildly, her rigging groaning and creaking at the strain.

Sebastian was flung forward, the bridge of his nose cracked against the edge of the cockpit and instantly twin jets of blood spurted from his nostrils to douse the front of his jacket.

The machine stood on her tail, propeller clawing ineffectively at the air, engine wailing in over rev. Then she dropped away on one wing and one side swooped sickeningly downwards.

Da Silva fought her, feeling the sloppiness of the stall in her controls come alive again as she regained air-speed. The fluffy tops of the mangroves rushed up to meet him, and desperately he tried to ease her off. She was trying to respond, the fabric wrinkling along her wings as they flexed to the enormous pressure. He felt her lurch again as she touched the top branches, heard above the howl of the engine the faint crackling brush of the vegetation against her belly. Then suddenly, miraculously, she was clear; flying straight and level, climbing slowly up and away from the hungry swamp.

She was sluggish and heavy, and there was something loose under her. It banged and thumped and slapped in the slipstream, jarring the whole fuselage. Da Silva could not dare to manoeuvre her. He held her on the course she had chosen, easing her nose slightly upwards, slowly gaining precious altitude.

At a thousand feet he brought her round in a wide gentle turn to the south, and banging and thumping, one wing

heavy, she staggered drunkenly through the sky towards her
rendezvous with Flynn O'Flynn.

– 62 –

Flynn stood up with slow dignity from where he had been leaning against the bole of the palm tree.

'Where are you going?' Rosa opened her eyes and looked up at him.

'To do something you can't do for me.'

'That's the third time in an hour!' Rosa was suspicious.

'That's why they call it the East African quickstep,' said Flynn, and moved off ponderously into the undergrowth. He reached the lantana bush, and looked around carefully. He couldn't trust Rosa not to follow him. Satisfied, he dropped to his knees and dug with his hands in the loose sand.

With the air of an old-time pirate unearthing a chest of doubloons, he lifted the bottle from its grave, and withdrew the cork.

The neck of the bottle was in his mouth, when he heard the muted beat of the returning aircraft. The bottle stayed there a while longer, Flynn's Adam's apple pulsing up and down his throat as he swallowed, but his eyes swivelled upwards and creased in concentration.

With a sigh of intense pleasure he recorked, and laid the bottle once more to rest, kicked sand over it, and set course for the beach.

'Can you see them?' he shouted the question at Rosa as he came down through the palms. She was standing out in the open. Her head was thrown back so that the long braid of her hair hung down to her waist behind. She did not answer him, but the set of her expression was hard and

293

strained with anxiety. The men standing about her were silent also, held by an expectant dread.

Flynn looked up and saw it coming in like a wounded bird, the engine stuttering and surging irregularly, streaming a long bluish streak of oily smoke from the exhaust manifold, the wings rocking crazily, and a loose tangle of wreckage hanging and swinging under the belly where one of the landing-wheels had been shot away.

It sagged wearily towards the beach, the broken beat of the engine failing so they could hear the whisper of the wind in her rigging.

The single landing-wheel touched down on the hard sand and for fifty yards she ran true, then with a jerk she toppled sideways. The port wing bit into the sand, slewing her towards the edge of the sea, the tail came up and over. There was a crackling, ripping, tearing sound; and in a dust storm of flying sand she cartwheeled, stern over stem.

The propeller tore into the beach, disintegrating in a blur of flying splinters, and from the forward cockpit a human body was flung clear, spinning in the air so that the outflung limbs were the spokes of a wheel. It fell with a splash in the shallow water at the edge of the beach, while the aircraft careened onwards, tearing herself to pieces. A lower wing broke off – the guy wires snapping with a sound like a volley of musketry. The body of the machine slowed as it hit the water, skidding to a standstill on its back, with the surf washing around it. Da Silva hung motionless in the back cockpit, suspended upside down by his safety-straps, his arms dangling.

The next few seconds of silence were appalling.

'Help the pilot! I'll get Sebastian.' Rosa broke it at last. Mohammed and two other Askari ran with her towards where Sebastian was lying awash, a piece of flotsam at the water's edge.

'Come on!' Flynn shouted at the men near him, and lumbered through the soft fluffy sand towards the wreck. They never reached it.

There was a concussion, a vast disturbance in the air that sucked at their eardrums, as the gasoline ignited in explosive combustion. The machine and the surface of the sea about it were instantly transformed into a roaring, raging sheet of flame.

They backed away from the heat. The flames were dark red laced with satanic black smoke, and they ate the canvas skin from the body of the aircraft, exposing the wooden framework beneath.

In the heart of the flames da Silva still hung in his cockpit, a blackened monkey-like shape as his clothing burned. Then the fire ate through the straps of his harness and he dropped heavily into the shallow water, hissing and sizzling as the flames were quenched.

The fire was still smouldering by the time Sebastian regained consciousness, and was able to lift himself on one elbow. Muzzily he stared down the beach at the smoking wreckage. The shadows of the palms lay like the stripes of a tiger on the sand that the low evening sun had softened to a dull gold.

'Da Silva?' Sebastian's voice was thick and slurred. His nose was broken and squashed across his face. Although Rosa had wiped most of the blood away, there were still little black crusts of it in his nostrils and at the corners of his mouth. Both his eyes were slits in the swollen plum-coloured bruises that bulged from the sockets.

'No!' Flynn shook his head. 'He didn't make it.'

'Dead?' whispered Sebastian.

'We buried him back in the bush.'

'What happened?' asked Rosa. 'What on earth happened out there?' She sat close beside him, protective as a mother over her child. Slowly Sebastian turned his head to look at her.

'We found the *Blücher*,' he said.

– 63 –

Captain Arthur Joyce, R.N., was a happy man. He stooped over his cabin desk, his hands placed open and flat on either side of the spread Admiralty chart. He glowed with satisfaction as he looked down at the hand-drawn circle in crude blue pencil as though it were the signature of the President of the Bank of England on a cheque for a million sterling.

'Good!' he said. 'Oh, very good,' and he pursed his lips as though he were about to whistle 'Tipperary'. Instead he made a sucking sound, and smiled across at Sebastian. Behind his flattened nose and blue-ringed eyes, Sebastian smiled back at him.

'A damn good show, Oldsmith!' Joyce's expression changed, the little lights of recognition sparkled suddenly in his eyes. 'Oldsmith?' he repeated. 'I say, didn't you open the bowling for Sussex in the 1911 cricket season?'

'That's right, sir.'

'Good Lord!' Joyce beamed at him. 'I'll never forget your opening over to Yorkshire in the first match of the season. You dismissed Graham and Penridge for two runs – two for two, hey?'

'Two for two, it was.' Sebastian liked this man.

'Fiery stuff! And then you made fifty-five runs?'

'Sixty-five,' Sebastian corrected him. 'A record ninth wicket partnership with Clifford Dumont of – one hundred and eighty-six!'

'Yes! Yes! I remember it well. Fiery stuff! You were damned unlucky not to play for England.'

'Oh, I don't know about that,' said Sebastian in modest agreement.

'Yes, you were.' Joyce pursed his lips again. '*Damned* unlucky.'

Flynn O'Flynn had not understood a word of this. He was thrashing around in his chair like an old buffalo in a trap, bored to the point of pain. Rosa Oldsmith had understood no more than he had, but she was fascinated. It was clear that Captain Joyce knew of some outstanding accomplishment of Sebastian's, and if a man like Joyce knew of it – then Sebastian was famous. She felt pride swell in her chest and she smiled on Sebastian also.

'I didn't know, Sebastian. Why didn't you tell me?' She glowed warmly at him.

'Some other time,' Joyce interrupted quickly. 'Now we must get on with this other business.' And he returned his attention to the chart on the desk.

'Now I want you to cast your mind back. Shut your eyes and try to see it again. Every detail you can remember, every little detail – it might be important. Did you see any signs of damage?'

Obediently Sebastian closed his eyes, and was surprised at how vividly the acid of fear had engraved the picture of *Blücher* on his mind.

'Yes,' he said. 'There were holes in her. Hundreds of holes, little black ones. And at the front end – the bows – there were trapezes hanging down on ropes, near the water. You know the kind that they use when they paint a high building . . .'

Joyce nodded at his secretary to record every word of it.

The single fan suspended over the table in the wardroom hummed quietly, the blades stirred the air that was moist and warm as the bedding of a malarial patient.

Except for the soft clink of cutlery on china, the only other sound was that of Commissioner Fleischer drinking his soup. It was thick, green pea soup, scalding hot, so that Fleischer found it necessary to blow heavily on each spoonful before ingesting it with a noise, not of the same volume, but with the delicate tonal quality, of a flushing water closet. During the pause while he crumbled a slice of black bread into his soup, Fleischer looked across the board at Lieutenant Kyller.

'So you did not find the enemy flying-machine, then?'

'No.' Kyller went on fiddling with his wine glass without looking up. For forty-eight hours he and his patrols had searched the swamps and channels and mangrove forests for the wreckage of the aircraft. He was exhausted and covered with insect bites.

'Ja,' Fleischer nodded solemnly. 'It fell only a short way, but it did not hit the trees. I was sure of that. I have seen sand-grouse do the same thing sometimes when you shoot them with a shot-gun. Pow! They come tumbling down like this . . .' He fluttered his hand in the air, letting it fall towards his soup, '. . . then suddenly they do this.' The hand took flight again in the direction of Commander (Engineering) Lochtkamper's rugged Neanderthal face. They all watched it.

'The little bird flies away home. It was bad shooting from so close,' said Fleischer, and ended the demonstration by picking up his soup spoon, and the moist warm silence once more gripped the wardroom.

Commander Lochtkamper stoked his mouth as though it were one of his furnaces. The knuckles of both his hands were knocked raw by contact with steel plate and wire rope. Even when Fleischer's hand had flown into his face, he had not been distracted from his thoughts. His mind was wholly occupied with steel and machinery, weights and points of balance. He wanted to achieve twenty degrees of starboard list on *Blücher*, so that a greater area of her bottom would be exposed to his welders. This meant displacing one thousand tons of dead weight. It seemed an impossibility – unless we flood the port magazines, he thought, and take the guns from their turrets and move them. Then we could rig camels under her . . .

'It was not bad shooting,' said the gunnery lieutenant. 'She was flying too close, the rate of track was . . .' He broke off, wiped the side of his long pointed nose with his forefinger, and regarded balefully the sweat that came away on it. This fat peasant would not understand, he would not waste energy in explaining the technicalities. He contented himself with repeating, 'It was not bad shooting.'

'I think we must accept that the enemy machine has returned safely to her base,' said Lieutenant Kyller. 'Therefore we can expect the enemy to mount some form of offensive action against us in the very near future.' Kyller enjoyed a position of privilege in the wardroom. No other of the junior officers would have dared to express his opinions so freely. Yet none of them would have made as much sense as Kyller. When he spoke his senior officers listened, if not respectfully, at least attentively. Kyller had passed out sword of honour cadet from Bremerhaven Naval Academy in 1910. His father was a Baron, a personal friend of the Kaiser's, and an Admiral of the Imperial Fleet. Kyller was wardroom favourite, not only because of his dark good looks and courteous manner – but also because of his appetite for hard work, his meticulous attention to detail, and his ready mind. He was a good officer to have aboard – a credit to the ship.

'What can the enemy do?' Fleischer asked with scorn. He did not share the general opinion of Ernst Kyller. 'We are safe here – what can he do?'

'A superficial study of naval history will reveal, sir, that the English can be expected to do what you least expect them to do. And that they will do it, quickly, efficiently and with iron purpose.' Kyller scratched the lumpy red insect bites behind his left ear.

'Bah!' said Fleischer, and sprayed a little pea soup with the violence of his disgust. 'The English are fools and cowards – at the worst, they will skulk off the mouth of the river. They would not dare come in here after us.'

'I have no doubt that time will prove you correct, sir.' This was Kyller's phrase of violent disagreement with a senior officer, and from experience Captain von Kleine and his commanders recognized it. They smiled a little.

'This soup is bitter,' said Fleischer, satisfied that he had carried the argument. 'The cook has used sea-water in it.'

The accusation was so outrageous, that even von Kleine looked up from his plate.

'Please do not let our humble hospitality delay you, Herr Commissioner. You must be anxious to return up-river to your wood-cutting duties.'

And Fleischer subsided quickly, hunching over his food. Von Kleine transferred his gaze to Kyller.

'Kyller, you will not be returning with the Herr Commissioner. I am sending Ensign Proust with him this trip. You will be in command of the first line of defence that I plan to place at the mouth of the delta, in readiness for the English attack. You will attend the conference in my cabin after this meal, please.'

'Thank you, sir.' His voice was husky with gratitude for

the honour his captain was conferring upon him. Von Kleine looked from him to his gunnery lieutenant.

'You also, please, Guns. I want to relieve you of your beloved upper deck pom-poms.'

'You mean to take them off their mountings, sir?' the gunnery lieutenant asked, looking at von Kleine dolefully over his long doleful nose.

'I regret the necessity,' von Kleine told him sympathetically.

– 65 –

'Well, Henry. We were right. *Blücher*'s there.'

'Unfortunately, sir.'

'Two heavy cruisers tied up indefinitely on blockade service.'

Admiral Sir Percy thrust out his lower lip lugubriously as he regarded the plaques of *Renounce* and *Pegasus* on the Indian Ocean plot. 'There is work for them elsewhere.'

'There is, at that,' agreed Henry Green.

'That request of Joyce's for two motor torpedo-boats . . .'

'Yes, sir?'

'We must suppose he intends mounting a torpedo attack into the delta.'

'It looks like it, sir.'

'It might work – worth a try anyway. What can we scratch together for him?'

'There is a full squadron at Bombay, and another at Aden, sir.'

For five seconds, Sir Percy Howe reviewed the meagre forces with which he was expected to guard two oceans. With this new submarine menace, he could not detach a single ship from the approaches to the Suez Canal – it would have to be Bombay. 'Send him an M. T. B. from the Bombay squadron.'

'He asked for two, sir.'

'Joyce knows full well that I only let him have half of anything he requests. He always doubles up.'

'What about this recommendation for a decoration, sir?'

'The fellow who spotted the *Blücher*?'

'Yes, sir.'

'A bit tricky – Portuguese irregular and all that sort of thing.'

'He's a British subject, sir.'

'Then he shouldn't be with the dagos,' said Sir Percy. 'Leave it over until the operation is completed. We'll think about it after we've sunk the *Blücher*.'

– 66 –

The sunset was blood and roses, nude pink and tarnished gold as the British blockade squadron stood in towards the land.

Renounce led with the commodore's penant flying at her masthead. In the smooth wide road of her wake, *Pegasus* slid over the water. Their silhouettes were crisp and black against the garish colours of the sunset. There was something prim and old-maidish about the lines of a heavy cruiser – none of the solid majesty of a battleship, nor the jaunty devil-may-care rake of a destroyer.

Close in under *Pegasus*'s beam, screened by her hull from the land, like a cygnet swimming beside the swan, rode the motor torpedo-boat.

Even in this light surface chop she was taking in water. Each wave puffed up over her bows and then streamed back greenish and cream along her decks. The spray rattled against the thin canvas that screened the open bridge.

Flynn O'Flynn crouched behind the screen and cursed the vaunting ambition that had led him to volunteer as pilot for this expedition. He glanced across at Sebastian who stood in the open wing of the bridge, behind the canvas-shrouded batteries of Lewis guns. Sebastian was grinning as the warm spray flew back into his face and trickled down his cheeks.

Joyce had recommended Sebastian for a Distinguished Service Order. This was almost more than Flynn could bear. He wanted one also. He had decided to go along now for that reason alone. Therefore Sebastian was directly to blame for Flynn's present discomfort, and Flynn felt a small warmth of satisfaction as he looked at the flattened, almost negroid contours of Sebastian's new nose. The young bastard deserved it, and he found himself wishing further punishment on his son-in-law.

'Distinguished Service Order and all . . .' he grunted. 'A half-trained chimpanzee could have done what he did. Yet who was it who found the wheels in the first place? No, Flynn Patrick, there just ain't no justice in this world, but we'll show the sons of bitches this time . . .'

His thoughts were interrupted by the small bustle of activity on the bridge around him. An Aldis lamp was winking from the high dark bulk of *Renounce* ahead of them.

The lieutenant commanding the torpedo-boat spelled the message aloud.

'Flag to YN2. D . . . P departure point. Good luck.' He was a dumpy amorphous figure in his duffle coat with the collar turned up. 'Thanks a lot, old chap – and one up your pipe also. No, Signaller, don't make that.' He went on quickly, 'YN2 to Flag. Acknowledged!' Then turning to the engine voice-pipe. 'Both engines stop,' he said.

The beat of her engines faded away, and she wallowed in the trough of the next wave. *Renounce* and *Pegasus* sailed on sedately, leaving the tiny vessel rolling crazily in the turbulence of their wakes. A lonely speck five miles off the mouth of the Rufiji delta, too far off for the shorewatchers to see her in the fading evening light.

– 67 –

Lieutenant Ernst Kyller watched through his binoculars as the two British cruisers turned in succession away from the land and coalesced with the darkness that fell so swiftly over the ocean and the land. They were gone.

'Every day it is the same.' Kyller let the binoculars fall against his chest and pulled his watch from the pocket of his tunic. 'Fifteen minutes before sunset, and again fifteen minutes before sun-up they sail past to show us that they are still waiting.'

'Yes, sir,' agreed the seaman who was squeezed into the crow's-nest beside Kyller.

'I will go down now. Moon comes up at 11.44 tonight – keep awake.'

'Yes, sir.'

Kyller swung his legs over the side and groped with his feet for the rungs of the rope ladder. Then he climbed down the palm tree to the beach fifty feet below. By the time he reached it the light had gone, and the beach was a vague white blur down to the green lights of phosphorus in the surf.

The sand crunched like sugar under his boots as he set off to where the launch was moored. As he walked, his mind was wholly absorbed with the details of his defence system.

There were only two of the many mouths of the Rufiji, up which the English could attack. They were separated by

304

a low wedge-shaped island of sand and mud and mangrove. It was on the seaward side of this island that Kyller had sited the four-pounder pom-poms taken from their mountings on *Blucher*'s upper deck.

He had sunk a raft of logs into the soft mud to give them a firm foundation on which to stand, and he had cut out the mangroves so they commanded an arc of fire across both channels. His search-lights he sited with equal care – so they could sweep left or right without blinding his gunners.

From Commander Lochtkamper he had solicited a length of four-inch steel hawser. This was rather like an unrehabilitated insolvent raising an unsecured loan from a money-lender, for Commander Locktkamper was not easily parted from his stores. Far up river Ensign Proust had diverted some of his axe-men to felling fifty giant African mahogany trees. They had floated the trunks down on the tide; logs the size of the columns of a Greek temple. With these and the cable Kyller had fashioned a boom that stretched across both channels, an obstacle so formidable that it would rip the belly out of even a heavy cruiser coming down on it at speed.

Not satisfied with this, for Kyller had highly developed the Teutonic capacity for taking infinite pains, he lifted the fat globular mines with their sinister horns that *Blücher* had sown haphazardly behind her on her journey up-river. These he rearranged into neat geometrical ranks behind his log boom, a labour that left his men almost prostrated with nervous exhaustion.

This work had taken ten days to complete, and immediately Kyller had begun building observation posts. He placed them on every hump of high ground that commanded a view of the ocean, he built them in the tops of the palm trees, and on the smaller islands that stood out at sea. He arranged a system of signals with his observers – flags and heliographs for the day, sky-rockets for the night.

During the hours of darkness, two whale boats rowed steadily back and forth along the log boom, manned by seamen who slapped steadily and sulkily at the light cloud of mosquitoes that haloed their heads, and made occasional brief but vitriolic statements about Lieutenant Kyller's ancestry, present worth and future prospects.

At 2200 hours on the moonless night of 16 June 1915, the British motor torpedo-boat YN2 crept with both engines running dead slow into the centre of Lieutenant Kyller's elaborate reception arrangements.

– 68 –

After the clean cool air on the open sea, the smell was like entering the monkey-house of London Zoo. The land masked the breeze, and the frolic of the surface chop died away. As the torpedo-boat groped its way into the delta, the miasma of the swamps spread out to meet her.

'My God, that smell.' Sebastian twitched his flattened nose. 'It brings back pleasant memories.'

'Lovely, isn't it?' agreed Flynn.

'We must be almost into the channel.' Sebastian peered into the night, sensing rather than seeing the loom of the mangroves ahead and on either hand.

'I don't know what the hell I'm doing on this barge,' grunted Flynn. 'This is raving bloody madness. We've got more chance of catching a clap than finding our way up to where *Blücher* is anchored.'

'Faith! Major O'Flynn, and shame on ye!' The commander of the torpedo-boat exclaimed in his best music-hall brogue. 'We put our trust in you and the Lord.' His tone changed and he spoke crisply to the helmsman beside him. 'Lay her off a point to starboard.'

The long nose of the boat, with the torpedo tubes lying like a rack of gigantic champagne bottles on her foredeck, swung fractionally. The commander cocked his head to listen to the whispered soundings relayed from the leadsman in the bows.

'Twelve fathoms,' he repeated thoughtfully. 'So far so good.' Then he turned back to Flynn.

'Now, Major, I heard you shooting the blarney to Captain Joyce about how well you know this river, I think your exact words were, "Like you know the way to your own Thunder Box." You don't seem so certain about it any longer. Why is that?'

'It's dark,' said Flynn sulkily.

'My, so it is. But that shouldn't fluster an old river pilot like you.'

'Well, it sure as hell does.'

'If we get into the channel and lay up until the moon rises, would that help?'

'It wouldn't do any harm.'

That exchange seemed to exhaust the subject and for a further fifteen minutes the tense silence on the bridge was spoiled only by the commander's quiet orders to the helm, as he kept his ship within the ten fathom line of the channel.

Then Sebastian made a contribution.

'I say, there's something dead ahead of us.'

A patch of deeper darkness in the night; a low blurred shape that showed against the faint sheen of the star reflections on the surface. A reef perhaps? No, there was a splash alongside it as an oar dipped and pulled.

'Guard boat!' said the commander, and stooped to the voice-pipe. 'Both engines full ahead together.'

The deck canted sharply under their feet as the bows lifted, the whisper of the engines rose to a dull bellow and the torpedo-boat plunged forward like a bull at the cape.

'Hold on! I'm going to ram it.' The commander's voice was pitched at conversational level, and a hubbub of shouts broke out ahead, oars splashed frantically as the guard boat tried to pull out of their line of charge.

'Steer for them,' said the commander pleasantly, and the helmsman put her over a little.

Flash and crack, flash and crack, someone in the guard boat fired a rifle just as the torpedo-boat struck her. It was a glancing blow, taken on her shoulder, that spun the little whale boat aside, shearing off the protruding oars with a crackling popping sound.

She scraped down the gunwale of the torpedo-boat, and then was left astern bobbing and rocking wildly as the larger vessel surged ahead.

Then abruptly it was no longer dark. From all around them sparkling trails of fire shot into the sky and burst in balls of blue, that lit it all with an eerie flickering glow.

'Sky rockets, be Jesus. Guy Fawkes, Guy,' said the commander.

They could see the banks of mangrove massed on either hand, and ahead of them the double mouths of the two channels.

'Steer for the southern channel.' This time the commander lifted his voice a little, and the ship plunged onward, throwing out white wings of water from under her bows, bucking and jarring as she leapt over the low swells pushed up by the out-flowing tide, so the men on the bridge hung on to the hand rail to steady themselves.

Then all of them gasped together in the pain of seared eyeballs as a solid shaft of dazzling white light struck them. It leapt out from the dark wedge of land that divided the two channels, and almost immediately two other searchlights on the outer banks of the channels joined in the hunt. Their beams fastened on the ship like the tentacles of a squid on the carcass of a flying fish.

'Get those lights!' This time the commander shouted the order at the gunners behind the Lewis guns at the corners of the bridge. The tracer that hosed out in a gentle arc towards the base of the searchlight beams was anaemic and pinkly pale, in contrast to the brilliance they were trying to quench.

The torpedo-boat roared on into the channel.

Then there was another sound. A regular thump, thump, thump like the working of a distant water pump. Lieutenant Kyller had opened up with his quick-firing pom-pom.

The four-pound tracer emanated from the dark blob of the island. Seeming to float slowly towards the torpedo-boat, but gaining speed as it approached, until it flashed past with the whirr of a rocketing pheasant.

'Jesus!' said Flynn as though he meant it. He sat down hurriedly on the deck and began to unlace his boots.

Still held in the cold white grip of the searchlights, the torpedo-boat roared on with four-pounder shell streaking around her, and bursting in flurries of spray on the surface near her. The long dotted tendrils of tracer from her own Lewis guns still arched out in delicate lines towards the shore, and suddenly they had effect.

The beam of one of the searchlights snapped off as a bullet shattered the glass, for a few seconds the filaments continued to glow dull red as they burned themselves out.

In the relief from the blinding glare, Sebastian could see ahead, and he saw a sea serpent. It lay across the channel, undulating in the swells, bellied from bank to bank by the push of the tide, showing its back at the top of the swells and then ducking into the troughs; long and sinuous and menacing, Lieutenant Kyller's log boom waited to welcome them.

'Good God, what's that?'

'Full port rudder!' the commander bellowed. 'Both engines full astern together.'

And before the ship could answer her helm or the drag of her propellers, she ran into a log four feet thick and a hundred feet long. A log as unyielding as a reef of solid granite that stopped her dead in the water and crunched in her bows.

The men in the well of her bridge were thrown into a heap of tangled bodies on the deck. A heap from which the bull figure of Flynn Patrick O'Flynn was the first to emerge. On stockinged feet he made for the side of the ship.

'Flynn, where are you going?' Sebastian shouted after him.

'Home,' said Flynn.

'Wait for me.' Sebastian scrambled to his knees.

The engines roaring in reverse pulled the torpedo-boat back off the log-boom, her plywood hull crackling and squeaking, but she was mortally wounded. She was sinking with a rapidity that amazed Sebastian. Already her cockpit was flooding.

'Abandon ship,' shouted the commander.

'You damned tooting,' said Flynn O'Flynn and leaped in an untidy tangle of arms and legs into the water.

Like a playful seal the torpedo-boat rolled over on its side, and Sebastian jumped. Drawing his breath while he was in the air, steeling himself against the cold of the water.

He was surprised at how warm it was.

– 69 –

From the bridge of H.M.S. *Renounce*, the survivors looked like a cluster of bedraggled water rats. In the dawn they floundered and splashed around the edge of the balloon of stained and filthy water where the Rufiji had washed them out, like the effluent from the sewer outlet of a city. *Renounce* found them before the sharks did, for there was no blood. There was one broken leg, a fractured collar bone and a few cracked ribs – but miraculously there was no blood. So from a crew of fourteen, *Renounce* recovered every man – including the two pilots.

They came aboard with their hair matted, their faces streaked, and their eyes swollen and inflamed with engine oil. With a man on either hand to guide them, leaving a trail of malodorous Rufiji water across the deck, they shuffled down to the sick-bay, a sodden and sorrowful-looking assembly of humanity.

'Well,' said Flynn O'Flynn, 'if we don't get a medal for *that*, then I'm going back to my old job – and the hell with them.'

'That,' said Captain Arthur Joyce, sitting hunched behind his desk, 'was not a roaring success.' He showed no inclination to whistle 'Tipperary'.

'It wasn't even a good try, sir,' agreed the torpedo-boat commander. 'The Boche had everything ready to throw at our heads.'

'A log boom—' Joyce shook his head, 'good Lord, they went out with the Napoleonic War!' He said it in a tone that implied that he was a victim of unfair play.

'It was extraordinarily effective, sir.'

'Yes, it must have been.' Joyce sighed. 'Well, at the very least we have established that an attack up the channel is not practical.'

'During the few minutes before the tide swept us away from the boom I looked beyond it, and I saw what I took to be a mine. I think it certain that the Boche have laid a minefield beyond the boom, sir.'

'Thank you, Commander,' Joyce nodded. 'I will see to it that their Lordships receive a full account of your conduct. I consider it excellent.' Then he went on, 'I would value your opinion of Major O'Flynn and his son – do you think they are reliable men?'

'Well . . .' the commander hesitated, he did not want to be unfair, ' – they can both swim and the young one seems to have good eyesight. Apart from that I am not really in a position to give a judgement.'

'No, I don't suppose you are. Still I wish I knew more about them. For the next phase in this operation I am going to rely quite heavily on them.' He stood up. 'I think I will talk to them now.'

'You mean you actually want someone to go on board *Blücher*!' Flynn was appalled.

'I have explained to you, Major, how important it is for me to know exactly what state she is in. I must be able to estimate when she is likely to break out of the delta. I must know how much time I have.'

'Madness,' whispered Flynn. 'Stark raving bloody madness.' He stared at Joyce in disbelief.

'You have told me how well organized is your intelligence system ashore, of the reliable men who work for you. Indeed it is through you that we know that the Germans are cutting cordwood and taking it aboard. We know that they have recruited an army of native labourers and are using them not only for wood-cutting, but also for heavy work aboard the *Blücher*.'

'So?' Into that single word Flynn put a wealth of caution.

'One of your men could infiltrate the labour gangs and get aboard *Blücher*.'

And Flynn perked up immediately; he had anticipated that Joyce would suggest that Flynn Patrick O'Flynn should personally conduct a survey of *Blücher*'s damage.

'It might be done.' There was a lengthy pause while

Flynn considered every aspect of the business. 'Of course, Captain, my men aren't fighting patriots like you and I. They work for money. They are . . .' Flynn searched for the word. 'They are . . .'

'Mercenaries?'

'Yes,' said Flynn. 'That's exactly what they are.'

'Hmm,' said Joyce. 'You mean they would want payment?'

'They'd want a big dollop of lolly – and you can't blame them, can you?'

'The person you send would have to be a first-class man.'

'He would be,' Flynn assured him.

'On behalf of His Majesty's Government, I could undertake to purchase a complete and competent report on the disposition of the German cruiser *Blücher*, for the sum of . . .' he thought about it a moment, '. . . one thousand pounds.'

'Gold?'

'Gold,' agreed Joyce.

'That would cover it nicely.' Flynn nodded, then allowed his eyes to move across the cabin to where Sebastian and Rosa sat side by side on the day couch. They were holding hands, and showing more interest in each other than in the bargainings of Flynn and Captain Joyce.

It was a good thing, Flynn decided, that the Wakamba tribe from which Commissioner Fleischer had recruited the majority of his labour force, affected clean-shaven pates. It would be impossible for a person of European descent to dress his straight hair to resemble the woollen cap of an African.

It was also a good thing about the M'senga tree. From the bark of the M'senga tree the fishermen of Central Africa decocted a liquid in which they soaked their nets. It toughened the fibres of the netting and it also stained the skin. Once Flynn had dipped his finger into a basin of the stuff, and despite constant scrubbing, it was fifteen days before the black stain faded.

It was finally a good thing about Sebastian's nose. Its new contours were decidedly negroid.

– 70 –

'A thousand pounds!' said Flynn O'Flynn as though it were a benediction, and he scooped another mugful of the black liquid and poured it over Sebastian Oldsmith's clean-shaven scalp. 'Think of it, Bassie, me lad, a thousand pounds! Your half share of that is five hundred. Why! You'll be in a position to pay me back every penny you owe me. You'll be out of debt at last.'

They were camped on the Abati river, one of the tributaries of the Rufiji. Six miles downstream was Commissioner Fleischer's wood-cutting camp.

'It's money for jam,' opined Flynn. He was sitting comfortably in a riempie chair beside the galvanized iron tub, in which Sebastian Oldsmith squatted with his knees drawn up under his chin. Sebastian had the dejected look of a spaniel taking a bath in flea shampoo. The liquid in which he sat was the colour and viscosity of strong Turkish coffee and already his face and body were a dark purply chocolate colour.

'Sebastian isn't interested in the money,' said Rosa Oldsmith. She knelt beside the tub and, tenderly as a mother bathing her infant, she was ladling the M'senga juice over Sebastian's shoulders and back.

'I know, I know!' Flynn agreed quickly. 'We are all doing our duty. We all remember little Maria – may the Lord bless and keep her tiny soul. But the money won't hurt us either.'

Sebastian closed his eyes as another mugful cascaded over his head.

'Rub it into the creases round your eyes – and under your chin,' said Flynn, and Sebastian obeyed. 'Now, let's go over it again, Bassie, so you don't get it all balled up. One of Mohammed's cousins is boss-boy of the gang loading the timber into the launches. They are camped on the bank of the Rufiji. Mohammed will slip you in tonight, and tomorrow his cousin will get you on to one of the launches going down with a load for *Blücher*. All you've got to do is keep your eyes open. Joyce just wants to know what work they are doing to repair her; whether or not they've got the boilers fired; things like that. You understand?'

Sebastian nodded glumly.

'You'll come back up-river tomorrow evening, slip out of camp soon as it's dark and meet us here. Simple as a pimple, right?'

'Right,' murmured Sebastian.

'Right then. Out you get and dry off.'

As the dry wind from the uplands blew over his naked body, the purply tint of the dye faded into a matt chocolate. Rosa had modestly moved away into the grove of Marula trees behind the camp. Every few minutes Flynn came across to Sebastian and touched his skin.

'Coming along nicely,' he said, and, 'Nearly done,' and, 'Jeez, you look better than real.' Then finally in Swahili, 'Right, Mohammed, mark his face.'

Mohammed squatted in front of Sebastian with a tiny gourd of cosmetics; a mixture of animal fat and ash and ochre. With his fingers he daubed Sebastian's cheeks and nose and forehead with the tribal patterns. His head held on one side in artistic concentration, making soft clucking sounds of concentration as he worked, until at last Mohammed was satisfied.

315

'He is ready.'

'Get the clothes,' said Flynn. This was an exaggeration. Sebastian's attire could hardly be called clothing.

A string of bark around his neck from which was suspended a plugged duiker horn filled with snuff, a cloak of animal skin that smelled of wood-smoke and man-sweat, draped over his shoulders.

'It stinks!' said Sebastian cringing from contact with the garment. 'And it's probably got lice.'

'The real thing,' agreed Flynn jovially. 'All right, Mohammed. Show him how to fit the istopo – the hat.'

'I don't have to wear that also,' Sebastian protested, staring in horror as Mohammed came towards him, grinning.

'Of course you've got to wear it.' Impatiently Flynn brushed aside his protest.

The hat was a hollow six-inch length cut from the neck of a calabash gourd. An anthropologist would have called it a penis-sheath. It had two purposes: firstly to protect the wearer from the scratches of thorns and the bites of insect pests, and secondly as a boost to his masculinity.

Once in position it looked impressive, enhancing Sebastian's already considerable muscular development.

Rosa said nothing when she returned. She took one long startled look at the hat and then quickly averted her gaze, but her cheeks and neck flared bright scarlet.

'For God's sake, Bassie. Act like you proud of it. Stand up straight and take your hands away.' Flynn coached his son-in-law.

Mohammed knelt to slip the rawhide sandals on to Sebastian's feet, and then hand him the small blanket roll tied with a bark string. Sebastian slung it over one shoulder, then picked up the long-handled throwing-spear.

Automatically he grounded the butt and leaned his weight on the shaft; lifting his left leg and placing the sole of his foot against the calf of his right leg, he stood in the stork posture of rest.

In every detail he was a Wakamba tribesman.

'You'll do,' said Flynn.

– 71 –

I n the dawn, little wisps of river mist swirled around Commissioner Fleischer's legs as he came down the bank and on to the improvised jetty of logs.

He ran his eyes over the two launches, checking the ropes that held down the cargoes of timber. The launches sat low in the water, their exhausts puttering and blowing pale blue smoke that drifted away across the slick surface of the river.

'Are you ready?' he called to his sergeant of Askari.

'The men are eating, Bwana Mkuba.'

'Tell them to hurry,' growled Fleischer. It was a futile order and he stepped to the edge of the jetty, unbuttoning his trousers. He urinated noisily into the river, and the circle of men who squatted around the three-legged pot on the jetty watched him with interest, but without interrupting their breakfast.

With leather cloaks folded around their shoulders against the chill air off the water, they reached in turn into the pot and took a handful of the thick white maize porridge, moulding it into a mouth-size ball and then with the thumb forming a cup in the ball, dipping the ball into the smaller enamel dish and filling the depression with the creamy yellow gravy it contained, a tantalizing mixture of stewed catfish and tree caterpillars.

It was the first time that Sebastian had tasted this delicacy. He sat with the others and imitated their eating routine, forcing himself to place a lump of the spiced maize

317

meal in his mouth. His gorge rose and gagged him, it tasted like fish oil and new-mown grass, not really offensive – it was just the thought of those fat yellow caterpillars. But had he been eating ham sandwiches, his appetite would not have been hearty.

His stomach was cramped with apprehension. He was a spy. A word from one of his companions, and Commissioner Fleischer would shout for the hanging ropes. Sebastian remembered the men he had seen in the monkey-bean tree on the bank of this same river, he remembered the flies clustered on their swollen, lolling tongues. It was not a mental picture conducive to enjoyment of breakfast.

Now, pretending to eat, he watched Commissioner Fleischer instead. It was the first time he had done so at leisure. The bulky figure in grey corduroy uniform, the pink-boiled face with pale golden eyelashes, the full petulant lips, the big freckled hands, all these revolted him. He felt his uneasiness swamped by a revival of the emotions that had possessed him as he stood beside the newly filled grave of his daughter on the heights above Lalapanzi.

'Black pig-animals,' shouted Herman Fleischer in Swahili, as he rebuttoned his clothing. 'That is enough! You do nothing but eat and sleep. It is time now for work.' He waddled across the logs of the jetty, into the little circle of porters. His first kick sent the three-legged pot clattering, his second kick caught Sebastian in the back and threw him forward on to his knees.

'Rasch!' He aimed another kick at one of them, but it was dodged, and the porters scattered to the launches.

Sebastian scrambled up. He had been kicked only once before in his life, and Flynn O'Flynn had learned not to do it again. For Sebastian there was nothing so humiliating as the contact of another man's foot against his person, also it had hurt.

Herman Fleischer had turned away to chivvy the others,

so he did not see the hatred nor the way that Sebastian snarled at him, crouching like a leopard. Another second and he would have been on him. He might have killed Fleischer before the Askari shot him down – but he never made the attempt.

A hand on his arm. Mohammed's cousin beside him, his voice very low.

'Come! Let it pass. They will kill us also.'

And when Fleischer turned back the two of them had gone to the launch.

On the run down-river, Sebastian huddled with the others. Like them, drawing his cloak over his head to keep off the sun, but unlike them, he did not sleep. Through half-hooded eyes he was still watching Herman Fleischer, and his thoughts were hate-ugly.

Even with the current, the run in the deep-laden launches took almost four hours, and it was noon before they chugged around the last bend in the channel and turned in towards the mangrove forests.

Sebastian saw Herman Fleischer swallow the last bite of sausage and carefully repack the remainder into his haversack. He stood up and spoke to the man at the rudder, and both of them peered ahead.

'We have arrived,' said Mohammed's cousin, and removed his cloak from over his head. The little huddle of porters stirred into wakefulness and Sebastian stood up with them.

This time he knew what to look for, and he saw the muzzy silhouette of the *Blücher* skulking under her camouflage. From low down on the water she looked mountainous, and Sebastian's spine tingled as he remembered when last he had seen her from this angle, driving down to ram them with those axe-sharp blows. But now she floated awry, listing heavily.

'The boat leans over to one side.'

'Yes,' agreed Mohammed's cousin. 'The Allemand wanted it so. There has been a great carrying of goods within her, they have moved everything to make the boat lean over.'

'Why?'

The man shrugged and pointed with his chin. 'They have lifted her belly from the water, see how they work with fire on the holes in her skin.'

Tiny as beetles, men swarmed on the exposed hull, and even in the bright glare of midday, the welding torches flared and sparkled with blue-white flame. The new plating was conspicuous in its coat of dull brown zinc oxide paint, against the battleship-grey of the original hull.

As the launch approached, Sebastian studied the work carefully. He could see that it was nearing completion, the welders were running closed the last seams in the new plating. Already there were painters covering the oxide red with the matt grey final coat.

The pock marks of the shell splinters in her upper-works had been closed, and here again men hung on the flimsy trapezes of rope and planks, their arms lifting and falling as they plied the paint brushes.

An air of bustle and intent activity gripped the *Blücher*. Everywhere men moved about fifty different tasks, while the uniforms of the officers were restless white spots roving about her decks.

'They have closed all the holes in her belly?' Sebastian asked.

'All of them,' Mohammed's cousin confirmed. 'See how she spits out the water that was in her womb.' And he pointed again with his chin. From a dozen outlet vents, *Blücher*'s pumps were expelling solid streams of brown water as she emptied the flooded compartments.

'There is smoke from her chimneys,' Sebastian

exclaimed, as he noticed for the first time the faint shimmer of heat at the mouths of her stacks.

'Yes. They have built fire in the iron boxes deep inside her. My brother Walaka works there now. He is helping to tend the fires. At first the fires were small, but each day they feed them higher.'

Sebastian nodded thoughtfully, he knew it took time to heat cold furnaces without cracking the linings of fireclay.

The launch nosed in and bumped against the cliff-high side of the cruiser.

'Come,' said Mohammed's cousin. 'We will climb up and work with the gangs carrying the wood down into her. You will see more up there.'

A new wave of dread flooded over Sebastian. He didn't want to go up there among the enemy. But already his guide was scrambling up the catwalk that hung down *Blücher's* flank.

Sebastian adjusted his penis-sheath, hitched up his cloak, took a deep breath and followed him.

– 72 –

'Sometimes it goes like that. In the beginning everything is an obscene shambles; nothing but snags and accidents and delays. Then suddenly everything drops into place and the job is finished.' Standing under the awning on the foredeck, Commander (Engineering) Lochtkamper was a satisfied man, as he looked around the ship. 'Two weeks ago it looked as though we would still be messing around when the war was over – but now!'

'You have done well,' von Kleine understated the facts. 'Again you have justified my confidence. But now I have another task to add to your burdens.'

'What is it, Captain?' Lochtkamper kept his voice non-committal, but there was a wariness in his eyes.

'I want to alter the ship's profile – change it to resemble that of a British heavy cruiser.'

'How?'

'A dummy stack abaft the radio office. Canvas on a wooden frame. Then mask "X" turret, and block in the dip of our waist. If we run into the British blockade squadron in the night, it may give us the few extra minutes that will make the difference between success or failure.' Von Kleine spoke again as he turned away, 'Come, I will show you what I mean.'

Lochtkamper fell in beside him and they started aft, an incongruous pair; the engineer swaddled in soiled overalls, long arms dangling, shambling along beside his captain like a trained ape. Von Kleine tall over him, his tropical whites crisp and sterile, hands clasped behind his back and golden beard bowed forward on to his chest, leaning slightly against the steeply canted angle of the deck.

He spoke carefully. 'When can I sail, Commander? I must know precisely. Is the work so far advanced that you can say with certainty?'

Lochtkamper was silent, considering his reply as they picked their way side by side through the milling jostle of seamen and native porters.

'I will have full pressure on my boilers by tomorrow night, another day after that to complete the work on the hull, two more days to adjust the trim of the ship and to make the alterations to the superstructure,' he mused aloud. Then he looked up. Von Kleine was watching him. 'Four days,' he said. 'I will be ready in four days.'

'Four days. You are certain of that?'

'Yes.'

'Four days,' repeated von Kleine, and he stopped in mid-stride to think. This morning he had received a message from Governor Schee in Dar es Salaam, a message relayed from the Admiralty in Berlin. Naval Intelligence reported that three days ago a convoy of twelve troop ships, carrying Indian and South African infantry, had left Durban harbour. Their destination was not known, but it was an educated guess that the British were about to open a new theatre of war. The campaign in German West Africa had been brought to a swift and decisive conclusion by the South Africans. Botha and Smuts had launched a double-pronged offensive, driving in along the railroads to the German capital of Windhoek. The capitulation of the German West African army had released the South African forces for work elsewhere. It was almost certain that those troopships were trundling up the east coast at this very moment, intent on a landing at one of the little harbours that dotted the coast of East Africa. Tanga perhaps, or Kilwa Kvinje – possibly even Dar es Salaam itself.

He must have his ship seaworthy and battle-ready to break out through the blockade squadron, and destroy that convoy.

'The big job will be readjusting the ship's trim. There is much to be done. Stores to be manhandled, shell from the magazines, the guns remounted . . .' Lochtkamper interrupted his thoughts. 'We will need labour.'

'I will order Fleischer to bring all his forced labour down to assist with the work,' von Kleine muttered. 'But we must sail in four days. The moon will be right on the night of the thirtieth, we must break out then.' The saintly face was ruffled by the force of his concentration, he paced slowly, the golden beard sunk on his chest as he formulated his plans, speaking aloud. 'Kyller has buoyed the channel. He must start clearing the minefield at the entrance. We can cut the boom at the last moment – and the current will sweep it aside.'

They had reached the waist of the cruiser. Von Kleine

was so deep in his thoughts that it took Lochtkamper's restraining hand on his arm, to return him to reality.

'Careful, sir.'

With a start von Kleine looked up. They had walked into a knot of African porters. Wild tribesmen, naked beneath their filthy leather cloaks, faces daubed with yellow ochre. They were man-handling the faggots of cordwood that were coming aboard from the launch that lay alongside *Blücher*. One of the heavy bundles was suspended from the boom of the derrick, it was swaying twenty feet above the deck and von Kleine had been about to walk under it. Lochtkamper's warning stopped him.

While he waited for them to clear away the faggot, von Kleine idly watched the native gang of workers.

One of the porters caught his attention. He was taller than his companions, his body sleeker, lacking the bunched and knotty muscle. His legs also were sturdier and finely moulded. The man lifted his head from his labours, and von Kleine looked into his face. The features were delicate; the lips not as full as, the forehead broader and deeper than, the typical African.

But it was the eyes that jerked von Kleine's attention back from the troop convoy. They were brown, dark brown and shifty. Von Kleine had learned to recognize guilt in the faces of his subordinates, it showed in the eyes. This man was guilty. It was only an instant that von Kleine saw it, then the porter dropped his gaze and stooped to take a grip on the bundle of timber. The man worried him, left him feeling vaguely uneasy, he wanted to speak with him – question him. He started towards him.

'Captain! Captain!' Commissioner Fleischer had come puffing up the catwalk from the launch, plump and sweaty; he was pawing von Kleine's arm.

'I must speak with you, Captain.'

'Ah, Commissioner,' von Kleine greeted him coolly,

324

trying to avoid the damp paw. 'One moment, please. I wish to . . .'

'It is a matter of the utmost importance. Ensign Proust . . .'

'In a moment, Commissioner.' Von Kleine pulled away, but Fleischer was determined. He stepped in front of von Kleine, blocking his path.

'Ensign Proust, the cowardly little prig . . .' and von Kleine found himself embroiled in a long report about Ensign Proust's lack of respect for the dignity of the Commissioner. He had been insubordinate, he had argued with Herr Fleischer, and further he had told Herr Fleischer that he considered him 'fat'.

'I will speak to Proust,' said von Kleine. It was a trivial matter and he wanted no part of it. Then Commander Lochtkamper was beside them. Would the Captain speak to the Herr Commissioner about labour for the handling of ballast? They fell into a long discussion and while they talked, the gang of porters lugged the bundle of timber aft and were absorbed by the bustling hordes of workmen.

Sebastian was sweating with fright; trembling, giddy with fright. Clearly he had sensed the German officer's suspicions. Those cold blue eyes had burned like dry ice. Now he stooped under his load, trying to shrink himself into insignificance, trying to overcome the grey clammy sense of dread that threatened to crush him.

'He saw you,' wheezed Mohammed's cousin, shuffling along beside Sebastian.

'Yes.' Sebastian bent lower. 'Is he still watching?'

The old man glanced back over his shoulder.

'No. He speaks with Mafuta, the fat one.'

'Good.' Sebastian felt a lift of relief. 'We must get back on the launch.'

'The loading is almost finished, but we must first speak with my brother. He waits for us.'

They turned the corner of the aft gun-turrets. On the deck was a mountain of cordwood. Stacked neatly and lashed down with rope. Black men swarmed over it, between them spreading a huge green tarpaulin over the wood pile.

They reached the wood pile and added the faggots they carried to the stack. Then, in the custom of Africa, they paused to rest and talk. A man clambered down from the wood pile to join them, a sprightly old gentleman with woolly grey hair, impeccably turned out in cloak and penis-sheath. Mohammed's cousin greeted him with courteous affection, and they took snuff together.

'This man is my brother,' he told Sebastian. 'His name is Walaka. When he was a young man he killed a lion with a spear. It was a big lion with a black mane.' To Sebastian this information seemed to be slightly irrelevant, his fear of discovery was making him nervously impatient. There were Germans all around them, big blond Germans bellowing orders as they chivvied on the labour gangs, Germans looking down on them from the tall superstructure above them, Germans elbowing them aside as they passed. Sebastian found it difficult to concentrate.

His two accomplices were involved in a family discussion. It seemed that Walaka's youngest daughter had given birth to a fine son, but that during his absence a leopard had raided Walaka's village and killed three of his goats. The new grandson did not seem to compensate Walaka for the loss of his goats. He was distressed.

'Leopards are the excrement of dead lepers,' he said, and would have enlarged on the subject but Sebastian interrupted him.

'Tell me of the things you have seen on this canoe. Say swiftly, there is little time. I must go before the Allemand comes for all of us with the ropes.'

Mention of the ropes brought the meeting to order, and Walaka launched into his report.

There were fires burning in the iron boxes in the belly of the canoe. Fires of such heat that they pained the eye when the door of the box was opened, fires with a breath like that of a hundred bush fires, fires that consumed . . .

'Yes, yes.' Sebastian cut short the lyrical description. 'What else?'

There had been a great carrying of goods, moving of them to one side of the canoe to make it lean in the water. They had carried boxes and bales, unbolted machinery and guns. See how they had been moved. They had taken from the rooms under her roof a great quantity of the huge bullets, also the white bags of powder for the guns and placed them in other rooms on the far side.

'What else?'

There was more, much more to tell. Walaka enthused about meat which came out of little tins, of lanterns that burned without wick, flame or oil, of great wheels that spun, and boxes of steel that screamed and hummed, of clean fresh water that gushed from the mouths of long rubber snakes, sometimes cold and at other times hot as though it had been boiled over a fire. There were marvels so numerous that it confused a man.

'These things I know. Is there nothing else that you have seen?'

Indeed there was. The Allemand had shot three native porters, lining them up and covering their eyes with strips of white cloth. The men had jumped and wriggled and fallen in a most comical fashion, and afterwards the Germans had washed the blood from the deck with water from the long snakes. Since then none of the other porters had helped themselves to blankets and buckets and other small movables – the price was exorbitant.

Walaka's description of the execution had a chilling

effect on Sebastian. He had done what he had come to do and now his urge to leave *Blücher* became overpowering. It was helped on by a German petty officer who joined the group uninvited.

'You lazy black baboons,' he bellowed. 'This is not a bloody Sunday-school outing – move, you swine, move!' And his boots flew. Led by Mohammed's cousin they left Walaka without farewell and scampered back along the deck. Just before they reached the entry port, Sebastian checked. The two German officers stood where he had left them, but now they were looking up at the high smoke stacks. The tall officer with the golden beard was describing sweeping motions with his outstretched hand, talking while the stocky one listened intently.

Mohammed's cousin scurried past them and disappeared over the side into the launch, leaving Sebastian hesitant and reluctant to run the gauntlet of those pale blue eyes.

'Manali, come quickly. The boat swims, you will be left!' Mohammed's cousin called from down below, his voice faint but urgent above the chug of the launch's engine.

Sebastian started forward again, his stomach a cold lump under his ribs. A dozen paces and he had reached the entry port.

The German officer turned and saw him. He challenged with raised voice, and came towards Sebastian, one arm outstretched as though to hold him.

Sebastian whirled and dived down the catwalk. Below him the launch was casting off her lines, water churning back from her propeller.

Sebastian reached the grating at the bottom of the catwalk. There was a gap of ten feet between him and the launch. He jumped, hung for a moment in the air, then hit the gunwale of the launch. His clutching fingers found a grip while his legs dangled in the warm water.

Mohammed's cousin caught his shoulder and dragged

him aboard. They tumbled together in a heap on the deck of the launch.

'Bloody kaffir,' said Herman Fleischer and stooped to cuff them both heavily around the ears. Then he went back to his seat in the stern, and Sebastian smiled at him with something close to affection. After those deadly blue eyes, Herman Fleischer seemed as dangerous as a teddy-bear.

Then he looked back at *Blücher*. The German officer stood at the top of the catwalk, watching them as they drew away, and set a course upstream. Then he turned away from the rail and disappeared.

– 73 –

Sebastian sat on the day couch in the master cabin of H.M.S. *Renounce*, he sagged against the arm-rest and fought off the grey waves of exhaustion that washed over his mind.

He had not slept in thirty hours. After his escape from *Blücher* there had been the long launch journey up-river during which he had remained awake and jittery with the after-effects of tension.

After disembarking he had sneaked out of Fleischer's camp, avoiding the Askari guards, and trotted through the moonlight to meet Flynn and Rosa.

A hurried meal, and then all three of them had mounted on bicycles supplied with the compliments of the Royal Navy, and ridden all night along a rough elephant path to where they had left a canoe hidden among the reeds on the bank of one of the Rufiji tributaries.

In the dawn they had paddled out of one of the unguarded channels of the delta and made their rendezvous with the little whaler from H.M.S. *Renounce*.

Two long days of activity without rest, and Sebastian

was groggy. Rosa sat beside him on the couch. She leaned across and touched his arm, her eyes dark with concern. Neither of them was taking any part in the conference in which the other persons in the crowded cabin were deeply involved.

Joyce sat as chairman, and beside him an older heavier man with bushy grey eyebrows and a truculent jaw, hair brushed in streaks across his pate in an ineffectual attempt to conceal his baldness. This was Armstrong, Captain of H.M.S. *Pegasus*, the other cruiser of the blockade squadron.

'Well, it looks as though *Blücher* has made good her damage, then. If she has fired her boilers, we can expect her to break out any day now – von Kleine would not burn up good fuel to keep his stokers warm.' He said it with relish, a fighting man anticipating a good hard fight. 'There's a message I'd like to give her from *Bloodhound* and *Orion* – an old account to settle.'

But Joyce also had a message, one that had its origin at the desk of Admiral Sir Percy Howe, Commander-in-Chief, South Atlantic and Indian Oceans. In part this message read:

'The safety of your squadron considered secondary to containing *Blücher*. Risk involved in delaying until *Blücher* leaves the delta before engaging her is too high. Absolutely imperative that she be either destroyed or blocked at her present anchorage. Consequences of *Blücher* running block-ade and attacking the troop convoy conveying landing forces to invasion of Tanga will be catastrophic. Efforts being made to send you two tramp steamers to act as block ships, but failing their arrival, and failing also effective offensive action against *Blücher* before 30 July 1915, you are hereby ordered to scuttle *Renounce* and *Pegasus* in the channel of the Rufiji to block *Blücher*'s exit.'

It was a command that left Captain Arthur Joyce sick

with dread. To scuttle his splendid ships – a thought as repulsive and loathsome as that of incest, of patricide, of human sacrifice. Today was 26 July, he had four days in which to find an alternative before the order became effective,

'She'll come out at night, of course, bound to!' Armstrong's voice was thick with battle lust. 'This time she'll not have an old girl and a baby like *Orion* and *Bloodhound* to deal with.' His tone changed slightly. 'We'll have to look lively. New moon in three days so *Blücher* will have dark nights. There could be a change in the weather . . .' Armstrong was looking a little worried now, '. . . we'll have to tighten up . . .'

'Read this,' said Joyce, and passed the flimsy to Armstrong. He read it.

'My God!' he gasped. 'Scuttle. Oh, my God!'

'There are two channels that *Blücher* could use.' Joyce spoke softly. 'We would have to block both of them – *Renounce* and *Pegasus*!'

'Jesus God!' swore Armstrong in horror. 'There must be another way.'

'I think there is,' said Joyce, and looked across at Sebastian. 'Mr Oldsmith,' he spoke gently, 'would it be possible for you to get on board the German cruiser once again?'

There were tiny lumps of yellow mucus in the corner of Sebastian's bloodshot eyes, but the stain that darkened his skin concealed the rings of fatigue under them.

'I'd rather not, old chap.' He ran his hand thoughtfully over his shaven scalp and the stubble of new hair rasped under his fingers. 'It was one of the most unpleasant hours of my life.'

'Quite,' said Captain Joyce. 'Quite so! I wouldn't have asked you, had I not considered it to be of prime importance.' Joyce paused and pursed his lips to whistle softly the first bar of Chopin's 'Funeral March', then he sighed and shook his head. 'If I were to tell you that you alone have it in your power to save both the cruisers of this squadron from destruction and to protect the lives of fifteen thousand British soldiers and seamen – how would you answer then?'

Glumly, Sebastian sagged back against the couch and closed his eyes.

'Can I have a few hours sleep first?'

– 74 –

It was exactly the size of a box of twenty-four Monte Cristo Havana Cigars, for that had been its contents before *Renounce*'s chief engine room artificer and the gunnery lieutenant had set to work on it.

It lay on the centre of Captain Joyce's desk, while the artificer explained its purpose to the respectful audience that stood around him.

'It's verra simple,' started the artificer in an accent that was as bracing as the fragrance of heather and highland whisky.

'It would have to be . . .' commented Flynn O'Flynn, '. . . for Bassie to understand it.'

'All you do is lift the lid.' The artificer suited action to the words, and even Flynn craned forward to examine the contents of the cigar box. Packed neatly into it were six yellow sticks of gelignite, looking like candles wrapped in grease-proof paper. There was also the flat dry cell battery from a bull's eye lantern, and a travelling-clock in a pigskin case. All of these were connected by loops and twists of fine copper wire. Engraved into the metal of the clock base were the words:

'To my dear husband Arthur,
With love,
Iris.
Christmas 1914.'

Captain Arthur Joyce stilled a sentimental pang of regret with the thought that Iris would understand.

'Then . . .' said the artificer, clearly enjoying the hold he had on his audience, '. . . you wind the knob on the clock.' He touched it with his forefinger, '. . . close the lid,' he closed it, '. . . wait twelve hours, and – Boom!' The enthusiasm with which the Scotsman simulated an explosion blew a fine spray of spittle across the desk, and Flynn withdrew hurriedly out of range.

'Wait twelve hours?' asked Flynn, dabbing at the droplets on his cheeks. 'Why so long?'

'I ordered a twelve-hour delay on the fusing of the charge.' Joyce answered the question. 'If Mr Oldsmith is to gain access to the *Blücher*'s magazines, he will have to infiltrate the native labour gangs engaged in transferring the explosives. Once he is a member of the gang he might find difficulty in extricating himself and getting away from the ship after he has placed the charge. I am sure that Mr Oldsmith would be reluctant to make this attempt unless we could ensure that there is time for him to escape from *Blücher*, when his efforts . . . ah,' he sought the correct phraseology, '. . . ah . . . come to fruition.' Joyce was pleased with this speech, and he turned to Sebastian for endorsement. 'Am I correct in my assumption, Mr Oldsmith?'

Not to be outdone in verbosity, Sebastian pondered his reply for a second. Five hours of deathlike sleep curled in Rosa's arms had refreshed his body and sharpened his wit to the edge of a Toledo steel blade.

'Indubitably,' he replied, and beamed in triumph.

They sat together in the time when the sun was dying and bleeding on the clouds. They sat together on a kaross of monkey skin in a thicket of wild ebony, at the head of one of the draws that wrinkled down into the valley of the Rufiji. They sat in silence. Rosa bent forward over her needlework, as she stitched a concealed pocket into the filthy cloak of leather that lay across her lap. The pocket would hold the cigar box. Sebastian watched her, and his eyes upon her were a caress. She pulled the last stitch tight, knotted it, then leaned forward to bite the thread.

'There!' she said. 'It's finished.' And looked up into his eyes.

'Thank you,' said Sebastian. They sat together quietly and Rosa reached out to touch his shoulder. The muscle under the black stained skin was rubber hard, and warm.

'Come,' she said and drew his head down to her so that their cheeks touched, and they held each other while the last light faded. The African dusk thickened the shadows in the wild ebony, and down the draw a jackal yipped plaintively.

'Are you ready?' Flynn stood near them, a dark bulky figure, with Mohammed beside him.

'Yes.' Sebastian looked up at him.

'Kiss me,' whispered Rosa, 'and come back safely.'

Gently Sebastian broke from her embrace. He stood tall above her, and draped the cloak over his naked body. The cigar box hung heavily between his shoulder blades.

'Wait for me,' he said, and walked away.

*

Flynn Patrick O'Flynn moved restlessly under his single blanket and belched. Heartburn moved acid sour in his throat, and he was cold. The earth under him had long since lost the warmth it had sucked from yesterday's sun. A small slice of the old moon gave a little silver light to the night.

Unsleeping he lay and listened to the soft sound of Rosa sleeping near him. The sound irritated him, he lacked only an excuse to waken her and make her talk to him. Instead he reached into the haversack that served as his pillow and his fingers closed round the cold smooth glass of the bottle.

A night-bird hooted softly down the draw, and Flynn released the bottle and sat up quickly. He placed two fingers between his lips and repeated the night-bird's cry.

Minutes later Mohammed drifted like a small black ghost into camp and came to squat beside Flynn's bed.

'I see you, Fini.'

'You I see also, Mohammed. It went well?'

'It went well.'

'Manali has entered the camp of the Allemand?'

'He sleeps now beside the man who is my cousin, and in the dawn they will go down the Rufiji, to the big boat of the Allemand once again.'

'Good!' grunted Flynn. 'You have done well.'

Mohammed coughed softly to signify that there was more to tell.

'What is it?' Flynn demanded.

'When I had seen Manali safely into the care of my cousin, I came back along the valley and . . .' he hesitated, '. . . perhaps it is not fitting to speak of such matters at a time when our Lord Manali goes unarmed and alone into the camp of the Allemand.'

'Speak,' said Flynn.

'As I walked without sound, I came to a place where this

335

valley falls down to the little river called Abati. You know the place?'

'Yes, about a mile down the draw from here.'

'That is the place.' Mohammed nodded. 'It was here that I saw something move in the night. It was as though a mountain walked.'

A silver of ice was thrust down Flynn's spine, and his breathing snagged painfully in his throat.

'Yes?' he breathed.

'It was a mountain armed with teeth of ivory that grew from its face to touch the ground as it walked.'

'*Plough the Earth*.' Flynn whispered the name, and his hand fell on to the rifle that lay loaded beside his bed.

'It was that one.' Mohammed nodded again. 'He feeds quietly, moving towards the Rufiji. But the voice of a rifle would carry down to the ears of the Allemand.'

'I won't fire,' whispered Flynn. 'I just want to have a look at him. I just want to see him again.' And the hand on the rifle shook like that of a man in high fever.

– 76 –

The sun pushed up and sat fat and fiery as molten gold, on the hills of the Rufiji basin. Its warmth lifted streamers of mist from the swamps and reed-beds that bounded the Abati river, and they smoked like the ashes of a dying fire.

Under the fever trees the air was still cool with the memory of the night, but the sun sent long yellow shafts of light probing through the branches to disperse and warm it.

Three old eland bulls came up from the river, bigger than domestic cattle, light bluey-brown in colour with faint chalk stripes across the barrel of their bodies, they walked in single file, heavy dewlaps swinging, thick stubby horns held erect, and the tuft of darker hair on their foreheads standing out clearly. They reached the grove of fever trees and the lead bull stopped, suddenly alert. For long seconds they stood absolutely still, staring into the open palisade of fever-tree trunks where the light was still vague beneath the canopy of interlaced leaves and branches.

The lead bull blew softly through his nostrils, and swung off the game path that led into the grove. Stepping lightly for such large animals, the three eland skirted the grove and moved away to blend into the dry thorn scrub higher up the slope.

'He is in there,' whispered Mohammed. 'The eland saw him, and turned aside.'

'Yes,' agreed Flynn. 'It is such a place as he would choose to lie up for the day.' He sat in the crotch of a M'banga tree, wedged securely ten feet above the ground, and peered across three hundred yards of open grassland at the dense stand of fever trees. The hands that held the binoculars to his eyes were unsteady with gin and excitement, and he was sweating, a droplet broke from his hair-line and slid down his cheek, tickling like an insect. He brushed it away.

'A wise man would leave him, and walk away even as the eland did.' Mohammed gave his opinion. He leaned against the base of the tree, holding Flynn's rifle across his chest. Flynn did not reply. He peered through the binoculars, swinging them slowly in an arc as he searched.

'He must be deep among the trees, I cannot see him from here.' And he loosened his leg grip from the crotch and clambered down to where Mohammed waited. He took his rifle and checked the load.

'Leave him, Fini,' Mohammed urged softly. 'There is no profit in it. We cannot carry the teeth away.'

'Stay here,' said Flynn.

'Fini, the Allemand will hear you. They are close – very close.'

'I will not shoot,' said Flynn. 'I must see him again – that is all. I will not shoot.'

Mohammed took the gin bottle from the haversack and handed it to him. Flynn drank.

'Stay here,' he repeated, his voice husky from the burn of the raw spirit.

'Be careful, Fini. He is an old one of evil temper – be careful.' Mohammed watched Flynn start out across the clearing. He walked with the slow deliberation of a man who goes in good time to a meeting that has long been prearranged. He reached the grove of fever trees and walked on into them without checking.

Plough the Earth was sleeping on his feet. His little eyes closed tightly in their wrinkled pouches. Tears had oozed in a long dark stain down his cheeks, and a fine haze of midges hovered about them. Tattered as battle-riven banners on a windless day, his ears lay back against his shoulders. His tusks were crutches that propped up the gnarled old head, and his trunk hung down between them, grey and slack and heavy.

Flynn saw him, and picked his way towards him between the trunks of the fever trees. The setting had an unreal quality, for the light effect of the low sun through the branches was golden beams reflected in shimmering misty green from the leaves of the fever trees. The grove was resonant with the whine of cicada beetles.

Flynn circled out until he was head on to the sleeping elephant, and then he moved in again. Twenty paces from him Flynn stopped. He stood with his feet set apart, the rifle held ready across one hip, and his head thrown back as he looked up at the unbelievable bulk of the old bull.

Up to this moment Flynn still believed that he would not shoot. He had come only to look at him once more, but it was as futile as an alcoholic who promised himself just one taste. He felt the madness begin at the base of his spine, hot and hard it poured into his body, filling him as though he were a container. The level rose to his throat and he tried to check it there, but the rifle was coming up. He felt the butt in his shoulder. Then he heard with surprise a voice, a voice that rang clearly through the grove and instantly stilled the whine of the cicadas. It was his own voice, crying out in defiance of his conscious resolve.

'Come on, then,' he shouted. And the old elephant burst from massive quiescence into full charge. It came down on him like a dynamited cliff of black rock. He saw it over the open rear sight of his rifle, saw it beyond the minute pip of the foresight that rode unwaveringly in the centre of the old bull's bulging brow – between the eyes, where the crease of skin at the base of its trunk was a deep lateral line.

The shot was thunderous, shattering into a thousand echoes against the boles of the fever trees. The elephant died in the fullness of his run. Legs buckled, and he came toppling forward, carried by his own momentum, a loose avalanche of flesh and bone and long ivory.

Flynn turned aside like a matador from the run of the bull, three quick dancing steps and then one of the tusks hit him. It took him across the hip with a force that hurled him twenty feet, the rifle spinning from his hands so that as he fell and rolled in the soft bed of loose trash and leaf mould, his lower body twisted away from his trunk at an impossible angle. His brittle old bones had broken like china; the ball of the femur snapping off in its socket, his pelvis fracturing clean through.

Lying face down, Flynn was mildly surprised that there was no pain. He could feel the jagged edges of bone rasping together deep in his flesh at his slightest movement, but there was no pain.

Slowly, pulling himself forward on his elbows so that his legs slithered uselessly after him, he crawled towards the carcass of the old bull.

He reached it, and with one hand stroked the yellowed shaft of ivory that had crippled him.

'Now,' he whispered, fondling the smoothly polished tusk the way a man might touch his firstborn son. 'Now, at last you are mine.'

And then the pain started, and he closed his eyes and cowered down, huddled beneath the hillock of dead and cooling flesh that had been *Plough the Earth*. The pain buzzed in his ears like cicada beetles, but through it he heard Mohammed's voice.

'Fini. It was not wise.'

He opened his eyes and saw Mohammed's monkey face puckered with concern.

'Call Rosa,' he croaked. 'Call Little Long Hair. Tell her to come.'

Then he closed his eyes again, and rode the pain. The tempo of the pain changed constantly – first it was drums, tom-toms that throbbed and beat within him. Then it was the sea, long undulating swells of agony. Then again it was night, cold black night that chilled him so he shivered and moaned – and the night gave way to the sun. A great fiery ball of pain that burned and shot out lances of blinding light that burst against his clenched eyelids. Then the drums began again.

Time was of no significance. He rode the pain for a minute and a million years, then through the beat of the drums of agony he heard movement near him. The shuffle of feet through the dead leaves, the murmur of voices that were not part of his consuming anguish.

'Rosa,' Flynn whispered, 'you have come!'

He rolled his head and forced his eyelids open.

Herman Fleischer stood over him. He was grinning. His face flushed as a rose petal, fresh sweat clinging in his pale eyebrows, breathing quickly and heavily with exertion as though he had been running, but he was grinning.

'So!' he wheezed. 'So!'

The shock of his presence was muted for Flynn by the haze of pain in which he lay. There were smears of dust dulling the gloss of Fleischer's jackboots, and dark patches of sweat had soaked through the thick grey corduroy tunic at the armpits. He held a Luger pistol in his right hand and with his left hand he pushed the slouch hat to the back of his head.

'Herr Flynn!' he said and chuckled. It was the fat infectious chuckle of a healthy baby.

Mildly Flynn wondered how Fleischer had found him so quickly in the broken terrain and thick bush. The shot would have alerted him, but what had led him directly to the grove of fever trees?

Then he heard a rustling fluting rush in the air above him, and he looked upwards. Through the lacework of branches he saw the vultures spiralling against the aching blue of the sky. They turned and dipped on spread black wings, cocking their heads sideways in flight to look down with bright beady eyes on the elephant carcass.

'Ja! The birds. We followed the birds.'

'Jackals always follow the birds,' whispered Flynn, and Fleischer laughed. He threw back his head and laughed with genuine delight.

'Good. Oh, ja. That is good.' And he kicked Flynn. He swung the jackboot lazily into Flynn's body, and Flynn shrieked. The laughter dried instantly in Fleischer's throat, and he bent quickly to examine Flynn.

He noticed for the first time how his lower body was grotesquely twisted and distorted. And he dropped to his knees beside him. Gently he touched Flynn's forehead, and deep concern flashed across his chubby features at the clammy cold feeling of the skin.

'Sergeant!' There was a desperate edge to his voice now. 'This man is badly injured. He will not last long. Be quick!

Get the rope! We must hang him before he loses consciousness.'

Rosa awoke in the dawn and found that she was alone. Beside Flynn's personal pack, his discarded blanket had been carelessly flung aside. His rifle was gone.

She was not alarmed, not at first. She guessed that he had gone into the bush on one of his regular excursions to be alone while he drank his breakfast. But an hour later when he had not returned she grew anxious. She sat with her rifle across her lap, and every bird noise or animal scuffle in the ebony thicket jarred her nerves.

Another hour and she was fretting. Every few minutes she stood up and walked to the edge of the clearing to listen. Then she went back to sit and worry.

Where on earth was Flynn? Why had Mohammed not returned? What had happened to Sebastian? Was he safe, or had he been discovered? Had Flynn gone to assist him? Should she wait here, or follow them down the draw?

Her eyes haunted, her mouth hard set with doubts, she sat and twisted the braid of her hair around one finger in a nervously restless gesture.

Then Mohammed came. Suddenly he appeared out of the thicket beside her, and Rosa jumped up with a low cry of relief. The cry died in her throat as she saw his face.

'Fini!' he said. 'He is hurt. The great elephant has broken his bones and he lies in pain. He asks for you.'

Rosa stared at him, appalled, not understanding.

'An elephant?'

'He followed *Plough the Earth*, the great elephant, and

killed him. But in dying the elephant struck him, breaking him.'

'The fool. Oh, the fool!' Rosa whispered. 'Now of all times. With Sebastian in danger, he must...' And then she caught herself and broke off her futile lament. 'Where is he, Mohammed? Take me to him.'

Mohammed led along one of the game paths, Rosa ran behind him. There was no time for caution, no thought of it as they hurried to find Flynn. They came to the stream of the Abati, and swung off the path, staying on the near bank. They plunged through a field of arrow grass, skirted around a tiny swamp and ran on into a stand of buffalo thorn. As they emerged on the far side Mohammed stopped abruptly and looked at the sky.

The vultures turned in a high wheel against the blue, like debris in a lazy whirlwind. The spot above which they circled lay half a mile ahead.

'Daddy!' Rosa choked on the word. In an instant all the hardness accumulated since that night at Lalapanzi disappeared from her face.

'Daddy!' she said again, and then she ran in earnest. Brushing past Mohammed, throwing her rifle aside so it clattered on the earth, she darted out of the buffalo thorn and into the open.

'Wait, Little Long Hair. Be careful.' Mohammed started after her. In his agitation he stepped carelessly, full on to a fallen twig from the buffalo thorn. There was a worn spot on the sole of his sandal, and three inches of cruel red-tipped thorn drove up through it and buried in his foot.

For a dozen paces he struggled on after Rosa, hopping on one leg, flapping his arms to maintain his balance and calling, but not too loudly.

'Wait! Be careful, Little Long Hair.'

But she took not the least heed, and went away from

him, leaving him at last to sink down and tend to his wounded foot.

She crossed the open ground before the fever-tree grove with the slack, blundering steps of exhaustion. Running silently, saving her breath for the effort of reaching her father. She ran into the grove, and a drop of perspiration fell into her eye, blurring her vision so she staggered against one of the trunks. She recovered her balance and ran on into the midst of them.

She recognized Herman Fleischer instantly. She had run almost against his chest, and his huge body towered over her. She screamed with shock and twisted away from the bear-like arms outspread to clutch her.

Two of the native Askari who were working over the crude litter on which lay Flynn O'Flynn, jumped up. As she ran they closed on her from either side, the way a pair of trained greyhounds will course a hare. They caught her between them, and dragged her struggling and screaming to where Herman Fleischer waited.

'Ah, so!' Fleischer nodded pleasantly in greeting. 'You have come in time for the fun.' Then he turned to his sergeant. 'Have them tie the woman.'

Rosa's screams penetrated the light mists of insensibility that screened Flynn's brain. He stirred on the litter, muttering incoherently, rolling his head from side to side, then he opened his eyes and focused them with difficulty. He saw her struggling between the Askari and he snapped back into full consciousness.

'Leave her!' he roared. 'Call those bloody animals off her. Leave her, you murderous bloody German bastard.'

'Good!' said Herman Fleischer. 'You are awake now.' Then he lifted his voice above Flynn's bellows. 'Hurry, Sergeant, tie the woman – and get the rope up.'

While they secured Rosa, one of the Askari shinned up

the smooth yellow trunk of a fever tree. With his bayonet he hacked the twigs from the thick horizontal branch above their heads. The sergeant threw the end of the rope up to him, and at the second attempt the Askari caught it and passed it over the branch. Then he dropped back to earth.

There was a hangman's knot fixed in the rope, ready for use.

'Set the knot,' said Fleischer, and the sergeant went to where Flynn lay. With poles cut from a small tree they had rigged a combination litter and splints. The poles had been laid down Flynn's flanks from ankle to armpit, with bark strips they had bound them firmly so that Flynn's body was held rigidly as that of an Egyptian mummy, only his head and neck were free.

The sergeant stooped over him, and Flynn fell silent, watching him venomously. As his hands came down with the noose to loop it over Flynn's head, Flynn moved suddenly. He darted his head forward like a striking adder and fastened his teeth in the man's wrist. With a howl the sergeant tried to pull away, but Flynn held on, his head jerking and wrenching as the man struggled.

'Fool,' grunted Fleischer, and strode over to the litter. He lifted his foot and placed it on Flynn's lower body. As he brought his weight down on it Flynn stiffened and gasped with pain, releasing the Askari's wrist.

'Do it this way.' Fleischer lunged forward and took a handful of Flynn's hair, roughly he yanked Flynn's head forward. 'Now, the rope, quickly.'

The Askari dropped the noose over Flynn's head and drew the slip-knot tight until it lay snugly under Flynn's ear.

'Good.' Fleischer stepped back. 'Four men on the rope,' he ordered. 'Gently. Do not jerk the rope. Walk away with it slowly. I don't want to break his neck.'

Rosa's hysteria had stilled into cold horror as she watched the preparations for the execution, and now she found her voice again.

'Please,' she whispered. 'He's my father. Please don't. Oh, no, please don't.'

'Hush, girl,' roared Flynn. 'You'd not shame me now by pleading with this fat bag of pus.' He swivelled his head, his eyes rolled towards the four Askari who stood ready with the rope end. 'Pull! You black sons of bitches. Pull! And damn you. I'll beat you to hell, and speak to the devil so he'll have you castrated and smeared with pig's fat.'

'You heard what Fini told you,' smiled Fleischer at his Askari. 'Pull!'

And they walked backwards in single file, shuffling through the dead leaves, leaning against the rope.

The litter lifted slowly at one end, came upright and then left the ground.

Rosa turned away and clenched her eyelids tight closed, but her hands were bound so she could not stop her ears, she could not keep out the sounds that Flynn Patrick O'Flynn made as he died.

When at last there was silence, Rosa was shivering. Hard spasms that shuddered through her whole body.

'All right,' said Herman Fleischer. 'That's it. Bring the woman. We can get back to camp in time for lunch if we hurry.'

When they were gone, the litter and its contents still hung in the fever tree. Swinging a little and turning slowly on the end of the rope. Near it lay the carcass of the elephant, and a vulture planed down slowly and made a flapping ungainly landing in the top branches of the fever tree. It sat hunched and suspicious, then suddenly squawked and launched again into noisy flight, for it had seen the man coming.

The little old man limped slowly into the grove. He stopped beside the dead elephant and looked up at the man who had been his master and his friend.

'Go in peace, Fini!' said Mohammed.

– 78 –

The alleyway was a narrow low-roofed corridor, the bulkheads were painted a pale grey that glistened in the harsh light of the electric globes set in small wire cages at regular intervals along the roof.

At the end of the corridor, a guard stood outside the heavy watertight door in the bulkhead that led through into the handling room of the forward magazine. The guard wore only a thin white singlet and white flannel trousers, but his waist was belted in a blancoed webbing from which hung a sheathed bayonet, and there was a Mauser rifle slung from his shoulder.

From his position he could look into the handling room, and he could keep the full length of the alleyway under surveillance.

A double file of Wakamba tribesmen filled the alleyway, living chains along one of which passed the cordite charges; along the other the nine-inch shells.

The Africans worked with the stoical indifference of draught animals, turning to grip the ugly cylindro-conical shells, hugging a hundred and twenty pounds' weight of steel and explosive to their chests while they moved it on to the next man in the chain.

The cordite charges, each wrapped in thick paper, were not so weighty and moved more swiftly along their line.

Each man bobbed and swung as he handled his load, so it seemed that the two ranks were sets in a complicated dance pattern.

From this mass of moving humanity rose clouds of warm body odour, that filled the alleyway and defeated the efforts of the air-conditioning fans.

Sebastian felt sweat trickling down his chest and back under the leather cloak, he felt also the tug of weight within the folds of the cloak each time he swung to receive a fresh cordite charge from his neighbour.

He stood just outside the door of the handling room, and each time he passed a charge through, he looked into the interior of the magazine where another gang was at work, packing the charges into the shelves that lined the bulkheads, and easing the nine-inch shells into their steel racks. Here there was another armed guard.

The work had been in progress since early that morning, with a half-hour's break at noon, so the German guards had relaxed their vigilance. They were restless in anticipation of relief. The one in the magazine was a fat middle-aged man who at intervals during the day had broken the monotony by releasing sudden ear-splitting posterior discharges of gas. With each salvo he had clapped the nearest African porter on the back and shouted happily.

'Have a bite at that one!' or, 'Cheer up – it doesn't smell.'

But at last he also was deflated. He slouched across the handling room, and leaned against the angle of the door to address his colleague in the alleyway.

'It's hot as hell, and smells like a zoo. These savages stink.'

'You've been doing your share.'

'I'll be glad when it's finished.'

'It's cooler in the magazine with the fans running – you are all right.'

'Jesus, I'd like to sit down for a few minutes.'

'Better not, Lieutenant Kyller is on the prowl.'

This exchange was taking place within a few feet of Sebastian. He followed the German conversation with more ease now that he had been able to exercise his rusty vocabulary, but he kept his head down in a renewed burst of energy. He was worried. In a short while the day's shift would end and the African porters would be herded on deck and into the launches to be transported to their camp on one of the islands. None of the native labour force were allowed to spend the night aboard *Blücher*.

He had waited since noon for an opportunity to enter the magazine and place the time charge. But he had been frustrated by the activities of the two German guards. It must be nearly seven o'clock in the evening now. It would have to be soon, very soon. He glanced once more into the magazine, and he caught the eye of Walaka, Mohammed's cousin. Walaka stood by the cordite shelves, supervising the packing, and now he shrugged at Sebastian in eloquent helplessness.

Suddenly there was a thud of a heavy object being dropped to the deck, and a commotion of shouts in the alleyway behind Sebastian. He glanced round quickly. One of the bearers had fainted in the heat and fallen with a shell in his arms, the shell had rolled and knocked down another man. Now there was a milling confusion clogging the alleyway. The two guards moved forward, forcing their way into the press of black bodies, shouting hoarsely and clubbing with the rifle butts. It was the opportunity for which Sebastian had waited.

He stepped over the threshold of the magazine, and went to Walaka beside the cordite shelves.

'Send one of your men to take my place,' he whispered, and reaching up into the folds of his cloak he brought out the cigar box.

349

With his back towards the door of the magazine, using the cloak as a screen to hide his movements, he slipped the catch of the box and opened the lid.

His hands trembled with haste and nervous agitation as he fumbled with the winder of the travelling-clock. It clicked, and he saw the second hand begin its endless circuit of the dial. Even over the shouts and scuffling in the alleyway, the muted ticking of its mechanism seemed offensively loud to Sebastian. Hastily he shut the lid and glanced guiltily over his shoulder at the doorway. Walaka stood there, and his face was sickly grey with the tension of imminent discovery, but he nodded to Sebastian, a signal that the guards were still occupied without.

Reaching up to the nearest shelf, Sebastian wedged the cigar box between two of the paper-wrapped cylinders of cordite. Then he packed others over it, covering it completely.

He stood back and found with surprise that he was panting, his breathing whistling in his throat. He could feel the little drops of sweat prickling on his shaven head. In the white electric light they shone like glass beads on his velvety, black-stained skin.

'Is it done?' Walaka croaked beside him.

'It is done,' Sebastian croaked back at him, and suddenly he was overcome with a driving compulsion to be out of this steel room, out of this box-packed room with the ingredients of violent death and destruction; out of the stifling press of bodies that had surrounded him all day. A dreadful thought seized his imagination, suppose the artificer had erred in his assembly of the time charge, suppose that even now the battery was heating the wires of the detonator and bringing them to explosion point. He felt panic as he looked wildly at the tons of cordite and shell around him. He wanted to run, to fight his way out and up into the open air. He made the first move, and then froze.

The commotion in the alleyway had subsided miraculously, and now only one voice was raised. It came from just outside the doorway, using the curt inflection of authority. Sebastian had heard that voice repeatedly during that long day, and he had come to dread it. It heralded danger.

'Get them back to work immediately,' snapped Lieutenant Kyller as he stepped over the threshold into the magazine. He drew a gold watch from the pocket of his tunic and read the time. 'It is five minutes after seven. There is still almost half an hour before you knock off.' He tucked the watch away, and swept the magazine with a gaze that missed no detail. He was a tall young man, immaculate in his tropical whites. Behind him the two guards were hurriedly straightening their dishevelled uniforms and trying to look efficient and intelligent.

'Yes, sir,' they said in unison.

For a moment Kyller's eyes rested on Sebastian. It was probably because Sebastian was the finest physical specimen among the bearers, he stood taller than the rest of them – as tall as Kyller himself. But Sebastian felt his interest was deeper. He felt that Kyller was searching beneath the stain on his skin, that he was naked of disguise beneath those eyes. He felt that Kyller would remember him, had marked him down in his memory.

'That shelf.' Kyller turned away from Sebastian and crossed the magazine. He went directly to the shelf on which Sebastian had placed his time charge, and he patted the cordite cylinders that Sebastian had handled. They were slightly awry. 'Have it repacked immediately,' said Kyller.

'Right away, sir,' said the fat guard.

Again Kyller's eyes rested on Sebastian. It seemed that he was about to speak, then he changed his mind. He stooped through the doorway and disappeared.

Sebastian stood stony still, appalled by the order that Kyller had given. The fat guard grimaced sulkily.

'Christ, that one is a busy bastard.' And he glared at the cordite shelf. 'There's nothing wrong there.' He crossed to it and fiddled ineffectually. After a moment he asked the guard at the door, 'Has Kyller gone yet?'

'Yes. He's gone down the companion-way into the sick-bay.'

'Good!' grunted the fat one. 'I'm damned if I'm going to waste half an hour repacking this whole batch.' He hunched his shoulders, and screwed up his face with effort. There was a bagpipe squeal, and the guard relaxed and grinned. 'That one was for Lieutenant Kyller, God bless him!'

– 79 –

Darkness was falling, and with it the temperature dropped a few degrees into the high eighties and created an illusion that the faint evening breeze was chilly. Sebastian hugged his cloak around his body, and shuffled along in the slow column of native labourers that dribbled over the side of the German battle cruiser into the waiting launches.

He was exhausted both in body and in mind from the strain of the day's labour in the magazine, so that he went down the catwalk and took his place in the whaler, moving in a state of stupor. When the boat shoved off and puttered up the channel towards the labour camp on the nearest island, Sebastian looked back at *Blücher* with the same dumb stare as the men who squatted beside him on the floorboards of the whaler. Mechanically he registered the fact that Commissioner Fleischer's steam launch was tied up alongside the cruiser.

'Perhaps the fat swine will be aboard when the whole lot blows to hell,' he thought wearily. 'I can at least hope for that.'

He had no way of knowing who else Herman Fleischer had taken aboard the cruiser with him. Sebastian had been below decks toiling in the handling room of the magazine when the launch arrived from up-river, and Rosa Oldsmith had been ushered up the catwalk by the Commissioner in person.

'Come along, Mädchen. We will take you to see the gallant captain of this fine ship.' Fleischer puffed jovially as he mounted the steps behind her. 'I am sure there are many interesting things that you can tell him.'

Bedraggled and exhausted with grief, pale with the horror of her father's death, and with cold hatred for the man who had engineered it, Rosa stumbled as she stepped from the catwalk on to the deck. Her hands were still bound in front of her so she could not check herself. She fell forward, letting herself fall uncaring, and with mild surprise felt hands hold and steady her.

She looked up at the man who had caught her, and in her confusion of mind she thought it was Sebastian. He was tall and dark and his hands were strong. Then she saw the peaked uniform cap with its golden insignia, and she jerked away from him in revulsion.

'Ah! Lieutenant Kyller.' Commissioner Fleischer spoke behind her. 'I have brought you a visitor – a lovely lady.'

'Who is she?' Kyller was appraising Rosa. Rosa could not understand a word that was spoken. She stood in quiet acceptance, her whole body drooping.

'This . . .' answered Fleischer proudly, '. . . is the most dangerous young lady in the whole of Africa. She is one of the leaders of the gang of English bandits that raided the column bringing down the steel plate from Dar es Salaam. It was she who shot and killed your engineer. I captured her and her father this morning. Her father was the notorious O'Flynn.'

'Where is he?' Kyller snapped.

353

'I hanged him.'

'You hanged him?' demanded Kyller. 'Without trial?'

'No trial was necessary.'

'Without interrogating him?'

'I brought in the woman for interrogation.'

Kyller was angry now, his voice crackled with it.

'I will leave it to Captain von Kleine to judge the wisdom of your actions,' and he turned to Rosa; his eyes dropped to her hands, and, with an exclamation of concern, he took her by the wrist.

'Commissioner Fleischer, how long has this woman been bound?'

Fleischer shrugged. 'I could take no chances on her escaping.'

'Look at this!' Kyller indicated Rosa's hands. They were swollen, the fingers puffy and blue, sticking out stiffly, dead-looking and useless.

'I could take no chances.' Fleischer bridled at the implied criticism.

'Give me your knife,' Kyller snapped at the petty officer in charge of the gangway, and the man produced a large clasp knife. He opened it and handed it to the lieutenant.

Carefully Kyller ran the blade between Rosa's wrists and sawed at the rope. As her bonds dropped away Rosa cried out in pain, fresh blood flowing into her hands.

'You will be lucky if you have not done her permanent damage,' Kyller muttered furiously as he massaged Rosa's bloated hands.

'She is a criminal. A dangerous criminal,' growled Fleischer.

'She is a woman, and therefore deserving of your consideration. Not of this barbarous treatment.'

'She will hang.'

'Her crimes she will answer for, in due course – but until she has stood trial she will be treated as a woman.'

354

Rosa did not understand the harsh German argument that raged around her. She stood quietly and her eyes were fastened on the knife in Lieutenant Kyller's hand.

The hilt brushed her fingers as he worked to restore the circulation of her blood. The blade was long and silver bright, she had seen how keen was its edge by the way in which it had cut through the rope. As she stared at it, it seemed to her fevered fancy that there were two names engraved in the steel of the blade. The names of the two persons she had loved. The names of her father and her child.

With an effort she tore her gaze from the knife and looked at the man she hated. Fleischer had come close up to her, as though to take her away from Lieutenant Kyller's attention. His face was flushed with anger and the fold of flesh under his chin wobbled flabbily as he argued.

Rosa flexed her fingers. They were still numb and stiff, but she could feel the strength flowing back into them. She let her gaze drop down to Fleischer's belly.

It jutted out round and full, soft-looking under the grey corduroy tunic, and again her fevered imagination formed a picture of the blade going into that belly. Slipping in silently, smoothly, burying itself to the hilt and then drawing upwards to open the flesh like a pouch. The picture was so vivid that Rosa shuddered with the intense sensual pleasure of it.

Kyller was completely occupied with Fleischer. He felt the girl's fingers slide into the cupped palm of his right hand, but before he could pull away she had scooped the knife deftly from his grip. He lunged at her, but she pirouetted lightly away from him. Her knife hand dropped and then darted forward, driven by the full weight of her body at the bulging belly of Herman Fleischer.

Rosa thought that because he was fat he would be slow.

She expected him to be stunned by the unexpected attack, to stand and take the knife in his vitals.

Herman Fleischer was fully alert before she even started her thrust. He was fast as a striking mamba, and strong beyond credibility. He did not make the mistake of intercepting the knife with his bare hands. Instead he struck her right shoulder with a clenched fist the size of a carpenter's mallet. The force of the blow knocked her sideways, deflecting the blade from its target. Her arm from the shoulder downwards was paralysed, and the knife flew from her hand and slithered away across the deck.

'Ja!' roared Fleischer triumphantly. 'Ja! So! Now you see how I was right to tie the bitch. She is vicious, dangerous.'

And he lifted the huge fist again to smash it into Rosa's face as she crouched, hugging her hurt shoulder and sobbing with pain and disappointment.

'Enough!' Kyller stepped between them. 'Leave her.'

'She must be tied up like an animal – she is dangerous,' bellowed Fleischer, but Kyller put a protective arm around Rosa's bowed shoulders.

'Petty Officer,' he said. 'Take this woman to the sick-bay. Have Surgeon Commander Buchholz see to her. Guard her carefully, but be gentle with her. Do you hear me?' And they took her away below.

'I must see Captain von Kleine,' Fleischer demanded. 'I must make a full report to him.'

'Come,' said Kyller, 'I will take you to him.'

80

Sebastian lay on his side beside the smoky little fire with his cloak draped over him. Outside he heard the night sounds of the swamp, the faint splash of a fish or a crocodile in the channel, the clink and boom of the tree frogs, the singing of insects, and the lap and sigh of wavelets on the mud bank below the hut.

The hut was one of twenty crude open-sided shelters that housed the native labour force. The earth floor was thickly strewn with sleeping bodies. The sound of their breathing was a restless murmur, broken by the cough and stir of dreamers.

Despite his fatigue, Sebastian was not sleeping, he could not relax from the state of tension in which he had been held all that day. He thought of the little travelling-clock ticking away in its nest of high explosive, measuring out the minutes and the hours, and then his mind side-stepped and went to Rosa. The muscles of his arms tightened with longing. Tomorrow, he thought, tomorrow I will see her and we will go away from this stinking river. Up into the sweet air of the highlands. Again his mind jumped. Seven o'clock, seven o'clock tomorrow morning and it will be over. He remembered Lieutenant Kyller's voice as he stood in the doorway of the magazine with the gold watch in his hand. '. . . The time is five minutes past seven . . .' he had said. So that Sebastian knew to within a few minutes when the time fuse would explode.

He must stop the porters going aboard *Blücher* in the morning. He had impressed on old Walaka that they must refuse to turn out for the next day's shift. They must . . .

'Manali! Manali!' his name was whispered close by in the gloom, and Sebastian lifted himself on one elbow. In the flickering light from the fire there was a shadowy figure, crawling on hands and knees across the earthen floor, and searching the faces of the sleeping men.

'Manali, where are you?'

'Who is it?' Sebastian answered softly, and the man jumped up and scurried to where he lay.

'It is I, Mohammed.'

'Mohammed?' Sebastian was startled. 'Why are you here? You should be with Fini at the camp on the Abati.'

'Fini is dead.' Mohammed's whisper was low with sorrow, so low that Sebastian thought he had misunderstood.

'What? What did you say?'

'Fini is dead. The Allemand came with the ropes. They hung him in the fever trees beside the Abati, and when he was dead they left him for the birds.'

'What talk is this?' Sebastian demanded.

'It is true,' mourned Mohammed. 'I saw it, and when the Allemand had gone, I cut the rope and brought him down. I wrapped him in my own blanket and buried him in an ant-bear hole.'

'Dead? Flynn dead? It isn't true!'

'It is true, Manali.' In the red glow of the camp-fire Mohammed's face was old and raddled and gaunt. He licked his lips. 'There is more, Manali. There is more to tell.'

But Sebastian was not listening. He was trying to force his mind to accept the reality of Flynn's death, but it balked. It would not accept the picture of Flynn swinging at the rope's end, Flynn with the rope burns at his throat and his face swollen and empurpled, Flynn wrapped in a dirty blanket and crammed into an ant-bear hole. Flynn dead? No! Flynn was too big, too vital – they could not kill Flynn.

'Manali, hear me.'

Sebastian shook his head, bemused, denying it. It could not be true.

'Manali, the Allemand, they have taken Little Long Hair. They have bound her with ropes and taken her.'

Sebastian winced, and jerked away as though he had been struck open-handed across the face.

'No!' He tried to close his mind against the words.

'They caught her this morning early as she went to Fini. They took her down-river in the small boat, and she is now on the great ship of the Allemand.'

'Blücher? Rosa is aboard the Blücher?'

'Yes. She is there.'

'No. Oh, God, no!'

In five hours Blücher would blow up. In five hours Rosa would die. Sebastian swung his head and looked out into the night, he looked through the open side of the hut, down the channel to where Blücher lay at her moorings half a mile away. There was a dim glow of light across the water from the hooded lanterns on Blücher's main deck. But her form was indistinguishable against the dark mass of the mangroves. Between her and the island, the channel was a smooth expanse of velvety blackness on which the reflections of the stars were scattered sequins of light.

'I must go to her,' said Sebastian. 'I cannot let her die there alone.' His voice gathered strength and resolve. 'I cannot let her die. I'll tell the Germans where to find the charge – I'll tell them . . .' Then he faltered. 'I can't. No, I can't. I'd be a traitor then, but, but . . .'

He threw aside his cloak.

'Mohammed, how did you come here? Did you bring the canoe? Where is it?'

Mohammed shook his head. 'No. I swam. My cousin brought me close to the island in the canoe, but he has gone away. We could not leave the canoe here, lest the Askari find it. They would have seen the canoe.'

'There isn't a boat on the island – nothing,' muttered Sebastian. The Germans were careful to guard against desertion. Each night the labour force was marooned on the island – and the Askari patrolled the mud banks.

'Mohammed, hear me now.' Sebastian reached across and laid his hand on the old man's shoulder. 'You are my friend. I thank you that you have come to tell me these things.'

'You are going to Little Long Hair?'

'Yes.'

'Go in peace, Manali.'

'Take my place here, Mohammed. When the guards count tomorrow morning, you will stand for me.' Sebastian tightened his grip on the bony shoulder. 'Stay in peace, Mohammed.'

His blackened body blending into the darkness, Sebastian crouched beneath the spread branches of a clump of pampa scrub, and the Askari guard almost brushed against him as he passed. The Askari slouched along with his rifle slung so that the barrel stood up behind his shoulder. The constant patrolling had beaten a path around the circumference of the island, the guard followed it mechanically. Half asleep on his feet, completely unaware of Sebastian's presence. He stumbled in the darkness and swore sleepily, and moved on.

Sebastian crossed the path on his hands and knees, then stretched out on his belly into a reptilian slither as he reached the mud bank. Had he tried to walk across it, the glutinous mud would have sucked so loudly around his feet that every guard within a hundred yards would have heard him.

The mud coated his chest and belly and legs with its coldly loathsome, clinging oiliness, and the reek of it filled his nostrils so he gagged. Then he was into the water. The water was blood warm, he felt the tug of the current and the bottom dropped away beneath him. He swam on his side, careful that neither legs nor arms should break the surface. His head alone showed, like the head of a swimming otter, and he felt the mud washing off his body.

He swam across the current, guided by the distant glimmer of *Blücher's* deck lights. He swam slowly, husbanding his strength, for he knew he would need all of it later.

His mind was filled with layers of awareness. The lowest layer was a lurking undirected terror of the dark water in which he swam, his dangling legs were vulnerable to the scaly predators which infested the Rufiji river. The current must be carrying his scent down to them. Soon they would come hunting up to find him. But he kept up the easy stroke of arms and legs. It was a chance, one chance of the many he was taking and he tried to ignore it and grapple with the practical problems of his attempt. When he reached *Blücher*, how was he to get aboard her? Her sides were fifty feet high, and the catwalks were the only means of access. These were both heavily guarded. It was a problem without solution, and yet he harried it.

Over this was a thick layer of hopeless sorrow. Sorrow for Flynn.

But the uppermost layer was thickest, strongest. Rosa, Rosa and Rosa.

He found with surprise that he was saying it aloud.

'Rosa!' with each forward thrust of his body through the water.

'Rosa!' each time he drew breath.

'Rosa!' as his legs kicked out and pushed him towards the *Blücher*.

He did not know what he would do if he reached her. Perhaps there was some half-formed idea of escaping with her, of fighting his way out of *Blücher* with his woman. Getting her away before that moment when the ship would vanish in a holocaust of flame. He did not know, but he swam on quietly.

Then he was under *Blücher's* side. The towering mass of steel blotted out the starry night sky, and he stopped swimming and hung in the warm water looking up at her.

There were small sounds. The hum of machinery within her, the faint clang of metal struck against metal, the low guttural murmur of voices at her gangway, the thump of a rifle butt against the wooden deck, the soft wash of water around the hull – and then a closer, clearer sound, a regular creak and tap, creak and tap.

He swam in towards the hull, searching for the source of this new sound. It came from near the bows, creak and tap. The creak of rope, and the tap of wood against the steel hull. He saw it then, just above his head. He almost cried out with joy.

The cradles! The platforms still suspended above the water on which the welders and the painters had worked.

He reached up and gripped the wooden edge and drew himself on to the platform. He rested a few seconds and then began to climb the rope. Hand over hand, gripping the rope between the insides of his bare feet, he went up.

His head came level with the deck and he hung there, searching carefully. Fifty yards away he saw two seamen at the gangway. Neither was looking his way.

At intervals the hooded lanterns threw puddles of yellow light upon the deck, but there were concealing shadows beyond them. It was dark around the base of the forward gun-turrets, and there were piles of material, abandoned welding equipment, heaps of rope and canvas in the shadows which would hide him when he had crossed the deck.

Once more he checked the two guards at the gangway, their backs were turned to him.

Sebastian filled his lungs and steeled himself to act. Then with one fluid movement he drew himself up and rolled over the side. He landed lightly on his feet and darted across the exposed deck into the shadows. He ducked down behind a pile of canvas and rope netting, and struggled to control his breathing. He could feel his legs trembling violently under him, so he sat down on the planking and huddled against the protecting pile of canvas. River water trickled from his shaven pate over his forehead and into his eyes. He wiped it away.

'Now what?' He was aboard Blücher, but what should he do next?

Where would they hold Rosa? Was there some sort of guard-room for prisoners? Would they put her in one of the officer's cabins? The sick-bay?

He knew roughly where the sick-bay was located. While he was working in the magazine he had heard the one German guard say, 'He has gone down the companion-way to the sick-bay.'

It must be somewhere just below the forward magazine – oh, God! If they had her there she would be almost at the centre of the explosion.

He came up on his knees, and peered over the pile of canvas. It was lighter now. Through the screen of camouflage netting, he could see the night sky had paled a little in the east. Dawn was not far off. The night had passed so swiftly, morning was on its way and there were but a few scant hours before the hands of the travelling-clock completed their journey, and made the electrical connection that would seal the Blücher's fate, and the fate of all those aboard her.

He must move. He rose slowly and then froze. The guards at the gangway had come to attention. They stood stiffly with their rifles at the slope, and into the light stepped a tall, white-clad figure.

There was no mistaking him. It was the officer that Sebastian had last seen in the forward magazine. Kyller, they had called him, Lieutenant Kyller.

Kyller acknowledged the salutes of the two guards, and he spoke with them a while. Their voices were low and indistinct. Kyller saluted again, and then left them. He came down the deck towards the bows; he walked briskly, and his face below the peak of his cap was in darkness.

Sebastian crouched down again, only his eyes lifted above the piled canvas. He watched the officer and he was afraid.

Kyller stopped in mid-stride. He half stooped to look at the deck at his feet, and then in the same movement, straightened with his right hand dropping to the holstered pistol on his belt.

'Guard!' he bellowed. 'Here! At the double!'

On the holystoned white planking, the wet footprints that Sebastian had left behind him glittered in the lantern light. Kyller stared in the direction that they led, coming directly towards Sebastian's hiding-place.

The boots of the two guards pounded heavily along the deck. They had unslung their rifles as they ran to join Kyller.

'Someone has come aboard here. Spread out and search...' Kyller shouted at them, as he closed in on Sebastian.

Sebastian panicked. He jumped up and ran, trying to reach the corner of the gun-turret.

'There he is!' Kyller's voice. 'Stop! Stop or I'll fire.'

Sebastian ran. His legs driving powerfully, his elbows pumping, head down, bare feet slapping on the planking, he raced through shadow.

'Stop!' Kyller was balanced on the balls of his feet, legs braced, right shoulder thrust forward and right arm outflung in the classic stance of the pistol marksman. The arm dropped slowly and then kicked up violently, as the shot spouted from the Luger in a bell of yellow flame. The bullet spanged against the plating of the turret and then glanced off in whining ricochet.

Sebastian felt the wind of the bullet pass his head and

he jinked his run. The corner of the turret was very close, and he dodged towards it.

Then Kyller's next shot blurted loudly in the night, and simultaneously something struck Sebastian a heavy blow under his left shoulder-blade. It threw him forward off balance and he reeled against the turret, his hands scrabbled at the smooth steel without finding purchase. His body flattened against the side of the turret, so that the blood from the exit hole that the bullet had torn in his breast sprayed on to the pale grey, painted turret.

His legs buckled and he slid down, slowly, still trying to find purchase with the hooked claws of his fingers, so that as his knees touched the deck he was in the attitude of devout prayer. Forehead pressed against the turret, kneeling, arms spread high and wide.

Then the arms sank down, and he slid sideways, collapsed onto the deck and rolled on to his back.

Kyller came and stood over him. The pistol hanging slackly in the hand at his side.

'Oh, my God,' there was genuine regret in Kyller's voice. 'It's only one of the porters. Why did the fool run! I wouldn't have fired if he had stood.'

Sebastian wanted to ask him where Rosa was. He wanted to explain that Rosa was his wife, that he loved her, and that he had come to find her.

He concentrated his vision on Kyller's face as it hung over him, and he summoned his school-boy German, marshalling the sentences in his mind.

But as he opened his mouth the blood welled up in his throat and choked him. He coughed, racking, and the blood bubbled through his lips in a pink froth.

'Lung shot!' said Kyller, and then to the guards as they came up, 'Get a stretcher. Hurry. We must take him down to the sick-bay.'

81

There were twelve bunks in *Blücher*'s sick-bay, six down each side of the narrow cabin. In eight of them lay German seamen; five malaria cases and three men injured in the work of repairing her bows.

Rosa Oldsmith was in the bunk farthest from the door. She lay behind a movable screen, and a guard sat outside the screen. He wore a pistol at his belt and was wholly absorbed in a year-old variety magazine, the cover of which depicted a buxom blonde woman in a black corset and high boots, with a horse whip in one hand.

The cabin was brightly lit and smelled of antiseptic. One of the malarial cases was in delirium, and he laughed and shouted. The medical orderly moved along the rows of bunks carrying a metal tray from which he administered the morning dosages of quinine. The time was 5 a.m.

Rosa had slept only intermittently during the night. She lay on top of the blankets and she wore a striped towelling dressing-gown over the blue flannel nightgown. The gown was many sizes too large and she had rolled back the cuffs of the sleeves. Her hair was loose on the pillows, and damp at the temples with sweat. Her face was pale and drawn, with bluish smudges of fatigue under her eyes, and her shoulder ached dully where Fleischer had struck her.

She was awake now. She lay staring up at the low roof of the cabin, playing over in her mind fragments from the happenings of the last twenty-four hours.

She recalled the interrogation with Captain von Kleine. He had sat opposite her in his luxuriously furnished cabin, and his manner had been kindly, his voice gentle, pronouncing the English words with blurring of the consonants and a hardening of the vowel sounds. His English was good.

'When did you last eat?' he asked her.

'I am not hungry,' she replied, making no attempt to conceal her hatred. Hating them all – this handsome, gentle man, the tall lieutenant who stood beside him, and Herman Fleischer who sat across the cabin from her, with his knees spread apart to accommodate the full hang of his belly.

'I will send for food.' Von Kleine ignored her protest and rang for his steward. When the food came, she could not deny the demands of her body and she ate, trying to show no enjoyment. The sausage and pickles were delicious, for she had not eaten since the previous noon.

Courteously von Kleine turned his attention to a discussion with Lieutenant Kyller until she had finished, but when the steward removed the empty tray he came back to her.

'Herr Fleischer tells me you are the daughter of Major O'Flynn, the commander of the Portuguese irregulars operating in German territory?'

'I was until he was hanged, murdered! He was injured and helpless. They tied him to a stretcher . . .' Rosa flared at him, tears starting in her eyes.

'Yes,' von Kleine stopped her, 'I know. I am not pleased. That is now a matter between myself and Commissioner Fleischer. I can only say that I am sorry. I offer you my condolence.' He paused and glanced at Herman Fleischer. Rosa could see by the angry blue of his eyes that he meant what he said.

'But now there are some questions I must ask you . . .'

Rosa had planned her replies, for she knew what he would ask. She replied frankly and truthfully to anything that did not jeopardize Sebastian's attempt to place the time fuse aboard *Blücher*.

What were she and Flynn doing when they were captured? Keeping the *Blücher* under surveillance. Waiting to signal her departure to the blockading cruisers.

How did the British know that Blücher *was in the Rufiji?* The steel plate, of course. Then confirmation by aerial reconnaissance.

Were they contemplating offensive action against Blücher? No, they would wait until she sailed.

What was the strength of the blockade squadron? Two cruisers that she had seen, she did not know if there were other warships waiting over the horizon.

Von Kleine phrased his questions carefully, and listened attentively to her replies. For an hour the interrogation continued, until Rosa was yawning openly, and her voice was slurred with exhaustion. Von Kleine realized that there was nothing to be learned from her, all she had told him he already knew or had guessed.

'Thank you,' he finished. 'I am keeping you aboard my ship. There will be danger here, for soon I will be going out to meet the British warships. But I believe that it will be better for you than if I handed you over to the German administration ashore.' He hesitated a moment and glanced at Commissioner Fleischer. 'In every nation there are evil men, fools and barbarians. Do not judge us all by one man.'

With distaste at her own treachery, Rosa found that she could not hate this man. A weary smile tugged her mouth and she answered him.

'You are kind.'

'Lieutenant Kyller will see you to the hospital. I am sorry I can offer you no better quarters, but this is a crowded vessel.'

When she had gone, von Kleine lit a cheroot and while he tasted its comforting fragrance, he allowed his eyes to rest on the portrait of the two golden women across the cabin. Then he sat up in his chair and his voice had lost its gentleness as he spoke to the man who lolled on the couch.

'Herr Fleischer, I find it difficult to express fully my extreme displeasure at your handling of this affair . . .'

After a night of fitful sleep, Rosa lay on her hospital bunk behind the screen and she thought of her husband. If things had gone well Sebastian must by now have placed the time charge and escaped from *Blücher*. Perhaps he was already on his way to the rendezvous on the Abati river. If this were so, then she would not see him again. It was her one regret. She imagined him in his ludicrous disguise, and she smiled a little. Dear lovable Sebastian. Would he ever know what had happened to her? Would he know that she had died with those whom she hated? She hoped that he would never know – that he would never torture himself with the knowledge that he had placed the instrument of her death with his own hands.

I wish I could see him just once more to tell him that my death is unimportant beside the death of Herman Fleischer, beside the destruction of this German warship. I wish only that when the time comes, I could see it. I wish there were some way I could know the exact time of the explosion so I could tell Herman Fleischer a minute before, when it is too late for him to escape, and watch him. Perhaps he would blubber, perhaps he would scream with fear. I would like that. I would like that very much.

The strength of her hatred was such that she could no longer lie still. She sat up and tied the belt of her gown around her waist. She was filled with a restless itchy exhilaration. It would be today – she felt sure – sometime today she would slake this burning thirst for vengeance that had tormented her for so long.

She threw her legs over the side of the bunk and pulled open the screen. The guard dropped his magazine and started up from his chair, his hand dropping to the pistol at his hip.

'I will not harm you...' Rosa smiled at him, '...not yet!'

She pointed to the door which led into the tiny shower cabinet and toilet. The guard relaxed and nodded acquiescence. He followed her as she crossed the cabin.

Rosa walked slowly between the bunks, looking at the sick men that lay in them.

'All of you,' she thought happily. 'All of you!'

She slid the tongue of the lock across, and was alone in the bathroom. She undressed, and leaned across the washbasin to the small mirror set above it. She could see the reflection of her head and shoulders. There was a purple and red bruise spreading down from her neck and staining the white swell of her right breast. She touched it tenderly with her finger-tips.

'Herman Fleischer,' she said the name gloatingly, 'it will be today – I promise you that. Today you will die.'

And then suddenly she was crying.

'I only wish you could burn as my baby burned – I wish you could choke and swing on the rope as my father did.' And the tears fell fat and slow, sliding down her cheeks to drop into the basin. She started to sob, dry convulsive gasps of grief and hatred. She turned blindly to the shower cabinet, and turned both taps full on so that the rush of the water would cover the sound of her weeping. She did not want them to hear it.

Later, when she had bathed her face and body and combed her hair and dressed again, she unlocked the door and stepped through it. She stopped abruptly and through puffy reddened eyes tried to make sense of what was happening in the sick-bay.

It was crowded. The surgeon was there, two orderlies, four German seamen, and the young lieutenant. All of them hovered about the stretcher that was being manoeuvred between the bunks. There was a man on the stretcher, she could see his form under the single grey blanket that covered him, but Lieutenant Kyller's back obscured her view of the man's face. There was blood on the blanket, and a brown smear of blood on the sleeve of Kyller's white tunic.

She moved along the bulkhead of the cabin and craned her head to see around Kyller, but at that moment one of the orderlies leaned across to swab the mouth of the man on the stretcher with a white cloth. The cloth obscured the wounded man's face. Bright frothy blood soaked through the material, and the sight of it nauseated Rosa. She averted her gaze and slipped away towards her own bunk at the end of the cabin. She reached the screen, and behind her somebody groaned. It was a low delirious groan, but the sound of it stopped Rosa instantly. She felt as though something within her chest was swelling to stifle her. Slowly, fearfully, she turned back.

They were lifting the man from the stretcher to lay him on an empty bunk. The head lolled sideways, and beneath its stain of bark juice Rosa saw that dear, well loved face.

'Sebastian!' she cried, and she ran to him, pushing past Kyller, throwing herself on to the blanket-draped body, trying to get her arms around him to hug him.

'Sebastian! What have they done to you!'

– 82 –

'Sebastian! Sebastian!' Rosa leaned across him and held her mouth to his ear.

'Sebastian!' She called his name quietly but urgently, then brushed his forehead with her lips. The skin was cold and damp.

He lay on his back with the bed clothes turned back to

his waist. His chest was swathed in bandages, and his breathing sawed and gurgled.

'Sebastian. It's Rosa. It's Rosa. Wake up, Sebastian. Wake up, it's Rosa.'

'Rosa?' At last her name had reached him. He whispered it painfully, wetly, and fresh blood stained his lips.

Rosa had been on the edge of despair. Two hours she had been sitting beside him. Since the surgeon had finished dressing the wound, she had sat with him – touching him, calling to him. This was the first sign of recognition he had given her.

'Yes! Yes! It's Rosa. Wake up, Sebastian.' Her voice lifted with relief.

'Rosa?' His eyelashes trembled.

'Wake up.' She pinched his cold cheek and he winced. His eyelids fluttered open.

'Rosa?' on a shallow, sawing breath.

'Here, Sebastian. I'm here.' His eyes rolled in their sockets, searching, trying desperately to focus.

'Here,' she said, leaning over him and taking his face between her hands. She looked into his eyes.

'Here, my darling, here.'

'Rosa!' His lips convulsed into a dreadful parody of a smile.

'Sebastian, did you set the bomb?'

His breathing changed, hoarser, and his mouth twitched with the effort.

'Tell them,' he whispered.

'Tell them what?'

'Seven. Must stop it.'

'Seven o'clock?'

'Don't – want – you—'

'Will it explode at seven o'clock?'

'You—' It was too much and he coughed.

'Seven o'clock? Is that it, Sebastian?'

'You will . . .' He squeezed his eyes closed, putting all his strength into the effort of speaking. 'Please. Don't die. Stop it.'

'Did you set it for seven o'clock?' In her impatience she tugged his head towards her. 'Tell me, for God's sake, tell me!'

'Seven o'clock. Tell them – tell them.'

Still holding him, she looked at the clock set high up on the bulkhead of the sick-bay.

On the white dial, the ornate black hands stood at fifteen minutes before the hour.

'Don't die, please don't die,' mumbled Sebastian.

She hardly heard the pain-muted pleading. A fierce surge of triumph lifted her – she knew the hour. The exact minute. Now she could send for Herman Fleischer, and have him with her.

Gently she laid Sebastian's head back on the pillow. On the table below the clock she had seen a pad and pencil among the bottles and jars, and trays of instruments. She went to it, and while the guard watched her suspiciously she scribbled a note.

'Captain,
My husband is conscious. He has a message of vital importance for Commissioner Fleischer. He will speak to no one but Commissioner Fleischer. The message could save your ship.

Rosa Oldsmith.'

She folded the sheet of paper and pushed it into the guard's hand.

'For the Captain. Captain.'

'Kapitän,' repeated the guard. 'Jawohl.' And he went to the door of the sick-bay. She saw him speak with the second guard outside the door, and then pass him the note.

Rosa sank down on the edge of Sebastian's bunk. She ran her hand tenderly over his shaven head. The new hair was stiff and bristly under her fingers.

'Wait for me. I'm coming with you, my darling. Wait for me.'

But he had lapsed back into unconsciousness. Crooning softly, she gentled him. Smiling to herself, happily, she waited for the minute hand of the clock to creep up to the zenith of the dial.

– 83 –

Captain Arthur Joyce had personally supervised the placing of the scuttling charges. Perhaps, long ago, another man had felt the way he did – hearing the command spoken from the burning bush, and knowing he must obey.

The charges were small, but laid in twenty places against the bare plating, they would rip *Renounce*'s belly out of her cleanly. The watertight bulkhead had been opened to let the water rush through her. The magazines had all of them been flooded to minimize the danger of explosion. The furnaces had been damped down, and he had blown the pressure on his boilers – retaining a head of steam, just sufficient to take *Renounce* in on her last run into the channel of the Rufiji.

The cruiser had been stripped of her crew. Twenty men left aboard her to handle the ship. The rest of them transshipped aboard *Pegasus*.

Joyce was going to attempt to force the log boom, take *Renounce* through the minefield, and sink her higher up, where the double mouth of the channel merged into a single thoroughfare.

If he succeeded he would effectively have blocked *Blücher*, and sacrificed a single ship.

If he failed, if *Renounce* sank in the minefield before she reached the confluence of the two channels, then Armstrong would have to take *Pegasus* in and scuttle her also. On his bridge Joyce sat hunched in his canvas deck chair, looking out at the land; the green line of Africa which the morning sun lit in harsh golden brilliance.

Renounce was running parallel to the coast, five miles off shore. Behind her *Pegasus* trailed like a mourner at a funeral.

'06.45 hours, sir.' The officer of the watch saluted.

'Very well.' Joyce roused himself. Until this moment he had hoped. Now the time had come and *Renounce* must die.

'Yeoman of Signals,' he spoke quietly, 'make this signal with *Pegasus* number "Plan A Effective".' This was the code that *Renounce* was to stand in for the channel. 'Stand by to pick up survivors.'

'*Pegasus* acknowledges, sir.'

Joyce was glad that Armstrong had not sent some inane message such as 'Good luck'. A curt acknowledgement, that was as it should be.

'All right, Pilot,' he said, 'take us in, please.'

– 84 –

It was a beautiful morning and a flat sea. The captain of the escort destroyer wished it were not, he would have forfeited a year's seniority for a week of fog and rain.

As his ship tore down the line of transports to administer a rebuke to the steamer at the end of the column for not keeping proper station, he looked out at the western horizon. Visibility was perfect, a German masthead would be able to pick out this convoy of fat sluggish transports at a distance of thirty miles.

Twelve ships, fifteen thousand men – and *Blücher* could be out. At any moment she could come hurtling up over the horizon, with those long nine-inch guns blazing. The thought gave him the creeps. He jumped up from his stool, and crossed to the port rail of his bridge to glower at the convoy.

Close alongside wallowed one of the transports. They were playing cricket on her afterdeck. As he watched, a sun-bronzed giant of a South African clad only in short khaki pants swung the bat and clearly he heard the crack as it struck the ball. The ball soared up and dropped into the sea with a tiny splash.

'Oh, good shot, sir!' applauded the lieutenant who stood beside the captain.

'This is not the members' enclosure at Lords, Mr Parkinson,' snarled the destroyer captain. 'If you have nothing to occupy you, I can find duties for you.'

The lieutenant retired hurt, and the captain glanced along the line of troopships.

'Oh, no!' he groaned. Number Three was making smoke again. Ever since leaving Durban harbour Number Three had been giving periodic impersonations of Mount Vesuvius. It would be a give-away to the lookout at *Blücher's* masthead.

He reached for his megaphone, ready to hurl the most scathing reprimand he could muster at Number Three as he passed her.

'This is worse than being a teacher in a kindergarten. They'll break me yet.' And he lifted the megaphone to his lips as Number Three came abreast.

The infantrymen that lined the troopship's rail cheered his eloquence to the echo.

'The fools. Let them cheer *Blücher* when she comes,'

growled the captain and crossed the bridge to gaze apprehensively into the west where Africa lay just below the horizon.

'Strength to *Renounce* and *Pegasus*.' He made the wish fervently. 'God grant they hold *Blücher*. If she gets through . . .'

– 85 –

'It's no use, Bwana. They won't move,' the sergeant of Askari reported to Ensign Proust.

'What is the trouble?' demanded Proust.

'They say there is a bad magic on the ship. They will not go to her today.'

Proust looked over the mass of black humanity. They squatted sullenly among the huts and palm trees, rank upon rank of them, huddled in their cloaks, faces closed and secretive.

Drawn up on the mud bank of the island were the two motor launches, ready to ferry the bearers downstream to the day's labour aboard *Blücher*. The German seamen tending the launches were watching with interest this charade of dumb rebellion, and Ensign Proust was very conscious of their attention.

Proust was at the age where he had an iron-clad faith in his own sagacity, the dignity of a patriarch, and pimples.

He was, in other words, nineteen years of age.

It was clear to him that these native tribesmen had embarked on their present course of action for no other reason than to embarrass Ensign Proust. It was a direct and personal attack on his standing and authority.

He lifted his right hand to his mouth and began to feed thoughtfully on his fingernails. His rather prominent Adam's apple moved in sympathy with the working of his jaws. Suddenly he realized what he was doing. It was a habit he was trying to cure, and he jerked his hand away and linked it with its mate behind his back, in a faithful imitation of Captain Otto von Kleine, a man whom he held in high admiration. It had hurt him deeply when Lieutenant Kyller had greeted his request for permission to grow a beard like Captain von Kleine's with ribald laughter.

Now he sank his bare chin on to his chest and began to pace solemnly up and down the small clearing above the mud bank. The sergeant of Askari waited respectfully with his men drawn up behind him for Ensign Proust to reach a decision.

He could send one of the launches back to *Blücher*, to fetch Commissioner Fleischer. After all, this was really the Herr Commissioner's shauri (Proust had taken to using odd Swahili words like an old Africa hand). Yet he realized that to call for Fleischer would be an admission that he was unable to handle the situation. Commissioner Fleischer would jeer at him, Commissioner Fleischer had shown an increasing tendency to jeer at Ensign Proust.

'No,' he thought, flushing so that the red spots on his skin were less noticeable, 'I will not send for that fat peasant.' He stopped pacing and addressed himself to the sergeant of Askari.

'Tell them . . .' he started, and his voice squeaked alarmingly. He adjusted the timbre to a deep throaty rumble, 'Tell them I take a very serious view of this matter.'

The sergeant saluted, did a showy about-face with much feet stamping, and passed on Ensign Proust's message in loud Swahili. From the dark ranks of bearers there was no reaction whatsoever, not so much as a raised eyebrow. The crews of the launches were more responsive. One of them laughed.

Ensign Proust's Adam's apple bobbed, and his ears chameleoned to the colour of a good burgundy.

'Tell them that it is *mutiny*!' The last word squeaked again, and the sergeant hesitated while he groped for the Swahili equivalent. Finally he settled for:

'Bwana Heron is very angry.' Proust had been nicknamed for his pointed nose and long thin legs. The tribesmen bore up valiantly under this intelligence.

'Tell them I will take drastic steps.'

Now, thought the sergeant, he is making sense. He allowed himself literary licence in his translation.

'Bwana Heron says that there are trees on this island for all of you – and he has sufficient rope.'

A sigh blew through them, soft and restless as a small wind in a field of wheat. Heads turned slowly until they were all looking at Walaka.

Reluctantly Walaka stood up to reply. He realized that it was foolhardy to draw attention to himself when there was talk of ropes in the air, but the damage had already been done. The hundreds of eyes upon him had singled him out to the Allemand. Bwana Intambu always hanged the man that everyone looked at.

Walaka began to speak. His voice had the soothing quality of a rusty gate squeaking in the wind. It went on and on, as Walaka attempted a one-man filibust.

'What is he talking about?' demanded Ensign Proust.

'He is talking about leopards,' the sergeant told him.

'What is he saying about them?'

'He says, among other things, that they are the excrement of dead lepers.'

Proust looked stunned, he had expected Walaka's speech to have at least some bearing on the business in hand. He rallied gamely.

'Tell him that he is a wise old man, and that I look to him to lead the others to their duties.'

And the sergeant gazed upon Walaka sternly.

'Bwana Heron says that you, Walaka, are the son of a

diseased porcupine and that you feed on offal with the vultures. He says further that you he has chosen to lead the others in the dance of the rope.'

Walaka stopped talking. He sighed in resignation and started down towards the waiting launch. Five hundred men stood up and followed him.

The two vessels chugged sedately down to *Blücher*'s moorings. Standing in the bows of the leading launch with his hands on his hips, Ensign Proust had the proud bearing of a Viking returning from a successful raid.

'I understand these people,' he would tell Lieutenant Kyller. 'You must pick out their leader and appeal to his sense of duty.'

He took his watch from his breast pocket.

'Fifteen minutes to seven,' he murmured. 'I'll have them aboard on the hour.' He turned and smiled fondly at Walaka who squatted miserably beside the wheelhouse.

'Good man, that! I'll bring his conduct to Lieutenant Kyller's attention.'

– 86 –

Lieutenant Ernst Kyller shrugged out of his tunic and sat down on his bunk. He held the tunic in his lap and fingered the sleeve. The smear of blood had dried, and as he rubbed the material between thumb and forefinger, the blood crumbled and flaked.

'He should not have run. I had to shoot.'

He stood up and hung the tunic in the little cupboard at the head of his bunk. Then he took his watch from the pocket and sat down again to wind it.

'Fifteen minutes to seven.' He noted the time mechanically, and laid the gold hunter on the flap table beside the bunk. Then he lay back and arranged the pillows under his head, he crossed his still-booted feet and regarded them dispassionately.

'He came aboard to try and rescue his wife. It was the natural thing to do. But that disguise – the shaven head, and stained skin – that must have been carefully thought out. It must have taken time to arrange.'

Kyller closed his eyes. He was tired. It had been a long and eventful watch. Yet there was something nagging him, a feeling that there was an important detail that he had overlooked, a detail of vital – no, of deadly importance.

Within two minutes of the girl's recognition of the wounded man, Kyller and the surgeon commander had established that he was not a native, but a white man disguised as one.

Kyller's English was sketchy, but he had understood the girl's cries of love and concern and accusation.

'You've killed him also. You've killed them all. My baby, my father – and now my husband. You murderers, you filthy murdering swines!'

Kyller grimaced and pressed his knuckles into his aching eyes. Yes, he had understood her.

When he had reported to Captain von Kleine, the captain had placed little importance on the incident.

'Is the man conscious?'

'No, sir.'

'What does the surgeon say his chances are?'

'He will die. Probably before midday.'

'You did the right thing, Kyller.' Von Kleine touched his shoulder in a show of understanding. 'Do not reproach yourself. It was your duty.'

'Thank you, sir.'

'You are off watch now. Go to your cabin and rest – that is an order. I want you fresh and alert by nightfall.'

'Is it tonight then, sir?'

'Yes. Tonight we sail. The minefield has been cleared

and I have given the order for the boom to be destroyed. The new moon sets at 11.47. We will sail at midnight.'

But Kyller could not rest. The girl's face, pale, smeared with her tears, haunted him. The strangled breathing of the dying man echoed in his ears, and that nagging doubt scratched against his nerves.

There was something he must remember. He flogged his tired brain, and it balked.

Why was the man disguised? If he came as soon as he had heard that his wife was a prisoner he would not have had time to effect the disguise.

Where had the man been when Fleischer had captured his wife? He had not been there to protect her. Where had he been? It must have been somewhere near at hand.

Kyller rolled on to his stomach and pressed his face into the pillow. He must rest. He must sleep now for tonight they would go out to break through the blockading English warships.

A single ship against a squadron. Their chances of slipping through unchallenged were small. There would be a night action. His imagination was heightened by fatigue, and behind his closed eyelids he saw the English cruisers, lit by the flashes of their own broadsides as they closed with *Blücher*. The enemy intent on vengeance. The enemy in overwhelming strength. The enemy strong and freshly provisioned, their coal-bunkers glutted, their magazines crammed with shell, their crews uncontaminated by the fever miasma of the Rufiji.

Against them a single ship with her battle damage hastily patched, half her men sick with malaria, burning green cordwood in her furnaces, her fire-power hampered by the desperate shortage of shell.

He remembered the tiers of empty shell racks, the depleted cordite shelves in the forward magazine.

The magazine? That was it! The magazine! It was

something about the magazine that he must remember. That was the thing that had been nagging him. The magazine!

'Oh, my God!' he shouted in horror. In one abrupt movement he had leapt from his prone position on the bunk to stand in the centre of the cabin.

The skin on his bare upper arms prickled with gooseflesh.

That was where he had seen the Englishman before. He had been with the labour party – in the forward magazine.

He would have been there for one reason only – sabotage.

Kyller burst from his cabin, and raced, half dressed, along the corridor.

'I must get hold of Commander Lochtkamper. We'll need a dozen men – strong men – stokers. There are tons of explosive to move, we'll have to handle it all to find whatever the Englishman placed there. Please, God, give us time. Give us time!'

– 87 –

Captain Otto von Kleine bit the tip from the end of his cheroot, and removed a flake of black tobacco from the tip of his tongue with thumb and fore-finger. His steward held a match for him and von Kleine lit the cheroot. At the wardroom table, the chairs of Lochtkamper, Kyller, Proust and one other were empty.

'Thank you, Schmidt,' he said through the smoke. He pushed his chair back and stretched out his legs, crossing his ankles and laying his shoulders against the padded back-rest. The breakfast had not been of gourmet standard; bread without butter, fish taken from the river and strong with the taste of the mud, washed down with black unsweetened coffee. Nevertheless, Herr Fleischer seemed to be enjoying it. He was beginning his third plateful.

Von Kleine found his appreciative snuffling distracting. This would be the last period of relaxation that von Kleine could anticipate in the next many days. He wanted to savour it along with his cheroot, but the wardroom was not the place to do so. Apart from the gusto with which the Herr Commissioner was demolishing his breakfast, and the smell of fish – there was a mood among his officers that was almost tangible. This was the last day and it was heavy with the prospect of what the night might bring. They were all of them edgy and tense. They ate in silence, keeping their attention on their plates, and it was obvious that most of them had slept badly. Von Kleine decided to finish his cheroot alone in his cabin. He stood up.

'Excuse me please, gentlemen.'

A polite murmur, and von Kleine turned to leave.

'Yes, Schmidt. What is it?' His steward was standing deferentially in his path.

'For you, sir.'

Von Kleine clamped the cheroot between his teeth and took the note in both hands, screwing up his eyes against the blue spiral of tobacco smoke. He frowned.

This woman, and the man she claimed was her husband, worried him. They were a drain on the attention which he should be devoting entirely to the problem of getting *Blücher* ready for tonight. Now this message – what could she mean by 'could save your ship'? He felt a prickle of apprehension.

He swung around.

'Herr Commissioner, a moment of your time, please.'

Fleischer looked up from his food with a smear of grease on his chin.

'Ja?'

'Come with me.'

'I will just finish . . .'

'Immediately, please.' And to avert argument von Kleine stooped out of the wardroom, leaving Herman Fleischer in

384

terrible indecision, but he was a man for the occasion, he took the remaining piece of fish on his plate and put it in his mouth. It was a tight fit, but he still found space for the half cup of coffee as well. Then he scooped up a slice of bread and wiped his plate hurriedly. With the bread in his hand he lumbered after von Kleine.

He was still masticating as he entered the sick-bay behind von Kleine. He stopped in surprise.

The woman sat on one of the bunks. She had a cloth in her hand and with it she wiped the mouth of a black man who lay there. There was blood on the cloth. She looked up at Fleischer. Her expression was soft with compassion and sorrow, but it changed the moment she saw Fleischer. She stood up quickly.

'Oh, thank God, you've come,' she cried with joy as though she were greeting a dear friend. Then incongruously she looked up at the clock.

Keeping warily away from her, Fleischer worked his way around to the opposite side of the bunk by which she stood. He leaned over and studied the face of the dying man. There was something very familiar about it. He chewed stolidly as he puzzled over it. It was the association with the woman that triggered his memory.

He made a choking sound, and bits of half chewed bread flew from his mouth.

'Captain!' he shouted. 'This is one of them – one of the English bandits.'

'I know,' said von Kleine.

'Why wasn't I told? This man must be executed immediately. Even now it might be too late. Justice will be cheated.'

'Please, Herr Commissioner. The woman has an important message for you.'

'This is monstrous. I should have been told . . .'

'Be still,' snapped von Kleine. Then to Rosa, 'You sent for me? What is it you have to tell us?'

385

With one hand Rosa was stroking Sebastian's head, but she was looking up at the clock.

'You must tell Herr Fleischer that the time is one minute before seven.'

'I beg your pardon?'

'Tell him exactly as I say it.'

'Is this a joke?'

'Tell him, quickly. There is very little time.'

'She says the time is one minute to seven,' von Kleine rattled out the translation. Then in English, 'I have told him.'

'Tell him that at seven o'clock he will die.'

'What is the meaning of that?'

'Tell him first. Tell him!' insisted Rosa.

'She says that you will die at seven o'clock.' And Fleischer interrupted his impatient gobbling over the prone form of Sebastian. He stared at the woman for a moment, then he giggled uncertainly.

'Tell her I feel very well,' he said, and laughed again, 'better than this one here.' He prodded Sebastian. 'Ja, much better.' And his laughter came full and strong, booming in the confined space of the sick-bay.

'Tell him my husband has placed a bomb in this ship, and it will explode at seven o'clock.'

'Where?' demanded von Kleine.

'Tell him first.'

'If this is true you are in danger also – where is it?'

'Tell Fleischer what I said.'

'There is a bomb in the ship.' And Fleischer stopped laughing.

'She is lying,' he spluttered. 'English lies.'

'Where is the bomb?' von Kleine had grasped Rosa's arm.

'It is too late,' Rosa smiled complacently. 'Look at the clock.'

'Where is it?' Von Kleine shook her wildly in his agitation.

'In the magazine. The forward magazine.'

'In the *magazine*! Sweet merciful Jesus!' von Kleine swore in German, and turned for the door.

'The magazine?' shouted Fleischer and started after him. 'It is impossible – it can't be.' But he was running, wildly, desperately, and behind him he heard Rosa Oldsmith's triumphant laughter.

'You are dead. Like my baby – dead, like my father. It is too late to run, much too late!'

– 88 –

Von Kleine went up the companion-way steps three at a time. He came out into the alleyway that led to the magazine, and stopped abruptly.

The alleyway was almost blocked by a mountain of cordite charges thrown haphazard from the magazine by a knot of frantically busy stokers.

'What are you doing?' he shouted.

'Lieutenant Kyller is looking for a bomb.'

'Has he found it?' von Kleine demanded as he brushed past them.

'Not yet, sir.'

Von Kleine paused again in the entrance to the magazine. It was a shambles. Led by Kyller, men were tearing at the stacks of cordite, sweeping them from the shelves, ransacking the magazine.

Von Kleine jumped forward to help.

'Why didn't you send for me?' he asked as he reached up to the racks above his head.

'No time, sir,' grunted Kyller beside him.

'How did you know about the bomb?'

'It's a guess – I could be wrong, sir.'

'You're right! The woman told us. It's set for seven o'clock.'

'Help us, God! Help us!' pleaded Kyller, and hurled himself at the next shelf.

'It could be anywhere – anywhere!' Captain von Kleine worked like a stevedore, knee-deep in spilled cylinders of cordite.

'We should clear the ship. Get the men off.' Kyller attacked the next rack.

'No time. We've got to find it.'

Then in the uproar there was a small sound, a muffled tinny buzz. The alarm bell of a travelling-clock.

'There!' shouted Kyller. 'That's it!' And he dived across the magazine at the same moment as von Kleine did. They collided and fell, but Kyller was up instantly, dragging himself on to his feet with hands clawing at the orderly rack of cordite cylinders.

The buzz of the alarm clock seemed to roar in his ears. He reached out and his hands fell on the smoothly paper-wrapped parcels of death, and at that instant the two copper terminals within the leather case of the clock which had been creeping infinitesimally slowly towards each other for the past twelve hours, made contact.

Electricity stored in the dry cell battery flowed through the circuit, reached the hair-thin filament in the detonator cap, and heated it white-hot. The detonator fired, transferring its energy into the sticks of gelignite that were packed into the cigar box. The wave of explosion leapt from molecule to molecule with the speed of light so that the entire contents of *Blücher's* magazine were consumed in one hundredth part of a second. With it were consumed Lieutenant Kyller and Captain von Kleine and the men about them.

In the centre of that fiery holocaust they burned to vapour.

The blast swept through *Blücher*. Downwards through two decks with a force that blew the belly out of her as easily as popping a paper bag, down through ten fathoms of water to strike the bottom of the river and the shock wave bounced up to raise fifteen-foot waves along the surface.

It blew sideways through *Blücher*'s watertight bulkheads, crumpling and tearing them like silver paper.

It caught Rosa Oldsmith as she lay across Sebastian's chest, hugging him. She did not even hear it come.

It caught Herman Fleischer just as he reached the deck, and shredded him to nothingness.

It swept through the engine room and burst the great boilers, releasing millions of cubic feet of scalding steam to race through the ship.

It blew upwards through the deck, lifting the forward gun-turret off its seating, tossing the hundreds of tons of steel high in a cloud of steam and smoke and debris.

It killed every single human being aboard. It did more than merely kill them, it reduced them to gas and minute particles of flesh or bone. Then still unsatisfied, its fury unabated, it blew outwards from *Blücher*'s shattered hulk, a mighty wind that tore the branches from the mangrove forest and stripped it of leaves.

It lifted a column of smoke and flame writhing and twisting into the bright morning sky above the Rufiji delta, and the waves swept out across the river as though from the eye of a hurricane.

They overwhelmed the two launches that were approaching *Blücher*, pouring over them and capsizing them, swirling them over and over and spilling their human cargo into the frightened frothing water.

And the shock waves rolled on across the delta to burst

thunderously against the far hills, or to dissipate out on the vastness of the Indian Ocean.

They passed over the British cruiser *Renounce* as she entered the channel between the mangroves. They rolled overhead like giant cannon-balls across the roof of the sky.

Captain Arthur Joyce leapt to the rail of his bridge, and he saw the column of agonized smoke rise from the swamps ahead of him. A grotesque living thing, unbelievable in its size, black and silver and shot through with flame.

'They've done it!' shouted Arthur Joyce. 'By Jove, they've done it!'

He was shaking; his whole body juddering, his face white as ice, and his eyes which he could not drag from that spinning column of destruction that rose into the sky, filled slowly with tears. He let them overflow his eyelids and run unashamedly down his cheeks.

– 89 –

Two old men walked into a grove of fever trees that stood on the south bank of the Abati river. They stopped beside a pile of gargantuan bones from which the scavengers had picked the flesh, leaving them scattered and white.

'The tusks are gone,' said Walaka.

'Yes,' agreed Mohammed, 'the Askari came back and stole them.'

Together they walked on through the fever trees and then they stopped again. There was a low mound of earth at the edge of the grove. Already it had settled and new grass was growing upon it.

'He was a man,' said Walaka.

'Leave me, my cousin. I will stay here a while.'

'Stay in peace, then,' said Walaka, and settled the string

of his blanket roll more comfortably over his shoulder before he walked on.

Mohammed squatted down beside the grave. He sat there unmoving all that day. Then in the evening Mohammed stood up and walked away towards the south.